T0109281

THE FIRST MAN IN ROME

By Colleen McCullough

The First Man in Rome
The Grass Crown
Fortune's Favorites
Caesar's Women
Caesar

Tim
The Ladies of Missalonghi
A Creed for the Third Millennium
An Indecent Obsession
The Thorn Birds

COLLEEN McCULLOUGH

THE FIRST MAN IN ROME

AVON

An Imprint of HarperCollins*Publishers*

First Avon Books paperback printing: August 1991.
First Avon Books International printing: May 1991.
First Avon A trade paperback printing: November 2008.

HarperCollins books may be purchased for educational, business, or sales promotional use. For information, please e-mail the Special Markets Department at SPsales@harpercollins.com.

Library of Congress Cataloging-in-Publication Data is available upon request.

ISBN 978-0-06-158241-7

23 24 25 26 27 LBC 15 14 13 12 11

*For Frederick T. Mason, dear friend, splendid colleague,
honest man, with love and gratitude.*

A note to the reader: to shed light on the world of ancient Rome, several maps and illustrations have been included throughout this book. Their locations are noted on page ix. A list of the main characters begins on page xix. An author's note appears on page 979. If you would like to know more about the historical background of *The First Man in Rome*, turn to page 983 for a glossary explaining some Latin words and unfamiliar terms. Readers who are interested in the pronunciations of Roman masculine names will find a guide on page 1105. A guide to the pronunciations of other names and terms begins on page 1115.

LIST OF MAPS
AND ILLUSTRATIONS

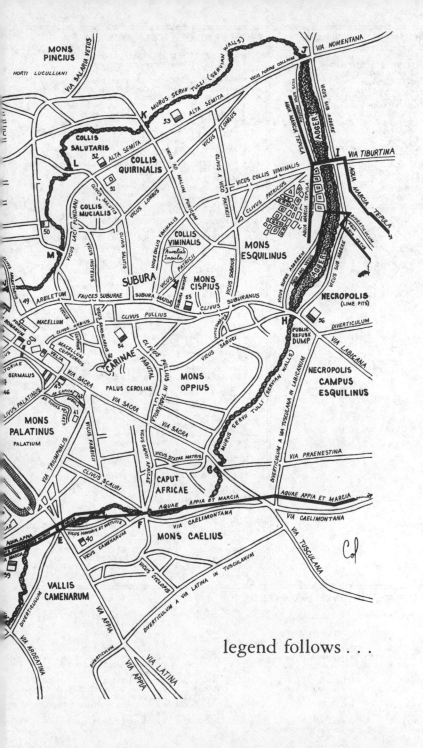

legend follows . . .

THE GATES IN THE SERVIAN WALLS

PORTA:
- A TRIGEMINA — Port of Rome
- B LAVERNALIS — Via Ostiensis
- C RAUDUSCULANA — Via Ostiensis
- D NAEVIA — Via Ardeatina
- E CAPENA — Via Appia & Via Latina
- F CAELIMONTANA — Via Tusculana
- G QUERQUETULANA — Via Praenestina
- H ESQUILINA — Via Labicana & Via Praenestina
- I VIMINALIS — Via Collatina & Via Tiburtina
- J COLLINA — Via Nomentana
- K QUIRINALIS — Via Salaria Vetus
- L SALUTARIS — Via Flaminia
- M SANQUALIS — Via Lata & Campus Martius
- N FONTINALIS — Campus Martius
- O TRIUMPHALIS — Triumphal Parades Only
- P CARMENTALIS — Circus Flaminius
- Q FLUMENTANA — Circus Flaminius

ROMA URBS
legend

TEMPLES & OTHER PLACES of SIGNIFICANCE

1 MAUSOLEUM OF THE JULII CAESARES (Hypothetically Sited)
2 T. VENUS VICTRIX (Atop Pompey's Auditorium)
3 POMPEY'S THEATER
4 PORTICUS OF POMPEY, with the Hundred-Pillared Colonnade
5 MEETING HALL of POMPEY'S COMPLEX (Site of Caesar's Murder)
6 T. HERCULIS MUSARUM (Hercules & the Nine Muses)
7 ⎰ FOUR TEMPLES   ? Juno Curitis (Juno of Meetings)
8 ⎱ ADJACENT TO   ? Fortunae Huiusce Diei (Today's Luck)
9 ⎰ POMPEY'S   ? FERONIA (Freedom For Slaves)
10 ⎱ THEATER COMPLEX   ? Lares Permarini (Lares of the Seafarer)
11 OLD PORTICUS MINUCIA IN THE CIRCUS FLAMINIUS
12 ⎰ TEMPLES   Vulcan (Fire, Earthquakes, Smiths)
13 ⎱ OF THE CIRCUS   Hercules Custos (Guardian of the Circus)
14 ⎱ FLAMINIUS   Mars Invictus (Undefeated Mars)
15 PORTICUS of the METELLI
16 T. APOLLO SOSIANUS (Medicine & Healing)
17 T. BELLONA & "ENEMY TERRITORY" (Foreign War)
18 T. JUNO REGINA (Juno the Ruler)
19 T. JUPITER STATOR (Stayer of Soldiers in Retreat)
20a POSSIBLE SITE OF NEW PORTICUS MINUCIA — OR POMPEY'S VILLA?
20b POSSIBLE SITE OF NEW PORTICUS MINUCIA — T. DIANA
21 FOUR TEMPLES — PIETAS, JANUS, SPES (Hope), JUNO SOSPITA
22 ⎰ TWO TEMPLES   T. FORTUNA (Chastity & Virginity)
23 ⎱ OF ALLIED CULTS   T. MATER MATUTA (Childbearing)
24 T. PORTUNUS (Ports & Port Trades)
25 T. JANUS (Doorways, Both In & Out, Beginnings & Ends)
26 ⎰ THREE CENTERS   HERCULES OLIVARIUS (Oil Merchants)
27 ⎰ FOR THE WORSHIP   ARA MAXIMA HERCULIS (Great Altar)
28 ⎱ OF HERCULES   HERCULES INVICTUS (Undefeated Hercules)
29 T. CERES (Bounty) — Headquarters of the Plebeian Aediles
30 T. FLORA (Vegetation)
31 ⎰ TWO TEMPLES FOR ALLIED   JUNO REGINA FOR WOMEN
32 ⎱ CULTS of the FREE CITIZEN   JUPITER LIBERTAS for MEN
33 SACRED PRECINCT of the ARMILUSTRIUM (Mars, the Army, the Salii)
34 T. DIANA (Protectress of Slaves)
35 T. LUNA (The Moon)
36 T. JUVENTAS (Coming of Age for Roman Citizen Males)
37 T. MERCURY (Trade) — Headquarters of Guild of Merchants
38 T. VENUS OBSEQUENS (Protectress of Prostitutes & Adulterers)
39 T. BONA DEA (Protectress of Women) & SAXUM SACRUM (Sacred Rock)
40 T. HONOS ET VIRTUS (A Cult for Military Commanders)
41 CURIAE VETERES — THE ANCIENT MEETING HALLS
42 BIRTHPLACE of GAIUS OCTAVIUS, LATER AUGUSTUS (Hypothetical)
43 T. JUPITER STATOR (Stayer of Soldiers in Retreat)
44 THE LUPERCAL (Cave of the Suckling Wolf of Romulus)
45 THE ROUND HUT OF ROMULUS (Carefully Preserved)
46 THE MUNDUS (A Vent of the Underworld)
47 T. MATER MAGNA (The Asian Great Goddess)
48 BASILICA JULIA (Replaced Basilicae Sempronia & Opimia)
49 FORUM JULIUM
50 T. SEMO SANCUS DIUS FIDIUS (Oaths & Treaties)
51 HOUSE OF TITUS POMPONIUS ATTICUS (Hypothetical)
52 T. SALUS (Good Health)
53 T. QUIRINUS (The Roman Citizen)
54 T. TELLUS (The Roman Earth Goddess)
55 T. JUNO LUCINA (Registry of Roman Citizen Births)
56 T. VENUS LIBITINA (Registry of Roman Citizen Deaths)—Hypothetical
57 T. AESCULAPIUS (Medicine) & SHIP of the PRECINCT ON THE INSULA
58 SEWER OUTLET FOR QUIRINAL & CAMPUS MARTIUS (R. Petronia)
59 CLOACA MAXIMA — SEWER OUTLET FOR SUBURA, Etc. (R. Spinon)
60 SEWER OUTLET FOR ESQUILINE, CIRCUS, Etc. (R. Nodinus)
61 TIGILLUM (Yoke), SHRINES of JUNO SORORIA (Puberty of Girls) & JANUS CURIATUS (Puberty of Boys) — Site Hypothetical

A TRANSLATION OF LATIN TERMS
(AS USED HEREIN)

CAMPUS	A Flat Expanse of Ground	SCALAE	A Flight of Steps
COLLIS	A Hill	VIA	A Main Road or Street
FAUCES	The Entrance to or Outlet of a Defile	VICUS	A Street or Lane
FLUMEN	A River	CLOACA	A Sewer
MONS	An Upland Spur or Ridge	AGGER	The Double Rampart of the Esquiline
PALUS	A Marshy Area with Many Springs	AQUA	A Water Channel, Above or Below Ground
VALLIS	A Depression in the Ground	BASILICA	Clerestory-Lit Hall for Courts or Business
HORTI	Gardens	CIRCUS	An Enclosure for Chariot Races and Games
MAIOR-MAJOR	Major	EMPORIUM	A Dockside Building for Trade Purposes
MAXIMUS-MAXIMA	The Biggest or Greatest	FORUM	An Open-Air Space for Public Business
MINOR	Minor	MACELLUM	An Open-Air Market of Booths and Stalls
NOVUS-NOVA	New	NECROPOLIS	A Burial Ground for Inhumation/Cremation
VETUS	Old	PONS	A Bridge
CLIVUS	A Hilly Street	PORTICUS	A Colonnaded Public Place of Business
DIVERTICULUM	A Road Connecting Main Roads	SAEPTA	The Centurate Voting Area

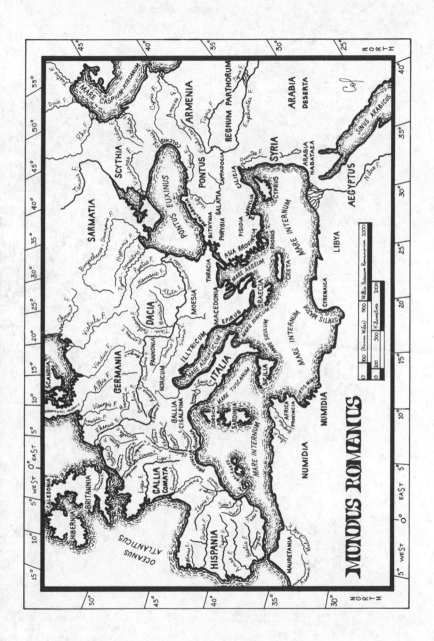

MUNDUS ROMANUS

CAMPUS MARTIUS

VIA LATA

CLIVUS ARGENTARIUS

MURUS SERVII TULLII (SERVIAN WALL)

CLIVUS ARGENTARIUS

OPEN SPACE
CALLED THE
VILLA PUBLICA

HERE ASSEMBLED THE
TRIUMPHAL PARADE —
ITS ROUTE IS MARKED
BY ARROWS INSOFAR AS
THE SCOPE OF THE
MAP PERMITS

VICUS PALLACINAE

ARX

SCALAE GEMONIAE

CAMPUS MARTIUS

VICUS TRIUMPHALIS

SCALAE ASYLI

ASYLUM
INTER DUOS
LUCOS

CLIVUS CAPITOLINUS

PARS
MEDIANA
ROMAE

legend follows...

CAPITOLIUM

VICUS TRIUMPHALIS

N

CAMPUS MARTIUS

0 20 40 60 80 100   METERS

EXTRAMURAL
FORUM
HOLITORIUM
(VEGETABLE MARKET)

HO
(VEGE

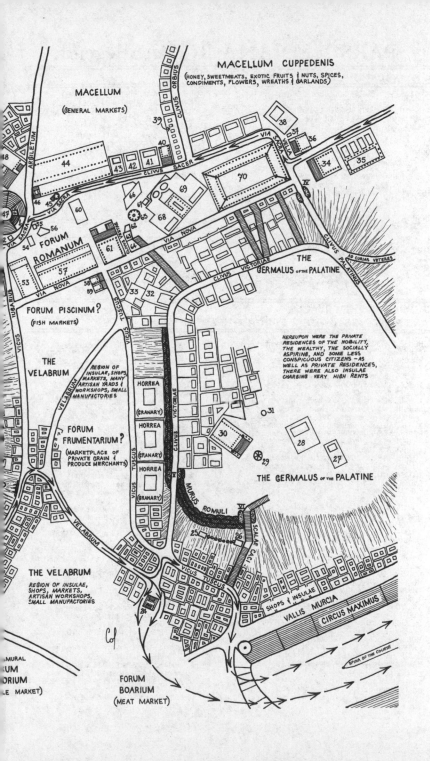

PARS MEDIANA ROMAE legend

A TRANSLATION of LATIN TERMS

ASYLUM	A SACRED PLACE or REFUGE
BASILICA	A CLERESTORY-LIT HALL FOR STATE BUSINESS & COMMERCE
CAMPUS	A FLAT EXPANSE OF GROUND
CIRCUS	AN ENCLOSURE FOR CHARIOT RACES & GAMES
CLIVUS	A HILLY STREET
DOMUS	A ONE-FAMILY CITY HOUSE (of One to Four Storeys)
DOMUS PUBLICUS	A STATE-OWNED DWELLING INHABITED BY A MAJOR PONTIFEX or FLAMEN
FORUM	AN OPEN-AIR GATHERING-PLACE FOR STATE BUSINESS OR PRIVATE COMMERCE
HORREA	A WAREHOUSE, also A GRANARY
INSULA	A BUILDING for MULTIPLE OCCUPANCY (Between Three & Twelve Storeys High)
MACELLUM	AN OPEN-AIR MARKET of STALLS & BOOTHS
MURUS	A DEFENSIVE WALL
PODIUM	A HIGH PLATFORM ELEVATING A TEMPLE, CONTAINING USABLE SPACE WITHIN IT

PORTA	A GATE IN A DEFENSIVE WALL
PORTICUS	A COLONNADED PLACE FOR PUBLIC BUSINESS & COMMERCE
SCALAE	A FLIGHT OF STEPS
VALLIS	A DEPRESSION IN THE GROUND
VIA	A MAIN STREET or ROAD
VICUS	A MINOR STREET or LANE
VILLA	A LARGE COUNTRY HOUSE

... IN THE SENSE USED HEREIN

GATES

I	CARMENTALIS	} IN THE
II	TRIUMPHALIS	} SERVIAN WALLS
III	FONTINALIS	
IV	MUGONIA	} IN THE ANCIENT WALLS
V	ROMULANA	} OF THE PALATINE
VI	CACANA	} CITY OF ROMULUS

TEMPLES, OTHER PLACES
AND BUILDINGS of INTEREST IN THE HEART OF ROME

1 HOUSE OF GAIUS MARIUS (Exact Site Unknown)
2 T. JUNO MONETA (Giver of Timely Warnings) THE MINT LAY BENEATH, INSIDE ITS PODIUM
3 T. VENUS ERUCINA (Protectress of Prostitutes)
4 T. MENS (Goddess of Proper Roman Thinking)
5 THE LAUTUMIAE PRISON
6 TULLIANUM or CARCER
7 T. CONCORD (Amicable Co-existence of Classes)
8 SENACULUM (Ambassadorial Reception Hall)
9 TABULARIUM (Repository of Records & Laws)
10 T. VEDIOVIS (Young Jupiter, God of Disappointments)
11 PORTICUS DEORUM CONSENTIUM (The Twelve Gods)
12 T. JUPITER FERETRIUS (Treaties & Armaments)
13 T. JUPITER OPTIMUS MAXIMUS
14 T. FORTUNA PRIMIGENIA (Protectress of First Born)
15 T. HONOS ET VIRTUS (Cult for Military Commanders)
16 T. OPS (Plenty) AN EMERGENCY FUND OF SILVER BULLION WAS STORED INSIDE ITS PODIUM
17 THE TARPEIAN ROCK
18 T. FIDES (Good Faith)
19 T. BELLONA (War with Foreign Powers)
20 "ENEMY TERRITORY"
21 T. APOLLO SOSIANUS (Medicine & Healing)
22 T. MATER MATUTA (Mothers & Childbearing)
23 T. FORTUNA (Virgins & Prepubescent Girls)
24 T. JANUS (Doorways, Beginnings & Ends)
25 SHRINE of the GENIUS LOCI (Procreative Power)
26 CAVE of the LUPERCAL (The Suckling She-Wolf)
27 HOUSE OF LUCIUS SERGIUS CATILINA (Exact Site Unknown)
28 HOUSE OF QUINTUS HORTENSIUS HORTALUS (Site Known)
29 THE ROUND HUT OF ROMULUS
30 T. MAGNA MATER (The Asian Great Goddess)
31 THE MUNDUS (A Vent of the Underworld)
32 HOUSE OF ① MARCUS LIVIUS DRUSUS ② MARCUS LICINIUS CRASSUS ③ MARCUS TULLIUS CICERO— EXACT SITE IS HYPOTHETICAL
33 HOUSE OF ① GNAEUS ② LUCIUS DOMITIUS AHENOBARBUS — SITE IS COMPLETELY IMAGINARY
34 T. JUPITER STATOR (Stayer of Army Retreats)
35 BATHS (Privately Owned) ? Senian Baths
36 T. PENATES (The Public Penates)
37 EQUESTRIAN STATUE of CLOELIA
38 DOMUS PUBLICUS of the REX SACRORUM— "THE KING'S HOUSE" (Site Approximate)
39 INN

40 T. LARES PRAESTITES (The Public Lares)
41 } THE DOMI PUBLICI of the THREE MAJOR
42 } FLAMINES — FLAMEN DIALIS, FLAMEN
43 } MARTIALIS, FLAMEN QUIRINALIS (Sites Are Purely Imaginary)
44 BASILICA AEMILIA (Business & Commercial Premises, Some Public Activities, Shops) Also Known as the Basilica Fulvia
45 T. VENUS CLOACINA (Purification of the Waters)
46 T. JANUS (Doorways, Beginnings & Ends)
47 THE WELL OF THE COMITIA & Its Inclusions ⓐ LAPIS NIGER ⓑ ROSTRA
48 OFFICES ATTACHED to the SENATE HOUSE
49 CURIA HOSTILIA (Senate House)
50 BASILICA PORCIA (Business & Commercial Premises, Particularly Banking — College of Tribunes of Plebs Headquartered Here)
51 T. SATURN (Unchanging Prosperity of the Roman State) THE TREASURY (Aerarium) LAY BENEATH, INSIDE THE PODIUM
52 ALTAR of the VOLCANAL (Vulcan Earthshaker)
53 BASILICA OPIMIA (Shops, Business, Courts)
54 TRIBUNAL of VARIOUS MAGISTRATES
55 SACRED TREES & STATUE of SATYR MARSYAS
56 LACUS CURTIUS (Pool of Curtius)
57 BASILICA SEMPRONIA (Shops, Courts, Business)
58 SHRINE of VOLUPIA & STATUE of DIVA ANGERONA
59 TOMB (Shrine) of LARENTIA
60 TRIBUNAL of the PRAETOR URBANUS — MAGISTRATES' STATION
61 T. CASTOR & POLLUX (Standard Weights & Measures Housed Within Podium, Also a Second Base for Tribunes of the Plebs)
62 FONS JUTURNA (Sacred Well of Juturna)
63 CULT SHRINE & STATUE of JUTURNA
64 ROOMS FOR USE OF PILGRIMS to JUTURNA
65 T. VESTA (Hearthfire of the State)
66 THE REGIA (Offices of PONTIFEX MAXIMUS)
67 CULT SHRINE & STATUE of VESTA
68 ATRIUM VESTAE of the DOMUS PUBLICUS (Home of the Vestal Virgins)
69 DOMUS PUBLICUS of the PONTIFEX MAXIMUS
70 PORTICUS MARGARITARIA (Jewelers, Pearl Vendors, Perfumiers, Luxury Shops & Stalls)

THE FIRST MAN IN ROME

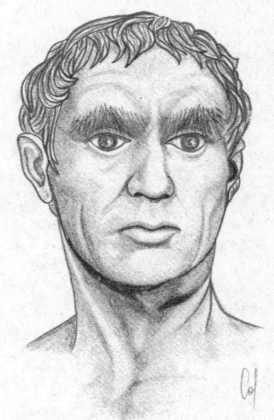

GAIUS MARIUS

THE MAIN CHARACTERS

Caepio

Quintus Servilius Caepio, consul 106 B.C.
Quintus Servilius Caepio Junior, his son
Servilia Caepionis, his daughter

Caesar

Gaius Julius Caesar, senator
Marcia of the Marcii Reges, his wife, mother of:
Sextus Julius Caesar, his older son
Gaius Julius Caesar Junior, his younger son
Julia Major (Julia), his older daughter
Julia Minor (Julilla), his younger daughter

Cotta

Marcus Aurelius Cotta, praetor (date unknown)
Rutilia, his wife; her first husband: his brother, Lucius
    Aurelius Cotta, consul 118 B.C. (died straight after)
Aurelia, his stepdaughter and niece
Lucius Aurelius Cotta, his stepson and nephew
Gaius, Marcus, and Lucius Aurelius Cotta, his sons by Rutilia

Decumius

Lucius Decumius, custodian of a crossroads college

Drusus

Marcus Livius Drusus Censor, consul 112 B.C., censor
109 B.C. (died in office)
Cornelia Scipionis, his estranged wife, mother of:
Marcus Livius Drusus, his older son
Mamercus Aemilius Lepidus Livianus, his younger son,
adopted out as a child
Livia Drusa, his daughter

Glaucia

Gaius Servilius Glaucia, tribune of the plebs 102 B.C., praetor
100 B.C.

Jugurtha

Jugurtha, King of Numidia, bastard son of Mastanabal
Bomilcar, his half brother and baron

Marius

Gaius Marius
Grania from Puteoli, his first wife
Martha of Syria, a prophetess

Metellus

Lucius Caecilius Metellus Dalmaticus Pontifex Maximus,
consul 119 B.C., older brother of:
Quintus Caecilius Metellus Numidicus, consul 109 B.C.,
censor 102 B.C.

Quintus Caecilius Metellus Pius, son of Numidicus
Caecilia Metella Dalmatica, niece and ward of Numidicus,
    daughter of Dalmaticus

Rutilius Rufus

Publius Rutilius Rufus, consul 105 B.C.
Livia of the Drusi, his deceased wife, sister of Marcus Livius
    Drusus Censor
Rutilia of the Rufi, his sister, widow of Lucius Aurelius Cotta,
    wife of Marcus Aurelius Cotta

Saturninus

Lucius Appuleius Saturninus, tribune of the plebs 103 and
    100 B.C.

Scaurus

Marcus Aemilius Scaurus Princeps Senatus, consul 115 B.C.,
    censor 109 B.C.
Marcus Aemilius Scaurus Junior, his son by his first wife

Sertorius

Quintus Sertorius, cadet and military tribune
Ria of the Marii, his mother, cousin of Gaius Marius

Sulla

Lucius Cornelius Sulla, quaestor 107 B.C., legate

Clitumna from Umbria, his stepmother, aunt of Lucius Gavius
   Stichus
Nicopolis the freedwoman, his mistress
Metrobius, an adolescent child star of the comedy theater

THE FIRST YEAR (110 B.C.):

In the Consulship of
Marcus Minucius Rufus
and
Spurius Postumius Albinus

LUCIUS CORNELIUS SULLA

Having no personal commitment to either of the new consuls, Gaius Julius Caesar and his sons simply tacked themselves onto the procession which started nearest to their own house, the procession of the senior consul, Marcus Minucius Rufus. Both consuls lived on the Palatine, but the house of the junior consul, Spurius Postumius Albinus, was in a more fashionable area. Rumor had it Albinus's debts were escalating dizzily, no surprise; such was the price of becoming consul.

Not that Gaius Julius Caesar was worried about the heavy burden of debt incurred while ascending the political ladder; nor, it seemed likely, would his sons ever need to worry on that score. It was four hundred years since a Julius had sat in the consul's ivory curule chair, four hundred years since a Julius had been able to scrape up that kind of money. The Julian ancestry was so stellar, so august, that opportunities to fill the family coffers had passed the succeeding generations by, and as each century finished, the family of Julius had found itself ever poorer. Consul? Impossible! Praetor, next magistracy down the ladder from consul? Impossible! No, a safe and humble backbencher's niche in the Senate was the inheritance of a Julius these days, including that branch of the family called Caesar because of their luxuriantly thick hair.

So the toga which Gaius Julius Caesar's body servant draped about his left shoulder, wrapped about his frame, hung about his left arm, was the plain white toga of a man who had never aspired to the ivory curule chair of high office. Only his dark red shoes, his iron senator's ring, and the five-inch-wide purple stripe on the right shoulder of his tunic distinguished his garb from that of his sons, Sextus and Gaius, who wore ordinary shoes, their seal rings only, and a thin purple knight's stripe on their tunics.

Even though dawn had not yet broken, there were little ceremonies to usher in the day. A short prayer and an offering of a salt cake at the shrine to the gods of the house in the atrium, and then, when the servant on door duty called out that he could see the torches coming down the hill, a reverence to Janus Patulcius, the god who permitted safe opening of a door.

Father and sons passed out into the narrow cobbled alley,

there to separate. While the two young men joined the ranks of the knights who preceded the new senior consul, Gaius Julius Caesar himself waited until Marcus Minucius Rufus passed by with his lictors, then slid in among the ranks of the senators who followed him.

It was Marcia who murmured a reverence to Janus Clusivius, the god who presided over the closing of a door, Marcia who dismissed the yawning servants to other duties. The men gone, she could see to her own little expedition. Where were the girls? A laugh gave her the answer, coming from the cramped little sitting room the girls called their own; and there they sat, her daughters, the two Julias, breakfasting on bread thinly smeared with honey. How lovely they were!

It had always been said that every Julia ever born was a treasure, for the Julias had the rare and fortunate gift of making their men happy. And these two young Julias bade fair to keep up the family tradition.

Julia Major—called Julia—was almost eighteen. Tall and possessed of grave dignity, she had pale, bronzy-tawny hair pulled back into a bun on the nape of her neck, and her wide grey eyes surveyed her world seriously, yet placidly. A restful and intellectual Julia, this one.

Julia Minor—called Julilla—was half past sixteen. The last child of her parents' marriage, she hadn't really been a welcome addition until she became old enough to enchant her softhearted mother and father as well as her three older siblings. She was honey-colored. Skin, hair, eyes, each a mellow gradation of amber. Of course it had been Julilla who laughed. Julilla laughed at everything. A restless and unintellectual Julia, this one.

"Ready, girls?" asked their mother.

They crammed the rest of their sticky bread into their mouths, wiggled their fingers daintily through a bowl of water and then a cloth, and followed Marcia out of the room.

"It's chilly," said their mother, plucking warm woolen cloaks from the arms of a servant. Stodgy, unglamorous cloaks.

Both girls looked disappointed, but knew better than to protest; they endured being wrapped up like caterpillars into cocoons, only their faces showing amid fawn folds of homespun. Identically swaddled herself, Marcia formed up her little convoy of daughters and servant escort, and led it through the door into the street.

They had lived in this modest house on the lower Germalus of the Palatine since Father Sextus had bestowed it upon his younger son, Gaius, together with five hundred *iugera* of good land between Bovillae and Aricia—a sufficient endowment to ensure that Gaius and his family would have the wherewithal to maintain a seat in the Senate. But not, alas, the wherewithal to climb the rungs of the *cursus honorum*, the ladder of honor leading up to the praetorship and consulship.

Father Sextus had had two sons and not been able to bear parting with one; a rather selfish decision, since it meant his property—already dwindled because he too had had a sentimental sire and a younger brother who also had to be provided for—was of necessity split between Sextus, his elder son, and Gaius, his younger son. It had meant that neither of his sons could attempt the *cursus honorum,* be praetor and consul.

Brother Sextus had not been as sentimental as Father Sextus; just as well! He and his wife, Popillia, had produced three sons, an intolerable burden for a senatorial family. So he had summoned up the necessary steel to part with his eldest boy, given him up for adoption to the childless Quintus Lutatius Catulus, thereby making a fortune for himself as well as ensuring that his eldest son would come into a fortune. Old Catulus the adopter was fabulously wealthy, and very pleased to pay over a huge sum for the chance to adopt a boy of patrician stock, great good looks, and a reasonable brain. The money the boy had brought Brother Sextus—his real father—had been carefully invested in land and in city property, and hopefully would produce sufficient income to allow both of Brother Sextus's younger sons a chance at the senior magistracies.

Strong-minded Brother Sextus aside, the whole trouble with the Julius Caesars was their tendency to breed more than one son, and then turn sentimental about the predicament more than one son embroiled them in; they were never able to rule their hearts, give up some of their too-profuse male offspring for adoption, and see that the children they kept married into lots of money. For this reason had their once-vast landholdings shrunk with the passing of the centuries, progressively split into smaller and smaller parcels to provide for two and three sons, and some of it sold to provide dowries for daughters.

Marcia's husband was just such a Julius Caesar—a sentimentally doting parent, too proud of his sons and too enslaved by his daughters to be properly, Romanly sensible. The older boy should have been adopted out and both girls should have been promised in marriage to rich men years ago; the younger son should also have been contracted to a rich bride. Only money made a high political career possible. Patrician blood had long become a liability.

It was not a very auspicious sort of New Year's Day. Cold, windy, blowing a fine mist of rain that slicked the cobbles dangerously and intensified the stale stench of an old burning in the air. Dawn had come, late because sunless, and this was one Roman holiday the ordinary people would prefer to spend in a cramped confinement indoors, lying on their straw pallets playing the ageless game they called Hide the Sausage.

Had the weather been fine, the streets would have been thronged with people from all walks of life going to a favorite vantage point from which to view the pomp in the Forum Romanum and on the Capitol; as it was, Marcia and her daughters found it easy walking, their servant escort not needing to use brute force in making a way for the ladies.

The tiny alley in which the house of Gaius Julius Caesar lay opened onto the Clivus Victoriae not far above the Porta Romulana, the ancient gate in the ancient Palatine city's walls, vast blocks of stone laid down by Romulus himself, now overgrown or built upon or carved up with the graffitic initials of six hundred years of tourists. Turning right to ascend the Clivus Victoriae toward the corner where the Palatine Germalus looked down upon the Forum Romanum, the ladies reached their destination five minutes later, a piece of vacant land occupying the best spot of all.

Twelve years earlier one of the finest houses in Rome had stood there. Nowadays the site bore little evidence of its previous dwelling, just an occasional stone half-buried in grass. The view was splendid; from where the servants set up campstools for Marcia and the two Julias, the women had an unobstructed vista before them of Forum Romanum and Capitol, with the seething declivity of the Subura adding definition to the northern hills of the city's horizon.

"Did you hear?" asked that Caecilia who was the wife of the merchant banker Titus Pomponius. Very pregnant, she was sitting nearby with her Aunt Pilia; they lived next but one down the street from the Caesars.

"No, what?" asked Marcia, leaning forward.

"The consuls and priests and augurs started just after midnight, to make sure they'd finish the prayers and rites in time—"

"They always do that!" said Marcia, interrupting. "If they make a mistake, they have to start all over again."

"I know, I know, I'm not *that* ignorant!" said Caecilia tartly, annoyed because she knew she was being put in her place by a praetor's daughter. "The thing is, they didn't make a mistake! The auspices were bad. Lightning four times on the right, and an owl inside the augural place screeching as if being murdered. And now the weather—it's not going to be a good year, *or* a good pair of consuls."

"Well, I could have told you that without benefit of owls or lightning," said Marcia, whose father had not lived to be consul, but as *praetor urbanus* had built the great aqueduct which brought sweet fresh water into Rome, and kept his memory green as one of the all-time greats in government. "A miserable assortment of candidates to begin with, and even then the electors couldn't pick the best of such a shabby lot. I daresay Marcus Minucius Rufus will try, but Spurius Postumius Albinus! They've always been inadequate."

"Who?" asked Caecilia, who wasn't very bright.

"The Postumius Albinus clan," said Marcia, her eyes darting to her daughters to make sure they were all right; they had spotted four girls belonging to two of the Claudius Pulchers—such a tribe of them, it was never possible to keep them all straight! And they usually weren't straight. But these girls gathered on the site of the Flaccus house had all gone to school together as children, and it was impossible to erect social barriers against a caste almost as aristocratic as the Julius Caesars. Especially when the Claudius Pulchers also perpetually battled the enemies of the old nobility, too many children allied to dwindling land and money. Now her two Julias had moved their campstools down to where the other girls sat unsupervised—where *were* their mothers? Oh. Talking to Sulla. Shady! That settled it.

"Girls!" Marcia called sharply.

Two draped heads turned to look at her.

"Come back here," she said, and added, "at once."

They came.

"Mama, please can't we stay with our friends?" asked young Julilla, eyes pleading.

"No," said Marcia, in the tone which indicated That Was That.

Down below in the Forum Romanum the procession was forming, as the long crocodile which had wended its way from the house of Marcus Minucius Rufus met up with the equally long crocodile originating at the house of Spurius Postumius Albinus. The knights came first, not as many as on a fine sunny New Year's Day, but a respectable enough gathering of seven hundred or so; as the light improved but the rain grew a trifle harder, they moved off up the slope of the Clivus Capitolinus to where, at the first bend in this short and hilly track, the priests and slaughter-men waited with two flawless white bulls on spangled halters, their horns gilded and their dewlaps garlanded. At the rear of the knights strolled the twenty-four lictors of the new consuls. After the lictors came the consuls themselves, and after them the Senate, those who had held senior magistracies in purple-bordered togas, the rest of the House in plain white togas. And last of all came those who did not by rights belong there, sightseers and a host of the consuls' clients.

Nice, thought Marcia. Perhaps a thousand men walked slowly up the ramp toward the temple of Jupiter Optimus Maximus, the Great God of Rome, rearing its impressive bulk in highest place of all on the more southerly of the two hills constituting the Capitol. The Greeks built their temples on the ground, but the Romans built theirs on lofty platforms with many steps, and the steps which led up to Jupiter Optimus Maximus were indeed many. Nice, thought Marcia again as the sacrificial animals and their escort joined the procession, and all went on together until at last they clustered as best they could in the restricted space before the great temple on high. Somewhere among them were her husband and her two sons, a part of the governing class of this mightiest of all cities of the world.

Somewhere among them too was Gaius Marius. As an ex-praetor, he wore the purple-bordered *toga praetexta,* and on his dark red senatorial shoes he wore the crescent-shaped buckle his praetorship permitted. Yet it wasn't enough. He had been a praetor five years earlier, should have been consul three years ago. But he knew now that he would never be allowed to run for the consulship. Never. Why? Because he wasn't good enough. That was the only reason why. Who had ever heard of a family called Marius? No one.

Gaius Marius was an upstart from the rural nowhere, a Military Man, someone who was said to have no Greek, and who still could be trapped by excitement or anger into putting upcountry inflections on his native Latin. It didn't matter that he could buy and sell half the Senate; it didn't matter that on a battlefield he could outgeneral both halves of the Senate. What did matter was blood. And his just wasn't good enough.

Gaius Marius hailed from Arpinum—not so many miles away

from Rome really, but dangerously close to the border between Latium and Samnium, and therefore a trifle suspect in its loyalties and leanings; the Samnites were still Rome's most obdurate enemies among the Italians. Full Roman citizenship had come late to Arpinum—only seventy-eight years ago—and the district still did not enjoy proper municipal status.

Ah, but it was so beautiful! Huddled in the foothills of the high Apennines, a fruitful valley cupping both the Liris and the Melfa rivers, where the grape grew with wonderful results for table as well as vintage, where the crops returned a hundred-and-fifty-fold, and the sheep were fat and the wool surprisingly fine. Peaceful. Green. Sleepy. Cooler than expected in summer, warmer than expected in winter. The water in both rivers was full of fish; the dense forests on the mountains ringing Arpinum's bowl around still yielded superb timber for ships and buildings. And there were pitch pines and torch pines, oaks to litter the ground with acorns for the pigs in autumn, fat hams and sausages and bacon fit to grace any noble table in Rome—which they often did.

Gaius Marius's family had been in Arpinum for centuries, prided itself upon its Latinity. Was Marius a Volscian name, a Samnite name? Did it have an Oscan ring to it, just because there were Samnites and Volsci called Marius? No! Marius was *Latin*. He, Gaius Marius, was as good as any of those lofty-nosed, haughty nobles who so delighted in putting him down. In fact— and this was what really hurt!—he was much better than any of them. His *feeling* told him so.

How could a man explain away a feeling? A feeling he hosted like a guest who refused to leave, no matter how inhospitably he behaved? It was a long, long time since that feeling had first moved inside his mind, time enough and more for the events of the ensuing years to have shown it its futility, prod it into moving out in despair. Yet it never had. It lived inside his mind today as vividly and indomitably as it had in the beginning, fully half a lifetime ago.

How strange the world was! thought Gaius Marius, looking closely into the glazed faces of the men wearing purple-bordered togas all around him in that dreary, mizzling hour after dawn. No, not a Tiberius or a Gaius Sempronius Gracchus among them! Pluck out Marcus Aemilius Scaurus and Publius Rutilius Rufus, and you were left with a gaggle of very little men. Yet all of them looked down on him—Gaius Marius—as a bumptious nobody with more gall than grace. Simply because they had the right blood in their veins. Any one of them knew if the right circumstances came into being, he might be entitled to call himself the First Man in Rome. Just as Scipio Africanus, Aemilius Paullus, Scipio Aemilianus, and perhaps a dozen others over the centuries of the Republic had been so called.

The First Man in Rome was not the best man; he was the first among other men who were his equals in rank and opportunity. And to be the First Man in Rome was something far better than kingship, autocracy, despotism, call it what you would. The First Man in Rome held on to that title by sheer pre-eminence, perpetually aware that his world was stuffed with others eager to supplant him—others who *could* supplant him, legally and bloodlessly, by producing a superior brand of pre-eminence. To be the First Man in Rome was more than being consul; consuls came and went at the rate of two a year. Where as the centuries of the Roman Republic passed, only the smallest handful of men would come to be hailed as the First Man in Rome.

At the moment Rome had no First Man; indeed, there had been no First Man since the death of Scipio Aemilianus nineteen years before. Marcus Aemilius Scaurus undoubtedly came closest, but he didn't have quite enough power—*auctoritas* they called it, a blend of power, authority, and fame peculiar to Rome—to merit the title, nor was the title applied to him. Save by himself!

There was a sudden reflexive stir and murmur among the crowd of senators; the senior consul, Marcus Minucius Rufus, was about to offer his white bull to the Great God, only it wasn't behaving itself, must have had the prescience to avoid its last manger of drugged fodder. Not a good year, everyone was saying it already. Poor omens during the night watch of the consuls, a miserable

day, and now the first of the two victims was snorting and plunging, had half a dozen sacerdotal underlings hanging on to his
horns and ears—silly fools, they should have put a ring through
his nose as a precaution. Stripped to the waist like the other attendants, the acolyte carrying the stunning hammer didn't wait
for the raising of the head toward the sky, followed by the dipping
of the head toward the earth; it could always be argued successfully later that the beast had lifted and lowered its head dozens of
times during its fight to survive. He stepped in and swung his iron
weapon up and down so quickly its shape was a blur. The dull
crack of the blow was followed immediately by another, the noise
of the bull's knees hitting the stone paving as it came down, all
sixteen hundred pounds of it. Then the half-naked axeman brought
his double-bladed instrument down into the neck and the blood
was pouring everywhere, some of it caught in the sacrificial cups,
most of it a steaming sticky river coursing off to nowhere, melting
and thinning amid the rain-soaked ground.

You could tell much about a man from how he reacted to the
shedding of blood, thought Gaius Marius, clinically remote, a half
smile curling the corners of his full mouth as he saw this one step
hastily aside, that one indifferent to the fact his left shoe was filling
up, another trying to pretend he wasn't on the verge of puking.

Ahhhhhh! *There* was the man to watch! The young yet fully
mature fellow on the outskirts of the knights, togate, yet minus
even a knight's stripe on the right shoulder of his tunic; he hadn't
been there long, and now he moved off again down the slope of
the Clivus Capitolinus toward the Forum. But not before Gaius
Marius had seen his extraordinary grey-white eyes glisten, flare,
drink up the sight of the blood redly, greedily. Positive he had
never seen the fellow before, Gaius Marius wondered who he
was; not a nobody, certainly. The kind of looks called epicene, a
beauty as much feminine as masculine, and such amazing coloring! Skin as white as milk, hair like the rising sun. Apollo incar-
nate. Was *that* who he had been? No. The god never existed with
eyes like the mortal man who had just left; his were the eyes of

someone who suffered, and there was no point in being a god if you had to suffer, was there?

Though the second bull was better drugged, it fought too, even harder. This time the hammerman didn't manage to strike true the first time, and the poor maddened creature turned in blind rage to charge. Then some thinking fellow grabbed the swaying bag of its scrotum, and in the single frozen instant his action afforded the slaughtermen, the hammerman and the axeman swung together. Down went the bull, spraying everyone within two dozen paces with blood, including both the consuls: Spurius Postumius Albinus was saturated; so was his younger brother, Aulus, standing just behind and to one side of him. Gaius Marius eyed them askance, wondering if the omen was what he thought it was. Bad news for Rome, anyway.

And still his unwelcome guest, the feeling, refused to go away; in fact, of late it had greatly increased in strength. As if the moment approached. The moment in which he, Gaius Marius, would become the First Man in Rome. Every particle of common sense in him—and there were many—screamed that his feeling was a traitor, a trap which would betray him and lead to ignominy and death. Yet he went on experiencing it, the ineradicable feeling that he would become the First Man in Rome. Ridiculous! argued the man of eminent good sense: he was forty-seven years old, he had limped in sixth and last among the six men elected as praetors five years ago, he was too old now to seek the consulship without benefit of name and a host of clients. His time had gone. Gone, gone, gone.

The consuls were finally being inaugurated; that pompous ass Lucius Caecilius Metellus Dalmaticus who rejoiced in the title of Pontifex Maximus was rattling off the concluding prayers, and soon the senior consul, Minucius Rufus, would have the herald call the Senate to meet inside the temple of Jupiter Optimus Maximus. There they would fix the date of the Latin Festival on the Alban Mount; discuss which of the provinces must receive new governors, and which prorogued governors; draw the lots apportioning the provinces, for the praetors as well as the consuls; some self-serving tribune of the plebs would start raving on about the People; Scaurus would squash the presumptuous fool like a beetle underfoot; and one of the many Caecilius Metelluses would drone interminably about the decline in the moral and ethical standards of Rome's younger generation, until dozens of voices from all around him told him to shut up and pull his head in. Same old Senate—same old People—same old Rome—same old Gaius Marius. Now forty-seven years old. Next year he'd be fifty-seven, the year after that sixty-seven, and then they'd shove him into the middle of a pyre of logs and kindling, and up he'd go in a puff of smoke. Goodbye, Gaius Marius, you upstart from the pigpens of Arpinum, you non-Roman.

Sure enough, the herald brayed his summons. Sighing, Gaius Marius began to move, lifting his head to see if there was anyone within footshot he could tread on heavily and feel good about doing so. No one. Of course. At which moment his eye caught the eye of Gaius Julius Caesar, who was smiling as if he knew exactly what Gaius Marius was thinking.

Arrested, Gaius Marius gazed back. Only a backbencher, but never mere lobby fodder, this most senior of the Julius Caesars left in the Senate now his older brother, Sextus, was dead. Tall, as erect as if he were a Military Man, wide in the shoulders still, his fine head of silver-gilt hair a fitting crown for his lined, handsome face. He wasn't young, had to be upward of fifty-five years old, but he looked as if he was going to become one of those desiccated ancients the patrician nobility produced with monotonous regularity, tottering off to every meeting of Senate or People at ninety-plus, and continuing to speak praiseworthy good sense. The sort you couldn't kill with a sacrificial axe. The sort who—when it was all boiled down—made Rome what Rome was, in spite of the plethora of Caecilius Metelluses. Better than the rest of the world put together.

"Which Metellus is going to harangue us today?" asked Caesar as they fell in beside each other and began to ascend the many steps of the temple.

"One still to earn his extra name," said Gaius Marius, his gigantic eyebrows leaping up and down like millipedes on pins. "Quintus Caecilius plain old Metellus, younger brother of our revered Pontifex Maximus."

"Why him?"

"Because he's going to run for consul next year, I think. So he's got to start making noises of the right kind now," said Gaius Marius, standing aside to permit the older man to precede him into the earthly dwelling place of the Great God, Jupiter Optimus Maximus—Jupiter Best and Greatest.

"I do believe you are correct," said Caesar.

The vast central room of the temple was reduced to semidarkness, so poor was the light outside, but the brick-red face of the Great God glowed as if illuminated from within. He was very old, made centuries before by the famous Etruscan sculptor Vulca out of terracotta, though gradually he had been gifted with an ivory robe, gold hair, gold sandals, gold thunderbolt, even silver skin on his arms and legs, and ivory nails on his fingers and toes. Only his face remained the color of that richly ruddy clay, clean-shaven in the Etruscan fashion Rome had inherited; his brainless shut-mouthed smile curved his lips up almost to his ears, and gave him the air of a fatuous parent determined to ignore the fact that his child was busy setting fire to the nursemaid.

On each side of the Great God's room opened another room, the left-hand one to house his daughter Minerva, the right-hand one to house his wife, Juno. Each lady had a wonderful statue of herself in gold and ivory within her *cella,* and each lady bore with resignation the presence of an uninvited guest, for when the temple was built two of the old gods refused to move out; Romans being Romans, they simply left the old gods there alongside the new.

"I wonder, Gaius Marius," said Caesar, "if you would care to share my dinner tomorrow afternoon?"

That was surprising! Gaius Marius blinked, using the fraction of time the action brought him to arrive at a conclusion. After something, was he? Undoubtedly. But it wouldn't be shoddy. And one thing no one could say about the Julius Caesars, that they were snobs. A Julius Caesar didn't need to be a snob. If you could trace your lineage straight back in the male line to Iulus, Aeneas, Anchises, and the goddess Venus, you were secure enough to find it no comedown to mix with anyone from a dockside worker to a Caecilius Metellus.

"Thank you, Gaius Julius," said Marius. "I would be very pleased to share your dinner."

Lucius Cornelius Sulla woke up before dawn on New Year's Day almost sober. He was lying exactly where he ought to be, he discovered, with his stepmother on his right side and his mistress on his left, but each lady—if one could be euphemistic enough so to call them—was turned with her back toward him, and fully clothed. This told him he had not been called upon to perform, a deduction reinforced by the fact that what had awakened him was a huge and exquisitely painful erection. For a moment he lay trying to stare his third eye looking straight up his belly at him out of its shameless countenance, but as usual he lost the unequal contest. Only one thing to do, gratify the ingrate. With this in mind, he put his right hand out and turned up the hem of his stepmother's robe, his left hand engaged upon the same business with his mistress. Whereupon both women, shamming sleep, reared up in the bed and began to belabor him with fists and tongues, drumming and drubbing unmercifully.

"What did I do?" he yelped, curling himself up into a defensive ball and shielding his groin, where his princely erection had collapsed like an empty wineskin.

They were only too eager to tell him—both at once. However, he was now remembering the reason for himself; just as well, for the two of them shrieking together made their explanation unintelligible. Metrobius, curse his eyes! Oh, but what eyes! Liquid-dark as polished jet, fringed with black lashes so long they could be curled around a finger. Skin like thick cream, black curls straying around his slender shoulders, and the sweetest arse in the world. Fourteen years old in time, a thousand years old in vice, the apprentice of old Scylax the actor—and a tease, a torment, a trollop, a tiger cub.

On the whole Sulla preferred women these days, but Metrobius was a case apart. The boy had come with Scylax to the party, dressed as Cupid to Scylax's raddled Venus, a ridiculous pair of little feathered wings strapped to his back and the tiniest skirt of Coan floss silk about his waist, dyed with some cheap imitation saffron that had run a little because the room was closely shuttered and stuffily hot, leaving orange-yellow stains down the insides of his thighs that served only to draw attention to what was hidden, but barely.

From that first glance he had fascinated Sulla, and Sulla had fascinated him. Well, how many men in the world besides Sulla had skin as white as snow and hair the color of the rising sun and eyes so pale they were almost white? Not to mention a face which had started a stampede in Athens a few years back, when an Aemilius who shall remain nameless had smuggled the penniless sixteen-year-old Sulla across on the packet to Patrae, and enjoyed his favors all the way from Patrae to Athens by the most prolonged route possible, right around the coast of the Peloponnese.

In Athens Sulla had been summarily dumped; the Aemilius was too important to have any slur attached to his masculinity. The Roman despised homosexuality; the Greek considered it the highest form of love. So what the one hid in fear and dread, the other flaunted before the eyes of his dazzled peers. As far as Sulla was concerned, however, the one soon turned out to be no better than the other, for there was absolutely no doubt that fear and dread added an element of spice—and a great deal more largesse. The Greeks, as he quickly learned, were loath to pay for what was readily available free of charge, even when the prize was as unusual as a Sulla. So he had blackmailed the Aemilius for a first-class fare back to Italy and Rome, and quit Athens forever.

Of course manhood had changed all that. Once his beard grew in sufficiently for him to have to shave daily, and he sprouted a chest of red-gold hair, his appeal to men faded—and the largesse along with it. Women, he discovered, were bigger fools and had a hankering to settle down which made them exploitable. As a child he had never really known many women, for his mother had died before he was old enough to form a memory of her he could cherish, and his father, an impoverished drunkard, cared little for either of his progeny. Sulla had a sister, Cornelia Sulla, two years older than he was; equally spectacular in looks, she had seized a chance of marriage with a very rich rustic from Picenum named Lucius Nonius, and gone north with him to enjoy whatever luxuries life in Picenum might hold. That left the sixteen-year-old Sulla to look after his father unaided, which affected the quality of their lives chiefly on the level of cleanliness.

Then when Sulla turned twenty-four, his father remarried. It was not the social event of the year, but it did bring a measure of relief to the young man, who had been used for years to having to find sufficient money to underwrite his father's bottomless thirst. For his father's new wife (by name Clitumna, by birth an Umbrian peasant) was the relict of a very rich merchant, and had managed to inherit all her dead husband's property by dint of destroying his will and packing his only child off to Calabria as the wife of an oil vendor.

Just what Clitumna saw in the decayed Sulla Senior at first was beyond his son; then Clitumna invited his son to share her commodious house on the Germalus of the Palatine, and promptly hopped out of her new husband's bed and into young Sulla's. Somewhere, he discovered at that moment, there did burn in him a small spark of loyalty and affection for his importunate parent, for he foisted Clitumna off as tactfully as possible and immediately moved out.

He had managed to save a very little, and found two rooms in a huge insula on the Esquiline near the Agger for a rent he could just afford: three thousand sesterces a year. This gave him a room for himself and another for his servant to sleep and cook in, plus the laundry labor of a girl who lived two floors higher up in the crumbling tenement and did for various tenants in all sorts of ways.

Once a week she took his dirty clothing down the alley to where a crossroads widened the maze of streets into a tiny, irregular square; in it were a shrine of the crossroads, a clubhouse where the crossroads sodality met, and a fountain spewing a continuous trickle of water out of the mouth of an ugly old Silanus into a stone-bottomed pool donated to the city—one of many—by that grand old man of history, Cato the Censor, a man as practical as he had been lowborn. Fighting for elbow room, she pounded Sulla's tunics on the stones, borrowed the assistance of another washerwoman to wring every garment bone-dry (having performed the same service for her fellow), and then brought him back his laundry neatly folded. Her price was simple; a quick in-and-out and none the wiser, especially the sour old bird she lived with.

At which point he met Nicopolis. Victory City, her name meant in her native Greek. She was certainly that to him, for she was a widow, comfortably off, and in love with him to the point of madness. The only trouble was that while she was happy to support him in lavish fashion, she was far too shrewd to give him an allowance. The twin, he recognized gloomily, of his stepmother, Clitumna. Women were fools, but they were clever fools. Either that, or he was far too transparent.

Two years after he had moved out of Clitumna's splendid house, his father died, having guzzled himself with unalloyed happiness into terminal liver disease; and if he had been the price Clitumna was prepared to pay in order to catch his son, then her ruse worked at last, especially after Sulla discovered that Clitumna was not at all averse to sharing his favors—and her bed—with Nicopolis the Greek tart. The three of them settled down into a cozy relationship in the house on the Palatine, a relationship which had only one occasional marring element, Sulla's weakness for young boys. It was not, he assured his two women, a serious weakness; he had no taste for the innocent, no desire to seduce the sons of senators as they cavorted on the exercise fields of the Campus Martius, playing at fencing with their wooden swords and vaulting on and off the backs of stuffed bolsters saddled just like real horses. No,

Sulla liked trollops, the professional pretty-boys up to every trick in town; the truth was, they reminded him of himself at the same age.

But because his women detested his trollops, and he was in spite of his sexual appetites very much a man, he resisted his urges in this direction for the sake of domestic harmony, or else made sure he indulged himself mighty far away from the ken of Clitumna and Nicopolis. Until New Year's Eve, the last hours of the consulship of Publius Cornelius Scipio Nasica and Lucius Calpurnius Bestia, the last hours before the commencement of the consulship of Marcus Minucius Rufus and Spurius Postumius Albinus. The Eve of Metrobius, it was likely to come to be called, if Clitumna and Nicopolis had anything to do with it.

The three of them adored the theater, but not the highbrow Greek stuff of Sophocles and Aeschylus and Euripides, all masks and groaning throbbing voices and high-flown poetry. No, they loved comedy—the giggle-gorged Latin larkery of Plautus and Naevius and Terence; and above all else the simple, maskless idiocy of the pure mime, with its naked strumpets, clumsy fools, clarion farts, elaborate practical jokes, improbable plots made up on the spur of the moment from traditional repertoires. Tall daisies stuck in arses wiggle-waggled; the movement of one finger was more eloquent than a thousand words; blindfolded fathers-in-law mistook tits for ripe melons; the adulteries were insane and the gods drunk—nothing was sacred in the name of Mimus.

They were friends with every comedic actor and director in Rome, didn't consider they threw a good party unless a cluster of "names" were present. As far as they were concerned, the tragic theater didn't exist—and in that they were true Romans, for Romans adored a good laugh.

So to the party at Clitumna's house on New Year's Eve were invited Scylax, Astera, Milo, Pedocles, Daphne, and Marsyas. It was of course a costume party; Clitumna reveled in dressing up, so did Nicopolis, and Sulla liked female impersonation of a certain kind, the kind where the onlooker can laugh at the antics of a patent man mocking women.

Sulla had therefore got himself up as Medusa the Gorgon, complete with a wig of genuine living snakelets that had the whole room screaming in terror every time he lowered his head and threatened to charge, and a flowing mass of draperies in Coan floss silk that showed the guests his biggest snake all too clearly. His stepmother came as an ape, which meant she capered and scratched in a hairy coat, and bared blue-painted buttocks. Rather more orthodox because she was rather more beautiful than Clitumna, Nicopolis tricked herself out as Diana of the Grove, thus exposing her long slender legs and one perfect breast as she cavorted about to make the tinny arrows in her quiver rattle in time to the music of flutes, pipes, bells, lyres, and drums.

The party got off to a swinging start. Sulla in his snaky getup was an undeniable success, but Clitumna the Ape was funniest. The wine flowed; the laughter and shrieks burst out of the peristyle-garden at the back of the house and drove all the conservative neighbors mad long before New Year's Eve became New Year's Day. Then, last guest to arrive, Scylax teetered through the door in cork-soled platform sandals, a golden-blonde wig, huge tits inflating his gorgeous gown, and the maquillage of an old whore. Poor Venus! In tow as his Cupid came Metrobius.

Sulla's biggest snake took one look and stood up in less than a second, which didn't please the Ape or Diana of the Grove. Nor for that matter did it please Venus Scylax. And there ensued scenes as frenzied as any that ever enlivened farce or mime: a bouncing blue bottom, a bouncing bared breast, a bouncing blonde wig, a bouncing biggest snake, and a bouncing befeathered boy. Culminating in the best bounce of all, which was Metrobius and Sulla enjoying a little buggery in a corner they had fancied more secluded than it actually was.

He had known, of course, that he was making a ghastly mistake; but knowing it didn't help in the least. From the moment he'd seen the dye running down those silky legs and the length of the lashes round those lustrous, night-dark eyes, Sulla had been finished, rolled up, hopelessly conquered. And when he brushed his hand across the little frilly skirt the boy wore and lifted it just enough to see how beautiful and hairless and dusky-hued was the endowment beneath, there was nothing else in the world he could do save what he did do, pull the boy into a corner behind a large pouffe and have him.

Farce almost turned into tragedy. Clitumna took up a rare goblet of Alexandrian glass, broke it, and went in real earnest for Sulla's face. Whereupon Nicopolis went for Clitumna with a wine jug, and Scylax went for Metrobius with one of his cork-soled platform sandals. Everyone else stopped partying to watch, enchanted. Luckily Sulla was not drunk enough to have lost his extraordinary physical competence, so he dealt with the lot of them briskly and harshly: gave Scylax a wallop on one lavishly painted eye that bruised it for a month, administered the sharp ends of a quiverful of arrows to Diana's long bare legs, and turned Clitumna upside down across his knee to make her bare buttocks as black as they were blue. After which he kissed the boy a lingering tongue-borne thank-you, and took himself off to bed in a mood of towering disgust.

It was only at dawn on New Year's Day that Sulla understood what was really the matter. Not farce. Not even comedy. A tragedy as strange and hideously convoluted as anything Sophocles ever imagined in his worst bout of despair at the antics of gods and men. Today, New Year's Day, was Sulla's birthday. He was exactly thirty years old.

And he turned then to look at the two brawling bawling women in the bed, no trace of his Medusa of the night before now remaining, and he looked at them with such icy anger and pain and loathing that they stilled immediately to stone, and sat incapable of moving while he dressed in a fresh white tunic and had a slave drape his toga around him, a garment he hadn't worn in years save to the theater. Only when he had gone did the women regain power to move, and then they stared at each other and blubbered noisy tears; not for their own grief, but for his, which they didn't even begin to understand.

The truth was that Lucius Cornelius Sulla, thirty today, was living a lie. Had always lived a lie. The world in which he had dwelled for thirty years—a world inhabited by drunkards and beggars, actors and whores, charlatans and freedmen—was not his world at all.

Rome was full of men bearing the family name Cornelius. But they had come to be called Cornelius because a father or a grandfather or however many generations back had once belonged, slave or peasant, to a patrician high aristocrat named Cornelius. When that patrician Cornelius emancipated them from their bondage in honor of a marriage or a birthday or a funeral, or because the purchase price of freedom had been saved up out of wages, they took his name, and so became Cornelius too. All those named Cornelius were clients of some patrician Cornelius because they owed him thanks for the citizenship which had come to them along with his name.

Excepting Clitumna and Nicopolis, the people Lucius Cornelius Sulla knew automatically assumed he was just such a Cornelius, the son or grandson or however many generations back of a Cornelian slave or peasant; with his barbaric coloring, more likely by far to be slave than peasant. After all, there were patrician noblemen called Cornelius Scipio and Cornelius Lentulus and Cornelius Merula, but who ever *heard* of a patrician Cornelius Sulla? No one even knew what the word "Sulla" meant!

But the truth was that Lucius Cornelius Sulla, enrolled by the censors according to his means among the *capite censi,* the Head Count masses of Rome owning absolutely no property, was a patrician nobleman, the son of a patrician nobleman, the grandson of a patrician nobleman, and so on through every generation going back to the days before the founding of Rome. His birth made Sulla eminently eligible for the full glory of the political ladder, the *cursus honorum.* By birth, the consulship was his.

His tragedy lay in his penuriousness, the inability of his father to provide either the income or the property necessary to enroll his son among even the lowest of the five economic classes; all his father had bequeathed him was the raw and simple citizenship itself. Not for Lucius Cornelius Sulla the purple stripe on the right shoulder of his tunic, knight-narrow or senator-broad. There were those who knew him had heard him say his tribe was the Cornelia, and laughed him to scorn. Assuming he was of slave origins, they knew his tribe had to be either urban Esquilina or urban Suburana. For rural Cornelia was one of the four oldest of the thirty-five Roman tribes, and did not number members of the Head Count among it.

On this thirtieth birthday Sulla should have been entering the Senate—either as an elected quaestor approved by the censors, or else as his birthright, appointed by the censors without their requiring him to be elected quaestor.

Instead, he was the kept plaything of two vulgar women, and there was not a single hope in the world that he would ever command the sort of fortune which would enable him to exercise his birthright. Next year was a censors' year—oh, to be able to present himself at the censors' tribunal in the Forum Romanum and show the censors proof that he had property yielding him an income of a million sesterces a year! That was the senator's minimum. Or even property yielding an income of four hundred thousand sesterces a year! That was the knight's minimum. As things stood in reality, he owned no property at all, and his income had never exceeded ten thousand sesterces in a year, even now he was kept by women. The definition of abject poverty in Rome was the inability to own one slave, and that meant that there had been times in his life when Sulla was abjectly poor. He, a patrician Cornelius.

During those two years of brave defiance when he had lived in the insula up the Esquiline near the Agger, he had been forced to seek work on the wharves of the Port of Rome below the Wooden Bridge, had humped jars of wine and emptied urns of wheat in order to keep that one slave who indicated to the world that he was not abjectly poor. For as he grew older, so did his pride increase—or rather, his consciousness of its utter humiliation. He had never succumbed to the urge to get a steady job, learn a trade in some foundry or carpenter's shop, or become a scribe, act as a merchant's secretary, or copy manuscripts for a publishing house or lending library. When a man labored on the wharves or in the market gardens or on some construction project, no one asked questions; when a man went to the same place of work each day, everyone asked questions. Sulla could not even enlist in the army—a man had to be propertied for that too. Entitled by his birth to lead an army, Sulla had never handled a sword, straddled a horse, or cast a spear, even on the training fields and exercise yards around the Villa Publica on the Campus Martius. He, a patrician Cornelius.

Perhaps had he gone to some remote patrician Cornelian relation and begged, the situation might have been remedied by the tendering of a massive loan. But pride—which could stomach being kept by vulgar women—balked at begging. For there were no patrician Cornelians of the Sullan branch left, only distant Cornelians indifferent to his plight. Better to be a nobody and owe nobody than a somebody groaning under the cliental obligations of a massive loan. He, a patrician Cornelius.

Exactly where he intended to go when he flung out of the door of his stepmother's house, he had no idea. Only to snuff the damp air, walk off his anguish. Clitumna had chosen an odd place to live, given her background: in a street of successful advocates and backbencher senators and middle-income knights, too low down on the Palatine Germalus to afford a view, yet conveniently close to the political and business hub of the city, the Forum Romanum and its surrounding basilicae and marketplaces and colonnades. Of course Clitumna liked the safety of this location, far from the stews of the Subura with its concomitant crime, but her noisy parties and dubious friends had led to many an irate deputation from her neighbors, who preferred peace and quiet. On one side of her was the exceedingly prosperous merchant banker and company director Titus Pomponius, and on the other side lived Gaius Julius Caesar, a senator.

Not that they saw much of each other. That was one of the benefits (or drawbacks, viewed conversely) of inward-looking houses, with their windowless outer walls and a central court— the peristyle-garden—shielded from the neighbors by the rooms entirely surrounding it. But there was no doubt that when Clitumna's parties spilled out of her dining room into the open court of the peristyle-garden, the cacophony penetrated far beyond the boundaries of her property, and made her the chief district nuisance.

Dawn had broken. Ahead of him Sulla could see Gaius Julius Caesar's women tittupping along on the high cork soles and higher cork heels of their winter shoes, sweet little feet elevated above the water in the middens. Going to watch the inauguration ceremony, he supposed, slowing his pace and regarding their closely wrapped forms with the unself-conscious appreciation of a man whose sexual urges were powerful and all-pervading. The wife was a Marcia, daughter of the builder of the Aqua Marcia, and not much above forty. Well, forty-five. Still slim and well cared for, tall, a brown lady with more than her share of good looks. Yet she couldn't rival her daughters. They were true Julias, blonde beauties both, though for Sulla's money it was the younger one took the laurels. For he had seen them from time to time going off to the market to shop with their eyes; their purses, as well he knew, were slender as their bodies. That was a family kept itself senatorial only by the skin of its teeth. The knight Titus Pomponius, Clitumna's neighbor on the other side, was more affluent by far.

Money. It ruled the world. Without it, a man was nothing. Little wonder then that when a man levered himself into any position where he could snatch at the chance to enrich himself, he always, always did. For a man to enrich himself through the medium of politics, he had to secure election as a praetor; his fortune was made in that moment, the years of outlay finally paid dividends. For the praetor went to govern a province, and there he was a god, he could help himself. If possible, he fought a little war against some barbarian tribe on the borders, took their gold and their sacred treasures, sold the captives of his sword into slavery, and pocketed the proceeds. But if the war prospects were dismal, there were other avenues: he could deal in grain and various staple commodities, he could lend money at exorbitant rates of interest (and use his army to collect the debt if necessary), he could doctor the account books when the taxes were gathered, he could dole out Roman citizenships for a price, he could accept illicit fees for everything from issuing government contracts to exempting some local city from its tribute to Rome.

Money. How to get it? How to get *enough* of it to enter the Senate? Dreams, Lucius Cornelius Sulla! Dreams!

When Caesar's women turned right onto the Clivus Victoriae, Sulla knew where they were going. To the *area Flacciana,* the site of Flaccus's house. By the time he halted on the street above its steep slope of tired winter grass, the Julian ladies were settling themselves upon campstools, and a sturdy Thracian-looking fellow who had led their slave escort was busy erecting an open-fronted tent of hide to shelter his mistress from the rain, marginally heavier. The two Julias, Sulla noted, spent a very brief time sitting demurely alongside their mother; when she began to speak to Titus Pomponius's very pregnant wife, they picked up their folding stools and scampered down to where four Claudius Pulcher girls were sitting a considerable distance away from their mothers. Their mothers? Ah! Licinia and Domitia. Both women he knew quite well, since he had managed to sleep with each of them. Looking neither left nor right, he walked down the slope to where the two women sat.

"Ladies," he said, inclining his head. "Miserable day."

Every woman on the hill knew who he was—a painfully interesting aspect of Sulla's predicament. His friends among the canaille always assumed he was one of them, but the Roman nobility didn't make that mistake. *They* knew he was the genuine article! *They* knew his history and his ancestry. Some were moved to pity him; a few like Licinia and Domitia would amuse themselves with him sexually; but none would *help* him.

The wind was blowing from the northeast, and it brought upon its breath a sour reek of dead fire, a smell compounded of wet charcoal, burned lime, buried rotted bodies in the high thousands. Last summer all of the Viminal and the upper Esquiline had gone up in flames, the worst fire anyone in Rome could remember. Perhaps a fifth of the city had burned before the united populace had managed to demolish a sufficiently wide swath of buildings to cut the conflagration off from the jam-packed tenement insulae of the Subura and the lower Esquiline; the wind and the width of the Vicus Longus had prevented its spreading to the sparsely settled outer Quirinal, the northernmost of the hills within the Servian Walls.

Even though half a year had elapsed since the fire, from where Sulla stood now on Flaccus's empty house site its terrible scar covered the heights beyond the Macellum market for a thousand paces, a full square mile of blackened ground, half-fallen buildings, desolation. How many people had died, no one knew. Sufficient anyway for there to have been no real housing shortage afterward. So the rebuilding was slow; only here and there did wooden scaffolds rear up a hundred and more feet, the sign of a new multistoreyed insula going up to fatten the purse of some city landlord.

Highly amused, Sulla sensed the tension in Licinia and Domitia the moment they realized who was greeting them; not for anything would he be merciful and leave them in peace. Let them suffer, silly sows! I wonder, does each of them know I've slept with both of them? he asked himself, and decided they did not. Which added a deliciously piquant tang to the encounter. Eyes dancing, he watched their covert glances toward each other and toward the few women like Marcia who shared the place with them. Oh, not *Marcia*! Pillar of rectitude! Monument of virtue!

"That was an awful week," said Licinia, voice pitched too high, her eyes fixed unswervingly upon the burned hills.

"Yes," said Domitia, clearing her throat.

"I was terrified!" babbled Licinia. "We lived on the Carinae then, Lucius Cornelius, and the fire kept rolling closer and closer. Naturally the moment it was out, I persuaded Appius Claudius to move over to this side of the city. Nowhere is safe from fire, but there can be no doubt it's better to have the Forum and the Swamp between oneself and the Subura!"

"It was beautiful," said Sulla, remembering how he had stood every night of that week at the top of the Vestal Steps to watch, pretending that what he saw in all its monstrous glory was an enemy city after a sack, and he the general of Rome who had ordered it. "Beautiful!" he repeated.

The gloating way in which he said the word made Licinia glance up at his face in spite of herself, and what she saw there made her glance away again very quickly, and bitterly regret ever placing herself in this man's power. Sulla was too dangerous, and not quite right in the head.

"Still, it's an ill wind blows nobody any good," she labored on brightly. "My cousins Publius and Lucius Licinius bought up a lot of the vacant land afterward. They say its value is bound to soar in years to come."

She was a Licinius Crassus, one of the millionaires many times over. Now why couldn't *he* find himself a rich bride, as her particular Appius Claudius Pulcher had done? Simple, Sulla! Because no father or brother or guardian of a rich noble girl would ever consent to such a match.

His delight in playing with the women vanished; without a word he turned on his heel and stalked up the slope toward the Clivus Victoriae. The two Julias, he noticed as he passed, had been called to order, and sat again beside their mother under the lee of the hide shelter. His strange eyes flicked over them, dismissing Julia Big Sister, but dwelling appreciatively on Julia Little Sister. Ye gods, she was lovely! A honey cake soaked in nectar, a dish fit for an Olympian. He had a pain in his chest, and rubbed himself under his toga to force it away. But he was aware nonetheless that Julia Little Sister had turned on her campstool to watch him until he disappeared.

He descended the Vestal Steps to the Forum Romanum and walked up the Clivus Capitolinus until he came to the back of the crowd in front of the temple of Jupiter Optimus Maximus. One of his peculiar talents was his ability to set up shivers of disquiet in people who surrounded him, so that they moved away from his vicinity; mostly he employed it to gain himself a good seat in the theater, but now he put his talent to opening up access to the front of the crowd of knights, where he stood with a perfect view of the place of sacrifice. Though he had no right to be there, he knew no one would ever evict him. Few of the knights knew who he was, and even among the senators were faces unfamiliar to him, but there were enough men present who did know him to ensure that his presence would be tolerated.

Some things no amount of isolation from the mainstream of noble public life could eradicate; perhaps they were, after so many generations—a thousand years of generations—actually inside the blood, little warning bells sounding knells of doom or disaster. Of choice he had never bothered to follow the political goings-on in the Forum Romanum, having concluded it was better to be ignorant than to chafe to participate in a life he could not have. And yet, standing at the front of the ranks of knights, he knew it was going to be a bad year. His blood told him this was to be another in what had proven to be a long line of bad years, ever since Tiberius Sempronius Gracchus had been murdered, and then, ten years later, his brother Gaius Gracchus forced to take his own life. Knives had flashed in the Forum, and Rome's luck was broken.

It was almost as if Rome was dwindling away, running out of political puff. A gathering, he thought, eyes sweeping over the assembled ranks, of mediocrities and nonentities. Men stood there, half-asleep on their feet despite the chilly drizzle, who had been responsible for the deaths of more than thirty thousand precious Roman and Italian soldiers in less than ten years, most in the name of personal greed. Money again. Money, money, money. Though power entered into it too. One should never forget or underestimate power. Which drove which? Which was the means, which the end? That probably depended upon the individual. But where in this sorry lot were the great ones, the ones who would enhance rather than diminish Rome?

The white bull was behaving badly. Little wonder, looking at the consuls of the year. I for one, he thought, would not willingly put *my* white neck under the chopper for the likes of Spurius Postumius Albinus, patrician though he might be. And where did they get their money from, anyway? Then he remembered. The Postumius Albinuses *always* married money. Curse their eyes.

Blood began to flow. There was a great deal of blood in a fully grown bull. What a waste. Potency, power, pile-driver force. But what a beautiful color, richly crimsoned, slick yet thick, coursing downhill among the feet. It fascinated him; he couldn't tear his gaze away. Was everything crammed with energy always some shade of red? Fire. Blood. Hair—*his* hair. Penises. Senatorial shoes. Muscle. Molten metal. Lava.

Time to go. Go where? Still full of the vision of so much blood, his eyes lifted, encountered the steady fierce stare of a tall senator in the *toga praetexta* of a senior magistrate. Amazing! Now that was a man! But *who*? He didn't have the look of any of the Famous Families; isolated from his kind though he was, Sulla yet knew their distinctive physical features unerringly.

Whoever the fellow was, he certainly didn't belong to a Famous Family. For one thing, his nose said he had a dollop of Celt in him; it was too short and straight to belong to a pure Roman. Picenum, then? And look at those gigantic eyebrows! Celt again. His face bore two battle scars, neither disfiguring. Yes, a formidable customer, fierce and proud and intelligent. A real eagle. *Who?* Not a consular, them Sulla knew down to the oldest one living. A praetor then. Not one of this year's praetors, however, for they were clotted together behind the consuls looking tremendously dignified and about as promising as an old queen with a bad dose of piles.

Aaaaaaah! Sulla turned abruptly and stalked away from all of it, including the ex-praetor with the mien of an eagle. Time to go. Go where? Where else was there to go save the only refuge he had, between the moistly ageing bodies of his stepmother and his mistress? He shrugged, sneered. There were worse fates, worse places. But not, said a voice at the back of his mind, for a man who should be entering the Senate today.

 The trouble with being an anointed sovereign visiting the city of Rome was that one could not cross its *pomerium,* its sacred boundary. So Jugurtha, King of Numidia, was forced to spend his New Year's Day kicking his heels in the outrageously expensive villa he was renting on the higher slopes of the Pincian Hill, overlooking the huge bend in the Tiber which enclosed the Campus Martius. The agent who had secured the villa for him had raved about its outlook, the view into the distance of the Janiculum and the Vatican Hill, the green sward of both the little Tiber-bounded plains, Martius and Vaticanus, the broad blue band of the big river. Bet there were no rivers the size of dear old Father Tiber in Numidia! the presumptuous little agent had burbled, all the while concealing the fact that he was acting for a senator who professed undying loyalty to Jugurtha's cause, yet was mighty anxious to close a deal for his villa that would keep him well supplied with the most costly of freshwater eels for months to come. Why did they think any man—let alone a king!—who was not a Roman was automatically a fool and a dupe? Jugurtha was well aware of who owned the villa, well aware too that he was being swindled in the matter of its rent; but there were times and places for frankness, and Rome at the moment when he closed the deal for the villa was not a place or a time for frankness.

From where he sat on the loggia in front of the vast peristyle-garden, his view was unimpeded. But to Jugurtha it was a small view, and when the wind was right the stench of the nightsoil fertilizing the market gardens of the outer Campus Martius around the Via Recta was strong enough to make him wish he had elected to live further out, somewhere around Bovillae or Tusculum. Used to the enormous distances of Numidia, he thought the fifteen-mile ride from Bovillae or Tusculum into Rome a mere trifle. And—since it turned out he could not enter the city anyway—what was the point in being housed close enough to spit over their accursed sacred boundary?

If he turned ninety degrees he could, of course, see the back cliffs of the Capitol and the wrong end of the mighty temple of Jupiter Optimus Maximus—in which, at this very moment, his agents assured him, the new consuls were holding the first senatorial meeting of their year in office.

How did one deal with the Romans? If he only knew that, he wouldn't be the worried man he admitted to himself he was.

In the beginning it had seemed simple enough. His grandfather had been the great Masinissa, who had forged the Kingdom of Numidia out of the wreckage left strewn up and down two thousand miles of North African coast by Rome's defeat of Punic Carthage. At first Masinissa's gathering of power to himself had been with the open connivance of Rome; though later, when he had grown uncomfortably powerful and the Punic flavor of his organization gave Rome flutters of disquiet about the rise of a new Carthage, Rome turned somewhat against him. Luckily for Numidia, Masinissa had died at the right moment, and, understanding only too well that a strong king is always succeeded by a weakling, he left Numidia to be divided by Scipio Aemilianus among his three sons. Clever Scipio Aemilianus! He didn't carve up Numidia's territory into thirds; he carved up the kingly duties instead. The eldest got custody of the treasury and the palaces; the middle son was appointed Numidia's war leader; and the youngest inherited all the functions of law and justice. Which meant the son with the army didn't have the money to foment rebellion, the son with the money didn't have the army to foment rebellion, and the son with the law on his side had neither money nor army to foment rebellion.

Before time and accumulating resentment might have fomented rebellion anyway, the two younger sons died, leaving the oldest son, Micipsa, to rule on alone. However, both his dead brothers had left children to complicate the future: two legitimate sons, and a bastard named Jugurtha. One of these young men would ascend the throne when Micipsa died—but which one? Then late in his life the hitherto childless Micipsa produced two sons of his own, Adherbal and Hiempsal. Thus did the court seethe with rivalries, for the ages of all these potential heirs were skewed exactly the wrong way around. Jugurtha the bastard was the oldest of them all, and the sons of the reigning King were mere babies.

His grandfather Masinissa had despised Jugurtha, not so much because he was a bastard as because his mother was of the humblest stock in the kingdom: she was a nomad Berber girl. Micipsa inherited Masinissa's dislike of Jugurtha, and when he saw what a fine-looking and intelligent fellow Jugurtha had grown into, he found a way to eliminate this oldest potential contender for the throne. Scipio Aemilianus had demanded that Numidia send auxiliary troops to assist him at the siege of Numantia, so Micipsa dispatched his military levy under the command of Jugurtha, thinking Jugurtha would die in Spain.

It didn't turn out that way. Jugurtha took to war as born warriors do; besides which, he made immediate friends among the Romans, two of whom he was to prize as his best and dearest friends. They were junior military tribunes attached to the staff of Scipio Aemilianus, and their names were Gaius Marius and Publius Rutilius Rufus. All three were the same age, twenty-three.

At the close of the campaign, when Scipio Aemilianus summoned Jugurtha into his command tent to deliver a homily on the subject of dealing honorably with Rome rather than with any particular Romans, Jugurtha managed to keep a straight face. For if his exposure to Romans during the siege of Numantia had taught him anything about them, it was that almost all Romans who aspired to high public office were chronically short of money. In other words, they could be bought.

On his return to Numidia, Jugurtha carried a letter from Scipio Aemilianus to King Micipsa. It extolled the bravery, good sense, and superior intelligence of Jugurtha so much that old Micipsa put away the dislike he had inherited from his father. And about the time that Gaius Sempronius Gracchus died in the Grove of Furrina beneath the Janiculan Hill, King Micipsa formally adopted Jugurtha and raised him to senior status among the heirs to the Numidian throne. However, he was careful to indicate that Jugurtha must never become king; his role was to assume the guardianship of Micipsa's own sons, now entering their early adolescence.

Almost as soon as he had set this situation up, King Micipsa died, leaving two underage heirs to his throne and Jugurtha as regent. Within a year Micipsa's younger son, Hiempsal, was assassinated at Jugurtha's instigation; the older son, Adherbal, escaped Jugurtha's net and fled to Rome, where he presented himself to the Senate and demanded that Rome settle the affairs of Numidia and strip Jugurtha of all authority.

"Why are we so afraid of them?" Jugurtha demanded, turning from his thoughts back to the present moment, the veil of soft rain drifting across the exercise fields and market gardens and obscuring the far bank of the Tiber completely.

There were some twenty men on the loggia, but all save one were bodyguards. These were not gladiatorial hirelings, but Jugurtha's own men of Numidia—the same men, in fact, who had brought Jugurtha the head of young Prince Hiempsal seven years before, and followed up that gift five years later with the head of Prince Adherbal.

The sole exception—and the man to whom Jugurtha had addressed his question—was a big, Semitic-looking man not far short of Jugurtha in size, sitting in a comfortable chair alongside his king. An outsider might have deemed them closely related by blood, which in actual fact they were; though it was a fact the King preferred to forget. Jugurtha's despised mother had been a simple nomad girl from a backward tribe of the Gaetuli Berbers, a mere nothing of a girl who by some quirk of fate had owned a face and a body akin to Helen of Troy's. And the King's companion on this miserable New Year's Day was his half brother, son of his humble mother and the court baron to whom Jugurtha's father had married her for the sake of convenience. The half brother's name was Bomilcar, and he was very loyal.

"Why are we so afraid of them?" Jugurtha asked again, more urgently, more despairingly.

Bomilcar sighed. "The answer's simple, I would think," he said. "It wears a steel helmet a bit like a basin turned upside down, a brownish-red tunic, and over that a long shirt of knitted chain mail. It carries a silly little short sword, a dagger almost as big, and one or two tiny-headed spears. It isn't a mercenary. It isn't even a pauper. It's called a Roman infantryman."

Jugurtha grunted, ended in shaking his head. "Only a part of the answer, Baron. Roman soldiers are perishable; they die."

"They die very hard," said Bomilcar.

"No, there's more to it than that. I don't understand! You can buy them like bread in a bakery, and that ought to mean they're as soft inside as bread. But they aren't."

"Their leaders, you mean?"

"Their leaders. The eminent Conscript Fathers of the Senate. They are utterly corrupt! Therefore they ought to be crawling with decay. Soft to melting, insubstantial. But they aren't. They're as hard as flint, as cold as ice, as subtle as a Parthian satrap. They never give up. Take hold of one, tame him to servility, and the next moment he's gone, you're dealing with a different face in a different set of circumstances."

"Not to mention that all of a sudden there's one you need whom you can't buy—not because he doesn't have a price, but because whatever his price is, you don't have it—and I'm not referring to money," said Bomilcar.

"I loathe them all," said Jugurtha between his teeth.

"So do I. Which doesn't get rid of them, does it?"

"Numidia is mine!" cried its king. "They don't even want it, you know! All they want to do is interfere. *Meddle!*"

Bomilcar spread out his hands. "Don't ask me, Jugurtha, because I don't know. All I do know is that you are sitting here in Rome, and the outcome is on the laps of the gods."

Indeed it is, thought the King of Numidia, returning to his thoughts.

When young Adherbal had escaped and gone to Rome six years ago, Jugurtha had known what to do, and had done it quickly. Off to Rome went a team of his ambassadors bearing gold, silver, jewels, works of art, whatever was likely to tickle a Roman noble's fancy. Interesting, that you could never bribe them with women or boys. Only with negotiable goods. The outcome of his embassage had been reasonably satisfactory, given the circumstances.

They were obsessed with committees and commissions, the Romans, and enjoyed nothing better than to send off a small party of officials to the remotest ends of the earth, there to investigate, pontificate, adjudicate, ameliorate. Anyone else would just march in at the head of an army, but the Romans would turn up in togas escorted only by lictors, nary a soldier within emergency call; they would proceed to issue their orders, and expect to be obeyed just as if they had arrived at the head of an army. And mostly they were obeyed.

Which returned him to his original question: why *are* we so afraid of them? Because we are. We are. But why? Maybe because there's always a Marcus Aemilius Scaurus among them?

It had been Scaurus who prevented the Senate from deciding in favor of Jugurtha when Adherbal had gone bleating to Rome. A lone voice in a body of three hundred men! Yet he had prevailed, kept hammering away at them until he, the lone voice, actually won the lot of them over to his side. Thus it had been Scaurus who forced a compromise acceptable neither to Jugurtha nor to Adherbal: a committee of ten Roman senators led by the consular Lucius Opimius was to travel to Numidia and there—after investigations made on the spot—decide what to do. So what did the committee do? It divided the kingdom. Adherbal got the eastern end with Cirta as his capital, more closely populated and commercialized than, yet not as rich as, the western end. The western end had gone to Jugurtha, who found himself sandwiched between Adherbal and the Kingdom of Mauretania. Pleased with their solution, the Romans went home. Jugurtha promptly settled down to watch his mouse Adherbal, waiting his moment to pounce. And to protect himself on his west, he married the daughter of the King of Mauretania.

He waited patiently for four years, then attacked Adherbal and his army between Cirta and its seaport. Beaten, Adherbal fell back on Cirta and organized its defense, assisted by the large and influential contingent of Roman and Italian merchants who formed the backbone of the business sector in Numidia. There was nothing odd about their presence in the country; wherever you went in the world, you would find a contingent of Roman and Italian businessmen running the local commercial sector, even in places with little connection to Rome and no protection.

Of course the news of the outbreak of war between Jugurtha and Adherbal had reached the ears of the Senate in short order; the Senate responded by dispatching a committee of three charming young sons of senators (it would give the younger generation a bit of valuable experience; there was nothing very important in this squabble) to rap the Numidian knuckles. Jugurtha got to them first, maneuvered them out of any contact with Adherbal or the inhabitants of Cirta, and sent them home laden with expensive gifts.

Then Adherbal managed to smuggle a letter out to Rome, a letter begging for help; always on Adherbal's side, Marcus Aemilius Scaurus immediately set out himself for Numidia, at the head of yet another committee of investigation. But so dangerous was the situation they found in all Africa that they were forced to remain inside the boundaries of the Roman African province, and eventually were obliged to return to Rome without interviewing either of the rivals for the throne, or influencing the course of the war. Jugurtha then went ahead and captured Cirta. Understandably, Adherbal was executed at once. Less understandably, Jugurtha took out his spleen at Rome by executing the Roman and Italian businessmen of Cirta down to the last man; for in so doing, he outraged Rome beyond any hope of conciliation.

News of the massacre of the Romans and Italians resident in Cirta had reached Rome fifteen months ago, during autumn. And one of the tribunes-elect of the plebs, Gaius Memmius, created such a howl in the Forum that no amount of bribing by Jugurtha could avert catastrophe. The junior consul-elect, Lucius Calpurnius Bestia, was ordered to go to Numidia at the beginning of his term in office to show Jugurtha that he could not freely slaughter Romans and Italians.

But Bestia had been a bribable man, so Jugurtha bribed, with the result that six months ago he had managed to negotiate a peace with Rome, and hand over thirty war elephants to Bestia along with a small gift of money for the Roman treasury—and a much larger, undisclosed sum which found its way into Bestia's private coffers. Rome appeared to be satisfied; Jugurtha was undisputed King of all Numidia at last.

But Gaius Memmius, oblivious to the fact that his term as a tribune of the plebs was finished, never shut up. Day after day he pursued his campaign to have the whole Numidian question gone into under the harshest light; day after day he accused Bestia of extorting money from Jugurtha in return for tenure of the throne; and finally Gaius Memmius achieved his aim, which was to browbeat the Senate into acting. Off to Numidia the Senate sent the praetor Lucius Cassius Longinus, under instructions to bring King Jugurtha in person to Rome, where he was to be made to provide Gaius Memmius with the names of all those he had bribed throughout the years. Had he been required to answer before the Senate, the situation would not have been so perilous; but Jugurtha was to answer before the People.

When Cassius the praetor arrived in Cirta and served the King with his summons, Jugurtha could not refuse to accompany him back to Rome. Only *why*? Why were they all so afraid? What could Rome actually do? Invade Numidia? There were always more Bestias in office than there were Gaius Memmiuses! Why then were they all so afraid? Was it the gall of the Romans, that they could calmly dispatch a single man to snap his fingers at the ruler of a great and rich land, and bring him to heel?

Jugurtha had come to heel, meekly packed his trunks, tapped a few barons on the shoulder to accompany him, selected the fifty best men in the Royal Numidian Guard, and taken ship with Cassius the praetor. That had been two months ago. Two months in which very little had happened.

Oh, Gaius Memmius had lived up to his word! He had summoned an Assembly of the Plebs in the Circus Flaminius, which lay outside the *pomerium,* the sacred boundary of the city, and therefore constituted a venue Jugurtha the anointed sovereign could attend in person. The purpose of the meeting was to enable every interested Roman from highest to lowest personally to hear the King of Numidia answer Gaius Memmius's questions: whom had he bribed, how much money had he paid over? Everyone in Rome knew exactly the sort of questions Gaius Memmius was going to ask. So the Assembly in the Circus Flaminius was extremely well attended, the arena crowded, with latecomers accommodated in the wooden tiers of seats hoping even at the distance to be able to hear.

However, Jugurtha still knew how to go about his defense; Spain and the years since had taught him too well ever to forget. He bought himself a tribune of the plebs.

On the face of it, tribunes of the plebs were junior in the magisterial hierarchy and in senatorial rank. Tribunes of the plebs had no imperium—now there was a word the Numidian language had no equivalent for! *Imperium!* Imperium meant—well, the kind of authority a god on earth might possess. It was why a lone praetor could summon a great king to go with him. Provincial governors had imperium. Consuls had imperium. Praetors had imperium. The curule aediles had imperium. But each possessed a different strength or kind of imperium. The only tangible evidence of imperium was the lictor. Lictors were professional attendants who walked ahead of the owner of imperium to clear a path for him, carrying on their left shoulders the *fasces,* the bundles of rods lashed together with crimson cords.

The censors didn't have imperium. Nor did the plebeian aediles. Nor did the quaestors. Nor—most important for Jugurtha's purposes—did the tribunes of the plebs. These last were the elected representatives of the plebs, that vast bulk of the Roman citizen body unable to claim the high distinction of being a *patricius,* a patrician. The patrician was the antique aristocrat, one whose family was listed among the Fathers of Rome. Four hundred years ago, when the Republic had been brand new, only the patrician had mattered. But as some plebeians gained money and power, and forced their way into Senate and curule chair, they wanted to be aristocrats too. The result: the *nobilis,* the nobleman.

Thus was the patrician joined by the nobleman in a dual aristocracy. To be a nobleman, all that was necessary was to have a consul in the family, and there was nothing to stop a plebeian's becoming consul. Plebeian honor—and ambition—were satisfied.

The plebs had their own assembly of government; no patrician could attend it, or vote in it. Yet so powerful had the plebs become—and so eclipsed the patricians—that this young body, the Plebeian Assembly, passed almost all the laws. Ten tribunes of the plebs were elected to look after the interests of the plebs. New ones every year. That was the worst feature of Roman government: its magistrates served for only a year, which meant you could never buy yourself one man who was going to last long enough to be of real service. Every year, you had to buy yourself another man. And usually you had to buy yourself several.

No, a tribune of the plebs didn't have imperium, nor was he a senior magistrate; on the surface, he didn't seem to count for much at all. And yet he had managed to make himself the most significant magistrate of the lot. In his hands was true power, for he alone possessed the power of the veto. His veto affected everyone; no one save a dictator was immune from it, and there had not been a dictator in office for nearly a hundred years. A tribune of the plebs could veto a censor, a consul, a praetor, the Senate, his fellow nine tribunes of the plebs, meetings, assemblies, elections—you name it, he could veto it—and probably had. Also, his person was sacrosanct, which meant he could not be physically impeded in the execution of his duties. Besides which, he made the laws. The Senate could not make a law; all the Senate could do was to recommend that a law be made.

Of course it was all designed to impose a system of checks and balances aimed at curbing the potential political power of any one body or any one individual. If the Romans had been a superior breed of political animal, the system would have worked too; but since they were not, it mostly didn't work. For of all the people in the history of the world, the Romans were the most adept at finding ostensibly legal ways around the law.

So King Jugurtha of Numidia bought himself a tribune of the

plebs—a nobody really, not a member of one of the Famous Families, nor a wealthy man. However, Gaius Baebius was a duly elected tribune of the plebs, and when the stream of silver denarii was poured out on the table in front of him, he silently scooped his treasure trove into a dozen big bags and became the property of the King of Numidia.

As the old year wore itself down, Gaius Memmius had convened his big meeting in the Circus Flaminius, and haled Jugurtha before it. Then, with the King standing submissively on the Flaminian rostra and the crowd of some thousands utterly silent, Gaius Memmius asked his first question.

"Did you bribe Lucius Opimius?" he asked the King.

And before the King could answer, Gaius Baebius piped up. "I forbid you to answer Gaius Memmius, King Jugurtha!" was all Gaius Baebius said. He didn't need to say a single word more.

It was a veto. Directed by a tribune of the plebs not to answer, Jugurtha could not legally be made to answer. So the Assembly of the Plebs broke up; the disappointed thousands went home muttering; Gaius Memmius was so angry his friends had to lead him away under restraint; and Gaius Baebius trotted off exuding an air of great virtue which fooled no one.

Yet the Senate hadn't given Jugurtha permission to return home, so here on New Year's Day he sat on his rented, hideously expensive loggia, cursing Rome, and cursing the Romans. Neither of the new consuls had yet given any indication that he might be interested in accepting a private donation; none of the new praetors was worth the effort of bribing, and the new tribunes of the plebs weren't inspiring either.

The trouble with bribery was that it could not just be cast upon the waters; your fish first had to rise to the surface and make gobbling motions, thus assuring you that he was interested in swallowing a gilded bait. If no one swam up to mouth his interest at you, then you had to float your line and sit back and wait with every ounce of patience you could possibly muster.

Yet—how *could* he sit back and wait patiently when his kingdom was already the target of several greedy pretenders? Gauda,

the legitimate son of Mastanabal, and Massiva, the son of Gu-
lussa, had strong claims, though they were by no means the only
claimants. To get home was vital. Yet here he sat, impotent. Were
he to leave without the Senate's permission, his departure might
be viewed as an act of war. As far as he knew, no one in Rome
wanted war, but he didn't have enough evidence to tell him which
way the Senate might jump if he did leave. And though it could
not pass laws, the Senate had all the say in foreign affairs, from
declaring war to governing the Roman provinces. His agents had
reported that Marcus Aemilius Scaurus was furious at Gaius
Baebius's veto. And Scaurus had enormous clout in the Senate,
had once already swung it around single-handedly. Scaurus was
of the opinion that Jugurtha boded no good for Rome.

Bomilcar the half brother sat quietly, waiting for Jugurtha to
abandon his brooding. He had news to impart, but he knew his
king better than to broach it while the storm signs were showing.
A wonderful man, Jugurtha. So much innate ability! And how
hard had his lot been because of the accident of his low birth.
Why did heredity matter so much? The Punic Carthaginian blood
in all the Numidian nobility was very marked in Jugurtha, but so
too was the Berber blood he got from his mother. Both were Se-
mitic peoples, but the Berber had lived far longer in North Africa
than the Punic.

In Jugurtha the two strains of Semite were perfectly married.
From his mother's Berber fairness he had inherited his light grey
eyes, his straight nose, and his long, gaunt-cheeked face, and
from her too he had inherited his height. But from his father Mastanabal's Punic blood came his corkscrew-curled black locks, his
dense black body hair, his swarthy skin, and his big-boned frame.
Perhaps that was why he was so impressive: the eyes were a shock
to see in one so dark, and frightening too. Hellenized by centuries of exposure to the Greeks, the Numidian upper classes wore
Greek dress, which did not really suit Jugurtha, who looked his
best in helmet and cuirass and greaves, sword at his side, war-horse
champing. A pity, thought Bomilcar, that the Romans in Rome

had never seen the King garbed for war; and then he shivered, horrified at the thought. A temptation of fate, to think that! Better offer the goddess Fortuna a sacrifice tomorrow, that the Romans never did see Jugurtha garbed for war.

The King was relaxing; his face had softened. Awful, to have to banish this hard-earned peace, burden him with a fresh worry. But better he should hear it from his loyalest baron, his own brother, than have the news blurted out to him by some idiot agent avid to cause a maximum of consternation.

"My lord king?" asked Bomilcar tentatively.

The grey eyes turned his way immediately. "Yes?"

"I heard a rumor yesterday, at the house of Quintus Caecilius Metellus."

That flicked Jugurtha on the raw, of course; Bomilcar could go where he liked inside Rome, for he wasn't an anointed king. It was Bomilcar who was invited to dine, not Jugurtha.

"What?" asked the King curtly.

"Massiva has turned up here in Rome. What's more, he's managed to interest the consul Spurius Postumius Albinus in his case, and intends to have Albinus petition the Senate."

The King sat up quickly, swinging his chair around so he could look directly into Bomilcar's face. "I wondered where the miserable little worm had wriggled off to," he said. "Now I know, don't I? But why him, and not me? Albinus must know I'll pay him more than Massiva ever could."

"Not according to my sources," said Bomilcar uneasily. "I suspect they've made a deal which depends upon Albinus's being awarded Africa Province as his governorship. You're stuck here in Rome; Albinus hies himself off to Africa Province with a neat little army, a quick march across the border to Cirta, and—all hail King Massiva of Numidia! I imagine King Massiva of Numidia will be very willing to pay Albinus pretty much what he asks."

"I've got to get home!" the King cried.

"I know! But how, tell me how?"

"You don't think there's any chance I could sway Albinus? I've still got money on hand, I can get more!"

Bomilcar shook his head emphatically. "The new consul does not like you," he said. "You neglected to send him a gift on his birthday, which was last month. Massiva didn't neglect to send him a gift. In fact, he sent Albinus a gift when he was elected consul, then another for the birthday."

"That's my agents, curse them!" Jugurtha bared his teeth. "They're beginning to think I'm going to lose, so they're not even trying." He chewed his lip, wet it with his tongue. "Am I going to lose?"

Bomilcar smiled. "You? Never!"

"I don't know. . . . Massiva! Do you realize I'd forgotten all about him? I thought he was in Cyrenaica with Ptolemy Apion." Jugurtha shrugged, visibly pulled himself together. "It might be a false rumor. Who exactly told you?"

"Metellus himself. He'd know. His ear's permanently to the ground these days, he's planning to run for consul next year. Not that he approves of the deal Albinus is making. If he did, he'd not have breathed a word of it to me. But you know Metellus—one of the upright virtuous Romans, not a bribe in mind. And he dislikes seeing kings camped on Rome's doorstep."

"Metellus can afford the luxury of virtuous uprightness!" said Jugurtha tartly. "What Caecilius Metellus isn't as rich as Croesus? They've carved up Spain and Asia between them. Well, they'll not carve up Numidia! Nor will Spurius Postumius Albinus, if I have anything to do with it." The King sat stiff in his chair. "Massiva is definitely here?"

"According to Metellus, yes."

"We must wait until we hear which consul is going out to govern Africa, and which to Macedonia."

Bomilcar snorted derisively. "Don't tell me you believe in the lots!"

"I don't know what I believe about the Romans," said the King somberly. "Maybe I think it's already decided, maybe I wonder if the drawing of the lots isn't that one time they're laughing at us, and actually have left it up to chance. So I will wait, Bomilcar. When I hear the result of the lots, I'll decide what to do."

With that, he turned his chair around again, and went back to his contemplation of the rain.

There had been three children in the old white stuccoed farmhouse near Arpinum: Gaius Marius was the eldest, then came his sister, Maria, and finally a second son, Marcus Marius. It was naturally expected that they would grow up to take a prominent place in the life of the district and its town, but no one dreamed any of the three would venture farther afield. They were rural nobility, old-fashioned bluff and hearty country squires, the Mariuses, seemingly destined forever to be important people only within their little domain of Arpinum. The idea that one of them would enter the Senate of Rome was unthinkable; Cato the Censor made sufficient stir because of his rustic origins, yet he had come from a place no farther afield than Tusculum, a mere fifteen miles from Rome's Servian Walls. So no Arpinate squire imagined that his son could become a Roman senator.

It wasn't a matter of money, for there was plenty of money; the Mariuses were most comfortably off. Arpinum was a rich locality many square miles in area, and most of its land was owned among three families—the Mariuses, the Gratidiuses, and the Tullius Ciceros. When an outsider was needed as wife or husband of a Marius or a Gratidius or a Tullius Cicero, feelers went out not to Rome but to Puteoli, where the Granius family lived; the Graniuses were a prosperous clan of seagoing merchants who had originally hailed from Arpinum.

Gaius Marius's bride had been arranged for him when he was still a little boy, and she waited patiently in the Granius household at Puteoli to grow up, for she was even younger than her betrothed. But when Gaius Marius fell in love, it was not with a woman. Or a man. He fell in love with the army—a natural, joyous, spontaneous recognition of the life's partner. Enrolled as a cadet on his seventeenth birthday and lamenting the fact that there were no important wars going on, he nonetheless managed to serve continuously in the ranks of the most junior officers of the consul's legions until, aged twenty-three, he was posted to the personal staff of Scipio Aemilianus before Numantia, in Spain.

It hadn't taken him long to befriend Publius Rutilius Rufus and Prince Jugurtha of Numidia, for they were all the same age, and all stood very high in the esteem of Scipio Aemilianus, who called them the Terrible Trio. None of the three was from the highest circles of Rome. Jugurtha was a complete outsider, Publius Rutilius Rufus's family hadn't been in the Senate more than a hundred years and had not so far managed to reach the consulship, and Gaius Marius was from a family of country squires. At this time, of course, none of the three was a bit interested in Roman politics; all they cared about was soldiering.

But Gaius Marius was a very special case. He was born to be a soldier, but more than that; he was born to lead soldiers.

"He just knows what to do and how to do it," said Scipio Aemilianus, with a sigh that might perhaps have been envy. Not that Scipio Aemilianus didn't know what to do and how to do it, but he had been listening to generals talk in the dining room since his early boyhood, and only he really knew the degree of innate spontaneity his own soldiering contained. Very little, was the truth. Scipio Aemilianus's great talent lay in his organization, not in his soldiering. He believed that if a campaign was thoroughly thrashed out in the planning room even before the first legionary was enlisted, soldiering had not much to do with the outcome.

Where Gaius Marius was a natural. At seventeen he had still been rather small and thin; a picky eater and a crochety child always, he had been pampered by his mother and secretly despised by his father. Then he lashed on his first pair of military boots and buckled the plates of a good plain bronze cuirass over his stout leather underdress. And grew in mind and body until he was bigger than everyone else physically, intellectually, in strength and courage and independence. At which point his mother began to reject him and his father swelled with pride in him.

In Gaius Marius's opinion there was no life like it, to be an integral part of the greatest military machine the world had ever known—the Roman legion. No route march was too arduous, no lesson in swordplay too long or too vicious, no humiliating task humiliating enough to stem the rising tide of his huge enthusiasm. He didn't care what they gave him to do, as long as he was soldiering.

It was at Numantia too that he met a seventeen-year-old cadet who had come from Rome to join Scipio Aemilianus's own select little band at Scipio Aemilianus's express request. This lad was Quintus Caecilius Metellus, the younger brother of that Caecilius Metellus who would, after a campaign against the tribesmen of the Dalmatian hills of Illyricum, adopt the last name of Dalmaticus and get himself appointed Pontifex Maximus, highest priest in the State religion.

Young Metellus was a typical Caecilius Metellus: a plodder, with no spark or flair for the work on hand, yet determined to do it and unshakably convinced he could do it superbly well. Though loyalty to his class prevented Scipio Aemilianus's saying so, perhaps the seventeen-year-old expert at everything irritated him, for not long after young Metellus arrived at Spanish Numantia, Scipio Aemilianus handed him over to the tender mercies of the Terrible Trio—Jugurtha, Rutilius Rufus, and Marius. Not old enough themselves to feel pity, they were as resentful as they were displeased at being given this self-opinionated millstone. And they took it out on young Metellus, not cruelly, just toughly.

While Numantia held out and Scipio Aemilianus was busy, the lad put up with his lot. Then Numantia fell. Was torn down, extirpated. And everyone from highest officer to merest ranker soldier was allowed to get drunk. The Terrible Trio got drunk. So did young Quintus Caecilius Metellus, for it happened to be his birthday; he turned eighteen. And the Terrible Trio thought it a great joke to throw the birthday boy into a pigsty.

He came out of the muck sober, spitting mad—and spitting spite. "You—you pathetic upstarts! Who do you think you are? Well, let me tell you! You're nothing but a greasy foreigner, Jugurtha! Not fit to lick a Roman's boots! And you're a jumped-up favor currier, Rutilius! As for you, Gaius Marius, you're nothing more than an Italian hayseed with no Greek! How dare you! How *dare* you! Don't you appreciate who I am? Don't you understand who my family is? *I* am a Caecilius Metellus, and we were kings in Etruria before Rome was ever thought of! For months I've suffered your insults, but no more! Treating *me* like an underling, as if *I* were the inferior! How dare you! How *dare* you!"

Jugurtha and Rutilius Rufus and Gaius Marius hung rocking gently on the pigsty fence, blinking like owls, faces slack. Then Publius Rutilius Rufus, who was that rare individual capable of scholarship as profound as his soldiering was practical, put a leg over the top of the fence and managed to balance himself astride it, a huge smile growing.

"Don't mistake me, I really do appreciate everything you're saying, Quintus Caecilius," he said, "but the trouble is that you've got a big fat pig turd on your head instead of a crown, O King of Etruria!" Out came a giggle. "Go and have a bath, then tell us again. We'll probably manage not to laugh."

Metellus reached up and brushed his head furiously, too enraged to take sensible advice, especially when it was tendered with such a smile. "Rutilius!" he spat. "What sort of name is that, to adorn the Senate rolls? Oscan nobodies, that's who you are! *Peasants!*"

"Oh, come now!" said Rutilius Rufus gently. "My Etruscan is quite good enough to translate the meaning of 'Metellus' into Latin, you know." He twisted where he sat on the fence and looked at Jugurtha and Marius. "It means, freed from service as a mercenary," he said to them gravely.

That was too much. Young Metellus launched himself at Rutilius Rufus and brought him crashing down into the aromatic mire, where the two of them rolled and wrestled and thumped without enough traction to harm each other until Jugurtha and Marius decided it looked good in there, and dived in after them. Howling with laughter, they sat in the mud amid the more impudent pigs, which in the manner of impudent pigs couldn't resist investigating them thoroughly. When the Terrible Trio stopped sitting on

Metellus and rubbing muck all over him, he floundered to his feet and escaped.

"You'll pay for this!" he said through his teeth.

"Oh, pull your head in!" said Jugurtha, and broke into fresh paroxysms of mirth.

But the wheel, thought Gaius Marius as he climbed out of his bath and picked up a towel to dry himself, turns full circle no matter what we do. Spite from the mouth of a half-grown sprig of a most noble house was no less true for being spiteful. Who were they in actual fact, the Terrible Trio of Numantia? Why, they were a greasy foreigner, a jumped-up favor currier, and an Italian hayseed with no Greek. That's who they were. Rome had taught them the truth of it, all right.

Jugurtha should have been acknowledged King of Numidia years ago, brought firmly yet kindly into the Roman fold of client-kings, kept there with sound advice and fair dealing. Instead, he had suffered the implacable enmity of the entire Caecilius Metellus faction, and was currently in Rome with his back against the wall, fighting a last-ditch stand against a group of Numidian would-be kings, forced to buy what his worth and his ability ought to have earned him free and aboveboard.

And dear little sandy-headed Publius Rutilius Rufus, the favorite pupil of Panaetius the philosopher, admired by the whole of the Scipionic Circle—writer, soldier, wit, politician of extraordinary excellence—had been cheated of his consulship in the same year Marius had barely managed a praetorship. Not only was Rutilius's background not good enough, he had also incurred the enmity of the Caecilius Metelluses, and that meant he—like Jugurtha—automatically became an enemy of Marcus Aemilius Scaurus, closely allied to the Caecilius Metelluses, and chief glory of their faction.

As for Gaius Marius—well, as Quintus Caecilius Metellus Piggle-wiggle would say, he had done better than any Italian hayseed with no Greek should. Why had he ever decided to go to Rome and try the political ladder anyway? Simple. Because Scipio Aemilianus (like most of the highest patricians, Scipio

Aemilianus was no snob) thought he must. He was too good a man to waste filling a country squire's shoes, Scipio Aemilianus had said. Even more important, if he didn't become a praetor, he could never command an army of Rome.

So Marius had stood for election as a tribune of the soldiers, got in easily, then stood for election as a quaestor, was approved by the censors—and found himself, an Italian hayseed with no Greek, a member of the Senate of Rome. How amazing that had been! How stunned his family back in Arpinum! He'd done his share of time serving and managed to scramble a little way upward. Oddly enough, it had been Caecilius Metellus support which had then secured him election as a tribune of the plebs in the severely reactionary time which had followed immediately after the death of Gaius Gracchus. When Marius had first sought election to the College of Tribunes of the Plebs, he hadn't got in; the year he did get in, the Caecilius Metellus faction was convinced it owned him. Until he showed it otherwise by acting vigorously to preserve the freedom of the Plebeian Assembly, never more threatened with being overpowered by the Senate than after the death of Gaius Gracchus. Lucius Caecilius Metellus Dalmaticus tried to push a law through that would have curtailed the ability of the Plebeian Assembly to legislate, and Gaius Marius vetoed it. Nor could Gaius Marius be cajoled, coaxed, or coerced into withdrawing his veto.

But that veto had cost him dearly. After his year as a tribune of the plebs, he tried to run for one of the two plebeian aedile magistracies, only to be foiled by the Caecilius Metellus lobby. So he had campaigned strenuously for the praetorship, and encountered Caecilius Metellus opposition yet again. Led by Metellus Dalmaticus, they had employed the usual kind of defamation—he was impotent, he molested little boys, he ate excrement, he belonged to secret societies of Bacchic and Orphic vice, he accepted every kind of bribe, he slept with his sister and his mother. But they had also employed a more insidious form of defamation more effectively; they simply said that Gaius Marius was not a Roman, that Gaius Marius was an upcountry Italian nobody, and that Rome could produce more than enough true sons of Rome to make it unnecessary for any Roman to elect a Gaius Marius to the praetorship. It was a telling point.

Minor criticism though it was compared to the rest, the most galling calumny of all as far as Gaius Marius was concerned was the perpetual inference that he was unacceptably crass because he had no Greek. The slur wasn't true; he spoke very good Greek. However, his tutors had been Asian Greeks—his pedagogue hailed from Lampsacus on the Hellespont, and his *grammaticus* from Amisus on the coast of Pontus—and they spoke a heavily accented Greek. Thus Gaius Marius had learned Greek with a twang to it that branded him improperly taught—as a common, underbred sort of fellow. He had been obliged to acknowledge himself defeated; if he said no Greek at all or if he said miles of Asian Greek, it came to the same thing. In consequence he ignored the slander by refusing to speak the language which indicated that a man was properly educated and cultured.

Never mind. He had scraped in last among the praetors, but he had scraped in nonetheless. *And* survived a trumped-up charge of bribery brought against him just after the election. Bribery! As if he could have! No, in those days he hadn't had the kind of money necessary to buy a magistracy. But luckily there were among the electors enough men who either knew firsthand of his soldierly valor, or had heard about it from those who did. The Roman electorate always had a soft spot for an excellent soldier, and it was that soft spot which won for him.

The Senate had posted him to Further Spain as its governor, thinking he'd be out of sight, out of mind, and perhaps handy. But since he was a quintessential Military Man, he thrived.

The Spaniards—especially the half-tamed tribes of the Lusitanian west and the Cantabrian northwest—excelled in a kind of warfare that didn't suit most Roman commanders any more than it suited the style of the Roman legions. Spaniards never deployed for battle in the traditional way, cared nothing for the universally accepted tenet that it was better to gamble everything you had on

the off chance of winning a decisive battle than to incur the hor-
rific costs of a prolonged war. The Spaniards already understood
that they were fighting a prolonged war, a war which they had to
continue so long as they desired to preserve their Celtiberian
identity; as far as they were concerned, they were engaged in an
ongoing struggle for social and cultural independence.

But, since they certainly didn't have the money to fight a prolonged war, they fought a civilian war. They never gave battle.
Instead, they fought by ambush, raid, assassination, and devastation of all Enemy property. That is, Roman property. Never appearing where they were expected, never marching in column,
never banding together in any numbers, never identifiable by the
wearing of uniforms or the carrying of arms. They just—pounced.
Out of nowhere. And then vanished without a trace into the formidable crags of their mountains as if they had never been. Ride
in to inspect a small town which Roman intelligence positively
stated was involved in some clever minor massacre, and it would
be as idle, as innocent, as unimpeachable as the most docile and
patient of asses.

A fabulously rich land, Spain. As a result, everyone had had a
go at owning it. The original Iberian indigenes had been inter-
mingling with Celtic elements invading across the Pyrenees for a
thousand years, and Berber-Moor incursions from the African
side of the narrow straits separating Spain from Africa had further enriched the local melting pot.

Then a thousand years ago came the Phoenicians from Tyre
and Sidon and Berytus on the Syrian coast, and after them came
the Greeks. Two hundred years ago had come the Punic Carthaginians, themselves descendants of the Syrian Phoenicians who
had founded an empire based on African Carthage; and the relative isolation of Spain was finished. For the Carthaginians came
to Spain to mine its metals. Gold, silver, lead, zinc, copper, and
iron. The Spanish mountains were loaded with all of them, and
everywhere in the world the demand for goods made out of some
and wealth made out of others was rapidly increasing. Punic
power was based upon Spanish ore. Even tin came from Spain,

though it wasn't found there; mined in the fabled Cassiterides, the Tin Isles somewhere at the ultimate limit of the livable globe, it arrived in Spain through little Cantabrian ports and traveled the Spanish trade routes down to the shores of the Middle Sea.

The seagoing Carthaginians had owned Sicily, Sardinia, and Corsica too, which meant that sooner or later they had to run foul of Rome, a fate that had overtaken them 150 years before. And three wars later—three wars which took over a hundred years to fight—Carthage was dead, and Rome had acquired the first of its overseas possessions. Including the mines of Spain.

Roman practicality had seen at once that Spain was best governed from two different locations; the peninsula was divided into the two provinces of Nearer Spain—Hispania Citerior—and Further Spain—Hispania Ulterior. The governor of Further Spain controlled all the south and west of the country from a base in the fabulously fertile hinterlands of the Baetis River, with the mighty old Phoenician city of Gades near its mouth. The governor of Nearer Spain controlled all the north and east of the peninsula from a base in the coastal plain opposite the Balearic Isles, and shifted his capital around as the whim or the need dictated. The lands of the far west—Lusitania—and the lands of the northwest—Cantabria—remained largely untouched.

Despite the object lesson Scipio Aemilianus had made out of Numantia, the tribes of Spain continued to resist Roman occupation by ambush, raid, assassination, and devastation of property. Well now, thought Gaius Marius, coming on this most interesting scene when he arrived in Further Spain as its new governor, I too can fight by ambush, raid, assassination, and devastation of property! And proceeded to do so. With great success. Out thrust the frontiers of Roman Spain into Lusitania and the mighty chain of ore-bearing mountains in which rose the Baetis, Anas, and Tagus rivers.

It was really not an exaggeration to say that as the Roman frontier advanced, the Roman conquerors kept tripping over richer and richer deposits of ore, especially silver, copper, and iron. And naturally the governor of the province—he who achieved the new frontiers in the name of Rome—was in the forefront of those who acquired grants of ore-bearing land. The Treasury of Rome took its cut, but preferred to leave the mine owning and actual mining in the hands of private individuals, who did it far more efficiently and with a more consistent brand of exploitative ruthlessness.

Gaius Marius got rich. Then got richer. Every new mine was either wholly or partly his; this in turn brought him sleeping partnerships in the great companies which contracted out their services to run all kinds of commercial operations—from grain buying and selling and shipping, to merchant banking and public works—all over the Roman world, as well as within the city of Rome itself.

He came back from Spain having been voted *imperator* by his troops, which meant that he was entitled to apply to the Senate for permission to hold a triumph; considering the amount of booty and tithes and taxes and tributes he had added to the general revenues, the Senate could not do else than comply with the wishes of his soldiers. And so he drove the antique triumphal chariot along its traditional route in the triumphal parade, preceded by the heaped-up evidence of his victories and depredations, the floats depicting tableaux and geography and weird tribal costumes; and dreamed of being consul in two years' time. He, Gaius Marius from Arpinum, the despised Italian hayseed with no Greek, would be consul of the greatest city in the world. And go back to Spain and complete its conquest, turn it into a peaceful, prosperous pair of indisputably Roman provinces. But it was five years since he had returned to Rome. *Five years!* The Caecilius Metellus faction had finally won: he would never be consul now.

"I think I'll wear the Chian outfit," he said to his body servant, standing waiting for orders. Many men in Marius's position would have lain back in the bath water and demanded that they be scrubbed, scraped, and massaged by slaves, but Gaius Marius preferred to do his own dirty work, even now. Mind you, at forty-seven he was still a fine figure of a man. Nothing to be ashamed of about his physique! No matter how ostensibly inert his days might be, he got in a fair amount of exercise, worked with the dumbbells and the closhes, swam if he could several times across the Tiber in the reach called the Trigarium, then ran all the way back from the far perimeter of the Campus Martius to his house on the flanks of the Capitoline Arx. His hair was getting a bit thin on top, but he still had enough dark brown curls to brush forward into a respectable coiffure. There. That would have to do. A beauty he never had been, never would be. A good face—even an impressive one—but no rival for Gaius Julius Caesar's!

Interesting. Why was he going to so much trouble with hair and dress for what promised to be a small family meal in the dining room of a modest backbencher senator? A man who hadn't even been aedile, let alone praetor. The *Chian* outfit he had elected to wear, no less! He had bought it several years ago, dreaming of the dinner parties he would host during his consulship and the years thereafter when he would be one of the esteemed ex-consuls, the consulars as they were called.

It was permissible to attire oneself for a purely private dinner party in less austere clothes than white toga and tunic, a bit of purple stripe their only decoration; and the Chian tapestry tunic with long drape to go over it was a spectacle of gold and purple lavishness. Luckily there were no sumptuary laws on the books at the moment that forbade a man to robe himself as ornately and luxuriously as he pleased. There was only a *lex Licinia,* which regulated the amount of expensive culinary rarities a man might put on his table—and no one took any notice of that. Besides which, Gaius Marius doubted that Caesar's table would be loaded down with licker-fish and oysters.

Not for one moment did it occur to Gaius Marius to seek out his wife before he departed. He had forgotten her years ago—if, in fact, he ever had remembered her. The marriage had been arranged during the sexless limbo of childhood and had lingered in the sexless limbo of an adult lack of love or even affinity for twenty-five childless years. A man as martially inclined and physically active as Gaius Marius sought sexual solace only when its absence was recollected by a chance encounter with some attractive woman, and his life had not been distinguished by many such. From time to time he enjoyed a mild fling with the attractive woman who had taken his eye (if she was available and willing), or a house girl, or (on campaign) a captive girl.

But Grania, his wife? Her he had forgotten, even when she was there not two feet from him, reminding him that she would like to be slept with often enough to conceive a child. Cohabitating with Grania was like leading a route march through an impenetrable fog. What you felt was so amorphous it kept squeezing itself into something different yet equally unidentifiable; occasionally you were aware of a change in the ambient temperature, patches of extra moistness in a generally clammy substrate. By the time his climax arrived, if he opened his mouth at all it was to yawn.

He didn't pity Grania in the least. Nor did he attempt to understand her. Simply, she was his wife, his old boiling fowl who had never worn the plumage of a spring chicken, even in her youth. What she did with her days—or nights—he didn't know, didn't worry about. Grania, leading a double life of licentious depravity? If someone had suggested to him that she might, he would have laughed until the tears came. And he would have been quite right to do so. Grania was as chaste as she was drab. No Caecilia Metella (the wanton one who was sister to Dalmaticus and Metellus Piggle-wiggle, and wife to Lucius Licinius Lucullus) about Grania from Puteoli!

His silver mines had bought the house high on the Arx of the Capitol just on the Campus Martius side of the Servian Walls, the most expensive real estate in Rome; his copper mines had bought the colored marbles with which its brick-and-concrete columns and divisions and floors were sheathed; his iron mines had bought the services of the finest mural painter in Rome to fill up the plastered spaces between pilasters and divisions with scenes of stag hunts and flower gardens and trompe l'oeil landscapes; his sleeping partnerships in several large companies had bought the statues and the herms, the fabulous citrus-wood tables on their gold-inlaid ivory pedestals, the gilded and encrusted couches and chairs, the gloriously embroidered hangings, the cast-bronze doors; Hymettus himself had landscaped the massive peristyle-garden, paying as much attention to the subtle combination of perfumes as he did to the colors of the blossoms; and the great Dolichus had created the long central pool with its fountains and fish and lilies and lotuses and superb larger-than-life sculptures of tritons, nereids, nymphs, dolphins, and bewhiskered sea serpents.

All of which, truth to tell, Gaius Marius did not give tuppence about. The obligatory show, nothing else. He slept on a camp bed in the smallest, barest room of the house, its only hangings his sword and scabbard on one wall and his smelly old military cape on another, its only splash of color the rather grimy and tattered *vexillum* flag his favorite legion had given him when their campaign in Spain was over. Ah, that was the life for a man! The only true value praetorship and consulship had for Gaius Marius was the fact that both led to military command of the highest order. But consul far more than praetor! And he knew he would never be consul, not now. They wouldn't vote for a nobody, no matter how rich he might be.

He walked in the same kind of weather the previous day had endured, a dreary mizzling rain and an all-pervading dampness, forgetting—which was quite typical—that he had a fortune on his back. However, he had thrown his old campaigning *sagum* over his finery—a thick, greasy, malodorous cape which could keep out the perishing winds of the alpine passes or the soaking days-long downpours of Epirus. The sort of garment a soldier needed. Its reek stole into his nostrils like a trickle of vapor from a bakery, hunger making, voluptuous on the gut, warmly friendly.

"Come in, come in!" said Gaius Julius Caesar, welcoming his guest in person at the door, and holding out his own finely made hands to receive the awful *sagum*. But having taken it, he didn't immediately toss it to the waiting slave as if afraid its smell might cling to his skin; instead, he fingered it with respect before handing it over carefully. "I'd say that's seen a few campaigns," he said then, not blinking an eye at the sight of Gaius Marius in all the vulgar ostentation of a gold-and-purple Chian outfit.

"It's the only *sagum* I've ever owned," said Gaius Marius, oblivious to the fact that his Chian tapestry drape had flopped itself all the wrong way.

"Ligurian?"

"Of course. My father gave it to me brand-new when I turned seventeen and went off to do my service as a cadet. But I tell you what," Gaius Marius went on, not noticing the smallness and simplicity of the Gaius Julius Caesar house as he strolled beside his host to the dining room, "when it came my turn to equip and outfit legions, I made sure my men all got the exact same cape—no use expecting men to stay healthy if they're wet through or chilled to the bone." He thought of something important, and added hastily, "Of course I didn't charge 'em more than the standard military-issue price! Any commander worth his salt ought to be able to absorb the extra cost from extra booty."

"And you're worth your salt, I know," said Caesar as he sat on the edge of the middle couch at its left-hand end, indicating to his guest that he take the place to the right, which was the place of honor.

Servants removed their shoes, and, when Gaius Marius declined to suffer the fumes of a brazier, offered socks; both men accepted, then arranged their angle of recline by adjusting the bolsters supporting their left elbows into comfortable position. The wine steward stepped forward, attended by a cup bearer.

"My sons will be in shortly, and the ladies just before we eat," said Caesar, holding his hand up to arrest the progress of the wine steward. "I hope, Gaius Marius, that you won't deem me a niggard with my wine if I respectfully ask you to take it as I intend to myself, well watered? I do have a valid reason, but it is one I do not believe can be explained away so early. Simply, the only reason I can offer you right now is that it behooves both of us to remain in full possession of our wits. Besides, the ladies become uneasy when they see their men drinking unwatered wine."

"Wine bibbing isn't one of my failings," said Gaius Marius,

relaxing and cutting the wine pourer impressively short, then ensuring that his cup was filled almost to its brim with water. "If a man cares enough for his company to accept an invitation to dinner, then his tongue should be used for talking rather than lapping."

"Well said!" cried Caesar, beaming.

"However, I am mightily intrigued!"

"In the fullness of time, you shall know it all."

A silence fell. Both men sipped at their wine-flavored water a trifle uneasily. Since they knew each other only from nodding in passing, one senator to another, this initial bid to establish a friendship could not help but be difficult. Especially since the host had put an embargo upon the one thing which would have made them more quickly comfortable—wine.

Caesar cleared his throat, put his cup down on the narrow table which ran just below the inside edge of the couch. "I gather, Gaius Marius, that you are not enthused about this year's crop of magistrates," he said.

"Ye gods, no! Any more than you are, I think."

"They're a poor lot, all right. Sometimes I wonder if we are wrong to insist that the magistracies last only one year. Perhaps when we're lucky enough to get a really good man in an office, we should leave him there longer to get more done."

"A temptation, and if men weren't men, it might work," said Marius. "But there is an impediment."

"An impediment?"

"Whose word are we going to take that a good man *is* a good man? His? The Senate's? The People's Assemblies'? The knights'? The voters', incorruptible fellows that they are, impervious to bribes?"

Caesar laughed. "Well, I thought Gaius Gracchus was a good man. When he ran for his second term as a tribune of the plebs I supported him wholeheartedly—and I supported his third attempt too. Not that my support could count for much, my being patrician."

"And there you have it, Gaius Julius," said Marius somberly. "Whenever Rome does manage to produce a good man, he's cut down. And why is he cut down? Because he cares more for Rome than he does for family, faction, and finances."

"I don't think that's particularly confined to Romans," said Caesar, raising his delicate eyebrows until his forehead rippled. "People are people. I see very little difference between Romans, Greeks, Carthaginians, Syrians, or any others you care to name, at least when it comes to envy or greed. The only possible way the best man for the job can keep it long enough to accomplish what his potential suggests he can accomplish is to become a king. In fact, if not in name."

"And Rome would never condone a king," said Marius.

"It hasn't for the last five hundred years. We grew out of kings. Odd, isn't it? Most of the world prefers absolute rule. But not we Romans. Nor the Greeks, for that matter."

Marius grinned. "That's because Rome and Greece are stuffed with men who consider they're all kings. And Rome certainly didn't become a true democracy when we threw our kings out."

"Of course not! True democracy is a Greek philosophic unattainable. Look at the mess the Greeks made of it, so what chance do we sensible Roman fellows stand? Rome is government of the many by the few. The Famous Families." Caesar dropped the statement casually.

"And an occasional New Man," said Gaius Marius, New Man.

"And an occasional New Man," agreed Caesar placidly.

The two sons of the Caesar household entered the dining room exactly as young men should, manly yet deferential, restrained rather than shy, not putting themselves forward, but not holding themselves back.

Sextus Julius Caesar was the elder, twenty-five this year, tall and tawny-bronze of hair, grey of eye. Used to assessing young men, Gaius Marius detected an odd shadow in him: there was the faintest tinge of exhaustion in the skin beneath his eyes, and his mouth was tight-lipped yet not of the right form to be tight-lipped.

Gaius Julius Caesar Junior, twenty-two this year, was sturdier than his brother and even taller, a golden-blond fellow with bright blue eyes. Highly intelligent, thought Marius, yet not a forceful or opinionated young man.

Together they were as handsome, Roman-featured, finely set-up a pair of sons as any Roman senator father might hope to sire. Senators of tomorrow.

"You're fortunate in your sons, Gaius Julius," Marius said as the young men disposed themselves on the couch standing at right angles to their father's right; unless more guests were expected (or this was one of those scandalously progressive houses where the women lay down to dine), the third couch, at right angles to Marius's left, would remain vacant.

"Yes, I think I'm fortunate," said Caesar, smiling at his sons with as much respect as love in his eyes. Then he turned on his elbow to look at Gaius Marius, his expression changing to a courteous curiosity. "You don't have any sons, do you?"

"No," said Marius unregretfully.

"But you are married?"

"I believe so!" said Marius, and laughed. "We're all alike, we military men. Our real wife is the army."

"That happens," said Caesar, and changed the subject.

The predinner talk was cultivated, good-tempered, and very considerate, Marius noticed; no one in this house needed to put down anyone else who lived here, everyone stood upon excellent terms with everyone else, no latent discord rumbled an undertone. He became curious to see what the women were like, for the father after all was only one half of the source of this felicitous result; espoused to a Puteolan pudding though he was, Marius was no fool, and he personally knew of no wife of the Roman nobility who didn't have a large input to make when it came to the rearing of her children. No matter whether she was profligate or prude, idiot or intellectual, she was always a person to be reckoned with.

Then they came in, the women. Marcia and the two Julias. Ravishing! Absolutely ravishing, including the mother. The servants set upright chairs for them inside the hollow center of the U formed by the three dining couches and their narrow tables, so that Marcia sat opposite her husband, Julia sat facing Gaius Marius, and Julilla sat facing her two brothers. When she knew her parents weren't looking at her but the guest was, Julilla stuck out her tongue at her brothers, Marius noted with amusement.

Despite the absence of licker-fish and oysters and the presence of heavily watered wine, it was a delightful dinner served by unobtrusive, contented-looking slaves who never shoved rudely between the women and the tables, nor neglected a duty. The food was plain but excellently cooked, the natural flavors of meats, fruits, and vegetables undisguised by fishy *garum* essences and bizarre mixtures of exotic spices from the East; it was, in fact, the kind of food the soldier Marius liked best.

Roast birds stuffed with simple blends of bread and onions and green herbs from the garden, the lightest of fresh-baked rolls, two kinds of olives, dumplings made of delicate spelt flour cooked with eggs and cheese, deliciously country-tasting sausages grilled over a brazier and basted with a thin coat of garlic and diluted honey, two excellent salads of lettuces, cucumbers, shallots, and celery (each with a differently flavored oil-and-vinegar dressing), and a wonderful lightly steamed medley of broccoli, baby squash, and cauliflower dashed over with oil and grated chestnut. The olive oil was sweet and of the first pressing, the salt dry, and the pepper—of the best quality—was kept whole until one of the diners signaled the lad who was its custodian to grind up a pinch in his mortar with his pestle, please. The meal finished with little fruit tarts, some sticky squares of sesame seed glued together with wild thyme honey, pastry envelopes filled with raisin mince and soaked in syrup of figs, and two splendid cheeses.

"Arpinum!" exclaimed Marius, holding up a wedge of the second cheese, his face with its preposterous eyebrows suddenly seeming years younger. "I know this cheese well! My father makes it. The milk is from two-year-old ewes, and taken only after they've grazed on the river meadow for a week, where the special milkgrass grows."

"Oh, how nice," said Marcia, smiling at him without a trace of affectation or selfconsciousness. "I've always been fond of this particular cheese, but from now on I shall look out for it especially.

The cheese made by Gaius Marius—your father is also a Gaius Marius?—of Arpinum."

The moment the last course was cleared away the women rose to take their leave, having had no sip of wine, but dined heartily on the food and drunk deeply of the water.

As she got up Julia smiled at him with what seemed genuine liking, Marius noted; she had made polite conversation with him whenever he initiated it, but made no attempt to turn the discourse between him and her father into a three-sided affair. Yet she hadn't looked bored, but had followed what Caesar and Marius talked about with evident interest and understanding. A truly lovely girl, a peaceful girl who yet did not seem destined to turn into a pudding.

Her little sister, Julilla, was a scamp—delightful, yes, but a regular handful too, suspected Marius. Spoiled and willful and fully aware of how to manipulate her family to get her own way. But there was something in her more disquieting; the assessor of young men was also a fairly shrewd assessor of young women. And Julilla caused his hackles to ripple ever so softly and slightly; somewhere in her was a defect, Marius was sure. Not exactly lack of intelligence, though she was less well read than her elder sister and her brothers, and clearly not a whit perturbed by her ignorance. Not exactly vanity, though she obviously knew and treasured her beauty. Then Marius mentally shrugged, dismissed the problem and Julilla; neither was ever going to be his concern.

The young men lingered for perhaps ten more minutes, then they too excused themselves and departed. Night had fallen; the water clocks began to drip away the hours of darkness, twice as long as the hours of daylight. This was midwinter, and for once the calendar was in step with the seasons, thanks to the fastidiousness of the Pontifex Maximus, Lucius Caecilius Metellus Dalmaticus, who felt date and season *ought* to coincide—quite Greek, really. What did it matter, so long as your eyes and temperature-sensing apparatus told you what season it was, and the official calendar displayed in the Forum Romanum told you what month and day it was?

When the servants came to light the lamps, Marius noticed that the oil was of top quality, and the wicks not coarse oakum, but made from properly woven linen.

"I'm a reader," said Caesar, following Marius's gaze and interpreting his thoughts with the same uncanny accuracy he had displayed at the outset of that chance meeting of eyes yesterday on the Capitol. "Nor, I'm afraid, do I sleep very well. Years ago now, when the children were first of an age to participate in family councils, we had a special meeting at which we decided each of us should be permitted one affordable luxury. Marcia chose to have a first-class cook, I remember—but since that directly benefited all of us, we voted that she should have a new loom, the latest model from Patavium, and always the kind of yarn she likes, even if it's expensive. Sextus chose to be able to visit the Fields of Fire behind Puteoli several times a year."

A look of anxiety settled momentarily upon Caesar's face; he sighed deeply. "There are certain hereditary characteristics in the Julius Caesars," he explained, "the most famous of which—aside from our fairness of coloring—is the myth that every Julia is born gifted with the ability to make her men happy. A present from the founder of our house, the goddess Venus—though I never heard that Venus made too many mortal men happy. Or Vulcan either, for that matter. Or Mars! Still, that's what the myth says about the Julian women. But there are other, less salubrious gifts visited upon some of us, including the one poor Sextus inherited. I'm sure you've heard of the malady he suffers from—the wheezes? When he gets one of his attacks, you can hear him wheezing from anywhere in the house, and in his worst attacks he goes black in the face. We've nearly lost him several times."

So that was what was written upon young Sextus's brow! He wheezed, poor fellow. It would slow his career down, no doubt.

"Yes," said Marius, "I do know the malady. My father says it's always worst when the air is full of chaff at harvest, or pollen in summer, and that those who suffer from it should stay away from the company of animals, especially horses and hounds. While he's on military service, keep him afoot."

"He found that out for himself," said Caesar, sighing again.

"Do finish your story about the family council, Gaius Julius," said Marius, fascinated; this much democracy they didn't have in the smallest *isonomia* in Greece! What an odd lot they were, these Julius Caesars! To an outsider's cursory gaze—perfectly correct, patrician pillars of the community. But to those on the inside—outrageously unorthodox!

"Well, young Sextus chose to go regularly to the Fields of Fire because the sulphur fumes seem to help him," said his father. "They still do, and he still goes."

"And your younger son?" asked Marius.

"Gaius said there was only one thing in the whole world he wanted as a privilege, though it couldn't be called a luxury. He asked to be allowed to choose his own wife."

Marius's eyebrows, hairily alive, danced up and down. "Ye gods! And did you grant him the privilege?"

"Oh, yes."

"But what if he does the usual boy's trick and falls in love with a tart, or an old trull?"

"Then he marries her, if such is his wish. However, I do not think young Gaius will be so foolish, somehow. His head is very well connected to his shoulders," said the doting father tranquilly.

"Do you marry in the old patrician way, *confarreatio*—for life?" pressed Marius, scarcely believing what he heard.

"Oh, yes."

"Ye gods!"

"My older girl, Julia, is also very level-headed," Caesar went on. "She elected membership in the library of Fannius. Now I had intended to ask for the exact same thing, but there didn't seem to be any sense in two of us belonging, so I gave the membership to her. Our baby, Julilla, alas, is not at all wise, but I suppose butterflies have no need of wisdom. They just"—he shrugged, smiled wryly—"brighten up the world. I would hate to see a world without butterflies, and since we were disgracefully improvident in having four children, it's nice that our butterfly didn't come along until last place. *And* had the grace to be female when she did come along."

"What did she ask for?" Gaius Marius smiled.

"Oh, about what we expected. Sweetmeats and clothes."

"And you, deprived of your library membership?"

"I chose the finest lamp oil and the best wicks, and struck a bargain with Julia. If I could borrow the books she borrowed, then she could use my lamps to read by."

Marius finished his smile at leisure, liking the author of this moral little tale enormously. What a simple, unenvious, happy life he enjoyed! Surrounded by a wife and children he actually strove to please, was interested in as individuals. No doubt he was spot-on in his character analyses of his offspring, and young Gaius wouldn't pick a wife out of a Suburan gutter.

He cleared his throat. "Gaius Julius, it has been an absolutely delightful evening. But now I think it's time you told me why I have had to stay a sober man."

"If you don't mind, I'll dismiss the servants first," Caesar said. "The wine is right here where we can reach it ourselves, and now that the moment of truth has arrived, we don't need to be so abstemious."

His scrupulousness surprised Marius, used now to the utter indifference with which the Roman upper classes viewed their household slaves. Oh, not in terms of treatment—they were usually good to their people—but they did seem to think that their people were stuffed and inanimate when it came to overhearing what ought to be private. This was a habit Marius had never become reconciled to himself; like Caesar, his own father had firmly believed in dismissing the servants.

"They gossip dreadfully, you know," said Caesar when they were alone behind a tightly closed door, "and we've nosy neighbors on either side. Rome might be a big place, but when it comes to the spread of gossip on the Palatine—why, it's a village! Marcia tells me there are several among her friends who actually stoop to paying their servants for items of gossip—*and* give bonuses when the gossip turns out to be accurate! Besides, servants have thoughts and feelings too, so it's better not to involve them."

"You, Gaius Julius, ought to have been consul, then turned into our most eminent consular, and been elected censor," said Marius with sincerity.

"I agree with you, Gaius Marius, I ought indeed! But I haven't the money to have sought higher office."

"I have the money. Is that why I'm here? And kept sober?"

Caesar looked shocked. "My dear Gaius Marius, of course not! Why, I'm closer to sixty than I am to fifty! At this late stage, my public career is ossified. No, it is my sons with whom I am concerned, and their sons when the time comes."

Marius sat up straight and turned on the couch to face his host, who did the same. Since his cup was empty, Marius picked up the jug and poured himself an unwatered draft, sipped it, and looked stunned. "Is this what I've been watering down to the merest taste all night?" he demanded.

Caesar smiled. "Dear me, no! That rich I'm not, I assure you. The wine we watered down was an ordinary vintage. This I keep for special occasions."

"Then I'm flattered." Marius looked at Caesar from under his brows. "What is it you want of me, Gaius Julius?"

"Help. In return, I will help you," said Caesar, pouring himself a cup of the superb vintage.

"And how is this mutual help to be accomplished?"

"Simple. By making you a member of the family."

"What?"

"I am offering you whichever of my two daughters you prefer," said Caesar patiently.

"A *marriage*?"

"Certainly a marriage!"

"Ohhhhhh! Now that's a thought!" Marius saw the possibilities at once. He took a deeper drink of the fragrant Falernian in his cup, and said no more.

"Everyone must take notice of you if your wife is a Julia," said Caesar. "Luckily you have no sons—or daughters, for that matter. So any wife you might take at this stage of your life must be young, and come from fertile stock. It is quite understandable that you might be seeking a new wife, no one will be surprised. But—if that wife is a Julia, then she is of the highest patrician stock, and your children will have Julian blood in their veins. Indirectly, marriage to a Julia ennobles you, Gaius Marius. Everyone will be forced to regard you quite differently from the way they regard you now. For your name will be enhanced by the vast *dignitas*—the public worth and standing—of Rome's most august family. Money we have not. *Dignitas* we have. The Julius Caesars are directly descended from the goddess Venus through her grandson Iulus, son of her son Aeneas. And some of our splendor will rub off on you."

Caesar put his cup down and sighed, but smilingly. "I do assure you, Gaius Marius, it *is* true! I am not, alas, the oldest son of my generation of the Julian house, but we do have the wax images in our cupboards, we do trace ourselves back for over a thousand years. The other name of the mother of Romulus and Remus, she who is called Rhea Silvia, was—Julia! When she cohabited with Mars and conceived her twin sons, *we* gave mortal form to Romulus, and so to Rome." His smile grew; a smile not of self-mockery, but of sheer pleasure in his illustrious forebears. "We were the kings of Alba Longa, the greatest of all Latin cities, for it was our ancestor Iulus who founded it, and when it was sacked by Rome, we were brought to Rome and elevated in Rome's hierarchy to add weight to Rome's claim to head the Latin race. And though Alba Longa was never rebuilt, to this day the Priest of the Alban Mount is a Julius."

He couldn't help himself; Marius sucked in a deep breath of awe. But said nothing, just listened.

"On a humbler level," Caesar went on, "I carry no small measure of clout myself, even though I have never had the money to stand for any higher office. My name makes me famous among the electors. I am wooed by social climbers—and the centuries which vote in the consular elections are full of social climbers, as you know—and I am highly respected by the nobility. My personal *dignitas* is above reproach, as was my father's before me," Caesar ended very seriously.

New vistas were opening up before Gaius Marius, who could not take his eyes off Caesar's handsome face. Oh yes, they were descended from Venus, all right! Every last one of them a beauty. Looks count—and throughout the history of the world, it has always been better to be blond. The children I sired of a Julia might be blond, yet have long, bumpy Roman noses too! They would look as right as they would look unusual. Which is the difference between the blond Julius Caesars from Alba Longa and the blond Pompeys from Picenum. The Julius Caesars look unmistakably Roman. Where the Pompeys look like Celts.

"You want to be consul," Caesar continued, "so much is clear to everyone. Your activities in Further Spain when you were praetor produced clients. But unfortunately you yourself are rumored to be a client, and that makes your clients the clients of your own patron."

The guest showed his teeth, which were large and white and strong looking. "It is a slander!" he said angrily. "I am nobody's client!"

"I believe you, but that is not what is generally believed," Caesar maintained, "and what is generally believed is far more important than what is actually the truth. Anyone with sense can discount the Herennius family's claim to hold you as their client—the Herennius clan is infinitely less Latin than the Marius clan of Arpinum. But the Caecilius Metelluses also claim to hold you in their patronage as their client. And the Caecilius Metelluses *are* believed. Why? For one thing, because your mother Fulcinia's family is Etruscan, and the Marius clan owns lands in Etruria. Etruria is the traditional fief of the Caecilius Metelluses."

"No Marius—or Fulcinius, for that matter!—has ever been in clientship to a Caecilius Metellus!" snapped Marius, growing angrier still. "They're far too wily to say I'm their client in any situation where they might be called upon to prove it!"

"That goes without saying," said Caesar. "However, they dislike you in a most personal manner, which lends considerable weight to their claim. The fact is remarked upon constantly. Men say it's too personal a dislike to stem merely from the way you tweaked their noses when you were a tribune of the plebs."

"Oh, it's personal!" said Marius, and laughed without humor. "Tell me."

"I once threw Dalmaticus's little brother—the same who is undoubtedly going to be consul next year—into a pigsty at Numantia. Actually three of us did—and none of the three of us has got very far with the Romans who wield the real influence since, that's certain."

"Who were the other two?"

"Publius Rutilius Rufus and King Jugurtha of Numidia."

"Ah! The mystery is solved." Caesar put his fingertips together and pressed them against his pursed lips. "However, the accusation that you are a dishonorable client is not the worst slur attached to your name, Gaius Marius. There is another, more difficult to deal with."

"Then before we go into that slur, Gaius Julius, how would you suggest I stop the client rumor?" asked Marius.

"By marrying one of my daughters. If you are accepted as a husband for one of my daughters, it will give the world to understand that I do not find any evidence of truth in the client story. And spread the tale of the Spanish pigsty! If possible, get Publius Rutilius Rufus to confirm it. Everyone will then have a more than adequate explanation for the personal quality of Caecilius Metellus dislike," said Caesar, smiling. "It must have been funny—a Caecilius Metellus brought down to the level of—why, not even *Roman* pigs!"

"It was funny," said Marius shortly, anxious to press on. "Now what's this other slur?"

"You must surely know it for yourself, Gaius Marius."

"I can't think of a single thing, Gaius Julius."

"It is said that you're in trade."

Marius gasped, stunned. "But—but how am I in trade differently from three quarters of the rest of the Senate? I own no stock in any company which entitles me to vote in or influence company affairs! I'm purely a sleeping partner, a provider of capital! Is *that* what's said of me, that I take an active part in trade?"

"Certainly not. My dear Gaius Marius, no one elaborates! You are dismissed with a general sneer, the simple phrase 'He's in trade.' The implications are legion, yet nothing concrete is ever *said*! So those without the wisdom to inquire further are led to believe that your family has been in trade for many generations, that you yourself run companies, farm taxes, get fat off the grain supply," said Caesar.

"I see," said Marius, tight-lipped.

"You had better see," said Caesar gently.

"I do nothing in business that any Caecilius Metellus does not! In fact, I'm probably less actively involved in business."

"I agree. But if I had been advising you all along, Gaius Marius," said Caesar, "I would have tried to persuade you to avoid any business venture that didn't involve owning land or property. Your mines are above reproach; they're good, solid real estate. But for a New Man—well, company dealings aren't at all wise. You should have stuck to only those ventures which are absolutely unimpeachable for a senator—land and property."

"You mean, my company activities are yet another indication that I am not and never can be a Roman nobleman," said Gaius Marius bitterly.

"Precisely!"

Marius squared his shoulders; to dwell upon the hurt of a manifest injustice was a waste of precious time and energy. Instead, he turned his thoughts to the alluring prospect of marrying a girl of the Julian house. "Do you really believe my marrying one of your daughters will improve my public image so much, Gaius Julius?"

"It can't not."

"A Julia . . . Why then shouldn't I apply to marry a Sulpicia—or a Claudia—or an Aemilia—or a Cornelia? A girl from any of the old patrician houses would surely do as well—no, even better! I'd have the ancient name plus a great deal more current political clout," said Marius.

Smiling, Caesar shook his head. "I refuse to be provoked, Gaius Marius, so don't bother trying. Yes, you could marry a Cornelia or an Aemilia. But everyone would know you simply bought the girl. The advantage of marrying a Julia lies in the fact that the Julius Caesars have *never* sold their daughters to rich nobodies desirous of carving public careers for themselves and a noble heritage for their progeny. The very fact that you have been *permitted* to marry a Julia will inform the world that you are deserving of every political honor, and that the slurs upon your name are pure malice. The Julius Caesars have always been above selling their daughters. It is a universally known fact." Caesar paused to think for a moment, then added, "Mind you, I shall strongly advise both my sons to make capital out of our quirkiness and marry *their* daughters to rich nobodies as fast as they can!"

Marius leaned back with a second full cup. "Gaius Julius, just why are you offering me this chance?" he asked.

Caesar frowned. "There are two reasons," he said. "The first is perhaps not very sensible, but out of it came my decision to reverse our traditional family reluctance to make financial capital out of our children. You see, when I noticed you yesterday at the inauguration, I was visited with a premonition. Now I am not a man who is premonition-prone, you must understand. But I swear by all the gods, Gaius Marius, that suddenly I *knew* that I was looking at a man who would—given the chance!—carry Rome on his back out of terrible danger. And I knew too that if you were not given the chance, Rome would cease to be." He shrugged, shivered. "Well, there's a strong streak of superstition in every Roman, and in the really old families, it's very highly developed. I believed what I felt. After the passage of a day, I still believe what I felt. And wouldn't it be lovely, I thought to myself, if I, a humble backbencher senator, gave Rome the man Rome is going to need so desperately?"

"I feel it too," said Marius abruptly. "I have ever since I went to Numantia."

"So there you are! Two of us."

"And your second reason, Gaius Julius?"

Caesar sighed. "I have reached an age where I must face the fact that I have not so far managed to provide for my children as a father should. Love they have had. Material comfort they have had, without the burden of too much material comfort. Education they have had. But this house, plus five hundred *iugera* of land in the Alban Hills, is all I own." He sat up, crossed his legs, leaned forward again. "I have *four* children. That's two too many, as you well know. Two sons, two daughters. What I own will not ensure the public careers of my sons, even as backbenchers like their father. If I divide what I have between my two boys, neither will qualify for the senatorial census. If I leave what I have to my elder boy, Sextus, he will survive after my fashion. But my younger boy, Gaius, will be so penurious he will not even qualify for the knights' census. In effect, I will make a Lucius Cornelius Sulla out of him—do you know Lucius Cornelius Sulla?" asked Caesar.

"No," said Marius.

"His stepmother is my next-door neighbor, a ghastly woman of low birth and no sense, but very rich. However, she has blood kin of her own who will inherit her money, a nephew, I believe. How do I know so much about her circumstances? The penalty of being a neighbor who also happens to be a senator. She badgered me to draw up her will for her, and never stopped talking. Her stepson, Lucius Cornelius Sulla, lives with her, according to her because he literally has nowhere else to go. Imagine it—a patrician Cornelius old enough to be in the Senate right now, but with absolutely no hope of ever entering the Senate. He is destitute! His branch of the family is long decayed, and his father had virtually nothing; to compound Lucius Cornelius's woes, the father turned to wine, and whatever might have been left was drunk up years ago. It was the father married my next-door neighbor, who has kept the son under her roof since her husband died, but is not prepared to do anything else for him. You, Gaius Marius, have been infinitely luckier than

Lucius Cornelius Sulla, for at least your family was affluent enough to give you the property and income of a senator when the opportunity came for you to enter the Senate. Your New Man status could not keep you out of the Senate when the opportunity came, where failure to meet the means test most certainly would have. Lucius Cornelius Sulla's birth is impeccable on both sides. But his penuriousness has effectively excluded him from his rightful position in the scheme of things. And I find I care too much for the welfare of my younger son to reduce him or his children or his children's children to the circumstances of a Lucius Cornelius Sulla," said Caesar with some passion.

"Birth is an accident!" said Marius with equal passion. "Why should it have the power to dictate the course of a life?"

"Why should money?" Caesar countered. "Come now, Gaius Marius, admit that it is the way of all men in all lands to value birth and money. Roman society I find more flexible than most, as a matter of fact—compared to the Kingdom of the Parthians, for example, Rome is as ideal as Plato's hypothetical Republic! In Rome, there have actually been cases where men managed to rise from nothing. Not, mind you, that I have ever personally admired any of them who have done so," said Caesar reflectively. "The struggle seems to ruin them as men."

"Then perhaps it's better that Lucius Cornelius Sulla stay right where he is," said Marius.

"Certainly not!" said Caesar firmly. "I admit that your being a New Man has inflicted an unkind and unjust fate upon you, Gaius Marius, but I am sufficiently a man of my class to deplore the fate of Lucius Cornelius Sulla!" He assumed an expression of businesslike decision. "However, what concerns me at the moment is the fate of my children. My daughters, Gaius Marius, are *dowerless*! I cannot even scrape together a pittance for them, because to do so would impoverish my sons. That means my daughters have absolutely no chance of marrying men of their own class. I apologize, Gaius Marius, if in saying that you deem I have insulted you. But I don't mean men like yourself, I mean"—he waved his hands about—"let me say that again. I mean I will have to marry my daughters to men I don't like, don't admire, have nothing in common with. I wouldn't marry them to men of their own class whom I didn't like, either! A decent, honorable, likable man is my desire. But I won't have the opportunity to discover him. The ones who will apply to me for my daughters' hands will be presumptuous ingrates I'd rather show the toe of my boot than the palm of my hand. It's similar to the fate of a rich widow; decent men will have none of her for fear of being deemed a fortune hunter, so that the only ones she is left to choose from are fortune hunters."

Caesar slid off the couch and sat on its back edge with his feet dangling. "Would you mind, Gaius Marius, if we took a stroll in the garden? It's cold out there, I know, but I can give you a warm wrap. It's been a long evening, and not an easy one for me. I'm beginning to feel my bones seizing up."

Without a word Marius levered himself off the couch, took Caesar's shoes and slipped them onto Caesar's feet, laced them with the swift efficiency of an organized mind. Then he did the same for himself, and stood up, his hand beneath Caesar's elbow.

"That's why I like you so much," said Caesar. "No nonsense, no pretenses."

It was a small peristyle, yet it had a certain charm few city garden-courtyards possessed. Despite the season, aromatic herbs still thrived and gave off delicious scents, and the plantings were mostly perennial evergreens. Small country habits died hard in the Julius Caesars, Marius noticed with a thrill of gratified warmth; along the edges of the eaves, where they would catch the sun yet not get wet, there hung hundreds of little bunches of fleabane drying, just as at his father's house in Arpinum. By the end of January they would be tucked into every clothes chest and corner from one end of the *domus* to the other, to discourage fleas, silverfish, vermin of all kinds. Fleabane was cut at the winter solstice for drying; Marius hadn't thought there was a household in Rome knew of it.

Because there had been a guest to dinner, the chandeliers which hung from the ceiling of the colonnade surrounding the peristyle all burned faintly, and the little bronze lamps which lit the paths of the garden glowed a delicate amber through the wafer-thin marble of their round sides. The rain had ceased, but fat drops of water coated every shrub and bush, and the air was vaporous, chill.

Neither man noticed. Heads together (they were both tall, so it was comfortable to lean their heads together), they paced down the walkways, and finally stood by the little pool and fountain at the middle of the garden, its quartet of stone dryads holding torches aloft. It being winter, the pool was empty and the fountain turned off.

This, thought Gaius Marius (whose pool and fountain were full of water all year round thanks to a system of heating), is *real*. None of my tritons and dolphins and gushing waterfalls move me as this little old relic does.

"Are you interested in marrying one of my daughters?" asked Caesar, not anxiously, yet conveying anxiety.

"Yes, Gaius Julius, I am," said Marius with decision.

"Will it grieve you to divorce your wife?"

"Not in the least." Marius cleared his throat. "What do you require of me, Gaius Julius, in return for the gift of a bride and your name?"

"A great deal, as a matter of fact," said Caesar. "Since you will be admitted into the family in the guise of a second father rather than as a son-in-law—a privilege of age!—I will expect you to dower my other daughter and contribute to the welfare of *both* my sons. In the case of the unlucky daughter and my younger son, money and property are necessarily a large part of it. But you must be willing to throw your weight behind both my boys when they enter the Senate and begin their journey toward the consulship. I want both my boys to be consuls, you see. My son Sextus is one year older than the elder of the two boys my brother, Sextus, kept for himself, so my son Sextus will be the first of this generation's Julius Caesars to be of age to seek the consulship. I want him consul in his proper year, twelve years after entering the Senate, forty-two after his birth. He will be the first Julian consul in four hundred years. I *want* that distinction! Otherwise, my brother Sextus's son Lucius will become the first Julian consul, in the following year."

Pausing to peer at Marius's dimly lit face, Caesar put out a reassuring hand. "Oh, there was never bad feeling between my brother and me while he was alive, nor is there now between me and mine, and his two sons. But a man should be consul in his proper year. It looks best."

"Your brother, Sextus, adopted his oldest boy out, didn't he?" asked Marius, striving to recollect what a Roman of the Romans would have known without stopping to think.

"Yes, a very long time ago. His name was Sextus too, it's the name we normally give to our eldest sons."

"Of course! Quintus Lutatius Catulus! I would have remembered if he used Caesar as part of his name, but he doesn't, does he? He'll surely be the first Caesar to attain the consulship, he's a lot older than any of the others."

"No," said Caesar, shaking his head emphatically. "He's not a Caesar anymore, he's a Lutatius Catulus."

"I gather that old Catulus paid well for his adopted son," said Marius. "There seems to be plenty of money in your late brother's family, anyway."

"Yes, he paid very dearly. As you will for your new wife, Gaius Marius."

"Julia. I'll take Julia," said Marius.

"Not the little one?" asked Caesar, sounding surprised. "Well, I admit I'm glad, for no other reason than I consider no girl should be married before she turns eighteen, and Julilla is still a year and a half off that. I think you've chosen rightly, as a matter of fact. Yet—I've always thought Julilla the more attractive and interesting of the two."

"You would, you're her father," said Marius, grinning. "No, Gaius Julius, your younger daughter doesn't tempt me in the least. If she isn't wild about the fellow she marries, I think she'll lead him a merry dance. I'm too old for girlish caprices. Where Julia seems to me to have sense as good as her looks. I liked everything about her."

"She'll make an excellent consul's wife."

"Do you honestly think I'll succeed in being consul?"

Caesar nodded. "Oh, certainly! But not straightaway. Marry Julia first, then let things—and people—settle down. Try to find yourself a decent war for a couple of years—it will help enormously if you've got a recent military success to your credit. Offer your services to someone as a senior legate. Then seek the consulship two or three years hence."

"But I'll be fifty years old," said Marius dismally. "They don't like electing men so far past the normal age."

"You're already too old, so what matter another two or three years? They'll stand you in good stead if you use them well. And you don't look your age, Gaius Marius, an important factor. If you were visibly running to seed, it would be quite different. Instead, you're the picture of health and vigor—and you're a big man in size, which always impresses the Centuriate electors. In fact, New Man or not, if you hadn't incurred the enmity of the Caecilius Metelluses, you would have been a strong contender for the consulship three years ago, in your proper time for it. Were you an insignificant-looking little chap with a skinny right arm, even a Julia mightn't help. As it is, you'll be consul, never fear."

"What exactly do you want me to do for your sons?"

"In terms of property?"

"Yes." said Marius, forgetting his Chian finery and sitting down on a bench of white unpolished marble. Since he sat there for some time and the bench was very wet, when he rose he left a mottled, oddly natural-looking pinkish-purple stain all over it. The purple dye from his outfit percolated into the porous stone and fixed itself, so that the bench became—in the fullness of time, a generation or two down the years—one of the most admired and prized pieces of furniture another Gaius Julius Caesar was to bring into the Domus Publicus of the Pontifex Maximus. To the Gaius Julius Caesar who concluded a marriage bargain with Gaius Marius, however, the bench was an omen; a wonderful, wonderful omen. When the slave came to tell him of the miracle in the morning and he saw it for himself (the slave was awed rather than horrified— everyone knew the regal significance of the color purple), he heaved a sigh of perfect satisfaction. For the purple bench told him that in striking this marriage bargain, he was advancing his family to the purple of highest office. And it became fused in his mind with that strange premonition; yes, Gaius Marius had a place in Rome's fate that Rome as yet did not dream of. Caesar removed the bench from the garden and put it in his atrium, but he never told a soul how exactly it had become overnight a richly mottled, delicately veined purple and pink. An omen!

"For my son Gaius, I need enough good land to ensure him a seat in the Senate," Caesar said now to his seated guest. "It so happens that there are six hundred *iugera* of excellent land for sale right at this moment, adjoining my own five hundred in the Alban Hills."

"The price?"

"Horrible, given its quality and proximity to Rome. It's a seller's market, unfortunately." Caesar took a deep breath. "Four million sesterces—a million denarii," he said heroically.

"Agreed," said Marius, as if Caesar had said four thousand sesterces rather than four million. "However, I do think it prudent if we keep our dealings secret for the moment."

"Oh, absolutely!" said Caesar fervently.

"Then I'll bring you the money tomorrow myself, in cash," said Marius, smiling. "And what else do you want?"

"I expect that before my elder son enters the Senate, you will have turned into a consular. You will have influence and power, both from this fact and from your marriage to my Julia. I expect you to use your influence and power to advance my sons as they stand for the various offices. In fact, if you do get a military legateship to tide you over the next two or three years, I expect you to take my sons with you to your war. They are not inexperienced, they've both been cadets and junior officers, but they need more military service to help their careers, and under you, they'll be under the best."

Privately Marius didn't think either young man was the stuff of which great commanders were made, but he did think they would be more than adequate officers, so he made no comment other than to say, "I'd be glad to have them, Gaius Julius."

Caesar ploughed on. "As regards their political careers, they have the grave disadvantage of being patricians. As you well know, that means they can't run for office as tribunes of the plebs, and to make a splash as a tribune of the plebs is far and away the most telling method of establishing a political reputation. My sons will have to seek the curule aedileship—punitively expensive! So I expect you to make sure both Sextus and Gaius are elected curule aediles, with enough money in their purses to put on the kind of games and shows the people will remember affectionately when they go to the polls to elect praetors. And if it should prove necessary for my sons to buy votes at any stage, I expect you to provide the money."

"Agreed," said Gaius Marius, and held out his right hand with commendable alacrity, considering the magnitude of Caesar's demands; he was committing himself to a union which would cost him at least ten million sesterces.

Gaius Julius Caesar took the hand, clasped it strongly, warmly. "Good!" he said, and laughed.

They turned to walk back into the house, where Caesar sent a sleepy servant to fetch the old *sagum* for its owner.

"When may I see Julia, talk to her?" asked Marius when his head emerged from the opening in the center of the *sagum*'s wagon-wheel-sized circle.

"Tomorrow afternoon," said Caesar, opening the front door himself. "Good night, Gaius Marius."

"Good night, Gaius Julius," said Marius, and stepped out into the piercing cold of a rising north wind.

He walked home without feeling it, warmer than he had been in a very long time. Was it possible that his unwelcome guest, the feeling, had been right to continue to dwell inside him? To be consul! To set his family's feet firmly on the hallowed ground of the Roman nobility! If he could do that, then it definitely behooved him to sire a son. Another Gaius Marius.

The Julias shared a small sitting room, in which they met the next morning to break their fast. Julilla was unusually restless, hopping from one foot to the other, unable to settle.

"What *is* the matter?" her sister asked, exasperated.

"Can't you tell? There's something in the wind, and I want to meet Clodilla in the flower market this morning—I promised her I would! But I think we're all going to have to stay home for another boring old family conference," said Julilla gloomily.

"You know," said Julia, "you really are unappreciative! How many other girls do you know who actually have the privilege of saying what they think at a family conference?"

"Oh, rubbish, they're boring, we never talk about anything interesting—just servants and unaffordables and tutors—I want to leave school, I'm fed up with Homer and boring old Thucydides! What use are they to a girl?"

"They mark her out as well educated and cultured," said Julia repressively. "Don't you want a good husband?"

Julilla giggled. "My notion of a good husband does *not* include Homer and Thucydides," she said. "Oh, I want to go out this morning!" And she jigged up and down.

"Knowing you, if you want to go out, you'll manage to go out," said Julia. "Now will you sit down and eat?"

A shadow darkened the door; both girls looked up, jaws dropping. Their father! Here!

"Julia, I want to talk to you," he said, coming in, and for once ignoring Julilla, his favorite.

"Oh, *tata*! Not even a good-morning kiss?" asked his favorite, pouting.

He glanced at her absently, pecked her on the cheek, and then recollected himself enough to give her a smile. "If you can find something to do, my butterfly, how about doing it?"

Her face was transformed into joy. "Thank you, *tata,* thank you! May I go to the flower market? And the Porticus Margaritaria?"

"How many pearls are you going to buy today?" her *tata* asked, smiling.

"Thousands!" she cried, and skipped out.

As she passed him, Caesar slipped a silver denarius into her left hand. "Not the price of the littlest pearl, I know, but it might buy you a scarf," he said.

"*Tata!* Oh, thank you, thank you!" cried Julilla, her arms sliding about his neck, her lips smacking his cheek. Then she was gone.

Caesar looked very kindly at his older daughter. "Sit down, Julia," he said.

She sat expectantly, but he said nothing more until Marcia came in and ranged herself on the couch alongside her daughter.

"What is it, Gaius Julius?" asked Marcia, curious but not apprehensive.

He didn't sit, stood shifting his weight from one foot to the other, then turned the full beauty of his blue eyes upon Julia. "My dear, did you like Gaius Marius?" he asked.

"Why yes, *tata,* I did."

"For what reasons?"

She considered the question carefully. "His plain but honest speaking, I think. And his lack of affectation. He confirmed what I have always suspected."

"Oh?"

"Yes. About the gossip one is always hearing—that he has no Greek, that he's a shocking oaf from the country, that his military reputation was got at the expense of others and the whim of Scipio Aemilianus. It always seemed to me that people talked *too* much—you know, too spitefully and constantly—for any of it to have been true. After meeting him, I'm sure I'm right. He's not an oaf, and I don't even think he acts like a rustic. He's very intelligent! And very well read. Oh, his Greek isn't very beautiful on the ear, but it's only his accent at fault. His construction and vocabulary are excellent. Just like his Latin. I thought his eyebrows were terrifically distinguished, didn't you? His taste in clothing is a bit ostentatious, but I expect that's his wife's fault." At which point Julia ran down, looking suddenly flustered.

"Julia! You *really* liked him!" said Caesar, a curious note of awe in his voice.

"Yes, *tata,* of course I did," she said, puzzled.

"I'm very glad to hear it, because you're going to marry him," blurted Caesar, his famous tact and diplomacy deserting him in this unfamiliar situation.

Julia blinked. "Am I?"

Marcia stiffened. "Is she?"

"Yes," said *tata,* and found it necessary to sit down.

"And just when did you arrive at this decision?" asked Marcia, with a dangerous note of umbrage in her voice. "Where has he seen Julia, to have asked for her?"

"He didn't ask for Julia," said Caesar, on the defensive. "I offered him Julia. Or Julilla. That's why I invited him to eat dinner with us."

Marcia was now staring at him with an expression on her face that clearly questioned his sanity. "*You* offered a New Man closer to your own age than our daughter's his choice of either of our daughters as his wife?" she asked, angry now.

"Yes, I did."

"*Why?*"

"Obviously you know who he is."

"Of course I know who he is!"

"So you must know he's one of the richest men in Rome?"

"Yes!"

"Look, girls," said Caesar seriously, lumping wife in with daughter, "you both know what we're facing. Four children, and not enough property or money to do the right thing by any of them. Two boys with the birth *and* the brains to go all the way to the top, and two girls with the birth *and* the beauty to marry only the best. But—no money! No money for the *cursus honorum,* and no money for dowries."

"Yes," said Marcia flatly. Because her father had died before she attained marriageable age, his children by his first wife had combined with the executors of his estate to make sure there was nothing worthwhile left for her. Gaius Julius Caesar had married her for love, and since she had only a tiny dowry, her family had been glad to assent to the union. Yes, they had married for love—and it had rewarded them with happiness, tranquillity, three extremely well adjusted children, and one gorgeous butterfly. But it had never ceased to humiliate Marcia that in marrying her, Caesar did no good financially.

"Gaius Marius needs a patrician wife of a family whose integrity and *dignitas* are as impeccable as its rank," Caesar explained. "He ought to have been elected consul three years ago, but the Caecilius Metelluses made sure he wasn't, and as a New Man with a Campanian wife, he doesn't have the family connections to defy them. Our Julia will force Rome to take Gaius Marius seriously. Our Julia will endow him with rank, enhance his *dignitas*—his public worth and standing will rise a thousandfold. In return, Gaius Marius has undertaken to ease our financial difficulties."

"Oh, Gaius!" said Marcia, eyes filling with tears.

"Oh, Father!" said Julia, eyes softening.

Now that he could see his wife's anger dissipating and his daughter beginning to glow, Caesar relaxed. "I noticed him at the inauguration of the new consuls the day before yesterday. The odd thing is that I've never really paid him any attention before, even when he was praetor, nor when he ran unsuccessfully for consul. But on New Year's Day, I—perhaps it would not be an exaggeration to say that the scales fell from before my eyes. I *knew* he was a great man! I knew Rome is going to need him. Just when I got the idea to help myself by helping him, I don't quite know. But by the time we entered the temple and stood together, it was there in my mind, fully formed. So I took the chance, and invited him to dine."

"And you really did proposition him, not the other way around?" asked Marcia.

"I did."

"Our troubles are over?"

"Yes," said Caesar. "Gaius Marius may not be a Roman of Rome, but in my opinion he's a man of honor. I believe he'll hew to his side of our bargain."

"What was his side of the bargain?" asked the practical mother, mentally reaching for her abacus.

"Today he will give me four million sesterces in cash to buy that land next door to ours at Bovillae. Which means that young Gaius will have enough property to ensure him a seat in the Senate without my needing to touch Sextus's inheritance. He will assist both of our boys to become curule aediles. He will assist both of our boys to do whatever they have to do in order to be elected consuls when their times come. And though we didn't discuss the details, he will dower Julilla handsomely."

"And what will he do for Julia?" asked Marcia crisply.

Caesar looked blank. "Do for Julia?" he echoed. "What more can he do for Julia than to marry her? There's no dowry going with her, after all, and it's certainly costing him a large fortune to make her his wife."

"Normally a girl has her dowry to make sure she retains a measure of financial independence after her marriage, especially in the event that she is divorced. Though some women are fools enough to hand their dowries over to their husbands, by no means all women do, and it has to be found when the marriage is over even if the husband has had the use of it. I insist that Gaius Marius dower Julia to a degree that will make sure she has enough to live on if at any time he divorces her," said Marcia, in a tone which brooked no argument.

"Marcia, I *can't* ask the man for more!" said Caesar.

"I'm afraid you must. In fact, I'm astonished you didn't think of it for yourself, Gaius Julius." Marcia heaved a sigh of exasperation. "I never can understand why the world labors under the fallacious belief that men have better business heads than women! They don't, you know. And you, my dear husband, are woollier in business matters than most men! Julia is the whole cause of our change in fortune, so we owe it to her to guarantee her future too."

"I admit you're right, my dear," said Caesar hollowly, "but I really can't ask the man for more!"

Julia looked from mother to father and back to mother; this was not the first time she had seen them differ, of course, especially over money matters, but it was the first time she had been the central issue, and it distressed her. So she put herself verbally between them by saying, "It's all right, truly it is! I'll ask Gaius Marius about a dowry myself, I'm not afraid to. He'll understand."

"Julia! You *want* to marry him!" gasped Marcia.

"Of course I do, Mama. I think he's wonderful!"

"My girl, he's just about thirty years older than you are! You'll be a widow before you know it."

"Young men are boring, they remind me of my brothers. I would much rather marry someone like Gaius Marius," said the scholarly daughter. "I'll be good to him, I promise. He will love me, and never regret the expense."

"Whoever would have thought it?" asked Caesar, of no one in particular.

"Don't be so surprised, *tata*. I'll be eighteen soon, I knew you would be arranging a marriage for me this year, and I must confess I've been dreading the prospect. Not marriage itself, exactly—just who my husband would be. Last night when I met Gaius Marius, I—I thought to myself immediately, wouldn't it be lovely if you found me someone like him?" Julia blushed. "He isn't a bit like you, *tata,* and yet he *is* like you—I found him fair, and kind, and honest."

Gaius Julius Caesar looked at his wife. "Isn't it a rare pleasure to discover that one genuinely likes one's child? To love one's child is natural. But liking? Liking has to be earned," he said.

Two encounters with women in the same day unnerved Gaius Marius more than the prospect of fighting an enemy army ten times bigger than his own. One encounter was his first meeting with his intended bride and her mother; the other was his last meeting with his present wife.

Prudence and caution dictated that he interview Julia before he saw Grania, to make sure there were no unforeseen hitches. So at the eighth hour of the day—midafternoon, that is—he arrived at the house of Gaius Julius Caesar, clad this time in his purple-bordered toga, unaccompanied and unburdened by the massive weight of a million silver denarii; the sum amounted to 10,000 pounds in weight, and that was 160 talents, or 160 men carrying a full load. Luckily "cash" was a relative term; Gaius Marius brought a bank draft.

In Gaius Julius Caesar's study he passed his host a small, rolled-up piece of Pergamum parchment.

"I've done everything as discreetly as possible," he said as Caesar unfurled the parchment and scanned the few lines written on it. "As you see, I've arranged for the deposit of two hundred talents of silver in your name with your bankers. There's no way the deposit can be traced to me without someone's wasting a good deal more of his time than any firm of bankers would allow for no better reason than to gratify curiosity."

"Which is just as well. It would look as if I've accepted a bribe! If I weren't such senatorial small fry, someone in my bank would be sure to alert the urban praetor," said Caesar, letting the parchment curl itself up and placing it to one side.

"I doubt anyone has ever bribed with so much, even to a consul with huge clout," said Marius, smiling.

Caesar held out his right hand. "I hadn't thought of it in talents," he said. "Ye gods, I asked you for the earth! Are you *sure* it hasn't left you short?"

"Not at all." Marius found himself unable to loosen his fingers from Caesar's convulsive grip. "If the land you want goes for the price you quoted me, then I've given you forty talents too much. They represent your younger daughter's dowry."

"I don't know how to thank you, Gaius Marius." Caesar let go Marius's hand at last, looking more and more uncomfortable. "I've kept telling myself I'm *not* selling my daughter, but at this moment it seems suspiciously like it to me! Truly, Gaius Marius, I wouldn't sell my daughter! I do believe her future with you and the status of her children of your begetting will be illustrious. I believe you'll look after her properly, and treasure her as I want my daughter treasured." His voice was gruff; not for another sum as large could he have done as Marcia wished, and demand yet more as a dowry for Julia. So he got up from behind his desk a little shakily, picking up the piece of parchment more casually than his heart or mind could ever hold it. Then he tucked it into the sinus of his toga, where the toga's folds looped beneath his free right arm and formed a capacious pocket. "I won't rest until this is lodged with my bank." He hesitated, then said, "Julia doesn't turn eighteen until the beginning of May, but I don't wish to delay your marriage until halfway through June, so—if you're agreeable—we can set the ceremony for some time in April."

"That will be acceptable," said Marius.

"I had already decided to do that," Caesar went on, more for the sake of talking, filling in the awkward gap his discomfort had created. "It's a nuisance when a girl is born right at the beginning of the only time of year when it's considered bad luck to marry. Though why high spring and early summer should be thought bad luck, I don't know." He shook himself out of his mood. "Wait here, Gaius Marius. I'll send Julia to you."

Now it was Gaius Marius's turn to be on edge, apprehensive; he waited in the small but tidy room with a terrifying anxiety. Oh, pray the girl was not too unwilling! Nothing in Caesar's demeanor had suggested she was unwilling, but he knew very well that there were things no one would ever tell him, and he found himself yearning for a truly willing Julia. Yet—how could she welcome a union so inappropriate to her blood, her beauty, her youth? How many tears had she shed when the news was broken to her? Did she already hanker after some handsome young aristocrat rendered ineligible by common sense and necessity? An elderly Italian hayseed with no Greek—what a husband for a Julia!

The door opening onto the colonnade at the house end of the peristyle-garden moved inward, and the sun entered Caesar's study like a fanfare of trumpets, blinding and brassy, golden-low. Julia stood in its midst, her right hand out, smiling.

"Gaius Marius," she said with pleasure, the smile clearly starting in her eyes.

"Julia," he said, moving close enough to take the hand, but holding it as if he didn't know what to do with it, or what to do next. He cleared his full throat. "Your father has told you?"

"Oh, yes." Her smile didn't fade; if anything, it grew, and there was nothing immature or girlishly bashful in her demeanor. On the contrary, she appeared in complete control of herself and the situation, regally poised, a princess in her power, yet subtly submissive.

"You don't mind?" he asked abruptly.

"I'm delighted," she said, her beautiful grey eyes wide and warm, the smile still in them; as if to reassure him, she curled her fingers around the edge of his palm, and gently squeezed it. "Gaius Marius, Gaius Marius, don't look so worried! I really, truly, honestly *am* delighted!"

He lifted his left hand, encumbered in folds of toga, and took hers between both of his, looking down at its perfect oval nails, its creamy tapered fingers. "I'm an old man!" he said.

"Then I must like old men, because I do like you."

"You *like* me?"

She blinked. "Of course! I would not otherwise have agreed to marry you. My father is the gentlest of men, not a tyrant. Much and all as he might have hoped I would be willing to marry you, he would never, never have forced me to it."

"But are you sure you haven't forced yourself?" he asked.

"It wasn't necessary," she said patiently.

"Surely there's some young man you like better!"

"Not at all. Young men are too like my brothers."

"But—but—" He cast round wildly for some objection, and finally said, "My eyebrows!"

"I think they're wonderful," she said.

He felt himself blush, helpless to control it, and was thus thrown even further off balance; then he realized that, collected and self-possessed though she was, she was nevertheless a complete innocent, and understood nothing of what he was enduring. "Your father says we may marry in April, before your birthday. Is that all right?" he asked.

She frowned. "Well, I suppose so, if that's what he says. But I'd rather put it forward to March, if you and he agree. I'd like to be married on the festival of Anna Perenna."

An appropriate day—yet an unlucky one too. The feast of Anna Perenna, held on the first full moon after the beginning of March, was all tied up with the moon, and the old New Year. In itself the feast day was lucky, but the day following it was not.

"Don't you fear starting your first proper day of marriage with poor omens?" he asked.

"No," said Julia. "There are none but good omens in marrying you."

She put her left hand beneath his right so that they were hand-fast, and looked up at him gravely.

"My mother has only given me a very short time to be alone with you," she said, "and there is one matter we must clarify between us before she comes in. My dowry." Now her smile did fade, replaced by a look of serious aloofness. "I do not anticipate an unhappy relationship with you, Gaius Marius, for I see nothing in you to make me doubt your temper or your integrity, and you will find mine all they should be. If we can respect each other, we will be happy. However, my mother is adamant about a dowry, and my father is most distressed at her attitude. She says I must be dowered in case you should ever decide to divorce me. But my father is already overwhelmed by your generosity, and loath to ask you for more. So I said *I* would ask, and I must ask before mama comes in. Because she's bound to say something."

There was no cupidity in her gaze, only concern. "Would it perhaps be possible to lay a sum aside on the understanding that if, as I expect, we find no need to divorce, it will be yours as well as mine? Yet if we do divorce, it would be mine?"

What a little lawyer she was! A true Roman. All so very carefully phrased, gracefully inoffensive, yet crystal-clear.

"I think it's possible," he said gravely.

"You must be sure I can't spend it while I'm married to you," she said. "That way, you'll know I'm honorable."

"If that's what you want, that's what I'll do," he said. "But it isn't necessary to tie it up. I'm quite happy to give you a sum now in your own name, to do with as you please."

A laugh escaped her. "Just as well you chose me and not Julilla! No, thank you, Gaius Marius. I prefer the honorable way," she said gently, and lifted her face. "Now will you kiss me before my mother comes?"

Her demand for a dowry hadn't discomposed him one bit, where this demand certainly did. Suddenly he understood how vitally important it was that he do nothing to disappoint her—or, worse still, give her a distaste for him. Yet what did he know about kisses, about lovemaking? His self-esteem had never required reassurances from his infrequent mistresses as to his competence as a lover, because it had never really mattered to him what they thought of his lovemaking or his kisses; nor did he have the faintest idea what young girls expected from their first lovers. Ought he to grab her and kiss her passionately, ought he to make this initial contact chastely light? Lust or respect, since love was at best a hope for the future? Julia was an unknown quantity, he had no clue as to what she expected—or what she wanted. All he did know was that pleasing her mattered greatly to him.

In the end he stepped closer to her without releasing her hands, and leaned his head down, not a very long way, for she was unusually tall. Her lips were closed and cool, soft and silky; natural instinct solved his dilemma for him when he shut his eyes and simply put himself on the receiving end of whatever she cared to offer. It was a totally new experience for her, one she desired without knowing what it would bring her, for Caesar and Marcia had kept their girls sheltered, refined, ignorant, yet not unduly inhibited. This girl, the scholarly one, had not developed along the lines of her young sister, but she was not incapable of strong feeling. The difference between Julia and Julilla was one of quality, not capacity.

So when her hands struggled to be free, he let go of them at once, and would have moved away from her had she not immediately lifted her arms and put them round his neck. The kiss warmed. Julia opened her lips slightly, and Marius employed his empty hands in holding her. Vast and many-folded, the toga prevented too intimate a contact, which suited them both; and the moment came quite naturally when this exquisite form of exploration found a spontaneous ending.

Marcia, entering noiselessly, could fault neither of them, for though they were embraced, his mouth was against her cheek, and she seemed, eyelids lowered, as satisfied yet unassailed as a cat discreetly stroked in just the right way.

Neither of them confused, they broke apart and turned to face the mother—who looked, thought Marius, distinctly grim. In her, not as ancient an aristocrat as the Julius Caesars, Marius sensed a certain grievance, and understood that Marcia would have preferred Julia to marry someone of her own class, even if it had meant no money came into the family. However, his happiness at that moment was complete; he could afford to overlook the umbrage of his future mother-in-law, some two years younger than he was himself. For in truth she was right: Julia belonged to someone younger and better than an elderly Italian hayseed with no Greek. Which was not to say that he intended for one moment to change his mind about taking her! Rather, it was up to him to demonstrate to Marcia that Julia was going to the best man of all.

"I asked about a dowry, Mama," said Julia at once, "and it's all arranged."

Marcia did have the grace to look uncomfortable. "That was my doing," she said, "not my daughter's—or my husband's."

"I understand," he said pleasantly.

"You have been most generous. We thank you, Gaius Marius."

"I disagree, Marcia. It's you who've been most generous. Julia is a pearl beyond price," said Marius.

A statement which stuck in his mind, so that when he left the house shortly after and found the tenth hour of daylight still in the lap of the future, he turned at the foot of the Vestal Steps to the right rather than to the left, and skirted the beautiful little round temple of Vesta to walk up the narrow defile between the Regia and the Domus Publicus. Which brought him out onto the Via Sacra at the foot of the little incline called the Clivus Sacer.

He strode up the Clivus Sacer briskly, anxious to reach the Porticus Margaritaria before the traders all went home. This big, airy shopping arcade built around a central quadrangle contained Rome's best jewelers. It had got its name from the pearl sellers who had established quarters in it when it had been newly erected; at that time the defeat of Hannibal had seen all the stringent sumptuary laws forbidding women to wear jewelry repealed, and in consequence the women of Rome spent wildly on every kind of gewgaw.

Marius wanted to buy Julia a pearl, and knew exactly where to go, as did all who lived in Rome: the firm of Fabricius Margarita. The first Marcus Fabricius had been the first of all the pearl vendors, and set up his shop when what pearls there were came from freshwater mussels, bluff and rock and mud oysters, and the sea pen, and were small and mostly dark in color. But Marcus Fabricius made such a specialty of pearls that he followed like a sniffer-hound down the tracks of legends, journeyed to Egypt and Arabia Nabataea in search of ocean pearls—and found them. In the beginning they had been still disappointingly small and irregular in shape, but they did have the true cream-white pearl color, and came from the waters of the Sinus Arabicus, far down near Aethiopia. Then as his name became known, he discovered a source of pearls from the seas around India and the pear-shaped island of Taprobane just below India. At which point he gave himself the last name of Margarita and established a monopoly of ocean pearl trade. Now, in the time of the consulship of Marcus Minucius Rufus and Spurius Postumius Albinus, his grandson—another Marcus Fabricius Margarita—was so well stocked that a rich man might be fairly sure if he went to Fabricius Margarita that he would find a suitable pearl in the shop right there and then.

Fabricius Margarita did indeed have a suitable pearl on hand, but Marius walked home without it, electing to have its perfect marble-sized roundness and moonlit color set upon a heavy gold necklace surrounded by smaller pearls, a process which would consume some days. The novelty of actually wanting to gift a woman with precious things possessed his thoughts, jostling there amid memories of her kiss, her willingness to be his bride. A great philanderer he was not, but he knew enough about women to recognize that Julia did not present the picture of a girl allying herself where she could not give her heart; and the very idea of owning a heart as pure, as young, as blue-blooded as Julia's filled him with the kind of gratitude that cried out to shower her with precious things. Her willingness he saw as a vindication, an omen for the future; she was his pearl beyond price, so to her must come pearls, the tears of a distant tropical moon that fell into the deepest ocean and, in sinking to its bottom, froze solid. And he would find her an Indian *adamas* stone harder than any other substance known and as big as a hazelnut, and a wonderful green *smaragdus* stone with blue flickers in its heart, all the way from northern Scythia . . . and a *carbunculus* stone, as bright and glistening as a blister full of new blood . . .

Grania was in, of course. When was she ever out? Waiting every day from the ninth hour onward to see if her husband would come home for dinner, postponing the meal a few minutes only at a time, she drove her appallingly expensive cook mad, and all too often ended in sniffling her way through a solitary repast designed to revive the vanished appetite of a glutton emerging from a fasting cure.

The culinary masterpiece produced by the artiste in the kitchen was always, always wasted, whether Marius dined out or at home; for Grania had outlaid a fortune for a cook qualified to cast the most discriminating Epicure into ecstasies. When Marius did stay home to dinner he was faced with fare like dormice stuffed with foie gras, the tiniest fig-pecker birds daintied beyond imagination, exotic vegetables and pungent arrays of sauces too rich for his tongue and his belly, if not his purse. Like most Military Men, he was happiest with a hunk of bread and a bowl of pease-pottage cooked with bacon, and didn't care if he missed a meal or two anyway. Food was fuel for the body to him, not fuel for pleasure. That after so many years of marriage Grania had still not worked this out for herself was symptomatic of the vast distance between them.

What Marius was about to do to Grania did not sit well with him, scant though his affection for her was. Their relationship had always been tinged with guilt on his side, for he was well aware that she had come to their marriage looking forward to a life of connubial bliss, cozy with children and shared dinners, a life centered on Arpinum, but with lots of trips to Puteoli, and perhaps a two-week holiday in Rome during the *ludi Romani* every September.

But from first sight of her to first night of her, she had left him so utterly unmoved that he couldn't even begin to counterfeit liking and desire. It wasn't that she was ugly, she wasn't; her round face was pleasant enough, it had even been described to him as beautiful, with its large well-opened eyes and small full mouth. It wasn't that she was a termagant, she wasn't; in fact, her behavior was tailored to please him in every way she knew. The trouble was, she couldn't please him, not if she filled his cup with Spanish fly and took one of the fashionable courses in lascivious dancing.

Most of his guilt stemmed from his knowledge that she did not have the faintest idea why she couldn't please him, even after many painful quizzes on the subject; he was never able to give her satisfactory answers, because he honestly didn't know why himself, and that was the real trouble.

For the first fifteen years she had made a praiseworthy attempt to keep her figure, which was not at all bad—full of breast, small of waist, swell of hip—and brushed her dark hair dry in the sun after washing it, to give it plenty of lustrous red highlights; and outlined her soft brown eyes with a black line of *stibium;* and made sure she never stank of sweat or menses.

If there was a change in him on this evening in early January when the door servant admitted him to his house, it was that he had finally found a woman who did please him, with whom he looked forward to marriage, a shared life. Perhaps in contrasting the two, Grania and Julia, he could find the elusive answer at last? And immediately he saw it. Grania was pedestrian, untutored, wholesome, domestic, the ideal wife for a Latin squire. Julia was aristocratic, scholarly, stately, political, the ideal wife for a Roman consul. In affiancing him to Grania, his family had naturally assumed he would lead the life of a Latin squire, this being the heritage of his blood, and chosen his wife accordingly. But Gaius Marius was an eagle, he flew the Arpinate coop. Adventurous and ambitious, formidably intelligent, a no-nonsense soldier who yet had vast imagination, he had come far and intended to go farther still, especially now he was promised a Julia of the Julius Caesars. *She* was the kind of wife he wanted! The kind of wife he *needed.*

"Grania!" he called, dropping the huge bulk of his toga on the magnificent mosaic floor of the atrium and stepping out of it before the servant scurrying to retrieve it could get there and save its whiteness from contact with the soles of Gaius Marius's muddy boots.

"Yes, dear?" She came running from her sitting room with pins and brooches and crumbs littering her wake, far too plump these days, for she had long learned to console her bitter loneliness with too many sweetmeats and syruped figs.

"In the *tablinum,* please," he flung over his shoulder as he strode toward the room.

Pattering quickly, she entered on his heels.

"Shut the door," he said, moving to where his favorite chair stood behind his big desk, seating himself in it, and thus compelling her to sit like a client on the opposite side of a great expanse of polished malachite edged with tooled gold.

"Yes, dear?" she asked, not fearfully, for he was never intentionally rude to her, nor did he ever ill-treat her in any way other than through the medium of neglect.

He frowned, turning an ivory abacus over between his hands; hands she had always loved, for they were as graceful as they were strong, square of palm but long of finger, and he used them like an expert, firmly decisive. Head on one side, she stared at him, the stranger to whom she had been married for twenty-five years. A fine-looking man, was her verdict now, no different from a thousand other verdicts. Did she love him still? How could she know? After twenty-five years, what she had come to feel was a complicated fabric with absolutely no pattern to it, so airy in some places the light of her mind shone through it, yet so dense in others that it hung like a curtain between her thoughts and her vague idea of who and what Grania the person was. Rage, pain, bewilderment, resentment, grief, self-pity—oh, so many, many emotions! Some felt so long ago they were almost forgotten, others fresh and new because she was now forty-five years old, her menses were dwindling, her poor unfruitful womb shrinking. If one emotion had come to dominate, it was ordinary, depressing, uninspiring disappointment; these days she even offered to Vediovis, the patron god of disappointments.

Marius's lips opened to speak; by nature they were full and sensuous, but he had already disciplined them to the contours of strength before she had met him. Grania leaned a little forward to hang upon what he would say, every fiber of her being strung to twanging point with the effort of concentrating.

"I am divorcing you," he said, and handed her the scrap of parchment upon which early this morning he had written the bill of divorcement.

What he said hardly penetrated; she spread the thick and slightly smelly rectangle of supple skin out on the surface of his desk and studied it presbyopically until its words kindled a response. Then she looked from parchment to husband.

"I have done nothing to deserve this," she said dully.

"I disagree," he said.

"What? What *have* I done?"

"You have not been a suitable wife."

"And it has taken you all of twenty-five years to come to this conclusion?"

"No. I knew it from the beginning."

"Why didn't you divorce me then?"

"It didn't seem important at the time."

Oh, one hurt after another, one insult after another! The parchment vibrated in her grasp, she flung it away and clenched her hands into hard little fists.

"Yes, that's about the sum of it!" she said, finally alive enough to be angry. "I never have been important to you. Not even important enough to divorce. So why are you doing it now?"

"I want to marry again," he said.

Incredulity drove out rage; her eyes widened. *"You?"*

"Yes. I've been offered a marriage alliance with a girl of a very old patrician house."

"Oh, come, Marius! The great despiser, turned snob?"

"No, I don't believe so," he said dispassionately, concealing his discomfort as successfully as his guilt. "Simply, this marriage means I will be consul after all."

The fire of indignation in her died, snuffed out by the cold wind of logic. How could one argue against that? How could one blame? How could one fight anything so inevitable? Though never once had he discussed his political rejection with her, nor complained of how lightly they held him, she knew it just the same. And had wept for him, burned for him, wished there were some way she could rectify the sin of their omission, those Roman noblemen who controlled Roman politics. Yet what could she do, a Grania from Puteoli? Wealthy, respectable, unimpeachable as wives went. But utterly lacking in clout, owning no relatives capable of rectifying the injustices doled out to him; if he was a Latin squire, she was a Campanian merchant's daughter, lowest of the low in a Roman nobleman's eyes. Until recently, her family hadn't held the citizenship.

"I see," she said tonelessly.

And he was merciful enough to leave it at that, not to hint to her of his excitement, the glowing little kernel of love busy germinating in his dormant heart. Let her think it was purely a match of political expediency.

"I *am* sorry, Grania," he said gently.

"So am I, so am I," she said, starting to shake again, but this time with the chill prospect of grasswidowhood, an even greater and more intolerable loneliness than the kind she was used to. Life without Gaius Marius? Unthinkable.

"If it's any consolation, the alliance was offered to me, I didn't actively seek it."

"Who is she?"

"The elder daughter of Gaius Julius Caesar."

"A Julia! That is looking high! You'll certainly be consul, Gaius Marius."

"Yes, I think so too." He fiddled with his favorite reed pen, the little porphyry bottle of blotting sand with its perforated gold cap, the inkwell made from a chunk of polished amethyst. "You have your dowry, of course, and it's more than adequate to meet your requirements. I invested it in more profitable enterprises than your father had, and since you've never touched it, it's now very large indeed." He cleared his throat. "I presume you'll want to live closer to your own family, but I wonder if—at your age—it's not advisable to have your own house, especially with your father dead, and your brother the *paterfamilias.*"

"You never slept with me often enough to give me a child," she said, aching to her core in the midst of this icy solitude. "Oh, I wish I had a child!"

"Well, I'm damned glad you don't! Our son would be my heir, and the marriage to Julia couldn't have its significance." He realized that didn't sound the proper note, and added, "Be sensible, Grania! Our children would be grown up by now, and living lives of their own. No comfort to you at all."

"There'd at least be grandchildren," she said, the tears starting to gather. "I wouldn't be so terribly alone!"

"I have been telling you for years, get yourself a little lapdog!" It wasn't said unkindly, it was merely sound advice; he thought of better advice still, and added, "What you ought to do is marry again, actually."

"Never!" she cried.

He shrugged. "Have it your own way. Getting back to where-

abouts you should live, I'm willing to buy a villa on the sea at
Cumae and install you in it. Cumae's a comfortable distance by
litter from Puteoli—close enough to visit your family for a day or
two, far enough away to assure you peace."

Hope had gone. "Thank you, Gaius Marius."

"Oh, don't thank me!" He got up and came round the desk to
help her to her feet with an impersonal hand under her elbow.
"You had better tell my steward what's happening, and think about
which slaves you want to take with you. I'll have one of my agents
find a suitable villa at Cumae tomorrow. I'll keep it in my name, of
course, but I'll deed you a life tenancy—or until you marry. All
right, all right! I know you said you wouldn't, but enterprising
suitors will smother you like flies a honey-pot. You're wealthy."
They had reached the door of her sitting room, and there he
stopped, taking his hand away. "I'd appreciate it if you'd be out of
here the day after tomorrow. In the morning, preferably. I imagine
Julia will want to make changes to the house before she moves in,
and we're to marry in eight weeks, which doesn't give me long to
make whatever changes she wants. So—the morning of the day
after tomorrow. I can't bring her here to inspect the place until
you've gone, it wouldn't be proper."

She started to ask him—something, anything—but he was already walking away.

"Don't wait dinner for me," he called as he crossed the vast
expanse of the atrium. "I'm going to see Publius Rutilius, and I
doubt I'll be back before you're in bed."

Well, that was that. It wouldn't break her heart to lose her oc-
cupancy of this huge barn of a house; she had always hated it, and
hated the urban chaos of Rome. Why he had chosen to live on the
damp and gloomy northern slope of the Arx of the Capitol had
always puzzled her, though she knew the site's extreme exclusivity had operated powerfully upon him. But there were so few
houses in the vicinity that visiting friends meant long walks up
many steps, and it was a residential political backwater; the neighbors, such as they were, were all terrific merchant princes with
little interest in politics.

She nodded at the servant standing by the wall outside her sitting room. "Please fetch the steward at once," she said.

The steward came, a majestic Greek from Corinth who had managed to get himself an education and then sold himself into slavery in order to make his fortune and eventually acquire the Roman citizenship.

"Strophantes, the master is divorcing me," she said without shame, for there was no shame attached. "I must be gone from here by the day after tomorrow, in the morning. Please see to my packing."

He bowed, hiding his amazement; this was one marriage he had never expected to see terminate sooner than death, for it had a mummified torpor about it rather than the kind of bitter warfare which usually led to divorce.

"Do you intend to take any of the staff, *domina*?" he asked, sure of his own continuance in this house, for he belonged to Gaius Marius, not to Grania.

"The cook, certainly. All the kitchen servants, otherwise he'll be unhappy, won't he? My serving girls, my seamstress, my hairdresser, my bath slaves, and both the page boys," she said, unable to think of anyone else she depended upon and liked.

"Certainly, *domina*." And he went away at once, dying to impart this fabulous piece of gossip to the rest of the staff, and especially looking forward to breaking the news of his move to the cook; that conceited master of the pots wouldn't welcome the exchange of Rome for Puteoli!

Grania wandered into her spacious sitting room and looked around at its comfortable air of dishevelment, at her paints and workbox, at the nail-studded trunk in which reposed her baby trousseau, hopefully gathered, heartbreakingly unused.

Since no Roman wife chose or bought the furniture, Gaius Marius would not be handing any of it over; her eyes brightened a little, the tears trickled inward instead of down her cheeks, and were not replaced. Really, she had only tomorrow before leaving Rome, and Cumae was not one of the world's greatest emporiums. Tomorrow she would go shopping for furniture to fill her new villa! How nice to be able to pick what *she* wanted! Tomorrow would be busy after all, no time for thinking, no empty hours to grieve. Much of the sting and shock began at once to evaporate; she could get through the coming night, now that she had a shopping spree to look forward to.

"Berenice!" she called, and then, when the girl appeared, "I'll dine now, tell the kitchen."

She found paper on which to compose her shopping list amid the clutter on her worktable, and left it where it sat ready for her to use as soon as she finished eating. And something else he had said to her—yes, that was it, the little lapdog. Tomorrow she would buy a little lapdog, first item on the list.

The euphoria lasted until Grania's solitary dinner was almost done, at which point she emerged from shock and promptly plunged into grief. Up went both hands to her hair, wrenching and pulling frenziedly; her mouth opened in a keening wail, the tears poured out in rivers. Every servant scattered, leaving her abandoned in the dining room to howl into the gold-and-purple tapestry covering her couch.

"Just listen to her!" said the cook bitterly, pausing in his packing-up of special pans, pots, tools; the sound of his mistress's agony came clearly into his domain at the far end of the peristyle-garden. "What's *she* got to cry about? I'm the one going into exile—she's been there for years, the fat silly old sow!"

The lot which gave the province of Roman Africa to Spurius Postumius Albinus was drawn on New Year's Day; not twenty-four hours later, he nailed his colors to the mast, and they were the colors of Prince Massiva of Numidia.

Spurius Albinus had a brother, Aulus, ten years younger than himself, newly admitted to the Senate, and eager to make a name. So while Spurius Albinus lobbied strenuously yet behind the scenes for his new client Prince Massiva, it fell to Aulus Albinus to escort

Prince Massiva through all the most important public places of the city, introducing him to every Roman of note, and whispering to Massiva's agents what sort of gift would be appropriate to send to every Roman of note Massiva met. Like most members of the Numidian royal house, Massiva was a well-set-up and good-looking Semite with a brain between his ears, capable of exerting charm, and lavish in the distribution of largesse. His chief advantage lay not in the undeniable legitimacy of his claim, but rather in the Roman delight of a divided camp; there was no thrill in a united Senate, no spice in a series of unanimous votes, no reputations to be made in amicable co-operation.

At the end of the first week of the New Year, Aulus Albinus formally presented the case of Prince Massiva to the House, and, on his behalf, claimed the throne of Numidia for the legitimate branch. It was Aulus Albinus's maiden speech, and a good one. Every Caecilius Metellus sat up and listened, then applauded at the end of it, and Marcus Aemilius Scaurus was delighted to speak in support of Massiva's petition. This, he said, was the answer to the vexed question as to what to do about Numidia—get it back on the right path with a lawful king at the reins, not a desperate pretender whose bloodline was not good enough to unite the whole country behind him, and who had established his tenure of the throne by murder and bribery. Before Spurius Albinus dismissed the meeting, the Senate was making noises indicating it was very ready to vote in favor of dismissing the present King, and replacing him with Massiva.

"We're up to our necks in boiling water," said Bomilcar to Jugurtha. "All of a sudden I'm not being invited to dine anywhere, and our agents can't find any ears prepared to listen."

"When is the Senate going to vote?" asked the King, his voice calm and steady.

"The fourteenth day before the Kalends of February is the next meeting scheduled for the House—that is seven days from tomorrow, sire."

The King straightened his shoulders. "It will go against me, won't it?"

"Yes, sire," said Bomilcar.

"In that case, it is pointless my trying to continue to do things the Roman way." Jugurtha was visibly growing in size, an awful majesty swelling him now that had been kept hidden since he came with Lucius Cassius to Italy. "From now on, I will do things *my* way—the Numidian way."

The rain had cleared, a cold sun shone; Jugurtha's bones longed for the warmer winds of Numidia, his body longed for the friendly and unavaricious comfort of his harem, his mind longed for the ruthless logic of Numidian plain dealing. Time to go home! Time to start recruiting and training an army, for the Romans were never going to let go.

He paced up and down the colonnade flanking the gigantic peristyle-garden, then beckoned to Bomilcar and strode with him to the center of the open air, by the loudly splashing fountain.

"Not even a bird can hear us," he said then.

Bomilcar stiffened, prepared himself.

"Massiva must go," said the King.

"*Here?* In Rome?"

"Yes, and within the next seven days. If Massiva is not dead before the Senate takes its vote, our task will be that much harder. With Massiva dead, there can be no vote. It will buy us time."

"I'll kill him myself," said Bomilcar.

But Jugurtha shook his head violently. "No! No! The assassin must be a Roman," he said. "Your job is to find the Roman assassin who will kill Massiva for us."

Bomilcar stared, aghast. "My lord king, we're in a foreign country! We don't know where or how, let alone who!"

"Ask one of our agents. Surely there's *one* we can trust," said Jugurtha.

That was more concrete; Bomilcar worked at it for some moments, nipping at the short hairs of his beard beneath his bottom lip with strong teeth. "Agelastus," he said at last. "Marcus Servilius Agelastus, the man who never smiles. His father is Roman, he was born and bred here. But his heart is with his Numidian mother, of that I'm sure."

"I leave it to you. Do it," said the King, and walked away down the path.

Agelastus looked stunned. "*Here?* In Rome?"

"Not only here, but within the next seven days," said Bomilcar. "Once the Senate votes for Massiva—as it will!—we'll have a civil war on our hands in Numidia. Jugurtha won't let go, you know that. Even if he were willing to let go, the Gaetuli wouldn't let him."

"But I haven't the faintest idea how to find an assassin!"

"Then do the job yourself."

"I couldn't!" wailed Agelastus.

"It has to be done! Surely in a city this size there are plenty of people willing to do murder for a good sum of money," Bomilcar persisted.

"Of course there are! Half the proletariat, if the truth is known. But I don't mix in those circles, I don't know any of the *proletarii*! After all, I can't just approach the first seedy-looking fellow I see, clink a bag of gold at him, and ask him to kill a prince of Numidia!" moaned Agelastus.

"Why not?" asked Bomilcar.

"He might report me to the urban praetor, that's why!"

"Show him the gold first, and I guarantee he won't. In this city, everyone has his price."

"Maybe that is indeed so, Baron," said Agelastus, "but I for one am not prepared to put your theory to the test."

And from that stand he would not be budged.

Everyone said the Subura was Rome's sink, so to the Subura Bomilcar went, clad inconspicuously, and without a single slave to escort him. Like every visitor of note to Rome, he had been warned never to venture into the valley northeast of the Forum Romanum, and now he understood why. Not that the alleys of the Subura were any narrower than those of the Palatine, nor were the buildings as oppressively high as those on the Viminal and upper Esquiline. No, what distinguished the Subura at first experience was people, more people than Bomilcar had ever seen. They leaned out of a thousand thousand windows screeching at each other, they elbowed their way through presses of bodies so great all movement was slowed to a snail's pace, they behaved in every rude and aggressive manner known to the race of men, spat and pissed and emptied their slops anywhere they fancied they saw a space open up, were ready to pick a fight with anyone who so much as looked at them sideways.

The second impression was of an all-prevailing squalor, an appalling stench. As he made his way from the civilized Argiletum to the Fauces Suburae, as the initial stretch of the main thoroughfare was known, Bomilcar was incapable of taking in anything beyond smell and dirt. Peeling and dilapidated, the very walls of the buildings oozed filth in runnels, as if the bricks and timber of which they were made had been mortared with filth. Why, he found himself wondering, hadn't they just let the whole district burn down last year, instead of fighting so hard to save it? Nothing and no one in the Subura was worth saving! Then as he penetrated deeper—careful as he walked not to turn off the Subura Major, as the main street was now called, into any of the gaps between the buildings on either side, for he knew if he did, he might never find his way out again—disgust was replaced by amazement. For he began to see the vitality and hardiness of the inhabitants, and experience a cheerfulness beyond his comprehension.

The language he heard was a bizarre mixture of Latin and Greek and a little Aramaic, an argot which probably couldn't be understood by anyone who didn't live in the Subura, for certainly in his extensive wanderings around the rest of Rome, he had never heard its like.

There were shops everywhere, foetid little snack bars all apparently doing a thriving trade—there was obviously money around somewhere—interspersed with bakeries, charcuteries, wine bars, and curious tiny shoplets which seemed (from what he could ascertain by peering into the gloom within) to sell every kind of thing from pieces of twine to cooking pots to lamps and tallow candles. However, clearly food was the best business to be in; at least two thirds of the shops were devoted to some aspect of the food trade. There were factories too: he could hear the thump of presses or the whir of grinding wheels or the clatter of looms, but these noises came from narrow doorways or from side alleys, and were hopelessly fused with what appeared to be tenement dwellings many storeys high. How did anyone ever survive here?

Even the little squares at the major crossroads were solid people; the way they managed to do their washing in the fountain basins and carry pitchers of water home astounded him. Cirta—of which city he as a Numidian was inordinately proud—he at last admitted was no more than a big village compared to Rome. Even Alexandria, he suspected, might have its work cut out to produce an ants' nest like the Subura.

However, there were places in which men gathered to sit and drink and pass the time of day. These seemed to be confined to major crossroads, but even of that he couldn't be sure, unwilling as he was to leave the main street. Everything kept happening very suddenly, in snatches of scenes that opened up before him and closed in a fresh throng of people, from a man beating a laden ass to a woman beating a laden child. But the dim interiors of the crossroads taverns—he didn't know what else to call them—were oases of relative peace. A big man in the pink of health, Bomilcar finally decided he would find out nothing more illuminating until he ventured inside one. After all, he had come to the Subura to find a Roman assassin, which meant he must find a venue where he could strike up a conversation with some of the local populace.

He left the Subura Major to walk up the Vicus Patricii, a main street leading onto the Viminal Hill, and found a crossroads tavern at the base of a triangular open space where the Subura Minor merged into the Vicus Patricii; the size of the shrine and the fountain told him this was a very important *compitum,* intersection. As he dipped his head to pass under the low lintel of the door, every face inside—and there must have been fifty of them—lifted and turned toward him, suddenly stony. The buzz of talk died.

"I beg your pardon," Bomilcar said, bearing unafraid, eyes busy trying to find the face belonging to the leader. Ah! There in the far left back corner! For as the initial shock of seeing a completely foreign-looking stranger enter wore off, the rest were turning to look at this one face—the face of the leader. A Roman rather than a Greek face, the property of a man of small size and perhaps thirty-five years. Bomilcar swung to look directly at him and addressed the rest of his remarks to him, wishing his Latin were fluent enough to speak in the native tongue, but forced to use Greek instead.

"I beg your pardon," he said again, "I seem to be guilty of trespass. I was looking for a tavern where I might be seated to drink a cup of wine. It's thirsty work, walking."

"This, friend, is a private club," said the leader in atrocious but understandable Greek.

"Are there no public taverns?" Bomilcar asked.

"Not in the Subura, friend. You're out of your ken. Go back to the Via Nova."

"Yes, I know the Via Nova, but I'm a stranger in Rome, and I always think one cannot get the real flavor of a city unless one goes into its most crowded quarter," said Bomilcar, steering a middle course between touristy fatuousness and foreign ignorance.

The leader was eyeing him up and down, shrewdly calculating. "Thirsty as all that, are you, friend?" he asked.

Gratefully Bomilcar seized upon the gambit. "Thirsty enough to buy everyone here a drink," he said.

The leader pushed the man sitting next to him off his stool, and patted it. "Well, if my honorable colleagues agree, we could make you an honorary member. Take the weight off your feet, friend." His head turned casually. "All in favor of making this gent an honorary member, say aye?"

"Aye!" came the chorus.

Bomilcar looked in vain for counter or vendor, drew a secret breath, and put his purse on the table so that one or two silver denarii spilled out of its mouth; either they would murder him for its contents, or he was indeed an honorary member. "May I?" he asked the leader.

"Bromidus, get the gent and the members a nice big flagon,"

said the leader to the minion he had unseated to make room for Bomilcar. "Wine bar we use is right next door," he explained.

The purse spilled a few more denarii. "Is that enough?"

"To buy one round, friend, it's plenty."

Out chinked more coins. "How about several rounds?"

A collective sigh went up; everyone visibly relaxed. The minion Bromidus picked up the coins and disappeared out the door followed by three eager helpers, while Bomilcar held out his right hand to the leader.

"My name is Juba," he said.

"Lucius Decumius," said the leader, shaking hands vigorously. "Juba! What sort of name is that?"

"It's Moorish. I'm from Mauretania."

"Maure-what? Where's it?"

"In Africa."

"Africa?" Clearly Bomilcar could as easily have said the Land of the Hyperboreans; it would have meant as much—or as little—to Lucius Decumius.

"A long way from Rome," the honorary member explained. "A place far to the west of Carthage."

"Oh, *Carthage*! Why didn't you say so in the first place?" Lucius Decumius turned to stare into this interesting visitor's face intently. "I didn't think Scipio Aemilianus left any of you lot alive," he said.

"He didn't. Mauretania isn't Carthage, it's far to the west of Carthage. Both of them are in Africa, is all," said Bomilcar patiently. "What used to be Carthage is now the Roman African province. Where this year's consul is going—you know, Spurius Postumius Albinus."

Lucius Decumius shrugged. "Consuls? They come and they go, friend, they come and they go. Makes no difference to the Subura, they don't live hereabouts, you comprehend. But just so long as you admit Rome's the top dog in the world, friend, you're welcome in the Subura. So are the consuls."

"Believe me, I know Rome is the top dog in the world," said Bomilcar with feeling. "My master—King Bocchus of Mauretania—

has sent me to Rome to ask the Senate to make him a Friend and Ally of the Roman People."

"Well, what do you know?" Lucius Decumius remarked idly.

Bromidus came back staggering under the weight of a huge flagon, followed by three others similarly burdened, and proceeded to dispense liquid refreshments to all; he started with Decumius, who gave him a wallop on his thigh that hurt.

"Here, idiot, got no manners?" he demanded. "Serve the gent who paid for it first, or I'll have your guts."

Bomilcar got a brimming beaker within seconds, and lifted it in a toast. "Here's to the best place and the best friends I've found so far in Rome," he said, and drank the awful vintage with feigned relish. Ye gods, they must have steel intestines!

Bowls of food also appeared, pickled vinegary gherkins and onions and walnuts, sticks of celery and slivers of carrots, a stinking mess of tiny salted fish that disappeared in a trice. None of it could Bomilcar eat.

"Here's to you, Juba, old friend!" said Decumius.

"Juba!" the rest chorused, in high good humor.

Within half an hour Bomilcar knew more about the workingman's Rome than he had ever dreamed of knowing, and found it fascinating; that he knew far less about the workingman's Numidia did not occur to him. All the members of the club worked, he discovered, learning that on each successive day a different group of men would use the club's facilities; most of them seemed to get every eighth day off work. About a quarter of the men in the room wore the little conical beanies on the backs of their heads that denoted they were freedmen, freed slaves; to his surprise, Bomilcar ascertained that some of the others were actually still slaves, yet nonetheless appeared to stand in the same stead as the rest of the members, worked in the same sorts of jobs for the same pay and the same hours and the same days off—which seemed very strange to him, but obviously was normal in the eyes of everyone else. And Bomilcar began to understand the real difference between a slave and a freeman: a freeman could come and go and choose his place and kind of work as he wanted, whereas a slave belonged to his employer, was his employer's property, so could not dictate his own life. Quite different from slavery in Numidia. But then, he reflected fairly, for he was a fair man, every nation has its different rules and regulations about slaves, no two the same.

Unlike the ordinary members, Lucius Decumius was a permanent fixture.

"I'm the club custodian," he said, sober as when he had sipped his first mouthful.

"What sort of club is it exactly?" Bomilcar asked, trying to eke out his drink as long as he could.

"I don't suppose you would know," said Lucius Decumius. "This, friend, is a crossroads club. A proper sodality, a sort of a college, really. Registered with the aediles and the urban praetor, blessed by the Pontifex Maximus. Crossroads clubs go back to the kings, before there was a republic. There's a lot of power in places where big roads cross. The proper *compita,* I'm talking about, not your little piddlyarse crossings of lanes and alleys. Yes, there's a lot of power in the crossroads. I mean—imagine you were a god and you looked down on Rome—you'd be a bit muddled if you wanted to chuck a thunderbolt or a dollop of plague, wouldn't you? If you go up onto the Capitol you'll get a good idea of what I mean—a heap of red roofs as close together as the tiles in a mosaic. But if you look hard, you can always see the gaps where the big roads cross, the *compita* like we've got outside these here premises. So if you were a god, that's where you'd chuck your thunderbolt or your dollop of plague, right? Only us Romans are clever, friend. Real clever. The kings worked out that we'd have to protect ourselves at the crossroads. So the crossroads were put under the protection of the Lares, shrines were built to the Lares at every crossroads even before there were fountains. Didn't you notice the shrine against the wall of the club outside? The little tower thingy?"

"I did," said Bomilcar, growing confused. "Who exactly are the Lares? More than one god?"

"Oh, there's Lares everywhere—hundreds—thousands," said

Decumius vaguely. "Rome's full of Lares. So's Italy, they say, though I've never been to Italy. I don't know any soldiers, so I can't say if the Lares go overseas with the legions too. But they're certainly here, everywhere they're needed. And it's up to us—the crossroads clubs—to take good care of our Lares. We keep the shrine in order and the offerings coming, we keep the fountain clean, we move broken-down wagons, dead bodies—mostly animals—and we shift the rubble when a building falls down. And around the New Year we have this big party, the Compitalia it's called. It only happened a couple of days ago, that's why we're so short on money for wine. We spend our funds and it takes time to save more."

"I see," said Bomilcar, who honestly didn't; the old Roman gods were an insoluble mystery to him. "Do you have to fund the party entirely among yourselves?"

"Yes and no," said Lucius Decumius, scratching his armpit. "We get some money from the urban praetor toward it, enough for a few pigs to roast—depends on who's urban praetor. Some are real generous. Other years they're so stingy their shit don't stink."

The conversation veered to curious questions about life in Carthage; it was impossible to get it through their heads that any other place in Africa existed, for their grasp of history and geography seemed to consist of what they gleaned from their visits to the Forum Romanum, not so far from their clubhouse in distance, but a remote place nonetheless. When they did visit the Forum Romanum, it was apparently because political unrest lent it interest and imparted a circusy flavor to Rome's governing center. Their view of Rome's political life was therefore somewhat skewed; its high point seemed to have been during the troubles culminating in the death of Gaius Sempronius Gracchus.

Finally the moment arrived. The members had all grown so used to his presence they didn't notice him, and they were besides fuddled from too much wine. Whereas Lucius Decumius was still sober, his alert inquisitive eyes never leaving Bomilcar's face. Not mere chance that this Juba fellow was here among his inferiors; he was after something.

"Lucius Decumius," said Bomilcar, leaning his head so close to the Roman that only the Roman could hear, "I have a problem, and I'm hoping you'll be able to tell me how to go about solving it."

"Yes, friend?"

"My master, King Bocchus, is very rich."

"I'd expect he's rich, him being a king."

"What worries King Bocchus is his prospect of remaining a king," said Bomilcar slowly. "He's got a problem."

"Same problem as yours, friend?"

"Exactly the same."

"How can I help?" Decumius plucked an onion out of the bowl of assorted pickles on the table and chewed at it reflectively.

"In Africa the answer would be simple. The King would simply give an order, and the man who constitutes our problem would be executed." Bomilcar stopped, wondering how long it would be before Decumius caught on.

"Aha! So the problem's got a name, has he?"

"That's right. Massiva."

"Sounds a bit more Latin than Juba," Decumius said.

"Massiva is a Numidian, not a Mauretanian." The lees of his wine seemed to fascinate Bomilcar, who stirred them into swirls with his finger. "The difficulty is, Massiva is living here in Rome. And making trouble for us."

"I can see where Rome makes it difficult," said Decumius, in a tone which lent his remark several different meanings.

Bomilcar looked at the little man, startled; here was a brain of subtlety as well as acuity. He took a deep breath. "My share of the problem is made more perilous because I'm a stranger in Rome," he said. "You see, I have to find a Roman who is willing to kill Prince Massiva. Here. In Rome."

Lucius Decumius didn't so much as blink. "Well, that's not hard," he said.

"It's not?"

"Money'll buy you anything in Rome, friend."

"Then can you tell me where to go?" asked Bomilcar.

"Seek no further, friend, seek no further," said Decumius,

swallowing the last of his onion. "I'd cut the throats of half the Senate for the chance to eat oysters instead of onions. How much does the job pay, like?"

"How many denarii are in this purse?" Bomilcar emptied it upon the table.

"Not enough to kill for."

"What about the same amount in gold?"

Decumius slapped his thigh hard. "*Now* you're talking! You have got yourself a deal, friend."

Bomilcar's head was spinning, but not from the wine, which he had been surreptitiously pouring on the floor for the last hour. "Half tomorrow, and half after the job is done," he said, pushing the coins back into the maw of the purse.

A stained hand with filthy nails arrested him. "Leave this here as evidence of good faith, friend. And come back tomorrow. Only wait outside by the shrine. We'll go to my flat to talk."

Bomilcar got up. "I'll be here, Lucius Decumius." As they walked to the door he stopped to look down into the club custodian's ill-shaven face. "Have you ever killed anyone?" he asked.

Up went Decumius's right forefinger against the right side of his nose. "A nod is as good as a wink to a blind barber, friend," he said. "In the Subura a man don't boast."

Satisfied, Bomilcar smiled at Decumius and walked off into the congestion of the Subura Minor.

Marcus Livius Drusus, who had been consul two years before, celebrated his triumph halfway through the second week of January. Assigned the province of Macedonia for his governorship in the year he was consul and lucky enough to have his command prorogued, he pursued a highly successful border war against the Scordisci, a tribe of clever and well-organized Celts who perpetually harassed Roman Macedonia. But in Marcus Livius Drusus they encountered a man of exceptional ability, and went down heavily. The result had been more beneficial than usual for Rome; Drusus was lucky enough to capture one of the largest Scordisci strongholds and find secreted within it a considerable part of the

Scordisci wealth. Most governors of Macedonia celebrated triumphs at the ends of their terms, but everyone agreed Marcus Livius Drusus deserved the honor more than most.

Prince Massiva was the guest of the consul Spurius Postumius Albinus at the festivities, and so was given a superb seat inside the Circus Maximus, from which vantage point he watched the long triumphal parade pass through the Circus, marveling as he discovered at first hand what he had always been told, that the Romans had real showmanship, knew better than any other people the art of staging a spectacle. His Greek of course was excellent, so he had understood his pretriumphal briefing, and was up from his seat ready to go before the last of Drusus's legions were out the Capena end of the vast arena. The whole consular party exited through a private door into the Forum Boarium, hurried up the Steps of Cacus onto the Palatine, and redoubled its pace. Steering the straightest course possible, twelve lictors led the way through almost deserted alleys, the hobnailed soles of their winter boots grinding against the cobblestones.

Ten minutes after leaving their seats in the Circus Maximus, Spurius Albinus's party clattered down the Vestal Steps into the Forum Romanum, heading for the temple of Castor and Pollux. Here, on the platform at the top of the steps of this imposing edifice, both consuls were to seat themselves and their guests to watch the parade come down the Via Sacra from the Velia toward the Capitol; in order to avoid insulting the triumphator, they had to be in position when the parade appeared.

"All the other magistrates and members of the Senate march at the head of the parade," Spurius Albinus had explained to Prince Massiva, "and the year's consuls are always formally invited to march, just as they're invited to the feast the triumphator gives afterward for the Senate inside the temple of Jupiter Optimus Maximus. But it isn't good form for the consuls to accept either invitation. This is the triumphator's great day, and he must be the most distinguished person in the celebrations, have the most lictors. So the consuls always watch from a position of importance, and the triumphator acknowledges them as he passes—yet they do not overshadow him."

The prince had indicated that he understood, though his extreme foreignness and his lack of exposure to the Romans limited his understanding of the overall picture he was having explained to him. Unlike Jugurtha, he had clung to non-Roman Africa all his life.

Once the consular party arrived at the junction of the Vestal Steps with the Via Nova, its onward progress was hindered by massive crowds. Rome had come out in its hundreds of thousands to see Drusus triumph, that astonishing grapevine which penetrated even into the meanest streets of the Subura having assured everyone that Drusus's triumph was going to be among the most splendid.

When on duty carrying the *fasces* within Rome, the lictors wore plain white togas; today their garb rendered them more anonymous than usual, for Rome going to a triumph whitened itself, every last citizen clad in his *toga alba* instead of just a tunic. In consequence the lictors had trouble forcing a passage for the consular party, which slowed down as the crowds pressed in. By the time it arrived alongside the temple of Castor and Pollux it had virtually disintegrated as a unit, and Prince Massiva, attended by a private bodyguard, lagged behind so badly that he lost all contact with the rest.

His sense of exclusivity and his un-Roman royalness stirred him to outrage at the familiar, disrespectful attitude of the hundreds thronging all around him; his bodyguards were elbowed aside, and he himself for a short moment lost sight of them.

It was the short moment Lucius Decumius had been waiting for; he struck with unerring accuracy, swift and sure and sudden. Crushed against Prince Massiva by a spontaneous surge of the crowd, he slid his specially sharpened dagger under the left side of the royal rib cage, turned it immediately upward with a brutal twist, let the haft go once he knew the blade was all the way in, and had slipped between a dozen bodies long before the first blood began to flow, or Prince Massiva knew enough to cry out. Indeed, Prince Massiva did not cry out; he simply fell where he was, and by the time his bodyguard had collected itself enough to shove people aside until they could surround their slain lord, Lucius Decimius was halfway across the lower Forum heading for the haven of the Argiletum, merely one droplet in a sea of white togas.

A full ten minutes passed before anyone thought to get the news to Spurius Albinus and his brother, Aulus, already installed upon the podium of the temple and unworried by Prince Massiva's nonappearance. Lictors rushed to cordon off the area, the crowd was pushed elsewhere, and Spurius and Aulus Albinus stood looking down at a dead man and ruined plans.

"It will have to wait," said Spurius at last. "We cannot offend Marcus Livius Drusus by disturbing his triumph." He turned to the leader of the bodyguard, which in Prince Massiva's case was composed of hired Roman gladiators, and spoke to the man in Greek. "Carry Prince Massiva to his house, and wait there until I can come," he said.

The man nodded. A rude stretcher was made from the toga given up by Aulus Albinus, the body rolled onto it and borne away by six gladiators.

Aulus took the disaster less phlegmatically than his older brother; to him had fallen the bulk of Massiva's generosity so far, Spurius feeling he could afford to wait for his share until his African campaign saw Massiva installed upon the throne of Numidia. Besides which, Aulus was as impatient as he was ambitious, and anxious to outstrip Spurius age for age.

"Jugurtha!" he said through his teeth. "Jugurtha did it!"

"You'll never get proof," said Spurius, sighing.

They climbed the steps of the temple of Castor and Pollux and resumed their seats just as the magistrates and senators appeared from behind the imposing bulk of the Domus Publicus, the State-owned house in which lived the Vestal Virgins and the Pontifex Maximus. It was a short glimpse only, but within half a moment they hove clearly into view, and the great procession rolled downhill to where the Via Sacra ended alongside the sunken well of the Comitia. Spurius and Aulus Albinus sat looking as if they had nothing on their minds beyond enjoyment of the spectacle and respect for Marcus Livius Drusus.

Bomilcar and Lucius Decumius met with noisy inconspicuousness, standing side by side at the counter of a busy snack bar on the upper corner of the Great Market until each was served a pasty filled with a savory loaf of garlicky sausage, and then moving very naturally aside to stand biting delicately into their goodies, which were very hot.

"Nice day for it, friend," said Lucius Decumius.

Wrapped in a hooded cloak which concealed his person, Bomilcar let out his breath. "I trust it remains a nice day," he said.

"This is one day, friend, that I can guarantee is going to end up perfect," said Lucius Decumius complacently.

Bomilcar fumbled beneath his cloak, found the purse holding the second half of Decumius's gold. "You're sure?"

"Sure as a man whose shoe stinks knows he's stepped in a turd," said Decumius.

The bag of gold changed hands invisibly. Bomilcar turned to go, heart light.

"I thank you, Lucius Decumius," he said.

"No, friend, the pleasure's all mine!" And Lucius Decumius stayed right where he was, biting with relish into his pasty until it was gone. "Oysters instead of onions," he said out loud, starting up the Fauces Suburae with a happy spring in his step and the bag of gold safely next to his skin.

Bomilcar left the city through the Fontinalis Gate, hurrying faster as the crowds diminished, down onto the Campus Martuns. He got inside the front door of Jugurtha's villa without encountering a person he knew, and flung off his cloak gladly. The King had been very kind this day and given every slave in the house time off to see Drusus triumph, and a present of a silver denarius each as well. So there were no alien eyes to witness Bomilcar's return, only the fanatically loyal bodyguards and Numidian servants.

Jugurtha was in his usual place, sitting on the loggia one floor up, above the entrance from the street.

"It's done," said Bomilcar.

The King gripped his brother's arm strongly. "Oh, good man!" he said, smiling.

"I'm glad it went so well," said Bomilcar.

"He's definitely dead?"

"My assassin assures me he is—sure as a man whose shoe stinks knows he stepped in a turd." Bomilcar's shoulders heaved with laughter. "A picturesque fellow, my Roman ruffian. But extraordinarily efficient, and quite nerveless."

Jugurtha relaxed. "The moment we hear for certain that my dear cousin Massiva is dead, we'd better call a conference with all our agents. We have to press for the Senate's recognition of my tenure of the throne, and for our return home." He grimaced. "I mustn't ever forget that I still have that pathetic professional invalid half brother of mine to contend with, sweet and beloved Gauda."

But there was one who did not appear when the summons came for Jugurtha's agents to assemble at his villa. The moment he learned of the assassination of Prince Massiva, Marcus Servilius Agelastus sought an audience with the consul Spurius Albinus. The consul pleaded through a secretary that he was too busy, but Agelastus stuck to his intention until in desperation the overworked secretary shunted him into the presence of the consul's younger brother, Aulus, who was galvanized when he heard what Agelastus had to say. Spurius Albinus was called, listened impassively as Agelastus repeated his story, then thanked him, took his address and a deposition to be certain, and dismissed him courteously enough to make most men smile; but not Agelastus.

"We'll take action through the *praetor urbanus,* as legally as we can under the circumstances," said Spurius as soon as he was alone with his young brother. "It's too important a matter to let Agelastus lay the charge—I'll do that myself—but he's vital to our case because he's the only Roman citizen among the lot if you exclude the mysterious assassin. It will be up to the *praetor ur-*

banus to decide exactly how Bomilcar will be prosecuted. Undoubtedly he'll consult the full Senate, seeking a directive to cover his arse. But if I see him personally and give it as my legal opinion that the fact of the crime's being committed inside Rome on a day of triumph by a Roman citizen assassin outweighs Bomilcar's noncitizen status—why, I think I can allay his fears. Especially if I reinforce the fact that Prince Massiva was the consul's client, and under his protection. It's vital that Bomilcar be tried and convicted in Rome by a Roman court. The sheer audacity of the crime will force Jugurtha's faction in the Senate to keep quiet. You, Aulus, can ready yourself to do the actual prosecuting in whichever court is decided upon. I'll make sure the *praetor peregrinus* is consulted, as he's normally the man concerned with lawsuits involving noncitizens. He may want to defend Bomilcar, just to keep things legal. But one way or another, Aulus, we are going to finish Jugurtha's chances to win Senate approval for his cause—and then see if we can't find another claimant to the throne."

"Like Prince Gauda?"

"Like Prince Gauda, poor material though he is. After all, he's Jugurtha's legitimate half brother. We'll just make sure Gauda never comes to Rome to plead in person." Spurius smiled at Aulus. "We are going to make our fortunes in Numidia this year, I swear it!"

But Jugurtha had abandoned any idea of fighting according to Rome's rules. When the urban praetor and his lictors arrived at the villa on the Pincian Hill to arrest Bomilcar on a charge of conspiracy to murder, for a moment the King was tempted to refuse outright to hand Bomilcar over, and see what happened after that. In the end he temporized by stating that, as neither the victim nor the accused was a Roman citizen, he failed to see what business it was of Rome's. The urban praetor responded by stating that the Senate had decided the accused must answer charges in a Roman court because there was evidence to indicate that the actual assassin procured was certainly a Roman citizen. One Marcus Servilius Agelastus, a Roman knight, had furnished much proof of this, and had sworn on oath that he himself had first been approached to do the murder.

"In which case," said Jugurtha, still fighting, "the only magistrate who can arrest my baron is the foreign praetor. My baron is not a Roman citizen, and my place of abode—which is also his—is outside the jurisdiction of the urban praetor!"

"You have been misinformed, sire," said the urban praetor smoothly. "The *praetor peregrinus* will be concerned, of course. But the imperium of the *praetor urbanus* extends as far as the fifth milestone from Rome, therefore your villa is within *my* jurisdiction, not the foreign praetor's. Now please produce Baron Bomilcar."

Baron Bomilcar was produced, and hied off at once to the cells of the Lautumiae, where he was to be held pending trial in a specially convened court. When Jugurtha sent his agents to demand that Bomilcar be released on bail—or at least that he be confined in the house of a citizen of good standing rather than in the tumbledown chaos of the Lautumiae—the request was refused. Bomilcar must remain resident inside Rome's only jail.

The Lautumiae had started existence several hundred years earlier as a quarry in the side of the Arx of the Capitol, and now was a haphazard collection of unmortared stone blocks which huddled in the cliff side just beyond the lower Forum Romanum. It could accommodate perhaps fifty prisoners in disgracefully dilapidated cells owning no sort of security; those imprisoned could wander anywhere they liked within its walls, and were kept from wandering out of it only by lictors on guard duty, or, on the rare occasions when someone truly dangerous was imprisoned, by manacles. Since the place was normally empty, the sight of lictors on guard duty was a great novelty; thus Bomilcar's incarceration rapidly became one of Rome's most widely disseminated news items thanks to the lictors, who were not at all averse to gratifying the curiosity of the passersby.

The lowliness of Lucius Decumius was purely social; it most definitely did not extend to his cerebral apparatus, which functioned extremely well. To gain the post of custodian of a crossroads college was no mean feat. So when a tendril of the gossip grapevine thrust its feeler deep into the heart of the Subura, Lucius Decumius put two of his fingers together with two more, and came up with an answer of four fingers. The name was Bomilcar, not Juba, and the nationality was Numidian, not Mauretanian. Yet he knew it was his man at once.

Applauding rather than condemning Bomilcar's deceit, off went Lucius Decumius to the Lautumiae cells, where he gained entrance by the simple expedient of grinning widely at the two lictors on door duty before rudely elbowing his way between them.

"Ignorant shit!" said one, rubbing his side.

"Eat it!" said Decumius, skipping nimbly behind a crumbling pillar and waiting for the grumbles at the door to subside.

Lacking any military or civil law-enforcement officers, Rome habitually obliged its College of Lictors to provide members for all kinds of peculiar duties. There were perhaps three hundred lictors all told, poorly paid by the State and therefore very dependent upon the generosity of the men they served; they inhabited a building and small piece of open land behind the temple of the Lares Praestites on the Via Sacra, and found the location satisfactory only because it also lay behind the long and sprawling premises of Rome's best inn, where they could always cadge a drink. Lictors escorted all the magistrates owning imperium and fought for the chance to serve on the staff of a governor going abroad, since they then shared in his share of the spoils and perquisites of office. Lictors represented the thirty divisions of Rome called *curiae*. And lictors might be called upon to assume guard duty at either the Lautumiae or the Tullianum next door, where those condemned to death waited scant hours for the strangler. Such guard duty was about the least desirable task a lictor could be given by the head man of his group of ten. No tips, no bribes, no nothing. Therefore neither lictor was interested in pursuing Lucius Decumius inside the building; their job description said they were there to guard the door, so that was all they were going to do, by Jupiter.

"Yoohoo, friend, where are you?" yelled Decumius in a voice loud enough to be heard by the bankers in the Basilica Porcia.

The hairs on Bomilcar's arms and neck rose; he leaped to his feet. This is it, this is the end, he thought, and waited numbly for Decumius to appear escorted by a troop of magistrates and other officials.

Decumius duly appeared. But quite alone. When he saw Bomilcar standing stiffly by the outside wall of his cell (which contained an unbarred and unshuttered opening quite large enough for a man to crawl through—that Bomilcar hadn't was evidence of his utter mystification at the way Romans thought and acted, for he could not believe the simple truth—that prison was a concept alien to the Romans), Decumius smiled at him jauntily and strolled into the doorless room.

"Who squealed on you, friend?" he asked, perching his skinny body on a fallen block of masonry.

Controlling his tendency to shake, Bomilcar licked his lips. "Well, if it wasn't you before, you fool, it certainly is now!" he snapped.

Eyes widening, Decumius stared at him; a slow comprehension was dawning. "Here, here, friend, don't you worry about things like that," he said soothingly. "There's no one to hear us, just a couple of lictors on the door, and that's twenty paces off. I heard you got arrested, so I thought I'd better come and see what went wrong."

"Agelastus," said Bomilcar. "Marcus Servilius Agelastus!"

"Want me to do the same to him I did to Prince Massiva?"

"Look, will you just get out of here?" cried Bomilcar, despairing. "Don't you understand that they'll start to wonder why you've come? If anyone caught a glimpse of your face near Prince Massiva, you're a dead man!"

"It's all right, friend, it's all right! Stop worrying—no one knows about me, and no one cares a fig that I'm here. This ain't no Parthian dungeon, friend, honest! They only put you in here to throw your boss into fits, that's all. They won't care a whole lot if you do a moonlight flit, it'll just brand you guilty." And he pointed to the gap in the outside wall.

"I can't run away," said Bomilcar.

"Suit yourself." Decumius shrugged. "Now, what about this Agelastus bird? Want him out of the way? I'll do it for the same price—payable on delivery this time; I trust you."

Fascinated, Bomilcar came by logical progression to the conclusion that not only did Lucius Decumius believe what he said, but he was undoubtedly correct to do so. If it hadn't been for Jugurtha, he would now have availed himself of that moonlit escape; but if he yielded to the temptation, only the gods knew what might happen to Jugurtha.

"You've got yourself another bag of gold," he said.

"Where's he live, this fellow who—judging by his name, anyway—never smiles?"

"On the Caelian Hill, in the Vicus Capiti Africae."

"Oh, nice new district!" said Decumius appreciatively. "Agelastus must be doing all right for himself, eh? Still, makes him easy to find, living out there where the birds sing louder than the neighbors. Don't worry, I'll do it for you straightaway. Then when your boss gets you out of here, you can pay me. Just send the gold to me at the club. I'll be there to take delivery."

"How do you know my boss will get me out of here?"

"Course he will, friend! They've only chucked you in here to give him a fright. Couple more days and they'll let him bail you out. But when they do, take my advice and go home as fast as you can. Don't stay around in Rome, all right?"

"Leaving the King here at their mercy? I couldn't!"

"Course you can, friend! What do you think they'll do to him here in Rome? Knock him on the head and chuck him in the Tiber? No! Never! That's not how they work, friend," said Lucius Decumius the expert counselor. "There's only one thing they'll murder for, and that's their precious Republic. You know, the laws and the Constitution and stuff like that. They might kill the odd tribune of the plebs or two, like they did Tiberius and Gaius Gracchus, but they'd never kill a foreigner, not in Rome. Don't you worry about your boss, friend. My bet is, they'll send him home too if you get away."

Bomilcar gazed at Decumius in wonder. "And yet, you don't

even know where Numidia is!" he said slowly. "You've never been to Italy! How do you know then the workings of Roman noblemen?"

"Well, that's different," said Lucius Decumius, getting up from his stone and preparing to depart. "Mother's milk, friend, mother's milk! We all drink it in along with mother's milk. I mean, aside from windfalls like you coming along, where else can a Roman get a thrill except in the Forum when there's no Games? And you don't even have to go there in the flesh to get the thrill. It comes to you, friend. Just like mother's milk."

Bomilcar held out his hand. "I thank you, Lucius Decumius. You are the only completely honest man I've met in Rome. I'll have your money sent to you."

"Don't forget, now, to the club! Oh, and"—his right forefinger went up to touch the right side of his nose—"if you've got any friends need a bit of practical help solving their little problems, let 'em know I take on a bit of outside contracting! I like this line of work."

Agelastus died, but since Bomilcar was in the Lautumiae and neither of the lictors thought to connect Decumius with the reason for Bomilcar's imprisonment, the case Spurius and Aulus Albinus were preparing against the Numidian baron weakened. They still possessed the deposition they had extracted from Agelastus, but there was no doubt his absence as chief witness for the prosecution was a blow. Seizing the opportunity the death of Agelastus afforded him, Jugurtha applied again to the Senate for bail for Bomilcar. Though Gaius Memmius and Scaurus argued passionately against its being granted, in the end Baron Bomilcar was released upon Jugurtha's handing over fifty of his Numidian attendants into Roman custody; they were distributed among the households of fifty senators, and Jugurtha was made to give over a large sum of money to the State, ostensibly to pay for the up-keep of his hostages.

His cause, of course, was irreparably damaged. However, he had ceased to care, for he knew he had no hope of ever obtaining

Roman approval of his kingship. Not because of the death of Massiva, but because the Romans had never intended to approve his kingship. They had been tormenting him for years, making him dance to their tune, and laughing at him behind their hands. So, with or without the consent of the Senate, he was going home. Home to raise an army and begin to train it to fight the legions which were bound to come.

Bomilcar fled to Puteoli the moment he was set free, took ship there for Africa, and got away clean. Whereupon the Senate washed its hands of Jugurtha. Go home, they said, giving him back his fifty hostages (but not his money). Get out of Rome, get out of Italy, get out of our lives.

The King of Numidia's last sight of Rome was from the top of the Janiculum, which he made his horse climb simply so he could look upon the shape of his fate. Rome. There it lay, rolling and rippling amid its sudden cliff faces, seven hills and the valleys between, a sea of orange-red roof tiles and brightly painted stuccoed walls, the gilded ornaments adorning temple pediments throwing shafts of light in glitters back into the sky, little highways for the gods to use. A vivid and colorful terracotta city, green with trees and grasses where the space permitted.

But Jugurtha saw nothing to admire. He looked for a long time, sure he would never see Rome again.

"A city for sale," he said then, "and when it finds a buyer, it will vanish in the twinkling of an eye."

And turned away toward the Via Ostiensis.

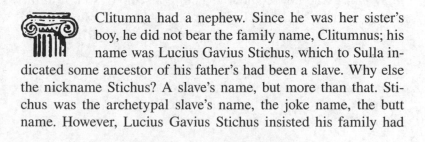 Clitumna had a nephew. Since he was her sister's boy, he did not bear the family name, Clitumnus; his name was Lucius Gavius Stichus, which to Sulla indicated some ancestor of his father's had been a slave. Why else the nickname Stichus? A slave's name, but more than that. Stichus was the archetypal slave's name, the joke name, the butt name. However, Lucius Gavius Stichus insisted his family had

earned the name because of their long association with slavery; like his father and his grandfather at least, Lucius Gavius Stichus dealt in slaves, ran a snug little agency for domestic servants situated in the Porticus Metelli on the Campus Martius. It was not a high-flying firm catering to the elite, but rather a well-established business catering to those whose purses did not run to more than three or four slave helpers.

Odd, thought Sulla when the steward informed him that the mistress's nephew was in the study, how he collected Gaviuses. There had been his father's boon drinking companion, Marcus Gavius Brocchus, and the dear old *grammaticus* Quintus Gavius Myrto. Gavius. It wasn't a very common family name, nor one of any distinction. Yet he had known three Gaviuses.

Well, the Gavius who had drunk with his father and the Gavius who had given Sulla no mean education aroused feelings in him he did not mind owning; but Stichus was very different. Had he suspected Clitumna was being honored by a visit from her awful nephew he wouldn't have come home, and he stood for a moment in the atrium debating what his next course of action should be—flight from the house, or flight to some part of it where Stichus did not stick his sticky beak.

The garden. With a nod and a smile for the steward's thoughtfulness in warning him, he bypassed the study and went into the peristyle, found a seat warmed a little by the weak sun, and sat gazing blindly at the dreadful statue of Apollo chasing a Daphne already more tree than dryad. Clitumna loved it, which was why she had bought it. But did the Lord of Light ever have such aggressively yellow hair, or eyes so putridly blue, or skin so cloyingly pink? And how could one admire a sculptor so lost to the criteria of asceticism that he turned all of Daphne's fingers into identical bright green twigs, and all of Daphne's toes into identical murky brown rootlets? The idiot had even—he probably considered it his master touch—bedaubed poor Daphne's one remaining humanoid breast with a trickle of purple sap oozing from her knotty nipple! To gaze at it blindly was the only way

Sulla had managed to preserve the work, when every part of his outraged senses screamed to take an axe to it.

"What am I doing here?" he asked poor Daphne, who ought to have looked terrified, and instead only managed to simper.

She didn't answer.

"What am I doing here?" he asked Apollo.

Apollo didn't answer.

He put up one hand to press its fingers against his eyes, and closed them; and began the all-too-familiar process of disciplining himself into—oh, not exactly acceptance, more a form of grim endurance. Gavius. Think of a different Gavius than Stichus. Think of Quintus Gavius Myrto, who had given him no mean education.

They had met not long after Sulla's seventh birthday, when the skinny but strong little boy had been helping his sodden father home to the single room on the Vicus Sandalarius where they had lived at the time. Sulla Senior collapsed on the street, and Quintus Gavius Myrto had come to the boy's rescue. Together they got the father home, with Myrto, fascinated by Sulla's appearance and the purity of the Latin he spoke, firing questions at him the whole way.

As soon as Sulla Senior was tipped onto his straw pallet, the old *grammaticus* sat himself down on the only chair and proceeded to extricate as much of his family history from him as the boy knew. And ended in explaining that he himself was a teacher, and offering to teach the boy to read and write for nothing. Sulla's plight appalled him: a patrician Cornelius with obvious potential stuck for the rest of his life in penury somewhere amid the stews of the poorest parts of Rome? It didn't bear thinking of. The boy should at least be equipped to earn a living as a clerk or a scribe! And what if by some miracle the Sullan luck changed, and he had the opportunity to espouse his rightful way of life, only to be prevented by illiteracy?

Sulla had accepted the offer to be taught, but scorned the gratis element. Whenever he could, he stole enough to slip old Quintus Gavius Myrto a silver denarius or a plump chicken, and when he was a little older, he sold himself to get that silver denarius. If Myrto suspected that these payments were gained at the cost of honor, he never said so; for he was wise enough to understand that in tendering them, the boy was demonstrating the value he placed upon this unexpected chance to learn. So he took the coins with every indication of pleasure and gratitude, and never gave Sulla reason to think that he worried himself sick over how they were come by.

To be taught rhetoric and walk in the train of a great advocate of the law courts was a dream Sulla knew he would never attain, which only gave added luster to the humbler efforts of Quintus Gavius Myrto. For thanks to Myrto, he could speak the purest Attic Greek, and acquired at least the basic rudiments of rhetoric. Myrto's library had been extensive, and so Sulla had read his Homer and his Pindar and his Hesiod, his Plato and his Menander and his Eratosthenes, his Euclid and his Archimedes. And he had read in Latin too—Ennius, Accius, Cassius Hemina, Cato the Censor. Ploughing through every scroll he could lay his hands on, he discovered a world where his own situation could be forgotten for a few precious hours, a world of noble heroes and great deeds, scientific fact and philosophical fantasy, the style of literature and the style of mathematics. Luckily the only asset his father had not lost long before Sulla was born was his beautiful Latin; thus of his Latin Sulla had no cause to be ashamed, but he also spoke the cant of the Subura perfectly, and a fairly correct yet lower class of Latin which meant he could move through any Roman sphere without comment.

Quintus Gavius Myrto's little school had always been held in a quiet corner of the Macellum Cuppedenis, the spice and flower markets which lay behind the Forum Romanum on its eastern side. Since he could not afford premises but must teach in the public domain, Myrto would say, what better place to pound knowledge into thick young Roman skulls than amid the heady perfumes of roses and violets, peppercorns and cinnamon?

Not for Myrto a post as live-in tutor to some pampered plebeian pup, nor even the exclusivity of half a dozen knightly scions
taught in a proper schoolroom decently cloistered from the racket
of the streets. No, Myrto simply had his lone slave set up his high
chair and the stools for his students where shoppers would not
trip over them, and taught his reading, writing, and arithmetic in
the open air amid the cries and bellows and sales pitches of the
spice and flower merchants. Had he not been well liked and had
he not given a small discount to boys and girls whose fathers
owned stalls in the Cuppedenis, he would soon have been intimidated into moving on; but as he was well liked and he did discount his teaching, he was allowed to hold his school in the same
corner until he died when Sulla was fifteen.

Myrto charged ten sesterces per week per student, and regularly dealt with ten or fifteen children (always more boys than
girls, yet he was never without several girls). His income was
about five thousand sesterces a year; he paid two thousand of that
for a very nice large single room in a house belonging to one of
his early students; it cost him about one thousand sesterces a year
to feed himself and his elderly but devoted slave quite well, and
the rest of his income he spent upon books. If he wasn't teaching
because it was a market day or a holiday, he could be found
browsing in the libraries and bookshops and publishing houses of
the Argiletum, a broad street which ran off the Forum Romanum
alongside the Basilica Aemilia and the Senate House.

"Oh, Lucius Cornelius," he was wont to say when he got the
boy on his own after lessons were over, desperate (though he
never let that desperation show) to keep the boy safe, to keep him
off the streets, "somewhere in this enormous world a man or a
woman has hidden the works of Aristotle! If you only knew how
much I long to read that man! Such a volume of work, such a
mind—imagine it, the tutor of Alexander the Great! They say he
wrote about absolutely everything—good and evil, stars and at-
oms, souls and hell, dogs and cats, leaves and muscles, the gods
and men, systems of thought and the chaos of mindlessness.
What a treat that would be, to read the lost works of Aristotle!"

And then he would shrug his shoulders, suck at his teeth in the irritating way he had that all his students for decades had mocked behind his back, strike his hands together in a little smack of frustration, and potter among the lovely leathery smell of book buckets and the acrid reek of best-quality paper. "Never mind, never mind," he would say as he went, "I shouldn't complain, when I have my Homer and my Plato."

When he died, which he did in the midst of a cold spell after his old slave had slipped on the icy stairs and broken his neck (amazing how when the line between two people is severed like that, thought Sulla at the time, both ends will go), it was easy to see how very well loved he had been. Not for Quintus Gavius Myrto the hideous indignity of a pauper's place in the lime pits beyond the Agger; no, he had a proper procession, professional mourners, a eulogy, a pyre scented with myrrh and frankincense and Jericho balsam, and a handsome stone tomb to house his ashes. The coin was paid to the custodians of the death records at the temple of Venus Libitina, courtesy of the excellent undertaker hired to manage Myrto's funeral. It had been organized and paid for by two generations of students, who wept for him with genuine grief.

Sulla had walked dry-eyed and high-headed in the throng which escorted Quintus Gavius Myrto out of the city to the burning place, thrown his bunch of roses into the fierce fire, and paid a silver denarius to the undertaker as his share. But later, after his father had crumpled in a wine-soaked heap and his unhappy sister had tidied things up as decently as she could, Sulla sat in his corner of the room in which the three of them lived at the time, and pondered his unexpected treasure trove in aching disbelief. For Quintus Gavius Myrto had arranged his death as tidily as he had his life; his will had been registered and lodged with the Vestal Virgins, a simple document, since he had no cash to bequeath. All that he had to leave—his books and his precious model of sun and moon and planets revolving around the earth—he left to Sulla.

Sulla had wept then, in drear and empty agony; his best and dearest and only real friend was gone, but every day of his life he would see Myrto's little library, and remember.

"One day, Quintus Gavius," he said through the pain of his spasming throat, "I will find the lost works of Aristotle."

Of course he hadn't managed to keep the books and the model long. One day he came home to find the corner where his straw pallet was lodged bare of everything save that pallet. His father had taken the lovingly accumulated treasures of Quintus Gavius Myrto and sold them all to buy wine. There followed the only occasion during Sulla's life with his father when he tried to commit parricide; luckily his sister had been present and put herself between them until sanity returned. It was very shortly afterward that she married her Nonius and went with him to Picenum. As for young Sulla, he never forgot, and he never forgave. At the end of his life, when he owned thousands of books and half a hundred models of the universe, he still would dwell upon the lost library of Quintus Gavius Myrto, and his grief.

The mental trick had worked; Sulla came back to the present moment and the garishly painted, clumsily executed group of Apollo and Daphne. When his eyes drifted past it and encountered the even more ghastly statue of Perseus holding up the Gorgon's head, he almost leaped to his feet, strong enough now to deal with Stichus. He stalked down the garden toward the study, which was the room normally reserved for the sole use of the head of the household; by default, it had been given over to Sulla, who functioned more or less as the man-about-the-house.

The pimply little fart was stuffing his face with candied figs when Sulla walked into the *tablinum,* poking his dirty sticky fingers through the rolls of books slowly accumulating in the pigeonholed walls.

"Ohhhhhhh!" Stichus whinnied at sight of Sulla, snatching his hands away.

"It's lucky I know you're too stupid to read," said Sulla, snapping his fingers at the servant in the doorway. "Here," he said to the servant, a costly pretty Greek not worth a tenth what Clitumna had paid, "get a bowl of water and a clean cloth, and wipe up the mess Master Stichus has made."

His eerie eyes stared at Stichus with the fixed malice of a goat in them, and he said to that unfortunate, who was trying to wipe the syrup off his hands by rubbing them on his expensive tunic, "I wish you'd get it out of your head that I keep a store of naughty picture books! I don't. Why should I? I don't need them. Naughty picture books are for people who don't have the guts to *do* anything. People like you, Stichus."

"One day," said Stichus, "this house and everything in it is going to be mine. You won't be so uppity then!"

"I hope you're offering plenty of sacrifices to postpone that day, Lucius Gavius, because it's likely to be your last. If it weren't for Clitumna, I'd cut you up into little pieces and feed you to the dogs."

Stichus stared at the toga on Sulla's powerful frame, raising his brows; he wasn't really afraid of Sulla, he'd known him too long, but he did sense that danger lurked inside Sulla's fiery head, therefore normally he trod warily. A mode of conduct reinforced by his knowledge that his silly old Auntie Clittie could not be swerved from her slavish devotion to the fellow. However, upon his arrival an hour earlier he had found his aunt and her boon companion Nicopolis in a fine state because their darling Lucius Cornelius had gone out in a rage wearing his toga. When Stichus dragged all of the story out of Clitumna, from Metrobius to the ensuing brawl, he was disgusted. Sickened.

So now he flopped himself down in Sulla's chair and said, "My, my, we are looking every inch the Roman today! Been to the inauguration of the consuls, have we? What a laugh! Your ancestry isn't half as good as mine."

Sulla picked him up out of the chair by clamping the fingers of his right hand on one side of Stichus's jaw and his right thumb on the other side, a hold so exquisitely painful that its victim couldn't even scream; by the time he recovered enough breath to do so, he had seen Sulla's face, and didn't, just stood as mute and graven as his aunt and her boon companion had at dawn that morning.

"My ancestry," said Sulla pleasantly, "is no business of yours. Now get out of my room."

"It won't be your room forever!" gasped Stichus, scuttling to the door and almost colliding with the returning slave, now bearing a bowl of water and a cloth.

"Don't count on it" was Sulla's parting shot.

The expensive slave sidled into the room trying to look demure. Sulla eyed him up and down sourly.

"Clean it up, you mincing flower," he said, and went to find the women.

Stichus had beaten Sulla to Clitumna, who was closeted with her precious nephew and was not to be disturbed, said the steward apologetically. So Sulla walked down the colonnade surrounding the peristyle-garden to the suite of rooms where his mistress Nicopolis lived. There were savory smells coming from the cookhouse at the far end of the garden, a site it shared with the bathroom and the latrine; like most houses on the Palatine, Clitumna's was connected to the water supply and the sewers, thus relieving the staff of the burden of fetching water from a public fountain and toting the contents of the chamber pots to the nearest public latrine or drain opening in the gutter.

"You know, Lucius Cornelius," said Nicopolis, abandoning her fancy work, "if you would only come down out of your aristocratic high-flies occasionally, you'd do a lot better."

He sat on a comfortable couch with a sigh, rugging himself up a little more warmly in his toga because the room was cold, and let the servant girl nicknamed Bithy remove his winter boots. She was a nice cheerful lass with an unpronounceable name, from the backwoods of Bithynia; Clitumna had picked her up cheap from her nephew and inadvertently acquired a treasure. When the girl finished unlacing the boots she bustled out of the room purposefully; in a moment she returned bearing a pair of thick warm socks which she smoothed carefully over Sulla's perfect, snow-white feet.

"Thank you, Bithy," he said, smiling at her and reaching out a careless hand to ruffle her hair.

She absolutely glowed. Funny little thing, he thought with a tenderness that surprised him, until he realized that she reminded him of the girl next door. Julilla . . .

"How do you mean?" he asked Nicopolis, who seemed as usual impervious to the cold.

"Why should that greedy little crawler Stichus inherit everything when Clitumna goes to join her dubious ancestors? If you would only change your tactics a fraction, Lucius Cornelius my very dear friend, she'd leave the lot to *you*. And she's got a lot, believe me!"

"What's he doing, bleating that I hurt him?" asked Sulla, taking a bowl of nuts from Bithy with another special smile.

"Of course he is! And lavishly embroidering it, I'm sure. I don't blame you in the least, he's detestable, but he is her only blood kin—and she loves him, so she's blind to his faults. But she loves you more, haughty wretch that you are! So when you see her next, don't go all icy and proud and refuse to justify yourself—spin her a story about Sticky Stichy even better than the one he's spinning about you."

Half-intrigued, half-skeptical, he stared at her. "Go on, she'd never be stupid enough to fall for it," he said.

"Oh, darling Lucius! When you want, you can make any woman fall for any line you care to toss them. Try it! Just this once? For my sake?" wheedled Nicopolis.

"No. I'd end up the fool, Nicky."

"You wouldn't, you know," Nicopolis persevered.

"There isn't enough money in the world to make me grovel to the likes of Clitumna!"

"She doesn't have all the money in the world, but she does have more than enough to see you into the Senate," whispered the temptress beguilingly.

"No! You're wrong, you really are. There's this house, admittedly, but she spends every penny she gets—and what she doesn't spend, Sticky Stichy does."

"Not so. Why do you think her bankers hang on her every word as if she were Cornelia the Mother of the Gracchi? She's got a very tidy fortune invested with them, and she doesn't spend half of her income. Besides which, give Sticky Stichy his due, he's not short of a sestertius either. As long as his late father's accountant and manager are capable of working, that business of Stichy's will continue to do very nicely."

Sulla sat up with a jerk, loosening the folds of toga. "Nicky, you wouldn't spin me a tale, would you?"

"I would, but not about this," she said, threading her needle with purple wool intertwined with gold bullion.

"She'll live to be a hundred," he said then, subsiding onto the couch and handing back the bowl of nuts to Bithy, no longer hungry.

"I agree, she might live to be a hundred," said Nicopolis, plunging her needle into the tapestry and drawing her glittering thread through very, very carefully. Her big dark eyes surveyed Sulla tranquilly. "But then again, she may not. Hers isn't a long-lived family, you know."

There were noises outside; Lucius Gavius Stichus was evidently taking his leave of his Aunt Clitumna.

Sulla stood up, let the servant girl slip backless Greek slippers onto his feet. The massive length and breadth of the toga slumped to the floor, but he seemed not to notice.

"All right, Nicky, just this once I'll try it," he said, and grinned. "Wish me luck!"

But before she could, he was gone.

The interview with Clitumna didn't go well; Stichus had done his work with cunning, and Sulla couldn't make himself humble his pride to plead, as Nicopolis had wanted.

"It's all your fault, Lucius Cornelius," said Clitumna fretfully, twisting the expensive fringe of her shawl between beringed fingers. "You won't make the slightest effort to be nice to my poor boy, where he always tries to meet you more than halfway!"

"He's a grubby little would-be-if-he-could-be," said Sulla between his teeth.

At which moment Nicopolis, listening outside the door, drifted gracefully through it and curled herself up on the couch beside Clitumna; she stared up at Sulla in resignation.

"What's the matter?" she asked, all innocence.

"It's both my Luciuses," said Clitumna. "They won't get on together, and I want them to so much!"

Nicopolis disentangled fringe from fingers, then unhooked a few threads which had caught on the roughnesses of gem settings, and lifted Clitumna's hand to rest its back against her cheek. "Oh, my poor girl!" she crooned. "Your Luciuses are a couple of roosters, that's the trouble."

"Well, they're going to have to learn to get on," said Clitumna, "because my darling Lucius Gavius is giving up his apartment and moving in with us next week."

"Then I'm moving out," said Sulla.

Both women began to squeal, Clitumna shrilly, Nicopolis like a small trapped kitten.

"Oh, be your age!" Sulla whispered, thrusting his face down until it was only inches from Clitumna's. "He knows the situation here more or less, but how do you think he's going to stomach living in the same house with a man who sleeps between two women, and one of them his aunt?"

Clitumna began to weep. "But he *wants* to come! How can I say no to my nephew?"

"Don't bother! I'll remove the cause of all his complaints by moving out," said Sulla.

As he began to withdraw Nicopolis stretched out her hand and clutched his arm. "Sulla, darling Sulla, don't!" she cried. "Look, you can sleep with me, and then whenever Stichus is out, Clitumna can come down and join us."

"Oh, very crafty!" said Clitumna, stiffening. "You want him all to yourself, you greedy sow!"

Nicopolis went white. "Well, what else do you suggest? It's your stupidity's got us into this mess!"

"Shut up, both of you!" snarled Sulla in the whisper all who knew him well had learned to dread more than any other man's shout. "You've been going to mimes so long you're beginning to live them. Grow up, don't be so vulgarly crass! I detest the whole wretched situation, I'm tired of being half a man!"

"Well, you're *not* half a man! You're two halves—half mine, and half Nicky's!" said Clitumna nastily.

There was no telling which hurt worse, the rage or the grief; perfectly poised on the very edge of madness, Sulla glared at his tormentors, unable to think, unable to see.

"I can't go on!" he said, wonder in his voice.

"Nonsense! Of course you can," said Nicopolis with the smugness of one who knew beyond any shadow of doubt that she had her man right where she wanted him—under her foot. "Now run away and do something constructive. You'll feel better tomorrow. You always do."

Out of the house, off to anywhere—anywhere *constructive*. Sulla's feet blundered up the alley rather than down, took him unaware across from the Germalus to the Palatium, that part of the Palatine which looked down toward the end of the Circus Maximus and the Capena Gate.

The houses were thinner here and there were many park-like spaces; the Palatium wasn't terribly fashionable, it lay too far from the Forum Romanum. Uncaring that it was very cold and he clad only in his house tunic, he sat upon a stone and looked at the view; not at the vacant bleachers of the Circus Maximus nor the lovely temples of the Aventine, but at the vista of himself stretched endlessly into a terrible future, a warped roadway of skin and bone that had absolutely no purpose. The pain was like a colic without the release of purgation; he shook with it until he could hear the grinding of his teeth, and did not know he groaned aloud.

"Are you ill?" asked the voice, small and timid.

At first when he looked up he saw nothing, his agony took the power from his eyes, but then they cleared, and so she swam slowly into focus from pointed chin to golden hairline, a heart-shaped face that was all eyes, huge and honey-colored, very afraid for him.

She knelt in front of him, wrapped in her homespun cocoon, just as he had seen her at the site of Flaccus's house.

"Julia," he said with a shudder.

"No, Julia's my older sister. They call me Julilla," she said, smiling at him. "Are you ill, Lucius Cornelius?"

"Not with anything a physician can heal." Sanity and memory were returning; he understood the galling truth of Nicopolis's last remark, he would feel better tomorrow. And hated that more than anything. "I would like so much—so very, very much!—to go mad," he said, "but it seems I can't."

Julilla remained where she was. "If you can't, then the Furies don't want you yet."

"Are you here on your own?" he asked, disapproving. "What are your parents about, to let you wander abroad at this hour?"

"My girl is with me," she said tranquilly, sinking back on her heels. A sudden light of mischief darted through her eyes, turned up the delicious corners of her mouth. "She's a good girl. The most loyal and discreet person."

"You mean she lets you go wherever you like and doesn't tell on you. But one day," said the man who was perpetually caught, "you'll be caught."

"Until I am, what's the use of worrying?"

Lapsing into silence, she studied his face with unselfconscious curiosity, clearly enjoying what she saw.

"Go home, Julilla," he said, sighing. "If you must get caught, don't let it be with me."

"Because you're a bad lot?" she asked.

That brought a faint smile. "If you like."

"*I* don't think you are!"

Oh, what god had sent her? Thank you, unknown god! His muscles were untwining themselves; he felt suddenly light, as if indeed some god had brushed by him, benign and good. A strange feeling for one who knew no good.

"I am a bad lot, Julilla," he said.

"Nonsense!" Her voice was firm and positive.

No novice, he recognized the symptoms of a girlish crush, and knew an impulse to dispel it by some coarse or frightening action. But he couldn't. Not to her, she didn't deserve it. For her, he would reach into his grab bag of tricks and produce the best Lucius Cornelius Sulla of them all, free from artifice, innocent of smut and smirch and smarm.

"Well, I thank you for your faith, young Julilla," he said a little lamely, unsure what she wanted to hear, anxious that it should reflect the best in him.

"I have some time," she said gravely. "Might we talk?"

He moved over on his rock. "All right. But sit here, the ground's too damp."

"They say," she said, "that you're a disgrace to your name. But I don't see how that's possible, when you haven't had a chance to prove different."

"I daresay your father's the author of that remark."

"Which remark?"

"That I'm a disgrace to my name."

She was shocked. "Oh, no! Not *tata*! He's the wisest man in the world."

"Where mine was the most foolish. We're at the opposite ends of Rome's spectrum, young Julilla."

She was plucking at the long grass around the base of the rock, pulling it out in long rhizomes, then wove with her nimble fingers until she had made a wreath of it. "Here," she said, and held it out to him.

His breath caught; the future spasmed, opened up to show him something, closed again with the glimpse too painfully short. "A crown of grass!" he said, wondering. "No! Not for me!"

"Of course it's for you," she insisted, and when he still made no move to take it, she leaned forward and put it on his head. "It should be flowers, but not at this time of year."

She didn't understand! Well, he wouldn't tell her. "You give a wreath of flowers only to a loved one," he said instead.

"You *are* my loved one," she said softly.

"Only for a little while, girl. It will pass."

"Never!"

He got up, laughed down at her. "Go on! You can't be more than fifteen," he said.

"Sixteen!" she said quickly.

"Fifteen, sixteen, what's the difference? You're a baby."

Flushed with indignation, her face grew set, sharp. "I am *not* a baby!" she cried.

"Of course you are." He laughed again. "Look at you, all swaddled up, a little roly-poly puppy." There! That was better! That ought to put her in her place.

It did, but more than that. She was blighted, withered, killed. The light died in her. "I'm not pretty?" she said. "I always thought I was."

"Growing up is a cruel business," said Sulla harshly. "I suppose almost all families tell their girl-children they're pretty. But the world judges by different standards. You'll be passable when you're older, you won't lack a husband."

"I only want you," she whispered.

"That's now. Anyway, disabuse yourself, my fat puppy. Run away before I pull your tail. Go on, shoo!"

She ran, her servant girl left far behind, calling after her vainly. Sulla stood watching until they both disappeared over the brow of the slope behind.

The grass crown was still on his head, its tawny color a subtle contrast to his fiery curls; he reached up and plucked it off, but didn't throw it away, stood holding it between his hands and staring at it. Then he tucked it in his tunic, and turned to go.

Poor little thing. He had hurt her after all. Still, she had to be discouraged; the last complication he needed in his life was Clitumna's next-door neighbor's daughter mooning over the wall, and she a senator's daughter.

With every step he took as he walked away the grass crown tickled his skin, reminding him. *Corona Graminea.* Grass crown. Given to him here on the Palatine, where hundreds of years before the original city of Romulus had stood, a bevy of oval thatched huts like the one still lovingly cared for near the Steps of Cacus. A grass crown given to him by a personification of Venus—truly one of Venus's girls, a Julia. An omen.

"If it comes to pass, I will build you a temple, Venus Victorious," he said aloud.

For he saw his way clear at last. Dangerous. Desperate. But for one with nothing to lose and everything to gain, possible nonetheless.

Winter twilight lay heavy when he was admitted back into Clitumna's house and asked where the ladies were. In the dining room, heads together, waiting for him before summoning the meal. That he had been the subject of their talk was obvious; they sprang apart on the couch, tried to look idly innocent.

"I want some money," he said baldly.

"Now, Lucius Cornelius—" Clitumna began, looking wary.

"Shut up, you pathetic old drab! I want money."

"But Lucius Cornelius!"

"I'm going away for a holiday," he said, making no move to join them. "It's up to you. If you want me back—if you want more of what I've got—then give me a thousand denarii. Otherwise, I'm quitting Rome forever."

"We'll give you half each," said Nicopolis unexpectedly, dark eyes fixed on his face.

"Now," he said.

"There may not be so much in the house," Nicopolis said.

"You'd better hope there is, because I'm not waiting."

When Nicopolis went to his room fifteen minutes later, she found him packing. Perching herself on his bed, she watched in silence until he should deign to notice her.

But it was she who broke down first. "You'll have your money, Clitumna's sent the steward to her banker's house," she said. "Where are you going?"

"I don't know, and I don't care. Just so long as it's away from here." He folded socks together, thrust them into closed-toe boots, every movement as economical as it was efficient.

"You pack like a soldier."

"How would you know?"

"Oh, I was the mistress of a military tribune once. I followed the drum, would you believe it? The things one does for love when one is young! I adored him. So I went with him to Spain, and then to Asia." She sighed.

"What happened?" he asked, rolling his second-best tunic around a pair of leather knee breeches.

"He was killed in Macedonia, and I came home." Pity stirred her heart, but not for her dead lover. Pity for Lucius Cornelius, trapped, a beautiful lion destined for some sordid arena. Why did one love at all? It hurt so much. So she smiled, not a pretty smile. "He left everything he had to me in his will, and I became quite rich. There was plenty of booty in those days."

"My heart bleeds," he said, wrapping his razors inside their linen sheath and sliding it down the side of a saddlebag.

Her face twisted. "This is a nasty house," she said. "Oh, I do hate it! All of us bitter and unhappy. How many truly pleasant things do we say to each other? Precious few. Insults and indignities, spite and malice. Why am I here?"

"Because, my dear, you're getting a bit frayed around the edges," he said, reinforcing her observation. "You're not the girl you used to be when you trudged all over Spain and Asia."

"And you hate us all," she said. "Is that where the atmosphere originates? In you? I swear it's getting worse."

"I agree, it is. That's why I'm going away for a while." He strapped the two bags, hefted them easily. "I want to be free. I want to spend big in some country town where no one knows my wretched face, eat and drink until I spew, get at least half a dozen girls pregnant, pick fifty fights with men who think they can take me with one arm tied behind their backs, find every pretty-boy between here and wherever I end up and give them sore arses." He smiled evilly. "And then, my dear, I promise I'll come tamely home to you and Sticky Stichy and Auntie Clittie, and we'll all live happily ever after."

What he didn't tell her was that he was taking Metrobius with him; and he wouldn't tell old Scylax, either.

Nor did he tell anyone, even Metrobius, just what he was up to.

For it wasn't a holiday. It was an investigative mission. Sulla was going to make inquiries into subjects like pharmacology, chemistry, and botany.

He didn't return to Rome until the end of April. Dropping Metrobius off at Scylax's elegant ground-floor apartment on the Caelian Hill outside the Servian Walls, he then drove down into the Vallis Camenarum to surrender the gig and mules he had hired from a stable there. Having paid the bill, he slung his saddlebags over his left shoulder and set out to walk into Rome. No servant had traveled with him; he and Metrobius had made do with the staff of the various inns and posting houses they had stayed in up and down the peninsula.

As he trudged up the Via Appia to where the Capena Gate interrupted the twenty-foot-high masonry of Rome's ramparts, the city looked very good to him. Legend had it that Rome's Servian Walls had been erected by King Servius Tullus before the Republic was established, but like most noblemen, Sulla knew these fortifications, at least, had not existed until three hundred years ago when the Gauls had sacked the city. The Gauls had poured down in teeming hordes from the western Alps, spreading across the huge valley of the Padus River in the far north, gradually working their way down peninsular Italy on both east and west. Many settled where they fetched up, especially in Umbria and Picenum, but those who came down the Via Cassia through Etruria headed purposely toward Rome—and having reached Rome, almost wrested the city permanently off her rightful owners. It was only after that the Servian Walls went up, while the Italian peoples of the Padus Valley, all Umbria, and northern Picenum mingled their blood with the Gauls, became despised half-castes. Never again had Rome suffered its walls to lapse into disrepair; the lesson had been a hard one, and the fear of barbarian invaders could still provoke horrified chills in every Roman.

Though there were a few expensive insula apartment towers on the Caelian Hill, the scene in the main was pastoral until Sulla reached the Capena Gate; the Vallis Camenarum outside it was given over to stockyards, slaughterhouses, smokehouses, and grazing fields for the animals sent to this greatest market in all Italy. Inside the Capena Gate lay the real city. Not the congested jumble of the Subura and the Esquiline, yet urban nonetheless. He strolled up along the Circus Maximus and took the Steps of Cacus onto the Germalus of the Palatine, after which it was only a short distance to the house of Clitumna.

Outside its door he took a deep breath, then sounded the knocker. And entered a world of shrieking women. That Nicopolis and Clitumna were delighted to see him was very plain. They wept and whinnied, draped themselves about his neck until he pushed them off, after which they kept circling close about him and would not leave him in peace.

"Where do I sleep these days?" he asked, refusing to hand his saddlebags to the servant itching to take them.

"With me," said Nicopolis, glittering triumphantly at the suddenly downcast Clitumna.

The door to the study was tightly shut, Sulla noted as he followed Nicopolis out onto the colonnade, leaving his stepmother standing in the atrium wringing her hands.

"I take it Sticky Stichy's well ensconced by now?" he asked Nicopolis as they reached her suite of rooms.

"Here," she said, ignoring his question, so bursting was she to show him his new quarters.

What she had done was to yield up her very spacious sitting room to him, leaving herself with a bedroom and a much smaller chamber. Gratitude filled him; he looked at her a little sadly, liking her in that moment more than he ever had.

"All mine?" he asked.

"All yours," she said, smiling.

He threw the saddlebags down on his bed. "Stichus?" he asked, impatient to know the worst.

Of course she wanted him to kiss her, make love to her, but she knew him well enough to understand that he was in no need of sexual solace simply because he had been away from her and

Clitumna. The lovemaking would have to wait; sighing, Nicopolis reconciled herself to the role of informant.

"Stichus is very well entrenched indeed," she said, and went over to the saddlebags to unpack for him.

He put her aside firmly, dropped the saddlebags down behind one of the clothes chests, and moved to his favorite chair, which stood behind a new desk. Nicopolis sat on his bed.

"I want all the news," he said.

"Well, Stichy's here, sleeping in the master's cubicle and using the study, of course. It's been better than expected in one way, really, because Stichy at close quarters every day is hard to take, even for Clitumna. A few more months, and I predict she'll throw him out. It was clever of you to go away, you know." Her hand smoothed the stack of pillows beside her absently. "I didn't think so at the time, I admit, but you were right and I was wrong. Stichy entered the place like a triumphing general, and you weren't here to dim his glory. Oh, things sailed around, I can tell you! Your books went into the rubbish bin—it's all right, the servants rescued them—and whatever else you left in the way of clothing and personal stuff went into the rubbish bin after the books. Since the staff like you and loathe him, nothing of yours was lost—it's all here in this room somewhere."

His pale eyes traveled around the walls, across the lovely mosaic floor. "This is nice," he said. And then, "Continue."

"Clitumna was devastated. She hadn't counted on Stichy's throwing your things out. In fact, I don't think she ever really wanted him to move in, but when he said he wanted to, she couldn't find a way to refuse. Blood and the last of her line and all the rest of it. Clitumna's not very bright, but she knew perfectly well his only reason for demanding to move in here was to get you moving in the direction of the street. Stichy's not hard up. But when you weren't even here to see your stuff being thrown out, it rather took the edge off Stichy's pleasure. No quarrels, no opposition, no—*presence*. Just a passively surly staff, a very weepy Auntie Clittie, and me—well, I just look through him as if he isn't there."

The little servant girl Bithy came sidling through the door bearing a plate of assorted buns, pasties, pies, and cakes, put it down on the corner of the desk with a shy smile for Sulla, and spied the leather band connecting the two saddlebags, poking up from behind the clothes chest. Off she went across the room to unpack.

Sulla moved so quickly Nicopolis didn't see him intercept the girl; one moment he was leaning back comfortably in his chair, the next the girl was being moved gently away from the clothes chest. Smiling at her, Sulla pinched Bithy gently on the cheek and thrust her out the door. Nicopolis stared.

"My, you are worried about those bags!" she said. "What's in them? You're like a dog guarding a bone."

"Pour me some wine," he said, sitting down again, and selecting a meat pasty from the plate.

She did as he asked, but she was not about to let go of the subject. "Come, Lucius Cornelius, what's in those bags that you don't want anyone to see?" A cup of unwatered wine was put in front of him.

Down went both corners of his mouth; he threw out his hands in a gesture indicating growing exasperation. "What do you think? I've been away from both my girls for almost four months! I admit I didn't think of you *all* the time, but I did think of you! Especially when I saw some little thing I thought might please one or the other of you."

Her face softened, glowed; Sulla was not a gift giver. In fact, Nicopolis could never remember his presenting her or Clitumna with a single gift, even of the cheapest kind, and she was a wise enough student of human nature to know this was evidence of parsimony, not of poverty; the generous will give, even when they have nothing to give.

"Oh, Lucius Cornelius!" she exclaimed, beaming. "Truly? When may I see?"

"When I'm good and ready," he said, turning his chair to glance through the big window behind him. "What's the time?"

"I don't know—about the eighth hour, I think. Dinner isn't due yet, anyway," she said.

He got up, went across to the clothes chest, and hooked the saddlebags out from behind it, slinging them over his shoulder. "I'll be back in time for dinner," he said.

Jaw dropped, she watched him go to the door. "*Sulla!* You are the most annoying creature in the entire world. I swear it! Just arrived home, and you're off somewhere! Well, I doubt you need to visit Metrobius, since you took him with you!"

That arrested his progress. Grinning, he stared at her. "Oh, I see! Scylax came a-calling to complain, did he?"

"You might say. He arrived like a tragedian playing Antigone, and left like a comedian playing the eunuch. Clitumna certainly put a squeak in his voice!" She laughed at the memory.

"Serves him right, the old whore. Do you know he'd deliberately prevented the boy's learning to read and write?"

But the saddlebags were gnawing again. "Don't trust us enough to leave them behind while you go out?" she asked.

"I'm not a fool," he said, and departed.

Female curiosity. He *was* a fool, to have overlooked it. So down to the Great Market he took himself and his saddlebags, and in the course of the next hour went on a concentrated shopping spree with the last of his thousand silver denarii, that remnant he had thought to save for the future. Women! Nosy, interfering sows! Why hadn't he thought of it?

The saddlebags weighed down with scarves and bangles, frivolous Eastern slippers and gewgaws for the hair, he was let back into Clitumna's house by a servant who informed him the ladies and Master Stichus were in the dining room, but had elected to wait a while before eating.

"Tell them I'll be there shortly," he said, and went to Nicopolis's suite.

There didn't seem to be anyone about, but to make sure, he closed the shutters on his window and then bolted his door. The hastily purchased presents he heaped on the desk, some new book rolls alongside them. The left-hand bag he ignored; the top layer of clothes in the right-hand bag he dumped out on the bed. Then from the depths of the right-hand bag he drew forth two pairs of rolled-up socks, and fiddled with them until they yielded two small bottles whose stoppers were heavily sealed with wax. Next emerged a plain wooden box, small enough to fit in his hand easily; as if unable to help himself, he lifted its lid, which fitted closely. The contents were uninspiring: just a few ounces of a sluggish off-white powder. Down went the lid; his fingers tamped it firmly into place. Then he looked around the room, frowning. Where?

A row of decrepit little wooden cupboards shaped like models of temples occupied the top of a long, narrow sideboard table: the relics of the House of Cornelius Sulla. All he had inherited from his father, all his father couldn't sell for wine, more likely for lack of a buyer than lack of the will to sell. Five cupboards, each a cube two feet by two feet by two feet; each had painted wooden doors in its front between an outer stand of columns: each had a pediment decorated with carved temple figures at apex and ends; and on the simple entablature running below the pediment, each had a man's name inscribed. One was the original ancestor common to all seven branches of the patrician House of Cornelius; one was Publius Cornelius Rufinus, consul and dictator over two hundred years earlier; one was his son, twice consul and once dictator during the Samnite wars, then expelled from the Senate for hoarding silver plate; one was the first Rutinus to be called Sulla, priest of Jupiter all his life; and the last was his praetor son, Publius Cornelius Sulla Rufinus, famous for his founding of the *ludi Apollinares,* the Games of Apollo.

It was the cupboard of the first Sulla which Sulla opened, very delicately, for the wood had been neglected for many years, and had grown frail. Once the paint had been bright, the tiny relief figures clearly outlined; now they were faded, chipped. One day he intended to find the money to restore his ancestral cupboards, and have a house with an imposing atrium in which he could display his cupboards proudly. However, for the moment it seemed appropriate to hide his two little bottles and his box of powder in the cupboard of Sulla the *flamen Dialis,* most sacred man in the Rome of his day, serving Jupiter Optimus Maximus.

The interior of the cupboard was filled with a life-size be-wigged wax mask, exquisitely lifelike, so well had the tints been applied to it. Eyes glared out at Sulla, blue rather than his own palest grey; the skin of Rufinus was fair, but not so fair as Sulla's; and the hair, thick and curling, was a carrot-red rather than a golden-red. Sufficient space lay around the mask to permit its removal, for it was fixed to a wooden head-shaped block from which it could be detached. The last time it had come out was at his father's funeral, which Sulla had paid for in a painful series of encounters with a man he detested.

Lovingly Sulla closed the doors, then plucked at the steps of the podium, which looked smooth and seamless. But, like a real temple, the podium of this ancestral cupboard was hollow; Sulla found the right spot, and out of the front steps there slid a drawer. It was not intended as a hiding place, but as a safe receptacle in which to store the written record of the ancestor's deeds, as well as a detailed description of his size, gait, posture, physical habits, and bodily distinguishing marks. For when a Cornelius Sulla died, an actor would be hired to don the mask and imitate the dead ancestor so accurately that he might be supposed to have come back to see this later scion of his noble house ushered out of the world he himself had once adorned.

The documents relating to Publius Cornelius Sulla Rufinus the priest were inside the drawer, but there was plenty of room for the bottles and the box; Sulla slipped them in, then pushed the drawer shut and made sure the closure was undetectable. His secret would be safe with Rufinus.

Feeling easier, Sulla opened up the window shutters and unbolted his door. And gathered up the heap of fripperies lying all over his desk, with a malicious grin at the scroll he also picked out from among the others stacked there.

Of course Lucius Gavius Stichus was occupying the host's place on the left-hand end of the middle couch; this was one of the few dining rooms where the women reclined rather than sat on upright chairs, since neither Clitumna nor Nicopolis was ruled by old-fashioned shibboleths.

"Here you are, girls," said Sulla, tossing his armful of gifts at the two adoring female faces following his progress into the room like flowers the sun. He had chosen well, things which might indeed have come from elsewhere than a market inside Rome, and things which neither woman would be ashamed to wear.

But before he slid artfully between Clitumna and Nicopolis on the first couch, he slapped the rolled-up book he was holding down in front of Stichus.

"A little something for you, Stichus," he said.

While Sulla settled himself between the two women, who responded with giggles and purrs, Stichus, startled at being the recipient of a gift, untied the tapes holding the book together, and unfurled it. Two scarlet spots flared in his sallow acne-pocked cheeks as his goggling eyes took in the beautifully drawn and painted male figures, penises erect as they performed all manner of athletic feats with each other upon the unsuspecting papyrus. With shaking fingers he rolled the thing up and tied it, then had of course to pluck up the courage to look at his benefactor. Sulla's frightful eyes were gleaming at him over the top of Clitumna's head, speaking silent volumes of contempt.

"Thank you, Lucius Cornelius," Stichus squeaked.

"You're very welcome, Lucius Gavius," said Sulla from the bottom of his throat.

At which moment the *gustatio*—the first course—came in, hastily augmented, Sulla suspected, in honor of his return; for besides the normal fare of olives, lettuce salad, and hard-boiled eggs, it contained some little pheasant sausages and chunks of tunnyfish in oil. Enjoying himself hugely, Sulla tucked in, sliding wicked sidelong glances at Stichus, alone on his couch while his aunt applied as much of her side to Sulla's side as she possibly could, and Nicopolis caressed Sulla's groin shamelessly.

"Well, and what's the news on the home front?" he asked as the first course was cleared away.

"Nothing much," said Nicopolis, more interested in what was happening under her hand.

Sulla turned his head toward Clitumna. "I don't believe her," he said, as he picked up Clitumna's hand and began to nibble its fingers. Then when he saw the look of distaste upon Stichus's face, he began to lick the fingers voluptuously. "Tell me, love"—lick—"because I refuse to believe"—lick—"nothing's happened." Lick, lick, lick.

Luckily the *fercula*—the main courses—arrived at that moment; greedy Clitumna snatched her hand away and stretched it out to grab at the roast mutton with thyme sauce.

"Our neighbors have been busy," she said between swallows, "to make up for how quiet we've been while you were away." A sigh. "Titus Pomponius's wife had a little boy in February."

"Ye gods, another boring money-hungry merchant banker for the future!" was Sulla's comment. "Caecilia Pilia is well, I trust?"

"Very! No trouble at all."

"And on the Caesar side?" He was thinking of delectable Julilla and the grass crown she had given him.

"Big news there!" Clitumna licked her own fingers. "They had a wedding—quite a society affair."

Something happened to Sulla's heart; it actually seemed to drop like a stone to the bottom of his belly, and sit there churning amid the food. The oddest sensation.

"Oh, really?" He kept his tone disinterested.

"Indeed! Caesar's elder daughter married none other than *Gaius Marius*! Disgusting, isn't it?"

"Gaius Marius . . ."

"What, don't you know him?" Clitumna asked.

"I don't think so. *Marius* . . . He must be a New Man."

"That's right. He was praetor five years ago, never made it to the consulship, of course. But he was governor of Further Spain, and made an absolute fortune out there. Mines and the like," said Clitumna.

For some reason Sulla remembered the man with the mien of

an eagle at the inauguration of the new consuls; he had worn a purple-bordered toga. "What does he look like?"

"Grotesque, my dear! The most enormous eyebrows! Like hairy caterpillars." Clitumna reached for the braised broccoli. "He's at least thirty years older than Julia, poor dear."

"What's so unusual about that?" demanded Stichus, feeling it time he had something to say. "At least half the girls in Rome marry men old enough to be their fathers."

Nicopolis frowned. "I wouldn't go so far as to say *half*, Stichy," she said. "A quarter would be more like it."

"Disgusting!" said Stichus.

"Disgusting, rubbish!" said Nicopolis vigorously, sitting up so she could glare at him more effectively. "Let me tell you, fart-face, that there's a lot to be said for older men as far as a young girl is concerned! At least older men have learned to be considerate and reasonable! My worst lovers were all under twenty-five. Think they know it all, but know nothing. Erk! Like being hit by a bull. Over before it starts."

Since Stichus was twenty-three years old, he bridled.

"Oh, you would! Think you know it all, don't you?" he sneered.

The look he got was level. "I know more than you do, fart-face," she said.

"Now, now, let's be happy tonight!" cried Clitumna. "Our darling Lucius Cornelius is back."

Their darling Lucius Cornelius promptly grabbed his stepmother and rolled her over on the couch, tickling her ribs until she screeched shrilly and kicked her legs in the air. Nicopolis retaliated by tickling Sulla, and the first couch became a melee.

This was too much for Stichus; clutching his new book, he slid off his couch and stalked out of the room, not sure they even noticed his going. How was he going to dislodge that man? Auntie Clittie was besotted! Even while Sulla was away, he had not managed to persuade her to send Sulla packing. She just wept that it was a pity her two darling boys couldn't get on.

Though he had eaten hardly anything, Stichus wasn't upset by the fact, for in his study he kept an interesting array of comestibles—a jar of his favorite figs in syrup, a little tray of honeyed pastry the cook was under orders to keep filled, some tongue-cloying perfumed jellies which came all the way from Parthia, a box of plumply juicy raisins, honey cakes, and honeyed wine. Roast mutton and braised broccoli he could live without; every tooth in his head was a sweet one.

Chin on his hand, a quintuple lamp chasing away the beginnings of evening, Lucius Gavius Stichus munched syruped figs while he carefully perused the illustrations of the book Sulla had given him, and read the short accompanying Greek text. Of course he knew the present was Sulla's way of saying *he* didn't need such books, because he'd done it all, but that couldn't stifle his interest; Stichus was not endowed with so much pride. Ah! Ah ah ah! Something was happening under his embroidered tunic! And he dropped his hand from chin to lap with a furtive innocence quite wasted upon its only audience, the jar of syruped figs.

Yielding to an impulse he despised himself for feeling, Lucius Cornelius Sulla walked next morning across the Palatine to the spot on the Palatium where he had encountered Julilla. It was high spring now, and the patches of parkland sported flowers everywhere, narcissus and anemone, hyacinths, violets, even an occasional early rose; wild apples and peaches were in full blossom, white and pink, and the rock upon which he had sat in January now was almost hidden by lushly green grass.

Her servant girl in attendance, Julilla was there, looking thinner, less honey-colored. And when she saw him, a wild triumphant joy suffused her from eyes to skin to hair—so *beautiful*! Oh, never in the history of the world had any mortal woman been so beautiful! Hackles rising, Sulla stopped in his tracks, filled with an awe akin to terror. Venus. She was Venus. Ruler of life and death. For what was life except the procreative principle, and what was death save its extinction? All else was decoration, the furbelows men invented to convince themselves life and death *must* mean more. She was Venus. But did that make him Mars, her equal in godhead—or was he merely Anchises, a mortal man she stooped to fancy for the space of one Olympian heartbeat?

No, he wasn't Mars. His life had equipped him for pure ornamentation, and even that of the cheapest gimcrack kind; who could he be but Anchises, the man whose only real fame lay in the fact that Venus stooped to fancy him for a moment? He shook with anger, directed his hateful frustration at her, and so pumped venom into his veins, creating an overwhelming urge to strike at her, reduce her from Venus to Julilla.

"I heard you came back yesterday," she said, not moving toward him.

"Got your spies out, have you?" he asked, refusing to move closer to her.

"That isn't necessary in our street, Lucius Cornelius. The servants know everything," she said.

"Well, I hope you don't think I came here looking for you today, because I didn't. I came here for a little peace."

Her beauty actually increased, though he hadn't thought it possible. My honey-girl, he thought. Julilla. It dropped like honey off the tongue. So did Venus.

"Does that mean I disturb your peace?" she asked, very sure of herself for one so young.

He laughed, contriving to make it sound light, amused, trifling. "Ye gods, baby girl, you have a lot of growing up to do!" he said, and laughed again. "I said I came here for peace. That means I thought I'd find it here, doesn't it? And by logical progression, the answer must be that you don't disturb my peace one iota."

She fought back. "Not at all! It might simply indicate that you didn't expect to find me here."

"Which leads straight back to indifference," he said.

It was an unequal contest, of course; before his eyes she was shrinking, losing her luster, an immortal turned mortal. Her face puckered, but she managed not to cry, just gazed at him bewildered, not able to reconcile how he looked and what he said with the true instinct of her heart, which told her in every beat that she had caught him in her toils.

"I love you!" she said, as if it explained everything.

Another laugh. "Fifteen! What would you know of love?"

"I'm sixteen!" she said.

"Look, baby girl," Sulla said, his tone cutting, "leave me alone! Not only are you a nuisance, you're rapidly becoming an embarrassment." And turned, and walked away without once looking back.

Julilla didn't collapse in floods of tears; it would have been better for her future welfare had she. For a passionate and painful bout of tears might have convinced her that she was wrong, that she stood no chance to capture him. As it was, she walked across to where Chryseis, her servant girl, was standing pretending to be absorbed in the prospect of an empty Circus Maximus. Her chin was up; so was her pride.

"He's going to be difficult," she said, "but never mind. Sooner or later I shall get him, Chryseis."

"I don't think he wants you," said Chryseis.

"Of course he wants me!" said Julilla scornfully. "He wants me *desperately*!"

Long acquaintance with Julilla put a curb on Chryseis's tongue; instead of trying to reason with her mistress, she sighed, shrugged. "Have it your own way," she said.

"I usually do," answered Julilla.

They began to walk home, the silence between them unusual, for they were much of an age, and had grown up together. But when they reached the great temple of Magna Mater, Julilla spoke, voice determined.

"I shall refuse to eat," she said.

Chryseis stopped. "And what do you think that's going to do?" she asked.

"Well, in January he said I was fat. And I am."

"Julilla, you're not!"

"Yes, I am. That's why I haven't eaten any sweetmeats since January. I'm a little thinner, but not nearly thin enough. He likes thin women. Look at Nicopolis. Her arms are like sticks."

"But she's *old*!" Chryseis said. "What looks good on you wouldn't look good on her. Besides, you'll worry your parents if you stop eating—they'll think you're sick!"

"Good," said Julilla. "If they think I'm sick, so will Lucius Cornelius. And he'll worry about me dreadfully."

Better and more convincing arguments Chryseis could not produce, for she was neither very bright nor very sensible. So she burst into tears, which pleased Julilla enormously.

Four days after Sulla returned to Clitumna's house, Lucius Gavius Stichus came down with a digestive disorder which prostrated him; alarmed, Clitumna called in half a dozen of the Palatine's most fashionable doctors, all of whom diagnosed an attack of food poisoning.

"Vomiting, colic, diarrhoea—a classic picture," said their spokesman, the Roman physician Publius Popillius.

"But he hasn't eaten anything the rest of us haven't!" protested Clitumna, her fears unallayed. "In fact, he isn't eating nearly as well as the rest of us, and that's what's worrying me most!"

"Ah, *domina,* I think you are quite wrong," lisped the nosiest of them, Athenodorus Siculus, a practitioner with the famous Greek investigative persistence; he had wandered off and poked into every room opening off the atrium, then into the rooms around the peristyle-garden. "Surely you are aware that Lucius Gavius has half a sweetmeat shop in his study?"

"Pish!" squeaked Clitumna. "Half a sweetmeat shop, indeed! A few figs and pastries, that's all. In fact, he hardly ever touches them."

The six learned medical men looked at each other. "*Domina,* he eats them all day and half the night, so your staff tell me," said Athenodorus the Greek from Sicily. "I suggest you persuade him to give up his confectioneries. If he eats better foods, not only will his digestive troubles clear up, but his general level of health will improve."

Lucius Gavius Stichus was privy to all this, lying on his bed too weak from the violence of his purging to defend himself, his slightly protruding eyes jumping from one face to another as the conversation jumped from one speaker to another.

"He has pimples, and his skin is a bad color," said a Greek from Athens. "Does he exercise?"

"He doesn't need to," said Clitumna, the first hint of doubt appearing in her tone. "He rushes about from place to place in the course of his business, it keeps him constantly on the run, I do assure you!"

"What is your business, Lucius Gavius?" asked the Spaniard.

"I'm a slaver," said Stichus.

Since all save Publius Popillius had started life in Rome as slaves, more jaundice appeared suddenly in their eyes than they could find in Lucius Gavius's, and they moved away from his vicinity under pretext that it was time to leave.

"If he wants something sweet, then let him confine himself to the honeyed wine," said Publius Popillius. "Keep him off solid foods for a day or two more, and then when he's feeling hungry again, let him have a normal diet. But mind—I said normal, *domina*! Beans, not sweetmeats. Salads, not sweetmeats. Cold collations, not sweetmeats."

Stichus's condition did improve over the next week, but he never got fully well. Eat nothing but nourishing and wholesome foods though he did, still he suffered from periodic bouts of nausea, vomiting, pain, and dysentery, none as severe as his initial attack, all debilitating. He began to lose weight, just a little at a time, so that no one in the house really noticed.

By the end of summer he couldn't drag himself as far as his office in the Porticus Metelli, and the days he fancied lying on a couch in the sun grew fewer and further apart. The fabulous illustrated book Sulla had given him ceased to interest him, and food of any kind became an ordeal to consume. Only the honeyed wine could he tolerate, and not always even that.

By September every medical practitioner in Rome had been called to see him, and many and varied were the diagnoses, not to mention the treatments, especially after Clitumna began to resort to quacks.

"Let him eat what he wants," said one doctor.

"Let him eat nothing and starve it out," said another.

"Let him eat nothing but beans," said a doctor of the Pythagorean persuasion.

"Be consoled," said the nosy Greek doctor, Athenodorus Siculus. "Whatever it is, it's obviously not contagious. *I* believe it is a malignancy in the upper bowel. However, make sure those who come in physical contact with him or have to empty his chamber pot wash their hands thoroughly afterward, and don't let them near the kitchen or the food."

Two days later, Lucius Gavius Stichus died. Beside herself with grief, Clitumna fled Rome immediately after the funeral, begging Sulla and Nicopolis to come with her to Circei, where she had a villa. But though Sulla escorted her down to the Campanian seashore, he and Nicopolis refused to leave Rome.

When he returned from Circei, Sulla kissed Nicopolis and moved out of her suite of rooms.

"I'm resuming tenancy of the study and my own sleeping cubicle," he said. "After all, now that Sticky Stichy is dead, I'm the closest thing she has to a son." He was sweeping the lavishly illustrated scrolls into a burning bucket; face twisting in disgust, he held up one hand to Nicopolis, who was watching from the doorway of the study. "Look at that! Not an inch of this room that isn't sticky!"

The carafe of honeyed wine stood in a caked ring on the priceless citrus-wood console against one wall. Lifting it, Sulla looked down at the permanently ingrained mark amid the exquisite whorls of the wood, and hissed between his teeth.

"What a cockroach! Goodbye, Sticky Stichy!"

And he pitched the carafe through the open window onto the

peristyle colonnade. But it flew farther than that, and broke into a thousand shards on the plinth of Sulla's favorite statue, Apollo pursuing the dryad Daphne. A huge star of syrupy wine marred the smooth stone, and began to trickle down in long runnels which soaked into the ground. Darting to the window to look, Nicopolis giggled.

"You're right," she said. "What a cockroach!" And sent her little serving maid Bithy to clean the pedestal with rag and water.

No one noticed the traces of white powder adhering to the marble, for it too was white. The water did its work: the powder vanished.

"I'm glad you missed the actual statue," said Nicopolis, sitting on Sulla's knee, both of them watching Bithy as she washed away.

"I'm sorry," said Sulla, but looked very pleased.

"Sorry? Lucius Cornelius, it would have ruined all that wonderful paintwork! At least the plinth is plain marble."

His upper lip curled back to show his teeth. "Bah! Why is it that I seem permanently surrounded by tasteless fools?" he asked, tipping Nicopolis off his lap.

The stain was completely gone; Bithy wrung out her rag and emptied her basin into the pansies.

"Bithy!" Sulla called. "Wash your hands, girl, and I mean wash them properly! You don't know what Stichus died of, and he was very fond of honeyed wine. Go on, off you go!"

Beaming because he noticed her, Bithy went.

"I discovered a most interesting young man today," said Gaius Marius to Publius Rutilius Rufus.

They were sitting in the precinct of the temple of Tellus on the Carinae, for it lay next door to Rutilius Rufus's house, and on this windy autumn day it offered some welcome sun.

"Which is more than my peristyle does," Rutilius Rufus had

explained as he conducted his visitor toward a wooden bench in the grounds of the spacious but shabby-looking temple. "Our old gods are neglected these days, especially my dear neighbor Tellus," he meandered on as they settled themselves. "Everyone's too busy bowing and scraping to Magna Mater of Asia to remember Rome is better served by her own earth goddess!"

It was to avert the looming homily upon Rome's oldest, most shadowy and mysterious gods that Gaius Marius chose to mention his encounter with the interesting young man. His ploy worked, of course; Rutilius Rufus was never proof against interesting people of any age or either sex.

"Who was that?" he asked now, lifting his muzzle to the sun in shut-eyed pleasure, old dog that he was.

"Young Marcus Livius Drusus, who must be all of—oh, seventeen or eighteen?"

"My nephew Drusus?"

Marius turned his head to stare. "*Is* he?"

"Well, he is if he's the son of the Marcus Livius Drusus who triumphed last January and intends to seek election as one of the censors for next year," said Rutilius Rufus.

Marius laughed, shook his head. "Oh, how embarrassing! Why don't I ever remember such things?"

"Probably," said Rutilius Rufus dryly, "because my wife, Livia—who, to refresh your bucolic memory, was the sister of your interesting young man's father—has been dead these many years, and never went out, and never dined with me when I entertained. The Livius Drususes have a tendency to break the spirits of their womenfolk, unfortunately. Nice little thing, my wife. Gave me two fine children, but never an argument. I treasured her."

"I know," said Marius uncomfortably, disliking being caught out—would he *never* get them all straight? But old friend though Rutilius Rufus was, Marius couldn't remember ever meeting his shy little wife. "You ought to marry again," he said, very enamored of marriage these days.

"What, just so you don't look so conspicuous? No, thank you! I find sufficient outlet for my passions in writing letters." One dark blue eye came open, peered at Marius. "Anyway, why do you think so highly of my nephew Drusus?"

"In the last week I've been approached by several groups of Italian Allies, all from different nations, and all bitterly complaining that Rome is misusing their soldier levies," said Marius slowly. "In my opinion they have good grounds for complaint. Almost every consul for a decade and more has wasted the lives of his soldiers—and with as little concern as if men were starlings or sparrows! And the first to perish have been Italian Allied troops, because it's become the custom to use them ahead of Romans in any situation where lives are likely to be lost. It's a rare consul who genuinely appreciates that the Italian Allied soldiers are men of property in their nations and are paid for by their nations, not by Rome."

Rutilius Rufus never objected to a roundabout discussion; he knew Marius far too well to assume that what he spoke of now bore no relationship to the nephew Drusus. So he answered this apparent digression willingly. "The Italian Allies came under Rome's military protection to unify defense of the peninsula," he said. "In return for donating soldiers to us, they were accorded special status as our allies and reaped many benefits, not the least of which was a drawing-together of the nations of the peninsula. They give their troops to Rome so that we all fight in a common cause. Otherwise, they'd still be warring one Italian nation against another—and undoubtedly losing more men in the process than any Roman consul has lost."

"That is debatable," said Marius. "They might have combined and formed one Italian nation instead!"

"Since the alliance with Rome is a fact, and has been a fact for two or three hundred years, my dear Gaius Marius, I fail to see where you're going at the moment," Rutilius said.

"The deputations who came to see me maintain that Rome is using their troops to fight foreign wars of absolutely no benefit to

Italy as a whole," Marius said patiently. "The original bait we dangled before the Italian nations was the granting of the Roman citizenship. But it's nearly eighty years since any Italian or Latin community has been gifted with the citizenship, as you well know. Why, it took the revolt of Fregellae to force the Senate to make concessions to the Latin Rights communities!"

"That is an oversimplification," said Rutilius Rufus. "We didn't promise the Italian Allies general enfranchisement. We offered them *gradual* citizenship in return for consistent loyalty—Latin Rights first."

"Latin Rights mean very little, Publius Rutilius! At best, they offer a rather tawdry second-class citizenship—no vote in any Roman elections."

"Well, yes, but in the fifteen years since Fregellae's revolt, you must admit things have improved for those with the Latin Rights," Rutilius Rufus said stubbornly. "Every man holding a magistracy in a Latin Rights town now automatically gains the full Roman citizenship for himself and his family."

"I know, I know, and that means there is now a considerable pool of Roman citizens in every Latin Rights town—an ever-growing pool, at that! Not to mention that the law provides Rome with new citizens of exactly the right type—men of property and great local importance—men who can be trusted to vote the right way in Rome," jeered Marius.

Up went Rutilius Rufus's brows. "And what's wrong with that?" he asked.

"You know, Publius Rutilius, open-minded and progressive though you are in many ways, at heart you're as stuffy a Roman nobleman as Gnaeus Domitius Ahenobarbus!" snapped Marius, still hanging on to his temper. "*Why* can't you see that Rome and Italy belong together in an equal union?"

"Because they don't," said Rutilius Rufus, his own sense of placid well-being beginning to fray. "Really, Gaius Marius! How can you sit here inside the walls of Rome advocating political equality between Romans of Rome and Italians? Rome is *not* Italy! Rome didn't stumble by accident into first place in the world, nor did she do it on Italian troops! Rome is different."

"Rome is superior, you mean," said Marius.

"Yes!" Rutilius Rufus seemed to swell. "Rome is Rome. Rome *is* superior."

"Hasn't it ever occurred to you, Publius Rutilius, that if Rome admitted the whole of Italy—even Italian Gaul of the Padus too!—into its hegemony, Rome would be enhanced?" Marius asked.

"Rubbish! Rome would cease to be Roman," said Rutilius.

"And therefore, you imply, Rome would be less."

"Of course."

"But the present situation is farcical," Marius persevered. "Italy is a checkerboard! Regions with the full citizenship, regions with the Latin Rights, regions with mere Allied status, all jumbled up together. Places like Alba Fucentia and Aesernia holding the Latin Rights completely surrounded by the Italians of the Marsi and the Samnites, citizen colonies implanted in the midst of the Gauls along the Padus—how can there be any real feeling of unity, of oneness with Rome?"

"Seeding Roman and Latin colonies through the Italian nations keeps them in harness to us," said Rutilius Rufus. "Those with the full citizenship or the Latin Rights won't betray us. It wouldn't pay them to betray us, considering the alternative."

"I think you mean war with Rome," said Marius.

"Well, I wouldn't go so far as to say that," Rutilius Rufus said. "More that it would entail a loss of privilege the Roman and Latin communities would find insupportable. Not to mention a loss of social worth and standing."

"*Dignitas* is all," said Marius.

"Precisely."

"So you believe the influential men of these Roman and Latin communities would carry the day against the thought of alliance with the Italian nations against Rome?"

Rutilius Rufus looked shocked. "Gaius Marius, why are you

taking this position? You're no Gaius Gracchus, and you are certainly no reformer!"

Marius got to his feet, paced up and down in front of the bench several times, then swung to direct those fierce eyes beneath their even fiercer brows upon the much smaller Rutilius, huddled in a distinctly defensive pose. "You're right, Publius Rutilius, I'm no reformer, and to couple my name with that of Gaius Gracchus is laughable. But I am a practical man, and I have, I flatter myself, more than my fair share of intelligence. Besides which, I am not a Roman of the Romans—as everyone who is a Roman of the Romans is at great pains to point out to me. Well, it may be that my bucolic origins endow me with a kind of detachment no Roman of the Romans can ever own. And I see trouble in our checkerboard Italy. I do, Publius Rutilius, I do! I listened to what the Italian Allies had to say a few days ago, and I smelled a change in the wind. For Rome's sake, I hope our consuls in the next few years are wiser in their use of Italian troops than the consuls of the previous decade."

"So do I, if not for quite the same reasons," said Rutilius Rufus. "Poor generalship is criminal, especially when it ends in wasting the lives of soldiers, Roman or Italian." He looked up at the looming Marius irritably. "Do sit down, I beg you! I'm getting a pain in the neck."

"You are a pain in the neck," said Marius, but sat down obediently, stretching his legs out.

"You're gathering clients among the Italians," said Rutilius Rufus.

"True." Marius studied his senator's ring, made of gold rather than of iron, for only the oldest senatorial families kept up the tradition of an iron ring. "However, I'm not alone in that activity, Publius Rutilius. Gnaeus Domitius Ahenobarbus has enlisted whole towns as his clients, mainly by securing remissions of their taxes."

"Or even securing removal of their taxes, I note."

"Indeed. Nor is Marcus Aemilius Scaurus above client gathering among the Italians of the north," said Marius.

"Yes, but admit he's less feral than Gnaeus Domitius," Rutilius Rufus objected; he was a Scaurus partisan. "At least he does good works for his client towns—drains a swamp, or erects a new meeting-house."

"I concede the point. But you mustn't forget the Caecilius Metelluses in Etruria. They're very busy."

Rutilius Rufus sighed a long-suffering sigh. "Gaius Marius, I wish I knew exactly what you're taking such an inordinately long time to say!"

"I'm not sure myself," said Marius. "Only that I sense a groundswell among the Famous Families, a new awareness of the importance of the Italian Allies. I don't think they're conscious of this importance in any way spelling danger to Rome, only acting on some instinct they don't understand. They—smell something in the wind?"

"*You* certainly smell something in the wind," said Rutilius Rufus. "Well, you're a remarkably shrewd man, Gaius Marius. And anger you though I may have done, I have also taken due note of what you've said. On the surface of it, a client isn't much of a creature. His patron can help him far more than he can help his patron. Until an election, or a threatened disaster. Perhaps he can assist only by refusing to support anyone acting against the interests of his patron. Instincts are significant, I agree with you. They're like beacons: they light up whole fields of hidden facts, often long before logic can. So maybe you're right about the groundswell. And maybe to enlist all the Italian Allies as clients in the service of some great Roman family is one way of dealing with this danger you insist is looming. I don't honestly know."

"Nor do I," said Marius. "But I'm gathering clients."

"And gathering wool," said Rutilius Rufus, smiling. "We started out, as I remember, to discuss my nephew Drusus."

Marius folded his legs beneath his knees and pushed himself to his feet so quickly the action startled Rutilius Rufus, who had resumed his shut-eyed repose. "That we did! Come, Publius Rutilius, we may not be too late for me to show you an example of the new feeling about the Italian Allies among the Famous Families!"

Rutilius got up. "I'm coming, I'm coming! But where?"

"To the Forum, of course," said Marius, setting out down the slope of the temple precinct toward the street. As they walked, Marius spoke. "There's a trial in progress, and if we're lucky we'll arrive before it ends."

"I'm surprised you noticed," said Rutilius Rufus dryly; Marius was not usually prone to pay attention to Forum trials.

"I'm surprised you haven't been attending it every day," Marius countered. "After all, it's the debut of your nephew Drusus as an advocate."

"No!" said Rutilius Rufus. "He made his debut months ago, when he prosecuted the chief tribune of the Treasury for recovery of certain funds which had mysteriously gone missing."

"Oh." Marius shrugged, speeded up his pace. "Then that accounts for what I thought was your delinquency. However, Publius Rutilius, you really ought to follow young Drusus's career more closely. If you had, my remarks about the Italian Allies would have made more sense to you."

"Enlighten me," said Rutilius Rufus, beginning to labor just a little; Marius always forgot his legs were longer.

"I noticed because I heard someone speaking the most beautiful Latin in an equally beautiful voice. A new orator, I thought, and stopped to see who it was. Your young nephew Drusus, no less! Though I didn't know who he was until I asked, and I'm still embarrassed that I didn't associate the name with your family."

"Who's he prosecuting this time?" asked Rutilius Rufus.

"That's the interesting thing, he's not prosecuting," said Marius. "He's defending, and before the foreign praetor, if you please! It's an important case; there's a jury."

"Murder of a Roman citizen?"

"No. Bankruptcy."

"That's unusual," panted Rutilius Rufus.

"I gather it's some sort of example," said Marius, not slowing down. "The plaintiff is the banker Gaius Oppius, the defendant a Marsic businessman from Marruvium called Lucius Fraucus. According to my informant—a real professional court-watcher—Oppius is tired of bad debts among his Italian accounts, and decided it was time he made an example of an Italian here in Rome. His object is to frighten the rest of Italy into keeping up what I suspect are exorbitant interest payments."

"Interest," huffed Rutilius Rufus, "is set at ten percent."

"*If* you're a Roman," said Marius, "and preferably a Roman of the upper economic classes."

"Keep on going, Gaius Marius, and you'll wind up like the Brothers Gracchi—very dead."

"Rubbish!"

"I would—much rather—go home," said Rutilius Rufus.

"You're getting soft," said Marius, glancing down at his trotting companion. "A good campaign would do wonders for your wind, Publius Rutilius."

"A good rest would do wonders for my wind." Rutilius Rufus slowed down. "I really don't see why we're doing this."

"For one thing, because when I left the Forum your nephew still had a good two and a half hours left in which to sum up his case," said Marius. "It's one of the experimental trials—you know, to do with changing trial procedures. So the witnesses were heard first, then the Prosecution was allowed two hours to sum up, and the Defense three hours, after which the foreign praetor will ask the jury for its verdict."

"There's nothing wrong with the old way," said Rutilius.

"Oh, I don't know, I thought the new way made the whole process more interesting for the spectators," said Marius.

They were descending the slope of the Clivus Sacer, the lower Forum Romanum just ahead, and the figures in the foreign praetor's court had not changed their distribution while Marius had been away.

"Good, we're in time for the peroration," said Marius.

Marcus Livius Drusus was still speaking, and his audience was still listening in rapt silence. Obviously well under twenty years of age, the shaveling advocate was of average height and stocky physique, black-haired and swarthy of complexion: not an advocate who would transfix by sheer physical presence, though his face was pleasant enough.

"Isn't he amazing?" asked Marius of Rutilius in a whisper. "He's got the knack of making you think he's speaking to you personally, not to anyone else."

He had. Even at the distance—for Marius and Rutilius Rufus stood at the back of the large crowd—his very dark eyes seemed to look deeply into their eyes, and into their eyes alone.

"Nowhere does it say that the fact a man is a Roman automatically puts him in the right," the young man was saying. "I do not speak for Lucius Fraucus, the accused—I speak for Rome! I speak for honor! I speak for integrity! I speak for justice! Not the kind of lip-service justice which interprets a law in its most literal sense, but the kind of justice which interprets a law in its most logical sense. The law should not be a huge and weighty slab which falls upon a man and squashes him into a uniform shape, for men are not uniform. The law should be a gentle sheet which falls upon a man and shows his unique shape beneath its blanketing sameness. We must always remember that we, the citizens of Rome, stand as an example to the rest of the world, especially in our laws and our courts of law. Has such sophistication ever been seen elsewhere? Such drafting? Such intelligence? Such care? Such wisdom? Do not even the Greeks of Athens admit it? Do not the Alexandrians? Do not the Pergamites?"

His rhetorical body language was superb, even with the severe disadvantages of his height and physique, neither lending itself to the toga; to wear the toga superlatively, a man had to be tall, wide of shoulder, and narrow of hip, and move with consummate grace. Marcus Livius Drusus did not qualify on any point. And yet he worked wonders with his body, from the smallest wiggle of a finger to the largest sweep of his whole right arm. The movements of his head, the expressions on his face, the changes in his walk—everything so *good*!

"Lucius Fraucus, an Italian from Marruvium," he went on, "is the ultimate victim, not the perpetrator. No one—including Lucius Fraucus!—disputes the fact that this very large sum of money advanced by Gaius Oppius is missing. Nor is it disputed that this very large sum of money must be restored to Gaius Oppius, together with the interest the loan has incurred. One way or another, it will be repaid. If necessary, Lucius Fraucus is willing to sell his houses, his lands, his investments, his slaves, his furniture—all he possesses! More than enough to constitute restitution!"

He walked up to the front row of the jury and glared at the men in its middle ranks. "You have heard the witnesses. You have heard my learned colleague the Prosecutor. Lucius Fraucus was the borrower. But he was not the thief. Therefore, say I, Lucius Fraucus is the real victim of this fraud, not Gaius Oppius, his banker. If you condemn Lucius Fraucus, conscript members of the jury, you subject him to the full penalty of the law as it applies to a man who is not a citizen of our great city, nor a holder of the Latin Rights. All of Lucius Fraucus's property will be put up for forced sale, and you know what that means. It will fetch nowhere near its actual value, and indeed might not even fetch enough to make restitution of the full sum." This last was said with a most speaking glance toward the sidelines, where the banker Gaius Oppius sat on a folding chair, attended by a retinue of clerks and accountants.

"Very well! Nowhere near its actual value! After which, conscript members of the jury, Lucius Fraucus will be sold into debt-bondage until he has made up the difference between the sum demanded and the sum obtained from the forced sale of all his property. Now, a poor judge of character in choosing his senior employees Lucius Fraucus may be, but in the pursuit of his business, Lucius Fraucus is a remarkably shrewd and highly successful man. Yet—how can he ever make good his debt if, propertyless and disgraced, he is handed over into bondage? Will he even be of use to Gaius Oppius as a clerk?"

The young man was now concentrating every scrap of his vigor and will upon the Roman banker, a mild-looking man in his fifties, who seemed entranced by what the young man said.

"For a man who is not a Roman citizen, conviction upon a criminal charge leads to one thing before all others. He must be flogged. Not chastised by the rods, as a Roman citizen is—a little sore, perhaps, but chiefly injured in his dignity. No! He must be flogged! Laid about with the barbed whip until nothing of skin and muscle is left, and he is maimed for life, scarred worse than any mine slave."

The hairs stood up on the back of Marius's neck; for if the young man was not looking straight at him—one of the biggest mine owners in Rome—then his eyes were playing tricks. Yet how could young Drusus have found a latecomer at the very back of such a huge crowd?

"We are Romans!" the young man cried. "Italy and its citizens are under our protection. Do we show ourselves to be mine owners of men who look to us as an example? Do we condemn an innocent man on a technicality, simply because his is the signature on the document of loan? Do we ignore the fact that he is willing to make complete restitution? Do we, in effect, accord him less justice than we would a citizen of Rome? Do we flog a man who ought rather to wear a dunce's cap upon his head for his foolishness in trusting a thief? Do we create a widow of a wife? Do we create orphans of children with a loving father? Surely not, conscript members of the jury! For we are Romans. We are a *better* brand of men!"

With a swirl of white wool the speaker turned and quit the vicinity of the banker, thus establishing an instant in which all eyes left the banker to follow, dazzled; all eyes, that is, save those of several jurymen in the front row, looking no different from the rest of the fifty-one members of the panel. And the eyes of Gaius Marius and Publius Rutilius Rufus. One juror gazed woodenly at Oppius, drawing his forefinger across the base of his throat as if it itched. The response followed instantly: the faintest shake of the great banker's head. Gaius Marius began to smile.

"Thank you, *praetor peregrinus,*" said the young man as he bowed to the foreign praetor, suddenly seeming stiff and shy, no longer possessed by whatever invaded him when he orated.

"Thank you, Marcus Livius," said the foreign praetor, and directed his glance toward the jury. "Citizens of Rome, please inscribe your tablets and permit the court your verdict."

There was a general movement throughout the court; the jurors all produced small squares of pale clay and pencils of charcoal. But they didn't write anything, instead sat looking at the backs of the heads in the middle of their front row. The man who had ghosted a question at Oppius the banker took up his pencil and drew a letter upon his clay tablet, then yawned mightily, his arms stretched above his head, the tablet still in his left hand, the multiple folds of his toga falling back toward his left shoulder as the arm straightened in the air. The rest of the jurors then scribbled busily, and handed in their tablets to the lictors who were going among them.

The foreign praetor did the counting himself; everyone waited, scarcely breathing, for the verdict. Glancing at each tablet, he tossed it into one of two baskets on the desk in front of him, most into one, a few into the other. When all fifty-one had been dealt with, he looked up.

"*ABSOLVO,*" he said. "Forty-three for, eight against. Lucius Fraucus of Marruvium, citizen of the Marsic nation of our Italian Allies, you are discharged by this court, but only on condition that you make full restitution as promised. I leave you to arrange matters with Gaius Oppius, your creditor, before this day is over."

And that was that. Marius and Rutilius Rufus waited for the crowds to finish congratulating the young Marcus Livius Drusus. Finally only the friends of Drusus were left clustered about him, very excited. But when the tall man with the fierce eyebrows and the little man everyone knew to be Drusus's uncle bore down on the group, everyone melted away bashfully.

"Congratulations, Marcus Livius," said Marius, extending his hand.

"I thank you, Gaius Marius."

"Well done," said Rutilius Rufus.

They turned in the direction of the Velia end of the Forum and began to walk.

Rutilius Rufus left the conversation to Marius and Drusus, pleased to see his young nephew was maturing so magnificently as an advocate, but well aware of the shortcomings beneath that stolidly stocky exterior. Young Drusus, thought his Uncle Publius, was a rather humorless pup, brilliant but oddly blighted, who would never have that lightness of being which could discern the shape of coming grotesqueries, and so as his life went on would fail to sidestep much of life's pain. Earnest. Dogged. Ambitious. Incapable of letting go once his teeth were fixed in a problem. Yes. But, for all that, Uncle Publius told himself, young Drusus was an honorable pup.

"It would have been a very bad thing for Rome if your Italian client had been convicted," Marius was saying.

"Very bad indeed. Fraucus is one of the most important men in Marruvium, and an elder of his Marsic nation. Of course he won't be nearly so important once he's paid back the money he owes Gaius Oppius, but he'll make more," said Drusus.

They had reached the Velia when "Do you ascend the Palatine?" young Drusus asked, pausing in front of the temple of Jupiter Stator.

"Certainly not," said Publius Rutilius Rufus, emerging from his thoughts. "Gaius Marius is coming home to dine with me, nephew."

Young Drusus bowed to his seniors solemnly, then began to ascend the slope of the Clivus Palatinus; from behind Marius and Rutilius Rufus emerged the unprepossessing form of Quintus Servilius Caepio Junior, young Drusus's best friend, running to catch up with young Drusus, who must have heard him, but didn't wait.

"That's a friendship I don't like," said Rutilius Rufus, standing watching the two young men dwindle in size.

"Oh?"

"They're impeccably noble and terrifically rich, the Servilius Caepios, but as short on brains as they're long on hauteur, so it's not a friendship between equals," said Rutilius Rufus. "My nephew seems to prefer the peculiar style of deference and syco-phancy young Caepio Junior offers to a more stimulating—not to mention deflating!—kind of fellowship with others among his peers. A pity. For I fear, Gaius Marius, that Caepio Junior's devo-tion will give young Drusus a false impression of his ability to lead men."

"In battle?"

Rutilius Rufus stopped in his tracks. "Gaius Marius, there *are* other activities than war, and other institutions than armies! No, I was referring to leadership in the Forum."

Later in that same week Marius came again to call upon his friend Rutilius Rufus, and found him distractedly packing.

"Panaetius is dying," explained Rutilius, blinking back his tears.

"Oh, that's too bad!" said Marius. "Where is he? Will you reach him in time?"

"I hope so. He's in Tarsus, and asking for me. Fancy his asking for me, out of all the Romans he taught!"

Marius's glance was soft. "And why shouldn't he? After all, you were his best pupil."

"No, no," said the little man, seeming abstracted.

"I'll go home," said Marius.

"Nonsense," said Rutilius Rufus, leading the way to his study, a hideously untidy room which seemed to be overfilled with desks and tables piled high with books, most of them at least par-tially unrolled, some anchored at one end and cascading onto the floor in a welter of precious Egyptian paper.

"Garden," said Marius firmly, perceiving no place to roost

amid the chaos, but well aware that Rutilius Rufus could put his hand on any book he owned in scant moments, no matter how buried it appeared to the uninitiated eye.

"What are you writing?" he asked, spotting a long screed of Fannius-treated paper on a table, already half-covered with Rutilius Rufus's unmistakable hand, as neat and easy to read as his room was disorganized.

"Something I'll have to consult you about," said Rutilius, leading the way outside. "A manual of military information. After our talk about the inept generals Rome has been fielding of late years, I thought it was time someone competent produced a helpful treatise. So far it's been all logistics and base planning, but now I move on to tactics and strategy, where you shine far brighter than I do. So I'm going to have to milk your brains."

"Consider them milked." Marius sat down on a wooden bench in the tiny, sunless, rather neglected garden, on the weedy side and with a fountain that didn't work. "Have you had a visit from Metellus Piggle-wiggle?" he asked.

"As a matter of fact, I have, earlier today," said Rutilius, coming to rest on a bench opposite Marius's.

"He came to see me this morning too."

"Amazing how little he's changed, our Quintus Caecilius Metellus Piggle-wiggle," laughed Rutilius Rufus. "If there'd been a pigsty handy, or my fountain was worthy of its name, I think I might have tossed him in all over again."

"I know how you feel, but I don't think that's a good idea," said Marius. "What did he have to say to you?"

"He's going to stand for consul."

"If we ever have any elections, that is! What on earth possessed those two fools to try to stand a second time as tribunes of the plebs when even the Gracchi came to grief?"

"It shouldn't delay the Centuriate elections—or the People's elections, for that matter," said Rutilius Rufus.

"Of course it will! Our two would-be second-termers will cause their colleagues to veto all elections," said Marius. "You know what tribunes of the plebs are like—once they get the bit between their teeth, no one can stop them."

Rutilius shook with laughter. "I should think I do know what tribunes of the plebs are like! I was one of the worst. And so were you, Gaius Marius."

"Well, yes. . . ."

"There'll be elections, never fear," said Rutilius Rufus comfortably. "My guess is that the tribunes of the plebs will go to the polls four days before the Ides of December, and all the others will follow just after the Ides."

"And Metellus Piggle-wiggle will be consul," said Marius.

Rutilius Rufus leaned forward, folding his hands together. "He knows something."

"You are not wrong, old friend. He definitely knows something we don't. Any guesses?"

"Jugurtha. He's planning a war against Jugurtha."

"That's what I think too," said Marius. "Only is he going to start it, or is Spurius Albinus going to?"

"I wouldn't have said Spurius Albinus had the intestinal fortitude. But time will tell," Rutilius said tranquilly.

"He offered me a job as senior legate with his army."

"He offered me the same position."

They looked at each other and grinned.

"Then we'd better make it our business to find out what's going on," said Marius, getting to his feet. "Spurius Albinus is supposed to arrive here any day to hold the elections, no one having told him there aren't going to be any elections for some time to come."

"He'd have left Africa Province before the news could have reached him, anyway," said Rutilius Rufus, bypassing the study.

"Are you going to accept Piggle-wiggle's offer?"

"I will, if you will, Gaius Marius."

"Good!"

Rutilius opened the front door himself. "And how is Julia? I won't have a chance to see her."

Marius beamed. "Wonderful—beautiful—glorious!"

"You silly old geezer," said Rutilius, and pushed Marius into the street. "Keep your ear to the ground while I'm away, and write to me if you hear any martial stirrings."

"I will. Have a good trip."

"In autumn? It'll be a charnel house on board ship and I might drown."

"Not you," said Marius, grinning. "Father Neptune wouldn't have you, he wouldn't be game to spoil Piggle-wiggle's plans."

Julia was pregnant, and very pleased to be so; the only stress she suffered was Marius's henlike concern for her.

"Truly, Gaius Marius, I am perfectly well," she said for the thousandth time; it was now November, and the baby was due about March of the next year, so she was beginning to look pregnant. However, she had bloomed the traditional prospective mother's bloom, untroubled by sickness or swelling.

"You're sure?" her husband asked anxiously.

"Go away, do!" she said, but gently, and smilingly.

Reassured, the fatuous husband left her with her servants in her workroom, and went to his study. It was the one place in the huge house where Julia's presence wasn't felt, the one place where he could forget her. Not that he tried to forget her; rather, there were times when he needed to think of other things.

Like what was happening in Africa. Sitting at his desk, he drew paper forward and began to write in his bald unvarnished prose to Publius Rutilius Rufus, safely arrived in Tarsus after a very speedy voyage.

> I am attending every meeting of both Senate and Plebs, and it finally looks as if there will be elections in the near future. About time. As you said, four days before the Ides of December. Publius Licinius Lucullus and Lucius Annius are beginning to collapse; I don't think they'll succeed in standing for second terms as tribunes of the plebs. In fact, the general im-

pression now is that they plotted to have everyone think it only in order to bring their names more forcibly before the eyes of the electors. They're both consul material, but neither managed to make a splash while tribune of the plebs—not surprising, considering they're not reformers. So what better way to make a splash than to inconvenience all of voting Rome? I must be turning into a Cynic. Is that possible for an Italian hayseed with no Greek?

As you know, things have been very quiet in Africa, though our intelligence sources report that Jugurtha is indeed recruiting and training a very large army—and in Roman style! However, things were far from quiet when Spurius Albinus came home well over a month ago to hold the elections. He gave his report to the Senate, this including the fact that he had kept his own army down to three legions, one made up of local auxiliaries, one of Roman troops already stationed in Africa, and one he had brought with him last spring from Italy. They are yet to be blooded. Spurius Albinus is not martially inclined, it would seem. I cannot say the same for Piggle-wiggle.

But what riled our venerable colleagues of the Senate was the news that Spurius Albinus had seen fit to appoint his little brother, Aulus Albinus, governor of Africa Province and commander of the African army in his absence! Imagine I suppose if Aulus Albinus had been his quaestor it might have passed scrutiny in the Senate, but—as I know you know, but I'm telling you again anyway—quaestor wasn't grand enough for Aulus Albinus, so he was put on his big brother's staff as a senior legate. Without the approval of the Senate! So there sits our Roman province of Africa, being governed in the governor's absence by a thirty-year-old hothead owning neither experience nor superior intelligence. Marcus Scaurus was spitting with rage, and served the consul a diatribe he won't forget in a hurry, I can tell you. But it's done. We can but hope Governor Aulus Albinus conducts himself properly. Scaurus doubts it. And so do I, Publius Rutilius.

That letter went off to Publius Rutilius Rufus before the elections were held; Marius had intended it to be his last, hoping that the New Year would see Rutilius back in Rome. Then came a letter from Rutilius informing him that Panaetius was still alive, and so rejuvenated at sight of his old pupil that he seemed likely to live for several months longer than the state of his malignancy had at first suggested. "Expect me when you see me, some time in the spring just before Piggle-wiggle embarks for Africa," Rutilius's letter said.

So Marius sat down again as the old year dwindled away, and wrote again to Tarsus.

Clearly you had no doubt Piggle-wiggle would be elected consul, and you were correct. However, the People and the Plebs got their share of the elections over before the Centuries polled, neither body producing any surprises. So the quaestors entered office on the fifth day of December and the new tribunes of the plebs on the tenth day—the only interesting-looking new tribune of the plebs is Gaius Mamilius Limetanus. Oh, and three of the new quaestors are promising—our famous young orators and forensic stars Lucius Licinius Crassus and his best friend, Quintus Mucius Scaevola, are two of them, but the third I find more interesting still: a very brash and abrasive fellow of a recent plebeian family, Gaius Servilius Glaucia, whom I'm sure you'll remember from his court days—it's being said these days that he's the best legal draftsman Rome has ever produced. I don't like him. Piggle-wiggle was returned first in the Centuriate polls, so will be the senior consul for next year. But Marcus Junius Silanus was not far behind him. The voting was conservative all the way, as a matter of fact. No New Men among the praetors. Instead, the six included two patricians and a patrician adopted into a plebeian family—none other than Quintus Lutatius Catulus Caesar. As far as the Senate is concerned, it was therefore an excellent vote and promises well for the New Year.

And then, my dear Publius Rutilius, the thunderbolt fell. It seems Aulus Albinus was tempted by rumors that a huge hoard of treasure was stored in the Numidian town of Suthul. So he waited just long enough to make sure his brother the consul was irrevocably on his way back to Rome to hold the elections, and then invaded Numidia! At the head of three paltry and inexperienced legions, if you please! His siege of Suthul was unsuccessful, of course—the townspeople just shut their gates and laughed at him from the top of their walls. But instead of admitting that he wasn't capable of waging a little siege, let alone a whole campaign, what did Aulus Albinus do? Return to the Roman province? I hear you ask, eminently sensible man that you are. Well, that may have been the choice you would have made were you Aulus Albinus, but it wasn't Aulus Albinus's choice. He packed up his siege and marched onward into western Numidia! At the head of his three paltry and inexperienced legions. Jugurtha attacked him in the middle of the night somewhere near the town of Calama, and defeated Aulus Albinus so badly that our consul's little brother surrendered unconditionally. And Jugurtha forced every Roman and auxiliary from Aulus Albinus on down to pass beneath the yoke. After which, Jugurtha extracted Aulus Albinus's signature upon a treaty giving himself everything he hadn't been able to get from the Senate!

We got the news of it in Rome not from Aulus Albinus but from Jugurtha, who sent the Senate a copy of the treaty with a covering letter complaining sharply about Roman treachery in invading a peacefully intentioned country that had not lifted so much as a warlike finger against Rome. When I say Jugurtha wrote to the Senate, I actually mean that he had the gall to write to his oldest and best enemy, Marcus Aemilius Scaurus, in Scaurus's role as Princeps Senatus. A calculated insult to the consuls, of course, to choose to address his correspondence to the Leader of the House. Oh, was Scaurus angry! He summoned a meeting of the Senate immediately, and compelled Spurius Albinus to divulge much that had been artfully concealed, including the fact that Spurius was not quite as ignorant of his little brother's plans as he at first protested. The House was stunned. Then it turned nasty, and the Albinus faction promptly changed sides, leaving Spurius on his own to admit that he had heard the news from Aulus in a letter he received several days earlier. From Spurius we learned that Jugurtha had ordered Aulus back to Roman Africa and forbidden Aulus to put a toenail across the Numidian border. So there waits greedy young Aulus Albinus, petitioning his brother for a directive as to what to do.

Marius sighed, flexed his fingers; what was a joy for Rutilius Rufus was a chore for him, no letter writer. "Get on with it, Gaius Marius," he said to himself. And got on with it.

Naturally what hurt the most was Jugurtha's forcing the Roman army to pass under the yoke. It happens rarely, but it never fails to stir up the whole city, from highest to lowest—this being my first experience with it, I found myself as stirred, as humiliated, as devastated as the most Roman Roman. I daresay it would have been equally painful for you, so I am glad you weren't here to witness the scenes, people in dark clothes weeping and tearing their hair, many of the knights without the narrow stripe on their tunics, senators wearing a narrow stripe instead of the wide one, the whole of Enemy Territory outside the temple of Bellona piled high with offerings to teach Jugurtha a lesson. Fortune has dropped a beautiful campaign into Piggle-wiggle's lap for next year, and you and I will have a field day—provided, that is, that we can learn to get along with Piggle-wiggle as our commanding officer!

The new tribune of the plebs Gaius Mamilius is in full cry after Postumius Albinus blood—he wants brother Aulus Albinus executed for treason, and brother Spurius Albinus tried for treason as well, if only for being stupid enough to appoint Aulus governor in his absence. In fact, Mamilius is calling for the institution of a special court, and wants to try every Roman who has ever had doubtful dealings with Jugurtha, from the time of Lucius Opimius on, if you please. Such is the mood of the Conscript Fathers of the Senate that he is likely to get his way. It's the passing under the yoke. Everyone agrees the army and its commander should have died where they fought sooner than submit their country to abject humiliation. In that I disagree, of course, as I think would you. An army is only as good as its commander, no matter how great its potential.

The Senate drafted and dispatched a stiff letter to Jugurtha, informing him that Rome could not and would not recognize a treaty extracted from a man who had no imperium and therefore no authority from the Senate and People of Rome to lead an army, govern a province, or make a treaty.

And, last but not least, Publius Rutilius, Gaius Mamilius did obtain a mandate from the Plebeian Assembly to set up a special court in which all those who have had or are suspected to have had dealings with Jugurtha are to be tried for treason. This is a postscript, written on the very last day of the old year. The Senate for once heartily endorsed the plebeian legislation, and Scaurus is busy compiling a list of the men who will face trial. Gleefully aided by Gaius Memmius, vindicated at last. What's more, in this special Mamilian court the chances of securing treason convictions are much greater than if it were done the traditional way, in trials conducted by the Centuriate Assembly. So far the names of Lucius Opimius, Lucius Calpurnius Bestia, Gaius Porcius Cato, Gaius Sulpicius Galba, Spurius Postumius Albinus, and his brother have come up for discussion. Blood tells, however. Spurius Albinus has assembled a formidable array of advocates to argue in the Senate that whatever his little brother, Aulus, may or may not have done, he cannot legally stand trial because he never legally possessed imperium. From that you gather that Spurius Albinus is going to assume Aulus's share of the guilt, and will certainly be convicted. I find it odd that if things go as I confidently expect they will, the prime mover, Aulus Albinus, will emerge from his passage beneath the yoke with his career unimpaired!

Oh, and Scaurus is to be one of the three presidents of the Mamilian Commission, as they are calling this new court. He accepted with alacrity.

And that is that for the old year, Publius Rutilius. A momentous year, all told. After hope was gone, my head has popped above the surface of Rome's political waters, buoyed up by my marriage to Julia. Metellus Piggle-wiggle is actually courting me, and men who never used to notice I was standing there are speaking to me as to an equal. Look after yourself on the voyage home, and make it soon.

THE SECOND YEAR
(109 B.C.):

In the Consulship of
Quintus Caecilius Metellus
and
Marcus Junius Silanus

GAIUS JULIUS CAESAR

Panaetius died in Tarsus halfway through February, which left Publius Rutilius Rufus little time to get home before the start of the campaigning season; originally he had planned to make the bulk of his journey overland, but urgency compelled him now to take his chances upon the sea.

"And I've been downright lucky," he said to Gaius Marius the day after he arrived in Rome, just before the Ides of March. "For once the winds blew in the direction I wanted."

Marius grinned. "I told you, Publius Rutilius, even Father Neptune wouldn't have the courage to spoil Piggle-wiggle's plans! Actually you've been lucky in more ways than that—if you'd been in Rome, you'd have had the unenviable task of going among the Italian Allies to persuade them to hand over troops."

"Which is what you've been doing, I take it?"

"Since early January, when the lots gave Metellus charge of the African war against Jugurtha. Oh, it wasn't difficult to recruit, not with all Italy burning to avenge the insult of passing beneath the yoke. But men of the right kind are getting very thin on the ground," said Marius.

"Then we had better hope that the future doesn't hold any more military disasters for Rome," said Rutilius Rufus.

"Indeed we had."

"How has Piggle-wiggle behaved toward you?"

"Quite civilly, all considered," said Marius. "He came to see me the day after he was inaugurated, and at least did me the courtesy of being blunt about his motives. I asked him why he wanted me—and you, for that matter—when we had made such a fool of him in the old days at Numantia. And he said he didn't care a fig for Numantia. What concerned him was winning this present war in Africa, and he couldn't think of a better way to do that than to avail himself of the services of the two men in all the world best equipped to understand Jugurtha's strategy."

"It's a shrewd idea," Rutilius Rufus said. "As the commander, he'll reap the glory. What matters who wins the war for him, when it's he who'll ride in the triumphal chariot and gather in all the accolades? The Senate won't offer you or me the new last name of Numidicus; they'll offer it to him."

"Well, he needs it more than we do. Metellus Piggle-wiggle is a Caecilius, Publius Rutilius! Which means his head rules his heart, especially where his skin is concerned."

"Oh, very aptly put!" said Rutilius Rufus appreciatively.

"He's already lobbying to have the Senate extend his command in Africa into next year," Marius said.

"Which just goes to show that he got sufficient of Jugurtha's measure all those years ago to realize beating Numidia into submission won't be easy. How many legions is he taking?"

"Four. Two Roman, two Italian."

"Plus the troops already stationed in Africa—say, two more legions. Yes, we ought to do it, Gaius Marius."

"I agree."

Marius got up from behind his desk and went to pour wine.

"What's this I hear about Gnaeus Cornelius Scipio?" asked Rutilius Rufus, accepting the goblet Marius held out to him just in time, for Marius shouted with laughter and spilled his own drink.

"Oh, Publius Rutilius, it was wonderful! Honestly, I never cease to be amazed at the antics of the old Roman nobles. There was Scipio, respectably elected a praetor, and awarded the governorship of Further Spain when the lots were drawn for the praetor's provinces. But what does he do? He gets up in the Senate and solemnly *declines* the honor of governing Further Spain! 'Why?' asks Scaurus, astonished—he supervised the drawing of the lots. 'Because,' says Scipio with an honesty I found quite endearing, 'I would rape the place.' It brought the House down—cheers, howls of mirth, feet stamping, hands clapping. And when the noise died down at last, Scaurus simply said, 'I agree, Gnaeus Cornelius, you would rape the place.' So now they're sending Quintus Servilius Caepio to govern Further Spain in Scipio's stead."

"He'll rape the place too," said Rutilius Rufus, smiling.

"Of course, of course! Everyone knew that, including Scaurus.

But Caepio at least has the grace to pretend he won't, so Rome can turn a blind eye Spainward and life can go on in the usual way," said Marius, back behind his desk. "I love this place, Publius Rutilius, I really do."

"I'm glad Silanus is being kept at home."

"Well, luckily someone has to govern Rome! What an escape! The Senate positively scrambled to prorogue Minucius Rufus's governorship of Macedonia, I can assure you. And that niche being filled, nothing was left for Silanus except Rome, where things are more or less self-perpetuating. Silanus at the head of an army is a prospect to make Mars himself blanch."

"Absolutely!" said Rutilius Rufus fervently.

"It's a good year so far, actually," Marius said. "Not only was Spain saved from the tender mercies of Scipio, and Macedonia from the tender mercies of Silanus, but Rome herself is considerably the lighter of villains, if I may be excused calling some of our consulars villains."

"The Mamilian Commission, you mean?"

"Precisely. Bestia, Galba, Opimius, Gaius Cato, and Spurius Albinus have all been condemned, and there are more trials scheduled, though no surprises. Gaius Memmius has been most assiduous in assisting Mamilius in gathering evidence of collusion with Jugurtha, and Scaurus is a ruthless president of the court. Though he did speak in defense of Bestia—then turned round and voted to condemn him."

Rutilius Rufus smiled. "A man has to be flexible," he said. "Scaurus had to acquit himself of his duty toward a fellow consular by speaking up for him, but it wouldn't swerve him from his duty toward the court. Not Scaurus."

"No, not Scaurus!"

"And where have the condemned gone?" Rutilius Rufus asked.

"Quite a few seem to be choosing Massilia as their place of exile these days, though Lucius Opimius went to western Macedonia."

"But Aulus Albinus survived."

"Yes. Spurius Albinus took all the blame, and the House voted to permit him," said Marius, and sighed. "It was a nice legal point."

Julia went into labor on the Ides of March, and when the midwives informed Marius that it was not going to be an easy birth, he summoned Julia's parents immediately.

"Our blood is too old and too thin," said Caesar fretfully to Marius as they sat together in Marius's study, husband and father bound together by a mutual love and fear.

"My blood isn't," said Marius.

"But that can't help *her*! It may help her daughter if she has one, and we must be thankful for that. I had hoped my marrying Marcia would infuse a little plebeian strength into my line—but Marcia is still too noble, it seems. Her mother was patrician, a Sulpicia. I know there are those who argue that the blood must be kept pure, but I have noticed time and time again that the girls of ancient family have a tendency to bleed in childbirth. Why else is the death rate among the girls of ancient family so much higher than it is among other girls?" And Caesar ran his hands through his silver-gilt hair.

Marius couldn't sit any longer; he got to his feet and began to pace up and down. "Well, she does have the best attention money can buy," he said, nodding in the direction of the confinement room, from which no noises of distress had yet begun to emanate.

"They couldn't save Clitumna's nephew last autumn," said Caesar, yielding to gloom.

"Who? Your unsatisfactory next-door neighbor, you mean?"

"Yes, that Clitumna. Her nephew died last September after a protracted illness. Only a young fellow, seemed healthy enough. The doctors did everything they could think of doing, but he died anyway. It's preyed on my mind since."

Marius stared at his father-in-law blankly. "Why on earth should it prey on your mind?" he asked. "What possible connection is there?"

Caesar chewed at his lip. "Things always happen in threes," he said cheerlessly. "The death of Clitumna's nephew was a death in close proximity to me and mine. There have to be two more deaths."

"If so, then the deaths will occur in that family."

"Not necessarily. There just have to be three deaths, all connected in *some* way. But until the second death happens, I defy a soothsayer to predict what the connection will be."

Out went Marius's hands, half in exasperation, half in despair. "Gaius Julius, Gaius Julius! Try to be optimistic, I beg of you! No one has yet come to say Julia is in danger of dying, I was simply told that the birth wouldn't be easy. So I sent for you to help me blunder through this awful waiting, not to make me so downcast I can't see a trace of light!"

Ashamed, Caesar made a conscious effort. "As a matter of fact, I'm glad Julia's time is here," he said more briskly. "I haven't wanted to bother her of late, but once she's over her delivery I'm hoping she will be able to spare the time to talk to Julilla."

Privately Marius considered what Julilla needed was a sore bottom from an unsparing parental hand, but he managed to look interested; after all, he had never been a parent himself, and now that (all going well) he was about to become a parent, he ought to admit to himself that he might turn out to be as doting a *tata* as Gaius Julius Caesar.

"What's the matter with Julilla?" he asked.

Caesar sighed. "She's off her food. We've had some difficulty in making her eat for a long time, but during the last four months it's worsened. She's lost pounds and pounds! And now she's prone to fainting fits, drops like a stone in her tracks. The doctors can find nothing wrong with her."

Oh, will I really get like this? Marius asked himself; there is nothing wrong with that spoiled young lady that a good dose of indifference wouldn't cure! However, he supposed she was something to talk about, so he tried to talk about her. "I gather you'd like Julia to get to the bottom of it?"

"Indeed I would!"

"She's probably in love with someone unsuitable," said Marius, utterly ignorant, but totally correct.

"Nonsense!" said Caesar sharply.

"How do you know it's nonsense?"

"Because the doctors thought of that, and I made full inquiries," said Caesar, on the defensive.

"Who did you ask? Her?"

"Naturally!"

"It might have been more practical to ask her girl."

"Oh, really, Gaius Marius!"

"She's not pregnant?"

"Oh, really, Gaius Marius!"

"Look, Father-in-law, there's no use starting to view me as an insect at this stage of things," said Marius unfeelingly. "I'm a part of the family, not an outsider. If I, with my extremely limited experience of young ladies of sixteen, can see these possibilities, so too ought you, and even more so. Get her girl into your study and wallop her until you get the truth out of her—I guarantee she's in Julilla's confidence, and I guarantee she'll break down if you question her properly—torture and death threats!"

"Gaius Marius, I couldn't do that!" said Caesar, aghast at even the thought of such Draconian measures.

"You wouldn't need to do more than cane her," said Marius patiently. "A smarting pair of buttocks and the mere mention of torture will produce everything she knows."

"I couldn't do that," Caesar repeated.

Marius sighed. "Have it your own way, then. But don't assume you know the truth just because you've asked Julilla."

"There has always been truth between me and mine," said Caesar.

Marius didn't answer, merely looked skeptical.

Someone knocked at the study door.

"Come!" called Marius, glad of the interruption.

It was the little Greek physician from Sicily, Athenodorus.

"*Domine,* your wife is asking to see you," he said to Marius, "and I think it would do her good if you came."

Down hurtled the contents of Marius's chest into his belly; he drew a sobbing breath, his hand going out. Caesar had jumped to his feet, and was staring at the doctor painfully.

"Is she—is she—?" Caesar couldn't finish.

"No, no! Rest easy, *domine,* she's doing well," said the Greek soothingly.

Gaius Marius had never been in the presence of a woman in labor, and now found himself terrified. It wasn't hard to look on those killed or maimed in battle; they were comrades of the sword, no matter which side they belonged to, and a man always knew he might but for Fortune be one of them. In Julia's case the victim was dearly beloved, someone to be shielded and protected, spared all possible pain. Yet now Julia was no less his victim than any enemy, put into her bed of pain because of him. Disturbing thoughts for Gaius Marius.

However, all looked very normal when he walked into the confinement chamber. Julia was indeed lying in a bed. The childing stool—the special chair on which she would be seated when she went into the final stage of her labor—was decently covered up in a corner, so he didn't even notice it. To his vast relief, she didn't look either worn out or desperately ill, and the moment she saw him she smiled at him radiantly, holding out both hands.

He took them and kissed them. "Are you all right?" he asked, a little foolishly.

"Of course I am! It's just going to take a long time, they tell me, and there's a bit of bleeding. But nothing to be worried about at this stage." A spasm of pain crossed her face; her hands closed on his with a strength he hadn't known she possessed, and clung there for perhaps a minute before she began to relax again. "I just wanted to see you," she resumed, as if there had been no interruption. "May I see you from time to time, or will it be too distressing for you?"

"I would much rather see you, my little love," he said, bending to kiss the line where brow and hair met, and a few fine, fluffy curls clustered. They were damp, his lips informed him, and her skin was damp too. Poor, sweet darling!

"It will be all right, Gaius Marius," she said, letting go of his hands. "Try not to worry too much. I *know* everything will be all right! Is *tata* still with you?"

"He is."

Turning to leave, he encountered a fierce glare from Marcia, standing off to one side in the company of three old midwives. Oh, ye gods! Here was one who wouldn't forgive him in a hurry for doing this to her daughter!

"Gaius Marius!" Julia called as he reached the door.

He looked back.

"Is the astrologer here?" she asked.

"Not yet, but he's been sent for."

She looked relieved. "Oh, good!"

Marius's son was born twenty-four hours later, in a welter of blood. He almost cost his mother's life, but her will to survive was very strong, and after the doctors packed her solid with swabs and elevated her hips the haemorrhaging slowed down, and eventually stopped.

"He will be a famous man, *dominus,* and his life will be full of great events and great adventures," said the astrologer, expertly ignoring those unpalatable aspects the parents of new sons never wished to hear about.

"Then he will live?" asked Caesar sharply.

"Undoubtedly he will live, *dominus.*" One long and rather grimy finger rested across a major Opposition, blocking it from sight. "He will hold the highest office in the land—it is here in his chart for all the world to see." Another long and grimy finger pointed to a Trine.

"My son will be consul," said Marius with huge satisfaction.

"Assuredly," said the astrologer, then added, "But he will not be as great a man as his father, says the Quincunx."

And that pleased Marius even more.

Caesar poured two goblets of the best Falernian wine, unwatered, and gave one to his son-in-law, beaming with pride. "Here's to your son and my grandson, Gaius Marius," he said. "I salute you both!"

Thus, when at the end of March the consul Quintus Caecilius Metellus sailed for the African province with Gaius Marius, Publius Rutilius Rufus, Sextus Julius Caesar, Gaius Julius Caesar Junior, and four promising legions, Gaius Marius could sail in the happy knowledge that his wife was out of all danger, and his son was thriving. Even his mother-in-law had deigned to speak to him again!

"Have a talk to Julilla," he said to Julia just before he departed. "Your father's very worried about her."

Feeling stronger and bursting with joy because her son was a magnificently large and healthy baby, Julia mourned but one thing: she was not yet well enough to accompany Marius to Campania, to have a few more days with him before he quit Italy.

"I suppose you mean this ridiculous starvation business," said Julia, leaning more comfortably into Marius's embrace.

"Well, I don't know any more than your father told me, but I did gather it was about that," said Marius. "You'll have to forgive me, I'm not really interested in young girls."

His wife, a young girl, smiled secretly; she knew he never thought of her as young, but rather as a person of his own age, equally mature and intelligent.

"I'll talk to her," said Julia, lifting her face for a kiss. "Oh, Gaius Marius, what a pity I'm not well enough to try for a little brother or sister for Young Marius!"

But before Julia could gird herself to talk to her ailing sister, the news of the Germans burst upon Rome, and Rome flew into a gabbling panic. Ever since the Gauls had invaded Italy three hundred years before, and almost vanquished the fledgling Roman state, Italy had lived in dread of barbarian incursions; it was to guard against them that the Italian Allied nations had chosen to link their fates to Rome's, and it was to guard against them that Rome and her Italian Allies fought perpetual border wars along the thousand miles of Macedonian frontier between the Adriatic Sea and the Thracian Hellespont. It was to guard against them that Gnaeus Domitius Ahenobarbus had forged a proper land route between Italian Gaul and the Spanish Pyrenees a mere ten years ago, and subdued the tribes which lived along the river Rhodanus with a view to weakening them by exposing them to Roman ways and putting them under Roman military protection.

Until five years ago, it was the barbarian Gauls and Celts had loomed largest in Roman fears; but then the Germans first came on the scene, and suddenly by comparison the Gauls and Celts seemed civilized, tame, tractable. Like all bogeys, these fears arose not out of what was known, but out of what was not known. The Germans had popped out of nowhere (during the consulship of Marcus Aemilius Scaurus), and after inflicting a hideous defeat upon a huge and superbly trained Roman army (during the consulship of Gnaeus Papirius Carbo) disappeared again as if they had never been. Mysterious. Incalculable. Oblivious to the normal patterns of behavior as understood and respected by all the peoples who dwelled around the margins of the Middle Sea. For why, when that ghastly defeat had spread the whole of Italy out before them as helpless as a woman in a sacked city, did the Germans turn away, disappear? It made no sense! But they *had* turned away, they *had* disappeared; and as the years since Carbo's hideous defeat accumulated, the Germans became little more than a Lamia, a Mormolyce—a bogey to frighten children. The old, old fear of barbarian invasion lapsed back into its normal condition, somewhere between a shiver of apprehension and a disbelieving smile.

And now, out of nowhere again, the Germans were back, pouring in their hundreds of thousands into Gaul-across-the-Alps where the river Rhodanus flowed out of Lake Lemanna; and the Gallic lands and tribes which owed Rome tribute—the lands of the Aedui and the Ambarri—were awash in Germans, all ten feet tall, pallidly pale, giants out of legends, ghosts out of some northern barbarian underworld. Down into the warm, fertile valley of the Rhodanus the Germans spilled, crushing every living thing in their way, from men to mice, from forests to ferns, as indifferent to crops in the field as they were to birds on the wing.

The news reached Rome just days too late to recall the consul Quintus Caecilius Metellus and his army, already landed in Africa Province. Thus, fool though he was, the consul Marcus Junius Silanus, kept in Rome to govern there where he could do least harm, now became the best the Senate could produce under the twin weights of custom and law. For a consul in office could not be passed over in favor of some other commander, if he indicated he was willing to undertake a war. And Silanus expressed himself delighted to undertake a war against the Germans. Like Gnaeus Papirius Carbo five years before him, Silanus envisioned German wagons loaded down with gold, and coveted that gold.

After Carbo had provoked the Germans into attacking him and gone down to crushing defeat, the Germans had failed to pick up the arms and armor the vanquished Romans had left behind, on their dead, or abandoned by those still living to accelerate the pace of their flight. Thus canny Rome rather than the oblivious Germans sent teams to collect every vestige of arms and gear, and bring it all back to Rome and store it. This military treasure trove still lay in warehouses all over the city, waiting to be used. The limited resources of manufactories to supply arms and gear at the start of the campaigning season had been exhausted by Metellus and his African expedition, so it was lucky indeed that Silanus's hastily levied legions could be equipped from this cache; though of course the recruits lacking arms and a set of armor had to buy them from the State, which meant that the State actually made a little profit from Silanus's new legions.

Finding troops to give Silanus was far more difficult. The recruiters labored mightily, and under an oppressive sense of urgency. Often the property qualifications were winked at; men anxious to serve who didn't own quite enough to qualify were hastily enlisted, their inability to arm and protect themselves rectified from Carbo's old cache, its cost deducted from their absentee compensation pay. Veterans who had retired were lured out of bucolic inertia—mostly with little trouble, as bucolic inertia did not suit many of the men who had done their ten seasons under the colors and therefore could not be called up again.

And finally it was done. Marcus Junius Silanus set off for Gaul-across-the-Alps at the head of a splendid army a full seven legions strong, and with a large cavalry arm of Thracians mixed with some Gauls from the more settled parts of the Roman Gallic province. The time was late May, a bare eight weeks after the news of the German invasion had reached Rome; in that time Rome had recruited, armed, and partially trained an army of fifty thousand men including the cavalry and noncombatants. Only a bogey as enormous as the Germans could have stimulated such a heroic effort.

"But nonetheless it's living proof of what we Romans can do when we've the will to do it," said Gaius Julius Caesar to his wife, Marcia, on their return; they had journeyed out to see the legions start their march up the Via Flaminia toward Italian Gaul, a dazzling sight, and a cheering one.

"Yes, provided Silanus can do the job," said Marcia, a true senator's wife, actively interested in politics.

"You don't think he can," said Caesar.

"Nor do you, if you'd only admit it. Still, watching so many booted feet march across the Mulvian Bridge made me very glad that we have Marcus Aemilius Scaurus and Marcus Livius Drusus as censors now," Marcia said with a sigh of satisfaction. "Marcus Scaurus is right—the Mulvian Bridge is tottering, and won't survive another flood. Then what would we do if all of our troops were south of the Tiber and needed to march north in a hurry? So I'm very glad he was elected, since he's vowed to rebuild the Mulvian Bridge. A wonderful man!"

Caesar smiled a little sourly, but said, trying to be fair, "Scaurus is becoming an institution, damn him! He's a showman, a dazzling trickster—and three parts sham. However, the one part which isn't sham just happens to be worth more than any other man's whole—and for that I must forgive all, I suppose. Besides which, he's right—we do need a new program of public works, and not only to keep employment levels up. All these penny-pinching perusers of the senatorial rolls we seem to have endured as censors for the last few years are hardly worth the cost of the paper they scribble out the census on! Give Scaurus his due: he intends to see to some items I know should have been attended to long ago. Though I cannot condone his draining of the fens around Ravenna, or his plans for a system of canals and dikes between Parma and Mutina."

"Oh, come now, Gaius Julius, be generous!" said Marcia a little sharply. "It's terrific that he's going to curb the Padus! With the Germans invading Gaul-across-the-Alps, we don't need to find our armies cut off from the alpine passes by the Padus in full spate!"

"I've already said I agree it's a good thing," said Caesar, then added with stubborn disapproval, "Yet I find it fascinating that on the whole he's managed to keep his program of public works firmly in those parts where he has clients galore—*and* is likely to sex-tuple their numbers by the time he's finished. The Via Aemilia goes all the way from Ariminum on the Adriatic to Taurasia in the foothills of the western Alps—three hundred miles of clients packed as solid as the paving stones in it!"

"Well, and good luck to him," said Marcia, equally stubborn. "I suppose you'll find something to deride about his surveying and paving the west coast road too!"

"You forgot to mention the branch to Dertona that will link up the west coast road with the Via Aemilia," gibed Caesar. "*And* he gets his name on the whole lot into the bargain! The Via Aemilia Scauri. Tchah!"

"Sourpuss," said Marcia.

"Bigot," said Caesar.

"There are definitely times when I wish I didn't like you so much," said Marcia.

"There are times when I can say the same," said Caesar.

At which point Julilla drifted in. She was extremely thin, but not quite skeletal, and had remained in much the same state now for two months. For Julilla had discovered an equilibrium which allowed her to look pitiable yet prevented her dropping to a point where death became a strong possibility, if not from pure starvation, then certainly from disease. Death was not part of Julilla's master plan, nor was her spirit troubled.

She had two objectives: one was to force Lucius Cornelius Sulla to admit he loved her, and the other was to soften up her family to breaking point, for only then, she knew, did she stand the remotest chance of securing her father's permission to marry Sulla. Very young and very spoiled though she was, she hadn't made the mistake of overestimating her power when compared to the power vested in her father. Love her to distraction he might, indulge her to the top limit of his monetary resources he might; yet when it came to deciding whom she would marry, he would follow his own wishes without regard for hers. Oh, if she was tractable enough to approve of his choice of a husband for her—as Julia had done—he would glow with a natural and simple pleasure, and she knew too that he would look for someone he felt sure would take care of her, love her, always treat her well and respectfully. But Lucius Cornelius Sulla as her husband? Never, never, never would her father consent to it, and no reason she—or Sulla—could put forward would change her father's mind. She could weep, she could beg, she could protest undying love, she could turn herself inside out, and still her father would refuse to give his consent. Especially now that she had a dowry of some forty talents—a million sesterces—in the bank, which made her eligible, and marred Sulla's chances of ever persuading her father that he wished to marry her for herself alone. That is, when he admitted that he wished to marry her.

As a child Julilla had never displayed any sign that she owned a streak of enormous patience, but now, when it was needed, she had it to hand. Patient as a bird hatching a sterile egg, Julilla embarked upon her master plan fully aware that if she was to get what she wanted—a marriage to Sulla—she must outwait and outendure everyone else she knew, from her victim, Sulla, to her controller, Gaius Julius Caesar. She was even aware of some of the pitfalls littering her path to success—Sulla, for instance, might marry elsewhere, or move away from Rome, or fall ill and die. But she did what she could to avert these possibilities, chiefly by using her apparent illness as a weapon aimed at the heart of a man she knew full well would not consent to see her. How did she know that? Because she had tried to see him many times during the first few months after he returned to Rome, only to suffer one rebuff after another, culminating in his informing her—hidden as they were behind a fat pillar in the Porticus Margaritaria—that if she didn't leave him alone, he would quit Rome forever.

The master plan had evolved slowly, its nuclear germ the result of that first meeting, when he had derided her puppy fat and shooed her away. She had ceased to gobble sweeties, and lost a little weight, and had no reward from him for her pains. Then when he came back to Rome and was even ruder to her, her resolve had hardened, and she began to forsake food. At first it had been very difficult, but then she discovered that when she adhered to this semistarvation for long enough without once succumbing to the urge to stuff herself, her capacity to eat diminished, and the hunger pangs entirely went away.

So by the time that Lucius Gavius Stichus had died of his lingering illness eight months ago, Julilla's master plan was more or less fully evolved; there remained only irritating problems to solve, from devising a way to keep herself in the forefront of Sulla's mind to discovering a way to maintain herself in a weight equilibrium which would allow her to live.

Sulla she dealt with by writing him letters.

> I love you, and I shall never tire of telling you so. If letters are the only way I can make you hear me, then letters there will be. Dozens. Hundreds. Thousands, if the years mount up. I will smother you in letters, drown you in letters, crush you in letters. What more Roman way is there than the writing of letters? We feed on them, as I feed upon writing to you. What does food mean, when you deny me the food my heart and spirit crave? My cruelest, most merciless, and unpitying be-

loved! How can you stay away from me? Break down the wall between our two houses, steal into my room, kiss me and kiss me and kiss me! But you will not. I can hear you saying it as I lie here too weak to leave my awful and hateful bed. What have I done to deserve your indifference, your coldness? Surely somewhere inside your white, white skin there curls the smallest of womannikins, my essence given into your keeping, so that the Julilla who lives next door in her awful and hateful bed is only a sucked-out and dried-up simulacrum growing steadily shadowier, fainter. One day I shall disappear, and all that will be left of me is that tiny womannikin under your white, white skin. Come and see me, look upon what you have done! Kiss me and kiss me and kiss me. For I love you.

The food equilibrium had been more difficult. Determined not to gain weight, she kept on losing it in spite of her efforts to remain static. And then one day the whole gang of physicians who had over the months paraded through the house of Gaius Julius Caesar, trying vainly to cure her, went to Gaius Julius Caesar and advocated that she be force-fed. But in the way of physicians, they had left it up to her poor family to do their dirty work. So the whole house had gathered up its courage and prepared itself for the effort, from the newest slave to the brothers, Gaius and Sextus, and Marcia, and Caesar himself. It had been an ordeal no one cared to remember afterward—Julilla screaming as if she were being murdered rather than resurrected, struggling feebly, vomiting back every mouthful, spitting and gagging and choking. When Caesar finally ordered the horror abandoned, the family had gone into council and agreed without one dissenting voice that no matter what might happen to Julilla in the future, force-fed she was not going to be.

But the racket Julilla had made during the attempt to force-feed her had let the cat out of the Caesar bag; the whole neighborhood now knew of the Caesar troubles. Not that the family had concealed its troubles from shame, only that Gaius Julius Caesar loathed gossip, and tried never to be a cause of it.

To the rescue came none other than Clitumna from next door, armed with a food she guaranteed Julilla would voluntarily ingest, and which would stay down once it was ingested. Caesar and Marcia welcomed her fervently, and sat listening fervently as she talked.

"Find a source of cow's milk," said Clitumna importantly, enjoying the novel experience of being the center of Caesarean attention. "I know it's not easy to come by, but I believe there are a couple of fellows out in the Camenarum Valley who do milk cows. Then for each cup of milk you break in one hen's egg and three spoons of honey. You beat it up until there's a froth on top, and add half a cup of strong wine right at the end. If you put the wine in before you beat it up, you won't get a nice froth on top. If you have a glass goblet, give it to her in that, because the drink's very pretty to look at—quite a rich pink, with a nice yellow top of froth. Provided she can keep it down, it will certainly keep her alive and fairly healthy," said Clitumna, who vividly remembered her sister's period of starvation after she had been prevented from marrying a most unsuitable fellow from Alba Fucentia—a snake charmer, no less!

"We'll try it," said Marcia, eyes full of tears.

"It worked for my sister," said Clitumna, and sighed. "When she got over the snake charmer, she married my dear, dear Stichus's father."

Caesar got up. "I'll send someone out to the Camenarum at once," he said, disappearing. Then his head came round the door. "What about the hen's egg? Ought it to be a tenth egg, or will an ordinary one do?" he asked.

"Oh, we just used ordinary ones," said Clitumna comfortably, relaxing in her chair. "The extra-large variety might upset the balance of the drink."

"And the honey?" Caesar persisted. "Ordinary Latin honey, or should we try to get Hymettan, or at any rate smokeless?"

"Ordinary Latin honey is quite good enough," said Clitumna

firmly. "Who knows? Maybe it was the smoke in the ordinary honey that did the trick. Let us not depart from the original recipe, Gaius Julius."

"Quite right." Caesar disappeared again.

"Oh, if only she can tolerate it!" said Marcia, her voice shaking. "Neighbor, we are at our wits' end!"

"I imagine you are. But don't make such a fuss about it, at least not in Julilla's hearing," advised Clitumna, who could be sensible when her heart wasn't involved, and would cheerfully have let Julilla die had she only known of those letters piling up in Sulla's room. Her face puckered. "We don't want a second death in these two houses," she said, and sniffled dolefully.

"We most certainly don't!" cried Marcia. Her sense of social fitness coming to the fore, she said delicately, "I do hope you're over the loss of your nephew a little, Clitumna? It's very difficult, I know."

"Oh, I manage," said Clitumna, who did grieve for Stichus on many levels, but upon one vital level had found her life a great deal easier without the friction between the deceased Stichus and her dear, darling Sulla. She heaved a huge sigh—sounding much like Julilla, had she only known it.

That encounter had proved to be the first of many, for when the drink actually worked, the Caesar household lay under a massive obligation to their vulgar neighbor.

"Gratitude," said Gaius Julius Caesar, who took to hiding in his study whenever he heard Clitumna's shrill voice in the atrium, "can be a wretched nuisance!"

"Oh, Gaius Julius, don't be such a curmudgeon!" said Marcia defensively. "Clitumna is really very kind, and we can't possibly hurt her feelings—which is what you're in danger of doing when you avoid her so persistently."

"I know she's terribly kind!" exclaimed the head of the household, goaded. "That's what I'm complaining about!"

Julilla's master plan had complicated Sulla's life to a degree which would have afforded her great satisfaction, had she only known. But she did not, for he concealed his torment from everyone save himself, and feigned an indifference to her plight which completely fooled Clitumna, always full of news about the situation next door now that she had donned the mantle of lifesaving miracle worker.

"I do wish you'd pop in and say hello to the poor girl," Clitumna said fretfully about the time that Marcus Junius Silanus led his seven magnificent legions north up the Via Flaminia. "She often asks after you, Lucius Cornelius."

"I've got better things to do than dance attendance on a female Caesar," said Sulla harshly.

"What arrant nonsense!" said Nicopolis vigorously. "You're as idle as any man could possibly be."

"And is that my fault?" he demanded, swinging round on his mistress with a sudden savagery that made her draw back in fright. "I could be busy! I could be marching with Silanus to fight the Germans."

"Well, and why didn't you go?" Nicopolis asked. "They've dropped the property qualifications so drastically that I'm sure with your name you could have managed to enlist."

His lips drew back from his teeth, revealing the overlong and sharply pointed canines which gave his smile a feral nastiness. "I, a patrician Cornelius, to march as a ranker in a legion?" he asked. "I'd sooner be sold into slavery by the Germans!"

"You might well be, if the Germans aren't stopped. Truly, Lucius Cornelius, there are times when you demonstrate only too well that you yourself are your own worst enemy! Here you are, when all Clitumna asked of you was a miserable little favor for a dying girl, grizzling that you have neither the time nor the interest—really, you do exasperate me!" A sly gleam crept into her eyes. "After all, Lucius Cornelius, you must admit your life here is vastly more comfortable since Lucius Gavius so conveniently expired." And she hummed the tune of a popular ditty under her breath, a song with words to the effect that the singer had murdered his rival in love and got away with it. "Con–veeeeeeniently ex–piiiiiiired!" she warbled.

His face became flinty, yet oddly expressionless. "My dear Nicopolis, why don't you stroll down to the Tiber and do me the *enormous* favor of jumping in?"

The subject of Julilla was prudently dropped. But it was a subject which seemed to crop up perpetually, and secretly Sulla writhed, aware of his vulnerability, unable to display concern. Any day that fool girl of Julilla's could be caught out carrying one of the letters, or Julilla herself caught in the deed of writing one—and then where would he be? Who would believe that he, with his history, was innocent of any kind of intrigue? It was one thing to have an unsavory past, but if the censors deemed him guilty of corrupting the morals of a patrician senator's daughter—he would never, never be considered for membership of the Senate. And he was determined he was going to reach the Senate.

What he yearned to do was to leave Rome, yet he didn't dare—what might the girl do in his absence? And, much though he hated having to admit it, he couldn't bring himself to abandon her while she was so ill. Self-induced her illness might be, but it was nonetheless a serious illness. His mind circled inside itself like a disorientated animal, unable to settle, unable to discipline itself to a sensible or logical path. He would drag the withered grass crown out from its hiding place in one of his ancestral cupboards and sit holding it between his hands, almost weeping in a frenzy of anxiety; for he knew where he was going and what he intended to do, and that wretched girl was an unbearable complication, and yet that wretched girl was the start of it all, with her grass crown—what to do, what to do? Bad enough to have to pick his way unerringly through the morass of his coming intentions, without the additional strain of Julilla.

He even contemplated suicide, he who was the last person in the world likely to do that deed—a fantasy, a delicious way out of everything, the sleep which has no end. And then back his thoughts would go to Julilla, always back to Julilla—*why?* He didn't love her, he wasn't capable of loving. Yet there were times when he hungered for her, craved to bite her and kiss her and impale her until she screamed in ecstatic pain; and there were other times, especially when he lay wakeful between his mistress and his step-mother, that he actively loathed her, wanting the feel of her skinny throat between his hands, wanting to see her empurpled face and goggling eyes as he squeezed the last vestige of her life out of her starving lungs. Then would come another letter—why didn't he just throw them away, or carry them to her father with a fierce look on his face and a demand that this harassment cease? He never did. He read them, those passionate and despairing pleas her girl kept slipping into the sinus of his toga in places too public to draw attention to her action; he read each one a dozen times, then put it away in his ancestral cupboards with the others.

But he never broke down in his resolve not to see her.

And spring turned into summer, and summer into the dog days of Sextilis, when Sirius the Dog Star shimmered sullenly over a heat-paralyzed Rome. Then, as Silanus was marching confidently up the Rhodanus toward the churning masses of the Germans, it began to rain in central Italy. And kept on raining. To the denizens of sunny Rome, a worse fate than the Sextilian dog days. Depressing, highly inconvenient, a worry in case of flood, a nuisance on all fronts. The marketplaces couldn't hope to open, political life was impossible, trials had to be postponed, and the crime rate soared. Men discovered their wives *in flagrante delicto* and murdered them, the granaries leaked and wetted the wheat stored therein, the Tiber rose just enough to ensure that some of the public latrines backfilled and floated excrement out of their doors, a vegetable shortage developed when the Campus Martius and the Campus Vaticanus were covered with a few inches of water, and shoddily built high-rise insulae began to crumble into total collapse or suddenly manifested huge cracks in walls and foundations. Everyone caught cold; the aged and infirm began to die of pneumonia, the young of croup and quinsy, all ages of that mysterious disease which paralyzed the body and, if survived, left an arm or a leg shriveled, wasted.

Clitumna and Nicopolis began to fight every day, and every day Nicopolis would remark to Sulla in a whisper how very convenient Stichus's death had been for him.

Then, after two full weeks of remorseless rain, the low clouds hauled their last tatters over the eastern horizon, and the sun came out. Rome steamed. Tendrils of vapor curled off the paving stones and roof tiles; the air was thick with it. Every balcony, loggia, peristyle-garden, and window in the city burgeoned with mouldy washing, contributing to the general fug, and houses where small babies dwelled—like the one of the merchant banker Titus Pomponius—suddenly found their peristyle-gardens filled with line upon line of drying diapers. Shoes had to be divested of mildew, every book in every literate house unrolled and inspected minutely for insidious fungus, the clothes chests and cupboards aired.

But there was one cheering aspect to this foetid dampness; mushroom season arrived with a phenomenal surplus. Always avid for the fragrant umbrellas after the normal summer dry, the whole city gobbled mushrooms, rich and poor alike.

And Sulla was once again loaded down with Julilla's letters, after a wonderful wet two weeks which had prevented Julilla's girl from finding him to drop them into his toga. His craving to quit Rome escalated until he knew if he didn't shake Rome's vaporous miasma off himself for the space of one little day, he would truly go mad at last. Metrobius and his protector, Scylax, were vacationing in Cumae, and Sulla didn't want to spend that day of respite alone. So he resolved that he would take Clitumna and Nicopolis on a picnic to his favorite spot outside the city.

"Come on, girls," he said to them on the third fine dawn in a row, "put on your glad rags, and I'll take you on a picnic!"

The girls—neither feeling at all girlish—looked at him with the sour derision of those in no mood to be jollied out of their doldrums, and declined to budge from the communal bed, though the humid night had left it sweatily soaked.

"You both need some fresh air," Sulla persisted.

"We are living on the Palatine because there is nothing wrong with the air up here," said Clitumna, turning her back.

"At the moment the air on the Palatine is no better than any other air in Rome—it's full of the stink of drains and washing," he said. "Come on, do! I've hired a carriage and we'll head off in the direction of Tibur—lunch in the woods—see if we can catch a fish or two—or buy a fish or two, and a good fat rabbit straight out of the trap—and come home before dark feeling a lot happier."

"No," said Clitumna querulously.

Nicopolis wavered. "Well . . ."

That was enough for Sulla. "Get ready, I'll be back in a few moments," he said, and stretched luxuriantly. "Oh, I am so tired of being cooped up inside this house!"

"So am I," said Nicopolis, and got out of bed.

Clitumna continued to lie with her face to the wall, while Sulla went off to the kitchen to command a picnic lunch.

"Do come," he said to Clitumna as he donned a clean tunic and laced on open boots.

She refused to answer.

"Have it your own way, then," he said as he went to the door. "Nicopolis and I will see you this evening."

She refused to answer.

Thus the picnic party consisted only of Nicopolis and Sulla and a big hamper of goodies the cook had thrown together at late notice, wishing he could go along himself. At the foot of the Steps of Cacus an open two-wheeled gig was waiting; Sulla helped Nicopolis up into the passenger's seat, then hoisted himself into the driver's seat.

"Away we go," he said happily, gathering in the reins and experiencing an extraordinary spurt of lightheartedness, a rare sense of freedom. He confessed to himself that he wasn't sorry Clitumna had declined to come. Nicopolis was company enough. "Gee up, you mules!" he cried.

The mules geed up nicely; the gig rattled down the Valley of Murcia in which the Circus Maximus lay, and left the city through the Capena Gate. Alas, the view at first was neither interesting nor cheering, for the ring road Sulla took in heading east crossed the great cemeteries of Rome. Tombstones and more tombstones— not the imposing mausolea and sepulchra of the rich and noble which flanked every arterial road out of the city, but the gravestones of simpler souls. Every Roman and Greek, even the poorest, even the slaves, dreamed that after his going he would be able to afford a princely monument to testify that he had once existed. For that reason, both poor and slaves belonged to burial clubs, and contributed every tiny mite they could afford to the club funds, carefully managed and invested; embezzlement was rife in Rome as in any place of human habitation, but the burial clubs were so jealously policed by their members that their executives had no choice save to be honest. A good funeral and a lovely monument *mattered*.

A crossroads formed the central point of the huge necropolis sprawled over the whole Campus Esquilinus, and there at the crossroads stood the massive temple of Venus Libitina, in the midst of a leafy grove of sacred trees. Inside the temple's podium lay the registers in which the names of Rome's dead citizens were inscribed, and there too lay chest after chest of money paid in over the centuries to register each citizen death. In consequence the temple was enormously rich, the funds belonging to the State, yet never touched. The Venus was that Venus who ruled the dead, not the living, that Venus who presided over the extinction of the procreative force. And her temple grove was the headquarters of Rome's guild of undertakers. Behind the precinct of Venus Libitina was an area of open space on which the funeral pyres were built, and beyond that was the paupers' cemetery, a constantly changing network of pits filled with bodies, lime, soil. Few, citizens or noncitizens, elected to be inhumed, apart from the Jews, who were buried in one section of the necropolis, and the aristocrats of the Famous Family Cornelius, who were buried along the Via Appia; thus most of the monuments transforming the Campus Esquilinus into a crowded little stone city housed urns of ashes rather than decomposing bodies. No one could be buried within Rome's sacred boundary, not even the greatest.

However, once the gig passed beneath the arches of the two aqueducts which brought water to the teeming northeastern hills of the city, the vista changed. Farmlands stretched in all directions, market gardens at first, then grass pastures and wheat fields.

Despite the effect the downpour had had on the Via Tiburtina (the densely packed layer of gravel, tufa dust, and sand on top of the paving stones had been eroded), the two in the gig were thoroughly enjoying themselves. The sun was hot but the breeze cooling, Nicopolis's parasol was large enough to shade Sulla's snow-white skin as well as her own olive hide, and the mules turned out to be a willingly tractable pair. Too sensible to force the pace, Sulla let his team find their own, and the miles trotted by delightfully.

To go all the way to Tibur and back was impossible in one day, but Sulla's favorite spot lay well short of the climb up to Tibur itself. Some distance out of Rome was a forest that stretched all the way into the ranges which rose, ever increasing in height, to the massif of the Great Rock, Italy's highest mountain. This forest cut diagonally across the route of the road for perhaps a mile before wandering off cross-country; the road then entered the Anio River valley, most fertile, eminently arable.

However, the mile or so of forest was harder ground, and here Sulla left the road, directing the mules down an unpaved wagon track which dived into the trees and finally petered out.

"Here we are," said Sulla, jumping down and coming round to help Nicopolis, who found herself stiff and a little sore. "I know it doesn't look promising, but walk a little way further with me and I'll show you a place well worth the ride."

First he unharnessed the mules and hobbled them, then he shoved the gig off the track into the shade of some bushes and took the picnic hamper out of it, hoisting it onto his shoulder.

"How do you know so much about dealing with mules and harness?" Nicopolis asked as she followed Sulla into the trees, picking her way carefully.

"Anyone does who's worked in the Port of Rome," said Sulla over his unburdened shoulder. "Take it slowly, now! We're not going far, and there's no hurry."

Indeed, they had made good time. Since the month was early September, the twelve hours of daylight were still on the long side at sixty-five minutes each; it still wanted two hours before noon when Sulla and Nicopolis entered the woods.

"This isn't virgin forest," he said, "which is probably why no one logs in it. In the old days this land was given over to wheat, but after the grain started coming from Sicily and Sardinia and Africa Province, the farmers moved into Rome and left the trees to grow back, for it's poor soil."

"You're amazing, Lucius Cornelius," she said, trying to keep up with Sulla's long, easy strides. "How is it that you know so many things about the world?"

"It's my luck. What I hear or read, I remember."

They emerged then into an enchanting clearing, grassy and filled with late-summer flowers—pink and white cosmos, great blooming jungles of pink and white rambling roses, and lupines in tall spikes, pink and white. Through the clearing flowed a stream in full spate from the rain, its bed filled with jagged rocks which divided its waters into deep still pools and foaming cascades; the sun glittered and flashed off its surface, amid dragonflies and little birds.

"Oh, how beautiful!" cried Nicopolis.

"I found it last year when I went away for those few months," he said, putting the hamper down in a patch of shade. "My gig cast a wheel right where that track runs into the forest, and I had to put Metrobius up on one of the mules and send him to Tibur for help. While I waited, I explored."

It gave Nicopolis no satisfaction to know that the despised and feared Metrobius had undoubtedly been shown this special place first, but she said nothing, simply flopped down in the grass and watched Sulla take a big skin of wine from the interior of the hamper. He immersed the wineskin in the stream where a natural fence of rocks anchored it, then took off his tunic and removed his open boots, all he wore.

Sulla's lighthearted mood still lay inside his bones, as warming as the sun upon his skin; he stretched, smiling, and looked about the glade with an affection which had nothing to do with Metrobius or Nicopolis. Simply, his pleasure came from a divorcement from the predicaments and frustrations which so hedged his normal life around, a place where he could tell himself that time did not move, politics did not exist, people were classless, and money an invention for the future. His moments of pure happiness were so few and dispersed so thinly along the route march of his life that he remembered every single one of them with piercing clarity—the day when the jumble of squiggles on a piece of paper suddenly turned into understandable thoughts, the hour in which an enormously kind and thoughtful man had shown him how perfect the act of love could be, the stunning emancipation of his father's death, and the realization that this clearing in a forest was the first piece of land he had ever been able to call his own, in that it belonged to no one who cared enough to visit it except for him. And that was all. The sum total. None was founded in an appreciation of beauty, or even of the process of living; they represented the acquisition of literacy, erotic pleasure, freedom from authority, and property. For those were the things Sulla prized, the things Sulla wanted.

Fascinated, Nicopolis watched him without even beginning to understand the source of his happiness, marveling at the absolute whiteness of his body in full sun—a sight she had never seen before—and the fiery gold of head and chest and groin. All far too much to resist; she doffed her own light robe and the shift she wore beneath it, its long back tail caught between her legs and pinned in front, until she too was naked and could relish the kiss of the sun.

They waded into one of the deep pools, gasping with the cold, stayed there long enough to warm up while Sulla played with her erect nipples and her beautiful breasts, then clambered out upon the thick soft grass and made love while they dried off. After which they ate their lunch, breads and cheeses and hard-boiled eggs and chicken wings, washed down with the chilly wine. She made a wreath of flowers for Sulla's hair, then made another for her own, and rolled over three times from the sheer voluptuous gratification of being alive.

"Oh, this is wonderful!" she sighed. "Clitumna doesn't know what she's missing."

"Clitumna never knows what she's missing," said Sulla.

"Oh, I don't know," said Nicopolis idly, the mischief-bee back buzzing inside her mind. "She's missing Sticky Stichy." And she began to hum the ditty about murder until she caught the flickering end of a glance from him that told her he was becoming angry. She didn't honestly believe Sulla had contrived at Stichus's death, but when she implied for the first time that Sulla had, she picked up interesting echoes of alarm from Sulla, and so kept it up from sheer idle curiosity.

Time to stop it. Leaping to her feet, she held out her hands to Sulla, still lying full length. "Come on, lazybones, I want to walk under the trees and cool off," she said.

He rose obediently, took her hand, and strolled with her under the eaves of the forest, where no undergrowth marred the carpet of sodden leaves, warm after the day's perfect portion of sun. Being barefoot was a treat.

And there they were! A miniature army of the most exquisite mushrooms Nicopolis had ever seen, every last one unmarked by insect hole or animal paw, purest white, fat and fleshy of canopy yet nicely slender of stalk, and giving off a heady aroma of earth.

"Oh, goody!" she cried, dropping to her knees.

Sulla grimaced. "Come on," he said.

"No, don't be mean just because *you* dislike mushrooms! Please, Lucius Cornelius, please! Go back to the hamper and find me a cloth—I'm going to take some of these home for my supper," said Nicopolis, voice determined.

"They mightn't be good ones," he said, not moving.

"Nonsense, of course they're good! Look! There's no membrane covering up the gills, no spots, no red color. They smell superb too. And this isn't an oak, is it?" She looked up at the tree in the base of which the mushrooms were growing.

Sulla eyed its deeply scalloped leaves and experienced a vision of the inevitability of fate, the pointing finger of his lucky goddess. "No, it's not an oak," he said.

"Then please! Please?" she wheedled.

He sighed. "All right, have it your own way."

A whole miniature army of mushrooms perished as Nicopolis selected her treasure trove, then wrapped it in the napkin Sulla had brought her and carefully laid it in the bottom of the hamper, where it would be protected from the heat as they drove home.

"I don't know why you and Clitumna don't like mushrooms," she said after they were ensconced in the gig again, and the mules were trotting eagerly in the direction of their stables.

"I never have liked them," said Sulla, not interested.

"All the more for me," she said, and giggled.

"What's so special about this lot, anyway?" Sulla asked. "At the moment you can buy mushrooms by the ton in the markets, and dirt-cheap too."

"These are *mine*," she tried to explain. "*I* found them, *I* saw how absolutely perfect they were, *I* picked them. The ones in the markets are any old how—full of grubs, holes, spiders, the gods know what. Mine will taste much better, I promise you."

They did taste better. When Nicopolis brought them into the kitchen the cook handled them suspiciously, but had to admit he couldn't fault them with eyes or nose.

"Fry them lightly in a little oil," said Nicopolis.

As it happened, the vegetable slave had brought home a huge basket of mushrooms from the markets that morning, so cheap that the entire staff was allowed to gorge on them, and had been doing so all day. Therefore no one was tempted to steal a few of the new arrivals; the cook was able to fry all of them just long enough to soften them and heat them through, then tossed them in a dish with a little freshly ground pepper and a squeeze of onion juice, and sent them to the dining room for Nicopolis. Who ate of them ravenously, her appetite sharpened by the day out—and by Clitumna's monumental fit of the sulks. For, of course, the moment it was too late to send a servant to catch them, Clitumna had regretted her decision not to go on the famous picnic. Subjected to a paean on the subject throughout dinner, she reacted badly, and ended her day by announcing that she would sleep alone.

It was eighteen hours later before Nicopolis experienced a pain in her belly. She became nauseated and was a little sick, but had no diarrhoea, and admitted the pain was bearable, she'd known worse. Then she urinated a small volume of fluid red with blood, and panicked.

Doctors were summoned at once; the household ran about distractedly; Clitumna sent servants out to look for Sulla, who had gone out early in the day without leaving any word of his destination.

When Nicopolis's heart rate went up and her blood pressure fell, the doctors looked grave. She had a convulsion, her respiration grew slow and shallow, her heart began to fibrillate, and she passed inexorably into coma. As it happened, no one even thought of mushrooms.

"Kidney failure," said Athenodorus of Sicily, now the most successful medical practitioner on the Palatine.

Everyone else concurred.

And about the time that Sulla came rushing home, Nicopolis died from a massive internal haemorrhage—the victim, said the doctors, of a complete systemic collapse.

"We should perform an autopsy," said Athenodorus.

"I agree," said Sulla, who didn't mention mushrooms.

"Is it catching?" asked Clitumna pathetically, looking old and ill and desperately alone.

Everyone said no.

The autopsy confirmed the diagnosis of renal and hepatic failure: kidneys and liver were swollen, congested, and full of haemorrhages. The envelope around Nicopolis's heart had bled, as had the linings of her stomach, her small intestine, and her colon. The innocent-looking mushroom called The Destroyer had done its subtle work well.

Sulla organized the funeral (Clitumna was too prostrated)

and walked in the procession as chief mourner, ahead of the stars of the Roman comedic and mimetic theaters; their presence assured a good attendance, which would have pleased Nicopolis.

And when Sulla returned to Clitumna's house afterward, he found Gaius Julius Caesar waiting for him. Throwing off his dark mourning toga, Sulla joined Clitumna and her guest in her sitting room. On few occasions had he set eyes on Gaius Julius Caesar, and knew the senator not at all; that the senator would visit Clitumna because of the untimely death of a Greek strumpet struck Sulla as very odd, so he was on his guard and punctiliously correct as he was introduced.

"Gaius Julius," he said, bowing.

"Lucius Cornelius," said Caesar, bowing also.

They did not shake hands, but when Sulla sat down, Caesar resumed his own seat with apparent tranquillity. He turned to the weeping Clitumna and spoke kindly.

"My dear, why stay?" he asked. "Marcia is waiting next door for you. Have your steward take you to her. Women stand in need of women's company in times of grief."

Without a word Clitumna rose and tottered to the door, while the visitor reached into his dark toga and produced a small roll of paper, which he then laid on the table.

"Lucius Cornelius, your friend Nicopolis had me draw up her will and lodge it with the Vestals a long time ago. The lady Clitumna is aware of its contents, which is why she did not need to stay to hear me read it."

"Yes?" asked Sulla, at a loss. He could find nothing further to say, and so sat dumbly, gazing at Caesar rather blankly.

Caesar moved to the crux of the matter. "Lucius Cornelius, the lady Nicopolis made you her sole heir."

Sulla's expression remained blank. "She did?"

"She did."

"Well, I suppose if I'd thought about it, I would have known she'd be bound to do that," said Sulla, recovering. "Not that it matters. Everything she had, she spent."

Caesar looked at him keenly. "She didn't, you know. The lady Nicopolis was quite wealthy."

"Rubbish!" said Sulla.

"Truly, Lucius Cornelius, she was quite wealthy. She owned no property, but she was the widow of a military tribune who did extremely well out of booty. What he left her, she invested. As of this morning, her estate is in excess of two hundred thousand denarii," said Caesar.

There could be no mistaking the genuineness of Sulla's shock. Whatever Caesar might have thought of him until that moment, he knew he was now looking at a man who possessed no inkling of this information; Sulla sat stupefied.

Then he sank back in his chair, put shaking hands up to his face, shuddered, and gasped. "So much! *Nicopolis?*"

"So much. Two hundred thousand denarii. Or eight hundred thousand sesterces, if you prefer. A knight's portion."

Down came Sulla's hands. "Oh, Nicopolis!" he said.

Caesar got to his feet, extending his hand. Sulla took it dazedly.

"No, Lucius Cornelius, don't get up," said Caesar warmly. "My dear fellow, I cannot tell you how delighted I am for you. I know it's difficult to salve your grief at this early stage, but I would like you to know that I've often wished with all my heart that one day you would better your fortune—and your luck. In the morning I'll commence probate. You had better meet me in the Forum at the second hour. By the shrine of Vesta. For now, I bid you good day."

After Caesar had gone, Sulla sat without moving for a long time. The house was as silent as Nicopolis's grave; Clitumna must have stayed next door with Marcia, and the servants were creeping about.

Perhaps as many as six hours went by before he finally got up, stiff and sore, and stretched a little. The blood began to flow, his heart to fill with fire.

"Lucius Cornelius, you are on your way at last," he said, and began to laugh.

Though it started very softly, his laughter swelled and rolled

into a shriek, a roar, a howl of mirth; the servants, listening terrified, debated among themselves as to which one was going to
venture into Clitumna's sitting room. But before they could reach
a decision, Sulla stopped laughing.

Clitumna aged almost overnight. Though her years numbered
only fifty, the death of her nephew had kicked the ageing process
into a gallop; now the death of her dearest friend—and her
lover—compounded her devastation. Not even Sulla had the
power to jolly her out of her megrims. Not mime nor farce could
lure her out of the house, nor could her regular visitors Scylax
and Marsyas provoke a smile. What appalled her was the shrinking world of her intimates as well as her own encroaching dotage;
if Sulla should abandon her—for his inheritance from Nicopolis
had freed him from economic dependence upon her—she would
be completely alone. A prospect she dreaded.

Soon after Nicopolis died, she sent for Gaius Julius Caesar.
"One cannot leave anything to the dead," she said to him, "and so
I must alter my will yet again."

The will was altered forthwith, and taken back to repose in the
Vestal pigeonholes.

Still she moped. Her tears dropped like rain, her once restless
hands were folded in her lap like two unbaked leaves of pastry
waiting for the cook to fill them. Everyone worried; everyone
understood there was nothing to be done save wait for time to
heal. If there was time.

For Sulla it was time.

Julilla's latest missive said:

> I love you, even though the months and now the
> years have shown me how little my love is returned,
> how little my fate matters to you. Last June I turned
> eighteen, by rights I should be married, but I have
> managed to postpone that evil necessity by making
> myself ill. I must marry you, you and no one but you,
> my most beloved, my dearest Lucius Cornelius. And

so my father hesitates, unable to present me to anyone as a suitable or desirable bride, and I shall keep it that way until you come to me and say that you will marry me. Once you said I was a baby, I would grow out of my immature love for you, but surely so long after—it is almost two years—I have proven my worth, I have proven that my love for you is as constant as the return of the sun from the south each spring. She is gone, your thin Greek lady I hated with every breath I drew, and cursed, and wished dead dead dead. You see how powerful I am, Lucius Cornelius? Why then do you not understand that you cannot escape me? No heart can be as full of love as mine and not generate reciprocation. You do love me, I know you love me. Give in, Lucius Cornelius, give in. Come and see me, kneel down beside my bed of pain and sorrow, let me draw down your head onto my breast, and offer me your kiss. Don't sentence me to die! Choose to let me live. Choose to marry me.

Yes, for Sulla it was time. Time to end many things. Time to slough off Clitumna, and Julilla, and all those other dreadful human commitments which tied his spirit down and cast such eerie shadows into the corners of his mind. Even Metrobius must go.

Thus midway through October Sulla went to knock on Gaius Julius Caesar's door at an hour when he could confidently expect the master of the house to be at home. And confidently expect that the women of the house would be banished to their quarters; Gaius Julius Caesar was not the kind of husband or father to permit his womenfolk to rub shoulders with his clients or his men friends. For though a part of his reason for knocking on Gaius Julius Caesar's door was to rid himself of Julilla, he had no wish to set eyes on her; every part of him, every thinking component, every source of energy, must be focused on Gaius Julius Caesar and what he had to say to Gaius Julius Caesar. What he had to say must be said without arousing any suspicion or mistrust.

He had already gone with Caesar to have Nicopolis's will probated, and come into his inheritance so easily, so free from reproach, that he was doubly wary. Even when he had presented himself to the censors, Scaurus and Drusus, everything went as smoothly as a well-orchestrated theatrical production, for Caesar had insisted upon going with him, and stood guarantor for the authenticity of all the papers he had had to produce for censorial scrutiny. At the end of it all, none other than Marcus Livius Drusus and Marcus Aemilius Scaurus had risen to their feet and shaken him by the hand and congratulated him sincerely. It was like a dream—but was it possible he would never again have to wake?

So, without the slightest need to contrive it, imperceptibly he had slipped into an acquaintance with Gaius Julius Caesar that ripened into a rather distant kind of friendly tolerance. To the Caesar house he never went; the acquaintance was pursued in the Forum. Both Caesar's sons were in Africa with their brother-in-law, Gaius Marius, but he had come to know Marcia a little in the weeks since Nicopolis had died, for she had made it her business to visit Clitumna. And it had not been hard to see that Marcia eyed him askance; Clitumna, he suspected, was not as discreet as she might have been about the bizarre relationship among Sulla and herself and Nicopolis. However, he knew very well that Marcia found him dangerously attractive, though her manner gave him to understand that she had classified his attractiveness somewhere between the alien beauty of a snake and a scorpion.

Thus Sulla's anxieties as he knocked on Gaius Julius Caesar's door halfway through October, aware that he did not dare postpone the next phase of his plans any further. He must act before Clitumna began to cheer up. And that meant he had to be sure of Gaius Julius Caesar.

The lad on door duty opened to him immediately, and did not hesitate to admit him, which indicated to Sulla that he had been placed on Caesar's list of those he was prepared to see anytime he was home.

"Is Gaius Julius receiving?" he asked.

"He is, Lucius Cornelius. Please wait," said the lad, and sped off toward Caesar's study.

Prepared to wait for a little while, Sulla strolled into the modest atrium, noting that this room, so plain and unadorned, contrived to make Clitumna's atrium look like the anteroom to an Eastern potentate's harem. And as he debated the nature of Caesar's atrium, Julilla walked into it.

For how long had she persuaded every servant likely to be given door duty that she must be told the moment Lucius Cornelius came to call? And how long would it be before the lad sped where he ought to have sped in the beginning, to tell Caesar who had come to call?

These two questions flew into Sulla's mind faster than it took a flicker of lightning to extinguish itself, faster than the responses of his body to the shock of the sight of her.

His knees gave way; he had to put out a hand to grab at the first object it could find, which happened to be an old silver-gilt ewer standing on a side table. Since the ewer was not anchored to the table, his frantic clutching at it unseated it, and it fell to the floor with a ringing, clanging crash just as Julilla, hands over her face, ran out of the room again.

The noise echoed like the interior of the Sibyl's cave at Cumae, and brought everyone running. Aware that he had lost every last vestige of what little color he owned, and that he had broken out in a chilling sweat of fear and anguish, Sulla elected to let his legs buckle completely, slid down the length of his toga to the floor, and sat there with his head between his knees and his eyes fast closed, trying to blot out the image of the skeleton wrapped in Julilla's golden skin.

When Caesar and Marcia got him to his feet and assisted him to walk into the study, he had reason to be thankful for the grey tinge in his face, the faint blueness about his lips; for he really did present the picture of a man genuinely ill.

A draft of unwatered wine brought him to a semblance of normality, and he was able to sit up on the couch with a sigh, wiping his brow with one hand. Had either of them seen? And where had Julilla gone? What to say? What to do?

Caesar looked very grim. So did Marcia.

"I'm sorry, Gaius Julius," he said, sipping again at the wine. "A faintness—I don't know what came over me."

"Take your time, Lucius Cornelius," said Caesar. "I know what came over you. You saw a ghost."

No, this was not the man to cheat—at least not blatantly. He was far too intelligent, far too perceptive.

"*Was* it the little girl?" he asked.

"Yes," said Caesar, and nodded a dismissal to his wife, who left at once, and without a look or a murmur.

"I used to see her several years ago around the Porticus Margaritaria in the company of her friends," said Sulla, "and I thought she was—oh, everything a young Roman girl should be—always laughing, never vulgar—I don't know. And then once on the Palatium—I was in pain—a pain of the soul, you understand—"

"Yes, I think I do," said Caesar.

"She thought I was ill, and asked if she could help me. I wasn't very nice to her—all I could think was that you wouldn't want her striking up an acquaintance with the likes of me. But she wouldn't be put off, and I just couldn't manage to be rude enough. Do you know what she did?" Sulla's eyes were even stranger than usual, for the pupils had dilated and now were huge, and around them were two thin rings of pallid grey-white, and two rings of grey-black outside of that; they gazed up at Caesar a little blindly, and did not look human.

"What did she do?" asked Caesar gently.

"She made me a grass crown! She made me a grass crown and she put it on my head. *Me!* And I saw—I saw—*something*!"

A silence fell. Because neither man could fathom how to break it, it lingered for many moments, moments during which each man assembled his thoughts and circled warily, wondering if the other was an ally or an adversary. Neither wanted to force the issue.

"Well," said Caesar finally, sighing, "what did you come to see me about, Lucius Cornelius?"

It was his way of saying that he accepted the fact of Sulla's innocence, no matter what interpretation he might have put upon the conduct of his daughter. And it was his way of saying that he wished to hear no more on the subject of his daughter; Sulla, whose thoughts had dwelled upon bringing up Julilla's letters, decided not to.

His original purpose in coming to see Caesar now seemed very far away, and quite unreal. But Sulla squared his shoulders and got off the couch, seated himself in the more manly chair on the client's side of Caesar's desk, and assumed the air of a client.

"Clitumna," he said. "I wanted to talk to you about her. Or it might be that I should talk to your wife about Clitumna. But the proper person to start with is you, certainly. She's not herself. Well, you're aware of that. Depressed—weepy—uninterested. Not at all the sort of behavior I'd call normal. Or even normal in this time of grief. The thing is, I don't know what to do for the best." He filled his chest with air. "I owe her a duty, Gaius Julius. Yes, she's a poor silly vulgar sort of woman and not exactly an adornment to the neighborhood, but I do owe her a duty. She was good to my father, and she's been good to me. And I don't know what to do for the best about her, I really don't."

Caesar sat back in his chair, conscious that something about this petition jarred. Nothing did he doubt in Sulla's story, for he had seen Clitumna himself, and listened often enough to Marcia on the subject. No, what perturbed him was Sulla's coming to him seeking advice; not in character for Sulla, thought Caesar, who very much doubted that Sulla was experiencing any uncertainty what to do about his stepmother, who gossip said was his mistress as well. About that, Caesar wasn't prepared to hazard a guess; if his coming here to seek help was any indication, it was probably a distorted lie, typical Palatine gossip. Just as was the rumor that Sulla's stepmother had been sexually involved with the dead woman, Nicopolis. Just as was the rumor that Sulla had been sexually involved with both of them—and at the same time, no less! Marcia had indicated that she thought there was something fishy about the situation, but, when pressed, hadn't been able to produce any concrete evidence. Caesar's disinclination to believe these rumors was not mere naïveté; it was due more to a personal fastidiousness which not only dictated his own behavior, but reflected itself in his beliefs about the behavior of others. Proof positive was one thing, hearsay quite another. In spite of which, something did not ring true about Sulla's coming here today to seek advice.

It was at this point that an answer occurred to Caesar. Not for one moment did he think there was anything established between Sulla and his younger daughter—but for a man of Sulla's character to faint upon seeing a starved-looking young girl—incredible! Then had come that odd story about Julilla's fashioning him a grass crown. Caesar of course understood the significance of that completely. Perhaps their congress had been limited to a very few times, and mostly in passing; but, decided Caesar, there was definitely something between them. Not shabby, not shoddy, not shifty either. Just something. Something worth watching carefully. Naturally he could not condone a relationship of any kind between them. And if they had an affinity for each other, that was too bad. Julilla must go to a man able to hold his head up in the circles to which the Caesars belonged.

While Caesar leaned back in his chair and considered these things, Sulla leaned back in his chair and wondered what was going through Caesar's mind. Because of Julilla, the interview had not gone according to plan, even remotely. How could he have had so little self-control? Fainting! He, Lucius Cornelius Sulla! After betraying himself so obviously, he had had little choice save to explain himself to this watchful father, and that in turn had meant telling a part of the truth; had it helped Julilla, he would have told all of the truth, but he didn't think Caesar would relish perusing those letters. I have made myself vulnerable to Gaius Julius Caesar, thought Sulla, and disliked the sensation very much.

"Have you any course of action in mind for Clitumna?" asked Caesar.

Sulla frowned. "Well, she has a villa at Circei, and I wondered if it might not be a good idea to persuade her to go down there and stay for a while," he said.

"Why ask me?"

The frown deepened; Sulla saw the gulf open beneath his feet, and endeavored to leap it. "You are quite right, Gaius Julius. Why ask you? The truth is, I'm caught between Scylla and Charybdis, and I was hoping you'd extend me an oar and rescue me."

"In what way can I rescue you? What do you mean?"

"I think Clitumna is suicidal," said Sulla.

"Oh."

"The thing is, how can I combat it? I'm a man, and with Nicopolis dead, there is literally no woman of Clitumna's house or family—or even among her servants—in a position of sufficient trust and affection to help Clitumna through." Sulla leaned forward, warming to his theme. "Rome isn't the place for her now, Gaius Julius! But how can I send her down to Circei without a woman to rely on? I'm not sure that I'm a person she wants to see at the moment, and besides, I—I—I have things to do in Rome at the moment! What I was wondering was, would your wife be willing to accompany Clitumna down to Circei for a few weeks? This suicidal mood won't last, I'm sure of that, but as of this moment, I'm very worried. The villa is very comfortable, and even though it's turning cold, Circei is good for the health at any time of the year. It might benefit your wife to breathe a bit of sea air."

Caesar visibly relaxed, looking as if an enormous load had suddenly vanished from his bowed back. "I see, Lucius Cornelius, I see. And I understand better than you think. My wife has indeed become the person Clitumna depends upon most. Unfortunately, I cannot spare her. You have seen Julilla, so you do not need to be told how desperate our situation is. My wife is needed at home. Nor would she consent to leave, fond of Clitumna though she is."

Sulla looked eager. "Well, why couldn't Julilla go down to Circei with them? The change might work wonders for her!"

But Caesar shook his head. "No, Lucius Cornelius, I am afraid it's out of the question. I myself am fixed in Rome until the spring. I could not countenance the absence of my wife and daughter from Rome unless I could be with them, not because I am selfish enough to deny them a treat, but because I would worry about them all the time they were away. If Julilla was well, it would be different. So—no."

"I understand, Gaius Julius, and I sympathize." Sulla got up to go.

"Send Clitumna to Circei, Lucius Cornelius. She'll be all right." Caesar walked his guest to the front door, and opened it himself.

"Thank you for bearing with my foolishness," said Sulla.

"It was no burden. In fact, I'm very glad you came. I think I can deal better with my daughter now. And I confess I like you the better for this morning's events, Lucius Cornelius. Keep me informed about Clitumna." And, smiling, Caesar held out his hand.

But the moment he closed the door behind Sulla, Caesar went to find Julilla. She was in her mother's sitting room, weeping desolately, her head buried in her arms as she slumped against the worktable. One hand to her lips, Marcia rose as Caesar appeared in the doorway; together they crept out and left her weeping.

"Gaius Julius, it is terrible," said Marcia, lips tight.

"Have they been seeing each other?"

A burning blush ran up under Marcia's pale-brown skin; she shook her head so savagely that the pins holding her hair in a prim bun loosened, and the bun dangled half-unrolled on the nape of her neck. "No, they haven't been seeing each other!" She struck her hands together, wrung them. "Oh, the shame of it! The *humiliation*!"

Caesar possessed himself of the writhing hands and held them gently but firmly still. "Calm yourself, wife, calm yourself! Nothing can possibly be so bad that you drive yourself into an illness. Now tell me."

"Such deceit! Such indelicacy!"

"Calm yourself. Start at the beginning."

"It's had nothing to do with him, it's all her own doing! Our daughter, Gaius Julius, has spent the last two years shaming herself and her family by—by—throwing herself at the head of a man who is not only unfit to wipe the mud off her shoes, but who doesn't even want her! And more than that, Gaius Julius, more than that! She has tried to capture his attention by starving herself and so forcing a guilt upon him he has done nothing to earn! Letters, Gaius Julius! Hundreds of letters her girl has delivered to him, accusing him of indifference and neglect, blaming him for her illness, pleading for his love the way a female dog grovels!" Marcia's eyes poured tears, but they were tears of disillusionment, of a terrible anger.

"Calm yourself," Caesar repeated yet again. "Come, Marcia, you can cry later. I must deal with Julilla, and you must see me deal with her."

Marcia calmed herself, dried her eyes; together they went back to her sitting room.

Julilla was still weeping, hadn't noticed that she was alone. Sighing, Caesar sat in his wife's favorite chair, hunting in the sinus of his toga as he did so, and finally bringing out his handkerchief.

"Here, Julilla, blow your nose and stop crying, like a good girl," he said, thrusting the cloth under her arm. "The waterworks are wasted. It's time to talk."

Most of Julilla's tears had their source in terror at being found out, so the reassuringly strong firm impartial tone of her father's voice enabled her to do as she was told. The waterworks turned off; she sat with her head down, her frail body shaken by convulsive hiccoughs.

"You have been starving yourself because of Lucius Cornelius Sulla, is that right?" her father asked.

She didn't answer.

"Julilla, you cannot avoid the question, and you'll get no mercy by maintaining silence. Is Lucius Cornelius the cause of all this?"

"Yes," she whispered.

Caesar's voice continued to sound strong, firm, impartial, but the words it framed burned into Julilla all the deeper for its level tone; so did he speak to a slave who had done him some unpardonable wrong, never did he speak to his daughter thus. Until now.

"Do you even begin to understand the pain, the worry, the fatigue you have caused this entire family for the past year and more? Ever since you began to waste away, you have been the pivot around which every one of us has turned. Not only me, your mother, your brothers, and your sister, but our loyal and admirable servants, our friends, our neighbors. You have driven us to the edge of dementia. And for what? Can you tell me for what?"

"No," she whispered.

"Nonsense! Of course you can! You've been playing a game with us, Julilla. A cruel and selfish game, conducted with a patience and intelligence worthy of a nobler purpose. You fell in love—*at sixteen years of age!*—with a fellow you knew was unsuitable, could never meet with my approval. A fellow who understood his unsuitability, and gave you absolutely no kind of encouragement. So you proceeded to act with deceit, with cunning, with an aim so manipulatory and exploitative—! Words fail me, Julilla," said Caesar unemotionally.

His daughter shivered.

His wife shivered.

"It seems I must refresh your memory, daughter. Do you know who I am?"

Julilla didn't answer, head down.

"Look at me!"

Her face came up at that; drowned eyes fixed themselves on Caesar, terrified and wild.

"No, I can see that you don't know who I am," said Caesar, still in conversational voice. "Therefore, daughter, it behooves me to tell you. I am the *paterfamilias,* the absolute head of this household. My very word is law. My actions are not actionable. Whatever I choose to do and say within the bounds of this household, I can do and I can say. No law of the Senate and People of Rome stands between me and my absolute authority over my household, my family. For Rome has structured her laws to ensure that the Roman family is above the law of all save the *paterfamilias*. If my wife commits adultery, Julilla, I can kill her, or have her killed. If my son is guilty of moral turpitude, or cowardice, or any other kind of social imbecility, I can kill him, or have him killed. If my daughter is unchaste, Julilla, I can kill her, or have her killed. If any member of my household—from my wife through my sons and my daughters to my mother, to my servants— transgresses the bounds of what *I* regard as decent conduct, I can kill him or her, or have him or her killed. Do you understand, Julilla?"

Her eyes had not swerved from his face. "Yes," she said.

"It grieves me as much as it shames me to inform you that you have transgressed the bounds of what I regard as decent conduct, daughter. You have made your family and the servants of this household—above all you have made its *paterfamilias*—your victim. Your puppet. Your plaything. And for what? For self-gratification, for personal satisfaction, for the most *abominable* of motives—yourself alone."

"But I love him, *tata*!" she cried.

Caesar reared up, outraged. "Love? What do you know of that peerless emotion, Julilla? How can you besmirch the word 'love' with whatever base imitation you have experienced? Is it love, to make your beloved's life a misery? Is it love, to force your beloved to a commitment he doesn't want, hasn't asked for? Well, is any of it love, Julilla?"

"I suppose not," she whispered, and then added, "but I thought it was."

The eyes of her parents met above her head; in both lay a wry and bitter pain as they finally understood Julilla's limitations, their own illusions.

"Believe me, Julilla, whatever it was you felt that made you behave so shabbily and dishonorably, it was not love," said Caesar, and stood up. "There will be no more cow's milk, no more eggs, no more honey. You will eat whatever the rest of your family eats. Or you will not eat. It is a matter of no moment to me. As your father and as *paterfamilias,* I have treated you from the time of your birth with honor, with respect, with kindness, with consideration, with tolerance. You have not thought well enough of me to reciprocate. I do not cast you off. And I am not going to kill you, or have you killed. But from this time on, whatever you make of yourself is entirely on your own head. You have injured me and mine, Julilla. Perhaps even more unpardonably, you have injured a man who owes you nothing, for he does not know you and is not related to you. Later on, when you are less appalling to look at, I shall require that you apologize to Lucius Cornelius Sulla. I do not require an apology from you for any of the rest of us, for you have lost our love and respect, and that renders apologies valueless."

He walked out of the room.

Julilla's face puckered; she turned instinctively toward her mother, and tried to hurl herself into her mother's arms. But Marcia drew back as if her daughter wore a poisoned robe.

"Disgusting!" she hissed. "All that for the sake of a man who isn't fit to lick the ground a Caesar walks on!"

"Oh, Mama!"

"Don't 'oh, Mama!' me! You wanted to be grown up, Julilla; you wanted to be woman enough to marry. Now live with it." And Marcia too walked out of the room.

Wrote Gaius Julius Caesar some days later to his son-in-law, Gaius Marius:

> And so, the unhappy business is finally wearing itself down. I wish I could say that Julilla has learned a lesson, but I very much doubt it. In later years, Gaius Marius, you too will face all the torments and dilemmas of parenthood, and I wish I could offer you the comfort of saying that you will learn by my mistakes. But you will not. For just as each and every child born into this world is different, and must be handled differently, so too is every parent different. Where did we go wrong with Julilla? I do not honestly know. I do not even know if we went wrong at all. Perhaps the flaw is

innate, intrinsic. I am bitterly hurt, and so too is poor Marcia, as best evidenced by her subsequent rejection of all Julilla's overtures of friendship and regret. The child suffers terribly, but I have had to ask myself whether we owe it to her to maintain our distance for the present, and I have decided we must do so. Love we have always given her, an opportunity to discipline herself we have not. If she is to gain any good out of all this, she must suffer.

Justice forced me to seek out our neighbor Lucius Cornelius Sulla, and tender him a collective apology which will have to do until Julilla's looks have improved and she can apologize to him in person. Though he didn't want to hand them over, I insisted that he return all of Julilla's letters—one of the few times being *paterfamilias* has had real value. I made Julilla burn them, but not until she had read every one of the silly things out to me and her mother. How awful, to have to be so hard upon one's own flesh and blood! But I very much fear that only the most personally galling of lessons will sink into Julilla's self-centered little heart.

There. Enough of Julilla and her schemes. Far more important things are happening. I may actually turn out to be the first to send this news to Africa Province, as I have a firm promise that this will go on a fast packet leaving Puteoli tomorrow. Marcus Junius Silanus has been shockingly defeated by the Germans. Over thirty thousand men are dead, the rest so demoralized and poorly led that they have scattered in all directions. Not that Silanus seems to care, or perhaps it would be more accurate to say that he seems to value his own survival ahead of his troops'. He brought the news to Rome himself, but in such a toned-down version that he stole a march on public indignation, and by the time that all the truth was known, he had stripped the disaster of much of its shock value. Of course what he's aiming for is to wriggle out of treason charges, and I think he'll succeed. If the Mamilian Commission were empowered to try him, a conviction might be possible. But a trial in the Centuriate Assembly, with all those antiquated rules and regulations, and so many jurors? It's not worth the effort of initiating proceedings, and so most of us feel.

And, I hear you ask, what of the Germans? Are they even now pouring down toward the coast of the Middle Sea, are the inhabitants of Massilia packing up in panic? No. For would you believe it, having annihilated Silanus's army, they promptly turned around again and went north. How can one deal with an enemy so enigmatic, so utterly unpredictable? I tell you, Gaius Marius, we shiver in our boots. For they will come. Later rather than sooner, it now seems, they will come. And we have no better commanders to oppose them than the likes of Marcus Junius Silanus. As usual these days, the Italian Allied legions took the brunt of the losses, though many Roman soldiers fell too. And the Senate is having to deal with a stream of complaints from the Marsi and the Samnites, and a host of other Italian nations.

But to finish on a lighter note, we are currently having a hilarious battle with our esteemed censor Marcus Aemilius Scaurus. The other censor, Marcus Livius Drusus, died very suddenly three weeks ago, which brought the *lustrum* of the censors to an abrupt end. Scaurus of course is obliged to stand down. Only he won't! And therein lies the hilarity. As soon as the funeral of Drusus was over, the Senate convened and directed Scaurus to lay aside his censorial duties so that the *lustrum* could be officially closed in the customary ceremony. Scaurus refused.

"I was elected censor, I'm in the middle of letting contracts for my building programs, and I cannot possibly abandon my work at this juncture," he said.

"Marcus Aemilius, Marcus Aemilius, it isn't up to you!" said Metellus Dalmaticus Pontifex Maximus. "The law says that when one censor dies in office, the *lustrum* is at an end, and his fellow censor must resign immediately."

"I don't care what the law says!" Scaurus replied. "I cannot resign immediately, and I will not resign immediately."

They begged and they pleaded, they shouted and they argued, all to no avail. Scaurus was determined to create a precedent by flouting convention and remaining censor. So they begged and they pleaded, they shouted and they argued all over again. Until Scaurus lost patience and temper.

"I piss on the lot of you!" he cried, and went right on with his contracts and his plans.

So Dalmaticus Pontifex Maximus called another meeting of the Senate, and forced it to pass a formal *consultum* calling for Scaurus's immediate resignation. Off went a deputation to the Campus Martius, and there interviewed Scaurus as he sat on the podium of the temple of Jupiter Stator, which edifice he had chosen for his office because it's right next door to the Porticus Metelli, where most of the building contractors have their headquarters.

Now as you know, I am not a Scaurus man. He's as crafty as Ulysses and as big a liar as Paris. But oh, I do wish you could have seen him make mincemeat out of them! How such an ugly, skinny, undersized specimen as Scaurus can do it, I do not know—he hasn't even got a hair left on his head! Marcia says it's his beautiful green eyes and his even more beautiful speaking voice and his wonderful sense of humor. Well, I will admit the sense of humor, but the charms of his ocular and vocal apparatus escape me. Marcia says I'm a typical man, though what her point about that is, I do not know. Women tend to seek refuge in such remarks when pinned down to logic, I have found. But there must also be some obscure logic to his success, and who knows? Perhaps Marcia has the right of it.

So there he sat, the little poseur, surrounded by all the utter magnificence of Rome's first marble temple, and those glorious statues of Alexander the Great's generals all mounted on horseback that Metellus Macedonicus pillaged from Alexander's old capital of Pella. Dominating the lot. How can that be possible, a hairless Roman runt outclassing Lysippus's quite superbly lifelike horses? I swear every time I see Alexander's generals, I expect them to step down from their plinths and ride away, each horse as different as Ptolemy is from Parmenion.

I digress. Back to business, then. When Scaurus saw the deputation he shoved contracts and contractors aside and sat spear-straight on his curule chair, toga perfectly draped, one foot extended in the classic pose.

"Well?" he asked, addressing his question to Dalmaticus Pontifex Maximus, who had been appointed the spokesman.

"Marcus Aemilius, the Senate has formally passed a *consultum* commanding that you resign your censorship at once," said this unhappy man.

"I won't do it," said Scaurus.

"You must!" bleated Dalmaticus.

"I mustn't anything!" said Scaurus, and turned his shoulder on them, beckoning the contractors to draw close again. "Now what was I saying before I was so rudely interrupted?" he asked.

Dalmaticus tried again. "Marcus Aemilius, please!"

But all he got for his pontifical pains was an "I piss on you! Piss, piss, piss!"

The Senate having shot its bolt, the whole problem was referred to the Plebeian Assembly, thereby making the Plebs responsible for a matter it hadn't created, considering that it is the Centuriate Assembly, a more exclusive body by far than the Plebeian Assembly, that elects the censors. However, the Plebs did hold a meeting to discuss Scaurus's stand, and handed its College of Tribunes one last duty for their year in office. They were instructed to remove Marcus Aemilius Scaurus from office as censor, one way or another.

So yesterday, the ninth day of December, saw all ten tribunes of the plebs march off to the temple of Jupiter Stator, Gaius Mamilius Limetanus in their lead.

"I am directed by the People of Rome, Marcus Aemilius, to depose you from office as censor," said Mamilius.

"As the People did not elect me, Gaius Mamilius, the People cannot depose me," said Scaurus, his hairless scone shining in the sun like a polished old winter apple.

"Nonetheless, Marcus Aemilius, the People are sovereign, and the People say you must step down," said Mamilius.

"I won't step down!" said Scaurus.

"In that case, Marcus Aemilius, I am authorized by the People to arrest you and cast you into prison until you formally resign," said Mamilius.

"Lay one hand on me, Gaius Mamilius, and you will revert to the soprano voice of your boyhood!" said Scaurus.

Whereupon Mamilius turned to the crowd which had naturally gathered to see the spectacle, and cried out to it, "People of Rome, I call you to witness the fact that I hereby interpose my veto against any further censorial activity by Marcus Aemilius Scaurus!" he declared.

And that of course was the end of the matter. Scaurus rolled up his contracts and handed everything over to his clerks, had his chair slave fold up his ivory seat, and stood bowing in all directions to the applauding throng, which loves nothing better than a good confrontation between its magistrates, and adores Scaurus wholeheartedly because he has the kind of courage all Romans admire in their magistrates. Then he strolled down the temple steps, gave Perdiccas's roan horse a pat in passing, linked his arm through Mamilius's, and left the field wearing all the laurels.

Caesar sighed, leaned back in his chair, and decided that he had better comment upon the news Marius—by no means such a wordy correspondent as his father-in-law—had sent from the Roman African province, where Metellus, it appeared, had succeeded in bogging the war against Jugurtha in a mire of inconsistent activity and poor generalship. Or at least that was Marius's version, though it did not tally with the reports Metellus kept sending the Senate.

You will shortly hear—if you have not heard already—that the Senate has prorogued Quintus Caecilius's command of the African province and the Jugurthine war. It will not in any way surprise you, I am sure. And I expect that, having leaped this biggest hurdle, Quintus Caecilius will step up his military activity, for once the Senate has prorogued a governor's command, he can be sure to retain that command until he considers the danger to his province over. It is a shrewd tactic to be inert until the consulship year is over and proconsular imperium is bestowed.

But yes, I do agree that your general was shockingly dilatory in not even starting his campaign until summer was almost over, especially considering that he arrived in early spring. But his dispatches say his army needed thorough training, and the Senate believes them. And yes, it escapes me as to why he appointed you, an infantryman, to lead his cavalry arm, just as it seems a waste of Publius Rutilius's talents to use him as *praefectus fabrum* when he would serve better in the field than running round dealing with supply columns and artillery repairs. However, it is the prerogative of the general to use his men as he likes, from his senior legates all the way down to his auxiliary rankers.

All Rome was delighted when the news of the capture of Vaga came, though I note your letter said the town surrendered. And—if you will forgive my playing Quintus Caecilius's advocate—I fail to see why you are so indignant at the appointment of Quintus Caecilius's friend Turpillius as the commander of the Vaga garrison. Is it important?

I am far more impressed with your version of the battle at the river Muthul than I am with the version contained in Quintus Caecilius's senatorial dispatch, which should console you somewhat for my hint of skepticism, and reassure you that I do indeed remain on your side. And I'm sure you're right in telling Quintus Caecilius that the best way to win the war against Numidia is to capture Jugurtha himself, for, like you, I believe him to be the fountainhead of all Numidian resistance.

I'm sorry this first year has been so frustrating for you, and that Quintus Caecilius has apparently decided he can win without properly using either your talents or those of Publius Rutilius. It will make your attempt to be elected consul the year after next much harder if you do not receive an opportunity to shine in the coming Numidian campaigns. But, Gaius Marius, I do not expect that you will take such cavalier treatment lying down, and I'm sure you'll find a way to shine in spite of the very worst Quintus Caecilius can do.

I shall close with one further Forum item. Due to the loss of Silanus's army in Gaul-across-the-Alps, the Senate has nullified one of the last surviving laws of Gaius Gracchus, namely the one limiting the number of times a man can enlist. Nor does he have to be seventeen anymore, nor do ten years under the colors exclude him from the levies anymore, nor do six campaigns exclude him anymore. A sign of the times. Both Rome and Italy are rapidly becoming denuded of men for the legions.

Do look after yourself, and write as soon as my mild attempts to play advocate for Quintus Caecilius have faded enough to allow you to think of me with affection. I am still your father-in-law, and I still think very well of you.

And that, decided Gaius Julius Caesar, was a letter well worth the sending, full of news and good advice and comfort. Gaius Marius would have it before the old year expired.

In the end it was almost halfway through December before Sulla escorted Clitumna down to Circei, all solicitude and tender kindness. Though he had worried that his plans might go awry because time would improve Clitumna's mood, the extraordinary change in his luck continued to bless him, for Clitumna remained deeply depressed, as Marcia would be bound to report to Caesar.

As villas on the Campanian coast went, Clitumna's version was not overlarge, but even so, it was far bigger than the house on the Palatine; vacationing Romans able to afford the luxury of owning country villas liked to feel surrounded by space. Standing atop a volcanic headland and having its own private beach, the villa lay some distance south of Circei, and had no close neighbors. One of the many speculation builders who frequented the Campanian coast had put it up during the course of the winter three years before, and Clitumna had bought it the moment she discovered the builder had a genius for plumbing, and had installed a shower bath as well as a proper bathing tub.

Thus the first thing Clitumna did after she arrived was to have a shower bath, after which she dined, after which she and Sulla went to bed in separate rooms, and alone. He remained at Circei for two days only, devoting all his time to Clitumna, who continued to be cheerless, though she didn't want Sulla to leave.

"I have a surprise for you," he said to her as he walked with her in the grounds of the villa early in the morning of the day he returned to Rome.

Even that hardly evoked a response. "Yes?" she asked.

"On the first night of the full moon you will receive your surprise," he said seductively.

"Night?" she asked, becoming the slightest bit interested.

"Night, *and* full moon! That is, provided it's a fine clear night and you can see the full moon."

They were standing beneath the tall front facade of the villa, which like most was built upon sloping ground, with a loggia atop the front section, where the villa dweller could sit to take in the view. Behind this narrow front facade was a vast peristyle-garden, and behind the peristyle-garden lay the villa proper, in which the bulk of the rooms were situated. The stables were located on the ground level of the front facade, with living quarters for the stable staff above, and the loggia above that again.

The land in front of Clitumna's villa sloped away in grass and tangles of rambling roses to the cliff top, and was most artfully planted on either flank with a grove of trees which ensured privacy should another villa go up on the next block of land.

Sulla pointed to the large clump of salt pines and pencil cypresses on their left.

"It's a secret, Clitumna," he said in what she called his "growly voice," always a sign of prolonged and particularly delicious love-making.

"What is a secret?" she asked, beginning to be eager.

"If I told you, it wouldn't be a secret any longer," he whispered, nibbling her ear.

She squirmed a little, cheered up a little. "Is the secret the same as the surprise on the night of the moon?"

"Yes. But you *must* keep everything a secret, including my promising you a surprise. Swear?"

"I swear," she said.

"What you must do is sneak out of the house at the beginning of the third hour of darkness, eight days from last night. You must come down here absolutely on your own, and hide in that grove of trees," said Sulla, stroking her flank.

Her listlessness was gone. "Ooooooooooh! Is it a nice surprise?" she asked, squeaking on the last word.

"It will be the biggest surprise of your entire life," said Sulla, "and that's not an idle promise, darling. But I do require a couple of conditions."

She wrinkled her nose girlishly and simpered, looking very silly. "Yes?"

"First of all, no one must know, not even little Bithy. If you do take anyone into your confidence, your chief surprise will be disappointment. And I will be very, very angry. You don't like it when I'm very, very angry, do you, Clitumna?"

She shivered. "No, Lucius Cornelius."

"Then keep our secret. Your reward will be amazing, a completely new and different kind of experience," he whispered. "In fact, if you can manage to seem specially downcast from now until you receive your surprise, it will turn out even better, I promise you."

"I'll be good, Lucius Cornelius," she said fervently.

He could see the way her mind was working, and knew that she had decided the surprise was a new and delectable companion—female, attractive, sexually willing, compatible, and a cozy gossipy talker for the passing of the long days between the lovely nights. But she knew Sulla well enough to understand that she must abide by his conditions, or he was just as likely to take whoever it was away again forever—perhaps install her in an apartment of her own, now that he had Nicopolis's money. Besides which, no one defied Sulla when he spoke in earnest, a reason why the servants of Clitumna's household held their tongues about what had gone on between Clitumna and Nicopolis and Sulla, and if they ever said anything at all, did so in a fear which robbed their words of much of their normal impact.

"There's a second condition," he said.

She snuggled against him. "Yes, darling Lucius?"

"If the night is not fine, the surprise cannot come. So you will have to respect the weather. If the first night is wet, wait for the next dry one."

"I understand, Lucius Cornelius."

Thus Sulla drove off to Rome in a hired gig leaving Clitumna faithfully hugging her secret, and trying assiduously to present a picture of acute depression. Even Bithy, with whom Clitumna had taken to sleeping, believed her mistress desolate.

Upon reaching Rome, Sulla summoned the steward of Clitumna's house on the Palatine; he was one staff member not relocated to Circei, as the villa there had its own steward, who acted as caretaker in his mistress's absence—and cheated her very cleverly. So did the steward of her Palatine house.

"How many servants did the mistress leave here, Iamus?" asked Sulla, sitting at his desk in the study; he was evidently making out some kind of list, for it lay beneath his hand.

"Just myself, two house boys, two house girls, a market boy, and the undercook, Lucius Cornelius," said the steward.

"Well, you're going to have to hire some extra help, because four days from now, Iamus, I am going to throw a party."

Sulla flapped his list at the astonished steward, who didn't know whether to protest that the lady Clitumna had given him no word of a party in her absence, or to go along with the idea and pray there were no ructions later, when the bills came in. Then Sulla relieved his mind.

"It's my show, so I'm paying for it," said Sulla, "and there'll be a big bonus in it for you on two conditions—one, that you co-operate fully in helping me put on the party, and two, that you make no mention of it to the lady Clitumna after she returns home, whenever that may be. Is that clear?"

"Fully, Lucius Cornelius," said Iamus, bowing deeply; largesse was a subject every slave risen high enough to be a steward understood almost as well as he understood how to doctor the household account books.

Off went Sulla to hire dancers, musicians, tumblers, singers, magicians, clowns, and other acts. For this was going to be the party to end all parties, one he intended would be heard far and wide across the Palatine. His last stop was the flat of Scylax the comedic actor.

"I want to borrow Metrobius," he said, erupting into the room Scylax had preferred to set up as a sitting room rather than as a study. It was the apartment of a voluptuary, redolent with incense and cassia wood, tapestried to death, overfurnished with couches and pouffes all stuffed with the finest wool.

Scylax sat up indignantly at the same moment Sulla was sinking into one of the sybaritically cushioned couches.

"Honestly, Scylax, you're as soft as custard pudding and as decadent as a Syrian potentate!" said Sulla. "Why don't you get a bit of ordinary horsehair furniture? This stuff makes a man feel as if he's sinking into the arms of a gigantic whore! Ugh!"

"I piss on your taste," lisped Scylax.

"As long as you hand over Metrobius, you can piss on anything you like."

"Why should I, you—you—savage?" Scylax ran his hands through his carefully arranged, dyed golden locks; he fluttered his long lashes, darkened with *stibium,* and rolled his eyes between them.

"Because the boy's not yours body and mind," said Sulla, testing a pouffe with his foot to see if it was less yielding.

"He *is* mine body and mind! And he hasn't been the same since you stole him from me and took him all over Italy with you, Lucius Cornelius! I don't know what you did to him, but you certainly spoiled him for me!"

Sulla grinned. "Made a man out of him, did I? Doesn't like eating your shit anymore, eh? Aaaaaaaah!" With which sound of disgust, Sulla lifted his head and roared, "Metrobius!"

The lad came flying through the door and launched himself straight at Sulla, covering his face with kisses.

Over the black head Sulla opened one pale eye at Scylax, and wiggled one ginger brow. "Give up, Scylax, your bum-boy just likes me better," he said, and demonstrated the truth of this by lifting the boy's skirt to display his erection. Scylax burst into tears, streaking his face with *stibium*.

"Come on, Metrobius," said Sulla, struggling to his feet. At the door he turned back to flip a folded paper at the blubbering Scylax. "Party at Clitumna's house in four days," he said. "It's going to be the best one ever, so swallow your spleen and come. You can have Metrobius back if you do."

Everyone was invited, including Hercules Atlas, who was billed as the world's strongest man, and hired himself out to fairs and fetes and festivals from one end of Italy to the other. Never seen outside his door unless wearing a moth-eaten lion skin and toting an enormous club, Hercules Atlas was a bit of an institution. However, he was rarely asked as a guest to the parties where he entertained with his strongman act, for when the wine flowed down his throat like water down the Aqua Marcia, Hercules Atlas became very aggressive and bad-tempered.

"You're touched in the head, to ask that bull!" said Metrobius, playing with Sulla's brilliant curls as he leaned over Sulla's shoulder to peer at yet another list. The real change in Metrobius that had occurred while he was away with Sulla was his literacy; Sulla had taught the lad to read and write. Willing to teach him every art he knew from acting to sodomy, Scylax had yet been too crafty to endow him with something as emancipating as letters.

"Hercules Atlas is a friend of mine," said Sulla, kissing the lad's fingers one by one with a great deal more pleasure than ever he felt kissing Clitumna's.

"But he's a madman when he's drunk!" Metrobius protested. "He'll tear this house apart, and very likely two or three of the guests as well! Hire his act by all means, but don't have him present as a guest!"

"I can't do that," said Sulla, seeming unworried. He reached up and pulled Metrobius down across his shoulder, settling the boy in his lap. And Metrobius wound his arms about Sulla's neck and lifted his face: Sulla kissed his eyelids very slowly, very tenderly.

"Lucius Cornelius, why won't you keep me?" Metrobius asked, settling against Sulla's arm with a sigh of utter content.

The kisses ceased. Sulla frowned. "You're far better off with Scylax," he said abruptly.

Metrobius opened huge dark eyes, swimming with love. "But I'm not, truly I'm not! The gifts and the acting training and the money don't matter to me, Lucius Cornelius! I'd much rather be with you, no matter how poor we were!"

"A tempting offer, and one I'd take you up on in a trice—*if* I intended to remain poor," said Sulla, holding the boy as if he cherished him. "But I am not going to remain poor. I have Nicopolis's money behind me now, and I'm busy speculating with it. One day I'll have enough to qualify for admission to the Senate."

Metrobius sat up. "The *Senate*!" Twisting, he stared into Sulla's face. "But you can't, Lucius Cornelius! Your ancestors were slaves like me!"

"No, they weren't," said Sulla, staring back. "I am a patrician Cornelius. The Senate is where I belong."

"I don't believe it!"

"It's the truth," said Sulla soberly. "That's why I can't avail myself of your offer, alluring though it is. When I do qualify for the Senate, I'm going to have to become a model of decorum—no actors, no mimes—and no pretty-boys." He clapped Metrobius on the back, and hugged him. "Now pay attention to the list, lad—and stop wriggling! It's not good for my concentration. Hercules Atlas is coming as a guest as well as performing, and that's final."

In fact, Hercules Atlas was among the first guests to arrive. Word of the revels to come had got out all up and down the street, of course, and the neighbors had steeled themselves to endure a night of howls, shrieks, loud music, and unimaginable crashes. As usual, it was a costume affair. Sulla had tricked himself out as the absent Clitumna, complete with fringed shawls, rings, and hennaed wig convoluted with sausagelike curls, and he constantly emitted uncanny imitations of her titters, her giggles, her loud whinnies of laughter. Since the guests knew her well, his performance was deeply appreciated.

Metrobius was equipped with wings again, but this night he was Icarus rather than Cupid, and had cleverly melted his large feathered fans along their outer edges, so that they drooped, and looked half-finished. Scylax came as Minerva, and contrived to make that stern, tomboyish goddess look like an old and over-made-up whore. When he saw how Metrobius hung all over Sulla, he proceeded to get drunk, and soon forgot how to manage his shield, his distaff, his stuffed owl, and his spear, and eventually tripped over them into a corner, where he wept himself to sleep.

Thus Scylax failed to see the endless succession of party turns, the singers who commenced with glorious melodies and stunning trills, and ended in warbling ditties like

> My sister Piggy Filler
> Got caught with Gus the Miller
> A-grinding of her flower
> Beneath the miller's tower.
> "Enough of this," said our dad.
> "It's clear that you've been had.
> Married you'd better be quick
> Or your arse will feel my stick!"

which were far more popular with the guests, who knew the words, and could sing along.

There were dancers who stripped to the buff with exquisite artistry, displaying pubes devoid of the smallest hair, and a man whose performing dogs could dance almost as well—if not as lubriciously—and a famous animal act from Antioch which consisted of a girl and her donkey—very, very popular with the audience, the male half of which was too intimidated by the donkey's endowments to proposition the girl afterward.

Hercules Atlas did his turn last of all, just before the party segregated into those too drunk to be interested in sex, and those drunk enough to be interested in nothing else. The revelers gathered around the colonnades of the peristyle-garden, in the midst of which Hercules Atlas had set himself up on a very sturdy dais. After warming up by bending a few iron bars and snapping a few thick logs like twigs, the strong man picked up squealing girls by the half dozen, piling them on his shoulders, on his head, and under each arm. Then he lifted an anvil or two in his hands and began to roar lustily, more fearsome than any lion in any arena. Actually he was having a wonderful time, for the wine was flowing down his throat like water down the Aqua Marcia, and his capacity to guzzle was as phenomenal as his strength. The trouble was, the more anvils he picked up, the more uncomfortable the girls became, until their squeals of joy became squeals of terror.

Sulla strolled out into the middle of the garden and tapped Hercules Atlas politely on his knee.

"Here, old fellow, do drop the girls," he said in the most friendly way. "You're squashing them with lumps of iron."

Hercules Atlas dropped the girls immediately. But he picked up Sulla instead, his hair-trigger temper let loose.

"Don't you tell me how to do my act!" he bellowed, and spun Sulla around his head like a priest of Isis his wand; wig, shawls, draperies fell from Sulla in a cascade.

Some of the partygoers began to panic; others decided to help by venturing out into the garden and pleading with the demented strong man to put Sulla down. But Hercules Atlas solved everyone's dilemma by shoving Sulla under his left arm as casually as a shopper a parcel, and leaving the festivities. There was no way he could be stopped. Ploughing through the bodies hurling themselves at him as if they were a cloud of gnats, he gave the door servant a shove in the face that sent him halfway across the atrium, and disappeared into the lane, still toting Sulla.

At the top of the Vestal Steps he halted. "All right? Did I do all right, Lucius Cornelius?" he asked, setting Sulla down very gently.

"You did perfectly," said Sulla, staggering a little because he was dizzy. "Come, I'll walk home with you."

"Not necessary," said Hercules Atlas, hitching up his lion skin and starting down the Vestal Steps. "Only a hop and a skip away from here, Lucius Cornelius, and the moon's just about full."

"I insist," said Sulla, catching him up.

"Have it your own way," shrugged Hercules Atlas.

"Well, it's less public if I pay you inside than out in the middle of the Forum," said Sulla patiently.

"Oh, right!" Hercules Atlas clapped a hand to his well-muscled head. "I forgot you haven't paid me yet. Come on, then."

He lived in four rooms on the third floor of an insula off the Clivus Orbius, on the fringes of the Subura, but in a better neighborhood by far. Ushered in, Sulla saw at a glance that his slaves had seized their opportunity and taken the night off, no doubt expecting that when their master came in, he would be in no state to take a head count. There did not seem to be a woman of the house, but Sulla checked anyway.

"Wife not here?" he asked.

Hercules Atlas spat. "Women! I hate 'em," he said.

A jug of wine and some cups stood on the table at which the two men seated themselves. Sulla pulled a fat purse from where he had secreted it inside a linen band around his waist. While Hercules Atlas poured two cups full of wine, Sulla loosened the strings holding the mouth of the purse shut, and deftly palmed a plump screw of paper he fished out of its interior. Then he tipped the purse up and sent a stream of bright silver coins tumbling across the tabletop. Too quickly; three or four rolled all the way to the far edge and fell to the floor, tinkling tinnily.

"Oh, hey!" cried Hercules Atlas, getting down on all fours to retrieve his pay.

While he was occupied in crawling about the floor, Sulla, taking his time, untwisted the paper he had palmed and tipped the white powder it contained into the further of the two cups; for want of any other instrument, he stirred the wine with his fingers until Hercules Atlas finally lumbered up from all fours to hind legs, and sat down.

"Good health," said Sulla, picking up the nearer cup and tipping it at the strong man in the friendliest manner.

"Good health and thanks for a terrific night," said Hercules Atlas, tilting his head back and his cup up, and draining it without pausing for breath. After which he refilled the cup and tossed a second drink back, it seemed on the same lungful of air.

Sulla got up, pushed his own cup under the strong man's hand, and took the other cup away, tucking it inside his tunic. "A little souvenir," he said. "Good night." And slipped out the door quietly.

The insula was asleep, its open concrete walkway around the central courtyard heavily screened to prevent refuse being tipped down the light well, and deserted. Very quickly and without making a sound, Sulla stole down three flights of stairs, and stepped into the narrow street unnoticed. The cup he had purloined went between the bars of a gutter drain; Sulla listened until he heard it splash far below, then thrust the screw of paper after it. At the Well of Juturna beneath the Vestal Steps he paused, dipped his hands and arms to the elbows in its still waters, and washed, and washed, and washed. There! That ought to rinse off whatever white powder might have adhered to his skin while he handled the paper and stirred the wine Hercules Atlas had devoured so satisfactorily.

But he didn't go back to the party. He bypassed the Palatine completely, heading up the Via Nova toward the Capena Gate. Outside the city he entered one of the many stables in the vicinity that hired out horses or vehicles to those resident inside Rome; few Roman houses kept mules, horses, transport. It was cheaper and easier to hire.

The stable he chose was good and reputable, but its idea of security was lax; the only groom in attendance was sound asleep in a mound of straw. Sulla assisted him into a far deeper sleep with a rabbit punch behind one ear, then took his time cruising up and down until he found a very strong-looking, amiable mule. Never having saddled a mount in his life, it took him some time to work out precisely what to do, but he had heard of an animal's holding its breath while the girth was being strapped tight, so he waited patiently until he was sure the mule's ribs were normal, then swung himself up into the saddle and kicked the beast gently in the flanks.

Though he was a novice rider, he wasn't afraid of horses or mules, and trusted to his luck in managing his mount. The four horns—one on each corner of the saddle—kept a man fairly securely upon the beast's back provided it wasn't prone to buck, and mules were more docile than horses in this respect. The only bridle he had managed to persuade the mule to take had a plain snaffle bit, but his steed seemed comfortable and placid chewing on it, so he headed down the moonlit Via Appia with every confidence in his ability to get quite a long way before morning. It was about midnight.

He found the ride exhausting, not being used to the activity. Ambling along beside Clitumna's litter was one thing, this hurried progress quite another. After a few miles his legs ached intolerably from hanging down unsupported, and his buttocks squirmed with the effort of keeping him straight in the saddle, and his balls felt every little jolt. However, the mule was a willing goer, and he got as far as Tripontium well before dawn.

From here he left the Via Appia and cut across country toward the coast, for there were a few rough roads traversing the bogs of the outer Pomptine Marshes, and it was much shorter—as well as much less public—than following the Via Appia down to Tarracina and then backtracking north to Circei. In a stand of trees some ten miles into the wilderness he stopped, for the ground felt dry and hard, and there didn't seem to be any mosquitoes. Tethering the mule on a long halter he had thought to purloin, he put the saddle down as a pillow under the shade of a pine, and slept dreamlessly.

Ten short daylight hours later, after giving himself and the mule a long drink in a nearby stream, Sulla resumed his ride. Covered from the gaze of any who might chance to see him by a hooded cloak he'd taken from the stable, he pattered along with considerably more grace than earlier, despite the ghastly ache in his spine and the deep soreness in rump and balls. So far he had eaten nothing, but felt no hunger; the mule had grazed on good grass, so was content enough, and remarkably fresh. And at dusk he came to the promontory on which sat Clitumna's villa, dismounting then with real relief. Once more he divested the mule of saddle and bridle; once more he tethered it so it could graze. But this time he left it by itself to rest.

His luck had held. The night was perfect, still and starry, not a cloud to be seen anywhere in the cold indigo vault. And then as the second hour of night began to drip away, the full moon rose over the hills far in the east and slowly drenched the landscape with its strange luminosity, a light which gave the eyes power to see, yet was of itself utterly invisible.

And the sense of his own inviolability swelled within Sulla, banished fatigue and pain, quickened the flow of his chilly blood and set his mind, curiously peacefully engaged, into a phase of sheer enjoyment. He was *felix;* he was lucky. Everything was going beautifully, and would continue to go beautifully. And that meant he could idle his way through in a haze of well-being; he could really *enjoy* himself. When the chance to rid himself of Nicopolis had presented itself so suddenly, so unexpectedly, there hadn't been time to enjoy it, only to make a lightning decision and wait out the hours. His investigations during his holiday with Metrobius had revealed The Destroyer to him, but Nicopolis it had been who chose the fashion of her own demise; he was involved only as catalyst. Luck had put her there. His luck. But tonight brain had put him where he was; luck would carry him through. As for fear—what was there to be afraid of?

Clitumna was there, waiting in the shadows of the salt pines, not yet impatient, but readying herself to turn impatient if her surprise was late. However, Sulla did not announce himself immediately; first he inspected the entire area to make sure she hadn't brought anyone with her. And yes, she was quite alone. Even the untenanted stables and rooms below the loggia were devoid of people, interested or uninterested.

As he approached her, he made enough noise to reassure her. Thus when she saw him emerge from the darkness she was prepared for it to be him, and held out her arms.

"Oh, it's just as you said!" she whispered, giggling into his neck. "My surprise! Where's my surprise?"

"A kiss first?" he asked, white teeth showing whiter than his skin for once, so strange was the moonlight, so magical the spell which bound him.

Starved for him, Clitumna offered her lips greedily. And was standing, her mouth glued to his, her feet up on their toes, when he broke her neck. It was so easy. Snap. Probably she never even knew, for he could see no hint of knowledge in her staring eyes when his hand pushed her head back to meet his other hand keeping her back straight, a movement as fast as a blow. Easy. Snap. The sound traveled, it was so sharp, so clear-cut on its edges. And as he released her, expecting her to sink to the ground, she rose up even higher on her toes and began to dance for him, arms akimbo, head lolling obscenely, jerks and hops and staccato heaves which culminated in her twirling round and round before she fell in a tangle of elbows and knees, ugly, utterly ungainly. The warm acrid smell of voided urine curled up to meet his distended nostrils then, and after it, the heavier stench of voided bowels.

He didn't scream. He didn't leap away. He enjoyed it all immensely, and while she danced for him, he watched in fascination, and when she fell, he watched in revulsion.

"Well, Clitumna," he said, "you died no lady."

It was necessary that he lift her, even though that meant he would be soiled, stained, smeared. There must be no marks in the tender moon-dewed grass, no sign of a body's being dragged—the main reason why he had stipulated that it be a fine night. So he lifted her, excrement and all, and carried her in his arms the short distance to the top of the cliff, her draperies gathered close to keep in the excrement, for he didn't want a trail of faeces across the grass either.

He had already found the right spot, and went to it without faltering because he had marked it with a pale stone days before, when he first brought her down. His muscles bunched, spasmed; in one beautiful drapery tracery he rejected her forever, threw her out and away in a flapping ghost-bird plummet all the way down to the rocks. There she spread herself, a shapeless drift of something the sea might have washed up beyond the reach of all but the wildest storms. For it was vital that she be found; he wanted no estate in limbo.

As at dawn, he had tethered the mule near running water, but before he went to bring it to drink, he waded into the stream fully clad in his woman's tunic, and washed away the last traces of his stepmother, Clitumna. After which there was one more thing to do, which he did the moment he left the water. On his belt was a small dagger in a sheath; using its pointed tip, he cut a very small gash in the skin of his left forehead about an inch below the hairline. It began to bleed immediately, as scalp cuts do, but that was only the start. Nothing about it could look neat or even. So he got the middle and ring fingers of each hand on either side of the nick and pulled until the flesh parted raggedly, considerably enlarging the wound. His bleeding increased dramatically, spattering his filthy, running-wet party garb in huge drops and runs that spread through the soaked fabric in a wonderfully gory way. There! Good! Out of his belt pouch he took a prepared pad of white linen and jammed it down hard on the tear in his brow, then bound it tightly with a ribbon of linen. Blood had run down into his left eye; he wiped it away with one hand, blinking, and then went to find the mule.

All through the night he rode, kicking the mule ruthlessly onward whenever it faltered, for it was very tired. However, it knew it was heading home to its stall, and, like all its kind, had a better heart and stouter sinews than a horse. It liked Sulla; that was the secret of its gallant response. It liked the comfort of the snaffle bit in a mouth more used to the pain of curbs; it liked his silence and economy; it liked his peacefulness. So for his sake it trotted, cantered, fell to a walk, picked up its stride again as soon as it was able, the steam rising from its shaggy coat in little trails that drifted behind them. For it knew nothing of the woman lying, neck broken ahead of her fall, on the cruel rocks below the great white villa. It took Sulla as it found him, and it found him interestingly kind.

A mile from the stables Sulla dismounted and removed the tack from the mule, throwing it aside into some bushes; then he smacked the animal on its rump and shooed it in the direction of its stables, sure it would find its way home. But when he began to plod toward the Capena Gate the mule followed him, and he was forced in the end to shy stones at it before it took the hint, swished its meager tail, and made off.

Muffled in his hooded cloak, Sulla entered Rome just as the eastern sky was pearling; in nine hours of seventy-four minutes each he had ridden from Circei to Rome, no mean feat for a tired mule and a man who had only really learned to ride on the journey.

The Steps of Cacus led from the Circus Maximus up onto the Germalus of the Palatine, and were surrounded by the most hallowed ground—the spirit of Romulus's original city lived thereabouts, and a small uninspiring cavelet and spring in the rock was the place where the she-wolf had suckled the twins Romulus and Remus after they had been abandoned. To Sulla, this seemed a fitting place to abandon his trappings, so the cloak and the bandage were carefully tucked into a hollow tree behind the monument to the Genius Loci. His wound immediately began to bleed again, but sluggishly; and thus those in Clitumna's street who were out and about early were stunned to see the missing man come staggering along in a bloodied woman's tunic, filthy and mauled.

Clitumna's household was astir, not having been to bed all at once since Hercules Atlas had blazed his way out of the place some thirty-two hours before. When the door servant admitted

Sulla, looking ghastly, people flew from all directions to succor him. He was put to bed, bathed and sponged, none other than Athenodorus of Sicily was summoned to inspect his wounded head, and Gaius Julius Caesar came from next door to ask him what had happened, for the whole of the Palatine had been searching for him.

"Tell me what you can," said Caesar, sitting by his bed.

Sulla looked totally convincing. There was a blue shade of pain and weariness about his lips, his colorless skin was even paler than usual, and his eyes, glazed with exhaustion, were red-rimmed and bloodshot.

"Silly," he said, slurring his words. "I shouldn't have tried to interfere with Hercules Atlas. But I'm strong, and I can look after myself. I just never counted on any man's being as strong as he turned out to be—I thought he'd got a good act together, was all. He was roaring drunk, and he—he just—carried me away with him! I couldn't do a thing to stop him. Somewhere or other he put me down. I tried to get away, and he must have clouted me, I really don't know. But I came to in some alley in the Subura. I must have lain there, out to it, for at least a whole day. But you know what the Subura's like—everyone left me to it. When I could move, I came home. That's all, Gaius Julius."

"You're a very lucky young man," said Caesar, lips tight. "Had Hercules Atlas carried you back to his flat, you might have shared his fate."

"His fate?"

"Your steward came to see me yesterday when you didn't come home, and asked me what he should do. After I learned the story, I took some hired gladiators to the strong man's lodgings, and found an absolute shambles. For whatever reason, Hercules Atlas had wrecked the place—splintered every piece of furniture, broken great holes in the walls with his fists, terrified the other residents of his insula so much that none of them had gone near. He was lying in the middle of the living room, dead. My personal belief is that he ruptured a blood vessel in his brain, and went mad with the agony of it. Either that, or some enemy poisoned him." An expression of distaste hovered on Caesar's face, and was resolutely ironed away. "He'd made a disgusting mess in dying. I think his servants found him first, but they'd gone long before I arrived. As we found no money whatsoever in the place, I presume they took whatever they could carry with them, and have run away. Did he, for instance, have a fee from your party? If so, it wasn't in the flat."

Sulla closed his eyes, not needing to feign tiredness. "I had paid him in advance, Gaius Julius, so I can't tell you if he had money there."

Caesar got to his feet. "Well, I have done all that I can." He looked down on the immobile figure in the bed sternly, knowing his look was wasted, for Sulla's eyes remained closed. "I do pity you deeply, Lucius Cornelius," he said, "but this conduct cannot go on, you know. My daughter nearly starved herself to death because of an immature emotional attachment to you, and has not even now recovered from that attachment. Which makes you a considerable nuisance to me as a neighbor, though I have to acquit you of encouraging my daughter, and must be fair enough to admit that she has made a considerable nuisance of herself to you. All of which suggests to me that you would do better if you lived elsewhere. I have sent to your stepmother in Circei and informed her what has transpired in her absence. I also informed her that she has long outworn her welcome in this street, and she might be more comfortable housed on the Carinae or the Caelian. We are a quiet body of people hereabouts. It would pain me to have to lodge a complaint—and a suit—with the urban praetor to protect our entitlement to peace, quiet, and physical well-being. But pain or no, I am prepared to lodge that suit if I have to, Lucius Cornelius. Like the rest of your neighbors, I have had enough."

Sulla didn't move, didn't open his eyes; as Caesar stood wondering how much of this homily had sunk in, his ears heard a snore. He turned at once and left.

But it was Sulla who got a letter from Circei first, not Gaius Julius Caesar. The next day a messenger came bearing a missive from Clitumna's steward, informing Sulla that the lady Clitumna's body had been found at the base of the cliff bordering her estate. Her neck had been broken in the fall, but there were no suspicious circumstances. As Sulla knew, said the steward, the lady Clitumna's mental state had been extremely depressed of late.

Sulla swung his legs out of bed and stood up.

"Run me a bath, and set out my toga," he said.

The little wound on his brow was healing nicely, but its edges were livid and swollen still; aside from that, there was nothing left to suggest his condition of the day before.

"Send for Gaius Julius Caesar," he said to Iamus the steward when he was dressed.

On this coming interview, Sulla understood with perfect clarity, all of his future hinged. Thank the gods that Scylax had taken Metrobius home from the party, protest though the lad did that he wanted to see what had happened to his beloved Sulla. That, and Caesar's early arrival on the scene, represented the only flaws in Sulla's plans. What an escape! Truly his luck was in its ascendancy! The presence of Metrobius in Clitumna's house when Caesar had been summoned by the worried Iamus would have cooked Sulla's goose forever. No, Caesar would never damn Sulla on hearsay, but the evidence of his own eyes would have put an entirely different complexion upon the situation. And Metrobius would not have been backward in coming forward. I am treading on eggshells, said Sulla to himself, and it is high time I stopped. He thought of Stichus, of Nicopolis, of Clitumna, and he smiled. Well, now he *could* stop.

He received Caesar looking every inch the patrician Roman, immaculate in white, the narrow knight's stripe adorning the right shoulder of his tunic, his magnificent head of hair cut and combed into a manly yet becoming style.

"I apologize for having to drag you here yet again, Gaius Julius," said Sulla, and handed Caesar a small roll of paper. "This has just arrived from Circei, and I thought you ought to see it at once."

Without a change of expression Caesar read it very slowly, his lips moving, but the sound of the words he said over to himself very quiet. He was weighing, Sulla knew, each and every word as he separated it from the uninterrupted flow of letters on the paper. Done, he laid the sheet down.

"It is the third death," said Caesar, and actually seemed happy about that fact. "Your household is sadly diminished, Lucius Cornelius. Please accept my condolences."

"I presumed that you had made Clitumna's will for her," Sulla said, standing very straight, "otherwise I assure you that I would not have bothered you."

"Yes, I have made several wills for her, the last one just after Nicopolis died." His handsome face, his direct blue eyes, everything about Caesar was carefully, legally noncommittal. "I would like you to tell me, Lucius Cornelius, what exactly you felt for your stepmother."

Here it was, the frailest eggshell yet. He must tread as surely and delicately as a cat on a windowsill strewn with broken shards a full twelve floors above the pavement. "I remember saying something to you before, Gaius Julius," he said, "but I'm glad to have the opportunity to speak at greater length about her. She was a very silly and stupid and vulgar woman, but as it happens, I was fond of her. My father"—and Sulla's face twisted—"was an incurable drunkard. The only life I ever remember with him—and for some years with my older sister too, until she married and escaped—was a nightmare. We were not impoverished gentry, Gaius Julius. We didn't live in a style in any way reminiscent of our origins. We were so poor we had no slave, not one. If it hadn't been for the charity of an old marketplace teacher, I, a patrician of the *gens* Cornelius, would not even have learned to read and write. I have never done my basic military training on the Campus Martius, nor learned to ride a horse, nor been the pupil of some advocate in the law courts. Of soldiering, of rhetoric, of public life, I know nothing. Such did my father do to me. And so—I was fond of her. She married my father, and she took him and me to live with her, and who knows? Perhaps, had my father and I gone on living in the Subura, I would one day have gone quite mad, and murdered him, and offended the gods beyond mercy. As it was, until he died she took the brunt of him, and I was liberated. Yes, I was fond of her."

"She was fond of you too, Lucius Cornelius," said Caesar. "Her will is simple and straightforward. It leaves everything she had to you."

Easy, easy! Not too much joy, but not too much grief either! The man he was facing was very intelligent and must have great experience of men.

"Did she leave me enough to enter the Senate?" he asked, looking into Caesar's eyes.

"More than enough."

Sulla visibly sagged. "I—can't—believe it!" he said. "Are you sure? I know she had this house and the villa at Circei, but I didn't think there was much else."

"On the contrary, she was an extremely wealthy woman— money invested, stocks and interests in all kinds of companies, as well as in a dozen merchant ships. I advise you to divest yourself of the ships and the company shares, and use the funds they realize to buy property. You'll need to have your affairs in exquisite order to satisfy the censors."

"It's a dream!" said Sulla.

"I can understand that you must find it so, Lucius Cornelius. But rest assured, it's all real enough." Caesar sounded tranquil, not repelled by Sulla's reaction, nor suspicious of feigned grief his common sense would have told him a Lucius Cornelius Sulla could never feel for a Clitumna, no matter how kind to his father she might have been.

"She might have gone on for years and years," said Sulla, voice wondering. "Mine is a happy fate after all, Gaius Julius. I never thought to be able to say that. I shall miss her. But I hope that in the years to come, the world will say that the greatest contribution she made to it was in her dying. For I intend to be an ornament to my class and to the Senate." Did that sound all right? Did it imply what he intended it to imply?

"I agree, Lucius Cornelius, that it would make her happy to

think you used her bequest fruitfully," said Caesar, taking what Sulla said exactly the right way. "And I trust there will be no more wild parties? No more dubious friends?"

"When a man can espouse the life his birth entitles him to, Gaius Julius, there is no need for wild parties or dubious friends." Sulla sighed. "They were a way of passing the time. I daresay that must seem inexplicable to you. But the life I have lived for over thirty years has hung on my neck like a huge millstone."

"Of course it has," said Caesar.

A horrifying thought occurred to Sulla. "But there are no censors! What can I do?"

"Well, though there is no need to elect more until four more years have elapsed, one of the conditions Marcus Scaurus put upon his voluntary resignation—such as it was—was that new censors be elected next April. You will just have to contain yourself until then," Caesar said comfortably.

Sulla girded himself, drew a deep breath. "Gaius Julius, I have one further request to make of you," he said.

The blue eyes held an expression Sulla found impossible to fathom, as if Caesar knew what was coming—yet how could that be, when the idea had just popped into his mind? The most brilliant idea yet, the luckiest. For if Caesar consented, Sulla's application to the censors would have far greater weight than mere money, far greater effect than the claim of birth, marred as it was by the kind of life he had led.

"What request is that, Lucius Cornelius?" asked Caesar.

"That you consider me as a husband for your daughter Julilla," he said.

"Even after she injured you so?"

"I—love her," said Sulla, and believed he meant it.

"At the moment Julilla is nowhere near well enough to contemplate marriage," said Caesar, "but I will take note of your request, Lucius Cornelius." He smiled. "Perhaps you deserve each other, after so much trouble."

"She gave me a grass crown," said Sulla. "And do you know, Gaius Julius, it was only after that my luck turned?"

"I believe you." Rising, he prepared to go. "Nonetheless, for the moment we will say nothing to anyone of your interest in marrying Julilla. Most particularly, I charge you to stay away from her. However you feel about her, she is still trying to find her way out of her predicament, and I want no easy solution presented to her."

Sulla accompanied Caesar to the door, and there held out his hand, smiling with his lips closed; for no one knew the effect of those overlong and oversharp canines better than their owner. Not for Gaius Julius Caesar any nasty chilling grins. No, Caesar was to be treasured and courted. Ignorant of the proposition Caesar had once put to Gaius Marius about a daughter, Sulla had come to the same conclusion. What better way to endear himself to the censors—and the electorate—than to have a Julia as his wife? Especially when there was one so close to hand she had nearly died for him.

"Iamus!" Sulla called when he had shut the door.

"Lucius Cornelius?"

"Don't bother with dinner. Put the house into mourning for the lady Clitumna, and see to the return of all her servants from Circei. I'm leaving at once to see to her funeral."

And, thought Sulla, packing quickly, I shall take young Metrobius with me, and say goodbye. Goodbye to every last trace of the old life, goodbye to Clitumna. None of it will I miss save Metrobius. And him I will miss. Badly.

THE THIRD YEAR
(108 B.C.):

In the Consulship of
Servius Sulpicius Galba
and
Quintus Hortensius

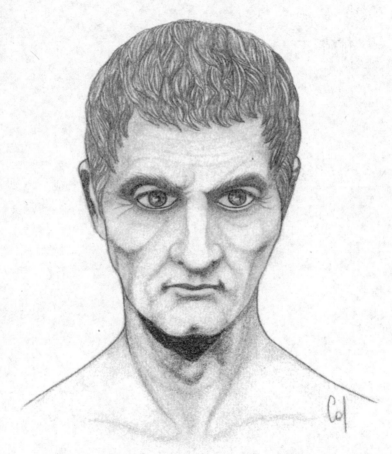

QUINTUS CAECILIUS METELLUS NUMIDICUS

With the coming of the winter rains, the war—such as it had been so far—against Numidia ground to a cheerless halt, neither side able to deploy its troops. Gaius Marius received his letter from his father-in-law, Caesar, and thought about what it contained, and wondered if the consul Quintus Caecilius Metellus Piggle-wiggle knew that he would become proconsul when the New Year arrived, his command successfully prorogued, a future triumph assured. Nor did anyone in the governor's headquarters at Utica mention the defeat of Marcus Junius Silanus by the Germans, or the loss of all those troops.

Which didn't mean, thought Marius resentfully, that these items were not known to Metellus; only that, as usual, his senior legate Gaius Marius would be the last man to be told. Poor Rutilius Rufus had been given the job of supervising the winter border garrisons, which put him out of touch with any developments short of the renewal of war; and Gaius Marius, recalled to duty in Utica, found himself the subordinate of Metellus Piggle-wiggle's *son!* That young man, all of twenty years old and a cadet in his father's personal train, enjoyed the task of commanding Utica's garrison and defenses, so that in any matter to do with Utica's military dispositions, Marius had to defer to the insufferably arrogant Piglet, as he soon came to be called—and not by Marius alone. Utica as a fortress aside, Marius's duties involved doing all the chores the governor didn't want to do—duties more suited to a quaestor than a senior legate.

Feelings in consequence were running high, and Marius's self-control was rapidly eroding, especially when Metellus Piglet amused himself at Marius's expense, something he liked to do now that his father had indicated it amused him too. The near defeat on the river Muthul had provoked both Rutilius Rufus and Marius into angry criticism of the general, and led Marius to tell him that the best way to win the war against Numidia was to capture Jugurtha himself.

"How can I do that?" Metellus had asked, sufficiently chastened by his first battle to listen.

"By subterfuge," Rutilius Rufus had said.

"What kind of subterfuge?"

"That," said Gaius Marius in conclusion, "you will have to work out for yourself, Quintus Caecilius."

But now that everyone was safely back in Africa Province enduring the boredom of wet days and routine tasks, Metellus Piggle-wiggle kept his own counsel. Until, that is, he made contact with a Numidian nobleman named Nabdalsa, and was obliged to call Marius into his interview with the man.

"Why?" asked Marius bluntly. "Can't do your own dirty work, Quintus Caecilius?"

"Believe me, Gaius Marius, if Publius Rutilius were here, I wouldn't be using you!" snapped Metellus. "But you know Jugurtha where I don't, and presumably that means you know a little more than I do about how Numidian minds work! All I want you to do is sit and watch this Nabdalsa, and tell me afterward what you think."

"I'm surprised you trust me enough to think I'll give you an honest opinion," said Marius.

Metellus raised his brows, genuinely taken aback. "You are here to fight against Numidia, Gaius Marius, why shouldn't you give me an honest opinion?"

"Then bring the fellow in, Quintus Caecilius, and I'll do my best to oblige."

Marius knew of Nabdalsa, though he had never met him; he was an adherent of the legitimate claimant to the Numidian throne, Prince Gauda, who was at present living in quasi-regal state not far from Utica, in the flourishing township which had grown up on the site of Old Carthage. Thus Nabdalsa had come from Prince Gauda in Old Carthage, and was received by Metellus in frosty audience.

Metellus explained himself; the best and quickest way to solve the Numidian question and put Prince Gauda on the throne was to effect the capture of Jugurtha himself. Did Prince Gauda—or Nabdalsa—have any idea how the capture of Jugurtha might be effected?

"Through Bomilcar, *dominus,* definitely," said Nabdalsa.

Metellus stared. "*Bomilcar?* But he's Jugurtha's half brother, his loyalest baron!"

"At the moment relations between them are rather strained," said Nabdalsa.

"Why?" asked Metellus.

"It's a question of the succession, *dominus.* Bomilcar wants to be designated regent in the event that anything should happen to Jugurtha, but Jugurtha refuses to consider it."

"Regent, not heir?"

"Bomilcar knows he could never be heir, *dominus.* Jugurtha has two sons. However, they are very young."

Frowning, Metellus tried to plumb the thought processes of alien minds. "Why is Jugurtha opposed? I should have thought that Bomilcar would represent an ideal choice."

"It is the bloodline, *dominus,*" said Nabdalsa. "Baron Bomilcar is not descended from King Masinissa, so does not belong to the royal house."

"I see." Metellus straightened. "Very well, then, see what you can do to persuade Bomilcar that he ought to ally himself with Rome." He turned to Marius. "How amazing! One would have thought that a man not noble enough to claim the throne would be the ideal choice for a regent."

"In our kind of society, yes," said Marius. "In Jugurtha's it's an invitation to murder of his sons. For how else could Bomilcar ascend the throne than by killing Jugurtha's heirs and founding a new dynasty?"

Metellus turned back to Nabdalsa. "I thank you, Baron Nabdalsa. You may go."

But Nabdalsa was not ready to go. "*Dominus,* I crave a small favor," he said.

"What?" asked Metellus, none too pleased.

"Prince Gauda is anxious to meet you, and wonders why he has not yet been offered the opportunity. Your year as governor of Africa Province is almost over, yet still Prince Gauda waits for an invitation to meet you."

"If he wants to meet me, what's to stop him?" asked the governor blankly.

"He cannot just present himself, Quintus Caecilius," said Marius. "You must extend a formal invitation."

"Oh! Well, if that's all there is to it, an invitation will be extended," said Metellus, hiding his smile.

And, the invitation duly extended the very next day, so that Nabdalsa could bear it back personally to Old Carthage, Prince Gauda came to call on the governor.

It was not a happy meeting; two more different men than Gauda and Metellus scarcely lived. Weak and sickly and not very bright, Gauda behaved in the manner he considered proper, and Metellus considered atrociously high-handed. For, having learned that an invitation must be extended before the royal guest in Old Carthage could come calling, Metellus assumed his visitor would be humble, even obsequious. Far from it. Gauda started proceedings off by flying into a temper when Metellus didn't rise to greet him, and ended the audience not many moments later by stalking out of the governor's presence.

"I am *royalty*!" Gauda bleated to Nabdalsa afterward.

"Everyone knows that, your Highness," soothed Nabdalsa. "However, the Romans are very odd about royalty. They regard themselves as superior to it because they deposed their kings many hundreds of years ago, and have chosen ever since to rule themselves without benefit of kings."

"I don't care if they worship shit!" said Gauda, his lacerated feelings still smarting. "I am my father's legitimate son, where Jugurtha is his bastard! And when I appear among these Romans, they should rise to greet me, they should bow down before me, they should give me a throne to sit on, and they should cull their soldiers for the hundred finest specimens and give them to me as a bodyguard!"

"True, true," said Nabdalsa. "I will see Gaius Marius. Perhaps Gaius Marius will be able to bring Quintus Caecilius to his senses."

Everyone Numidian knew about Gaius Marius and Publius Rutilius Rufus, for Jugurtha had spread their fame in the days when he had first returned from Numantia, and had seen both of them frequently during his recent visit to Rome.

"Then see Gaius Marius," said Gauda, and retired in a monumental huff back to Old Carthage, there to brood upon the wrongs done him by Metellus in Rome's name, while Nabdalsa unobtrusively sought an interview with Gaius Marius.

"I'll do what I can, Baron," said Marius, sighing.

"*I* would appreciate it, Gaius Marius," said Nabdalsa with feeling.

Marius grinned. "Your royal master taking it out on you, is he?"

Nabdalsa's answer was a speaking look.

"The trouble is, my friend, that Quintus Caecilius considers himself infinitely better born than any Numidian prince. I very much doubt that anyone, especially I, could convince him to change his tune. But I'll try, because I want you free to seek out Bomilcar. That's a lot more important than squabbles between governors and princes," said Marius.

"The Syrian prophetess says that the family Caecilius Metellus is riding for a fall," said Nabdalsa thoughtfully.

"Syrian prophetess?"

"A woman called Martha," said the Numidian. "Prince Gauda found her in Old Carthage, where it seems she was abandoned some years ago by a sea captain who believed she had successfully put a curse upon his ship. At first only the humble consulted her, but now her fame is very large, and Prince Gauda has taken her into his court. She has prophesied that Prince Gauda will indeed become King of Numidia, after the fall of Jugurtha. Though that fall, she says, will not be yet."

"And what about the family Caecilius Metellus?"

"She says the whole family Caecilius Metellus is past the zenith of its power, and will grow less in number and less in wealth, surpassed by—among others—you yourself, *dominus*."

"I want to see this Syrian prophetess," said Marius.

"It can be arranged. But you must come to Old Carthage, for she will not leave Prince Gauda's house," said Nabdalsa.

An audience with Martha the Syrian prophetess involved an audience with Prince Gauda first; resignedly Marius listened to the litany of complaints about Metellus, and made promises he hadn't the faintest idea how he was going to keep.

"Rest assured, your Highness, that when I am in a position to do so, I will make sure you are treated with all the respect and deference to which your birth entitles you," he said, bowing as low as even Gauda could have wished.

"That day will come!" said Gauda eagerly, grinning to reveal very bad teeth. "Martha says you will be the First Man in Rome, and before very long. For that reason, Gaius Marius, I wish to enroll myself among your clients, and I will make sure that my supporters in the Roman African province also enroll themselves as your clients. What is more, when I am King of Numidia, the whole of Numidia will be in your clientship."

To this Marius listened amazed; he, a mere praetor, was being offered the kind of clients even a Caecilius Metellus might long for in vain! Oh, he had to meet this Martha, this Syrian prophetess!

Not many moments later he was given the chance, for she had asked to see him, and Gauda had him conducted to her apartments within the huge villa he was using as a temporary palace. A cursory glance was enough to assure Marius, bidden wait in her sitting room, that she was indeed held in high esteem, for the apartment was fabulously furnished, its walls painted with some of the finest murals he had ever been privileged to see, and its floors paved with mosaics equally as good as the murals.

When she came in she was wearing purple, another signal honor not normally accorded to one whose birth was not royal. And royal she certainly was not. A little, shriveled, skinny old lady who stank of stale urine and whose hair hadn't been washed in what Marius suspected were literal years. She looked foreign, great beaky thin-bladed nose dominating a face of a thousand wrinkles, and a pair of black eyes whose light was as fierce and proud and vigilant as any eagle's. Her breasts had sagged like two empty socks with toes full of pebbles, and swung visibly beneath the thin Tyrian purple shift which was all she wore above the waist. A Tyrian purple shawl was tied about her hips, her hands and feet were almost black with henna, and she tinkled when she walked from a myriad of bells, bracelets, rings, and trinkets, all of solid gold. Secured by a solid gold comb, a gauze veil of Tyrian purple covered the back of her head and fell over her spine like a windless flag.

"Sit down, Gaius Marius," she said, pointing at a chair with one long-taloned finger, its gnarled length glittering from the many rings adorning it.

Marius did as he was told, unable to take his eyes from her ancient brown face. "Prince Gauda tells me that you have said I will be the First Man in Rome," he said, and was forced to clear his throat. "I would like to hear more."

She actually began to cackle a classic crone's cackle, revealing gums toothless save for one yellowed incisor in her upper jaw. "Oh, yes, I'm sure you would," she said, and clapped her hands for a servant. "Bring us an infusion of the dried leaves and some of those little cakes I like," she ordered. Then to Gaius Marius she said, "It won't be long. When it comes, we will talk. Until then, we will sit in silence."

Not willing to offend her, he sat as he was bidden—in silence—and, when the steaming brew came, sipped at the cup of it she gave him, his nose suspicious, his instincts wary. It didn't taste too bad, but as he wasn't used to hot drinks, he burned his tongue and put the cup aside. She, clearly an expert, took birdlike sips at her own cup, downing each one with an audible gulp of pleasure.

"Delicious stuff, though I daresay you'd prefer wine."

"No, not at all," he murmured politely.

"Have a cake," she mumbled, mouth full.

"Thank you, but no."

"All right, all right, I can take a hint!" she said, and rinsed her mouth with another draft of the hot liquid. Out came one claw imperiously. "Give me your right hand."

He gave. She took.

"Yours is a great destiny, Gaius Marius," she said, eyes devouring the multiplicity of creases in his palm. "What a hand! It shapes whatever it puts itself to. And what a head line! It rules your heart, it rules your life, it rules everything except the ravages of time, Gaius Marius, for those no one can withstand. But you will withstand much that other men cannot. There is a terrible illness. . . . But you will overcome it the first time it appears, and even the second time. . . . There are enemies, enemies by the score. . . . But you will overcome them. . . . You will be consul the year after this one just beginning, which is to say, next year. . . . And after that, you will be consul six more times. . . . Seven times in all will you be consul, and you will be called the Third Founder of Rome, for you will save Rome from the greatest of all her perils!"

He was conscious of his face burning, burning, hot as a spear thrust into the fire. And of a whirling roaring inside his head. Of his heart pounding away like a *hortator* drumming at ramming speed. Of a thick red veil in front of his eyes. For she spoke the truth. He knew it.

"You have the love and respect of a great woman," Martha went on, pawing now at the minor folds in his skin, "and her nephew will be the greatest of all the Romans for all time."

"No, that's me," he said at once, his bodily responses calming into normality at this less palatable piece of news.

"No, it's her nephew," said Martha stubbornly. "A much greater man than you, Gaius Marius. He has the same first name as you, Gaius. But his family is her family, not yours."

The fact was filed; he would not forget it. "What of my son?" he asked.

"Your son will be a great man too. But not as great as his father, nor will he live nearly as long in the number of his years. However, he will still be alive when your time comes."

She pushed his hand away and tucked her dirty bare feet—toes a-tinkle with bells, ankles a-clash with bracelets—under her on the couch where she sat.

"I have seen all there is to see, Gaius Marius," she said, leaned back, and closed her eyes.

"I thank you, Martha Prophetess," he said, getting to his feet and pulling out his purse. "How much . . . ?"

She opened her eyes, wickedly black, evilly alive. "For you there is no fee. It is enough to be in the company of the truly great. Fees are for the likes of Prince Gauda, who will never be a great man, though he will be a king." Came the cackle again. "But you know that, Gaius Marius, as surely as I do, for all that you have no gift to look into the future. Your gift is to see into the hearts of men, and Prince Gauda has a small heart."

"Then once again I must thank you."

"Oh, I do have a favor to ask of you," she called to his back as he went to the door.

He turned immediately. "Yes?"

"When you are consul for the second time, Gaius Marius, bring me to Rome and treat me with honor. I have a wish to see Rome before I die."

"You shall see Rome," he said, and left her.

Consul seven times! The First Man in Rome! The Third Founder of Rome! What greater destiny could there be than that? How could another Roman surpass that? Gaius . . . She must mean the son of his younger brother-in-law, Gaius Julius Caesar Junior. Yes, his son would be Julia's nephew—the only one to be named Gaius, certainly.

"Over my dead body," said Gaius Marius, and climbed on his horse to ride back to Utica.

He sought an interview with Metellus the next day, and found the consul poring over a sheaf of documents and letters from Rome, for a ship had come in overnight, long delayed by stormy seas.

"Excellent news, Gaius Marius!" said Metellus, for once affable. "My command in Africa is prorogued, with proconsular imperium, and every likelihood of continued prorogation should I need more time." That sheet of paper was dropped, another picked up, both for show, since he had obviously read them before Marius arrived; no one just scanned words on paper in silence and with a lightning glance of comprehension, for they had to be disentangled from each other and read aloud to aid the disentanglement process.

"It is just as well my army is intact, because it seems the general shortage of manpower in Italy has become acute, thanks to Silanus in Gaul. Oh, you don't know about that, do you? Yes, my consular colleague was defeated by the Germans. Shocking loss of life." He grabbed at another roll, held it up. "Silanus writes that there were upward of half a million German giants on the field." Down went the scroll, the one he still held was brandished at Marius. "Here is the Senate notifying me that it has nullified the *lex Sempronia* of Gaius Gracchus limiting the numbers of campaigns a man must complete. High time! We can call up thousands of veterans if ever we need them." Metellus sounded pleased.

"That is a very bad piece of legislation," said Marius. "If a veteran wishes to retire, after ten years *or* six full campaigns, he should be entitled to do so without fear that he will ever again be mustered under the colors. We are eroding the smallholders, Quintus Caecilius! How *can* a man leave his little farm for what might now be twenty years of service in the legions, and expect to see it prosper in his absence? How can he sire sons to take his place, both on his little farm and in our legions? More and more it has become the duty of his barren wife to oversee their land, and women do not have the strength, the foresight, or the aptitude. We should be looking elsewhere for our soldiers—and we should be protecting them against bad generalship!"

Metellus had pokered up, lips thin. "It is not your place, Gaius Marius, to criticize the wisdom of the most illustrious governing body in our society!" he said. "Just who *do* you think you are?"

"I believe you once told me who I was, Quintus Caecilius, very many years ago. As I remember, an Italian hayseed with no Greek was how you put it. And that may be true. But it does not disqualify me from commenting upon what I still deem a very bad

piece of legislation," said Marius, keeping his voice even. "We—
and by 'we' I mean the Senate, of which illustrious body I am no
less a member than you!—are allowing a whole class of citizens
to die out because we haven't got the courage or the presence of
mind to put a stop to all these so-called generals we've been fielding now for years! The blood of Roman soldiers is not for wasting, Quintus Caecilius, it's for living and healthy use!"

Marius got to his feet, leaning across Metellus's desk, and continued his diatribe. "When we originally designed our army, it was
for campaigns within Italy, so that men could go home again each
winter, and manage their farms, and sire their sons, and supervise
their women. But when a man enlists or is levied nowadays, he's
shipped overseas, and instead of a campaign lasting a single summer, it runs into years during which he never manages to go home,
so that his six campaigns might take him twelve or even fifteen
years to complete—in some place other than his homeland! Gaius
Gracchus legislated to try to curtail that, and to stop the smallholdings of Italy becoming the prey of big-time speculating graziers!" He drew a sobbing breath, eyed Metellus ironically. "Oh,
but I forgot, didn't I, Quintus Caecilius? You're one of those
big-time speculating graziers yourself, aren't you? And how you
do love to see the smallholdings fall into your grasp because the
men who ought to be home running them are dying on some foreign field through sheer aristocratic greed and carelessness!"

"Aha! Now we come to it!" cried Metellus, jumping to his feet
and thrusting his face into Marius's. "There it is! Aristocratic
greed and carelessness, eh? It's the aristocrat sticks in your craw,
isn't it? Well, let me tell you a thing or two, Gaius Marius Upstart! Marrying a Julia of the Julians can't turn you into an aristocrat!"

"I wouldn't want it to," snarled Marius. "I despise the lot of
you—save for the single exception of my father-in-law, who by
some miracle has managed to remain a decent man in spite of his
ancestry!"

Their voices had risen to shouts long since, and in the outer
office all ears were turned their way.

"Go to it, Gaius Marius!" said a tribune of the soldiers.

"Hit him where it hurts, Gaius Marius!" said another.

"Piss all over the arrogant *fellator,* Gaius Marius!" said a third, grinning.

Which made it manifest that everyone liked Gaius Marius a great deal more than they liked Quintus Caecilius Metellus, all the way down to the ranker soldiers.

But the shouting had penetrated even further than the outer office; when the consul's son, Quintus Caecilius Metellus Junior, burst in, the consul's staff tried to look all efficiency and busy activity. Without sparing them a glance, Metellus Piglet opened the door to his father's room.

"Father, your voices can be heard for miles!" said the young man, casting a glare of loathing at Marius.

He was very like his father physically, of average height and size, brown-haired, brown-eyed, modestly good-looking in a Roman way, and having nothing about him to make him stand out in a Roman crowd.

The interruption sobered Metellus, though it did little to diminish Marius's rage. Neither of the antagonists made any move to sit down again. Young Metellus Piglet stood to one side, alarmed and upset, passionately devoted to his father but out of his depth, especially when he bethought himself of the indignities he had heaped upon the head of Gaius Marius ever since his father had appointed him commander of the Utica garrison. For he now saw for the first time a different Gaius Marius: physically enormous, of a bravery and courage and intelligence beyond the capacity of any Caecilius Metellus.

"I see no point in continuing this conversation, Gaius Marius," said Metellus, hiding the trembling of his hands by pressing them, palms down, on the desk. "What did you come to see me about, anyway?"

"I came to tell you that I intend to leave service in this war at the end of next summer," Marius said. "I'm going back to Rome to seek election as consul."

Metellus looked as if he couldn't believe his ears. "You are *what*?"

"I'm going to Rome to contest the consular elections."

"No, you are not," said Metellus. "You signed on as my senior legate—and with a propraetor's imperium at that!—for the duration of my term as governor of Africa Province. My term has just been extended. Which means so has yours."

"You can release me."

"If I wish to release you. But I do not wish to," said Metellus. "In fact, if I had my way, Gaius Marius, I'd bury you here in the provinces for the rest of your life!"

"Don't make me do anything nasty, Quintus Caecilius," Marius said, in quite a friendly voice.

"Make you do anything *what*? Oh, get out of here, Marius! Go and do something useful—stop wasting my time!" Metellus caught his son's eye and grinned at him like a conspirator.

"I insist that I be released from service in this war so that I may stand for consul in Rome this coming autumn."

Emboldened by his father's growing air of lordly and indifferent superiority, Metellus Piglet began to break into muffled giggles, which fueled his father's wit.

"I tell you what, Gaius Marius," he said, smiling, "you are now almost fifty years of age. My son is twenty. Might I suggest that you stand for election as consul in the same year he does? By then you might just have managed to learn enough to pass muster in the consul's chair! Though I'm sure my son would be delighted to give you a few pointers."

Young Metellus burst into audible laughter.

Marius looked at them from under his bristling eyebrows, his eagle's face prouder and haughtier by far than theirs. "I will be consul," he said. "Rest assured, Quintus Caecilius, that I will be consul—not once, but seven times."

And he left the room, leaving the two Metelluses gazing after him in mingled puzzlement and fear. Wondering why they could find nothing amusing in that preposterous statement.

The next day Marius rode back to Old Carthage and sought an audience with Prince Gauda.

Admitted into the princely presence, he went down on one knee and pressed his lips to Gauda's clammy limp hand.

"Rise, Gaius Marius!" cried Gauda delightedly, charmed by the sight of this magnificent-looking man doing him homage in such a genuinely respectful, admiring way.

Marius began to rise, then sank down on both knees, his hands outstretched. "Your royal Highness," he said, "I am not worthy to stand in your presence, for I come before you as the most humble of petitioners."

"Rise, rise!" squealed Gauda, more delighted still. "I will not hear of your asking me for anything on your knees! Here, sit by me and tell me what it is you want."

The chair Gauda indicated was indeed by him—but one step lower than the princely throne. Bowing deeply all the way to the chair, Marius seated himself on its very edge, as if awed into discomfort by the radiance of the only being comfortably seated, namely Gauda himself.

"When you enrolled yourself as my client, Prince Gauda, I accepted the amazing honor you did me because I felt that I would be able to advance your cause in Rome. For I had intended to seek election as consul in the autumn." Marius paused, sighed profoundly. "But, alas, it is not to be! Quintus Caecilius Metellus remains in Africa Province, his term as governor prorogued—which means that I, as his legate, may not leave his service without his permission. When I told him I wished to seek election as consul, he refused to allow me to leave Africa one day ahead of himself."

The noble scion of the Numidian royal house went rigid with the easy rage of a pampered invalid; well did he remember Metellus refusing to rise to greet him, refusing to bow low to him, refusing to permit him a throne in the governor's presence, refusing him a Roman escort. "But this is beyond all reason, Gaius Marius!" he exclaimed. "How may we force him to change his mind?"

"Sire, your intelligence—your grasp of the situation—I am awed!" cried Marius. "That is exactly what we have to do, force him to change his mind." He paused. "I know what you are going to suggest, but perhaps it might be better coming from my lips than yours, for it is a sordid business. So do, I beg you, allow me to say it!"

"Say it," said Gauda loftily.

"Your royal Highness, Rome and the Senate, even the People through their two Assemblies, must be swamped with letters! Letters from you—and from every single burgher, pastoralist, grain grower, merchant, and broker in the entire Roman African province—letters informing Rome how inefficient, how grossly incompetent Quintus Caecilius Metellus's conduct of this war against the Numidian enemy has been, letters explaining that the few successes we have enjoyed have all been my doing, not Quintus Caecilius Metellus's. *Thousands* of letters, my prince! And not just written once, but written over and over again, until Quintus Caecilius Metellus relents, and grants me leave to go to Rome to seek election as consul."

Gauda whinnied blissfully. "Isn't it simply astonishing, Gaius Marius, how much in concert our two minds are? Letters are *exactly* what I was going to suggest!"

"Well, as I said, I knew that," said Marius deprecatingly. "But is it possible, sire?"

"Possible? Of course it's possible!" said Gauda. "All it takes is time and influence and money—and I think, Gaius Marius, that between the two of us we can get together a great deal more time and influence and money than Quintus Caecilius Metellus, don't you?"

"I'm certainly hoping so," said Marius.

Of course Marius didn't leave it there. He went in person to every Roman, Latin, and Italian man of note from one end of Africa Province to the other, pleading his duties on Metellus's behalf as his reason for needing to travel so far afield, so constantly. With him he carried a secret mandate from Prince Gauda, promising all sorts of concessions in Numidia once he was its king. And asking everyone to enroll as a client of Gaius Marius's. Rain and mud and rivers overflowing their banks couldn't stop Gaius Marius; he went on his way enlisting clients and gathering promises of letters, letters, and more letters. Thousands upon thousands of letters. Letters enough to sink Quintus Caecilius Metellus's ship of state to the bottom of the sea of political extinction.

By February the letters from the Roman African province to every important man or body of men in Rome began to arrive, and continued to arrive by every ship thereafter. Said one of the early ones, from Marcus Caelius Rufus, Roman citizen owner of hundreds of *iugera* of land in the Bagradas River valley, producer of 240-fold wheat crops for the Roman market:

> Quintus Caecilius Metellus has done very little in Africa save look after his own interests. It is my considered opinion that his intention is to prolong this war to increase his own personal glory and further his craving for power. Last autumn he gave out that it was his policy to weaken King Jugurtha's position by burning Numidian crops and raiding Numidian towns, especially those containing treasure. As a result, my lands and the lands of many other Roman citizens in this province have been placed in jeopardy, for Numidian raiding parties are now retaliating inside the Roman province. The entire Bagradas Valley, so vital to Rome's grain supply, lives in fear and trembling from one day to the next.
> Furthermore, it has come to my ears, as it has to many others, that Quintus Caecilius Metellus cannot even manage his legates, let alone his army. He has deliberately wasted the potential of men as senior and capable as Gaius Marius and Publius Rutilius Rufus, putting the one to commanding his unimportant cavalry unit, and the other to work as his *praefectus fabrum*. His behavior toward Prince Gauda, regarded by the Senate and People of Rome as the rightful ruler of Numidia, has been insufferably arrogant, thoughtless, and sometimes cruel.

In conclusion, may I say that what little success last year's campaigns produced is purely due to the efforts of Gaius Marius and Publius Rutilius Rufus. I am aware that they have been accorded no credit or thanks for their endeavors. May I recommend Gaius Marius and Publius Rutilius Rufus to your notice, and condemn most strongly the conduct of Quintus Caecilius Metellus?

This missive was addressed to one of the largest and most important grain merchants in Rome, a man whose influence among senators and knights was legion. Naturally, once he was apprised of Metellus's shameful conduct of the war, his indignation waxed loud; his voice dinned in all sorts of interesting ears, with immediate effect. And as the days went by and the spate of letters kept coming, his voice was joined by many other voices. Senators began to flinch when they saw a merchant banker or maritime plutocrat coming their way, and the complacent satisfaction of the enormously powerful Caecilius Metellus clan was rapidly tumbling into dismay.

Off went letters from the Caecilius Metellus clan to its esteemed member Quintus Caecilius, proconsul of Africa Province, begging that he tone down his arrogance toward Prince Gauda, treat his senior legates with more consideration than he did his son, and try to drum up a couple of really impressive victories in the field against Jugurtha.

Then there broke the scandal of Vaga, which, having surrendered to Metellus in the late autumn, now rebelled and executed most of its Italian businessmen; the revolt had been fomented by Jugurtha—with the connivance of none other than Metellus's personal friend, the garrison commander Turpilius. Metellus made the mistake of defending Turpilius when Marius demanded loudly that he be courtmartialed for treason, and by the time the story reached Rome via hundreds of letters, it appeared that Metellus himself was as guilty of treason as was Turpilius. Off went more letters from the Caecilius Metellus clan to their esteemed

Quintus Caecilius in Utica, begging that he choose his friends better, if he was going to insist upon defending them on treason charges.

Many weeks passed before Metellus could be brought to believe that Gaius Marius was the author of the Roman letter campaign; and even when he was forced to believe it, he was slow to understand the significance of this epistolary war—and even slower to counter it. He, a Caecilius Metellus, brought into disrepute in Rome on the word of a Gaius Marius and a sniveling pretender and a few vulgar colonial merchants? Impossible! Rome didn't work that way. Rome belonged to *him,* not to Gaius Marius.

Once every eight days, regular as the calendar, Marius presented himself to Metellus and demanded to be released from service at the end of Sextilis; just as regularly, Metellus turned him down.

In all fairness to Metellus, he had other things on his mind than Marius and a few paltry letters turning up in Rome; most of his energies were taken up with Bomilcar. It had taken Nabdalsa many days to arrange an interview between himself and Bomilcar, then many more days to set up a secret meeting between Bomilcar and Metellus. But late in March the latter finally happened, in a small annex attached to the governor's residence in Utica, to which Bomilcar was smuggled.

They knew each other fairly well, of course, for it was Metellus who had kept Jugurtha informed through Bomilcar during those last despairing days in Rome, Bomilcar rather than his king who had availed himself of Metellus's hospitality, contained as it had been within the city's *pomerium.*

However, there were few social niceties about this new meeting; Bomilcar was edgy, afraid his presence inside Utica would be detected, and Metellus was uncertain of himself in this new role of spymaster.

So Metellus didn't mince matters. "I want to conclude this war with as few losses in men and matériel as possible, and in as short a time as possible," he said. "Rome needs me elsewhere than an outpost like Africa."

"Yes, I heard about the Germans," said Bomilcar smoothly.

"Then you understand the haste," said Metellus.

"Indeed I do. However, I fail to see what I personally can do to shorten the hostilities here."

"I have been led to believe—and after considerable thought, I find myself convinced—that the quickest and best way to decide the fate of Numidia in a way favorable to Rome is to eliminate King Jugurtha," the proconsul said.

Bomilcar considered the proconsul thoughtfully. No Gaius Marius, he knew well; not even a Rutilius Rufus. Prouder, haughtier, far more conscious of his station, yet not as competent or detached. As always to a Roman, Rome mattered. But the concept of Rome cherished by a Caecilius Metellus was very different from the concept of Rome cherished by Gaius Marius. What puzzled Bomilcar was the difference between the old Metellus of days in Rome and the Metellus who governed Africa Province; for though he knew about the letters, he had no appreciation of their importance.

"It's true that Jugurtha is the wellhead for Numidian resistance to Rome," Bomilcar said. "However, you may not be aware of the unpopularity of Gauda within Numidia. Numidia will never consent to be ruled by Gauda, legitimate or not."

At the mention of Gauda's name, an expression of distaste appeared on Metellus's face. "Faugh!" he exclaimed, waving one hand. "A nothing! An apology for a man, let alone a ruler." His light brown eyes dwelled shrewdly upon Bomilcar's heavy face. "*If* anything should happen to King Jugurtha, I—and Rome, of course—was thinking more along the lines of putting a man on the Numidian throne whose good sense and experience have taught him to believe that Numidia's interests are best served in a dutiful client kingship to Rome."

"I agree; I think Numidia's interests are best served in that way." Bomilcar paused, wet his lips. "Would you consider me a possible King of Numidia, Quintus Caecilius?"

"Most definitely!" said Metellus.

"Good! In that case I shall happily work toward the elimination of Jugurtha."

"Soon, I hope," said Metellus, smiling.

"As soon as may be. There is no point in an assassination attempt. Jugurtha is too careful. Besides, he has the total loyalty of his royal guard. Nor do I think a coup would succeed. Most of the nobility are well satisfied with the way Jugurtha has ruled Numidia—and with his conduct of this war. If Gauda were a more attractive alternative, things might be different. I"—Bomilcar grimaced—"do not have the blood of Masinissa in my veins, which means I will need all of Rome's support to ascend the throne successfully."

"Then what *is* to be done?" demanded Metellus.

"I think the only way to do it is to maneuver Jugurtha into a situation where he can be captured by a Roman force—I don't mean in a battle, I mean in an ambush. Then, you can kill him on the spot, or take him into custody and do what you like with him later," said Bomilcar.

"All right, Baron Bomilcar. I take it you'll get word to me in plenty of time to set up this ambush?"

"Of course. Border raids are the ideal opportunity, and Jugurtha plans to lead many of them as soon as the ground is dry enough. Though be warned, Quintus Caecilius. You may fail several times before you succeed in capturing someone as wily as Jugurtha. After all, I cannot afford to jeopardize my own survival—I am no use to Rome or myself if I'm dead. Rest assured, eventually I'll manage to lead him into a good trap. Not even Jugurtha can lead a charmed life forever."

All in all, Jugurtha was well satisfied with the way things were going. Though he had suffered considerably from Marius's raids into the more settled parts of his realm, he knew—none better—that the sheer size of Numidia was his greatest advantage and protection. And the settled parts of Numidia, unlike other nations, mattered less to the King than the wilderness. Most of Numidia's soldiers, including the light-armed cavalry so famous throughout the world, were recruited among the peoples who lived a seminomadic existence far within the interior of the country, even on the far side of the mighty mountains in which the patient Atlas held up the sky on his shoulders; these peoples were known as Gaetuli and Garamantes; Jugurtha's mother belonged to a tribe of the Gaetuli.

After the surrender of Vaga, the King made sure he kept no money or treasure in any town likely to be along the line of a Roman route march; everything was transferred to places like Zama and Capsa, remote, difficult to infiltrate, built as citadels atop unscalable peaks—and surrounded by the fanatically loyal Gaetuli. And Vaga turned out to be no Roman victory; once again Jugurtha had bought himself a Roman, the garrison commander, Turpilius. Metellus's friend. Ha!

However, something was changed. As the winter rains began to dwindle, Jugurtha became more and more convinced of this. The trouble was, he couldn't put his finger on what was changed. His court was a mobile affair; he moved constantly from one citadel to another, and distributed his wives and concubines among all of them, so that wherever he went, he could be sure of loving faces, loving arms. And yet—something was wrong. Not with his dispositions, nor with his armies, nor with his supply lines, nor with the loyalty of his many towns and districts and tribesmen. What he sensed was little more than a whiff, a twitch, a tingling sensation of danger from some source close to him. Though never once did he associate his premonition with his refusal to appoint Bomilcar regent.

"It's in the court," he said to Bomilcar as they rode from Capsa to Cirta at the end of March, walking their horses at the head of a huge train of cavalry and infantry.

Bomilcar turned his head and looked straight into his half brother's pale eyes. "The court?"

"There's mischief afoot, brother. Sown and cultivated by that slimy little turd Gauda, I'd be willing to bet," said Jugurtha.

"Do you mean a palace revolution?"

"I'm not sure what I mean. It's just that something is wrong. I can feel it in my bones."

"An assassin?"

"Perhaps. I really don't honestly know, Bomilcar! My eyes are going in a dozen different directions at once, and my ears feel as if they're rotating, they're so busy—yet only my nose has discovered anything wrong. What about you? Do you feel nothing?" he asked, supremely sure of Bomilcar's affection, trust, loyalty.

"I have to say I feel nothing," said Bomilcar.

Three times did Bomilcar maneuver the unwitting Jugurtha into a trap, and three times did Jugurtha manage to extricate himself unharmed. Without suspecting his half brother.

"They're getting too clever," said Jugurtha after the failure of the third Roman ambush. "This is Gaius Marius or Publius Rutilius at work, not Metellus." He grunted. "I have a spy in my camp, Bomilcar."

Bomilcar managed to look serene. "I admit the possibility. But who would dare?"

"I don't know," said Jugurtha, his face ugly. "But rest assured, sooner or later I will know."

At the end of April, Metellus invaded Numidia, persuaded by Rutilius Rufus to content himself at first with a slighter target than the capital, Cirta; the Roman forces marched on Thala instead. A message came from Bomilcar, who had lured Jugurtha in person to Thala, and Metellus made a fourth attempt to capture the King. But as it wasn't in Metellus to go about the storming of Thala with the speed and decision the job needed, Jugurtha escaped, and the assault became a siege. A month later Thala fell, and much to Metellus's gratified surprise, yielded a large hoard of treasure Jugurtha had brought to Thala with him, and had been obliged to leave behind when he fled.

As May slid into June, Metellus marched to Cirta, where he received another pleasant surprise. For the Numidian capital surrendered without a fight, its very large complement of Italian and Roman businessmen a significantly pro-Roman force in town politics. Besides which, Cirta did not like Jugurtha any more than he liked Cirta.

The weather was hot and very dry, normal for that time of the year; Jugurtha moved out of reach of the slipshod Roman intelligence network by going south to the tents of the Gaetuli, and then to Capsa, homeland of his mother's tribe. A small but heavily fortified mountain citadel in the midst of the Gaetulian remoteness, Capsa contained a large part of Jugurtha's heart, for it was here his mother had actually lived since the death of her husband, Bomilcar's father. And it was here that Jugurtha had stored the bulk of his treasure.

It was here in June that Jugurtha's men brought Nabdalsa, caught coming away from Roman-occupied Cirta after Jugurtha's spies in the Roman command finally obtained enough evidence of Nabdalsa's treachery to warrant informing the King. Though always known as Gauda's man, Nabdalsa had not been prevented from moving freely within Numidia; a remote cousin with Masinissa's blood in him, he was tolerated and considered harmless.

"But I now have proof," said Jugurtha, "that you have been actively collaborating with the Romans. If the news disappoints me, it's chiefly because you've been fool enough to deal with Metellus rather than Gaius Marius." He studied Nabdalsa, clapped in irons upon capture, and visibly wearing the signs of harsh treatment at the hands of Jugurtha's men. "Of course you're not in this alone," he said thoughtfully. "Who among my barons has conspired with you?"

Nabdalsa refused to answer.

"Put him to the torture," said Jugurtha indifferently.

Torture in Numidia was not sophisticated, though like all Eastern-style despots, Jugurtha did avail himself of dungeons and long-term imprisonment. Into one of Jugurtha's dungeons, buried in the base of the rocky hill on which Capsa perched, and entered only through a warren of tunnels from the palace within the citadel's walls, was Nabdalsa thrown, and there the subhumanly brutish soldiers who always seemed to inherit such positions applied the torture.

Not very long afterward, it became obvious why Nabdalsa had chosen to serve the inferior man, Gauda; he talked. All it had taken was the removal of his teeth and the fingernails of one hand. Summoned to hear his confession, the unsuspecting Jugurtha brought Bomilcar with him.

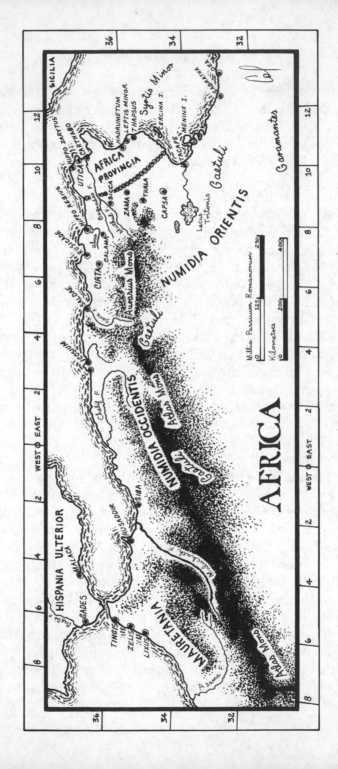

Knowing that he would never leave the subterranean world he was about to enter, Bomilcar gazed into the illimitable heights of the rich blue sky, sniffed the sweet desert air, brushed the back of his hand against the silky leaves of a flowering bush. And strove to carry the memories with him into the darkness.

The poorly ventilated chamber stank; excrement, vomitus, sweat, blood, stagnant water, and dead tissue clubbed together to form a miasma out of Tartarus, an atmosphere no man could breathe without experiencing fear. Even Jugurtha entered the place with a shiver.

The inquisition proceeded under terrible difficulties, for Nabdalsa's gums continued to bleed profusely, and a broken nose prevented attempts to stanch the haemorrhage by packing the mouth. Stupidity, thought Jugurtha, torn by a mixture of horror at the sight of Nabdalsa and anger at the thoughtlessness of his brutes, beginning in the one place they ought to have kept free and clear of their attentions.

Not that it mattered a great deal. Nabdalsa uttered the one vital word on Jugurtha's third question, and it was not too difficult to understand as it was mumbled out through the blood.

"Bomilcar."

"Leave us," said the King to his brutes, but was prudent enough still to order them to remove Bomilcar's dagger.

Alone with the King and the half-conscious Nabdalsa, Bomilcar sighed. "The only thing I regret," he said, "is that this will kill our mother."

It was the cleverest thing he could have said under the circumstances, for it earned him a single blow from the executioner's axe instead of the slow, lingering dying his half brother the King yearned to inflict upon him.

"*Why?*" asked Jugurtha.

Bomilcar shrugged. "When I grew old enough to start weighing up the years, brother, I discovered how much you had cheated me. You have held me in the same contempt you might have held a pet monkey."

"What did you want?" Jugurtha asked.

"To hear you call me brother in front of the whole world."

Jugurtha stared at him in genuine wonder. "And raise you above your station? My dear Bomilcar, it is the sire who matters, not the dam! Our mother is a Berber woman of the Gaetuli, and not even the daughter of a chief. She has no royal distinction to convey. If I were to call you brother in front of the whole world, all who heard me do so would assume that I was adopting you into Masinissa's line. And that—since I have two sons of my own who are legal heirs—would be imprudent, to say the very least."

"You should have appointed me their guardian and regent," said Bomilcar.

"And raise you again above your station? My dear Bomilcar, our mother's blood negates it! Your father was a minor baron, a relative nobody. Where my father was Masinissa's legitimate son. It is from my father I inherit my royalty."

"But you're not legitimate, are you?"

"I am not. Nevertheless, the blood is there. And blood tells."

Bomilcar turned away. "Get it over and done with," he said. "I failed—not you, but myself. Reason enough to die. Yet—beware, Jugurtha."

"Beware? Of what? Assassination attempts? Further treachery, other traitors?"

"Of the Romans. They're like the sun and the wind and the rain. In the end they wear everything down to sand."

Jugurtha bellowed for the brutes, who came tumbling in ready for anything, only to find nothing untoward, and stood waiting for orders.

"Kill them both," said Jugurtha, moving toward the door. "But make it quick. And send me both their heads."

The heads of Bomilcar and Nabdalsa were nailed to the battlements of Capsa for all to see. For a head was more than a mere talisman of kingly vengeance upon a traitor; it was fixed in some public place to show the people that the right man had died, and to prevent the appearance of an imposter.

Jugurtha told himself he felt no grief, just felt more alone than ever before. It had been a necessary lesson: that a king could trust no man, even his brother.

However, the death of Bomilcar had two immediate results. One was that Jugurtha became completely elusive, never staying more than two days in any one place, never informing his guard where he was going next, never allowing his army to know what his plans for it were; authority was vested in the person of the King, no one else. The other result concerned his father-in-law, King Bocchus of Mauretania, who had not actively aided Rome against his daughter's husband, but had not actively aided Jugurtha against Rome either; the feelers went out from Jugurtha to Bocchus at once, and Jugurtha put increased pressure upon Bocchus to ally himself with Numidia, eject Rome from all of Africa.

By the end of summer, Quintus Caecilius Metellus's position in Rome had been totally undermined. No one there could find a kindly word to say about him or his conduct of the war. And still the letters kept coming, steady, relentless, influential in the extreme.

After the capture of Thala and the surrender of Cirta, the Caecilius Metellus faction had managed to gain some ground among the knights' lobbies, but then came further news from Africa that made it clear neither Thala nor Cirta would ensure an end to the war; and after that came reports of endless, pointless skirmishes, of advances further into the Numidian west achieving nothing, of funds misused and six legions kept in the field at huge cost to the Treasury and with no end to the expense in sight. Thanks to Metellus, the war against Jugurtha would certainly drag on for at least another year.

The consular elections were scheduled for mid-October, and Marius's name—now on everyone's lips—was constantly bruited about as a candidate. Yet time went on, and still he didn't appear in Rome. Metellus remained obdurate.

"I insist upon going," said Marius to Metellus for what must have been the fiftieth time.

"Insist all you like," said Metellus. "You're not going."

"Next year I *will* be consul," said Marius.

"An upstart like you consul? Impossible!"

"You're afraid the voters would elect me, aren't you?" asked Marius smugly. "You won't let me go because you know I will be elected."

"I cannot believe any true Roman would vote for you, Gaius Marius. However, you're an extremely rich man, and that means you can buy votes. Should you ever at any time in the future be elected consul—and it won't be next year!—you may rest assured that I will gladly expend every ounce of energy I possess in proving in a court of law that you bought office!"

"I don't need to buy office, Quintus Caecilius, I never have bought office. Therefore feel free to try," said Marius, still annoyingly smug.

Metellus tried a different tack. "I am not letting you go—reconcile yourself to that. As a Roman of the Romans, I would betray my class if I did let you go. The consulship, Gaius Marius, is an office far above anyone of your Italian origins. The men who sit in the consul's ivory chair must fit it by birth, by the achievements of their ancestors as much as by their own. I would rather be disgraced and dead than see an Italian from the Samnite borderlands—a semiliterate boor who ought never even have been praetor!—sit in the consul's ivory chair! Do your worst—or do your best! It makes not one iota of difference to me. I would rather be disgraced and dead than give you permission to go to Rome."

"If necessary, Quintus Caecilius, you will be both," said Marius, and left the room.

Publius Rutilius Rufus attempted to bring both men to reason, his motives concern for Rome as well as for Marius.

"Leave politics out of it," he said to them. "The three of us are here in Africa to beat Jugurtha, but neither of you is interested in devoting your energies to that end. You're more concerned with getting the better of each other than you are of Jugurtha, and I, for one, am fed up with the situation!"

"Are you accusing me of dereliction of duty, Publius Rutilius?" asked Marius, dangerously calm.

"No, of course I'm not! I'm accusing you of withholding that streak of genius I know you to possess in warfare. I am your equal tactically. I am your equal logistically. But when it comes to strategy, Gaius Marius—the long-term look at war—you have no equal at all anywhere. Yet have you devoted any time or thought to a strategy aimed at winning this war? No!"

"And where do I fit into this paean of praise for Gaius Marius?" asked Metellus, tight-lipped. "For that matter, where do I fit into this paean of praise for Publius Rutilius Rufus? Or am I not important?"

"You are important, you unmitigated snob, because you are the titular commander in this war!" snapped Rutilius Rufus. "And if you think you're better at tactics and logistics than I, or better at tactics and logistics and strategy than Gaius Marius, do not feel backward at coming forward about it, I beg you! Not that you would. But if it's praise you want, I am prepared to give you this much—you're not as venal as Spurius Postumius Albinus, nor as ineffectual as Marcus Junius Silanus. Your main trouble is that you're just not as good as you think you are. When you displayed sufficient intelligence to enlist me and Gaius Marius as your senior legates, I thought the years must have improved you. But I was wrong. You've wasted our talents as well as the State's money. We're not winning this war, we're engaged in an extremely expensive impasse. So take my advice, Quintus Caecilius! Let Gaius Marius go to Rome, let Gaius Marius stand for consul—and let *me* organize our resources and devise our military maneuvers. As for you—devote your energies to undermining Jugurtha's hold over his people. You are welcome to every scrap of public glory as far as I'm concerned, provided that within these four walls you're willing to admit the truth of what I'm saying."

"I admit nothing," said Metellus.

And so it went on, all through late summer and well into autumn. Jugurtha was impossible to pin down, indeed seemed to have disappeared from the face of the earth. When it became obvious even to the least ranker legionary that there was not going to be a confrontation between the Roman army and the Numidian army, Metellus withdrew from far western Numidia and went into camp outside Cirta.

Word had come that Bocchus of Mauretania had finally yielded to Jugurtha's pressure tactics, formed up his army, and marched to join his son-in-law somewhere to the south; united, rumor had it, they planned to move on Cirta. Hoping to join battle at last, Metellus made his dispositions and listened with more interest than usual to Marius and Rutilius Rufus. But it was not to be. The two armies lay some miles apart, with Jugurtha refusing to be drawn. Impasse descended again, the Roman position too strongly defended for Jugurtha to attack, and the Numidian position too ephemeral to tempt Metellus out of his camp.

And then, twelve days before the consular elections in Rome, Quintus Caecilius Metellus Piggle-wiggle formally released Gaius Marius from his service as senior legate in the campaign against Jugurtha.

"Off you go!" said Metellus, smiling sweetly. "Rest assured, Gaius Marius, that I will make all of Rome aware that I *did* release you before the elections."

"You think I won't get there in time," said Marius.

"I think—nothing, Gaius Marius."

Marius grinned. "That's true enough, at any rate," he said, and snapped his fingers. "Now where's the piece of paper that says I'm formally released? Give it to me."

Metellus handed over Marius's marching orders, his smile somewhat fixed, and as Marius reached the door he said, not raising his voice, "By the way, Gaius Marius, I have just had some wonderful news from Rome. The Senate has extended my governorship of Africa Province and my command in the Numidian war into next year."

"That's nice of the Senate," said Marius, and vanished.

"I piss on him!" Marius said to Rutilius Rufus moments later.

"He thinks he's cooked my goose and saved his own. But he's wrong. I'm going to beat him, Publius Rutilius, you wait and see! I'm going to be in Rome in time to stand for consul, and then I'm going to have his prorogued command torn off him. And have it given to myself."

Rutilius Rufus eyed him thoughtfully. "I have a great deal of respect for your ability, Gaius Marius," he said, "but in this case, time is going to prove Piggle-wiggle the winner. You'll never make it to Rome for those elections."

"I will," said Marius, sounding supremely confident.

He rode from Cirta to Utica in two days, pausing to snatch a few hours' sleep en route, and ruthlessly commandeering a fresh horse at every opportunity. Before nightfall of the second day he had hired a small, fast ship he found in Utica harbor. And at dawn of the third day he set sail for Italy, having offered a costly sacrifice to the Lares Permarini on the seashore just as light began to filter into the eastern rim of the world.

"You sail to an unimaginably great destiny, Gaius Marius," said the priest who made the offering to the gods who protect all those who voyage on the sea. "I have never seen better omens than today."

His words were no surprise to Marius. Ever since Martha the Syrian prophetess had told him what his future held, he had remained unshaken in his conviction that things would turn out just as she predicted. So as the ship crept from Utica harbor, he leaned tranquilly on the rail and waited for a wind. It came out of the southwest at a steadily brisk twenty sea miles, and it blew the ship from Utica to Ostia in just three days, a perfect following wind in a perfect following sea, no need to hug the coast, no need to put in anywhere for shelter or provisions. All the gods were on his side, as Martha had foretold.

News of the miraculous voyage beat him into Rome, even though he delayed in Ostia only long enough to pay for his ship and reward its captain generously; so when he rode into the Forum Romanum and dismounted before the consul Aurelius's electoral table, a crowd had gathered. A crowd which cheered and applauded him wildly, and gave him to understand that he was the hero of the hour. Surrounded by people clapping him on the back, beaming at his magical appearance, Marius stepped up to the *consul suffectus* who had taken the place of Servius Sulpicius Galba, condemned by the Mamilian Commission, and laid Metellus's letter down on the table.

"If you will excuse the fact that I have not waited to change into the whitened toga, Marcus Aurelius," he said, "I am here to lodge my name as a candidate in the consular contest."

"Provided you can prove that Quintus Caecilius has freed you from your obligation to him, Gaius Marius, I will accept your name gladly," said the suffect consul, stirred by the crowd's welcome and aware that the most influential knights in the city were hurrying from every basilica and porticus around as the news of Marius's unexpected arrival spread.

How Marius had grown! How wonderfully substantial he looked as he stood half a head taller than those around him, smiling his fierce smile! How wide his shoulders, to take the burden of the consulship upon them! For the first time in his long career the Italian hayseed with no Greek experienced genuine political adulation; not the wholesome faithful esteem of soldiers, but the fickle self-serving adoration of the Forum masses. And Gaius Marius loved it, not because his image of himself needed it, but because it was so alien, so tainted, so inexplicable.

He plunged into the five most hectic days of his life, with neither the time nor the energy to give Julia more than a quick hug, and never home at an hour when his son might have been shown to him. For that hysterical welcome when he declared his candidacy was not an indication that he could win; the enormously influential Caecilius Metellus faction joined hands with every other aristocratic faction, patrician and plebeian, in a last-ditch effort to keep the Italian hayseed with no Greek out of the consul's ivory curule chair. His strength lay among the knights, thanks to his Spanish connections and to Prince Gauda's promises of coming concessions in a Gaudane Numidia, but there were many knights whose ties were to the various factions allied against him.

And people talked, people argued, people questioned, people debated: would it truly be a good thing for Rome to elect the New Man Gaius Marius consul? New Men were a risk. New Men didn't know the noble life. New Men made mistakes noblemen did not. New Men were New Men were New Men. . . . Yes, his wife was a Julia of the Julians. Yes, his military record was an adornment to Rome. Yes, he was so rich he could confidently be expected to keep himself above corruption. But who had ever seen him in the law courts? Who had ever heard him speak about laws and lawmaking? Wasn't it true that he had been a disruptive element in the College of Tribunes of the Plebs all those years ago, with his defiance of those who knew Rome and Rome's needs better than he, and that obnoxious law which had narrowed the voting bridges in the *saepta*? And look at his age! He would be a full fifty years old if he became consul, and old men made poor consuls.

And over and above all these speculations and objections, the Caecilius Metellus faction made meaty capital out of the most repellent aspect of Gaius Marius as consul. He was not a Roman of the Romans. He was an Italian. Was Rome so devoid of suitable Roman noblemen that the consulship should go to an Italian New Man? Surely among the candidates were half a dozen men more worthy than Gaius Marius! Romans all. Good men all.

Of course Marius spoke, to small groups and to large ones, in the Forum Romanum, in the Circus Flaminius, from the podiums of various temples, in the Porticus Metelli, in all the basilicae. And he was a good speaker, well trained in rhetoric, though he had not used his skills until after he entered the Senate. Scipio Aemilianus had seen to his oratical polish. He held his audiences; no one walked away or dismissed him as a poor sort of speaker, though he couldn't rival Lucius Cassius or Catulus Caesar. Many were the questions thrown at him, some from those who simply wanted to know, some from those he himself had put up to ask, some from those his enemies had put up to ask, and some from those who were interested to hear the differences between his answers and Metellus's reports to the Senate.

The election itself was a quiet and orderly one, held in the voting grounds out on the Campus Martius, at the place called the *saepta*. Elections in the thirty-five tribes could be called in the well of the Comitia in the Forum Romanum, for it was easy to organize tribal voters in a relatively confined space; but the elections of the Centuriate Assembly were massively unwieldy in size, requiring as they did the deployment of the Centuries in the Five Classes.

As the vote of each century was called, starting with the First Century of the First Class, the pattern began to emerge: Lucius Cassius Longinus was going to be the choice of every century, but their choices of the second consul were rich and varied. Sure enough, the First and Second Classes voted so solidly for Lucius Cassius Longinus that he was returned in first place without missing a century, and so was designated the senior consul, who held the *fasces* for the month of January. But the name of the junior consul wasn't known until almost the end of the Third Class, so close was the contest between Gaius Marius and Quintus Lutatius Catulus Caesar.

And then it happened. The successful candidate for junior consul was Gaius Marius. The Caecilius Metelluses were still able to influence Centuriate voting—but not enough to keep Gaius Marius out. And that could be classified as a great triumph for Gaius Marius, the Italian hayseed with no Greek. He was a genuine New Man, the first of his family to hold a seat in the Senate, the first of his family to make his home inside the city of Rome, the first of his family to make a huge fortune, the first of his family to make a mark in the army.

Late in the afternoon of election day, Gaius Julius Caesar held a celebratory dinner, a family affair. His contact with Marius had been confined to a quick handshake in the Forum and another quick handshake on the Campus Martius when the centuries had assembled, so desperate had Marius's five-day election campaign been.

"You've had unbelievable luck," said Caesar, leading his guest of honor to the dining room while his daughter Julia went off to find her mother and younger sister.

"I know it," said Marius.

"We're very thin as to men today," Caesar went on, "with both my sons still in Africa, but I can offer you one more man as moral support, so we do equal the women."

"I have letters from Sextus and Gaius Julius, and plenty of news about their exploits," Marius said as they arranged themselves comfortably on the couch.

"Later will do."

The promised third man entered the dining room, and Marius started in surprise; for he recognized the young yet mature man who had been standing among the knights almost three years before while the sacrificial bull of the new consul Minucius Rufus had so fought its dying. How could one forget that face, that hair?

"Gaius Marius," said Caesar with a little constraint, "I would like you to meet Lucius Cornelius Sulla, not only my next-door neighbor, but also my fellow senator, and soon to be my other son-in-law."

"Well!" exclaimed Marius, extending his hand and shaking Sulla's with great warmth. "You're a lucky man, Lucius Cornelius."

"I'm well aware of it," said Sulla with feeling.

Caesar had chosen to be a trifle unorthodox in his dining arrangements, keeping the top couch for himself and Marius, and relegating Sulla to the second couch; not an insult, as he was careful to explain, but to make the group look a little larger, and give everyone plenty of room.

How interesting, thought Marius with a mental frown; I have never before seen Gaius Julius Caesar feeling at a disadvantage. But this oddly beautiful fellow upsets him in some way, throws him off balance. . . .

And then the women came in, seated themselves on straight chairs opposite their partners, and the dinner got under way.

Try as he would not to present the picture of a doting elderly husband, Marius found his eyes constantly drawn to his Julia, who had grown in his absence into a ravishing young matron, gracious, unafraid of her new responsibilities, an excellent mother and chatelaine—and the most ideal of wives. Whereas, decided Marius, Julilla had not grown up satisfactorily at all. Of course he had not seen her in the worst throes of her wasting illness—which had ceased to plague her some time before, yet had left her with what he could only call a thin attitude to life—thin of body, thin of intellect, thin of experience, thin of contentment. Feverish in her talk, fluttery in her manner, she was prone to jump from fright, and could not stay settled on her chair; nor could she restrain herself from dominating her betrothed's attention, so that he often found himself excluded from the conversation between Marius and Caesar.

He bore it well, Marius noted, and seemed genuinely devoted to Julilla, fascinated no doubt by the way she focused her emotions upon him. But that, the practical Marius decided, would not last beyond six months of marriage. Not with a Lucius Cornelius Sulla the bridegroom! Nothing about him suggested a natural preference for female company, or an uxorious inclination.

At the end of the meal Caesar announced that he was taking Gaius Marius off to his study for a private talk. "Stay here if you like, or go about your various ways," he said calmly. "It is too long since Gaius Marius and I have met."

"There have been changes in your household, Gaius Julius," said Marius as they got comfortable in the *tablinum*.

"Indeed there have—and therein lies most of my reason for wanting to get you on your own without delay."

"Well, I'm consul on New Year's Day next, and that's my life disposed of tidily," said Marius, smiling. "I owe it all to you—and not the least do I owe you the happiness of a perfect wife, an ideal partner in my enterprises. I've had little time to give her since my return, but now that I am elected, I intend to rectify that. Three days from now I'm taking Julia and my son to Baiae, and we're going to forget the whole world for a month."

"It pleases me more than you can know to hear you speak with such affection and respect of my daughter."

Marius leaned back a little more comfortably in his chair. "Very well. Now to Lucius Cornelius Sulla. I remember some words you had to say about an aristocrat without the money to take up the life his birth entitled him to, and the name was his, your son-in-law to be. What happened to change things?"

"According to him, luck. He says if it goes on the way it has since he met Julilla, he's going to have to add a second nickname—Felix—to the name he inherited from his father. Who was a drunkard and a wastrel, but who married the wealthy Clitumna fifteen years ago or more, and died not long after. Lucius Cornelius met Julilla on New Year's Day almost three years ago, and she gave him a grass crown without knowing the significance of what she had done. He maintains that from that moment, his luck changed. First Clitumna's nephew died, who was her heir. Then a woman called Nicopolis died and left Lucius Cornelius a small fortune—she was, I gather, his mistress. And not many moons after that, Clitumna committed suicide. Having no heirs of her own blood, she left her whole fortune—the house next door, a villa at Circei, and some ten million denarii—to Lucius Cornelius."

"Ye gods, he does deserve to add Felix to his name," said Marius, rather dryly. "Are you being naïve about this, Gaius Julius, or have you proved to your satisfaction that Lucius Cornelius Sulla didn't help any of the dead into Charon's ferry across the Styx?"

Caesar acknowledged the shaft with a raised hand, but grinned. "No, Gaius Marius, I assure you I have not been naive. I cannot implicate Lucius Cornelius in any of the three deaths. The nephew expired after a long bowel and stomach disorder, where the Greek freedwoman Nicopolis died of massive kidney failure within—I don't know, a day, two days, certainly no longer. Both were autopsied, and nothing suspicious was found. Clitumna was morbidly depressed before she killed herself. It happened at Circei, at a time when Lucius Cornelius was most definitely here in Rome. I've subjected all Clitumna's household slaves, both here and in

Circei, to exhaustive questioning, and it is my considered opinion that there is nothing more to know about Lucius Cornelius Sulla." He grimaced. "I have always been against torturing slaves to find evidence of crime because I don't think evidence produced by torture is worth a spoonful of vinegar. But I genuinely do not believe Clitumna's slaves would have a tale to tell even if they were tortured. So I elected not to bother."

Marius nodded. "I agree with you, Gaius Julius. Slave testimony is of value only if it is freely given—and is as logical as it is patently truthful."

"So the upshot of all this was that Lucius Cornelius went from abject poverty to decent wealth over the course of two months," Caesar went on. "From Nicopolis he inherited enough to be admitted to the knights' census, and from Clitumna enough to be admitted to the Senate. Thanks to Scaurus's fuss about the absence of censors, a new pair were elected last May. Otherwise Lucius Cornelius would have had to wait for admission to the Senate for several years."

Marius laughed. "Yes, what did actually happen? Didn't anyone want the censors' jobs? I mean, to some extent Fabius Maximus Eburnus is logical, but Licinius *Getha*? He was thrown out of the Senate by the censors eight years ago for immoral behavior, and only got back into the Senate by getting himself elected a tribune of the plebs!"

"I know," said Caesar gloomily. "No, I think what happened was that everyone was reluctant to stand for fear of offending Scaurus. To want to be censor seemed like a want of respect and loyalty for Scaurus, so the only ones who stood were quite incapable of that kind of sensitivity. Mind you, Getha's easy enough to deal with— he's only in it for the status and a few silver handshakes from companies bidding for State contracts. Where Eburnus—well, we all know he's not right in the head, don't we, Gaius Marius?"

Yes, thought Gaius Marius, we do indeed! Immensely old and of an aristocracy surpassed only by the Julius clan, the Fabius Maximus line had died out, and was kept going only by a series of adoptions. The Quintus Fabius Maximus Eburnus who had been elected censor was an adopted Fabius Maximus; he had sired only one son, and then five years earlier, he had executed this one son for unchastity. Though there was no law to prevent Eburnus from executing his son when acting as *paterfamilias,* the execution of wives or children under the protective shelter of family law had long fallen into disuse. Therefore, Eburnus's action had horrified the whole of Rome.

"Mind you, it's just as well for Rome that Getha has an Eburnus as his colleague," said Marius thoughtfully. "I doubt he'll get away with much, not with Eburnus there."

"I'm sure you're right, but oh, that poor young man, his son! Mind you, Eburnus is really a Servilius Caepio, and the Servilius Caepio lot are all rather strange when it comes to sexual morality. Chaster than Artemis of the Forest, and vocal about it too. Which really makes one wonder."

"So which censor persuaded which to let Lucius Cornelius Sulla into the Senate?" asked Marius. "One hears he hasn't exactly been a pillar of sexual morality, now that I can associate his name with his face."

"Oh, I think the moral laxity was mostly boredom and frustration," said Caesar easily. "However, Eburnus did look down his knobby little Servilius Caepio nose and mutter a bit, it's true. Where Getha would admit a Tingitanian ape if the price was right. So in the end they agreed Lucius Cornelius might be enrolled—but only upon conditions."

"Oh?"

"Yes. Lucius Cornelius is conditionally a senator—he has to stand for election as a quaestor and get in the first time. If he fails, then he's no longer a senator."

"And will he get in?"

"What do you think, Gaius Marius?"

"With a name like his? Oh, he'll get in!"

"I hope so." But Caesar looked dubious. Uncertain. A little embarrassed? He drew a breath and leveled a straight blue gaze at his son-in-law, smiling ruefully. "I vowed, Gaius Marius, that after your generosity when you married Julia, I would never ask you for another favor. However, that's a silly sort of vow. How can one know what the future will need? Need. I need. I need another favor from you."

"Anything, Gaius Julius," said Marius warmly.

"Have you had sufficient time with your wife to find out why Julilla nearly starved herself to death?" asked Caesar.

"No." The stern strong eagle's face lit up for a moment in pure joy. "What little time we've had together since I returned home hasn't been wasted in talking, Gaius Julius!"

Caesar laughed, sighed. "I wish my younger daughter was cast in the same mould as my older! But she isn't. It is probably my fault, and Marcia's. We spoiled her, and excused her much the three older children were not excused. On the other hand, it is my considered opinion that there is an innate lack in Julilla as well. Just before Clitumna died, we found out that the silly girl had fallen in love with Lucius Cornelius, and was trying to force him—or us—or both him and us—it is very difficult to know just what she intended, if ever she really knew herself—anyway, she wanted Lucius Cornelius, and she knew I would never give my consent to such a union."

Marius looked incredulous. "And knowing there was a clandestine relationship between them, you've allowed the marriage to go ahead?"

"No, no, Gaius Marius, Lucius Cornelius was never in any way implicated!" Caesar cried. "I assure you, he had nothing to do with what she did."

"But you said she gave him a grass crown two New Years ago," Marius objected.

"Believe me, the meeting was innocent, at least on his part. He didn't encourage her—in fact, he tried to discourage her. She brought disgrace upon herself and us, because she actually attempted to suborn him into declaring feelings for her which he knew I would never condone. Let Julia tell you the whole story, and you'll see what I mean," said Caesar.

"In which case, how is it they're getting married?"

"Well, when he inherited his fortune and was able to take up his proper station in life, he asked me for Julilla's hand. In spite of the way she had treated him."

"The grass crown," said Marius thoughtfully. "Yes, I can understand how he'd feel bound to her, especially when her gift changed his luck."

"I understand it too, which is why I have given my consent." Again Caesar sighed, more heavily. "The trouble is, Gaius Marius, that I feel none of the liking for Lucius Cornelius that I do for you. He's a very strange man—there are things in him that set my teeth on edge, and yet I have no idea in the world what those things are. And one must always strive to be fair, to be impartial in judgments."

"Cheer up, Gaius Julius, it will all turn out well in the end," said Marius. "Now what can I do for you?"

"Help Lucius Cornelius get elected quaestor," said Caesar, speech crispening now he had a man's problem to deal with. "The trouble is that no one knows him. Oh, everyone knows his *name*! Everyone knows he's a genuine patrician Cornelius. But the *cognomen* Sulla isn't one we hear of these days, and he never had the opportunity to expose himself in the Forum and the law courts when he was a very young man, nor did he ever do military service. In fact, if some malicious noble chose to make a fuss about it, the very fact that he's never done military service could keep him out of office—and out of the Senate. What we're hoping is that no one will ask too closely, and in that respect this pair of censors are ideal. It didn't occur to either of them that Lucius Cornelius was not able to train on the Campus Martius or join the legions as a junior military tribune. And luckily it was Scaurus and Drusus who enrolled Lucius Cornelius as a knight, so our new censors simply assume the old censors went into everything a great deal more thoroughly than they actually did. Scaurus and Drusus were understanding men, they felt Lucius Cornelius should be given his chance. And besides, the Senate wasn't in question at the time."

"Do you want me to bribe Lucius Cornelius into office?" Marius asked.

Caesar was old-fashioned enough to look shocked. "Most definitely not! I can see where bribing might be excusable if the consulship was the prize, but *quaestor*? Never! Also, it would be too risky. Eburnus has his eye on Lucius Cornelius, he'll be watching for any opportunity to disqualify him—and prosecute him. No, the favor I want is far different and less comfortable for you if he turns out to be hopeless. I want you to ask for Lucius Cornelius as your personal quaestor—give him the accolade of a personal appointment. As you well know, once the electorate realizes a candidate for the quaestorship has already been asked for by a consul-elect, he is certain to be voted in."

Marius didn't answer immediately; he was busy digesting the implications. No matter really whether Sulla was innocent of any complicity in the deaths of his mistress and his stepmother, his testamentary benefactresses. It was bound to be said later on that he had murdered them if he made sufficient political mark to be consular material; someone would unearth the story, and a whispering campaign that he had murdered to get his hands on enough money to espouse the public career his father's poverty had denied him would be a gift from the gods in the hands of his political rivals. Having a daughter of Gaius Julius Caesar to wive would help, but nothing would scotch the slur entirely. And in the end there would be many who believed it, just as there were many who believed Gaius Marius had no Greek. That was the first objection. The second lay in the fact that Gaius Julius Caesar couldn't quite bring himself to like Sulla, though he had no concrete grounds for the way he felt. Was it a matter of Smell rather than Thought? Animal instincts? And the third objection was the personality of Julilla. His Julia, he knew now, would never have married a man she considered unworthy, no matter how desperate the Julius Caesar financial plight. Where Julilla had shown that she was flighty, thoughtless, selfish—the kind of girl who couldn't pick a worthy mate if her life depended upon it. Yet she had picked Lucius Cornelius Sulla.

Then he let his mind go far from the Caesars, cast it back to that early drizzly morning on the Capitol when he had covertly watched Sulla watching the bulls bleed to death. And then he knew what was the right thing to do, what he was going to answer. Lucius Cornelius Sulla was *important*. Under no circumstances must he be allowed to slide back into obscurity. He must inherit his birthright.

"Very well, Gaius Julius," he said without the slightest hesitation in his voice, "tomorrow I shall request the Senate to give me Lucius Cornelius Sulla for my quaestor."

Caesar beamed. "Thank you, Gaius Marius! Thank you!"

"Can you marry them before the Assembly of the People meets to vote for the quaestors?" he asked.

"It shall be done," said Caesar.

And so, less than eight days later Lucius Cornelius Sulla and Julia Minor, younger daughter of Gaius Julius Caesar, were married in the old-style *confarreatio* ceremony, two patricians bound together for life. Sulla's career was off with a bound; personally requested by the consul-elect Gaius Marius as his quaestor, and united in wedlock to a family whose *dignitas* and integrity were above reproach, it seemed he couldn't lose.

In which jubilant spirit he approached his wedding night, he who had never really fancied being tied down to a wife and family responsibilities. Metrobius had been dismissed before Sulla applied to the censors for enrollment as a senator, and though the parting had been more fraught with emotion than he could cope with easily—for the boy loved him dearly, and was heartbroken—Sulla was firm in his resolution to put all such activities behind him forever. Nothing was going to jeopardize his rise to fame.

Besides which, he knew enough about his emotional state to understand that Julilla was very precious to him, and not merely because she symbolized his luck, though in his thoughts he classified his feelings for her around that luck. Simply, Sulla was incapable of defining his feelings for any human being as love. Love to Sulla was something other, lesser people felt. As defined by these other, lesser people, it seemed a very odd business, filled with illusions and delusions, at times noble to the point of imbecility and at other times base to the point of amorality. That Sulla could not recognize it in himself was due to his conviction that love negated common sense, self-preservation, enlightenment of the mind. In the years to come he did not ever see that his patience and forbearance in the matter of his flighty, labile wife were all the evidence of love he actually needed. Instead, he put the patience and forbearance down as virtues intrinsic to his own character, and so failed to understand himself or love, and so failed to grow.

A typical Julius Caesar wedding, it was more dignified by far than it was bawdy, though the weddings Sulla had attended were bawdier by far than they were dignified, so he endured the business rather than enjoyed it. However, when the time came there were no drunken guests outside his bedroom door, no wasting of his time having to forcibly eject them from his house. When the short journey from one front door to the next was over, and he picked Julilla up—how airy she felt, how ephemeral!—to carry her over the threshold, the guests who had accompanied them melted away.

As immature virgins had never formed a part of his life, Sulla experienced no misgivings about how events ought to go, and so saved himself a lot of unnecessary worry. For whatever the clinical status of her hymen, Julilla was as ripe, as easy to peel, as a peach caught dropping of its own volition from the tree. She watched him shed his wedding tunic and pull off the wreath of flowers on his head, as fascinated as she was excited. And pulled off her own layers upon layers without being asked, cream and flame and saffron bridal layers, the seven-tiered tiara of wool upon her head, all the special knots and girdles.

They gazed at each other then in complete satisfaction, Sulla beautifully put together, Julilla too thin, yet retaining a willowy grace of line which did much to soften what in someone else would have been angular and ugly. And it was she who moved to him, put her hands on his shoulders and with exquisitely natural and spontaneous voluptuousness inched her body against his, sighing in delight as his arms slid round her and began to stroke her back in long, hard sweeps of both hands.

He adored her lightness, the acrobatic suppleness with which she responded as he lifted her high above his head, let her twine herself about him. Nothing he did alarmed or offended her, and everything he did to her which she could in reciprocation do to him, she did. Teaching her to kiss took seconds; and yet through all their years together, she never stopped learning how to kiss. A wonderful, beautiful, ardent woman, anxious to please him, but greedy for him to please her. All his. Only his. And which of them that night could ever imagine that things might change, be less perfect, less wanted, less welcome?

"If you ever so much as look at anyone else, I'll kill you," he said as they lay on his bed, resting between their bouts of activity.

"I believe you," she said, remembering her father's bitter lesson on the rights of the *paterfamilias;* for now she had moved out from under her father's authority, replaced his with Sulla's. A patrician, she was not and never could be her own mistress. The likes of Nicopolis and Clitumna were infinitely better off.

There was very little difference in their heights, for Julilla was quite tall for a woman, and Sulla almost exactly average for a man. So her legs were somewhat longer than his, and she could twist them through his knees, marveling at the whiteness of his skin compared to the deep gold of hers.

"You make me look like a Syrian," she said, holding her arm along his, both in the air so she could see the contrast, increased by the lamplight.

"I'm not normal," he said abruptly.

"That's good," she laughed, leaning over to kiss him.

After which it was his turn to study her, the contrast and slenderness of her, scarcely escaping boyishness. With one hand he flipped her over quickly, pushed her face into the pillow and studied the lines of back and buttocks and thighs. Lovely.

"You're as beautiful as a boy," he said.

She tried to bounce up indignantly, was held where she lay. "I like that! Don't make it sound as if you *prefer* boys to girls, Lucius

Cornelius!" It was said in all innocence, amid giggles muffled by the soft pillow beneath her mouth.

"Well, until I met you, I think I did," he said.

"Fool!" she laughed, taking his remark as a joke, then breaking free of him and clambering on top of him to straddle his chest and kneel on his arms. "For saying that, you can take a very close look at my little piggle-wiggle and tell me if it's anything like a hard old spear!"

"Only a look?" he asked, pulling her up round his neck.

"A boy!" The idea still amused her. "You are a fool, Lucius Cornelius!" And then she forgot all about it in the delirious discovery of fresh pleasures.

The Assembly of the People duly elected Sulla a quaestor, and even though his year of office was not due to commence until the fifth day of December (though, as with all the personal quaestors, he would not be required until the New Year, when his superior would enter office), Sulla presented himself the day after the elections at the house of Marius.

November was under way, so dawn was growing later, a fact for which Sulla was profoundly thankful; his nightly excesses with Julilla made early rising more difficult than of yore. But he knew he had to present himself before the sun rose, for Marius's requesting him as personal quaestor had subtly changed Sulla's status.

Though it was not a traditional clientship lasting for life, Sulla was now technically Marius's client for the duration of his quaestorship, which ran as long as Marius kept his imperium, rather than for the normal year. And a client did not lie abed with his new wife into the daylight hours; a client presented himself as the first light infused the sky at the house of his patron, and there offered his services to his patron in whatever manner his patron wished. He might find himself courteously dismissed; he might be asked to go with his patron into the Forum Romanum or one of the basilicae to conduct a day's public or private business; he might be deputed to perform some task for his patron.

Though he was not untimely enough to deserve rebuke, the

vast atrium of Marius's house was packed with clients more timely than Sulla; some, Sulla decided, must actually have slept in the street outside Marius's door, for normally they were seen in the order in which they had arrived. Sighing, Sulla made for an inconspicuous corner and prepared for a long wait.

Some great men employed secretaries and *nomenclatores* to sort the morning's catch of clients, dismissing the sprats needful only of being noted as present, and sending none but big or interesting fish in to see the great man himself. But Gaius Marius, Sulla noted with approval, acted as his own culler of the catch; there was not an aide to be seen. This particular great man, consul-elect and therefore of enormous importance to many in Rome, did his own dirty work with calm expedition, separating the needful from the dutiful more efficiently than any secretary Sulla knew of. Within twenty minutes the four hundred men clustered in the atrium and spilling onto the peristyle colonnade had been sorted out and tidied up; over half were happily departing, each freedman client or freeman client of lowly status clutching a donative pressed into his hand by a Marius all smiles and deprecating gestures.

Well, thought Sulla, he may be a New Man and he may be more an Italian than a Roman, but he knows how to behave, all right. No Fabius or Aemilius could have performed the role of patron better. It wasn't necessary to bestow largesse upon clients unless they specifically asked for it, and even then it lay within the discretion of the patron to refuse; but Sulla knew from the attitude of those waiting their turns as Marius moved from man to man that Marius made a habit of bestowing largesse, while giving out a subtle message in his manner that woe betide any man being plain greedy.

"Lucius Cornelius, you've no need to wait out here!" said Marius when he arrived in Sulla's corner. "Go into my study, sit down, and make yourself comfortable. I'll be with you shortly, and we can talk."

"Not at all, Gaius Marius," Sulla said, and smiled with his mouth shut. "I am here to offer you my services as your new quaestor, and I'm happy to wait my turn."

"Then you can wait your turn seated in my study. If you are to function properly as my quaestor, you'd better see how I conduct my affairs," said Marius, put a hand on Sulla's shoulder, and escorted him into the *tablinum*.

Within three hours the throng of clients was dealt with, patiently yet swiftly; their petitions ranged from some sort of assistance to requests to be considered among the first when Numidia was reopened to Roman and Italian businessmen. Nothing was ever asked of them in return, but the implication was nonetheless patent—have yourself ready to do whatever your patron wishes at any time, be it tomorrow or twenty years from tomorrow.

"Gaius Marius," said Sulla when the last client was gone, "since Quintus Caecilius Metellus has already had his command in Africa prorogued for next year, how can you hope to help your clients into businesses when Numidia is reopened?"

Marius looked pensive. "Why, that's true, Quintus Caecilius *does* have Africa next year, doesn't he?"

As this was clearly a rhetorical question, Sulla didn't attempt to answer it, just sat fascinated with the way Marius's mind worked. No wonder he'd got as far as consul!

"Well, Lucius Cornelius, I've been thinking about the problem of Quintus Caecilius in Africa, and it's not insoluble."

"But the Senate will never replace Quintus Caecilius with you," Sulla ventured. "I'm not deeply acquainted with the political nuances inside the Senate as yet, but I have certainly experienced your unpopularity among the leading senators, and it seems far too strong to permit you to swim against it."

"Very true," said Marius, still smiling pleasantly. "I am an Italian hayseed with no Greek—to quote Metellus, whom I had better inform you I always call Piggle-wiggle—and unworthy of the consulship. Not to mention that I'm fifty years old, which is far too late into office, an age thought beyond great military commands. The dice are loaded against me in the Senate. But then, they always have been, you know. And yet—here I am, consul at fifty! A bit of a mystery, isn't it, Lucius Cornelius?"

Sulla grinned, which meant he looked a little feral; Marius did not seem perturbed. "Yes, Gaius Marius, it is."

Marius leaned forward in his chair and folded his beautiful hands together on the fabulous green stone of his desk top. "Lucius Cornelius, many years ago I discovered how very many different ways there are to skin a cat. While others proceeded up the *cursus honorum* without a hiccough, I marked time. But it was not time wasted. I spent it cataloguing all the ways of skinning that cat. Among other equally rewarding things. You see, when one is kept waiting beyond one's proper turn, one watches, assesses, puts pieces together. I was never a great lawyer, never an expert on our unwritten Constitution. While Metellus Piggle-wiggle was trailing around the courts behind Cassius Ravilla and learning how to secure condemnations of Vestal Virgins—well, I mean it in an apocryphal sense only, the time frame is quite wrong—I was soldiering. And I continued to soldier. It's what I do best. Yet, I would not be wrong if I made the boast that I have come to know more about the law and the Constitution than half a hundred Metellus Piggle-wiggles. I look at things from the outside, my brain hasn't been channeled into a rut by training. So I say to you now, I am going to tumble Quintus Caecilius Metellus Piggle-wiggle from the high horse of his African command, and I myself am going to replace him there."

"I believe you," said Sulla, drawing a breath. "But how?"

"They're all legal simpletons," said Marius scornfully, "that's how. Because by custom the Senate has always doled out the governorships, it never occurs to anyone that senatorial decrees do not, strictly speaking, have any weight at law. Oh, they all know that fact if you get them to rattle it off, but it's never sunk in, even after the lessons the Brothers Gracchi tried to teach them. Senatorial decrees only have the force of custom, of tradition. *Not* of law! It's the Plebeian Assembly makes the law these days, Lucius Cornelius. And I wield a great deal more power in the Plebeian Assembly than any Caecilius Metellus."

Sulla sat absolutely still, awed and a little afraid, two odd sensations in him. Awesome though Marius's brainpower might be, Marius's brainpower was not what awed Sulla; no, what awed Sulla was the novel experience of being drawn into a vulnerable man's complete confidence. How did Marius know he, Sulla, was to be trusted? Trust had never been a part of his reputation, and Marius would have made it his business to explore Sulla's reputation thoroughly. Yet here was Marius baring his future intentions and actions for Sulla's inspection! And putting all his trust in his unknown quaestor, just as if that trust had already been earned.

"Gaius Marius," he said, unable not to say it, "what's to stop me from turning into the house of any Caecilius Metellus after I leave here this morning, and telling that Caecilius Metellus everything you're telling me?"

"Why, nothing, Lucius Cornelius," said Marius, undismayed by the question.

"Then why are you making me privy to all this?"

"Oh, that's easy," said Marius. "Because, Lucius Cornelius, you strike me as a superbly able and intelligent man. And any superbly able and intelligent man is superbly able to use his intelligence to work out for himself that it's not at all intelligent to throw in his lot with a Caecilius Metellus when a Gaius Marius is offering him the stimulation and the excitement of a few years of interesting and rewarding work." He drew a huge breath. "There! I got that out quite well."

Sulla began to laugh. "Your secrets are safe with me, Gaius Marius."

"I know that."

"Still and all, I would like you to know that I appreciate your confidence in me."

"We're brothers-in-law, Lucius Cornelius. We're linked, and by more than the Julius Caesars. You see, we share another commonality. Luck."

"Ah! Luck."

"Luck is a sign, Lucius Cornelius. To have luck is to be beloved of the gods. To have luck is to be chosen." And Marius looked at his new quaestor in perfect contentment. "I am chosen. And I chose you because I think you too are chosen. We are important to Rome, Lucius Cornelius. We will both make our mark on Rome."

"I believe that too," said Sulla.

"Yes, well . . . In another month, there will be a new College of Tribunes of the Plebs in office. Once the college is in, I'll make my move regarding Africa."

"You're going to use the Plebeian Assembly to pass a law to topple the senatorial decree giving Metellus Piggle-wiggle another year in Africa," said Sulla certainly.

"I am indeed," said Marius.

"But is it really legal? Will such a law be allowed to stand?" asked Sulla; and to himself he began to appreciate how a very intelligent New Man, emancipated from custom, could turn the whole system upside down.

"There's nothing on the tablets to say it isn't legal, and therefore nothing to say that it can't be done. I have a burning desire to emasculate the Senate, and the most effective way to do that is to undermine its traditional authority. How? By legislating its traditional authority out of existence. By creating a precedent."

"Why is it so important that you get the African command?" Sulla asked. "The Germans have reached as far as Tolosa, and the Germans are far more important than Jugurtha. Someone is going to have to go to Gaul to deal with them next year, and I'd far rather it was you than Lucius Cassius."

"I won't get the chance," said Marius positively. "Our esteemed colleague Lucius Cassius is the senior consul, and he wants the Gallic command against the Germans. Anyway, the command against Jugurtha is vital for my political survival. I've undertaken to represent the interests of the knights, both in Africa Province and in Numidia. Which means I must be in Africa when the war ends to make sure my clients get all the concessions I've promised them. Not only will there be a vast amount of superb grain-growing land to partition up in Numidia, but there have been recent discoveries of a unique first-quality marble, and large deposits of copper as well. Added to which, Numidia yields two rare gemstones and a lot of gold. And since Jugurtha became king, Rome has had no share in any of it."

"All right, Africa it is," said Sulla. "What can I do to help?"

"Learn, Lucius Cornelius, *learn*! I am going to need a corps of officers who are something more than merely loyal. I want men who can act on their own initiative without ruining my grand design—men who will add to my own ability and efficiency, rather than drain me. I don't care about sharing the credit, there's plenty of credit and glory to go around when things are well run and the legions are given a chance to show what they can do."

"But I'm as green as grass, Gaius Marius."

"I know that," said Marius. "But, as I've already told you, I think you have great potential. Stick with me, give me loyalty and hard work, and I'll give you every opportunity to develop that potential. Like me, you're late starting. But it's never *too* late. I'm consul at last, eight years beyond the proper age. You're in the Senate at last, three years beyond the proper age. Like me, you're going to have to concentrate upon the army as a way to the top. I'll help you in every way I can. In return, I expect you to help me."

"That sounds fair, Gaius Marius." Sulla cleared his throat. "I'm very grateful."

"You shouldn't be. If I didn't think I'd get a good return from you, Lucius Cornelius, you wouldn't be sitting here now." And Marius held out his hand. "Come, let's agree that there'll be no gratitude between us! Just loyalty and the comradeship of the legions."

Gaius Marius had bought himself a tribune of the plebs, and picked himself a good man at that. For Titus Manlius Mancinus didn't sell his tribunician favors entirely for money. Mancinus was out to make a splash as a tribune of the plebs, and needed a cause better than the only one which mattered to him—the casting of every impediment he could think of in the path of the patrician Manlius family, of which he was not a member. His hatred of the Manliuses, he found, easily spread to encompass all the great aristocratic and noble families, including the Caecilius Metelluses. So he was able to accept Marius's money with a clear conscience, and espouse Marius's plans with premonitory glee.

The ten new tribunes of the plebs went into office on the third day before the Ides of December, and Titus Manlius Mancinus wasted no time. On that very day he introduced a bill into the Assembly of the Plebs that purported to remove the African command from Quintus Caecilius Metellus, and give it instead to Gaius Marius.

"The People are sovereign!" Mancinus shouted to the crowd. "The Senate is the servant of the People, not the People's master! If the Senate enacts its duties with proper respect for the People of Rome, then by all means it should be allowed to go on doing so. But when the Senate enacts its duties to protect its own leading members at the expense of the People, it must be stopped. Quintus Caecilius Metellus has proven derelict in his command, he has accomplished precisely *nothing*! Why then has the Senate extended his command for a second time, into this coming year? Because, People of Rome, the Senate is as usual protecting its own leading lights at the expense of the People. In Gaius Marius, duly elected consul for this coming year, the People of Rome have a leader worthy of that name. But according to the men who run the Senate, Gaius Marius's name isn't good enough! Gaius Marius, People of Rome, is a mere New Man—an upstart—a nobody, not a noble!"

The crowd was rapt; Mancinus was a good speaker, and felt passionately about senatorial exclusivity. It was some time since the Plebs had tweaked the Senate's nose, and many of the unelected but influential leaders of the Plebs were worried that their arm of Rome's government was losing ground. So on that day at that moment in time, everything ran in Gaius Marius's favor— public sentiment, knightly disgruntlement, and ten tribunes of the plebs in a mood to tweak the Senate's nose, not one of them on the Senate's side.

The Senate fought back, marshaling its best orators of plebeian status to speak in the Assembly, including Lucius Caecilius Metellus Dalmaticus Pontifex Maximus—ardent in his young brother Piggle-wiggle's defense—and the senior consul-elect, Lucius

Cassius Longinus. But Marcus Aemilius Scaurus, who might have tipped the scales in the Senate's favor, was a patrician, and therefore could not speak in the Plebeian Assembly. Forced to stand on the steps of the Senate House looking down into the jam-packed tiered circular well of the Comitia, in which the Plebeian Assembly met, Scaurus could only listen impotently.

"They'll beat us," he said to the censor Fabius Maximus Eburnus, another patrician. "Piss on Gaius Marius!"

Pissed on or not, Gaius Marius won. The remorseless letter campaign had succeeded brilliantly in turning the knights and the middle classes away from Metellus, smearing his name, quite destroying his political clout. Of course in time he would recover; his family and connections were too powerful. But at the moment the Plebeian Assembly, ably led by Mancinus, took his African command off him, his name in Rome was muddier than the pigsty of Numantia. And take his African command off him the People did, passing a precedent-setting law which replaced him with Gaius Marius by name. And once the law—strictly, a plebiscite—was engraved on the tablets, it lay in an archive under a temple as an example and a recourse for others in the future to try the same thing—others who might perhaps not have either the ability of Gaius Marius, or his excellent reasons.

"However," said Marius to Sulla as soon as the law was passed, "Metellus will never leave me his soldiers."

Oh, how many things were there to learn, things he, a patrician Cornelius, ought to know, yet didn't? Sometimes Sulla despaired of learning enough, but then would contemplate his luck in having Gaius Marius as his commander, and rest easier. For Marius was never too busy to explain things to him, and thought no less of him for his ignorance. So now Sulla increased his knowledge by asking, "But don't the soldiers belong to the war against King Jugurtha? Oughtn't they stay in Africa until the war is won?"

"They could stay in Africa—but only if Metellus wanted them to stay. He would have to announce to the army that it had signed on for the duration of the campaign, and therefore his removal from the command did not affect its fate. But there's nothing to stop him taking the position that *he* recruited them, and that their term finishes simultaneously with his. Knowing Metellus, that's the position he'll take. So he'll discharge them, and ship them straight back to Italy."

"Which means you'll have to recruit a new army," said Sulla. "I see." Then he asked, "Couldn't you wait until he brings his army home, then re-enlist it in your name?"

"I could," said Marius. "Unfortunately I won't get the chance. Lucius Cassius is going to Gaul to deal with the Germans at Tolosa. A job which has to be done—we don't want half a million Germans sitting within a hundred miles of the road to Spain, and right on the borders of our own province. So I would imagine that Cassius has already written to Metellus and asked him to re-enlist his army for the Gallic campaign before it even departs from Africa."

"So that's how it works," said Sulla.

"That's how it works. Lucius Cassius is the senior consul, he takes precedence over me. Therefore he has first choice of whatever troops are available. Metellus will bring six highly trained and seasoned legions back to Italy with him. And they will be the troops Cassius takes to Gaul-across-the-Alps, no doubt of it. And that means I am going to have to start from the beginning—recruit raw material, train it, equip it, fill it with enthusiasm for the war against Jugurtha." Marius pulled a face. "It will mean that in my year as consul I won't be given enough time to mount the kind of offensive against Jugurtha I could mount if Metellus left his troops behind for me. In turn, that means I'll have to make sure my own command in Africa is extended into the following year, or I'll fall flat on my arse and wind up looking worse than Piggle-wiggle."

"And now there's a law on the tablets that creates a precedent for someone to take your command off you exactly as you took the command off Metellus." Sulla sighed. "It isn't easy, is it? I never dreamed of the difficulties a man could face just ensuring his own survival, let alone advancing the majesty of Rome."

That amused Marius; he laughed delightedly, and clapped Sulla on the back. "No, Lucius Cornelius, it isn't ever easy. But that's what makes it so worth doing! What man of true excellence and worth honestly wants a smooth path? The rougher the path, the more obstacles in the way, the more satisfaction there is."

This constituted an answer on a personal plane, perhaps, but it didn't solve Sulla's main problem. "Yesterday you told me Italy is completely exhausted," he said. "So many men have died that the levies can't be filled among the citizens of Rome, and Italian resistance to the levies is hardening day by day. Where then can you possibly find enough raw material to form into four good legions? Because—as you've said yourself—you can't defeat Jugurtha with fewer than four legions."

"Wait until I'm consul, Lucius Cornelius, and you'll see," was all Sulla could get out of him.

It was the feast of the Saturnalia undid Sulla's resolutions. In the days when Clitumna and Nicopolis had shared the house with him, this time of holiday and merrymaking had been a wonderful end to the old year. The slaves had lain around snapping their fingers while the two women had run giggling to obey their wishes, everyone had drunk too much, and Sulla had yielded up his place in the communal bed to whichever slaves fancied Clitumna and Nicopolis—on condition that he enjoyed the same privileges elsewhere in the house. And after the Saturnalia was over, things went back to normal as if nothing untoward had ever happened.

But this first year of his marriage to Julilla saw Sulla experience a very different Saturnalia: he was required to spend the waking hours of it next door, in the midst of the family of Gaius Julius Caesar. There too for the three days the festival lasted, everything was upside down—the slaves were waited on by their owners, little gifts changed hands, and a special effort was exerted to provide food and wine as delectable as plentiful. But nothing *really* changed. The poor servants lay as stiff as statues on the dining couches and smiled shyly at Marcia and Caesar as they hurried back and forth between *triclinium* and kitchen, no one would have dreamed of getting drunk, and certainly no one would have dreamed of doing or saying anything which might have led to embarrassment when the household reverted to normal.

Gaius Marius and Julia attended also, and seemed to find the proceedings perfectly satisfactory; but then, thought Sulla resentfully, Gaius Marius was too anxious to be one of them to contemplate putting a foot wrong.

"What a treat it's been," said Sulla as he and Julilla said their farewells at the door on the last evening, and so careful had he become that no one, even Julilla, realized he was being heavily sarcastic.

"It wasn't too bad at all," said Julilla as she followed Sulla into their own house, where—in lieu of the master and mistress's presence—the slaves had simply been given a three-day rest.

"I'm glad you think so," said Sulla, bolting the gate.

Julilla sighed and stretched. "And tomorrow is the dinner for Crassus Orator. I must say I'm looking forward to that."

Sulla stopped halfway across the atrium and turned to stare at her. "You're not coming," he said.

"What do you mean?"

"Just what I said."

"But—but—I thought wives were invited too!" she cried, face puckering.

"*Some* wives," said Sulla. "Not you."

"I want to go! Everyone's talking about it, all my friends are so envious—I *told* them I was going!"

"Too bad. You're not going, Julilla."

One of the house slaves met them at the study door, a little drunk. "Oh, good, you're home!" he said, staggering. "Fetch me some wine, and be quick about it!"

"The Saturnalia is over," said Sulla very softly. "Get out, you fool."

The slave went, suddenly sober.

"Why are you in such a beastly mood?" Julilla demanded as they entered the master's sleeping cubicle.

"I'm not in a beastly mood," he said, and went to stand behind her, slip his arms about her.

She pulled away. "Leave me alone!"

"*Now* what's the matter?"

"I want to go to Crassus Orator's dinner!"

"Well, you can't."

"Why?"

"Because, Julilla," he said patiently, "it isn't the kind of party your father would approve of, and the few wives who are going are not women your father approves of."

"I'm not in my father's hand anymore, I can do anything I like," she said.

"That's not true, and you know it. You passed from your father's hand to my hand. And *I* say you're not going."

Without a word Julilla picked up her clothes from the floor, and flung a robe about her thin body. Then she turned and left the room.

"Please yourself!" Sulla called after her.

In the morning she was cold to him, a tactic he ignored, and when he left for Crassus Orator's dinner, she was nowhere to be found.

"Spoiled little baggage," he said to himself.

The tiff ought to have been amusing; that it wasn't had nothing to do with the tiff, but came from somewhere much deeper within Sulla than the space Julilla occupied. He wasn't the slightest bit excited at the prospect of dining at the opulent mansion of the auctioneer Quintus Granius, who was giving the dinner party. When he had first received the invitation, he had been quite absurdly pleased, interpreting it as an overture of friendship from an important young senatorial circle; then he heard the gossip about the party, and understood that he had been invited because he had a shady past, would add a touch of the exotic to liven the aristocratic male guest list.

Now as he plodded along he was in better case to gauge what kind of trap had closed about him when he married Julilla and entered the ranks of his natural peers. For it was a trap. And there was no relief from its jaws while he was forced to live in Rome. All very well for Crassus Orator, so entrenched he could be party to a party deliberately designed to defy the sumptuary edict of his own father, so secure in his tenure of Senate and a new tribunate of the plebs that he could afford even the luxury of pretending to be vulgar and underbred, accept the blatant favor currying of a mushroom like Quintus Granius the auctioneer.

When he entered Quintus Granius's vast dining room, he saw Colubra smiling at him from over the top of a jeweled golden beaker, saw her pat the couch beside her invitingly. I was right, I'm here as a freak, he said silently, gave Colubra a brilliant smile, and yielded up his person to the attentions of a crowd of obsequious slaves. No intimate function, this! The dining room was filled with couches—sixty guests would recline to celebrate Crassus Orator's entry upon the tribunate of the plebs. But, thought Sulla as he climbed up beside Colubra, Quintus Granius doesn't have the slightest idea how to throw a *real* party.

When he left six hours later—which meant he left well ahead of any other guest—he was drunk, and his mood had plummeted from acceptance of his lot to the kind of black depression he had thought he would never experience again once he entered his rightful sphere. He was frustrated, powerless—and, he realized suddenly, intolerably lonely. From his heart to his head to his fingers and toes he ached for congenial and loving company, someone to laugh with, someone free from ulterior motives, someone entirely *his*. Someone with black eyes and black curls and the sweetest arse in the world.

And he walked, gifted with wings on his feet, all the way out to the apartment of Scylax the actor without once allowing himself to remember how fraught with peril this course was, how imprudent, how foolish, how—it didn't matter! For Scylax would be there; all he'd be able to do was sit and drink a cup of watered wine, and mouth inanities with Scylax, and let his eyes feast upon his boy. No one would be in a position to say a thing. An innocent visit, nothing more.

But Fortune still smiled. Metrobius was there alone, left behind as punishment when Scylax departed to visit friends in Antium. *Metrobius was there alone.* So glad to see him! So filled with love, with hunger, with passion, with grief. And Sulla, the passion and hunger sated, put the boy on his knees and hugged him, and almost wept.

"I spent too long in this world," he said. "Ye gods, how I miss it!"

"How I miss you!" said the boy, snuggling down.

A silence fell; Metrobius could feel Sulla's convulsive swallows against his cheek, and yearned to feel Sulla's tears. But them, he knew, he would not feel. "What's the matter, dear Lucius Cornelius?" he asked.

"I'm bored," said Sulla's voice, very detached. "These people at the top are such hypocrites, so *deadly* dull! Good form and good manners on every public occasion, then furtively dirty pleasures whenever they think no one's watching—I'm finding it hard tonight to disguise my contempt."

"I thought you'd be happy," said Metrobius, not displeased.

"So did I," said Sulla wryly, and fell silent again.

"Why come tonight?"

"Oh, I went to a party."

"No good?"

"Not by your or my lights, lovely lad. By theirs, it was a brilliant success. All *I* wanted to do was laugh. And then, on the way home, I realized I had no one to share the joke with. No one!"

"Except me," said Metrobius, and sat up straight. "Well then, aren't you going to tell me?"

"You know who the Licinius Crassuses are, don't you?"

Metrobius studied his nails. "I'm a child star of the comedy theater," he said. "What do I know about the Famous Families?"

"The family Licinius Crassus has been supplying Rome with consuls and the occasional Pontifex Maximus for—oh, centuries! It's a fabulously rich family, and it produces men of two sorts—the frugal sort, and the sybaritic sort. Now this Crassus Orator's father was one of the frugal sort, and put that ridiculous sumptuary law on the tablets—you know the one," said Sulla.

"No gold plate, no purple cloths, no oysters, no imported wine—is that the one?"

"It is. But Crassus Orator—who it seems didn't get on with his father—adores to be surrounded by every conceivable luxury. And Quintus Granius the auctioneer needs a political favor from Crassus Orator now that he's a tribune of the plebs, so Quintus Granius the auctioneer threw a party tonight in honor of Crassus Orator. The theme," said Sulla, a little expression creeping into his voice, "was 'Let's ignore the *lex Licinia sumptuaria*!' "

"Was that why you were invited?" asked Metrobius.

"I was invited because it appears in the highest circles—the circles of Crassus Orator, that is, even if not of Quintus Granius the auctioneer—I am regarded as a fascinating fellow—life as low as birth was high, I think they thought I'd strip off all my clothes and sing a few dirty ditties while I humped the daylights out of Colubra."

"Colubra?"

"Colubra."

Metrobius whistled. "You *are* moving in exalted circles! I hear she charges a silver talent for *irrumatio*."

"She might, but she offered it to me for nothing," said Sulla, grinning. "I declined."

Metrobius shivered. "Oh, Lucius Cornelius, don't go making enemies now that you're in your rightful world! Women like Colubra wield enormous power."

An expression of distaste settled upon Sulla's face. "Tchah! I piss on them!"

"They'd probably like that," said Metrobius thoughtfully.

It did the trick; Sulla laughed, and settled down to tell his story more happily.

"There were a few wives there—the more adventurous kind, with husbands pecked almost to death—two Claudias, and a lady in a mask who insisted on being called Aspasia, but who I know very well is Crassus Orator's cousin Licinia—you remember, I used to sleep with her occasionally?"

"I remember," said Metrobius a little grimly.

"The place absolutely dripped gold and Tyrian purple," Sulla went on. "Even the dishrags were Tyrian purple over-sewn with gold! You should have seen the dining steward waiting until his master wasn't looking, and then whipping out an ordinary dish-rag to mop up someone's spilled Chian wine—the gold-and-purple rags were useless, of course."

"You hated it," said Metrobius.

"I hated it," said Sulla, sighed, and resumed his story. "The couches were encrusted with pearls. They really were! And the guests fiddled and plucked until they managed to denude the couches of their pearls, popped them into a corner of the gold-and-purple napkins, knotted the corner up carefully—and there wasn't one among the men at least who couldn't have bought what he stole without noticing the expense."

"Except you," said Metrobius softly, and pushed the hair off Sulla's white brow. "*You* didn't take any pearls."

"I'd sooner have died," said Sulla. He shrugged. "They were only little river blisters, anyway."

Metrobius chuckled. "Don't spoil it! I like it when you're insufferably proud and noble."

Smiling, Sulla kissed him. "That bad, am I?"

"That bad. What was the food like?"

"Catered. Well, not even Granius's kitchens could have turned out enough food for sixty—ooops, fifty-nine!—of the worst gluttons I've ever seen. Every hen egg was a tenth egg, most of them double-yolked. There were swan eggs, goose eggs, duck eggs, seabird eggs, and even some eggs with gilded shells. Stuffed udders of nursing sows—fowls fattened on honey cakes soaked in vintage Falernian wine—snails specially imported from Liguria—oysters driven up from Baiae in a fast gig—the air was so redolent with the most expensive peppers that I had a sneezing fit."

He needed to talk very badly, Metrobius realized; what a strange world Sulla's must be now. Not at all as he had imagined it, though how exactly he had imagined it before it happened was something Metrobius did not know. For Sulla was not a talker, never had been a talker. Until tonight. Out of nowhere! The sight of that beloved face was a sight Metrobius had reconciled himself never to see again, save at a distance. Yet there on the doorstep he'd stood, looking—*ghastly*. And needing love. Needing to talk. Sulla! How lonely he must be, indeed.

"What else was there?" Metrobius prompted, anxious to keep him talking.

Up went one red-gold brow, its darkening of *stibium* long gone. "The best was yet to come, as it turned out. They bore it in shoulder-high on a Tyrian purple cushion in a gem-studded golden dish, a huge licker-fish of the Tiber with the same look on its face as a flogged mastiff. Round and round the room they paraded it, with more ceremony than the twelve gods are accorded at a *lectisternium*. A *fish*!"

Metrobius knitted his brows. "What sort of fish was it?"

Sulla pulled his head back to stare into Metrobius's face. "You know! A licker-fish."

"If I do, I don't remember."

Sulla considered, relaxed. "I daresay you mightn't, at that. Licker-fish are a far cry from a comics' feast. Let me just say, young Metrobius, that every gastronomic fool in Rome's upper stratum passes into a swoon of ecstasy at the very thought of a licker-fish of the Tiber. Yet—there they cruise between the Wooden Bridge and the Pons Aemilius, laving their scaly sides in the outflow from the sewers, and so full from eating Rome's shit that they can't even be bothered nosing a bait. They smell of shit and they taste of shit. Eat them, and, in my opinion, you're eating shit. But Quintus Granius and Crassus Orator raved and drooled as if a licker-fish of the Tiber was a compound of nectar and ambrosia instead of a shit-eating drone of a freshwater bass!"

Metrobius couldn't help himself; he gagged.

"Well said!" cried Sulla, and began to laugh. "Oh, if you could only have seen them, all those puffed-up fools! Calling themselves Rome's best and finest, while Rome's shit dribbled down their chins—" He stopped, sucked in a hissing breath. "I couldn't take it another day. Another hour." He stopped again. "I'm drunk. It was that awful Saturnalia."

"*Awful* Saturnalia?"

"Boring—awful—it doesn't matter. A different upper stratum

than Crassus Orator's party crowd, Metrobius, but just as dreadful. Boring. Boring, boring, boring!" He shrugged. "Never mind. Next year I'll be in Numidia, with something to sink my teeth into. I can't wait! Rome without you—without my old friends—I can't bear it." A shiver rolled visibly down him. "I'm drunk, Metrobius. I shouldn't be here. But oh, if you knew how good it is to be here!"

"I only know how good it is to have you here," said Metrobius loudly.

"Your voice is breaking," said Sulla, surprised.

"And not before time. I'm seventeen, Lucius Cornelius. Luckily I'm small for my age, and Scylax has trained me to keep my voice high. But sometimes these days I forget. It's harder to control. I'll be shaving soon."

"Seventeen!"

Metrobius slid off Sulla's lap and stood looking down at him gravely, then held out one hand. "Come! Stay with me a little while longer. You can go home before it's light."

Reluctantly Sulla got up. "I'll stay," he said, "this time. But I won't be back."

"I know," said Metrobius, and lifted his visitor's arm until it lay across his shoulders. "Next year you'll be in Numidia, and you'll be happy."

THE FOURTH YEAR (107 B.C.):

In the Consulship of
Lucius Cassius Longinus
and
Gaius Marius (I)

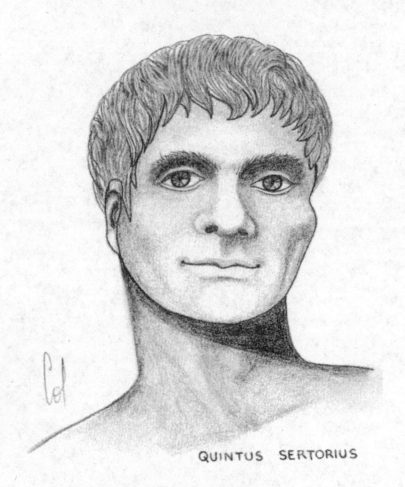

QUINTUS SERTORIUS

No consulship ever mattered to its owner the way Gaius Marius's first consulship mattered to him. He proceeded to his inauguration on New Year's Day secure in the knowledge that his night watch for omens had been unimpeachable, and that his white bull had gorged itself on drugged fodder. Solemn and aloof, Marius stood looking every inch the consul, splendidly tall, far more distinguished than any of those around him in the crisp fine early morning air; the senior consul, Lucius Cassius Longinus, was short and stocky, didn't look imposing in a toga, and was completely overshadowed by his junior colleague.

And at long last Lucius Cornelius Sulla walked as a senator, the broad purple stripe on the right shoulder of his tunic, attending his consul, Marius, in the role of quaestor.

Though he didn't have the *fasces* for the month of January, those crimson-tied bundles of rods being the property of the senior consul, Cassius, until the Kalends of February, Marius nevertheless summoned the Senate for a meeting the following day.

"At the moment," he said to the assembled senators, almost all of whom elected to attend, for they didn't trust Marius, "Rome is being called upon to fight wars on at least three fronts, and that excludes Spain. We need troops to combat King Jugurtha, the Scordisci in Macedonia, and the Germans in Gaul. However, in the fifteen years since the death of Gaius Gracchus we have lost *sixty thousand* Roman soldiers, dead on various fields of battle. Thousands more have been rendered unfit for further military service. I repeat the length of the period, Conscript Fathers of the Senate—fifteen years. Not even half a generation in length."

The House was very silent; among those who sat there was Marcus Junius Silanus, who had lost more than a third of that total less than two years earlier, and was still fending off treason charges. No one had ever dared before to say the dreaded total number in the House, yet all present knew very well that Marius's figures erred on the side of conservatism. Numbed by the sound of the figures pronounced in Marius's upcountry Latin, the senators listened.

"We cannot fill the levies," Marius went on, "for one cogent reason. We no longer have enough men. The shortage of Roman citizen and Latin Rights men is frightening, but the shortage of Italian men is worse. Even conscripting in every district south of the Arnus, we stand no hope of recruiting the troops we need to field this year. I would presume the African army, six legions strong, trained and equipped, will return to Italy with Quintus Caecilius Metellus, and be used by my esteemed colleague Lucius Cassius in Further Gaul of the Tolosates. The Macedonian legions are also properly equipped and of veteran status, and will, I am sure, continue to do well under Marcus Minucius and his young brother."

Marius paused to draw breath; the House continued to listen. "But there remains the problem of a new African army. Quintus Caecilius Metellus has had six full-strength legions at his disposal. I anticipate being able to reduce that total to four legions if I have to. However, Rome doesn't *have* four legions in reserve! Rome doesn't even have *one* legion in reserve! To refresh your memories, I will give you the precise numbers a four-legion army contains."

There was no need for a Gaius Marius to refer to notes; he simply stood there on the consuls' dais slightly in front of his ivory curule chair and gave the figures out of his memory. "At full strength: 5,120 infantrymen per legion, plus 1,280 noncombatant freemen and another 1,000 noncombatant slaves per legion. Then we have the cavalry: a force of 2,000 mounted troops, with a further 2,000 noncombatant freemen and slaves to support the horse. I am therefore faced with the task of finding 20,480 infantrymen, 5,120 noncombatant freemen, 4,000 noncombatant slaves, 2,000 cavalry troopers, and 2,000 noncombatant cavalry support men."

His eyes traveled the House. "Now the noncombatant forces have never been difficult to recruit, and will not be difficult to recruit, I predict—there is no property qualification upon the noncombatant, who can be as poor as a foothills sharecropper. Nor will the cavalry be difficult, as it is many generations since Rome fielded mounted troopers of Roman or Italian origin. We will as always find the men we want in places like Macedonia,

Thrace, Liguria, and Gaul-across-the-Alps, and they bring their own noncombatants with them, as well as their horses."

He paused for a longer space of time, noting certain men: Scaurus and the unsuccessful consular candidate Catulus Caesar, Metellus Dalmaticus Pontifex Maximus, Gaius Memmius, Lucius Calpurnius Piso Caesoninus, Scipio Nasica, Gnaeus Domitius Ahenobarbus. Whichever way these men jumped, the senatorial sheep would follow.

"Ours is a frugal state, Conscript Fathers. When we threw out the kings, we abrogated the concept of fielding an army largely paid for by the State. For that reason, we limited armed service to those with sufficient property to buy their own arms, armor, and other equipment, and that requirement was for all soldiers— Roman, Latin, Italian, no difference. A man of property has property to defend. The survival of the State and of his property matter to him. He is willing to put his heart into fighting. For that reason, we have been reluctant to assume an overseas empire, and have tried time and time again to avoid owning provinces.

"But after the defeat of Perseus, we failed in our laudable attempt to introduce self-government into Macedonia because the Macedonians could not understand any system save autocracy. So we had to take Macedonia over as a province of Rome because we couldn't afford to have barbarian tribes invading the west coast of Macedonia, so close to our own Italy's east coast. The defeat of Carthage forced us to administer Carthage's empire in Spain, or risk some other nation's taking possession. We gave the bulk of African Carthage to the kings of Numidia and kept only a small province around Carthage itself in the name of Rome, to guard against any Punic revival—and yet, look at what has happened because we gave so much away to the kings of Numidia! Now we find ourselves obliged to take over Africa in order to protect our own small province and crush the blatantly expansionist policies of one man, Jugurtha. For all it takes, Conscript Fathers, is one man, and we are undone! King Attalus willed us Asia when he died, and we are still trying to avoid our provincial responsibilities there! Gnaeus Domitius Ahenobarbus opened up the whole coast of Gaul between Liguria and Nearer Spain so that we had a safe, properly Roman corridor between Italy and Spain for our armies—but out of that, we found ourselves obliged to create yet another province."

He cleared his throat; such a silence! "Our soldiers now fight their campaigns outside of Italy. They are away for long periods, their farms and homes are neglected, their wives unfaithful, their children unsired. With the result that we see fewer and fewer volunteers, are forced increasingly to call up men in the levies. No man who farms the land or conducts a business wants to be away from it for five or six or even seven years! And when he is discharged, he is liable to be called up again the moment the volunteers don't volunteer."

The deep voice grew somber. "But more than anything else, so many of these men have *died* during the past fifteen years! And they have not replaced themselves. The whole of Italy is empty of men with the necessary property qualifications to form a Roman army in the traditional mould."

The voice changed again, was raised to echo round the naked rafters of the ancient hall, built during the time of King Tullus Hostilius. "Well, ever since the time of the second war against Carthage, the recruiting officers have had to wink an eye at the property qualifications. And after the loss of the younger Carbo's army six years ago, we have even admitted to the ranks men who couldn't afford to buy their own armor, let alone equip themselves in other ways. But it has been covert, unapproved, and always a last resort.

"Those days are over, Conscript Fathers. I, Gaius Marius, consul of the Senate and People of Rome, am hereby serving notice upon the members of this House that I intend to *recruit* my soldiers, not conscript them—I want willing soldiers, not men who would rather be at home! And where am I going to find some twenty thousand volunteers, you ask? Why, the answer's simple! I am going to seek them among the Head Count, the absolute bottom of the social strata, too poor to be admitted to one of the Five Classes—I am going to seek my volunteers among those who have no money, no property, and very often no steady job—I am going to seek my volunteers among those who never before have been offered the opportunity to fight for their country, to fight for Rome!"

A swelling murmur arose, and increased, and increased, until the whole House was thundering: "No! No! No!"

Showing no anger, Marius waited patiently, even as the anger of others beat around him tangibly in shaking fists and purpling faces, the scraping of more than two hundred folding stools as the swishing togas of men leaping to their feet pushed them across the old stone floor, buffed by the passage of centuries of feet.

Finally the noise died down; roused to ire though they were, they knew they hadn't yet heard it all, and curiosity was a powerful force, even in the irate.

"You can scream and yell and howl until vinegar turns into wine!" shouted Marius when he could make himself heard. "But I am serving notice upon you here and now that this is what I am going to do! And I don't need your permission to do it, either! There's no law on the tablets says I cannot do it—but within a matter of days there will be a law on the tablets says I *can* do it! A law which says that any lawfully elected senior magistrate in need of an army may seek it among the *capite censi*—the Head Count—the *proletarii*. For I, senators, am taking my case to the People!"

"Never!" cried Dalmaticus.

"Over my dead body!" cried Scipio Nasica.

"No! No! No!" cried the whole House, thundering.

"Wait!" cried the lone voice of Scaurus. "Wait, wait! Let me refute him!"

But no one heard. The Curia Hostilia, home of the Senate since the foundation of the Republic, shuddered to its very foundations from the noise of infuriated senators.

"Come on!" said Marius, and swept out of the House, followed by his quaestor, Sulla, and his tribune of the plebs, Titus Manlius Mancinus.

The Forum crowds had gathered at the first rumblings of the storm, and found the well of the Comitia already packed with Marius's supporters. Down the steps of the Curia and across to

the rostra along the back of the Comitia marched the consul
Marius and the tribune of the plebs Mancinus; the quaestor Sulla,
a patrician, remained on the Senate House steps.

"Hear ye, hear ye!" roared Mancinus. "The Assembly of the
Plebs is called into session! I declare a *contio,* a preliminary discussion!"

Forth to the speaker's platform at the front of the rostra stepped
Gaius Marius, and turned so that he partially faced the Comitia
and partially the open space of the lower Forum; those on the
steps of the Senate House mostly saw his back, and when all the
senators save the few patricians began to move down the tiers of
the Comitia to where from its floor they could look straight at
Marius and harass him, the ranks of his clients and supporters
who had been summoned to the Comitia in readiness suddenly
blocked their onward passage, and would not let them through.
There were scuffles and punches, teeth were bared and tempers
flared, but the Marian lines held. Only the nine other tribunes of
the plebs were allowed to proceed to the rostra, where they stood
along its back with stern faces and silently debated whether it was
going to be possible to interpose a veto and live.

"People of Rome, they say I cannot do what is necessary to
ensure the survival of Rome!" Marius shouted. "Rome needs soldiers, Rome needs soldiers desperately! We are surrounded on all
fronts by enemies, yet the noble Conscript Fathers of the Senate
as usual are more concerned with preserving their inherited right
to rule than ensuring the survival of Rome! It is they, People of
Rome, who have sucked the blood of Romans and Latins and Italians dry by their indifferent exploitation of the classes of men
who have traditionally been Rome's soldiers! For I say to you,
there are none of these men left! Those who haven't died on some
battlefield thanks to the greed, the arrogance, and the stupidity of
some consular commander are either too maimed to be of further
use as soldiers, or currently serving in the legions!

"But there is an alternative source of soldiers, a source ready
and eager to volunteer to serve Rome as soldiers! I am referring to
the men of the Head Count, the citizens of Rome or of Italy who

are too poor to have a vote in the Centuries, too poor to own land or businesses, too poor to buy soldiers' gear! But it is time, People of Rome, that the thousands upon thousands of these men should be called upon to do more for Rome than queue up whenever cheap grain is offered, push and shove their way into the Circus on holidays in search of gratification, breed sons and daughters they cannot feed! The fact that they have no worth should not make them worthless! Nor do I for one believe that they love Rome any less than any man of substance! In fact, I believe their love for Rome is purer by far than the love displayed by most of the honorable members of the Senate!"

Marius raised himself up in swelling indignation, threw wide his arms to embrace, it seemed, the whole of Rome. "I am here with the College of Tribunes at my back to seek a mandate from you, the People, which the Senate will not give me! I am asking you for the right to call upon the military potential of the Head Count! I want to turn the men of the Head Count from useless insignificants into soldiers of Rome's legions! I want to offer the men of the Head Count gainful employment—a profession rather than a trade!—a future for themselves and their families with honor and prestige and an opportunity to advance! I want to offer them a consciousness of dignity and worth, a chance to play no mean part in the onward progress of Rome the Mighty!"

He paused; the Comitia stared up at him in profound silence, all eyes fixed on his fierce face, his glaring eyes, the indomitable thrust of chin and chest. "The Conscript Fathers of the Senate are denying these thousands upon thousands of men their chance! Denying *me* the chance to call upon their services, their loyalty, their love of Rome! And for what? Because the Conscript Fathers of the Senate love Rome more than I do? No! Because they love themselves and their own class more than they love Rome or anything else! So I have come to you, the People, to ask you to give me—and give Rome!—what the Senate will not! Give me the *capite censi,* People of Rome! Give me the humblest, the lowliest! Give me the chance to turn them into a body of citizens Rome can be proud of, a body of citizens Rome can make use of instead of merely enduring, a body of citizens equipped and trained and paid by the State to serve the State with hearts and bodies as soldiers! Will you give me what I ask? Will you give Rome what Rome needs?"

And the shouting began, the cheering, the stamping of feet, the audible breaking of a tradition ten centuries old. Nine tribunes of the plebs looked sideways at each other, and agreed without speaking not to interpose a veto; for all of them liked living.

"Gaius Marius," said Marcus Aemilius Scaurus in the House when the *lex Manlia* had been passed, empowering the consuls of the day to call for volunteers among the *capite censi,* "is a ravening, slavering wolfshead, running amok! Gaius Marius is a pernicious ulcer upon the body of this House! Gaius Marius is the single most obvious reason why, Conscript Fathers, we should close our ranks against New Men, never even permit them a seat at the very back of this venerable establishment! What, I ask you, does a Gaius Marius know about the nature of Rome, the imperishable ideals of its traditional government?

"I am Princeps Senatus—the Leader of the House—and in all my many years within this body of men I love as the manifestation of the spirit of Rome it is, never have I seen a more insidious, dangerous, piratical individual than Gaius Marius! Twice within three months he has taken the hallowed prerogatives of the Senate and smashed them on the uncouth altar of the People! First he nullified our senatorial edict giving Quintus Caecilius Metellus an extended command in Africa. And now, to gratify his own ambitions, he exploits the ignorance of the People to grant him powers of recruitment of soldiers that are unnatural, unconscionable, unreasonable, and unacceptable!"

The meeting was heavily attended; of the 300 living senators, over 280 had come to this session of the House, winkled out of their homes and even their sickbeds by Scaurus and the other leaders. And they sat upon their little folding stools in the three rising tiers along either side of the Curia Hostilia like a huge flock of snowy hens gone to roost on their perches, only the purple-

bordered togas of those who had been senior magistrates to relieve that blinding, shadowless mass of white. The ten tribunes of
the plebs sat upon their long wooden bench on the floor of the
House, to one side of the only other magistrates accorded the distinction of isolation from the main body—two curule aediles, six
praetors, and two consuls—all seated upon their beautiful carved
ivory chairs raised up on a dais at the far end of the hall, opposite
the pair of huge bronze doors which gave entrance to the chamber.

On that dais sat Gaius Marius, next to and slightly behind the
senior consul, Cassius, his isolation purely one of the spirit; Marius appeared calm, content, almost catlike, and he listened to
Scaurus without dismay, without anger. The deed was done. He
had his mandate. He could afford to be magnanimous.

"This House must do whatever it can to limit the power Gaius
Marius has just given the Head Count. For the Head Count must
remain what it has always been—a useless collection of hungry
mouths we who are more privileged must care for, feed, and
tolerate—without ever asking it for any service in return. For
while it does no work for us and has no use, it is no more and no
less than a simple dependant, Rome's wife who toils not, and has
no power, and no voice. It can claim nothing from us that we are
not willing to give it, for it does nothing. It simply *is*.

"But thanks to Gaius Marius we now find ourselves faced with
all the problems and grotesqueries of what I must call an army of
professional soldiers—men who have no other source of income,
no other way of making a living—men who will want to stay on in
the army from campaign to campaign—men who will cost the
State enormous sums of money. And, Conscript Fathers, men who
will claim they now have a voice in Rome's scheme of things, for
they do Rome a service, they work for Rome. You heard the People.
We of the Senate, who administer the Treasury and apportion out
Rome's public funds, must dig into Rome's coffers and find the
money to equip Gaius Marius's army with arms, armor, and all the
other gear of war. We are also directed by the People to pay these
soldiers on a regular basis instead of at the very end of a campaign,

when booty is available to help defray the outlay. The cost of fielding armies of insolvent men will financially break the back of the State, there can be no doubt of it."

"Nonsense, Marcus Aemilius!" Marius interjected. "There is more money in Rome's Treasury than Rome knows what to do with—because, Conscript Fathers, you never spend any of it! All you do is hoard it."

The rumbling began, the faces started to mottle, but Scaurus held up his right arm for silence, and got it. "Yes, Rome's Treasury is full," he said. "That is how a treasury should be! Even with the cost of the public works I instituted while censor, the Treasury remains full. But in the past there have been times when it was very empty indeed. The three wars we fought against Carthage brought us to the very brink of fiscal disaster. So what, I ask you, is wrong with making sure that never happens again? While her Treasury is full, Rome is prosperous."

"Rome will be more prosperous because the men of her Head Count have money in their purses to spend," said Marius.

"That is not true, Gaius Marius!" cried Scaurus. "The men of the Head Count will fritter their money away—it will disappear from circulation and never grow."

He walked from where he stood at his stool in the front row of the seated tiers, and positioned himself near the great bronze doors, where both sides of the House could see as well as hear him.

"I say to you, Conscript Fathers, that we must resist with might and main in the future whenever a consul avails himself of the *lex Manlia* and recruits among the Head Count. The People have specifically ordered us to pay for Gaius Marius's army, but there is nothing in the law as it has been inscribed to compel us to pay for the equipping of whichever is the next army of paupers! And that is the tack we must take. Let the consul of the future cull all the paupers he wants to fill up the ranks of his legions—but when he applies to us, the custodians of Rome's monies, for the funds to pay his legions as well as to outfit them, we must turn him down.

"The State cannot afford to field an army of paupers, it is that simple. The Head Count is feckless, irresponsible, without respect for property or gear. Is a man whose shirt of mail was given to him free of charge, its cost borne by the State, going to look after his shirt of mail? No! Of course he won't! He'll leave it lying about in salt air or downpours to rust, he'll pull up stakes in a camp and forget to take it with him, he'll drape it over the foot of the bed of some foreign whore and then wonder why she stole it in the night to equip her Scordisci boyfriend! And what about the time when these paupers are no longer fit enough to serve in the legions? Our traditional soldiers are owners of property, they have homes to return to, money invested, a little solid, tangible worth to them! Where pauper veterans will be a menace, for how many of them will save any of the money the State pays them? How many will bank their share of the booty? No, they will emerge at the end of their years of paid service without homes to go to, without the wherewithal to live. Ah yes, I hear you say, but what's strange about that, to them? They live from hand to mouth always. But, Conscript Fathers, these military paupers will grow used to the State's feeding them, clothing them, housing them. And when upon retirement all that is taken away, they will grumble, just as any wife who has been spoiled will grumble when the money is no longer there. Are we then going to be called upon to find a pension for these pauper veterans?

"It must not be allowed to happen! I repeat, fellow members of this Senate I lead, that our future tactics must be designed to pull the teeth of those men conscienceless enough to recruit among the Head Count by adamantly refusing to contribute one sestertius toward the cost of their armies!"

Gaius Marius rose to reply. "A more shortsighted and ridiculous attitude would be hard to find in a Parthian satrap's harem, Marcus Aemilius! Why won't you understand? If Rome is to hold on to what is even at this moment Rome's, then Rome must invest in *all* her people, including the people who have no entitlement to vote in the Centuries! We are wasting our farmers and small businessmen by sending them to fight, especially when we dower them with brainless incompetents like Carbo and Silanus—oh, are you there, Marcus Junius Silanus? I *am* sorry!"

"What's the matter with availing ourselves of the services of a very large section of our society which until this time has been about as much use to Rome as tits on a bull? If the only real objection we can find is that we're going to have to be a bit freer with the mouldering contents of the Treasury, then we're as stupid as we are shortsighted! You, Marcus Aemilius, are convinced that the men of the Head Count will prove dismal soldiers. Well, I think they'll prove wonderful soldiers! Are we to continue to moan about paying them? Are we going to deny them a retirement gift at the end of their active service? That's what you want, Marcus Aemilius!

"But I would like to see the State part with some of Rome's public lands so that upon retirement, a soldier of the Head Count can be given a small parcel of land to farm or to sell. A pension of sorts. And an infusion of some badly needed new blood into the more than decimated ranks of our smallholding farmers. How can that be anything but good for Rome? Gentlemen, gentlemen, why can't you see that Rome can grow richer only if Rome is willing to share its prosperity with the sprats in its sea as well as the whales?"

But the House was on its feet in an uproar, and Lucius Cassius Longinus, the senior consul, decided prudence was the order of the day. So he closed the meeting, and dismissed the Conscript Fathers of the Senate.

Marius and Sulla set out to find 20,480 infantrymen, 5,120 noncombatant freemen, 4,000 noncombatant slaves, 2,000 cavalry troopers, and 2,000 noncombatant cavalry support men.

"I'll do Rome; you can do Latium," said Marius, purring. "I very much doubt that either of us will have to go as far afield as Italy. We're on our way, Lucius Cornelius! In spite of the worst they could do, we're on our way. I've conscripted Gaius Julius, our father-in-law, to deal with arms and armor manufactories and contractors, and I've sent to Africa for his sons—we can use them. I don't find either Sextus or Gaius Junior the stuff true leaders are made of, but they're excellent subordinates, as hardworking and intelligent as they are loyal."

He led the way into his study, where two men were waiting. One was a senator in his middle thirties whose face Sulla vaguely knew, the other was a lad of perhaps eighteen.

Marius proceeded to introduce them to his quaestor.

"Lucius Cornelius, this is Aulus Manlius, whom I've asked to be one of my senior legates." That was the senator. One of the patrician Manliuses, thought Sulla; Marius did indeed have friends and clients from all walks.

"And this young man is Quintus Sertorius, the son of a cousin of mine, Maria of Nersia, always called Ria. I'm seconding him to my personal staff." A Sabine, thought Sulla; they were, he had heard, of tremendous value in an army—a little unorthodox, terrifically brave, indomitable of spirit.

"All right, it's time to get to work," said the man of action, the man who had been waiting over twenty years to implement his ideas as to what the Roman army ought to be.

"We will divide our duties. Aulus Manlius, you're in charge of getting together the mules, carts, equipment, noncombatants, and all the staples of supply from food to artillery. My brothers-in-law, the two Julius Caesars, will be here any day now, and they'll assist you. I want you ready to sail for Africa by the end of March. You can have any other help you think you may need, but might I suggest you start by finding your noncombatants, and cull the best of them to pitch in with you as you go? That way, you'll save money, as well as begin to train them."

The lad Sertorius was watching Marius, apparently fascinated, while Sulla found the lad Sertorius more fascinating than he did Marius, used as he was by now to Marius. Not that Sertorius was sexually attractive, he wasn't; but he did have a power about him that was odd in one so young. Physically he promised to be immensely powerful when he reached maturity, and maybe that contributed to Sulla's impression, for though he was tall, he was already so solidly muscular that he gave an impression of being short; he had a square, thick-necked head and a pair of remarkable eyes, light brown, deep-set, and compelling.

"I myself intend to sail by the end of April with the first group of soldiers," Marius went on, gazing at Sulla. "It will be up to you, Lucius Cornelius, to continue organizing the rest of the legions, and find me some decent cavalry. If you can get it all done and sail by the end of Quinctilis, I'll be happy." He turned his head to grin at young Sertorius. "As for you, Quintus Sertorius, I'll keep you on the hop, rest assured! I can't have it said that I keep relatives of mine around doing nothing."

The lad smiled, slowly and thoughtfully. "I like to hop, Gaius Marius," he said.

The Head Count flocked to enlist; Rome had never seen anything like it, nor had anyone in the Senate expected such a response from a section of the community it had never bothered to think about save in times of grain shortages, when it was prudent to supply the Head Count with cheap grain to avoid troublesome rioting.

Within scant days the number of volunteer recruits of full Roman citizen status had reached 20,480—but Marius declined to stop recruiting.

"If they're there to take, we'll take them," he said to Sulla. "Metellus has six legions, I don't see why I ought not to have six legions. Especially with the State funding the costs! It won't ever happen again, if we are to believe dear Scaurus, and Rome may have need of those two extra legions, my instincts tell me. We won't get a proper campaign mounted this year anyway, so we'll do better to concentrate on training and equipping. The nice thing is, these six legions will all be Roman citizen legions, not Italian auxiliaries. That means we still have the Italian *proletarii* to tap in years to come, as well as plenty more Roman Head Count."

It all went according to plan, which was not surprising when Gaius Marius was in the command tent, Sulla found out. By the end of March, Aulus Manlius was en route from Neapolis to Utica, his transports stuffed with mules, ballistae, catapults, arms, tack, and all the thousand and one items which gave an army teeth. The moment Aulus Manlius was landed in Utica, the transports returned to Neapolis and picked up Gaius Marius, who

sailed with only two of his six legions. Sulla remained behind in
Italy to get the other four legions outfitted and into order, and find
the cavalry. In the end he went north to the regions of Italian Gaul
on the far side of the Padus River, where he recruited magnificent
horse troopers of Gallo-Celtic background.

There were other changes in Marius's army, above and beyond
its Head Count composition. For these were men who had no tradition of military service, and so were completely ignorant of
what it entailed. And so were in no position to resist change, or to
oppose it. For many years the old tactical unit called the maniple
had proven too small to contend with the massive, undisciplined
armies the legions often had to fight; the cohort—three times the
size of the maniple—had been gradually supplanting it in actual
practice. Yet no one had officially regrouped the legions into cohorts rather than maniples, or restructured its centurion hierarchy
to deal with cohorts rather than maniples. But Gaius Marius did,
that spring and summer of the year of his first consulship. Except
as a pretty parade-ground unit, the maniple now officially ceased
to exist; the cohort was supreme.

However, there were unforeseen disadvantages in fielding an
army of *proletarii*. The old-style propertied soldiers of Rome
were mostly literate and numerate, so had no difficulty recognizing flags, numbers, letters, symbols. Marius's army was mostly
illiterate, barely numerate. Sulla instituted a program whereby
each unit of eight men who tented and messed together had at
least one man in it who could read and write, and for the reward
of seniority over his fellows, was given the duty of teaching his
comrades all about numbers, letters, symbols, and standards, and
if possible was to teach them all to read and write. But progress
was slow; full literacy would have to wait until the winter rains in
Africa rendered campaigning impossible.

Marius himself devised a simple, highly emotive new rallying
point for his legions, and made sure all ranks were indoctrinated
with superstitious awe and reverence for his new rallying point.
He gave each legion a beautiful silver spread-winged eagle upon
a very tall, silver-clad pole; the eagle was to be carried by the

aquilifer, the man considered the best specimen in his whole legion, exclusively clad in a lion skin as well as silver armor. The eagle, said Marius, was the legion's symbol for Rome, and every soldier was obliged to swear a dreadful oath that he would die rather than allow his legion's eagle to fall into the hands of the Enemy.

Of course he knew exactly what he was doing. After half a lifetime under the colors—and being the kind of man he was—he had formed firm opinions and knew a great deal more about the actual individual ranker soldiers than any high aristocrat. His ignoble origins had put him in a perfect position to observe, just as his superior intelligence had put him in a perfect position to make deductions from his observations. His personal achievements underrated, his undeniable abilities mostly used for the advancement of his betters, Gaius Marius had been waiting for a very long time before his first consulship arrived—and thinking, thinking, thinking.

Quintus Caecilius Metellus's reaction to the vast upheaval Marius had provoked in Rome surprised even his son, for Metellus was always thought a rational, controlled kind of man. Yet when he got the news that his command in Africa had been taken away from him and given to Marius, he went publicly mad, weeping and wailing, tearing his hair, lacerating his breast, all in the marketplace of Utica rather than the privacy of his offices, and much to the fascination of the Punic population. Even after the first shock of his grief passed, and he withdrew to his residence, the merest mention of Marius's name was enough to bring on another bout of noisy tears—and many unintelligible references to Numantia, some trio or other, and some pigs.

The letter he received from Lucius Cassius Longinus, senior consul-elect, did much to cheer him up, however, and he spent some days organizing the demobilization of his six legions, having obtained their consent to re-enlist for service with Lucius Cassius the moment they reached Italy. For, as Cassius told him in the letter, Cassius was determined that he was going to do a great deal better in Gaul-across-the-Alps against the Germans and their allies the Volcae Tectosages than Marius the Upstart could possibly do in Africa, troopless as he would be.

Ignorant of Marius's solution to his problem (in fact, he would not learn of it until he arrived back in Rome), Metellus quit Utica at the end of March, taking all six of his legions with him. He chose to go to the port of Hadrumetum, over a hundred miles to the southeast of Utica, and there sulked until he heard that Marius had arrived in the province to assume command. In Utica to wait for Marius he left Publius Rutilius Rufus.

So when Marius sailed in, it was Rutilius who greeted him on the pier, Rutilius who formally handed over the province.

"Where's Piggle-wiggle?" asked Marius as they strolled off to the governor's palace.

"Indulging in a monumental snit way down in Hadrumetum, along with all his legions," said Rutilius, sighing. "He has taken a vow to Jupiter Stator that he will not see you or speak to you."

"Silly fool," said Marius, grinning. "Did you get my letters about the *capite censi* and the new legions?"

"Of course. And I'm a trifle tender around the ears due to the paeans of praise Aulus Manlius has sung about you since he got here. A brilliant scheme, Gaius Marius." But when he looked at Marius, Rutilius didn't smile. "They'll make you pay for your temerity, old friend. Oh, how they'll make you pay!"

"They won't, you know. I've got them right where I want them—and by all the gods, I swear that's the way I'm going to keep them until the day I die! I am going to grind the Senate into the dust, Publius Rutilius."

"You won't succeed. In the end, it's the Senate will grind you into the dust."

"Never!"

And from that opinion Rutilius Rufus could not budge him.

Utica was looking its best, its plastered buildings all freshly whitewashed after the winter rains, a gleaming and spotless town of modestly high buildings, flowering trees, a languorous warmth, a colorfully clad people. The little squares and plazas were thronged with street stalls and cafés; shade trees grew in their centers; the cobbles and paving stones looked clean and swept. Like most Roman, Ionian Greek, and Punic towns, it was provided with a good system of drains and sewers, had public baths for the populace and a good water supply aqueducted in from the lovely sloping mountains blue with distance all around it.

"Publius Rutilius, what are you going to do?" asked Marius once they reached the governor's study, and were settled, both of them amused at the way Metellus's erstwhile servants now bowed and scraped to Marius. "Would you like to stay on here as my legate? I didn't offer Aulus Manlius the top post."

Rutilius shook his head emphatically. "No, Gaius Marius, I'm going home. Since Piggle-wiggle is leaving, my term is up, and I've had enough of Africa. Quite candidly, I don't fancy seeing poor Jugurtha in chains—and now that you're in command, that's how he's going to end up. No, it's Rome and a bit of leisure for me, a chance to do some writing and cultivate friends."

"What if one day not so far in the future, I were to ask you to run for the consulship—with me as your colleague?"

Rutilius threw him a puzzled yet very keen glance. "*Now* what are you plotting?"

"It has been prophesied, Publius Rutilius, that I will be consul of Rome no less than seven times."

Any other man might have laughed, or sneered, or simply refused to believe. But not Publius Rutilius Rufus. He knew his Marius. "A great fate. It raises you above your equals, and I'm too Roman to approve of that. But if such is the pattern of your fate, you cannot fight it, any more than I can. Would I like to be consul? Yes, of course I would! I consider it my duty to ennoble my family. Only save me for a year when you're going to need me, Gaius Marius."

"I will indeed," said Marius, satisfied.

When the news of the elevation of Marius to the command of the war reached the two African kings, Bocchus took fright and bolted home to Mauretania immediately, leaving Jugurtha to face

Marius unsupported. Not that Jugurtha was cowed by his father-in-law's desertion, any more than he was cowed by the idea of Marius's new position; he recruited among the Gaetuli and bided his time, leaving it to Marius to make the first move.

By the end of June four of his six legions were in the Roman African province, and Marius felt pleased enough with their progress to lead them into Numidia. Concentrating on sacking towns, plundering farmlands, and fighting minor engagements, he blooded his lowly recruits and welded them into a formidable little army. However, when Jugurtha saw the size of the Roman force and understood the implications of its Head Count composition, he decided to risk the chance of battle, recapture Cirta.

But Marius arrived before the city could fall, leaving Jugurtha no option save a battle, and at last the Head Count soldiers were offered the opportunity to confound their Roman critics. A jubilant Marius was able afterward to write home to the Senate that his pauper troops had behaved magnificently, fought not one iota less bravely or enthusiastically because they had no vested property interests in Rome. In fact, the Head Count army of Marius defeated Jugurtha so decisively that Jugurtha himself was obliged to throw away his shield and spear in order to escape uncaptured.

The moment King Bocchus heard of it, he sent an embassage to Marius begging that he be allowed to re-enter the Roman client fold; and when Marius failed to respond, he sent more embassages. Finally Marius did consent to see a deputation, which hurried home to tell the King that Marius didn't care to do business with him on any level. So Bocchus was left to chew his nails down to the quick and wonder why he had ever succumbed to Jugurtha's blandishments.

Marius himself remained wholly occupied in removing from Jugurtha every square mile of settled Numidian territory, his aim being to make it impossible for the King to seek recruits or supplies in the rich river valleys and coastal areas of his realm. And make it impossible for the King to accrue additional revenues. Only among the Gaetuli and Garamantes, the inland Berber tribes, could Jugurtha now be sure of finding shelter and soldiers, be sure his armaments and his treasures were safe from the Romans.

Julilla gave birth to a sickly seven-months baby girl in June, and in late Quinctilis her sister, Julia, produced a big, healthy, full-term baby boy, a little brother for Young Marius. Yet it was Julilla's miserable child who lived, Julia's strong second son who died, when the foetid summer vapors of Sextilis curled their malignant tentacles among the hills of Rome, and enteric fevers became epidemic.

"A girl's all right, I suppose," said Sulla to his wife, "but before I leave for Africa you're going to be pregnant again, and this time you're going to have a boy."

Unhappy herself at having given Sulla a puling, puking girl-baby, Julilla entered into the making of a boy with great enthusiasm. Oddly enough, she had survived her first pregnancy and the actual birth of her tiny daughter better by far than her sister, Julia, had, though she was thin, not well, and perpetually fretful. Where Julia, better built and better armed emotionally against the tempests of marriage and maternity, suffered badly that second time.

"At least we have a girl to marry off to someone we need when the time comes," said Julilla to Julia in the autumn, after the death of Julia's second son, and by which time Julilla knew she was carrying another child. "Hopefully this one will be a boy." Her nose ran; she sniffled, hunted for her linen handkerchief.

Still grieving, Julia found herself with less patience and sympathy for her sister than of yore, and understood at last why their mother, Marcia, had said—and grimly—that Julilla was permanently damaged.

Funny, she thought now, that you could grow up with someone, yet never really understand what was happening to her. Julilla was ageing at the gallop—not physically, not even mentally—a process of the spirit, rather, intensely self-destructive. The starvation had undermined her in some way, left her unable to lead a happy kind of life. Or maybe this present Julilla had always been there beneath the giggles and the silliness, the enchanting girlish tricks which had so charmed the rest of the family.

One wants to believe the illness caused this change, she thought sadly; one *needs* to find an external cause, for the alternative is to admit that the weakness was always there.

She would never be anything save beautiful, Julilla, with that magical honey-amber coloring, her grace of movement, her flawless features. But these days there were circles beneath her huge eyes, two lines already fissuring her face between cheeks and nose, a mouth whose dented corners now turned down. Yes, she looked weary, discontented, restless. A faint note of complaint had crept into her speech, and still she heaved those enormous sighs, a habit quite unconscious but very, very irritating. As was her tendency to sniffle.

"Have you got any wine?" Julilla asked suddenly.

Julia blinked in simple astonishment, aware that she was faintly scandalized, and annoyed at herself for such a priggish reaction. After all, women did drink wine these days! Nor was it regarded as a sign of moral collapse anymore, save in circles Julia herself found detestably intolerant and sanctimonious. But when your young sister, barely twenty years old and brought up in the house of Gaius Julius Caesar, asked you for wine in the middle of the morning without a meal or a man in sight—yes, it was a shock!

"Of course I have wine," she said.

"I'd love a cup," said Julilla, who had fought against asking; Julia was bound to comment, and it was unpleasant to expose oneself to the disapproval of one's older, stronger, more successful sister. Yet she hadn't been able to refrain from asking. The interview was difficult, the more so because it was overdue.

These days Julilla found herself out of patience with her family, uninterested in them, bored by them. Especially by the admired Julia, wife of the consul, rapidly becoming one of Rome's most esteemed young matrons. Never put a foot wrong, that was

Julia. Happy with her lot, in love with her ghastly Gaius Marius, model wife, model mother. How boring indeed.

"Do you usually drink wine in the mornings?" Julia asked, as casually as she could.

A shrug, a flapping and fluttering of hands, a brightly burning look that acknowledged the shaft, yet refused to take it seriously. "Well, Sulla does, and he likes to have company."

"*Sulla?* Do you call him by his *cognomen?*"

Julilla laughed. "Oh, Julia, you are old-fashioned! Of course I call him by his *cognomen!* We don't live inside the Senate House, you know! Everyone in our circles uses the *cognomen* these days, it's chic. Besides, Sulla likes me to call him Sulla—he says being called Lucius Cornelius makes him feel a thousand years old."

"Then I daresay I am old-fashioned," said Julia, making an effort to be casual. A sudden smile lit her face; perhaps it was the light, but she looked younger than her younger sister, and more beautiful. "Mind you, I do have some excuse! Gaius Marius doesn't have a *cognomen.*"

The wine came. Julilla poured a glass of it, but ignored the alabaster decanter of water. "I've often wondered about that," she said, and drank deeply. "Surely after he's beaten Jugurtha he'll find a really impressive *cognomen* to assume. Trust that stuck-up sourpuss Metellus to talk the Senate into letting him celebrate a triumph, *and* assume the *cognomen* Numidicus! Numidicus ought to have been kept for Gaius Marius!"

"Metellus Numidicus," said Julia with punctilious regard for facts, "qualified for his triumph, Julilla. He killed enough Numidians and brought home enough booty. And if he wanted to call himself Numidicus, and the Senate said he might, then that's that, isn't it? Besides, Gaius Marius always says that the simple Latin name of his father is good enough for him. There's only one Gaius Marius, where there are dozens of Caecilius Metelluses. You wait and see—my husband isn't going to need to distinguish himself from the herd by a device as artificial as a *cognomen.* My husband is going to be the First Man in Rome—and by dint of nothing except superior ability."

Julia eulogizing the likes of Gaius Marius was quite sickening; Julilla's feelings about her brother-in-law were a mixture of natural gratitude for his generosity, and a contempt acquired from her new friends, all of whom despised him as an upstart, and in consequence despised his wife. So Julilla refilled her cup, and changed the subject.

"This isn't a bad wine, sister. Mind you, Marius has the money to indulge himself, I daresay." She drank, but less deeply than from her first cup. "Are you in love with Marius?" she asked, suddenly realizing that she honestly didn't know.

A blush! Annoyed at betraying herself, Julia sounded defensive when she answered. "*Of course* I'm in love with him! And I miss him dreadfully, as a matter of fact. Surely there's nothing wrong with that, even among those in your circles. Don't you love Lucius Cornelius?"

"Yes!" said Julilla, who now found herself on the defensive. "But I do not miss him now he's gone, I can assure you! For one thing, if he stays away for two or three years, I won't be pregnant again the minute this one is born." She sniffled. "Waddling around weighing a talent more than I ought is not my idea of happiness. I like to float like a feather, I *hate* feeling *heavy*! I've either been pregnant or getting over a pregnancy the whole time I've been married. Ugh!"

Julia held her temper. "It's your job to be pregnant," she said coolly.

"Why is that women never have any choice in a job?" asked Julilla, beginning to feel tearful.

"Oh, don't be ridiculous!" Julia snapped.

"Well, it's an awful way to have to live one's life," said Julilla mutinously, feeling the effects of the wine at last. And it made her cheer up; she summoned a conscious effort, and smiled. "Let's not quarrel, Julia! It's bad enough that Mama can't find it in herself to be civil to me."

And that was true, Julia acknowledged; Marcia had never forgiven Julilla for her conduct over Sulla, though quite why was a mystery. Their father's frostiness had lasted a very few days, after which he treated Julilla with all the warmth and joy her beginning recovery inspired. But their mother's frostiness persisted. Poor, poor Julilla! Did Sulla really like her to drink wine with him in the mornings, or was that an excuse? Sulla, indeed! It lacked respect.

Sulla arrived in Africa at the end of the first week in September with the last two legions and two thousand magnificent Celtic cavalrymen from Italian Gaul. He found Marius in the throes of mounting a major expedition into Numidia, and was hailed gladly, and put immediately to work.

"I've got Jugurtha on the run," Marius said jubilantly, "even without my full army. Now that you're here, we'll see some real action, Lucius Cornelius."

Sulla passed over letters from Julia and from Gaius Julius Caesar, then screwed up his courage to offer condolences for the death of Marius's unseen second son.

"Please accept my sympathy for the passing of your little Marcus Marius," he said, awkwardly aware that his own ratlike daughter, Cornelia Sulla, was doggedly continuing to survive.

A shadow crossed Marius's face, then was resolutely wiped away. "I thank you, Lucius Cornelius. There's time to make more children, and I have Young Marius. You left my wife and Young Marius well?"

"Very well. As are all the Julius Caesars."

"Good!" Private considerations were shelved; Marius put his mail on a side table and moved to his desk, where a huge map painted on specially treated calfskin was spread out. "You're just in time to sample Numidia at first hand. We're off to Capsa in eight days' time." The keen brown eyes searched Sulla's face, peeling and splotchy. "I suggest, Lucius Cornelius, that you explore the Utican marketplaces until you find a really strong hat with as wide a brim as possible. It's obvious you've been out and around in Italy all summer. But the sun of Numidia is even hotter and harsher. You'll burn like tinder here."

It was true; Sulla's flawless white complexion, hitherto sheltered by a life lived largely indoors, had suffered during his
months of traveling throughout Italy, exercising troops, and
learning himself as surreptitiously as possible. Pride had not
permitted him to skulk in the shade while others braved the
light, and pride had dictated that he wear the Attic helmet of his
high estate, headgear which did nothing to save his skin. The
worst of the sunburn was now over, but so little pigment did he
possess that there was no deepening of his color, and the healed
and healing areas were as white as ever. His arms had fared better than his face; it was possible that after sufficient exposure,
arms and legs would manage to survive assault by the sun. But
his face? Never.

Some of this did Marius sense as he watched Sulla's reaction
to his suggestion of a hat; he sat down and pointed to the tray of
wine. "Lucius Cornelius, I have been laughed at for one thing or
another since I first entered the legions at seventeen. At first I was
too scrawny and undersized, then I was too big and clumsy. I had
no Greek. I was an Italian, not a Roman. So I understand the humiliation you feel because you have a soft white skin. But it is
more important to me, your commanding officer, that you maintain good health and bodily comfort, than that you present what
you consider the proper image to your peers. Get yourself that
hat! Keep it tied on with a woman's scarf, or ribbons, or a gold-
and-purple cord if such is all you can find. And laugh at *them*!
Cultivate it as an eccentricity. And soon, you'll find, no one even
notices it anymore. Also, I recommend that you find some sort of
ointment or cream thick enough to lessen the amount of sun your
skin drinks up, and smear it on. And if the right one stinks of
perfume, what of it?"

Sulla nodded, grinned. "You're right, and it's excellent advice.
I'll do as you say, Gaius Marius."

"Good."

A silence fell; Marius was edgy, restless, but not for any reason
connected with Sulla, his quaestor understood. And all of a sudden

Sulla knew what the reason was—hadn't he labored under the same feeling himself? Wasn't all of Rome laboring under it?

"The Germans," Sulla said.

"The Germans," Marius said, and reached out a hand to pick up his beaker of well-watered wine. "Where have they come from, Lucius Cornelius, and where are they going?"

Sulla shivered. "They're going to Rome, Gaius Marius. That is what we all feel in our bones. Where they come from, we don't know. A manifestation of Nemesis, perhaps. All we know is that they have no home. What we fear is that they intend to make our home theirs."

"They'd be fools if they didn't," said Marius somberly. "These forays into Gaul are tentative, Lucius Cornelius—they're simply biding their time, gathering up their courage. Barbarians they may be, but even the least barbarian knows that if he wants to settle anywhere near the Middle Sea, he must first deal with Rome. The Germans will come."

"I agree. But you and I are not alone. That's the feeling from one end of Rome to the other these days. A ghastly worry, a worse fear of the inevitable. And our defeats don't help," said Sulla. "Everything conspires to help the Germans. There are those, even in the Senate, who walk round speaking of our doom as if it had already happened. There are those who speak of the Germans as a divine judgment."

Marius sighed. "Not a judgment. A test." He put down his beaker and folded his hands. "Tell me what you know about Lucius Cassius. The official dispatches give me nothing to think about, they're so rarefied."

Sulla grimaced. "Well, he took the six legions which came back from Africa with Metellus—how do you like the 'Numidicus,' by the way?—and he marched them all the way down the Via Domitia to Narbo, which it seems he reached about the beginning of Quinctilis, after eight weeks on the road. They were fit troops, and could have moved faster, but no one blames Lucius Cassius for going easy on them at the start of what promised to be a hard campaign. Thanks to Metellus Numidicus's determination not to leave a single man behind in Africa, all Cassius's legions were over strength by two cohorts, which meant he had close to forty thousand infantrymen, plus a big cavalry unit he augmented with tame Gauls along the way—about three thousand altogether. A big army."

Marius grunted. "They were good men."

"I know. I saw them, as a matter of fact, while they were marching up through the Padus Valley to the Mons Genava Pass. I was recruiting cavalry at the time. And though you may find this hard to believe, Gaius Marius, I had never before seen a Roman army on the march, rank after rank after rank, all properly armed and equipped, and with a decent baggage train. I'll never forget the sight of them!" He sighed. "Anyway . . . the Germans it seems had come to an understanding with the Volcae Tectosages, who claim to be their kinsmen, and had given them land to the north and east of Tolosa."

"I admit the Gauls are almost as mysterious as the Germans, Lucius Cornelius," said Marius, leaning forward, "but according to the reports, Gauls and Germans are not of the same race. How could the Volcae Tectosages call the Germans kinsmen? After all, the Volcae Tectosages aren't even long-haired Gauls—they've been living around Tolosa since before we've had Spain, and they speak Greek, and they trade with us. So *why*?"

"I don't know. Nor it seems does anyone," said Sulla.

"I'm sorry, Lucius Cornelius, I interrupted. Continue."

"Lucius Cassius marched up from the coast at Narbo along our decent road Gnaeus Domitius made, and got his army into final fighting trim on good ground not far from Tolosa itself. The Volcae Tectosages had allied themselves completely with the Germans, so we faced a mighty force. However, Lucius Cassius brought them to battle in the right place, and beat them soundly. Typical barbarians, they didn't linger in the vicinity once they lost. Germans and Gauls alike ran for their lives away from Tolosa and our army."

He paused, frowning, sipped more wine, put the beaker down. "I had this from Popillius Laenas himself, actually. They brought him across from Narbo by sea just before I sailed."

"Poor wretch, he'll be the Senate's scapegoat," said Marius.

"Of course," said Sulla, lifting his ginger brows.

"The dispatches say Cassius followed the fleeing barbarians," Marius prompted.

Sulla nodded. "Quite right, he did. They'd gone down both banks of the Garumna toward the ocean—when Cassius saw them leave Tolosa, they were in complete disorder, as one would expect. I daresay he despised them as simple, rather oafish barbarians, because he didn't even bother to deploy our army in proper formation when he gave chase."

"He didn't put his legions into a defensive marching order?" asked Marius incredulously.

"No. He treated the pursuit like an ordinary route march, and took every bit of his baggage with him, including all the plunder he'd picked up when the Germans fled, leaving their wagons behind. As you know, our Roman-made road stops at Tolosa, so progress down the Garumna into alien territory was slow, and Cassius was mainly concerned that the baggage train be adequately protected."

"Why didn't he leave the baggage in Tolosa?"

Sulla shrugged. "Apparently he didn't trust what Volcae Tectosages remained behind in Tolosa. Anyway, by the time he'd penetrated down the Garumna as far as Burdigala, the Germans and the Gauls had had at least fifteen days to recover from their trouncing. They went to earth inside Burdigala, which is, it seems, far larger than the usual Gallic *oppidum,* and heavily fortified, not to mention stuffed with armaments. The local tribesmen didn't want a Roman army in their lands, so they helped the Germans and the Gauls in every way they could, from contributing more troops to offering them Burdigala. And then they set a very clever ambush for Lucius Cassius."

"The fool!" said Marius.

"Our army had camped not far to the east of Burdigala, and when Cassius decided to move on to attack the *oppidum* itself, he left the baggage train behind in the camp, under a guard of about half a legion—sorry, I mean five cohorts—one of these days I'll get the terminology right!"

Marius found a smile. "You will, Lucius Cornelius, I guarantee it. But continue."

"It seems Cassius was supremely confident he would encounter no organized resistance, so he marched our army toward Burdigala without even tightening ranks, or making the men march in square, or even sending out scouts. Our whole army fell into a perfect trap, and the Germans and the Gauls literally annihilated us. Cassius himself fell on the field—so did his senior legate. All told, Popillius Laenas estimates thirty-five thousand Roman soldiers died at Burdigala," said Sulla.

"Popillius Laenas himself had been left in command of the baggage train and camp, I understand?" asked Marius.

"That's right. He heard the racket from the battlefield, of course, it drifted downwind for miles, and he was downwind of it. But the first he knew of the disaster was when no more than a handful of our men appeared, running for their lives to shelter in the camp. And though he waited and waited, no more of our men ever came. Instead, the Germans and the Gauls arrived. He says there were thousands upon thousands upon thousands of them, milling around the camp as thick as a plague of mice on a threshing floor. The ground was one mass of moving barbarians in a victory frenzy, lifted out of themselves, brandishing Roman heads on their spears and screaming war chants, all of them giants, their hair standing up stiff with clay, or hanging in great yellow braids down over their shoulders. A terrifying sight, Laenas said."

"And one we're going to see a lot more of in the future, Lucius Cornelius," said Marius grimly. "Go on."

"It's true that Laenas could have resisted them. But for *what*? It seemed more sensible to him to save his pitiful remnant of our army, for our future use if possible. So that's what he did. He ran up the white flag and walked out himself to meet their chieftains, with his spear reversed and his scabbards empty. And they spared

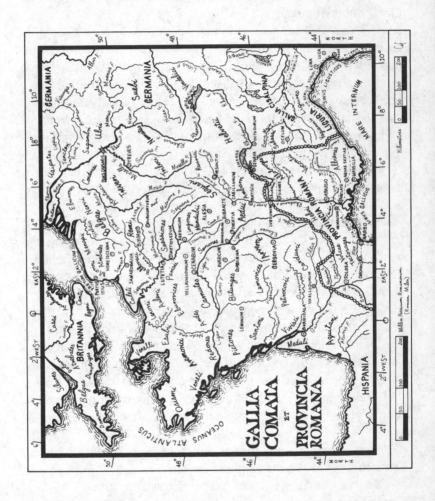

him, and they spared all of our surviving men. Then to show us what a greedy lot they thought we were, they even left us the baggage train! All they took from it were their own treasures which Cassius had looted." He drew a breath. "However, they did make Popillius Laenas and the rest pass under the yoke. After which they escorted them as far as Tolosa, and made sure they went on to Narbo."

"We've passed under the yoke too often of late years," said Marius, clenching his fists.

"Well, that is the chief reason for the general fury of indignation in Rome against Popillius Laenas, certainly," said Sulla. "He'll face treason charges, but from what he was saying to me, I doubt he'll stay to be tried. I think he plans to get together what portable valuables he has, and go into a voluntary exile at once."

"It's the sensible move, at least he'll salvage something out of his ruin that way. If he waits to be tried, the State will confiscate the lot." Marius thumped the map. "But the fate of Lucius Cassius is not going to be our fate, Lucius Cornelius! By fair means or foul, we're going to rub Jugurtha's face in the mud—and then we're going home to demand a mandate from the People to fight the Germans!"

"Now that, Gaius Marius, is something I'll drink to!" said Sulla, lifting his beaker.

The expedition against Capsa was successful beyond all expectations, but—as everyone admitted—only thanks to Marius's brilliant management of the campaign. His legate Aulus Manlius, whose cavalry Marius didn't quite trust, because among its ranks were some Numidians claiming they were Rome's and Gauda's men, tricked his cavalry into thinking that Marius was on a foraging expedition. So what news Jugurtha got was completely misleading.

Thus when Marius appeared with his army before Capsa, the King thought him still a hundred miles away; no one had reported to Jugurtha that the Romans had stocked up on water and grain in order to cross the arid wastelands between the Bagradas River and

Capsa. When the ostensibly impregnable fortress found itself looking down on a sea of Roman helmets, its inhabitants surrendered it
without a fight. But once again Jugurtha managed to escape.

Time to teach Numidia—and especially the Gaetuli—a lesson,
decided Gaius Marius. So in spite of the fact that Capsa had offered
him no resistance, he gave his soldiers permission to loot it, rape it,
and burn it; every adult, male and female, was put to the sword. Its
treasures, and Jugurtha's huge hoard of money, were loaded into
wagons; Marius then brought his army safely out of Numidia into
winter quarters near Utica, well before the rains began.

His Head Count troops had earned their rest. And it gave him
intense pleasure to write a dulcet letter to the Senate (to be read
out by Gaius Julius Caesar) lauding the spirit, courage, and morale of his Head Count army; nor could he resist adding that after
the appallingly bad generalship of Lucius Cassius Longinus, his
senior colleague in the consulship, it was certain Rome would
need more armies made up of the *capite censi.*

Said Publius Rutilius Rufus in a letter to Gaius Marius toward
the end of the year:

> Oh, so many red faces! Your father-in-law roared
> your message out in impressively stentorian tones, so
> that even those who covered their ears were still
> obliged to listen. Metellus Piggle-wiggle—also known
> as Metellus Numidicus these days—looked murder-
> ous. As well he might—his old army dead along the
> Garumna, and your raggle-taggle crew heroes of the
> living kind. "There is no justice!" he was heard to say
> afterward, whereupon I turned round and said, very
> sweetly, "That is true, Quintus Caecilius. For if justice
> did exist, you wouldn't be calling yourself Numidi-
> cus!" He was not amused, but Scaurus fell about laugh-
> ing, of course. Say what you will about Scaurus, he
> has the keenest sense of humor, not to mention sense
> of the ridiculous, of any man I know. Since this is not
> something I can say of any of his cronies, I sometimes

wonder if he doesn't choose his cronies so he can laugh at their posturing in secret.

What amazes me, Gaius Marius, is the strength of your fortunate star. I know you weren't worried, but I can tell you now that I didn't think you stood a chance of having your command in Africa prorogued for next year. Then what happens? Lucius Cassius gets himself killed, along with Rome's biggest and most experienced army, leaving the Senate and its controlling faction helpless to oppose you. Your tribune of the plebs, Mancinus, went to the Assembly of the Plebs and procured you a plebiscite extending your governorship of Africa Province without any trouble at all. The Senate lay silent, it being too apparent, even to them, that you are going to be needed. For Rome is a very uneasy place these days. The threat of the Germans hangs over it like a pall of doom, and there are many who say no man is going to arise capable of averting that doom. Where are the Scipio Africanuses, the Aemilius Paulluses, the Scipio Aemilianuses? they ask. But you have a loyal band of devoted followers, Gaius Marius, and since the death of Cassius they are saying, louder and louder, that you are that man who will arise and turn back the German tide. Among them is the accused legate from Burdigala, Gaius Popillius Laenas.

Since you are a backward Italian hayseed with no Greek, I shall tell you a little story.

Once upon a time, there was a very bad and nasty King of Syria named Antiochus. Now because he was not the first King of Syria to be named Antiochus, nor the greatest (his father claimed the distinction of calling himself Antiochus the Great), he had a number after his name. He was Antiochus IV, the fourth King Antiochus of Syria. Even though Syria was a rich kingdom, King Antiochus IV lusted after the neighboring kingdom of Egypt, where his cousins Ptolemy

Philometor, Ptolemy Euergetes Gross Belly, and Cleopatra (being the second Cleopatra, she had a number
after her name also, and was known as Cleopatra II)
ruled together. I wish I could say they ruled in happy
harmony, but they did not. Brothers and sister, husband and wife (yes, in Oriental kingdoms incest is
quite permissible), they had been fighting between
themselves for years, and had almost succeeded in ruining the fair and fertile land of the great river Nilus.
So when King Antiochus IV of Syria decided to conquer Egypt, he thought he would have a very easy time
of it thanks to the squabbles of his cousins the two
Ptolemies and Cleopatra II.

But, alas, the minute he turned his back on Syria, a
few unpleasantly seditious incidents compelled him to
turn around and go home again to chop off a few heads,
dismember a few bodies, pull a few teeth, and probably
tear out someone's womb. And it was four years before
sufficient heads, arms, legs, teeth, and wombs were
plucked from their owners, and King Antiochus IV
could start out a second time to conquer Egypt. This
time, Syria in his absence remained very quiet and
obedient, so King Antiochus IV invaded Egypt, captured Pelusium, marched down the Delta to Memphis,
captured that, and began to march up the other side of
the Delta toward Alexandria.

Having ruined the country and the army, the brothers Ptolemy and their sister-wife, Cleopatra II, had no
choice but to appeal to Rome for help against King
Antiochus IV, Rome being the best and greatest of all
nations, and everyone's hero. To the rescue of Egypt,
the Senate and People of Rome (being in better accord
in those days than we would believe possible now—or
so the storybooks say) sent their noble brave consular
Gaius Popillius Laenas. Now any other country would
have given its hero a whole army, but the Senate and

People of Rome gave Gaius Popillius Laenas only twelve lictors and two clerks. However, because it was a foreign mission, the lictors were allowed to wear the red tunics and put the axes in their bundles of rods, so Gaius Popillius Laenas was not quite unprotected. Off they sailed in a little ship, and came to Alexandria just as King Antiochus IV was marching up the Canopic arm of the Nilus toward the great city wherein cowered the Egyptians.

Clad in his purple-bordered toga and preceded by his twelve crimson-clad lictors, all bearing the axes in their bundles of rods, Gaius Popillius Laenas walked out of Alexandria through the Sun Gate, and kept on walking east. Now he was not a young man, so as he went he leaned upon a tall staff, his pace as placid as his face. Since only the brave and heroic and noble Romans built decent roads, he was soon walking along through thick dust. But was Gaius Popillius Laenas deterred? No! He just kept on walking, until near the huge hippodrome in which the Alexandrians liked to watch the horse races, he ran into a wall of Syrian soldiers, and had to stop.

King Antiochus IV of Syria came forward, and went to meet Gaius Popillius Laenas.

"Rome has no business in Egypt!" the King said, frowning awfully and direfully.

"Syria has no business in Egypt either," said Gaius Popillius Laenas, smiling sweetly and serenely.

"Go back to Rome," said the King.

"Go back to Syria," said Gaius Popillius Laenas.

But neither of them moved a single inch.

"You are offending the Senate and People of Rome," said Gaius Popillius Laenas after a while of staring into the King's fierce face. "I have been ordered to make you return to Syria."

The King laughed and laughed and laughed. "And

how are you going to make me go home?" he asked. "Where is your army?"

"I have no need of an army, King Antiochus IV," said Gaius Popillius Laenas. "Everything that Rome is, has been, and will be, is standing before you here and now. I am Rome, no less than Rome's largest army. And in the name of Rome, I say to you a further time, go home!"

"No," said King Antiochus IV.

So Gaius Popillius Laenas stepped forward, and moving sedately, he used the end of his staff to trace a circle in the dust all the way around the person of King Antiochus IV, who found himself standing inside Gaius Popillius Laenas's circle.

"Before you step out of this circle, King Antiochus IV, I advise you to think again," said Gaius Popillius Laenas. "And when you do step out of it—why, be facing east, and go home to Syria."

The King said nothing. The King did not stir. Gaius Popillius Laenas said nothing. Gaius Popillius Laenas did not stir. Since Gaius Popillius Laenas was a Roman and did not need to hide his face, his sweet and serene countenance was on full display. But King Antiochus IV hid his face behind a curled and wired wig-beard, and even then could not conceal its thunder. Time went on. And then, still inside the circle, the mighty King of Syria turned on his heel to face east, and stepped out of the circle in an easterly direction, and marched back to Syria with all his soldiers.

Now on his way to Egypt, King Antiochus IV had invaded and conquered the isle of Cyprus, which belonged to Egypt. Egypt needed Cyprus, because Cyprus gave it timber for ships and buildings, and grain, and copper. So after he left the cheering Egyptians in Alexandria, Gaius Popillius Laenas sailed to Cyprus, where he found a Syrian army of occupation.

"Go home," he said to it.

And home it went.

Gaius Popillius Laenas went home himself to Rome, where he said, very sweetly and serenely and simply, that he had sent King Antiochus IV home to Syria, and saved Egypt and Cyprus from a cruel fate. I wish I could end my little story by assuring you that the Ptolemies and their sister, Cleopatra II, lived—and ruled—happily ever after, but they didn't. They just went on fighting among themselves, and murdering a few close relatives, and ruining the country.

What in the name of all the gods, I can hear you asking, am I telling children's stories for? Simple, my dear Gaius Marius. How many times at your mother's knee did you get told the story of Gaius Popillius Laenas and the circle around the King of Syria's feet? Well, maybe in Arpinum mothers don't tell that one. But in Rome, it's standard issue. From highest to lowest, every Roman child gets told the story of Gaius Popillius Laenas and the circle around the feet of the King of Syria.

So how, I ask you, could the great-grandson of the hero of Alexandria proceed into exile without risking his all by standing trial? To proceed into exile voluntarily is to admit guilt—and I for one consider that our Gaius Popillius Laenas did the sensible thing at Burdigala. The upshot of it was that our Popillius Laenas remained and stood trial.

The tribune of the plebs Gaius Coelius Caldus (acting on behalf of a senatorial clique which shall be nameless—but you are allowed to guess—a clique determined to transfer the blame for Burdigala elsewhere than on Lucius Cassius's shoulders, naturally) vowed that he would see Laenas condemned. However, since the only special treason court we have is limited to those dealing with Jugurtha, the trial had to take place in the Centuriate Assembly. Glaringly public, what with each Century's spokesman shouting out his Century's verdict for all the world to hear. *"CONDEMNO!"* *"ABSOLVO!"* Who, after hearing the story of Gaius Popillius Laenas and the circle around the King of Syria's feet at his mother's knee, would dare to shout, *"CONDEMNO!"*?

But did that stop Caldus? Certainly not. He introduced a bill in the Plebeian Assembly which extended the secret ballot of elections to cover treason trials as well. That way, the Centuries called upon to vote could be sure that each man's opinion wasn't known. The bill passed; all seemed in good train.

And as the month of December started, Gaius Popillius Laenas was tried in the Centuriate Assembly on a charge of treason. The ballot was a secret one, just as Caldus wanted. But all a few of us did was slip among the gargantuan jury, and whisper, "Once upon a time there was a noble, brave consular named Gaius Popillius Laenas . . ." and that was the end of it.

When they counted the votes, they all said, *"ABSOLVO."*

So, you might say, if justice was done, it was entirely thanks to the nursery.

THE FIFTH YEAR
(106 B.C.):

In the Consulship of
Quintus Servilius Caepio
and
Gaius Atilius Serranus

PUBLIUS RUTILIUS RUFUS

When Quintus Servilius Caepio was given a mandate to march against the Volcae Tectosages of Gaul and their German guests—now happily resettled near Tolosa—he was fully aware he was going to get that mandate. It happened on the first day of the New Year, during the meeting of the Senate in the temple of Jupiter Optimus Maximus after the inauguration ceremony. And Quintus Servilius Caepio, making his maiden speech as the new senior consul, announced to the packed assemblage that he would not avail himself of the new kind of Roman army.

"I shall use Rome's traditional soldiers, not the paupers of the Head Count," he said, amid cheers and wild applause.

Of course there were senators present who did not cheer; Gaius Marius did not exist alone amid a totally inimical Senate. A good number of the backbenchers were sufficiently enlightened to see the logic behind Marius's stand against entrenched opinion, and even among the Famous Families there were some independent-thinking men. But the clique of conservatives who sat in the front row of the House around the person of Scaurus Princeps Senatus were the men who dictated senatorial policy; when they cheered, the House cheered, and when they voted a certain way, the House voted a similar way.

To this clique did Quintus Servilius Caepio belong, and it was the active lobbying of this clique that prodded the Conscript Fathers to authorize an army eight full legions strong for the use of Quintus Servilius Caepio in teaching the Germans that they were not welcome in the lands of the Middle Sea, and the Volcae Tectosages of Tolosa that it did not pay to welcome Germans.

About four thousand of Lucius Cassius's troops had come back fit to serve, but all save a few of the noncombatants in Cassius's army had perished along with the actual troops, and the cavalry who survived had scattered to their homelands, taking their horses and their noncombatants with them. Thus Quintus Servilius Caepio was faced with the task of finding 41,000 infantrymen, plus 12,000 free noncombatants, plus 8,000 slave noncombatants, plus 5,000 cavalry troopers and 5,000 noncombatant cavalry servants.

All this in an Italy denuded of men with the property qualifications, be they Roman, Latin, or Italian in origin.

Caepio's recruitment techniques were appalling. Not that he himself participated in them, or even bothered to acquaint himself with how the men were going to be found; he paid a staff and set his quaestor in charge, while he himself turned his hand to other things, things more worthy of a consul. The levies were enforced ruthlessly. Men were pressed into service not only without their consent, but as victims of kidnap, and veterans were hauled willy-nilly from their homes. A mature-looking fourteen-year-old son of a pressed smallholding farmer was also pressed, as was his youthful-looking sixty-year-old grandfather. And if such a family could not produce the money to arm and equip its pressed members, someone was on hand to write down the price of the gear, and take the smallholding as payment; Quintus Servilius Caepio and his backers acquired a large amount of land. When, even so, neither Roman nor Latin citizens could provide anything like enough men, the Italian Allies were hounded remorselessly.

But in the end Caepio got his forty-one thousand infantrymen and his twelve thousand noncombatant freemen the traditional way, which meant that the State didn't have to pay for their arms, armor, or equipment; and the preponderance of Italian Allied auxiliary legions put the financial burdens of upkeep upon the Italian Allied nations rather than Rome. As a result, the Senate offered Caepio a vote of thanks, and was delighted to open its purse wide enough to hire horse troopers from Thrace and the two Gauls. While Caepio looked even more self-important than usual, Rome's conservative elements spoke of him in laudatory terms wherever and whenever they could find ears to listen.

The other things to which Caepio personally attended while his press-gangs roamed throughout the Italian peninsula were all to do with returning power to the Senate; one way or another, the Senate had been suffering since the time of Tiberius Gracchus, almost thirty years before. First Tiberius Gracchus, then Fulvius Flaccus, then Gaius Gracchus, and after them a mixture of New Men and reforming noblemen had steadily whittled away at senatorial participation in the major law courts and the making of laws.

If it hadn't been for Gaius Marius's recent assaults upon senatorial privilege, possibly Caepio would have been less imbued with zeal to put the state of affairs right, and less determined. But Marius had stirred up the senatorial hornets' nest, and the result during the first weeks of Caepio's consulship was a dismaying setback for the Plebs and the knights who controlled the Plebs.

A patrician, Caepio summoned the Assembly of the People, from which he was not disbarred, and forced through a bill that removed the extortion court from the knights, who had received it from Gaius Gracchus; once more the juries in the extortion court were to be filled solely from the Senate, which could confidently be expected to protect its own. It was a bitter battle in the Assembly of the People, with the handsome Gaius Memmius leading a strong group of senators opposed to Caepio's act. But Caepio won.

And, having won, in late March the senior consul led eight legions and a big force of cavalry in the direction of Tolosa, his mind filled with dreams, not so much of glory as of a more private form of self-gratification. For Quintus Servilius Caepio was a true Servilius Caepio, which meant that the opportunity to increase his fortune from a term as governor was more alluring by far than mere military fortune. He had been a praetor-governor in Further Spain, when Scipio Nasica had declined the job on the grounds that he was not to be trusted, and he had done very well for himself. Now that he was a consul-governor, he expected to do even better.

If it was routinely possible to send troops from Italy to Spain by water, then Gnaeus Domitius Ahenobarbus would not have needed to open up the land route along the coast of Gaul-across-the-Alps; as it was, the prevailing winds and sea currents made water transportation too risky. So Caepio's legions, like Lucius Cassius's the year before, were obliged to walk the thousand-plus miles from Campania to Narbo. Not that the legions minded the walk; every last one of them hated and feared the sea, and dreaded the thought of a hundred miles of sailing far more than the reality of a thousand miles of walking. For one thing, their muscles were laid on from infancy in the right way to facilitate swift and end-less walking, and walking was the most comfortable form of lo-comotion.

The journey from Campania to Narbo took Caepio's legions a little over seventy days, which meant they averaged less than fif-teen miles a day—a slow pace, hampered as they were not only by a large baggage train, but by the many private animals and vehicles and slaves the old-style propertied Roman soldier knew himself entitled to carry with him to ensure his own comfort.

In Narbo, a little seaport Gnaeus Domitius Ahenobarbus had reorganized to serve the needs of Rome, the army rested just long enough to recover from its march, yet not long enough to soften up again. In early summer Narbo was a delightful place, its pel-lucid waters alive with shrimp, little lobsters, big crabs, and swimmy fish of all kinds. And in the mud at the bottom of the saltwater pools around the mouths of the Atax and the Ruscino were not only oysters, but dug-mullets. Of all the fish the legions of Rome had catalogued worldwide, dug-mullets were considered the most delicious. Round and flat like plates, with both eyes on one side of their silly thin heads, they lurked under the mud, had to be dug out, and then were speared as they floundered about trying to dig themselves back into the mud.

The legionary didn't get sore feet. He was too used to walking, and his thick-soled, ankle-supporting sandals had hobnails to raise him still further off the ground, absorb some of the shock, and keep pebbles out. However, it was wonderful to swim in the sea around Narbo, easing aching muscles, and those few soldiers who had managed to escape so far being taught to swim were here discovered, and the omission rectified. The local girls were no different from girls all over the world—crazy for men in uniform—and for the space of sixteen days Narbo hummed with irate fathers, vengeful brothers, giggling girls, lecherous legion-aries, and tavern brawls, keeping the provost marshals busy and the military tribunes in a foul temper.

Then Caepio packed his men up and moved them out along the excellent road Gnaeus Domitius Ahenobarbus had built between the coast and the city of Tolosa. Where the river Atax bent at right angles as it flowed from the Pyrenees away to the south, the grim fortress of Carcasso frowned from its heights; from this point the legions marched over the hills dividing the headwaters of the huge Garumna River from the short streams emptying into the Middle Sea, and so came down at last to the lush alluvial plains of Tolosa.

Caepio's luck was amazing, as usual; for the Germans had quarreled bitterly with their hosts, the Volcae Tectosages, and been ordered by King Copillus of Tolosa to leave the area. Thus Caepio found that the only enemies his eight legions had to deal with were the hapless Volcae Tectosages, who took one look at the steel-shirted ranks coming down from the hills like an endless snake, and decided discretion was by far the better part of valor. King Copillus and his warriors departed for the mouth of the Garumna, there to alert the various tribes of the region and wait to see if Caepio was as foolish a general as Lucius Cassius had been last year. Left in the care of old men, Tolosa itself surrendered at once. Caepio purred.

Why did he purr? Because Caepio knew about the Gold of Tolosa. And now he would find it without even having to fight a battle. Lucky Quintus Servilius Caepio!

A hundred and seventy years before, the Volcae Tectosages had joined a migration of the Gauls led by the second of the two famous Celtic kings called Brennus. This second Brennus had overrun Macedonia, poured down into Thessaly, turned the Greek defense at the pass of Thermopylae, and penetrated into central Greece and Epirus. He had sacked and looted the three richest temples in the world—Dodona in Epirus, Olympian Zeus, and the great sanctuary of Apollo and the Pythoness at Delphi.

Then the Greeks fought back, the Gauls retreated north with their plunder, Brennus died as the result of a wound, and his master plan fell apart. In Macedonia his leaderless tribes decided to cross the Hellespont into Asia Minor; there they founded the Gallic outpost nation called Galatia. But perhaps half of the Volcae Tectosages wanted to go home to Tolosa rather than cross the

Hellespont; at a grand council, all the tribes agreed that these homesick Volcae Tectosages should be entrusted with the riches of half a hundred pillaged temples, including the riches of Dodona, Olympia, and Delphi. It was just that, a trust. The home-bound Volcae Tectosages would hold the wealth of that whole migration in Tolosa against the day when all the tribes would return to Gaul, and claim it.

They melted everything down, to make their journey home easier: bulky solid-gold statues, silver urns five feet tall, cups and plates and goblets, golden tripods, wreaths made of gold or silver—into the crucibles they went, a small piece at a time, until a thousand laden wagons rolled westward through the quiet alpine valleys of the river Danubius, and came at last after several years down to the Garumna and Tolosa.

Caepio had heard the story while he had been governor of Further Spain three years before, and had dreamed ever since of finding the Gold of Tolosa, even though his Spanish informant had assured him the treasure trove was commonly regarded as a myth. There was no gold in Tolosa, every visitor to the city of the Volcae Tectosages swore to that fact; the Volcae Tectosages had no more wealth than their bountiful river and wonderful soil. But Caepio knew his luck. He *knew* the gold was there in Tolosa. Otherwise, why had he heard the story in Spain, and then got this commission to follow in the footsteps of Lucius Cassius to Tolosa—and found the Germans gone when he got there, the city his without a fight? Fortune was working her will, all in his cause.

He shed his military gear, put on his purple-bordered toga, and walked the rather rustic alleys of the town, poked through every nook and niche inside the citadel, wandered into the pastures and fields which encroached upon the outskirts in a manner more Spanish than Gallic. Indeed, Tolosa had little Gallic feel to it—no Druids, no typical Gallic dislike for an urban environment. The temples and temple precincts were laid out in the fashion of Spanish cities, a picturesque parkland of artificial lakes and rivulets, fed from and going back to the Garumna. Lovely!

Having found nothing on his walks, Caepio put his army to looking for the gold, a treasure hunt in a gala atmosphere conducted by troops who were released from the anxiety of facing an enemy, and who smelled a share in fabulous booty.

But the gold couldn't be found. Oh, the temples yielded a few priceless artifacts, but only a few, and no bullion. And the citadel was a complete disappointment, as Caepio had already seen for himself; nothing but weapons and wooden gods, horn vessels and plates of fired clay. King Copillus had lived with extreme simplicity, nor were there secret storage vaults under the plain flags of his halls.

Then Caepio had a bright idea, and set his soldiers to digging up the parks around the temples. In vain. Not one hole, even the deepest, revealed a sign of a gold brick. The gold diviners brandished their forked withies without finding one tiny signal to set the palms of their hands tingling or the withies bending like bows. From the temple precincts, the search spread into the fields and into the streets of the town, and still nothing. While the landscape came more and more to resemble the demented burrowing of a gigantic mole, Caepio walked and thought, thought and walked.

The Garumna was alive with fish, including freshwater salmon and several varieties of carp, and since the river fed the temple lakes, they too teemed with fish. It was more comfortable for Caepio's legionaries to catch fish in the lakes than in the river, wide and deep and swift flowing, so as he walked, he was surrounded by soldiers tying flies and making rods out of willow canes. Down to the biggest lake he walked, deep in thought. And as he stood there, he absently watched the play of light on the scales of lurking fish, glitters and gleams flickering in and out of the weeds, coming and going, ever changing. Most of the flashes were silver, but now and then an exotic carp would slide into view, and he would catch a gleam of gold.

The idea invaded his conscious mind slowly. And then it struck, it exploded inside his brain. He sent for his corps of engineers and told them to drain the lakes—not a difficult job, and one which certainly paid off. For the Gold of Tolosa lay at the bottom of these sacred pools, hidden by mud, weeds, the natural detritus of many decades.

When the last bar was rinsed off and stacked, Caepio came to survey the hoard, and gaped; that he had not watched as the gold was retrieved was a quirk of his peculiar nature, for he wanted to be surprised. He *was* surprised! In fact, he was flabbergasted. There were roughly 50,000 bars of gold, each weighing about 15 pounds; 15,000 talents altogether. And there were 10,000 bars of silver, each weighing 20 pounds; 3,500 talents of silver altogether. Then the sappers found other silver in the lakes, for it turned out that the only use the Volcae Tectosages had made of their riches was to craft their millstones out of solid silver; once a month they hauled these silver millstones from the river and used them to grind a month's supply of flour.

"All right," said Caepio briskly, "how many wagons can we spare to transport the treasure to Narbo?" He directed his question at Marcus Furius, his *praefectus fabrum,* the man who organized supply lines, baggage trains, equipment, accoutrements, fodder, and all the other necessities entailed in maintaining an army in the field.

"Well, Quintus Servilius, there are a thousand wagons in the baggage train, about a third of which are empty at this stage. Say three hundred and fifty if I do a bit of shuffling around. Now if each wagon carries about thirty-five talents—which is a good but not excessive load—then we'll need about three hundred and fifty wagons for the silver, and four hundred and fifty wagons for the gold," said Marcus Furius, who was not a member of the ancient Famous Family Furius, but the great-grandson of a Furian slave, and now was a client of Caepio's, as well as a banker.

"Then I suggest that we ship the silver first, in three hundred and fifty wagons, unload it in Narbo, and bring the wagons back to Tolosa to transport the gold," said Caepio. "In the meantime, I'll have the troops unload an extra hundred wagons, so that we have sufficient to send the gold off in one convoy."

By the end of Quinctilis, the silver had made its way to the coast and been unloaded, and the empty wagons sent back to To-losa for the gold; Caepio, as good as his word, had found the extra hundred wagons during the interval.

While the gold was loaded, Caepio wandered around deliri-ously from one stack of rich bricks to another, unable to resist stroking one or two in passing. He chewed the side of his hand, thinking hard, and finally sighed. "You had better go with the gold, Marcus Furius," he said then. "Someone very senior will have to stay with it in Narbo until every last brick is safely loaded on board the last ship." He turned to his Greek freedman Bias. "The silver is already on its way to Rome, I trust?"

"No, Quintus Servilius," said Bias smoothly. "The transports which brought heavy goods across on the winter winds at the be-ginning of the year have dispersed. I could only locate a dozen good vessels, and I thought it wiser to save them for the gold. The silver is under heavy guard in a warehouse and is quite safe. The sooner we ship the gold to Rome, the better, I think. As more de-cent ships come in, I'll hire them for the silver."

"Oh, we can probably send the silver to Rome by road," Caepio said easily.

"Even with the risk of a ship's foundering, Quintus Servilius, I would rather trust to the sea for every single brick, gold and sil-ver," said Marcus Furius. "There are too many hazards by road from raiding alpine tribes."

"Yes, you're quite right," agreed Caepio, and sighed. "Oh, it's almost too good to be true, isn't it? We are sending more gold and silver to Rome than there is in every one of Rome's treasuries!"

"Indeed, Quintus Servilius," said Marcus Furius, "it is remark-able."

The gold set out from Tolosa in its 450 wagons midway through Sextilis. It was escorted by a single cohort of legionaries, for the Roman road was a civilized one passing through civilized country that had not seen a hand lifted in anger in a very long time, and Caepio's agents had reported that King Copillus and his warriors were still within Burdigala, hoping to see Caepio venture down the same road Lucius Cassius had taken to his death.

Once Carcasso was reached, the road was literally downhill all the way to the sea, and the pace of the wagon train increased. Everyone was pleased, no one worried; the cohort of soldiers began to fancy that they could smell the salt of the shore. By nightfall, they knew, they would be clattering into the streets of Narbo; their minds were on oysters, dug-mullets, and Narbonese girls.

The raiding party, over a thousand strong, came whooping out of the south from the midst of a great forest bordering the road on either side, spilling in front of the first wagon and behind the last wagon some two miles further back, where the halves of the cohort were distributed. Within a very short space of time not a single Roman soldier was left alive, and the wagon drivers too lay in jumbled heaps of arms and legs.

The moon was full, the night fine; during the hours when the wagon train had waited for darkness, no one had come along the Roman road from either direction, for provincial Roman roads were really for the movement of armies, and trade in this part of the Roman Province was scant between coast and interior, especially since the Germans had come to settle around Tolosa.

As soon as the moon was well up, the mules were again harnessed to the wagons and some of the raiders climbed up to drive, while others walked alongside as guides. For when the forest ceased to march alongside the road, the wagon train turned off it onto a stretch of hard coastal ground suited only to the nibbling mouths of sheep. By dawn Ruscino and its river lay to the north; the wagon train resumed tenure of the Via Domitia and crossed the pass of the Pyrenees in broad daylight.

South of the Pyrenees its route was circuitous and not within sight of any Roman road until the wagon train crossed the Sucro River to the west of the town of Saetabis; from there it headed straight across the Rush Plain, a desolate and barren stretch of country which dived between two of the greatest of the chains of Spanish mountains, yet was not used as a short cut because of its waterlessness. After which the trail petered out, and further progress of the Gold of Tolosa was never ascertained by Caepio's investigators.

It was the misfortune of a dispatch rider carrying a message from Narbo to find the tumbled heaps of looted corpses alongside the road through the forest just to the east of Carcasso. And when the dispatch rider reported to Quintus Servilius Caepio in Tolosa, Quintus Servilius Caepio broke down and wept. He wept loudly for the fate of Marcus Furius, he wept loudly for the fate of that cohort of Roman soldiers, he wept loudly for wives and families left orphaned in Italy; but most of all he wept loudly for those glittering heaps of ruddy bricks, the loss of the Gold of Tolosa. It wasn't fair! What had happened to his luck? he cried. And wept loudly.

Clad in a dark toga of mourning, his tunic dark and devoid of any stripe on its right shoulder, Caepio wept again when he called his army to an assembly, and told them the news they had already learned through the camp grapevine.

"But at least we still have the silver," he said, wiping his eyes. "It alone will ensure a decent profit for every man at the end of the campaign."

"I'm thankful for small mercies, myself," said one veteran ranker to his tentmate and messmate; they had both been pressed off their farms in Umbria, though each had already served in ten campaigns over a period of fifteen years.

"You are?" asked his companion, somewhat slower in his thought processes, due to an old head wound from a Scordisci shield boss.

"Too right I am! Have you ever known a general to share *gold* with us scum-of-the-earth soldiers? Somehow he always finds a reason why he's the only one gets it. Oh, and the Treasury gets some, that's how he manages to hang on to most of it, he buys the Treasury off. At least we're going to get a share of the silver, and there was enough silver to make a mountain of. What with all the fuss about the gold going missing, the consul don't have much choice except to be fair about dishing out the silver."

"I see what you mean," said his companion. "Let's catch a nice fat salmon for our supper, eh?"

Indeed, the year was wearing down and Caepio's army had not had to do any fighting at all, save for that one unlucky cohort deputed to guard the Gold of Tolosa. Caepio wrote off to Rome with the whole story from the decamped Germans to the lost gold, asking for instructions.

By October he had his answer, which was much as he had expected: he was to remain in the neighborhood of Narbo with his entire army, winter there, and wait for fresh orders in the spring. Which meant that his command had been extended for a year; he was still the governor of Roman Gaul.

But it wasn't the same without the gold. Caepio fretted and moped, and often wept, and it was noted by his senior officers that he found it difficult to settle, kept on walking back and forth. Typical of Quintus Servilius Caepio, was the general feeling; no one really believed that the tears he shed were for Marcus Furius, or the dead soldiers. Caepio wept for his lost gold.

One of the main characteristics of a long campaign in a foreign land is the way the army and its chain of command settle into a life-style which regards the foreign land as at least a semipermanent home. Despite the constant movements, the campaigns, the forays, the expeditions, base camp takes on all the aspects of a town: most of the soldiers find women, many of the women produce babies, shops and taverns and traders multiply outside the heavily fortified walls, and mud-brick houses for the women and babies mushroom through a haphazard system of narrow streets.

Such was the situation in the Roman base camp outside Utica, and to a lesser extent the same thing occurred in the base camp outside Cirta. Since Marius chose his centurions and military tribunes very carefully, the period of the winter rains—which saw no fighting—was used not only for drills and exercises, but for sorting out the troops into congenial octets expected to tent and mess together, and dealing with the thousand and one disciplinary problems which naturally occur among so many men cooped up together for long stretches of time.

However, the arrival of the African spring—warm, lush, fruitful, and dry—always saw a great stirring within the camp, a little like the rolling shiver which starts at one end of a horse's skin and proceeds all the way to the other end. Kits were sorted out for the coming campaigns, wills made and lodged with the legion's clerks, mail shirts oiled and polished, swords sharpened, daggers honed, helmets padded with felt to withstand heat and chafing, sandals carefully inspected and missing hobnails attended to, tunics mended, imperfect or worn-out gear shown to the centurion and then turned in to the army stores for replacement.

Winter saw the arrival of a Treasury quaestor from Rome bearing pay for the legions, and a spate of activity among the clerks as they compiled their accounts and paid the men. Because his soldiers were insolvent, Marius had instituted two compulsory funds into which some of every man's pay was channeled—a fund for burial in respectable fashion for the legionary who died while away but not actually in battle (if he died in battle, the State paid for his burial), and a savings bank which would not release the legionary's money until he was discharged.

The army of Africa knew great things were planned for it in the spring of the year of Caepio's consulship, though only the very highest levels of command knew what. Orders went out for light marching order, which meant there would be no miles-long baggage train of ox-drawn wagons, only mule-drawn wagons able to keep up with and camp within each night's camp. Each soldier was now obliged to carry his gear on his back, which he did very cleverly, slung from a stout Y-shaped rod he bore on his left shoulder—shaving kit, spare tunics, socks, cold-weather breeches, and thick neckerchiefs to avoid chafing where the mail shirt rubbed against the neck, all rolled inside his blanket and encased in a hide cover; *sagum*—his wet-weather circular cape—in a leather bag; mess kit and cooking pot, water bag, a minimum of three days' rations; one precut, notched stake for the camp palisade, whichever entrenching tool he had been allocated, hide bucket, wicker basket, saw, and sickle; and cleaning compounds for the care of his arms and armor. His shield, encased in a supple kidskin protective cover, he slung across his back beneath his gear, and his helmet, its long dyed horsehair plume removed and stowed away carefully, he either added to the clutter depending from his carrying pole, or slung high on his right chest, or wore on his head if he marched in expectation of attack. He always donned his mail shirt for the march, its twenty-pound weight removed from his shoulders because he kilted it tightly around his waist with his belt, thus distributing its load on his hips. On the right side of his belt he fixed his sword in its scabbard, on the left side his dagger in its scabbard, and he wore both on the road. His two spears he did not carry.

Each eight men were issued with a mule, on which were piled their leather tent, its poles, and their spears, together with extra rations if no fresh issue was to be made every three days. Eighty legionaries and twenty noncombatants made up each century, officered by the centurion. Every century had one mule cart allocated to it, in which rode all the men's extra gear—clothing, tools, spare weapons, wicker breastwork sections for the camp's fortifications, rations if no issues were to be made for very long periods, and more. If the whole army was on the move and didn't expect to double back on its tracks at the end of a campaign, then every single thing it owned from plunder to artillery was carried in oxcarts which plodded miles to the rear under heavy guard.

When Marius set out for western Numidia in the spring, he left this heavy baggage behind in Utica, of course; it was nonetheless an imposing parade, seeming to stretch illimitably, for each legion and its mule carts and artillery took up a mile of road, and Marius led six legions west, plus his cavalry: The cavalry, however, he disposed on either side of the infantry, which kept the total length of his column to about six miles.

In open country there was no possibility of ambush, an enemy could not string himself out enough to attack all parts of the column simultaneously without being seen, and any attack on a part of the column would immediately have resulted in the rest of the column's turning in on the attackers and surrounding them, the act of wheeling bringing them into battle rank and file automatically.

And yet, every night the order was the same—make a camp. Which meant measuring and marking an area large enough to hold every man and animal in the army, digging deep ditches, fixing the sharpened stakes called *stimuli* in their bottoms, raising earthworks and palisades; but at the end of it, every man save the sentries could sleep like the dead, secure in the knowledge that no enemy could get inside quickly enough to take the camp by surprise.

It was the men of this army, the first composed entirely of the Head Count, who christened themselves "Marius's mules" because Marius had loaded them like mules. In an old-style army composed of propertied men, even ranker soldiers had marched with their effects loaded onto a mule, a donkey, or a slave; those who could not afford the outlay hired carrying space from those who could. In consequence, there was little control over the number of wagons and carts, as many were privately owned. And in consequence, the old-style army marched more slowly and less efficiently than did Marius's African Head Count army—and the many similar armies which were to follow in its wake for the next six hundred years.

Marius had given the Head Count useful work and a wage for doing it. But he did them few favors otherwise, save to lop the curved top and curved bottom off the old five-foot-tall infantryman's shield, for a man couldn't have carried that on his back beneath his loaded pole; at its new reduced height of three feet, it didn't collide with his burdens, or clip the backs of his ankles as he strode along.

And so they marched into western Numidia six miles long, singing their marching songs at the tops of their voices to keep their pace even and feel the comfort of military camaraderie, moving together, singing together, a single mighty human machine rolling irresistibly along. Midway down the column marched the general Marius with all his staff and the mule carts

carrying their gear, singing with the rest; none of the high command rode, for it was uncomfortable as well as conspicuous,
though they did have horses close by in case of attack, when the
general would need the additional height of horseback to see to
his dispositions and send out his staff with orders.

"We sack every town and village and hamlet we encounter,"
Marius said to Sulla.

And this program was faithfully carried out, with some addi-
tions: granaries and smokehouses were pillaged to augment the
food supply, local women were raped because the soldiers were
missing their own women, and homosexuality was punishable by
death. Most of all, everyone kept his eyes peeled for booty, which
was not allowed to be taken as private property, but was contributed to the army's haul.

Every eighth day the army rested, and whenever it reached a
point where the coastline intersected the march route, Marius
gave everyone three days of rest to swim, fish, eat well. By the
end of May they were west of Cirta, and by the end of Quinctilis
they had reached the river Muluchath, six hundred miles further
west again.

It had been an easy campaign; Jugurtha's army never appeared,
the settlements were incapable of resisting the Roman advance, and
at no time had they run short of either food or water. The inevitable
regimen of hardtack bread, pulse porridge, salty bacon, and salty
cheese had been varied by enough goat meat, fish, veal, mutton,
fruit, and vegetables to keep everyone in good spirits, and the sour
wine with which the army was occasionally issued had been augmented with Berber barley beer and some good wine.

The river Muluchath formed the border between western Numidia and eastern Mauretania; a roaring torrent in late winter, by
midsummer the big stream had dwindled to a string of water
holes, and by the late autumn it dried up completely. In the midst
of its plain not far from the sea there reared a precipitous volcanic
outcrop a thousand feet high, and on top of it Jugurtha had built
a fortress. In it, so Marius's spies had informed him, there was a

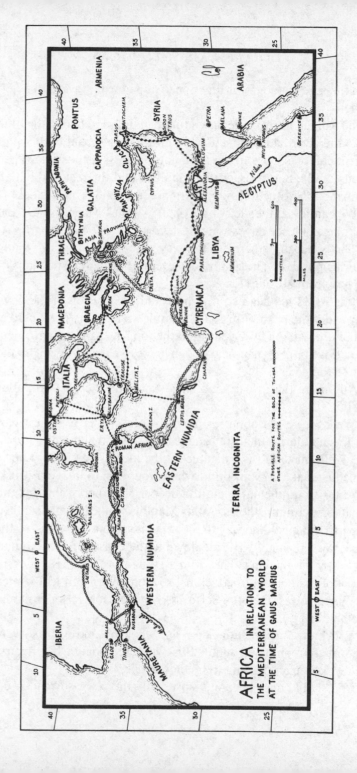

AFRICA IN RELATION TO
THE MEDITERRANEAN WORLD
AT THE TIME OF GAIUS MARIUS

A POSSIBLE ROUTE FOR THE GOLD OF TOLOSA ○○○○○○○○○○
OTHER AFRICAN ROUTES ●━━━●━━━●

great treasure stored, for it functioned as Jugurtha's western head-quarters.

The Roman army came down to the plain, marched to the high banks the river had cut itself when in full spate, and built a permanent camp as close to the mountain fortress as possible. Then Marius, Sulla, Sertorius, Aulus Manlius, and the rest of the high command took time to study the impregnable-looking citadel.

"We can forget the idea of a frontal assault," Marius said, "and I, for one, can't see any way to besiege it."

"That's because there isn't a way to besiege it," said young Sertorius positively; he had made several thorough inspections of the peak from all sides.

Sulla lifted his head so that he could see the top of the peak from under the brim of his hat. "I think we're going to sit here at the bottom without ever getting to the top," he said, and grinned. "Even if we built a gigantic wooden horse, we'd never get it up the track to the gates."

"Any more than we'd get a siege tower up there," said Aulus Manlius.

"Well, we've got about a month before we have to turn east again," said Marius finally. "I suggest we spend that month camped here. We'll make life as palatable for the men as possible—Lucius Cornelius, make up your mind where you want to take our drinking water from, then allocate the deeper river pools downstream of that for swimming holes. Aulus Manlius, you can organize fishing parties to go all the way to the sea—it's about ten miles, so the scouts say. You and I will ride down to the coast ourselves tomorrow to spy out the land. They're not going to run the risk of coming out of that citadel to attack us, so we may as well let the men enjoy themselves. Quintus Sertorius, you can forage for fruit and vegetables."

"You know," said Sulla later on, when he and Marius were alone in the command tent, "this whole campaign has been a holiday. When am I going to be blooded?"

"You should have been at Capsa, only the place surrendered," said Marius, and gave his quaestor a searching glance. "Are you becoming bored, Lucius Cornelius?"

"Actually, no," said Sulla, frowning. "I wouldn't have believed how interesting this kind of life is—there's always something interesting to do, interesting problems to wrestle. I don't even mind the bookkeeping! It's just that I need to be blooded. Look at you. By the time you were my age, you'd been in half a hundred battles. Whereas look at me—a tyro."

"You'll be blooded, Lucius Cornelius, and hopefully soon."

"Oh?"

"Certainly. Why do you think we're here, so far from anywhere important?"

"No, don't tell me, let me work it out!" said Sulla quickly. "You're here because . . . because you're hoping to give King Bocchus a big enough fright to ally himself with Jugurtha . . . because if Bocchus does ally himself with Jugurtha, Jugurtha will feel strong enough to attack."

"Very good!" said Marius, smiling. "This land is so vast we could spend the next ten years marching up and down it, and never so much as smell Jugurtha on the wind. If he didn't have the Gaetuli, smashing the settled areas would smash his ability to resist, but he does have the Gaetuli. However, he's too proud to like the idea of a Roman army on the loose among his towns and villages, and there's no doubt he must be feeling the pinch of our raids, particularly in his grain supply. Yet he's too crafty to risk a pitched battle while I'm in command. Unless we can push Bocchus to his aid. The Moors can field at least twenty thousand good troops, and five thousand excellent cavalry. So if Bocchus does join him, Jugurtha will move against us, nothing surer."

"Don't you worry that with Bocchus, he'll outnumber us?"

"No! Six Roman legions properly trained and properly led can contend with any enemy force, no matter how large."

"But Jugurtha learned his warfare with Scipio Aemilianus at Numantia," said Sulla. "He'll fight the Roman way."

"There are other foreign kings who fight the Roman way," said

Marius, "but their troops aren't Roman. Our methods were evolved to suit the minds and temperaments of our people, and I make no distinction in this regard between Roman and Latin and Italian."

"Discipline," said Sulla.

"And organization," said Marius.

"Neither of which is going to get us to the top of that mountain out there," said Sulla.

Marius laughed. "True! But there's always one intangible, Lucius Cornelius."

"What's that?"

"Luck," said Marius. "Never forget luck."

They had become good friends, Sulla and Marius, for though there were differences between them, there were also basic similarities: neither man was an orthodox thinker, both men were unusual, adversity had honed each of them finely, and each was capable of great detachment as well as great passion. Most important similarity of all, both men liked to get on with the job, and liked to excel at it. The aspects of their natures which might have driven them apart were dormant during those early years, when the younger man could not hope to rival the older in any way, and the younger man's streak of cold-bloodedness did not need to be exercised, any more than did the older man's streak of iconoclasm.

"There are those who maintain," said Sulla, stretching his arms above his head, "that a man makes his own luck."

Marius opened his eyes wide, an action which sent his eyebrows flying upward. "But of course! Still, isn't it nice to know one has it?"

Publius Vagiennius, who hailed from back-country Liguria and was serving in an auxiliary squadron of cavalry, found himself with a great deal more to do than he liked to do after Gaius Marius established camp along the banks of the river Muluchath. Luckily the plain was covered with a long, dense growth of native grass turned silver by the summer sun, so that grazing for the army's several thousand mules was not a problem. However, horses were fussier eaters than mules, and nudged half-heartedly at this hard strappy ground cover—with the result that the cavalry's horses had to be moved to the north of the citadel mountain in the midst of the plain, to a place where underground soaks had stimulated the growth of more tender grasses.

If the commander were other than Gaius Marius, thought Publius Vagiennius resentfully, the whole of the cavalry might have been permitted to camp separately, in close proximity to decent grazing for their horses. But no. Gaius Marius wanted no temptations offered the dwellers in the Muluchath citadel, and had issued orders that every last man had to camp within the main compound. So every day the scouts had first to ascertain that no Enemy lurked in the vicinity; then the cavalry troopers were allowed to lead their horses out to graze, and every evening were obliged to lead their horses back again to the camp. This meant every horse had to be hobbled to graze, otherwise catching it would have been impossible.

Every morning therefore Publius Vagiennius had to ride one of his two mounts and lead the other across the plain from the camp to the good grass, hobble them for a good day's browsing, and plod the five miles back to the camp, where (it seemed to him, at any rate) his hours of leisure had just begun when it was time to plod out to pick up his horses again. Added to which, not a cavalry trooper born liked walking.

However, there was nothing to say a man had to walk back to camp after turning his animals out to graze; therefore Publius Vagiennius made some adjustments to his schedule. Since he rode bareback and without a bridle—only a fool would leave his precious saddle and bridle parked in open country for the day—he got into the habit of slinging a water bag over his shoulder and a lunch pouch on his belt when starting out from the camp. Then, having liberated his two animals close to the base of the citadel mountain, he would retire to a shady spot to while away his day.

On his fourth trip, he settled comfortably with water bag and lunch pouch in a fragrant flower-filled dell surrounded by sheer crags, sat down with his back against a grassy shelf, closed his eyes, and dozed. Then came a moist little puff of wind spinning dizzily down the funnels and grooves of the mountain, and on its breath a very strong, curious smell. A smell which made Publius Vagiennius, eyes gleaming excitedly, sit up with a jerk. For it was a smell he knew. Snails. Big, fat, juicy, sweet, succulent, ambrosiac snails!

In the towering coastal alps of Liguria and in the higher alps behind—whence came Publius Vagiennius—there were snails. He had grown up on snails. He had become addicted to putting garlic in everything he ate thanks to snails. He had become one of the world's most knowledgeable connoisseurs of snails. He dreamed one day of breeding snails for the market, even of producing a brand-new breed of snails. Some men's noses were tuned to wines, other men's noses were tuned to perfumes, but the nose of Publius Vagiennius was tuned to snails. And that whiff of snails which came borne on the wind off the citadel mount told him that somewhere up aloft dwelled snails of an unparalleled deliciousness.

With the industry of a pig on the trail of truffles, he got to work following the evidence of his olfactory apparatus, prowling the flanges of rock for a way up to the snail colony. Not since coming to Africa with Lucius Cornelius Sulla in September of the year before had he so much as tasted a snail. African snails were held to be the best in the world, but wherever they lived he hadn't found out, and those which came into the markets of Utica and Cirta went straight to the tables of the military tribunes and the legates—if they didn't go straight to Rome, that is.

Anyone less motivated would not have found the ancient fumarole, its volcanic vapors long since spent, for it lay behind a seemingly uninterrupted wall of basalt formed in tall columnar crystals; nose down, Publius Vagiennius sniffed his way around an optical illusion and found a huge chimney. During the passage of millions of years of inactivity, dust blown in by winds had filled the vent to the level of the ground outside and was piling up against the leeward wall higher and higher, but it was still possible for a man to gain access to the interior of this natural cavity. It measured some twenty feet across, and perhaps two hundred feet upward there gleamed a patch of sky. The walls were vertical, and to almost all observers appeared unscalable. But Publius Vagiennius was an alpine man; he was also a snail gastronome on the track of a superlative taste experience. So he climbed the fumarole—not without difficulty, but certainly without ever being in real danger of falling.

And at its top he emerged onto a grassy shelf perhaps a hundred feet long and fifty feet wide at its widest point, which was where the chimney came to its termination. Because all of this occurred on the north face of the rugged volcanic outcrop—actually the eroded remnant of the lava plug, for the outer mountain itself had disappeared aeons before—the shelf was permanently wet from seepage, some of which dripped over the rim of the fumarole, but most of which ran down the rocks on the outside at the point where the shelf sloped to form a fissure. A great crag some hundred feet above overhung most of the shelf, and the cliff between shelf and overhang was hollowed out into an open-fronted cave wet with seepage, a wonderful wall of ferns, mosses, liverworts, and sedges; at one place so much water was being squeezed out of the rock by the enormous pressures of the upper mountain that a tiny rivulet twinkled and fell with copious splashes along its way, and ran off with the other seepage over the edge of the shelf. Clearly this was the reason why the grass on the plain at the northern base of the outcrop was sweeter.

Where the great cave now yawned had once been a deposit of mud agglomerate which penetrated much deeper into the lava plug, gathered water, and emerged to the surface only to be greedily chewed away by wind and frosts. One day, the expert mountain man Publius Vagiennius knew, the basalt crag teetering so ominously overhead would become undermined enough to break off; shelf and cave would be buried, as would the old volcanic chimney.

The great cave was perfect snail country, permanently damp, a pocket of humid air in a notoriously dry land, stuffed with all the decayed plant matter and minute dead insects snails adored, always shady, protected from the brunt of the winds by a crag from below that reared up much higher than the shelf for a third of its length, and curved outward, thus deflecting the winds.

The whole place reeked of snails, but not snails of any kind known to Publius Vagiennius, said his nose. When he finally saw one, he gaped. Its shell was as big as the palm of his hand! Having seen one, he soon distinguished dozens, and then hundreds, none of them shorter in the shell than his index finger, some of them longer than his outstretched hand. Hardly believing his eyes, he climbed up into the cave, scouted it with ever-increasing amazement, and finally arrived at its far edge, where he found a way up and up and up; not a snake path, he thought in amusement, but a snail path!

The path dived into a crevice which opened into a smaller, more enclosed, ferny cave. The snails kept getting more numerous. And then he found himself around the side of the overhang, discovered it was in itself over a hundred feet thick, kept on climbing until, with a heave, he came out of Snail Paradise into Snail Tartarus, the dry and windswept lava plug atop the overhang. He gasped, panicked, ducked quickly behind a rock; for there not five hundred feet above him was the fortress. So easy was the incline he could have walked up it without a staff, and so low was the citadel wall he could have pulled himself over it without a helping shove from beneath.

Publius Vagiennius descended back to the snail path, got down into the lower reaches of the cave, and there paused to pop half a dozen of the largest snails into the bloused chest section of his tunic, each well wrapped in wet leaves. Then he began the serious descent, hindered by his precious cargo yet inspired by it to superhuman feats of rock climbing. And finally emerged into his little flower-filled dell.

A long drink of water, and he felt better; his snails were snug, slimy, safe. Not intending to share them with anyone, he transferred them from his tunic to his lunch pouch, complete with wet leaves and a few chunks of much drier humus collected in the dell, moistened from his water bag. The lunch pouch he tied securely to prevent the snails' escape, and put it in a shady place.

The next day he dined superbly, having brought a kettle with him in which to steam two of his catches, and some good oil-and-garlic sauce. Oh, what snails! Size in a snail most definitely did not mean toughness. Size in a snail simply meant additional nuances of flavor and more to eat with a lot less fiddling about.

He dined on two snails each day for six days, making one more trip up the fumarole to fetch down the second half dozen. But on the seventh day his conscience began to gnaw at him; had he been a more introspective sort of fellow, he might have come to the conclusion that his pangs of conscience were increasing in linear proportion to his pangs of snail-sated indigestion. At first all he thought was that he was a selfish *mentula*, to hoard the snails entirely for himself when he had good friends among his squadron's members. And then he began to think about the fact that he had discovered a way to scale the mountain.

For three more days he battled his conscience, and finally suffered from an attack of gastritis which quite killed all his appetite for snails and made him wish he had never heard of them. That made up his mind.

He didn't bother about reporting to his squadron commander; he went straight to the top.

Roughly in the center of the camp, where the *via praetoria* connecting the main and rear gates intersected with the *via principalis* connecting the two side gates, sat the general's command tent and its flagpole, with an open space on either flank for assemblies. Here, in a hide structure substantial enough to warrant a proper wooden framework, Gaius Marius had his command headquarters and his living quarters; under the shade of a long awning which extended in front of the main entrance was a table and chair, occupied by the military tribune of the day. It was his duty to screen those wanting to see the general, or to route inquiries about this or that to the proper destinations. Two sentries stood one to either side of the entrance, at ease but vigilant, the monotony of this duty alleviated by the fact that they could overhear all conversation between the duty tribune and those who came to see him.

Quintus Sertorius was on duty, and enjoying himself enormously. Solving conundrums of supply, discipline, morale, and men appealed to him, and he loved the increasingly complex and responsible tasks Gaius Marius gave him. If ever there was a case of hero worship, it existed in Quintus Sertorius, its object Gaius Marius; the embryonic master-soldier recognizing the mature form. Nothing Gaius Marius could have asked of him would have seemed a distasteful chore to Quintus Sertorius, so where other junior military tribunes loathed desk duty outside the general's tent, Quintus Sertorius welcomed it.

When the Ligurian horse trooper lurched up with the gait peculiar to men who straddle horses with their legs hanging down unsupported all their lives, Quintus Sertorius regarded him with interest. Not a very prepossessing sort of fellow, he had a face only his mother could have thought beautiful, but his mail shirt was buffed up nicely, his soft-soled Ligurian felt riding shoes were adorned with a pair of sparkling spurs, and his leather knee breeches were respectably clean. If he smelled a little of horses, that was only to be expected; all troopers did, it was ingrained, and had nothing to do with how many baths they took or how often they washed their clothes.

One pair of shrewd brown eyes looked into another pair, each liking what it saw.

No decorations yet, thought Quintus Sertorius, but then, the cavalry hadn't really seen any action yet, either.

Young for this job, thought Publius Vagiennius, but a real neat-looking soldier, if ever I saw one—typical Roman footslogger, though, no taste for horses.

"Publius Vagiennius, Ligurian cavalry squadron," said Publius Vagiennius. "I'd like to see Gaius Marius."

"Rank?" asked Quintus Sertorius.

"Trooper," said Publius Vagiennius.

"Your business?"

"That's private."

"The general," said Quintus Sertorius pleasantly, "doesn't see ordinary troopers of auxiliary cavalry, especially escorted by no one save themselves. Where's your tribune, trooper?"

"He don't know I'm here," said Publius Vagiennius, looking mulish. "My business is private."

"Gaius Marius is a very busy man," said Quintus Sertorius.

Publius Vagiennius leaned both hands on the table and thrust his head closer, almost asphyxiating Sertorius with the smell of garlic. "Now listen, young sir, you tell Gaius Marius I've got a proposition of great advantage to him—but I'm not going to spill it to anyone else, and that's final."

Keeping his eyes aloof and his face straight while he was dying to burst out laughing, Quintus Sertorius got to his feet. "Wait here, trooper," he said.

The interior of the tent was divided into two areas by a leather wall sliced up its center to form a flap. The back room formed Marius's living quarters, the front room his office. This front room was by far the bigger of the two, and held an assortment of folding chairs and tables, racks of maps, some models of siege-works the engineers had been playing with regarding Muluchath Mountain, and portable sets of pigeonholed shelves in which reposed various documents, scrolls, book buckets, and loose papers.

Gaius Marius was sitting on his ivory curule chair to one side of the big folding table he called his personal desk, with Aulus Manlius, his legate, on its other side, and Lucius Cornelius Sulla, his quaestor, between them. They were clearly engaged in the activity which they detested most, but which was dear to the hearts of the bureaucrats who ran the Treasury—going through the accounts and keeping the books. That this was a preliminary conference was easy to see for a Quintus Sertorius; if it had been serious, several clerks and scribes would also have been in attendance.

"Gaius Marius, I apologize for interrupting you," said Sertorius, rather diffidently.

Something in his tone made all three men lift their heads to look at him closely.

"You're forgiven, Quintus Sertorius. What is it?" asked Marius, smiling.

"Well, it's probably a complete waste of your time, but I've got a trooper of Ligurian cavalry outside who insists on seeing you, Gaius Marius, but won't tell me why."

"A trooper of Ligurian cavalry," said Marius slowly. "And what does his tribune have to say?"

"He hasn't consulted his tribune."

"Oh, top secret, eh?" Marius surveyed Sertorius shrewdly. "Why should I see this man, Quintus Sertorius?"

Quintus Sertorius grinned. "If I could tell you that, I'd be a lot better at my job," he said. "I don't know why, and that's an honest answer. But—I don't know, I'm probably wrong, but—I think you should see him, Gaius Marius. I've got a feeling about it."

Marius laid down the paper in his hand. "Bring him in."

The sight of all the Senior Command sitting together did not even dent Publius Vagiennius's confidence; he stood blinking in the dimmer light, no fear on his face.

"This is Publius Vagiennius," said Sertorius, preparing to leave again.

"Stay here, Quintus Sertorius," said Marius. "Well now, Publius Vagiennius, what have you to say to me?"

"Quite a lot," said Publius Vagiennius.

"Then spit it out, man!"

"I will, I will!" said Publius Vagiennius, uncowed. "The thing is, I'm just going through my options first. Do I lay my information, or put up my business proposition?"

"Does one hinge upon the other?" asked Aulus Manlius.

"It most certainly do, Aulus Manlius."

"Then let's have the business proposition first," said Marius, poker-faced. "I like the oblique approach."

"Snails," said Publius Vagiennius.

All four Romans looked at him, but no one spoke.

"My business proposition," said Publius Vagiennius patiently. "It's snails. The biggest, juiciest snails you ever seen!"

"So that's why you reek of garlic!" said Sulla.

"Can't eat snails without garlic," said Vagiennius.

"How can we help you with your snails?" asked Marius.

"I want a concession," said Vagiennius, "and I want a introduction to the right people in Rome to market them."

"I see." Marius looked at Manlius, Sulla, Sertorius. No one was smiling. "All right, you've got your concession, and I imagine between us we can scrape up the odd introduction. Now what's the information you want to lay?"

"I found a way up the mountain."

Sulla and Aulus Manlius sat up straight.

"You found a way up the mountain," said Marius slowly.

"Yes."

Marius got up from behind the table. "Show me," he said.

But Publius Vagiennius backed away. "Well, I will, Gaius Marius, I will! But not until we sort out my snails."

"Can't it wait, man?" asked Sulla, looking ominous.

"No, Lucius Cornelius, it can't!" said Publius Vagiennius, thereby demonstrating that he knew all the names of the Senior Command when he saw them. "The way to the top of the mountain goes straight through the middle of my snail patch. And it's *my* snail patch! The best snails in the whole world too! Here." He unslung his lunch pouch from its rather incongruous resting place athwart his long cavalry sword, opened it, and carefully withdrew an eight-inch-long snail shell, which he put on Marius's desk.

They all looked at it fixedly, in complete silence. Since the surface of the table was cool and sleek, after a moment or two the snail ventured out, for it was hungry, and it had been jolted around inside Publius Vagiennius's lunch pouch for some time, deprived of tranquillity. Now it rabbited out of its hat as snails do, not emerging like a tortoise, but rather jacking its shell up into the air and expanding into existence under it via slimy amorphous lumps. One such lump formed itself into a tapering tail, and the opposite lump into a stumpy head which lifted bleary stalks into the air by growing them out of nothing. Its metamorphosis complete, it began to chomp quite audibly upon the mulch Publius Vagiennius had wrapped around it.

"Now that," said Gaius Marius, "is what I call a *snail*."

"Rather!" breathed Quintus Sertorius.

"You could feed an army on those," said Sulla, who was a conservative eater, and didn't like snails any more than he liked mushrooms.

"That's it!" yelped Publius Vagiennius. "That's just it! I don't want them greedy *mentulae*"—his audience winced—"pinching my snails! There's a lot of snails, but five hundred soldiers'd see the end of them! Now I want to bring them to some place handy to Rome and breed them, and I don't want my snail patch ruined either. I want that concession, and I want my snail patch kept safe from all the *cunni* in this here army!"

"It's an army of *cunni* all right," said Marius gravely.

"It so happens," drawled Aulus Manlius in his extremely upper-class accent, "that I can help you, Publius Vagiennius. I have a client from Tarquinia—Etruria, you know—who has been getting together a very exclusive and lucrative little business in the Cuppedenis markets—Rome, you know—selling snails. His name is Marcus Fulvius—not a noble Fulvius, you know—and I advanced him a little money to get himself started a couple of years ago. He's doing well. But I imagine he'd be very happy to come to some sort of agreement with you, looking at this magnificent—truly magnificent, Publius Vagiennius!—snail."

"You got a deal, Aulus Manlius," said the trooper.

"*Now* will you show us the way up the mountain?" demanded Sulla, still impatient.

"In a moment, in a moment," said Vagiennius, turned to where Marius was lacing on his boots. "First I want to hear the general say my snail patch will be safe."

Marius finished with his boots and straightened up to look Publius Vagiennius in the eye. "Publius Vagiennius," he said, "you are a man after my own heart! You combine a sound busi-

ness head with a staunchly patriotic spirit. Fear not, you have my
word your snail patch will be kept safe. Now lead us to the mountain, if you please."

When the investigative party set out shortly thereafter, it had
been augmented by the chief of engineers. They rode to save
time, Vagiennius on his better horse, Gaius Marius on the elderly
but elegant steed he saved mostly for parades, Sulla adhering to
his preference for a mule, and Aulus Manlius and Quintus Sertorius and the engineer on ponies out of the general compound.

The fumarole represented no difficulties to the engineer.
"Easy," he said, gazing up the chimney. "I'll build a nice wide
staircase all the way up, there's room."

"How long will it take you?" asked Marius.

"I just happen to have a few cartloads of planks and small
beams with me, so—oh, two days, if I work day and night," said
the engineer.

"Then get to it at once," said Marius, gazing at Vagiennius
with renewed respect. "You must be three parts goat to be able to
climb up this," he said.

"Mountain born, mountain bred," said Vagiennius smugly.

"Well, your snail patch will be safe until the staircase is done,"
Marius said as he led the way back to the horses. "Once your
snails come under threat, I'll deal with it myself."

Five days later the Muluchath citadel belonged to Gaius Marius, together with a fabulous hoard of silver coins, silver bars, and
a thousand talents in gold; there were also two small chests, one
stuffed with the finest, reddest *carbunculus* stones anyone had
ever seen, and the other stuffed with stones no one had ever seen,
long naturally faceted crystals carefully polished to reveal that
they were deep pink at one end, shading through to dark green at
the other.

"A fortune!" said Sulla, holding up one of the parti-colored
stones the locals called *lychnites.*

"Indeed, indeed!" gloated Marius.

As for Publius Vagiennius, he was decorated at a full assembly
of the army, receiving a complete set of nine solid-silver *phalerae,*

these being big round medallions sculpted in high relief and joined together in three rows of three by chased, silver-inlaid straps so that they could be worn on the chest over the top of the cuirass or mail shirt. He quite liked this distinction, but he was far better pleased by the fact that Marius had honored his word, and protected the snail patch from predators by fencing off a route for the soldiers to take to the top of the mountain. This passageway Marius had then screened with hides, so that the soldiers never knew what succulent goodies cruised rheumily through the cave of ferns. And when the mountain was taken, Marius ordered the staircase demolished immediately. Not only that, but Aulus Manlius had written off to his client the ignoble Marcus Fulvius, setting a partnership in train for when the African campaign was over, and Publius Vagiennius had his discharge.

"Mind you, Publius Vagiennius," said Marius as he strapped on the nine silver *phalerae*, "the four of us expect a proper reward in years to come—free snails for our tables, with an extra share for Aulus Manlius."

"It's a deal," said Publius Vagiennius, who had discovered to his sorrow that his liking for snails had permanently gone since his illness. However, he now regarded snails with the jealous eye of a preserver rather than a destroyer.

By the end of Sextilis the army was on its way back from the borderlands, eating very well off the land because the harvest was in. The visit to the edge of King Bocchus's realm had had the desired effect; convinced that once he had Numidia conquered, Marius was not going to stop, Bocchus decided to throw in his lot with his son-in-law, Jugurtha. He therefore hustled his Moorish army to the Muluchath River and there met Jugurtha, who waited until Marius was gone, then reoccupied his denuded mountain citadel.

The two kings followed in the wake of the Romans as they headed east, not in any hurry to attack, and keeping far enough back to remain undetected. And then when Marius was within a hundred miles of Cirta, the kings struck.

It was just on dusk, and the Roman army was busy pitching camp. Even so, the attack did not catch the men completely off-guard, for Marius pitched camp with scrupulous attention to safety. The surveyors came in and computed the four corners, which were staked out, then the whole army moved with meticulous precision into the future camp's interior, knowing by rote exactly where each legion was to go, each cohort of each legion, each century of each cohort. No one tripped over anyone else; no one went to the wrong place; no one erred as to the amount of ground he was to occupy. The baggage mule train was brought inside too, the noncombatants of each century took charge of each octet's mules and the century's cart; and the train attendants saw to stabling of the animals and storage of the carts. Armed with digging tools and palisade stakes from their backpacks, the soldiers, still completely armed, went to the sections of boundary always designated to them. They worked in their mail shirts and girt with swords and daggers; their spears were planted firmly in the ground and their shields propped against them, after which their helmets were hooked by their chin straps around the spears and over the fronts of the shields so that a wind could not blow the erections over. In that way, every man's helmet, shield, and spear were within reach while the laboring went on.

The scouts did not find the Enemy, but came in reporting all clear, then went to do their share of pitching camp. The sun had set. And in the brief lustrous dimness before darkness fell, the Numidian and Mauretanian armies spilled out from behind a nearby ridge and descended upon the half-finished camp.

All the fighting took place during darkness, a desperate business which went against the Romans for some hours. But Quintus Sertorius got the noncombatants kindling torches until finally the field was lit up enough for Marius to see what was happening, and from that point on, things began to improve for the Romans. Sulla distinguished himself mightily, rallying those troops who began to flag or panic, appearing everywhere he was needed—as if by magic, but in reality because he had that inbuilt military eye which could discern where the next weak spot was going to develop before it actually did. Sword blooded, blood up, he took to battle like a veteran—brave in attack, careful in defense, brilliant in difficulties.

And by the eighth hour of darkness, victory went to the Romans. The Numidian and Mauretanian armies drew off in fairly good order, yet left several thousands of their soldiers behind on the field, where Marius had lost surprisingly few.

In the morning the Roman army moved on, Marius having decided rest for his men was out of the question. The dead were properly cremated, and the Enemy dead were left for the vultures. This time the legions marched in square, with the cavalry disposed at front and at back of the compressed column, and the mules as well as the baggage mule train right in the middle. If a second attack occurred on the march, all the soldiers had to do was face outward in each square, while the cavalry was already placed to form wings. Each man now wore his helmet on his head, its colored horse's-tail plume fixed to its top; he carried his shield uncovered by its protective hide, and he also carried both his spears. Not until Cirta was reached would vigilance be relaxed.

On the fourth day, with Cirta the coming night's destination, the kings struck again. This time Marius was ready. The legions formed into squares, each square formed part of a vaster square with the baggage in its middle, and then each small square dissolved into rank and file to double its thickness facing the Enemy. As always, Jugurtha counted upon his many thousands of Numidian horse to unsettle the Roman front; superb riders, they used neither saddle nor bridle, and wore no armor, relying for their punch and power upon fleetness, bravery and their deadly accuracy with javelin and long-sword. But neither his cavalry nor Bocchus's could break through into the center of the Roman square, and their infantry forces broke against a solid wall of legionaries undismayed by horse or foot.

Sulla fought in the front line with the leading cohort of the leading legion, for Marius was in control of tactics and the element of surprise was negligible; when Jugurtha's infantry lines finally broke, it was Sulla who led the charge against them, Sertorius not far behind.

Sheer desperation to be rid of Rome for once and for all kept Jugurtha in the battle too long. When he did decide to withdraw, it was already too late to do so, and he had no choice but to struggle on against a Roman force sensing victory. So the Roman victory when it came was complete, rounded, whole. The Numidian and Mauretanian armies were destroyed, most of their men dead on the field. Jugurtha and Bocchus got away.

Marius rode into Cirta at the head of an exhausted column, every man in it jubilant; there would be no more war on a grand scale in Africa—the least soldier knew it. This time Marius quartered his army within Cirta's walls, unwilling to risk exposure outside. His troops were billeted upon hapless Numidian civilians, and hapless Numidian civilians made up the work parties he sent out the next day to clean up the field of battle, burn the mountains of African dead, and bring in the far fewer Roman dead for the proper obsequies.

Quintus Sertorius found himself placed in charge of all the decorations which Marius intended to award at a special assembly of the army following the cremation of the fallen; he was also placed in charge of organizing the ceremony. As it was the first such ceremony he had ever attended, he had no idea how to go about his task, but he was intelligent and resourceful. So he found a veteran *primus pilus* centurion, and asked him.

"Now what you got to do, young Sertorius," said this old stager, "is get all of Gaius Marius's own decorations out, and display them on the general's dais so the men can see what sort of soldier he was. These are good boys of ours, Head Count or not, but they don't know nothing about the military life, and they don't come from families with a military tradition. So how do they know what sort of soldier Gaius Marius was? I do! That's because I been with Gaius Marius in every campaign he fought since—oh, Numantia."

"But I don't think he has his decorations with him," said Sertorius, dismayed.

"Course he has, young Sertorius!" said the veteran of a hundred battles and skirmishes. "They're his luck."

Sure enough, when applied to, Gaius Marius admitted that he did have his decorations along on the campaign. Looking a little embarrassed, until Sertorius told him of the centurion's remark about luck.

All of Cirta turned out to ogle, for it was an impressive ceremony, the army in full parade regalia, each legion's silver eagle wreathed with the laurels of victory, each maniple's standard of a silver hand wreathed with the laurels of victory, each century's cloth *vexillum* banner wreathed with the laurels of victory. Every man wore his decorations, but since this was a new army of new men, only a few of the centurions and a half-dozen soldiers sported armbands, neck rings, medallions. Of course Publius Vagiennius wore his set of silver *phalerae*.

Ah, but Gaius Marius himself reigned supreme! So thought the dazzled Quintus Sertorius, standing waiting to be awarded his Gold Crown for a single combat upon the field; Sulla too was waiting to be awarded a Gold Crown.

There they were, ranged behind him on the high dais, Gaius Marius's decorations. Six silver spears for killing a man in single combat on six different occasions; a scarlet *vexillum* banner embroidered in gold and finished with a fringe of gold bullion for killing several men in single combat on the same occasion; two silver-encrusted shields of the old oval pattern for holding hotly contested ground against odds. Then there were the decorations he wore. His cuirass was of hardened leather rather than the normal silver-plated bronze of a senior officer, for over it he wore all his *phalerae* on their gold-encrusted harnesses—no less than three full sets of nine in gold, two on the front of the cuirass, one on the back; six gold and four silver tores depended from little straps across shoulders and neck; his arms and wrists glittered with gold and silver *armillae* bracelets. Then there were his crowns. On his head he wore one *Corona Civica,* which was the crown of oak leaves awarded only to a man who had saved the lives of his fellows and held the ground on which he had done the deed for the rest of the battle. Two more oak-leaf crowns hung from two of the silver spears, indicating that he had won the *Corona Civica* no fewer than three times; on two more of the silver spears hung two Gold Crowns for conspicuous bravery, crowns made of gold hammered into the shape of laurel leaves; on the fifth spear hung a *Corona Muralis,* a gold crown with a crenellated battlement awarded for being the first man to scale the walls of an enemy town; and on the sixth spear hung a *Corona Vallaris,* a gold crown awarded for being the first man into an enemy camp.

What a man! thought Quintus Sertorius, mentally cataloguing these talismans. Yes, the only awards he hadn't won were the naval crown, given for valor in a sea battle—Marius had never fought at sea, so that omission was logical—and the *Corona Graminea,* the simple wreath of common grass awarded to a man who literally by his own valor and initiative saved a whole legion, or even a whole army. The grass crown had been given only a handful of times during the whole history of the Republic, the first time to the legendary Lucius Siccius Dentatus, who had won no less than twenty-six different crowns—but only one *Corona Graminea.* To Scipio Africanus during the second war against Carthage. Sertorius frowned, dredging up the rest of the winners. Oh, Publius Decius Mus had won it during the first Samnite war! And Quintus Fabius Maximus Verrucosis Cunctator had won it for stalking Hannibal up and down Italy, thus preventing Hannibal's gaining the confidence to attack Rome herself.

Then Sulla was called to receive his Gold Crown, and a full set of nine gold *phalerae* as well, for his valor during the first of the two battles against the kings. How pleased he looked, how—*enhanced.* Quintus Sertorius had heard that he was a cold sort of fellow, and had a cruel streak; but not once in their time together in Africa had he seen evidence to substantiate these accusations, and surely if they were true, Gaius Marius would not have liked him as well as he clearly did. For of course Quintus Sertorius did not understand that when life was going well, and was enjoyable, and held enough mental and physical challenge, coldness and cruelty could be buried, however temporarily; he also did not understand that

Sulla was quite shrewd enough to know Gaius Marius was not the man to whom to show the baser, darker side of himself. In fact, Lucius Cornelius Sulla had been on his very best behavior ever since Marius had asked for him as his quaestor—and had not found it at all difficult to be so, either.

"Oh!" Quintus Sertorius jumped. He had been so deep in his thoughts that he hadn't heard his name called, and got a dig in the ribs from his servant, almost as proud of Quintus Sertorius as Quintus Sertorius was of himself. Up onto the dais he stumbled, and stood there while the great Gaius Marius placed the Gold Crown on his head, then suffered the cheers of the army, and had his hand shaken by Gaius Marius and Aulus Manlius.

And after all the torcs and bracelets and medallions and banners were handed out, and some of the cohorts got group awards of gold or silver wreaths for their standard poles, Gaius Marius spoke.

"Well done, men of the Head Count!" he cried, the dazed recipients of decorations standing gathered around him. "You have proven yourselves braver than the brave, more willing than the willing, harder working than the hardworking, more intelligent than the intelligent! There's many a naked standard pole which now can be adorned with the decorations won by its owners! When we walk in triumph through Rome, we'll give them all something to look at! And in future, let no Roman say that the men of the Head Count don't care enough about Rome to win battles for her!"

November was just beginning to promise rain when an embassage arrived in Cirta from King Bocchus of Mauretania. Marius let its members stew for several days, ignoring their pleas of urgency.

"They'll be soft as cushions," he said to Sulla when finally he consented to see them.

"I'm not going to forgive King Bocchus," he said as his opening gambit, "so go home! You're wasting my time."

The spokesman was a younger brother of the King, one Bogud,

and now Prince Bogud stepped forward quickly, before Marius could wave at his lictors to eject the embassage.

"Gaius Marius, Gaius Marius, my brother the King is only too aware of the magnitude of his transgressions!" said the prince. "He isn't asking for forgiveness, nor is he asking that you recommend to the Senate and People of Rome that he be reinstated as a Friend and Ally of the Roman People. What he does ask is that in the spring you send two of your most senior legates to his court in Tingis beyond the Pillars of Hercules. There he will explain to them most carefully why he allied himself with King Jugurtha, and he asks only that they listen to him with open ears. They are not to say one word to him in reply—they are to report what he has said to you, so that you may reply. Do, I entreat you, grant my brother the King this favor!"

"What, send two of my top men all the way to Tingis at the start of the campaigning season?" asked Marius with well-feigned incredulity. "No! The best I'll do is send them as far as Saldae." This was a small seaport not far to the west of Cirta's seaport, Rusicade.

The whole embassage threw up hands in horror. "Quite impossible!" cried Bogud. "My brother the King wishes to avoid King Jugurtha at all costs!"

"Icosium," said Marius, naming another seaport, this one about two hundred miles to the west of Rusicade. "I'll send my senior legate, Aulus Manlius, and my quaestor, Lucius Cornelius Sulla, as far as Icosium—but *now,* Prince Bogud, not in the spring."

"Impossible!" cried Bogud. "The King is in Tingis!"

"Rubbish!" said Marius scornfully. "The King is on his way back to Mauretania with his tail between his legs. If you send a fast rider after him, I'll guarantee he has no trouble reaching Icosium about the same moment as my legates sail in." He glared at Bogud balefully. "That is my best—and only!—offer. Take it or leave it."

Bogud took it. When the embassage embarked two days later, it sailed together with Aulus Manlius and Sulla upon a ship bound for Icosium, having sent that fast rider to catch up with the tattered remnants of the Moorish army.

"He was waiting for us when we sailed in, just as you said," Sulla reported a month later, upon his return.

"Where's Aulus Manlius?" asked Marius.

Sulla's eyes twinkled. "Aulus Manlius isn't well, so he decided to come back overland."

"A serious indisposition?"

"I've never seen a poorer sailor," said Sulla reminiscently.

"Well, I never knew that about him!" said Marius, amazed. "I take it then that you did most of the careful listening, not Aulus Manlius?"

"Yes," said Sulla, and grinned. "He's a funny little man, Bocchus. Round like a ball from too many sweeties. Very pompous on the surface, very timid underneath."

"It's a combination goes together," said Marius.

"Well, it's clear enough that he's afraid of Jugurtha; I don't think he's lying about that. And if we were to give him strong guarantees that we have no intention of removing him from rule in Mauretania, I think he'd be delighted to serve Rome's interests. But Jugurtha works on him, you know."

"Jugurtha works on everyone. Did you adhere to Bocchus's rule about saying nothing, or did you speak up?"

"Oh, I let him talk himself out first," said Sulla, "but then I spoke up. He tried to get all royal and dismiss me, so I told him his had been a one-sided bargain that did not bind your representatives as far as you were concerned."

"What did you have to say?" asked Marius.

"That if he was a clever little king, he'd ignore Jugurtha in the future and stick by Rome."

"How did he take that?"

"Quite well. Certainly I left him in a chastened mood."

"Then we'll wait and see what happens next," said Marius.

"One thing I did find out," added Sulla, "was that Jugurtha has come to the end of his recruiting tether. Even the Gaetuli are refusing to give him more men. Numidia is very tired of the war, and hardly anyone in the kingdom, be he a dweller in the settled regions or a nomad of the inland, now feels there's the remotest chance of winning."

"But will they hand over Jugurtha?"

Sulla shook his head. "No, of course they won't!"

"Never mind," said Marius, showing his teeth. "Next year, Lucius Cornelius! Next year we'll get him."

Shortly before the old year ended, Gaius Marius received a letter from Publius Rutilius Rufus, long delayed en route by a series of appalling storms.

> I know you wanted me to stand for consul in tandem with you, Gaius Marius, but an opportunity has come up which I'd be a fool to ignore. Yes, I intend to stand for the consulship of next year, and am lodging my name as a candidate tomorrow. The well seems to have run temporarily dry, you see. No one of any note is standing. What, not Quintus Lutatius Catulus Caesar again? I hear you ask. No, he's lying very low these days, as he belongs too obviously to that faction which has defended all our consuls responsible for the loss of so many soldier lives. So far the best nominee is a New Man of sorts—Gnaeus Mallius Maximus, no less. He's not a bad sort of fellow, I could certainly work with him—but if he's the best candidate in the field, I'm just about a certainty. Your own command is prorogued for the coming year, as you probably already know.
>
> Rome is really a very boring place at the moment; I have hardly any news to give you, and precious little by way of scandal. Your family are all well, Young Marius being a joy and a delight, very domineering and ahead of his years, into every sort of mischief and driving his mother mad, just as a small boy ought. However, your father-in-law, Caesar, is not well,

though of course, being Caesar, he never complains. There's something wrong with his voice, and no amount of honey seems to fix it.

And that really is the end of the news! How frightful. What can I talk about? Barely a page filled, and bare is right. Well, there's my niece Aurelia. And who on the face of this earth is Aurelia? I hear you ask. Nor are you one bit interested, I'll warrant. Never mind. You can listen; I'll be brief. I'm sure you know the story of Helen of Troy, even if you are an Italian hayseed with no Greek. She was so beautiful every single king and prince in all of Greece wanted to marry her. Of like kind is my niece. So beautiful that everyone of any note in Rome wants to marry her.

All the children of my sister, Rutilia, are handsome, but Aurelia is more than merely handsome. When she was a child, everyone deplored her face—it was too bony, too hard, too everything. But now she's turning eighteen, everyone is lauding exactly the same face.

I love her very much, as a matter of fact. Now why? I hear you ask. True, I am not normally interested in the female offspring of my many close relatives, even my own daughter and my two granddaughters. But I know why I prize my darling Aurelia. Because of her serving maid. For when she turned thirteen, my sister and her husband, Marcus Aurelius Cotta, decided she ought to have a permanent maidservant who would also function as companion and watchdog. So they bought a very good girl, and gave the girl to Aurelia. Who after a very short time announced that she didn't want this particular girl.

"Why?" asked my sister, Rutilia.

"Because she's lazy," said the thirteen-year-old.

Back the parents went to their dealer, and, after even more care, chose another girl. Whom Aurelia also refused.

"Why?" asked my sister, Rutilia.

"Because she thinks she can dominate me," said Aurelia.

And back the parents went a third time, and they combed Spurius Postumius Glycon's books for another girl. All three, I add, were highly educated, Greek, and vocally intelligent.

But Aurelia didn't want the third girl either.

"Why?" asked my sister, Rutilia.

"Because she's got an eye for the main chance; she's already fluttering her lashes at the steward," said Aurelia.

"All right, go and pick your own maidservant!" said my sister, Rutilia, refusing to have anything more to do with the whole business.

When Aurelia came home with her choice, the family was appalled. For there stood this sixteen-year-old girl of the Gallic Arverni, a vastly tall and skinny creature with a horrid round pink short-nosed face, faded blue eyes, cruelly cropped hair (it had been sold to make a wig when her previous master needed money), and the most enormous hands and feet I have ever seen on anyone, male or female. Her name, announced Aurelia, was Cardixa.

Now as you know, Gaius Marius, I am always intrigued with the backgrounds of those we bring into our houses as slaves. For, it has always struck me, we spend considerably more time deciding upon the menu for a dinner party than we do upon the people whom we trust to care for our clothes, our persons, our children, and even our reputations. Whereas, it struck me immediately, my thirteen-year-old niece Aurelia had chosen this ghastly Cardixa girl for precisely the right reasons. She wanted someone loyal, hardworking, submissive, and well intentioned, rather than someone who looked good, spoke Greek like a native (don't they all?), and could hold up her end of a conversation.

Thus I made it my business to find out about Cardixa, which was very simple. I merely asked Aurelia, who knew the girl's whole history. She had been sold into captivity with her mother when she was four years old, after Gnaeus Domitius Ahenobarbus had conquered the Arverni and carved out our province of Gaul-across-the-Alps. Not long after the pair arrived in Rome, the mother died, it appears of homesickness. So the child became a kind of page girl, trotting back and forth with chamber pots, pillows, and pouffes. She was sold several times after she lost her toddler's prettiness and began to grow into the gangling homely weed I saw when Aurelia brought her home. One master had sexually molested her when she was eight; another master had flogged her every time his wife complained; a third master had her taught to read and write along with his daughter, a recalcitrant student.

"So your pity was stirred, and you wanted to bring this poor creature into a kind home," I said to Aurelia.

And here, Gaius Marius, is why I love this girl more than I love my own daughter.

For my comment did not please her at all. She reared back a little like a serpent, and said, "Certainly not! Pity is admirable, Uncle Publius, for so all our books tell us, and our parents too. But I would find pity a poor reason for choosing a maidservant! If Cardixa's life has not been ideal, that is no fault of mine. Therefore I am in no way morally bound to rectify her misfortunes. I chose Cardixa because I am sure she will prove loyal, hardworking, submissive, and well intentioned. A pretty bucket is no guarantee that the book it contains is worth reading."

Oh, don't you love her too, Gaius Marius, just a little? Thirteen years old she was at the time! And the strangest part about it was that though in my atrocious handwriting now, what she said may sound priggish, or even unfeeling, I knew she was neither prig nor cold-heart. Common sense, Gaius Marius! My niece has common sense. And how many women do you know with such a wonderful gift as that? All these fellows here want to marry her because of her face and her figure and her fortune, where I would rather give her to someone who prized her common sense. But how does one decide whose suit to favor? That is the burning question we are all asking each other.

When he laid the letter down, Gaius Marius picked up his pen and drew a sheet of paper toward him. He dipped his stylus in his inkpot, and wrote without hesitation.

Of course I understand. Go to it, Publius Rutilius! Gnaeus Mallius Maximus will need all the help he can get, and you will prove an excellent consul. As to your niece, why don't you let her pick her own husband? She seems to have done all right with her maidservant. Though I can't honestly see what all the fuss is about. Lucius Cornelius tells me he is the father of a son, but he had the news from Gaius Julius, not from Julilla. Would you do me the favor of keeping an eye on that young lady? For I do not think Julilla is like your niece in the matter of common sense, and I do not know whom else to ask, considering that I cannot very well ask her *tata* to keep an eye on her. I thank you for telling me Gaius Julius is unwell. I hope when you receive this, you are a new consul.

THE SIXTH YEAR
(105 B.C.):

In the Consulship of
Publius Rutilius Rufus
and
Gnaeus Mallius Maximus

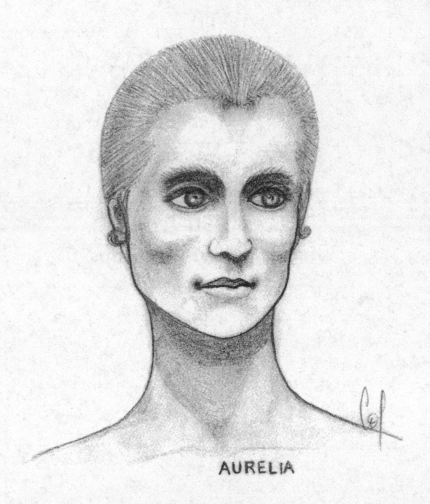

AURELIA

Though Jugurtha was not yet a fugitive in his own country, its more settled and eastern parts had certainly come to terms with the specter of the Romans, and accepted the inevitability of Roman dominance. However, Cirta, the capital, was situated in the center, so Marius decided it might be prudent to winter there himself, rather than in Utica. Cirta's inhabitants had never demonstrated any great fondness for the King, but Marius knew Jugurtha well enough to understand that he was at his most dangerous—and his most charming—when pressed; it would not be politic to leave Cirta open to seduction by the King. Sulla was left in Utica to govern the Roman province, while Aulus Manlius was released from service and allowed to go home. With him to Rome Manlius took the two sons of Gaius Julius Caesar, neither of whom had wanted to leave Africa. But Rutilius's letter had perturbed Marius; he had a feeling that it might be wise to give Caesar back his sons.

In January of the New Year, King Bocchus of Mauretania made up his mind at last; despite his blood and marital ties to Jugurtha, he would formally ally himself with Rome—*if* Rome would deign to have him. So he moved from Iol to Icosium, the place where he had interviewed Sulla and the seasick Manlius two months earlier, and sent a small embassage off from Icosium to treat with Marius. Unfortunately it did not occur to him that Marius would winter anywhere save in Utica; as a result, the little delegation made Utica its goal, thus passing well to the north of Cirta and Gaius Marius.

There were five Moorish ambassadors, including the King's younger brother Bogud once again, and one of his sons as well, but the party traveled in very little state and without a military escort; Bocchus wished no difficulties with Marius, and no intimations of martial intentions. He also wanted to bypass attention from Jugurtha.

In consequence, the cavalcade looked exactly like a group of prosperous merchants heading home with the proceeds of a season's good trading, and was irresistibly tempting to the gangs of armed bandits who had taken advantage of the fragmentation of Numidia and the impotence of its king by helping themselves to other people's property. As the group crossed the river Ubus not far south of Hippo Regius, it was set upon by outlaws and robbed of everything save the clothes its members wore; even its retinue of slaves and servants was taken for resale in some distant market.

Quintus Sertorius and his exquisitely tuned cerebral apparatus were on duty with Marius, which meant that Sulla was served by less perceptive officers. Knowing this, however, he had made it his practice to keep an eye on what was happening at the gates of the governor's palace in Utica; and, as luck would have it, he personally saw the raggle-taggle cluster of poor itinerants who stood trying fruitlessly to gain admission.

"But we must see Gaius Marius!" Prince Bogud was insisting. "We are the ambassadors of King Bocchus of Mauretania, I do assure you!"

Sulla recognized at least three of the group, and strolled over. "Bring them in, idiot," he said to the duty tribune, then took Bogud's arm to help him along, for he was clearly footsore. "No, the explanations can wait, Prince," he said firmly. "You need a bath, fresh clothes, food, and a rest."

Some hours later he heard Bogud's story.

"We have been much longer getting here than we expected," Bogud said in conclusion, "and I fear the King my brother will have despaired. May we see Gaius Marius?"

"Gaius Marius is in Cirta," said Sulla easily. "I advise you to tell me what it is your king wants, and leave it to me to get word to Cirta. Otherwise, there will be more delays."

"We are all blood relatives of the King, who asks Gaius Marius to send us onward to Rome, where we are to beg the Senate in person to reinstate the King in Rome's service," said Bogud.

"I see." Sulla rose to his feet. "Prince Bogud, please make yourself comfortable and wait. I'll send to Gaius Marius at once, but it will be some days before we hear."

Said Marius's letter, which turned up in Utica four days later:

Well, well, well! This could be quite useful, Lucius Cornelius. However, I must be extremely careful. The new senior consul, Publius Rutilius Rufus, tells me that our dear friend Metellus Numidicus Piggle-wiggle is going around informing anyone who will listen that he intends to prosecute me for extortion and corruption in my provincial administration. Therefore I can do nothing to give him ammunition. Luckily he'll have to manufacture his evidence, as it has never been my practice to extort or corrupt—well, you know that better than most, I imagine. So here is what I want you to do.

I shall give audience to Prince Bogud in Cirta, which means you will have to bring the embassage here. However, before you start out, I want you to gather up every single Roman senator, tribune of the Treasury, official representative of the Senate or People of Rome, and important Roman citizen, in the whole of the Roman African province. Bring them all to Cirta with you. For I am going to interview Bogud with every single Roman notable I can find listening to every word I say, and approving in writing of whatever I decide to do.

Shouting with laughter, Sulla put the letter down. "Oh, superbly done, Gaius Marius!" he remarked to the four walls of his office, and went to scatter havoc among his tribunes and administrative officials by ordering them to scour the whole province for Roman notables.

Because of its importance to Rome as a supplier of grain, Africa Province was a place the more globe-trotting members of the Senate liked to visit. It was also exotic and beautiful, and at this early time of the year, the prevailing winds being from the northern quadrant, it was a safer sea route to the east than passage across the Adriatic Sea—for those who had the extra time. And though it was the rainy season, that did not mean that every day it rained; between rains the climate was deliciously balmy compared to winter-struck Europa, and cured the visitor's chilblains immediately.

Thus Sulla was able to gather two globe-trotting senators and two visiting absentee landowners (including the biggest, Marcus Caelius Rufus), plus one senior Treasury official on winter vacation, and one plutocrat from Rome who had a huge business buying grain, and was currently in Utica to dabble a little in wheat futures.

"But the great coup," he said to Gaius Marius the moment he arrived in Cirta fifteen days later, "was none other than Gaius Billienus, who fancied taking a look at Africa on his way to govern Asia Province. Thus I am able to offer you a praetor with proconsular imperium, no less! We also have a Treasury quaestor, Gnaeus Octavius Ruso, who fortunately happened to sail into Utica harbor just before I set out, bearing the army's wages. So I dragooned him too."

"Lucius Cornelius, you're a man after my own heart!" said Marius, grinning broadly. "Oh, but you do catch on fast!"

And before he saw the Moorish embassage, Marius called a council of his Roman notables.

"I want to explain the situation to all of you august gentlemen exactly as it exists, and then after I have seen Prince Bogud and his fellow ambassadors in your presence, I want us to arrive at a joint decision as to what I ought to do about King Bocchus. It will be necessary for each of you to put down his opinion in writing, so that when Rome is informed, everyone can see that I did not exceed the limits of my authority," said Marius to senators, landowners, businessmen, one tribune of the Treasury, one quaestor, and one governor of a province.

The outcome of the meeting was exactly what Marius had wanted; he had put his case to the Roman notables with care as well as eloquence, and was vehemently supported by his quaestor, Sulla. A peace agreement with Bocchus was highly desirable, the notables concluded, and might best be accomplished if three of the Moors were sent onward to Rome escorted by the Treasury quaestor Gnaeus Octavius Ruso, and the two remaining Moors were returned to Bocchus forthwith as evidence of Rome's good faith.

So Gnaeus Octavius Ruso shepherded Bogud and two of his cousins onward to Rome, where they arrived early in March, and were heard at once by the Senate in a specially convened meeting. This was held in the temple of Bellona because the matter involved a foreign war with a foreign ruler; Bellona being Rome's own goddess of war and therefore far older than Mars, her temple was the place of choice for war meetings of the Senate.

The consul Publius Rutilius Rufus delivered the Senate's verdict with the temple doors wide open to permit those who clustered outside to hear him.

"Tell King Bocchus," Rutilius Rufus said in his high, light voice, "that the Senate and People of Rome remember both an offense and a favor. It is clear to us that King Bocchus rues his offense sincerely, so it would be unduly churlish of us, the Senate and People of Rome, to withhold our forgiveness. Therefore is he forgiven. However, the Senate and People of Rome now require that King Bocchus do us a favor of similar magnitude, for to date we have no favor to remember alongside the offense. We make no stipulations as to what this favor should be, we leave it entirely up to King Bocchus. And when the favor has been shown to us as unequivocally as the offense was, the Senate and People of Rome will be happy to give King Bocchus of Mauretania a treaty of friendship and alliance."

Bocchus got this answer at the end of March, delivered in person by Bogud and the two other ambassadors. Terror of Roman reprisals had outweighed the King's fears for his person, so rather than retreat to far-off Tingis beyond the Pillars of Hercules, Bocchus had elected to remain in Icosium. Gaius Marius, he reasoned, would treat with him from this distance, but no further. And to protect himself from Jugurtha, he brought a new Moorish army to Icosium, and fortified the tiny port settlement as best he could.

Off went Bogud to see Marius in Cirta.

"My brother the King begs and beseeches Gaius Marius to tell him what favor he can do Rome of similar magnitude to his offense." asked Bogud, on his knees.

"Get up, man, get up!" said Marius testily. "I am not a king! I am a proconsul of the Senate and People of Rome! No one grovels to me, it demeans me as much as it does the groveler!"

Bogud clambered to his feet, bewildered. "Gaius Marius, help us!" he cried. "What favor can the Senate want?"

"I would help you if I could, Prince Bogud," said Marius, studying his nails.

"Then send one of your senior officers to speak to the King! Perhaps in personal discussion, a way might be found."

"All right," said Marius suddenly. "Lucius Cornelius Sulla can go to see your king. Provided that the meeting place is no further from Cirta than Icosium."

"Of course it's Jugurtha we want as the favor," said Marius to Sulla as his quaestor prepared to ship out. "Ah, I'd give my eyeteeth to be going in your place, Lucius Cornelius! But since I cannot, I'm very glad I'm sending a man with a decent pair of eyeteeth."

Sulla grinned. "Once they're in, I find it hard to let go," he said.

"Then sink them in, twice as deep for me! And if you can, bring me Jugurtha!"

So it was with swelling heart and iron determination that Sulla set sail from Rusicade; with him he had a cohort of Roman legionaries, a cohort of light-armed Italian troops from the tribe of the Paeligni in Samnium, a personal escort of slingers from the Balearic Isles, and one squadron of cavalry, Publius Vagiennius's unit from Liguria. The time was mid-May.

All the way to Icosium he chafed, in spite of the fact that he was a good sailor, and had discovered in himself a great liking for the sea and ships. This expedition was a lucky one. And a significant one for himself. He knew it, as surely as if he too had received a prophecy. Oddly enough, he had never sought an interview with Martha the Syrian, though Gaius Marius urged him to it often; his refusal had nothing to do with disbelief, or lack of the necessary superstition. A Roman, Lucius Cornelius Sulla was riddled with superstitions. The truth was, he was too afraid. Yearn though he did to have some other human being confirm his own suspicions about his high destiny, he knew too much about his weaknesses and his darknesses to go as serenely into prognostication as had Marius.

But now, sailing into Icosium Bay, he wished he had gone to see Martha. For his future seemed to press down on him as heavily as a blanket, and he did not know, could not feel, just what it held. Great things. But evil too. Almost alone among his peers, Sulla understood the tangible brooding presence of evil. The Greeks argued about its nature interminably, and many argued indeed that it did not exist at all. But Sulla knew it existed. And he very much feared it existed in himself.

Icosium Bay craved some majestic city, but instead owned only a small township huddled in its back reaches, where a rugged range of coastal mountains came right down to the shore, and rendered it both sheltered and remote. During the winter rains many streamlets discharged themselves into the water, and more than a dozen islands floated like wonderful ships with the tall local cypresses appearing as masts and sails upon them. A beautiful place, Icosium, thought Sulla.

On the shore adjacent to the town there waited perhaps a thousand Moorish Berber horse troopers, equipped as were the Numidians—no saddles, no bridles, no body armor—just a cluster of spears held in one hand, and long-swords, and shields.

"Ah!" said Bogud as he and Sulla landed from the first lighter. "The King has sent his favorite son to meet you, Lucius Cornelius."

"What's his name?" asked Sulla.

"Volux."

The young man rode up, armed like his men, but upon a bedizened horse bearing both saddle and bridle. Sulla found himself liking the way his hand was shaken, and liking Prince Volux's manner; but where was the King? Nowhere could his practised eye discern the usual clutter and scurrying confusion which surrounded a king in residence.

"The King has retreated south about a hundred miles into the mountains, Lucius Cornelius," the prince explained as they walked to a spot where Sulla could supervise the unloading of his troops and equipment.

Sulla's skin prickled. "That was no part of the King's bargain with Gaius Marius," he said.

"I know," said Volux, looking uneasy. "You see, King Jugurtha has arrived in the neighborhood."

Sulla froze. "Is this a trap, Prince Volux?"

"No, no!" cried the young man, both hands going out. "I swear to you by all our gods, Lucius Cornelius, that it is not a trap! But Jugurtha smells a dead thing, because he was given to understand that the King my father was going back to Tingis, yet still the King my father lingers here at Icosium. So Jugurtha has moved into the hills with a small army of Gaetuli—not enough men to attack us, but too many for us to attack him. The King my father decided to withdraw from the sea in order to make Jugurtha believe that if he expects someone from Rome, he expects his visitor to travel on the road. So Jugurtha followed him. Jugurtha knows nothing of your arrival here, we are sure. You were wise to come by sea."

"Jugurtha will find out I'm here soon enough," said Sulla grimly, thinking of his inadequate escort, fifteen hundred strong.

"Hopefully not, or at least, not yet," said Volux. "I led a thousand of my troopers out of the King my father's camp three days ago as if on maneuvers, and came up to the coast. We are not officially at war with Numidia, so Jugurtha has little excuse to attack us, but he's not sure what the King my father intends to do either, and he dare not risk an outright breach with us until he knows more. I do assure you that he elected to remain watching our camp in the south, and that his scouts will not get anywhere near Icosium while my troopers patrol the area."

Sulla rolled a skeptical eye at the young man, but said nothing of his feelings; they were not a very practical lot, these Moorish royals. Fretting too at the painful slowness of the disembarkation —for Icosium possessed no more than twenty lighters all told, and he could see that it would be this time tomorrow before the process was complete—he sighed, shrugged. No point in worrying; either Jugurtha knew, or did not know.

"Whereabouts is Jugurtha located?" he asked.

"About thirty miles from the sea, on a small plain in the midst of the mountains, due south of here. On the only direct path between Icosium and the King my father's camp," said Volux.

"Oh, that's delightful! And how am I to get through to the King your father without fighting Jugurtha first?"

"I can lead you around him in such a way that he'll never know," said Volux eagerly. "Truly I can, Lucius Cornelius! The King my father trusts me—I beg that you will too!" He thought for a moment, and added, "However, I think it would be better if you left your men here. We stand a much better chance if our party is very small."

"Why should I trust you, Prince Volux?" Sulla asked. "I don't know you. For that matter, I don't really know Prince Bogud—or the King your father, either! You might have decided to go back on your word and betray me to Jugurtha—I'm quite a prize! My capture would be a grave embarrassment for Gaius Marius, as you well know."

Bogud had said nothing, only looked grimmer and grimmer, but the young Volux was not about to give up.

"Then give me a task which will prove to you that I and the King my father are trustworthy!" he cried.

Sulla thought about that, smiling wolfishly. "All right," he said with sudden decision. "You've got me by the balls anyway, so what have I got to lose?" And he stared at the Moor, his strange light eyes dancing like two fine jewels under the brim of his wide straw hat—an odd piece of headgear for a Roman soldier, but one famous these days clear from Tingis to Cyrenaica, anywhere the deeds of the Romans were told over by campfires and hearths: the albino Roman hero in his hat.

I must trust to my luck, he was thinking to himself, for I feel nothing inside me that warns me my luck will not hold. This is a test, a trial of my confidence in myself, a way of showing everyone from King Bocchus and his son to the man in Cirta that I am equal to—no, superior to!—anything Fortune can toss in my way. A man cannot find out what he's made of by running away. No, I go forward. I have the luck. For I have made my luck, and made it well.

"As soon as darkness falls this night," he said to Volux, "you and I and a very small cavalry escort are going to ride for the King your father's camp. My own men will stay here, which means that if Jugurtha does discover a Roman presence, he'll naturally assume it is limited to Icosium, and that the King your father will be coming here to see us."

"But there's no moon tonight!" said Volux, dismayed.

"I know," said Sulla, smiling in his nastiest manner. "That is the test, Prince Volux. We will have the light of the stars, none other. And you are going to lead me straight through the middle of Jugurtha's camp."

Bogud's eyes bulged. "That's insanity!" he gasped.

Volux's eyes danced. "Now that's a real challenge," he said, and smiled with genuine pleasure.

"Are you game?" Sulla asked. "Right through the middle of Jugurtha's camp—in one side without the Watch seeing us or hearing us—down the middle on the *via praetoria* without disturbing one sleeping man or one dozing horse—and out the other side without the Watch seeing us or hearing us. You do that, Prince Volux, and I will *know* I can trust you! And in turn trust the King your father."

"I'm game," said Volux.

"You're both mad," said Bogud.

Sulla decided to leave Bogud behind in Icosium, not sure that this member of the Moorish royal family was to be trusted. His detention was courteous enough, but he had been left in the charge of two military tribunes who were under orders not to let him out of their sight.

Volux found the four best and surest-footed horses in Icosium, and Sulla produced his mule, still of the opinion that a mule was a better beast by far than any horse. He also packed his hat. The party had been fixed at Sulla, Volux, and three Moorish nobles, so all save Sulla were used to riding without saddles or bridles.

"Nothing metal to jingle and betray us," said Volux.

However, Sulla elected to saddle his mule, and put a rope halter around nose and ears. "They may creak, but if I fall, I'll make a lot more noise," he said.

And at full darkness the five of them rode out into the stunning blackness of a moonless night. But the sky glowed with light, for no wind had come up to stir the African dust into the air; what at first glance seemed misty straggling clouds were actually vast conglomerations of stars, and the riders had no difficulty in seeing. All the animals were unshod, and pattered rather than clattered over the stony track which traversed a series of ravines in the range of hills around Icosium Bay.

"We'll have to trust to our luck that none of our mounts goes lame," said Volux after his horse stumbled, righted itself.

"You may trust to my luck at least," said Sulla.

"Don't talk," said one of the three escorts. "On windless nights like this, your voices can be heard for miles."

Thence they rode in silence, the remarkable devices of their eyes adjusted to pick up the smallest particle of light, the miles going by. So when the orange glow of dying campfires from the little basin where Jugurtha lay began to appear over the crest before them, they knew where they were. And when they looked down upon the basin, it seemed as brilliant as a city, its layout manifest.

Down from their mounts slid the five; Volux put Sulla aside, and set to work. Waiting patiently, Sulla watched as the Moors proceeded to fit specially adapted hippo shoes over every hoof; normally these had wooden soles and were used on loose ground to keep the tender underside of the hoof around the frog clear of stones, but Volux's hippo shoes had been soled with thick felt. They were held on with two supple leather straps fixed to their fronts; these crossed over, looped under a hinged metal hook at the back, and were brought forward again to buckle over the front of the hoof.

Everyone rode his mount around for a while to get it used to the hippo shoes, then Volux headed off on the last half mile between them and Jugurtha's camp. Presumably there were sentries and a mounted patrol, but the five riders saw no one wakeful, no one moving. Roman trained, naturally Jugurtha had based the construction of his camp upon the Roman pattern, but—an aspect of foreigners which fascinated Gaius Marius, Sulla knew—had not been able to summon up the patience or the willingness to reproduce the original properly. Thus Jugurtha, well aware Marius and his army were in Cirta and Bocchus not strong enough to attempt aggression, had not bothered to entrench himself; he had merely raised a low earthen wall so easy to ride a horse up and over that Sulla suspected it was more to keep animals in than humans out. But had Jugurtha been a Roman, rather than Roman trained, his camp would have had its full complement of trenches, stakes, palisades, and walls no matter how safe he felt himself.

The five riders came to the earthen wall some two hundred paces east of the main gate, which was really just a wide gap, and urged their mounts up and over it easily. On the inside, each rider turned his steed abruptly to walk parallel with the wall and hugging it; in the freshly dug soil, not a sound did they make as they headed for the main gate. Here they could discern guards, but the men faced outward and were far enough in front of the gap not to hear the five riders wheel onto the broad avenue running down the center of the camp, from the front gate to the back gate. Sulla and Volux and the three Moorish nobles rode all the way down the half-mile-long *via praetoria* at a walk, turned off it to hug the inside of the wall when they reached its far end, and then crossed to the outside of the camp and freedom as soon as they judged themselves far enough away from the back gate guard.

A mile further on, they removed the hippo shoes.

"We did it!" whispered Volux fiercely, teeth flashing at Sulla in a triumphant grin. "Do you trust me now, Lucius Cornelius?"

"I trust you, Prince Volux," said Sulla, grinning back.

They rode on at a pace between a walk and a trot, careful not to lame or exhaust their unshod beasts, and shortly after dawn found a Berber camp. The four tired horses Volux offered to trade for fresh ones were superior to any the Berbers owned, and the mule was a bit of a novelty, so five horses were forthcoming, and the ride continued remorselessly through the day. Since he had brought along his shady hat, Sulla hid beneath its brim and sweated.

Just after dark they reached the camp of King Bocchus, not unlike Jugurtha's in construction, but bigger. And here Sulla balked, reining in on his awkward halter well out of sentry distance.

"It isn't lack of trust, Prince Volux," he said, "it's more a pricking of my fingers. You're the King's son. You can ride in and out any time of day or night without question. Where I am obviously a foreign stranger, an unknown quantity. So I'm going to lie down here in as much comfort as I can manage, and wait until you see your father, make sure all is well, and return to fetch me."

"I wouldn't lie down," said Volux.

"Why?"

"Scorpions."

The hair stood up on Sulla's neck, he had to discipline himself not to leap instinctively; since Italy was free of all venomous insects, not a Roman or an Italian lived who did not abominate spiders and scorpions. Silently he drew breath, ignoring the beads of cold sweat on his brow, and turned a disinterested starlit face to Volux.

"Well, I'm certainly not going to stand up for however many hours it's going to take for you to return, and I am not climbing back up on that animal," he said, "so I'll take my chances with the scorpions."

"Suit yourself," said Volux, who already admired Sulla to the point of hero worship, and now brimmed over with awe.

Sulla lay down amid a patch of soft and sandy earth, dug a

hollow for his hip, shaped a mound for the back of his neck, said a mental prayer and promised an offering to Fortune to keep the scorpions away, closed his eyes, and fell instantly asleep. When Volux came back four hours later he found Sulla thus, and could have killed him. But Fortune belonged to Sulla in those days; Volux was a genuine friend.

The night was cold; Sulla hurt everywhere. "Oh, this creeping around like a spy is a younger man's profession!" he said, extending a hand to Volux for help in getting to his feet. Then he discerned a shadowy form behind Volux, and stiffened.

"It's all right, Lucius Cornelius, this is a friend of the King my father's. His name is Dabar," said Volux quickly.

"Another cousin of the King your father, I presume?"

"Actually no. Dabar is a cousin of Jugurtha's, and like Jugurtha, he's the bastard of a Berber woman. That's how he came to throw in his lot with us—Jugurtha prefers to be the only royal bastard at his court."

A flask of rich sweet unwatered wine was passed over; Sulla drained it without pausing to breathe, and felt the pain lessen, the cold vanish in a huge glow. Honey cakes followed, a piece of highly spiced kid's meat, and another flask of the same wine, which seemed at that moment the best Sulla had ever tasted in all his life.

"Oh, I feel better!" he said, flexing his muscles and stretching enormously. "What's the news?"

"Your pricking fingers cautioned you well, Lucius Cornelius," said Volux. "Jugurtha got to my father first."

"Am I betrayed?"

"No, no! But the situation has changed nonetheless. I will leave it to Dabar to explain, he was there."

Dabar squatted down on his haunches to join Sulla. "It seems Jugurtha heard of a deputation from Gaius Marius to my king," he said, low-voiced. "Of course he assumed that was why my king had not gone back to Tingis, so he decided to be close by, putting himself between my king and any embassage from Gaius Marius by road or by sea. And he sent one of his greatest barons,

Aspar, to sit by my king's right hand and listen to all congress between my king and the expected Romans."

"I see," said Sulla. "What's to do, then?"

"Tomorrow Prince Volux will escort you into my king's presence as if you have ridden together from Icosium—Aspar did not see the prince come in tonight, fortunately. You will speak to my king as if you had come from Gaius Marius at the order of Gaius Marius, rather than at my king's behest. You will ask my king to abandon Jugurtha, and my king will refuse, but in a prevaricating way. He will order you to camp nearby for ten days while he thinks about what you have said. You will go to that camp and wait. However, my king will come to see you privately tomorrow night at a different place, and then you can talk together without fear." Dabar looked at Sulla keenly. "Is that satisfactory, Lucius Cornelius?"

"Entirely," said Sulla, yawning mightily. "The only problem is, where can I stay tonight, and where can I find a bath? I stink of horse, and there are things crawling in my crotch."

"Volux has had a comfortable camp pitched for you not far away," said Dabar.

"Then lead me to it," said Sulla, getting to his feet.

The next day Sulla went through his farcical interview with Bocchus. It wasn't difficult to tell which one of the nobles present was Jugurtha's spy, Aspar; he stood on the left of Bocchus's majestic chair—far more majestic than its occupant—and nobody ventured near him nor looked at him with the ease of long familiarity.

"What am I to do, Lucius Cornelius?" wailed Bocchus that night after dark, meeting Sulla undetected at a distance from both his camp and Sulla's.

"A favor for Rome," said Sulla.

"Just tell me what favor Rome wants, and it shall be done! Gold —jewels—land—soldiers—cavalry—wheat—only name it, Lucius Cornelius! You're a Roman, you must know what the Senate's cryptic message means! For I swear I do not!" Bocchus quivered in fear.

"Every commodity you have named, Rome can find without being cryptic, King Bocchus," said Sulla scornfully.

"Then *what*? Only tell me what!" pleaded Bocchus.

"I think you must already have worked it out for yourself, King Bocchus. But you won't admit that," said Sulla. "I can understand why. *Jugurtha!* Rome wants you to hand Jugurtha over to Rome peacefully, bloodlessly. Too much blood has already been shed in Africa, too much land torn up, too many towns and villages burned, too much wealth frittered away. But while ever Jugurtha continues at large, this terrible waste will go on. Crippling Numidia, inconveniencing Rome—and crippling Mauretania too. So give me Jugurtha, King Bocchus!"

"You ask me to betray my son-in-law, the father of my grandchildren, my kinsman through Masinissa's blood?"

"I do indeed," said Sulla.

Bocchus began to weep. "I cannot! Lucius Cornelius, I cannot! We are Berber as well as Punic, the law of the tented people binds us both. Anything, Lucius Cornelius, I will do *anything* to earn that treaty! Anything, that is, except betray my daughter's husband."

"Anything else is unacceptable," said Sulla coldly.

"My people would never forgive me!"

"Rome will never forgive you. And that is worse."

"I cannot!" Bocchus wept, genuine tears wetting his face, glistening amid the strands of his elaborately curled beard. "Please, Lucius Cornelius, please! I cannot!"

Sulla turned his back contemptuously. "Then there will never be a treaty," he said.

And each day for the next eight days the farce continued, Aspar and Dabar riding back and forth between Sulla's pleasant little camp and the King's pavilion, bearing messages which bore no relation to the real issue. That remained a secret between Sulla and Bocchus, and was discussed only in the nights. However, it was plain Volux knew of the real issue, Sulla decided, for Volux now avoided him as much as possible, and whenever he did see him looked angry, hurt, baffled.

Sulla was enjoying himself, discovering that he liked the sensation of power and majesty being Rome's envoy gave him; and more than that, enjoyed being the relentless drip of water that wore down this so-called royal stone. He, who was no king, yet had dominion over kings. He, a Roman, had the real power. And it was heady, enormously satisfying.

On the eighth night, Bocchus summoned Sulla to the secret meeting place.

"All right, Lucius Cornelius, I agree," said the King, his eyes red from weeping.

"Excellent!" said Sulla briskly.

"But how can it be done?"

"Simple," said Sulla. "You send Aspar to Jugurtha and offer to betray me to him."

"He won't believe me," said Bocchus desolately.

"Certainly he will! Take my word for it, he will. If the circumstances were different, it's precisely what you might be doing, King."

"But you're only a quaestor!"

Sulla laughed. "What, are you trying to say that you do not think a Roman quaestor is as valuable as a Numidian king?"

"No! No, of course not!"

"Let me explain, King Bocchus," said Sulla gently. "I am a Roman quaestor, and it is true that all the title signifies in Rome is the lowest man on the senatorial ladder. However, I am also a patrician Cornelius—my family is the family of Scipio Africanus and Scipio Aemilianus, and my bloodline is far older, far nobler than either yours or Jugurtha's. If Rome was ruled by kings, those kings would probably be members of the Cornelian family. And—last but by no means least—I happen to be Gaius Marius's brother-in-law. Our children are first cousins. Does that make it more understandable?"

"Jugurtha—does Jugurtha know all this?" whispered the King of Mauretania.

"There's very little escapes Jugurtha," Sulla said, and sat back, and waited.

"Very well, Lucius Cornelius, it shall be as you say. I will send

Aspar to Jugurtha and offer to betray you." The King drew himself up, dignity a little threadbare. "However, you must tell me exactly how I am to go about it."

Sulla leaned forward and spoke crisply. "You will ask for Jugurtha to come here the night after next, and promise him that you will hand over to him the Roman quaestor Lucius Cornelius Sulla. You will inform him that this quaestor is alone in your camp, endeavoring to persuade you to ally yourself with Gaius Marius. He knows it to be true, because Aspar has been reporting to him. He also knows there are no Roman soldiers within a hundred miles, so he won't bother to bring his army with him. And he thinks he knows you, King Bocchus. So he won't dream that it is he who will be yielded up rather than me." Sulla pretended not to see Bocchus wince. "It's not you or your army Jugurtha is afraid of. He's only afraid of Gaius Marius. Rest assured, he'll come, and he'll come believing every word Aspar tells him."

"But what will I do when Jugurtha never returns to his own camp?" asked Bocchus, shivering anew.

Sulla smiled a nasty smile. "I strongly recommend, King Bocchus, that the moment you have turned Jugurtha over to me, you strike camp and march for Tingis as fast as you can."

"But won't you need my army to keep Jugurtha prisoner?" The King stared at Sulla, palpitating; never was a man more patently terrified. "You have no men to help you take him to Icosium! And his camp is there in between."

"All I want is a good set of manacles and chains, and six of your fastest horses," said Sulla.

Sulla found himself looking forward to the confrontation, and did not experience one twinge of self-doubt or trepidation. Yes, it would be his name linked to the capture of Jugurtha forever! Little matter that he acted under Gaius Marius's orders; it was his valor and intelligence and initiative which effected the deed, and that could not be taken away from him. Not that he thought Gaius Marius would try to take the credit. Gaius Marius wasn't greedy for glory, he knew he had more than his fair share. And he would not oppose the leaking of the story of Jugurtha's capture. For a patrician, the kind of personal fame necessary to ensure election as consul was hampered by the fact that a patrician could not be a tribune of the plebs. Therefore a patrician had to find other ways of earning approbation, making sure the electorate knew he was a worthy scion of his family. Jugurtha had cost Rome dearly. And all of Rome would know that it was Lucius Cornelius Sulla, indefatigable quaestor, who had single-handedly achieved the capture of Jugurtha.

So when he joined Bocchus to go to the appointed place, he was confident, exhilarated, eager to get it done.

"Jugurtha isn't going to expect to see you in chains," said Bocchus. "He's under the impression that you've asked to see him, with the intention of persuading him to surrender. And he has instructed *me* to bring sufficient men to make you captive, Lucius Cornelius."

"Good," said Sulla shortly.

When Bocchus rode in with Sulla beside him and a strong troop of Moorish cavalry at his back, Jugurtha was waiting, escorted only by a handful of his barons, including Aspar.

Pricking his mount, Sulla forged ahead of Bocchus and trotted straight to Jugurtha, then slid to the ground and held out his hand in the universal gesture of peace and friendship.

"King Jugurtha," he said, and waited.

Jugurtha looked down at the hand, then dismounted to take hold of it. "Lucius Cornelius."

While this was going on, the Moorish cavalry had silently formed a ring around the central participants, and while Sulla and Jugurtha stood with hands joined, the capture of Jugurtha was effected as neatly and smoothly as even Gaius Marius could have wished. The Numidian barons were overcome without a sword being drawn; Jugurtha was taken too firmly to struggle, and borne to the ground. When he was set upon his feet again, he wore heavy manacles on both wrists and ankles, all connected to chains just long enough to permit that he shuffle along bowed over in a crouch.

His eyes, Sulla noted in the torchlight, were very pale in so dark a man; he was big too, and well preserved. But his years sat heavily upon his beaky face, so he looked much older than Gaius Marius. Sulla knew he could manage to get him as far as he had to without an escort.

"Put him up on the big bay," he instructed Bocchus's men, and stood watching closely as the chains were snapped to special loops on the modified saddle. Then he checked the girth and the locks. After that he accepted a hoist up onto another bay, and took the bridle of Jugurtha's horse, and secured it to his own saddle; if Jugurtha took it into his head to kick his mount into bolting, it would have no leeway, nor could the reins be wrested from Sulla. The four spare mounts were tethered together and tied by a fairly short line to Jugurtha's saddle. He was now doubly handicapped. And finally, to make absolutely sure, another length of chain was snapped to Jugurtha's right wrist's manacle, and its other end was fastened to a manacle on Sulla's own left wrist.

Sulla had said not a word to the Moors from the time Jugurtha was taken; now, still silent, he kicked his horse and rode off, Jugurtha's horse following docilely enough as the reins and the chain linking him to Sulla drew taut. The four spare horses followed. And in very few moments all the mounts had disappeared into the shadows between the trees.

Bocchus wept. Volux and Dabar watched helplessly.

"Father, let me catch him!" pleaded Volux suddenly. "He can't travel fast so trammeled—I can catch him!"

"It is too late." Taking the fine handkerchief his servant gave him, King Bocchus dried his eyes and blew his nose. "He will never let himself be caught, that one. We are as helpless babes compared to Lucius Cornelius Sulla, who is a Roman. No, my son, poor Jugurtha's fate is out of our hands. We have Mauretania to think of. It's time to go home to our beloved Tingis. Perhaps we don't belong in the world of the Middle Sea."

For perhaps a mile Sulla rode without speaking or letting his pace slacken. All his jubilance, his fantastic pleasure in his own brilliance, he kept as tightly reined as he did his prisoner, Jugurtha.

Yes, if he did the dissemination properly, and without detracting from the achievements of Gaius Marius, the story of his capture of Jugurtha would join those other wonderful stories mothers told their children—the leap of young Marcus Curtius into the chasm in the Forum Romanum, the heroism of Horatius Cocles when he held the Wooden Bridge against Lars Porsenna of Clusium, the drawing of the circle around the King of Syria's feet by Gaius Popillius Laenas, the killing of his treasonous sons by Lucius Junius Brutus, the killing of Spurius Maelius the would-be King of Rome by Gaius Servilius Ahala—yes, the capture of Jugurtha by Lucius Cornelius Sulla would join all those and many more bedtime stories, for it had all the necessary elements, including the ride through the middle of Jugurtha's camp.

But he was not by nature a romancer, a dreamer, a builder of fantasies, so he found it easy to abandon these thoughts when it came time to halt, to dismount. Keeping well clear of Jugurtha, he went to the lead holding the four spare horses, and cut it, then sent the animals careering in all directions with a shower of well-placed stones.

"I see," said Jugurtha, watching Sulla scramble astride his bay by grabbing at its mane. "We have to ride a hundred miles on the same horses, eh? I was wondering how you were going to manage to transfer me from one beast to another." He laughed jeeringly. "My cavalry will catch you, Lucius Cornelius!"

"Hopefully not," said Sulla, and jerked his prisoner's mount forward.

Instead of proceeding due north to the sea, he headed due east across a small plain, and rode for ten miles through the breathless night of early summer, his way lit up by a sliver of moon in the west. Then in the far distance reared a range of mountains, solidly black; in front of it and much closer was a huddle of gigantic round rocks piled in jumbled heaps, looming above the sparse and stunted trees.

"Right where it ought to be!" Sulla exclaimed joyously, and whistled shrilly.

His own Ligurian cavalry squadron spilled out of the shelter afforded by the boulders, each man encumbered by two spare mounts; silently they rode to meet Sulla and his prisoner, and produced two extra horses. And two mules.

"I sent them here to wait for me six days ago, King Jugurtha," Sulla said. "King Bocchus thought I came to his camp alone, but as you see, I didn't. I had Publius Vagiennius following close behind me, and sent him back to bring up his troop to wait for me here."

Freed from his encumbrances, Sulla supervised the remounting of Jugurtha, who now was chained to Publius Vagiennius. And soon they were riding away, bearing northeast to skirt Jugurtha's camp by many miles.

"I don't suppose, your royal Majesty," said Publius Vagiennius with delicate diffidence, "that you would be able to tell me whereabouts I'd find snails around Cirta? Or around anywhere else in Numidia, for that matter?"

By the end of June the war in Africa was over. For a little while Jugurtha was housed in appropriately comfortable quarters within Utica, as Marius and Sulla tidied up. And there his two sons, Iampsas and Oxyntas, were brought to keep him company while his court disintegrated and the scrabbling for places of influence under the new regime began.

King Bocchus got his treaty of friendship and alliance from the Senate, and Prince Gauda the invalid became King Gauda of a considerably reduced Numidia. It was Bocchus who reaped the extra territory from a Rome too busy elsewhere to expand her African province by many hundreds of miles.

And as soon as a small fleet of good ships and stable weather ensured a smooth passage, Marius loaded King Jugurtha and his sons on board one of these hired vessels, and sent them to Rome for safekeeping. The Numidian threat vanished over the horizon with the passing of Jugurtha.

With them sailed Quintus Sertorius, determined that he was going to see action against the Germans in Gaul-across-the-Alps. He had applied to his cousin Marius for permission to leave.

"I am a fighting man, Gaius Marius," said the grave young

contubernalis, "and the fighting here is finished. Recommend me to your friend Publius Rutilius Rufus, and let him give me duty in Further Gaul!"

"Go with my thanks and blessings, Quintus Sertorius," said Marius with rare affection. "And give my regards to your mother."

Sertorius's face lit up. "I will, Gaius Marius!"

"Remember, young Sertorius," said Marius on the day that Quintus Sertorius and Jugurtha sailed for Italy, "that I will need you again in the future. So guard yourself in battle if you're fortunate enough to find one. Rome has honored your bravery and skill with the Gold Crown, with *phalerae* and torcs and bracelets—all of gold. A rare distinction for one so young. But don't be rash. Rome is going to need you alive, not dead."

"I'll stay alive, Gaius Marius," Quintus Sertorius promised.

"And don't go off to your war quite the moment you arrive in Italy," Marius admonished. "Spend some time with your dear mother first."

"I will, Gaius Marius," Quintus Sertorius promised.

When the lad took his leave, Sulla looked at his superior ironically. "He makes you as clucky as an old hen sitting on one lone egg."

Marius snorted. "Rubbish! He's my cousin on his mother's side, and I'm fond of her."

"Certainly," said Sulla, grinning.

Marius laughed. "Come now, Lucius Cornelius, admit that you're as fond of young Sertorius as I am!"

"I admit it freely. Nonetheless, Gaius Marius, he does *not* make me clucky!"

"Mentulam caco!" said Marius.

And that was the end of the subject.

 Rutilia, who was the only sister of Publius Rutilius Rufus, enjoyed the unusual distinction of being married to each of two brothers. Her first husband had been Lucius Aurelius Cotta, colleague in the consulship with Metellus Dalmaticus Pontifex Maximus some fourteen years earlier; it was the same year Gaius Marius had been tribune of the plebs, and defied Metellus Dalmaticus Pontifex Maximus.

Rutilia had gone to Lucius Aurelius Cotta as a girl, whereas he had been married before, and already had a nine-year-old son named Lucius, like himself. They were married the year after Fregellae was leveled to the ground for rebelling against Rome, and in the year of Gaius Gracchus's first term as a tribune of the plebs, they had a daughter named Aurelia. Lucius Cotta's son was then ten years old, and very pleased to have acquired a little half sister, for he liked his stepmother, Rutilia, very much.

When Aurelia turned five years old, her father, Lucius Aurelius Cotta, died suddenly, only days after the end of his consulship. The widow Rutilia, twenty-four years old, clung for comfort to Lucius Cotta's younger brother, Marcus, who had not yet found a wife. Love grew between them, and with her father's and her brother's permission, Rutilia married her brother-in-law, Marcus Aurelius Cotta, eleven months after the death of Lucius Cotta. With her into Marcus's care, Rutilia brought her stepson and Marcus's nephew, Lucius Junior, and her daughter and Marcus's niece, Aurelia. The family promptly grew: Rutilia bore Marcus a son, Gaius, less than a year later, then another son, Marcus Junior, the year after that, and finally a third son, Lucius, seven years later.

Aurelia remained the only girl her mother bore, fascinatingly situated; by her father, she had a half brother older than herself, and by her mother, she had three half brothers younger than herself who also happened to be her first cousins because her father had been their uncle, where their father was her uncle. It could prove very, very bewildering to those not in the know, especially if the children explained it.

"She's my cousin," Gaius Cotta would say, pointing to Aurelia.

"He's my brother," Aurelia would riposte, pointing to Gaius Cotta.

"He's my brother," Gaius Cotta would then say, pointing to Marcus Cotta.

"She's my sister," Marcus Cotta would say in his turn, pointing to Aurelia.

"He's my cousin," Aurelia would say last of all, pointing to Marcus Cotta.

They could keep it up for hours; little wonder most people never worked it out. Not that the complex blood links worried any of that strong-minded, self-willed cluster of children, who liked each other as well as loved each other, and all basked in a warm relationship with Rutilia and her second Aurelius Cotta husband, who also happened to adore each other.

The family Aurelius was one of the Famous Families, and its branch Aurelius Cotta was respectably elderly in its tenure of the Senate, though new to the nobility bestowed by the consulship. Rich because of shrewd investments, huge inheritances of land, and many clever marriages, the Aurelius Cottas could afford to have multiple sons without worrying about adopting some of them out, and to dower the daughters more than adequately.

The brood which lived under the roof of Marcus Aurelius Cotta and his wife, Rutilia, was therefore financially very eligible marriage material, but also possessed great good looks. And Aurelia, the only girl, was the best-looking of them all.

"Flawless!" was the opinion of the luxury-loving yet restlessly brilliant Lucius Licinius Crassus Orator, who was one of the most ardent—and important—suitors for her hand.

"Glorious!" was the way Quintus Mucius Scaevola—best friend of and first cousin of Crassus Orator—put it; he too had entered his name on the list of suitors.

"Unnerving!" was Marcus Livius Drusus's comment; he was Aurelia's cousin, and very anxious to marry her.

"Helen of Troy!" was how Gnaeus Domitius Ahenobarbus Junior described her, suing for her hand.

Indeed, the situation was exactly as Publius Rutilius Rufus had described it to Gaius Marius in his letter; everyone in Rome

wanted to marry his niece Aurelia. That quite a few of the applicants had wives already neither disqualified nor dishonored
them—divorce was easy, and Aurelia's dowry was so large a man
didn't need to worry about losing the dowry of an earlier wife.

"I really do feel like King Tyndareus when every important
prince and king came to sue for Helen's hand," Marcus Aurelius
Cotta said to Rutilia.

"He had Odysseus to solve his dilemma," Rutilia commented.

"Well, I wish I did! No matter whom I give her to, I'm going to
offend everyone who doesn't get her."

"Just like Tyndareus," nodded Rutilia.

And then Marcus Cotta's Odysseus came to dinner, though
properly he was Ulysses, being a Roman of the Romans, Publius
Rutilius Rufus. After the children—including Aurelia—had gone
to bed, the conversation turned as always to the subject of Aurelia's
marriage. Rutilius Rufus listened with interest, and when the moment came, offered his answer; what he didn't tell his sister and
brother-in-law was that the real unraveler of the conundrum was
Gaius Marius, whose terse letter he had just received from Africa.

"It's simple, Marcus Aurelius," he said.

"If it is, then I'm too close to see," said Marcus Cotta. "Enlighten me, Ulysses!"

Rutilius Rufus smiled. "No, I can't see the point of making a
song and dance about it, the way Ulysses did," he said. "This is
modern Rome, not ancient Greece. We can't slaughter a horse, cut
it up into four pieces, and make all Aurelia's suitors stand on it to
swear an oath of fealty to you, Marcus Aurelius."

"Especially not *before* they know who the lucky winner is!"
said Cotta, laughing. "What romantics those old Greeks were!
No, Publius Rutilius, I fear what we have to deal with is a collection of litigious-minded, hairsplitting Romans."

"Pre-*cisely,*" said Rutilius Rufus.

"Come, brother, put us out of our misery and tell us," urged
Rutilia.

"As I said, my dear Rutilia, simple. Let the girl pick her own
husband."

Cotta and his wife stared.

"Do you really think that's wise?" asked Cotta.

"In this situation, wisdom fails, so what have you got to lose?" asked Rutilius Rufus. "You don't need her to marry a rich man, and there aren't any notorious fortune hunters on your list of suitors, so limit her choice to your list. Nor are the Aurelians, the Julians, or the Cornelians likely to attract social climbers. Besides which, Aurelia is full of common sense, not a scrap sentimental, and certainly not a romantic. She won't let you down, not my girl!"

"You're right," said Cotta, nodding. "I don't think there's a man alive could turn Aurelia's head."

So the next day Cotta and Rutilia summoned Aurelia to her mother's sitting room, with the intention of telling her what had been decided about her future.

She walked in; she didn't drift, undulate, stride, mince. Aurelia was a good plain walker, moved briskly and competently, disciplined hips and bottom to a neat economy, kept shoulders back, chin tucked in, head up. Perhaps her figure erred on the spare side, for she was tall and inclined to be flat-chested, but she wore her draperies with immaculate neatness, did not affect high cork heels, and scorned jewelry. Thick and straight, her palest-icy-brown hair was dragged severely back into a tight bun positioned right where it could not be seen from the front full face, giving her no softening frame of hair. Cosmetics had never sullied her dense and milky skin, without a blemish, faintly pinked across her incredible cheekbones and deepening to a soft rose within the hollows below. As straight and high-bridged as if Praxiteles had chiseled it, her nose was too long to incur animadversions about Celtic blood, and therefore could be forgiven its lack of character—in other words, its lack of truly Roman humps and bumps. Lushly crimsoned, deliciously creased at its corners, her mouth had that folded quality which drove men mad to kiss it into blooming. And in all this wonderful heart-shaped face, with its dented chin and its broad high forehead and its widow's peak, there dwelled an enormous pair of eyes everyone insisted were not dark blue, but *purple,* framed in long and thick black lashes, and surmounted by thin, arched, feathery black brows.

Many were the debates at men's dinner parties (for it could confidently be predicted that among the guests would be two or three of her gazetted suitors) as to what exactly constituted Aurelia's appeal. Some said it all lay in those thoughtful, detached purple eyes; some insisted it was the remarkable purity of her skin; others plumped for the carved starkness of her facial planes; a few muttered passionately about her mouth, or her dented chin, or her exquisite hands and feet.

"It's none of those things and yet it's all of those things," growled Lucius Licinius Crassus Orator. "Fools! She's a Vestal Virgin on the loose—she's *Diana,* not Venus! Unattainable. And therein lies her fascination."

"No, it's those purple eyes," said Scaurus Princeps Senatus's young son, another Marcus like his father. "Purple is *the* color! Noble! She's a living, breathing omen."

But when the living, breathing omen walked into her mother's sitting room looking as sedate and immaculate as always, there entered no atmosphere of high drama with her; indeed, the character of Aurelia did not encourage high drama.

"Sit down, daughter," said Rutilia, smiling.

Aurelia sat and folded her hands in her lap.

"We want to talk to you about your marriage," said Cotta, and cleared his throat, hoping she would say something to help him elucidate.

He got no help at all; Aurelia just looked at him with a kind of remote interest, nothing more.

"How do you feel about it?" Rutilia asked.

Aurelia pursed her lips, shrugged. "I suppose I just hope you'll pick someone I like," she said.

"Well, yes, we hope that too," said Cotta.

"Who *don't* you like?" asked Rutilia.

"Gnaeus Domitius Ahenobarbus Junior," Aurelia said without any hesitation, giving him his whole name.

Cotta saw the justice of that. "Anyone else?" he asked.

"Marcus Aemilius Scaurus Junior."

"Oh, that's too bad!" cried Rutilia. "I think he's very nice, I really do."

"I agree, he's very nice," said Aurelia, "but he's timid."

Cotta didn't even try to conceal his grin. "Wouldn't you like a timid husband, Aurelia? You could rule the roost!"

"A good Roman wife does not rule the roost."

"So much for Scaurus. Our Aurelia has spoken." Cotta waggled head and shoulders back and forth. "Anyone else you don't fancy?"

"Lucius Licinius."

"What's the matter with him?"

"He's fat." The pursed mouth pursed tighter.

"Unappealing, eh?"

"It indicates a lack of self-discipline, Father." There were times when Aurelia called Cotta Father, other times when he was Uncle, but her choice was never illogical; when their discourse revealed that he was acting in a paternal role, he was Father, and when he was acting in an avuncular role, he was Uncle.

"You're right, it does," said Cotta.

"Is there anyone you would prefer to marry above all the others?" asked Rutilia, trying the opposite tack.

The pursed mouth relaxed. "No, Mother, not really. I'm quite happy to leave the decision to you and Father."

"What do you hope for in marriage?" asked Cotta.

"A husband befitting my rank who adores his . . . several fine children."

"A textbook answer!" said Cotta. "Go to the top of the class, Aurelia."

Rutilia glanced at her husband, only the faintest shadow of amusement in her eyes. "Tell her, Marcus Aurelius, do!"

Cotta cleared his throat again. "Well, Aurelia, you're causing us a bit of a problem," he said. "At last count I have had thirty-seven formal applications for your hand in marriage. Not one of these hopeful suitors can be dismissed as ineligible. Some of them are of rank far higher than ours, some of fortune far greater than ours—and some even have rank *and* fortune far in excess of ours! Which puts us in a quandary. If *we* choose your husband, we are going to make a lot of enemies, which may not worry us unduly, but will make life hard for your brothers later on. I'm sure you can see that."

"I do, Father," said Aurelia seriously.

"Anyway, your Uncle Publius came up with the only feasible answer. *You* will choose your husband, my daughter."

And for once she was thrown off-balance. She gaped. *"I?"*

"You."

Her hands went up to press at her reddened cheeks; she stared at Cotta in horror. "But I can't do that!" she cried. "It isn't—it isn't *Roman!*"

"I agree," said Cotta. "Not Roman. Rutilian."

"We needed a Ulysses to tell us the way, and luckily we have one right in the family," said Rutilia.

"Oh!" Aurelia wriggled, twisted. "Oh, oh!"

"What is it, Aurelia? Can't you see your way clear to a decision?" asked Rutilia.

"No, it's not that," said Aurelia, her color fading to normal, then fading beyond it, and leaving her white-faced. "It's just—oh, well!" She shrugged, got up. "May I go?"

"Indeed you may."

At the door she turned to regard Cotta and Rutilia very gravely. "How long do I have to make up my mind?" she asked.

"Oh, there's no real hurry," said Cotta easily. "You're eighteen at the end of January, but there's nothing to say you have to marry the moment you come of age. Take your time."

"Thank you," she said, and went out of the room.

Her own little room was one of the cubicles which opened off the atrium, and so was windowless and dark; in such a careful and caring family bosom, the only daughter would not have been permitted to sleep anywhere less protected. However, being the only daughter amid such a collection of boys, she was also much indulged, and could easily have grown into a very spoiled young lady did she have the germ of such a flaw in her. Luckily she did not. The consensus of family opinion was that it was utterly impossible to spoil Aurelia, for she had not an avaricious or envious atom in her. Which didn't make her sweet-natured, or even lovable; in fact, it was a lot easier to admire and respect Aurelia than it was to love her, for she did not give of herself. As a child she would listen impassively to the vainglorious posturing of her older brother or one of her first two younger brothers, then when she had had enough, she would thump him across the ear so hard his head rang, and walk away without a word.

Because as the only girl she needed, her parents felt, a domain of her own marked off-limits to all the boys, she had been given a modestly large and brilliantly sunny room off the peristyle-garden for her own, and a maidservant of her own, the Gallic girl Cardixa, who was a gem. When Aurelia married, Cardixa would go with her to her new husband's home.

One quick glance at Aurelia's face when she walked into her workroom told Cardixa that something of importance had just occurred; but she said nothing, nor did she expect to be told what it was, for the kind and comfortable relationship between mistress and maidservant contained no girlish confidences. Aurelia clearly needed to be alone, so Cardixa departed.

The tastes of its owner were emblazoned on the room, most of the walls of which were solidly pigeonholed and held many rolls of books; a desk held scrolls of blank paper, reed pens, wax tablets, a quaint bone stylus for inscribing the wax, cakes of compressed sepia ink waiting to be dissolved in water, a covered inkwell, a full shaker of fine sand for blotting work in progress, and an abacus.

In one corner was a full-sized Patavian loom, the walls behind it pegged to hold dozens of long hanks of woolen thread in a myriad of thicknesses and colors—reds and purples, blues and greens, pinks and creams, yellows and oranges—for Aurelia wove the fabric for all her clothes, and loved brilliant hues. On the loom was a wide expanse of misty-thin flame-colored textile woven from wool spun hair-fine; Aurelia's wedding veil, a real challenge. The saffron material for her wedding dress was already completed, and lay folded upon a shelf until the time came to make it up; it was unlucky to start cutting and sewing the dress until the groom was fully contractually committed.

Having a talent for such work, Cardixa was halfway through making a carved fretwork folding screen out of some striking African cabinet-wood; the pieces of polished sard, jasper, carnelian, and onyx with which she intended to inlay it in a pattern of leaves and flowers were all carefully wrapped within a carved wooden box, an earlier example of her skill.

Aurelia went along the room's exposed side closing the shutters, the grilles of which she left open to let in fresh air and a muted light; the very fact that the shutters were closed was signal enough that she did not wish to be disturbed by anyone, little brother or servant. Then she sat down at her desk, greatly troubled and bewildered, folded her hands on its top, and thought.

What would Cornelia the Mother of the Gracchi do?

That was Aurelia's criterion for everything. What would Cornelia the Mother of the Gracchi do? What would Cornelia the Mother of the Gracchi think? How would Cornelia the Mother of the Gracchi feel? For Cornelia the Mother of the Gracchi was Aurelia's idol, her exemplar, her ready-reckoner of conduct in speech and deed.

Among the books lining the walls of her workroom were all of Cornelia the Mother of the Gracchi's published letters and essays, as well as any work by anyone else which so much as mentioned the name Cornelia the Mother of the Gracchi.

And who was she, this Cornelia the Mother of the Gracchi? Everything a Roman noblewoman ought to be, from the moment of her birth to the moment of her death. That was who.

The younger daughter of Scipio Africanus—who rolled up Hannibal and conquered Carthage—she had been married to the great nobleman Tiberius Sempronius Gracchus in her nineteenth year, which was his forty-fifth year; her mother, Aemilia Paulla, was the sister of the great Aemilius Paullus, which made Cornelia the Mother of the Gracchi patrician on both sides.

Her conduct while wife to Tiberius Sempronius Gracchus was unimpeachable, and patiently over the almost twenty years of their marriage, she bore him twelve children. Gaius Julius Caesar would probably have maintained that it was the endlessly inter-married bloodlines of two very old families—Cornelius and Aemilius—that rendered her babies sickly, for sickly they all were. But, indefatigable, she persisted, and cared for each child with scrupulous attention and great love; and actually succeeded in rearing three of them. The first child who lived to be grown up was a girl, Sempronia; the second was a boy, who inherited his father's name, Tiberius; and the third was another boy, Gaius Sempronius Gracchus.

Exquisitely educated and a worthy child of her father, who adored everything Greek as the pinnacle of world culture, she herself tutored all three of her children (and those among the nine dead who lived long enough to need tutoring) and oversaw every aspect of their upbringing. When her husband died, she was left with the fifteen-year-old Sempronia, the twelve-year-old Tiberius Gracchus, and the two-year-old Gaius Gracchus, as well as several among the nine dead who had survived infancy.

Everyone lined up to marry the widow, for she had proven her fertility with amazing regularity, and she was still fertile; she was also the daughter of Africanus, the niece of Paullus, and the relict of Tiberius Sempronius Gracchus; and she was fabulously wealthy.

Among her suitors was none other than King Ptolemy Euergetes Gross Belly—at that moment in time, late King of Egypt, current King of Cyrenaica—who was a regular visitor to Rome in the years between his deposition in Egypt and his reinstatement as its sole ruler nine years after the death of Tiberius Sempronius Gracchus. He would turn up to bleat incessantly in the Senate's weary ear, and agitate and bribe to be let climb back upon the Egyptian throne.

At the time of Tiberius Sempronius Gracchus's death, King Ptolemy Euergetes Gross Belly was eight years younger than the thirty-six-year-old Cornelia the Mother of the Gracchi—and considerably thinner in his middle regions than he would be later, when Cornelia the Mother of the Gracchi's first cousin and son-in-law, Scipio Aemilianus, boasted that he had made the indecently clad, hideously fat King of Egypt *walk*! He sued as persistently and incessantly for her hand in marriage as he did for reinstatement on the Egyptian throne, but with as little success. Cornelia the Mother of the Gracchi could not be had by a mere foreign king, no matter how incredibly rich or powerful.

In fact, Cornelia the Mother of the Gracchi had resolved that a true Roman noblewoman married to a great Roman nobleman for nearly twenty years had no business remarrying at all. So suitor after suitor was refused with gracious courtesy; the widow struggled on alone to rear her children.

When Tiberius Gracchus was murdered during his tribunate of the plebs, she carried on living with head unbowed, holding herself steadfastly aloof from all the innuendo about her first cousin Scipio Aemilianus's implication in the murder; and held herself just as steadfastly aloof from the marital hideousnesses which existed between Scipio Aemilianus and his wife, her own daughter, Sempronia. Then when Scipio Aemilianus was found mysteriously dead and it was rumored that he too had been murdered—by his wife, no less, her own daughter—still she held herself steadfastly aloof. After all, she was left with one living son to nurture and encourage in his blossoming public career, her dear Gaius Gracchus.

Gaius Gracchus died with great violence about the time she turned seventy years of age, and everyone assumed that here at last was the blow strong enough to break Cornelia the Mother of the Gracchi. But no. Head unbowed, she carried on living, widowed, minus her splendid sons, her only surviving child the embittered and barren Sempronia.

"I have my dear little Sempronia to bring up," she said, referring to Gaius Gracchus's daughter, a tiny babe.

But she did retire from Rome, though never from life or from the pursuit of it. She went to live permanently in her huge villa at Misenum, it no less than her a monument to everything of taste and refinement and splendor Rome could offer the world. There she collected her letters and essays and graciously permitted old Sosius of the Argiletum to publish them, after her friends beseeched her not to let them go unknown to posterity. Like their author, they were sprightly, full of grace and charm and wit, yet very strong and deep; in Misenum they were added to, for Cornelia the Mother of the Gracchi never lost intellect or erudition or interest as she piled up the total of her years.

When Aurelia was sixteen and Cornelia the Mother of the Gracchi eighty-three, Marcus Aurelius Cotta and his wife, Rutilia, paid a duty call—no duty call really, it was an event eagerly looked forward to—upon Cornelia the Mother of the Gracchi as they were passing through Misenum. With them they had the full tribe of children, even including the lofty Lucius Aurelius Cotta, who naturally at twenty-six did not consider himself a true member of the tribe. Everyone was issued orders to be quiet as mice, demure as Vestals, still as cats before the pounce—no fidgeting, no jiggling, no kicking the chair legs—under pain of death by indescribably agonizing torture.

But Cotta and Rutilia needn't have bothered issuing threats foreign to their natures. Cornelia the Mother of the Gracchi knew just about everything there was to know of little boys and big boys too, and her granddaughter, Sempronia, was a year younger than Aurelia. Delighted to be surrounded by such interesting and vivid children, she had a wonderful time, and for much longer than her household of devoted slaves thought wise, for she was frail by this time, and permanently blue about the lips and earlobes.

And the girl Aurelia came away captured, inspired—when she grew up, she vowed, she was going to live by the same standards of Roman strength, Roman endurance, Roman integrity, Roman patience, as Cornelia the Mother of the Gracchi. It was after this that her library grew rich in the old lady's writings; then that the pattern of a life to be equally remarkable was laid down.

The visit was never repeated, for the following winter Cornelia the Mother of the Gracchi died, sitting up straight in a chair, head unbowed, holding her granddaughter's hand. She had just informed the girl of her formal betrothal to Marcus Fulvius Flaccus

Bambalio, only survivor of that family of the Fulvius Flaccuses who had died supporting Gaius Gracchus; it was fitting, she told the young Sempronia, that as sole heiress to the vast Sempronian fortune, she should bring that fortune as her gift to a family stripped of its fortune in the cause of Gaius Gracchus. Cornelia the Mother of the Gracchi was also pleased to be able to tell her granddaughter that she still possessed enough clout in the Senate to procure a decree waiving the provisions of the *lex Voconia de mulierum hereditatibus,* just in case some remote male cousin appeared and lodged a claim to the vast Sempronian fortune under this antiwoman law. The waiver, she added, extended to the next generation, just in case another woman should prove the only direct heir.

The death of Cornelia the Mother of the Gracchi happened so quickly, so mercifully, that the whole of Rome rejoiced; truly the gods had loved—and sorely tried—Cornelia the Mother of the Gracchi! Being a Cornelian, she was inhumed rather than cremated; alone among the great and small families of Rome, the members of the *gens* Cornelius kept their bodies intact after death. A magnificent tomb on the Via Latina became her monument, and was never without offerings of fresh flowers laid all around it. And with the passing of the years it became both shrine and altar, though the cult was never officially recognized. A Roman woman in need of the qualities associated with Cornelia the Mother of the Gracchi would pray to her, and leave her fresh flowers. She had become a goddess, but of a kind new to any pantheon; a figure of unconquerable spirit in the face of bitter suffering.

What would Cornelia the Mother of the Gracchi do? For once Aurelia had no answer to that question; neither logic nor instinct could graft Aurelia's predicament onto one whose parents would never, never, never have given her the freedom to choose her own husband. Of course Aurelia could appreciate the reasons why her crafty Uncle Publius had suggested it; her own classical education was more than broad enough to appreciate the parallel between herself and Helen of Troy, though Aurelia did not think of herself as fatally beautiful—more as irresistibly eligible.

Finally she came to the only conclusion Cornelia the Mother of the Gracchi would have approved; she must sift through her suitors with painstaking care, and choose the best one. That did not mean the one who attracted her most strongly. It meant the one who measured up to the Roman ideal. Therefore he must be well-born, of a senatorial family at least—and one whose *dignitas,* whose public worth and standing in Rome went down the generations since the founding of the Republic without slur or smear or scar; he must be brave, untempted by excesses of any kind, contemptuous of monetary greed, above bribery or ethical prostitution, and prepared if necessary to lay down his life for Rome or for his honor.

A tall order! The trouble was, how could a girl of her sheltered background be sure she was judging aright? So she decided to talk to the three adult members of her immediate family—to Marcus Cotta and to Rutilia and to her elder half brother, Lucius Aurelius Cotta—and ask them for their candid opinions about each of the men on the list of suitors. The three applied to were taken aback, but they tried to help as best they could; unfortunately, each of them when pressed admitted to personal prejudices likely to warp judgment, so Aurelia ended up no better off.

"There's no one she really fancies," said Cotta to his wife gloomily.

"Not a solitary one!" said Rutilia, sighing.

"It's unbelievable, Rutilia! An eighteen-year-old girl without a hankering for *anyone*? What's the matter with her?"

"How should I know?" asked Rutilia, feeling unfairly put on the defensive. "She doesn't get it from *my* side of the family!"

"Well, she certainly doesn't get it from mine!" snapped Cotta, then shook himself out of his exasperation, kissed his wife to make up, and slumped back into simple depression. "I would be willing to bet, you know, that she ends up deciding none of them are any good!"

"I agree," said Rutilia.

"What are we going to do, then? If we're not careful, we'll end up with the first voluntary spinster in the entire history of Rome!"

"We'd better send her to see my brother," Rutilia said. "She can talk to him about it."

Cotta brightened. "An excellent idea!" he said.

The next day Aurelia walked from the Cotta mansion on the Palatine to Publius Rutilius Rufus's house on the Carinae, escorted by her maidservant, Cardixa, and two big Gallic slaves whose duties were many and varied, but all demanded plenty of physical strength; neither Cotta nor Rutilia had wanted to handicap the congress between Aurelia and her uncle with the presence of parents. An appointment had been made, for as consul kept to administer Rome—thus freeing up Gnaeus Mallius Maximus to recruit the very large army he intended to take to Gaul-across-the-Alps in late spring—Rutilius Rufus was a busy man. Never too busy, however, to deal with the few items of a family nature which came his way.

Marcus Cotta had called to see his brother-in-law just before dawn, and explained the situation—which seemed to amuse Rutilius Rufus mightily.

"Oh, the little one!" he exclaimed, shoulders shaking. "A virgin through and through. Well, we'll have to make sure she doesn't make the wrong decision and remain a virgin for the rest of her life, no matter how many husbands and children she might have."

"I hope you have a solution, Publius Rutilius," said Cotta. "I can't even see a tiny gleam of light."

"I know what to do," said Rutilius Rufus smugly. "Send her over to me just before the tenth hour. She can have some dinner with me. I'll send her home in a litter under strong guard, never fear."

When Aurelia arrived, Rutilius Rufus sent Cardixa and the two Gauls to his servants' quarters to eat dinner and wait upon his pleasure; Aurelia he conducted to his dining room, and saw her comfortably ensconced upon a straight chair where she could converse with equal ease with her uncle and whoever might recline to his left.

"I'm only expecting one guest," he said, getting himself organized on his couch. "Brrr! Chilly, isn't it? How about a nice warm pair of woolly socks, niece?"

Any other eighteen-year-old female might have considered death a preferable fate to wearing something as unglamorous as a nice warm pair of woolly socks, but not Aurelia, who judiciously weighed the ambient temperature of the room against her own state of being, then nodded. "Thank you, Uncle Publius," she said.

Cardixa was summoned and bidden obtain the socks from the housekeeper, which she did with commendable promptness.

"What a sensible girl you are!" said Rutilius Rufus, who really did adore Aurelia's common sense as any other man might adore the perfect ocean pearl he found inside a whiskery whelk on the Ostia mud flats. No great lover of women, he never paused to reflect that common sense was a commodity just as rare in men as in women; he simply looked for its lack in women and consequently found it. Thus was Aurelia, his miraculous ocean pearl, found on the mud flats of womankind, and greatly did he treasure her.

"Thank you, Uncle Publius," said Aurelia, and gave her attention to Cardixa, who was kneeling to remove shoes.

The two girls were engrossed in pulling on socks when the single guest was ushered in; neither of them bothered to look up at the sounds of greeting, the noises of the guest being settled to his host's left.

As Aurelia straightened again, she looked into Cardixa's eyes and said, "Thank you," with one of her very rare smiles.

So when she was fully upright and gazing across the table at her uncle and his guest, the smile still lingered, as did the additional flush bending down had imparted to her cheeks; she looked breathtaking.

The guest's breath caught audibly. So did Aurelia's.

"Gaius Julius, this is my sister's girl, Aurelia," said Publius

Rutilius Rufus suavely. "Aurelia, I would like you to meet the son of my old friend Gaius Julius Caesar—a Gaius like his father, but not the eldest son."

Purple eyes even larger than usual, Aurelia looked at the shape of her fate, and never thought once of the Roman ideal, or Cornelia the Mother of the Gracchi. Or perhaps on some deeper level she did; for indeed he measured up, though only time would prove it to her. At this moment of meeting, all she saw was his long Roman face with its long Roman nose, the bluest of eyes, thickly waving golden hair, beautiful mouth. And, after all that internal debate, all that careful yet fruitless deliberation, she solved her dilemma in the most natural and satisfying way possible. She fell in love.

Of course they talked. In fact, they had a most enjoyable dinner. Rutilius Rufus leaned back on his left elbow and let them have the floor, tickled at his own cleverness in working out which young man among the hundreds he knew would be the one to appeal to his precious ocean pearl. It went without saying that he liked young Gaius Julius Caesar enormously, and expected good things of him in future years; he was the very finest type of Roman. But then, he came from the finest type of Roman family. And, being a Roman of the Romans himself, Publius Rutilius Rufus was particularly pleased that if the attraction between young Gaius Julius Caesar and his niece came to full flower—as he confidently expected it would—a quasi-familial bond would be forged between himself and his old friend Gaius Marius. The children of young Gaius Julius Caesar and his niece Aurelia would be the first cousins of the children of Gaius Marius.

Normally too diffident to quiz anyone, Aurelia forgot all about manners, and quizzed young Gaius Julius Caesar to her heart's content. She found out that he had been in Africa with his brother-in-law Gaius Marius as a junior military tribune, and been decorated on several occasions—a *Corona Muralis* for the battle at the Muluchath citadel, a banner after the first battle outside Cirta, nine silver *phalerae* after the second battle outside Cirta. He had sustained a severe wound in the upper leg during this second battle, and had been sent home, honorably discharged. None of this had she found easy to prise out of him, for he was more interested in telling her of the exploits of his elder brother, Sextus, in the same campaigns.

This year, she found out, he was appointed a moneyer, one of three young men who in their presenatorial years were given an opportunity to learn something of how Rome's economy worked by being put in charge of the minting of Rome's coins.

"Money disappears from circulation," he said, never before having had an audience as fascinating as fascinated. "It's our job to make more money—but not at our whim, mind you! The Treasury determines how much new money is to be minted in a year; we only mint it."

"But how can something as solid as a coin disappear?" asked Aurelia, frowning.

"Oh, it might fall down a drain hole, or be burned up in a big fire," said young Caesar. "Some coins just plain wear out. But most coins disappear because they're hoarded. And when money is hoarded, it can't do its proper job."

"What is its proper job?" asked Aurelia, never having had much to do with money, for her needs were simple and her parents sensitive to them.

"To change hands constantly," said young Gaius Caesar. "That's called circulation. And when money circulates, every hand it passes through has been blessed by it. It buys goods, or work, or property. But it must keep on circulating."

"So you have to make new money to replace the coins someone is hoarding," said Aurelia thoughtfully. "However, the coins being hoarded are still there, really, aren't they? What happens, for instance, if suddenly a huge number of them which have been hoarded are—are—*un*-hoarded?"

"Then the value of money goes down."

Having had her first lesson in simple economics, Aurelia moved on to find out the physical side of coining money.

"We actually get to choose what goes on the coins," said young Gaius Caesar eagerly, captivated by his rapt listener.

"You mean the Victory in her *biga*?"

"Well, it's easier to get a two-horse chariot on a coin than a four-horse one, which is why Victory rides in a *biga* rather than a *quadriga*," he answered. "But those of us with a bit of imagination like to do something more original than just Victory, or Rome. If there are three issues of coins in a year—and there mostly are—then each of us gets to pick what goes on one of the issues."

"And will you pick something?" Aurelia asked.

"Yes. We drew lots, and I got the silver denarius. So this year's denarius will have the head of Iulus the son of Aeneas on one side, and the Aqua Marcia on the other, to commemorate my grandfather Marcius Rex," said young Caesar.

After that, Aurelia discovered that he would be seeking election as a tribune of the soldiers in the autumn; his brother, Sextus, had been elected a tribune of the soldiers for this year, and was going to Gaul with Gnaeus Mallius Maximus.

When the last course was eaten, Uncle Publius packed his niece off home in the well-protected litter, as he had promised. But his masculine guest he persuaded to stay a little longer.

"Have a cup or two of unwatered wine," he said. "I'm so full of water I'm going to have to go out now and piss a whole bucket."

"I'll join you," said the guest, laughing.

"And what did you think of my niece?" asked Rutilius Rufus after they had been served with an excellent vintage of Tuscania.

"That's like asking whether I like living! Is there any alternative?"

"Liked her that much, eh?"

"Liked her? Yes, I did. But I'm in love with her too," said young Caesar.

"Want to marry her?"

"Of course I do! So, I gather, does half of Rome."

"That's true, Gaius Julius. Does it put you off?"

"No. I'll apply to her father—her Uncle Marcus, I mean. And try to see her again, persuade her to think kindly of me. It's worth a try, because I know she liked me."

Rutilius Rufus smiled. "Yes, I think she did too." He slid off the couch. "Well, you go home, young Gaius Julius, tell your father what you plan to do, then go and see Marcus Aurelius tomorrow. As for me, I'm tired, so I'm going to bed."

Though he had made himself sound confident enough to Rutilius Rufus, young Gaius Caesar walked home in less hopeful mood. Aurelia's fame was widespread. Many of his friends had applied for her hand; some Marcus Cotta had refused to add to his list, others were entered on it. Among the successful applicants were names more august than his, if only because those names were allied to enormous fortunes. To be a Julius Caesar meant little beyond a social distinction so secure even poverty could not destroy its aura. Yet how could he compete against the likes of Marcus Livius Drusus, or young Scaurus, or Licinius Orator, or Mucius Scaevola, or the elder of the Ahenobarbus brothers? Not knowing that Aurelia had been given the opportunity to choose her own husband, young Caesar rated his chances extremely slender.

When he let himself in through the front door and walked down the passageway to the atrium, he could see the lights still burning in his father's study, and blinked back sudden tears before going quietly to the half-open door, and knocking.

"Come," said a tired voice.

Gaius Julius Caesar was dying. Everyone in the house knew it, including Gaius Julius Caesar, though not a word had been spoken. The illness had started with difficulty in swallowing, an insidious thing which crept onward, so slowly at first that it was hard to tell whether there actually was a worsening. Then his voice had begun to croak, and after that the pain started, not unbearable at first. It had now become constant, and Gaius Julius Caesar could no longer swallow solid food. So far he had refused to see a doctor, though every day Marcia begged him to.

"Father?"

"Come and keep me company, young Gaius," said Caesar, who turned sixty this year, but in the lamplight looked more like eighty. He had lost so much weight his skin hung on him, the planes of his skull were just that, a skull, and constant suffering had bleached the life out of his once-intense blue eyes. His hand went out to his son; he smiled.

"Oh, Father!" Young Caesar tried manfully to keep the emotion out of his voice, but could not; he crossed the room to Caesar, took the hand, and kissed it, then stepped closer and gathered his father to him, arms about the skinny shoulders, cheek against the lifeless silver-gilt hair.

"Don't cry, my son," Caesar croaked. "It will soon be over. Athenodorus Siculus is coming tomorrow."

A Roman didn't cry. Or wasn't supposed to cry. To young Caesar that seemed a mistaken standard of behavior, but he mastered his tears, drew away, and sat down near enough to his father to retain his clasp of the clawlike hand.

"Perhaps Athenodorus will know what to do," he said.

"Athenodorus will know what all of us know, that I have an incurable growth in my throat," said Caesar. "However, your mother hopes for a miracle, and I am far enough gone now for Athenodorus not to even think of offering her one. I have gone forward with living for only one reason, to make sure all the members of my family are properly provided for, and to assure myself they are happily settled." Caesar paused, his free hand groping for the cup of un-watered wine which was now his only physical solace. A minute sip or two, and he continued.

"You are the last, young Gaius," he whispered. "What am I to hope for you? Many years ago I gave you one luxury, which you have not yet espoused—the luxury of choosing your own wife. Now I think the time is here for you to exercise your option. It would make me rest easier if I knew you were decently settled."

Young Gaius Caesar lifted his father's hand and laid it against his cheek, leaning forward and taking all the weight of his father's arm. "I've found her, Father," he said. "I met her tonight—isn't that strange?"

"At Publius Rutilius's?" asked Caesar incredulously.

The young man grinned. "I think he was playing matchmaker!"

"An odd role for a consul."

"Yes." Young Caesar drew a breath. "Have you heard of his niece—Marcus Cotta's stepdaughter, Aurelia?"

"The current beauty? I think everyone must have."

"That's her. She's the one."

Caesar looked troubled. "Your mother tells me there's a line of suitors clear around the block, including the richest and noblest bachelors in Rome—and even some who are not bachelors, I hear."

"All absolutely true," said young Gaius. "But *I* shall marry her, never fear!"

"If your instincts about her are right, then you're going to make a rod for your own back," said the caring father very seriously. "Beauties of her caliber don't make good wives, Gaius. They're spoiled, capricious, willful, and pert. Let her go to some other man, and choose a girl of humbler kind." He bethought himself of a comforting fact, and relaxed. "Luckily you're a complete nobody compared to Lucius Licinius Orator or Gnaeus Domitius Junior, even if you are a patrician. Marcus Aurelius won't even consider you, of that I'm sure. So don't set your heart on her to the exclusion of all others."

"She'll marry me, *tata,* wait and see!"

And from that contention Gaius Julius Caesar did not have the strength to budge his son, so he let himself be helped to the bed where he had taken to sleeping alone, so restless and transient were his periods of sleep.

Aurelia lay on her stomach within the closely curtained litter as it jiggled and joggled her up and down the hills between her Uncle Publius's house and her Uncle Marcus's house. Gaius Julius Caesar Junior! How wonderful he was, how perfect! But would he want to marry her? What would Cornelia the Mother of the Gracchi think?

Sharing the litter with her mistress, Cardixa watched her with great curiosity; this was an Aurelia she had never seen before.

Bolt upright in a corner and carefully holding a candle shielded by thin alabaster so that the interior of the litter was not completely darkened, she noted symptoms of a marked change. Aurelia's quick tense body was utterly relaxed in a sprawl, her mouth was held less tightly, and creamy eyelids hid whatever lurked in her eyes. Being of excellent intelligence, Cardixa knew exactly the reason for the change; the terribly good-looking young man Publius Rutilius had produced almost like a main course. Oh, cunning old villain that he was! And yet—Gaius Julius Caesar Junior was a very special person, just right for Aurelia. Cardixa knew it in her bones.

Whatever Cornelia the Mother of the Gracchi might have done in a similar situation, by the time she arose next morning Aurelia knew her course of action. The first thing she did was to send Cardixa around to the Caesar house with a note for her young man.

"Ask to marry me," it said baldly.

After which she did nothing at all, simply hid herself in her workroom and appeared for meals as inconspicuously as possible, aware herself that she was changing, and not wanting her vigilant parents to see it before she made her move.

The following day she waited until Marcus Cotta's clients had been attended to, in no hurry because Cotta's secretary had informed her there were no meetings of Senate or People for him to attend; he would certainly remain at home for an hour or two after the last client departed.

"Father?"

Cotta looked up from the papers on his desk. "Ah! It's Father today, is it? Come in, daughter, come in." He smiled at her warmly. "Would you like your mother here too?"

"Yes, please."

"Then go and fetch her."

Off she went, reappearing a moment later with Rutilia.

"Sit down, ladies," said Cotta.

They disposed themselves side by side on a couch.

"Well, Aurelia?"

"Have there been any new applicants?" she asked abruptly.

"As a matter of fact, yes. Young Gaius Julius Caesar came to see me yesterday, and as I have nothing against him, I added him to the list. Which makes my total thirty-eight."

Aurelia blushed. Fascinated, Cotta stared at her, never having seen her discomposed in his entire acquaintance of her. The tip of a pink tongue came out, wetted her lips. Rutilia, he noted, had swiveled on the couch to observe her daughter, and was equally intrigued by the blush and the discomposure.

"I've made up my mind," Aurelia said.

"Excellent! Tell us," prompted Cotta.

"Gaius Julius Caesar Junior."

"What?" asked Cotta blankly.

"Who?" asked Rutilia blankly.

"Gaius Julius Caesar Junior," Aurelia repeated patiently.

"Well, well! The last horse entered in the race," said Cotta, amused.

"My *brother's* late entry," said Rutilia. "Ye gods, he's clever! How did he know?"

"He's a remarkable man," said Cotta to his wife, then said to his stepdaughter, "You met Gaius Julius Junior at your uncle's the day before yesterday—was that for the very first time?"

"Yes."

"But he's the one you want to marry."

"Yes."

"My darling girl, he's a relatively poor man," said the mother. "There won't be any luxury for you as the wife of young Gaius Julius, you know."

"One doesn't marry in order to live in luxury."

"I'm glad you have the good sense to know that, my child. However, he's not the man I would have chosen for you," said Cotta, not really pleased.

"I'd like to know why, Father," said Aurelia.

"It's a strange family. Too—too unorthodox. And they're bound ideologically as well as maritally to Gaius Marius, a man I absolutely detest," said Cotta.

"Uncle Publius likes Gaius Marius," said Aurelia.

"Your Uncle Publius is sometimes a little misguided," Cotta answered grimly. "However, he's not so besotted that he'd vote against his own class in the Senate just for the sake of Gaius Marius—where I cannot say the same of the Julians of Gaius's branch! Your Uncle Publius soldiered with Gaius Marius for many years, and that creates an understandable bond. Where old Gaius Julius Caesar welcomed Gaius Marius with open arms, and has taught his whole family to esteem him."

"Didn't Sextus Julius marry one of the lesser Claudias not long ago?" asked Rutilia.

"I believe so."

"Well, that's an unimpeachable union, at any rate. Maybe the sons are not so attached to Gaius Marius as you think."

"They're brothers-in-law, Rutilia."

Aurelia interjected, "Father and Mother, you left it up to me," she said sternly. "I am going to marry Gaius Julius Caesar, and that's that." It was said with great firmness, but not insolently.

Cotta and Rutilia gazed at her in consternation, finally understanding; the coolly sensible Aurelia was in love.

"That's true, we did," said Cotta briskly, deciding there was no alternative save to make the best of it. "Well, off with you!" He waved dismissal to his wife and niece. "I have to get the scribes onto writing thirty-seven letters. And then I had better walk round to see Gaius Julius—father and son, I suppose."

The general letter Marcus Aurelius Cotta sent out said:

> After careful consideration, I decided that I would permit my niece and ward, Aurelia, to choose her own husband. My wife, her mother, agreed. This is to announce that Aurelia has made her choice. Her husband is to be Gaius Julius Caesar Junior, younger son of the Conscript Father Gaius Julius Caesar. I trust you will join with me in offering the couple all felicitations for their coming marriage.

His secretary looked at Cotta with wide eyes.

"All right, don't just sit there, get onto it!" said Cotta rather gruffly for such an even-tempered man. "I want thirty-seven copies of that within the hour, each one headed to a man on this list." He shoved the list across the table. "I'll sign them myself, then they are to be delivered by hand immediately."

The secretary got to work; so did the gossip grapevine, which easily beat the letters to their recipients. Many were the sore hearts and new grudges when the news got round, for clearly Aurelia's choice was an emotional one, not an expedient one. Somehow that made it less forgivable; none of the starters on Aurelia's list of suitors liked being pipped on the post by the younger son of a mere backbencher, no matter how august his lineage. Besides which, the lucky man was far too good-looking, and that was generally felt to be an unfair advantage.

After she recovered from the initial shock, Rutilia was inclined to approve of her daughter's choice. "Oh, think of the children she'll have!" she purred to Cotta as he stood being draped in his purple-bordered toga so he could venture forth to visit the Julius Caesar household, situated in a less fashionable part of the Palatine. "If you leave money out of it, it's a splendid match for an Aurelius, let alone a Rutilius. The Julians are the very top of the tree."

"You can't dine off an ancient bloodline," growled Cotta.

"Oh, come now, Marcus Aurelius, it isn't that bad! The Marius connection has advanced the Julian fortune mightily, and no doubt it will continue to do so. I can't see any reason why young Gaius Julius won't be consul. I've heard he's very bright, as well as very capable."

"Handsome is as handsome does," said Cotta, unconvinced.

However, he set out in togate magnificence, a handsome man himself, though with the florid complexion all the Aurelius Cottas possessed; it was a family whose members did not live to be very old, for they were subject to apoplexy.

The younger Gaius Julius Caesar was not at home, he was

informed, so he asked for the old man, and was surprised when the steward looked grave.

"If you will excuse me, Marcus Aurelius, I will make inquiries," the steward said. "Gaius Julius is not well."

This was the first Cotta had heard of an illness, but upon reflection he realized that indeed the old man had not been in the Senate House in some time. "I'll wait," he said.

The steward came back quickly. "Gaius Julius will see you," he said, conducting Cotta to the study. "I should warn you that his appearance will shock you."

Glad he had been warned, Cotta concealed his shock as the bony fingers managed the enormous task of poking forward to offer a handshake.

"Marcus Aurelius, it is a pleasure," Caesar said. "Sit down, do! I'm sorry I cannot rise, but my steward will have told you I am not well." A faint smile played around the fine lips. "A euphemism. I'm dying."

"Oh, surely not," said Cotta uneasily, seating himself on the edge of a chair with twitching nostrils; there was a peculiar smell in the room, of something unpleasant.

"Surely so. I have a growth in my throat. It was confirmed this morning by Athenodorus Siculus."

"It grieves me to hear you say it, Gaius Julius. Your presence in the House will be sorely missed, especially by my brother-in-law Publius Rutilius."

"He's a good friend." Caesar's red-rimmed eyes blinked tiredly. "I can guess why you're here, Marcus Aurelius, but please tell me."

"When the list of my niece and ward Aurelia's suitors got so long—and so filled with powerful names—that I had to fear the choosing of her husband would leave my sons with more enemies than friends, I permitted her to choose her own spouse," said Cotta. "Two days ago she met your younger son at the house of her uncle, Publius Rutilius, and today she tells me she has chosen him."

"And you dislike it as much as I do," said Caesar.

"I do." Cotta sighed, shrugged. "However, I passed my word on the matter, so I shall adhere to it."

"I made the same concession to my younger son many years ago," said Caesar, and smiled. "We will agree to make the best of it then, Marcus Aurelius, and hope that our children have more sense than we do."

"Indeed, Gaius Julius."

"You will want to know my son's circumstances."

"He told me when he applied for her hand."

"He may not have been forthcoming enough. There is more than sufficient land to ensure his seat in the Senate, but at the moment, nothing more," said Caesar. "Unfortunately, I am not in a position to purchase a second house in Rome, and that is a difficulty. This house goes to my older son, Sextus, who married recently and lives here with his wife, now in the early stages of her first pregnancy. My death is imminent, Marcus Aurelius. After my death, it is Sextus who becomes the *paterfamilias,* and upon his marriage my younger son will have to find another place to live."

"I'm sure you know Aurelia is heavily dowered," said Cotta. "Perhaps the most sensible thing to do is to invest her dowry in a house." He cleared his throat. "She inherited a large sum from her father, my brother, which has been invested for some years now. In spite of the market ups and downs, it stands at the moment at about one hundred talents. Forty talents will buy a more than respectable house on the Palatine or the Carinae. Naturally the house would be put in your son's name, but if at any time a divorce should occur, your son would have to replace the sum the house cost. But divorce aside, Aurelia would still have a sufficient sum left in her own right to ensure she doesn't want."

Caesar frowned. "I dislike the thought that my son will live in a private dwelling funded by his wife," he croaked. "It would be a presumption on his part. No, Marcus Aurelius, I think something is called for that will safeguard Aurelia's money better than the purchasing of a house she will not own. A hundred talents will buy an insula in excellent condition anywhere on the Esquiline. It should be bought for her, in *her* name. The young couple can live rent-free in one of the ground-floor apartments, and your niece can enjoy an income from renting the rest of the apartments, an income larger than she can get from other kinds of investments. My son will have to strive of his own volition to earn the money to buy a private house, and that will keep his courage and ambitions high."

"I couldn't allow Aurelia to live in an insula!" said Cotta, aghast. "No, I'll slice off forty talents to buy a house, and leave the other sixty talents safely invested."

"An insula in her own name," said Caesar stubbornly. He gasped, choked, leaned forward fighting for breath.

Cotta poured a cup of wine and placed it in the clutching hand, assisting the hand to Caesar's lips.

"Better," said Caesar in a little while.

"Perhaps I ought to come back," said Cotta.

"No, let's thrash this out now, Marcus Aurelius. We do agree, you and I, that this match is not the one we would have chosen for either participant. Very well then, let us not make it too easy for them. Let us teach them the price of love. If they belong together, a little hardship can only strengthen their bond. If they do not, a little hardship will accelerate the break. We will ensure that Aurelia keeps all of her dowry, and we will not injure my son's pride any more than we can help. An insula, Marcus Aurelius! It must be of the best construction, so make sure you employ honest men to inspect it. And," the whispering voice went on, "don't be too fussy about its location. Rome is growing rapidly, but the market for inexpensive housing is far steadier than for housing of those moving upward. When times are hard, those moving upward slide down, so there are always tenants looking for cheaper rent."

"Ye gods, my niece would be a common landlady!" cried Cotta, revolted by the idea.

"And why not?" asked Caesar, smiling tiredly. "I hear she's a colossal beauty. Won't the two roles marry? If they won't, perhaps she should think twice about marrying my son."

"It is true that she's a colossal beauty," said Cotta, smiling broadly at a secret joke. "I shall bring her to meet you, Gaius Julius, and let you make of her what you will." He got to his feet, leaned over to pat the thin shoulder. "My last word is this: it shall be left to Aurelia to decide what happens to her dowry. You put your proposition of the insula to her yourself, and I shall put my suggestion of a house forward. Is it a deal?"

"It's a deal," said Caesar. "But send her quickly, Marcus Aurelius! Tomorrow, at noon."

"Will you tell your son?"

"Indeed I will. He can fetch her to me tomorrow."

Under normal circumstances Aurelia didn't dither about what she was going to wear; she loved bright colors and she liked to mix them, but the decision was as crisp and no-nonsense as was all else about her. However, having been notified that she was to be fetched by her betrothed to meet her prospective parents-in-law, she dithered. Finally she chose an underdress of fine cerise wool, and overlaid it with a drapery of rose-pink wool, fine enough to let the deeper color below show through, and overlaid that with a second drapery of palest pink, as fine as her wedding veil. She bathed, then scented herself with attar of roses, but her hair was dragged back into its uncompromising bun, and she refused her mother's offering of a little rouge and *stibium*.

"You're too pale today," Rutilia protested. "It's the tension. Go on, look your best, please! Just a dab of rouge on your cheeks, and a line around your eyes."

"No," said Aurelia.

Pallor turned out not to matter, anyway, for when Gaius Julius Caesar Junior called to fetch her, Aurelia produced all the color her mother could have wished.

"Gaius Julius," she said, holding out her hand.

"Aurelia," he said, taking it.

After that, they didn't know what to do.

"Well, go on, goodbye!" said Rutilia irritably; it felt so odd to be losing her first child to this extremely attractive young man, when she only felt eighteen herself.

They set off, Cardixa and the Gauls trailing behind.

"I should warn you that my father isn't well," said young Caesar with tight control. "He has a malignant growth in his throat, and we fear he will not be with us much longer."

"Oh," said Aurelia.

They turned a corner. "I got your note," he said, "and hurried to see Marcus Aurelius immediately. I can't believe you chose me!"

"I can't believe I found you," she said.

"Do you think Publius Rutilius did it deliberately?"

That triggered a smile in her. "Definitely."

They walked the rest of the block, turned a corner. "I see you're not a talker," said young Caesar.

"No," said Aurelia.

And that was all the conversation they managed before the Caesar residence was reached.

One look at his son's chosen bride caused Caesar to change his thinking somewhat. This was no spoiled, capricious beauty! Oh, she was everything he had heard she was—colossally beautiful—but not in any accepted mode. Then again, he reasoned, that was probably why to her alone did they append the hyperbole "colossal." What wonderful children they would have! Children he would not live to see.

"Sit down, Aurelia." His voice was scarcely audible, so he pointed to a chair right alongside his own, but enough to the front for him to see her. His son he placed upon his other side.

"What did Marcus Aurelius tell you about the talk we had?" he asked then.

"Nothing," said Aurelia.

He went right through the discussion of her dowry he had had with Cotta, making no bones about his own feelings, or about Cotta's.

"Your uncle your guardian says the choice is yours. Do you want a house or an insula?" he asked, eyes on her face.

What would Cornelia the Mother of the Gracchi do? This time she knew the answer: Cornelia the Mother of the Gracchi would do the most honorable thing, no matter how hard. Only now she had two honors to consider, her beloved's as well as her own. To choose the house would be more comfortable and familiar by far, but it would injure her beloved's pride to know his wife's money provided their house.

She took her gaze off Caesar and stared at his son very gravely. "Which would you prefer?" she asked him.

"It's your decision, Aurelia," he said.

"No, Gaius Julius, it's your decision. I am to be your wife. I intend to be a proper wife, and know my proper place. You will be the head of our house. All I ask in return for yielding the first place to you is that you always deal with me honestly and honorably. The choice of where we live is yours. I will abide by it, in deed as well as word."

"Then we will ask Marcus Aurelius to find you an insula, and register the deeds of ownership in your name," young Caesar said without hesitation. "It must be the most profitable and well-built real estate he can find, and I agree with my father—its location is of no moment. The income from the rents will be yours. We will live in one of its ground floor apartments until I am in a position to buy us a private dwelling. I will support you and our children from the income of my own land, of course. Which means that you will have the full responsibility for your insula—I will not be a part of it."

She was pleased, it showed at once, but she said nothing.

"You're not a talker!" said Caesar, amazed.

"No," said Aurelia.

Cotta got to work with a will, though his intention was to find his niece a snug property in one of the better parts of Rome. However, it was not to be; look though he would, the wisest and shrewdest investment was a fairly big insula in the heart of the Subura. Not a new apartment block (it had been built by its single owner some thirty years before, and since this owner had lived in the larger of its two ground-floor apartments, he had built to last), it had stone-and-concrete footings and foundations up to fifteen feet in depth and five feet in width; the outer and load-bearing walls were two feet thick, faced on either side with the irregular brick-and-mortar called *opus incertum,* and filled with a stout mixture of cement and small-stone aggregate; the windows were all relief-arched in brick; the whole was reinforced with wooden beams at least a foot square and up to fifty feet in length; foot-square wooden beams supported floors of concrete aggregate in the lower storeys and wooden planks in the upper storeys; the generous light-well was load-bearing yet retained its open nature through a system of two-foot-thick square pillars every five feet around its edge, joined at every floor by massive wooden beams.

At nine storeys of nine feet each in height including the foot-thick floors, it was quite modest—most of the insulae in the same neighborhood were two to four storeys higher—but it occupied the whole of a small triangular block where the Subura Minor ran into the Vicus Patricii. Its blunted apex faced the crossroads, its two long sides ran one down the Subura Minor and the other down the Vicus Patricii, and its base was formed by a lane which ran through from one street to the other.

Their first sight of it had come at the end of a long string of other properties; Cotta, Aurelia, and young Caesar were by this inured to the patter of a small, glib salesman of impeccably Roman ancestry—no Greek freedman sales staff for the real-estate firm of Thorius Postumus!

"Note the plaster on the walls, both inside and out," droned the agent. "Not a crack to be seen, foundations as firm as a miser's grip on his last bar of gold . . . eight shops, all under long lease, no trouble with the tenants or the rents . . . two apartments ground-floor with reception rooms two storeys high . . . two apartments only next floor up . . . eight apartments per floor to the sixth floor . . . twelve apartments on the seventh, twelve on the eighth . . . shops all have an upper floor for living in . . . additional storage above false, ceilings in the sleep cubicles of the ground-floor apartments . . ."

On and on he extolled the virtues of the property; after a while Aurelia shut him out and concentrated upon her own thoughts.

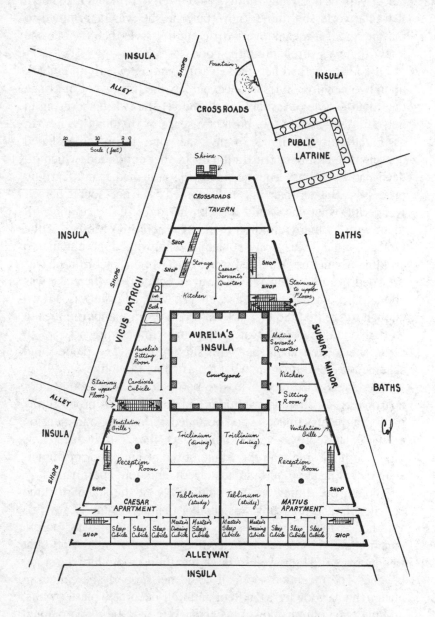

Uncle Marcus and Gaius Julius could listen to him and take heed. It was a world she didn't know, but one she was determined to master, and if it meant a very different life-style than the one she knew, that was surely all to the good.

Of course she had her fears, wasn't panting eagerly to embark upon two new life-styles at once, namely the lifestyle of marriage and the life-style of insula living. And yet she was discovering in herself a fearlessness too, born of a sense of freedom too new to assimilate fully. Ignorance of any other kind of life had excluded conscious boredom or frustration during her childhood, which indeed had been busy enough, involving as it had many learning processes. But as marriage had loomed, she had found herself wondering what she would do with her days if she couldn't fill them with as many children as had Cornelia the Mother of the Gracchi—and it was a rare nobleman who wanted more than two children. By nature Aurelia was a doer, a worker; by birth she was excluded from very much in the way of action. Now here she was about to become a landlady as well as a wife, and she was shrewd enough to see that the first at least promised rare opportunities to work. Not only work, but interesting and stimulating work.

So she looked about her with shining eyes, and plotted and schemed, tried to imagine what it was going to be like.

There was a difference in size between the two ground-floor apartments, for the owner-builder had done himself proud in the matter of the apartment he had occupied. After the Cotta mansion on the Palatine it was very small; in fact, the Cotta mansion was bigger in floor area than the whole of the ground floor of this insula, including shops, crossroads tavern, and both apartments.

Though the dining room would barely fit the standard three couches in, and the study was smaller than any study in any private house, they were lofty; the wall between them was more a partition and did not reach the ceiling, thus enabling air and light to flow from the light-well through the dining room into the study beyond. The reception room (it could not properly be called an atrium) had a good terrazzo floor and well-decorated plaster walls, and the two columns down its center were of solid wood painted to look like fancifully colored marble; air and light came in from the street through a huge iron grille high up on the outside wall between the end of a shop along its front and the stairwell which led to the upper floors. Three typically windowless sleeping cubicles led off the reception room, and two more, one of them larger, off the study. There was a little room she could use as her sitting room, and between it and the stairwell was a smaller room Cardixa could have. But the greatest relief of all was to discover that the apartment contained a bathroom and a latrine—for, as the agent gleefully explained, the insula lay right athwart one of Rome's main sewers, and was legally supplied with an adjutage to the water supply.

"There's a public latrine right opposite on the Subura Minor, and the Subura Baths are right next door to that," said the agent. "Water is no problem. You're at an ideal height here, low enough to get good feed from the Agger reservoirs, but too high to be troubled by backwashes when the Tiber floods, and the size of the adjutage into the mains is larger than the water companies are supplying now—*if* the new blocks can even get connected to the mains, that is! Naturally the previous owner kept the water and sewer for himself—the tenants are well served because of the crossroads just outside, and the latrine and baths opposite."

Aurelia listened to this fervently, for she had heard that her new life-style would not include the luxuries of laid-on water and a latrine; if any aspect of living in an insula had dismayed her, it was the idea of going without her private bath and her private excretions. None of the other insulae they had inspected provided either water or sewer, even though most of them had been in better districts. If Aurelia had not made up her mind this insula was the right one before, she now certainly did.

"How much rent can we expect?" asked young Caesar.

"Ten talents a year—a quarter of a million sesterces."

"Good, good!" said Cotta, nodding.

"Upkeep on the building is negligible because it was built to top standards," said the agent. "That in itself means it is never without a full complement of tenants—so many of these insulae come tumbling down, you know, or go up like dry bark. Not this place! *And* it has a street frontage on two of its three sides as well as a somewhat wider than usual lane behind, which means it is less likely to catch fire if a neighboring building does go up. Yes, this place is as sound as a Granius ship. I can say it with truth."

Since it was senseless to battle through the Subura encumbered by a litter or a sedan chair, Cotta and young Caesar had brought along the pair of Gauls as extra protection, and undertook to escort Aurelia safely on foot. Not that there was much risk involved, for it was high noon, and everyone on the jam-packed streets seemed more interested in his or her own business than in molesting the beautiful Aurelia.

"What do you think?" Cotta asked her as they came down the slight slope of the Fauces Suburae into the Argiletum and prepared to cross the lower end of the Forum Romanum.

"Oh, Uncle, I think it's ideal!" she said, then turned to look at young Caesar. "Do you agree, Gaius Julius?"

"I think it will suit us very well," he said.

"All right then, I'll close the deal this afternoon. At ninety-five talents, it's a good buy, if not a bargain. And you'll have five talents left to use on furniture."

"No," said young Caesar firmly, "the furniture is my responsibility—and I'm not destitute, you know! My land at Bovillae brings me in a good income."

"I know it does, Gaius Julius," said Cotta patiently. "You told me, remember?"

He didn't remember. All young Caesar could think about these days was Aurelia.

They were married in April, on a perfect spring day, with every omen auspicious; even Gaius Julius Caesar seemed better.

Rutilia wept and Marcia wept, the one because this was the first of her children to enter the married state, the other because this was the last of her children to do so. Julia and Julilla were there, as was Sextus's wife, Claudia, but none of their husbands were; Marius and Sulla were still in Africa, and Sextus Caesar was recruiting in Italy, unable to get leave from the consul Gnaeus Mallius Maximus.

Cotta had wanted to rent a house on the Palatine for the young couple for their first month together. "Get used to being married first, then get used to living in the Subura," he said, most concerned for his only girl.

But the young couple resolutely refused, so the wedding walk was a very long one, and the bride was cheered by—or so it seemed—the whole of the Subura. Young Caesar was profoundly glad the veil hid his bride's face, but took his own share of the casually obscene raillery in excellent part, smiling and bowing as they walked.

"It's our new neighborhood, we'd best learn to get on with them," he said. "Just close your ears."

"I'd rather you steered clear of them," muttered Cotta, who had wanted to hire gladiators to escort the bridal party; the teeming masses and the crime rate worried him sick, as did the language.

By the time they reached Aurelia's insula they had quite a gathering tacked on behind, hopeful it seemed that there would be plenty of wine at the end of the road, and determined to invade the festivities. However, when young Caesar got the big door unlocked and swung his new wife off her feet to carry her across the threshold, Cotta, Lucius Cotta, and the two Gauls managed to keep the throng at bay for long enough for young Caesar to get inside and slam the door. Amid howls of protest, Cotta marched away down the Vicus Patricii with his head up.

Only Cardixa was present inside the apartment; Aurelia had decided to use her leftover dowry money to buy household servants, but had postponed this duty until after her marriage, for she wanted to do it all by herself, not suffer the presence and advice of her mother or her mother-in-law. Young Caesar too had servants to buy—the steward, the wine steward, his secretary, a clerk, and a valet—but Aurelia had more: two heavy-duty cleaning maids, a laundress, a cook and assistant cook, two general-purpose servants, and a strong man. Not a large household by any means, but adequate.

It was growing dark outside, but the apartment was far darker, something the high noon of their only previous visit had not indicated. Light percolating down the nine floors of the central well dimmed early, as did light coming in from the street, a defile of tall insulae. Cardixa had lit what lamps they had, but they were far too few to banish black corners; she herself had retired to her little room, to leave the newlyweds decently alone.

The noise was what amazed Aurelia. It came from everywhere—the street outside, the stairwell leading to the upper floors, the central light-well—even the ground seemed to rumble. Cries, curses, crashes, shouted conversations, screamed altercations and vituperations, babies crying, children wailing, men and women hawking and spitting, a band of musicians banging away at drums and cymbals, snatches of song, oxen bellowing, sheep bleating, mules and asses wheezing, carts endlessly trundling, howls of laughter.

"Oh, we won't be able to hear ourselves think!" she said, blinking away sudden tears. "Gaius Julius, I'm so sorry! I never thought of the noise!"

Young Caesar was wise enough and sensitive enough to know that a part at least of this uncharacteristic outburst was due not to the noise, but to an unacknowledged nervousness brought on by the hectic events of the past few days, the sheer strain of getting married. He had felt it himself; how much greater then must it be for his new little wife?

So he laughed cheerfully and said, "We'll get used to it, never fear. I guarantee that in a month we won't even notice it. Besides, it's bound to be less in our bedroom." And he took her by the hand, feeling it tremble.

Sure enough, the master's sleeping cubicle, reached through his study, was quieter. It was also pitch-black and utterly airless unless the door to the study was left open, for it had been given a false ceiling for storage purposes.

Leaving Aurelia standing in the study, young Caesar went and fetched a lamp from the reception room. Hand in hand, they entered the cubicle, and stood enchanted. Cardixa had decked it out in flowers, strewn scented petals all over the double sleeping couch, and stood every height of vase along the walls, then stuffed them with roses, stocks, violets; on a table reposed a flagon of wine, one of water, two golden cups, and a big plate of honey cakes.

Neither of them was shy. Being Romans, they were properly enlightened about sexual matters, yet modest. Every Roman who could afford it preferred privacy for intimate activities, especially if the body was to be bared; yet they were not inhibited. Of course young Caesar had had his share of adventures, though his face belied his nature; the one was strikingly noticeable, the other quietly inconspicuous. For with all his undeniable gifts, young Caesar was basically a retiring man, lacking the push and shove of an aggressive and political personality; a man others could rely upon, but who was more likely to advance their careers than his own.

Publius Rutilius Rufus's instincts had been exactly right. Young Caesar and Aurelia fitted together beautifully. He was tender, considerate, respectful, warmly loving rather than full of fire; perhaps had he burned with passion, she might have kindled from him, but that neither of them would ever know. Their lovemaking was delicate in its touch, soft in its kisses, slow in its pace. It satisfied them; it even inspired them. And Aurelia was able to tell herself that she had surely earned the unqualified approval of Cornelia the Mother of the Gracchi, for she had done her duty exactly as Cornelia the Mother of the Gracchi must have done hers, with a pleasure and contentment that guaranteed the act itself would never rule her life or dictate her conduct outside the marriage bed—yet also guaranteed that she would never come to dislike the marriage bed.

 During the winter which Quintus Servilius Caepio spent in Narbo grieving for his lost gold, he received a letter from the brilliant young advocate Marcus Livius Drusus, one of Aurelia's most ardent—and most disappointed—suitors.

I was but nineteen when my father the censor died, and left me to inherit not only all his property, but also the position of *paterfamilias*. Perhaps luckily, my only onerous burden was my thirteen-year-old sister, deprived as she was of both father and mother. At the time, my mother, Cornelia, asked to take my sister into her household, but of course I declined. Though there was never any divorce, you are I know aware of the coolness between my parents that came to a head when my father agreed that my young brother should be adopted out. My mother was always far fonder of him than of me, so when my brother became Mamercus Aemilius Lepidus Livianus, she pleaded his young age as an excuse, and went with him to his new household, where indeed she found a kind of life far freer and more licentious than ever she could have lived under my father's roof. I refresh your memory about these things as a point of honor, for I feel my honor touched by my mother's shabby and selfish behavior.

I have, I flatter myself, brought up my sister, Livia Drusa, as befits her great position. She is now eighteen years old, and ready for marriage. As, Quintus Servilius, am I, even at my young age of twenty-three. I know it is more customary to wait until after twenty-five to marry, and I know there are many who prefer to wait until after they enter the Senate. But I cannot. I am the *paterfamilias,* and the only male Livius Drusus of my generation. My brother, Mamercus Aemilius Lepidus Livianus, can no longer claim the Livius Drusus name or any share of the Livius Drusus fortune. Therefore it behooves me to marry and procreate, though I decided at the time of my father's death that I would wait until my sister was old enough to marry.

The letter was as stiff and formal as the young man, but Quintus Servilius Caepio had no fault to find with that; he and the young man's father had been good friends, just as his son and the young man were good friends.

> Therefore, Quintus Servilius, I wish as the head of my family to propose a marriage alliance to you, the head of your family. I have not, incidentally, thought it wise to discuss this matter with my uncle, Publius Rutilius Rufus. Though I have nothing against him as husband of my Aunt Livia, nor as father of her children, I do not consider either his blood or his temperament sufficiently weighty to make his counsel of any value. Only recently, for instance, it came to my ears that he actually persuaded Marcus Aurelius Cotta to allow his stepdaughter, Aurelia, to choose her own husband. A more un-Roman act is hard to imagine. And of course she chose a pretty-boy Julius Caesar, a flimsy and impoverished fellow who will never amount to anything.

There. That disposed of Publius Rutilius Rufus. On ploughed Marcus Livius Drusus, sore of heart, but also sore of *dignitas*.

> In electing to wait for my sister, I thought to relieve my own wife of the responsibility of housing my sister, and being answerable for her conduct. I can see no virtue in transmitting one's own duties to others who cannot be expected to share the same degree of concern.
> What I now propose, Quintus Servilius, is that you permit me to marry your daughter, Servilia Caepionis, and permit your son, Quintus Servilius Junior, to marry my sister, Livia Drusa. It is an ideal solution for both of us. Our ties through marriage go back many generations, and both my sister and your daughter have dowries of exactly the same size, which means

that no money needs to change hands, an advantage in
these times of cash-flow shortages.
Please let me know your decision.

There was really nothing to decide; it was the match Quintus
Servilius Caepio had dreamed of, for the Livius Drusus fortune
was vast, as was the Livius Drusus nobility. He wrote back at
once:

My dear Marcus Livius, I am delighted. You have
my permission to go ahead and make all the arrangements.

And so Drusus broached the matter with his friend Caepio Junior, anxious to prepare the ground for the letter he knew would
soon arrive from Quintus Servilius Caepio to his son; better that
Caepio Junior saw his coming marriage as desirable than the result of a direct order.

"I'd like to marry your sister," he said to Caepio Junior, a little
more abruptly than he had meant to.

Caepio Junior blinked, but didn't answer.

"I'd also like to see you marry my sister," Drusus went on.

Caepio Junior blinked several times, but didn't answer.

"Well, what do you say?" asked Drusus.

Finally Caepio Junior marshaled his wits (which were not
nearly as great as either his fortune or his nobility), and said, "I'd
have to ask my father."

"I already have," said Drusus. "He's delighted."

"Oh! Then I suppose it's all right," said Caepio Junior.

"Quintus Servilius, Quintus Servilius, I want to know what
you think!" cried Drusus, exasperated.

"Well, my sister likes you, so that's all right. . . . And I like
your sister, but . . ." He didn't go on.

"But what?" demanded Drusus.

"I don't think your sister likes me."

It was Drusus's turn to blink. "Oh, rubbish! How could she not

like you? You're my best friend! Of course she likes you! It's the
ideal arrangement, we'll all stay together."

"Then I'd be pleased," said Caepio Junior.

"Good!" said Drusus briskly. "I discussed all the things which
had to be discussed when I wrote to your father—dowry payments and the like. Nothing to worry about."

"Good," said Caepio Junior.

They were sitting on a bench under a splendid old oak tree
growing beside the Pool of Curtius in the lower Forum Romanum, for they had just eaten a delicious lunch of unleavened bread
pockets stuffed with a spicy mixture of lentils and minced pork.

Rising to his feet, Drusus handed his large napkin to his body
servant, and stood while the man made sure his snowy toga was
unsullied by the food.

"Where are you off to in such a hurry?" asked Caepio Junior.

"Home to tell my sister," said Drusus. He lifted one sharply
peaked black brow. "Don't you think you ought to go home to
your sister and tell her?"

"I suppose so," said Caepio Junior dubiously. "Wouldn't you
rather tell her yourself? She likes you."

"No, you have to tell her, silly! You're *in loco parentis* at the
moment, so it's your job—just as it's my job to tell Livia Drusa."
And off went Drusus up the Forum, heading for the Vestal Steps.

His sister was at home—where else would she be? Since
Drusus was the head of the family and their mother, Cornelia,
was forbidden the door, Livia Drusa could not leave the house for
a moment without her brother's permission. Nor would she ever
have dared to sneak out, for in her brother's eyes she was potentially branded with her mother's shame, and seen as a weak and
corruptible female creature who could not be allowed the smallest latitude; he would have believed the worst of her, even on no
evidence at all beyond escape.

"Please ask my sister to come to the study," he said to his steward when he arrived at his house.

It was commonly held to be the finest house in all Rome, and had only just been completed when Drusus the censor died. The view from the loggia balcony across the front of its top storey was magnificent, for it stood on the very highest point of the Palatine cliff above the Forum Romanum. Next door to it was the *area Flacciana,* the vacant block once containing the house of Marcus Fulvius Flaccus, and on the far side of that was the house of Quintus Lutatius Catulus Caesar.

In true Roman style, even on the side of the vacant block its outside walls were windowless, for when a house was built there again, its outside walls would fuse to Drusus's. A high wall with a strong wooden door in it as well as a pair of freight gates fronted onto the Clivus Victoriae, and was actually the back of the house; the front of the house overlooked the view, was three storeys high, and was built out on piers fixed firmly in the slope of the cliff. The top floor, level with the Clivus Victoriae, housed the noble family; the storage rooms and kitchens and servants' quarters were below, and did not run the full depth of the block because of its abrupt slope.

The freight gates in the wall along the street opened directly into the peristyle-garden, which was so large it contained six wonderful, fully grown lotus trees imported as saplings from Africa ninety years before by Scipio Africanus, who had owned the site at the time. Every summer they bloomed a drooping rain of blossom—two red, two orange, and two deep yellow—that lasted for over a month and filled the whole house with perfume; later they were gracefully provided with a thin cover of pale-green fernlike compound leaves; and in winter they were bare, permitting every morsel of sunlight tenure in the courtyard. A long thin shallow pool faced with pure-white marble had four beautiful matching bronze fountains by the great Myron, one on each corner, and other full-scale bronze statues by Myron and Lysippus ranged down the length of either side of the pool—satyrs and nymphs, Artemis and Actaeon, Dionysos and Orpheus. All these bronzes were painted in startlingly lifelike verisimilitude, so that the courtyard at first glance suggested a congress of woodsy immortals.

A Doric colonnade ran down either side of the peristyle-garden and across the side opposite the street wall, supported by wooden columns painted yellow, their bases and capitals picked out in bright colors. The floors of the colonnade were of polished terrazzo, the walls along its back vividly painted in greens and blues and yellows, and hung in the spaces between earth-red pilasters were some of the world's greatest paintings—a child with grapes by Zeuxis, a "Madness of Ajax" by Parrhasius, some nude male figures by Timanthes, one of the portraits of Alexander the Great by Apelles, and a horse by Apelles so lifelike it seemed tethered to the wall when viewed from the far side of the colonnade.

The study opened onto the back colonnade to one side of big bronze doors; the dining room opened onto it to the other side. And beyond that was a magnificent atrium as large as the whole Caesar house, lit by a rectangular opening in the roof supported by columns at each of the four corners and on the long sides of the pool below. The walls were painted in trompe l'oeil realism to simulate pilasters, dadoes, entablatures, and between these were panels of black-and-white cubes so three-dimensional they leaped out at the beholder, and panels of swirling flowerlike patterns; the colors were vivid, mostly reds, with blues and greens and yellows.

The ancestral cupboards containing the wax masks of the Livius Drusus ancestors were all perfectly kept up, of course; painted pedestals called herms because they were adorned with erect male genitalia supported busts of ancestors, or gods, or mythical women, or Greek philosophers, all exquisitely painted to appear real. Full-length statues, each painted to simulate life, stood around the *impluvium* pool and the walls, some on marble plinths, some on the ground. Great silver and gold chandeliers dangled from the ornate plaster ceiling an immense distance above (it was painted to resemble a starlit sky between ranks of gilded plaster flowers), or stood seven and eight feet tall on the floor, which was a colored mosaic depicting the revels of Bacchus and his Bacchantes dancing and drinking, feeding deer, teaching lions to quaff wine.

Drusus didn't notice any of the magnificence, for he was inured

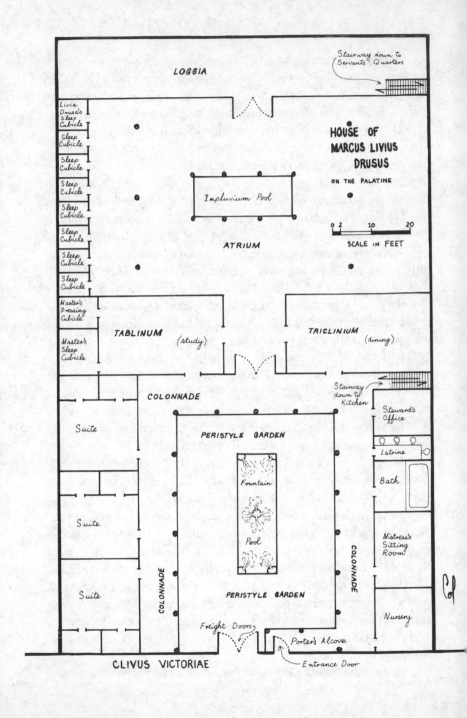

to it, and rather impervious to it as well; it had been his father and his grandfather who dabbled with perfect taste in works of art.

The steward found Drusus's sister outside on the loggia, which opened off the front of the atrium. She was always alone, Livia Drusa, and always lonely. The house was so big she couldn't even plead that she needed the exercise of walking on the streets outside, and when she fancied a shopping spree, her brother simply summoned several whole shops and stalls to his house, and had the vendors spread out their wares in some of the suites along the colonnade, and ordered the steward to pay for whatever Livia Drusa chose. Where both the Julias had trotted all over the more respectable parts of Rome under the eye of their mother or trusted servants, and Aurelia visited relatives and school friends constantly, and the Clitumnas and Nicopolises of Rome lived so free a life they even reclined to dine, Livia Drusa was absolutely cloistered, the prisoner of a wealth and exclusivity so great it forbade its women any egress; she was also the victim of her mother's escape, her mother's present freedom to do as she liked.

Livia Drusa had been ten years old when her mother—a Cornelia of the Scipios—had left the house the Livius Drusus family had then lived in; she had passed then into the complete care of her indifferent father—who preferred to walk slowly along his colonnades looking at his masterpieces—and a series of maidservants and tutors who were all far too afraid of the Livius Drusus power to make themselves her friends. Her older brother, fifteen at the time, she hardly saw at all. And three years after her mother had departed with her little brother, Mamercus Aemilius Lepidus Livianus, as he now had to be called, they had moved from the old house to this vast mausoleum; and she was lost, a tiny atom moving aimlessly amid an eternity of empty space, deprived of love, conversation, companionship, notice. When her father died almost immediately after the move, his passing made no difference.

So unacquainted was she with laughter that when from time to time it floated up from the servants' crowded airless cells below, she wondered what it was, why they did it. The only world she had found to love lay within the cylinders of books, for no one stopped her reading and writing. So she did both for a great deal of every one of her days, thrilling to the repercussions of the wrath of Achilles and the deeds of Greeks and Trojans, lit up by tales of heroes, monsters, gods, and the mortal girls they seemed to hanker after as more desirable than immortals. And when she had managed to deal with the awful shock of the physical manifestations of puberty—for there was no one to tell her what was the matter or what to do—her hungry and passionate nature discovered the wealth of poetry written about love. As fluent in Greek as in Latin, she discovered Alcman—who had invented the love poem (or so it was said)—and passed to Pindar's maiden songs, and Sappho, and Asclepiades. Old Sosius of the Argiletum, who occasionally simply bundled up whatever he had and sent the buckets of books to Drusus's house, had no idea who the reader was; he just assumed the reader was Drusus. So shortly after Livia Drusa turned seventeen, he began to send her the works of the new poet Meleager, who was very much alive and very much attracted to lust as well as love. More fascinated than shocked, Livia Drusa found the literature of eroticism, and thanks to Meleager sexually awoke at last.

Not that it did her any good; she went nowhere, saw no one. In that house, it would have been unthinkable to make overtures to a slave, or for a slave to make overtures to Livia Drusa. Sometimes she met the friends of her brother Drusus, but only in passing. Except, that is, for his best friend, Caepio Junior. And Caepio Junior—short-legged, pimply faced, homely by any standard—she identified with the buffoons in Menander's plays, or the loathsome Thersites whom Achilles slew with one blow from his hand after Thersites accused the great hero of making love to the corpse of the Amazon queen Penthesileia.

It wasn't that Caepio Junior ever did anything to remind her forcibly of either buffoons or Thersites; only that in her starved imagination she had gifted these types of men with the face of Caepio Junior. Her favorite ancient hero was King Odysseus (she thought of him in Greek, so gave him the Greek version of his name), for she liked his brilliant way of solving everybody else's dilemmas, and found his wooing of his wife and then his wife's twenty-year duel of wits with her suitors as she waited for Odysseus to come home the most romantic and satisfying of all the Homeric love stories. And Odysseus she had gifted with the face of the young man she had seen once or twice only on the loggia of the house below Drusus's. This was the house of Gnaeus Domitius Ahenobarbus, who had two sons; but neither of his sons was the young man on his loggia, for them she had met in passing when they came to visit her brother.

Odysseus had red hair, and he was left-handed (though had she read a little more intently and discovered that he owned a pair of legs far too short for his trunk, she might have lost her enthusiasm for him, as short legs were Livia Drusa's pet hate); so too the strange young man on Domitius Ahenobarbus's loggia. He was very tall, his shoulders were wide, and his toga sat upon him in a way suggesting that the rest of his body was powerfully slender. In the sun his red hair glittered, and his head on its long neck was very proud, the head of a king like Odysseus. Even at the distance from which she had seen him, the young man's masterfully beaked nose was apparent, but she could distinguish nothing else of his face—even so, she knew in her bones that his eyes would be large and luminous and grey, as were the eyes of King Odysseus of Ithaca.

So when she read the scorching love poems of Meleager, she insinuated herself into the role of the girl or the young boy being assaulted by the poet, and always the poet was the young man on Ahenobarbus's balcony. If she thought of Caepio Junior at all, it was with a grimace of distaste.

"Livia Drusa, Marcus Livius wants to see you in his study at once," said the steward, breaking into her dream, which was of remaining on the loggia long enough to see the red-haired stranger emerge onto the loggia thirty feet below.

But of course the summons pre-empted her wishes; she turned and followed the steward inside.

Drusus was studying a paper on his desk, but looked up as

soon as his sister entered the room, his face displaying a calm, indulgent, rather remote interest.

"Sit down," he said, indicating the chair on the client's side of his table.

She sat and watched him with equal calm and equal lack of humor; she had never heard Drusus laugh, and rarely seen him smile. The same could he have said of her.

A little alarmed, Livia Drusa realized that he was studying her with more intentness than usual. His interest was a proxy affair, an inspection of her carried out on Caepio Junior's behalf, which of course she could not know.

Yes, she was a pretty little thing, he thought, and though in stature she was small, she had at least escaped the family taint of short legs. Her figure was delightful, full and high of breast, narrow-waisted, nicely hipped; her feet and hands were quite delicate and thin—a sign of beauty—and she did not bite her nails, but kept them well manicured. Her chin was pointed, her forehead broad, her nose reasonably long and a little aquiline. In mouth and eyes she fulfilled every criterion of true beauty, for the eyes were very large and well opened, and the mouth was small, a rosebud. Thick and becomingly dressed, her hair was black, as were eyes, brows, and lashes.

Yes indeed, Livia Drusa was pretty. No Aurelia, however. His heart contracted painfully; it still did whenever he thought of Aurelia. How very quickly he had written to Quintus Servilius once he learned of Aurelia's impending marriage! It was all for the best; there was nothing *wrong* with the Aurelians, but neither in wealth nor in social standing could they equal the patrician Servilians. Besides which, he had always been fond of young Servilia Caepionis, and had no qualms about making her his wife.

"My dear, I've found a husband for you," he said without preamble, and looking highly pleased with himself.

It obviously came as a shock to her, though she kept her face impassive enough. She licked her lips, then managed to ask, "Who, Marcus Livius?"

He became enthusiastic. "The very best of good fellows, a wonderful friend! Quintus Servilius Junior."

Her face froze into a look of absolute horror; she parted her dry lips to speak, but couldn't.

"What's the matter?" he asked, genuinely puzzled.

"I can't marry him," Livia Drusa whispered.

"Why?"

"He's disgusting—revolting!"

"Don't be ridiculous!"

She began to shake her head, and kept on shaking it with increasing vehemence. "I won't marry him, I won't!"

An awful thought occurred to Drusus, ever conscious of his mother; he got up, came round the table, and stood over his sister. "Have you been meeting someone?"

The motion of her head ceased, she lifted it to stare up at him, outraged. "*Me?* How could I possibly meet anyone, stuck in this house every single day of my life? The only men I see come here with you, and I don't even get the opportunity to converse with them! If you have them to dinner, you don't ask me—the only time I'm permitted to come to dinner is when you have that frightful oaf Quintus Servilius Junior!"

"How dare you!" he said, growing angry; it had never occurred to him that she would judge his best friend differently than he did.

"I won't marry him!" she cried. "I'd rather be dead!"

"Go to your room," he said, looking flinty.

She got up at once, and walked toward the door which opened onto the colonnade.

"Not your sitting room, Livia Drusa. Your bedroom. And there you will stay until you come to your senses."

A burning look was her only answer, but she turned around and left by the door to the atrium.

Drusus remained by her vacant chair, and tried to deal with his anger. It was preposterous! How dare she defy him!

After some moments his emotions quietened; he was able to grasp the tail of this spitting cat, even though he had no idea what to do with it. In all his life no one had ever defied him; no one had ever put him in a position from which he could see no logical way out. Used to being obeyed, and to being treated with a degree of respect and deference not normally accorded to one so young, he had no idea what to do. If he had known his sister better—and he now had to admit that he knew her not at all—if his father were alive—if his mother—oh, what a pickle! And what to do?

Soften her up a bit, came the answer; he sent for his steward at once.

"The lady Livia Drusa has offended me," he said with admirable calm and no expression of ire, "and I have ordered her to her bedroom. Until you can fit a bolt to it, you will keep someone on guard outside her door at all times. Send a woman in to attend to her wants whom she doesn't know. For no reason whatsoever is she to be permitted to leave her bedroom, is that clear?"

"Perfectly, Marcus Livius," said the steward woodenly.

And so the duel began. Livia Drusa was sent to a smaller prison than she was used to, not so dark or airless as most sleeping cubicles because it lay adjacent to the loggia, and so had a grille high up on the outside wall. But a dismal prison nonetheless. When she asked for books to read and paper to write upon, she found out just how dismal a prison it was, for her request was refused. Four walls enclosing a space some eight feet by eight feet, a bed, a chamber pot, and dreary unpalatable meals on a tray brought by a woman she had never seen before; that was now Livia Drusa's lot.

In the meantime, Drusus was faced with the task of keeping his sister's unwillingness from his best friend, and lost no time commencing. The moment he had issued his orders regarding Livia Drusa, he donned his toga again and went around the corner to see Caepio Junior.

"Oh, good!" beamed Caepio Junior.

"I thought I'd better have a further word with you," said Drusus, making no attempt to sit down, and having no real idea what the further word was going to be.

"Well, before you do, Marcus Livius, go and see my sister, will you? She's very anxious."

That at least was a good sign; she must have accepted the news of her betrothal if not with joy, at least with equanimity, thought the disillusioned Drusus.

He found her in her sitting room, and was left in no doubt at all that his suit was welcome, for she jumped to her feet the moment he filled the doorway, and cast herself upon his chest, much to his discomfort.

"Oh, Marcus Livius!" she said, gazing up at him with a melting adoration.

Why hadn't Aurelia ever looked at him like this? But resolutely he put that thought away, and smiled down at the palpitating Servilia Caepionis. She wasn't a beauty and she had the family's short legs, but she had at least escaped the family tendency to acne—as had his sister—and she had a singularly beautiful pair of eyes, soft and tender in their expression, satisfyingly large, liquidly dark. Though he was not in love with her, he thought that in time he could love her, and he certainly had always liked her.

So he kissed her on her soft mouth, was surprised and gratified by her response, and stayed long enough with her to have a few sentences of conversation.

"And your sister, Livia Drusa, is pleased?" asked Servilia Caepionis when he got up to leave.

Drusus stood very still. "Very pleased," he said, then added, the words popping out of nowhere, "Unfortunately she isn't well at the moment."

"Oh, that's too bad! Never mind, tell her that as soon as she feels up to visitors, I'm coming to see her. We are to be sisters-in-law twice over, but I'd rather we were friends."

That drew a smile from him. "Thank you," he said.

Caepio Junior was waiting impatiently in his father's study, which he occupied in his father's absence.

"I am delighted," said Drusus, sitting down. "Your sister is pleased at the match."

"I told you she liked you," said Caepio Junior. "But how did Livia Drusa take the news?"

He was well prepared now. "She was delighted," he lied blandly. "Unfortunately I found her taken to her bed with a fever.

The doctor was already there, and he's a little worried. Apparently there are complications, and he fears whatever it is might be contagious."

"Ye gods!" Caepio Junior exclaimed, face paling.

"We'll wait and see," said Drusus soothingly. "You like her very much, Quintus Servilius, don't you?"

"My father says I can't do better than Livia Drusa. He says I have excellent taste. Did you tell him I liked her?"

"I did." Drusus smiled faintly. "It's been rather obvious for a couple of years now, you know."

"I got my father's letter today, it was waiting when I got home. He says Livia Drusa is as rich as she is noble. He likes her too," said Caepio Junior.

"Well, as soon as she's feeling better we'll all have dinner together, and talk about the wedding. The beginning of May, eh? Before the unlucky time." Drusus got up. "I can't stay, Quintus Servilius, I'll have to get back and see how my sister is."

Both Caepio Junior and Drusus had been elected tribunes of the soldiers, and were to go to Further Gaul with Gnaeus Mallius Maximus. But rank and wealth and political conformity told; where the relatively obscure Sextus Caesar couldn't even get leave from his recruiting duties to attend his brother's wedding, neither Drusus nor Caepio Junior had yet been called up. Certainly Drusus envisioned no difficulty in planning a double wedding for early May, even though by then both the bridegrooms would be involved with army duties, even if the army itself was already on its way to Further Gaul; they could always catch it up.

He issued orders to his entire household in case Caepio Junior or his sister should come inquiring after Livia Drusa's health, and cut Livia Drusa's diet back to unleavened bread and water. For five days he left her completely alone, then sent for her to his study.

She came blinking a little in the brighter light, her feet not quite steady, her hair inexpertly combed. That she had not been sleeping was manifest in the state of her eyes, but her brother could detect no evidence of prolonged tears. Her hands trembled, she had trouble controlling her mouth, and the bottom lip was bitten raw.

"Sit down," said Drusus curtly.

She sat.

"How do you feel now about marrying Quintus Servilius?"

Her whole body began to shake; what little color she had preserved now faded completely. "Don't want to," she said.

Her brother leaned forward, his hands clasped together. "Livia Drusa, I am the head of our family. I have absolute control over your life. I even have absolute control over your death. It so happens I'm very fond of you. That means I dislike hurting you, and it distresses me greatly to see you suffer. You are suffering now. I am distressed. But we are both Romans. That fact means everything to me. It means more to me than you do. Than *anyone* does! I am very sorry that you cannot like my friend Quintus Servilius. However, you will marry him! It is your duty as a Roman woman to obey me. As you know. Quintus Servilius is the husband our father intended for you, just as his father intended Servilia Caepionis to be my wife. For a while I considered taking a wife of my own choice, but events have only gone to prove that my father—may his shade be appeased—was wiser than I. Besides all of that, we have the embarrassment of a mother who has not proven an ideal Roman woman. Thanks to her, the responsibility which rests on you is much greater. Nothing you do or say can be allowed to give anyone room to think her flaw is also present in you."

Livia Drusa dragged in a huge breath, and said again, but more shakily still, "Don't *want* to!"

"Want has nothing to do with it," said Drusus sternly. "Who do you think you are, Livia Drusa, to hold your personal wants as more important than our family's honor and standing? Make up your mind to it, you will marry Quintus Servilius, and no other. If you persist in this defiance, you will marry no one at all. In fact, you will never leave your bedroom again as long as you live. There you will stay, without company or diversion, day in and day out, forever." His eyes stared at her with less feeling than two cold black stones. "I mean what I say, sister. No books, no paper, no food other than bread and water, no bath, no mirror, no maidservants, no clean clothes, no fresh bedding, no brazier during winter, no extra blankets, no shoes or slippers for your feet, no belts or girdles or ribbons whereby to hang yourself, no scissors to cut your nails or your hair, no knives to use to stab yourself—and if you try to starve yourself, I will have the food shoved forcibly down your throat."

He snapped his fingers, a small sharp sound that brought the steward in with the kind of suspicious alacrity that suggested he had been listening at the door. "Take my sister back to her room. And bring her to me at dawn tomorrow before you admit any clients to my house."

The steward had to help her to her feet, one hand beneath her arm, and guide her out of the room.

"I will expect your answer tomorrow," Drusus said.

Not one word did the steward say to her as he led her across the atrium; firmly but gently he put her inside her bedroom door, stepped back, closed the door, and shot the bolt Drusus had ordered fitted to its outside.

Darkness was falling; Livia Drusa could tell that she had no more than two hours left to her before the pall of black, empty nothingness enfolded her for the duration of the long late-winter night. So far she hadn't wept. A strong consciousness that she was in the right coupled with a burning indignation had sustained her for the first three days and nights, and after that she had taken solace from the plights of all the heroines she had discovered through her reading. Penelope's twenty-year wait came top of the list, of course, but Danaë had been shut up in her bedroom by her father, and Ariadne had been abandoned by Theseus on the seashore of Naxos. . . . In every case, things had changed for the better. Odysseus came home, Perseus was born, and Ariadne was rescued by a god. . . .

But with her brother's words still echoing inside her thoughts, Livia Drusa began to understand the difference between great literature and real life. Great literature was never intended to be either facsimile or echo of real life; it was meant to shut out real life for a while, to free the harried mind from mundane considerations, so that the mind could holiday amid glorious language and vivid word-pictures and inspiring or alluring ideas. At least Penelope had enjoyed the freedom of her own palace halls, and the company of her son; and Danaë had been dazzled by showers of gold; and Ariadne had suffered no more than the pinprick of Theseus's rejection before one far greater than Theseus espoused her. But in real life Penelope would have been raped and forcibly married and her son murdered, and Odysseus would never have come home at all; and Danaë and her baby would have floated in their chest until the sea drowned them; and Ariadne would have been left pregnant by Theseus, and died in a lonely childbirth. . . .

Would Zeus appear in a shower of gold to enliven the long imprisonment of a Livia Drusa of modern-day Rome? Or Dionysos drive through her frigid little dark hole of a room in his chariot drawn by leopards? Or Odysseus string his great bow and slay her brother and Caepio Junior with the same shaft he had sent through the hollows of the axes? No! Of course not! They had all lived more than a thousand years ago—if they had ever lived at all, save in some poet's indelible lines. Was that the meaning of immortality, to have life through some poet's indelible lines rather than because the flesh had ever quickened?

Somehow she had clung to the thought that her red-haired hero from the balcony of Ahenobarbus thirty feet below would learn of her plight, and break in through the grille in her wall, and spirit her away to live on some enchanted isle in the wine-dark sea. And she had dreamed the awful hours away seeing him in her mind's eye, so tall and Odysseus-like, brilliant, innovative, fantastically courageous. What a tiny obstacle he would find the house of Marcus Livius Drusus once he discovered she lay captive within it!

Ah, but tonight was different. Tonight was the real beginning of a confinement that had no happy ending, no miraculous deliverance. Who knew she was imprisoned, save her brother and his servants? And who among his servants would dare to flout her brother's orders, or pity her more than they feared him? He was not a cruel man; she understood that very well. But he was used to being obeyed, and she, his young sister, was as much his creature as the least of his slaves, or the dogs he kept in his hunting lodge in Umbria. His word was her law. His wishes her commands. What she wanted had no validity, and therefore no existence outside her own mind.

She felt an itching beneath her left eye, and then a hot, itching trail down her left cheek. Something splashed onto the back of her hand. The right eye itched, the right cheek was seared; the splashes grew more frequent, like short summer rain getting started, the drops falling faster and faster. Livia Drusa wept, for her heart was broken. Rocked back and forth; mopped her face, her streaming eyes, and her running nose; and wept again, for her heart was truly broken. Many hours she wept, alone in an ocean of Stygian gloom, the prisoner of her brother's will and her own unwillingness to do his will.

But when the steward came to unbolt her door and admit the blinding glare of his lamp into the smelly coldness of her bedroom, she was sitting on the edge of her bed, dry-eyed and calm. And rose to her feet and walked out of the room ahead of him, across the vast vivid atrium to her brother's study.

"Well?" asked Drusus.

"I will marry Quintus Servilius," she said.

"Good. But I require more of you, Livia Drusa."

"I will endeavor to please you in everything, Marcus Livius," she said steadily.

"Good." He snapped his fingers, the steward obeyed the summons immediately. "Send some hot honeyed wine and some honey cakes to the lady Livia Drusa's sitting room, and tell her maidservant to prepare a bath."

"Thank you," she said colorlessly.

"It is my genuine pleasure to make you happy, Livia Drusa—so long as you behave like a proper Roman woman, and do what is expected of you. I expect you to behave toward Quintus Servilius as any young woman would who welcomed her marriage. You will let him know that you are pleased, and you will treat him with unfailing deference, respect, interest, and concern. At no time—even in the privacy of your bedroom after you are married—will you give Quintus Servilius the slightest indication that he is not the husband of your choice. Do you understand?" he asked sternly.

"I understand, Marcus Livius," she said.

"Come with me."

He led her into the atrium, where the great rectangle in the roof was beginning to pale and a pearly light stole inside, purer than the lamps, fainter yet more luminous. In the wall was a small shrine to the household gods, the Lares and the Penates, flanked on either side by the exquisitely painted miniature temples which housed the *imagines* of the famous men of the Livius Drusus family, from her dead father the censor all the way back to the beginning. And there Marcus Livius Drusus made her swear a terrible oath to terrible Roman gods who had no statues and no mythologies and no humanity, who were personifications of qualities inside the mind, not divine men and women; under pain of their displeasure she swore to be a warm and loving wife to Quintus Servilius Caepio Junior.

After it was done he dismissed her to her sitting room, where the hot honeyed wine and honey cakes were waiting. She got some of the wine down and felt the benefit of it at once, but her throat closed up at the very thought of swallowing the cakes, so she put them to one side with a smile at her maid, and rose to her feet.

"I want my bath," she said.

And that afternoon Quintus Servilius Caepio Junior and his sister, Servilia Caepionis, came to dine with Marcus Livius Drusus and his sister, Livia Drusa, a cozy quartet with marriages to plan. Livia Drusa abided by her oath, thanking every god that she did not belong to a smiling family; no one thought it a bit odd that she remained absolutely solemn, for they all did. Low-voiced and interested, she conversed with Caepio Junior while her brother concentrated upon Servilia Caepionis, and slowly Caepio Junior's inchoate fears subsided. Why had he ever thought Livia Drusa didn't like him? Wan from her illness she might be, but there could be no mistaking the gentle enthusiasm with which she greeted her masterful brother's plans for a double wedding at the beginning of May, before Gnaeus Mallius Maximus began his march across the Alps.

Before the unlucky time. But every time is the unlucky time for me, thought Livia Drusa. However, she did not say it.

 Wrote Publius Rutilius Rufus to Gaius Marius in June, before the news of the capture of Jugurtha and the end of the war in Africa had reached Rome:

> We have had a very uneasy winter, and a rather panic-stricken spring. The Germans are definitely on the move, and south at that, into our province along the river Rhodanus. We had been getting urgent letters from our Gallic allies the Aedui since before the end of last year, saying that their unwanted guests the Germans were going to move on. And then in April came the first of the Aeduan deputations to tell us that the Germans had cleaned out the Aeduan and Ambarric granaries, and were loading up their wagons. However, they had given out their destination as Spain, and those in the Senate who think it wiser to play down the threat of the Germans were quick to spread the news.
>
> Luckily Scaurus is not of their number, nor is Gnaeus Domitius Ahenobarbus. So pretty soon after Gnaeus Mallius and I began our consulship, there was a strong faction urging that a new army be recruited for any emergency, and Gnaeus Mallius was directed to assemble six new legions.

Rutilius Rufus found himself stiffening as if to ward off a Marian tirade, and smiled ruefully.

Yes, I know, I know! Hold on to your temper, Gaius Marius, and let me put my case before you start jumping up and down upon my poor head—and I do not mean that lump of bone and flesh on top of my neck! It should by rights have been me directed to recruit and command this new army; I am well aware of it. I am the senior consul, I have had a long and highly successful military career, and am currently even enjoying some degree of fame because my manual of military practice has been published at last. Whereas my junior colleague, Gnaeus Mallius, is almost completely untried.

Well, it's all your fault! My association with you is general knowledge, and your enemies in the House would sooner, I think, that Rome perish under a flood tide of Germans than gratify you and yours in any way. So Metellus Numidicus Piggle-wiggle got up and made a magnificent speech to the effect that I was far too old to lead an army, and that my undeniable talents could be better used if I remained in Rome to govern. They followed him like sheep the leader who betrays them to the slaughter, and passed all the necessary decrees. Why did I not fight them? I hear you ask. Oh, Gaius Marius, I am not you! I just do not have that streak of destructive hatred for them that you have, nor do I have your phenomenal energy. So I contented myself with insisting that Gnaeus Mallius be provided with some truly able and experienced senior legates. And at least this has been done. He has Marcus Aurelius Scaurus to back him up—yes, I did say Aurelius, not Aemilius. All he shares in common with our esteemed Leader of the House is a *cognomen*. However, I suspect that his military ability is considerably better than the famous Scaurus's. At least, for Rome's sake and Gnaeus Mallius's sake, I hope so!

And, all told, Gnaeus Mallius has done fairly well. He elected to recruit among the Head Count, and could point to your African army as proof of the Head Count's effectiveness. By the end of April, when the news came that the Germans would be heading south into our Roman province, Gnaeus Mallius had six legions enlisted, all of Roman or Latin Head Count. But then the delegation arrived from the Aedui, and for the first time the House had definite estimates of the actual number of Germans involved in the migration. We discovered, for instance, that the Germans who killed Lucius Cassius in Aquitania—we knew they numbered about a quarter of a million—were only about a third of the total number, if that. So according to the Aedui, something like eight hundred thousand German warriors, women, and children are at present traveling toward the Gallic coast of the Middle Sea. It mazes the mind, does it not?

The House gave Gnaeus Mallius the authority to recruit four more legions, bringing his force up to a total of ten legions plus five thousand cavalry. And by this, the news of the Germans was out all over Italy, try though the House did to calm everyone down. We are very, very worried, especially because we have not so far actually won one engagement against the Germans. From the time of Carbo, our history has been defeat. And there are those, especially among the ordinary people, who are now saying that our famous adage that six good Roman legions can beat a quarter of a million undisciplined barbarians is so much *merda*. I tell you, Gaius Marius, the whole of Italy is afraid! And I, for one, do not blame Italy.

I imagine because of the general dread, several of our Italian Allies reversed their policy of recent years, and have voluntarily contributed troops to Gnaeus Mallius's army. The Samnites have sent a legion of

light-armed infantry, and the Marsi have sent a wonderful legion of standard Roman-style infantry. There
is also a composite auxiliary legion from Umbria,
Etruria, and Picenum. So, as you may imagine, our
fellow Conscript Fathers are like the cat which got to
the fish—very smug and self-satisfied. Of the four extra legions, three are being paid for and kept up by the
Italian Allies.

That is all positive. But there is an opposite side, of
course. We have a frightful shortage of centurions,
which means that none of the newly enlisted Head
Count troops have undergone a proper training program, and the one legion of Head Count men in the
last four legions just put together is almost totally un-
prepared. His legate Aurelius suggested that Gnaeus
Mallius split the experienced centurions up evenly
among his seven Head Count legions, and that means
no more than 40 percent of the centurions in any one
legion have undergone anything like battle conditions.
Military tribunes are well and good, but I do not need
to tell you that it is the centurions who hold the centuries and cohorts together.

Quite frankly, I fear for the result. Gnaeus Mallius
is not a bad sort of fellow, but I do not think him capable of waging war against the Germans. This opinion Gnaeus Mallius himself reinforced, when he got
up in the House at the end of May and said that he
couldn't ensure every man in his force would know
what to do on a battlefield! There are *always* men who
don't know what to do on a battlefield, but you don't
get up in the House and say so!

And what did the House do? It sent orders to Quintus Caepio in Narbo to transfer himself and his army
across to the Rhodanus immediately, and join up with
Gnaeus Mallius's army when it reaches the Rhodanus.
For once the House didn't procrastinate—the message

went off by mounted courier, and got from Rome to Narbo in less than two weeks. Nor did Quintus Servilius procrastinate in answering! We got his answer yesterday. And what an answer it was.

Naturally the senatorial orders had said that Quintus Caepio would subordinate himself and his troops to the imperium of the year's consul. All perfectly normal and aboveboard. Last year's consul may have a proconsular imperium, but in any joint enterprise, the consul of the year takes the senior command.

Oh, Gaius Marius, that did not sit well with Quintus Caepio! Did the House honestly think that he—a patrician Servilius directly descended from Gaius Servilius Ahala, the savior of Rome—would act as the subordinate of an upstart New Man without a single face in an ancestral cupboard, a man who had only reached the consulship because no one of better origins had stood for election? There were consuls and there were consuls, said Quintus Caepio. Yes, I swear to you that he really did say all this! In his year the field of candidates had been respectable, but in this present year the best Rome could do was a broken-down old minor noble (me) and a presumptuous parvenu with more money than taste (Gnaeus Mallius). So, Quintus Caepio's letter ended, he would certainly march at once for the Rhodanus—but by the time he got there, he expected to find a senatorial courier waiting for him with the news that he would be the supreme commander in this joint venture. With Gnaeus Mallius working as his subordinate, he was sure, said Quintus Caepio, that all would go superbly.

His hand was beginning to cramp; Rutilius Rufus laid his reed pen down with a sigh, and sat massaging his fingers, staring frowningly into nothing. Presently his eyelids began to droop, and his head fell forward, and he dozed; when he woke with a jerk, his hand at least felt better, so he resumed his writing.

Oh, such a long, long letter! But no one else will give you an honest account of what has happened, and you must know it all. Quintus Caepio's letter had been directed to Scaurus Princeps Senatus rather than to me, and of course you know our beloved Marcus Aemilius Scaurus! He read the whole dreadful letter out to the House with every evidence of ghoulish enjoyment. In fact, he drooled. Oh, and did it put the cat among the pigeons! There were purple faces, flying fists, and a brawl between Gnaeus Mallius and Metellus Piggle-wiggle which I stopped by calling in the lictors from the Curia vestibule—an action which Scaurus did not appreciate. Oh, what a day for Mars! A pity we couldn't bottle all that hot air and just blow the Germans away with the most poisonous weapon Rome can manufacture.

The upshot of it was that there will indeed be a courier waiting for Quintus Caepio on the banks of the Rhodanus—but the new orders will be exactly the same as the old ones. He is to subordinate himself to the legally elected consul of the year, Gnaeus Mallius Maximus. Such a pity the silly fool dowered himself with a *cognomen* like Maximus, isn't it? A bit like awarding yourself a Grass Crown after your men saved you, not the other way around. Not only is it the height of crassness to give yourself a pat on the back, but if you are not a Fabius, the *cognomen* Maximus is horribly presumptuous. Of course he maintains his great-grandmother was a Fabia Maxima, and his grandfather used it, but all I know is that his father never did. And I doubt the Fabia Maxima story very much.

Anyway, here I am like a war-horse turned out to pasture, itching to be in Gnaeus Mallius's shoes, and burdened instead with earthshaking decisions like whether we can afford to give the State granaries a new coat of pitch inside this year, after paying to equip seven new Head Count legions. Would you believe that with the whole of Rome talking Germans, Germans, Germans, the House argued for eight days about that one? Drive a man insane, it would!

I do have an idea, though, and I'm going to implement it. Come victory or defeat in Gaul, I'm going to implement it. With not one man left in all Italy whom I would call a centurion's bootlaces, I am going to recruit drill instructors and other training personnel from the gladiator schools. Capua is full of gladiator schools—and the best ones at that—so what could be more convenient, considering that Capua is also our base camp for all new troops? If Lucius Tiddlypuss can't hire enough gladiators to put on a good show at his granddad's funeral, hard luck! Rome's need is greater than Lucius Tiddlypuss's, say I! This plan also tells you that I am going to continue to recruit among the Head Count.

I'll keep you informed, of course. How goes it in the land of the lotus-eaters, sirens, and enchanted isles? Not managed to put leg-irons on Jugurtha yet? It isn't far off, I'll bet. Metellus Numidicus Piggle-wiggle is in a trifle of a dither these days, actually. He can't make up his mind whether to concentrate on you or on Gnaeus Mallius. Naturally he gave a magnificent speech supporting Quintus Servilius's elevation to commander-in-chief. It gave me inordinate pleasure to sink his case with a few well-placed shafts.

Ye gods, Gaius Marius, how they do get me down! Trumpeting the feats of their wretched ancestors when what Rome needs right now is a living, breathing military genius! Hurry up and come home, will you? We need you, for I am not up to battling the whole of the Senate, I just am not.

There was a postscriptum:

There have been a couple of peculiar incidents in Campania, by the way. I don't like them, yet I fail to see why they happened, either. At the beginning of May there was a slave revolt at Nuceria—oh, easily put down, and all it really meant was that thirty poor creatures from all over the world were executed. But then three days ago another revolt broke out, this time in a big holding camp outside Capua for low-grade male slaves waiting for buyers in need of a hundred wharf laborers or quarry fodder or treadmill plodders. Almost 250 slaves were involved this time. It was put down at once, as there were several cohorts of recruits in camp around Capua. About fifty of the insurgents perished in the fighting, and the rest were executed forthwith. But I don't like it, Gaius Marius. It's an omen. The gods are against us at the moment; I feel it in my bones.

And a second postscriptum:

Some sad news for you has this very moment come to hand. As my letter to you was already arranged through Marcus Granius of Puteoli to go on his fast packet sailing for Utica at the end of the week, I have volunteered to tell you what has happened. Your much-loved father-in-law; Gaius Julius Caesar, died this afternoon. As you know, he has been suffering from a malignancy in the throat for some time. And this afternoon he fell on his sword. He chose the best alternative, as I'm sure you will agree. No man should linger to be a burden to his loved ones, especially when it detracts from his dignity and integrity as a man. Is there one among us who prefers life to death when life means lying in one's own excrement, or being cleaned of that excrement by a slave? No, when a man cannot command either his bowels or his gorge, it is time to go. I think Gaius Julius would have chosen to go sooner, except that he worried about his younger son, who as I'm sure you know married recently. I went to see Gaius Julius only two days ago, and he managed to whisper through the thing choking him that all his doubts about the suitability of young Gaius Julius's marriage were now allayed, for the beautiful Aurelia—the darling of my own heart, I admit—was just the right wife for his boy. So it is *ave atque vale*, Gaius Julius Caesar.

At the very end of June the consul Gnaeus Mallius Maximus left on the long march north and west, his two sons on his personal staff, and all twenty-four of the elected tribunes of the soldiers for that year distributed among seven of his ten legions. Sextus Julius Caesar, Marcus Livius Drusus, and Quintus Servilius Caepio Junior marched with him, as did Quintus Sertorius, taken on as a junior military tribune. Of the three Italian Allied legions, the one sent by the Marsi was the best trained and most soldierly legion of all ten; it was commanded by a twenty-five-year-old Marsic nobleman's son named Quintus Poppaedius Silo—under supervision by a Roman legate, of course.

Because Mallius Maximus insisted upon lugging enough State-purchased grain to feed his entire force for two months, his baggage train was huge and his progress painfully slow; by the end of the first sixteen days he hadn't even reached the Adriatic at Fanum Fortunae. Talking very hard and passionately, the legate Aurelius then managed to persuade him to leave his baggage train in the escort of one legion, and push on with his nine others, his cavalry, and light baggage only. It had proven very difficult to convince Mallius Maximus that his troops were not going to starve before they got to the Rhodanus, and that sooner or later the heavy baggage would arrive safely.

Having a much shorter march over level ground, Quintus Servilius Caepio reached the huge river Rhodanus ahead of Mallius Maximus. He took only seven of his eight legions with him—the eighth he shipped to Nearer Spain—and no cavalry, having disbanded it the previous year as an unnecessary expense. Despite his orders and the urging of legates, Caepio had refused to move from Narbo until an expected overseas communication from Smyrna came. Nor was he in a good mood; when he could be deflected from complaining about the disgraceful tardiness of this contact between Smyrna and Narbo, he complained about the insensitivity of the Senate in thinking that he would yield supreme command of the Grand Army to a mushroom like Mallius Maximus. But in the end, he was obliged to march without his letter, leaving explicit instructions behind in Narbo that it was to be forwarded as soon as it came.

Even so, Caepio still beat Mallius Maximus to their target destination comfortably. At Nemausus, a small trading town on the western outskirts of the vast salt marshes around the delta of the Rhodanus, he was met by the Senate's courier, who gave him the Senate's new orders.

It had never occurred to Caepio that his letter would fail to move the Conscript Fathers, especially when none other than Scaurus read it out to the House. So when he opened the cylinder and scanned the Senate's brief reply, he was outraged. Impossible! Intolerable! He, a patrician Servilius, tugging his forelock at the whim of Mallius Maximus the New Man? Never!

Roman intelligence reported that the Germans were now on their way south, rolling along through the lands of the Celtic Allobroges, inveterate Roman-haters caught in a cleft stick; Rome was the enemy they knew, the Germans the enemy they didn't know. And the Druidic confraternity had been telling every tribe in Gaul for two years now that there wasn't room for the Germans to settle anywhere in Gaul. Certainly the Allobroges were not about to yield enough of their lands to make a new homeland for a people far more numerous than they were themselves. And they were close enough to the Aedui and the Ambarri to know well what a shambles the Germans had made out of the lands of these intimidated tribes. So the Allobroges retreated into the towering foothills of their beloved Alps, and concentrated upon harrying the Germans as much as they could.

The Germans breached the Roman province of Gaul-across-the-Alps to the north of the trading post of Vienne late in June, and surged on, unopposed. The whole mass, over three quarters of a million strong, traveled down the eastern bank of the mighty river, for its plains were wider and safer, less exposed to the fierce highland tribes of central Gaul and the Cebenna.

Learning of this, Caepio deliberately turned off the Via Domitia at Nemausus, and instead of crossing the delta marshes on the long causeway Ahenobarbus had built, he marched his army northward on the western bank, thus keeping the river between himself and the path of the Germans. It was the middle of the month Sextilis.

From Nemausus he had sent a courier hotfoot to Rome with another letter for Scaurus, declaring that he would not take orders from Mallius Maximus, and that was final. After this stand, the only route he could take with honor was west of the river.

On the eastern bank of the Rhodanus, some forty miles north of the place where the Via Domitia crossed the river on a long causeway terminating near Arelate, was a Roman trading town of some importance; its name was Arausio. And on the western bank ten miles north of Arausio, Caepio put his army of forty thousand foot soldiers and fifteen thousand noncombatants into a strong camp. And waited for Mallius Maximus to appear on the opposite bank—and waited for the Senate to reply to his latest letter.

Mallius Maximus arrived ahead of the Senate's reply, at the end of Sextilis. He put his fifty-five thousand infantry and his thirty thousand noncombatants into a heavily fortified camp right on the edge of the river five miles north of Arausio, thus making the river serve as part of his defenses as well as his water source.

The ground just to the north of the camp was ideal for a battle, thought Mallius Maximus, envisioning the river as his greatest protection. This was his first mistake. His second mistake was to detach his five thousand cavalry from his camp, and send them to act as his advance guard thirty miles further north. And his third mistake was to appoint his most able legate, Aurelius, to command the horse, thereby depriving himself of Aurelius's counsel. All the mistakes were part of Mallius Maximus's grand strategy; he intended to use Aurelius and the cavalry as a brake on the German advance—not by offering battle, but by offering the Germans their first sight of Roman resistance. For Mallius Maximus wanted to treat, not fight, hoping to turn the Germans peacefully back into central Gaul, well away from southward progress through the Roman province. All the earlier battles fought between the Germans and Rome had been forced on the Germans by Rome, and only after the Germans had indicated they were willing to turn back peacefully from Roman territory. So Mallius Maximus had high hopes for his grand strategy, and they were not without foundation.

However, his first task was to get Caepio from the west bank of the river to the east bank. Still smarting from the insulting, insensitive letter from Caepio that Scaurus had read out in the House, Mallius Maximus dictated a curt and undisguised direct order to Caepio: get yourself and your army across the river and inside my camp *at once*. He gave it to a team of oarsmen in a boat, thus ensuring quick delivery.

Caepio used the same boat to send Mallius Maximus his answer. Which said with equal curtness that he, a patrician Servilius, would not take orders from any pretentious mushroom of a tradesman, and would stay right where he was, on the western bank.

Said Mallius Maximus's next directive:

> As your supreme commander in the field, I repeat my order to transfer yourself and your army across the river without an hour's delay. Please regard this, my second such order, as my last. Should you persist in defying me, I shall institute legal proceedings against

you in Rome. The charge will be high treason, and your own high-flown actions will have convicted you.

Caepio responded with an equally litigious reply:

I do not admit that you are the supreme commander in the field. By all means institute treason proceedings against me. I will certainly be instituting treason proceedings against you. Since we both know who will win, I demand that you turn the supreme command over to me forthwith.

Mallius Maximus replied with even greater hauteur. And so it went until midway through September, when six senators arrived from Rome, utterly exhausted by the speed and discomfort of their trip. Rutilius Rufus, the consul in Rome, had pushed successfully to send this embassage, but Scaurus and Metellus Numidicus had managed to pull the embassage's teeth by refusing to allow the inclusion of any senator of consular status or real political clout. The most senior of the six senators was a mere praetor of moderately noble background, none other than Rutilius Rufus's brother-in-law, Marcus Aurelius Cotta. Scant hours after the embassage arrived at Mallius Maximus's camp, Cotta at least understood the gravity of the situation.

So Cotta went to work with great energy and a passion normally alien to him, concentrating upon Caepio. Who remained obdurate. A visit to the cavalry camp thirty miles to the north sent him back to the fray with redoubled determination, for the legate Aurelius had led him under cover to a high hill, from which he was able to see the leading edge of the German advance.

Cotta looked, and turned white. "You ought to be inside Gnaeus Mallius's camp," he said.

"If a fight was what we wanted, yes," said Aurelius, his calm unimpaired, for he had been looking at the German advance for days, and had grown used to the sight. "Gnaeus Mallius thinks we can repeat earlier successes, which have always been diplomatic.

When the Germans have fought, it's only been because we pushed them to it. I have absolutely no intention of starting anything—and that will mean, I'm sure, that they won't start anything either. I have a team of competent interpreters here, and I've been indoctrinating them for days as to what I want to say when the Germans send their chiefs to parley, as I'm sure they will, once they realize that there's a Roman army of huge size waiting for them."

"But surely they know that now!" said Cotta.

"I doubt it," said Aurelius, unperturbed. "They don't move in a military fashion, you know. If they've heard of scouts, they certainly haven't bothered to employ them so far. They just—roll on! Taking, it seems to Gnaeus Mallius and me, whatever comes to them when it comes."

Cotta turned his horse. "I must get back to Gnaeus Mallius as soon as possible, cousin. Somehow we've *got* to get that stiff-necked imbecile Caepio across the river, or we may as well not even have his army in the vicinity."

"I agree," said Aurelius. "However, Marcus Aurelius of the Cottae, if feasible I would like you to return to me here the moment I send you word that a German delegation has arrived to parley. *With* your five colleagues! The Germans will be impressed that the Senate has sent six representatives all the way from Rome to treat with them." He smiled wryly. "We certainly won't let them know that the Senate has sent six representatives all the way from Rome to treat with our own fools of generals!"

The stiff-necked imbecile Quintus Servilius Caepio was— rather inexplicably—in a much better mood and more prone to listen to Cotta when he had himself rowed across the Rhodanus the next day.

"Why the sudden lightheartedness, Quintus Servilius?" asked Cotta, puzzled.

"I've just had a letter from Smyrna," said Caepio. "A letter I should have had months ago." But instead of going on to explain what any letter from Smyrna might contain to make him so much happier, Caepio got down to business. "All right," he said, "I'll come across to the east bank tomorrow." He pointed to his map with an ivory wand topped by a gold eagle he had taken to carrying to indicate the high degree of his imperium; he still had not consented to see Mallius Maximus in person. "Here is where I'll cross."

"Wouldn't it be more prudent to cross south of Arausio?" asked Cotta dubiously.

"Certainly not!" said Caepio. "If I cross to the north, I'll be closer to the Germans."

True to his word, Caepio struck camp at dawn the next day, and marched north to a ford twenty miles above Mallius Maximus's fortress, a scant ten miles south of the place where Aurelius was encamped with his cavalry.

Cotta and his five senatorial companions rode north too, intending to be in Aurelius's camp when the German chieftains arrived to treat. En route they encountered Caepio on the east bank, most of his army across the river. But the sight that met their eyes struck fresh dismay into their hearts, for all too obviously Caepio was preparing to dig a heavily fortified camp right where he was.

"Oh, Quintus Servilius, Quintus Servilius, you *can't* stay here!" cried Cotta as they sat their horses on a knoll above the new campsite, where scurrying figures dug trenches and piled excavated earth up into ramparts.

"Why not?" asked Caepio, raising his brows.

"Because twenty miles to the south of you is a camp already made—and made large enough to accommodate your legions as well as the ten at present inside it! *There* is where you belong, Quintus Servilius! Not here, too far away from Aurelius to the north of you and Gnaeus Mallius to the south of you to be of any help to either—or they to you! Please, Quintus Servilius, I beg of you! Pitch an ordinary marching camp here tonight, then head south to Gnaeus Mallius in the morning," said Cotta, putting every ounce of urgency he could into his plea.

"I *said* I'd cross the river," Caepio announced, "but I did not give any sort of undertaking as to what I'd do when I did cross the river! I have seven legions, all trained to the top of their bent, and all experienced soldiers. Not only that, but they're men of property—*true* Roman soldiers! Do you seriously think that I would consent to share a camp with the rabble of Rome and the Latin countryside—sharecroppers and laborers, men who can't read or write? Marcus Cotta, I would sooner be dead!"

"You might well be," said Cotta dryly.

"Not my army, and not me," said Caepio, adamant. "I'm twenty miles to the north of Gnaeus Mallius and his loathsome rabble. Which means that I shall encounter the Germans first. And I shall beat them, Marcus Cotta! A solid million barbarians couldn't defeat seven legions of *true* Roman soldiers! Let that— that *tradesman* Mallius have one iota of the credit? No! Quintus Servilius Caepio will hold his second triumph through the streets of Rome as the sole victor! Mallius will have to stand there looking on."

Leaning forward in his saddle, Cotta put his hand out and grasped Caepio's arm. "Quintus Servilius," he said, more earnestly and seriously than he had ever spoken in his entire life, "I beg of you, *join forces with Gnaeus Mallius*! Which means more to you, Rome victorious or Rome's nobility victorious? Does it matter who wins, so long as Rome wins? This isn't a little border war against a few Scordisci, nor is it a minor campaign against the Lusitani! We are going to need the best and biggest army we've ever fielded, and your contribution to that army is vital! Gnaeus Mallius's men haven't had the time or the training under arms that your men have. Your presence among them will steady them, give them an example to follow. For I say to you very sternly, there *will* be a battle! I feel it in my bones. No matter how the Germans have behaved in the past, this time is going to be different. They've tasted our blood and liked it, they've felt our mettle and found it weak. *Rome* is at stake, Quintus Servilius, not Rome's nobility! But if you persist in remaining isolated from the other army, I tell you straight, the future of Rome's nobility will indeed be at stake. In your hands you hold the future of Rome and your own kind. Do the right thing by both, please! March tomorrow to Gnaeus Mallius's camp, and ally yourself with him."

Caepio dug his horse in the ribs and moved away, wrenching free of Cotta's grip. "No," he said. "I stay here."

So Cotta and his five companions rode on north to the cavalry camp, while Caepio produced a smaller but identical copy of Mallius Maximus's camp, right on the edge of the river.

The senators found themselves only just in time, for the German treating party rode into Aurelius's camp slightly after dawn of the next day. There were fifty of them, aged somewhere between forty and sixty, thought the awestruck Cotta, who had never seen men so large—not one of them looked to be under six feet in height, and most were six inches taller than that. They rode enormous horses, shaggy-coated and unkempt to Roman eyes, with big hooves skirted in long hair, and manes falling over their mild eyes; none was encumbered by a saddle, but all were bridled.

"Their horses are like war elephants," said Cotta.

"Only a few," Aurelius answered comfortably. "Most ride ordinary Gallic horses—these men take their pick, I suppose."

"Look at the young one!" Cotta exclaimed, watching a fellow no older than thirty slide down from his mount's back and stand, his pose superbly confident, gazing about him as if he found nothing he saw remarkable.

"Achilles," said Aurelius, undismayed.

"I thought the Germans went naked save for a cloak," Cotta said, taking in the sight of leather breeches.

"They do in Germania, so they say, but from what we've seen of these Germans so far, they're trousered like the Gauls."

Trousered they were, but none wore a shirt in this fine hot weather. Many sported square gold pectorals which sat on their chests from nipple to nipple, and all carried the empty scabbards of long-swords on shoulder baldrics. They wore much gold—the pectorals, their helmet ornaments, sword scabbards, belts, baldrics, buckles, bracelets, and necklaces—though none wore a Celtic neck torc. Cotta found the helmets fascinating: rimless and pot-shaped, some were symmetrically adorned above the ears with magnificent horns or wings or hollow tubes holding bunches of stiffly upright feathers, while others were fashioned to resemble serpents or dragon heads or hideous birds or pards with gaping jaws.

All were clean-shaven and wore their uniformly flaxen hair long, either braided or hanging loose, and they had little if any chest hair. Skins not as pink as Celtic skins, Cotta noted—more a pale gold. None was freckled; none had red hair. Their eyes were light blue, and held no grey or green. Even the oldest among them had kept himself in magnificent trim, flat-bellied and warriorlike, no evidence of self-indulgence; though the Romans were not to know it, the Germans killed men who let themselves go to seed.

The parley went on through Aurelius's interpreters, who were mostly Aedui and Ambarri, though two or three of them were Germans captured by Carbo in Noricum before he was defeated. What they wanted, the German thanes explained, was a peaceful right-of-way through Gaul-across-the-Alps, for they were going to Spain. Aurelius himself conducted the first phase of the talks, clad in full military-parade armor—a torso-shaped silver cuirass, scarlet-plumed Attic helmet of silver, and the double kilt of stiff leather straps called *pteryges* over a crimson tunic. As a consular he wore a purple cloak lashed to the shoulders of his cuirass, and a crimson girdle ritually knotted and looped around his cuirass just above the waist was the badge of his general's rank.

Cotta watched spellbound, now more afraid than he had ever dreamed he could be, even in the depths of despair. For he knew he was looking at Rome's doom. In months to come they haunted his sleep, those German thanes, so remorselessly that he stumbled red-eyed and thick-witted through his days, and even after sheer custom reduced their capacity to keep him wakeful, he would find himself sitting bolt upright in his bed, mouth agape, because they rode their gigantic horses into some less important nightmare. Intelligence reported their numbers at well over three quarters of a million, and that meant at least three hundred thousand gargantuan warriors. Like most men of his eminence, Cotta had seen his share of barbarian warriors, Scordisci and Iapudes, Salassi and Carpetani; but never had he seen men like the Germans. Everyone had deemed the Gauls giants. But they were as ordinary men alongside the Germans.

And, worst terror of all, they spelled Rome's doom because Rome did not take them seriously enough to heal the discord between the Orders; how could Rome hope to defeat them when two Roman generals refused to work with each other, and called each other snob and upstart, and damned each other's very soldiers? If Caepio and Mallius Maximus would only work as a team, Rome would field close to one hundred thousand men, and that was an acceptable ratio if morale was high and training complete and leadership competent.

Oh, Cotta thought, his bowels churning, I have seen the shape of Rome's fate! For we cannot survive this blond horde. Not when we cannot survive ourselves.

Finally Aurelius broke off the talk, and each side stepped back to confer.

"Well, we've learned something," said Aurelius to Cotta and the other five senators. "They don't call themselves Germans. In fact, they think of themselves as three separate peoples whom they call the Cimbri, the Teutones, and a rather polyglot third group made up of a number of smaller peoples who have joined up with the Cimbri and the Teutones during their wanderings—the Marcomanni, Cherusci, and Tigurini—who, according to my German interpreter, are more Celt than German in origins."

"Wanderings?" asked Cotta. "How long have they wandered?"

"They don't seem to know themselves, but for many years, at least. Perhaps a generation. The young sprig who looks like a barbarian Achilles was a small child when his tribe, the Cimbri, left its homeland."

"Do they have a king?" asked Cotta.

"No, a council of tribal chieftains, the largest part of which you are currently looking at. However, that same young sprig who looks like a barbarian Achilles is moving up in the council very fast, and his adherents are beginning to call him a king. His name is Boiorix, and he's by far the most truculent among them. He's not really interested in all this begging for our permission to move south—he believes might is right, and he's all for abandoning talks with us in favor of just going south no matter what."

"Dangerously young to be calling himself a king. I agree, he's trouble," said Cotta. "And who is that man over there?" He unobtrusively indicated a man of about forty who wore a glittering gold pectoral, and several pounds more of gold besides.

"That's Teutobod of the Teutones, the chief of their chiefs. He too is beginning to like being called a king, it seems. As with Boiorix, he thinks might is right, and they should simply keep on going south without worrying about whether Rome agrees or not. I don't like it, cousin. Both my German interpreters from Carbo's day tell me that the mood is very different than it was then—they've gathered confidence in themselves, and contempt for us." Aurelius chewed at his lip. "You see, they have been living among the Aedui and the Ambarri for long enough now to have learned a lot about Rome. And what they've heard has lulled their fears. Not only that, but so far—if you exclude that first engagement of Lucius Cassius's, and who finds exclusion difficult, considering the sequel?—they have won every encounter with us. Now Boiorix and Teutobod are telling them they have absolutely no reason to fear us just because we're better armed and better trained. We are like children's bogeys, all imagination and air. Boiorix and Teutobod *want* war. With Rome a thing of the past, they can wander where they choose, settle where they like."

The parley began again, but now Aurelius drew forward his six guests, all clad in togas, escorted by twelve lictors wearing the crimson tunics and broad gold-embossed belts of duty outside Rome itself, and carrying axed *fasces*. Of course every German eye had noticed them, but now that introductions were performed, they stared at the billowing white robes—so unmartial!—in wonder. *This* was what Romans looked like? Cotta alone wore the purple-bordered *toga praetexta* of the curule magistrate, and it was to him that all the strange-sounding, unintelligible harangues were directed.

He held up well under the pressure: proud, aloof, calm, soft-spoken. It seemed no disgrace to a German to become puce with rage, spit gobbets of saliva to punctuate his words, pound the fist of one hand into the palm of the other, but there could be no mistaking the fact that they were puzzled and made ill at ease by the unassailable tranquillity of the Romans.

From the beginning of his participation in the parley until its end, Cotta's answer was the same: no. No, the migration could not continue south; no, the German people could not have a right of way through any Roman territory or province; no, Spain was not a feasible destination unless they intended to confine themselves to Lusitania and Cantabria, for the rest of Spain was Roman. Turn north again, was Cotta's constant retort; preferably go home, wherever home might be, but otherwise retreat across the Rhenus into Germania itself, and settle there, among their own peoples.

It was not until dusk was fading into night that the fifty German thanes hauled themselves up on their horses and rode away. Last of all to leave were Boiorix and Teutobod, the younger man turning his head over his shoulder to see the Romans for as long as he could. His eyes held neither liking nor admiration. Aurelius is right, he is Achilles, thought Cotta, though at first the parallel's rightness was a mystery. Then he realized that in the young German's handsome face lay all the pigheaded, mercilessly vengeful power of Achilles. Here too was a man who would kick his heels by his ships while the rest of his countrymen died like flies, all for the sake of the merest pinprick in the skin of his honor. And Cotta's heart thudded, despaired; for wasn't that equally true of Quintus Servilius Caepio?

There was a full moon two hours after nightfall; freed from the encumbrance of their togas, Cotta and his five very soberly silent companions ate at Aurelius's table, then got ready to ride south.

"Wait until morning," begged Aurelius. "This isn't Italy, there are no trusty Roman roads, and you know nothing of the lay of the land. A few hours can't make any difference."

"No, I intend to be at Quintus Servilius's camp by dawn," said Cotta, "and try to persuade him yet again to join Gnaeus Mallius.

I shall certainly apprise him of what's happened here today. But no matter what Quintus Servilius decides to do, I'm riding all the way back to Gnaeus Mallius tomorrow, and I don't intend to sleep until I've seen him."

They shook hands. As Cotta and the senators with their escort of lictors and servants rode away into the dense shadows cast by the moon, Aurelius stood clearly delineated by firelight and moonlight, his arm raised in farewell.

I shall not see him again, thought Cotta; a brave man, the very best kind of Roman.

Caepio wouldn't even hear Cotta out, let alone listen to the voice of reason.

"Here is where I stay" was all he said.

So Cotta rode on without pausing to slake his thirst in Caepio's half-finished camp, determined that he would reach Gnaeus Mallius Maximus by noon at the latest.

At dawn, while Cotta and Caepio were failing to see eye to eye, the Germans moved. It was the second day of October, and the weather continued to be fine, no hint of chill in the air. When the front ranks of the German mass came up against Aurelius's camp walls, they simply rolled over them, wave after wave after wave. Aurelius hadn't really understood what was happening; he naturally assumed there would be time to get his cavalry squadrons into the saddle—that the camp wall, extremely well fortified, would hold the Germans at bay for long enough to lead his entire force out the back gate of the camp, and to attempt a flanking maneuver. But it was not to be. There were so many fast-moving Germans that they were around all four sides of the camp within moments, and poured over every wall in thousands. Not used to fighting on foot, Aurelius's troopers did their best, but the engagement was more a debacle than a battle. Within half an hour hardly a Roman or an auxiliary was left alive, and Marcus Aurelius Scaurus was taken captive before he could fall on his sword.

Brought before Boiorix, Teutobod, and the rest of the fifty who had come to parley, Aurelius conducted himself superbly. His bearing was proud, his manner insufferably haughty; no indignity or pain they could inflict upon him bowed his head or caused him to flinch. So they put him in a wicker cage just large enough to hold him, and made him watch while they built a pyre of the hottest woods, and set fire to it, and let it burn. Aurelius watched, legs straight, no tremor in his hands, no fear on his face, not even clinging to the bars of his little prison. It being no part of their plan that Aurelius should die from inhaling smoke—or that he should die too quickly amid vast licks of flame—they waited until the pyre had died down, then winched the wicker cage over its very center, and roasted Aurelius alive. But he won, though it was a lonely victory. For he would not permit himself to writhe in agony, or cry out, or let his legs buckle under him. He died every inch the Roman nobleman, determined that his conduct would show them the real measure of Rome, make them take heed of a place which could produce men such as he, a Roman of the Romans.

For two days more the Germans lingered by the ruins of the Roman cavalry camp, then the move southward began again, with as little planning as before. When they came level with Caepio's camp they just kept on walking south, thousands upon thousands upon thousands, until the terrified eyes of Caepio's soldiers lost all hope of counting them, and some decided to abandon their armor and swim for the west bank of the river, and safety. But that was a last resort Caepio intended to keep exclusively for himself; he burned all but one of his small fleet of boats, posted a heavy guard all the way down the riverbank, and executed any men who tried to escape. Marooned in a vast sea of Germans, the fifty-five thousand soldiers and noncombatants in Caepio's camp could do nothing but wait to see if the flood would pass them by unharmed.

By the sixth day of October, the German front ranks had reached the camp of Mallius Maximus, who preferred not to keep his army pent up within its walls. So he formed up his ten legions and marched them out onto the ground just to the north before the Germans, clearly visible, could surround his camp. He arrayed his troops across the flat ground between the riverbank and the first rise in the ground which heralded the tips of the tentacles of the Alps, even though their foothills were almost a hundred miles away to the east. The legions stood, all facing north, side by side for a distance of four miles, Mallius Maximus's fourth mistake; not only could he easily be outflanked—since he possessed no cavalry to protect his exposed right—but his men were stretched too thin.

Not one word had come to him of conditions to the north, of Aurelius or of Caepio, and he had no one to disguise and send out into the German hordes, for all the available interpreters and scouts had been sent north with Aurelius. Therefore he could do nothing except wait for the Germans to arrive.

Logically his command position was atop the highest tower of his fortified camp wall, so there he positioned himself, with his personal staff mounted and ready to gallop his orders to the various legions; among his personal staff were his own two sons, and the youthful son of Metellus Numidicus Piggle-wiggle, the Piglet. Perhaps because Mallius Maximus deemed Quintus Poppaedius Silo's legion of Marsi best disciplined and trained—or perhaps because he deemed its men more expendable than Romans, even Roman rabble—it stood furthest east of the line, on the Roman right, and devoid of any cavalry protection. Next to it was a legion recruited early in the year commanded by Marcus Livius Drusus, who had inherited Quintus Sertorius as his second-in-charge. Then came the Samnite auxiliaries, and next in line another Roman legion of early recruits; the closer the line got to the river, the more ill trained and inexperienced the legions became, and the more tribunes of the soldiers were there to stiffen them. Caepio Junior's legion of completely raw troops was stationed along the riverbank, with Sextus Caesar, also commanding raw troops, next to him.

There seemed to be a slight element of plan about the German attack, which commenced two hours after dawn on the sixth day of October, more or less simultaneously upon Caepio's camp and upon Mallius Maximus's line of battle.

None of Caepio's fifty-five thousand men survived when the Germans all around them simply turned inward on the three landward perimeters of the camp and spilled into it until the crush of men was so great the wounded were trampled underfoot along with the dead. Caepio himself didn't wait. As soon as he saw that his soldiers had no hope of keeping the Germans out, he hustled himself down to the water, boarded his boat, and had his oarsmen make for the western bank of the Rhodanus at racing speed. A handful of his abandoned men tried to swim to safety, but there were so many Germans hacking and hewing that no Roman had the time or the space to shed his twenty-pound shirt of mail or even untie his helmet, so all those who attempted the swim drowned. Caepio and his boat crew were virtually the sole survivors.

Mallius Maximus did little better. Fighting valiantly against gargantuan odds, the Marsi perished almost to the last man, as did Drusus's legion fighting next to the Marsi. Silo fell, wounded in the side, and Drusus was knocked senseless by a blow from the hilt of a German sword not long after his legion engaged; Quintus Sertorius tried to rally the men from horseback, but there was no holding the German attack. As fast as they were chopped down, fresh Germans sprang in to replace them, and the supply was endless. Sertorius fell too, wounded in the thigh at just the place where the great nerves to the lower leg were most vulnerable; that the spear shore through the nerves and stopped just short of the femoral artery was nothing more nor less than the fortunes of war.

The legions closest to the river turned and took to the water, most of them managing to doff their heavy gear before wading in, and so escape by swimming the Rhodanus to its far side. Caepio Junior was the first to yield to temptation, but Sextus Caesar was cut down by one of his own soldiers when he tried desperately to stop their retreat, and subsided into the melee with a mangled left hip.

In spite of Cotta's protests, the six senators had been ferried across to the western bank before the battle began; Mallius Maximus had insisted that as civilian observers they should leave the field and observe from some place absolutely safe.

"If we go down, you must survive to bring the news to the Senate and People of Rome," he said.

It was Roman policy to spare the lives of all they defeated, for able-bodied warriors fetched the highest prices as slaves destined for labor, be it in mines, on wharves, in quarries, on building projects. But neither Celts nor Germans spared the lives of the men they fought, preferring to enslave those who spoke their languages, and only in such numbers as their unstructured way of life demanded.

So when, after a brief inglorious hour of battle, the German host stood victorious on the field, its members passed among the thousands of Roman bodies and killed any they found still alive. Luckily this act wasn't disciplined or concerted; had it been, not one of the twenty-four tribunes of the soldiers would have survived the battle of Arausio. Drusus lay so deeply unconscious he seemed dead to every German who looked him over, and all of Quintus Poppaedius Silo showing from beneath a pile of Marsic dead was so covered in blood he too went undiscovered. Unable to move because his leg was completely paralyzed, Quintus Sertorius shammed dead. And Sextus Caesar, entirely visible, labored so loudly for breath and was so blue in the face that no German who noticed him could be bothered dispatching a life so clearly ending of its own volition.

The two sons of Mallius Maximus perished as they galloped this way and that bearing their distracted father's orders, but the son of Metellus Numidicus Piggle-wiggle, young Piglet, was made of sterner stuff; when he saw the inevitability of defeat, he hustled the nerveless Mallius Maximus and some half-dozen aides who stood with him across the top of the camp ramparts to the river's edge, and there put them into a boat. Metellus Piglet's actions were not entirely dictated by motives of self-preservation, for he had his share of courage; simply, he preferred to turn that courage in the direction of preserving the life of his commander.

It was all over by the fifth hour of the day. And then the Germans turned north again, and walked the thirty miles back to where their many thousands of wagons stood all around the camp of the dead Aurelius. In Mallius Maximus's camp—and in Caepio's—they had made a wonderful discovery: huge stores of wheat, plus other foodstuffs, and sufficient vehicles and mules and oxen to carry all of it away. Gold, money, clothing, even arms and armor didn't attract them in the least. But Mallius Maximus's and Caepio's food was irresistible, so that they plundered the last rasher of bacon and the last pot of honey. And some hundreds of *amphorae* of wine.

One of the German interpreters, captured when Aurelius's camp was overwhelmed and restored to the bosom of his Cimbri people, had not been back among his own kind more than a very few hours when he realized that he had been among the Romans far too long to have any love left for barbarian living. So when no one was looking, he stole a horse and headed south for Arausio town. His route passed well to the east of the river, for he had no wish to encounter the aftermath of the terrible Roman defeat, even by smelling its unburied corpses.

On the ninth day of October, three days after the battle, he walked his tired steed down the cobbled main street of the prosperous town, looking for someone to whom he could tell his news, but finding no one. The whole populace seemed to have fled before the advance of the Germans. And then at the far end of the main street he spied the villa of Arausio's most important personage—a Roman citizen, of course—and there he discerned activity.

Arausio's most important personage was a local Gaul named Marcus Antonius Meminius because he had been given the coveted citizenship by a Marcus Antonius, for his services to the army of Gnaeus Domitius Ahenobarbus seventeen years before. Exalted by this distinction and helped by the patronage of the Antonius family to gain trade concessions between Gaul-across-the-Alps and Roman Italy, Marcus Antonius Meminius had prospered exceedingly. Now the chief magistrate of the town, he had tried to persuade its people to stay in their houses at least long enough to see whether the battle being fought to the north went for or against Rome. Not succeeding, he had nonetheless elected to stay himself, merely acting prudently by sending his children off in the care of their pedagogue, burying his gold, and concealing the trapdoor to his wine cellar by moving a large stone slab across it. His wife announced that she preferred to stay with him than go with the children, and so the two of them, attended by a loyal handful of servants, had listened to the brief cacophony of anguish which had floated on the heavy air between Mallius Maximus's camp and the town.

When no one came, Roman or German, Meminius had sent one of his slaves to find out what had happened, and was still reeling with the news when the first of the senior Roman officers to save their own skins came into town. They were Gnaeus Mallius Maximus and his handful of aides, behaving more like drugged animals on their way to ritual slaughter than high Roman military men; this impression of Meminius's was heightened by the behavior of Metellus Numidicus's son, who herded them with the sharpness and bite of a small dog. Meminius and his wife came out personally to lead the party into their villa, then gave them food and wine, and tried to obtain a coherent account of what had happened. But all their attempts failed; for the only rational one, young Metellus Piglet, had developed a speech impediment so bad he couldn't get two words out, and Meminius and his wife had no Greek, and only the most basic Latin.

More dragged themselves in over the next two days, but pitifully few, and no ranker soldiers, though one centurion was able to say that there were some thousands of survivors on the west bank of the river, wandering dazed and leaderless. Caepio came in last of all, accompanied by his son, Caepio Junior, whom he had found on the western bank as he came down it toward Arausio. When Caepio learned that Mallius Maximus was sheltering inside Meminius's house, he refused to stay, electing instead to press onward to Rome, and take his son with him. Meminius gave him two gigs harnessed to four-mule teams, and sent him on his way with food and drivers.

Bowed over with grief at the death of his sons, Mallius Maximus was unable until the third day to ask whereabouts the six senators were; until then Meminius hadn't even known of them, but when Mallius Maximus pressed for a search party to find them, Meminius demurred, afraid that the Germans were still in possession of the field of battle, and more concerned with making sure that he and his wife and all his shocked guests were readied for a quick flight to safety.

Such was the situation when the German interpreter rode into Arausio and located Meminius. It was immediately clear to Meminius that the man was big with news of some kind, but unfortunately neither of them could understand the other's Latin, and it did not occur to Meminius to ask Mallius Maximus to see the man. Instead, he gave him shelter, and told him to wait until someone came with both the language and the state of mind to interview him.

Under Cotta's leadership, the missing senatorial embassage had ventured back across the river in their boat the moment the Germans turned back into the north, and began to search that awful carnage for survivors. With their lictors and servants counted in, they numbered twenty-nine all told, and labored without regard for their safety should the Germans return. As the time passed, no one came to help them.

Drusus had come to his senses with darkness, lain half-conscious through the night, and with the dawn recovered enough to crawl in search of water, his only thought; the river was three miles away, the camp almost as far, so he struck off to the east, hoping to find a stream where the ground began to rise. Not more than a few feet away he found Quintus Sertorius, who flapped a hand at sight of him.

"Can't move," said Sertorius, licking cracked lips. "Leg dead. Waiting for someone. Thought it would be German."

"Thirsty," croaked Drusus. "Find water, then be back."

The dead were everywhere, acres upon acres of them, but they chiefly lay behind the route of Drusus's unsteady walk in search of water, for he had fallen in the true front line at the very beginning of the battle, and the Romans had not advanced an inch, only fallen back and back and back. Like himself, Sertorius had remained in the front line; had he lain among the tumbled heaps and mounds of Roman dead scant feet to his rear, Drusus would never have seen him.

His heavy Attic helmet gone, Drusus was bareheaded; a little puff of wind came and blew one single strand of hair across the great lump above his right eye, and so swollen, so stretched was the skin and tissue beneath, so bloodied the frontal bone, that the touch of that single strand of hair brought Drusus to his knees in agony.

But the will to live is very strong. Drusus climbed sobbing to his feet and continued his walk east, and even remembered that he had nothing in which to carry water, and that there would be some like Sertorius in sore need of water. Groaning with the immensity of the pain produced by bending over, he pulled the helmets off two dead Marsic soldiers and walked on, carrying the helmets by their chin straps.

And there among the field of Marsic dead stood a little water donkey, blinking its gentle, long-lashed eyes at the carnage, but unable to move away because its halter was wound round and round the arm of a man buried beneath other corpses. It had tried to tug itself free, but only succeeded in tightening the rope until tubes of blackening flesh protruded between the coils. Still wearing his dagger, Drusus cut the rope where it entered the lifeless arm and tied it to his sword belt, so that if he fainted the donkey would not be able to get away. But at the moment he found it, it was very glad to see a living man, and stood patiently while Drusus slaked his thirst, then was quite happy to follow wherever Drusus led.

On the outskirts of the huge confusion of bodies around the water donkey were two moving legs; amid renewed groans from Drusus that the donkey echoed sadly, Drusus managed to shove sufficient of the dead aside to uncover a Marsic officer who was still very much alive. His bronze cuirass was stove in along its right side just below and in front of the man's right arm, and a hole in the middle of the great dent oozed pink fluid rather than blood.

Working as delicately as he could, Drusus got the officer out of the press of bodies onto a patch of trampled grass and began to unbuckle the cuirass where its front and back plates met along the left side. The officer's eyes were closed, but a pulse in his neck was beating strongly, and when Drusus pried the shell of the cuirass off the chest and abdomen it had been designed to protect, he cried out sharply.

Then, "Go easy!" said an irritable voice in purest Latin.

Drusus stopped for a moment, then resumed unbuckling the leather underdress. "Lie still, you fool!" he said. "I'm only trying to help. Want some water first?"

"Water," echoed the Marsic officer.

Drusus fed it to him out of a helmet, and was rewarded with the unshuttering of two yellow-green eyes, a sight that reminded him of snakes; the Marsi were snake worshipers, and danced with them, and charmed them, and even kissed them tongue to tongue. Easy to believe, looking at those eyes.

"Quintus Poppaedius Silo," the Marsic officer said. "Some *irrumator* about eight feet tall caught me on the hop." He closed his eyes; two tears rolled down his bloodied cheeks. "My men—they're all dead, aren't they?"

"Afraid so," said Drusus gently. "Along with mine—and everybody else's, it seems. My name is Marcus Livius Drusus. Now hold on, I'm going to lift your jerkin off."

The wound had stanched itself, thanks to the woolen tunic the force of the German long-sword had pushed into its narrow mouth; Drusus could feel broken pieces of ribs moving under his hands, but cuirass, leather jerkin, and ribs had managed to prevent the blade invading the interior of chest and belly.

"You'll live," said Drusus. "Can you get up if I help you? I have a comrade back in my own legion who needs me. So it's either stay here and make your own way to me when you can, or come with me now on your own two feet." Another lone strand of hair blew across his pulped right forehead, and he screamed with the pain of it.

Quintus Poppaedius Silo considered the situation. "You'll never cope with me in your state," he said. "See if you can give me my dagger, I'm going to cut a bit off the bottom of my tunic and use it to bind this gash. Can't afford to start bleeding again in this Tartarus."

Drusus gave him the dagger and moved off with his donkey.

"Where will I find you?" Silo asked.

"Over yonder, next legion down," said Drusus.

Sertorius was still conscious. He drank gratefully, then managed to sit up. His wound was actually the worst of the three of them, and clearly he could not be moved until Drusus got help from Silo. So for the time being Drusus sank down next to Sertorius and rested, moving only when Silo appeared an hour later. The sun was getting up into the sky, and it was growing hot.

"The two of us will have to move Quintus Sertorius far enough away from the dead to give his leg less chance of being infected," said Silo. "Then I suggest we rig up some sort of shade shelter for him, and see if there's anyone else alive out here."

All this was done with frustrating slowness and too much pain, but eventually Sertorius was made as comfortable as possible, and Drusus and Silo set off on their quest. They hadn't gone very far when Drusus became nauseated, and sank down in a retching huddle on the battered dusty ground, each convulsion of diaphragm and stomach coming amid frantic screams of agony. In little better case, Silo subsided near him, and the donkey, still tethered to Drusus's belt, waited patiently.

Then Silo rolled over and inspected Drusus's head. He grunted. "If you can stand it, Marcus Livius, I think your pain might be much less if I broke open that lump with my knife and let some of the fluid out. Are you game?"

"I'd brave the hydra-headed monster if I thought it might fix me up!" gasped Drusus.

Before he applied the tip of his dagger to the lump, Silo muttered some charm or incantation in an ancient tongue Drusus could not identify; not Oscan, for that he understood well. A snake spell, that's what he's whispering, thought Drusus, and felt oddly comforted. The pain was blinding. Drusus fainted. And while he was unconscious Silo squeezed as much of the dammed-up blood and fluid out of the lump as he could, mopping up the mess with a chunk he tore off Drusus's tunic, and then helping himself to another chunk as Drusus stirred, came around.

"Feel any better?" asked Silo.

"Much," said Drusus.

"If I bind it, you'll only hurt more, so here, use this to mop up the muck when it blinds you. Sooner or later it will stop draining." Silo glanced up into the pitiless sun. "We've got to move into some shade, or we won't last—and that means young Sertorius won't last either," he said, getting to his feet.

The closer they staggered to the river, the more signs that men lived among the carnage began to appear; faint cries for help, movements, moans.

"This is an offense against the gods," said Silo grimly. "No battle was ever worse planned. We were executed! I curse Gnaeus Mallius Maximus! May the great light-bearing Snake wrap himself around Gnaeus Mallius Maximus's dreams!"

"I agree, it was a fiasco, and we were no better generaled than Cassius's men at Burdigala. But the blame has to be apportioned fairly, Quintus Poppaedius. If Gnaeus Mallius is guilty, how much more so is Quintus Servilius Caepio?" Oh, how that hurt to say! His wife's father, no less.

"*Caepio?* What did he have to do with it?" asked Silo.

The head wound was feeling much better; Drusus found he could turn to look at Silo easily. "Don't you know?" he asked.

"What does any Italian ever know about Roman command decisions?" Silo spat derisively on the ground. "We Italians are just here to fight. We don't get a say in *how* we are to fight, Marcus Livius."

"Well, since the day he arrived here from Narbo, Quintus Servilius has refused to work with Gnaeus Mallius." Drusus shivered. "He wouldn't take orders from a New Man."

Silo stared at Drusus; yellow-green eyes fixed on black eyes. "You mean Gnaeus Mallius *wanted* Quintus Servilius here in this camp?"

"Of course he did! So did the six senators from Rome. But Quintus Servilius wouldn't serve under a New Man."

"You're saying it was Quintus Servilius who kept the two armies separate?" Silo couldn't seem to believe what he was hearing.

"Yes, it was Quintus Servilius." It had to be said. "He is my father-in-law, I am married to his only daughter. How can I bear it? His son is my best friend, and married to my sister—fighting here today with Gnaeus Mallius—dead, I suppose." The fluid Drusus mopped from his face was mostly tears. "Pride, Quintus Poppaedius! Stupid, useless pride!"

Silo had stopped walking. "Six thousand soldiers of the Marsi and two thousand Marsic servants died here yesterday—now you tell me it was because some overbred Roman idiot bore a grudge against some underbred Roman idiot?" The breath hissed between Silo's teeth, he shook with rage. "May the great light-bearing Snake have them both!"

"Some of your men may be alive," said Drusus, not to excuse his superiors, but in an effort to comfort this man, whom he knew he liked enormously. And he was awash in pain, pain that had nothing to do with any physical wound, pain all bound up in a terrible grief. He—Marcus Livius Drusus—who had not known any of life's realities until now—wept for shame at the thought of a Rome led by men who could cause so much pain all for the sake of a class-conscious quarrel.

"No, they're dead," said Silo. "Why do you think it took me so long to join you where Quintus Sertorius lay? I went among them looking. Dead. All dead!"

"And mine," said Drusus, weeping still. "We took the brunt of it on the right, and not a cavalry trooper to be seen."

It was shortly after that they saw the senatorial party in the distance, and called for help.

Marcus Aurelius Cotta brought the tribunes of the soldiers into Arausio himself, plodding the five miles behind oxen because the pace and the kind of cart made it an easier journey; his fellows he left trying to organize some kind of order out of the chaos. Marcus Antonius Meminius had managed to persuade some of the local Gallic tribesmen who lived on farmsteads around Arausio to go out to the battlefield and do what they could to help.

"But," said Cotta to Meminius when he arrived at the local magistrate's villa, "this is the evening of the third day, and somehow we have to dispose of the dead."

"The townspeople are gone, and the farmers convinced the Germans will be back—you've no idea how hard I had to talk to get anyone to go out there and help you," said Meminius.

"I don't know where the Germans are," said Cotta, "and I can't work out why they headed back into the north. But so far, I haven't seen a sign of them. Unfortunately I don't have anyone to send out to scout, the battlefield is more important."

"Oh!" Meminius clapped his hand to his brow. "A fellow came in about four hours ago, and from what I can gather—I can't understand him—he's one of the German interpreters who were attached to the cavalry camp. He has Latin, but his accent is too thick for me. Would you talk to him? He might be willing to scout for you."

So Cotta sent for the German, and what he learned changed everything.

"There has been a terrible quarrel, the council of thanes is split, and the three peoples have gone their separate ways," the man said.

"A quarrel among the thanes, you mean?" asked Cotta.

"Well, between Teutobod of the Teutones and Boiorix of the Cimbri, at least in the beginning," said the interpreter. "The warriors went back to get the wagons started, and the council met to divide the spoils. There was much wine taken from the three camps of the Romans, and the council drank it. Then Teutobod said he had had a dream while he rode back to the wagons of his people, and was visited by the great god Ziu, and Ziu told him that if his people kept marching south into the Roman lands, the Romans would inflict a defeat upon them that would see all the warriors, the women, and the children slain or sold into slavery. So Teutobod said he was going to take the Teutones to Spain through the lands of the Gauls, not the lands of the Romans. But Boiorix took great exception to this, accused Teutobod of cowardice, and announced that the Cimbri would go south through the Roman lands, no matter what the Teutones did."

"Are you sure of all this?" Cotta asked, hardly able to believe it. "How do you know? From hearsay? Or were you there?"

"I was there, *dominus.*"

"Why were you there? How were you there?"

"I was waiting to be taken to the Cimbri wagons, since I am Cimbric. And they were all very drunk, so no one noticed me. I found I did not want to be a German anymore, so I thought I would learn what I could, and escape."

"Go on, then, man!" said Cotta eagerly.

"Well, the rest of the thanes joined in the argument, and then Getorix, who leads the Marcomanni and Cherusci and Tigurini, proposed that the matter be settled by remaining among the Aedui and Ambarri. But no one except his own people wanted to do that. The Teutonic thanes sided with Teutobod, and the Cimbric thanes with Boiorix. So the council ended yesterday with the three peoples all wanting different things. Teutobod has ordered the Teutones to travel into far Gaul, and make their way to Spain through the lands of the Cardurci and Petrocorii. Getorix and his people are going to stay among the Aedui and Ambarri. And Boiorix is going to lead the Cimbri to the other side of the great river Rhodanus, and travel to Spain along the outskirts of the Roman lands, rather than through them."

"So that's why there's been no sign of them!" said Cotta.

"Yes, *dominus*. They will not be coming south through the Roman lands," said the German.

Back went Cotta to Marcus Antonius Meminius, and told him the news, smiling broadly.

"Spread the word, Marcus Meminius, and as quickly as possible! For you must get all those bodies burned, otherwise your ground and your water will be contaminated, and disease will do more damage to the people of Arausio than the Germans could," said Cotta. He frowned, chewed his lip. "Where is Quintus Servilius Caepio?"

"Already on his way to Rome, Marcus Aurelius."

"*What?*"

"He left with his son to bring the news to Rome as quickly as he could," said Meminius, puzzled.

"Oh, I'll just bet he did!" said Cotta grimly. "Is he going by road?"

"Of course, Marcus Aurelius. I gave him four-mule gigs out of my own stables."

Cotta stood up, bone tired but filled with new vigor. "*I* will bring the news of Arausio to Rome," he said. "If I have to grow wings and fly, I'll beat Quintus Servilius, I swear it! Marcus Meminius, give me the best horse you can find. I start for Massilia at the crack of dawn."

He rode at the gallop for Massilia, unescorted, commandeered a fresh horse in Glanum, and another in Aquae Sextiae, and got to Massilia seven hours after leaving Arausio. The great seaport founded by the Greeks centuries before had heard not one word about the great battle fought four days earlier; Cotta found the city—so sleek and Greek, so white and bright—in a fever of apprehension at the coming of the Germans.

The house of the *ethnarch* pointed out to him, Cotta walked in with all the arrogance and haste of a Roman curule magistrate on urgent business. As Massilia enjoyed ties of friendship with Rome without submitting to Roman rule, Cotta could have been politely shown the door. But of course he was not. Especially after the *ethnarch* and a few of his councillors living close by had heard what Cotta had to say.

"I want the fastest ship you've got, and the best sailors and oarsmen in Massilia," he said. "There's no cargo to slow the ship down, so I'll carry two spare teams of oarsmen in case we have to row against the wind and into a head sea. Because I swear to you, *Ethnarch* Aristides, that I will be in Rome in three days, if it means rowing the whole way! We're not going to hug the coast—we're going in as straight a line for Ostia as the best navigator in Massilia can sail. When's the next tide?"

"You will have your ship and your crew by dawn, Marcus Aurelius, and that happens to coincide with the tide," said the *ethnarch* gently. He coughed with great delicacy. "Who will be paying?"

Typical Massiliote Greek, thought Cotta, but didn't say so aloud. "Write me out a bill," he said. "The Senate and People of Rome will be paying."

The bill was written at once; Cotta looked down at the outrageous price and grunted. "It's a tragedy," he said to *Ethnarch* Aristides, "when bad news costs enough to fight another war against the Germans. I don't suppose you'd lop a few drachmae off?"

"I agree, it is a tragedy," said the *ethnarch* smoothly. "However, business is business. The price stands, Marcus Aurelius. Take it or leave it."

"I'll take it," said Cotta.

Caepio and his son didn't bother to take the detour a visit to Massilia would have meant for a road traveler. No one knew better than Caepio—veteran of a year in Narbo and a year in Spain when he had been praetor—that the winds *always* blew the wrong way across the Sinus Gallicus. He would take the Via Domitia up the valley of the Druentia River, cross into Italian Gaul through the Mons Genava Pass, and hurry as fast as he could down the Via Aemilia and the Via Flaminia. Hopefully he could average seventy miles a day if he managed to commandeer decent animals often enough, and he expected his proconsular imperium to do that for him. It did; as the miles flew by Caepio began to feel confident that he would beat even the senatorial courier to Rome. So rapid had his crossing of the Alps been that the Vocontii, always on the lookout for vulnerable Roman travelers on the Via Domitia, were unable to organize an attack on the two galloping gigs.

By the time he reached Ariminum and the end of the Via Aemilia, Caepio knew he would make it from Arausio to Rome in seven days, assisted by good roads and plenty of fresh mules. He began to relax. Exhausted he might be, a headache of huge proportions he might have, but his version of what had happened at Arausio would be the first version Rome heard, and that was nine tenths of the battle. When Fanum Fortunae appeared and the gigs turned onto the Via Flaminia for the crossing of the Apennines and the descent into the Tiber Valley, Caepio knew he had won. His was the version of Arausio Rome would believe.

But Fortune had a greater favorite; Marcus Aurelius Cotta sailed the Sinus Gallicus from Massilia to Ostia in winds that veered between perfect and nonexistent, a better passage by far than could have been predicted. When the wind dropped, the professional oarsmen took their places in the outriggers, the *hortator* started to mark the stroke on his drum, and thirty muscled backs bent to the task. It was a small ship, built for speed rather than cargo, and looked suspiciously like a Massiliote fighting ship to Cotta, though the Massiliotes were not supposed to have any without Roman approval. Its two banks of oars, fifteen to a side, were housed in outriggers surmounted by decks that could easily have been fenced with a row of good stout shields and turned into fighting platforms in the twinkling of an eye, and the crane rigged on the afterdeck seemed rather haphazard in construction; perhaps, thought Cotta, a hefty catapult normally sits there. Piracy was a profitable industry, and rife from one end of the Middle Sea to the other.

However, he was not the man to question a gift from Fortune, so Cotta nodded blandly when the captain explained that he specialized in passengers, and that the outrigger decks were a *nice* place for the passengers to stretch their legs, since cabin accommodation was a bit primitive. Before they sailed Cotta had been persuaded by the captain that two extra teams of oarsmen were excessive, for his men were the best in the business and would keep up a top pace with only one extra team. Now Cotta was glad he had agreed, for they were the lighter in weight because they carried fewer men, and the wind provided enough puff to rest both teams of rowers just when it looked as if exhaustion was going to set in.

The ship had sailed out of Massilia's magnificent harbor at dawn on the eleventh day of October, and came to anchor in Ostia's dismally poor harbor at dawn on the day before the Ides, exactly three days later. And three hours later Cotta walked into the consul Publius Rutilius Rufus's house, scattering clients before him like hens before a fox.

"Out!" he said to the client seated in the chair at Rutilius Rufus's desk, and threw himself wearily into the chair as the startled client scuttled to the door.

By noon the Senate had been summoned to an emergency meeting in the Curia Hostilia; Caepio and his son were at that same moment trotting briskly down the last stretch of the Via Aemilia.

"Leave the doors open," said Publius Rutilius Rufus to the chief clerk. "This is one meeting the People must hear. And I want it taken down verbatim and transcribed for the records."

Given the short notice, it was a fairly full House; for in the unfathomable way that news has of percolating ahead of official dissemination, the rumor was already spreading through the city that there had been a great disaster against the Germans in Gaul. The well of the Comitia near the foot of the Curia Hostilia steps was rapidly filling with people; so were the steps and all the level spaces nearby.

Fully privy to Caepio's letters protesting against Mallius

Maximus as well as demanding the supreme authority, and fearing a fresh round of arguments, the Conscript Fathers were edgy. Not having heard in weeks from Caepio, the doughty Marcus Aemilius Scaurus was at a disadvantage, and knew it. So when the consul Rutilius Rufus commanded that the House doors remain open, Scaurus made no move to insist they be closed. Nor did Metellus Numidicus. All eyes were riveted on Cotta, given a chair in the front row in close proximity to the dais on which stood his brother-in-law Rutilius Rufus's ivory chair.

"Marcus Aurelius Cotta arrived in Ostia this morning," Rutilius Rufus said. "Three days ago he was in Massilia, and the day before that, he was in Arausio, near which our armies stationed themselves. I call upon Marcus Aurelius Cotta to speak, and give the House notice that this meeting is being transcribed verbatim for the records."

Of course Cotta had bathed and changed, but there could be no mistaking the grey tinge of fatigue in his normally highly colored face, and every line of his body as he got to his feet indicated the immensity of that fatigue.

"On the day before the Nones of October, Conscript Fathers, a battle was fought at Arausio," said Cotta, not needing to project his voice, for the House was utterly still. "The Germans annihilated us. *Eighty thousand* of our soldiers are dead."

No one exclaimed, no one murmured, no one moved; the House sat in a silence as profound as that inside the Sibyl's cave at Cumae. "When I say eighty thousand soldiers, I mean just that. The noncombatant dead number some twenty-four thousand more. And the cavalry dead are separate again."

His voice expressionlessly level, Cotta went on to tell the senators exactly what had happened from the time he and his five companions arrived at Arausio—the fruitless dickering with Caepio; the atmosphere of confusion and unrest Caepio's flouting of orders created within Mallius Maximus's chain of command, some of whom sided with Caepio, like Caepio's son; the stranding of the consular Aurelius and the cavalry too far away to act as part of a military machine. "Five thousand troopers, all their noncombatants, and every single animal in Aurelius's camp perished. The legate Marcus Aurelius Scaurus was taken prisoner by the Germans and used as a deliberate example. They burned him alive, Conscript Fathers. He died, I was told by a witness, with extreme courage and bravery."

There were ashen faces among the senators now, for most had sons or brothers or nephews or cousins in one or the other of the armies; men wept silently, heads muffled in their togas, or sat forward, faces hidden in their hands. Scaurus Princeps Senatus alone remained erect, two fierce spots of color in his cheeks, mouth a hard line.

"All of you here today must take a part of the blame," said Cotta. "Your delegation did not contain one consular, and I—a mere ex-praetor!—was the only curule magistrate among the six. With the result that Quintus Servilius Caepio refused to speak with us as his equals in birth or seniority. Or even experience. Instead, he took our insignificance, our lack of clout, as a message from the Senate that it was behind him in his stand against Gnaeus Mallius Maximus. And he was *right* to do so, Conscript Fathers! If you had seriously intended to see that Quintus Servilius obeyed the law by subordinating himself to the consul of the year, you would have *stuffed* your delegation with consulars! But you did not. You deliberately sent five *pedarii* and one ex-praetor to deal with one of the House's most obdurately elitist, most senior members!"

Not a head came up; more and more were now shrouded in folds of toga. But Scaurus Princeps Senatus continued to sit bolt upright, his blazing eyes never leaving Cotta's face.

"The rift between Quintus Servilius Caepio and Gnaeus Mallius Maximus prevented the amalgamation of their forces. Instead of a tightly bound single army comprising no less than seventeen legions and over five thousand horse, Rome fielded two armies twenty miles apart, with the smaller one closer to the German advance, and the body of cavalry separate again. Quintus Servilius Caepio personally told me that he would not share his triumph with Gnaeus Mallius Maximus, and so had deliberately put his army too far north of Gnaeus Mallius's to allow it any participation in *his* battle."

Cotta drew in a rasping breath which sounded so loud in the silence that Rutilius Rufus jumped. Scaurus did not. Beside Scaurus, Metellus Numidicus poked his head slowly out of his toga, straightened to reveal a stony face.

"Even leaving aside the disastrous rift between them, the truth is, Conscript Fathers, that neither Quintus Servilius nor Gnaeus Mallius had sufficient military talent to win against the Germans! However, of the two commanders, it is Quintus Servilius who must take the brunt of the blame. For not only was he as poor a general as Gnaeus Mallius, but he flouted the law as well. *He put himself above the law,* he deemed the law a device for lesser mortals than himself! A true Roman, Marcus Aemilius Scaurus Princeps Senatus"—this was said directly to the Leader of the House, who didn't move—"holds the law paramount, knowing that under the law there is no true social distinction, only a system of checks and balances we have deliberately designed to ensure that *no man* can consider himself above his peers. Quintus Servilius Caepio behaved like the First Man in Rome. But under the law, there cannot *be* a First Man in Rome! So I say to you that Quintus Servilius broke the law, where Gnaeus Mallius was simply an inadequate general."

The stillness and the silence continued; Cotta sighed. "Arausio is a worse disaster than Cannae, my fellow senators. The flower of our men is perished. I know, for I was there. Perhaps thirteen thousand soldiers survived, and they—the greenest troops of all—fled without any order to retreat, leaving their arms and armor behind on the field, and swimming the Rhodanus to safety. They are still wandering unmustered to the west of the river somewhere, and, from some reports I have had, are so frightened of the Germans that they intend to go to earth rather than run the risk of being collected and put back into a Roman army. When he tried to stop this rout, the tribune Sextus Julius Caesar was cut down by his own soldiers. I am pleased to say he lives, for I found him on the field myself, left for dead by the Germans. I and my companions—twenty-nine, all told—were the only people available to succor the wounded, and for nearly three days no others came to help. Though the vast majority of those left lying on the field were dead, there can be no doubt that some died who might not have died were there people on hand to give them aid after the battle."

In spite of iron control, Metellus Numidicus moved, his hand going out in dreadful query. Cotta caught the gesture, and looked at Gaius Marius's enemy, who was his own friend; for Cotta had no love to lay on Gaius Marius's altar.

"Your son, Quintus Caecilius Metellus Numidicus, survived unharmed, but not as a coward. He rescued the consul Gnaeus Mallius and some of his personal staff. However, both the sons of Gnaeus Mallius were killed. Of the twenty-four elected tribunes of the soldiers, only three survived—Marcus Livius Drusus, Sextus Julius Caesar, and Quintus Servilius Caepio Junior. Marcus Livius and Sextus Julius were severely wounded. Quintus Servilius Junior—who commanded the greenest legion of troops, closest to the river—survived unharmed by swimming to safety, in what circumstances of personal integrity I do not know."

Cotta paused to clear his throat, wondering if the vast relief in Metellus Numidicus's eyes was mostly for the simple survival of his son, or for the news that his son had been no coward. "But these casualty figures pale when compared to the fact that *not one centurion of any experience in either army* is now alive. Rome is officerless, Conscript Fathers! And the great army of Gaul-across-the-Alps no longer exists." He waited for a moment, then added, "It never did exist, thanks to Quintus Servilius Caepio."

Outside the great bronze doors of the Curia Hostilia the news was being disseminated by those close enough to hear to those too far away to hear, an ever-widening audience that was still gathering, now spreading up the Argiletum and the Clivus Argentarius, and across the lower Forum Romanum behind the well of the Comitia. The crowds were immense. But they were quiet crowds. The only sounds were the sounds of tears. Rome had lost the crucial battle. And Italy was open to the Germans.

Before Cotta could sit down, Scaurus spoke.

"And where are the Germans now, Marcus Aurelius? How much farther south of Arausio were they when you left to bring us the news? And how much farther south might they be now, this very moment?" he asked.

"I honestly do not know, Princeps Senatus. For when the battle was over—and it only took about an hour—the Germans turned back into the north, apparently to fetch their wagons and women and children, left just to the north of the cavalry camp. But when I departed, they had not come back. And I interviewed a German man whom Marcus Aurelius Scaurus had employed as one of his interpreters when the German chiefs came to parley. This man was captured, recognized as a German, and so was not harmed. According to him, the Germans quarreled, and have—for the moment, anyway—split up into three separate groups. It seems none of the three groups is confident enough to press on alone south into our territory. So they are going to Spain by various routes through Long-haired Gaul. But the quarrel was induced by Roman wine taken as part of the spoils. How long the rift will persist, no one can predict. Nor can I be sure that the man I interviewed was telling all the truth. Or even part of the truth, for that matter. He *says* he escaped and came back because he doesn't want to live as a German anymore. But it may be that he was sent back by the Germans to lull our fears and make us even easier prey. All I can tell you for certain is that when I left, there was no sign of a southward German movement," said Cotta, and sat down.

Rutilius Rufus rose to his feet. "This is not the occasion for a debate, Conscript Fathers. Nor is it an occasion for recriminations, yet more quarrels. Today is an occasion for *action*."

"Hear, hear!" said a voice from the back.

"Tomorrow is the Ides of October," Rutilius Rufus went on. "That means the campaign season is just about over. But we have very little time left to us if we are to prevent the Germans invading Italy anytime they feel like doing so. I have formulated a plan of action which I intend to present to you now, but first I am going to give you a solemn warning. At the slightest sign of argument, dissension, or any other conceivable polarization of this House, I will take my plan to the People and have it approved in the Plebeian Assembly. Thereby depriving you, Conscript Fathers, of your prerogative to take the lead in all matters pertaining to the defense of Rome. The conduct of Quintus Servilius Caepio points up the greatest weakness of our senatorial order—namely, its unwillingness to admit that Chance and Fortune and Luck occasionally combine to throw up men from the lower ranks with far greater abilities than all of us who regard ourselves as entitled by birth and tradition to govern the People of Rome—and command Rome's armies."

He had turned his person and pitched his voice toward the open doors, and the great high sound of it floated out into the air above the Comitia.

"We are going to need every able-bodied man in all of Italy, so much is sure. From the Head Count clear through the orders and classes to the Senate, *every* able-bodied man! I therefore require a decree from you directing the Plebs to enact a law immediately forbidding any man between the ages of seventeen and thirty-five—*any* man, be he Roman or Latin or Italian—to leave the shores of Italy, or cross the Arnus or the Rubico into Italian Gaul. By tomorrow I want couriers riding at the gallop to every port in our peninsula with orders that no ship or boat is to accept an able-bodied free man as crew or passenger. The penalty will be death, both for the man trying to avoid military service and the man accepting him."

No one in the House said a word—not Scaurus Princeps Senatus, not Metellus Numidicus, not Metellus Dalmaticus Pontifex Maximus, not Ahenobarbus Senior, not Catulus Caesar, not Scipio Nasica. Good, thought Rutilius Rufus. They'll not oppose that law, anyway.

"All available personnel will be set to recruiting soldiers of any class from Head Count to Senate. And that means, Conscript Fathers, that those among you aged thirty-five or younger will automatically be inducted into the legions, no matter how many campaigns you have served in previously. We will get soldiers if we enforce this law rigorously. However, I very much fear we won't get enough. Quintus Servilius cleaned out the last pockets of those throughout Italy owning property, and Gnaeus Mallius took almost seventy thousand men of the Head Count, either as soldiers or as noncombatants.

"So we must look to what other armies we have available. In Macedonia: two legions only, both of auxiliaries, which cannot possibly be spared duty there. In Spain: two legions in the further province, and one in the nearer province—two of these legions are Roman, one auxiliary—and not only will they have to stay in Spain, but they must be heavily reinforced, for the Germans say they intend to invade Spain." He paused.

And Scaurus Princeps Senatus came to life at last. "Get on with it, Publius Rutilius!" he said testily. "Get to Africa—and Gaius Marius!"

Rutilius Rufus blinked, feigning surprise. "Why, thank you, Princeps Senatus, thank you! If you hadn't mentioned it, I might have forgotten! Oh, truly are you called the watchdog of the Senate! What *would* we do without you?"

"Spare me the sarcasm, Publius Rutilius!" Scaurus snarled. "Just get on with it!"

"Certainly! There are three aspects of Africa which I think must be mentioned. The first is a war successfully concluded—an enemy completely rolled up, an enemy king and his family at this very moment waiting for retribution right here in Rome, as houseguests of our noble Quintus Caecilius Metellus Piggle-wiggle—oooops, I do beg your pardon, Quintus Caecilius!—*Numidicus,* I mean!—well, here in Rome, certainly.

"The second aspect," he went on, "is an army six legions strong—composed of the Head Count, admittedly!—but superbly well trained, and valiant, and brilliantly officered from the most junior centurion and cadet-tribune clear through to its legates. With it is a cavalry force two thousand strong, of equally experienced and valorous men."

Rutilius Rufus stopped, rocked on his heels, grinned all around him wolfishly. "The third aspect, Conscript Fathers, is a man.

One single man. I refer of course to the proconsul Gaius Marius, commander-in-chief of the African army, and sole engineer of a victory so complete it ranks with the victories of Scipio Aemilianus. Numidia will not rise again. The threat in Africa to Rome's citizens, property, province, and grain supply is now nonexistent. In fact, Gaius Marius is bequeathing us an Africa so subjugated and pacified that it is not even necessary to put a garrison legion there."

He left the dais on which stood the curule chairs, stepped down onto the black-and-white flagging of the ancient floor, and walked toward the doors, standing so that the main volume of his voice went outside into the Forum.

"Rome's need for a general is even greater than her need for soldiers or centurions. As Gaius Marius once said in this very House, thousands upon thousands of Rome's soldiers have perished in the few years since the death of Gaius Gracchus—due *solely* to the incompetence of the men who led them and their centurions! And at the time Gaius Marius spoke, Italy was still the richer by a hundred thousand men than Italy is right at this moment. But how many soldiers, centurions, and noncombatants has Gaius Marius himself lost? Why, Conscript Fathers, virtually none! Three years ago he took six legions with him to Africa, and he still has those legions alive and well. Six *veteran* legions, six legions with *centurions!*"

He paused, then roared at the top of his voice, "Gaius Marius is the answer to Rome's need for an army—*and* a competent general!"

His small spare figure showed briefly against the press of listeners outside on the porch when he turned to walk back up the length of the House to his dais. There he stopped.

"You have heard Marcus Aurelius Cotta say that there has been a quarrel among the Germans, and that at the moment they seem to have abandoned their intention of migrating through our province of Gaul-across-the-Alps. But we cannot possibly let ourselves relax because of this report. We must be skeptical of it, not emboldened by it to indulge in further stupidity. However, one

fact seems fairly sure. That we do have the coming winter to prepare. And the first phase of preparation must be to appoint Gaius
Marius proconsul in Gaul, with an imperium that cannot be re-
scinded until the Germans are beaten."

There was a general murmur, a harbinger of coming protest.
Then came the voice of Metellus Numidicus.

"Give Gaius Marius the governorship of Gaul-across-the-Alps
with a proconsular imperium for anything up to *years*?" he asked
incredulously. "Over my dead body!"

Rutilius Rufus stamped his foot, shook his fist. "Oh, ye gods,
there you go!" he cried. "Quintus Caecilius, Quintus Caecilius,
do you not *yet* understand the magnitude of our plight? We need
a general of Gaius Marius's caliber!"

"We need his troops," said Scaurus Princeps Senatus loudly.
"We do *not* need Gaius Marius! There are others here as good."

"Meaning your friend Quintus Caecilius Piggle-wiggle, Marcus Aemilius?" Rutilius Rufus blew a rude noise. "Rubbish! For
two years Quintus Caecilius fiddled about in Africa—I know, because I was there! I worked with Quintus Caecilius, and
Piggle-wiggle is an apt name for that gentleman, because he's as
turgidly calculating as any woman's piggle-wiggle! I have also
worked with Gaius Marius. And perhaps it is not too much to hope
that some of the members of this House remember about me that I
am no mean Military Man myself! I should have been given the
command in Gaul-across-the-Alps, not Gnaeus Maximus! But that
is past, and I do not have the time to waste in recriminations.

"I say to you now, Conscript Fathers, that Rome's plight is too
huge and urgent to pander to a few individuals at the top of our
noble tree! I say to you now, Conscript Fathers—all you who sit
on the middle tiers of both sides of the House, and all you who sit
on the back tiers of both sides of this House!—that there is only
one man with the ability to lead us out of our peril! And that one
man is Gaius Marius! What matter, that he isn't in the studbook?
What matter, that he isn't a Roman of Rome? Quintus Servilius
Caepio *is* a Roman of Rome, and look where he's put us! Do you
know where he's put us? *Right in the middle of the shit!*"

Rutilius Rufus was roaring, angry and afraid, sure now that they wouldn't see the reason of his proposal. "Honorable members of this House—Good Men all—fellow senators! I beseech you to put aside your prejudices just this once! We *must* give Gaius Marius proconsular power in Gaul-across-the-Alps for however long it is going to take to shove the Germans back to Germania!"

And this last passionate plea worked. He had them. Scaurus knew it; Metellus Numidicus knew it.

The praetor Manius Aquillius rose to his feet; a man noble enough, but coming from a family whose history was checkered with more deeds of cupidity than deeds of glory; his father it was who, in the wars after King Attalus of Pergamum willed his kingdom to Rome, had sold the whole land of Phrygia to the fifth King Mithridates of Pontus for a huge sum of gold, and thereby let the inscrutable Orient into western Asia Minor.

"Publius Rutilius, I wish to speak," he said.

"Speak, then," said Rutilius Rufus, and sat down, spent.

"*I* wish to speak!" said Scaurus Princeps Senatus angrily.

"After Manius Aquillius," said Rutilius Rufus sweetly.

"Publius Rutilius, Marcus Aemilius, Conscript Fathers," Aquillius began correctly, "I agree with the consul that there is only one man with the genius to extricate us from our plight, and I agree that man is Gaius Marius. But the answer our esteemed consul has proposed is not the right one. We cannot handicap Gaius Marius with a proconsular imperium limited to Gaul-across-the-Alps. First of all, what happens if the war moves out of Gaul-across-the-Alps? What if its theater shifts to Italian Gaul, or Spain, or even to Italy itself? Why, the command will automatically shift to the appropriate governor, or to the consul of the year! Gaius Marius has many enemies in this House. And I for one am not sure that those enemies will hold Rome dearer than their grudges. The refusal of Quintus Servilius Caepio to collaborate with Gnaeus Mallius Maximus is a perfect example of what happens when a member of the old nobility holds his *dignitas* more important than Rome's *dignitas*."

"You are mistaken, Manius Aquillius," Scaurus interjected. "Quintus Servilius held his *dignitas* identical to Rome's!"

"I thank you for the correction, Princeps Senatus," said Aquillius smoothly, and with a little bow no one could honestly call ironic. "You are absolutely correct to correct me. The *dignitas* of Rome and that of Quintus Servilius Caepio *are* identical! But why do you hold the *dignitas* of Gaius Marius as so inferior to Quintus Servilius Caepio's? Surely Gaius Marius's *personal* share is quite as high, if not higher, even if his ancestors owned not a scrap! Gaius Marius's personal career has been illustrious! And does any member of this House seriously believe that Gaius Marius thinks of Arpinum first, Rome second? Does any member of this House seriously believe Gaius Marius thinks of Arpinum in any other way than that it is a part of Rome? All of us have ancestors who were once New Men! Even Aeneas—who came to Latium from far-off Ilium, after all!—was a New Man! Gaius Marius has been praetor and consul. He has therefore ennobled himself, and his descendants to the very end of time will be noble."

Aquillius's eyes roved across the white-clad ranks. "I see several Conscript Fathers here today who bear the name of Porcius Cato. Now their grandfather was a New Man. But do we today think of these Porcii Catones as anything save pillars of this House, noble descendants of a man who in his own day had much the same effect on men with the name of Cornelius Scipio as Gaius Marius has today on men with the name of Caecilius Metellus?"

He shrugged, got down from the dais, and emulated Rutilius Rufus by striding down the floor of the House to a position near the open doors.

"It is Gaius Marius and no other who must retain supreme command against the Germans. No matter *where* the theater of war might be! Therefore it is not enough to invest Gaius Marius with a proconsular imperium limited to Gaul-across-the-Alps."

He turned to face the House, and thundered his words. "As is evident, Gaius Marius is not here to give his personal opinion, and time is galloping away as fast as a bolting horse. Gaius Marius must be consul. That is the only way we can give him the power he is going to need. He must be put up as a candidate for the coming consular elections—a candidate *in absentia*!"

The House was growling, murmuring, but Manius Aquillius carried on, and carried their attention. "Can anyone here deny that the men of the Centuries are the finest flower of the People? So I say to you, let the men of the Centuries decide! By either electing Gaius Marius consul *in absentia,* or not electing him! For this decision of the supreme command is too big for this House to make. And it is also too big for the Assembly of the Plebs or even of the Whole People to make. I say to you, Conscript Fathers, that the decision of the supreme command against the Germans must be handed to that section of the Roman People who matter the most—the men of the First and the Second Classes of citizens, voting in their centuries in their own Assembly, the Comitia Centuriata!"

Oh, here is Ulysses! thought Rutilius Rufus. I would never have thought of this! Nor do I approve. But he's got the Scaurus faction by the balls just the same. No, it would never have worked to take the vexed question of Gaius Marius's imperium to the People in their tribes, have the whole thing conducted by the tribunes of the plebs in an atmosphere of shouting, yelling, even rioting crowds! To men like Scaurus, the Plebeian Assembly is an excuse for the rabble to run Rome. But the men of the First and Second Classes? Oh, they're a very different breed of Roman! Clever, clever Manius Aquillius!

First you do something unheard of, by proposing that a man be elected consul when he isn't even here to stand for office, and then you let the Scaurus faction know that you are willing to have the whole question decided by Rome's finest! If Rome's finest don't want Gaius Marius, then all they have to do is organize the First and Second Classes of the Centuries to vote for two other men. If they do want Gaius Marius, then all they have to do is vote for him and one other man. And I'd be willing to bet that the Third Class doesn't even get a chance to vote! Exclusivity is satisfied.

The real legal quibble is the *in absentia* proviso. Manius Aquillius will have to go to the Plebeian Assembly for that, though, because the Senate won't give it to him. Look at the tribunes of the plebs wriggling with glee on their bench! There won't be a veto among them—they'll take the *in absentia* dispensation to the Plebs, and the Plebs, dazzled by the vision of ten tribunes of the plebs in accord, will pass a special law enabling Gaius Marius to be elected consul *in absentia*. Of course Scaurus and Metellus Numidicus and the others will argue the binding power of the *lex Villia annalis,* which says that no man can stand a second time for the consulship until ten years have elapsed. And Scaurus and Metellus Numidicus and the others will lose.

This Manius Aquillius needs watching, thought Rutilius Rufus, turning in his chair to watch. Amazing! he thought. They can sit there for years as demure and tractable as a new little Vestal Virgin, and then all of a sudden the opportunity presents itself, and off comes the sheep's disguise, forth stands the wolf. You, Manius Aquillius, are a wolf.

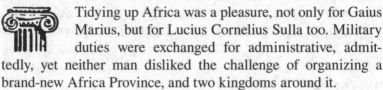

Tidying up Africa was a pleasure, not only for Gaius Marius, but for Lucius Cornelius Sulla too. Military duties were exchanged for administrative, admittedly, yet neither man disliked the challenge of organizing a brand-new Africa Province, and two kingdoms around it.

Gauda was now King of Numidia; not much of a man himself, he had a good son in Prince Hiempsal—who would be king, Marius thought, fairly quickly. Reinstated as an official Friend and Ally of the Roman People, Bocchus of Mauretania found his realm enormously enlarged by the gift of most of western Numidia; where once the river Muluchath had been his eastern boundary, this now lay only fifty miles to the west of Cirta and Rusicade. Most of eastern Numidia went into a much bigger Africa Province to be governed by Rome, so that Marius could dower all the knights and landowners in his clientele with the rich

coastal lands of the Lesser Syrtis, including the old and still powerful Punic town of Leptis Magna, as well as Lake Tritonis and
the port of Tacape. For his own uses, Marius kept the big, fertile
islands of the Lesser Syrtis; he had plans for them, particularly
for Meninx and Cercina.

"When we get round to discharging the army," Marius said to
Sulla, "there comes the problem of what to do with them. They're
all Head Count, which means they have no farms or businesses to
go back to. They'll be able to enlist in other armies, and I suspect
a lot of them will want to do that, but some won't. However, the
State owns their equipment, which means they won't be allowed
to keep it, and that means the only armies they'll be able to enlist
in will be Head Count armies. With Scaurus and Piggle-wiggle
opposing financing of Head Count armies in the House, there's a
distinct possibility Head Count armies of the future will be rare
birds, at least after the Germans are dealt with—oh, Lucius Cornelius, wouldn't it be grand to be in that campaign? But they'll
never agree to it, alas."

"I'd give my eyeteeth," said Sulla.

"You could spare them," said Marius.

"Go on with what you were saying about the men who will
want their discharges," Sulla prompted.

"I think the State owes Head Count soldiers a little more than
their share of the booty at the end of a campaign. I think the State
should gift each man with a plot of land to settle on when he
elects to retire. Make decent, modestly affluent citizens of them,
in other words."

"A military version of the land settlements the Brothers Gracchi tried to introduce?" asked Sulla, frowning slightly.

"Precisely. You don't approve?"

"I was thinking of the opposition in the House."

"Well, I've been thinking that the opposition would be much
less if the land involved wasn't *ager publicus*—in Rome's public
domain. Start even talking about giving away the *ager publicus,*
and you're asking for trouble. Too many powerful men are leasing it. No, what I plan to do is secure permission from the

House—or the People, if the House won't do it—hopefully, it won't come to that—to settle Head Count soldiers on nice big plots of land on Cercina and Meninx, right here in the African Lesser Syrtis. Give each man, say, a hundred *iugera,* and he will do two things for Rome. First of all, he and his companions will form the nucleus of a trained body of men who can be called up for duty in the event of any future war in Africa. And secondly, he and his companions will bring Rome to the provinces—Rome's thoughts, customs, language, way of life."

But Sulla frowned. "I don't know, Gaius Marius—it seems wrong to me to want to do the second thing. Rome's thoughts, customs, language, way of life—those things belong to Rome. To graft them onto Punic Africa, with its Berbers and Moors beneath that again—well, to me it seems a betrayal of Rome."

Marius rolled his eyes toward the roof. "There is no doubt, Lucius Cornelius, that you are an aristocrat! Live a low life you might have done, but think low you don't." He reverted to the task at hand. "Have you got those lists of all the odds and ends of booty? The gods help us if we forget to itemize the last gold-headed nail—and in quintuplicate!"

"Treasury clerks, Gaius Marius, are the dregs of the Roman wine flagon," said Sulla, hunting through papers.

"Of anybody's wine flagon, Lucius Cornelius."

On the Ides of November a letter came to Utica from the consul Publius Rutilius Rufus. Marius had got into the habit of sharing these letters with Sulla, who enjoyed Rutilius Rufus's racy style even more than Marius did, being better with words than Marius was. However, Marius was alone when the letter was brought to his office, which fact pleased him; for he liked the opportunity to go through it first to familiarize himself with the text, and when Sulla sat listening to him mutter his way across the endless squiggles trying to divide them up into separate words, it tended to put him off.

But he had hardly begun to read it aloud to himself when he

jumped, shivered, leaped to his feet. *"Jupiter!"* he cried, and ran for Sulla's office.

He burst in, white-faced, brandishing the scroll. "Lucius Cornelius! A letter from Publius Rutilius!"

"What? What is it?"

"A hundred thousand Roman dead," Marius began, reading out important snatches of what he had already read himself. "Eighty thousand of the dead are soldiers. . . . The Germans annihilated us. . . . That fool Caepio refused to join camps with Mallius Maximus . . . insisted on staying twenty miles to the north. . . . Young Sextus Caesar was badly wounded, so was young Sertorius. . . . Only three of the twenty-four tribunes of the soldiers survived. . . . No centurions left. . . . The soldiers who did survive were the greenest, and have deserted. . . . A whole legion of propertied Marsi dead, and the nation of the Marsi has already lodged a protest with the Senate . . . claiming huge damages, in court if necessary. . . . The Samnites are furious too. . . ."

"Jupiter!" breathed Sulla, flopping back into his chair.

Marius read on to himself for a moment, murmuring a little too softly for Sulla to hear; then he made a most peculiar noise. Thinking Marius was about to have some sort of seizure, Sulla got quickly to his feet, but didn't have time to get around his desk before the reason came out.

"I—am—consul!" gasped Gaius Marius.

Sulla stopped in his tracks, face slack. "Jupiter!" he said again, could think of nothing else to say.

Marius began to read Rutilius Rufus's letter out loud to Sulla, for once beyond caring how much he stumbled as he sorted the squiggles into words.

"The day wasn't over before the People got the bit between their teeth. Manius Aquillius didn't even have time to resume his seat before all ten tribunes of the plebs were off their bench and streaming out the door toward the rostra, with what looked like half of Rome jammed into the Comitia well, and the other half filling the whole of the lower Forum. Of course the whole House followed the tribunes of the plebs, leaving Scaurus and our dear friend Piggle-wiggle shouting to nothing more than a couple of hundred capsized stools.

"The tribunes of the plebs convened the Plebeian Assembly, and within no time flat, two plebiscites were tabled. It always amazes me that we can manage to trot out something better phrased and drafted in the twinkling of an eye than we can after several months of everyone and his uncle having a go at it. Just goes to show that everyone and his uncle do little else than fragment good laws into bad.

"Cotta had told me that Caepio was on his way to Rome as fast as he could to get his version in first, but intended to keep his imperium by staying beyond the *pomerium* and having his son and his agents go to work on his behalf inside the city. That way, he thought he would be safe and snug with his imperium wrapped protectively around him until his version of events became the official version. I imagine he thought—and no doubt correctly—that he'd manage to have his governorship prorogued, and so retain his imperium and his tenure of Gaul-across-the-Alps for long enough to let the stench dissipate.

"But they got him, did the Plebs! They Voted overwhelmingly to strip Caepio of his imperium at once. So when he does reach the outskirts of Rome, he's going to find himself as naked as Ulysses on the beach at Scheria. The second plebiscite, Gaius Marius, directed the electoral officer—me—to enter your name as a candidate for the consulship, despite your inability to be present in Rome for the elections."

"This is the work of Mars and Bellona, Gaius Marius!" said Sulla. "A gift from the gods of war."

"Mars? Bellona? No! This is the work of Fortune, Lucius Cornelius. Your friend and mine, Lucius Cornelius. *Fortune!*"

He read on.

"The People having ordered me to get on with the elections, I had little choice but to do so.

"Incidentally, after the plebiscites were tabled, none other than Gnaeus Domitius Ahenobarbus—feeling a proprietary interest because he regards himself as the founder of our province of Gaul-across-the-Alps, I imagine—tried to speak from the rostra against the plebiscite allowing you to stand for consul *in absentia*. Well, you know how choleric that family are—arrogant lot of bad-tempered so-and-sos, all of them!—and Gnaeus Domitius was literally spitting with rage. When the crowd got fed up with him and shouted him down, he tried to shout the crowd down! I think being Gnaeus Domitius he had a fair chance of succeeding too. But something gave way inside his head or his heart, for he keeled over right there on the rostra as dead as last week's roast duck. It rather put a damper on things, so the meeting broke up and the crowd went home. The important work was done, anyway.

"The plebiscites were passed the next morning, without one dissenting tribe. Leaving me to get the elections under way. I let no grass grow beneath my feet, I can tell you. A polite request to the College of Tribunes of the Plebs got everything going. They polled the new college within days. A very likely-looking and superior lot stood too, I imagine because of matters like warring generals. We have the late lamented Gnaeus Domitius Ahenobarbus's elder son, and the late lamented Lucius Cassius Longinus's elder son. I gather Cassius is out to prove that not every member of his family is an irresponsible killer of Roman soldiers, so he ought to be good value as far as you're concerned, Gaius Marius. And Lucius Marcius Philippus got in, and—ho-hum!—a Clodius of the Very Many Claudius-Clodius brigade. Ye gods, how they do breed!

"The Centuriate Assembly polled yesterday, with the result that—as I said a few columns back—Gaius Marius was returned as senior consul by every single century in the First Class, plus all of the Second Class required to make up the numbers. Certain senior senators would have loved to destroy your chances, but you are far too well known as a patron of honor and sincere supporter of big business (especially after your scrupulous honoring of all your promises in Africa). The voting knights had no qualms of conscience about details such as running for consul a second time within three years, or standing for consul *in absentia*."

Marius looked up from the scroll exultantly. "How's that for a mandate from the People, Lucius Cornelius? Consul a second time, and I didn't even know I was standing!" He stretched his arms above his head as if reaching for the stars. "I shall bring Martha the prophetess to Rome with us. She shall see with her own eyes my triumph and my inauguration as consul on one and the same day, Lucius Cornelius! For I have just made up my mind. I'll triumph on New Year's Day."

"And we'll be off to Gaul," said Sulla, more interested in this development by far. "That is, Gaius Marius, if you will have me."

"My dear fellow, I couldn't do without you! Or without Quintus Sertorius!"

"Finish the letter," said Sulla, finding that he needed more time to assimilate all this staggering news before it became necessary to discuss it at length with Marius.

"So when I see you, Gaius Marius, it will be to hand over the trappings of my office to you. I wish I could say I was glad with every tiniest part of me. For Rome's sake, it was vital that you be given the German command, but oh, I wish it could have been done in a more orthodox way! I think of the enemies you will add to those you have already made, and my whole body quails. You have caused too many changes in the way our lawmaking machinery functions. Yes, I know every single one was necessary if you were to survive. But, as it was said by the Greeks about their Odysseus, the strand of his life was so strong it rubbed all the life-strands it crossed until they snapped. I think Marcus Aemilius Scaurus Princeps Senatus has some right on his side in this present situation, for I acquit him of the narrow-minded bigotry of men like Numidicus Piggle-wiggle. Scaurus sees the passing of the old way Rome operated, as indeed do I. And yes, I understand Rome is busy building its own funeral pyre, that if the Senate could be trusted to leave you alone to deal with the Germans in your own way and your own time, none of these startling, extraordinary, unorthodox, and novel measures would be necessary. But I grieve none-theless."

Marius's voice hadn't wavered, nor his decision to read it all out to Sulla, even though the conclusion was less satisfying, and took the keenest edge off his pleasure.

"There's a little more," he said. "I'll read it."

"Your candidacy, I must add in closing, frightened all of honor and repute away. Some decent fellows had got as far as putting their names up for consul, but they all withdrew. As did Quintus Lutatius Catulus Caesar, declaring he wouldn't work with you as his colleague any more than he would with his lapdog had it been elected. Consequently your colleague in the consulship is a man of straw. Which may not dismay you unduly, for he certainly won't give you any battles. I know you're dying to hear who he is, but grant me my little tittle! I would only say of him, he's venal, though I think you already know that about him. His name? Gaius Flavius Fimbria."

Sulla snorted. "Oh, I know him," he said. "A visiting thrill seeker in the stews of a Rome that was mine, not his. And as crooked as a dog's hind leg." The white teeth showed, not the striking sight they would have been in a face even a little darker. "Which means, Gaius Marius, don't let him cock that leg and piss on you."

"I shall leap very fast and well to the side," said Marius gravely. He stretched out his hand to Sulla, who took it at once. "A pledge, Lucius Cornelius. That we will beat the Germans, you and I."

The army of Africa and its commander sailed from Utica to Puteoli toward the end of November, in high fettle. The sea was calm for the time of year, and neither the North Wind, Septentrio, nor the Northwest Wind, Corus, disturbed their passage. Which was exactly what Marius expected; his career was in its ascendancy, Fortune was his to command as surely as his soldiers were. Besides, Martha the Syrian prophetess had predicted a quick smooth voyage. She was with Marius in his flagship, replete with honor and gummy cackles, an ancient bag of bones the sailors—a superstitious lot, always—eyed askance and avoided fearfully. King Gauda had not been keen to part with her; then she spat upon the marble floor in front of his throne and threatened to put the Evil Eye upon him and all his house. After that, he couldn't get rid of her fast enough.

In Puteoli, Marius and Sulla were met by one of the brand-new Treasury quaestors, very brisk and anxious to have the tally of booty, but very deferential too. It pleased Marius and Sulla to be graciously helpful, and as they were possessed of admirable account books, everyone was pleased. The army went into camp outside Capua, surrounded by new recruits being drilled by Rutilius Rufus's gladiatorial conscripts. Now Marius's skilled centurions were put to helping. The saddest part, however, was the scarcity of these new recruits. Italy was a dry well, and would be until the younger generation turned seventeen in sufficient numbers to swell the ranks once more. Even the Head Count was exhausted, at least among the Roman citizens.

"And I very much doubt if the Senate will condone my recruiting among the Italian Head Count," said Marius.

"They haven't much choice," said Sulla.

"True. *If* I push them. But right at the moment it's not in my interests—or Rome's interests—to push them."

Marius and Sulla were splitting up until New Year's Day. Sulla of course was free to enter the city, but Marius, still endowed with his proconsular imperium, could not cross the sacred boundary of the city without losing it. So Sulla was going to Rome, whereas Marius was going to his villa at Cumae.

Cape Misenum formed the formidable north headland of what was called Crater Bay, a huge and very safe anchorage dotted with seaports—Puteoli, Neapolis, Herculaneum, Stabiae, and Surrentum. A tradition so old it went back far before lore or memory held that once Crater Bay had been a gigantic volcano, which exploded and let the sea in. There was evidence of that volcanic activity, of course. The Fields of Fire lit up the night skies behind Puteoli sullenly as flames belched out of cracks in the ground, and mud pools boiled with sluggish plops, and vivid yellow encrustations of sulphur lay everywhere; vents roaring columns of steam popped up anywhere, and either closed up again or got bigger; and then there was Vesuvius—a rugged, almost sheer pinnacle of rock many thousands of feet high, said once to have been an active volcano—though no one knew when that might have been, for Vesuvius had slept peacefully throughout recorded history.

Two little towns lay one on either side of the narrow neck of Cape Misenum, along with a series of mysterious lakes. On the seaward side was Cumae, on the Crater Bay side was Baiae, and the lakes were of two kinds—one with water so pure and mildly warm it was perfect for growing oysters, one palpably hot and curling wisps of sulphur-tainted steam. Of all the Roman seaside resorts, Cumae was the most expensive, where Baiae was relatively undeveloped. In fact, Baiae seemed to be becoming a commercial fish-farming place, for half a dozen enthusiastic fellows were trying to devise a way to farm oysters, their leader the impoverished patrician aristocrat Lucius Sergius, who hoped to revive his family's fortunes by producing and shipping cultivated oysters to Rome's more affluent Epicureans and gastronomes.

Marius's villa stood atop a great sea cliff at Cumae and looked out toward the islands of Aenaria, Pandataria, and Pontia, three peaks with slopes and plains at ever-increasing distance, like mountaintops poking through a sheet of pale-blue mist. And here in Marius's villa, Julia waited for her husband.

It was over two and a half years since they had last seen each other; Julia was now almost twenty-four years old, and Marius was fifty-two. That she was desperately anxious to see him he knew, for she had come down from Rome to Cumae at a time of year when the seaside was squally and bitter, and Rome the most comfortable place to be. Custom forbade her traveling anywhere with her husband, especially if he was on any sort of official public business; she could not accompany him to his province, nor even on any of his journeys within Italy unless he formally invited her, and it was considered poor form to issue such invitations. In the summer, when a Roman nobleman's wife went to the seaside, he came down to join her whenever he could, but they made their journeys separately; and if he fancied a few days on the farm or at one of his multiple villas outside Rome, he rarely took his wife with him.

Julia wasn't exactly apprehensive; she had written to Marius once a week throughout his time away, and he had written back just as regularly. Neither of them indulged in gossip, so their correspondence tended to be brief and purely filled with family matters, but it was unfailingly affectionate and warm. Of course it was none of her business whether he might have had other women during his time away, and Julia was far too well bred and well trained to contemplate inquiring; nor did she expect him to tell her of his own accord. Such things were a part of the realm of men, and had nothing to do with wives. In that respect, as her mother, Marcia, had been careful to tell her, she was very lucky to be married to a man thirty years older than she was; for his sexual appetites—said Marcia—would be more continent than those of a younger man, just as his pleasure in seeing his wife again would be greater than that of a younger man.

But she had missed him acutely, not merely because she loved him, but also because he pleased her. In fact, she *liked* him, and that liking made the separations harder to bear, for she missed her friend as much as she missed her husband and lover.

When he walked into her sitting room unannounced, she got clumsily to her feet only to find that her knees would not support her, and collapsed back into her chair. How tall he was! How brown and fit and full of life! He didn't look a day older—rather, he looked younger than she remembered. There was a wide white smile for her—his teeth were as good as ever—those fabulously lush eyebrows were glittering with points of light from the dark eyes hidden beneath them, and his big, well-shaped hands were stretched out to her. And she unable to move! What would he think?

He thought kindly, it seemed, for he walked across to her chair and drew her gently to her feet, not making any move to embrace her, merely standing looking down at her with that big wide white smile. Then he put his hands up to cup her face between them, and tenderly kissed her eyelids, her cheeks, her lips. Her arms stole round him; she leaned into him and buried her face in his shoulder.

"Oh, Gaius Marius, I am so glad to see you!" she said.

"No gladder than I to see you, wife." His hands stroked her back, and she could feel them trembling.

She lifted her face. "Kiss me, Gaius Marius! Kiss me properly!"

And so their meeting was everything each of them had looked forward to, warm with love, fraught with passion. Not only that; there was the delicious delight of Young Marius, and the private sorrow both parents could now indulge for the death of their second boy.

Much to his father's gratified surprise, Young Marius was magnificent—tall, sturdy, moderately fair in coloring, and with a pair of large grey eyes which assessed his father fearlessly. Insufficient discipline had been administered, Marius suspected, but all that would change. A father, the scamp would soon discover, was not someone to be dominated and manipulated; a father was someone to reverence and respect, just as he, Gaius Marius, reverenced and respected his own dear father.

There were other sorrows than the dead second son; Julia he knew had lost her father, but he now learned through Julia's sensitive telling that his own father was dead. Not before due time, and not until after the elections which had seen his oldest son become consul for the second time in such amazing circumstances. His death had been swift and merciful, a stroke that happened while the old man was busy talking to friends about the welcome Arpinum was going to put on for its most splendid citizen.

Marius put his face between Julia's breasts and wept, and was comforted, and afterward was able to see that everything happened at the right moment. For his mother, Fulcinia, had died seven years before, and his father had been lonely; if Fortune had not been kind enough to permit him the sight of his son again, the goddess had at least permitted him to know of his son's extraordinary distinction.

"So there's no point in my going to Arpinum," said Marius to Julia later. "We'll stay right here, my love."

"Publius Rutilius is coming down soon. After the new tribunes of the plebs settle a bit, he said. I think he fears they may prove a difficult lot—some of them are very clever."

"Then until Publius Rutilius arrives, my dearest, sweetest, most beautiful and darling wife, we won't even think about exasperating things like politics."

Sulla's homecoming was very different. For one thing, he journeyed toward it with none of Marius's simple, unconcealed, eager pleasure. Though why that should be, he didn't want to know, for, like Marius, he had been sexually continent during his two years in the African province—admittedly for reasons other than love of his wife, yet continent nevertheless. The brand-new and pristine page with which he had covered up his old life must never be sullied; no graft, no disloyalty to his superior, no intriguing or maneuvering for power, no intimations of fleshly weaknesses, no lessening of his Cornelian honor or *dignitas*.

An actor to the core, he had thrown himself absolutely into the new role his term as Marius's quaestor had given him, lived it inside his mind as well as in all his actions, looks, words. So far it hadn't palled, for it had offered him constant diversion, enormous challenges, and a huge satisfaction. Unable to commission his own *imago* in wax until he became consul, or sufficiently famous or distinguished in some other way to warrant it, he could still look forward to commissioning Magius of the Velabrum to make a splendid mounting for his war trophies, his Gold Crown and *phalerae* and torcs, and look forward to being there supervising the installation of this testament to his prowess in the atrium of his house. For the years in Africa had been a vindication; though he would never turn into one of the world's great equestrians, he *had* turned into one of the world's natural soldiers, and the Magius trophy in his atrium would stand there to tell Rome of this fact.

And yet . . . everything from the old life was there just the same, and he knew it. The yearning to see Metrobius, the love of grotesquery—of dwarves and transvestites and raddled old whores and outrageous characters—the intractable dislike of women using their powers to dominate him, the capacity to snuff out a life when intolerably threatened, the unwillingness to suffer fools, the gnawing, consuming ambition . . . The actor's African theatrical run was over, but he wasn't looking at a prolonged rest; the future held many parts. And yet . . . Rome was the stage upon which his old self had postured; Rome spelled anything from ruin to frustration to discovery. So he journeyed toward Rome in wary mood, aware of the profound changes in himself, but also aware that very little had actually changed. The actor between parts, never a truly comfortable creature.

And Julilla waited for him very differently than Julia waited for Marius, sure that she loved Sulla far more than Julia loved Marius. To Julilla, any evidence whatsoever of discipline or self-control was proof positive of an inferior brand of love; love of the highest order should overwhelm, invade, shake down the spiritual walls, drive out all vestige of rational thought, roar tempestuously, trample down everything in its path as if some vast elephant. So she waited feverishly, unable to settle to anything other than the wine flask, her costume changed several times a day, her hair now up, now down, now sideways, her servants driven mad.

And all this she threw over Sulla like a pall woven from the most clinging and tentacular cobwebs. When he walked into the atrium, she was there running wildly across the room to him, arms outstretched, face transfigured; before he could look at her or collect himself to feel anything, she had glued her mouth to his like a leech on an arm, sucking, devouring, wriggling, wet, all blood and blackness. Her hands were groping after his genitals, she made noises of the most lascivious pleasure, then she actually began to wind her legs about him as he stood in that most unprivate place, watched by the derisive eyes of a dozen slaves, most of whom were total strangers to him.

He couldn't help himself; his hands came up and wrenched her arms down, his head went back and ripped her mouth away.

"Recollect yourself, madam!" he said. "We are *not* alone!"

She gasped as if he had spat in her face, but it sobered her into conducting herself more sedately; with pitifully casual artlessness she linked her arm through his and walked with him to the peristyle, then down to where her sitting room was, in Nicopolis's old suite of rooms.

"Is this private enough?" she asked, a little spitefully.

But the mood had been spoiled for him long before this spurt of spite; he didn't want her mouth or her hands probing their way into the most sequestered corners of his being without regard for the sensitivity of the layers they pierced.

"Later, later!" he said, moving to a chair.

She stood, poor frightened and bewildered Julilla, as if her world had ended. More beautiful than ever, but in a most frail and brittle way, from the sticklike arms poking out of what he recognized at once as draperies in the height of fashion—a man with Sulla's background never lost his instinct for line or style—to the enormous, slightly mad-looking eyes sunk deep into their orbits amid dense blue-black shadows.

"I—don't—understand!" she cried to him then, not daring to move from where she stood, her gaze drinking him in not avidly anymore, but rather as the mouse drinks in the smile on the face of the cat: are you friend or enemy?

"Julilla," he said with what patience he could muster, "I am tired. I haven't had time to regain my land legs. I hardly know any of the faces in this house. And since I'm not in the least drunk, I have all a sober man's inhibitions about the degree of physical license a married couple should allow themselves in public."

"But I *love* you!" she protested.

"So I should hope. Just as I love you. Even so, there are boundaries," he said stiffly, wanting everything within his Roman sphere to be exactly right, from wife and domicile to Forum career.

When he had thought of Julilla during his two years away, he hadn't honestly remembered what sort of *person* she was—only how she looked, and how frantically, excitingly passionate she was in their bed. In fact, he had thought of her as a man thought of his mistress, not his wife. Now he stared at the young woman who was his wife, and decided she would make a far more satisfactory mistress—someone he visited upon his terms, didn't have to share his home with, didn't have to introduce to his friends and associates.

I ought never to have married her, he thought. I got carried away by a vision of my future seen through the medium of her eyes—for that was all she did, serve as a vessel to pass a vision through on its way from Fortune to Fortune's chosen one. I didn't stop to think that there would be dozens of young noblewomen available to me more suitable than a poor silly creature who tried to starve herself to death for love of me. That in itself is an excess. I don't mind excess—but not an excess I'm the object of. Only excess I'm the perpetrator of, thank you! *Why* have I spent my life tangled up with women who want to suffocate me?

Julilla's face altered. Her eyes slid away from the two pale inflexible orbs dwelling upon her in a clinical interest holding nothing of love, or of lust. There! Oh, what would she do without it? Wine, faithful trusty wine . . . Without stopping to think what he might think, she moved to a side table and poured herself a full goblet of unwatered wine, and downed it in one draft; only then did she remember him, and turn to him with a question in her gaze.

"Wine, Sulla?" she asked.

He was frowning. "You put that away mighty quick! Do you normally toss your wine back like that?"

"I needed a drink!" she said fretfully. "You're being very cold and depressing."

He sighed. "I daresay I am. Never mind, Julilla. I'll improve. Or maybe you should—yes, yes, give me the wine!" He almost snatched the goblet she had been extending mutely for some moments and drank from it, but not at a gulp, and by no means the entire contents. "When last I heard from you—you're not much of a letter writer, are you?"

The tears were pouring down Julilla's face, but she didn't sob; just wept soundlessly. "I hate writing letters!"

"That much is plain," he said dryly.

"Anyway, what about them?" she asked, pouring herself a second goblet and drinking it down as quickly as her first.

"I was going to say, when last I heard from you, I thought we had a couple of children. A girl and a boy, wasn't it? Not that you bothered to tell me of the boy; I had to find that out from your father."

"I was ill," she said, still weeping.

"Am I not to see my children?"

"Oh, down there!" she cried, pointing rather wildly toward the back of the peristyle.

He left her mopping at her face with a handkerchief and back at the wine flagon to refill her empty goblet.

His first glimpse of them was through the open window of their nursery, and they didn't see him. A woman's murmuring voice was in the background, but she was invisible; all of his sight was filled with the two little people he had generated. A girl—yes, she'd be half past two now—standing over a boy—yes, he'd be half past one!

She was enchanting, the most perfect tiny doll he had ever seen—head crowned with a mass of red-gold curls, skin of milk and roses, dimples in her plump pink cheeks, and under soft red-gold brows, a pair of the widest blue eyes, happy and smiling and full of love for her little brother.

He was even more enchanting, this son Sulla had never seen. Walking—that was good—not a stitch of clothing on him—that was what his sister was on at him about, so he must do it often—and talking—he was giving his sister back as good as she was giving him, the villain. And he was laughing. He looked like a Caesar—the same long attractive face, the same thick gold hair, the same vivid blue eyes as Sulla's dead father-in-law.

And the dormant heart of Lucius Cornelius Sulla didn't just awaken with a leisurely stretch and a yawn, it leaped into the world of feeling as Athene must have leaped fully grown and fully armed from the brow of Zeus, clanging and calling a clarion. In the doorway he went down on his knees and held out both arms to them, eyes shimmering.

"*Tata* is here," he said. "*Tata* has come home."

They didn't even hesitate, let alone shrink away, but ran into the circle of his arms and covered his rapt face with kisses.

Publius Rutilius Rufus turned out not to be the first magistrate to visit Marius at Cumae; the returned hero had scarcely settled into a routine when his steward came inquiring if he would see the noble Lucius Marcius Philippus. Curious as to what Philippus wanted—for he had never met the man, and knew the family only in the most cursory way—Marius bade his man bring the visitor into his study.

Philippus didn't prevaricate; he got straight to the reason for his call. A rather soft-looking fellow, thought Marius—too much flabby flesh around his waist, too much jowl beneath his chin—but with all the arrogance and self-assurance of the Marcius clan, who claimed descent from Ancus Marcius, the fourth King of Rome, and builder of the Wooden Bridge.

"You don't know me, Gaius Marius," he said, his dark brown eyes looking directly into Marius's own, "so I thought I would take the earliest opportunity to rectify the omission—given that you *are* next year's senior consul, and that I am a newly elected tribune of the plebs."

"How nice of you to want to rectify the omission," said Marius, his smile devoid of any irony.

"Yes, I suppose it is," said Philippus blandly. He sat back in his chair and crossed his legs, an affectation Marius had never cared for, deeming it unmasculine.

"What may I do for you, Lucius Marcius?"

"Actually, quite a lot." Philippus poked his head forward, his face suddenly less soft, distinctly feral. "I find myself in a bit of financial bother, Gaius Marius, and I thought it behooved me to—shall we say—offer my services to you as a tribune of the plebs. I wondered, for instance, if there was a small trifle of legislation you'd like passed. Or perhaps you would just like to know that you have a loyal adherent among the tribunes of the plebs back in Rome while you're away keeping the German wolf from our door. Silly Germans! They haven't yet realized that Rome is a wolf, have they? But they will, I'm sure. If anyone can teach them the wolfish nature of Rome, you will."

The mind of Marius had moved with singular speed during this preamble. He too sat back, but didn't cross his legs. "As a matter of fact, my dear Lucius Marcius, there *is* a small trifle I'd like passed through the Plebeian Assembly with a minimum of fuss or attention. I would be delighted to assist you to extricate yourself from your financial bother if you can spare me any legislative bother."

"The more generous the donation to my cause, Gaius Marius, the less fuss or attention my law will receive," said Philippus with a broad smile.

"Splendid! Name your price," said Marius.

"Oh, dear! Such *bluntness!*"

"Name your price," Marius repeated.

"Half a million," said Philippus.

"Sesterces," said Marius.

"Denarii," said Philippus.

"Oh, I'd want a lot more than just a trifle of legislation for half a million denarii," said Marius.

"For half a million denarii, Gaius Marius, you will get a lot more. Not only my services during my tribunate, but thereafter as well. I do pledge it."

"Then we have a deal."

"How easy!" exclaimed Philippus, relaxing. "Now what is it I can do for you?"

"I need an agrarian law," said Marius.

"*Not* easy!" Philippus sat up straight, looking stunned. "What on this earth do you want a land bill for? I need money, Gaius Marius, but only if I am to live to spend what's left over after I pay my debts! It is no part of my ambitions to be clubbed to death on the Capitol, for I assure you, Gaius Marius, that a Tiberius Gracchus I am not!"

"The law is agrarian in nature, yes, but not contentious," said Marius soothingly. "I assure *you*, Lucius Marcius, that I am not a reformer or a revolutionary, and have other, better uses for the poor of Rome than to gift them with Rome's precious *ager publi-cus*! I'll enlist them in the legions—and make them work for any land I give them! No man should get anything for nothing, for a man is not a beast."

"But what other land is there to give away than the *ager publi-cus*? Unless you intend that the State should buy more of it? Or acquire more of it? But that means finding money," said Philip-pus, still very uneasy.

"There's no need to be alarmed," said Marius. "The land con-cerned is already in Rome's possession. While ever I retain my proconsular imperium over Africa, it is in my province to nomi-nate a use for land confiscated from the Enemy. I can lease it to my clients, or auction it to the highest bidder, or give it to some foreign king as a part of his domains. All I have to do is make sure the Senate confirms my dispositions."

Marius shifted, leaned forward, and continued. "But I have no intention of baring my arse for the likes of Metellus Numidicus to sink his teeth into, so I intend to go on as I have always gone on in the past—strictly according either to law, or general practice and precedent. Therefore on New Year's Day, I intend to yield up my proconsular imperium over Africa without giving Metellus Numidicus so much as a glance at my bare arse.

"All the main dispositions of territory I acquired in the name of the Senate and People of Rome have already been given sena-torial sanction. But there is one matter I do not intend to broach myself. It is a matter so delicate, in fact, that I intend to accom-plish my purpose in two separate stages. One this coming year, one the year after.

"Your job, Lucius Marcius, will be to implement the first stage. Briefly, I believe that if Rome is to continue fielding decent armies, then the legions must become an *attractive* career for a man of the Head Count, not just an alternative he is pushed to by patriotic zeal in emergencies, or boredom at other times. If he is offered the routine inducements—a small wage and a small share in whatever booty a campaign produces—he may not be attracted.

But if he is assured a piece of good land to settle on or sell up when he retires, the inducement to become a soldier is powerful. However, it cannot be land within Italy. Nor do I see why it should be land in Italy."

"I think I begin to see what you want, Gaius Marius," Philippus said, chewing at his full lower lip. "Interesting."

"I think so. I have reserved the islands in the Lesser Syrtis of Africa as places on which I can settle my Head Count soldiers after their discharge—which, thanks to the Germans, is not going to be for some time. This time I shall use to secure the People's approval for allocating land on Meninx and Cercina to my soldiers. But I have many enemies who will try to stop me, if for no other reason than that they've made whole careers out of trying to stop me," said Marius.

Philippus nodded his head up and down like a sage. "It is certainly true that you have many enemies, Gaius Marius."

Not sure that sarcasm underlay this remark, Marius gave Philippus a withering look, then went on. "Your job, Lucius Marcius, is to table a law in the Plebeian Assembly reserving the islands of the African Lesser Syrtis in the Roman *ager publicus* without lease or subdivision or sale unless by further plebiscites. You will not mention soldiers, and you will not mention the Head Count. All you have to do is—very casually and quietly—make sure that these islands are put into a storage cupboard well enough locked to keep greedy hands off them. It is vital that my enemies do not suspect that I am behind your little law."

"Oh, I think I can manage," said Philippus more cheerfully.

"Good. On the day that the law goes into effect, I will have my bankers deposit half a million denarii in your name in such a way that your change in fortune cannot be traced back to me," said Marius.

Philippus rose to his feet. "You have bought yourself a tribune of the plebs, Gaius Marius," he said, and held out a hand. "What is more, I shall continue to be your man throughout my political career."

"I'm glad to hear it," said Marius, shaking the hand. But as soon as Philippus had taken his leave, Marius sent for warm water, and washed both his hands.

"Just because I make use of bribery does not mean I have to like the men I bribe," said Gaius Marius to Publius Rutilius Rufus when he arrived in Cumae five days later.

Rutilius Rufus pulled a face of resignation. "Well, he was as true as his word," he said. "He authored your modest little agrarian law as if he'd thought of it all by himself, and he made it sound so logical that no one even argued for the sake of argument. Clever fellow, Philippus, in a slimy sort of way. Accorded himself laurels for patriotism by telling the Assembly that he felt some tiny, insignificant part of the great African land distribution ought to be saved—'banked' was the word he used!—for the Roman People's future. There were even those among your enemies who thought he was only doing it to irritate you. The law passed without a murmur."

"Good!" said Marius, sighing in relief. "For a while I can be sure the islands will be waiting for me, untouched. I need more time to prove the worth of the Head Count legionary before I dare give him a retirement gift of land. Can't you hear it now? The old-style Roman soldier didn't have to be bribed with a present of land, so why should the new-style soldier get preferential treatment?" He shrugged. "Anyway, enough of that. What else has happened?"

"I've passed a law enabling the consul to appoint extra tribunes of the soldiers without holding an election whenever a genuine emergency faces the State," said Rutilius.

"Always thinking of what tomorrow might bring! And have you picked any tribunes of the soldiers under your law?"

"Twenty-one. The same number who died at Arausio."

"Including?"

"Young Gaius Julius Caesar."

"Now that *is* good news! Relatives mostly aren't. Do you remember Gaius Lusius? Fellow my brother-in-law's sister Gratidia married?"

"Vaguely. Numantia?"

"That's him. Awful wart! But very rich. Anyway, he and Gratidia produced a son and heir, now aged twenty-five. And they're begging me to take him with me to fight the Germans. Haven't even met the sprog, but had to say yes all the same, otherwise my brother, Marcus, would never have heard the end of it."

"Speaking of your vast collection of relatives, you'll be pleased to know young Quintus Sertorius is at home in Nersia with his mother, and will be fit enough to go to Gaul with you."

"Good! As well Cotta went to Gaul *this* year, eh?"

Rutilius Rufus blew a rudely expressive noise. "I ask you, Gaius Marius! One ex-praetor and five backbenchers to form a delegation charged with reasoning with the likes of Caepio? But I knew my Cotta, where Scaurus and Dalmaticus and Pigglewiggle did not. I had no doubt that whatever could be salvaged out of it, Cotta would."

"And Cacpio, now he's back?"

"Oh, his chin's above water, but he's paddling mighty hard to stay afloat, I can tell you. I predict that as time goes on, he'll tire until only his nostrils are showing. There's a huge swell of public feeling running against him, so his friends on the front benches are unable to do nearly as much for him as they'd like."

"Good! He ought to be thrown into the Tullianum and left to starve to death," said Marius grimly.

"Only after hand-cutting the wood for eighty thousand funeral pyres," said Rutilius Rufus, teeth showing.

"What of the Marsi? Quietened down?"

"Their damages suit, you mean? The House threw it out of the courts, of course, but didn't make any friends for Rome in so doing. The commander of the Marsic legion—name's Quintus Poppaedius Silo—came to Rome intending to testify, and I'll bet you can't guess who was prepared to testify for him too," said Rutilius Rufus.

Marius grinned. "You're right, I can't. Who?"

"None other than my nephew—young Marcus Livius Drusus! It seems they met after the battle—Drusus's legion was next to Silo's in the line, apparently. But it came as a shock to Caepio when my nephew—who happens to be his son-in-law—put his name up to testify in a case which has direct bearing on Caepio's own conduct."

"He's a pup with sharp teeth," said Marius, remembering young Drusus in the law court.

"He's changed since Arausio," said Rutilius Rufus. "I'd say he's grown up."

"Then Rome may have a good man for the future," said Marius.

"It seems likely. But I note a marked change in all those who survived Arausio," said Rutilius Rufus sadly. "They've not yet succeeded in mustering all the soldiers who escaped by swimming the Rhodanus, you know. I doubt they ever will."

"I'll find them," said Marius grimly. "They're Head Count, which means they're my responsibility."

"That's Caepio's tack, of course," said Rutilius Rufus. "He's trying to shift the blame onto Gnaeus Mallius and the Head Count rabble, as he calls that army. The Marsi are not pleased at being labeled Head Count, nor are the Samnites, and my young nephew Marcus Livius has come out in public and sworn on oath that the Head Count had nothing to do with it. He's a good orator, and a better showman."

"As Caepio's son-in-law, how can he criticize Caepio?" Marius asked curiously. "I would have thought even those most against Caepio would be horrified at such lack of family loyalty."

"He's not criticizing Caepio—at least not directly. It's very neat, really. He says nothing about Caepio at all! He just refutes Caepio's charge that the defeat was due to Gnaeus Mallius's Head Count army. But I notice that young Marcus Livius and young Caepio Junior aren't quite as thick as they used to be, and that's rather difficult, since Caepio Junior is married to my niece, Drusus's sister," said Rutilius Rufus.

"Well, what can you expect when all you wretched nobles insist upon marrying each other's cousins rather than letting some new blood in?" Marius demanded, and shrugged. "But enough of that! Any more news?"

"Only about the Marsi, or rather, the Italian Allies. Feelings are running high against us, Gaius Marius. As you know, I've been trying to recruit for months. But the Italian Allies refuse to co-operate. When I asked them for Italian Head Count—since they insist they've no propertied men left of an age for service—they said they had no Head Count either!"

"Well, they're rural peoples, I suppose it's possible," said Marius.

"Nonsense! Sharecroppers, shepherds, migrating field workers, free farm laborers—when has any rural community not had plenty of their like? But the Italian Allies *insist* there is no Italian Head Count! Why? I asked them in a letter. Because, they said, any Italian men who *might* have qualified as Head Count were now all Roman slaves, mostly taken for debt bondage. Oh, it is very bitter!" said Rutilius Rufus gravely. "Every Italian nation has written in strong terms to the Senate protesting at its treatment by Rome—not just official Rome, mark you, but private Roman citizens in positions of power too. The Marsi—the Paeligni—the Picentines—the Umbrians—the Samnites—the Apulians—the Lucanians—the Etrurians—the Marrucini—the Vestini—the list is complete, Gaius Marius!"

"Well, we've known there's trouble brewing for a long time," said Marius. "My hope is that the common threat of the Germans knits up our rapidly unraveling peninsula."

"I don't think it will," said Rutilius Rufus. "All the nations say that Rome has taken to keeping their propertied men away from home so long that their farms or businesses have fallen into bankruptcy from inadequate care, and all the men lucky enough to have survived a career fighting for Rome have come home to find themselves in debt to Roman landowners or local businessmen with the Roman citizenship. Thus, they say, Rome already owns their Head Count—as slaves scattered from one end of the Middle

Sea to the other! Particularly, they say, where Rome needs slaves with agricultural skills—Africa, Sardinia, Sicily."

Marius began to look equally uneasy. "I had no idea things had come to such a pass," he said. "I own a lot of land in Etruria myself, and it includes many farms confiscated for debt. But what else can one do? If *I* didn't buy the farms, Piggle-wiggle or his brother, Dalmaticus, would! I inherited estates in Etruria from my mother Fulcinia's family, which is why I've concentrated on Etruria. But there's no getting away from the fact that I'm a big landowner there."

"And I'll bet you don't even know what your agents did about the men whose farms you confiscated," said Rutilius.

"You're right, I don't," said Marius, looking uncomfortable. "I had no idea there were so many Italians enslaved to us. It's like enslaving Romans!"

"Well, we do that too when Romans fall into debt."

"Less and less, Publius Rutilius!"

"True."

"I shall see to the Italian complaint the moment I'm in office," said Gaius Marius with decision.

Italian dissatisfaction hovered darkly in the background that December, its nucleus the warlike tribes of the central highlands behind the Tiber and Liris valleys, led by the Marsi and the Samnites. But there were other rumblings as well, aimed more at the privileges of the Roman nobility, and generated by other Roman nobles.

The new tribunes of the plebs were very active indeed. Smarting because his father was one of those incompetent generals held in such odium at the moment, Lucius Cassius Longinus tabled a startling law for discussion in a *contio* meeting of the Plebeian Assembly. All those men whom the Assembly had stripped of their imperium must also lose their seats in the Senate. That was declaring war upon Caepio with a vengeance! For of course it was generally conceded that Caepio, if and when tried for treason under the present system, would be acquitted. Thanks to his power and wealth, he held too many knights in the First and Second Classes in his sway not to be acquitted. But the Plebeian Assembly law stripping him of his seat in the Senate was something quite different. And fight back though Metellus Numidicus and his colleagues did, the bill proceeded on its way toward becoming law. Lucius Cassius was not going to share his father's odium.

And then the religious storm broke, burying all other considerations under its fury; since it had its funny side, this was inevitable, given the Roman delight in the ridiculous. When Gnaeus Domitius Ahenobarbus had dropped dead on the rostra during the row about Gaius Marius's standing for the consulship *in absentia,* he left one loose end behind that it was not in his power to tie up. He was a *pontifex,* a priest of Rome, and his death left a vacancy in the College of Pontifices. At the time, the Pontifex Maximus was the ageing Lucius Caecilius Metellus Dalmaticus, and among the priests were Marcus Aemilius Scaurus Princeps Senatus, and Publius Licinius Crassus, and Scipio Nasica.

New priests were co-opted by the surviving members of the college, a plebeian being replaced by a plebeian, and a patrician by a patrician; the colleges of priests and of augurs normally stood at half-plebeian, half-patrician. According to tradition, the new priest would belong to the same family as the dead priest, thus enabling priesthoods and augurships to pass from father to son, or uncle to nephew, or cousin to cousin. The family honor and *dignitas* had to be preserved. And naturally Gnaeus Domitius Ahenobarbus Junior, now the head of his branch of the family, expected to be asked to take his father's place as a priest.

However, there was a problem, and the problem's name was Scaurus. When the College of Pontifices met to co-opt its new member, Scaurus announced that he was not in favor of giving the dead Ahenobarbus's place to his son. One of his reasons he did not mention aloud, though it underlay everything he said, and loomed equally large in the minds of the thirteen priests who listened to him; namely, that Gnaeus Domitius Ahenobarbus had been a pigheaded, argumentative, irascible, and unlikable man, and had sired a son who was even worse. No Roman nobleman minded the idiosyncrasies of his peers, and every Roman nobleman was prepared to put up with quite a gamut of the less admirable character traits; provided, that is, that he could get away from these fellows. But the priestly colleges were close-knit and met within the cramped confines of the Regia, the little office of the Pontifex Maximus—and young Ahenobarbus was only thirty-three years old. To those like Scaurus who had suffered his father for many years, the idea of suffering the son was not at all attractive. And, as luck would have it, Scaurus had two valid reasons to offer his fellow priests when moving that the new place not go to young Ahenobarbus.

The first was that when Marcus Livius Drusus the censor had died, his priesthood had not gone to his son, nineteen at the time. This had been felt to be just a little too underage. The second was that young Marcus Livius Drusus was suddenly displaying alarming tendencies to abandon his natural inheritance of intense conservatism; Scaurus felt that if he was given his father's priesthood, it would draw him back into the fold of his tradition-bound ancestors. His father had been an obdurate enemy of Gaius Gracchus, yet the way young Drusus was carrying on in the Forum Romanum, he sounded more like Gaius Gracchus! There were extenuating circumstances, Scaurus argued, particularly the shock of Arausio. So, what nicer and better way could there be than to co-opt young Drusus into his father's priestly college?

The thirteen other priests, including Dalmaticus Pontifex Maximus, thought this was a splendid way out of the Ahenobarbus dilemma, particularly because old Ahenobarbus had secured an augurship for his younger son, Lucius, not long before he died. The family could not therefore argue that it was utterly devoid of priestly clout.

But when Gnaeus Domitius Ahenobarbus the younger heard that his expected priesthood was going to Marcus Livius Drusus, he was not pleased. In fact, he was outraged. At the next meeting of the Senate he announced that he was going to prosecute Marcus Aemilius Scaurus Princeps Senatus on charges of sacrilege. The occasion had been the adoption of a patrician by a plebeian, this complicated affair needing a sanction from the College of Pontifices as well as the Lictors of the Thirty Curiae; young Ahenobarbus alleged that Scaurus had not attended to the requirements properly. Well aware of the real reason behind this sudden espousal of sacerdotal punctiliousness, the House was not a bit impressed. Nor was Scaurus, who simply got to his feet and looked down his nose at the puce-faced Ahenobarbus.

"Do you, Gnaeus Domitius—not even a *pontifex!*—accuse me, Marcus Aemilius, *pontifex* and Leader of the House, of *sacrilege?*" asked Scaurus in freezing tones. "Run away and play with your new toys in the Plebeian Assembly until you finally grow up!"

And that seemed the end of the matter. Ahenobarbus flounced out of the House amid roars of laughter, catcalls, cries of "Sore loser!"

But Ahenobarbus wasn't beaten yet. Scaurus had told him to run away and play with his new toys in the Plebeian Assembly, so that was precisely what he would do! Within two days he had tabled a new bill, and before the old year was done he had pushed it through the discussion and voting processes into formal law. In future, new members for priesthoods and for augurships would not be co-opted by the surviving members, said the *lex Domitia de sacerdotiis;* they would be elected by a special tribal assembly, and anyone would be able to stand.

"Ducky," said Metellus Dalmaticus Pontifex Maximus to Scaurus. "Just ducky!"

But Scaurus only laughed and laughed. "Oh, Lucius Caecilius, admit he's twisted our pontifical tails beautifully!" he said, wiping his eyes. "I like him the better for it, I must say."

"The next one of us to pop off, he's going to be running for election," said Dalmaticus Pontifex Maximus gloomily.

"And why not? He's earned it," said Scaurus.

"But what if it's me? He'd be Pontifex Maximus as well!"

"What a wonderful comeuppance for all of us that would be!" said Scaurus, impenitent.

"I hear he's after Marcus Junius Silanus now," said Metellus Numidicus.

"That's right, for illegally starting a war with the Germans in Gaul-across-the-Alps," said Dalmaticus Pontifex Maximus.

"Well, he can have the Plebeian Assembly try Silanus for that, where a treason charge means going to the Centuries," said Scaurus, and whistled. "He's good, you know! I begin to regret that we didn't co-opt him to take his father's place."

"Oh, rubbish, you do not!" said Metellus Numidicus. "You are enjoying every moment of this ghastly fiasco."

"And why shouldn't I?" asked Scaurus, feigning surprise. "This is *Rome,* Conscript Fathers! Rome as Rome ought to be! All of us noblemen engaged in healthy competition!"

"Rubbish, rubbish, rubbish!" cried Metellus Numidicus, still seething because Gaius Marius would be consul very soon. "Rome as we know it is dying! Men elected consul a second time within three years and who weren't even present in Rome to show themselves in the *toga candida*—the Head Count admitted into the legions—priests and augurs elected—the Senate's decisions about who will govern what overturned by the People—the State paying out fortunes to field Rome's armies—New Men and recent arrivals running things—tchah!"

THE SEVENTH YEAR
(104 B.C.):

**In the Consulship of
Gaius Marius (II)
and
Gaius Flavius Fimbria**

THE EIGHTH YEAR
(103 B.C.):

**In the Consulship of
Gaius Marius (III)
and
Lucius Aurelius Orestes**

THE NINTH YEAR
(102 B.C.):

**In the Consulship of
Gaius Marius (IV)
and
Quintus Lutatius Catulus Caesar**

QUINTUS LUTATIUS CATULUS CAESAR

It had been left to Sulla to organize Marius's triumphal parade; he followed orders scrupulously despite his inner misgivings, these being due to the result of Marius's instructions.

"I want the triumph over and done with quick-smart," Marius had said to Sulla in Puteoli when they had first landed from Africa. "Up on the Capitol by the sixth hour of day at the very latest, then straight into the consular inaugurations and the meeting of the Senate. Rush through the lot, because I've decided it's the *feast* must be memorable. After all, it's my feast twice over, I'm a triumphing general as well as the new senior consul. So I want a first-class spread, Lucius Cornelius! No hard-boiled eggs and run-of-the-mill cheeses, d'you hear? Food of the best and most expensive sort, dancers and singers and musicians of the best and most expensive sort, the plate gold and the couches purple."

Sulla had listened to all this with a sinking heart. He will never be anything but a peasant with social aspirations, Sulla thought; the hurried parade and hasty consular ceremonies followed by a feast of the kind he's ordered is poor form. Especially that vulgarly splashy feast!

However, he followed instructions to the letter. Carts carrying clay tanks waxed inside to make them waterproof trundled trays of Baiae oysters and Campanian crayfish and Crater Bay shrimps into Rome, while other carts similarly fitted out trundled freshwater eels and pikes and bass from the upper reaches of the Tiber; a team of expert licker-fishermen were stationed around Rome's sewer outlets; fattened on a diet of honey cakes soaked in wine, capons and ducks, piglets and kids, pheasants and baby deer were sent to the caterers for roasting and stuffing, forcing and larding; a big consignment of giant snails had come from Africa with Marius and Sulla, compliments of Publius Vagiennius, who wanted a report on Roman gourmet reactions.

So Marius's triumphal parade Sulla kept businesslike and brisk, thinking to himself that when *his* triumph came, he'd make it so big it took three days to travel the ancient route, just like Aemilius Paullus. For to expend time and splendor upon a triumph was the mark of the aristocrat, anxious to have the people share in the treat; whereas to expend time and splendor upon the feast in the temple of Jupiter Optimus Maximus that followed was the mark of the peasant, anxious to impress a privileged few.

Nevertheless, Sulla succeeded in making the triumphal parade memorable. There were floats showing all the highlights of the African campaigns, from the snails of Muluchath to the amazing Martha the Syrian prophetess; she was the star of the pageant displays, reclining on a purple-and-gold couch atop a huge float arranged as a facsimile of Prince Gauda's throne room in Old Carthage, with an actor portraying Gaius Marius, and another actor filling Gauda's twisted shoes. On a lavishly ornamented flat-topped dray, Sulla caused all of Marius's personal military decorations to be carried. There were cartloads of plunder, cartloads of trophies consisting of enemy suits of armor, cartloads of important exhibits—all of these arranged so that the onlookers could see and exclaim over individual items—plus cartloads of caged lions, apes and bizarre monkeys, and two dozen elephants to walk flapping their vast ears. The six legions of the African army were all to march, but had to be deprived of spears and daggers and swords, carrying instead wooden staves wreathed in victory laurels.

"And pick up your heels and march, you *cunni!*" cried Marius to his soldiers on the scuffed sward of the Villa Publica as the parade was ready to move off. "I have to be on the Capitol by the sixth hour myself, so I won't be able to keep an eye on you. But no god will help you if you disgrace me—hear me, *fellatores?*"

They loved it when he talked to them obscenely; but then, reflected Sulla, they loved him no matter how he talked to them.

Jugurtha marched too, clad in his kingly purple robes, his head bound for the last time with the tasseled white ribbon called the diadem, all his golden jeweled necklaces and rings and bracelets flashing in the early sun, for it was a perfect winter's day, neither unspeakably cold nor inconveniently windy. Both Jugurtha's sons were with him, purple clad too.

When Marius had returned Jugurtha to Rome Jugurtha could hardly believe it, so sure had he been when he and Bomilcar quit Rome that he would never, never be back. The terracotta city of the brilliant colors—painted columns, vivid walls, statues everywhere looking so lifelike the observer expected them to start orating or fighting or galloping or weeping. Nothing whitely African about Rome, which did not build much in mud brick anymore, and never whitewashed its walls, but painted them instead. The hills and cliffs, the parklike spaces, the pencil cypresses and the umbrella pines, the high temples on their tall podiums with winged Victories driving four-horsed *quadrigae* on the very crests of the pediments, the slowly greening scar of the great fire on the Viminal and upper Esquiline. Rome, the city for sale. And what a tragedy, that he'd not been able to find the money to buy it! How differently things might have turned out, had he.

Quintus Caecilius Metellus Numidicus had taken him in, an honored houseguest who yet was not permitted to step outside the house. It had been dark when they smuggled him in, and there for months he had remained, disbarred from the loggia which overlooked the Forum Romanum and the Capitol, limited to pacing up and down the peristyle-garden like the lion he felt himself. His pride would not let him go to seed; every day he ran in one spot, he touched his toes, he shadowboxed, he lifted himself up until his chin touched the bough he had chosen as a bar. For when he walked in Gaius Marius's triumphal parade, he wanted them to admire him, those ordinary Romans—wanted to be sure they took him for a formidable opponent, not a flabby Oriental potentate.

With Metellus Numidicus he had kept himself aloof, declining to pander to one Roman's ego at the expense of another's—a great disappointment to his host, he sensed at once. Numidicus had hoped to gather evidence that Marius had abused his position as proconsul. That Numidicus got nothing instead was a secret pleasure to Jugurtha, who knew which Roman he had feared, and which Roman he was glad had been the one to beat him. Certainly Numidicus was a great noble, and had integrity of a sort, but as a man and a soldier he couldn't even reach up to touch Gaius Marius's bootlaces. Of course, as far as Metellus Numidicus was concerned, Gaius Marius was little better than a bastard; so Jugurtha, who knew all about bastardy, remained committed to Gaius Marius in a queer and pitiless comradeship.

On the night before Gaius Marius was to enter Rome in triumph and as consul for the second time, Metellus Numidicus and his speech-bereft son had Jugurtha and his two sons to dinner. The only other guest was Publius Rutilius Rufus, for whom Jugurtha had asked. Of those who had fought together at Numantia under Scipio Aemilianus, only Gaius Marius was absent.

It was a very odd evening. Metellus Numidicus had gone to enormous lengths to produce a sumptuous feast—for, as he said, he had no intention of eating at Gaius Marius's expense after the inaugural meeting of the Senate in the temple of Jupiter Optimus Maximus.

"But there's scarcely a crayfish or an oyster left to buy, or a snail, or anything extra-special," said Numidicus as they prepared to dine. "Marius cleaned the markets out."

"Can you blame him?" asked Jugurtha, when Rutilius Rufus would not.

"I blame Gaius Marius for everything," said Numidicus.

"You shouldn't. If you could have produced him from your own ranks of the high nobility, Quintus Caecilius, well and good. But you could not. *Rome* produced Gaius Marius. I don't mean Rome the city or Rome the nation—I mean Roma, the immortal goddess, the genius of the city, the moving spirit. A man is needed. A man is found," said Jugurtha of Numidia.

"There are those of us with the right birth and background who could have done what Gaius Marius has done," said Numidicus stubbornly. "In fact, it ought to have been me. Gaius Marius stole my imperium, and tomorrow is reaping my rewards." The faint look of incredulity on Jugurtha's face annoyed him, and he added, a little waspishly, "For instance, it wasn't really Gaius Marius who captured *you,* King. Your captor had the right birth and ancestral background—Lucius Cornelius Sulla. It could be said—and in the form of a valid syllogism!—that Lucius Cornelius ended the war, not Gaius Marius." He drew a breath, and sacrificed his own claim to pre-eminence upon the more logical aristocratic altar named Lucius Cornelius Sulla. "In fact, Lucius Cornelius has all the earmarks of a right-thinking, properly Roman Gaius Marius."

"No!" scoffed Jugurtha, aware that Rutilius Rufus was watching him fixedly. "He's a pard with very different spots, that one. Gaius Marius is *straighter,* if you know what I mean."

"I don't have the remotest idea what you mean," said Numidicus stiffly.

"I know exactly what you mean," said Rutilius Rufus, and smiled delightedly.

Jugurtha grinned the old Numantia grin at Rutilius Rufus. "Gaius Marius is a freak," he said, "a perfect fruit from an overlooked and ordinary tree growing just outside the orchard wall. Such men cannot be stopped or deflected, my dear Quintus Caecilius. They have the heart, the guts, the brains, and the streak of immortality to surmount every last obstacle set in their way. The gods *love* them! On them, the gods lavish all of Fortune's bounty. So a Gaius Marius travels straight, and when he is compelled to walk crookedly, his path is still straight."

"How right you are!" said Rutilius Rufus.

"Luh-Luh-Lucius Cor-Cor-Cornelius is buh-buh-buh-better!" young Metellus Piglet said angrily.

"No!" said Jugurtha, shaking his head for emphasis. "Our friend Lucius Cornelius has the brains . . . and the guts . . . and maybe the heart . . . but I don't think he has the streak of immortality inside his mind. The crooked way feels natural to him; he sees it as the straighter way. There's no war elephant about a man who's happier astride a mule. Oh, brave as a bull! In a battle, there's no one quicker to lead a charge, or form up a relief column, or dash into a gap, or turn a fleeing century around. But Lucius Cornelius doesn't hear Mars. Where Gaius Marius never not hears Mars. I presume, by the way, that 'Marius' is some Latin distortion of 'Mars'? The son of Mars, perhaps? You don't know? Nor do you want to know, Quintus Caecilius, I suspect! A pity. It's an extremely powerful-sounding language, Latin. Very crisp, yet rolling."

"Tell me more about Lucius Cornelius Sulla," said Rutilius Rufus, choosing a piece of fresh white bread and the plainest-looking egg.

Jugurtha was wolfing down snails, not having tasted one since his exile began. "What's to tell? He's a product of his class. Everything he does, he does well. Well enough that nine out of ten witnesses will never be able to fathom whether he's a natural at what he's doing, or just a very intelligent and thoroughly schooled unnatural. But in the time I spent with him, I never got a spark out of him that told me what was his natural bent—or his proper sphere, for that matter. Oh, he will win wars and run governments, of that I have no doubt—but never with the spirit side of his mind." The garlic-and-oil sauce was slicked all over the guest of honor's chin; he ceased talking while a servant scrubbed and polished shaven and bearded parts, then belched enormously, and continued. "He'll always choose expedience, because he's lacking in the sticking power only that streak of immortality inside the mind can give a man. If two alternatives are presented to Lucius Cornelius, he'll pick the one he thinks will get him where he wants to be with the least outlay. He's just not as thorough as Gaius Marius—or as clear-sighted, I suspect."

"Huh-huh-huh-how duh-duh-do you know so muh-muh-muh-much about Luh-Luh-Luh-Lucius Cornelius?" asked Metellus Piglet.

"I shared a remarkable ride with him once," said Jugurtha reflectively, using a toothpick. "And then we shared a voyage along the African coast from Icosium to Utica. We saw a lot of each other." And the way he said that made all the others wonder just how many meanings it contained. But no one asked.

The salads came out, and then the roasts. Metellus Numidicus and his guests set to again, and with relish, save for the two young princes Iampsas and Oxyntas.

"They want to die with me," Jugurtha explained to Rutilius Rufus, low-voiced.

"It wouldn't be countenanced," said Rutilius Rufus.

"So I've told them."

"Do they know where they're going?"

"Oxyntas to the town of Venusia, wherever that might be, and Iampsas to Asculum Picentum, another mystery town."

"Venusia's south of Campania, on the road to Brundisium, and Asculum Picentum is northeast of Rome, on the other side of the Apennines. They'll be comfortable enough."

"How long will their detention last?" Jugurtha asked.

Rutilius Rufus pondered that, then shrugged. "Hard to tell. Some years, certainly. Until the local magistrates write a report to the Senate saying they're thoroughly indoctrinated with Roman attitudes, and won't be a danger to Rome if they're sent home."

"Then they'll stay for life, I'm afraid. Better they die with me, Publius Rutilius!"

"No, Jugurtha, you can't say that with complete assurance. Who knows what the future holds for them?"

"True."

The meal went on through more roasts and salads, and ended with sweetmeats, pastries, honeyed confections, cheeses, the few fruits in season, and dried fruits. Only Iampsas and Oxyntas failed to do the meal justice.

"Tell me, Quintus Caecilius," said Jugurtha to Metellus Numidicus when the remains of the food were borne away, and unwatered wine of the best vintage was produced, "what will you do if one day another Gaius Marius should appear—only this time with all Gaius Marius's gifts and vigor and vision—and streak of immortality inside his mind!—wearing a patrician Roman skin?"

Numidicus blinked. "I don't know what you're getting at, King," he said. "Gaius Marius is Gaius Marius."

"He's not necessarily unique," said Jugurtha. "What would you do with a Gaius Marius who came from a patrician family?"

"He couldn't," said Numidicus.

"Nonsense, of course he could," said Jugurtha, rolling the superb Chian wine around his tongue.

"I think what Quintus Caecilius is trying to say, Jugurtha, is that Gaius Marius is a product of his class," said Rutilius Rufus gently.

"A Gaius Marius may be of any class," Jugurtha insisted.

Now all the Roman heads were shaking a negative in unison. "No," said Rutilius Rufus, speaking for the group. "What you are saying may be true for Numidia, or for any other world. But never true of Rome! *No* patrician Roman could ever think or act like Gaius Marius."

So that was that. After a few more drinks the party broke up, Publius Rutilius Rufus went home to his bed, and the inhabitants of Metellus Numidicus's house scattered to their various beds. In the comfortable aftermath of excellent food, wine, and company, Jugurtha of Numidia slept deeply, peacefully.

When he was woken by the slave appointed to serve his needs as valet about two hours before the dawn, Jugurtha got up refreshed and invigorated. He was permitted a hot bath, and great care was devoted to his robing; his hair was coaxed into long, sausagelike curls with heated tongs, and his trim beard curled and then wound about with strings of gold and silver, the clean-shaven areas of cheeks and chin scraped closely. Perfumed with costly unguents, the diadem in place, and all his jewelry (which had already been catalogued by the Treasury clerks, and would go to the dividing of the spoils on the Campus Martius the day after the triumph) distributed about his person, King Jugurtha came out of his chambers the picture of a Hellenized sovereign, and regal from fingertips to toes to top of head.

"Today," he said to his sons as they traveled in open sedan chairs to the Campus Martius, "I shall see Rome for the first time in my life."

Sulla himself received them amid what seemed a chaotic confusion lit only by torches; but dawn was breaking over the crest of the Esquiline, and Jugurtha suspected the turmoil was due only to the number of people assembled at the Villa Publica, that in reality a streamlined order existed.

The chains placed on his person were merely token; where in all Italy could a Punic warrior-king go?

"We were talking about you last night," said Jugurtha to Sulla conversationally.

"Oh?" asked Sulla, garbed in glittering silver cuirass and *pteryges,* silver greaves cushioning his shins, a silver Attic helmet crested with fluffy scarlet feathers, and a scarlet military cloak. To Jugurtha, who knew him in a broad-brimmed straw hat, he was a stranger. Behind him, his personal servant carried a frame upon which his decorations for valor were hung, an imposing enough collection.

"Yes," said Jugurtha, still conversationally. "There was a debate about which man actually won the war against me—Gaius Marius or you."

The whitish eyes lifted to rest on Jugurtha's face. "An interesting debate, King. Which side did you take?"

"The side of right. I said Gaius Marius won the war. His were the command decisions, his the men involved, including you. And his was the order which sent you to see my father-in-law, Bocchus." Jugurtha paused, smiled. "However, my only ally was my old friend Publius Rutilius. Quintus Caecilius and his son both maintained that you won the war because you captured me."

"You took the side of right," said Sulla.

"The side of right is relative."

"Not in this case," said Sulla, his plumes nodding in the direction of Marius's milling soldiers. "I will never have his gift of dealing with *them.* I have no fellow feeling for them, you see."

"You hide it well," said Jugurtha.

"Oh, they know, believe me," said Sulla. "He won the war, with them. My contribution could have been done by anyone of legatal rank." He drew a deep breath. "I take it you had a pleasant evening, King?"

"Most pleasant!" Jugurtha jiggled his chains, and found them very light, easy to carry. "Quintus Caecilius and his stammering son put on a kingly feast for me. If a Numidian was asked which food he would want the night before he died, he would always ask for snails. And last night I had snails."

"Then your belly's nice and full, King."

Jugurtha grinned. "Indeed it is! The right way to go to the strangler's loop, I'd say."

"No, that's *my* say," said Sulla, whose toothy grin was far darker in his far fairer face.

Jugurtha's own grin faded. "What do you mean?"

"I'm in charge of the logistics of this triumphal parade, King Jugurtha. Which means I'm the one to say how you die. Normally you'd be strangled with a noose, that's true. But it isn't regulation, there is an alternative method. Namely, to shove you down the hole inside the Tullianum, and leave you to rot." Sulla's grin grew. "After such a kingly meal—and especially after trying to sow discord between me and my commanding officer—I think it would be a pity if you weren't permitted to finish digesting your snails. So there will be no strangler's noose for you, King! You can die by inches."

Luckily his sons were standing too far away to hear; the King watched as Sulla flicked a salute of farewell to him, then watched as the Roman strode to his sons, and checked their chains. He gazed around at the panic all about him, the seething masses of servants doling out head wreaths and garlands of victory laurel leaves, the musicians tuning up their horns and the bizarre horse-headed trumpets Ahenobarbus had brought back from Long-haired Gaul, the dancers practising last-moment twirls, the horses snuffling and blowing snorting breaths as they stamped their hooves impatiently, the oxen hitched to carts in dozens with horns gilded and dewlaps garlanded, a little water donkey wearing a straw hat ludicrously wreathed in laurel and its ears poking up rampant through holes in the crown, a toothlessly raddled old hag with swinging empty breasts and clad from head to foot in purple and gold being hoisted up onto a pageant dray, where she spread herself on a purple-draped litter like the world's greatest courtesan, and stared stared stared straight down into his eyes with eyes like the Hound of Hades—surely she should have had three heads. . . .

Once it got going, the parade hustled. Usually the Senate and all the magistrates except the consuls marched first, and then some musicians, then dancers and clowns aping the famous; then there came the booty and display floats, after which came more dancers and musicians and clowns escorting the sacrificial animals and their priestly attendants; next came the important prisoners, and the triumphing general driving his antique chariot; and, in last place, the general's legions marched. But Gaius Marius changed the sequence around a bit, preceding his booty and his pageants and his floats, so that he would arrive on the Capitol and sacrifice his beasts in time to be inaugurated afterward as consul, hold the inaugural meeting of the Senate, and then preside at his feast in the temple of Jupiter Optimus Maximus.

Jugurtha found himself able to enjoy his first—and last— journey on foot through the streets of Rome. What mattered it how he died? A man had to die sooner or later, and his had been a most satisfying life, even if it had ended in defeat. He'd given them a good run for their money, the Romans. His dead brother, Bomilcar . . . He too had died in a dungeon, come to think of it. Perhaps fratricide displeased the gods, no matter how valid the reason. Well, only the gods had kept count of the number of his blood kin who had perished at his instigation, if not by his own hands. Did that lack of personal participation make his hands clean?

Oh, how tall the apartment buildings were! The parade jogged briskly into the Vicus Tuscus of the Velabrum, a part of the city stuffed with insulae, leaning as if they tried to embrace across the narrow alleys by falling on each other's bricky chests. Every window held faces, every face cheered, and he was amazed that they cheered for him too, urged him on to his death with words of encouragement and best wishes.

And then the parade skirted the edges of the Meat Market, the Forum Boarium, where the statue of naked Hercules Triumphalis was all decked out for the day in the general's triumphal regalia—purple-and-gold *toga picta,* palm-embroidered purple *tunica palmata,* the laurel branch in one hand and the eagle-topped ivory scepter in the other, and his face painted bright red with *minim.* The meaty business of the day was clearly suspended, for the magnificent temples on the borders of the huge marketplace were cleared of booths and stalls. There! The temple of Ceres, called the most beautiful in the entire city—and beautiful it was in a garish way, painted in reds and blues and greens and yellows, high on a podium like all Roman temples; it was, Jugurtha knew, the headquarters of the Plebeian Order, and housed their records and their aediles.

The parade now turned into the interior of the Circus Maximus, a greater structure than he had ever seen; it stretched the whole length of the Palatine, and seated about a hundred and fifty thousand people. Every one of its stepped wooden tiers was packed with cheering onlookers for Gaius Marius's triumphal parade; from where he walked not far in front of Marius, Jugurtha could hear the cheers swell to screams of adulation for the general. No one minded the hasty pace, for Marius had sent out his clients and agents to whisper to the crowds that he hurried because he cared for Rome; he hurried so he could leave all the quicker for Gaul-across-the-Alps and the Germans.

The leafy spaces and magnificent mansions of the Palatine were thronged with watchers too, above the level of the herd, safe from assault and robbery, women and nursemaids and girls and boys of good family mostly, he had been told. They turned out of the Circus Maximus into the Via Triumphalis, which skirted the far end of the Palatine and had rocks and parklands above it on the left, and on the right, clustering below the Caelian Hill, yet another district of towering apartment blocks. Then came the Palus Ceroliae—the swamp below the Carinae and the Fagutal— and finally a turn into the Velia and the downhill trip to the Forum Romanum along the worn cobbles of the ancient sacred way, the Via Sacra.

At last he would see it, the center of the world, just as in olden days the Acropolis had been the center of the world. And then he set eyes on it, the Forum Romanum, and was hugely disappointed. The buildings were little and old, and they didn't face a logical way, for they were all skewed to the north, where the Forum itself was oriented northwest to southeast; the overall effect was slipshod, and the whole place wore an air of dilapidation. Even the newer buildings—which did at least face the Forum at a proper angle—were not kept up well. In fact, the buildings along the way had been far more imposing, and the temples along the way bigger, richer, grander. The houses of the priests did sport fairly new coats of paint, admittedly, and the little round temple of Vesta was pretty, but only the very lofty temple of Castor and Pollux and the vast Doric austerity of the temple of Saturn were at all eye-catching, admirable examples of their kind. A drab and cheerless place, sunk down in a queer valley, damp and unlovely.

Opposite the temple of Saturn—from the podium of which the senior Treasury officials watched the parade—Jugurtha and his sons and those among his barons and his wives who had been captured were led out of the procession and put to one side; they stood to watch the lictors of the general, his dancers and musicians and censer bearers, his drummers and trumpeters, his legates, and then the chariot-borne general himself, remote and unrecognizable in all his regalia and with his *minim*-painted red face, pass by. They all went up the hill to where the great temple of Jupiter Optimus Maximus presented its pillared side to the Forum, for it too was skewed north-south. Its front looked south. South to Numidia.

Jugurtha looked at his sons. "Live long and live well," he said to them; they were going into custody in remote Roman towns, but his barons and his wives were going home to Numidia.

The guard of lictors who surrounded the King nudged his chains a little, and he walked across the crowded flags of the lower Forum, beneath the trees around the Pool of Curtius and the statue of the satyr Marsyas blowing his oboe, around the edge of the vast tiered well which saw meetings of the Tribes, and up to the start of the Clivus Argentarius. Above was the Arx of the Capitol and the temple of Juno Moneta, where the mint was housed. And there was the ancient shabby Senate House across the far side of the Comitia, and beyond it the small shabby Basilica Porcia, built by Cato the Censor.

But that was as far as his walk through Rome took him. The Tullianum stood in the lap of the Arx hill just beyond the Steps of Gemonia, a very tiny grey edifice built of the huge unmortared stones men all over the world called Cyclopean; it was only one storey high and had only one opening, a doorless rectangular gap in the stones. Fancying himself too tall, Jugurtha ducked his head as he came to it, but passed inside with ease, for it turned out to be taller than any mortal man.

His lictors stripped him of his robes, his jewels, his diadem, and handed them to the Treasury clerks waiting to receive them; a docket changed hands, officially acknowledging that this State property was being properly disposed of. Jugurtha was left only the loincloth Metellus Numidicus had advised him to wear, for Metellus Numidicus knew the rite. The fountainhead of his physical being decently covered, a man could go to his death decently.

The only illumination came from the aperture behind him, but by its light Jugurtha could see the round hole in the middle of the roundish floor. Down there was where they would put him. Had he been scheduled for the noose, the strangler would have accompanied him into the lower regions with sufficient helpers to restrain him, and when the deed was done, and his body tossed down into one of the drain openings, those who still lived would have climbed up a ladder to Rome and their world.

But Sulla must have found time to countermand the normal procedure, for no strangler was present. Someone produced a ladder, but Jugurtha waved it aside. He stepped up to the edge of the hole, then stepped into space without a sound issuing from his lips; what words were there to mark this event? The thud of his landing was almost immediate, for the lower cell was not deep. Having heard it, the escort turned in silence and left the place. No one lidded the hole; no one barred the entrance. For no one ever climbed out of the awful pit beneath the Tullianum.

Two white oxen and one white bull were Marius's share of the sacrifices that day, but only the oxen belonged to his triumph. He left his four-horse chariot at the foot of the steps up to the temple of Jupiter Optimus Maximus, and ascended them alone. Inside the main room of the temple he laid his laurel branch and his laurel wreaths at the foot of the statue of Jupiter Optimus Maximus, after which his lictors filed inside and their laurel wreaths too were offered to the god.

It was just noon. No triumphal parade had ever gone so quickly; but the rest of it—which was the bulk of it—was proceeding at a more leisurely pace, so the people would have plenty of time to see the pageants, floats, booty, trophies, soldiers. Now came the real business of Marius's day. Down the steps to the assembled senators came Gaius Marius, face painted red, toga purple and gold, tunic embroidered with palm fronds, and in his right hand the ivory scepter. He walked briskly, his mind bent upon getting the inauguration over, his costume a minor inconvenience he could endure.

"Well, let's get on with it!" he said impatiently.

Utter silence greeted this directive. No one moved, no one betrayed what he was thinking by an expression on his face. Even Marius's colleague Gaius Flavius Fimbria and the outgoing consul Publius Rutilius Rufus (Gnaeus Mallius Maximus had sent word that he was ill) just stood there.

"What's the matter with you?" Marius asked testily.

Out of the crowd stepped Sulla, no longer martial in his silver parade armor, but properly togate. He was smiling broadly, his hand outstretched, every inch of him the helpful and attentive quaestor.

"Gaius Marius, Gaius Marius, you've forgotten!" he cried loudly, reaching Marius and swinging him round with unexpected strength in his grip. *"Get home and change, man!"* he whispered.

Marius opened his mouth to argue, then he caught a secret look of glee on Metellus Numidicus's face, and with superb timing he put his hand up to his face, brought it down to look at its reddened palm. "Ye gods!" he exclaimed, face comical. "I do apologize, Conscript Fathers," he said as he moved toward them again. "I know I'm in a hurry to get to the Germans, but this is ridiculous! Please excuse me. I'll be back as soon as I possibly can. The general's regalia—even triumphal!—cannot be worn to a meeting of the Senate within the *pomerium*." And as he marched away across the Asylum toward the Arx, he called over his shoulder, "I thank you, Lucius Cornelius!"

Sulla broke away from the silent spectators and ran after him, not something every man could do in a toga; but he did it well, even made it look natural.

"I *do* thank you," said Marius to him when Sulla caught up. "But what on earth does it really matter? Now they've all got to stand around in the freezing wind for an hour while I wash this stuff off and put on my *toga praetexta!*"

"It matters to them," said Sulla, "and I do believe it matters to me too." His shorter legs were moving faster than Marius's. "You're going to need the senators, Gaius Marius, so *please* don't antagonize them any further today! They weren't impressed at being obliged to share their inauguration with your triumph, to start with. So don't rub their noses in it!"

"All right, all right!" Marius sounded resigned. He took the steps that led from the Arx to the back door of his house three at a time, and charged through the door so violently that its custodian fell flat on his face and started to shriek in terror. "Shut up, man, I'm not the Gauls and this is now, not three hundred years ago!" he said, and started to yell for his valet, and his wife, and his bath servant.

"It's all laid out ready," said that queen among women, Julia, smiling peacefully. "I thought you'd arrive in your usual hurry. Your bath is hot, everyone is waiting to help, so off you go, Gaius Marius." She turned to Sulla with her lovely smile. "Welcome, my brother. It's turned cold, hasn't it? Do come into my sitting room and warm yourself by the brazier while I find you some mulled wine."

"You were right, it is freezing," said Sulla, taking the beaker from his sister-in-law when she came back bearing it. "I've got used to Africa. Chasing after the Great Man, I thought I was hot, but now I'm perished."

She sat down opposite him, head cocked inquisitively. "What went wrong?" she asked.

"Oh, you are a *wife*," he said, betraying his bitterness.

"Later, Lucius Cornelius," she said. "Tell me what went wrong first."

He smiled wryly, shaking his head. "You know, Julia, I do love that man as much as I can love any man," he said, "but at times I could toss him to the Tullianum strangler as easily as I could an enemy!"

Julia chuckled. "So could I," she said soothingly. "It is quite normal, you know. He's a Great Man, and they're very hard to live with. What did he do?"

"He tried to participate in the inauguration wearing his full triumphal dress," said Sulla.

"Oh, my dear brother! I suppose he made a fuss about the waste of time, and antagonized them all?" asked the Great Man's loyal but lucid wife.

"Luckily I saw what he was going to do even through all that red paint on his face." Sulla grinned. "It's his eyebrows. After three years with Gaius Marius, anyone except a fool reads his mind from the antics of his eyebrows. They wriggle and bounce in code—well, you'd know, you're certainly no fool!"

"Yes, I do know," she said with an answering grin.

"Anyway, I got to him first, and yelled out something or other to the effect that he'd forgotten. Phew! I held my breath for a moment or two, though, because it was on the tip of his tongue to tell me to take a running jump into the Tiber. Then he saw Quintus Caecilius Numidicus just waiting, and he changed his mind. What an actor! I imagine everyone except Publius Rutilius was fooled into thinking he had genuinely forgotten what he was wearing."

"Oh, thank you, Lucius Cornelius!" said Julia.

"It was my pleasure," he said, and meant it.

"More hot wine?"

"Thank you, yes."

When she returned, she bore a plate of steaming buns as well. "Here, these just came out of the pot. Yeasty and filled with sausage. They're awfully good! Our cook makes them for Young Marius all the time. He's going through that dreadful stage where he won't eat anything he should."

"My two eat anything that's put in front of them," Sulla said, face lighting up. "Oh, Julia, they're lovely! I never realized anything living could be so—so—*perfect!*"

"I'm rather fond of them myself," said their aunt.

"I wish Julilla was," he said, face darkening.

"I know," said Julilla's sister softly.

"What *is* the matter with her? Do you know?"

"I think we spoiled her too much. Father and Mother didn't want a fourth child, you know. They'd had two boys, and when I came along they didn't mind a girl to round the family out. But Julilla was a shock. And we were too poor. So then when she grew up a little, everyone felt sorry for her, I think. Especially Mother and Father, because they hadn't wanted her. Whatever she did, we found an excuse for. If there was a spare sestertius or two, she got them to fritter away, and was never chided for frittering them away. I suppose the flaw was there all along, but we didn't help her to cope with it—where we should have taught her patience and forbearance, we didn't. Julilla grew up fancying herself the most important person in the world, so she grew up selfish and self-centered and self-excusing. We are largely to blame. But poor Julilla is the one who must suffer."

"She drinks too much," said Sulla.

"Yes, I know."

"And she hardly ever bothers with the children."

The tears came to Julia's eyes. "Yes, I know."

"What can I do?"

"Well, you *could* divorce her," said Julia, the tears now trickling down her face.

Out went Sulla's hands, smeared with the contents of a bun. "How can I do that when I'm going to be away from Rome myself for however long it takes to defeat the Germans? And she's the mother of my children. I *did* love her as much as I can love anyone."

"You keep saying that, Lucius Cornelius. If you love—you love! Why should you love any less than other men?"

But that was too near the bone. He closed up. "I didn't grow up with any love, so I never learned how," he said, trotting out his conventional excuse. "I don't love her anymore. In fact, I think I hate her. But she's the mother of my daughter and my son, and until the Germans are a thing of the past at least, Julilla is all they have. If I divorced her, she'd do something theatrical—go mad, or kill herself, or triple the amount of wine she drinks—or some other equally desperate and thoughtless alternative."

"Yes, you're right, divorce isn't the answer. She would definitely damage the children more than she can at present." Julia sighed, wiped her eyes. "Actually there are two troubled women in our family at the moment. May I suggest a different solution?"

"Anything, please!" cried Sulla.

"Well, my mother's the second troubled woman, you see. She isn't happy living with Brother Sextus and his wife and their son. Most of the trouble between her and my Claudian sister-in-law is because my mother still regards herself as the mistress of the house. They fight constantly. Claudians are headstrong and domineering, and all the women of that family are brought up to rather despise the old female virtues, where my mother is the exact opposite," Julia explained, shaking her head sadly.

Sulla tried to look intelligent and at ease with all this female logic, but said nothing.

Julia struggled on. "Mama changed after my father's death. I don't suppose any of us ever realized how strong the bond was between them, or how heavily she relied on his wisdom and his direction. So she's become crotchety and fidgety and fault finding—oh, sometimes intolerably critical! Gaius Marius saw how unhappy the situation was at home, and offered to buy Mama a villa on the sea somewhere so poor Sextus could have peace. But she flew at him like a spitting cat, and said she knew when she wasn't wanted, and may she be treated like an oath breaker if she gave up residence in *her* house. Oh, dear!"

"I gather you're suggesting that I invite Marcia to live with Julilla and me," said Sulla, "but why should this suggestion appeal to her when the villa by the sea didn't work?"

"Because she knew Gaius Marius's suggestion was simply a way of getting rid of her, and she's far too cantankerous these days to oblige poor Sextus's wife," said Julia frankly. "To invite her to live with you and Julilla is quite different. She would be living next door, for one thing. And for another, she'd be wanted. Useful. And she could keep an eye on Julilla."

"Would she want to?" Sulla asked, scratching his head. "I gather from what Julilla's said that she never comes to visit at all, in spite of the fact she's living right next door."

"She and Julilla fight too," said Julia, beginning to grin as her worry faded. "Oh, do they! Julilla only has to set eyes on her coming through the front door, and she orders her home again. But if *you* were to invite her to make her home with you, then Julilla can't do a thing."

Sulla was grinning too. "It sounds as if you're determined to make my house a Tartarus," he said.

Julia lifted one brow. "Will that worry you, Lucius Cornelius? After all, you'll be away."

Dipping his hands in the bowl of water a servant was holding out to him, Sulla lifted one of his own brows. "I thank you, sister-in-law." He got up, leaned over, and kissed Julia on the cheek. "I shall see Marcia tomorrow, and ask her to come and live with us. And I will be absolutely outspoken about my reasons for wanting her. So long as I know my children are being loved, I can bear being separated from them."

"Are they not well cared for by your slaves?" Julia asked, rising too.

"Oh, the slaves pamper and spoil them," said their father. "I will say this, Julilla acquired some excellent girls for the nursery. But that's to make them into slaves, Julia! Little Greeks or Thracians or Celts or whatever other nationality the nurserymaids might happen to be. Full of outlandish superstitions and customs, thinking first in other languages than Latin, regarding their parents and relatives as some sort of remote authority figures. I want my children reared *properly*—in the Roman way, by a Roman woman. It ought to be their mother. But since I doubt that will happen, I cannot think of a better alternative than their stout-hearted Marcian grandmother."

"Good," said Julia.

They moved toward the door.

"Is Julilla unfaithful to me?" he asked abruptly.

Julia didn't pretend horror or experience anger. "I very much doubt that, Lucius Cornelius. Wine is her vice, not men. You're a man, so you deem men a far worse vice than wine. I do not agree. I think wine can do your children more damage than infidelity. An unfaithful woman doesn't stop noticing her children, nor does she burn her house down. A drunken woman does." She flapped her hand. "The important thing is, let's put Mama to work!"

Gaius Marius erupted into the room, respectably clad in purple-bordered toga and looking every inch the consul. "Come on, come on, Lucius Cornelius! Let's get back and finish the performance before the sun goes down and the moon comes up!"

Wife and brother-in-law exchanged rueful smiles, and off went the two men to the inauguration.

Marius did what he could to mollify the Italian Allies. "They are not Romans," he said to the House on the occasion of its first proper meeting, on the Nones of January, "but they are our closest allies in all our enterprises, and they share the peninsula of Italy with us. They also share the burden of providing troops to defend Italy, and they have not been well served. Nor has Rome. As you are aware, Conscript Fathers, at the moment a sorry business is working itself out in the Plebeian Assembly, where the consular Marcus Junius Silanus is defending himself against a charge brought against him by the tribune of the plebs Gnaeus Domitius. Though the word 'treason' has not been used, the implication is clear: Marcus Junius is one of those consular commanders of recent years who lost a whole army, including legions of Italian Allied men.''

He turned to look straight at Silanus, in the House today because the Nones were *fasti*—days of holiday or business—and the Plebeian Assembly could not meet. "It is not my place today to level any kind of charge at Marcus Junius. I simply state a fact. Let other bodies and other men deal with Marcus Junius in litigation. I simply state a fact. Marcus Junius has no need to speak in defense of his actions here today because of me. I simply state a fact."

Deliberately he cleared his throat, the pause offering Silanus an opportunity to say something, anything; but Silanus sat in stony silence, pretending Marius didn't exist. "I simply state a fact, Conscript Fathers. Nothing more, nothing less. A fact is a fact."

"Oh, *do* get on with it!" said Metellus Numidicus wearily.

Marius bowed grandly, his smile wide. "Why, thank you, Quintus Caecilius! How could I not get on with it, having been invited to do so by such an august and notable consular as yourself?"

"'August' and 'notable' mean the same thing, Gaius Marius," said Metellus Dalmaticus Pontifex Maximus, with a weariness quite the equal of his younger brother's. "You would save this House considerable time if you spoke a less tautologous kind of Latin."

"I do beg the august and notable consular Lucius Caecilius's pardon," said Marius with another grand bow, "but in this highly democratic society of ours, the House is open to all Romans, even those—like myself—who cannot claim to be august and notable." He pretended to search his mind, the eyebrows meeting in hairy abandon across his nose. "Now where was I? Oh, yes! The burden the Italian Allies share with us Romans, of providing troops to defend Italy. One of the objections to providing troops raised in the current spate of letters from the magistrates of the Samnites, the Apulians, the Marsi, and others"—he took a sheaf of small rolls from one of his clerks and showed it to the House—"concerns the legality of our asking the Italian Allies to provide troops for campaigns outside the borders of Italy and Italian Gaul. The Italian Allies, august and notable Conscript Fathers, maintain that they have been providing troops—and losing many, many thousands of these troops!—for Rome's—and I quote the letters—'foreign wars'!"

The senators mumbled, rumbled.

"That allegation is completely unfounded!" snapped Scaurus. "Rome's enemies are also Italy's enemies!"

"I only quote the letters, Marcus Aemilius Princeps Senatus," said Marius soothingly. "We should all be aware of what is in them, for the simple reason that I imagine this House will shortly be obliged to receive embassages from all the Italian nations who have expressed their discontent in these very many letters."

His voice changed, lost its mildly bantering tone. "Well, enough of this skirmishing! We are living in a peninsula cheek by jowl with our Italian friends—who are not Romans, and never can be Romans. That they have been elevated to their present position of importance in the world is due purely to the great achievements of Rome and Romans. That Italian nationals are present in large numbers throughout the provinces and spheres of Roman influence is due purely to the great achievements of Rome and Romans. The bread on their tables, the winter fires in their cellars, the health and number of their children, they owe to Rome and Romans. Before Rome, there was chaos. Complete disunity. Before Rome, there were the cruel Etruscan kings in the north of the peninsula, and the greedy Greeks in the south. Not to mention the Celts of Gaul."

The House had settled down. When Gaius Marius spoke in serious vein everybody listened, even those who were his most obdurate enemies. For the Military Man—blunt and forthright though he was—was a powerful orator in his native Latin, and so long as his feelings were governed, his accent was not noticeably different from Scaurus's.

"Conscript Fathers, you and the People of Rome have given me a mandate to rid us—*and* Italy!—of the Germans. As soon as possible, I will be taking the propraetor Manius Aquillius and the valiant senator Lucius Cornelius Sulla with me as my legates to Gaul-across-the-Alps. If it costs us our lives, we will rid you of the Germans, and make Rome—*and* Italy!—safe forever. So much I pledge you, in my own name and in the names of my legates, and in the names of every last one of my soldiers. Our duty is sacred to us. No stone will be left unturned. And before us we will carry the silver eagles of Rome's legions and be victorious!"

The anonymous clusters of senators in the back of the House began to cheer and stamp their feet, and after a moment the front ranks of senators began to clap, even Scaurus. But not Metellus Numidicus.

Marius waited for silence. "However, before I leave, I must beg this House to do what it can to alleviate the concern of our Italian Allies. We can give no credence to these allegations that Italian troops are being used to fight in campaigns which do not concern the Italian Allies. Nor can we cease to levy the soldiers all the Italian Allies formally agreed per treaty to give us. The Germans threaten the whole of our peninsula, and Italian Gaul as well. Yet the dreadful shortage of men suitable to serve in the legions affects the Italian Allies as much as it affects Rome. The well has run dry, my fellow senators, and the level of the table feeding it will take time to rise. I would like to give our Italian Allies my personal assurance that so long as there is breath left in this un-august and un-notable body, never again will Italian—*or* Roman!—troops waste their lives on a battlefield. Every life of every man I take with me to defend my homeland I will treat with more reverence and respect than I do my own! So do I pledge it."

The cheers and the stamping of feet began again, and the front

ranks were quicker to start applauding. But not Metellus Numidicus. And not Catulus Caesar.

Again Marius waited for silence. "A reprehensible situation has
been drawn to my attention. That we, the Senate and People of
Rome, have taken into debt bondage many thousands of Italian
Allied men, and sent them as our slaves throughout the lands we
control around the Middle Sea. Because the majority of them have
farming backgrounds, the majority of them are currently working
out their debts in our grainlands of Sicily, Sardinia, Corsica, and
Africa. That, Conscript Fathers, is an injustice! If we do not en-
force slavery upon Roman debtors anymore, nor should we on our
Italian Allies. No, they are not Romans. No, they never can be
Romans. But they are our little brothers of the Italian Peninsula.
And no Roman sends his little brother into debt bondage."

He didn't give the few big grainland-owning senators time to
protest; he swept on to his peroration. "Until I can give our grainland farmers their source of labor back in the form of German
slaves, they must look for other labor than Italian debt slaves. For
we, Conscript Fathers, must today enact a decree—and the Assembly of the People must ratify that decree—freeing all slaves
of Italian Allied birth. We *cannot* do to our oldest and loyalest
allies what we do not do to ourselves. These slaves *must* be freed!
They must be brought home to Italy, and made to do what is their
natural duty to Rome—serve in Rome's auxiliary legions.

"I am told there is no *capite censi* population in any Italian nation anymore, because it is enslaved. Well, my fellow senators,
the Italian *capite censi* can be better employed than in working
the grainlands. We cannot field our traditional armies anymore,
for the men of property who served in them are either too old, too
young—*or too dead*! For the time being, the Head Count is our
only source of military manpower. My valiant African army—
entirely Roman Head Count!—has proved that the men of the
Head Count can be turned into superb soldiers. And, just as history has demonstrated that the propertied men of the Italian nations are not one iota inferior as soldiers to the propertied men of

Rome, so too will the next few years show Rome that the Head Count men of the Italian nations are not one iota inferior as soldiers to the Head Count men of Rome!"

He stepped down from the curule dais and walked to the middle of the floor. "I want that decree, Conscript Fathers! Will you give it to me?"

It had been supremely well done. Borne away on the force of Marius's oratory, the House stampeded to a Division, while Metellus Numidicus, Metellus Dalmaticus Pontifex Maximus, Scaurus, Catulus Caesar, and others shouted vainly to be heard.

"But how," asked Publius Rutilius Rufus as he and Marius strolled the few short paces to Marius's house after the Senate had been dismissed, "are you going to reconcile the grainland owners to this decree? You realize, I hope, that you're treading heavily on the toes of exactly that group of knights and businessmen you depend upon most for support. All the favors you doled out in Africa to these men will seem very hollow. Do you understand how many of the grain slaves are Italian? Sicily *runs* on them!"

Marius shrugged. "My agents are at work already; I'll survive. Besides which, just because I've been sitting down at Cumae for the last month doesn't say I've been idle. I had a survey done, and the results are highly informative, not to mention interesting. Yes, there *are* many thousands of Italian Allied grain slaves. But in Sicily, for instance, the vast majority of the grain slaves are Greeks. And in Africa I've sent to King Gauda for replacement labor when the Italians are freed. Gauda is my client; he doesn't have any choice but to do as I ask. Sardinia is the most difficult, for in Sardinia almost all the grain slaves are Italian. However, the new governor—our esteemed propraetor Titus Albucius—can be persuaded to do his level best in my cause, I'm sure."

"He's got a pretty arrogant quaestor in Pompey Cross-eyes from Picenum," said Rutilius Rufus dubiously.

"Quaestors are like gnats," said Marius contemptuously, "not experienced enough to head for parts unknown when a man starts clapping round his head."

"That's not a very complimentary observation to make about Lucius Cornelius!"

"He's different."

Rutilius Rufus sighed. "I don't know, Gaius Marius, I'm sure! I just hope it all turns out as you think it will."

"Old Cynic," said Marius affectionately.

"Old Skeptic, if you please!" said Rutilius Rufus.

Word came to Marius that the Germans showed no sign of moving south into the Roman province of Gaul-across-the-Alps, save for the Cimbri, who had crossed to the western bank of the Rhodanus and were keeping clear of the Roman sphere. The Teutones, said Marius's agent's report, were wandering off to the northwest, and the Tigurini-Marcomanni-Cherusci were back among the Aedui and Ambarri looking as if they never intended to move. Of course, the report admitted, the situation could change at any moment. But it took time for eight hundred thousand people to gather up their belongings, their animals, and their wagons, and start moving. Gaius Marius need not expect to see any Germans coming south down the Rhodanus before May or June. *If* they came at all.

It didn't really please Gaius Marius, that report. His men were excited and primed for a good fight, his legates were anxious to do well, and his officers and centurions had been toiling to produce a perfect military machine. Though Marius had known since landing in Italy the previous December that there was a German interpreter saying the Germans were at loggerheads with each other, he hadn't really believed they would not resume their southward progress through the Roman province. The Germans having annihilated an enormous Roman army, it was logical, natural, and proper for them to take advantage of their victory and move into the territory they had in effect won by force of arms. Settle in it, even. Otherwise, why give battle at all? Why emigrate? Why *anything*?

"They are a complete mystery to me!" he cried, chafing and frustrated, to Sulla and Aquillius after the report came.

"They're barbarians," said Aquillius, who had earned his place as senior legate by suggesting that Marius be made consul, and now was very eager to go on proving his worth.

But Sulla was unusually thoughtful. "We don't know nearly enough about them," he said.

"I just remarked about that!" snapped Marius.

"No, I was thinking along different lines. But"—he slapped his knees—"I'll go on thinking about things for a bit longer, Gaius Marius, before I speak. After all, we don't really know what we'll find when we cross the Alps."

"That one thing we do have to decide," said Marius.

"What?" asked Aquillius.

"Crossing the Alps. Now that we've been assured the Germans are not going to prove a threat before May or June at the very earliest, I'm not in favor of crossing the Alps at all. At least, not by the usual route. We're moving out at the end of January with a massive baggage train. So we're going to be slow. The one thing I'll say for Metellus Dalmaticus as Pontifex Maximus is that he's a calendar fanatic, so the seasons and the months are in accord. Have you felt the cold this winter?" he asked Sulla.

"Indeed I have, Gaius Marius."

"So have I. Our blood is thin, Lucius Cornelius. All that time in Africa, where frosts are short-lived, and snow is something you see on the highest mountains. Why should it be any different for the troops? If we cross through the Mons Genava Pass in winter, it will go very hard on them."

"After furlough in Campania, they'll need hardening," said Sulla unsympathetically.

"Oh, yes! But not by losing toes from frostbite and the feeling in their fingers from chilblains. They've got winter issue—but will the cantankerous *cunni* wear it?"

"They will, if they're made."

"You are determined to be difficult," said Marius. "All right then, I won't try to be reasonable—I'll simply issue orders. We are not taking the legions to Gaul-across-the-Alps by the usual route. We're going to march along the coast the whole long way."

"Ye gods, it'll take an eternity!" said Aquillius.

"How long is it since an army traveled to Spain or Gaul along the coast?" Marius asked Aquillius.

"I can't remember an occasion when an army has!"

"And there you have it, you see!" said Marius triumphantly. "That's why we're going to do it. I want to see how difficult it is, how long it takes, what the roads are like, the terrain—everything. I'll take four of the legions in light marching order, and you, Manius Aquillius, will take the other two legions plus the extra cohorts we've managed to scrape together, and escort the baggage train. If when they do turn south, the Germans head for Italy instead of for Spain, how do we know whether they'll go over the Mons Genava Pass into Italian Gaul, or whether they'll head—as they'll see it, anyway—straight for Rome along the coast? They seem to have precious little interest in discovering how our minds work, so how are they going to know that the quickest and shortest way to Rome is not along the coast, but over the Alps into Italian Gaul?"

His legates stared at him.

"I see what you mean," said Sulla, "but why take the whole army? You and I and a small squadron could do it better."

Marius shook his head vigorously. "No! I don't want my army separated from me by several hundred miles of impassable mountains. Where I go, my whole army goes."

So at the end of January Gaius Marius led his whole army north along the coastal Via Aurelia, taking notes the entire way, and sending curt letters back to the Senate demanding that repairs be made to this or that stretch of the road forthwith, bridges built or strengthened, viaducts made or refurbished.

"This is Italy," said one such missive, "and all available routes to the north of the peninsula and Italian Gaul and Liguria must be kept in perfect condition; otherwise we may rue the day."

At Pisae, where the river Arnus flowed into the sea, they crossed from Italy proper into Italian Gaul, which was a most peculiar area, neither officially designated a province nor governed like Italy proper. It was a kind of limbo. From Pisae all the

way to Vada Sabatia the road was brand-new, though work on it
was far from finished; this was Scaurus's contribution when he
had been censor, the Via Aemilia Scauri. Marius wrote to Marcus
Aemilius Scaurus Princeps Senatus:

> You are to be commended for your foresight, for I
> regard the Via Aemilia Scauri as one of the most sig-
> nificant additions to the defense of Rome and Italy
> since the opening-up of the Mons Genava Pass, and
> that is a very long time ago, considering that it was
> there for Hannibal to use. Your branch road to Der-
> tona is vital strategically, for it represents the only way
> across the Ligurian Apennines from the Padus to the
> Tyrrhenian coast—Rome's coast.
>   The problems are enormous. I talked to your engi-
> neers, whom I found to be a most able group of men,
> and am happy to relay to you their request that addi-
> tional funds be found to increase the work force on this
> piece of road. It needs some of the highest viaducts—not
> to mention the longest—I have ever seen, more indeed
> like aqueduct construction than road building. Luckily
> there are local quarry facilities to provide stone, but the
> pitifully small work force is retarding the pace at which
> I consider the work must progress. With respect, may I
> ask that you use your formidable clout to pry the money
> out of the House and Treasury to speed up this project?
> If it could be completed by the end of this coming sum-
> mer, Rome may rest easier at the thought that a mere
> fifty-odd miles of road may save an army several hun-
> dreds.

"There," said Marius to Sulla, "that ought to keep the old boy
busy and happy!"

"It will, too," said Sulla, grinning.

The Via Aemilia Scauri ended at Vada Sabatia; from that point
on there was no road in the Roman sense, just a wagon trail which

followed the line of least resistance through an area where very high mountains plunged into the sea.

"You're going to be sorry you chose this way," said Sulla.

"On the contrary, I'm glad. I can see a thousand places where ambush is possible, I can see why no one in his right mind goes to Gaul-across-the-Alps this way, I can see why our Publius Vagiennius—who hails from these parts—could climb a sheer wall to find his snail patch, and I can see why we need not fear that the Germans will choose this route. Oh, they might start out along the coast, but a couple of days of this and a fast horseman going ahead will see them turn back. If it's difficult for us, it's impossible for them. Good!"

Marius turned to Quintus Sertorius, who, in spite of his very junior status, enjoyed a privileged position nothing save merit had earned him.

"Quintus Sertorius, my lad, whereabouts do you think the baggage train might be?" he asked.

"I'd say somewhere between Populonia and Pisae, given the poor condition of the Via Aurelia," Sertorius said.

"How's your leg?"

"Not up to that kind of riding." Sertorius seemed always to know what Marius was thinking.

"Then find three men who are, and send them back with this," said Marius, drawing wax tablets toward him.

"You're going to send the baggage train up the Via Cassia to Florentia and the Via Annia to Bononia, and then across the Mons Genava Pass," said Sulla, sighing in satisfaction.

"We might need all those beams and bolts and cranes and tackle yet," said Marius. He smacked the backs of his fingers down on the wax to produce a perfect impression from his seal ring, and closed the hinged leaves of the tablet. "Here," he said to Sertorius. "And make sure it's tied and sealed again; I don't want any inquisitive noses poking inside. It's to be given to Manius Aquillius himself, understood?"

Sertorius nodded and left the command tent.

"As for this army, it's going to do a bit of work as it goes,"

Marius said to Sulla. "Send the surveyors out ahead. We'll make a reasonable track, if not a proper road."

In Liguria, like other regions where the mountains were pre-cipitous and the amount of arable land small, the inhabitants tended to a pastoral way of life, or else made a profession out of banditry and piracy, or like Publius Vagiennius took service in Rome's auxiliary legions and cavalry. Wherever Marius saw ships and a village clustered in an anchorage and deemed the ships more suited to raiding and boarding than to fishing, he burned both ships and village, left women, old men, and children behind, and took the men with him to labor improving the road. Mean-while the reports from Arausio, Valentia, Vienne, and even Lug-dunum made it increasingly clear as time went on that there would be no confrontation with the Germans this year.

At the beginning of June, after four months on the march, Marius led his four legions onto the widening coastal plains of Gaul-across-the-Alps and came to a halt in the well-settled coun-try between Arelate and Aquae Sextiae, in the vicinity of the town of Glanum, south of the Druentia River. Significantly, his baggage train had arrived before him, having spent a mere three and a half months on the road.

He chose his campsite with extreme care, well clear of arable land; it was a large hill having steep and rocky slopes on three sides, several good springs on top, and a fourth side neither too steep nor too narrow to retard swift movement of troops in or out of a camp atop the hill.

"This is where we are going to be living for many moons to come," he said, nodding in satisfaction. "Now we're going to turn it into Carcasso."

Neither Sulla nor Manius Aquillius made any comment, but Sertorius was less self-controlled.

"Do we need it?" he asked. "If you think we're going to be in the district for many moons to come, wouldn't it be a lot easier to billet the troops on Arelate or Glanum? And why stay here? Why not seek the Germans out and come to grips with them before they can get this far?"

"Well, young Sertorius," said Marius, "it appears the Germans have scattered far and wide. The Cimbri, who seemed all set to follow the Rhodanus to its west, have now changed their minds and have gone—to Spain, we must presume—around the far side of the Cebenna, through the lands of the Arverni. The Teutones and the Tigurini have left the lands of the Aedui and gone to settle among the Belgae. At least, that's what my sources say. In reality, I imagine it's anyone's guess."

"Can't we find out for certain?" asked Sertorius.

"How?" asked Marius. "The Gauls have no cause to love us, and it's upon the Gauls we have to rely for our information. That they've given it to us so far is simply because they don't want the Germans in their midst either. But on one thing you can rely: when the Germans reach the Pyrenees, they'll turn back. And I very much doubt that the Belgae will want them any more than the Celtiberians of the Pyrenees. Looking at a possible target from the German point of view, I keep coming back to Italy. So here we stay until the Germans arrive, Quintus Sertorius. I don't care if it takes years."

"If it takes years, Gaius Marius, our army will grow soft, and you will be ousted from the supreme command," Manius Aquillius pointed out.

"Our army is not going to grow soft, because I am going to put it to work," said Marius. "We have close to forty thousand men of the Head Count. The State pays them; the State owns their arms and armor; the State feeds them. When they retire, I shall see to it that the State looks after them in their old age. But while they serve in the State's army, they are nothing more nor less than employees of the State. As consul, I represent the State. Therefore they are my employees. And they are costing me a very large amount of money. If all they are required to do in return is sit on their arses waiting to fight a battle, compute the enormity of the cost of that battle when it finally comes." The eyebrows were jiggling up and down fiercely. "They didn't sign a contract to sit on their arses waiting for a battle, they enlisted in the army of the State to do whatever the State requires of them. Since the State is paying them, they owe the State work. And that's what they're going to do. *Work!* This year they're going to repair the Via Domitia all the way from Nemausus to Ocelum. Next year they're going to dig a ship canal all the way from the sea to the Rhodanus at Arelate."

Everyone was staring at him in fascination, but for a long moment no one could find anything to say.

Then Sulla whistled. "A soldier is paid to fight!"

"If he bought his gear with his own money and he expects nothing more from the State than the food he eats, then he can call his own tune. But that description doesn't fit my lot," said Gaius Marius. "When they're not called upon to fight, they'll do much-needed public works, if for no other reason than it will give them to understand that they're in service to the State in exactly the same way as a man is to any employer. And it will keep them fit!"

"What about us?" asked Sulla. "Do you intend to turn us into engineers?"

"Why not?" asked Marius.

"I'm not an employee of the State, for one thing," said Sulla, pleasantly enough. "I give my time as a gift, like all the legates and tribunes."

Marius eyed him shrewdly. "Believe me, Lucius Cornelius, it's a gift I appreciate," he said, and left it at that.

Sulla left the meeting dissatisfied nonetheless. Employees of the State, indeed! True for the Head Count, perhaps, but not for the tribunes and legates, as he had pointed out. Marius had taken the point, and backed away. But what Sulla had left unsaid was true just the same. Monetary rewards for the tribunes and legates would be shares in the booty. And no one had any real idea how much booty the Germans were likely to yield. The sale of prisoners into slavery was the general's perquisite—he did not share it with his legates, his tribunes, his centurions, or his troops—and somehow Sulla had a feeling that at the end of this however-many-years-long campaign, the pickings would be lean except in slaves.

Sulla had not enjoyed the long, tedious journey to the Rhodanus. Quintus Sertorius had snuffled his way like a hound on a leash, tail wagging, all of himself aquiver with pleasure at the slightest whiff of any kind of job. He had taught himself to use the *groma,* the surveyor's instrument; he had settled down to watch how the corps of engineers dealt with rivers in spate, or fallen bridges, or landslides; he had led a century or two of soldiers to winkle out a nest of pirates from some mean cove; he had done duty with the gangs on road repairs; he had gone ranging ahead to spy out the land; he had even cured and tamed a young eagle with a broken wing, so that it still came back to visit him from time to time. Yes, everything was grist to Quintus Sertorius's mill. If in nothing else, in that one could see that he was related to Gaius Marius.

But Sulla needed *drama.* He had gained sufficient insight into himself to understand that now he was a senator, this represented a flaw in his character, yet at thirty-six years of age, he didn't think he was going to be able to excise a facet of himself so innate. Until that dreary interminable journey along the Via Aemilia Scauri and through the Maritime Alps, he had thoroughly enjoyed his military career, finding it full of action and challenge, be it the action and challenge of battle or of carving out a new Africa. But making roads and digging canals? That wasn't what he had come to Gaul-across-the-Alps to do! Nor would he!

And in late autumn there would be a consular election, and Marius would be replaced by someone inimical, and all that he'd have to show for his much-vaunted second consulship was a magnificently upkept road already bearing someone else's name. How could the man remain so tranquil, so unworried? He hadn't even bothered to answer that half of Aquillius's statement, to the effect that he would be ousted from his command. What was the Arpinate fox up to? *Why* wasn't he worried?

Suddenly Sulla forgot these vexed questions, for he had spied something which promised to be deliciously piquant; his eyes began to dance with interest and amusement.

Outside the senior tribunes' mess tent two men were in

conversation. Or at least that was what it looked like to a casual observer. To Sulla it looked like the opening scene of a wonderful farce. The taller of the two men was Gaius Julius Caesar. The shorter was Gaius Lusius, nephew (by marriage only, Marius had been quick to say) of the Great Man.

I wonder, does it take one to know one? Sulla asked himself as he strolled up to them. Caesar obviously didn't know one when he saw one, and yet it was clear to Sulla that every instinct in Caesar was clanging an alarm.

"Oh, Lucius Cornelius!" whinnied Gaius Lusius. "I was just asking Gaius Julius whether he knew what sort of night life there is in Arelate, and if there is any, whether he'd care to sample it with me."

Caesar's long, handsome face was an expressionless mask of courtesy, but his anxiety to be away from his present company showed itself in a dozen ways, thought Sulla; the eyes that tried to remain focused on Lusius's face but drifted aside, the minimal movements his feet made inside his military boots, the little flicks his fingers were making, and more.

"Perhaps Lucius Cornelius knows better than I do," said Caesar, beginning to make his bolt for freedom by shifting all his weight onto one foot, and poking the other forward a trifle.

"Oh no, Gaius Julius, don't go!" Lusius protested. "The more the merrier!" And he actually giggled.

"Sorry, Gaius Lusius, I have to go on duty," said Caesar, and was away.

More Lusius's own height, Sulla put his hand on Lusius's elbow and drew him further away from the tent. His hand fell immediately.

Gaius Lusius was very good-looking. His eyes were long-lashed and green, his hair a tumbled mass of darkish red curls, his brows finely arched and dark, his nose rather Greek in its length, high bridge, and straightness. Quite the little Lord Apollo, thought Sulla, unmoved and untempted.

He doubted whether Marius had so much as set eyes on the young man; that would not have been Marius's way. Having been pressured by his family into accepting Gaius Lusius into his military family—he had appointed Lusius an unelected tribune of the soldiers because his age was correct—Marius would prefer to forget the young man's existence. Until such time as the young man intruded himself upon his notice, hopefully via some deed of valor or extraordinary ability.

"Gaius Lusius, I'm going to offer you a word of advice," said Sulla crisply.

The long-lashed eyelids fluttered, lowered. "I am grateful for *any* advice from you, Lucius Cornelius."

"You joined us only yesterday, having made your own way from Rome," Sulla began.

Lusius interrupted. "Not from Rome, Lucius Cornelius. From Ferentinum. My uncle Gaius Marius gave me special leave to remain in Ferentinum because my mother was ill."

Aha! thought Sulla. That explains some of Marius's gruff offhandedness about this nephew by marriage! How he would hate to trot out that reason for the young man's tardy arrival, when he would never have used it to excuse himself!

"My uncle hasn't asked to see me yet," Lusius was busy complaining now. "When may I see him?"

"Not until he asks, and I doubt he'll ask at all. Until you prove your worth, you're an embarrassment to him, if for no other reason than that you claimed extra privilege before the campaign even started—you came late."

"But my mother was ill!" said Lusius indignantly.

"We all have mothers, Gaius Lusius—or we all did have mothers. Many of us have been obliged to go off to military service when our mothers were ill. Many of us have learned of a mother's death when on military service very far away from her. Many of us are deeply attached to our living mothers. But a mother's illness is not normally considered an adequate excuse for turning up late on military service. I suppose you've already told all your tentmates why you're tardy?"

"Yes," said Lusius, more and more bewildered.

"A pity. You'd have done better to have said nothing at all, and let your tentmates guess in the dark. They won't think the better of you for it, and your uncle knows they won't think the better of him for allowing it. But blood family is blood family, and often unfair." Sulla frowned. "However, that is not what I wanted to say to you. This is the army of Gaius Marius, not the army of Scipio Africanus. Do you know what I am referring to?"

"No," said Lusius, completely out of his depth.

"Cato the Censor accused Africanus and his senior officers of running an army riddled with moral laxity. Well, Gaius Marius is a lot closer in his thinking to Cato the Censor than he is to Scipio Africanus. Am I making myself understood?"

"No," said Lusius, the color fading from his cheeks.

"I think I am, really," said Sulla, smiling to show his long teeth unpleasantly. "You're attracted to handsome young men, not to pretty young women. I can't accuse you of overt effeminacy, but if you go on fluttering your eyelashes at the likes of Gaius Julius—who happens to be your uncle's brother-in-law, as indeed am I—you'll find yourself in boiling water up to the neck. Preferring one's own sex is not considered a Roman virtue. On the contrary, it is considered—especially in the legions!—an undesirable vice. If it wasn't, perhaps the women of the towns near which we camp wouldn't make so much money, nor the women of the enemies we conquer find rape their first taste of our Roman swords. But you must know *some* of this, at least!"

Lusius writhed, torn between a feeling of inexplicable inferiority and a burning sense of injustice. "Times are changing," he protested. "It isn't the social solecism it was!"

"You mistake the times, Gaius Lusius, probably because you want them to change, and have been associating with a group of your peers who feel the same way. So you gather together and you compare notes, seizing upon any remark to support your contention. I can assure you," Sulla said very seriously, "that the more you go about the world into which you were born, the more you will come to see that you are deluding yourself. And *nowhere* is there less forgiveness for preferring your own sex than in Gaius

Marius's army. And no one will crack down on you harder than Gaius Marius if he learns of your secret."

Almost weeping, Lusius wrung his hands together in futile anguish. "I'll go mad!" he cried.

"No, you won't. You'll discipline yourself, you'll be extremely careful in whatever overtures you make, and as soon as you can, you'll learn the signals that operate here between men of your own persuasion," said Sulla. "I can't tell you the signals because I don't indulge in the vice myself. If you're ambitious to succeed in public life, Gaius Lusius, I strongly advise you not to indulge in the vice. But if—you are young, after all—you find you cannot restrain your appetites, make very sure you pick on the right man." And with a kinder smile, Sulla turned on his heel and walked away.

For a while he simply strolled about aimlessly, hands behind his back, scarcely noticing the orderly activity all around him. The legions had been instructed to build a temporary camp, in spite of the fact that there wasn't an enemy force inside the province; simply, no Roman army slept unprotected. The permanent hilltop camp was already being tackled by the surveyors and engineers, and those troops not detailed to construct the temporary camp were put onto the first stages of fortifying the hill. This consisted in procuring timber for beams, posts, buildings. And the lower Rhodanus Valley possessed few forests, for it had been populous now for some centuries, ever since the Greeks founded Massilia, and Greek—then Roman—influence spread inland.

The army lay to the north of the vast salt marshes which formed the Rhodanus delta and spread both west and east of it; it was typical of Marius that he had chosen untilled ground whereon to build his camps, both temporary and permanent.

"There's no point in antagonizing one's potential allies," he said. "Besides which, with fifty thousand extra mouths in the area to feed, they're going to need every inch of arable land they've got."

Marius's grain and food procurators were already riding out to conclude contracts with farmers, and some of the troops were building granaries atop the hill to hold sufficient grain to feed fifty thousand men through the twelve months between one harvest and the next. The heavy baggage contained all manner of items Marius's sources of information had said would either be unobtainable in Gaul-across-the-Alps, or would be scarce—pitch, massive beams, block-and-tackle, tools, cranes, treadmills, lime, and quantities of precious iron bolts and nails. At Populonia and Pisae, the two ports which received the rough-smelted bloom-iron "sows" from the isle of Ilva, the *praefectus fabrum* had purchased every sow available and carted them along too in case the engineers had to make steel; in the heavy baggage were anvils, crucibles, hammers, fire bricks, all the tools necessary. Already a group of soldiers were fetching timber to make a large cache of charcoal, for without charcoal it was impossible to get a furnace hot enough to melt iron, let alone steel it.

And by the time that he turned back toward the general's command tent, he had decided that the time had come; for Sulla had an answer to boredom already thoroughly thought out, an answer which would give him all the drama he could ask for. The idea had germinated while he was still in Rome, and grown busily all the way along the coast, and now could be permitted to flower. Yes, time to see Gaius Marius.

The general was alone, writing industriously.

"Gaius Marius, I wonder if you have an hour to spare? I would like your company on a walk," Sulla said, holding open the flap between the tent and the hide awning under which the duty officer sat. An inquisitive beam of light had stolen in behind him, and so he stood surrounded by an aura of liquid gold, his bare head and shoulders alive with the fire of his curling hair.

Looking up, Marius eyed this vision with disfavor. "You need a haircut," he said curtly. "Another couple of inches and you'll look like a dancing girl!"

"How extraordinary!" said Sulla, not moving.

"I'd call it slipshod," said Marius.

"No, what's extraordinary is that you haven't noticed for months, and right at this moment, when it's in the forefront of my mind, you suddenly do notice. You may not be able to read minds,

Gaius Marius, but I think you are attuned to the minds of those you work with."

"You sound like a dancing girl as well," said Marius. "Why do you want company on a walk?"

"Because I need to speak to you privately, Gaius Marius, somewhere that I can be sure neither the walls nor the windows have ears. A walk should provide us with such a place."

Down went the pen, the roll of paper was furled; Marius rose at once. "I'd much rather walk than write, Lucius Cornelius, so let's go," he said.

They strode briskly through the camp, not talking, and unaware of the curious glances which followed them from parties of soldiers, centurions, cadets, and more soldiers; after three years of campaigning with Gaius Marius and Lucius Cornelius Sulla, the men of these legions had developed an inbuilt sense of sureness about their commanders that told them whenever there was something important in the offing. And today was such an occasion; every man sensed it.

It was too late in the day to contemplate climbing the hill, so Marius and Sulla stopped where the wind blew their words away.

"Now, what's the matter?" asked Marius.

"I started growing my hair long in Rome," said Sulla.

"Never noticed until now. I take it the hair has something to do with what you want to talk to me about?"

"I'm turning myself into a Gaul," Sulla announced.

Marius looked alert. "Oho! Talk on, Lucius Cornelius."

"The most frustrating aspect of this campaign against the Germans is our abysmal lack of reliable intelligence about them," Sulla said. "From the very beginning, when the Taurisci first sent us their request for aid and we discovered that the Germans were migrating, we've been handicapped by the fact that we know absolutely nothing about them. We don't know who they are, where they come from, what gods they worship, why they migrated from their homelands in the first place, what sort of social organization they enjoy, how they are led. Most important of all, we don't know why they keep defeating us and then turning away from Italy, when you wouldn't have stopped Hannibal or Pyrrhus with a barricade of a million war elephants."

His eyes were looking ninety degrees away from Marius, and the last shafts of the sun shone through them from side to side, filling Marius with an uneasy awe; on rare occasions he was struck by a facet of Sulla normally hidden, the facet he thought of as Sulla's *inhumanity,* and he didn't use that word for any of its more accepted connotations. Simply, Sulla could suddenly drop a veil and stand revealed as no man—but no god either—a different invention of the gods than a man. A quality reinforced at this moment, with the sun bound up inside his eyes as if it belonged there.

"Go on," said Marius.

Sulla went on. "Before we left Rome, I bought myself two new slaves. They've traveled with me; they're with me now. One is a Gaul of the Carnutes, the tribe which controls the whole Celtic religion. It's a strange sort of worship—they believe trees are animate, in that they have spirits, or shades, or something of the kind. Difficult to relate to our own ideas. The other man is a German of the Cimbri, captured in Noricum at the time Carbo was defeated. I keep them isolated from each other. Neither man knows of the other's existence."

"Haven't you been able to find out about the Germans from your German slave?" asked Marius.

"Not a thing. He pretends to have no knowledge of who they are or where they come from. My inquiries lead me to believe that this ignorance is a general characteristic in the few Germans we have managed to capture and enslave, though I very much doubt that any other Roman owner has actively tried to obtain information. That is now irrelevant. My purpose in buying my German was to obtain information, but when he proved recalcitrant—and there doesn't seem to be much point in torturing someone who stands there like a gigantic ox—I had a better idea. Information, Gaius Marius, is usually secondhand. And for our purposes, secondhand isn't good enough."

"True," said Marius, who knew where Sulla was going now, but had no wish to hurry him.

"So I began to think that if war with the Germans was not imminent, it behooved us to try to obtain information about them at first hand," said Sulla. "Both my slaves have been in service to Romans for long enough to have learned Latin, though in the case of the German, it's a very rudimentary sort of Latin. Interestingly, from my Carnutic Gaul I learned that once away from the Middle Sea and into Longhaired Gaul, the second language among the Gauls is Latin, not Greek! Oh, I don't mean to imply that the Gauls walk round exchanging Latin quips, only that thanks to contacts between the settled tribes like the Aedui and ourselves—be it in the guise of soldiers or traders—there is an occasional Gaul who has a smattering of Latin, and has learned to read and write. Since their own languages are not written, when they read and write, they do so in Latin. Not in Greek. Fascinating, isn't it? We're so used to thinking of Greek as the lingua franca of the world that it's quite exhilarating to find one part of the world preferring Latin!"

"Not being either scholar or philosopher, Lucius Cornelius, I must confess to some lack of excitement. However," said Marius, smiling faintly, "I am extremely interested in finding out about the Germans!"

Sulla lifted his hands in mock surrender. "Point taken, Gaius Marius! Very well, then. For nearly five months I have been learning the language of the Carnutes of central Long-haired Gaul, and the language of the Cimbric Germans. My tutor in Carnute is far more enthusiastic about the project than my tutor in German—but then, he's also a brighter specimen." Sulla stopped to consider that statement, and found himself dissatisfied with it. "My impression that the German is duller may not necessarily be correct. He may be—since the shock of separation from his own kind is far greater than for the Gaul—merely living at a mental remoteness from his present plight. Or, given the luck of the grab bag and the fact that he was foolish enough to let himself be captured in a war his people won, he may just be a dull German."

"Lucius Cornelius, my patience is not inexhaustible," said Marius, not snappishly, more in tones of resignation. "You are showing all the signs of a particularly peripatetic Peripatetic!"

"My apologies," Sulla said with a grin, and turned now to look at Marius directly. The light died out of his eyes, and he seemed once again quite human.

"With my hair and skin and eyes," Sulla said crisply, "I can pass very easily for a Gaul. I intend to become a Gaul, and travel into areas where no Roman would dare go. Particularly, I intend to shadow the Germans on their way to Spain, which I gather means the people of the Cimbri for certain, and perhaps the other peoples. I now know enough Cimbric German to at least understand what they say, which is why I will concentrate upon the Cimbri." He laughed. "My hair actually ought to be considerably longer than a dancing girl's, but it will have to do for the moment. If I'm quizzed about its shortness, I shall say I had a disease of the scalp, and had to shave it all off. Luckily it grows very fast."

He fell silent. For some moments Marius didn't speak, just put his foot up on a handy log and his elbow on his knee and his chin on his fist. The truth was that he couldn't think of what to say. Here for months he had been worrying that he was going to lose Lucius Cornelius to the fleshpots of Rome because the campaign was going to be too boring, and all the time Lucius Cornelius was fastidiously working out a plan sure not to be boring. What a plan! What a man! Ulysses had been the first recorded spy, donning the guise of some Trojan nobody and sneaking inside the walls of Ilium to pick up every scrap of information he could—and one of the favorite debates a boy's *grammaticus* concocted was whether or not Calchas had defected to the Achaeans because he was genuinely fed up with the Trojans, or because he wanted to spy for King Priam, or because he wanted to sow discord among the kings of Greece.

Ulysses had had red hair too. Ulysses had been highborn too. And yet—Marius found it impossible to think of Sulla as some latter-day Ulysses. He was his own man, complete and rounded. Just as was his plan. There was no fear in him, so much was plain; he was approaching this extraordinary mission in a businesslike and—and—*invulnerable* way. In other words, he was approaching it like the Roman aristocrat he was. He harbored no doubts that he would succeed, because he knew he was better than other men.

Down came the fist, the elbow, the foot. Marius drew a breath, and asked, "Do you honestly think you can do it, Lucius Cornelius? You're such a Roman! I'm consumed with admiration for you, and it's a brilliant, brilliant plan. But it will call for you to shed every last trace of the Roman, and I'm not sure any Roman can do that. Our culture is so enormously strong, it leaves ineradicable marks on us. You'll have to live a lie."

One red-gold brow lifted; the corners of the beautiful mouth went down. "Oh, Gaius Marius, I have lived one kind of lie or another all my life!"

"Even now?"

"Even now."

They turned to commence walking back.

"Do you intend to go on your own, Lucius Cornelius?" Marius asked. "Don't you think it might be a good idea to have company? What if you need to send a message back to me urgently, but find you cannot leave yourself? And mightn't it be a help to have a comrade to serve as your mirror, and you as his?"

"I've thought of all that," said Sulla, "and I would like to take Quintus Sertorius with me."

At first Marius looked delighted, then a frown gathered. "He's too dark. He'd never pass for a Gaul, let alone a German."

"True. However, he could be a Greek with Celtiberian blood in him." Sulla cleared his throat. "I gave him a slave when we left Rome, as a matter of fact. A Celtiberian of the tribe Illergetes. I didn't tell Quintus Sertorius what was in the wind, but I did tell him to learn to speak Celtiberian."

Marius stared. "You're well prepared. I approve."

"So I may have Quintus Sertorius?"

"Oh, yes. Though I still think he's too dark, and I wonder if that fact mightn't undo you."

"No, it will be all right. Quintus Sertorius is extremely valuable to me, and his darkness will, I fancy, turn out to be an asset. You see, Quintus Sertorius has animal magic, and men with animal magic are held in great awe by all barbarian peoples. His darkness will contribute to his shaman-power."

"Animal magic? What exactly do you mean?"

"Quintus Sertorius can summon wild creatures to him. I noticed it in Africa, when he actually whistled up a pard-cat and fondled it. But I only began to work out a role for him on this mission when he made a pet out of the eagle chick he cured, yet didn't kill its natural wish to be free and wild. So now it lives as it was meant to, yet it still remains his friend, and comes to visit him, and sits on his arm and kisses him. The soldiers reverence him. It is a great omen."

"I know," said Marius. "The eagle is the symbol of the legions, and Quintus Sertorius has reinforced it."

They stood looking at the place where six silver eagles upon silver poles ornamented with crowns and *phalerae* medals and torcs were driven into the ground; a fire in a tripod burned before them, sentries stood to attention, and a togate priest with folds pulled up to cover his head threw incense on the coals in the tripod as he said the sundown prayers.

"What exactly is the importance of this animal magic?" Marius asked.

"The Gauls are highly superstitious about the spirits which dwell in all wild things, and so I gather are the Cimbric Germans. Quintus Sertorius will masquerade as a shaman from a Spanish tribe so remote even the tribes of the Pyrenees will not know much about him," said Sulla.

"When do you intend to set out?"

"Very soon now. But I'd prefer it if you told Quintus Sertorius," said Sulla. "He'll want to come, but his loyalty to you is complete. So it's better that you tell him." He blew through his nostrils. "No one is to know. *No one!*"

"I couldn't agree more," said Marius. "However, there are three slaves who know a little something, since they've been giving you language lessons. Do you want them sold and shipped overseas somewhere?"

"Why go to so much trouble?" asked Sulla, surprised. "I intended to kill them."

"An excellent idea. But you'll lose money on the deal."

"Not a fortune. Call it my contribution to the success of the campaign against the Germans," said Sulla easily.

"I'll have them killed the moment you're gone."

But Sulla shook his head. "No, I'll do my own dirty work. And now. They've taught me and Quintus Sertorius as much as they know. Tomorrow I'll send them off to Massilia to do a job for me." He stretched, yawned voluptuously. "I'm good with a bow and arrow, Gaius Marius. And the salt marshes are very desolate. Everyone will simply assume they've run away. Including Quintus Sertorius."

I'm too close to the earth, thought Marius. It isn't that I mind sending men to extinction, even in cold blood. To do so is a part of life as we know it, and vexes no god. But he is one of the old patrician Romans, all right. Too far above the earth. Truly a demigod. And Marius found himself turning in his mind to the words of the Syrian prophetess Martha, now luxuriating as an honored guest in his house in Rome. A far greater Roman than he, a Gaius too, but a Julius, not a Marius . . . Was that what it needed? That semi-divine drop of patrician blood?

 Said Publius Rutilius Rufus in a letter to Gaius Marius dated the end of September:

Well, Publius Licinius Nerva has nerved himself at last to write to the Senate with complete candor about the situation in Sicily. As senior consul, you are being sent the official dispatches, of course, but you will hear my version first, for I know you'll choose to read my letter ahead of boring old dispatches, and I've cadged a place for my letter in the official courier's bag.

But before I tell you about Sicily, it is necessary to go back to the beginning of the year, when—as you know—the House recommended to the People in their tribes that a law should be passed freeing all slaves of Italian Allied nationality throughout our world. But you will not know that it had one unforeseen repercussion—namely, that the slaves of other nationalities, particularly those nations officially designated as Friends and Allies of the Roman People, either assumed that the law referred to them as well, or else were mighty displeased that it did not. This is particularly true of Greek slaves, who form the majority of Sicily's grain slaves, and also form the majority of slaves of all kinds in Campania.

In February, the son of a Campanian knight and full Roman citizen named Titus Vettius, aged all of twenty years old, apparently went mad. The cause of his madness was debt; he had committed himself to pay seven silver talents for—of all things!—a Scythian slave girl. But the elder Titus Vettius being a tightwad of the first order, and too old to be the father of a twenty-year-old besides, young Titus Vettius borrowed the money at exorbitant interest, pledging his entire inheritance as collateral. Of course he was as helpless as a plucked chicken in the hands of the moneylenders, who insisted he pay them at the end of thirty days. Naturally he could not, and he did obtain an extension of a further thirty days. But when again he had no hope of paying them, the moneylenders went to his father and demanded their loan—with exorbitant interest. The father refused, and disowned his son. Who went mad.

The next thing, young Titus Vettius had put on a diadem and a purple robe, declared himself the King of Campania, and roused every slave in the district to rebellion. The father, I hasten to add, is one of the good old-fashioned bulk farmers—treats his slaves well, and has no Italians among them. But just down the road was one of the new bulk farmers, those dreadful men who buy slaves dirt-cheap, chain them up to work, don't ask questions about their origins, and lock them in *ergastulum* barracks to sleep. This despicable fellow's name was Marcus Macrinus Mactator, and he turns out to have been a great friend of your junior colleague in the consulship, our wonderfully upright and honest Gaius Flavius Fimbria.

The day young Titus Vettius went mad, he armed his slaves by buying up five hundred sets of old show-arms a gladiatorial school was auctioning off, and down the road the little army marched to the well of servile pain run by Marcus Macrinus Mactator. And proceeded to torture and kill Mactator and his family, and free a very large number of slaves, many of whom turned out to be of Italian Allied nationality, and therefore were illegally detained.

Within no time at all, young Titus Vettius the King of Campania had an army of slaves over four thousand strong, and had barricaded himself into a very well fortified camp atop a hill. And the servile recruits kept pouring in! Capua barred its gates, brought all the gladiatorial schools into line, and appealed to the Senate in Rome for help.

Fimbria was very vocal about the affair, and mourned the loss of his friend Mactator Slaughterman until the Conscript Fathers were fed up enough to depute the *praetor peregrinus,* Lucius Licinius Lucullus, to assemble an army and quash the servile uprising. Well, you know what a colossal aristocrat Lucius Licinius Lucullus is! He didn't take at all kindly to being ordered by a cockroach like Fimbria to clean up Campania.

And now a mild digression. I suppose you know that Lucullus is married to Metellus Piggle-wiggle's sister, Metella Calva. They have a pair of sons about fourteen and twelve years of age who are commonly rumored to be extremely promising, and now that Piggle-wiggle's son, the Piglet, can't manage to get two words out straight, the whole family is rather pinning its hopes on young Lucius and young Marcus Lucullus. Now stop it, Gaius Marius! I can hear you ho-humming from Rome! All this is important stuff, if only you could be brought to believe it. How can you possibly conduct yourself unscathed through the labyrinth of Roman public life if you won't bother to learn all the family ramifications and gossip? Lucullus's wife—who is Piggle-wiggle's sister—is notorious for her immorality. First of all, she conducts her affairs of the heart in blazingly public fashion, complete with hysterical scenes in front of popular jeweler's shops, and the occasional attempted suicide by stripping off all her clothes and trying to hop over the wall into the Tiber. But secondly, poor Metella Calva does not philander with men of her own class, and that's what really hurts our lofty Piggle-wiggle. Not to mention the haughty Lucullus. No, Metella Calva likes handsome slaves, or hulking laborers she picks up on the wharves of the Port of Rome. She is therefore a dreadful burden to Piggle-wiggle and Lucullus, though I believe she is an excellent mother to her boys.

End of digression. I mention it to sprinkle this whole episode with a little much-needed spice. And to make you understand why Lucullus went off to Campania smarting at having to take orders from precisely the sort of man Metella Calva might well have fancied were he poorer—rougher he could not be! There is something very fishy going on with Fimbria, incidentally. He has struck up a friendship with Gaius Memmius, of all people, and the two of them are as thick as thieves, and a lot of money is changing hands, though for what purpose is unclear.

Anyway, Lucullus soon cleaned up Campania. Young Titus Vettius was executed, as were his officers and the members of his slave army. Lucullus was commended for his work, and went back to hearing the assizes in places like Reate.

But didn't I tell you some time ago that I had a feeling about those tiny little servile uprisings in Campania last year? My nose was right. First we had Titus Vettius. And now we have a full-scale slave war on our hands in Sicily!

I have always thought Publius Licinius Nerva looked and acted like a mouse, but who could ever have dreamed that it would be dangerous to send him as praetor-governor to Sicily? He's so squeaky-meticulous the job should have suited him down to the ground. Scurrying here, scurrying there, laying in his stores for winter, writing copiously detailed accounts with the tip of his tail dipped in ink, whiskers twitching.

Of course all would have gone well, had it not been for this wretched law about freeing the Italian Allied slaves. Our praetor-governor Nerva scurried off to Sicily and began to manumit the Italians, who number about a quarter of the total grain slaves. And he got started in Syracuse, while his quaestor got started at the other end of the island, in Lilybaeum. It went slowly and precisely, Nerva being Nerva—he did, by the way, evolve an excellent system to catch out slaves claiming to be Italian who were not Italian, by quizzing them in Oscan and local geography of our peninsula. But he published his decree in Latin only, thinking this too would weed out potential imposters. With the result that those reading Greek had to rely upon others to translate, and the confusion grew, and grew, and grew. . . .

The two weeks at the end of May saw Nerva free

some eight hundred Italian slaves in Syracuse, while his quaestor in Lilybaeum marked time, waiting for orders. And there arrived in Syracuse a very angry deputation of grain farmers, all the members of which threatened to do things to Nerva if he went on freeing their slaves that ranged from emasculation to litigation. Nerva panicked at sight of this spitting cat, and shut down his tribunal at once. No more slaves were to be freed. This directive reached his quaestor in Lilybaeum a little too late, unfortunately, for his quaestor had grown tired of waiting, and set up his tribunal in the marketplace. Now, having barely got started, he too shut down. The slaves lined up in the marketplace were quite literally mad with rage, and went home to do murder.

The result was an outright revolt at the western end of the island. It started with the murder of a couple of wealthy brothers who farmed a huge grain property near Halicyae, and it went on from there. All over Sicily slaves in hundreds and then thousands left their farms, some of them only after murdering their overseers and even their owners, and converged on the Grove of the Palici, which lies, I believe, some forty miles southwest of Mount Aetna. Nerva called up his militia, and thought he had crushed the revolt when he stormed and took an old citadel filled with refugee slaves. So he disbanded his militia, and sent them all to their various homes.

But the revolt was only just beginning. It flared up next time near Heracleia Minoa, and when Nerva tried to get his militia together again, everyone became extremely deaf. He was forced to fall back on a cohort of auxiliaries stationed at Enna, quite a distance from Heracleia Minoa, but the closest force of any size nonetheless. This time Nerva didn't win. The whole cohort perished, and the slaves acquired arms.

While this was going on, the slaves produced a leader, predictably an Italian who had not been freed before Nerva closed down his tribunals. His name is Salvius, and he's a member of the Marsi. His profession when a free man, it seems, was a snake-charming flute player, and he was enslaved because he was caught playing the flute for women involved in the Dionysiac rites which so worried the Senate a few years ago. Salvius now calls himself a king, but being an Italian, his idea of a king is Roman, not Hellenic. He wears the *toga praetexta* rather than a diadem, and is preceded by lictors bearing the *fasces,* complete with axes.

At the far end of Sicily, somewhere around Lilybaeum, a second slave-king then appeared, a Greek this time, named Athenion, and he too raised an army. Both Salvius and Athenion converged on the Grove of the Palici, and there had a conference. The result of this is that Salvius (who now calls himself King Tryphon) has become the ruler of the whole lot, and has chosen for his headquarters an impregnable place called Triocala, in the lap of the mountains above the coast opposite Africa, about halfway between Agrigentum and Lilybaeum.

Right at this moment, Sicily is a very *Iliad* of woes. The harvest is lying trampled into the ground aside from what the slaves harvested to fill their own bellies, and Rome will get no grain from Sicily this year. The cities of Sicily are groaning at the seams to contain the enormous numbers of free refugees who have sought shelter within the safety of walls, and starvation and disease are already stalking the streets. An army of over sixty thousand well-armed slaves—and five thousand slave cavalry—is running wild anywhere it likes from one end of the island to the other, and when

threatened, retires to this impregnable fortress of Triocala. They have attacked and taken Murgantia, and all
but succeeded in taking Lilybaeum, which fortunately
was saved by some veterans who heard about the trouble and sailed across from Africa to help.

And here comes the ultimate indignity. Not only is
Rome looking at a drastic grain shortage, but it very
much seems that someone attempted to manipulate
events in Sicily to *manufacture* a grain shortage! The
slave uprising has turned what would have been a spu-
rious shortage into a real one, but our esteemed Princeps Senatus, Scaurus, is nose-down on a trail leading,
he hopes, to the culprit or culprits. I suspect he sus-
pects our despicable consul Fimbria and Gaius Memmius. Why would a decent and upright man like
Memmius ally himself with the likes of Fimbria? Well,
yes, I can answer that one, I think. He should have
been praetor years ago but has only just got there now,
and he doesn't have the kind of money to run for consul. And when lack of money keeps a man out of the
chair he thinks he's entitled to sit in, he can do many
imprudent things.

Gaius Marius laid the letter down with a sigh, pulled the official dispatches from the Senate toward him, and read those too,
comfortably alone, and therefore able to labor aloud over the
hopeless fusion of words at the top of his lungs if he so wished.
Not that there was any disgrace in it, everyone read aloud; but
everyone else was assumed to know Greek.

Publius Rutilius was right, as always. His own extremely long
letter was infinitely more informative than the dispatches, though
they contained the text of Nerva's letter, and were full of statistics.
They just weren't as compelling nor as newsy. Nor could they put
a man right in the middle of the picture the way Rutilius did.

He had no trouble in imagining the consternation in Rome. A
drastic grain shortage meant political futures at stake, and a

growling Treasury, and aediles scrambling to find alternative sources of grain. Sicily was the breadbasket, and when Sicily didn't deliver a good harvest, Rome stared famine in the face. Neither Africa nor Sardinia sent half as much grain to Rome as Sicily did. *Combined* they didn't! This present crisis would see the People blaming the Senate for sending an inadequate governor to Sicily, and the Head Count would blame both the People and the Senate for their empty bellies.

The Head Count was not a political body; it was not interested in governing any more than it was interested in being governed. The sum total of its participation in public life was seats at the games and free handouts at the festivals. Until its belly was empty. And then the Head Count was a force to be reckoned with.

Not that the Head Count got its grain free; but the Senate through its aediles and quaestors made sure the Head Count was sold grain at a reasonable price, even if in times of shortage that meant buying expensive grain and letting it go at the same reasonable price, much to the chagrin of the Treasury. Any Roman citizen resident within Rome could avail himself of the State's price-frozen grain ration, no matter how rich he was, provided he was willing to join the huge line at the aedile's desk in the Porticus Minucia and obtain his chits; these, when presented at one of the State granaries lining the Aventine cliffs above the Port of Rome, would permit him to buy his five *modii* of cheap grain. That few of means bothered was purely convenience; it was so much easier to shop in the grain market of the Velabrum and leave it to the merchants to fetch the grain from the privately owned granaries lining the bottom of the Palatine cliffs on the Vicus Tuscus.

Knowing himself caught in what could be a precarious political position, Gaius Marius frowned his wonderful eyebrows together. The moment the Senate asked the Treasury to open its cobwebbed vaults to buy in expensive grain for the Head Count, the howling would begin; the chiefs of the *tribuni aerarii*—the Treasury bureaucrats—would start expostulating that they couldn't possibly afford to pay out huge sums for grain when a

Head Count army six legions strong was currently employed in Gaul-across-the-Alps doing public works! That in turn would shift the onus onto the Senate, which would have to do hideous battle with the Treasury to get the extra grain; and then the Senate would complain to the People that, as usual, the Head Count were a mighty costly nuisance.

Wonderful! How was he going to get himself elected consul *in absentia* for a second year in a row, when he led a Head Count army, and Rome was at the mercy of a hungry Head Count? May Publius Licinius Nerva rot! And every grain speculator along with him!

Only Marcus Aemilius Scaurus Princeps Senatus had sensed something wrong ahead of the crisis; with a fresh harvest due, the grain price within Rome normally fell a little at the end of summer. Whereas this year it had steadily risen. The reason seemed apparent; the freeing of the Italian grain slaves would limit the amount of planted grain being harvested. But then the grain slaves had not been freed, and the harvest was predicted normal. At which point, the price should have fallen dramatically. But it didn't. It kept on rising.

To Scaurus, the evidence pointed conclusively to a grain manipulation stemming from the Senate, and his own observations pointed to the consul Fimbria and the urban praetor Gaius Memmius, who had been desperately raising money throughout the spring and summer. To buy grain cheaply and sell it at an enormous profit, Scaurus concluded.

And then came the news of the slave uprising in Sicily. Whereupon Fimbria and Memmius began frantically selling everything they owned aside from their houses on the Palatine and sufficient land to ensure that they remained on the senatorial census. Therefore, Scaurus deduced, whatever the nature of their business venture might have been, it could not have had anything to do with the grain supply.

His reasoning was specious, but pardonably so; had the consul and the urban praetor been involved in the escalation of the grain price, they would now be sitting back picking their teeth content-edly rather than chasing their tails to find the cash to pay back loans. No, not Fimbria and Memmius! He must look elsewhere.

After Publius Licinius Nerva's letter confessing the extent of the crisis in Sicily reached Rome, Scaurus began to hear one senatorial name bruited about among the grain merchants; his sensitive pro-boscis smelled fresher—and gamier—game than the false scent of Fimbria and Memmius. Lucius Appuleius Saturninus. The quaestor for the port of Ostia. Young and new to the Senate, but holding the most sensitive position a new young senator could, if he was inter-ested in grain prices. For the quaestor at Ostia supervised grain shipment and storage, knew and conversed with everybody in-volved with the whole gamut of the grain supply, was privy to all kinds of information well ahead of the rest of the Senate.

Further investigations convinced Scaurus that he had found his culprit, and he struck his blow for the good name of the Senate at a meeting of that body early in October. Lucius Appuleius Sat-urninus was the prime mover behind the premature rise in the price of grain which had prevented the Treasury's acquiring ad-ditional stocks for the State granaries at anything like a reason-able price, said Scaurus Princeps Senatus to a hushed House. And the House had found its scapegoat; amid great indignation, the senators voted overwhelmingly to dismiss Lucius Appuleius Sat-urninus from his post as quaestor, thereby depriving him of his seat in the House, and leaving him open to massive prosecutions for extortion.

Summoned from Ostia to appear in the House, Saturninus could do little more than deny Scaurus's charges. Of actual proof there was none—either for or against—and that meant the issue boiled down to which one of the men involved was more worthy of being believed.

"Give me proof I am implicated!" cried Saturninus.

"Give me proof you are *not* implicated!" sneered Scaurus.

And naturally the House believed its Princeps Senatus, for Scaurus on the trail of wrongdoing was above reproach, everyone knew it. Saturninus was stripped of everything.

But he was a fighter, Lucius Appuleius Saturninus. In age he was exactly right for the job of quaestor and a new senatorial seat, being thirty; which in turn meant that no one really knew much about him, since he had not starred in a great courtroom drama as a youth, and had not shone out luminously during his military apprenticeship, and came from a senatorial family originating in Picenum. Little choice did he have about losing his post as quaestor, or his seat in the Senate; he could not even protest when the House turned around and gave his beloved job in Ostia to none other than Scaurus Princeps Senatus for the rest of the year! But he was a fighter.

No one in Rome believed him innocent. Wherever he went he was spat upon, jostled, even stoned, and the outside wall of his house was smothered in graffiti—PIG, PEDERAST, ULCER, WOLFS-HEAD, MONSTER, PENIS GOBBLER, and other slurs jostled each other for prominence on the plastered surface. His wife and his young daughter were ostracized, and spent most of their days in tears. Even his servants looked askance at him, and were slow to respond whenever he made a request, or—temper tried—barked an order.

His best friend was a relative nobody, Gaius Servilius Glaucia. Some years older than Saturninus, Glaucia enjoyed mild fame as an advocate in the courts and a brilliant legal draftsman; but he did not enjoy the distinction of being a patrician Servilius, nor even an important plebeian Servilius. Save for his reputation as a lawyer, Glaucia was about on a par with another Gaius Servilius who had made money and scrambled into the Senate on the edge of his patron Ahenobarbus's toga; this other plebeian Servilius, however, had not yet acquired a *cognomen,* where "Glaucia" was quite a respectable one, for it referred to the family's beautiful grey-green eyes.

They were a good-looking pair, Saturninus and Glaucia, the one very dark indeed, the other very fair, each in the best physical mould of his type. The basis for their friendship was an equal sharpness of mind and depth of intellect, as well as the avowed purpose of reaching the consulship and ennobling their families forever. Politics and lawmaking fascinated them, which meant they were eminently suited to the kind of work their birth made mandatory.

"I'm not beaten yet," said Saturninus to Glaucia, mouth set hard. "There's another way back into the Senate, and I am going to use it."

"Not the censors," said Glaucia.

"Definitely not the censors! No, I shall stand for election as a tribune of the plebs," said Saturninus.

"You'll never get in." Glaucia was not being unduly gloomy, just realistic.

"I will if I can find myself a powerful enough ally."

"Gaius Marius."

"Who else? He's got no love for Scaurus or Numidicus or any of the Policy Makers," Saturninus said. "I'm sailing for Massilia in the morning to explain my case to the only man who might be prepared to listen to me, and to offer him my services."

Glaucia nodded. "Yes, it's a good tactic, Lucius Appuleius. After all, you have nothing to lose." A thought occurring to him, he grinned. "Think of the fun you can have making old Scaurus's life a misery when you're a tribune of the plebs!"

"No, he's not the one I want!" said Saturninus scornfully. "He acted as he saw fit; I can't quarrel with that. Someone deliberately set me up as a decoy, and that's the someone I want. And if I'm a tribune of the plebs, I can make *his* life a misery. That is, if I can find out who it was."

"You go to Massilia and see Gaius Marius," said Glaucia. "In the meantime, I'll start work on the grain culprit."

In the autumn it was possible to sail to the west, and Lucius Appuleius Saturninus had a good passage to Massilia. From there he journeyed on horseback to the Roman camp outside Glanum, and sought an audience with Gaius Marius.

It had not been a gross exaggeration on Marius's part to tell his senior staff that he planned to build another Carcasso, though this was a wood-and-earth version of Carcasso's stone. The hill upon which the vast Roman camp stood bristled with fortifications; Saturninus appreciated at once that a people like the Germans, unskilled in siege, would never be able to take it, even if they stormed it with every man they had at their disposal.

"But," said Gaius Marius as he took his unexpected guest upon a tour of the dispositions, "it isn't really here to protect my army, you know. It's here to delude the Germans into thinking it is."

This man isn't supposed to be subtle! thought Saturninus, suddenly appreciating the quality of Gaius Marius's intellect. If anyone can help me, he can.

They had taken a spontaneous liking to each other, sensing a kindred ruthlessness and determination, and perhaps a certain un-Roman iconoclasm. Saturninus was profoundly glad to discover that—as he had hoped—he had beaten the news of his disgrace from Rome to Glanum. However, it was difficult to tell how long he might have to wait to unfold his tale of disaster, for Gaius Marius was the commander-in-chief of a mighty enterprise, and his life, including his debatable leisure, was not his own for many moments at a stretch.

Expecting a crowded dining room, Saturninus was surprised to discover that he and Manius Aquillius were the only two who would share Gaius Marius's meal.

"Is Lucius Cornelius in Rome?" he asked.

Unperturbed, Marius helped himself to a stuffed egg. "No, he's off on a special job," he said briefly.

Understanding that there was no point in concealing his plight from Manius Aquillius, who had conclusively proven himself Marius's man the previous year—and who would be bound to get letters from Rome with all the tittle-tattle in them—Saturninus embarked upon his story as soon as the meal was over. The two men listened in silence until it was done, not interrupting with even a single question, which made Saturninus feel that he must have outlined events with clarity and logic.

Then Marius sighed. "I'm very glad you came in person to see me," he said. "It lends considerable strength to your case, Lucius Appuleius. A guilty man might have resorted to many ploys, but not that of coming to see me in person. I am not deemed a gullible man. Nor is Marcus Aemilius Scaurus, for that matter. But, like you, I think whoever had investigated this tortuous situation would have been led by a series of illusions to you. After all, as quaestor at Ostia, you're a perfect decoy."

"If the case against me falls down anywhere, Gaius Marius, it is in the fact that I don't have the kind of money to buy grain in bulk," Saturninus said.

"True, but it doesn't automatically exonerate you, either," Marius said. "You could as easily have done it for a very big bribe, or taken out a loan."

"Do you think I did?"

"No. I think you're the victim, not the perpetrator."

"So do I," said Manius Aquillius. "It's too simple."

"Then will you help me secure election as a tribune of the plebs?" asked Saturninus.

"Oh, certainly," said Marius without hesitation.

"I shall reciprocate in whatever way I can."

"Good!" said Marius.

After which things happened in a hurry. Saturninus had no time to waste, as the tribunician elections were scheduled for early November, and he had to get back to Rome in time to have himself declared a candidate and line up the support Marius had promised him. So, armed with a bulky packet of letters from Marius to various people in Rome, Saturninus set off toward the Alps in a fast gig drawn by four mules, and with a purse large enough to make sure he could hire animals along the way as good as the four which started him on his journey.

As he was leaving, an extraordinary trio came in on foot through the camp's main gates. Three Gauls. *Barbarian* Gauls! Never having set eyes upon a barbarian in his life, Saturninus gaped. One was apparently the prisoner of the other two, for he was manacled. Oddly enough, he was less barbaric in his garb and appearance than the other two! A medium-sized fellow, fairish but not spectacularly so, his hair worn long but cut like a Greek, clean-shaven, clad in the trousers of a Gaul and in a Gallic coat of hairy wool bearing a faint and complicated check in its weave. The second fellow was very dark, but he wore a towering headdress of black feathers and golden wire which proclaimed him some Celtiberian outlander—and little else by way of clothing, displaying instead a body bulging with muscles. The third man was obviously the leader, a true barbarian Gaul, the bare skin of his chest white as milk yet weathered, his trousers bound with thongs like a German or one of the mythical Belgae; long red-gold hair hung down his back, long red-gold moustaches fell one on either side of his mouth, and around his neck he wore a massive dragonheaded torc of what looked like real gold.

The gig started to move; as he swept by the little group at even closer quarters, Saturninus encountered the cold white gaze of the leader, and shivered in spite of himself. Now *he* was a complete barbarian!

The three Gauls continued on up the slope inside the camp's main gates, challenged by no one until they reached the duty officer's table under the shelter of the awning outside the general's substantial timber house.

"Gaius Marius, please," said the leader in flawless Latin.

The duty officer didn't even blink. "I'll see if he's receiving," he said, getting up. Within a moment he was out again. "The general says to go in, Lucius Cornelius," he said, smiling widely.

"Smart," said Sertorius under his breath as he brushed past the duty officer with waggling headdress. "Just keep your mouth shut about this, hear me?"

When he set eyes upon his two lieutenants, Marius stared as intently at them as had Saturninus, but with less amazement.

"About time you came home," he said to Sulla, grasping his hand warmly, then reaching to greet Sertorius.

"We're not here for very long," said Sulla, jerking his captive forward. "All we came back to do was deliver you a gift for your triumphal parade. Meet King Copillus of the Volcae Tectosages, the same who connived at the annihilation of Lucius Cassius's army at Burdigala."

"Ah!" Marius looked the prisoner over. "Doesn't look much like a Gaul, does he? You and Quintus Sertorius look far more impressive."

Sertorius grinned; Sulla answered.

"Well, with his capital at Tolosa, he's been exposed to civilization for a long time. He speaks Greek well, and he's probably only about half Gallic in his thinking. We caught him outside Burdigala."

"Is he really worth so much trouble?" Marius asked.

"You'll think so when I tell you," said Sulla, smiling in his most tigerish fashion. "You see, he has a curious tale to tell—*and* he can tell it in a tongue Rome understands."

Arrested by the look on Sulla's face, Marius stared at King Copillus more closely. "What tale?"

"Oh, about ponds once full of gold. Gold that was loaded into Roman wagons and sent down the road from Tolosa to Narbo during the time when a certain Quintus Servilius Caepio was proconsul. Gold that mysteriously disappeared not far from Carcasso, leaving a cohort of Roman soldiers dead along the road, with their arms and armor stripped from them. Copillus was near Carcasso when that gold disappeared—after all, the gold was rightfully in his charge, according to his way of thinking. But the party of men who took the gold south into Spain was far too large and well armed to attack, for Copillus had only a few men with him. The interesting thing is that there *was* a Roman survivor—Furius, the *praefectus fabrum*. And a Greek freedman survivor—Quintus Servilius Bias. But Copillus wasn't near Malaca several months later as the wagons full of gold rolled into a fish factory owned by one of Quintus Servilius Caepio's clients, nor was he near Malaca when the gold sailed away to Smyrna labeled 'Garum of Malaca, on Consignment for Quintus Servilius Caepio.' But Copillus has a friend who has a friend who has a friend who well knows a Turdetanian bandit named Brigantius, and according to this Brigantius, he was hired to steal the gold and get it to Malaca. By the agents of none other than Quintus Servilius Caepio, namely Furius and the freedman Bias, who paid Brigantius with the wagons, the mules—and six hundred sets of good Roman arms and armor, taken from the men Brigantius killed. When the gold went east, Furius and Bias went with it."

Never before, thought Sulla, have I seen Gaius Marius looking utterly stunned, even when he read the letter that said he was elected consul *in absentia*—that just winded him, whereas this tries his credulity.

"Ye gods!" Marius whispered. "He wouldn't dare!"

"He dared, all right," said Sulla contemptuously. "What matter that the price was six hundred good Roman soldier lives? After all, there were fifteen thousand talents of gold in those wagons! It turns out that the Volcae Tectosages do not regard themselves as the owners of the gold, only as its guardians. The wealth of Delphi, Olympia, Dodona, and a dozen other smaller sanctuaries, which the second Brennus took as the property of all the Gallic tribes. So now the Volcae Tectosages are accursed, and King Copillus doubly accursed. The wealth of Gaul is gone."

His shock evaporating, Marius now looked more at Sulla than at Copillus. It was a little story told in richly ringing tones, yes, but more than that; it was a little story told by a Gallic bard, not by a Roman senator.

"You are a great actor, Lucius Cornelius," he said.

Sulla looked absurdly pleased. "My thanks, Gaius Marius."

"But you're not staying? What about the winter? You'd be more comfortable here." Marius grinned. "Especially young Quintus Sertorius, if he's got no more in his clothes chest than a feathered crown."

"No, we're off again tomorrow. The Cimbri are milling around the foothills of the Pyrenees, with the local tribesmen throwing every last thing they can find to throw down on them from every ledge, crag, rock, and cliff. The Germans seem to have a fascination for alps! But it's taken Quintus Sertorius and me all these months to get close to the Cimbri—we've had to establish our identities with half of Gaul and Spain, it seems," said Sulla.

Marius poured out two cups of wine, looked at Copillus, and

poured a third, which he handed to the prisoner. As he gave Sertorius his drink, he eyed his Sabine relative up and down gravely. "You look like Pluto's rooster," he said.

Sertorius took a sip of the wine and sighed blissfully. "Tusculan!" he said, then preened. "Pluto's rooster, eh? Well, better that than Proserpina's crow."

"What news do you have of the Germans?" Marius asked.

"In brief—I'll tell you more over dinner—very little. It's too early yet to be able to give you information about where they come from, or what drives them. Next time. I'll get back well ahead of any move they might make in the direction of Italy, never fear. But I can tell you where they all are at this very moment. The Teutones and the Tigurini, Marcomanni, and Cherusci are trying to cross the Rhenus into Germania, while the Cimbri are trying to cross the Pyrenees into Spain. I don't think either group will succeed," said Sulla, putting down his cup. "Oh, that wine was good!"

Marius called for his duty officer. "Send me three reliable men, would you?" he asked. "And see if you can find comfortable quarters for King Copillus here. He'll have to be locked up, unfortunately, but only until we can get him away to Rome."

"I wouldn't put him in Rome," said Sulla thoughtfully, when the duty officer had departed. "In fact, I'd be very quiet about where I did put him, anyway."

"Caepio? He wouldn't dare!" said Marius.

"He purloined the gold," said Sulla.

"All right, we'll put the King in Nersia," said Marius briskly. "Quintus Sertorius, has your mother got any friends who wouldn't mind housing the King for a year or two? I'll make sure the money's good."

"She'll find someone," said Sertorius confidently.

"What a piece of luck!" crowed Marius. "I never thought we'd get the evidence to send Caepio into well-deserved exile, but King Copillus is *it*. We'll keep it very quiet until we're all back in Rome after the Germans are beaten, then we'll arraign Caepio on charges of extortion *and* treason!"

"Treason?" asked Sulla, blinking. "Not with the friends he's got in the Centuries!"

"Ah," said Marius blandly, "but friends in the Centuries can't help him when he's tried in a special treason court manned only by knights."

"What are you up to, Gaius Marius?" Sulla demanded.

"I've got myself *two* tribunes of the plebs for next year!" said Marius triumphantly.

"They mightn't get in," said Sertorius prosaically.

"They'll get in!" said Marius and Sulla in chorus.

Then all three laughed, and the prisoner continued to stand with great dignity, pretending he could understand their Latin, and waiting for whatever was to befall him next.

At which point Marius remembered his manners and shifted the conversation from Latin to Greek, drawing Copillus warmly into the group, and promising that his chains would soon be struck off.

"Do you know, Quintus Caecilius," said Marcus Aemilius Scaurus Princeps Senatus to Metellus Numidicus, "I am thoroughly enjoying my stint as the quaestor of Ostia? Here I am, fifty-five years old, bald as an egg, lines on my face so deep my barber can't give me a really clean shave anymore—and I'm feeling like a boy again! Oh, and the *ease* with which one solves the problems! At thirty, they loomed like insurmountable alps—I remember it well. At fifty-five, they're piddling little cobblestones."

Scaurus had come back to Rome for a special meeting of the Senate convened by the *praetor urbanus* Gaius Memmius to discuss a matter of some concern regarding Sardinia; the junior consul, Gaius Flavius Fimbria, was indisposed—a common occurrence these days, it seemed to many.

"Did you hear the rumor?" asked Metellus Numidicus as the two of them strolled up the steps of the Curia Hostilia and passed inside; the herald had not yet summoned the House to convene, but most senators who arrived early didn't bother waiting outside—they went straight in and continued their talk until the meeting started with the convening magistrate offering a sacrifice and prayers.

"What rumor?" asked Scaurus a little inattentively; his mind these days tended to be absorbed with the grain supply.

"Lucius Cassius and Lucius Marcius have clubbed together and intend to put it to the Plebeian Assembly that Gaius Marius be allowed to stand for consul again—*in absentia,* no less!"

Scaurus stopped a few feet short of where his personal attendant had set up his stool in its customary front-rank position next to the stool of Metellus Numidicus, and with Metellus Dalmaticus Pontifex Maximus on his other side. His eyes rested on Numidicus's face, wide with shock.

"They wouldn't dare!" he said.

"Oh yes they would! Can you imagine it? A third term as consul is unprecedented—it's to make the man a long-term dictator! Why else on those rare occasions when Rome needed a dictator was the term of a dictator limited to six months, if not to make sure that the man holding the office got no inflated idea of his own supremacy? And now, here we are with this—this—*peasant* making up his own rules as he goes along!" Metellus Numidicus was spitting in rage.

Scaurus sank down onto his stool like an old man. "It's our own fault," he said slowly. "We haven't had the courage of our predecessors and rid ourselves of this noxious mushroom! Why is it that Tiberius Gracchus and Marcus Fulvius and Gaius Gracchus were eliminated, where Gaius Marius survives? He ought to have been cut down years ago!"

Metellus Numidicus shrugged. "He's a peasant. The Gracchi and Fulvius Flaccus were noblemen. Noxious mushroom is the right way to describe him—he pops up somewhere overnight, but by the time you arrive to weed him out, he's gone somewhere else."

"It has to stop!" cried Scaurus. "*No one* can be elected to the consulship *in absentia,* let alone twice running! That man has tampered in more ways with Rome's traditions of government than any man in the entire history of the Republic. I am beginning to believe that he wants to be King of Rome, not the First Man in Rome."

"I agree," said Metellus Numidicus, sitting down. "But how can we rid ourselves of him, I ask you? He's never here for long enough to assassinate!"

"Lucius Cassius and Lucius Marcius," said Scaurus in tones of wonder. "I don't understand! They're noblemen from the finest, oldest plebeian families! Can't someone appeal to their sense of fitness, of—of—decency?"

"Well, we all know about Lucius Marcius," said Metellus Numidicus. "Marius bought up all his debts; he's solvent for the first time in his rather revolting life. But Lucius Cassius is different. He's become morbidly sensitive about the People's opinion of incompetent generals like his late father, and morbidly aware of Marius's reputation among the People. I think he thinks that if he's seen helping Marius rid us of the Germans, he'll retrieve his family's reputation."

"Humph!" was all Scaurus said to this piece of theorizing.

Further discussion was impossible; the House convened, and Gaius Memmius—looking very haggard these days, and in consequence handsomer than ever—rose to speak.

"Conscript Fathers," he said, a short document in his hand, "I have received a letter from Gnaeus Pompeius Strabo in Sardinia. It was addressed to me rather than to our esteemed consul Gaius Flavius because, as urban praetor, it is my duty to supervise the law courts of Rome."

He paused to glare fiercely at the back ranks of senators, and contrived to appear almost ugly; the back ranks of senators got the message, and put on their most attentive expressions.

"To remind those of you at the back who hardly ever bother to honor this House with your presence, Gnaeus Pompeius Strabo is quaestor to the governor of Sardinia, who—to remind you!—is Titus Annius Albucius this year. Now do we all understand these complicated relationships, Conscript Fathers?" he asked, voice dripping sarcasm.

There was a general mumble, which Memmius took as assent.

"Good!" he said. "Then I shall read out Gnaeus Pompeius's letter to me. Are we all listening?"

Another mumble.

"Good!" Memmius unfurled the paper in his hand and held it out before him, then began to read with a clear, crisp diction no one afterward could have faulted.

> "I write, Gaius Memmius, to request that I be allowed to prosecute Titus Annius Albucius, governor *propraetore* of our province of Sardinia, immediately upon our return to Rome at the end of the year. As the House is aware, one month ago Titus Annius reported that he had succeeded in stamping out brigandage in his province, and requested an ovation for his work. His request for an ovation was refused, and rightly so. Though some nests of these pernicious fellows were eradicated, the province is by no means free of brigands. But the reason I wish to prosecute the governor lies in his un-Roman conduct after he learned that his request for an ovation had been denied. Not only did he refer to the members of the Senate as a pack of unappreciative *irrumatores,* but he proceeded—at great expense—to celebrate a mock triumph through the streets of Carales! I regard his actions as threats to the Senate and People of Rome, and his triumph as treasonous. In fact, so strongly do I feel that I am adamant no one other than myself shall conduct the prosecution. Please answer me in good time."

Memmius laid the letter down amid a profound silence. "I would appreciate an opinion from the learned Leader of the House, Marcus Aemilius Scaurus," he said, and sat down.

His lined face grim, Scaurus walked to the middle of the floor.

"How strange," he began, "that I was speaking of matters not unlike this just before the House convened. Of matters indicating the erosion of our time-honored systems of government and personal conduct in government. In recent years, this august body composed of Rome's greatest men has suffered the loss not only of its power, but of its dignity as Rome's senior arm in government. We—Rome's greatest men!—are no longer permitted to direct the path Rome treads. We—Rome's greatest men!—have become used to the People—fickle, untrained, greedy, thoughtless, part-time and good-time amateur politicians at best—have become used to the People grinding our faces into the mud! We—Rome's greatest men!—are held of no account! Our wisdom, our experience, the distinction of our families over the many generations since the founding of the Republic, all have ceased to matter. Only the People matter. And I say to you, Conscript Fathers, that the People are *not qualified* to govern Rome!"

He turned toward the open doors, and threw his voice in the direction of the well of the Comitia. "What segment of the People runs the Plebeian Assembly?" he bellowed. "The men of the Second and Third and even Fourth Classes—minor knights ambitious to run Rome like their businesses, shopkeepers and smallholding farmers, even *artisans* grown large enough to run 'multiple sculpturals,' as I saw one yard describe itself! And men who call themselves advocates, but who must hawk for clients among the bucolic and the imbecilic, and men who call themselves agents, but can never quite describe what they are agents for! Their private activities bore them, so they frequent the Comitia flattering themselves that they in their precious tribes can run Rome better than we in our Curiate exclusivity! Political cant dribbles off their tongues as noisome and lumpy as vomit, and they prate of entertaining this or that tribune of the plebs, and applaud when senatorial prerogatives are handed over to the knights! They are middlemen, these fellows! Neither great enough to belong to the First Class of the Centuries, nor lowly enough to mind their own business like the Fifth Class and the Head Count! I say to you again, Conscript Fathers, that the People are *not qualified* to govern Rome! Too much power has been accorded to them, and in their overweening arrogance—aided and abetted, I might add, by sundry members of this House when tribunes of the plebs!—they now presume to ignore our advice, our directives, and our persons!"

This, everyone recognized, was going to be one of Scaurus's more memorable speeches; his own secretary and several other scribes were busy scribbling his words down verbatim, and he was speaking slowly enough to make sure his words were properly recorded.

"It is high time," he went on sonorously, "that we of the Senate reversed this process. It is high time that we showed the People that *they* are the juniors in our joint governing venture!" He drew a breath, and spoke conversationally. "Of course the origins of this erosion of senatorial power are easy to pinpoint. This august body has admitted too many parvenus, too many noxious mushrooms, too many New Men into its senior magistracies. What does the Senate of Rome honestly mean to a man who had to wipe the pig-shit off his face before he came to Rome to try his political luck? What does the Senate of Rome mean to a man who is at best a half Latin from the Samnite borderlands—who rode into his first consulship on the skirts of a patrician woman he *bought*? And what does the Senate of Rome mean to a cross-eyed hybrid from the Celt-infested hills of northern Picenum?"

Naturally Scaurus was going to attack Marius, that was to be expected; but his approach was tangential enough to be refreshing, and the House felt itself properly rebuked. So the House listened on in a spirit of interest as well as duty.

"Our sons, Conscript Fathers," said Scaurus sadly, "are timid creatures, growing up in a political atmosphere which suffocates the Senate of Rome even as it breathes life into the People of Rome. How can we expect our sons to lead Rome in their turn, when the People cow them? I say to you—if you have not already begun, today you *must* begin to educate your sons to be strong for the Senate, and merciless to the People! Make them understand the natural superiority of the Senate! And make them prepared to fight to maintain that natural superiority!"

He had moved away from the doors, and now addressed his speech to the tribunes' bench, which was full. "Can anyone tell me why a member of this august House would deliberately set out to undermine it? *Can* anyone? Because it happens all the time! There they sit, calling themselves senators—members of this august House!—yet also calling themselves tribunes of the plebs! Serving two masters these days! I say, let them remember they are senators first, and tribunes of the plebs only after that. Their real duty toward the plebs is to educate the plebs in a subordinate role. But do they do that? No! Of course they don't! Some of these tribunes remain loyal to their rightful order, I acknowledge, and I commend them highly. Some, as is always the way in the annals of men, accomplish nothing for Senate or for People, too afraid that if they sit to either end of the tribunes' bench, the rest will get up, and they will be tipped on the ground and turn themselves into laughingstocks. But some, Conscript Fathers, deliberately set out to undermine this august body, the Senate of Rome. Why? What could possibly lead them to destroy their own order?"

The ten on the bench sat in various attitudes which clearly reflected their political attitudes: the loyal senatorial tribunes were glowing, upright, smug; the men on the middle of the bench wriggled a little, and kept their eyes on the floor; and the active tribunes sat with eyes and faces hard, defiant, impenitent.

"I can tell you why, fellow senators," said Scaurus, voice oozing contempt. "Some allow themselves to be bought like pinchbeck gewgaws on a cheap market stall—those men we all understand! But others have more subtle reasons, and of these men the first was Tiberius Sempronius Gracchus. I speak of the kind of tribune of the plebs who sees in the plebs a tool to further his own ambitions, the kind of man who craves the status of the First Man in Rome without earning it among his peers, as Scipio Aemilianus did, and Scipio Africanus, and Aemilius Paullus, and—if I may beg your collective pardon for my presumption—Marcus Aemilius Scaurus Princeps Senatus! We have borrowed a word from the Greeks to describe the Tiberius and Gaius Gracchus style of tribune of the plebs: we call them demagogues. However, we do not use it in precisely the way that the Greeks do. Our demagogues don't bring the whole city into the Forum screaming for blood, and tear down senators bodily from the steps of the Curia, and work their will through mass violence. Our demagogues content themselves with inflaming the habitual frequenters of the Comitia, and work their will through legislation. Oh, there is violence from time to time, but more often than not, it is we of the Senate who have had to resort to violence to reestablish the status quo. For our demagogues are legislators and legal draftsmen, more subtle, more vindictive, more dangerous by far than simple inciters of riots! They corrupt the People to further their own ambitions. And that, Conscript Fathers, is beneath contempt. Yet every day it is done, and every day it grows more prevalent. The shortcut to power, the easy road to pre-eminence."

He broke off, took a turn about the floor, clutched the massive folds of his purple-bordered toga with his left hand as they fell forward over his left shoulder and cuddled into his neck, flexed his bare right arm so it could continue to emphasize his words by gestures.

"The shortcut to power, the easy road to pre-eminence," he repeated sonorously. "Well, we all know these men, don't we? First among them is Gaius Marius, our esteemed senior consul, who I hear is about to have himself elected consul yet again, and yet again *in absentia*! By *our* wish? No! Through the medium of the People, of course! How else could Gaius Marius have got where he is today, except through the medium of the People? Some of us have fought him, and fought him tooth and nail, and fought him to exhaustion, and fought him with every legal weapon in our constitutional arsenal! To no avail. Gaius Marius has the support of the People, the ear of the People, and pours money into the purses of some of the tribunes of the plebs. In this day and age, those are enough. Rich as Croesus, he can buy what he cannot get any other way. Such is Gaius Marius. But it is not Gaius Marius I rose to discuss. You will forgive me, Conscript Fathers, for allowing my emotions to carry me too far from the main thrust of my oration."

He walked back to his original position, and turned to face the dais whereon sat the curule magistrates, and addressed his remarks to Gaius Memmius.

"I rose to speak about another upstart, a less noticeable sort of upstart than Gaius Marius. The sort of upstart who claims ancestors in the Senate, and can speak good Greek, and has been educated, and lives in his home with a vastness of power ensuring that his eyes have never rested upon pigshit—if, that is, his eyes could see anything at all! *Not* a Roman of the Romans, for all he claims otherwise. I speak of the quaestor Gnaeus Pompeius Strabo, deputed by this august House to serve the governor of Sardinia, Titus Annius Albucius.

"Now who is this Gnaeus Pompeius Strabo? A Pompey, who claims blood relationship to the Pompeys in this House for some generations, though it would be interesting to discover just how close the blood links are. Rich as Croesus, half of northern Italy in his clientship, a king inside the borders of his own lands. That's who is this Gnaeus Pompeius Strabo."

Scaurus's voice rose to a roar. "Members of the Senate, what is this august body coming to, when a brand-new senator in the guise of a quaestor has the temerity and the—the—*crassness* to indict his superior? How short of young Roman men are we, that we cannot put Roman arses on a mere three hundred seats? *I—am—scandalized!* Does this Pompey Cross-eyes really possess so little education in the niceties of behavior expected from a member of the Senate that he could even *dream* of indicting his superior? What is the matter with us, that we are letting the likes of this Pompey Cross-eyes put his uncouth arse on a senatorial stool? And what is the matter with him, that he could do such a thing? Ignorance and lack of breeding, that's what's the matter with him! Some things, Conscript Fathers, are just—not—done! Things like indicting one's superior or one's close relatives, including relatives by marriage. *Not done!* Crass —bovine—ill-mannered—underbred—presumptuous— stupid—our Latin language does not possess sufficient scathing

epithets whereby to catalogue the shortcomings of such a noxious mushroom as this Gnaeus Pompeius Strabo, this Pompey
Cross-eyes!"

A voice came from the tribunes' bench. "Are you inferring,
Marcus Aemilius, that Titus Annius Albucius is to be lauded for
his behavior?" asked Lucius Cassius.

The Princeps Senatus drew himself up like a cobra, and just as
venomously. "Oh, grow up, Lucius Cassius!" he said. "The issue
here is not Titus Annius. Naturally he will be dealt with in the
appropriate manner, which in his case is prosecution. If he is
found guilty, he will incur the proper punishment the law pre-
scribes. The issue here is protocol, politesse, etiquette—in plain
words, Lucius Cassius, *manners*! Our noxious mushroom Pompey
Cross-eyes is guilty of a flagrant breach of manners!"

He faced the House. "I move, Conscript Fathers, that Titus Annius Albucius answer charges of a treasonable nature—but that
the *praetor urbanus* shall at the same time write a very stiff letter
to the quaestor Gnaeus Pompeius Strabo informing him that, one,
under no circumstances will he be permitted to prosecute his superior, and that, two, he has the manners of a boor."

The House voted with a flourishing flapping of hands, making
a Division unnecessary.

"I think, Gaius Memmius," said Lucius Marcius Philippus in a
nasal drawl of vastly aristocratic superiority (he was smarting at
Scaurus's inference that Marius had bought his services), "that
the House should at this time appoint a prosecutor to deal with
the case of Titus Annius Albucius."

"Do I hear any objections?" asked Memmius, looking around.

No one objected.

"Very well, let it be tabled that the House will appoint a prosecutor in the case of the State versus Titus Annius Albucius. Do I
hear any names?" asked Memmius.

"Oh, my dear *praetor urbanus,* there is only one possible
name!" said Philippus, still drawling.

"Then speak it, Lucius Marcius."

"Why, our learned young man of the courts Caesar *Strabo*," said Philippus. "I mean, let us not utterly deprive Titus Annius of the sensation that he is being hounded by a voice from his past! I do think his prosecutor *must* be cross-eyed!"

The House fell about laughing, Scaurus hardest of all; and when the hilarity died down, voted unanimously to appoint the cross-eyed young Gaius Julius Caesar Strabo—youngest brother of Catulus Caesar and Lucius Caesar—as Titus Annius Albucius's prosecutor. And in so doing, revenged itself tellingly upon Pompey Strabo. When Pompey Strabo received the Senate's stiff letter (plus a copy of Scaurus's speech, thrown in by Gaius Memmius to rub salt into the wound), he got the message. And vowed that one day he would have all those high-and-mighty aristocrats on the hop, needing him more than he needed them.

Fight strenuously though they did, neither Scaurus nor Metellus Numidicus could swing enough votes in the Plebeian Assembly to avert the nomination of Gaius Marius as a candidate for the consulship *in absentia*. Nor could they sway the Centuriate Assembly, for the Second Class of voters was still smarting at Scaurus's inference during his memorable speech that they were mere middlemen, and as reprehensible as the Third and Fourth Classes. The Centuriate Assembly gave Gaius Marius a continued mandate to stop the Germans, and would not hear of any other man's taking his place. Elected senior consul for the second time in a row, Gaius Marius was the man of the hour, and might without fear of contradiction claim to be the First Man in Rome.

"But not *primus inter pares*—first among equals," said Metellus Numidicus to young Marcus Livius Drusus, returned to the law courts after his short-lived military career of the year before. They had encountered each other in front of the urban praetor's tribunal, where Drusus was standing with his friend and brother-in-law, Caepio Junior.

"I am afraid, Quintus Caecilius," said Drusus without an ounce of apology in his tone, "that for once I did not subscribe to the thinking of my peers. I voted *for* Gaius Marius—yes, that stops you in your tracks, doesn't it? Not only did I vote for Gaius Marius, but I prevailed upon most of my friends and all my clients to vote for him as well."

"You're a traitor to your class!" snapped Numidicus.

"Not at all, Quintus Caecilius. You see, I was at Arausio," said Drusus quietly. "I saw at first hand what can happen when senatorial exclusivity overcomes the dictates of good sound Roman common sense. And I say to you flatly that if Gaius Marius was as cross-eyed as Caesar Strabo, as crass as Pompey Strabo, as lowborn as a laborer in the Port of Rome, as vulgar as the knight Sextus Perquitienus—*still* I would have voted for him! I do not believe we have another military man of his caliber, and I will not countenance placing a consul over him who would treat him as Quintus Servilius Caepio treated Gnaeus Mallius Maximus!"

And Drusus walked away with great dignity, leaving Metellus Numidicus staring after him openmouthed.

"He's changed," said Caepio Junior, who still followed Drusus about, but with less enthusiasm since their return from Gaul-across-the-Alps. "My father says that if Marcus Livius isn't careful, he'll turn into a demagogue of the worst kind."

"He *couldn't!*" cried Metellus Numidicus. "Why, his father the censor was Gaius Gracchus's most obdurate foe—young Marcus Livius has been brought up in the most conservative way!"

"Arausio changed him," maintained Caepio Junior. "Maybe it was the blow to his head—that's what my father thinks, anyway. Ever since he came back, he's stayed as thick as thieves with the Marsic fellow Silo he befriended after the battle." He snorted. "Silo comes down from Alba Fucentia and lords it around Marcus Livius's house as if he owns it, and they sit for hours and hours talking, and they never ask me to join in."

"A regrettable affair, Arausio," said Metellus Numidicus, laboring a little, since he was passing these remarks to the son of the man who had incurred most of the blame.

Caepio Junior escaped as soon as he could, and walked home conscious of a vague dissatisfaction which had wrapped him round from the time—oh, he didn't know really, but somewhere about the time he had married Drusus's sister, and Drusus had married his sister. There was no reason why he should feel this way; he just did. And things had changed so since Arausio! His father wasn't the same man either; one moment he would be chuckling gleefully at a joke Caepio Junior didn't understand, the next moment he would be down in the depths of despair at the swelling tide of public resentment for Arausio, and only moments later he would be shouting in rage at the injustice of it all—what he meant by "it all" Caepio Junior had not been able to work out.

Nor could Caepio Junior's feelings about Arausio ever be free from guilt; while Drusus and Sertorius and Sextus Caesar and even that Silo fellow lay on the field given up for dead, he had run away across the river like a kicked cur, no less anxious to survive than the least Head Count raw recruit in his legion. Naturally this had never been spoken to anyone, even his father; it was Caepio Junior's awful secret. Yet every day when he met Drusus, he wondered what Drusus suspected.

His wife, Livia Drusa, was in her sitting room, her infant daughter on her knee, for she had just finished breast-feeding the mite. As always, his advent produced a smile, and that should have warmed him. But it never did. Her eyes were at odds with the rest of her face, for no smile ever reached inside them, and no interest ever flared out of them. Whenever she spoke to him or listened to him speaking, Caepio Junior was aware that her eyes never looked into his, even for a moment. And yet, no man was ever blessed with a nicer, more accommodating wife. She was never too tired or unwell to receive his sexual advances, nor did she object to any sexual request he made of her. Of course at such times he couldn't see her eyes; how then could he know so positively they held not a scrap of pleasure?

A more perceptive and intelligent man would have gently taxed Livia Drusa with these things, but Caepio Junior tended to put it all down to his own imagination, having too little imagination to understand he lacked it. Mentally acute enough to know there was something radically wrong, he was not mentally acute enough to make the correct assumptions. Certainly it never occurred to him that she didn't love him, though before they married he had been sure she positively disliked him. But that had been his imagination. For she could not have disliked him, when she had proven a model Roman wife. Therefore—she must love him.

His daughter, Servilia, was an object rather than a human creature to Caepio Junior, disappointed that he hadn't been dowered with a son. So now he sat down while Livia Drusa gave the baby a few rubs on the back, then handed her over to her Macedonian nursemaid.

"Did you know that your brother actually voted for Gaius Marius in the consular elections?" he asked.

Livia Drusa's eyes widened. "No. Are you sure?"

"He said so today, to Quintus Caecilius Metellus Numidicus. While I was there. Waffled on about being at Arausio. Oh, I wish my father's enemies would let that die a natural death!"

"Give it time, Quintus Servilius."

"It's getting worse," said Caepio Junior despondently.

"Are you in to dinner?"

"No, on my way out again, actually. Going to eat at Lucius Licinius Orator's house. Marcus Livius will be there too."

"Oh," said Livia Drusa flatly.

"Sorry, did mean to tell you this morning. Just forgot," said her husband, getting up. "You don't mind, do you?"

"No, of course not," said Livia Drusa tonelessly.

Of course she did mind, not because she craved her husband's company, but because a little forethought on his part might have saved both money and effort in the kitchen. They lived with Caepio the father, who was forever complaining about the size of the household bills, and forever blaming Livia Drusa for not being a more careful housekeeper. It never occurred to Caepio the father any more than it did to his son that neither of them bothered to apprise her of their movements, and so every day she was obliged to make sure a proper dinner was prepared, even if no one turned up to eat it, and it went back almost untouched to slide down the gullets of Caepio the father's ecstatic slaves.

"*Domina,* shall I take the baby back to the nursery?" the Macedonian girl asked.

Livia Drusa started out of her reverie, nodded. "Yes," she said, not even giving the child a glance in passing as the maid carried her off. That she was breast-feeding her daughter was not out of any consideration for the welfare of baby Servilia; it was because she knew while ever she gave the baby her milk, she would not conceive again.

She didn't care for baby Servilia very much; every time she looked at the mite, she saw a miniature copy of the mite's father—short legs, a darkness so dark it was disquieting, a dense coat of black hair along spine, arms and legs, and a shock of coarse black head hair which grew low down on the forehead and the back of the neck like an animal's pelt. To Livia Drusa, little Servilia possessed no virtues whatsoever. She didn't even attempt to list the baby's assets, which were by no means contemptible, for she had a pair of black eyes so big and dark that they promised great beauty later on, and the tiniest rosebud of a mouth, still and secretive, another harbinger of beauty.

The eighteen months of her marriage had not reconciled Livia Drusa to her fate, though never once did she disobey her brother Drusus's orders; her courtesy and demeanor were perfect. Even in the midst of her frequent sexual encounters with Caepio Junior, she behaved impeccably. Luckily her high birth and status precluded an ardent response; Caepio Junior would have been appalled if she had moaned in ecstasy or thrown herself around in the bed as if she enjoyed herself in the manner of a mistress. All she was obliged to do, she did in the manner her wifehood dictated—flat on her back, no fancy hipwork, a suitable meed of warmth, and unassailable modesty. Oh, but it was difficult! More difficult than any other aspect of her life, for when her husband touched her she wanted to scream rape and violation, and vomit in his face.

There was no room in her to pity Caepio Junior, who in actual fact had never really done anything to deserve the passionate revulsion she felt for him. By now, he and her brother Drusus had merged indissolubly into a single vast and threatening presence capable of reducing her to far worse circumstances; hideously afraid of them, she moved on day by day toward death aware that she was never going to know what it was like to live.

Worst of all was her geographical exile. The Servilius Caepio house was on the Circus Maximus side of the Palatine, looked across to the Aventine, and had no houses below it, just a steep and rocky cliff. There were no more chances to stand on Drusus's loggia watching the balcony of the house underneath for a glimpse of her red-haired Odysseus.

And Caepio the father was a singularly unpleasant man who grew steadily more unpleasant as time went on; he didn't even have a wife to lighten Livia Drusa's burden, though so remote was he and so remote was her relationship with his son that she never found the courage to ask either of them whether the wife/mother was alive or dead. Of course Caepio the father's temper was tried more and more as time went on because of his part in the disaster at Arausio. First he had been stripped of his imperium, then the tribune of the plebs Lucius Cassius Longinus had succeeded in passing a law stripping his seat in the Senate from him, and now hardly a month went by without some enterprising would-be crowd pleaser trying to prosecute him on thinly veiled treason charges. Virtually confined to his house by the virulent hatred of the People and his own lively sense of self-preservation, Caepio the father spent a good deal of his time watching Livia Drusa—and criticizing her remorselessly.

However, she didn't help matters by doing some very silly things. One day her father-in-law's mania for watching her made her so angry that she marched out into the middle of the peristyle-garden where no one could overhear what she said, and began to talk to herself aloud. The moment the slaves began to gather beneath the colonnade and whisper debates as to what she might be doing, Caepio the father erupted out of his study with a face like flint.

Down the path he came and stood over her fiercely. "What do you think you're doing, girl?" he demanded.

Her big dark eyes opened guilessly wide. "I'm reciting the lay of King Odysseus," she said.

"Well, don't!" snarled her father-in-law. "You're making a spectacle of yourself! The servants are saying you've gone off your head! If you must recite Homer, then do it where people can *hear* it's Homer! Though why you'd want to beats me."

"It passes the time," she said.

"There are better ways to pass the time, girl. Set up your loom, or sing to your baby, or do whatever else women do. Go on, go on, go away!"

"I don't know what women do, Father," she said, getting to her feet. "What do women do?"

"Drive men insane!" he said, went back into his study and shut the door with a snap.

After that she went even further, for she took Caepio the father's advice and set up her loom. The only trouble was, she began to weave the first of a whole series of funeral dresses, and as she worked she talked very loudly to an imaginary King Odysseus, pretending that he had been away for years and she was weaving funeral dresses to stave off the day when she must choose a new husband; every so often she would pause in her monologue and sit with head cocked to one side, as if she were listening to someone speak.

This time Caepio the father sent his son to find out what was the matter.

"I'm weaving my funeral dress," she said calmly, "and trying to find out when King Odysseus is coming home to rescue me. He will rescue me, you know. One day."

Caepio Junior gaped. "*Rescue* you? What are you talking about, Livia Drusa?"

"I never set foot outside this house," she said.

Flinging his hands up, Caepio Junior made a small sound of exasperation. "Well, what's to stop you going out if you want to, for Juno's sake?"

Her jaw dropped; she could think of nothing to say except "I don't have any money."

"You want money? I'll *give* you money, Livia Drusa! Just stop worrying my father!" cried Caepio Junior, goaded from two directions. "Go out whenever you want! Buy whatever you want!"

Face wreathed in smiles, she walked across the room and kissed her husband on the cheek. "Thank you," she said, and meant it so sincerely that she actually hugged him.

It had been as easy as that! All those years of enforced isolation were gone. For it had not occurred to Livia Drusa that in passing from the authority of her brother to the authority of her husband and his father, the rules might have changed a little.

When Lucius Appuleius Saturninus was elected a tribune of the plebs, his gratitude to Gaius Marius knew no bounds. Now he could vindicate himself! Nor was he completely without allies, as he soon discovered; one of the other tribunes of the plebs was a client of Marius's from Etruria, one Gaius Norbanus, who had considerable wealth but no senatorial clout because he had no senatorial background. And there was a Marcus Baebius, one of the ever-tribuning Baebius clan who were justly notorious for their bribe taking; he might be bought if it proved necessary.

Unfortunately the opposite end of the tribunes' bench was occupied by three formidably conservative opponents. On the very end of the bench was Lucius Aurelius Cotta, son of the dead consul Cotta, nephew of the ex-praetor Marcus Cotta, and half brother of Aurelia, the wife of young Gaius Julius Caesar. Next to him sat Lucius Antistius Reginus, of respectable but not spectacular background, and rumored to be a client of the consular Quintus Servilius Caepio, therefore faintly smeared with Caepio's odium. The third man was Titus Didius, a very efficient and quiet man whose family had originally hailed from Campania, and who had made himself a considerable reputation as a soldier.

Those in the middle of the bench were very humble tribunes of the plebs, and seemed to think that their chief role throughout the coming year was going to be keeping the opposite ends of the bench from tearing each other's throats out. For indeed there was no love lost between the men Scaurus would have apostrophized as demagogues and the men Scaurus commended for never losing sight of the fact that they were senators before they were tribunes of the plebs.

Not that Saturninus was worried. He had swept into office at the top of the college, followed closely by Gaius Norbanus, which gave the conservatives notice that the People had lost none of their affection for Gaius Marius—and that Marius had thought it worthwhile to spend a great deal of his money buying votes for Saturninus and Norbanus. It was necessary that Saturninus and Norbanus strike swiftly, for interest in the Plebeian Assembly waned dramatically after some three months of the year had gone by; this was partly due to boredom on the part of the People, and partly due to the fact that no tribune of the plebs could keep up the pace for longer than three months. The tribune of the plebs spent himself early, like Aesop's hare, while the old senatorial tortoise kept plodding on at the same rate.

"All they'll see is my dust," Saturninus said to Glaucia as the tenth day of the month of December drew near, the day upon which the new college would enter office.

"What's first?" asked Glaucia idly, a little put out that he, older than Saturninus, had not yet found the opportunity to seek election as a tribune of the plebs.

Saturninus grinned wolfishly. "A little agrarian law," he said, "to help my friend and benefactor Gaius Marius."

With great care in his planning and through the medium of a magnificent speech, Saturninus tabled for discussion a law to distribute the *ager Africanus insularum,* reserved in the public domain by Lucius Marcius Philippus one year before; it was now to be divided among Marius's Head Count soldiers at the end of their service in the legions, at the rate of a hundred *iugera* per man. Oh, how he enjoyed it! The howls of approbation from the People, the howls of outrage from the Senate, the fist that Lucius

Cotta raised, the strong and candid speech Gaius Norbanus made in support of his measure.

"I never realized how interesting the tribunate of the plebs can be," he said after the *contio* meeting was dissolved, and he and Glaucia dined alone at Glaucia's house.

"Well, you certainly had the Policy Makers on the defensive," said Glaucia, grinning at the memory. "I thought Metellus Numidicus was going to rupture a blood vessel!"

"A pity he didn't." Saturninus lay back with a sigh of content, eyes roaming reflectively over the patterns sooty smoke from lamps and braziers had made on the ceiling, which was badly in need of new paint. "Odd how they think, isn't it? Even breathe the words 'agrarian bill' and they're up in arms, yelling about the Brothers Gracchi, horrified at the idea of giving something away for nothing to men without the wit to acquire anything. Even the Head Count doesn't approve of giving something away for nothing!"

"Well, it's a pretty novel concept to all right-thinking Romans, really," said Glaucia.

"And after they got over that, they started to yell about the huge size of the allotments—ten times the size of a smallholding in Campania, moaned the Policy Makers. You'd think they'd know without being told that an island in the African Lesser Syrtis isn't one tenth as fertile as the worst smallholding in Campania, nor the rainfall one tenth as reliable," said Saturninus.

"Yes, but the debate was really about so many thousands of new clients for Gaius Marius, wasn't it?" asked Glaucia. "That's where the shoe actually pinches, you know. Every retired veteran in a Head Count army is a potential client for his general— especially when his general has gone to the trouble of securing him a piece of land for his old age. He's *beholden*! Only he doesn't see that it's the State that is his true benefactor, since the State has to find the land. He thanks his general. He thanks Gaius Marius. And that's what the Policy Makers are up in arms about."

"Agreed. But fighting it isn't the answer, Gaius Servilius. The answer is to enact a general law covering all Head Count armies for all time—ten *iugera* of good land to every man who completes his time in the legions—say, fifteen years? Twenty, even? Given irrespective of how many generals the soldier serves under, or how many different campaigns he sees."

Glaucia laughed in genuine amusement. "That's too much like good sound common sense, Lucius Appuleius! And think of the knights a law like that would alienate. Less land for them to lease—not to mention our esteemed pastoralist senators!"

"If the land was in Italy, I'd see it," said Saturninus. "But the islands off the coast of Africa? I ask you, Gaius Servilius! Of what conceivable use are they to these dogs guarding their stinking old bones? Compared to the millions of *iugera* Gaius Marius gave away in the name of Rome along the Ubus and the Chelif and around Lake Tritonis—and all to exactly the same men currently screaming!—this is a pittance!"

Glaucia rolled his long-lashed grey-green eyes, lay flat on his back, flapped his hands like a stranded turtle his flippers, and started to laugh again. "I liked Scaurus's speech best, though. He's clever, that one. The rest of them don't matter much apart from their clout." He lifted his head and stared at Saturninus. "Are you prepared for tomorrow in the Senate?" he asked.

"I believe so," said Saturninus happily. "Lucius Appuleius returns to the Senate! And this time they can't throw me out before my term in office is finished! It would take the thirty-five tribes to do that, and they won't do that. Whether the Policy Makers like it or not, I'm back inside their hallowed portals as angry as a wasp—and just as nasty."

He entered the Senate as if he owned it, with a sweeping obeisance to Scaurus Princeps Senatus, and flourishes of his right hand to each side of the House, which was almost full, a sure sign of a coming battle. The outcome, he decided, did not matter very much, for the arena in which the real conflict would be decided lay outside the Curia Hostilia's doors, down in the well of the Comitia; this was brazening-it-out day, the disgraced grain quaestor transmogrified into the tribune of the plebs, a bitter surprise indeed for the Policy Makers.

And for the Conscript Fathers of the Senate he took a new tack, one he fully intended to present later in the Plebeian Assembly; this would be a trial run.

"Rome's sphere of influence has not been limited to Italy for a very long time," he said. "All of us know the trouble King Jugurtha caused Rome. All of us are forever grateful to the esteemed senior consul, Gaius Marius, for settling the war in Africa so brilliantly—and so *finally*. But how can we in Rome today guarantee the generations to come that our provinces will be peaceful and their fruits ours to enjoy? We have a tradition concerning the customs of peoples not Roman, though they live in our provinces—they are free to pursue their religious practices, their trade practices, their political practices. *Provided* these pursuits do not hamper Rome, or offer a threat to Rome. But one of the less desirable side effects of our tradition of noninterference is ignorance. Not one of our provinces further from Italy than Italian Gaul and Sicily knows enough about Rome and Romans to favor co-operation over resistance. Had the people of Numidia known more about us, Jugurtha would never have managed to persuade them to follow him. Had the people of Mauretania known more about us, Jugurtha would never have managed to persuade King Bocchus to follow him."

He cleared his throat; the House was taking it well so far—but then, he hadn't reached his conclusion. Now he did. "Which brings me to the matter of the *ager Africanus insularum*. Strategically these islands are of little importance. In size they are modest. None of us here in this House will miss them. They contain no gold, no silver, no iron, no exotic spices. They are not particularly fertile when compared to the fabulous grainlands of the Bagradas River, where quite a few of us here in this House own properties, as do many knights of the First Class. So why *not* give them to Gaius Marius's Head Count soldiers upon their retirement? Do we really want close to forty thousand Head Count veterans frequenting the taverns and alleys of Rome? Jobless, aimless, penniless after they've spent their tiny shares of the army's booty? Isn't it better for them—and for Rome!—to settle them on the *ager Africanus insularum*? For, Conscript Fathers, there is one job left that they in their retirement can do. They can bring Rome to the province of Africa! Our language, our customs, our gods, our very way of life! Through these brave and cheerful expatriate Roman soldiers, the peoples of Africa Province can come to understand Rome better, for these brave and cheerful expatriate Roman soldiers are *ordinary*—no richer, no brighter, no more privileged than many among the native peoples they will mingle with on a day-to-day basis. Some will marry local girls. All will fraternize. And the result will be less war, greater peace."

It was said persuasively, reasonably, without any of the grander periods and gestures of Asianic rhetoric, and as he warmed to his peroration Saturninus began to believe that he would make them, the pigheaded members of this elite body, see at last where the vision of men like Gaius Marius—and himself!—would lead their beloved Rome.

And when he moved back to his end of the tribunes' bench, he sensed nothing in the silence to gainsay his conviction. Until he realized that they were waiting. Waiting for one of the Policy Makers to point the way. Sheep. Sheep, sheep, sheep. Wretched woolly pea-brained sheep.

"May I?" asked Lucius Caecilius Metellus Dalmaticus Pontifex Maximus of the presiding magistrate, the junior consul, Gaius Flavius Fimbria.

"You have the floor, Lucius Caecilius," said Fimbria.

He took the floor, his anger, well concealed until that moment, breaking the bounds of control with the sudden flare of tinder. "Rome is exclusive!" he trumpeted, so loudly that some of the listeners jumped. "How dare any Roman elevated to membership of this House propose a program aimed at turning the rest of the world into imitation Romans?"

Dalmaticus's normal pose of superior aloofness had vanished; he swelled up, empurpled, the veins beneath his plump pink cheeks no darker than those selfsame cheeks. And he trembled, he vibrated almost as quickly as the wings of a moth, so angry was he. Fascinated, awed, every last man present in the House sat forward to listen to a Dalmaticus Pontifex Maximus no one had ever dreamed existed.

"Well, Conscript Fathers, we all know this particular Roman, don't we?" he brayed. "Lucius Appuleius Saturninus is a thief—an exploiter of food shortages—an effeminate vulgarity—a polluter of little boys who harbors filthy lusts for his sister and his young daughter—a puppet manipulated by the Arpinate dollmaster in Gaul-across-the-Alps—a cockroach out of Rome's vilest stew—a pimp—a pansy—a pornographer—the creature on the end of every *verpa* in town! What does he know of Rome, what does his peasant dollmaster from Arpinum know of Rome? Rome is exclusive! Rome cannot be tossed to the world like shit to sewers, like spit to gutters! Are we to endure the dilution of our race through hybrid unions with the raggle-taggle women of half a hundred nations? Are we in the future to journey to places far from Rome and have our Roman ears defiled by a bastard Latin argot? Let them speak Greek, I say! Let them worship Serapis of the Scrotum or Astarte of the Anus! What does that matter to us? But *we* are to give them *Quirinus*? Who are the Quirites, the children of Quirinus? *We* are! For who is this Quirinus? Only a Roman can know! Quirinus is the spirit of the Roman citizenship; Quirinus is the god of the assembly of Roman men; Quirinus is the unconquered god because Rome has never been conquered— *and never will be conquered,* fellow Quirites!"

The whole House erupted into screaming cheers; while Dalmaticus Pontifex Maximus staggered to his stool and almost fell onto it, men wept, men stamped their feet, men clapped until their hands were numb, men turned to each other with the tears streaming down their faces, and embraced.

But so much emotion uncontained spent itself like sea foam on basaltic rock, and when the tears dried and the bodies ceased to shake, the men of the Senate of Rome found themselves with nothing more to give that day, and dragged their leaden feet home to live again in dreams that one magical moment when they actually saw the vision of faceless Quirinus rear up to throw his numinous toga over them as a father over his truehearted and unfailingly loyal sons.

The House was nearly empty when Crassus Orator, Quintus Mucius Scaevola, Metellus Numidicus, Catulus Caesar, and Scaurus Princeps Senatus recollected themselves enough to break off their euphoric conversation and think about following in the footsteps of the rest. Lucius Caecilius Metellus Dalmaticus Pontifex Maximus was still sitting on his stool, back straight, hands folded in his lap as neatly as a well-bred girl's. But his head had fallen forward, chin on chest, the thinning wisps of his greying hair blowing gently in a little breeze through the open doors.

"Brother of mine, that was the greatest speech I have ever heard!" cried Metellus Numidicus, putting his hand out to squeeze Dalmaticus's shoulder.

Dalmaticus sat on, and did not speak or move; only then did they discover he was dead.

"It's fitting," said Crassus Orator. "I'd die a happy man to think I gave my greatest speech on the very threshold of death."

But not the speech of Metellus Dalmaticus Pontifex Maximus nor the passing of Metellus Dalmaticus Pontifex Maximus nor all the ire and power of the Senate could prevent the Plebeian Assembly from passing Saturninus's agrarian bill into law. And the tribunician career of Lucius Appuleius Saturninus was off to a resounding start, a curious compound of infamy and adulation.

"I love it," said Saturninus to Glaucia over dinner late in the afternoon of the day the agrarian *lex Appuleia* was voted into law. They often did dine together, and usually at Glaucia's house; Saturninus's wife had never properly recovered from the awful events following Scaurus's denunciation of Saturninus when the quaestor at Ostia. "Yes, I do love it! Just think, Gaius Servilius, I might have had quite a different kind of career if it hadn't been for that nosy old *mentula,* Scaurus."

"The rostra suits you, all right," said Glaucia, eating hot-house grapes. "Maybe there is something shapes our lives after all."

Saturninus snorted. "Oh, you mean *Quirinus!*"

"You can sneer if you want. But I maintain that life is a very bizarre business," said Glaucia. "There's more pattern and less chance to it than there is in a game of *cottabus*."

"What, no element of Stoic or Epicure, Gaius Servilius? Neither fatalism nor hedonism? You'd better be careful, or you might confound all the old Greek killjoys who maintain so loudly that we Romans will never produce a philosophy we didn't borrow from them," laughed Saturninus.

"Greeks *are*. Romans *do*. Take your pick! I never met a man yet who managed to combine both states of being. We're the opposite ends of the alimentary canal, we Greeks and Romans. Romans are the mouth—we shove it in. Greeks are the arsehole—they shove it out. No disrespect to the Greeks intended, simply a figure of speech," said Glaucia, punctuating his statement by popping grapes into the Roman end of the alimentary canal.

"Since one end has no job to do without the contributions of the other, we'd better stick together," said Saturninus.

Glaucia grinned. "There speaks a Roman!" he said.

"Through and through, despite Metellus Dalmaticus's saying I'm not one. Wasn't that a turnup for the books, the old *fellator* up and dying so very timely? If the Policy Makers were more enterprising, they might have made an undying example of him. Metellus Dalmaticus—the New Quirinus!" Saturninus swirled the lees in his cup and tossed them expertly onto an empty plate; the splatter they made was counted according to the number of arms radiating out of the central mass. "Three," he said, and shivered. "That's the death number."

"And where's our Skeptic now?" gibed Glaucia.

"Well, it's unusual, only three."

Glaucia spat expertly, and destroyed the form of the splash with three grape seeds. "There! Three done in by three!"

"We'll both be dead in three years," said Saturninus.

"Lucius Appuleius, you're a complete contradiction! You are as white as Lucius Cornelius Sulla, and with far less excuse. Come, it's only a game of *cottabus!*" said Glaucia, and changed the subject. "I agree, life on the rostra is far more exciting than life as a darling of the Policy Makers. It's a great challenge, politically manipulating the People. A general has his legions. A demagogue has nothing sharper than his tongue." He chuckled. "And wasn't it a pleasure to watch the crowd chase Marcus Baebius from the Forum this morning, when he tried to interpose his veto?"

"A sight to cure sore eyes!" grinned Saturninus, the memory banishing ghostly fingers, three or thirty-three.

"By the way," said Glaucia with another abrupt change of subject, "have you heard the latest rumor in the Forum?"

"That Quintus Servilius Caepio stole the Gold of Tolosa himself, you mean?" asked Saturninus.

Glaucia looked disappointed. "Dis take you, I thought I'd got in first!"

"I had it in a letter from Manius Aquillius," Saturninus said. "When Gaius Marius is too busy, Aquillius writes to me instead. And I confess I don't repine, since he's a far better man of letters than the Great Man."

"From Gaul-across-the-Alps? How do they know?"

"That's where the rumor began. Gaius Marius has acquired a prisoner. The King of Tolosa, no less. And *he* alleges that Caepio stole the gold—all fifteen thousand talents of it."

Glaucia whistled. "Fifteen thousand talents! Mazes the mind, doesn't it? A bit much, though—I mean, everyone understands that a governor is entitled to his perquisites, but more gold than there is in the Treasury? A trifle excessive, surely!"

"True, true. However, the rumor will work very well for Gaius Norbanus when he brings his case against Caepio, won't it? The story of the gold will be around the whole city in less time than it takes Metella Calva to lift her dress for a lusty gang of navvies."

"I like your metaphor!" said Glaucia. And suddenly he looked very brisk. "Enough of this idle chatter! You and I have work to do on treason bills and the like. We can't afford to let anything go unnoticed."

The work Saturninus and Glaucia did on treason bills and the like was as carefully planned and co-ordinated as any grand military strategy. They intended to remove treason trials from the province of the Centuries and the impossible sequence of dead ends and stone walls this entailed; after which, they intended to remove extortion and bribery trials from the control of the Senate by replacing the senatorial juries with juries composed entirely of knights.

"First, we have to see Norbanus convict Caepio in the Plebeian Assembly on some permissible charge—as long as the charge isn't worded to say treason, we can do that right now, with popular feeling running so high against Caepio because of the stolen gold," said Saturninus.

"It's never worked before in the Plebeian Assembly," said Glaucia dubiously. "Our hot-headed friend Ahenobarbus tried it when he charged Silanus with illegally causing a war against the Germans—no mention of treason there! But the Plebeian Assembly still threw the case out. The problem is that no one *likes* treason trials."

"Well, we keep working on it," said Saturninus. "In order to get a conviction out of the Centuries, the accused has to stand there and say out of his own mouth that he deliberately connived at ruining his country. And no one is fool enough to say that. Gaius Marius is right. We have to clip the wings of the Policy Makers by showing them that they're not above either moral reproach or the law. And we can only do that in a body of men who are not senators."

"Why not pass your new treason law at once, then try Caepio in its special court?" asked Glaucia. "Yes, yes, I know the senators will squeal like trapped pigs—don't they always?"

Saturninus grimaced. "We want to live, don't we? Even if we do only have three more years, that's better than dying the day after tomorrow!"

"You and your three years!"

"Look," Saturninus persevered, "if we can actually get Caepio convicted in the Plebeian Assembly, the Senate will take the hint we're aiming to give it—that the People are fed up with senators sheltering fellow senators from just retribution. That there's not one law for senators and another for everybody else. It's time the People woke up! And I'm the boy to administer the whack that will wake them up. Since this Republic began, the Senate has gulled the People into believing that senators are a better breed of Roman, entitled to do and say whatever they want. Vote for Lucius Tiddlypuss—his family gave Rome her first consul! And does it matter that Lucius Tiddlypuss is a self-seeking gold-hungry incompetent? No! Lucius Tiddlypuss has the family name, and the family tradition of service in Rome's public sphere. The Brothers Gracchi were right. Take the courts away from the Lucius Tiddlypuss cohort by giving them to the knights!"

Glaucia was looking thoughtful. "Something has just occurred to me, Lucius Appuleius. The People are at least a responsible and well-educated lot. Pillars of Roman tradition. But—what if one day someone starts talking about the Head Count the way you're talking about the People?"

Saturninus laughed. "As long as their bellies are full, and the aediles put on a good show at the games, the Head Count are happy. To make the Head Count politically conscious, you'd have to turn the Forum Romanum into the Circus Maximus!"

"Their bellies aren't quite as full as they ought to be this winter," said Glaucia.

"Full enough, thanks to none other than our revered Leader of the House, Marcus Aemilius Scaurus himself. You know, I don't mourn the fact that we'll never persuade Numidicus or Catulus Caesar to see things our way, but I can't help thinking it a pity we'll never win Scaurus over," said Saturninus.

Glaucia was gazing at him curiously. "You never have held it against Scaurus for throwing you out of the House, have you?"

"No. He did what he thought was right. But one day, Gaius Servilius, I'll find out who the real culprits were, and then—they'll wish they had as easy a time of it as Oedipus!" said Saturninus savagely.

Early in January the tribune of the plebs Gaius Norbanus arraigned Quintus Servilius Caepio in the Plebeian Assembly on a charge that was phrased as "the loss of his army."

Feelings ran high from the very beginning, for by no means all of the People were opposed to senatorial exclusivity, and the Senate was there in its full plebeian numbers to fight for Caepio. Long before the tribes were called upon to vote, violence flared and blood flowed. The tribunes of the plebs Titus Didius and Lucius Aurelius Cotta stepped forward to veto the whole procedure, and were hauled down from the rostra by a furious crowd. Stones flew viciously, clubs cracked around ribs and legs; Didius and Lucius Cotta were manhandled out of the Comitia well and literally forced by the pressure of the throng into the Argiletum, then kept there. Bruised and shocked though they were, they tried screaming their vetos across a sea of angry faces, but were shouted down again and again.

The rumor about the Gold of Tolosa had tipped the balance against Caepio and the Senate, there could be no doubt of it; from Head Count clear to First Class, the whole city shrieked imprecations at Caepio the thief, Caepio the traitor, Caepio the self-seeker. People—women included—who had never evinced any kind of interest in Forum or Assembly events came to see this man Caepio, a criminal on a scale hitherto unimaginable; there were debates about how high the mountain of gold bricks must have been, how heavy, how many. And the hatred was a tangible presence, for no one likes to see a single individual make off with money deemed the property of everyone. Especially so much money.

Determined the trial would proceed, Norbanus ignored the peripheral turmoil, the brawls, the chaos when habitual Assembly attenders impinged upon the crowds who had come solely to see and abuse Caepio, standing on the rostra amid a guard of lictors deputed to protect him, not detain him. The senators whose patrician rank meant they could not participate in the Plebeian Assembly were clustered on the Curia Hostilia steps hectoring Norbanus, until a segment of the crowd began to pelt them with stones. Scaurus fell, inanimate, bleeding from a wound on his head. Which didn't stop Norbanus, who continued the trial without even pausing to discover whether the Princeps Senatus was dead or merely unconscious.

The voting when it came was very fast; the first eighteen of the thirty-five tribes all condemned Quintus Servilius Caepio, which meant no more tribes were called upon to vote. Emboldened by this unprecedented indication of the degree of hatred felt for Caepio, Norbanus then asked the Plebeian Assembly to impose a specific sentence by vote—a sentence so harsh that every senator present howled a futile protest. Again the first eighteen tribes chosen by lot all voted the same way, to visit dreadful punishment upon Caepio. He was stripped of his citizenship, forbidden fire and water within eight hundred miles of Rome, fined fifteen thousand talents of gold, and ordered confined in the cells of the Lautumiae under guard and without speech with anyone, even the members of his own family, until his journey into exile began.

Amid shaking fists and triumphant yells that he was not going to get the chance to see his brokers or his bankers and bury his personal fortune, Quintus Servilius Caepio, ex–citizen of Rome, was marched between his guard of lictors across the short distance between the well of the Comitia and the tumbledown cells of the Lautumiae.

Thoroughly satisfied with the final events of what had been a deliciously exciting and unusual day, the crowds went home, leaving the Forum Romanum to the tenure of a few men, all senatorial in rank.

The ten tribunes of the plebs were standing in polarized groups: Lucius Cotta, Titus Didius, Marcus Baebius, and Lucius Antistius Reginus huddled gloomily together, the four middlemen looked helplessly from their left to their right, and an elated Gaius Norbanus and Lucius Appuleius Saturninus talked with great animation and much laughter to Gaius Servilius Glaucia, who had strolled over to congratulate them. Not one of the ten tribunes of the plebs still wore his toga, torn away in the melee.

Marcus Aemilius Scaurus was sitting with his back against the plinth of a statue of Scipio Africanus while Metellus Numidicus and two slaves tried to stanch the blood flowing freely from a cut on his temple; Crassus Orator and his boon companion (and first cousin) Quintus Mucius Scaevola were hovering near Scaurus, looking shaken; the two shocked young men Drusus and Caepio Junior were standing on the Senate steps, shepherded by Drusus's uncle Publius Rutilius Rufus, and by Marcus Aurelius Cotta; and the junior consul, Lucius Aurelius Orestes, not a well man at the best of times, was lying full length in the vestibule being tended by an anxious praetor.

Rutilius Rufus and Cotta both moved quickly to support Caepio Junior when he suddenly sagged against the dazed and white-faced Drusus, who had one arm about his shoulders.

"What can we do to help?" asked Cotta.

Drusus shook his head, too moved to speak, while Caepio Junior seemed not to hear.

"Did anyone think to send lictors to guard Quintus Servilius's house from the crowds?" asked Rutilius Rufus.

"I did," Drusus managed to say.

"The boy's wife?" asked Cotta, nodding at Caepio Junior.

"I've had her and the baby sent to my house," Drusus said, lifting his free hand to his cheek as if to discover whether he actually existed.

Caepio Junior stirred, looking at the three around him in wonder. "It was only the gold," he said. "All they cared about was the gold! They didn't even think of Arausio. They didn't condemn him for Arausio. All they cared about was the gold!"

"It is human nature," said Rutilius Rufus gently, "to care more about gold than about men's lives."

Drusus glanced at his uncle sharply, but if Rutilius Rufus had spoken in irony, Caepio Junior didn't notice.

"I blame Gaius Marius for this," said Caepio Junior.

Rutilius Rufus put his hand under Caepio Junior's elbow.

"Come, young Quintus Servilius, Marcus Aurelius and I will take you to young Marcus Livius's house."

As they moved off the Senate steps, Lucius Antistius Reginus broke away from Lucius Cotta, Didius, and Baebius. He strode across to confront Norbanus, who backed away and took up a stance of aggressive self-defense.

"Oh, don't bother!" spat Antistius. "I wouldn't soil my hands with the likes of you, you cur!" He drew himself up, a big man with obvious Celt in him. "I'm going to the Lautumiae to free Quintus Servilius. No man in the history of our Republic has ever been thrown into prison to await exile, and I will not let Quintus Servilius become the first! You can try to stop me if you like, but I've sent home for my sword, and by living Jupiter, Gaius Norbanus, if you try to stop me, I'll kill you!"

Norbanus laughed. "Oh, take him!" he said. "Take Quintus Servilius home with you and wipe his eyes—not to mention his arse! I wouldn't go near *his* house, though, if I were you!"

"Make sure you charge him plenty!" Saturninus called in the wake of Antistius's diminishing figure. "He can afford to pay in gold, you know!"

Antistius swung round and flipped up the fingers of his right hand in an unmistakable gesture.

"Oh, I will not!" yelled Glaucia, laughing. "Just because you're a queen doesn't mean the rest of us are!"

Gaius Norbanus lost interest. "Come on," he said to Glaucia and Saturninus, "let's go home and eat dinner."

Though he was feeling very sick, Scaurus would sooner have died than demean himself by vomiting in public, so he forced his churning mind to dwell upon the three men walking away, laughing, animated, victorious.

"They're werewolves," he said to Metellus Numidicus, whose toga was stained with Scaurus's blood. "Look at them! Gaius Marius's tools!"

"Can you stand yet, Marcus Aemilius?" Numidicus asked.

"Not until I'm feeling surer of my stomach."

"I see Publius Rutilius and Marcus Aurelius have taken Quintus Servilius's two young men home," said Numidicus.

"Good. They'll need someone to keep an eye on them. I've never seen a crowd so out for noble blood, even in the worst days of Gaius Gracchus," said Scaurus, drawing deep breaths. "We will have to go very quietly for a while, Quintus Caecilius. If we push, those werewolves will push us harder."

"Rot Quintus Servilius and the gold!" snapped Numidicus.

Feeling better, Scaurus allowed himself to be helped to his feet. "So you think he took it, eh?"

Metellus Numidicus looked scornful. "Oh, come, don't try to hoodwink me, Marcus Aemilius!" he said. "You know him as well as I do. Of course he took it! And I'll never forgive him for taking it. It belonged to the Treasury."

"The trouble is," said Scaurus as he began to walk on what felt like a series of very uneven clouds, "that we have no internal system whereby men like you and me can punish those among our own who betray us."

Metellus Numidicus shrugged. "There can be no such system, you are aware of that. To institute one would be to admit that our own men do sometimes fall short of what they should be. And if we show our weaknesses to the world, we're finished."

"I'd rather be dead than finished," said Scaurus.

"And I." Metellus Numidicus sighed. "I just hope our sons feel as strongly as we do."

"That," said Scaurus wryly, "was an unkind thing to say."

"Marcus Aemilius, Marcus Aemilius! Your boy is very young! I can't see anything very wrong with him, truly."

"Then shall we exchange sons?"

"No," said Metellus Numidicus, "if for no other reason than that the gesture would kill your son. His worst handicap is that he knows very well he lives under your disapproval."

"He's a weakling," said Scaurus the strong.

"Perhaps a good wife might help," said Numidicus.

Scaurus stopped and turned to face his friend. "Now that's a thought! I hadn't earmarked him for anyone yet, he's so—grossly immature. Have you someone in mind?"

"My niece. Dalmaticus's girl, Metella Dalmatica. She'll be eighteen in about two years. I'm her guardian now that dear Dalmaticus is dead. What do you say, Marcus Aemilius?"

"It's a deal, Quintus Caecilius! A deal!"

Drusus had sent his steward Cratippus and every physically fit slave he owned to the Servilius Caepio house the moment he realized that Caepio the father was going to be convicted.

Unsettled by the trial and the very little she had managed to overhear of conversation between Caepio Junior and Caepio the father, Livia Drusa had gone to work at her loom for want of something else to do; no book could keep her enthralled, even the love poetry of the spicy Meleager. Not expecting an invasion by her brother's servants, she took alarm from the expression of controlled panic on Cratippus's face.

"Quick, *dominilla,* get together anything you want to take away with you!" he said, glancing around her sitting room. "I have your maid packing your clothes, and your nanny taking care of the baby's needs, so all you have to do is show me what you want to bring away for yourself—books, papers, fabrics."

Eyes enormous, she stared at the steward. "What is it? What's the matter?"

"Your father-in-law, *dominilla.* Marcus Livius says the court is going to convict him," said Cratippus.

"But why should that mean I have to leave?" she asked, terrified at the thought of going back to live in the prison of her brother's house now that she had discovered freedom.

"The city is out for his blood, *dominilla.*"

What color she still retained now fled. "His *blood*? Are they going to kill him?"

"No, no, nothing quite as bad as that," Cratippus soothed. "They'll confiscate his property. But the crowd is so angry that your brother thinks it likely when the trial is over that many of the most vengeful may come straight here to loot."

Within an hour Quintus Servilius Caepio's house was devoid of servants and family, its outer gates bolted and barred; as Cratippus led Livia Drusa away down the Clivus Palatinus, a big squad of lictors came marching up it, clad only in tunics and bearing clubs instead of *fasces*. They were going to take up duty outside the house and keep any irate crowds at bay, for the State wanted Caepio's property intact until it could be catalogued and auctioned.

Servilia Caepionis was there at Drusus's door to bring her sister-in-law inside, her face as pale as Livia Drusa's.

"Come and look," she said, hurrying Livia Drusa through peristyle-garden and house, guiding her out to the loggia, which overlooked the Forum Romanum.

And there it was, the end of the trial of Quintus Servilius Caepio. The milling throng was sorting itself out into tribes to vote about the sentence of far-away exile and huge damages, a curious swaying series of surging lines which were orderly enough in the well of the Comitia, but became chaotic where the huge crowds of onlookers fused into them. Knots indicated fights in progress, eddies revealed where the fights had begun to escalate into something approaching riot nuclei; on the Senate steps many men were clustered, and on the rostra at the edge of the well of the Comitia stood the tribunes of the plebs and a small, lictor-hedged figure Livia Drusa presumed was her father-in-law, the accused.

Servilia Caepionis had begun to weep; too numb yet to feel like crying, Livia Drusa moved closer to her.

"Cratippus said the crowd might go to Father's house to loot it," she said. "I didn't know! Nobody told me anything!"

Dragging out her handkerchief, Servilia Caepionis dried her tears. "Marcus Livius has feared it all along," she said. "It's that wretched story about the Gold of Tolosa! Had it not got around, things would have been different. But most of Rome seems to have judged Father before his trial—and for something he's not even on trial for!"

Livia Drusa turned away. "I must see where Cratippus has put my baby."

That remark provoked a fresh flood of tears in Servilia Caepionis, who so far had not managed to become pregnant, though she wanted a baby desperately. "Why haven't I conceived?" she asked Livia Drusa. "You're so lucky! Marcus Livius says you're going to have a second baby, and I haven't even managed to start my first one!"

"There's plenty of time," Livia Drusa comforted. "They were away for months after we were married, don't forget, and Marcus Livius is much busier than my Quintus Servilius. It's commonly said that the busier the husband is, the harder his wife finds it to conceive."

"No, I'm barren," Servilia Caepionis whispered. "I know I'm barren; I can feel it in my bones! And Marcus Livius is so kind, so forgiving!" She broke down again.

"There, there, don't fret about it so," said Livia Drusa, who had managed to get her sister-in-law as far as the atrium, where she looked about her for help. "You won't make it any easier to conceive by becoming distraught, you know. Babies like to burrow into placid wombs."

Cratippus appeared.

"Oh, thank the gods!" cried Livia Drusa. "Cratippus, fetch my sister's maid, would you? And perhaps you could show me whereabouts I am to sleep, and whereabouts little Servilia is?"

In such an enormous house, the accommodation of several additional important people was not a problem; Cratippus had given Caepio Junior and his wife one of the suites of rooms opening off the peristyle-garden, and Caepio the father another, while baby Servilia had been located in the vacant nursery along the far colonnade.

"What shall I do about dinner?" the steward came to ask Livia Drusa as she began to direct the unpacking.

"That's up to my sister, Cratippus, surely! I'd much rather not do anything to usurp her authority."

"She's lying down in some distress, *dominilla*."

"Oh, I see. Well, best have dinner ready in an hour—the men might want to eat. But be prepared to postpone it."

There was a stir outside in the garden; Livia Drusa went out to see, and found her brother Drusus supporting Caepio Junior along the colonnade.

"What is it?" she asked. "How may I help?" She looked at Drusus. "What is it?" she repeated.

"Quintus Servilius our father-in-law is condemned. Exile no closer than eight hundred miles from Rome, a fine of fifteen thousand talents of gold—which means confiscation of every lamp wick and dead leaf the whole of his family owns—and imprisonment in the Lautumiae until Quintus Servilius can be deported," said Drusus.

"But everything Father owns won't amount to a hundred talents of gold!" said Livia Drusa, aghast.

"Of course. So he'll never be able to come home again."

Servilia Caepionis came running, looking, thought Livia Drusa, like Cassandra flying from the conquering Greeks, hair wild, eyes huge and blurred with tears, mouth agape.

"What is it, what is it?" she cried.

Drusus coped with her firmly but kindly, dried her tears, forbade her to cast herself on her brother's chest. And under this treatment she calmed with magical swiftness.

"Come, let's all go to your study, Marcus Livius," she said, and actually led the way.

Livia Drusa hung back, terrified.

"What's the matter with you?" asked Servilia Caepionis.

"We can't sit in the study with the men!"

"Of course we can!" said Servilia Caepionis impatiently. "This is no time to keep the women of the family in ignorance, as Marcus Livius well knows. We stand together, or we fall together. A strong man must have strong women around him."

Head spinning, Livia Drusa tried to assimilate all the mood twists of the previous moments, and understood at last what a mouse she had been all her life. Drusus had expected a wildly disturbed wife to greet him, but then expected her to calm down and become extremely practical and supportive; and Servilia Caepionis had behaved exactly as he expected.

So Livia Drusa followed Servilia Caepionis and the men into the study, and managed not to look horrified when Servilia Caepionis poured unwatered wine for the whole company. Sitting sipping the first undiluted liquor she had ever tasted, Livia Drusa hid her storm of thoughts. And her anger.

At the end of the tenth hour Lucius Antistius Reginus brought Quintus Servilius Caepio to Drusus's house. Caepio looked exhausted, but more annoyed than depressed.

"I took him out of the Lautumiae," said Antistius, tightlipped. "No Roman consular is going to be incarcerated while I'm a tribune of the plebs! It's an affront to Romulus and Quirinus as much as it is to Jupiter Optimus Maximus. How dare they!"

"They dared because the People encouraged them, and so did all those neck-craning refugees from the games," said Caepio, downing his wine at a gulp. "More," he said to his son, who leaped to obey, happy now his father was safe. "I'm done for in Rome," he said then, and stared with black snapping eyes first at Drusus, only second at his son. "It is up to you young men from now on to defend the right of my family to enjoy its ancient privileges and its natural pre-eminence. With your last breaths, if necessary. The Mariuses and the Saturninuses and the Norbanuses must be exterminated—by the knife if that is the only way, do you understand?"

Caepio Junior was nodding obediently, but Drusus sat with his wine goblet in his hand and a rather wooden look on his face.

"I swear to you, Father, that our family will never suffer the loss of its *dignitas* while I am *paterfamilias*," said Caepio Junior solemnly; he appeared more tranquil now.

And, thought Livia Drusa, loathing him, more like his detestable father than ever! Why do I hate him so much? Why did my brother make me marry him?

Then her own plight faded, for she saw an expression on Drusus's face which fascinated her, puzzled her. It wasn't that he disagreed with anything their father-in-law said, more as if he qualified it, filed it away inside his mind along with a lot of other things, not all of which made sense to him. And, Livia Drusa decided suddenly, my brother dislikes our father-in-law intensely! Oh, he had changed, had Drusus! Where Caepio Junior would never change, only become more what he had always been.

"What do you intend to do, Father?" Drusus asked.

A curious smile blossomed on Caepio's face; the irritation died out of his eyes, and was replaced by a most complex meld of triumph, slyness, pain, hatred. "Why, my dear boy, I shall go into exile as directed by the Plebeian Assembly," he said.

"But where, Father?" asked Caepio Junior.

"Smyrna."

"How will we manage for money?" Caepio Junior asked. "Not so much me—Marcus Livius will help me out—but you yourself. How will you be able to afford to live comfortably in exile?"

"I have money on deposit in Smyrna, more than enough for my needs. As for you, my son, there is no need to worry. Your mother left a great fortune, which I have held in trust for you. It will sustain you more than adequately," said Caepio.

"But won't it be confiscated?"

"No, for two reasons. First of all, it's already in your name, not in mine. And secondly, it's not on deposit in Rome. It's in Smyrna, with my own money." The smile grew. "You must live here in Marcus Livius's house with him for several years, after which I'll begin to send your fortune home. And if anything should happen to me, my bankers will carry on the good work. In the meantime, son-in-law, keep an account of all the monies you expend on my son's behalf. In time he will repay you every last sestertius."

A silence fraught with so much energy and emotion it was almost visible fell upon the entire group, while each member of it realized what Quintus Servilius Caepio was not saying; that he *had* stolen the Gold of Tolosa, that the Gold of Tolosa was in Smyrna, and that the Gold of Tolosa was now the property of Quintus Servilius Caepio, free and clear, safe and sound. That Quintus Servilius Caepio was very nearly as rich as Rome.

Caepio turned to Antistius, silent as the rest. "Have you considered what I asked you on the way here?"

Antistius cleared his throat loudly. "I have, Quintus Servilius. And I'd like to accept."

"Good!" Caepio looked at his son and his son-in-law. "My dear friend Lucius Antistius has agreed to escort me to Smyrna, to give me both the pleasure of his company and the protection of a tribune of the plebs. When we reach Smyrna, I shall endeavor to persuade Lucius Antistius to remain there with me."

"I haven't decided about that yet," said Antistius.

"There's no hurry, no hurry at all," said Caepio smoothly. He rubbed his hands together as if to warm them. "I do declare, I'm hungry enough to eat a baby! Is there any dinner?"

"Of course, Father," said Servilia Caepionis. "If you men go into the dining room, Livia Drusa and I will see to things in the kitchen."

That, of course, was a gross inaccuracy; Cratippus saw to things in the kitchen. But the two women did search for him, and finally found him on the loggia squinting down into the Forum Romanum, where the shadows of dusk were growing.

"Look at that! Did you ever see such a mess?" the steward asked indignantly, pointing. "Litter everywhere! Shoes, rags, sticks, half-eaten food, wine flagons—it's a disgrace!"

And there he was, her red-haired Odysseus, standing with Gnaeus Domitius Ahenobarbus on the balcony of the house below; like Cratippus, the two of them seemed to be waxing in anger about the litter.

Livia Drusa shivered, licked her lips, stared in starved anguish at the young man so near to her—and yet so far. The steward rushed away toward the kitchen stairs; now was her chance, now while it would seem a casual inquiry.

"Sister," she asked, "who is that red-haired man on the terrace with Gnaeus Domitius? He's been visiting there for years, but I don't know who he is, I just can't place him. Do you know? Can you tell me?"

Servilia Caepionis snorted. "Oh, him! That's Marcus Porcius Cato," she said, voice ringing contemptuously.

"Cato? As in Cato the Censor?"

"The same. Upstarts! He's Cato the Censor's grandson."

"But wouldn't his grandmother have been Licinia, and his mother Aemilia Paulla? Surely that makes him acceptable!" objected Livia Drusa, eyes shining.

Servilia Caepionis snorted again. "Wrong branch, my dear. He's no son of Aemilia Paulla's—if he were, he'd have to be years older than he is. No, no! He's not a Cato Licinianus! He's a Cato Salonianus. And the great-grandson of a slave."

Livia Drusa's imaginary world shifted, grew a network of tiny cracks. "I don't understand," she said, bewildered.

"What, you don't know the story? He's the son of the son of Cato the Censor's *second* marriage."

"To the daughter of a *slave*?" gasped Livia Drusa.

"The daughter of his slave, to be exact. Salonia, her name was. I think it's an absolute disgrace that they're allowed the same license to mingle with us as the descendants of Cato the Censor's first wife, Licinia! They've even wormed their way into the Senate. Of course," Servilia Caepionis said, "the Porcii Catones Liciniani don't speak to them. Nor do we."

"Why does Gnaeus Domitius suffer him, then?"

Servilia Caepionis laughed, sounding very much like her insufferable father. "Well, the Domitii Ahenobarbi aren't such an illustrious lot, are they? More money than ancestors, in spite of all the tales they tell about Castor and Pollux touching their beards with red! I don't know exactly why he's accepted among them. But I can guess. My father worked it out."

"Worked out what?" asked Livia Drusa, heart in her feet.

"Well, it's a red-haired family, Cato the Censor's second lot. Cato the Censor was red-haired himself, for that matter. But Licinia and Aemilia Paulla were both dark, so their sons and daughters have brown hair and brown eyes. Whereas Cato the Censor's slave Salonius was a Celtiberian from Salo in Nearer Spain, and he was fair.

His daughter Salonia was very fair. And that's why the Catones Saloniani have kept the red hair and the grey eyes." Servilia Caepionis shrugged. "The Domitii Ahenobarbi have to perpetuate the myth they started about the red beards they inherited from the ancestor touched by Castor and Pollux. So they always marry red-haired women. Well, red-haired women are scarce. And if there's no better-born red-haired woman about, I imagine a Domitius Ahenobarbus would marry a Cato Salonianus. They're so stuck up they think their own blood capable of absorbing any old rubbish."

"So Gnaeus Domitius's friend must have a sister?"

"He has a sister." Servilia Caepionis shook herself. "I must go inside. Oh, what a day! Come, dinner will be there."

"You go ahead," said Livia Drusa. "I'll have to feed my daughter before I feed myself."

Mention of the baby was enough to send poor child-hungry Servilia Caepionis hurrying off; Livia Drusa returned to the balustrade and looked over it. Yes, they were still there, Gnaeus Domitius and his visitor. His visitor with a slave for a great-grandfather. Perhaps the burgeoning gloom was responsible for the dimming of the hair on the man below, for the diminishing of his height, the width of his shoulders. His neck now looked slightly ridiculous, too long and skinny to be really Roman. Four tears dropped to star the yellow-painted railing, but no more.

I have been a fool as usual, thought Livia Drusa. I have dreamed and mooned for four whole years over a man who turns out to be the recent descendant of a slave—a fact-slave, not a myth-slave. I confabulated him into a king, noble and brave as Odysseus. I made myself into patient Penelope, waiting for him. And now I find out he's not noble. Not even *decently* born! After all, who was Cato the Censor but a peasant from Tusculum befriended by a patrician Valerius Flaccus? A genuine harbinger of Gaius Marius. That man on the terrace below is the recent descendant of a Spanish slave and a Tusculan peasant. What a fool I am! What a stupid, stupid idiot!

When she reached the nursery she found little Servilia thriving and hungry, so she sat for fifteen minutes and fed the small one, whose regular routine had been thrown out of kilter this momentous day.

"You'd better find her a wet nurse," she said to the Macedonian nanny as she prepared to leave. "I'd like a few months of rest before I bear again. And when this new baby comes, you can get in wet nurses from the start. Feeding a child oneself obviously doesn't prevent conception, or I wouldn't be pregnant right now."

She slipped into the dining room just as the main courses were being served, and sat down as inconspicuously as she could on a straight chair opposite Caepio Junior. Everyone seemed to be making a good meal; Livia Drusa discovered she too was hungry.

"Are you all right, Livia Drusa?" asked Caepio Junior, a trifle anxiously. "You look sort of sick."

Startled, she stared at him, and for the first time in all the many years she had known him, the sight of him did not arouse all those inchoate feelings of revulsion. No, he did not have red hair; no, he did not have grey eyes; no, he was not tall and graceful and broad-shouldered; no, he would never turn into King Odysseus. But he was her husband; he had loved her faithfully; he was the father of her children; and he was a patrician Roman nobleman on *both* sides.

So she smiled at him, a smile which reached her eyes. "I think it's only the day, Quintus Servilius," she said gently. "In myself, I feel better than I have in years."

Encouraged by the result of the trial of Caepio, Saturninus began to act with an arbitrary arrogance that rocked the Senate to its foundations. Hard on the heels of Caepio's trial, Saturninus himself prosecuted Gnaeus Mallius Maximus for "loss of his army" in the Plebeian Assembly, with a similar result: Mallius Maximus, already deprived of his sons by the battle of Arausio, was now deprived of his Roman citizenship and all his property, and sent into exile a more broken man by far than the gold-greedy Caepio.

Then late in February came the new treason law, the *lex Appuleia de maiestate,* which took treason trials off the cumbersome Centuries and put them into a special court staffed entirely by knights. The Senate was to have no part in this court at all. In spite of which, the senators said little derogatory about the bill during their obligatory debate, nor attempted to oppose its passage into law.

Monumental though these changes were, and of an unimaginable importance to the future government of Rome, they could not capture the interest of Senate or People the way the pontifical election held at the same time did. The death of Lucius Caecilius Metellus Dalmaticus Pontifex Maximus had left not one, but two vacancies in the College of Pontifices; and yet, since these two vacancies were held by one and the same man, there were those who argued only one election was necessary. But, as Scaurus Princeps Senatus pointed out, voice wobbling dangerously, mouth quivering, that would only be possible if the man who was elected ordinary *pontifex* was also a candidate for the big job. Finally it was agreed that the Pontifex Maximus would be elected first.

"Then we shall see what we shall see," said Scaurus, taking deep breaths, and only once hooting with laughter.

Both Scaurus Princeps Senatus and Metellus Numidicus had put their names up as candidates for Pontifex Maximus, as had Catulus Caesar. And Gnaeus Domitius Ahenobarbus.

"If I am elected, or Quintus Lutatius is elected, then we must hold a second poll for the ordinary *pontifex,* as we are both already in the college," said Scaurus, voice control heroic.

Among this field were a Servilius Vatia, an Aelius Tubero, and Metellus Numidicus. And Gnaeus Domitius Ahenobarbus.

The new law stipulated that seventeen of the thirty-five tribes be chosen by casting the lots, and that they alone vote. So the lots were cast, and the seventeen tribes which would vote determined. All this was done in a spirit of high good humor and great tolerance; no violence in the Forum Romanum that day! For many more than Scaurus Princeps Senatus were enjoying a wonderful chuckle. Nothing appealed to the Roman sense of humor more than a squabble involving the most august names on the censors' rolls, especially when the aggrieved party had managed so neatly to turn the tables on those who had caused the grievance.

Naturally Gnaeus Domitius Ahenobarbus was the hero of the hour. So no one was very surprised when Gnaeus Domitius Ahenobarbus was elected Pontifex Maximus, and thereby made a second election unnecessary. Amid cheers and flying ropes of flowers, Gnaeus Domitius Ahenobarbus scored the perfect revenge on those who had given his dead father's priesthood to young Marcus Livius Drusus.

Scaurus rolled about in paroxysms of laughter the moment the verdict came in—much to the disgust of Metellus Numidicus, who couldn't see the funny side at all.

"Really, Marcus Aemilius, you are the *limit*! It's an outrage!" he bleated. "That bad-tempered and dirty-livered *pipinna* as Pontifex Maximus? After my dear brother, Dalmaticus? And versus you? Or me?" He pounded his fist against one of the Volscian ship's beaks which had given the rostra its name. "Oh, if there is any time when I *detest* Romans, it's when their perverted sense of the ridiculous overcomes their normal sense of fitness! I can forgive the passage of a Saturninus law easier than I can forgive this! At least in a Saturninus law, people's deep-rooted opinions are involved. But this—this farce? Sheer irresponsibility! I feel like joining Quintus Servilius in his exile, I'm so ashamed."

But the greater the fury Metellus Numidicus worked himself into, the harder Scaurus laughed. Finally, clutching his sides and looking at Metellus Numidicus through a curtain of tears, he managed to gasp, "Oh, stop behaving like an old Vestal confronted by a pair of hairy balls and a stiff prick! It is hilarious! And we deserve everything he's dished out to us!" Off he went again into a fresh convulsion; emitting a noise like a squeezed kitten, Metellus Numidicus stalked off.

Said Gaius Marius in a rare letter to Publius Rutilius Rufus, which its recipient got in September:

> I know I ought to write more often, old friend, but the trouble is, I'm not a comfortable correspondent. Now your letters are like a piece of cork thrown to a

drowning man, full of yourself as you are—no frills, no fringes, no formality. There! I managed a little bit of style, but at what price you wouldn't believe.

No doubt you've been going to the Senate to endure our Piggle-wiggle oink-oinking against the cost to the State of keeping up a Head Count army through a second year of inertia on the far side of the Alps? And how am I going to get myself elected to a fourth term as consul, for the third time in a row? That of course is what I have to do. Otherwise—I lose everything I stand to gain. Because next year, Publius Rutilius, is going to be the year of the Germans. I know it in my bones. Yes, I admit I have no real basis yet for this feeling, but when Lucius Cornelius and Quintus Sertorius return, I am sure that is what they're going to say. I haven't heard from either of them since they came last year to bring me King Copillus. And though I'm glad my two tribunes of the plebs managed to convict Quintus Servilius Caepio, I'm still rather sorry I didn't have the chance to do the job myself, with Copillus testifying. Never mind. Quintus Servilius got his just reward. A pity however that Rome will never lay eyes on the Gold of Tolosa. It would have paid for many a Head Count army.

Life goes on here much as always. The Via Domitia is now in mint condition all the way from Nemausus to Ocelum, which will make it a great deal easier for legions on the march in the future. It had been let go to ruin. Parts of it had not been touched since our new Pontifex Maximus's *tata* was through here nearly twenty years ago. Floods and frosts and the runoff from sudden cloudbursts had taken an awful toll. Of course it's not like building a new road. Once the stones are fitted into place in the roadbed, the base is there forever. But you can't expect men to march and wagons to roll and hooves to trot safely across the ups and downs of outsized cobbles, now can you? The top

surface of sand and gravel and quarry dust has to be
kept as smooth as an egg, and watered until it packs
down like concrete. Take it from me, the Via Domitia
at the moment is a credit to my men.

We also built a new causeway across the Rhodanus
marshes all the way from Nemausus to Arelate, by the
way. And we've just about finished digging a new ship
canal from the sea to Arelate, to bypass the swamps
and mud flats and sandbars of the natural waterway.
All the big Greek fish in Massilia are groveling with
their noses pressed against my arse in thanks—slimy
gang of hypocrites they are! Gratitude hasn't caused
any price cuts in whatever they sell my army, I note!

In case you should come to hear of it and the story
gets distorted—as stories about me and mine always
seem to—I will tell you what happened with Gaius Lusius. You remember, my sister-in-law's sister's boy?
Came to me as a tribune of the soldiers. Only it turned
out that wasn't what he wanted to be of the soldiers. My
provost marshal came to me two weeks ago with what
he thought was going to be a very bad piece of personal
news. Gaius Lusius had been found dead down in the
rankers' barracks, split from gizzard to breadbasket by
the neatest bit of sword work any commander could ask
for from a ranker. The guilty soldier had given himself
up—nice young chap too—finest type, his centurion
told me. Turns out Lusius was a pansy and took a fancy
to this soldier. And he kept on pestering, wouldn't let
up. Then it became a joke in the century, with everyone
mincing around flapping their hands and fluttering their
eyelashes. The poor young ranker couldn't win.
Result—murder. Anyway, I had to court-martial the
soldier, and I must say it gave me great pleasure to acquit him with praise, a promotion, and a purse full of
money. There. Did it again, got in a bit of literary style.

The business turned out well for me too. I was able

to prove that Lusius wasn't a blood relation, first off. And in close second place, it was a chance for me to show the rankers that their general sees justice done as justice should be done, no favoritism for members of the family. I suppose there must be jobs a pansy can do, but the legions are no place for him, that's definite, eh, Publius Rutilius? Can you imagine what we'd have done to Lusius at Numantia? He wouldn't have got off with a nice clean death; he'd have been singing soprano. Though you grow up eventually. I'll never forget what a shock I got listening to some of the things that were said about Scipio Aemilianus at his funeral! Well, he never put the hard word on me, so I still don't know. Odd fellow, but—I think these stories get around when men don't sire children.

And that's about it. Oh, except I made a few changes in the *pilum* this year, and I expect my new version will become standard issue. If you've got any spare cash, go out and buy some shares in one of the new factories bound to spring up to make them. Or found a factory yourself—as long as you own the building, the censors can't accuse you of unsenatorial practices, can they, now?

Anyway, what I did was change the design of the junction between the iron shaft and the wooden shaft. The *pilum* is such an efficient piece of work compared to the old *hasta*-type spear, but there's no doubt they're a lot more expensive to make—little properly barbed head instead of big leafy head, long iron shaft, and then a wooden shaft shaped to suit the throwing action instead of the old *hasta* broom handle. I've noticed over the years that the Enemy love to get their fingers on a *pilum*, so they deliberately provoke our green troops into throwing when there's no chance of hitting anything other than an Enemy shield. Then they either keep the *pilum* for another day, or they throw it back at us.

What I did was work out a way of joining the iron shaft to the wooden shaft with a weak pin. The minute the *pilum* hits anything, the shafts break apart where they join, so the Enemy can't throw them back at us, or make off with them. What's more, if we retain the field at the end of a battle, the armorers can go round and pick up all the broken bits, and fix them together again. Saves us money because it saves us losing them, and saves us lives because they can't be thrown back at us by the Enemy.

And that's definitely all the news. Write soon.

Publius Rutilius Rufus laid the letter down with a smile. Not too grammatical, not too graceful, not at all stylish. But then, that was Gaius Marius. He too was like his letters. This obsession about the consulship was worrying, however. On the one hand he could understand why Marius wanted to remain consul until the Germans were defeated—Marius knew no one else could defeat the Germans. On the other hand, Rutilius Rufus was too much a Roman of his class to approve, even taking the Germans into account. Was a Rome so altered by Marian political innovations it was no longer the Rome of Romulus really worth it? Rutilius Rufus wished he knew. It was very difficult to love a man the way he loved Marius, yet live with the trail of blasted traditions he left in his wake. The *pilum,* for Juno's sake! Could he leave *nothing* the way he found it?

Still, Publius Rutilius Rufus sat down and replied to the letter at once. Because he did love Gaius Marius.

This being a rather sluggish kind of summer, I'm afraid I haven't a great deal to report, dear Gaius Marius. Nothing of moment, anyway. Your esteemed colleague Lucius Aurelius Orestes, the junior consul, isn't well, but then, he wasn't well when he was elected. I don't understand why he stood, except I suppose he felt he deserved the office. It remains to be seen whether the office has deserved him. Somehow I doubt the latter.

A couple of juicy scandals are about all the news, but I know you'll enjoy them as much as I did. Interestingly enough, both involve your tribune of the plebs, Lucius Appuleius Saturninus. An extraordinary fellow, you know. A mass of contradictions. Such a pity, I always think, that Scaurus singled him out like that. Saturninus entered the Senate, I am sure, with the avowed intention of becoming the first Appuleius to sit in the consul's chair. Now he burns to tear the Senate down to the point where the consuls are no more effective than a wax mask. Yes, yes, I can hear you saying I'm being unduly pessimistic, and I'm exaggerating, and my view of things is warped by my love of the old ways. But I'm right, all the same! You will excuse me, I hope, that I refer to everyone by *cognomen* only. This is going to be a long letter, and I'll save a few words that way.

Saturninus has been vindicated. What do you think about that? An amazing business, and one which has redounded very much to the credit of our venerated Princeps Senatus, Scaurus. You must admit he's a far finer man than his boon companion, Piggle-wiggle. But then, that's the difference between an Aemilius and a Caecilius.

You know—I know you know because I told you—that Scaurus has continued in his role as curator of the grain supply, and spends his time shuttling between Ostia and Rome, making life thoroughly miserable for the grain lords, who can get away with nothing. We have only one person to thank for the remarkable stability of grain prices these last two harvests, in spite of the shortages. Scaurus!

Yes, yes, I'll cease the panegyric and get on with the story. It seems that when Scaurus was down in

Ostia about two months ago, he ran into a grain-buying agent normally stationed in Sicily. There's no need to fill you in on the slave revolt there, since you get the Senate's dispatches regularly, except to say that I do think we sent the right man to Sicily as governor this year. He might be a pokered-up aristocrat with a mouth like a cat's arsehole, but Lucius Licinius Lucullus is as punctilious over matters like his reports to the House as he is in tidying up his battlefields.

Would you believe, incidentally, that an idiot praetor—one of the more dubiously antecedented (isn't that a good phrase?) plebeian Servilians who managed to buy himself election as an augur on the strength of his patron Ahenobarbus's money and now calls himself Gaius Servilius Augur, if you please!—actually had the gall the other day to stand up in the House and accuse Lucullus of deliberately prolonging the war in Sicily to ensure that his command is pro-rogued into next year?

On what grounds did he make this astonishing charge? I hear you ask. Why, because after Lucullus defeated the slave army so decisively, he didn't rush off to storm Triocala, leaving thirty-five thousand dead slaves on the field and all the pockets of servile resis-tance in the area of Heracleia Minoa to grow into fresh sores in our Roman hide! Lucullus did the job prop-erly. Having defeated the slaves in battle, he then took a week to dispose of the dead, and flush out those pockets of servile resistance, before he moved on to Triocala, where the slaves who survived the battle had gone to earth. But Servilius the Augur says Lucullus should have flown like the birds of the sky straight to Triocala from the battle, for—alleges Servilius the Augur—the slaves who did go to earth in Triocala were in such a state of panic that they would have sur-rendered to him immediately! Where, as things turned out in the real world, by the time that Lucullus did get to Triocala, the slaves had got over their panic and decided to keep on fighting. Now from whom does Servilius the Augur get his information, you ask? Why, from his auguries, naturally! How else could he know what sort of state of mind a crowd of rebel slaves shut inside an impregnable fortress were in? And did you ever find Lucullus sufficiently devious to fight a huge battle, then work out a plan whereby he ensured that his term as governor was prorogued? What a mountain of rubbish! Lucullus did as his nature dictated—he tidied up alpha before he proceeded to start beta.

I was disgusted by Servilius the Augur's speech, and even more disgusted when Ahenobarbus Pontifex Maximus started roaring out his support for Servilius the Augur's preposterous tissue of completely unsubstantiated allegations! Of course, all the armchair generals on the back benches who wouldn't know one end of a battlefield from the other thought the disgrace was Lucullus's! We shall see what we shall see, but do not be surprised if you hear that the House decides, one, not to prorogue Lucullus, and two, to give the job as governor of Sicily next year to none other than Servilius the Augur. Who only started this treason hunt in order to have himself made next year's governor of Sicily! It's a peachy post for someone as inexperienced and addled as Servilius the Augur, because Lucullus has really done all the work for him. The defeat at Heracleia Minoa has driven what slaves there are left inside a fortress they can't leave because Lucullus has them under siege, Lucullus managed to push enough farmers back onto their land to ensure that there'll be a harvest of some kind this year, and the open countryside of Sicily is no longer being ravaged by the slave army. Enter the new governor Servilius the Augur onto this already settled stage, bowing to right and to left as he collects the accolades. I tell you, Gaius Marius, ambition allied to no talent is the most dangerous thing in the world.

Edepol, edepol, that was quite a digression, wasn't it? My indignation at the plight of Lucullus got the better of me. I do feel desperately sorry for him. But on with the tale of Scaurus down at Ostia, and the chance meeting with the grain-buying agent from Sicily. Now when it was thought that one quarter of Sicily's grain slaves would be freed before the harvest of last year, the grain merchants calculated that one quarter of the harvest would remain lying on the ground due to lack of hands to reap the wheat. So no one bothered to buy that last quarter. Until the two-week period during which that rodent Nerva freed eight hundred Italian slaves. And Scaurus's grain-buying agent was one of a group who went around Sicily through those two weeks, frantically buying up the last quarter of the harvest at a ridiculously cheap price. Then the growers bullied Nerva into closing down his emancipation tribunals, and all of a sudden Sicily was given back enough labor to ensure that the complete harvest would be gathered in. So the last quarter, bought for a song from a marketplace beggar, was now in the ownership of a person or persons unknown, and the reason for a massive hiring of every vacant silo between Puteoli and Rome was becoming apparent. The last quarter was to be stored in those silos until the following year, when Rome's insistence that the Italian slaves be freed would indeed have produced a smaller than normal Sicilian harvest. And the price of grain would be high.

What those enterprising persons unknown didn't count upon was the slave revolt. Instead of all four quarters of the crop being harvested, none of it was. So the grand scheme to make an enormous profit from the last quarter came to nothing, and those waiting empty silos remained empty.

However, to go back to the frantic two weeks during which Nerva freed some Italian slaves and the group of grain buyers scrambled to purchase the last quarter of the crop, the moment this was done and the tribunals were closed, our group of grain buyers was set upon by armed bandits, and every last man was killed. Or so the bandits thought. But one of them, the fellow who talked to Scaurus in Ostia, shammed dead, and so survived.

Scaurus sniffed a gigantic rat. What a nose he has! And what a mind! He saw the pattern at once, though the grain buyer had not. And how I do love him, in spite of his hidebound conservatism. Burrowing like a terrier, he discovered that the persons unknown were none other than your esteemed consular colleague of last year, Gaius Flavius Fimbria, and this year's governor of Macedonia, Gaius Memmius! They had laid a false scent for our terrier Scaurus last year that very cleverly led straight to the quaestor of Ostia—none other than our turbulent tribune of the plebs Lucius Appuleius Saturninus.

Once he had assembled all his evidence, Scaurus got up and apologized to Saturninus twice—once in the House, once in the Comitia. He was mortified, but lost no *dignitas,* of course. All the world loves a sincere and graceful apologist. And I must say that Saturninus never singled Scaurus out when he returned to the House as a tribune of the plebs. Saturninus got up too, once in the House and once in the Comitia, and told Scaurus that he had never borne a grudge because he had understood how very crafty the real villains were, and he was now extremely grateful for the recovery of his reputation. So Saturninus lost no *digni-*

tas either. All the world loves a modestly gracious recipient of a handsome apology.

Scaurus also offered Saturninus the job of impeaching Fimbria and Memmius in his new treason court, and naturally Saturninus accepted. So now we look forward to lots of sparks and very little obscuring smoke when Fimbria and Memmius are brought to trial. I imagine they will be convicted in a court composed of knights, for many knights in the grain business lost money, and Fimbria and Memmius are being blamed for the whole Sicilian mess. And what it all boils down to is that sometimes the real villains do get their just desserts.

The other Saturninus story is a lot funnier, as well as a lot more intriguing. I still haven't worked out what our vindicated tribune of the plebs is up to.

About two weeks ago, a fellow turned up in the Forum and climbed up on the rostra—it was vacant at the time, there being no Comitial meeting and the amateur orators having decided to take a day off—and announced to the whole bottom end of the Forum that his name was Lucius Equitius, that he was a freedman Roman citizen from Firmum Picenum, and—now wait for it, Gaius Marius, it's glorious!—that he was the natural son of none other than Tiberius Sempronius Gracchus!

He had his tale off pat, and it does hang together, as far as it goes. Briefly, it goes like this: his mother was a free Roman woman of good though humble standing, and fell in love with Tiberius Gracchus, who also fell in love with her. But of course her birth wasn't good enough for marriage, so she became his mistress, and lived in a small yet comfortable house on one of Tiberius Gracchus's country estates. In due time Lucius Equitius—his mother's name was Equitia—was born.

Then Tiberius Gracchus was murdered and Equitia died not long after, leaving her small son to the care of Cornelia the Mother of the Gracchi. But Cornelia the Mother of the Gracchi was not amused at being appointed the guardian of her son's bastard, and put him in the care of a slave couple on her own estates at Misenum. She then had him sold as a slave to people in Firmum Picenum.

He didn't know who he was, he says. But if he has done the things he says he has, then he was no infant when his father, Tiberius Gracchus, died, in which case he's lying. Anyway, sold into slavery in Firmum Picenum, he worked so diligently and became so beloved of his owners that when the *paterfamilias* died, he was not only manumitted, but fell heir to the family fortunes, there being no heirs of the flesh, so to speak. His education was excellent, so he took his inheritance and went into business. Over the next however many years, he served in our legions and made a fortune. To hear him talk, he ought to be about fifty years old, where in actual fact he looks about thirty.

And then he met a fellow who made a great fuss about his likeness to Tiberius Gracchus. Now he had always known he was Italian rather than foreign, and he had wondered greatly, he says, about his parentage. Emboldened by the discovery that he looked like Tiberius Gracchus, he traced the slave couple with whom Cornelia the Mother of the Gracchi had boarded him for a while, and learned from them the story of his begetting. Isn't it glorious? I haven't made up my mind yet whether it's a Greek tragedy or a Roman farce.

Well, of course our gullible sentimental Forum-frequenters went wild, and within a day or two Lucius Equitius was being feted everywhere as Tiberius Gracchus's son. A pity his legitimate sons are all dead, isn't it? Lucius Equitius does, by the way, bear a most remarkable resemblance to Tiberius Gracchus—quite uncanny, as a matter of fact. He speaks like him, walks like him, grimaces like him, even picks his nose the same way. I think the thing that puts me off Lucius Equitius the most is that the likeness is too perfect. A twin, not a son. Sons don't resemble their fathers in every detail, I've noticed it time and time again, and there's many a woman brought to bed of a son who is profoundly thankful for that fact, and expends a great deal of her postpartum energy assuring the sprog's *tata* that the sprog is a dead ringer for her great-uncle Lucius Tiddlypuss. Oh, well!

Then the next thing all we old fogies of the Senate know, Saturninus takes this Lucius Equitius up, and starts climbing onto the rostra with him, and encourages Equitius to build a following. Thus, not a week had gone by before Equitius was the hero of everyone in Rome on an income lower than a tribune of the Treasury and higher than the Head Count—tradesmen, shopkeepers, artisans, smallholding farmers—the flower of the Third and Fourth and Fifth Classes. You know the people I mean. They worshiped the ground the Brothers Gracchi walked on, all those little honest hardworking men who don't often get to vote, but vote in their tribes often enough to feel a distinct cut above freedmen and the Head Count. The sort who are too proud to take charity, yet not rich enough to survive astronomical grain prices.

The Conscript Fathers of the Senate, particularly those wearing purple-bordered togas, began to get a bit upset at all this popular adulation—and a bit worried too, thanks to the participation of Saturninus, who is the real mystery. Yet what could be done about it? Finally none other than our new Pontifex Maximus, Ahenobarbus (he's got a new nickname and it's sticking—*pipinna*!), proposed that the sister of the

Brothers Gracchi (and the widow of Scipio Aemilianus, as if we could ever forget the brawls that particular married couple used to have!) should be brought
to the Forum and hied up onto the rostra to confront
the alleged imposter.

Three days ago it was done, with Saturninus standing off to one side grinning like a fool—only he isn't a
fool, so what's he up to?—and Lucius Equitius gazing
blankly at this wizened-up old crab apple of a woman.
Ahenobarbus Pipinna struck a maximally pontifical
pose, took Sempronia by the shoulders—she didn't
like that a bit, and shook him off like a hairy-legged
spider—and asked in tones of thunder, "Daughter of
Tiberius Sempronius Gracchus Senior and Cornelia
Africana, do you recognize this man?"

Of course she snapped that she'd never seen him
before in her life, and that her dearest, most beloved
brother Tiberius would never, never, never loosen the
stopper of his wine flask outside the sacred bonds of
marriage, so the whole thing was utter nonsense. She
then began to belabor Equitius with her ivory and eb-
ony walking stick, and it really did turn into the most
outrageous mime you ever saw—I kept wishing Lucius Cornelius Sulla had been there. He would have
reveled in it!

In the end Ahenobarbus Pipinna (I do love that
nickname! Given to him by none other than Metellus
Numidicus!) had to haul her down off the rostra while
the audience screamed with laughter, and Scaurus fell
about hooting himself to tears and only got worse
when Pipinna and Piggle-wiggle and Piglet accused
him of unsenatorial levity.

The minute Lucius Equitius had the rostra to himself
again, Saturninus marched up to him and asked him if
he knew who the old horror was. Equitius said no, he

didn't, which proved either that he hadn't been listening when Ahenobarbus roared out his introduction, or he was lying. But Saturninus explained to him in nice short words that she was his Auntie Sempronia, the sister of the Brothers Gracchi. Equitius looked amazed, said he'd never set eyes on his Auntie Sempronia in all his astonishingly full life, and then said he'd be very surprised if Tiberius Gracchus had ever told his sister about the mistress and child in a snug little love nest down on one of the Sempronius Gracchus farms.

The crowd appreciated the good sense of this answer, and goes merrily on believing implicitly that Lucius Equitius is the natural son of Tiberius Gracchus. And the Senate—not to mention Ahenobarbus—is fulminating. Well, all except Saturninus, who smirks; Scaurus, who laughs; and me. Three guesses what I'm doing!

Publius Rutilius Rufus sighed and stretched his cramped hand, wishing that he could feel as uncomfortable writing a letter as Gaius Marius did; then perhaps he might not be driven to putting in all the delicious details which made the difference between a five-column missive and a fifty-five-column missive.

And that, dear Gaius Marius, is positively all. If I sit here a moment longer I'll think of more entertaining tales, and end in falling asleep with my nose in the inkpot. I do wish there was a better—that is, a more traditionally Roman—way of going about safeguarding your command than running yet again for the consulship. Nor do I see how you can possibly pull it off. But I daresay you will. Keep in good health. Remember, you're no spring chicken anymore, you're an old boiler, so don't go tail over comb and break any bones. I will write again when something interesting happens.

Gaius Marius got the letter at the beginning of November, and had just got it worked out so he could read it through with real enjoyment when Sulla turned up. That he was back for good he demonstrated by shaving off his now enormously long and drooping moustaches, and having his hair barbered. So while Sulla soaked blissfully in the bath, Marius read the letter out to him, and was ridiculously happy at having Sulla back to share such pleasures.

They settled in the general's private study, Marius having issued instructions that he was not to be disturbed, even by Manius Aquillius.

"Take off that wretched torc!" Marius said when the properly Roman, tunic-clad Sulla leaned forward and brought the great gold thing into view.

But Sulla shook his head, smiling and fingering the splendid dragon heads which formed the ends of the torc's almost complete circle. "No, I don't think I ever will, Gaius Marius. Barbaric, isn't it?"

"It's wrong on a Roman," grumbled Marius.

"The trouble is, it's become my good-luck talisman, so I can't take it off in case my luck goes with it." He settled himself on a couch with a sigh of voluptuous ease. "Oh, the bliss of reclining like a civilized man again! I've been carousing bolt upright at tables with my arse on hard wooden benches for so long that I'd begun to think I had only dreamed there were races lay down to eat. And how good it is to be *continent* again! Gauls and Germans alike, they do everything to excess—eat and drink until they spew all over each other, or else starve half to death because they went out to raid or do battle without thinking to pack a lunch. Ah, but they're fierce, Gaius Marius! *Brave!* I tell you, if they had one tenth of our organization and self-discipline, we couldn't hope to beat them."

"Luckily for us, they don't have as much as a hundredth of either, so we can beat them. At least I think that's what you're saying. Here, drink this. It's Falernian."

Sulla drank deeply, yet slowly. "Wine, wine, wine! Nectar of the gods, balm for the sore heart, glue for the shredded spirit! How did I ever exist without it?" He laughed. "I don't care if I never see another horn of beer or tankard of mead in all the rest of my life! Wine is *civilized*. No belches, no farts, no distended belly—on beer, a man becomes a walking cistern."

"Where's Quintus Sertorius? All right, I hope?"

"He's on his way, but we traveled separately, and I wanted to brief you alone, Gaius Marius," said Sulla.

"Any way you want it, Lucius Cornelius, as long as I hear it," said Marius, watching him with affection.

"I hardly know where to start."

"At the beginning, then. Who are they? Where do they come from? How long has their migration been going on?"

Relishing his wine, Sulla closed his eyes. "They don't call themselves Germani, and they don't regard themselves as a single people. They are the Cimbri, the Teutones, the Marcomanni, the Cherusci, and the Tigurini. The original homeland of the Cimbri and the Teutones is a long, wide peninsula lying to the north of Germania, vaguely described by some of the Greek geographers, who called it the Cimbrian Chersonnese. It seems the half farthest north was the home of the Cimbri, and the half joining onto the mainland of Germania was the home of the Teutones. Though they regard themselves as separate peoples, it's very difficult to see any physical characteristics peculiar to either people, though the languages are somewhat different—they can understand each other, however.

"They weren't nomads, but they didn't grow crops, and didn't farm in our sense. It would seem that their winters were more wet than snowy, and that the soil produced wonderful grass all year round. So they lived with and off cattle, eked out by a little oats and rye. Beef eaters and milk drinkers, a few vegetables, a little hard black bread, and porridge.

"And then about the time that Gaius Gracchus died—almost twenty years ago, at any rate—they had a year of inundations. Too much snow on the mountains feeding their great rivers, too much rain from the skies, ferocious gales, and very high tides.

The ocean Atlanticus covered the whole peninsula. And when the sea receded, they found the soil too saline to grow grass, and their wells brackish. So they built an army of wagons, gathered together the cattle and horses which had survived, and set off to find a new homeland."

Marius was stiff with interest and excitement, sitting very straight in his chair, his wine forgotten. "All of them? How many were there?" he asked.

"Not all of them, no. The old and the feeble were knocked on the head and buried in huge barrows. Only the warriors, the younger women, and the children migrated. As far as I can estimate, about six hundred thousand started to walk southeast down the valley of the great river we call the Albis."

"But I believe that part of the world is hardly peopled," said Marius, frowning. "Why didn't they stay along the Albis?"

Sulla shrugged. "Who knows, when they don't? They just seem to have given themselves into the hands of their gods, and waited for some sort of divine signal to tell them they had found a new homeland. Certainly they didn't seem to encounter much opposition as they walked, at least along the Albis. Eventually they came to the sources of the river, and saw high mountains for the first time in the memory of the race. The Cimbrian Chersonnese was flat and low-lying."

"Obviously, if the ocean could flood it," said Marius, and lifted a hand hastily. "No, I didn't mean that sarcastically, Lucius Cornelius! I'm not good with words, or very tactful." He got up to pour more wine into Sulla's cup. "I take it that the mountains affected them powerfully?"

"Indeed. Their gods were sky gods, but when they saw these towers tickling the underbellies of the clouds, they began to worship the gods they were sure lived beneath the towers, and shoved them up out of the ground. They've never really been very far from mountains since. In the fourth year they crossed an alpine watershed, and passed from the headwaters of the Albis to the headwaters of the Danubius, a river we know more about, of course. And they turned east to follow the Danubius toward the plains of the Getae and the Sarmatae."

"Was that where they were going, then?" Marius asked. "To the Euxine Sea?"

"It appears so," said Sulla. "However, they were blocked by the Boii from entering the basin of northern Dacia, and so were forced to keep following the course of the Danubius where it bends sharply south into Pannonia."

"The Boii are Celts, of course," said Marius thoughtfully. "Celt and German didn't mix, I take it."

"No, they certainly didn't. But the interesting thing is that nowhere have the Germans decided to stay put and fight for land. At the least sign of resistance from the local tribes, they've moved on. As they did away from the lands of the Boii. Then somewhere near the confluence of the Danubius with the Tisia and the Savus, they ran up against another wall of Celts, this time the Scordisci."

"Our very own enemies, the Scordisci!" Marius exclaimed, grinning. "Well, isn't it comforting to find out now that we and the Scordisci have a common enemy?"

One red-gold brow went up. "Considering that it happened about fifteen years ago and we knew nothing of it, it's hardly comforting," Sulla said dryly.

"I'm not saying anything right today, am I? Forgive me, Lucius Cornelius. You've been living it; I'm merely sitting here so excited at finding out at last that my tongue has developed a forest of thumbs," said Marius.

"It's all right, Gaius Marius, I do understand," said Sulla, smiling.

"Go on, go on!"

"Perhaps one of their greatest problems was that they had no leader worthy of the name. Nor any semblance of a—a—master plan, for want of a better phrase to describe it. I think they just waited for the day when some great king would give them permission to settle down on some of his vacant land."

"And of course great kings are not prone to do that," said Marius.

"No. Anyway, they turned back and began to travel west," Sulla went on, "only they left the Danubius. They followed the Savus first, then skewed a little north, and picked up the course of the Dravus, which they then tracked toward its sources. By this time they had been walking for over six years without staying for more than a few days anywhere."

"They don't travel on the wagons?" asked Marius.

"Rarely. They're harnessed to cattle, so they're not driven, just guided. If someone is ill or near term with a child, the wagon becomes a vehicle of transport, not otherwise," said Sulla. He sighed. "And of course we all know what happened next. They entered Noricum, and the lands of the Taurisci."

"Who appealed to Rome, and Rome sent Carbo to deal with the invaders, and Carbo lost his army," said Marius.

"And, as always, the Germans turned away from trouble," said Sulla. "Instead of invading Italian Gaul, they walked right into the high mountains, and came back to the Danubius a little to the east of its confluence with the Aenus. The Boii weren't going to let them go east, so they headed west along the Danubius, through the lands of the Marcomanni. For reasons I haven't been able to fathom, a large segment of the Marcomanni joined the Cimbri and the Teutones in this seventh year of the migration."

"What about the thunderstorm?" Marius asked. "You know, the one which interrupted the battle between the Germans and Carbo, and saved at least some of Carbo's men. There were those who believed the Germans took the storm as a sign of divine wrath, and that that was what saved us from invasion."

"I doubt it," said Sulla tranquilly. "Oh, I'm sure when the storm broke, the Cimbri—it was the Cimbri who fought Carbo; they were closest to his position—fled in terror, but I don't believe it deflected them from Italian Gaul. The real answer seems simply to be that they never liked waging war to win territory for themselves."

"How fascinating! And here we see them as slavering hordes

of barbarians just thirsting for Italy." Marius looked at Sulla keenly. "And what happened next?"

"Well, they followed the Danubius right to its sources this time. In the eighth year they were joined by a group of real Germans, the Cherusci, who came down from their lands around the Visurgis River, and in the ninth year by a people of Helvetia called the Tigurini, who seem to have lived to the east of Lake Lemanna, and are definitely Celts. As are, I believe, the Marcomanni. However, both the Marcomanni and the Tigurini are very Germanic Celts."

"They don't dislike the Germans, you mean?"

"Far less than they dislike their fellow Celts!" Sulla grinned. "The Marcomanni had been warring with the Boii for centuries, and the Tigurini with the Helvetii. So I suppose when the German wagons rolled through, they thought it might be a pleasant change to head for parts unknown. By the time the migration crossed through the Jura into Gallia Comata, there were well over eight hundred thousand participants."

"Who all descended upon the poor Aedui and Ambarri," said Marius. "And stayed there."

"For over three years." Sulla nodded. "The Aedui and Ambarri were softer people, you see. *Romanized*, Gaius Marius! Teeth pulled by Gnaeus Domitius so that our province of Gaul-across-the-Alps would be safe—er. And the Germans were developing a taste for our fine white bread. Something to spread their butter on! And sop up their beef juice with. And mix into their awful blood puddings."

"You speak feelingly, Lucius Cornelius."

"I do, I do!" Smile fading, Sulla studied the surface of his wine reflectively, then looked up at Marius, his light eyes gleaming. "They've elected themselves an overall king," he said abruptly.

"Oho!" said Marius softly.

"His name is Boiorix, and he's Cimbric. The Cimbri are the most numerous people."

"It's a Celtic name, though," said Marius. "Boiorix—Boii. A very formidable nation. There are colonies of Boii all over the

THE TREK OF THE 𝕲ermans

BATTLES

CIMBRI ●●●●●●●●●●●●●●
TEUTONES ▬ ▬ ▬ ▬ ▬ ▬ ▬ ▬
TIGURINI - MARCOMANNI - CHERUSCI ········

1 CARBO	5 CAEPIO-MALLIUS
2 SILANUS	6 CATULUS CAESAR
3 L. CASSIUS	7 MARIUS
4 L. CASSIUS	8 MARIUS – CATULUS

place—Dacia, Thrace, Long-haired Gaul, Italian Gaul, Helvetia. Who knows? Maybe a long time ago they planted a colony among the Cimbri. After all, if this Boiorix says he's Cimbric, then he's Cimbric. They can't be so primitive that they have no genealogical lore."

"Actually they have very little genealogical lore," said Sulla, propping himself on his elbow. "Not because they're particularly primitive, but because their whole structure is different from ours. Different from any people scattered around the Middle Sea, for that matter. They're not farmers, and when men don't own land and farm down the generations, they don't develop a sense of *place*. That means they don't develop a sense of family either. Tribal life—group life, if you prefer—is more important. They tend to eat as a community, which for them is more sensible. When houses are huts for sleeping and have no kitchens, or home is on wheels and has no kitchen, it's easier to kill whole beasts, spit them, roast them whole, and feed the tribe as a single group.

"Their genealogical lore relates to the tribe, or even to the collection of individual tribes which make up the people as a whole. They have heroes they sing about, but they embroider their doings out of all proportion to what must have been actual fact—a chieftain only two generations back behaves like Perseus or Hercules, he's become so shadowy as a man. Their concept of place is shadowy too. And the position—chief or thane or priest or shaman—takes precedence over the identity of the individual man filling it. The individual man *becomes* the position! He moves apart from his family, and his family doesn't rise with him. And when he dies, the position goes to someone the tribe selects without regard to what we would call family entitlements. Their ideas about family are very different from ours, Gaius Marius." Sulla lifted himself off his elbow to pour more wine.

"You've actually been living with them!" gasped Marius.

"Oh, I had to!" Sipping enough from his cup to diminish the level of the wine, Sulla added water. "I'm not used to it," he said, sounding surprised. "Never mind, my head will return, no doubt." He frowned. "I managed to infiltrate the Cimbri while they were still trying to fight their way across the Pyrenees. It would have been November of last year, the moment I returned from seeing you."

"How?" asked Marius, fascinated.

"Well, they were beginning to suffer what any people in a protracted war suffer—including us, especially after Arausio. Since the whole nation save for the old and infirm is moving as a unit, every warrior who dies is likely to leave a widow and orphans. These women become a liability unless their male children are old enough to become warriors fairly quickly. So the widows have to scramble to find new husbands among the warriors not old enough or enterprising enough to have acquired women already. If a woman succeeds in attaching herself and her offspring to another warrior, she's allowed to continue as before. Her wagon is her dowry. Though not all the widowed women have wagons. And not all the widowed women find new mates. Owning a wagon definitely helps. They're given a certain amount of time to make fresh arrangements. Three months—that is, one season. After that, they're killed—along with their children—and the members of their tribe who don't have wagons cast lots for vacant wagons. They kill those who are deemed too old to contribute productively to the welfare of the tribe, and excess girl-children are killed."

Marius grimaced. "And I thought we were hard!"

But Sulla shook his head. "What's hard, Gaius Marius? The Germans and the Gauls are like any other peoples. They structure their society to survive as a people. Those who become a drain on the community that it simply cannot afford must go. And which is better—to set them adrift without men to look after them, or hit them on the head? To die slowly of starvation and cold, or quickly and without pain? That's how they look at it. That's how they *have* to look at it."

"I suppose so," said Marius reluctantly. "Personally I take great delight in our old. Listening to them is worth giving them food and shelter."

"But that's because we can *afford* to keep our old, Gaius

Marius! Rome is very rich. Therefore Rome can afford to support some at least of those who contribute nothing productive to the community. But we don't condemn the exposing of unwanted children, do we?" Sulla asked.

"Of course not!"

"So what's the difference, really? When the Germans find a homeland, they'll become more like the Gauls. And the Gauls exposed to Greeks or Romans become more like Greeks or Romans. Having a homeland will enable the Germans to relax the rules; they'll acquire sufficient wealth to feed their old and their widows burdened with children. They're not city dwellers, they're country folk. Cities have different rules again, haven't you noticed? Cities breed disease to remove the old and the infirm, and cities decrease the farmer's sense of place and family. The bigger Rome gets, the closer to the Germans it gets."

Marius scratched his head. "I'm lost, Lucius Cornelius. Get back to the subject, please! What happened to you? Did you find yourself a widow and tack yourself onto a tribe as a warrior?"

Sulla nodded. "Exactly so. Sertorius did the same thing in a different tribe, which is why we haven't seen a great deal of each other, only occasionally to compare notes. We each found a woman with a wagon who hadn't managed to find a new mate. That was after establishing ourselves within our tribes as warriors, of course. We'd done that before we set out to see you last year, and we found our women as soon as we got back."

"Didn't they reject you?" asked Marius. "After all, you were posing as Gauls, not as Germans."

"True. But we fight well, Quintus Sertorius and I. No tribal chief sneezes at good warriors," said Sulla, grinning.

"At least you haven't been called upon to kill Romans! Though no doubt you would have, had it been necessary."

"Certainly," said Sulla. "Wouldn't you?"

"Of course I would. Love is for the many. Sentiment is for the few," said Marius. "A man must fight to save the many, never the few." He brightened. "Unless, that is, he has the opportunity to do both."

"I was a Gaul of the Carnutes serving as a Cimbric warrior," Sulla said, finding Marius's philosophizing as confusing as Marius found his. "In the very early spring there was a big council composed of all the chiefs of all the tribes. The Cimbri by then had moved as far west as they could, hoping to penetrate Spain where the Pyrenees are lowest. The council was held on the banks of the river the Aquitanians call the Aturis. Definite word had come, you see, that every tribe of the Cantabri, Astures, Vettones, western Lusitani, and Vascones had gathered on the Spanish side of the mountains to contend German passage into their lands. And at this council, all of a sudden, completely unexpected— Boiorix emerged!"

"I remember the report Marcus Cotta filed after Arausio," Marius said. "He was one of the two leaders who fell out, and the other was Teutobod of the Teutones."

"He's very young," said Sulla, "about thirty, no more. Monstrously tall, and built like Hercules. Feet that look as big as licker-fish. But the interesting thing is that he's got a mind akin to ours. Both the Gauls and the Germans have patterns of thinking so different from any people of the Middle Sea that to us they seem—barbarian! Whereas Boiorix has shown himself these past nine months to be a very different kind of barbarian. For one thing, he's had himself taught to read and write—in Latin, not in Greek. I think I've already told you that when a Gaul is literate, he tends to be literate in Latin, not in Greek—"

"Boiorix, Lucius Cornelius!" said Marius. *"Boiorix!"*

Smiling, Sulla resumed. "Back to Boiorix it is. He's been strong in the councils for perhaps four years, but this spring he overcame all opposition, and got himself appointed paramount chief—we'd call him a king, certainly, because he's reserved the final decision in all situations for himself, and he isn't afraid to disgree with his council."

"How did he get himself appointed?" Marius asked.

"The old way," said Sulla. "Neither Germans nor Gauls hold elections, though they do sometimes vote in council. But council decisions are more likely to be made by whoever remains sober the longest, or has the loudest voice. As for Boiorix, he became king by right of combat. He took on all comers, and killed them. Not in a single engagement—merely one a day until there were no more challengers left. All told, eleven thanes disputed his right. And bit the dust, in good old Homeric fashion."

"King by killing one's rivals," said Marius thoughtfully. "Where's the satisfaction in that? Truly barbaric! Kill a rival in debate or court, and he'll live to fight again. No man should be without rivals. Alive, he shines against them because he's better than they are. Dead, he has no one to shine against at all."

"I agree," said Sulla. "But in a barbarian world—or an Eastern one, for that matter—the whole idea is to kill all one's rivals. It's safer."

"What happened to Boiorix after he became king?"

"He told the Cimbri they were not going to Spain. There were far easier places, he said. Like Italy. But first, he said, the Cimbri were going to join up with the Teutones, the Tigurini, the Marcomanni, and the Cherusci. And then he would be king of the Germans as well as the Cimbri."

Sulla refilled his cup, well watered. "We spent the spring and the summer moving north through Long-haired Gaul. We crossed the Garumna, the Liger, and the Sequana, and then we entered the lands of the Belgae."

"The Belgae!" breathed Marius. "You've *seen* them?"

"Yes, of course," said Sulla, looking casual.

"There must have been war to the death."

"Not at all. King Boiorix, you see, has taken to what you or I would call opening up negotiations. Until our summer journey through Long-haired Gaul, the Germans had revealed no interest in negotiating. Every time they've encountered one of our armies barring their progress, for instance, they've sent an embassage to us asking for permission to pass through our territory. We've always said no, naturally. So they ride away and they never come back for a second try. They've never dickered, or asked to sit down at a bargaining table, or attempted to find out if there was anything we'd be prepared to take from them in order to open up a fresh round of propositions. Whereas Boiorix has behaved very differently. He *negotiated* a passage through Long-haired Gaul for the Cimbri."

"Did he now? What did he bargain with?"

"He bought the Gauls and the Belgae off with meat, milk, butter—and work in the fields. He bartered his cattle for their beer and their wheat, and offered his warriors to help plough extra ground to grow enough for everyone," said Sulla.

Marius's eyebrows worked furiously. "Clever barbarian!"

"Indeed he is, Gaius Marius. And so in complete peace and amity we followed the Isara River north from the Sequana, and came finally to the lands of a tribe of Belgae called the Atuatuci. Basically, the Atuatuci are Germans who live along the Mosa River just downstream from the Sabis, and who also live on the edge of a vast forest they call the Arduenna. It stretches east from the Mosa all the way to the Mosella, and unless you're a German, it's impenetrable. The Germans of Germania proper live inside the forests, and use them in much the same way as we use fortifications."

Marius was thinking hard, for his eyebrows continued to writhe as if they had life of their own. "Continue, Lucius Cornelius. I'm finding the German Enemy more and more interesting."

Sulla inclined his head. "I thought you would. The Cherusci actually come from a part of Germania not so very far from the lands of the Atuatuci, and claim the Atuatuci are their kinsmen. So they had persuaded the Teutones, the Tigurini, and the Marcomanni to go with them to the lands of the Atuatuci while the Cimbri were away south looking up at the Pyrenees. But when we of the Cimbri came upon the scene late in Sextilis, it wasn't a happy scene at all. The Teutones had antagonized the Atuatuci *and* the Cherusci to the point where there had been a lot of skirmishing, quite a few deaths, and an ill feeling that we Cimbri could see almost visibly growing."

"But King Boiorix fixed all that," said Marius.

"King Boiorix fixed all that!" Sulla said with a grin. "He settled the Atuatuci down and then called a grand council of the migrant Germans—Cimbri, Teutones, Tigurini, Cherusci, and Marcomanni. At the council he announced that he was not only the King of the Cimbri, but the King of all the Germans. He had to fight a few duels, but not with his only serious rivals, Teutobod of the Teutones and Getorix of the Tigurini. They thought a bit like Romans themselves, because they both decided they liked living and would have considerably more nuisance value to King Boiorix alive than dead."

"And how did you find all this out?" asked Marius. "Had you become a chieftain by this? Did you sit listening?"

Sulla tried to look modest, humility being a little too out of character. "As a matter of fact, I had become a thane. Not a very big thane, you understand, just big enough to be invited to the councils. My wife Hermana—she's actually a member of the Cherusci, not the Cimbri—bore twin boys just as we reached the Mosa, and it was considered such a good omen that my status as tribal chief was elevated to group thane just in time to participate in the grand council of all the Germans."

Marius roared with laughter. "Do you mean to say that in years to come, some poor Roman is going to come up against a couple of little Germans who look like you?"

"It's possible," said Sulla, grinning.

"And a few little Quintus Sertoriuses as well?"

"One, at least."

Marius sobered. "Continue, Lucius Cornelius."

"He's very, very clever, our lad Boiorix. Whatever we do, we mustn't underrate him because he's a barbarian. Because he came up with a grand strategy *you* would have been proud to have thought of yourself. I do not exaggerate, believe me."

Marius tensed. "I believe you! What's his grand strategy?"

"As soon as the weather permits it next year—March at the latest—the Germans intend to invade Italy on three fronts," said Sulla. "When I say March, I mean that's when the whole eight hundred thousand of them are going to leave the lands of the Atuatuci. Boiorix has given everyone six months to complete the journey from the Mosa River to Italian Gaul."

Both Marius and Sulla leaned forward.

"He's divided them into three separate forces. The Teutones are to invade Italian Gaul from the west. They represent some quarter million of the total number. They'll be led by their king, Teutobod, and at this stage they plan to travel down the Rhodanus and along the Ligurian coast toward Genua and Pisae. It's my guess, however, that with Boiorix in charge of the whole invasion, before they start they'll have changed their route to the Via Domitia and the Mons Genava Pass. Which will bring them out on the Padus at Taurasia."

"He's learning some geography as well as some Latin, is he?" asked Marius grimly.

"I told you, Boiorix is a reader. He's also put Roman captives to the torture—not quite all of those we lost at Arausio died. If they fell to the Cimbri, Boiorix kept them alive until he found out what he wanted to know. One cannot blame our men for co-operating." Sulla pulled a face. "The Germans routinely resort to torture."

"So that means the Teutones will be following the same route as the whole host took before Arausio," said Marius. "How are the others planning to enter Italian Gaul?"

"The Cimbri are the most numerous of the three great German divisions," said Sulla. "All told, four hundred thousand of them at least. Where the Teutones go straight down the Mosa to the Arar and the Rhodanus, the Cimbri will move down the Rhenus all the way to Lake Brigantinus, go north of the lake over the watershed and down to the source of the Danubius. They'll go east along the Danubius until they reach the Aenus, then down the Aenus and cross into Italian Gaul through the Pass of Brennus. Which will put them on the Athesis, near Verona."

"Led by King Boiorix himself," said Marius, and humped his head into his shoulders. "I like it less and less."

"The third group is the smallest and least cohesive," Sulla went on. "The Tigurini, Marcomanni, and Cherusci. About two hundred thousand of them. They'll be led by Getorix of the Tigurini. At first Boiorix was going to send them in a straight line through the great German forests—the Hercynian, Gabreta, and so on—and have them strike south through Pannonia into Noricum. Then I think he wondered if they'd stick to it, and decided to make them travel with him down the Danubius to the Aenus. From there they'll keep on going east along the Danubius until they reach Noricum, and turn south. They'll enter Italian Gaul over the Carnic Alps, which will put them at Tergeste, with Aquileia not far away."

"And each segment has six months to make the journey, you say?" Marius asked. "Well, I can see the Teutones doing it, but the Cimbri have a much longer journey, and the hybrids the longest journey of all."

"And there you are mistaken, Gaius Marius," said Sulla. "In actual fact, from the point on the Mosa where all three divisions start out, the distance each division travels is much the same. All involve crossing the Alps, but only the Teutones will cross through country they haven't traversed before. The Germans have wandered *everywhere* through the Alps during the last eighteen years! They've been down the Danubius from its sources to Dacia; they've been down the Rhenus from its sources to the Helella; they've been down the Rhodanus from its sources to Arausio. They're alpine veterans."

The breath hissed between Marius's teeth. "Jupiter, Lucius Cornelius, it's brilliant! But can they really do it? I mean, Boiorix has to bank on each division reaching Italian Gaul by—October?"

"I think the Teutones and the Cimbri will certainly do it. They're well led and strongly motivated. About the others, I can't be sure. Nor, I suspect, can Boiorix."

Sulla slid off the couch and began to pace the floor. "There's one more thing, Gaius Marius, and it's a very serious thing. After eighteen years of homeless wandering, the Germans are tired. And they're desperate to settle down. A huge number of children have grown old enough to become young warriors without ever knowing a homeland. There's actually even been talk of going back to the Cimbrian Chersonnese. The sea has retreated long since, and the ground is sweet again."

"I wish they would!" said Marius.

"It's too late for that," Sulla said, pacing up and down restlessly. "They've grown to like crusty white bread, you see, to put their butter on, and sop up their beef juice, and put into their awful blood puddings. They like the warmth of the southern sun and the proximity of the great white mountains. First Pannonia and Noricum, then Gaul. Ours is a richer world. And now that they've got Boiorix, they've made up their minds they'll take it."

"Not while I'm in charge, they won't," said Marius, and sagged in his chair. "Is that all?" he asked.

"All, yet nothing," Sulla said, a little sadly. "I could talk about them for days. But that's as much as you need to know as a beginning, certainly."

"What about your wife, your sons? Have you left them to be knocked on the head because they've no warrior to support them?"

"Isn't it funny?" Sulla asked himself, wondering. "I couldn't do that! When the time came to go, I found I just—couldn't. So I took Hermana and the boys to the Cherusci of Germania. They live to the north of the Chatti, along the Visurgis River. Her tribe is a part of the Cherusci, though it's called the Marsi. Odd, don't you find? We have our Marsi. The Germans have theirs. The name is pronounced exactly the same way. Makes you wonder. . . . How did we all come to be where we are? Is it in the nature of men to wander in search of fresh homelands? Will we of Rome grow tired of Italy one day, and migrate elsewhere? I've thought a great deal about the world since I joined the Germans, Gaius Marius."

For a reason he couldn't quite grasp, this last speech of Sulla's moved Marius almost to tears; so he said in a gentler voice than usual, "I'm glad you didn't leave her to die."

"So am I, even though I couldn't afford the time. I was worried that I wouldn't reach you before the consular elections were due, because I thought my news would be a terrific help." He cleared his throat. "Actually I took it upon myself—in your name, of course—to conclude a treaty of peace and friendly alliance with the Marsi of Germania. In some way, I thought, my German sons would then have the faintest whiff of Rome under their short

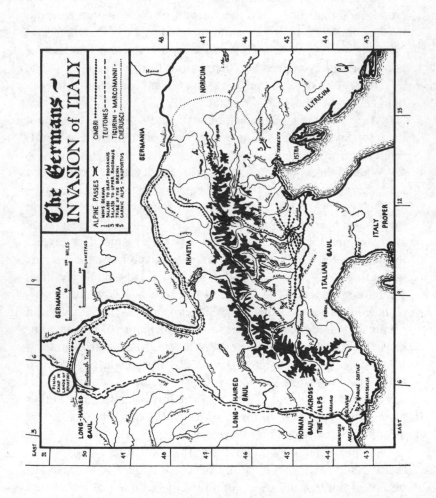

The Germans ~ INVASION of ITALY

ALPINE PASSES

CIMBRI ········
TEUTONES ·········
TIGURINI — MARCOMANNI —
CHERUSCI ········

1 MNS SEVAVA
2 PASS TO ISAR - RHODANUS
3 SALASSI TO UPPER RHODANUS
4 TRIBE OF THE BRENNI
5 CARNIC ALPS - MAUPORTUS

GERMANIA

0 50 100 MILES
0 50 100 KILOMETRES

straight Cherusci noses. Hermana has promised to raise them to think kindly of Rome."

"Won't you ever see her again?" asked Marius.

"Of course not!" said Sulla briskly. "Nor the twins. I do not intend ever again, Gaius Marius, to grow my hair or my moustaches, nor journey away from the lands around the Middle Sea. A diet of beef and milk and butter and oaten porridge does not agree with my Roman stomach, nor do I like going without a bath, nor do I like *beer*. I've done what I could for Hermana and the boys by putting them where their lack of a warrior will not mean they have to die. But I've told Hermana she must try to find another man. It's sensible and proper. All going well, they'll survive. And my boys will grow up to be good Germans. Fierce warriors, I hope! And bigger than me by far, I hope! Yet—if Fortune doesn't intend them to survive—why, I'll not know about it, will I?"

"Quite so, Lucius Cornelius." Marius looked down at his hands where they curled about his cup, and seemed surprised that their knuckles were white.

"The only time I ever take credence of Metellus Numidicus Piggle-wiggle's allegations about your vulgar origins," said Sulla, sounding nothing but amused, "is when some incident rouses your dormant peasant sentimentality."

Marius glared. "The worst of you—*Sulla!*—is that I will never know what makes you work! What makes your legs go up and down, what makes your arms swing, why you smile like a wolf. And what you really think. That I'll never, never know."

"If it's any consolation, brother-in-law, nor will anyone else. Even me," said Sulla.

 It looked, that November, as if Gaius Marius would never succeed in becoming consul for the following year. A letter from Lucius Appuleius Saturninus drove out all hope of a plebiscite authorizing him to stand *in absentia* a third time.

The Senate won't stand by idly again, because most of Rome is now convinced the Germans won't come at all. Ever. In fact, the Germans have turned into a new Lamia, a monster employed to strike terror into every heart so often and for so long that eventually she holds no terror.

Naturally your enemies have made a great deal out of the fact that this is your second year in Gaul-across-the-Alps repairing roads and digging ship canals, and that your presence there with a large army is costing the State more than it can afford, especially with the price of wheat what it is.

I've tested the electoral water in the matter of your standing *in absentia* a third time, and the toe I dipped in has dropped off from the frost. Your chances would be somewhat better if you came to Rome to stand in person. But of course if you do that, your enemies will argue that the so-called emergency in Gaul-across-the-Alps does not actually exist.

However, I've done what I can for you, mainly lining up support in the Senate so you will at least have your command prorogued with proconsular status. This will mean next year's consuls will be your superiors. And as a final note of cheer, the favored consular candidate for next year is Quintus Lutatius Catulus. The electors are so fed up with his standing every single year that they've decided to get rid of him by voting him in. I trust this finds you well.

When Marius finished reading Saturninus's short missive, he sat frowning for a long time. Though the news it imparted was cheerless, there was yet a faintly jaunty feel to the letter; as if Saturninus too was deciding Gaius Marius was a man of the past, and was busy realigning his priorities. Gaius Marius had no polling appeal. No more knight clout. For the Germans were much less of a threat than the Sicilian slave war and the grain supply; Lamia the monster was dead.

Well, Lamia the monster wasn't dead, and Lucius Cornelius Sulla was alive to prove it. Only what was the point of sending Sulla to Rome to testify to this fact when he, Gaius Marius, had no excuse to accompany Sulla to Rome? Without support and power, Sulla wouldn't prevail; he'd have to tell his whole story to too many men alienated from his commander, men who would find the idea of a Roman aristocrat masquerading as a Gaul for almost two years so disturbing they would end in having Rome dismiss Sulla's story as unstable, unreliable, unacceptable. No, either both of them journeyed to Rome, or neither of them did.

Out came blank paper, pen, ink: Gaius Marius wrote to Lucius Appuleius Saturninus.

> Vindicated you may be, Lucius Appuleius, but remember it was I who enabled you to survive until you were vindicated. You are still beholden to me, and I expect a clientlike loyalty from you.
>
> Do not assume I cannot come to Rome. An opportunity may still arise. Or at least, I expect you to act as if I will indeed appear in Rome. Therefore here is what I want. The most immediate necessity is to postpone the consular elections, a job you and Gaius Norbanus as tribunes of the plebs are well able to do. You will do it. Wholeheartedly. Throwing all your energy into the job. After that, I expect you to use the brain you were born with to seize upon the first opportunity which will enable you to put pressure on the Senate and People to call me to Rome.
>
> I will get to Rome, never doubt it. So if you want to rise a great deal higher than the tribunate of the plebs, it behooves you to remain Gaius Marius's man.

And by the end of November an east wind blew Gaius Marius a smacking kiss from the goddess Fortuna, in the shape of a second letter from Saturninus that arrived by sea two days before the Senate courier and his dispatches reached Glanum. Saturninus said, very humbly:

> I do not doubt you will reach Rome. Not one day after I received your chastening note, your esteemed colleague Lucius Aurelius Orestes, the junior consul, died suddenly. And, still feeling the lash of your displeasure, I seized upon this opportunity to force the Senate into recalling you. That had not been the plan formulated by the Policy Makers, who through the agency of the Leader of the House recommended that the Conscript Fathers choose a *consul suffectus* to fill the ivory chair left vacant by Orestes. But—amazing luck!—only the day before, Scaurus had delivered a long speech in the House to the effect that your presence in Gaul-across-the-Alps was an affront to the credulity of all Good Men, that you had manufactured the German panic to get yourself elected a virtual dictator. Of course the moment Orestes died, Scaurus changed his tune completely—the House did not dare recall you to exercise the electoral functions of the consul with the German menace threatening Italy, so the House must appoint a suffect consul to get the elections under way.
>
> Having had no time to start using my tribunate to postpone any elections, I now found it unnecessary to do so. Instead, I rose in the House and made a very fine speech to the effect that our esteemed Princeps Senatus couldn't have it both ways. Either there was a German menace, or there was not. And I chose to accept his speech of the day before as his honest opinion—there was no German menace, therefore there was no need to fill the dead junior consul's chair with a *suffectus*. No, I said, Gaius Marius must be recalled; Gaius Marius must finally do the job he had been elected to do—carry out

the duties of a consul. I didn't need to accuse Scaurus of altering his viewpoint to fit the new set of circumstances in his second speech; everyone got the message.

Hopefully this will beat the courier. The time of year favors the sea over the road. Not that you are not perfectly capable of working out what must have been the sequence of events the moment you get the Senate's communication! Only that if I do beat the courier, you have a little extra time to plan your campaign in Rome. I am starting things moving among the electors, naturally, and by the time you reach Rome you should have a most respectable deputation of leading lights of the People begging you to stand for the consulship.

"We're on our way!" said Marius jubilantly to Sulla, tossing him Saturninus's letter. "Pack your things—there's no time to lose. You are going to tell the House that the Germans will invade Italy on three separate fronts in the autumn of next year, and I am going to tell the electors that I am the only man capable of stopping them."

"How far do I go?" asked Sulla, startled.

"Only as far as you have to. I'll introduce the subject, and state the findings. You'll testify to their truth, but not in a way which gives the House to understand that you became a barbarian yourself." Marius looked rueful. "Some things, Lucius Cornelius, are best left unsaid. They don't know you well enough yet to understand what kind of man you are. Don't give them information they can use against you later on. You're a patrician Roman. So let them think your daring deeds were done inside a patrician Roman skin."

Sulla shook his head. "It's manifestly impossible to go prowling among the Germans looking like a patrician Roman!"

"They don't know that," said Marius with a grin. "Remember what Publius Rutilius said in his letter? The armchair generals on the back benches, he called them. Well, they're armchair spies too, on the front benches as well as the back. They would not know the rules for spying if the rules ran up their arses!" And he began to laugh. "In fact, I wish I'd asked you to keep your moustaches and long hair for a little while. I'd have dressed you as a German and paraded you around the Forum. And you know what would happen, don't you?"

Sulla sighed. "Yes. No one would recognize me."

"Correct. So we won't put unbearable strain on their Roman imaginations. I'll be speaking first, and you take your cue from me," said Marius.

To Sulla, Rome offered none of the political vigor or domestic warmth it did to Gaius Marius. In spite of his brilliant quaestorship—under Marius—and his brilliant career as a spy—under Marius—he was just another one of the Senate's young up-and-coming men, walking in the shadow of the First Man in Rome. Nor was his future political career going anywhere fast enough, especially considering his late entry into the Senate; he was patrician and therefore not permitted to become a tribune of the plebs, he didn't have the money to run for curule aedile, and he hadn't been in the Senate long enough to run for praetor. That was the political side of things. At home he found a bitter and enervating atmosphere polluted by a wife who drank too much and neglected her children, and by a mother-in-law who disliked him quite as much as she disliked her situation. That was the domestic side of things.

Well, the political climate would improve for him, he was not so depressed he couldn't see it; but the climate in his home could do nothing else than deteriorate. And what made it harder coming to Rome this time was that he was passing from his German wife to his Roman one. For just about a year he had lived with Hermana in the midst of an environment more alien to his aristocratic world than the old world of the Suburan stews had been. And Hermana was his solace, his fortress, his one normal point of reference in that bizarre barbarian society.

Tacking himself onto the Cimbric comet's tail had not been difficult, for Sulla was more than just another brave and physically strong warrior; he was a warrior who thought. In bravery and physical strength many of the Germans left him far behind. But where they were an unalloyed metal, he was the tempered finality—cunning as well as brave, slippery as well as strong. Sulla was the small man facing the giant, the man who, in order to excel in armed combat, had no other way of going about it than to *think*. Therefore he had been noticed on the field against the Spanish tribes of the Pyrenees at once, and accepted into the warrior confraternity.

Then he and Sertorius had agreed that if they were to blend into this strange world to the point where they would rise high enough to be privy to German policies (such as they were), they would have to be more than useful soldiers. They would have to carve themselves niches in tribal life. So they had separated, chosen different tribes, and then taken women from among the ranks of those women recently widowed.

His eye had lighted upon Hermana because she was an outsider herself, and because she had no children. Her man had been the chief of his Cimbric tribe; otherwise the women of the tribe would never have tolerated her foreign presence among them when, in effect, she usurped a place which ought to have been filled by a Cimbric woman. And the angry women were already clubbing her to death inside their minds when Sulla—a meteor among the warriors—climbed into her wagon and thereby established his claim to her. They would be foreigners together. There was no sentiment or attraction of any kind in his selection of the Cheruscic Hermana; simply, she needed him more than a Cimbric woman would have within the tribal enclave, and also owed the tribe far less than a Cimbric woman would have. Thus if she should discover his Roman origins, Hermana would be far less likely to report him than a Cimbric woman.

As German women went, she was very ordinary. Most were tall, strongly yet gracefully built, with long legs and high breasts, flaxen hair, the bluest of eyes—and fair of face if one could forgive the ugliness of wide mouths and straight little noses. Hermana was a great deal shorter even than Sulla (who as Romans went was a respectable height at about three inches less than six feet—Marius, an inch over six feet, was very tall), and plumper than most of her fellows. Though her hair was extremely thick and long, it was definitely of that indeterminate shade universally known as mouse, and her eyes were a darkish grey-fawn to match her hair. For the rest, she was German enough—the bones of her skull were well defined, and her nose was like a short straight blade, fine and thin. She was thirty years old, and had been barren; if her man had not been the chief, and autocratic to the point of refusing to cast her off, Hermana would have died.

What made her distinctive enough to have been the choice of two men of superior quality in succession was not obvious on the surface. Her first man had called her different and interesting, but could be no more specific; Sulla thought her a natural aristocrat, a finicky aloof lady who yet radiated a powerfully sexual message.

They fitted together very well in every way, for she was intelligent enough to be undemanding, sensible enough not to trammel him, passionate enough to make bedding her a pleasure, articulate enough to make her an interesting communicant, and industrious enough to give him no additional work. Hermana's beasts were always herded together properly, branded properly, milked properly, mated properly, medicined properly. Hermana's wagon was always in tiptop condition, its canopy kept taut and patched or mended, its wooden tray oiled and chinked, its big wheels greased with a mixture of butter and beef drippings along the axle junctions and linch-pins, and never missing spokes or segments of their rims. Hermana's pots and crocks and vessels were kept clean; her provisions were carefully stored against damp and marauders; her clothing and rugs were aired and darned; her killing and quartering knives were superbly sharp; her oddments were never put away in some place she forgot. Hermana, in fact, was everything Julilla was not. Except a Roman of blood as good as his own.

When she discovered she was pregnant—in fact, she fell at once—both of them were delighted, Hermana for one extra reason. She was now vindicated in the eyes of the tribe to which she did not belong, and the blame for her previous sterility was now thrown squarely upon the shoulders of her dead chieftain. A fact which didn't please the women of the tribe one little bit, for they had long hated her. Not that there was much they could do about it, because by spring, when the Cimbri set off on their trek northward to the lands of the Atuatuci, Sulla was the new chief. Hermana, it might safely be inferred, had more than her share of luck.

And then in Sextilis, after a wearying yet uncomplaining gestation, Hermana gave birth to twin boys, big and healthy and red-haired; Sulla called one Herman, and the other Cornel. He had racked his brains to think of a name which would in some way perpetuate his *gens,* Cornelius, yet wouldn't sound too odd in the German tongue. "Cornel" was his solution.

The babies were everything twin boys ought to be: so alike it was difficult to tell them apart, even for their mother and father; content to be together; more interested in thriving than crying. Twins were rare, and their birth to this strange outlander couple was considered an omen important enough to secure Sulla the thaneship of a whole group of small tribes. In consequence, he went to the grand council Boiorix called of all the Germans of all three peoples after the King of the Cimbri settled Atuatuci-Teutonic friction without bloodshed.

For some time, of course, Sulla had known he would soon have to leave, but he put off his departure until after that grand council, aware that he worried over what should have been a very minor consideration—what would happen to Hermana and his sons once he was gone? The men of his tribe he might possibly have trusted, but the women were not to be trusted, and in any domestic tribal situation, the women would prevail. The moment he disappeared, Hermana would die under the clubs, even if her sons were allowed to survive.

It was September, and time was of the essence. Yet Sulla made a decision which ran counter both to self-interest and Rome's interest. Though he could ill afford the time, before he returned to

Marius he would take Hermana back to her own people in Germania. That meant he had to tell her who and what he was. She was more fascinated than surprised; he saw her eyes turn to their sons with wonder in them, as if now she truly understood how important they were, these sons of a demigod. No grief appeared on her face when he told her he would have to leave her forever, but gratitude did when he told her he would first deliver her to the Marsi of Germania, in the hope that among her own settled people she would be protected and allowed to live.

At the beginning of October they left the gargantuan enclave of Germans wagons, during the first hours of darkness, having chosen a site for their wagons and beasts from which their departure was less likely to attract notice. When day broke they were still wending their way between German wagons, but no one paid them any attention, and two days after that they finally drew clear of the encampment.

The distance from the Atuatuci to the Marsi was no more than a hundred miles, and the countryside was fairly flat. But between Long-haired Gaul of the Belgae and Germania flowed the biggest river in all of western Europa: the Rhenus. Somehow Sulla had to get his wife's wagon across it. And somehow he had to protect his family from marauders. He did it the Sullan way, very simply and directly, by trusting to his bond with the goddess Fortuna, who did not desert him.

When they reached the Rhenus, they found its banks populous and the people not interested in preying upon one lone wagon and one lone German, especially with red-haired twin boys sitting one in each of their mother's arms. A barge big enough to carry the wagon plied the great river regularly, the price a jar of most precious wheat; since the summer had been relatively dry, the water was at its quietest, and Sulla for the payment of three jars of wheat was able to get all Hermana's beasts across as well as the wagon.

Once into Germania they made brisk progress, for the land this far downstream of the Rhenus was cleared of vast forests, and some simple growing was attempted, more for winter cattle fodder than human consumption. During the third week of October Sulla found Hermana's tribe of the Marsi, and delivered her into their care. And concluded his treaty of peace and friendship between the German Marsi and the Senate and People of Rome.

Then when the moment of actual parting came, they wept in dreadful grief, finding it harder by far than either of them had dreamed. Carrying the twins, Hermana followed Sulla on foot until the legs of his horse wore her to a standstill, and there she stood, howling, long after he had passed out of her sight forever. While Sulla rode his horse southwest, so blinded by tears he had to trust to the instincts of this horse for many miles.

Hermana's people had given him a good mount, so that he was able to trade it for another good mount at the end of the day, and so continued well mounted for the twelve days it took him to ride from the sources of the river Amisia, where lay the Marsi settlements, to Marius's camp outside Glanum. He cut cross-country the whole way, avoiding the high mountains and thickest forests by following the great rivers—Rhenus to Mosella, Mosella to Arar, Arar to Rhodanus.

His heart lay so heavy within him that he had to force himself to take note of the country and peoples he traversed, though once he caught himself listening with amazement to himself speaking the Gallic of the Druids, and thought, I am fluent in German of several dialects and fluent in Carnutic Gallic—I, Lucius Cornelius Sulla, senator of Rome!

But what neither he nor Quintus Sertorius discovered of the German dispositions among the Atuatuci did not transpire until the following spring, long after both Sulla and Sertorius were gone from their lives and wives of Germania. For when the wagons began to roll in their thousands upon thousands and the three great hosts divided up to invade Italy, the Cimbri and the Teutones and the Tigurini and the Cherusci and the Marcomanni left something behind for the Atuatuci to guard against their return. They left a force of six thousand of their finest men to ensure that the Atuatuci suffered no incursions from other tribes; and they left every last tribal treasure they owned—gold statues, gold chariots, gold harness, gold votives, gold coins, gold bullion, several tons of finest amber, and various other treasures they had picked up along their migration to swell what had been theirs for many generations. The only gold which moved with the Germans as they started out was gold they wore on their bodies. All the rest remained hidden among the Atuatuci, in much the same way as the Volcae Tectosages of Tolosa had minded the gold of the Gallic peoples.

So when Sulla saw Julilla again, he contrasted her with Hermana, and found her slipshod, careless, intellectually untutored, disordered and unmethodical, and—*hateful.* She had at least learned enough from their previous reunion not to throw herself at him immodestly under the gaze of their servants. But, he thought wearily over dinner on that first day home, his being spared that particular ordeal was more likely to have been due to the presence of Marcia in the house rather than a wish on Julilla's part to please him. For Marcia was quite a presence—stiff, straight, unsmiling, unloving, unforgiving. She hadn't aged gracefully, and after so many years of happiness as the wife of Gaius Julius Caesar, her widowhood was a great burden to her. Also, Sulla suspected, she loathed being the mother of a daughter as unsatisfactory as Julilla.

Little wonder in that. He loathed being married to a wife as unsatisfactory as Julilla. Yet it was not politic to cast her off, for she was no Metella Calva, coupling indiscriminately with the lowborn, nor did she couple with the highborn. Fidelity had become perhaps her only virtue. Unfortunately the drinking had not progressed to the point where everyone in Rome knew her as a wine bibber; Marcia had worked indefatigably to conceal it. Which meant that a *diffarreatio* divorce (even had he been willing to undergo its hideousness) was out of the question.

And yet she was impossible to live with. Her physical demands within the bedroom were so starved and scratchy that he could experience no emotion more scorching than a ghastly, all-pervading embarrassment; he only had to set eyes on Julilla, and every iota of erectile tissue belonging to his body shrank inside itself like one of Publius Vagiennius's snails. He didn't want to touch her, and he didn't want her touching him.

It was easy for a woman to counterfeit sexual desire, sexual pleasure too, but a man couldn't counterfeit sexual desire any more than he could sexual pleasure. If men were by nature more truthful than women, thought Sulla, it was surely because they carried a tattletale truth teller between their legs into every sexual encounter, and this colored all aspects of masculine life. And if there was a reason why men were drawn to men, it lay in the fact that the act of love required no accompanying act of faith.

None of these cogitations boded well for Julilla, who had no idea what her husband thought, but was devastated by the all-too-evident little he felt. For two nights in succession she found herself pushed away, while Sulla's patience frayed and his excuses grew more perfunctory, less convincing. And on the third morning Julilla rose even earlier than Sulla so that she could have a copious breakfast of wine, only to be caught in the act by her mother.

The result was a quarrel between the two women so bitter and acrimonious that the children wept, the slaves fled, and Sulla shut himself inside his *tablinum* calling down curses upon the heads of all women. What snatches of the argument he overheard indicated that the subject was not new, nor this confrontation the first. The children, Marcia alleged in a voice loud enough to be heard as far away as the temple of Magna Mater, were being completely ignored by their mother. Julilla retorted in a scream audible as far away as the Circus Maximus that Marcia had stolen the children's affections, so what could she expect?

The battle raged for longer than any altercation so verbally violent should have—another indication, Sulla decided, that the subject and the argument had been thoroughly explored on many earlier occasions. They were proceeding almost by rote. It ended in the atrium just outside Sulla's study door, where Marcia informed Julilla that she was taking the children and their nanny for a long walk, and she didn't know when she'd be back, but Julilla had better be sober when she did come back.

Hands pressed over his ears to shut out the pathetic sobs and pleas for peace both children were making of their mother and grandmother, Sulla tried to concentrate upon what beautiful children they were. He was still filled with the delight of seeing them again after so long; Cornelia Sulla was over five now, and little Lucius Sulla was four. People in their own right—and quite old enough to suffer, as he well knew from the memories of his own childhood, buried yet never forgotten. If there was any mercy in his abandonment of his German twin sons, it lay in the fact that when he left them they were still very young babies, heads nodding up and down, mouths blowing bubbles, every kink in every bone from head to toe stuffed with dimples. It would be far harder to part with his Roman children because they were old enough to be people. He pitied them deeply. And loved them deeply too, a very different kind of feeling from any he had ever experienced for either man or woman. Selfless and pure, untainted and rounded.

His door burst open; Julilla rushed into the room with draperies swirling, her fists knotted, her face dyed a dark rose from rage. And wine.

"Did you hear that?" she demanded.

Sulla laid his pen down. "How could I help hearing it?" he asked in a tired voice. "The whole Palatine heard."

"That old turnip! That dried-up old troublemaker! How dare she accuse me of neglecting my children?"

Do I, or don't I? asked Sulla of himself. Why am I putting up with her? Why don't I get out my little box of white powder from the Pisae foundry and dose her wine until her teeth fall out of her head and her tongue curls up into a smoking string and her tits swell up like puffballs and explode? Why don't I find a nice wet oak tree and harvest a few flawless mushrooms and feed them to her until she pours blood from every orifice? Why don't I give her the kiss she's panting for, and snap her skinny nasty neck the way I did Clitumna's? How many men have I killed with sword, dagger, arrow, poison, stone, axe, club, thong, hands? What does she have none of those others had? He found the answer at once, of course. Julilla had given him his dream. Julilla had given him his luck. And she was a patrician Roman, blood of his blood. He'd sooner kill Hermana.

Even so, words couldn't kill her, this tough, sinewy Roman madam, so words he could use.

"You do neglect your children," he said. "That's why I brought your mother to live here in the first place."

She gasped stagily, choked, wrapped her hands about her throat. "Oh! Oh! How dare you? I have never neglected my children, never!"

"Rubbish. You've never cared a scrap for them," he said in the same tired patient voice he seemed to have adopted since he set foot in this awful, blighted house. "The only thing you care about, Julilla, is a flagon of wine."

"And who can blame me?" she asked, hands falling. "Who can honestly blame me? Married to a man who doesn't want me, who can't even get it up when we're in the same bed and I've got it in my mouth sucking and licking until my jaws crack!"

"If we're going to be explicit, would you please close the door?" he asked.

"Why? So the precious servants can't hear? What a filthy hypocrite you are, Sulla! And whose is the shame, yours or mine? Why isn't it ever yours? Your reputation as a lover is far too well established in this town for my miserable failure to have you classified impotent! It's only *me* you don't want! *Me!* Your own wife! I've never so much as looked at another man, and what thanks do I get? After nearly two years away, you can't even get it up when I turn myself into an *irrumator*!" The huge hollow yellow eyes were bleeding tears. "What did I ever do? Why don't you love me? Why don't you even want me? Oh, Sulla, look at me with eyes of love, touch me with hands of love, and I will never need another sip of wine as long as I live! How *can* I love you the way I love you without striking so much as one tiny little spark in return?"

"Perhaps that's a part of the problem," he said, clinically detached. "I don't like being loved excessively. It's not right. In fact, it's unhealthy."

"Then tell me *how* to stop loving you!" she wept. "*I* don't know how! Do you think if I could stop, I wouldn't? In less time than it takes to strike that spark from a good dry flint, I'd stop! I *pray* to stop! I yearn to stop! But I can't stop. I love you more than I love life itself."

He sighed. "Perhaps the answer is to finish growing up. You look and act like an adolescent. In mind and body, you're still sixteen. Only you're not, Julilla. You're twenty-four. You have a child of five, and another going on for four."

"Maybe sixteen was the last time I was ever happy," she said, rubbing her palms around her running cheeks.

"If you haven't been happy since you were sixteen, the blame for it can hardly be laid at my door," said Sulla.

"Nothing's *ever* your fault, is it?"

"Absolutely true," he said, looking superior.

"Well, what about other women?"

"What about them?"

"Is it possible that one of the reasons why you haven't shown any interest in me since you came back is because you've got a woman tucked away in Gaul?"

"Not a woman," he corrected gently, "a wife. And not in Gaul. In Germania."

Her mouth dropped open, she gaped. "*A wife?*"

"Well, according to the German custom, anyway. And twin boys about four months old now." He closed his eyes, the pain in them too private a thing to let her see. "I miss her badly. Isn't that odd?"

Julilla managed to shut her mouth and swallow convulsively. "Is she that beautiful?" she whispered.

His pale eyes opened, surprised. "Beautiful? *Hermana?* No, not at all! She's dumpy and in her thirties. Not even one hundredth as beautiful as you. Not even as blonde. Not even the daughter of a chief, let alone a king. Just a barbarian."

"Why?"

Sulla shook his head. "I don't know. Except that I liked her a great deal."

"What does she have that I haven't?"

"A good pair of breasts," said Sulla, shrugging, "but I'm not partial to breasts, so it can't be that. She worked hard. She never complained. She never expected anything of me—no, that's not it. Better to say, she never expected me to be what I'm not." He nodded, smiled with obvious fondness. "Yes, I think that must be it. She belonged to herself, and so she didn't burden me with herself. You're a lead weight chained about my neck. Hermana was a pair of wings strapped to my feet."

Without another word Julilla turned and walked out of the study. Sulla got up, followed her to the door, and closed it.

But not enough time elapsed for Sulla to compose himself sufficiently to resume his doodling—for write sensibly he couldn't that morning—before the door opened again.

His steward stood there, giving a superb imitation of an inanimate block of wood.

"Yes?"

"A caller, Lucius Cornelius. Are you in?"

"Who is it?"

"I would have given you his name, *dominus,* if I knew it," said the steward stiffly. "The caller preferred to charge me with a message for you. 'Scylax sends greetings.'"

Sulla's face cleared like a breath from the surface of a polished mirror; a delighted smile dawned. One of the old gang! One of the mimes, the comedians, the actors he used to know! Oh, terrific! This nincompoop steward Julilla had bought wouldn't know, of course he wouldn't know. Clitumna's slaves weren't good enough for Julilla. "Well, bring him in!"

He would have known who it was anywhere, anytime. And yet—how much he had changed! From boy into man.

"Metrobius," Sulla said, getting to his feet, his eyes flicking to the door automatically to make sure it was shut. It was. The windows were not shut, but they didn't matter, for there was an ironclad rule in Sulla's house: that no one was ever to stand where they could see into Sulla's study through the colonnade windows.

He must be twenty-two now, thought Sulla. Quite tall for a Greek. The long mane of black curls had been barbered neatly into a manly cap, and where the skin of his cheeks and chin had once been milky-smooth, now it displayed the blue shadow of a heavy beard kept closely shaven. He still had a profile like a Praxiteles Apollo, and something of the same epicene repose, a Nicias painted marble so true to life it might step down from its plinth and begin to walk, yet remained still folded away within itself, keeping the secret of its mystery, its wellsprings.

The marmoreal control of perfect beauty held perfectly broke then; Metrobius looked at Sulla with perfect love, and smilingly extended his arms.

The tears stood forth in Sulla's eyes; his mouth shook. As he came around it, the corner of his desk struck his hip, but Sulla didn't notice. He just walked into Metrobius's arms and let them close about him, and put his chin on Metrobius's shoulder, and his arms about Metrobius's back. And felt as if he had come home at last. So the kiss when it happened was exquisite, the understanding heart grown up, the act of faith made without cognizance, without pain of any kind.

"My boy, my beautiful boy!" said Sulla, and wept in simple gratitude that some things did not change.

Outside Sulla's open study windows Julilla stood and watched her husband walk into the lovely young man's arms, watched them kiss, heard the words of love which passed between them, watched as they moved together to the couch and sank upon it, and began the initial intimacies of a relationship so old and so satisfying to them both that this was merely a homecoming. No one needed to tell her that here was the real reason for her husband's neglect, and for her own drinking, and for her revenge in neglecting her children. Her husband's children.

Before they could loosen each other's clothing Julilla turned away, and walked with head held high and eyes tearless into the bedroom she shared with Lucius Cornelius Sulla. Her husband. Beyond it was a smaller cubicle they used as a clothes repository, more cluttered now that Sulla was home again, for his dress-parade armor was suspended from a T-shaped frame, its helmet on a special stand, and his sword with its ivory eagle's head handle hung upon the wall complete with scabbard and baldric.

Getting the sword down was easy; getting it free from its sheath and belt was more difficult. But she managed at last, and drew in her breath sharply when the blade sheared her hand open to the bone, so well honed was it. She experienced a twinge of surprise that she could actually feel physical pain at this moment, then dismissed both surprise and pain as irrelevant. Without hesitation she picked up the sword by its ivory eagle, turned it in upon herself, and walked into the wall.

It was badly done. She fell in a sprawling tangle of blood and draperies with the sword buried in her belly, her heart beating, beating, beating, the rasp of her own breathing heavy in her ears like someone stealing up behind her to take life or virtue. Neither virtue nor life did she own anymore, so what could it matter? She felt the dreadful agony of it then, and the warmth of her own blood on her skin as it quit her. But she was a Julius Caesar; she would not cry out for help, or regret this decision for what little time she had remaining. Not a thought of her two little children crossed her mind; all she could think of was her own foolishness, that for many years she had loved a man who loved men.

Sufficient reason to die. She wouldn't live to be laughed at, jeered at, made a mockery of by all those lucky lucky women out there who were married to men who loved women. As the blood flowed away carrying life along with it, her burning mind began to cool, and slow, and petrify. Oh, how wonderful, to stop loving him at last! No more torment, no more anguish, no more humiliation, no more wine. She had asked him to show her how to stop loving him, and he had shown her. So kind to her he had finally been, her darling Sulla. Her last lucid moments of thought were about her children; at least in them, something of herself she would leave behind. So she waded into the sweet shallows of the ocean Death wishing her children long life, and much happiness.

Sulla returned to his desk and sat down. "There's wine; pour me some," he said to Metrobius.

How like the boy the man was, once animation stole into his face! Easier then to remember that once the boy had offered to give up every luxury for the chance to live in penury with his darling Sulla.

Smiling softly, Metrobius brought the wine and sat down in the client's chair. "I know what you're going to say, Lucius Cornelius. We can't make a habit of this."

"Yes. Among other things." Sulla sipped his wine, then looked at Metrobius sternly. "It *isn't* possible, dearest lad. Just sometimes, when the need or the pain or whatever it is becomes too much to bear. I'm the width of a whisker away from everything I want, which means I can't have you too. If this were Greece, yes. But it isn't. It's Rome. If I were the First Man in Rome, yes. But I'm not. Gaius Marius is."

Metrobius pulled a face. "I understand."

"Are you still in the theater?"

"Of course. Acting's all I know. Besides, Scylax was a good teacher, give him his due. So I don't lack parts, and I don't rest very often." He cleared his throat and looked a little self-conscious. "The only change is, I've become serious."

"Serious?"

"That's right. It turned out, you see, that I didn't have the true comedic touch. I was all right when I was a child star, but once I grew out of the Cupid's wings and the mirthful imps, I discovered my real talent lay in tragedy, not comedy. So now I play Aeschylus and Accius instead of Aristophanes and Plautus. I don't repine."

Sulla shrugged. "Oh well, at least that means I'll be able to go to the theater without betraying myself because you're there play-ing the hapless ingenue. Are you a citizen?"

"No, alas."

"I'll see what I can do." Sighing, Sulla put his goblet down and folded his hands together like a banker. "Let us meet by all means—but not too often—and never again here. I have a rather mad wife whom I can't trust."

"It would be wonderful if we could meet occasionally."

"Do you have a reasonably private place of your own, or are you still living with Scylax?"

Metrobius looked surprised. "I thought you knew! But of course, how could you, when it's years since you've lived in Rome? Scylax died six months ago. And he left me everything he owned, including his apartment."

"Then that's where we'll meet." Sulla got up. "Come, I'll show you out myself. And I'll enroll you as my client, so that if you should ever need to come here, you'll have a valid reason for do-ing so. I'll send a note to your place before I call round."

A kiss looked out of the beautiful dark eyes when they parted at the outside door, but nothing was said, and nothing done to in-dicate to either the hovering steward or the door porter that the amazingly good-looking young man was anything more than a new client from the old days.

"Give my love to everyone, Metrobius."

"I daresay you won't be in Rome for the theatrical games?"

"Afraid not," said Sulla, smiling casually. "Germans."

And so they parted, just as Marcia came down the street shep-herding the children and their nanny. Sulla waited for her and acted as porter himself.

"Marcia, come into my study, please."

Eyes wary, she sidled into the room ahead of him and went to the couch, where, Sulla saw with horror, there was a wet patch glaring at him like a beacon.

"In the chair, if you don't mind," he said.

She sat down, glowering at him with her chin up and her mouth set hard.

"Mother-in-law, I'm well aware that you don't like me, and I have no intention of trying to woo you," Sulla began, making sure he appeared at his ease, unworried. "I didn't ask you to come and live here because I liked you, either. My concern was for my children. It still is. And I must thank you with all my heart for your good offices there. You've done a wonderful job in caring for them. They're little Romans again."

She thawed a little. "I'm glad you think so."

"In consequence, the children are no longer my main worry. Julilla is. I heard your altercation with her this morning."

"The whole world heard it!" snapped Marcia.

"Yes, that's true. . . ." He sighed heavily. "After you took the children out, she had an altercation with me which the whole world also heard—or at least heard her half of it. I wondered if you had any idea what we can do."

"Unfortunately not enough people know she drinks to divorce her on those grounds, which are really your only grounds," said Marcia, knowing full well she had concealed it. "I think you just have to be patient. Her drinking is increasing, I won't be able to hide it for much longer. The moment it's general knowledge, you can put her away without condemnation," said Julilla's mother.

"What if that stage should arrive while I'm away?"

"I'm her mother; I can put her away. If it happens in your absence, I'll send her to your villa at Circei. Then when you return, you can divorce her and shut her up elsewhere. In time she'll drink herself to death." Marcia got up, anxious to be gone, and giving no hint as to the degree of pain she felt. "I do not like you, Lucius Cornelius," she said, "but I do not blame you for Julilla's plight."

"Do you like any of your in-laws?" he asked.

She snorted. "Only Aurelia."

He walked out into the atrium with her. "I wonder where Julilla is?" he asked, suddenly realizing that he had neither heard nor seen her since the arrival of Metrobius. A frisson of alarm skimmed up his spine.

"Lying in wait for one or the other of us, I imagine," she said.

"Once she starts the day with a quarrel, she usually continues to quarrel until she becomes so drunk she passes out."

Sulla's distaste pulled his lips down. "I haven't seen her since she ran out of my study. An old friend called to see me not a moment later, and I was just letting him out when you came back with the children."

"She's not normally so backward," said Marcia, and looked at the steward. "Have you seen your mistress?" she asked.

"The last I did see of her, she was going into her sleeping cubicle," he said. "Shall I ask her maid?"

"No, don't bother." Marcia glanced sideways at Sulla. "I think we ought to see her together right now, Lucius Cornelius. Maybe if we tell her what will happen unless she pulls herself out of her pigsty, she might see reason."

And so they found Julilla, twisted and still. Her fine woolen draperies had acted like a blotter and soaked up much of the blood, so that she was clad in wet, rusting scarlet, a Nereid out of some volcano.

Marcia clutched at Sulla's arm, staggering; he put the arm about her and held her upright.

But Quintus Marcius Rex's daughter made the effort and brought herself under iron control. "This is one solution I did not expect," she said levelly.

"Nor I," said Sulla, used to slaughter.

"What *did* you say to her?"

Sulla shook his head. "Nothing to provoke this, as far as I can remember—we can probably find out from the servants; they heard her half of it at least."

"No, I do not think it advisable to ask them," Marcia said, and turned suddenly within Sulla's arm, seeking shelter against his body. "In many ways, Lucius Cornelius, this is the best solution of all. I'd rather the children suffered the shock of her death than the slow disillusionment of her drinking. They're young enough to forget now. But any later, and they'd remember." She laid her cheek against Sulla's chest. "Yes, it's by far the best way." A tear oozed beneath her closed eyelid.

"Come, I'll take you to your room," he said, guiding her out of the blood-drenched cubicle. "I never even thought of my sword, fool that I am!"

"Why should you?"

"Hindsight," said Sulla, who knew exactly why Julilla had found his sword and used it; she had looked through his study windows at his reunion with Metrobius. Marcia was right. This was the best way by far. And *he* hadn't had to do it.

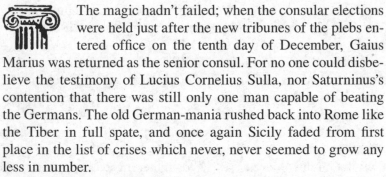 The magic hadn't failed; when the consular elections were held just after the new tribunes of the plebs entered office on the tenth day of December, Gaius Marius was returned as the senior consul. For no one could disbelieve the testimony of Lucius Cornelius Sulla, nor Saturninus's contention that there was still only one man capable of beating the Germans. The old German-mania rushed back into Rome like the Tiber in full spate, and once again Sicily faded from first place in the list of crises which never, never seemed to grow any less in number.

"For as fast as we eliminate one, a new one pops up out of nowhere," said Marcus Aemilius Scaurus to Quintus Caecilius Metellus Numidicus Piggle-wiggle.

"Including Sicily," said Lucullus's brother-in-law with venom in his voice. "How *could* Gaius Marius lend his support to that *pipinna* Ahenobarbus when he insisted Lucius Lucullus must be replaced as governor of Sicily? By *Servilius the Augur,* of all people! He's nothing but a New Man skulking in the guise of an old name!"

"He was tweaking your tail, Quintus Caecilius," Scaurus said. "Gaius Marius doesn't give a counterfeit coin who governs Sicily, not now that the Germans are definitely coming. If you wanted Lucius Lucullus to remain there, you would have done better to have kept quiet; then Gaius Marius wouldn't have remembered that you and Lucius Lucullus matter to each other."

"The senatorial rolls need a stern eye to look them over," said Numidicus. "I shall stand for censor!"

"Good thinking! Who with?"

"My cousin Caprarius."

"Oh, more good thinking, by Venus! He'll do exactly as you tell him."

"It's time we weeded the Senate out, not to mention the knights. I shall be a stringent censor, Marcus Aemilius, have no fear!" said Numidicus. "Saturninus is going, and so is Glaucia. They're dangerous men."

"Oh, don't!" cried Scaurus, flinching. "If I hadn't falsely accused him of peculation in grain, he might have turned into a different kind of politician. I can never rid myself of guilt about Lucius Appuleius."

Numidicus raised his brows. "My dear Marcus Aemilius, you are in strong need of a tonic! What if anything caused that wolfshead Saturninus to act the way he does is immaterial. All that matters at this present moment is that he is what he is. And he has to go." He blew through his nostrils angrily. "We are not finished as a force in this city yet," he said. "And at least this coming year Gaius Marius is saddled with a real man as his colleague, instead of those straw men Fimbria and Orestes. We'll make sure Quintus Lutatius is put into the field with an army, and every tiny success Quintus Lutatius has with his army, we'll trumpet through Rome like triumphs."

For the electorate had also voted in Quintus Lutatius Catulus Caesar as consul, junior to Marius admittedly, but, "A thorn in my side," said Marius.

"Your young brother's in as a praetor," said Sulla.

"And going to Further Spain, nicely out of the way."

They caught up with Marcus Aemilius Scaurus, who had parted company with Numidicus at the bottom of the Senate steps.

"I must thank you personally for your industry and enterprise in the matter of the grain supply," said Marius civilly.

"As long as there's wheat to be bought somewhere in the world,

Gaius Marius, it's not a very difficult job," said Scaurus, also civilly. "What worries me is the day when there's no wheat to be had anywhere."

"Not likely at the moment, surely! Sicily will be back to normal next harvest, I imagine."

Scaurus struck immediately. "Provided, that is, we don't lose everything we've gained once that prating fool Servilius Augur takes office as governor!" he said tartly.

"The war in Sicily is over," said Marius.

"You'd better hope so, consul. I'm not so sure."

"And where have you been getting the wheat these past two years?" Sulla asked hastily, to avert an open disagreement.

"Asia Province," said Scaurus, willing enough to be sidetracked, for he genuinely did love being *curator annonae,* the custodian of the grain supply.

"But surely they don't grow much surplus?" prompted Sulla.

"Hardly a *modius,* as a matter of fact," said Scaurus smugly. "No, we can thank King Mithridates of Pontus. He's very young, but he's mighty enterprising. Having conquered all of the northern parts of the Euxine Sea and gained control of the grainlands of the Tanais, the Borysthenes, the Hypanis, and the Danastris, he's making a very nice additional income for Pontus by shipping this Cimmerian surplus down to Asia Province, and selling it to us. What's more, I'm going to follow my instincts, and buy again in Asia Province next year. Young Marcus Livius Drusus is going as quaestor to Asia, and I've commissioned him to act for me in the matter."

Marius grunted. "No doubt he'll visit his father-in-law, Quintus Servilius Caepio, in Smyrna while he's there?"

"No doubt," said Scaurus blandly.

"Then have young Marcus Livius send the bills for the grain to Quintus Servilius Caepio," said Marius. "He's got more money to pay for it than the Treasury has!"

"That's an unfounded allegation."

"Not according to King Copillus."

An uneasy silence fell for a simmering moment before Sulla

said, "How much of that Asian grain reaches us, Marcus Aemilius? I hear the pirate problem grows worse every year."

"About half, no more," Scaurus said grimly. "Every hidden cove and harbor on the Pamphylian and Cilician coasts shelters pirates. Of course by trade they're slavers, but if they can steal grain to feed the slaves they steal, then they're sure of huge profits, aren't they? And whatever grain they have left over, they sell back to us at twice the price we originally paid for it, if for no other reason than they guarantee it will reach us without being pirated—again."

"Amazing," said Marius, "that even among pirates there are middlemen. Because that's what they are! Steal it, then sell it back to us. Pure profit. It's time we did something, Princeps Senatus, isn't it?"

"It certainly is," said Scaurus fervently.

"What do you suggest?"

"A special commission for one of the praetors—a roving governorship, if there is such an animal. Give him ships and marines, and charge him with flushing out every nest of pirates along the whole Pamphylian and Cilician coast," said Scaurus.

"We could call him the governor of Cilicia," said Marius.

"What a good idea!"

"All right, Princeps Senatus, let's call the Conscript Fathers together as soon as possible, and do it."

"Let's," said Scaurus, oozing charity. "You know, Gaius Marius, I may loathe everything you stand for, but I do love your capacity to act without turning the whole business into a new set of circus games."

"The Treasury will scream like a Vestal invited to dinner in a brothel," said Marius, grinning.

"Let it! If we don't eradicate the pirates, trade between East and West will cease to be. Ships and marines," said Scaurus thoughtfully. "How many, do you think?"

"Oh, eight or ten full fleets, and, say—ten thousand trained marines. If we have that many," said Marius.

"We can get them," Scaurus said confidently. "If necessary we can hire some at least from Rhodes, Halicarnassus, Cnidus, Athens, Ephesus—don't worry, we'll find them."

"It ought to be Marcus Antonius," said Marius.

"What, not your own brother?" asked Scaurus, aping surprise.

But Marius grinned, unruffled. "Like me, Marcus Aemilius, my brother Marcus Marius is a landlubber. Where all the Antonii like going to sea."

Scaurus laughed. "When they're not all *at* sea!"

"True. But he's all right, our praetor Marcus Antonius. He'll do the job, I think."

"I think he will too."

"And in the meantime," said Sulla, smiling, "the Treasury is going to be so busy whining and complaining about Marcus Aemilius's grain purchases and pirate chasers that it won't even notice how much money it's paying out for Head Count armies. Because Quintus Lutatius will have to enlist a Head Count army too."

"Oh, Lucius Cornelius, you've been too long in the service of Gaius Marius!" said Scaurus.

"I was thinking the same thing," said Marius unexpectedly. But more than that he would not say.

Sulla and Marius left for Gaul-across-the-Alps late in February, having dealt with the obsequies and aftermath of Julilla; Marcia had agreed to remain in Sulla's house to look after the children for the time being.

"But," she said in minatory tones, "you can't expect me to be here forever, Lucius Cornelius. Now that I'm getting into my fifties, I have a fancy to move to the Campanian coast. My bones don't like the damp city weather. You had better marry again, give those children a proper mother and some half brothers or half sisters to play with."

"It will have to wait until the Germans are dealt with," Sulla said, trying to keep his voice courteous.

"Well, all right then, after the Germans," said Marcia.

"Two years hence," he warned.

"*Two?* One, surely!"

"Perhaps, though I doubt it. Plan on two, Mother-in-law."

"Not a moment longer, Lucius Cornelius."

Sulla looked at her, one brow lifting quizzically. "You had better start looking for a suitable wife for me."

"Are you joking?"

"No, I'm not joking!" Sulla cried, his patience worn a trifle thin of late. "How do you think I can go away to fight the Germans and also look inside Rome for a new wife? If you want to move out as soon as I'm home, then you'd better have a wife picked out and willing to be picked out."

"What sort of wife?"

"I don't care! Just make sure she'll be kind to my little ones," said Sulla.

For this and other reasons, Sulla was very glad to leave Rome. The longer he remained there, the greater became his hunger to see Metrobius, and the more he saw Metrobius, the more he suspected he would want to see Metrobius. Nor could he exert the same influence and control over the grown Metrobius that he had over the boy; Metrobius was now of an age to feel that he too had something to say about how the relationship was to progress. Yes, it was best to be far from Rome! Only his children would he miss, dear little people they were. Enchanting. Utterly, uncritically loving. He would be away for many moons, but the moment he reappeared, they welcomed him with open arms and millions of kisses. Why shouldn't adult love be like that? But the answer, he thought, was simple. Adult love was too concerned with self and with thinking.

Sulla and Marius had left the junior consul, Quintus Lutatius Catulus Caesar, in the throes of recruiting another army, and complaining loudly because it would have to be Head Count in composition.

"Of course it has to be Head Count!" said Marius shortly. "And don't come grizzling and mewling to me about it—it wasn't I lost eighty thousand soldiers at Arausio, nor any of the rest we've wasted in battle!"

That of course shut Catulus Caesar up, but in a tightlipped, aristocratic way.

"I wish you wouldn't cast the crimes of his own sort in his face," said Sulla.

"Then let him stop casting the Head Count in my face!" growled Marius.

Sulla gave up.

Luckily things in Gaul were very much as they ought to be; Manius Aquillius had kept the army in good condition with more construction of bridges and aqueducts and plenty of drills. Quintus Sertorius had come back, but then returned to the Germans because, he said, he could be of better use there; he would go with the Cimbri on their trek, and report to Marius whenever he could. And the troops were beginning to quiver with eager anticipation at the thought that this year they'd see action.

That year should have seen an extra February intercalated— inserted—into the calendar, but the difference between the old Pontifex Maximus, Dalmaticus, and Ahenobarbus, the new, now showed itself: Ahenobarbus could see no virtue in keeping the calendar in time with the seasons. So when the calendar March came around, it was still winter, for the calendar now began to move ahead of the actual seasons. In a year of only 355 days, an extra 20-day month had to be intercalated each two years, traditionally at the end of February. But it was a decision made by the College of Pontifices, and if the members were not kept up to the mark by a conscientious Pontifex Maximus, the calendar fell by the wayside, as it did now.

Happily a letter arrived from Publius Rutilius Rufus not long after Sulla and Marius settled back into the routine of life in an army camp on the far side of the Alps.

> This is definitely going to be an event-filled year, so my main problem is knowing where to start. Of course everyone was just waiting for you to get out of the way, and I swear you hadn't got as far as Ocelum before there were mice and rats cavorting all over the lower

end of the Forum. What a lovely play they're having, O Cat!

All right then, I'll start with our precious pair of censors, Piggle-wiggle and his tame cousin Billy Goat. Piggle-wiggle has been going about for some time—well, since he was elected, really, only he was careful not to talk in your vicinity—saying that he intends to "purge the Senate," I think he put it.

One thing you can say for them, they're not going to be a venal pair of censors, so all the State contracts will be gone into properly, and let according to price combined with merit. However, they've antagonized the Treasury already by demanding a large sum of money to repair and redecorate some of the temples not rich enough to pay themselves, not to mention fresh paint and marble latrine benches in the three State houses of the major *flamines,* also the houses of the Rex Sacrorum and the Pontifex Maximus. Personally I like my wooden latrine bench. Marble is so cold and hard! There was quite a lively little squabble when Piggle-wiggle mentioned the Domus Publicus of the Pontifex Maximus, the Treasury being of the opinion that our new P.M. is rich enough to donate paint and marble latrine benches.

They then proceeded to let all the ordinary contracts—and did very well, I consider. Tenders were plentiful, bidding was brisk, and I doubt there'll be much chicanery.

They had moved with almost unheard-of speed to this point because what they really wanted to do, of course, was review the roll of senators and the roll of knights. Not two days after the contracts were all finished—I swear they've done eighteen months of work in less than one month!—Piggle-wiggle called a *contio* of the Assembly of the People to read out the censors' findings on the moral plenitude or turpitude

of the Conscript Fathers of the Senate. However, someone must have told Saturninus and Glaucia ahead of
time that their names were going to be missing, because when the Assembly met, it was stuffed with
hired gladiators and other bully-boys not normally to
be found attending meetings of the Comitia.

And no sooner did Piggle-wiggle announce that he
and the Billy Goat were removing Lucius Appuleius
Saturninus and Gaius Servilius Glaucia from the roll
of senators, than the place erupted. The gladiators
charged the rostra and hauled poor Piggle-wiggle
down off it, then passed him from man to man slap-
ping him viciously across the face with their huge and
horny open hands. It was a novel technique—no clubs
or billets of wood, just open hands. On the theory I
suppose that hands cannot kill unless bunched into
fists. Minimal violence, I heard it being called. How
pathetic. It all happened so quickly and was so well
organized that Piggle-wiggle had been passed all the
way to the start of the Clivus Argentarius before Scaurus, Ahenobarbus, and a few other Good Men managed to pick him up and race him to asylum within the
temple of Jupiter Optimus Maximus. There they found
his face twice its normal size, both eyes closed, his
lips split in a dozen places, his nose spurting like a
fountain, his ears mangled, and his brows cut. He
looked for all the world like an old-time Greek boxer
at the Olympic games.

How do you like the word they're attaching to the
archconservative faction, by the way? *Boni*—the Good
Men. Scaurus is going round claiming to have invented
it after Saturninus began calling the archconservatives
the Policy Makers. But he ought to remember that
there are plenty of us old enough to know that both
Gaius Gracchus *and* Lucius Opimius called the men
of their factions the *boni*. Now back to my story!

After he learned Cousin Numidicus was safe, Cousin Caprarius managed to restore order in the Comitia. He had his heralds blow their trumpets, then shouted out that he didn't agree with his senior colleague's findings, therefore Saturninus and Glaucia would remain on the senatorial rolls. You'd have to say Piggle-wiggle lost the engagement, but I don't like friend Saturninus's methods of fighting. He simply says he had nothing to do with the violence, but that he's grateful the People are so vehemently on his side.

You might be pardoned for thinking that was the end of it. But no! The censors then began their financial assessment of the knights, having had a handsome new tribunal built near the Pool of Curtius—a wooden structure, admittedly, but designed for their purpose, with a flight of steps up each side so those being interviewed are kept orderly—up one side, across the front of the censors' desk, and down the other side. Well done. You know the routine—each knight or would-be knight must furnish documentary evidence of his tribe, his birthplace, his citizenship, his military service, his property and capital, and his income.

Though it takes several weeks to discover whether in truth these applicants do have an income of at least 400,000 sesterces a year, the show always draws a good crowd on its first couple of days. As it did when Piggle-wiggle and the Billy Goat began to go through the equestrian rolls. He did look a sight, poor Piggle-wiggle! His bruises were more bilious-yellow than black, and the cuts had become a network of congested dark lines. Though his eyes had opened enough to see. He must have wished they hadn't, when he saw what he saw in the afternoon of that first day on the new tribunal!

None other than Lucius Equitius, the self-proclaimed bastard son of Tiberius Gracchus! The fellow strolled up the steps when his turn came, and stood in front of Numidicus, not Caprarius. Piggle-wiggle just froze as he took in the sight of Equitius attended by a small army of scribes and clerks, all loaded down with account books and documents. Then he turned to his own secretary and said the tribunal was closing for the day, so please to dismiss this creature standing in front of him.

"You've got time to see me," said Equitius.

"All right then, what do you want?" he asked ominously.

"I want to be enrolled as a knight," said Equitius.

"Not in this censors' *lustrum,* you're not!" snarled our Good Man Piggle-wiggle.

I must say Equitius was patient. He said, rolling his eyes toward the crowd standing around the base of the tribunal—and it then became apparent that the gladiators and bully-boys were back—"You can't turn me down, Quintus Caecilius. I fulfill all the criteria."

"You do not!" said Numidicus. "You are disqualified on the most basic ground of all—you are not a Roman citizen."

"But I am, esteemed censor," said Equitius in a voice everyone could hear. "I became a Roman citizen on the death of my master, who bestowed it upon me in his will, along with all his property, and his name. That I have gone back to my mother's name is immaterial. I have the proof of my manumission and adoption. Not only that, but I have served in the legions for ten years—and as a Roman citizen legionary, not an auxiliary."

"I will not enroll you as a knight, and when we commence the census of the Roman citizens, I will not enroll you as a Roman citizen," said Numidicus.

"But I am entitled," said Equitius, very clearly. "I am a Roman citizen—my tribe is Suburana—I served

my ten years in the legions—I am a moral and respectable man—I own four insulae, ten taverns, a hundred *iugera* of land at Lanuvium, a thousand *iugera*
of land at Firmum Picenum, a market porticus in Firmum Picenum—and I have an income of over four
million sesterces a year, so I also qualify for the Senate." And he snapped his fingers at his head clerk, who
snapped his fingers at the minions, all of whom stepped
forward holding out huge collections of papers. "I have
proof, Quintus Caecilius."

"I don't care how many bits of paper you produce,
you vulgar lowborn mushroom—and I don't care who
you bring forward to witness for you, you sucking bag
of greed!" cried Piggle-wiggle. "I will not enroll you
as a citizen of Rome, let alone as a member of the
Ordo Equester! I piss on you, pimp! Now be off!"

Equitius turned to face the crowd, spread his arms
wide—he was wearing a toga—and spoke. "Do you
hear that?" he asked. "I, Lucius Equitius, son of Tiberius Sempronius Gracchus, am denied my citizenship
as well as my knight's status!"

Piggle-wiggle got to his feet so fast and moved so
fast that Equitius didn't even see him coming; the next
thing, our valiant censor landed a right on Equitius's
jaw, and down Equitius went on his arse, sitting gaping up with his brains rattling round in their bone-box.
Then Piggle-wiggle followed the punch with a kick
that sent Equitius slithering off the edge of the tribunal into the crowd.

"I piss on the lot of you!" he roared, shaking his
fists at the spectators and gladiators. "Be off with you,
and take that non-Roman turd with you!"

So it happened all over again, only this time the
gladiators didn't touch Piggle-wiggle's face. They
dragged him off the tribunal and took to his body with
fists, nails, teeth, and boots. In the end it was Saturninus

and Glaucia—I forgot to tell you that they were lurking in the background—who stepped forward and pulled Numidicus out of the ranks of his attackers. I imagine it was no part of their plan to have Numidicus dead. Then Saturninus climbed up on the tribunal and quietened everyone enough for Caprarius to make himself heard.

"I do not agree with my colleague, and I will take it upon myself to admit Lucius Equitius into the ranks of the *Ordo Equester!*" he yelled, white-faced, poor fellow. I don't think he ever saw so much violence on any of his military campaigns.

"Enter Lucius Equitius's name!" roared Saturninus.

And Caprarius entered the name in the rolls.

"Home, everyone!" said Saturninus.

And everyone promptly went home, carrying Lucius Equitius on their shoulders.

Piggle-wiggle was a mess. Lucky not to be dead, is my opinion. Oh, he was angry! And went at Cousin Billy Goat like a shrew for giving in yet again. Poor old Billy Goat was just about in tears, and quite incapable of defending his actions.

"Maggots! Maggots, the lot of them!" Piggle-wiggle kept saying, over and over, while we all tried to bind up his ribs—he had several broken ones—and discover what other injuries his toga was hiding. And yes, it was all very foolish, but ye gods, Gaius Marius, one has to admire Piggle-wiggle's courage!

Marius looked up from the letter, frowning. "I wonder exactly what Saturninus is up to?" he asked.

But Sulla's mind was dwelling upon a far less important point. "Plautus!" he said suddenly.

"What?"

"The *boni,* the Good Men! Gaius Gracchus, Lucius Opimius, and our own Scaurus claim to have invented *boni* to describe their factions, but *Plautus* applied *boni* to plutocrats and other patrons a hundred years ago! I remember hearing it in a production of Plautus's *Captivi*—put on while Scaurus was curule aedile, by Thespis! I was just old enough to be a playgoer."

Marius was staring. "Lucius Cornelius, stop worrying about who coined pointless words, and pay attention to what really matters! Mention theater to you, and everything else is forgotten."

"Oooops, sorry!" said Sulla impenitently.

Marius resumed reading.

> We now move from the Forum Romanum to Sicily, where all sorts of things have been happening, none of them good, some of them blackly amusing, and some downright incredible.

> As you know, but I shall refresh your memory anyway because I loathe ragged stories, the end of last year's campaigning season saw Lucius Licinius Lucullus sit down in front of the slave stronghold of Triocala, to starve the rebels out. He'd thrown terror into them by having a herald retell the tale of the Enemy stronghold which sent the Romans a message saying they had food enough to last for ten years, and the Romans sent the reply back that in that case, they'd take the place in the eleventh year.

> In fact, Lucullus did a magnificent job. He hemmed in Triocala with a forest of siege ramps, towers, shelter sheds, rams, catapults, and barricades, and he filled in a huge chasm which lay like a natural defense in front of the walls. Then he built an equally magnificent camp for his men, so strongly fortified that even if the slaves could have got out of Triocala, they couldn't have got into Lucullus's camp. And he settled down to wait the winter out, his men extremely comfortable, and he himself sure that his command would be prorogued.

> Then in January came the news that Gaius Servilius Augur was the new governor, and with the official

dispatch came a letter from our dear Metellus Numidicus Piggle-wiggle, which filled in the nasty details, the scandalous way in which the deed had been done by Ahenobarbus and his arse-boy the Augur.

You don't know Lucullus all that well, Gaius Marius. But I do. Like so many of his kind, he presents a cool, calm, detached, and insufferably haughty face to the world. You know, "I am Lucius Licinius Lucullus, a noble Roman of most ancient and prestigious family, and if you're very lucky, I might deign to notice you from time to time." But underneath the facade is a very different man—thin-skinned, fanatically conscious of slights, filled with passion, awesome in rage. So when Lucullus got the news, he took it on the surface with exactly the degree of calm and composed resignation you might expect. Then he proceeded to tear out every last piece of artillery, the siege ramp, the siege tower, the tortoise, the shelter sheds, the rubble-filled defile, the walled-in mountain shelves, everything. And he burned the lot he could burn, and carried every bucketload of rubble, fill, earth, whatever, far away from Triocala in a thousand different directions. After which he demolished his own camp, and destroyed the materials it contained too.

You think that's enough? Not for Lucullus, who was only just getting started! He destroyed every single record of his administration in both Syracuse and Lilybaeum, and he marched his seventeen thousand men to the port of Agrigentum.

His quaestor proved terrifically loyal, and connived at everything Lucullus wanted to do. The pay had come for his army, and there was money in Syracuse from spoils taken after the battle of Heracleia Minoa. Lucullus then proceeded to fine every non–Roman citizen in Sicily for putting too much strain upon Publius Licinius Nerva, the previous governor, and added that money to the rest. After which he used some of the new shipment of money which had arrived for the use of Servilius the Augur in hiring a fleet of ships to transport his soldiers.

On the beach at Agrigentum he discharged his men, and gave them every last sestertius he had managed to scrape up. Now Lucullus's men were a motley collection, and proof positive that the Head Count in Italy is as exhausted these days as all the other classes when it comes to providing troops. Aside from the Italian and Roman veterans he'd got together in Campania, he had a legion and a few extra cohorts from Bithynia, Greece, and Macedonian Thessaly—it was his demanding these from King Nicomedes of Bithynia which had led the King to say he had no men to give, because the Roman tax farmers had enslaved them all. A rather impertinent reference to our freeing the Italian Allied slaves—Nicomedes thought his treaty of friendship and alliance with us should extend the emancipation to Bithynian slaves! Lucullus rolled him up, of course, and got his Bithynian soldiers.

Now the Bithynian soldiers were sent home, and the Roman and Italian soldiers were sent home to Italy and Rome. With their discharge papers. And having removed every last trace of his governorship from the annals of Sicily, Lucullus himself sailed away.

The moment he was gone, King Tryphon and his adviser Athenion spilled out of Triocala, and began to plunder and pillage Sicily's countryside all over again. They are now absolutely convinced that they'll win the war, and their catch-cry is "Instead of being a slave, *own* a slave!" No crops have been planted, and the cities are overflowing with rural refugees. Sicily is a very *Iliad* of woes once more.

Into this delightful situation came Servilius the Augur. Of course he couldn't believe it. And started to bleat in letter after letter to his patron, Ahenobarbus Pipinna.

In the meantime, Lucullus arrived back in Rome, and began to make preparations for the inevitable. When Ahenobarbus taxed him in the House with deliberate destruction of Roman property—siegeworks and camps especially—Lucullus simply looked down his nose and said he thought the new governor would want to start in his own way. He himself, said Lucullus, liked to leave everything the way he found it, and that was precisely what he had done in Sicily at the end of his term—he had left Sicily the way he had found it. Servilius the Augur's chief grievance was the lack of an army—he had simply assumed Lucullus would leave his legions behind. But he hadn't bothered to make a formal request of Lucullus about the troops. So Lucullus maintained that in the absence of any request from Servilius the Augur, his troops were his to do what he wanted with. And he felt they were due for discharge.

"I left Gaius Servilius Augur a new tablet, wiped clean of everything I might have done," said Lucullus in the House. "Gaius Servilius Augur is a New Man, and New Men have their own ways of doing everything. I considered therefore that I was doing him a favor."

Without an army there's very little Servilius the Augur can do in Sicily, of course. Nor, with Catulus Caesar sifting what few recruits Italy can drop into his net, is there any likelihood of another army for Sicily this year. Lucullus's veterans are scattered far and wide, most of them with plump purses, and not anxious to be found.

Lucullus is well aware he's left himself wide open to prosecution. I don't think he honestly cares. He's had the infinite satisfaction of completely destroying any chance Servilius the Augur might have had to steal his thunder. And that matters more to Lucullus than avoiding prosecution. So he's busy doing what he can to protect his sons, for it's plain he thinks Aheno-barbus and the Augur will utilize Saturninus's new knight-run treason court to initiate a suit against him, and secure a conviction. He has transferred as much of his property as he possibly can to his older son, Lucius Lucullus, and given out his younger son, aged thirteen now, to be adopted by the Terentii Varrones. There is no Marcus Terentius Varro in this generation, and it's an extremely wealthy family.

I heard from Scaurus that Piggle-wiggle—who is very upset by all this, as well he might be, for if Lucul-lus is convicted, he'll have to take his scandal-making sister, Metella Calva, back—says the two boys have taken a vow to have their revenge upon Servilius the Augur as soon as they're both of age. The older boy, Lucius Lucullus Junior, is particularly bitter, it seems. I'm not surprised. He looks like his father on the out-side, so why not on the inside as well? To be cast into disgrace by the overweening ambition of the noisome New Man Augur is anathema.

And that's all for the moment. I'll keep you in-formed. I wish I could be there to help you with the Germans, not because you need my help, but because I'm feeling left out of it.

It was well into April of the calendar year before Marius and Sulla had word that the Germans were packing up and beginning to move out of the lands of the Atuatuci, and another month be-fore Sertorius came in person to report that Boiorix had kept the Germans together as a people sufficiently to ensure his plan was going to be put into effect. The Cimbri and the mixed group led by the Tigurini started off to follow the Rhenus, while the Teu-tones wandered southeast down the Mosa.

"We have to assume that in the autumn the Germans will indeed arrive in three separate divisions on the borders of Italian Gaul," said Marius, breathing heavily. "I'd like to be there in person to greet Boiorix himself when he comes down the Athesis, but it isn't sensible. First, I have to take on the Teutones and render them impotent. Hopefully the Teutones will travel the fastest of the three groups, at least as far as the Druentia, because they don't have any alpine territory to cross until later. If we can beat the Teutones here—and do it properly—then we ought to have time to cross the Mons Genava Pass and intercept Boiorix and the Cimbri before they actually enter Italian Gaul."

"You don't think Catulus Caesar can deal with Boior on his own?" asked Manius Aquillius.

"No," said Marius flatly.

Later, alone with Sulla, he enlarged upon his feelings about his junior colleague's chances against Boiorix; for Quintus Lutatius Catulus was leading his army north to the Athesis as soon as it was trained and equipped.

"He'll have about six legions, and he has all spring and summer to get them into condition. But a real general he's not," said Marius. "We must hope Teutobod comes earliest, that we beat Teutobod, cross the Alps in a tearing hurry, and join up with Catulus Caesar before Boiorix reaches Lake Benacus."

Sulla raised an eyebrow. "It won't happen that way," he said, voice certain.

Marius sighed. "I knew you were going to say that!"

"I knew you knew I was going to say that," said Sulla, grinning. "It isn't likely that either of the two divisions traveling without Boiorix himself will make better time than the Cimbri. The trouble is, there's not going to be enough time for you to be in each place at the right moment."

"Then I stay here and wait for Teutobod," said Marius, making up his mind. "This army knows every blade of grass and twig of tree between Massilia and Arausio, and the men need a victory badly after two years of inaction. Their chances of victory are very good here. So here I must stay."

"I note the 'I,' Gaius Marius," said Sulla gently. "Do you have something else for me to do?"

"I do. I'm sorry, Lucius Cornelius, to cheat you of a well-deserved chance to swipe a few Teutones, but I think I must send you to serve Catulus Caesar as his senior legate. He'll stomach you in that role; you're a patrician," said Marius.

Bitterly disappointed, Sulla looked down at his hands. "What help can I possibly be when I'm serving in the wrong army?"

"I wouldn't worry so much if I didn't see all the symptoms of Silanus, Cassius, Caepio, and Mallius Maximus in my junior consul. But I do, Lucius Cornelius, I do! Catulus Caesar has no grasp either of strategy or of tactics—he thinks the gods popped them into his brain when they ordained his high birth, and that when the time comes, they'll be there. But it isn't like that, as you well know!"

"Yes, I do," said Sulla.

"If Boiorix and Catulus Caesar meet before I can get across Italian Gaul, Catulus Caesar is going to commit some ghastly military blunder, and lose his army. And if he's allowed to do that, I don't see how we can win. The Cimbri are the best led of the three branches, and the most numerous. Added to which, I don't know the lie of the land anywhere in Italian Gaul on the far side of the Padus. If I can beat the Teutones with less than forty thousand men, it's because I know the country."

Sulla tried to stare his superior out of countenance, but those eyebrows defeated him. "But what do you expect me to do?" he asked. "Catulus Caesar is wearing the general's cape, not Cornelius Sulla! What do you *expect* me to do?"

Marius's hand went out and closed fast about Sulla's arm above the wrist. "If I knew that, I'd be able to control Catulus Caesar from here," he said. "The fact remains, Lucius Cornelius, that you survived over a year of living among a barbarian enemy as one of them. Your wits are as sharp as your sword, and you use both superbly well. I have no doubt that whatever you might have to do to save Catulus Caesar from himself, you will do."

Sulla sucked in a breath. "So my orders are to save his army at all costs?"

"At *all* costs."

"Even the cost of Catulus Caesar?"

"Even the cost of Catulus Caesar."

Spring wore itself out in a smother of flowers and summer came in as triumphantly as a general on his victory parade, then stretched itself out, hot and dry. Teutobod and his Teutones came steadily down through the lands of the Aedui and into the lands of the Allobroges, who occupied all the area between the upper Rhodanus and the Isara River, many miles to the south. They were warlike, the Allobroges, and had an abiding hatred for Rome and Romans; but the German host had journeyed through their lands three years earlier, and they did not want the Germans as their overlords. So there was hard fighting, and the Teutonic advance slowed down. Marius began to pace the floor of his command house, and wonder how things were with Sulla, now a part of Catulus Caesar's army in Italian Gaul, camped along the Padus.

Catulus Caesar had marched up the Via Flaminia at the head of six understrength new legions late in June; the manpower shortage was so acute he could recruit no more. When he got to Bononia on the Via Aemilia, he took the Via Annia to the big manufacturing town of Patavium; this was well to the east of Lake Benacus, but a better route for an army on the march than the side roads and lanes and tracks with which Italian Gaul was mostly provided. From Patavium he marched on one of these poorly kept-up side roads to Verona, and there established his base camp.

Thus far Catulus Caesar had done nothing Sulla could fault, yet he understood better now why Marius had transferred him to Italian Gaul and what he had thought at the time was the lesser task. Militarily it might well be—yet Marius, Sulla thought, had not mistaken the cut of Catulus Caesar. Superbly aristocratic, arrogant, overconfident, he reminded Sulla vividly of Metellus Numidicus. The trouble was, the theater of war and the enemy Catulus Caesar faced were very much more dangerous than those Metellus Numidicus had faced; and Metellus Numidicus had owned Gaius Marius and Publius Rutilius Rufus as legates, besides harboring the memory of a salutary experience in a pigsty at Numantia. Whereas Catulus Caesar had never encountered a Gaius Marius on his way up the chain of military command; he had served his requisite terms as a cadet and then as a tribune of the soldiers with lesser men engaged in lesser wars—Macedonia, Spain. War on a grand scale had always eluded him.

His reception of Sulla had not been promising, as he had sorted out his legates before leaving Rome, and when he reached Bononia found Sulla waiting for him with a directive from the commander-in-chief, Gaius Marius, to the effect that Lucius Cornelius Sulla was appointed senior legate and second-in-command. The action was arbitrary and highhanded, but of course Marius had had no choice; Catulus Caesar's manner toward Sulla was freezing, and his conduct obstructive. Only Sulla's birth stood him in good stead, but even that was weakened by his past history of low living. There was also a tiny streak of envy in Catulus Caesar, for in Sulla he saw a man who had not only seen major actions in major theaters, but had also pulled off a brilliant coup in spying on the Germans. Had he only known of Sulla's real role in that spying, he would have been even more mistrustful and suspicious of Sulla than he already was.

In fact, Marius had displayed his usual genius in sending Sulla rather than Manius Aquillius, who might also have proven his worth as a watchdog-cum-guardian; for Sulla grated on Catulus Caesar's nerves, rather as if out of the corner of Catulus Caesar's eye he was always conscious that a white pard stalked him—yet when he turned to confront the thing, it wasn't there. No senior legate was ever more helpful; no senior legate was ever more willing to take the burdens of day-to-day administration and supervision of the army from a busy general's shoulders. And yet—and yet—Catulus Caesar *knew* something was wrong. Why should Gaius Marius have sent this fellow at all, unless he was up to something devious?

It was no part of Sulla's plan to settle Catulus Caesar down, allay his fears and suspicions; on the contrary, what Sulla aimed to do was keep Catulus Caesar fearful and suspicious, and thus gain a mental ascendancy over him which when necessary—*if* necessary—he could bring to bear. And in the meantime he made it his business to get to know every military tribune and centurion in the army, and a great many of the ranker soldiers as well. Left to his own devices by Catulus Caesar in the matter of routine training and drilling once camp was established near Verona, Sulla became the senior legate everyone below the rank of legate knew, respected, trusted. It was very necessary that this happen, in case he was obliged to eliminate Catulus Caesar.

Not that he had any intention of killing or maiming Catulus Caesar; he was enough of a patrician to want to protect his fellow noblemen, even from themselves. Affection for Catulus Caesar he could not feel; affection for that man's class he did.

The Cimbri had done well under the leadership of Boiorix, who had guided both his own division and that of Getorix as far as the confluence of the Danubius with the Aenus; at that point he left Getorix with a relatively short journey to complete on his own, while the Cimbri turned south down the Aenus. Soon they were passing through the alpine lands peopled by a tribe of Celts called the Brenni, after the first Brennus. They controlled the Pass of Brennus, the lowest of all the passes into Italian Gaul, but were in no condition to prevent Boiorix and his Cimbri from using it.

In late Quinctilis of the calendar, the Cimbri reached the Athesis River where it joined the Isarcus, the stream they had followed down from the Pass of Brennus. Here in verdant alpine meadows they spread out a little, and looked up to the height of the mountains against a rich and cloudless sky. And here the scouts Sulla had sent out discovered them.

Though he had thought himself prepared for every contingency, Sulla hadn't dreamed of the one he now was called upon to cope with; for he didn't yet know Catulus Caesar well enough to predict how he would react to the news that the Cimbri were at the head of the Athesis Valley and about to invade Italian Gaul.

"So long as I live, no German foot will touch Italian soil!" said

Catulus Caesar in ringing tones when the matter was discussed in council. "No German foot will touch Italian soil!" he said again, rising majestically from his chair and looking at each of his senior officers in turn. "We march."

Sulla stared. "We march?" he asked. "We march where?"

"Up the Athesis, of course," said Catulus Caesar, with a look on his face that said he considered Sulla a fool. "I shall turn the Germans back across the Alps before an early snow makes that impossible."

"How far up the Athesis?" Sulla asked.

"Until we meet them."

"In a narrow valley like the Athesis?"

"Certainly," said Catulus Caesar. "We'll be in much better case than the Germans. We're a disciplined army; they're a vast and unorganized mob. It's our best chance."

"Our best chance is where the legions have room to deploy," said Sulla.

"There's more than enough room along the Athesis for as much deployment as we'll need." And Catulus Caesar would hear no further argument.

Sulla left the council with mind reeling, the plans he had formulated to deal with the Cimbri all worse than useless; he had rehearsed how he would go about feeding whichever one of his alternatives would work the best to Catulus Caesar so that Catulus Caesar thought the scheme was his. Now Sulla found himself with no plan, and could formulate no plan. Not until he managed to persuade Catulus Caesar to change his mind.

But Catulus Caesar would not change his mind. He uprooted the army and made it march upstream along the Athesis where that river flowed a few miles to the east of Lake Benacus, the biggest of the exquisite alpine lakes which filled the laps of the foothills of the Italian Alps. And the further the little army—it contained twenty-two thousand soldiers, two thousand cavalry, and some eight thousand noncombatants—marched northward, the narrower and more forbidding the valley of the Athesis grew.

Finally Catulus Caesar reached the trading post called Tridentum. Here three mighty alps reared up, three jagged broken fangs which had given the area its name of Three Teeth. The Athesis now ran very deep and fast and strong, for its sources lay in mountains where the snows never melted fully, and so fed the river all year round. Beyond Tridentum the valley closed in even more, the road which wound down it to the village petering out where the river roared in full spate beneath a long wooden bridge set on stone piers.

Riding ahead with his senior officers, Catulus Caesar sat his horse gazing around him, and nodding in satisfaction.

"It reminds me of Thermopylae," he said. "This is the ideal place to hold the Germans back until they give up and turn north again."

"The Spartans holding Thermopylae all died," said Sulla.

Catulus Caesar raised his brows haughtily. "And what does that matter, if the Germans are pushed back?"

"But they're not going to turn back, Quintus Lutatius! Turn back at this time of year, with nothing but snow to their north, their provisions low, and all the grass and grain of Italian Gaul not many miles away to their south?" Sulla shook his head vehemently. "We won't stop them here," he said.

The other officers stirred restlessly; all of them had caught Sulla's jitters since the march up the Athesis began and their common sense screamed that Catulus Caesar's actions were foolish. Nor had Sulla concealed his jitters from them; if he had to prevent Catulus Caesar from losing his army, he would need the support of Catulus Caesar's senior staff.

"We fight here," Catulus Caesar said, and would not be budged. His mind was full of visions of the immortal Leonidas and his tiny band of Spartans; what did it matter if the body died untimely, when the reward was enduring fame?

The Cimbri were very close. It would have been impossible for the Roman army to have marched further north than Tridentum, even if Catulus Caesar had wished it. Despite this, Catulus Caesar insisted upon crossing the bridge with his whole force, and putting it into camp on the wrong side of the river, in a place so narrow the camp stretched for miles north to south, for each legion was strung behind its neighbor, with the last legion bivouacking near the bridge.

"I have been atrociously spoiled," said Sulla to the *primus pilus* centurion of the legion closest to the bridge, a sturdy steady Samnite from Atina named Gnaeus Petreius; his legion was Samnite too, composed of Samnite Head Count, and classified as an auxiliary.

"How've you been spoiled?" asked Gnaeus Petreius, staring at the flashing water from the side of the bridge; it had no railing, just a low kerb made from logs.

"I've soldiered under none but Gaius Marius," Sulla said.

"Half your luck," said Gnaeus Petreius. "I was hoping I'd get the chance." He grunted, a derisive sound. "But I don't think any of us will, Lucius Cornelius."

They were standing with a third man, the commander of the legion, who was an elected tribune of the soldiers. None other than Marcus Aemilius Scaurus Junior, son of the Leader of the House—and a keen disappointment to his doughty father. Scaurus Junior turned now from his own contemplation of the river to look at his chief centurion.

"What do you mean, none of us will?" he asked.

Gnaeus Petreius grunted again. "We're all going to die here, *tribunus*."

"Die? All of us? Why?"

"Gnaeus Petreius means, young Marcus Aemilius," said Sulla grimly, "that we have been led into an impossible military situation by yet another highborn incompetent."

"No, you're quite mistaken!" cried young Scaurus eagerly. "I noticed that you didn't seem to understand Quintus Lutatius's strategy, Lucius Cornelius, when he explained it to us."

Sulla winked at the centurion. "*You* explain it, then, *tribunus militum*! I'm all agog."

"Well, there are four hundred thousand Germans, and only twenty-four thousand of us. So we can't possibly face them on an open battlefield," said young Scaurus, emboldened by the intent stares of these two Military Men. "The only way we can possibly beat them is to squeeze them up into a front no wider than our own army can span, and hammer at that front with all our superior skill. When they realize we won't be budged—why, they'll do the usual German thing, and turn back."

"So that's how you see it," said Gnaeus Petreius.

"That's how it *is*!" said young Scaurus impatiently.

"*That's* how it is!" said Sulla, beginning to laugh.

"That's how it is," said Gnaeus Petreius, laughing too.

Young Scaurus stood watching them in bewilderment, their amusement filling him with fear. "Please, why is it so funny?"

Sulla wiped his eyes. "It's funny, young Scaurus, because it's hopelessly naïve." His hand went up, swept the mountain flanks on either side like a painter's brush. "Look up there! What do you see?"

"Mountains," said young Scaurus, bewilderment increasing.

"Footpaths, bridle tracks, cattle trails, that's what *we* see!" said Sulla. "Haven't you noticed those frilly little terraces that make the mountains look like Minoan skirts? All the Cimbri have to do is take to the heights along the terraces and they'll outflank us in three days—and then, young Marcus Aemilius, we'll be between the hammer and the anvil. Squashed flatter than a beetle underfoot."

Young Scaurus turned so white that Sulla and Petreius moved automatically to make sure he didn't pitch overboard into the water, for nothing falling into that stream would survive.

"Our general has made a bad plan," said Sulla harshly. "We should have waited for the Cimbri between Verona and Lake Benacus, where we would have had a thousand alternatives to trap them properly, and enough ground to spring our trap."

"Why doesn't someone *tell* Quintus Lutatius, then?" young Scaurus whispered.

"Because he's just another stiff-rumped consul," said Sulla. "He doesn't want to hear anything except the gibberish inside his own head. If he were a Gaius Marius, he'd listen. But that's a non sequitur—Gaius Marius wouldn't have needed telling! No, young Marcus Aemilius, our general Quintus Lutatius Catulus Caesar thinks it best to fight as at Thermopylae. And if you remember your history, you'll know that *one* little footpath around the mountain was enough to undo Leonidas."

Young Scaurus gagged. "Excuse me!" he gasped, and bolted for his tent.

Sulla and Petreius watched him weave along trying to hold his gorge.

"This isn't an army, it's a fiasco," said Petreius.

"No, it's a good little army," Sulla contradicted. "The leaders are the fiasco."

"Except for you, Lucius Cornelius."

"Except for me."

"You've got something in your mind," Petreius said.

"Indeed I do." And Sulla smiled to show his long teeth.

"Am I allowed to ask what it is?"

"I think so, Gnaeus Petreius. But I'd rather answer you at—dusk, shall we say? In the assembly forum of your own Samnite legion's camp," said Sulla. "You and I are going to spend the rest of the afternoon summoning every *primus pilus* and chief cohort centurion to a meeting there at dusk." He calculated swiftly under his breath. "That's about seventy men. But they're the seventy who really count. Now on your way, Gnaeus Petreius! You take the three legions at this end of the valley, and I'll hop on my trusty mule and take the three at the far end."

The Cimbri had arrived that same day just to the north of Catulus Caesar's six legions, boiling into the valley far ahead of their wagons to be brought up short by the ramparts of a Roman camp. And there remained, boiling, while the word flew through the legions and sightseers made their way north to peer over the wicker breastworks at the chilling sight of more men than any Roman had ever seen—and gigantic men at that.

Sulla's meeting in the assembly forum of the Samnite legion's camp took very little time. When it was over, there was still sufficient light in the sky for those who attended it to follow Sulla across the bridge and into the village of Tridentum, where Catulus Caesar had established his headquarters in the local magistrate's house. Catulus Caesar had called a meeting of his own to discuss the arrival of the Cimbri, and was busy complaining about the absence of his second-in-command when Sulla walked into the crowded room.

"I would appreciate punctuality, Lucius Cornelius," he said frigidly. "Please sit down, then we can get down to the business of planning our attack tomorrow."

"Sorry, but I haven't time to sit down," said Sulla, who wasn't wearing a cuirass, but was clad in his leather undersuit and *pteryges*, and had sword and dagger belted about him.

"If you have more important things to do, then go!" said Catulus Caesar, face mottling.

"Oh, I'm not going anywhere," said Sulla, smiling. "The important things I have to do are right here in this room, and the most important thing of all is that there will be no battle tomorrow, Quintus Lutatius."

Catulus Caesar got to his feet. "No battle? Why?"

"Because you have a mutiny on your hands, and I'm its instigator." Sulla drew his sword. "Come in, *centuriones!*" he called. "It'll be a bit of a crush, but we'll all fit."

None of the original inhabitants of the room said a word, Catulus Caesar because he was too angry, the rest either because they were too relieved—not all the senior staff were happy about the projected battle of the morrow—or too bewildered. Seventy centurions filed through the door and stood densely packed behind and to both sides of Sulla, thus leaving about three feet of vacant space between themselves and Catulus Caesar's senior staff—who were now all standing, literally with their backs against the wall.

"You'll be thrown off the Tarpeian Rock for this!" said Catulus Caesar.

"If I have to, so be it," said Sulla, and sheathed his sword. "But when is a mutiny really a mutiny, Quintus Lutatius? How far can a soldier be expected to go in blind obedience? Is it true patriotism to go willingly to death when the general issuing the orders is a military imbecile?"

It was nakedly obvious that Catulus Caesar just did not know what to say, could not find the perfect rejoinder to such brutal honesty. On the other hand, he was too proud to splutter inarticulate expostulations, and too sure of his ground to make no reply at all. So in the end he said, with cold dignity, "This is untenable, Lucius Cornelius!"

Sulla nodded. "I agree, it is untenable. In fact, our whole presence here in Tridentum is untenable. Tomorrow the Cimbri are going to find the hundreds of paths along the slopes of the mountains made by cattle, sheep, horses, wolves. Not *one* Anopaea, but hundreds of Anopaeas! You are not a Spartan, Quintus Lutatius, you're a Roman, and I'm surprised your memories of Thermopylae are Spartan rather than Roman! Didn't you learn how Cato the Censor used the Anopaea footpath to outflank King Antiochus? Or did your tutor feel Cato the Censor was too lowborn to serve as an example of anything beyond hubris? It's Cato the Censor at Thermopylae *I* admire, not Leonidas and his royal guard, dying to the last man! The Spartans were willing to die to the last man simply to delay the Persians long enough for the Greek fleet to ready itself at Artemisium. Only it didn't work, Quintus Lutatius. *It—didn't—work!* The Greek fleet perished, and Leonidas died for nothing. And did Thermopylae influence the course of the war against the Persians? Of course it didn't! When the next Greek fleet won at Salamis, there was no prelude at Thermopylae. Can you honestly say you prefer the suicidal gallantry of Leonidas to the strategic brilliance of Themistocles?"

"You mistake the situation," said Catulus Caesar stiffly, his personal pride in tatters thanks to this red-haired Ulyssean trickster; for the truth was that he cared more to extricate himself with *dignitas* and *auctoritas* unimpaired than he did about the fate of either his army or the Cimbri.

"No, Quintus Lutatius, *you* mistake the situation," said Sulla. "Your army is now my army by right of mutiny. When Gaius Marius sent me here"—he dropped the name with dulcet clarity into the pool of silence—"I came with only one order. Namely, to make sure this army survives intact until Gaius Marius can take it into his personal care—and he cannot do that until he has defeated the Teutones. Gaius Marius is our commander-in-chief, Quintus Lutatius, and I am acting under his orders at this very moment. When his orders conflict with yours, I obey his orders, not yours. If I permit this foolhardy escapade to continue, this army will lie dead on the field of Tridentum. Well, there is not going to be a field of Tridentum. This army is going to retreat tonight. In one piece. And live to fight another day, when the chances of victory are infinitely better."

"I vowed no German foot would tread on Italian soil," said Catulus Caesar, "and I will not be forsworn."

"The decision isn't yours to make, Quintus Lutatius, so you are not forsworn," said Sulla.

Quintus Lutatius Catulus Caesar was one of those oldguard senators who refused to wear a golden ring as an insignia of his senatorship; instead, he wore the ancient iron ring all senators had once worn, so when he moved his right hand imperiously at the ogling men filling the room, his index finger didn't flash a yellow beam—it wrote a dull grey blur upon the air. Utterly still until they saw that grey blur, the men now stirred, moved, sighed.

"Leave us, all of you," said Catulus Caesar. "Wait outside. I wish to speak alone with Lucius Cornelius."

The centurions turned and filed out, the tribunes of the soldiers followed, and Catulus Caesar's personal staff, and his senior legates. When only Catulus Caesar and Sulla remained, Catulus Caesar returned to his chair and sat down heavily.

He was caught in a cleft stick, and he knew it. Pride had led him up the Athesis; not pride in Rome or in his army, but that pride of person which had prompted him to announce no German foot should tread Italian soil—and then prevented his recanting, even for the sake of Rome or for his army. The further he had penetrated up the valley, the stronger his feeling became that he had blundered; and yet pride of person would not allow him to admit the blunder. Higher and higher up the river Athesis, lower and lower his spirits. So when he came to Tridentum and thought how like Thermopylae it was—though of course in strictly geographic terms it was not like Thermopylae at all—he conceived a *worthy* death for all concerned, and thereby salvaged his honor, that fatal personal pride. Just as Thermopylae rang down the ages, so too would Tridentum. The fall of the gallant few confronted with the overwhelming many. *Stranger, go tell the Romans that here we lie in obedience to their command!* With a magnificent monument, and pilgrimages, and immortal epic poems.

The sight of the Cimbri spilling into the northern end of the valley brought him to his senses, then Sulla completed the process. For of course he did have eyes, and there *was* a brain behind them, even if it was a brain too easily clouded by the vastness of his own *dignitas;* the eyes had taken note of the many terraces making giant steps out of the steep green slopes above, and the brain had understood how quickly the Cimbric warriors could outflank them. This was no gorge with cliffs; it was simply a narrow alpine valley unsuitable for deploying an army because its pastures sloped upward at an angle quite impossible for troops to take in rank and file, let alone wheel and turn in proper maneuvers.

What he hadn't been able to see was how to extricate himself from his dilemma without losing face, and at first Sulla's invasion of his pre-battle conference had seemed the perfect answer; he could blame it on a mutiny, and thunder in the House, and arrange for the treason trials of every officer involved, from Sulla down to the least centurion. But that solution hadn't lasted more than a very few moments. Mutiny was the most serious crime in the military manual, but a mutiny which saw him standing alone against every other officer in his entire army (he had quickly seen from their faces that none of the men who had been closeted with him when Sulla walked in would refuse to join the mutiny) smacked a great deal more of common sense overcoming monumental stupidity. If there had never been an Arausio—if Caepio and Mallius Maximus had not forever besmirched the concept of the Roman general's imperium in the eyes of the Roman People—and even some factions within the Senate—then it might have been different. As it was, he understood very quickly after Sulla's appearance that were he to continue to insist a mutiny had taken place, it was he himself who would suffer in the eyes of the Roman world, he himself who might well end in being arraigned in the special treason court set up by Saturninus.

Consequently, Quintus Lutatius Catulus Caesar drew a deep breath and embarked upon conciliation. "Let me hear no more talk of mutiny, Lucius Cornelius," he said. "There was no need for you to make your feeling so public. You should have come to see me privately. Had you only done so, matters could have been sorted out between the two of us alone."

"I disagree, Quintus Lutatius," said Sulla smoothly. "If I had come to you privately, you'd have sent me about my business. You needed an object lesson."

Catulus Caesar's lips tightened; he looked down his long Roman nose, a handsome member of a handsome clan, fair of hair and blue of eye, his hauteur armed for battle. "You've been with Gaius Marius far too long, you know," he said. "This sort of conduct doesn't accord with your patrician status."

Sulla slapped his hand against his leather skirt of straps so loudly its fringes and metal ornaments clattered. "Oh, for the sake of all the gods, let's forget this family claptrap, Quintus Lutatius! I'm fed up to vomit-point with exclusivity! And before you start ranting on about our mutual superior, Gaius Marius, let me remind you that when it comes to soldiering *and* generaling, he outshines us the way the Alexandrian lighthouse dims a single piddling candle! You're not a natural military man any more than I am! But where I have the advantage of you is that I learned my craft in apprenticeship to the lighthouse of Alexandria, so my candle burns brighter than yours!"

"That man is overrated!" said Catulus Caesar between his clenched teeth.

"Oh no, he's not! Bleat and bellow about it as hard as you like, Quintus Lutatius, Gaius Marius is the First Man in Rome! The man from Arpinum took on the lot of you single-handed, and beat you hollow."

"I'm surprised you're such an adherent—but I promise you, Lucius Cornelius, that I won't ever forget it."

"I'll bet you won't," said Sulla grimly.

"I do advise you, Lucius Cornelius, to change your loyalties somewhat in years to come," Catulus Caesar said. "If you don't, you'll never become praetor, let alone consul!"

"Oh, I do like naked threats!" said Sulla conversationally. "Who are you trying to fool? I have the birth, and if the time should come when it's to your advantage to woo me, woo me you will!" He looked at Catulus Caesar slyly. "One day, you know, I'll be the First Man in Rome. The tallest tree in the world, just like Gaius Marius. And the thing about trees so tall is that no one can chop them down. When they fall, they fall because they rot from within."

Catulus Caesar did not answer, so Sulla flung himself into a chair and leaned forward to pour himself wine.

"Now about our mutiny, Quintus Lutatius. Disabuse yourself of any belief you might be cherishing that I don't have the gumption to follow this through to its bitterest end."

"I admit I don't know you at all, Lucius Cornelius, but I've got sufficient measure of your steel these last couple of months to understand there's very little you're unwilling to do to get your own way," said Catulus Caesar. He looked down at his old iron senator's ring as if he could draw inspiration from it. "I said before, and I say it again now, let there be no more talk of mutiny." He swallowed audibly. "I shall abide by the army's decision to retreat. On one condition. That the word 'mutiny' is never mentioned to anyone ever again."

"On behalf of the army, I agree," said Sulla.

"I would like to order the retreat personally. After that—I presume your strategy is already worked out?"

"It's absolutely necessary that you order the retreat personally, Quintus Lutatius. Including to the men waiting outside for us to emerge," said Sulla. "And yes, I do have a strategy worked out. A very simple strategy. At dawn the army will pull up stakes and move out as quickly as it possibly can. Everyone must be over the bridge and south of Tridentum before tomorrow's nightfall. The Samnite auxiliaries are lying closest to the bridge, therefore they can guard it until everyone else is over, then cross it themselves in last place. I need the entire corps of engineers immediately, because the moment the last Samnite is over the bridge, it must come down. The pity of it is that it's built on stone piers we won't have the opportunity to dismantle, so the Germans will be able to rebuild the bridge. However, they're not engineers, and that means the job will take them far longer than it would us, and their structure may fall apart a few times as Boiorix brings his people across. If he wants to go south, he has to cross the river here at Tridentum. So we must slow him down."

Catulus Caesar rose to his feet. "Then let's get this farce over and done with." He walked outside and stood calmly, completely in control of his outer self; the repairing of *dignitas* and *auctoritas* was already beginning. "Our position here is untenable, so I am ordering a full retreat," he said, crisply and clearly. "I have given Lucius Cornelius full instructions as to how to proceed, so you will take your orders from him. However, I wish to make it plain that the word 'mutiny' has never been spoken. Is that understood?"

The officers murmured assent, profoundly glad that the word "mutiny" could be forgotten.

Catulus Caesar turned to go back inside. "You are dismissed," he said over his shoulder.

As the group scattered, Gnaeus Petreius fell in beside Sulla, and walked with him toward the bridge. "That went pretty well, I consider, Lucius Cornelius. He did better than I thought he would. Better than others of his kind, I swear."

"Oh, he has a brain behind all that grand manner," said Sulla easily. "But he's right, 'mutiny' is a word never spoken."

"You won't hear it from my lips!" said Petreius fervently.

It was fully dark, but the bridge was lit by torches, so they crossed its chinked logs without difficulty. At its far end Sulla ran ahead of the centurions and tribunes following him and Petreius, and turned round to face them.

"All troops ready to roll at the first sign of light," he said. "Corps of engineers and all centurions are to report to me here one hour before first light. Tribunes of the soldiers, come with me now."

"Oh, I'm glad we've got him!" said Gnaeus Petreius to his second centurion.

"So am I, but I'm not a bit glad we've got *him*," said the second centurion, pointing in the direction of Marcus Aemilius Scaurus Junior, hurrying after Sulla and his fellow tribunes.

Petreius grunted. "I agree, he is a bit of a worry. Still, I'll keep an eye on him tomorrow. 'Mutiny' may be a word none of us has heard, but our men of Samnium aren't going to be misled by a Roman idiot, no matter who his father is."

At dawn the legions began to move out. The retreat began—as all maneuvers did among well-trained Roman troops—with remarkable silence and no confusion whatsoever. The legion farthest from the bridge crossed it first, then was followed by the legion next farthest from the bridge, so that the army in effect rolled itself up like a carpet. Luckily the baggage train and all the beasts of burden save a handful of horses reserved for the use of the most senior officers had been kept to the south of the village and the bridge; Sulla got these started down the road at first light well ahead of the legions, and had issued orders that half of the army would bypass the baggage train when it caught up, while the other half followed it all the way down to Verona. For if they got clear of Tridentum, Sulla knew the Cimbri wouldn't move fast enough to see their dust.

As it turned out, the Cimbri were so busy scouting the tracks terracing the mountainsides that it was a full hour after the sun rose before they realized the Roman force was in retreat. Then confusion reigned until Boiorix arrived in person and got his enormous mass of men into some semblance of order. In the meantime the Roman column had indeed moved fast; when the

Cimbri finally formed up to attack, the farthest legion from the bridge was already marching at the double across it.

The corps of engineers had worked feverishly among the beams and struts beneath the causeway from well before dawn.

"It's always the same!" complained the chief of engineers to Sulla when he came to see how the work was progressing. "I always have to deal with a properly built Roman bridge just when I want the wretched thing to fall apart with a gentle tug."

"Can you do it?" asked Sulla.

"Hope so, *legatus*! There's not a bit of lashing or a bolt in the thing, though. Proper sockets and tongues, everything rabbeted together to hold it down, not up. So I can't pull it apart in a hurry without a bigger crane than any we've got with us, even if I had time to assemble a crane that big, which I don't. No, it's the hard way, I'm afraid, and that means it's going to be a bit wobbly when the last of our men are tramping across it," said the chief engineer.

Sulla frowned. "What's the hard way?"

"We're sawing through the main struts and beams."

"Then keep at it, man! I've got a hundred oxen coming to give you that gentle tug—enough?"

"It'll have to be," said the chief engineer, and moved off to look at the job from a different angle.

The Cimbric cavalry came shrieking and screaming down the valley, taking the deserted hurdles of five Roman camps in their stride, for these were routine walls and ditches; there hadn't been sufficient time to build anything else. Only the Samnite legion was left on the far side of the bridge, and was actually in the process of marching out of the main gate of its camp when the Cimbri flashed between them and the bridge, cutting them off. The Samnites turned files into ranks and prepared to withstand the coming charge, spears at the ready, faces set.

Watching helplessly from the opposite side of the bridge, Sulla waited for the first rush of cavalry to go by and wheel their horses, straining to see what the Samnite legion commander was going to do. This was young Scaurus, and now Sulla began to fret that he hadn't removed this timid son of an intrepid father and taken over command himself. But it was too late now; he couldn't recross the bridge because he didn't have enough men with him, and he didn't trust Catulus Caesar to see to the retreat, which meant he himself had to survive. Nor did he want to draw the Cimbri's attention to the existence of the bridge, for if they turned their barbarian eyes toward it, there plain to see were five Roman legions and a baggage train marching south and begging for pursuit. If necessary, he decided, he would have the oxen start to haul on the chains connecting them to the undermined bridge; but the moment he did that, there was no hope for the Samnite legion.

"Lead a charge, young Scaurus, lead a charge north!" he found himself muttering. "Roll them back, get your men to the bridge!"

The Cimbric cavalry was turning, its front ranks carried far past the Samnite camp by the impetus of their charge, and the ranks in the rear pulled back on their mounts to give the front ranks room to turn and gallop back; the whole press would then fall upon the Samnite camp, leap their horses up and over, and trample everything down so that the hordes of foot warriors could finish things off. From that point on, the cavalry would turn itself into a giant scoop, pushing the Samnites north into the mass of Cimbric infantry.

The only chance the Samnites had was to drive across the front of the rear ranks of horsemen and cut the front ranks off from this reinforcement, then bring down the mounts of both ranks with their spears, while those not engaged made a dash for the bridge. But where was young Scaurus? Why wasn't he doing it? A few moments more, and it would be too late!

The cheering of the three centuries of men Sulla had with him actually preceded his own view of the Samnite charge, for he was looking for a horse-mounted tribune of the soldiers, while the charge was led by a man on foot. Gnaeus Petreius, the Samnite *primus pilus* centurion.

Yelling along with the rest of his men, Sulla hopped and danced from one foot to the other as the Samnites not engaged began to stream across the bridge at a run, packing their numbers so close together that they gave the Cimbri no room to cut them off a second

time. The front ranks of Cimbric horses were falling in hundreds
before the rain of Samnite spears, warriors struggling to free themselves from fallen steeds, tangling themselves into an ever-increasing
chaos as more Samnite spears hurtled to stick into heaving equine
sides, chests, rumps, necks, flanks; and the rear ranks of Cimbric
horse penned on the other side of the Samnites fared no better. In
the end it was their own fallen cavalry which kept the Cimbric foot
away. And Gnaeus Petreius came across the bridge behind the last
of his men with hardly a German in pursuit.

The oxen had been putting their shoulders to the job long before this happened, for the hundred beasts harnessed two abreast
couldn't gather impetus in under many moments, the lead beasts
pulling, then the next, and so on down the fifty pairs until the
chains tightened and the bridge began to feel the strain. Being a
good stout Roman bridge, it held for much longer than even the
chief of engineers—a pessimistic fellow, like all his breed—had
thought; but eventually one of the struts parted company with its
companions, and amid groans, snaps, pops, and roars the Triden-
tine bridge across the Athesis gave way. Its timbers tumbled into
the torrent and whirled away downstream like straws bobbing
about in a garden fountain.

Gnaeus Petreius was wounded in the side, but not badly; Sulla
found him sitting while the legion's surgeons peeled away his
mail shirt, his face streaked with a mixture of mud, sweat, and
horse dung, but looking remarkably fit and alert nonetheless.

"Don't touch that wound until you've got him clean, you *mentulae!*" Sulla snarled. "Wash every last bit of dung off him first!
He's not going to bleed to death, are you, Gnaeus Petreius?"

"Not Gnaeus Petreius!" said the centurion, grinning broadly.
"We did it, eh, Lucius Cornelius? We got 'em all across, and only
a handful of dead on the other side!"

Sulla sank down beside him and leaned his head too close to
the centurion's to permit of anyone's overhearing. "What happened to young Scaurus?"

Down went Petreius's lips. "Got a dose of the shits while he
should have been thinking, then when I kept pushing him as to

what to do, he passed out on me. Just fell over in a faint. He's all right, poor young chap; some of the lads carried him over the bridge. Pity, but there it is. None of his dad's guts, none at all. Ought to have been a librarian."

"I can't tell you how glad I am you were there, and not some other *primus pilus*. I just didn't think! The moment I did, I kicked myself because I didn't relieve him of the command myself," said Sulla.

"Doesn't matter, Lucius Cornelius, it all worked out in the end. At least this way, he knows his limitations."

The surgeons were back with enough water and sponges to wash off a dozen men; Sulla got up to let them get to work, extending his right arm. Gnaeus Petreius held up his own, and the two men expressed everything they felt in that handshake.

"It's the grass crown for you," said Sulla.

"No!" said Petreius, looking embarrassed.

"But yes. You saved a whole legion from death, Gnaeus Petreius, and when a man single-handedly saves a whole legion from death, he wears the grass crown. I shall see to it myself," said Sulla.

Was that the grass crown Julilla had seen in his future all those years ago? wondered Sulla as he headed off down the slope to the town to organize wagon transportation for Gnaeus Petreius, the hero of Tridentum. Poor Julilla! Poor, poor Julilla . . . She never had managed to do anything right, so perhaps that extended to her brushes against the strange manifestations of Fortune. The sole Julia not born with the gift of making her men happy, that had been Julilla. Then his mind passed to other, more important things; Lucius Cornelius Sulla was not about to start blaming himself for Julilla. Her fate had nothing to do with him; she brought it on herself.

Catulus Caesar had his army back in the camp outside Verona before Boiorix was able to get the last of his wagons across the last of several rickety bridges, and commence the downhill trek to the lush plains of the Padus River. At first Catulus Caesar had insisted they stand and fight the Cimbri near Lake Benacus, but Sulla, firmly in the saddle now, would not countenance it. Instead, he made Catulus Caesar send word to every city and town and village from Aquileia in the east to Comum and Mediolanum in the west: Italian Gaul-across-the-Padus was to be evacuated by all Roman citizens, Latin Rights holders, and Gauls unwilling to fraternize with the Germans. The refugees were to move south of the Padus and leave Italian Gaul-across-the-Padus completely to the Cimbri.

"They'll be like pigs in acorn mush," said Sulla confidently, veteran of a year of living among the Cimbri. "When they get a taste of the pastures and the peace between Lake Benacus and the north bank of the Padus, Boiorix won't be able to hold his people together. They'll scatter in a hundred different directions, you wait and see."

"Looting, wrecking, burning," said Catulus Caesar.

"That—*and* forgetting what they're supposed to be doing, namely, invading Italy. Cheer up, Quintus Lutatius! At least it's the most Gallic of the Gauls on the Italian side of the Alps, and they won't cross the Padus until they've picked it as clean as a hungry man a chicken's carcass. Our own people will be gone well ahead of the Germans, carrying everything they value. Their land will keep; we'll get it back when Gaius Marius comes."

Catulus Caesar winced, but held his tongue; he had learned how biting was Sulla's tongue. But more than that, he had learned how ruthless was Sulla. How cold, how inflexible, how determined. An odd intimate for Gaius Marius, despite the fact they were brothers-in-law. Or had been brothers-in-law. Did Sulla get rid of his Julia too? wondered Catulus Caesar, who in the many hours of thought he expended upon Sulla had remembered a rumor that had circulated among the Julius Caesar brothers and their families around the time Sulla had emerged out of obscurity into public life, and married his Julia-Julilla. That he had found the money to enter public life by murdering his—mother?—stepmother? —mistress?—nephew? Well, when the time came to return to

Rome, thought Catulus Caesar, he would make a point of making inquiries about that rumor. Oh, not to use it blatantly, or even right away; just to have ready for the future, when Lucius Cornelius might hope to run for praetor. Not aedile, let him have the joy of that—and the ruinous drain on his purse. Praetor. Yes, praetor.

When the legions had marched into camp outside Verona, Catulus Caesar knew the first thing he had to do was send word posthaste to Rome of the disaster up the Athesis; if he didn't, he suspected Sulla would via Gaius Marius, so it was important that his be the first version Rome absorbed. With both the consuls in the field, a dispatch to the Senate was addressed to the Leader of the House, so to Marcus Aemilius Scaurus Princeps Senatus did Catulus Caesar send his report, including with it a private letter which more accurately detailed what had actually occurred. And he entrusted the report and letter, heavily sealed, to young Scaurus, son of the Princeps Senatus, ordering him to take the packet to Rome at the gallop.

"He's the best horseman we've got," Catulus Caesar said blandly to Sulla.

Sulla eyed him with the same ironic, superior derision he had shown during their interview about the mutiny. "You know, Quintus Lutatius, you own the most exquisitely refined kind of cruelty I've ever encountered," Sulla said.

"Do you wish to countermand the order?" asked Catulus Caesar, sneering. "You have the clout to do so."

But Sulla shrugged, turned away. "It's your army, Quintus Lutatius. Do what you like."

And he had done what he liked, sent young Marcus Aemilius Scaurus posthaste to Rome bearing the news of his own disgrace.

"I have given you this duty, Marcus Aemilius Junior, because I cannot think of a worse punishment for a coward of your family background than to bring to his own father the news of both a military failure and a personal failure," said Catulus Caesar in measured, pontifical tones.

Young Scaurus—pallid, hangdog, pounds lighter in weight than he had been two weeks earlier—stood to attention and tried not to look at his general. But when Catulus Caesar named the task, young Scaurus's eyes—a paler, less beautiful version of his father's green—dragged themselves unwillingly to Catulus Caesar's haughty face.

"Please, Quintus Lutatius!" he gasped. "Please, I beg of you, send someone else! Let me face my father in my own time!"

"Your time, Marcus Aemilius Junior, is Rome's time," said Catulus Caesar icily, the contempt welling up in him. "You will ride at the gallop to Rome, and give the Princeps Senatus my consular dispatch. A coward in battle you may be, but you are one of the best horsemen we possess, and you have a name sufficiently illustrious to procure you good mounts all the way. You need have no fear, you know! The Germans are well to the north of us, so you'll find none to threaten you in the south."

Young Scaurus rode like a sack of meal in the saddle for mile after mile after mile, down the Via Annia and the Via Cassia to Rome, a shorter journey but a rougher. His head bobbed up and down in time to the gait of his horse, his teeth clicking together in a kind of heartbeat, curiously comforting. At times he talked to himself.

"If I had any courage there to screw up, don't you think I would have found it?" he asked the phantom listeners in wind and road and sky. "What can I do when there is no courage in me, Father? Where does courage come from? Why did I not receive my share? How can I tell you of the pain and fear, the *terror* I felt when those awful savages came shrieking and screaming like the Furies? I couldn't move! I couldn't even control my bowels, let alone my heart! It swelled up and up and up until it burst, until I fell down inanimate, glad I was dead! And then I woke to find myself alive after all, still full of terror—my bowels still loose—the soldiers who carried me to safety washing themselves free of my stinking shit in the river under my very eyes, with such contempt, such loathing! Oh, Father, what is courage? Where did my share go? Father, *listen* to me, let me try to explain! How can you blame me for something I do not possess? Father, *listen* to me!"

But Marcus Aemilius Scaurus Princeps Senatus did not listen. When his son arrived with the packet from Catulus Caesar he was in the Senate, and when he came home his son had bolted himself in his room, leaving a message with the steward for his father that he had brought a packet from the consul and would wait in his room until his father read it, and sent for him.

Scaurus chose to read the dispatch first, grim-faced, but thankful at least that the legions were safe. Then he read Catulus Caesar's letter, lips uttering word after dreadful word out loud, shrinking further and further into his chair until he seemed but half his normal size, and the tears gathered in his eyes and fell with great blurry splashes onto the paper. Of course he had Catulus Caesar's measure; that part did not surprise him, and he was profoundly thankful that a legate as strong and unafraid as Sulla had been on hand to protect those precious troops.

But he had thought his son would discover in the throes of a vital, last-ditch emergency that courage, that bravery Scaurus truly believed lived inside all men. Or all men named Aemilius, anyway. The boy was the only son he had sired—the only child, for that matter. And now his line would end in such disgrace, such ignominy—! Fitting it did, if such was the mettle of his son, his only child.

He drew a breath, and came to a decision. There would be no disguise, no coat of whitewash, no excuses, no dissimulation. Leave that kind of ploy to Catulus Caesar. His son was a proven coward; he had deserted his troops in their hour of gravest danger in a way more craven, more humiliating than mere flight—he had shit himself and fainted. His troops carried *him* to safety, when it should have been the other way around. The shame Scaurus resolved to bear with that courage he himself had always possessed. Let his son feel the scourge of a whole city's scorn!

His tears dried, his face composed, he clapped his hands for his steward, and when the man came he found his master sitting erect in his chair, his hands folded loosely on the desk.

"Marcus Aemilius, your son is most anxious to see you," said the steward, very aware something was wrong, for the young man was acting strangely.

"You may take a message to Marcus Aemilius Scaurus Junior," said Scaurus stiffly, "to the effect that though I disown him, I will not strip him of our name. My son is a coward—a white-livered mongrel dog—but all of Rome shall know him a coward under our name. I will never see him again as long as I live, you will tell him. And tell him too that he is not welcome in this house, even as a beggar at its door. Tell him! Tell him I will never have him come into my presence again as long as I shall live! Go, tell him! Tell him!"

Shivering from the shock of it and weeping for the poor young man, of whom he was fond—and about whom he could have told the father any time during these past twenty years that his son had no courage, no strength, no internal resources—the steward went and told young Scaurus what his father had said.

"Thank you," said young Scaurus, and closed his door, but did not bolt it.

When the steward ventured into his room several hours later because Scaurus had demanded to know whether his no-son had quit the house yet, he found young Scaurus dead upon the floor. The only quarry his sword deemed too unworthy to live turned out to be himself, so he bloodied it at last upon himself.

But Marcus Aemilius Scaurus Princeps Senatus remained true to his words. He refused to see his son, even in death. And in the Senate he gave the litany of the disasters in Italian Gaul with all of his customary energy and spirit, including the hideously frank, unvarnished story of his son's cowardice and suicide. He didn't spare himself, nor did he show grief.

When after the meeting Scaurus made himself wait on the Senate steps for Metellus Numidicus, he did wonder if perhaps the gods had meted out so much courage to him that there was none left in the family cupboard for his son, so great was the fund of courage it took to wait there for Metellus Numidicus while the senators hustled themselves past him, pitying, anxious, shy, unwilling to stop.

"Oh, my dear Marcus!" cried Metellus Numidicus as soon as there were no ears to hear. "My dear, dear Marcus, what can I possibly *say*?"

"About my son, nothing," said Scaurus, a thin splinter of warmth piercing the icy wastes inside his chest; how good it was to have friends! "About the Germans, how do we manage to keep Rome from panicking?"

"Oh, don't worry your head about Rome," said Metellus Numidicus comfortably. "Rome will survive. Panic today and tomorrow and the day after tomorrow, and by the next market day—business as usual! Have you ever known people to move because the place where they're living is unusually prone to suffer earthquakes, or there's a volcano belching outside the back door?"

"That's true, they don't. At least, not until a rafter falls down and squashes Granny, or the old girl falls into a pool of lava," said Scaurus, profoundly glad to find that he could conduct a normal discussion, and even smile a little.

"We'll survive, Marcus, never fear." Metellus Numidicus swallowed, then demonstrated that he too was not without his share of courage by saying manfully, "Gaius Marius is still waiting for his share of the Germans to come. Now if *he* goes down to defeat—*then* we had better worry. Because if Gaius Marius can't beat them, nobody can."

Scaurus blinked, deeming Metellus Numidicus's gesture so heroic he had better not comment; furthermore, he had better instruct his memory to forget for all eternity that Metellus Numidicus had ever ever ever admitted Gaius Marius was Rome's best chance—and best general.

"Quintus, there is one thing I must mention about my son, and then we can close that book," said Scaurus.

"What's that?"

"Your niece—your ward, Metella Dalmatica. This wretched

episode has caused you—and her—great inconvenience. But tell her she's had a lucky escape. It would have been no joy to a Caecilia Metella to find herself married to a coward," said Scaurus gruffly.

Suddenly he found himself walking alone, and turned to see Metellus Numidicus standing looking thunderstruck.

"Quintus? Quintus? Is anything the matter?" Scaurus asked, returning to his friend's side.

"The *matter*?" asked Metellus Numidicus, returning to life. "Good Amor, no, nothing's the *matter*! Oh, my dear, dear Marcus! I have just been visited by a splendid idea!"

"Oh?"

"Why don't *you* marry my niece Dalmatica?"

Scaurus gaped. *"I?"*

"Yes, you! Here you are, a widower of long standing, and now with no child to inherit your name or your fortune. That, Marcus, is a tragedy," said Metellus Numidicus in tones of great warmth and urgency. "She's a sweet little girl, and so pretty! Come, Marcus, bury the past, start all over again! She's *very* rich, into the bargain."

"I'd be no better than that randy old goat Cato the Censor," said Scaurus, just enough doubt in his voice to signal Metellus Numidicus that he might be won round if the offer was really a serious one. "Quintus, I am fifty-five years old!"

"You look good for another fifty-five years."

"Look at me! Go on, look at me! Bald—a bit of a paunch—more wrinkled than Hannibal's elephant—getting stooped—plagued by rheumatics and haemorrhoids alike—no, Quintus, no!"

"Dalmatica is young enough to think a grandfather exactly the right sort of husband," said Metellus Numidicus. "Oh, Marcus, it would please me so much! Come on, what do you say?"

Scaurus clutched at his hairless pate, gasping, yet also beginning to feel a new wellspring trickle through him. "Do you honestly think it *could* work? Do you think I could have another family? I'd be dead before they grew up!"

"Why should you die young? You look like one of those Egyptian things to me—preserved well enough to last another thousand years. When you die, Marcus Aemilius, Rome will shake to her very foundations."

They began to walk across the Forum toward the Vestal Steps, deep in their discussion, right hands waving emphasis.

"Will you look at that pair?" asked Saturninus of Glaucia. "Plotting the downfall of all demagogues, I'll bet."

"Coldhearted old shit, Scaurus," said Glaucia. "How could he get up and speak that way about his own son?"

Saturninus lifted his lip. "Because family matters more than the individuals who make up family. Still, it was brilliant tactics. He showed the world his *family's* not lacking in courage! His son almost lost Rome a legion, but no one is going to blame Marcus Aemilius, nor hold it against his family."

By the middle of September the Teutones had passed through Arausio, and were nearing the confluence of the Rhodanus and the Druentia; spirits in the Roman fortress outside Glanum rose higher and higher.

"It's good," said Gaius Marius to Quintus Sertorius as they did a tour of inspection.

"They've been waiting years for this," said Sertorius.

"Not a bit afraid, are they?"

"They trust you to lead them well, Gaius Marius."

The news of the fiasco at Tridentum had come with Quintus Sertorius, who had abandoned his Cimbric guise for the time being; he had seen Sulla in secret, and picked up a letter for Marius which described events graphically, and concluded by informing Marius that Catulus Caesar's army had gone into a winter camp outside Placentia. Then came a letter from Publius Rutilius Rufus in Rome, giving Rome's view of the affair.

I presume it was your personal decision to send Lucius Cornelius to keep an eye on our haughty friend Quintus Lutatius, and I applaud it heartily. There are all kinds of peculiar rumors floating about, but what the truth is, no one seems able to establish, even the *boni*. No doubt you already know through the offices of Lucius Cornelius—later on, when all this German business is over, I shall claim sufficient friendship with you to be given the true explanation. So far I've heard mutiny, cowardice, bungling, and every other military crime besides. The most fascinating thing is the brevity and—dare I say it?—honesty of Quintus Lutatius's report to the House. But *is* it honest? A simple admission that when he encountered the Cimbri he realized Tridentum was not a suitable place for a battle, and so turned round and retreated to save his army, having first destroyed a bridge and delayed the German advance? There has to be more to it than that! I can see you smiling as you read.

This is a very dead place without the consuls. I was extremely sorry for Marcus Aemilius, of course, and I imagine you are too. What does one do when one finally realizes one has sired a son not worthy to bear one's name? But the scandal died a quick death, for two reasons. The first, that everyone respects Scaurus (this is going to be a long letter, so you will forgive the use of the *cognomen*) enormously, whether they like him or not, and whether they agree with his politics or not. The second reason is far more sensational. The crafty old *culibonia* (how's that for a pun?) provided everyone with a new talking point. He's married his son's betrothed, Caecilia Metella Dalmatica, now in the ward of Metellus Numidicus Piggle-wiggle. Aged *seventeen,* if you please! If it wasn't so funny, I'd weep. Though I've not met her, I hear she's a dear little thing, very gentle and thoroughly nice—a trifle hard to believe coming out of that stable, but I believe, I do believe! You ought to see Scaurus—how you'd chuckle! He's positively prancing. I am seriously thinking of taking a prowl through Rome's better-type schoolrooms in search of a nubile maiden to be the new Mrs. Rutilius Rufus!

We face a serious grain shortage this winter, O senior consul, just to remind you of the duties attached to your office the Germans have rendered it impossible for you to deal with. However, I hear that Catulus Caesar will be leaving Sulla in command at Placentia shortly, and will return to Rome for the winter. No news as far as you're concerned, I'm sure. The business at Tridentum has strengthened your own candidacy *in absentia* for yet another consulship, but Catulus Caesar won't be holding any elections until after you meet your Germans! It must be very difficult for him, hoping for Rome's sake that you have a great victory, yet hoping for his own sake that you fall flat on your peasant *podex*. If you win, Gaius Marius, you will certainly be consul next year. It was a clever move, by the way, to free Manius Aquillius to stand for consul. The electorate was terrifically impressed when he came, declared his candidacy, and then said very firmly that he was going back to you to face the Germans, even if that meant he wouldn't be in Rome for the elections, and so missed out on standing after all. If you defeat the Germans, Gaius Marius—and you send Manius Aquillius back immediately afterward—you will have a junior colleague you can actually work with for a change.

Gaius Servilius Glaucia, boon companion of your quasi-client Saturninus—unkind comment, I know! —has announced that he will run for tribune of the plebs. What a great big furry grey cat among the pigeons he'll be! Talking of Serviliuses and getting back to the grain shortage, Servilius the Augur continues to do abysmally in Sicily. As I told you in an earlier missive, he really did expect that Lucullus would meekly hand over everything he'd worked so hard to establish.

Now the House gets a letter once every market day, as regular as a prune eater's bowel movements, in which Servilius the Augur bemoans his lot and reiterates that he'll be prosecuting Lucullus the minute he gets back to Rome. The slave-king is dead—Salvius or Tryphon, he called himself—and another has been elected, the Asian Greek named Athenion. He's cleverer than Salvius/Tryphon. If Manius Aquillius gets in as your junior consul, it might be an idea to send him off to Sicily and end that business once and for all. At the moment King Athenion is ruling Sicily, not Servilius the Augur. However, my real complaint about the Sicilian mess is purely semantic. Do you know what that despicable old *culibonia* had the gall to say in the House the other day? Scaurus, I am referring to, may his procreative apparatus drop off from overuse in overjuice! "Sicily," he roared, "is become a very *Iliad* of woes!" And everyone rushed up to him after the meeting and poured syrupy praise all over him for coining such a neat epigram! Well, as you know from *my* earlier missive, that's my neat epigram! He must have heard me say it, rot his entire back and front everythings.

Now I leap lightly back to the subject of tribunes of the plebs. They have been a most dismal and uninspiring lot this year—one reason why, though I shudder as I say it, I'm rather glad Glaucia is standing for next year. Rome is a very boring place without a decent brawl or two going on in the Comitia. But we have just had one of the oddest of all tribunician incidents, and the rumors are absolutely whizzing around.

About a month ago some twelve or thirteen fellows arrived in town, clad in remarkable raiment—coats of brilliant colors interwoven with pure gold flowing about their feet—jewels dripping from their beards and curls and earlobes—heads trailing gorgeous em-

broidered scarves. I felt as if I was in the midst of a
pageant! They presented themselves as an embassage,
and asked to see the Senate in a special sitting. But
after our revered rejuvenated phrase-pinching Scaurus
Princeps Senatus friskily examined their credentials,
he denied them an audience on the grounds that they
had no official status. They purported to have come
from the sanctuary of the Great Goddess at Pessinus
in Anatolian Phrygia, and to have been sent to Rome
by the Great Goddess herself to wish Rome well in her
struggle against the Germans! Now why, I can hear
you asking, should the Anatolian Great Goddess give
tuppence about the Germans? It has us all scratching
our heads, and I'm sure that's why Scaurus refused to
have anything to do with these gaudy fellows.

Yet no one can work out what they're after. Orien-
tals are such confidence tricksters that any Roman
worth his salt sews his purse shut and straps it into his
left armpit the moment he encounters them. However,
not this lot! They're going around Rome distributing
largesse as if their own purses were bottomless. Their
leader is a splendidly showy specimen called Battaces.
The eye positively glazes in beholding him, for he's
clad from head to foot in genuine cloth of gold, and
wears a huge solid-gold crown on his head. I'd heard
of cloth of gold, but I never thought I'd live to see it
unless I took a trip to see King Ptolemy or the King of
the Parthians.

The women of this silly city of ours went wild over
Battaces and his entourage, dazzled at the sight of so
much gold and holding their greedy little hands out for
any stray pearls or carbuncles which might happen to
fall off a beard or a—say no more, Publius Rutilius! I
merely add with exquisite delicacy that they are not—
repeat, not!—eunuchs.

Anyway, whether because his own wife was one of

the bedazzled Roman ladies or for more altruistic motives, the tribune of the plebs Aulus Pompeius got up
on the rostra and accused Battaces and his fellow
priests of being charlatans and imposters, and called
for their forcible ejection from our fair city—preferably
riding backward on asses and bedaubed with pitch and
feathers. Battaces took great exception to Aulus Pompeius's diatribe, and marched off to complain to the
Senate. A few wives within that worthy body must
have been infected—or injected—with enthusiasm for
the ambassadors, for the House promptly ordered Aulus Pompeius to cease and desist his badgering of these
Important Personages. The purists among us Conscript Fathers sided with Aulus Pompeius because it is
not the province of the Senate to discipline a tribune
of the plebs for his conduct within the Comitia. There
was then a row about whether Battaces and his gang
were an embassage or not an embassage, despite Scaurus's previous ruling. Since no one could find
Scaurus—I presume he was either looking up my old
speeches for more epigrams, or looking up his wife's
skirts for more epidermis—the point remained unre-
solved.

So Aulus Pompeius went on roaring like a lion from
the rostra, and accusing Rome's ladies of cupidity as
well as unchastity. The next thing, Battaces himself
comes striding down to the rostra trailing gorgeous
priests and gorgeous Roman ladies behind him like a
fishmonger stray cats. Luckily I was there—well, you
know what Rome's like! I was tipped off, of course, as
was half the rest of the city—and witnessed a terrific
farce, much better than anything Sulla could hope for
in a theater. Aulus Pompeius and Battaces went at
it—alas, verbally only—faster than Plautus, our noble
tribune of the plebs insisting his opponent was a moun-
tebank, and Battaces insisting Aulus Pompeius was

dicing with danger because the Great Goddess didn't like hearing her priests insulted. The scene ended with Battaces pronouncing a blood-curdling curse of death upon Aulus Pompeius—in Greek, which meant everyone understood it. I would have thought she liked being hailed in Phrygian.

Here comes the best bit, Gaius Marius! The moment the curse was pronounced, Aulus Pompeius began to choke and cough. He tottered off the rostra and had to be helped home, where he took to his bed for the next three days, growing sicker and sicker. And at the end of three days—he died! Turned up his toes and breathed no more. Well, you can imagine the effect it's had upon everyone from the Senate to the ladies of Rome. Battaces can go where he likes, do what he likes. People hop out of his path as if he suffered from a kind of golden leprosy. He gets free dinners, the House changed its mind and received his embassage formally (still no sign of Scaurus!), the women hang all over him, and he smiles and waves his hands about in blessing and generally acts like Zeus.

I am amazed, disgusted, sickened, and about a thousand other equally unpalatable things. The big question is, how did Battaces do it? Was it divine intervention, or some unknown poison? I am betting on the last, but then, I am of the Skeptic persuasion—if not an out-and-out Cynic.

Gaius Marius laughed himself sore in the sides, then went out to deal with the Germans.

A quarter of a million Teutones crossed the Druentia River just east of the spot where it entered the Rhodanus, and began to stream toward the Roman fortress. The ragged column was spread out for miles, its flanks and vanguard made up of the warriors, one hundred and thirty thousand strong, its meandering tail a vast congregation of wagons and cattle and horses shepherded by the women and children; there were few old men, fewer still old women. In the foreground of the fighting men there strode the tribe called the Ambrones, fierce, proud, valorous. The very last group of wagons and animals were twenty-five miles to their rear.

German scouts had found the Roman citadel, but Teutobod the King was confident. They would march to Massilia in spite of Rome, for in Massilia—the biggest city aside from Rome any of them had ever heard of—they would find women, slaves, food, luxuries. After the satisfaction of sacking and burning it, they would turn east along the coast for Italy, for though Teutobod had discovered the Via Domitia over the Mons Genava Pass was in excellent condition, he still believed the coastal route would get him to Italy faster.

The harvest still stood in the fields, and so was trampled down by the passing of the host; to none of them, even Teutobod, did it seem to matter that a modicum of care might have preserved the grain for reaping and storing against the coming winter. The wagons were full of provisions plundered from all who had been in the German path; as for the crops in the field, what human foot had trodden down could still be chewed by bovine and equine mouths. Unharvested crops simply meant grazing fodder.

When the Ambrones reached the foot of the hill upon which the Roman fortress perched, nothing happened. Marius didn't stir, nor did the Germans bother storming him. But he did present a mental barrier, so the Ambrones stopped and the rest of the warriors piled up behind until Germans milled like ants all about the hill, and Teutobod himself arrived. First they tried to tempt the Roman army out by catcalls, boos, jeers, and a parade of captured civilians who had all been put to the torture. No Roman answered; no Roman ventured out. Then the host attacked en masse, a simple frontal assault which broke and ebbed away fruitlessly against the magnificent fortifications of Marius's camp; the Romans hurled a few spears at easy targets, but did nothing else.

Teutobod shrugged. His thanes shrugged. Let the Romans stay

there, then! It didn't really matter. So the German host rolled around the base of the hill like a syrupy sea around a great rock and disappeared to the south, the thousands of wagons creaking in its wake for seven days, every German woman and child staring up at the apparently lifeless citadel as the cavalcade plodded on toward Massilia.

But the last wagon had scarcely dipped below the horizon when Marius moved with all six overstrength legions, and moved at the double. Quiet, disciplined, overjoyed at the prospect of battle at last, the Roman column skirted the Germans undetected as they pushed and jostled along the road from Arelate to Aquae Sextiae, from which point Teutobod intended to lead his warriors down to the sea. Crossing the river Ars, Marius took up a perfect position on its south bank at the top of a strong, sloping ridge surrounded by gently rolling hills, and there dug himself in, looking down on the river.

Still in the lead, thirty thousand Ambrone warriors came to the ford and looked up to find a Roman camp bristling with plumed helmets and spears. But this was an ordinary camp, easy meat; without waiting for reinforcements, the Ambrones took the shallow stream at a run and attacked. Uphill.

The Roman legionaries simply stepped over their wall along its entire front length and moved downhill to meet a shrieking horde of undisciplined barbarians. First they cast their *pila* with devastating effect, then they drew their swords and swung their shields around and waded into battle like the intermeshed components of one gigantic machine. Hardly an Ambrone lived to stagger back across the ford; thirty thousand Ambrone dead sprawled along the sloping ridge. Of casualties, Marius suffered almost none.

The action was over in less than half an hour; within an hour the Ambrone bodies had been piled into a denuded rampart— swords, torcs, shields, bracelets, pectorals, daggers, and helmets were thrown into the Roman camp—along the edge of the ford; the first obstacle the next wave of Germans would have to surmount was this rampart of their own dead.

The far bank of the Ars was now a roiling mass of Teutones,

gazing in confusion and anger at the huge wall of dead Ambrones, and the Roman camp atop the ridge beyond lined with
thousands of jeering, whistling, singing, booing, hissing, whooping soldiers, lifted out of themselves in a victory euphoria; for
this was the first time a Roman army had killed great numbers of
German Enemy.

It was, of course, only a preliminary engagement. The major
action was yet to come. But it would come, nothing surer. To
complete his plan, Marius peeled off three thousand of his best
troops and sent them that evening under the command of Manius
Aquillius way downstream to cross the river; they were to wait
until the general engagement took place, then fall upon the Germans from behind when the battle was at its height.

Hardly a legionary slept that night, so great was the elation;
but when the next day brought no aggressive move on the part of
the Germans, tiredness didn't matter. The barbarian inactivity
worried Marius, who didn't want the outcome postponed because
the Germans decided not to attack. He needed a decisive victory,
and he was determined to have it. But on the far bank of the river
the Teutones had camped in their myriad thousands, unfortified
save by sheer numbers, while Teutobod—so tall on his little Gallic horse that his dangling feet nearly brushed the ground—prowled
the ford accompanied by a dozen of his thanes. Up and down and
back and forth he walked his miserably overloaded steed all that
day, two great flaxen braids straying across his golden breastplate, the golden wings on his helmet above each ear glittering in
the sun. Even at the distance, anxiety and indecision could be
discerned upon his clean-shaven face.

The following morning dawned as cloudless as the days before, promising a degree of heat which would turn the area into a
seething mass of Ambrone putrefaction all too soon; it was no
part of Marius's plan to remain where he was until disease became a greater threat than the Enemy.

"All right," he said to Quintus Sertorius, "we'll risk it. If they
won't attack, I'll induce the battle by coming out myself and
moving to attack them. We'll lose the advantage of their charge

uphill, but even so, our chances are better here than anywhere else, and Manius Aquillius is in position. Sound the bugles, marshal the troops, and I'll address them."

That was standard practice; no Roman army ever went into a major action unharangued. For one thing, it gave everyone a good look at the general in his war gear; for another, it served as a morale booster; and finally, it was the general's only opportunity to inform even the least legionary how he intended to win. The battle never went strictly according to plan—everyone understood that—but the general's address did give the soldiers an idea of what the general wanted them to do; and if more confusion than normal reigned, it enabled the troops to think for themselves. Many a Roman army had won its battle because its soldiers knew what the general wanted of them, and did it without a tribune in earshot.

The defeat of the Ambrones had acted like a tonic. The legions were out to win, in perfect physical condition down to the last man, arms and armor polished, equipment immaculate. Massed in the open space they called their assembly forum, the ranks stood in file to listen to Gaius Marius. They would have followed him into Tartarus, of course, for they adored him.

"All right, you *cunni,* today's the day!" Marius shouted from his makeshift rostra. "We were too good, that's our trouble! Now they don't want to fight! So we're going to make them so hopping mad they'd fight the legions of the dragon's teeth! We're going across our wall and down the slope, and then we're going to start pushing dead bodies around! We're going to kick their dead, spit on their dead, piss on their dead if we have to! And make no mistake, they're going to come across that ford in more thousands than you ignorant *mentulae* can count in units! And we won't have the advantage of sitting up here like cocks on a fence; we're going to have to take them on eye to eye—and that means looking *up*! Because they're bigger than us! They're *giants*! Does that worry us? Does it?"

"No!" they roared with one voice. "No, no, no!"

"No!" echoed Marius. "And why? Because we're the legions of

Rome! We're following the silver eagles to death or glory! Romans are the best soldiers the world has ever seen! And you—Gaius Marius's own soldiers of the Head Count—are the best soldiers *Rome* has ever seen!"

They cheered him for what seemed an eternity, hysterical with pride, tears running down their faces, every fiber of their beings geared to an unbearable pitch of readiness.

"All right, then! We're going over the wall and we're going into a slogging match! There's no other way to win this war than to beat those mad-eyed savages to their knees! It's fight, men! It's keep going until there's not one madeyed savage left on his gigantic feet!" He turned to where six men wrapped in lion skins—fanged muzzles engulfing their helmets, empty clawed paws knotted across their mail-shirted chests—stood with their hands clasped about the polished silver shafts of standards bearing six open-winged silver eagles. "There they are, your silver eagles! Emblems of courage! Emblems of Rome! Emblems of my legions! Follow the eagles for the glory of Rome!"

Even in the midst of such exaltation there was no loss of discipline; ordered and unhurried, Marius's six legions moved out of the camp and down the slope, turning to protect their own flanks, as this was not a site for cavalry. Like a sickle they presented their ranks to the Germans, who made up King Teutobod's mind for him at the first demonstration of Roman contempt for the Ambrone dead. Through the ford they came, into the Roman front, which didn't even falter. Those in the German forefront fell to a volley of *pila* thrown with stunning accuracy; for Marius's troops had been practising for over two years against this day.

The battle was long and grueling, but the Roman lines could not be broken, nor the silver eagles borne by their six *aquiliferi* be taken. The German dead piled up and up, joining their Ambrone fellows, and still more Germans kept coming across the ford to replace the fallen. Until Manius Aquillius and his three thousand soldiers descended upon the German rear, and slaughtered it.

By the middle of the afternoon, the Teutones were no more. Fueled by the military tradition and glory of Rome and led by a

superb general, thirty-seven thousand properly trained and properly equipped Roman legionaries made military history at Aquae
Sextiae by defeating well over a hundred thousand German warriors in two engagements. Eighty thousand corpses joined the
thirty thousand Ambrones along the river Ars; very few of the
Teutones had elected to live, preferring to die with pride and
honor intact. Among the fallen was Teutobod. And to the victors
went the spoils, many thousands of Teutonic women and children, and seventeen thousand surviving warriors. When the slave
traders swarmed up from Massilia to buy the spoils, Marius donated the proceeds to his soldiers and officers, though by tradition money from the sale of slave-prisoners belonged solely to the
general.

"I don't need the money, and they earned it," he said. He
grinned, remembering the colossal sum the Massiliotes had
charged Marcus Aurelius Cotta for a single ship to take him to
Rome bearing the news of Arausio. "I see the magistrates of
Massilia have sent us a vote of thanks for saving their fair city. I
think I'll send them a bill for saving it."

To Manius Aquillius he gave his report to the Senate, and sent
him at the gallop for Rome.

"You can bring the news, and stand for the consulship," he
said. "Only don't delay!"

Manius Aquillius didn't delay, reaching Rome by road in seven
days. The letter was handed to the junior consul, Quintus Lutatius
Catulus Caesar, to read out to the assembled Senate, a wooden
Manius Aquillius having refused to say a word.

> I, Gaius Marius, senior consul, find it my duty to
> report to the Senate and People of Rome that this day
> on the field of Aquae Sextiae in the Roman province
> of Gaul-across-the-Alps, the legions under my com
> mand have defeated the entire nation of the German
> Teutones. The German dead are numbered at one hun
> dred and thirteen thousand, the German captives at
> seventeen thousand men, and one hundred and thirty

thousand women and children. Of wagons there are thirty-two thousand, of horses forty-one thousand, of cattle two hundred thousand. I have decreed that all the spoils including those sold into slavery are to be divided up in the correct proportions among my men. Long live Rome!

The whole of Rome went mad with joy, its streets filled with weeping, dancing, cheering, embracing hordes of people, from slaves to the most august. And Gaius Marius was voted senior consul for the next year *in absentia,* with Manius Aquillius his junior colleague. The Senate voted him a thanksgiving of three days, and the People two days more.

"Sulla referred to it," Catulus Caesar remarked to Metellus Numidicus after the fuss died down.

"Oho! You don't like our Lucius Cornelius! 'Sulla,' eh? What did he refer to?"

"He said something to the effect that the tallest tree in the world couldn't be cut down by anyone. He has all the luck, Gaius Marius. I couldn't persuade my army to fight, while he defeats a whole nation and hardly loses a man doing it," said Catulus Caesar gloomily.

"He's always had the luck," said Metellus Numidicus.

"Luck, nothing!" said the eavesdropping Publius Rutilius Rufus vigorously. "Give credit where credit's due!"

Which left them with little more to say [wrote Rutilius Rufus to Gaius Marius]. As you well know, I cannot condone all these consecutive consulships, nor some of your more wolfy friends. But I do confess to exasperated annoyance when I am faced with envy and spite from men who ought to be big enough to be magnanimous. Aesop summed them up nicely—sour grapes, Gaius Marius. Did you ever hear such nonsense as attributing your success and their lack of success to luck? A man makes his luck, and that's the truth of it. I could spit when I hear them depreciating your wonderful victory.

Enough about that, I'll give myself an apoplexy. Speaking of your more wolfy friends, Gaius Servilius Glaucia—having entered into his tribunate of the plebs eight days ago—is already stirring up a nice little storm in the Comitia. He has called his first *contio* to discuss a new law he proposes to promulgate, his intent being to undo the work of that hero of Tolosa, Quintus Servilius Caepio, may his exile in Smyrna last forever. I do not like that man; I never did like that man! Glaucia is going to give the extortion court back to the knights, with all sorts of frills attached to it too. From now on—if the law is passed, which I suppose it will be—the State will be able to recover damages or misappropriated property or peculated funds from their ultimate recipients as well as from the original culprits. So where before a rapacious governor could sign his ill-gotten gains over to his Auntie Liccy or his wife's *tata* Lucius Tiddlypuss or even someone as obvious as his son, under Glaucia's new law Auntie Liccy and Lucius Tiddlypuss and the son will have to cough up as well.

I suppose there is some justice in it, but where does legislation like this lead, Gaius Marius? It gives the State too much power, not to mention too much money! It breeds demagogues and bureaucrats, that's what! There is something terribly reassuring about being in politics to enrich oneself. It's normal. It's human. It's forgivable. It's understandable. The ones to watch are the ones who are in politics to change the world. They do the real damage, the power-men and the altruists. It isn't healthy to think about other people ahead of oneself. Other people are not as deserving. Did I tell you I was a Skeptic? Well, I am. Though sometimes—just sometimes!—I wonder if I'm not becoming a little bit of a Cynic too.

We hear that you'll be back in Rome briefly. I cannot wait! I want to see Piggle-wiggle's face at the instant he first sets eyes on you. Catulus Caesar has been made proconsul of Italian Gaul, as you might have expected, and has already gone to rejoin his army in Placentia. Watch him, he'll try to take the credit of the next victory off you if he can. I hope your Lucius Cornelius Sulla is as loyal as he used to be, now Julilla's dead.

On the diplomatic front, Battaces and his priests have finally seen fit to go home, and the wails from various highborn ladies can be heard at least as far as Brundisium. Now we are playing host to a much less awesome and infinitely more ominous embassage. It's come from none other than that very dangerous young man who has managed to collar most of the territory around the Euxine Sea—King Mithridates of Pontus. He's asking for a treaty of friendship and alliance. Scaurus is not in favor. I wonder why? Could it possibly have something to do with the fierce lobbying of the agents of King Nicomedes of our friendly allied Bithynia? *Edepol, edepol,* there goes that dreadful Skeptic streak again! No, Gaius Marius, it is not a Cynical streak! Not yet, anyway.

To conclude, a little gossip and personal news. The Conscript Father Marcus Calpurnius Bibulus has a little son and heir, giving rise to great expressions of joy on the part of various Domitii Ahenobarbi and Servilii Caepiones, though I note the Calpurnii Pisones have managed to maintain their air of indifference. And while it may be the fate of some venerable elders to marry schoolgirls, it is a more usual fate to yield to the arms of Death. Our very own literary giant Gaius Lucilius is dead. I'm quite sorry about it, really. He was a horrible bore in the flesh, but oh he was witty on paper! I am also sorry—and with deep sincerity this time—that your old Syrian seer Martha is dead. No news to you, I know Julia wrote, but I shall miss the old harridan. Piggle-wiggle used to foam at the mouth whenever he saw her being toted around Rome in her lurid purple litter. Your dear wonderful Julia vows she'll miss Martha too. I hope you appreciate the treasure you married, by the way. It isn't every wife I know would grieve at the passing of a houseguest who came for a month and stayed for the duration, especially a houseguest who thought it etiquette to spit on the floor and piss in the fishpond.

I close by echoing your own remark. How could you, Gaius Marius? "Long live Rome!" indeed! What a conceit!

THE TENTH YEAR (101 B.C.):

In the Consulship of
Gaius Marius (V)
and
Manius Aquillius

THE ELEVENTH YEAR (100 B.C.):

In the Consulship of
Gaius Marius (VI)
and
Lucius Valerius Flaccus

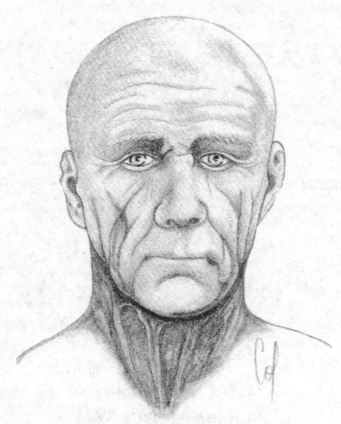

MARCUS AEMILIUS SCAURUS

Sulla was right: the Cimbri weren't even interested in crossing the Padus. Like cows let loose in a huge river-flat pasture, they browsed contentedly across the eastern half of Italian Gaul-across-the-Padus, surrounded by so much agricultural and pastoral plenty that they took no heed of the exhortations of their king. Alone among them Boiorix worried; alone among them Boiorix was deeply depressed when he got the news of the defeat of the Teutones at Aquae Sextiae. When to this was joined the news that the Tigurini-Marcomanni-Cherusci had grown discouraged and turned back toward their original homelands, Boiorix despaired. His grand strategy had been ruined by a combination of Roman superiority in arms and German fecklessness, and now he was beginning to doubt his ability to control his people, the Cimbri.

He still felt they, the most numerous of the three divisions, could conquer Italy unaided—but only if he could teach them the priceless lessons of collective unity and individual self-discipline.

All through the winter following Aquae Sextiae he kept to himself, understanding that he could accomplish nothing until his people either tired of this place, or ate it out. Since they were not farmers, the second possibility was a probability, but nowhere on his travels had Boiorix seen such fertility, such a capacity to feed, and keep on feeding. If Italian Gaul-across-the-Padus was in the fief of the Romans, no wonder Rome was so great. Unlike Long-haired Gaul, here no vast forests were left standing; instead, carefully culled stands of oaks provided a bounteous crop of acorns for many thousands of pigs let loose to graze among them during the winter. The rest of the countryside was tilled: millet where the Padus made the ground too boggy, wheat where the ground was dry enough; chick-peas and lentils, lupines and beans in every kind of soil. Even when in the spring the farmers were either fled or too afraid to sow their crops, still the crops came up, so many seeds already lay dormant on the ground.

What Boiorix failed to understand was the physical structure of Italy; had he done so, he might have elected after all to announce

that here in Gaul-across-the-Padus was the new Cimbric homeland; and had he done that, it may have suited Rome to let him be,
since Italian Gaul-across-the-Padus was not considered of vital
importance, and its populace was mostly Celtic. For the physical
structure of Italy largely prevented the incredible riches of the
Padus River valley being of any use to the Italian peninsula itself.
All the rivers ran between east and west, west and east, and the
daunting mountain chain of the Apennines divided peninsular
Italy from Italian Gaul all the way from the Adriatic seaboard to
the coast of Liguria. In effect, Italian Gaul-of-the-Padus was a
separate country divided itself into two countries, north of the
great river and south of the great river.

As it was, Boiorix regained his purpose when spring slid into
summer and the first tiny evidences of an eaten-out land began to
appear. Crops had indeed sown themselves, but they were thin
and did not seem to be forming ears or pods or tufts; crafty in the
extreme, being intelligent creatures, the pigs conserved their
dwindling numbers by disappearing completely; and the half-
million beasts the Cimbri themselves had brought with them had
trampled what they hadn't grazed into chaffy dust.

It was time to move on; when Boiorix went among his thanes
and stirred them up, they in turn went among the people, stirring.
And so in early June the cattle were driven in, the horses mustered, the wagons hitched up. The Cimbri, united once more into
a single vast mass, moved westward upstream along the north
bank of the Padus, heading for the more Romanized regions
around the big town of Placentia.

In Placentia lay the Roman army, fifty-four thousand strong.
Marius had donated two of his legions to Manius Aquillius, who
had gone to Sicily early in the year to deal with the slave-king
Athenion; so thoroughly had the Teutones been vanquished that it
was not even necessary to leave any soldiers behind to garrison
Gaul-across-the-Alps.

The situation had certain parallels to the command situation at
Arausio: again the senior commander was a New Man, again the

junior commander was a formidable aristocrat. But the difference between Gaius Marius and Gnaeus Mallius Maximus was enormous; the New Man Marius was not the man to take any nonsense from the aristocrat Catulus Caesar. Catulus Caesar was brusquely told what to do, where to go, and why he was doing and going. All that was required of him was that he obey, and he knew exactly what would happen if he didn't obey, because Gaius Marius had taken the time to tell him. Very frankly.

"You might say I've drawn a line for you to tread, Quintus Lutatius. Put one toe either side of it, and I'll have you back in Rome so fast you won't know how you got there," said Marius. "I'll have no Caepio tricks played on me! I'd much prefer to see Lucius Cornelius in your boots anyway, and that's who will go into them if you so much as think of deviating from your line. Understood?"

"I am not a subaltern, Gaius Marius, and I resent being treated like one," said Catulus Caesar, a crimson spot burning in each cheek.

"Look, Quintus Lutatius, I don't *care* what you feel!" said Marius with exaggerated patience. "All I care about is what you do. And what you do is what I tell you to do, nothing else."

"I do not anticipate any difficulty following your orders, Gaius Marius. They're as specific as they are detailed," said Catulus Caesar, curbing his temper. "But I repeat, there is no need to speak to me as if I were a junior officer! I am your second-in-command."

Marius grinned unpleasantly. "I don't like you either, Quintus Lutatius," he said. "You're just another one of the many upper-class mediocrities who think they've got some sort of divine right to rule Rome. My opinion of you as an individual is that you couldn't run a wine bar sitting between a brothel and a men's club! So this is how you and I are going to collaborate—I issue the instructions; you follow them to the letter."

"Under protest," said Catulus Caesar.

"Under protest, but do it," said Marius.

"Couldn't you have been a little more tactful?" asked Sulla of Marius later that day, having endured Catulus Caesar striding up and down his tent ranting about Marius for a full hour.

"What for?" asked Marius, genuinely surprised.

"Because in Rome he *matters*, that's what for! And he also matters here in Italian Gaul!" snapped Sulla. His spurt of anger died, he looked at the unrepentant Gaius Marius and shook his head. "Oh, you're impossible! And getting worse, I swear."

"I'm an old man, Lucius Cornelius. Fifty-six. The same age as our Princeps Senatus, whom everybody calls an old man."

"That's because our Princeps Senatus is a bald and wrinkled Forum fixture," said Sulla. "You still represent the vigorous commander in the field, so no one thinks of you as old."

"Well, I'm too old to suffer fools like Quintus Lutatius gladly," said Marius. "I do not have the time to spend hours smoothing down the ruffled feathers of cocks-on-dungheaps just to keep them thinking well of themselves."

"Don't say I didn't warn you!" said Sulla.

By the second half of Quinctilis the Cimbri were massed at the foot of the western Alps, spread across a plain called the Campi Raudii, not far from the small town of Vercellae.

"Why here?" asked Marius of Quintus Sertorius, who had been mingling with the Cimbri off and on as they moved westward.

"I wish I knew, Gaius Marius, but I've never managed to get close to Boiorix himself," said Sertorius. "The Cimbri seem to think they're going home to Germania, but a couple of the thanes I know think Boiorix is still determined to go south."

"He's too far west," said Sulla.

"The thanes think he's trying to placate the people by leading them to believe they'll be crossing the Alps back into Long-haired Gaul very soon, and next year will be home again in the Cimbrian Chersonnese. But he's going to keep them in Italian Gaul just long enough to close the alpine passes, and then present them with a pretty poor alternative—stay in Italian Gaul and starve through the winter, or invade Italy."

"That's a very complicated maneuver for a barbarian," said Marius skeptically.

"The three-pronged fish spear into Italian Gaul wasn't your typical barbarian strategy either," Sulla reminded him.

"They're like vultures," said Sertorius suddenly.

"How?" asked Marius, frowning.

"They pick the bones of wherever they are clean, Gaius Marius. That's really why they keep moving, it seems to me. Or maybe a plague of locusts is a better comparison. They eat everything in sight, then move on. It will take the Aedui and the Ambarri twenty years to repair the ravages of playing host to the Germans for four years. And the Atuatuci were looking very dismayed when I left, I can tell you."

"Then how did they manage to stay in their original homeland without moving for so long?" asked Marius.

"There were less of them, for one thing. The Cimbri had their huge peninsula, the Teutones all the land to the south of it, the Tigurini were in Helvetia, the Cherusci were along the Visurgis in Germania, and the Marcomanni lived in Boiohaemum," said Sertorius.

"The climate is different," said Sulla when Sertorius fell silent. "North of the Rhenus, it rains all year round. So the grass grows very quickly, and it's juicy, sweet, tender grass. Nor are the winters so very hard, it seems—at least as close to Oceanus Atlanticus as the Cimbri, the Teutones, and the Cherusci were. Even at dead of winter they get more rain than snow and ice. So they can graze rather than grow. I don't think the Germans live the way they do because it's their nature. I think the Germans live the way their original homelands dictated."

Marius looked up from beneath his brows. "So if, for instance, they fetched up long enough in Italy, they'd learn to farm, you think?"

"Undoubtedly," said Sulla.

"Then we'd better force a conclusive fight this summer, and make an end to it—and them. For nearly fifteen years Rome has been living under their shadow. I can't rest peacefully in my bed if the last thing I think of before I close my eyes is half a million Germans wandering around Europa looking for an Elysium they left behind somewhere north of the Rhenus. The German migration has to stop. And the only way I can be sure it's stopped is to stop it with Roman swords."

"I agree," said Sulla.

"And I," said Sertorius.

"Haven't you got a sprog among the Cimbri somewhere?" asked Marius of Sertorius.

"I have."

"Do you know where?"

"Yes."

"Good. After it's over, you can send the sprog and his mother wherever you want, even Rome."

"Thank you, Gaius Marius. I'll send them to Nearer Spain," said Sertorius, smiling.

Marius stared. "Spain? Why Spain?"

"I liked it there, when I was learning to be a Celtiberian. The tribe I stayed with will look after my German family."

"Good! Now, good friends, let's see how we can bring on a battle with the Cimbri."

Marius brought on his battle; the date was the last day of Quinctilis by the calendar, and it had been formally fixed at a conference between Marius and Boiorix. For Marius was not the only one fed up with years of indecision. Boiorix too was keen to see an end to it.

"To the victor goes Italy," said Boiorix.

"To the victor goes the *world*," said Marius.

As at Aquae Sextiae, Marius fought an infantry engagement, his scant cavalry drawn up to protect two massive infantry wings made up of his own troops from Gaul-across-the-Alps, split up into two lots of fifteen thousand. Between them he put Catulus Caesar and his twenty-four thousand less experienced men to form the center; the veteran troops in the wings would keep them steady and contained. He himself commanded the left wing, Sulla the right wing, and Catulus Caesar the center.

Fifteen thousand Cimbric cavalry began the battle, magnificently clad and equipped, and riding the huge northern horses rather than little Gallic ponies. Each German trooper wore a towering helmet shaped like a mythical monster's head with gaping jaws, stiff tall feathers on either side to give the rider even more height; he wore an iron breastplate and a long-sword, and carried a round white shield as well as two heavy lances.

The horsemen massed four deep along a line nearly four miles long, with the Cimbric infantry directly behind them, but when they charged they swung to their right, and drew the Romans with them; a tactic designed to move the Roman line far enough to the Roman left to enable the Cimbric infantry to outflank Sulla's right, and take the Romans from behind.

So eager were the legions to come to grips that the German plan very nearly succeeded; then Marius managed to pull his troops to a halt and took the brunt of the cavalry charge, leaving Sulla to deal with the first onslaught of the Cimbric foot, while Catulus Caesar in the middle battled horse and foot.

Roman fitness, Roman training, and Roman guile won on the field of Vercellae, for Marius had banked on a battle fought mostly before noon, and thus formed up with his lines facing west. It was the Cimbri who had the morning sun in their eyes, the Cimbri who couldn't keep up the pace. Used to a cooler, kinder climate—and having breakfasted as always upon huge amounts of meat—they fought the Romans two days after the summer solstice beneath a cloudless sky and in a choking pall of dust. To the legionaries it was a mild inconvenience, but to the Germans it was a pitiless furnace. They went down in thousands upon thousands upon thousands, tongues parched, armor as fiery as the hair shirt of Hercules, helmets a roasting burden, swords too heavy to lift.

And by noon the fighting men of the Cimbri were no more. Eighty thousand fell on the field, including Boiorix; the rest fled to warn the women and children in the wagons, and take what they could across the Alps. But fifty thousand wagons couldn't be driven away at a gallop, nor half a million cattle and horses mustered in an hour or two. Those closest to the alpine passes of the

Vale of the Salassi escaped; the rest did not. Many of the women rejected the thought of captivity and killed themselves and their children; some of the women killed the fleeing warriors as well. Even so, sixty thousand live Cimbric women and children were sold to the slavers, as were twenty thousand warriors.

Of those who fled up the Vale of the Salassi and got away to Gaul-across-the-Alps through the Lugdunum Pass, few succeeded in running the gauntlet of the Celts. The Allobroges assailed them with fierce delight, as did the Sequani. Perhaps two thousand Cimbri finally rejoined the six thousand warriors left among the Atuatuci; and there where the Mosa received the Sabis, the last remnants of a great migration settled down for good, and in time came to call themselves Atuatuci. Only the vast accumulation of treasure reminded them that they had once been a German host more than three quarters of a million strong; but the treasure was not theirs to spend, only theirs to guard against the coming of other Romans.

Catulus Caesar came to the council Marius called after Vercellae girt for war of a different kind, and found a mellow, affable Marius only too happy to grant his every request.

"My dear fellow, of *course* you shall have a triumph!" said Marius, clapping him on the back.

"My dear fellow, take *two thirds* of the spoils! After all, my men have the spoils from Aquae Sextiae as well, and I donated the proceeds from sale of slaves to them, so they'll come out of the campaign far ahead of your fellows, I imagine—unless you too intend to donate the slave money—? No? *Perfectly* understandable, my dear Quintus Lutatius!" said Marius, pushing a plate of food into his hands.

"My dear fellow, I wouldn't *dream* of taking all the credit! Why should I, when your soldiers fought with equal skill and enthusiasm?" said Marius, taking the plate of food off him and replacing it with a brimming goblet of wine. "Sit down, sit down! A great day! I can sleep in peace."

"Boiorix is dead," said Sulla, smiling contentedly. "It is all over, Gaius Marius. Definitely, definitely over."

"And your woman and child, Quintus Sertorius?" asked Marius.

"Safe."

"Good. Good!" Marius looked around the crowded general's tent, even his eyebrows seeming to beam. "And who wants to bring the news of Vercellae to Rome?" he asked.

Two dozen voices answered; several dozen more said nothing but put eager expressions on their faces. Marius looked them over one by one, and finally let his eyes rest where he had already made up his mind.

"Gaius Julius," he said, "you shall have the job. You are my quaestor, but I have even better grounds. In you is vested a part of all of us in senior command. We must stay in Italian Gaul until everything is properly tidied up. But you are the brother-in-law of Lucius Cornelius and myself; our children have your family's blood in their veins. And Quintus Lutatius here is a Julius Caesar by birth. So it's fitting that a Julius Caesar should bring the news of victory to Rome." He turned to look at everyone present. "Is that fair?" he asked.

"It's fair," everyone said in chorus.

"What a lovely way to enter the Senate," said Aurelia, unable to take her eyes off Caesar's face; how brown he was, how very much a man! "I'm glad now that the censors didn't admit you before you left to serve Gaius Marius."

He was still elated, still half-living those glorious moments when, after handing Marius's letter to the Leader of the House, he had actually seen with his own eyes the Senate of Rome receive the news that the threat of the Germans was no more. The applause, the cheers, the senators who danced and the senators who wept, the sight of Gaius Servilius Glaucia, head of the College of Tribunes of the Plebs, running with toga hugged about himself from the Curia to the Comitia to scream the news from the rostra, august presences like Metellus Numidicus and Ahenobarbus Pontifex Maximus solemnly shaking each other's hands and trying to be more dignified than excited.

"It's an omen," he said to his wife, eyes dwelling upon her in besotted admiration. How beautiful she was, how unmarked by her more than four years of living in the Subura and acting as the landlady of an insula.

"You'll be consul one day," she said confidently. "Whenever they think of our victory at Vercellae, they'll remember that it was you who brought the news to Rome."

"No," he said fairly, "they'll think of Gaius Marius."

"And you," the doting wife insisted. "Yours was the face they saw; you were his quaestor."

He sighed, snuggled down on the dining couch, and patted the vacant space next to himself. "Come here," he said.

Sitting correctly on her straight chair, Aurelia looked toward the door of the *triclinium*. "Gaius Julius!" she said.

"We're alone, my darling wife, and I'm not such a stickler that on my first evening home I like being separated from you by the width of a table." Another pat for the couch. "Here, woman! Immediately!"

When the young couple had first made their home in the Subura, their arrival was sufficiently remarkable to have made them the object of ongoing curiosity to everyone who lived within several streets of Aurelia's insula. Aristocratic landlords were common enough, but not resident aristocratic landlords; Gaius Julius Caesar and his wife were rare birds, and as such came in for more than the usual amount of attention. In spite of its mammoth size, the Subura was really a teeming, gossipy village which liked nothing better than a new sensation.

All the predictions were that the young couple would never last; the Subura, that great leveler of pretensions and pride, would soon show them up for what they were, Palatine people. What hysterical seizures milady was going to throw! What sniffy tantrums milord was going to throw! Ha, ha. So said the hard cases of the Subura. And waited gleefully.

None of it ever happened. Milady, they discovered, was not above doing her own marketing—nor above being explicitly obnoxious to any leering fellow who tried to proposition her—nor frightened when a group of local women surrounded her as she crossed the Vicus Patricii and tried to tell her to go back to the Palatine where she belonged. As for milord, he was—and there could be no other word applied to him—a true gentleman: unruffled, polite, interested in everything said to him by every element in the community, helpful about wills and leases and contracts.

Very soon they were respected. Eventually they were loved. Many of their qualities were novelties, like their tendency to mind their own business and not inquire into everyone else's business; they never complained or criticized, and they never held themselves better than those around them. Speak to them, and you could be sure of a ready and genuine smile, true interest, courtesy, and sensitivity. Though at first this was deemed an act, in the end the residents of their part of the Subura came to understand that Caesar and Aurelia were exactly what they seemed to be.

For Aurelia this local acceptance was more important by far than for Caesar; she was the one engaged in Suburan affairs, and she was the landlady of a populous apartment building. It hadn't been easy in the beginning, though it wasn't until after Caesar left Rome that she fully understood why. At first she deemed her difficulties the result of unfamiliarity and lack of experience. The agents who had sold the insula offered to act on her behalf when it came to collecting the rents and dealing with the tenants, and Caesar had thought this a good idea, so the obedient new wife agreed. Nor did Caesar grasp the unconscious message she relayed to him a month after they had moved in, when she told him all about their tenants.

"It's the variety I find hardest to believe," she said, face animated, her customary composure not so noticeable.

He humored her by asking, "Variety?"

"Well, the two top floors are mostly freedmen—Greek in the main—who all seem to eke out a living running after their ex-masters, and have terrific worry lines on their faces, and more boyfriends than wives. On the main floors there are all sorts—a fuller and his family—Roman; a potter and his family—Roman; a shepherd and his family—did you realize there were shepherds in *Rome*? He looks after the sheep out on the Campus Lanatarius while they wait to be sold for slaughter, isn't that fascinating? I asked him why he didn't live closer to his job, but he said he and his wife were both Suburans, and couldn't think of living anywhere else, and he doesn't mind the walk at all," said Aurelia, becoming more animated still.

But Caesar frowned. "I am not a snob, Aurelia, yet I'm not sure it's a good thing to strike up conversations with any of your tenants. You're the wife of a Julius, and you have certain standards of conduct. One must never be peremptory or uncivil to these people, nor above being interested in them, but I'll be going away soon, and I don't want my wife making friends out of acquaintances. You must keep yourself a little aloof from the people who rent living accommodation from you. That's why I'm glad the agents are acting as your rent collectors and business consultants."

Her face had dropped, she was staring at him in dismay, and stammered, "I—I'm sorry, Gaius Julius, I—I didn't think. Truly I've made no real advances; I just thought it would be interesting to find out what everyone did."

"Of course it is," he soothed, aware that in some way he had blighted her. "Tell me more."

"There's a Greek rhetor and his family, and a Roman school-teacher and his family—he's interested in renting the two rooms next door to his apartment when they fall vacant, so he can conduct his school on the premises." She shot Caesar a quick look, and added, "The agents told me," thereby telling her first lie to her husband.

"That sounds satisfactory," he said. "Who else have we got, my love?"

"The next floor up from us is very odd. There's a spice merchant with a frightfully superior wife, and an *inventor*! He's a bachelor, and his flat is absolutely stuffed with all these amazing little working models of cranes and pumps and mills," she said, her tongue getting the better of her again.

"Do you mean to say, Aurelia, that you have been inside the apartment of a bachelor?" asked Caesar.

She told her second lie, heart beating uncomfortably. "No, Gaius Julius, truly! The agent thought it would be a good thing if I accompanied him on his rounds, and inspected the tenants as well as how they live."

Caesar relaxed. "Oh, I see! Of course. What does our inventor invent?"

"Brakes and pulleys mostly, I gathered. He did show me how they work on a model of a crane, but I don't have a technical mind, he said, so I'm afraid it didn't make any sense to me."

"His inventing obviously pays him well, if he can afford to live on the next floor up," said Caesar, uncomfortably aware that his wife had lost a great deal of her original animation, but having insufficient intuition to see whose fault that was.

"For his pulleys he has a deal with a foundry that does a lot of work for big building contractors, where his brakes he manufactures in tiny premises of his own somewhere down the street from here." She drew a rather shaky breath, and passed on to her most unusual tenants. "And we have a whole floor of Jews, Gaius Julius! They like to live surrounded by other Jews, they were telling me, because they have so many rules and regulations—which, incidentally, they seem to have inflicted upon themselves. Very *religious* people! I can understand the xenophobia—they make the rest of us look a shabby lot morally. They're all self-employed, chiefly because they rest every seventh day. Isn't that a strange system? With Rome having a market holiday every eighth day, and then the feasts and festivals, they can't fit in with non-Jewish employers. So they contract themselves out, rather than take regular jobs."

"How extraordinary!" said Caesar.

"They're all artisans and scholars," said Aurelia, careful to keep her voice disinterested. "One of the men—his name's Shimon, I think—is the most exquisite scribe. Beautiful work, Gaius Julius, truly beautiful! He works in Greek only. None of them has a very good grasp of Latin. Whenever a publisher or an author has a special edition of a work to put out at a higher than normal price, he goes to Shimon, who has four sons all learning to be scribes too. They're going to school with our Roman teacher as well as to their own religious school, because Shimon wants them to be as fluent in Latin as in Greek and Aramaic and—Hebrew, I think he said. Then they'll have plenty of work in Rome forever."

"Are all the Jews scribes?"

"Oh, no, only Shimon. There's one who works with gold, and contracts himself out to some of the shops in the Porticus Margaritaria. And we have a portrait sculptor—a tailor—an armorer—a textile maker—a mason—and the last one is a balsam merchant."

"Surely not all working upstairs?" asked Caesar, alarmed.

"Only the scribe and the goldsmith, Gaius Julius. The armorer has a workshop at the top of the Alta Semita, the sculptor rents space from a big firm in the Velabrum, and the mason has a yard near the marble wharves in the Port of Rome." In spite of herself, Aurelia's purple eyes began to shine. "They sing a lot. Religious, I gather. It's a very *strange* sort of singing—you know, Oriental and tuneless? But it's a nice change from crying babies."

Caesar reached out a hand to tuck back a strand of hair which had fallen forward onto her face; she was all of eighteen years old, this wife of his. "I take it our Jews like living here?" he asked.

"Actually everyone seems to like living here," she said.

That night after Caesar had fallen asleep, Aurelia lay beside him and sprinkled her pillows with a very few tears. It hadn't occurred to her that Caesar would expect the same sort of conduct from her here in an insula of the Subura as he would have from a Palatine wife; didn't he understand that in these cramped quarters there were not the diversions or hobbies available to a woman of the Palatine? No, of course he didn't. His time was taken up with his burgeoning public career, so his days were spent between the law courts, important senators like Marcus Aemilius Scaurus Princeps Senatus, the mint, the Treasury, the various arcades and colonnades where an incipient senator went to learn his profession. A gentler, more kindly disposed and considerate husband did not live; but Gaius Julius Caesar still regarded his wife as a special case.

The truth was that Aurelia had conceived a wish to run the insula herself, and dispense with the agents. So she had taken herself around to every tenant of every floor, and chatted with them, and discovered what kind of people they were. She had liked them, couldn't see any reason why she should not deal with them personally. Until she talked to her husband, and understood that the precious person of his wife was a woman apart, a woman high on the plinth of Julian *dignitas;* she would never be permitted to do anything which might detract from his family. Her own background was sufficiently like his for her to appreciate this, and understand it; but oh, how was she going to fill her days? She didn't dare think about the fact that she had told her husband two lies. Instead, she sniffled herself to sleep.

Luckily her dilemma was temporarily solved by a pregnancy. It slowed her down somewhat, though she suffered none of the traditional ailments. In the pink of health and youth, she had enough relatively new blood in her from both sides to ensure that she didn't possess the frailty of purely old-nobility girls; besides which, she had got into the habit of walking miles each day to keep herself from going mad with boredom, her gigantic serving maid, Cardixa, more than adequate protection on the streets.

Caesar was seconded to the service of Gaius Marius in Gaul-across-the-Alps before their first child was born, and fretted at leaving behind a wife so heavy, so vulnerable.

"Don't worry, I'll be perfectly all right," she said.

"Make sure you go home to your mother's house well ahead of your time," he instructed.

"Leave all that to me, I'll manage" was as far as she would commit herself.

Of course she didn't go home to her mother; she had her baby in her own apartment, attended by no fashionable Palatine practitioners, only the local midwife and Cardixa. An easy and fairly short labor produced a girl, yet another Julia, and as blonde and blue-eyed and gorgeous as any Julia needed to be.

"We'll call her 'Lia' for short," she said to her mother.

"Oh, no!" cried Rutilia, deeming "Lia" too commonplace and unimposing. "How about 'Julilla'?"

Aurelia shook her head very firmly. "No, that's an unlucky diminutive," she said. "Our girl will be 'Lia.'"

But Lia didn't thrive; she cried and cried and cried for six solid weeks, until Shimon's wife, Ruth, came marching down to Aurelia's apartment and sniffed scornfully at Aurelia's tales of doctors, worried Cottae grandparents, colic, and colds.

"You just got a hungry baby there," said Ruth in her heavily accented Greek. "You got no milk, silly girl!"

"Oh, where *am* I going to put a wet nurse?" asked Aurelia, profoundly relieved at what she instantly saw was the truth, but at her wits' end to persuade the staff they must share the servants' quarters with yet another body.

"You don't need no wet nurse, silly girl," said Ruth. "This building's full of mothers feeding babies. Don't you worry, we'll all give the little one a drink."

"I can pay you," Aurelia offered tentatively, sensitive enough to know that she ought not sound patronizing.

"For what, nature? You leave it to me, silly girl. *And* I make sure they all wash their teats first! The little one's got some catching up to do; we don't want her sick," said Ruth.

So little Lia acquired a whole insula of wet nurses, and the bewildering array of nipples popped into her mouth seemed to worry the baby's feelings as little as the mixture of Greek milk, Roman milk, Jewish milk, Spanish milk, and Syrian milk worried her digestion. Little Lia began to thrive.

As did her mother, once she was recovered from the birth process and the worry of a perpetually crying baby. For with Caesar gone, Aurelia's true character began to assert itself. First she made mincemeat of her male relatives, all of whom had been charged by Caesar to keep an eye on her.

"If I do need you, Father," she said to Cotta firmly, "I will send for you."

"Uncle Publius, leave me alone!" she said to Rutilius Rufus.

"Sextus Julius, go away to Gaul!" she said to her husband's older brother.

Then she looked at Cardixa and rubbed her hands together gleefully. "My life is my own at last!" she said. "Oh, there are going to be some changes!"

She started within the walls of her own apartment, where the slaves she and Caesar had bought just after their marriage were running the young couple rather than the other way around. Led by the steward, a Greek named Eutychus, they worked well enough that Aurelia found herself without sufficient grounds to impeach them to Caesar; for she had learned that Caesar did not see things as she saw them, and was absent-minded enough not to see some things at all, especially domestic things. But within the space of a single day Aurelia had the servants hopping to her tune, working her will upon them with a speech first and a schedule after that. Gaius Marius would have approved the speech mightily, for it was short and breathtakingly frank, delivered in the tone and manner of a general.

"Oooooo-er!" said the cook, Murgus, to the steward, Eutychus. "And I thought she was a nice little thing!"

The steward rolled his long-lashed beguiling eyes. "What about *me*? I thought I might just sneak into her bedroom and console her a bit during Gaius Julius's absence—what an escape! I'd sooner crawl into bed with a lion."

"Do you really think she'd have the guts to take such a terrible financial loss by selling us all with bad references?" asked the cook, Murgus, shivering at the very thought.

"She'd have the guts to crucify us," said the steward.

"Oooooo-er!" wailed the cook.

From this encounter, Aurelia went straight to deal with the tenant of the other ground-floor apartment. That initial conversation with Caesar about the tenants had robbed her of all her original resolve to be rid of the ground-floor tenant immediately; in the end she hadn't mentioned the man to her husband, realizing that he wouldn't see the situation the way she did. But now she could act, and act she did.

The other ground-floor apartment was accessible from within the insula; all Aurelia had to do was walk across the courtyard at the bottom of the light-well. However, that would give her visit an informality she definitely didn't want. So she approached through her tenant's front door. This meant that she was obliged to go out her own front door onto the Vicus Patricii, turn right, and walk up along the row of shops she rented out, to the apex of the building where the crossroads tavern stood; from there she turned right into the Subura Minor and walked down the other row of shops she rented out, until she finally came to the front door of the second ground-floor apartment.

Its tenant was a famous actor named Epaphroditus, and according to the books, he had been living there for well over three years.

"Tell Epaphroditus that his landlady wishes to see him," said Aurelia to the porter.

While she waited in the reception room—as large as the one in her own apartment—she assessed its condition with an eye grown expert in the matter of cracks, chips, peeling paint, and the like, and sighed; it was better than her own reception room, and had recently been frescoed with swathes of fruit and flowers dangled by dimpled Cupids between convincing-looking painted purple curtains.

"I don't believe it!" cried a beautiful voice, in Greek.

Aurelia swung round to face her tenant. He was much older than voice or reputation upon the stage or the view across the courtyard suggested, a fiftyish man with a golden-yellow wig upon his head and an elaborately made-up face, wearing a floating robe of Tyrian purple embroidered with clusters of golden stars. Though many wearers of purple pretended it was Tyrian, this was the real thing, a color as much black as purple, of a luster which changed its hue as the light changed, suffusing it with sheens of plum and deepest crimson; in tapestry one saw it, but only once in her life had Aurelia seen genuine Tyrian purple raiment, on her visit to the villa of Cornelia the Mother of the Gracchi, who had displayed with pride a robe taken from King Perseus of Macedonia by Aemilius Paullus.

"You don't believe what?" asked Aurelia, also in Greek.

"*You,* darling! I'd heard our landlady was beautiful and owned a pair of purple eyes, but the reality pales what I had imagined from the distance across the courtyard!" he fluted; his voice was more melodious than ridiculous, despite the effeminate accent. "Sit down, sit down!" he said.

"I prefer to stand."

He stopped in his tracks and turned back toward her, his thin plucked black brows lifting. "You mean business!"

"I certainly do."

"How may I assist you, then?" he asked.

"You can move out," said Aurelia.

He gasped; he staggered; his hands flew to clutch at his chest; an expression of horror fell upon his face. *"What?"*

"I'm giving you eight days' notice," said the landlady.

"But you can't! My rent's paid up and it always has been! I look after this place as if I owned it! Give me your grounds, *domina,*" he said, voice now very hard, and a look about him which made the painted face seem an utterly masculine lie.

"I don't like the way you live," said Aurelia.

"The way I live is my business," said Epaphroditus.

"Not when I have to bring up my family looking across a courtyard into scenes not fit for my eyes, let alone a child's," she said. "Not when the harlots of both sexes spill out into the courtyard to continue their activities."

"Put up curtains," said Epaphroditus.

"I'll do no such thing. Nor will it satisfy me if you put up curtains. My household has ears as well as eyes."

"Well, I'm very sorry you feel this way, but it can make no difference," he said briskly. "I refuse to leave."

"In that case, I shall hire bailiffs and evict you."

Using his considerable arts to grow in stature until he seemed to tower over her, Epaphroditus came closer to her, and succeeded in reminding the uncowed Aurelia of Achilles hiding in the harem of King Lycomedes of Skyros.

"Now listen to me, little lady," he said, "I've spent a fortune turning this place into my kind of place, and I have no intention of leaving it. If you try any tricks like sending bailiffs in, I'll sue you for everything you've got. In fact, after I've ushered you off *my* premises, I'm going straight to the tribunal of the urban praetor to lay charges against you."

The purple of her eyes made a cheap mockery of Tyrian imitations; so did the look on her face. "Do that!" she said sweetly. "His name is Gaius Memmius, and he's a cousin of mine. However, it's a busy time for litigation at the moment, so you will have to see his assistant first. He's a new senator, but I know him well. Ask for him by name, do! Sextus Julius Caesar. He's my brother-in-law." She moved away and inspected the newly decorated walls, the expensive mosaic floor no rented apartment ever boasted. "Yes, this is all very nice! I'm glad your taste in interior design is superior to your taste in companions. But you realize, of course, that any improvements made to rented premises belong to the landlord, and that the landlord is not obliged under the law to pay a single penny's compensation."

Eight days later Epaphroditus was gone, calling down curses upon the heads of women, and unable to do what he had fully intended to do, namely to deface his frescoes and dig up his mosaic floor; Aurelia had installed a pair of hired gladiators inside the apartment.

"Good!" she said, dusting off her hands. "Now, Cardixa, I can find a decent tenant."

The process whereby an apartment was let occurred in any of several ways; the landlord hung a notice upon his front door and more notices on the walls of his shops, did the same thing outside the baths and public latrines and any wall owned by friends, then spread the news of a vacancy by word of mouth as well. Because

Aurelia's insula was known as a particularly safe one, there was no shortage of prospective tenants, whom she interviewed herself. Some she liked; some she felt were trustworthy; some she wouldn't have rented to had they been the only applicants. But none proved to be what she was after, so she kept on looking and interviewing.

It was seven weeks before she found her ideal tenant. A knight and the son of a knight, his name was Gaius Matius; he was the same age as Caesar, and his wife was the same age as Aurelia; both were cultivated and educated; they had married about the same time as Caesar and Aurelia; they had a baby girl the same age as Lia; and they were comfortably off. His wife was called Priscilla, which must have derived from her father's *cognomen* rather than his *gens,* but in all the many years the family Matius was to live there, Aurelia never did find out Priscilla's proper name. The Matius family business was in brokerage and the handling of contracts, and Gaius Matius's father lived with a second wife and younger children in a commodious house on the Quirinal. Aurelia was careful to check all this, and when her inquiries confirmed it, she rented Gaius Matius her ground-floor apartment for the welcome sum of ten thousand denarii a year; Epaphroditus's expensive murals and mosaic floor helped secure the contract, as did Aurelia's promise that all her future leasing contracts would be handled by the firm of Gaius Matius and Gaius Matius.

For there were to be no more agents collecting the rents; from now on, Aurelia intended to run her insula herself. All the flats would be let by written lease, with an option to renew every two years. Penalty clauses for damage to the property were inserted, as well as clauses to protect the tenants from extortion by the landlord.

She converted her sitting room into an office stacked high with account books, kept only her loom from all her old hobbies, and set to work to discover the complexities of being a landlady. After she collected the insula's paperwork from the erstwhile agents, Aurelia discovered there were files for all manner of things—masons, painters, plasterers, vendors of many kinds, water rates, taxes, land titles, bills as well as receipts. A good deal of the incoming, she learned, would have to be almost immediately outgoing. As well as charging for the water and sewer laid on, the State took a small contribution for every window the insula possessed, and every door opening onto the street, and every staircase leading to every floor. And though it was undeniably a stoutly built insula, there were repairs going on all the time. Among the tradesmen listed were several carpenters; conning the dates, Aurelia found one man who seemed to have done the most work and lasted the longest. So she sent for him, and ordered him to remove the wooden screens boxing in the light-well.

This project she had cherished from the time she and Caesar first moved into the insula; Aurelia had discovered in herself a longing to make a garden, and dreamed of transforming the ill-kept central courtyard into an oasis which would be a pleasure to everyone living in the building. But everything had conspired against her, starting with the problem of Epaphroditus, also entitled to use the courtyard. Caesar had never seen for himself the goings-on of Epaphroditus; the actor was cunning enough to make sure his debaucheries occurred only when Caesar was out. And Caesar, she learned, thought all women tended to exaggerate.

Irksomely dense wooden screens were fixed between the columns of the balconies which looked down into the courtyard from every upper floor. Therefore, no one who lived upstairs could gain a glimpse of it. Admittedly these screens did keep the courtyard private—and helped stem the constant torrent of noise which emanated from every flat—but they also converted the light-well into a dreary brown chimney nine storeys high, and the courtyard into its equally dreary hearth, and rendered it impossible for any of the upper floors to obtain much light or much fresh air.

Thus as soon as possible after Caesar left, Aurelia sent for her carpenter and told him to tear down every screen.

He stared at her as if she had gone mad.

"What's the matter?" she asked, bewildered.

"*Domina,* you'll be knee-deep in shit and piss inside three days," he said, "not to mention anything else they want to toss out, from the dead dog to the dead granny to the girl-babies."

She felt a tide of red suffuse her face until even her ears were on fire. It wasn't the unvarnished truth of the carpenter's statement mortified her, but her own naïveté. Fool, fool, fool! Why hadn't she thought of that? Because, she answered herself, a lifetime of passing the doorways and staircases of apartment buildings could not give one who had always lived in a large private dwelling the remotest idea of what went on inside. Her Uncle Cotta would not have divined the purpose of that wooden screen any quicker than she had.

She pressed her hands to her glowing cheeks and gave the carpenter such an adorable look of confused amusement that he dreamed of her for almost a year, called round regularly to see how things were, and improved the standard of his work by at least 100 percent.

"Thank you!" she said to him fervently.

The departure of the revolting Epaphroditus did give her the opportunity to start making a garden in the courtyard, however, and then the new tenant, Gaius Matius, revealed that he too had a passion for gardening.

"Let me help!" he pleaded.

It was difficult to say no when she had spent so long searching for these ideal tenants. "Of course you can help."

Which led to yet another lesson. Through Gaius Matius, Aurelia learned that it was one thing to dream of making a wonderful garden, but quite another to actually do it. For she herself didn't have the eye or the art, whereas Gaius Matius did. In fact, he had a genius for gardening. Once the Caesar bathwater had gurgled down into the sewers, but now it was ducted to a small cistern in the courtyard, and fed the plants Gaius Matius produced with bewildering rapidity—purloined, he informed Aurelia, from his father's Quirinal mansion in the main, but also from anyone else who owned a likely bush or vine or tree or ground cover. He knew how to graft a weakly plant onto strong rootstock of the same kind; he knew which plants liked a little lime, which Rome's naturally acidic soil; he knew the correct times of the year for sowing seed, bedding out, pruning. Within twelve months the courtyard—all thirty feet by thirty feet of it—was a bower, and creepers were wending their way steadily up lattices on the columns toward the patch of sky high above.

Then one day Shimon the Jewish scribe came to see her, looking very strange to her Roman eyes in his long beard and with his long ringlets of hair curling around his little skullcap.

"*Domina* Aurelia, the fourth floor has a very special favor to ask of you," he said.

"If I can grant it, Shimon, be sure I will," she said gravely.

"We will understand if you decline, for what we ask is an invasion of your privacy," said Shimon, picking his phrases with a delicacy he usually reserved for his work. "But—if we pledge you our word that we will never abuse the privilege by tossing refuse or ordure—might we remove the wooden screens from around our light-well balcony? We could breathe better air, and look down on your beautiful garden."

Aurelia beamed. "I'm very happy to grant you this favor," she said. "However, I can't condone the use of the windows onto the street for disposing of refuse and ordure, either. You must promise me that all your wastes will be carried across the road to the public latrine, and tipped into the sewer."

Delighted, Shimon promised.

Down came the screens around the light-well balcony on the fourth floor, though Gaius Matius begged that they be retained where they covered the columns, so that his creepers could continue to grow upward. The Jewish floor started a fashion; the inventor and the spice merchant on the first floor just above asked next if they could take away their screens, and then the third floor asked, and the sixth, and the second, and the fifth, until finally only the freedman warrens of the two top floors were screened in.

In the spring before the battle of Aquae Sextiae, Caesar made a hurried trip across the Alps bearing dispatches for Rome, and his brief visit resulted in a second pregnancy for Aurelia, who bore a second girl the following February, again in her own home, again attended by no one save the local midwife and Cardixa. This time she was alerted to her lack of milk, and the second little Julia—who was to suffer all her life under the babyish sobriquet of "Ju-Ju"—was put immediately onto the breasts of a dozen lactating mothers scattered through the various floors of the insula.

"That's good," said Caesar in response to her letter telling him of Ju-Ju's birth, "we've got the two traditional Julian girls over and done with. The next set of dispatches I bring for the Senate, we'll start on the Julian boys."

Which was much what her mother, Rutilia, had said, thinking to offer Aurelia comfort for bearing girls.

"You might have known you were wasting your words," said Cotta, amused.

"Yes, well—!" said Rutilia irritably. "Honestly, Marcus Aurelius, that girl of mine baffles me! When I tried to cheer her up, all she did was raise her brows and remark that it was a matter of complete indifference to her which sex her babies were, as long as she had good babies."

"But that's a wonderful attitude!" protested Cotta. "As those of us who can afford to feed the little things gave up exposing girl-babies at birth a good four or five hundred years ago, it's better that a mother welcomes her girls, surely."

"Of course it is! It's the only attitude!" snapped Rutilia. "No, it's not her composure I'm complaining about, it's that maddening way she has of making you feel a fool for stating the obvious!"

"I love her," chuckled Publius Rutilius Rufus, party to this exchange.

"You would!" said Rutilia.

"Is it a nice little girl-baby?" Rutilius asked.

"Exquisite, what else could you expect? That pair couldn't have an ugly baby if they stood on their heads to make it," said the goaded Rutilia.

"Now, now, who's supposed to be a proper Roman noblewoman?" Cotta chided, winking at Rutilius Rufus.

"I hope your teeth fall out!" said Rutilia, and pitched her cushions at them.

Shortly after the birth of Ju-Ju, Aurelia was obliged to deal with the crossroads tavern at last. It was a task she had avoided, for though it was housed in her insula, she could collect no rent, as it was regarded as the meeting place of a religious brotherhood; while it didn't have temple or *aedes* status, it was nonetheless "official," and registered on the urban praetor's books.

But it was a nuisance. Activity around it and in it never seemed to abate, even during the night, and some of its frequenters were very quick to push people off the sidewalk outside it, yet very slow to clean up the constant accumulation of refuse on that same section of sidewalk.

Cardixa it was who first learned of a blacker aspect to the religious brotherhood of the crossroads tavern. She had been sent to the small shop alongside Aurelia's front door to purchase ointment for Ju-Ju's bottom, and found the proprietor—an old Galatian woman who specialized in medicines and tonics, remedies and panaceas—backed against the wall while two villainous-looking men debated with each other as to which set of jars and bottles they were going to smash first. Thanks to Cardixa, they smashed nothing; Cardixa smashed them instead. After the men had fled, howling imprecations, she got the tale out of the terrified old woman, who had been unable to pay her protection fee.

"Every shop has to pay the crossroads brotherhood a fee to remain open," Cardixa told Aurelia. "They *say* they're providing a service to protect the shopkeepers from robbery and violence, but the only robbery and violence the shopkeepers suffer is at their hands when the protection fee isn't paid. Poor old Galatia buried her husband not long ago, as you know, *dominilla,* and she buried him very well. So she doesn't have any money at the moment."

"That settles it!" said Aurelia, girding herself for war. "Come on, Cardixa, we'll soon fix this."

Out her front door she marched, down past her shops on the

Vicus Patricii, stopping at each one to force its proprietor into telling her about the brotherhood's protection fees. From some she discovered that the brotherhood's business extended far beyond her own insula's shops, and so she ended in walking the entire neighborhood, unraveling an amazing tale of blatant extortion. Even the two women who ran the public latrine on the opposite side of the Subura Minor—under contract to the firm which held the contract from the State—were forced to pay the brotherhood a percentage of the money they received from patrons well off enough to afford a sponge on a stick to clean themselves after defaecating; when the brotherhood discovered that the two women also ran a service collecting chamber pots from various apartments for emptying and cleaning, and had not revealed this, every chamber pot was broken, and the women were obliged to buy new ones. The baths next door to the public latrine were privately owned—as were all baths in Rome—but did a lucrative trade nonetheless. Here too the brotherhood levied fees which assured that the customers were not held under the water until they nearly drowned.

By the time Aurelia finished her investigation, she was so angry she thought it wise to go home and calm down before confronting the brotherhood in their lair.

"Out of my house!" she said to Cardixa. "*My* house!"

"Don't you worry, Aurelia, we'll give them their comeuppance," Cardixa comforted.

"Where's Ju-Ju?" asked Aurelia, taking deep breaths.

"Upstairs on the fourth floor. It's Rebeccah's turn to give her a drink this morning."

Aurelia wrung her hands. "Why can't I seem to make milk? I'm as dry as a crone!"

Cardixa shrugged. "Some women make milk; others don't. No one knows why. Now don't get down in the dumps—it's this brotherhood business that's really upsetting you. No one minds giving Ju-Ju a drink, you know that. I'll send one of the servants upstairs to ask Rebeccah to keep Ju-Ju for a little while, and we'll go down and sort these wretches out."

Aurelia rose to her feet. "Come on, then, let's get it over and done with."

The interior of the tavern was very dim; Aurelia stood in the doorway outlined in light, at the peak of a beauty which lasted all of her life. The din inside subsided at once, but began again angrily when Cardixa loomed behind her mistress.

"That's the great elephant beat us up this morning!" said a voice out of the gloom.

Benches scraped. Aurelia marched in and stood looking about, Cardixa hovering watchfully at her back.

"Who's responsible for you louts?" Aurelia demanded.

Up he got from a table in one back corner, a skinny little man in his forties with an unmistakably Roman look to him. "That's me," he said, coming forward. "Lucius Decumius, at your service."

"Do you know who I am?" asked Aurelia.

He nodded.

"You are tenanting—rent-free!—premises which I own," she said.

"You don't own this here premises, madam," said Lucius Decumius, "the State do."

"The State does not," she said, and gazed about her now that her eyes were getting used to the poor light. "This place is a downright disgrace. You don't look after it at all. I am evicting you."

A collective gasp went up. Lucius Decumius narrowed his eyes and looked alert.

"You can't evict us," he said.

"Just watch me!"

"I'll complain to the urban praetor."

"Do, by all means! He's my cousin."

"Then there's the Pontifex Maximus."

"So there is. He's my cousin too."

Lucius Decumius snorted, a sound which might have been contempt—or laughter. "They can't *all* be your cousins!"

"They can, and they are." Aurelia's formidable jaw jutted forward. "Make no mistake, Lucius Decumius, you and your dirty ruffians are going."

He stood gazing at her reflectively, one hand scratching his chin, what could have been a smile lurking at the back of his clear grey eyes; then he stepped aside and bowed toward the table where he had been sitting. "How about we discuss our little problem?" he asked, smooth as Scaurus.

"There's nothing to discuss," said Aurelia. "You're going."

"Pooh! There's always room for discussion. Come on, now, madam, let's you and me sit down," wheedled Lucius Decumius.

And Aurelia found that an awful thing was happening to her; she was starting to *like* Lucius Decumius! Which was manifestly ridiculous. Yet a fact, nonetheless.

"All right," she said. "Cardixa, stand behind my chair."

Lucius Decumius produced the chair, and sat himself on a bench. "A drop of wine, madam?"

"Certainly not."

"Oh."

"Well?"

"Well what?" asked Lucius Decumius.

"It's you wanted to discuss things," she pointed out.

"S'right, so it was." Lucius Decumius cleared his throat. "Now what precisely was you objecting to, madam?"

"Your presence under my roof."

"Now, now, that's a bit broad in scope, ain't it? I mean, we can come to some sort of arrangement—you tell me what you don't like, and I'll see if I can't fix it," said Decumius.

"The dilapidation. The filth. The noise. The assumption that you own the street as well as these premises, when neither is the truth," Aurelia began, ticking her points off on her fingers. "*And* your little neighborhood business! Terrorizing harmless shop-keepers into paying you money they can't afford! What a despicable thing to do!"

"The world, madam," said Decumius, leaning forward with great earnestness, "is divided into sheep and wolves. It's natural. If it weren't natural, there wouldn't be a lot more sheep than there are wolves, where we all know for every wolf there's at least a thousand sheep. Think of us inside here as the local wolves. We're not bad as wolves go. Only little teeth, a bite or two, no necks broken."

"That is a revolting metaphor," said Aurelia, "and it doesn't sway me one little bit. Out you go."

"Oh, deary me!" said Lucius Decumius, leaning backward. "Deary, deary me." He shot her a look. "Are they *really* all your cousins?"

"My father was the consul Lucius Aurelius Cotta. My uncle is the consul Publius Rutilius Rufus. My other uncle is the praetor Marcus Aurelius Cotta. My husband is the quaestor Gaius Julius Caesar." Aurelia sat back in her chair, lifted her head a little, closed her eyes, and said smugly, "And what is more, Gaius Marius is my brother-in-law."

"Well, *my* brother-in-law is the King of Egypt, ha ha!" said Lucius Decumius, supersaturated with names.

"Then I suggest you go home to Egypt," said Aurelia, not a bit annoyed at this feeble sarcasm. "The consul Gaius Marius *is* my brother-in-law."

"Oh, yes, and of course Gaius Marius's sister-in-law is going to be living in an insula way up the Subura's arse-end!" countered Lucius Decumius.

"This insula is *mine*. It's my dowry, Lucius Decumius. My husband is a younger son, so we live here in my insula for the time being. Later on, we'll be living elsewhere."

"Gaius Marius really is your brother-in-law?"

"Down to the last hair in his eyebrows."

Lucius Decumius heaved a sigh. "I like it here," he said, "so we'd better do some negotiating."

"I want you out," said Aurelia.

"Now look, madam, I do have *some* right on my side," said Lucius Decumius. "The members of this here lodge are the custodians of the crossroads shrine. Legitimate, like. You may think all them cousins means you own the State—but if we go, another lot are only going to move in, right? It's a crossroads college, madam, official on the urban praetor's books. And I'll let you in on a little secret." He leaned forward again. "*All* of us crossroads brethren are wolves!" He thrust his neck out, rather like a tortoise. "Now you and me can come to an agreement, madam. We keep this place clean, we slap a bit of paint on the walls, we tippy-toe around after dark, we help old ladies across the drains and gutters, we cease and desist our little neighborhood operation—in fact, we turn into pillars of society! How does that take your fancy?"

Try though she might to suppress it, that smile would tug at the corners of her mouth! "Better the evil I know, eh, Lucius Decumius?"

"*Much* better!" he said warmly.

"I can't say I'd look forward to going through all of this again with a different lot of you," she said. "Very well, Lucius Decumius, you're on trial for six months." She got up and went to the door, Lucius Decumius escorting her. "But don't think for one moment that I lack the courage to get rid of you and break in a new lot," she said, stepping into the street.

Lucius Decumius walked with her down the Vicus Patricii, clearing a path for her through the crowds with magical ease. "I assure you, madam, we will be pillars of society."

"But it's very difficult to do without an income after you've grown used to spending it," said Aurelia.

"Oh, that's no worry, madam!" said Lucius Decumius cheerfully. "Rome's a big place. We'll just shift our income-making operation far enough away not to annoy you—the Viminal—the Agger—the factory swamps—plenty of places. Don't you worry your lovely little head about Lucius Decumius and his brothers of the sacred crossroads. We'll be all right."

"That's no kind of answer!" said Aurelia. "What's the difference between terrorizing our own neighborhood, and doing the same thing somewhere else?"

"What the eye don't see and the ear don't hear, the heart don't grieve about," he said, genuinely surprised at her denseness. "That's a fact, madam."

They had reached her front door. She stopped and looked at him ruefully. "I daresay you'll do as you see fit, Lucius Decumius.

But don't ever let me find out whereabouts you've transferred your—operation, as you call it."

"Mum, madam, I swear! Mum, dumb, numb!" He reached past her to knock on her door, which was opened with suspicious alacrity by the steward himself. "Ah, Eutychus, haven't seen you in the brotherhood for a few days now," said Lucius Decimius blandly. "Next time madam gives you a holiday, I'll expect to see you in the lodge. We're going to wash the place out and give it a bit of a paint to please madam. Got to keep the sister-in-law of Gaius Marius happy, eh?"

Eutychus looked thoroughly miserable. "Indeed," he said.

"Oho, holding out on us, were you? Why didn't you tell us who madam was?" asked Lucius Decimius in tones of silk.

"As you will have noticed over the years, Lucius Decimius, I do *not* talk about my family at all," said Eutychus grandly.

"Wretched Greeks, they're all the same," said Lucius Decimius, giving his lank brown hair a tug in Aurelia's direction. "Good day to you, madam. Very nice to make your acquaintance. Anything the lodge can do to help, let me know."

When the door had closed behind her, Aurelia looked at the steward expressionlessly. "And what have you got to say for yourself?" she asked.

"*Domina*, I *have* to belong!" he wailed. "I'm the steward of the landlords—they wouldn't *not* let me belong!"

"You realize, Eutychus, that I could have you flogged for this," said Aurelia, still expressionless.

"Yes," he whispered.

"A flogging is the established punishment, is it not?"

"Yes," he whispered.

"Then it is well for you that I am my husband's wife and my father's daughter," said Aurelia. "My father-in-law, Gaius Julius, put it best, I think. Shortly before he died he said that he could never understand how any family could live in the same house with people they flogged, be it their sons or their slaves. However, there are other ways of dealing with disloyalty and insolence. Never think I am not prepared to take the financial loss of selling you with bad references. And you know what that would mean. Instead of a price of ten thousand denarii on your head, it would be a thousand sesterces. And your new owner would be so vulgarly low he'd flog you unmercifully, for you would come to him tagged as a bad slave."

"I understand, *domina.*"

"Good! Go on belonging to the crossroads brotherhood—I can appreciate your predicament. I also commend you for your discretion about us." She went to move away, then stopped. "Lucius Decumius. Does he have a job?"

"He's the lodge caretaker," said Eutychus, looking more uneasy than ever.

"You're keeping something back."

"No, no!"

"Come on, give me all of it!"

"Well, *domina,* it's only a rumor," said Eutychus. "No one really *knows,* you understand. But he has been heard to say it himself—though that could be idle boasting. Or he could be saying it to frighten us."

"Saying *what*?"

The steward blanched. "He says he's an assassin."

"*Ecastor!* And who has he assassinated?" she asked.

"I believe he takes credit for that Numidian fellow who was stabbed in the Forum Romanum some years ago," said Eutychus.

"Will wonders never cease!" said Aurelia, and went off to see what her babies were doing.

"They broke the mould when they made her," said Eutychus to Cardixa.

The huge Gallic maidservant put out a hand and hurled it down on the pretty steward's shoulder much as a cat might have tethered a mouse by putting a paw on its tail. "They did indeed," she said, giving Eutychus an ostensibly friendly shake. "That's why we've *all* got to look after her."

It was not so very long after this that Gaius Julius Caesar came home from Italian Gaul bearing Marius's message from Vercellae.

He simply knocked on the door and was admitted by the steward, who then helped Caesar's orderly in with his baggage while Caesar went to find his wife.

She was in the courtyard garden tying little gauze bags around the ripening grapes on Gaius Matius's arbor, and didn't bother to turn when she heard a footfall. "You wouldn't think the Subura was so full of birds, would you?" she asked whoever it was. "But this year I'm determined we'll get to eat the grapes, so I'm going to see if this works."

"I'll look forward to the grapes," said Caesar.

She spun round, her handful of gauze bags fluttering to the ground, her face transformed with joy. "Gaius Julius!"

He held out his arms, she ran into them. Never had a kiss been more loving, nor followed so quickly by a dozen more. The sound of applause brought them back to reality; Caesar looked up the height of the light-well to find the railings of the balconies lined with beaming people, and waved up to them.

"A great victory!" he called. "Gaius Marius has annihilated the Germans! Rome need never fear them again!"

Leaving the tenants to rejoice and spread the news through the Subura before either Senate or People were informed, Caesar slipped an arm about Aurelia's shoulders and walked with her into the narrow hallway which ran between the reception room and the kitchen area; he turned in the direction of his study, approving of the neatness, the cleanliness, the tasteful yet inexpensive decor. There were vases of flowers everywhere, a new side to Aurelia's housekeeping, he thought, and wondered anxiously if she could afford so many blooms.

"I have to see Marcus Aemilius Scaurus right away," he said, "but I wasn't going to go to his house before I visited mine. How good it is to be home!"

"It's wonderful," said Aurelia shakily.

"It will be more wonderful still tonight, wife, when you and I start making our first boy," he said, kissing her again. "Oh, I do miss you! No other woman has any appeal after you, and that's the truth. Is there any chance of a bath?"

"I saw Cardixa duck in there a moment ago, so I expect it's being run for you already." Aurelia snuggled against him with a sigh of pleasure.

"And you're sure it isn't too much for you, running our house, looking after our girls, and this whole barn of a place?" he asked. "I know you always tell me the agents took more commission than they should, but—"

"It is no trouble, Gaius Julius. This is a very orderly residence, and our tenants are superior," she said firmly. "I've even sorted out the little difficulty I had with the crossroads tavern, so that's very quiet and clean these days." She laughed up at him, passing it off casually, lightly. "You've no idea how co-operative and well behaved everyone is when they find out I'm Gaius Marius's sister-in-law!"

"All these flowers!" said Caesar.

"Aren't they beautiful? They're a perpetual gift I receive every four or five days."

His arms tightened about her. "Do I have a rival, then?"

"I don't think you'll be worried after you meet him," said Aurelia. "His name is Lucius Decumius. He's an assassin."

"A *what*?"

"No, dearest love, I'm only joking," she soothed. "He says he's an assassin, I suspect to maintain his ascendancy over his fellow brethren. He's the caretaker of the tavern."

"Where does he get the flowers?"

She laughed softly. "Never look a gift horse in the mouth," she said. "In the Subura, things are different."

 It was Publius Rutilius Rufus who apprised Gaius Marius of events in Rome immediately after Caesar delivered the victory letter.

There's a very nasty feeling in the air, arising chiefly out of the fact that you've succeeded in what you set out to do, namely eliminate the Germans, and the People are so grateful that if you stand for the consulship, you'll get in yet again. The word on every highborn lip is "dictator" and the First Class at least is starting to sit up and echo it. Yes, I know you have many important knight clients and friends in the First Class, but you must understand that the whole of Rome's political and traditional structure is designed to depress the pretensions of men who stand above their peers. The only permissible "first" is the first among equals, but after five consulships, three of them *in absentia,* it is getting extremely difficult to disguise the fact that you tower over your so-called equals. Scaurus is disgusted, but him you could deal with if you had to. No, the real turd in the bottom of the punch bowl is your friend and mine, Piggle-wiggle, ably assisted by his stammering son, the Piglet.

From the moment you moved east of the Alps to join Catulus Caesar in Italian Gaul, Piggle-wiggle and the Piglet have made it their business to blow Catulus Caesar's contributions to the campaign against the Cimbri out of all proportion to the fact. So when the news of the victory at Vercellae came, and the House met in the temple of Bellona to debate things like triumphs and votes of thanksgiving, there were a lot of ears ready to listen when Piggle-wiggle got up to speak.

Briefly, he moved that only two triumphs be held— one by you, for Aquae Sextiae, and one by Catulus Caesar, for Vercellae! Completely ignoring the fact that you were the commander on the field of Vercellae, *not* Catulus Caesar! His argument is purely legalistic— two armies were involved, one commanded by the consul, you, and the other by the proconsul, Catulus Caesar. The amount of spoils involved, said Pigglewiggle, was disappointingly small, and would look ridiculously inadequate were three triumphs to be celebrated. Therefore, since you hadn't yet celebrated the triumph voted you for Aquae Sextiae, why, you could have that, and Catulus Caesar could have the triumph he was entitled to for Vercellae. A second Vercellae triumph celebrated by you would be a superfluity.

Lucius Appuleius Saturninus got up at once to object, and was howled down. Since he is a *privatus* this year, he holds no office that might have compelled the Conscript Fathers to pay him more attention. The House voted two triumphs, yours to be solely for Aquae Sextiae—last year's battle, therefore less significant—and Vercellae—this year's battle, therefore the big one in everybody's eyes—solely the prerogative of Catulus Caesar. In effect, as the Vercellae triumph wends its way through the city, it will be telling the people that you had absolutely nothing to do with the defeat of the Cimbri in Italian Gaul, that Catulus Caesar was the hero. Your own idiocy in handing him most of the spoils and all the German standards captured on the field has clinched the matter. When your mood is expansive and your natural generosity is allowed to come to the fore, you commit your worst blunders, and that is the truth.

I don't know what you can do about it—the whole thing is cut and dried, officially voted upon, and recorded in the archives. I am very angry about it, but the Policy Makers (as Saturninus calls them) or the *boni* (as Scaurus calls them) have won the engagement resoundingly, and you will never quite have as much prestige for the defeat of the Germans as you ought. It amused us all those years ago at Numantia to perpetuate the mud bath Metellus took among his porky friends by tagging him with a porky nickname that also happens to be nursery slang for a little girl's genitalia, but it is my considered opinion now that the man is no piggle-wiggle—he's a full-grown *cunnus*. As for the Piglet, he's not going to be a little girl all his life, either. Another full-grown *cunnus*.

Enough, enough, I'll give myself that apoplexy yet! I shall conclude this missive by telling you that Sicily is looking good. Manius Aquillius is doing a superb job, which only makes Servilius the Augur look smaller. However, he did what he promised: he indicted Lucullus in the new treason court. Lucullus insisted upon conducting his own defense, and did his cause no good with all those farting blow-my-nose-between-my-fingers knights, for he stood there with all that freezing hauteur of his showing, and the entire jury thought he was directing it at them. He was, he was! Another stubborn idiot, Lucullus. Naturally they condemned him—*DAMNO* written upon every tile, I believe. And the savagery of the sentence was unbelievable! His place of exile can be no closer to Rome than a thousand miles, which leaves him only two places of any size at all—Antioch or Alexandria. He has chosen to honor King Ptolemy Alexander over King Antiochus Grypus. And the court took everything he owned off him—houses, lands, investments, city property.

He didn't wait for them to hound him to leave. In fact, he didn't even wait to see how much his possessions fetched, but commended his trollop of a wife to the care of her brother, Piggle-wiggle—that'll punish him a little!—and left his elder son, now sixteen and a man in the eyes of the State, to his own devices. Interesting, that he didn't commend this very gifted boy to Piggle-wiggle's care, isn't it? The younger—now fourteen—is adopted. Marcus Terentius Varro Lucullus.

Scaurus was telling me that both boys have vowed

to prosecute Servilius the Augur as soon as Varro Lucullus is old enough to don the toga of manhood; the parting with their father was heartrending, as you might imagine. Scaurus says Lucullus will get himself to Alexandria, and then choose to die. And that both boys think that's what their *tata* will do too. What hurts the Licinii Luculli most is the fact that all this pain and poverty has been inflicted upon them by a jumped-up nobody New Man like Servilius the Augur. You New Men have not made yourselves any friends when it comes to Lucullus's sons.

Anyway, when the Lucullus boys are old enough to prosecute Servilius the Augur in tandem, it will be in the new extortion court as set up by yet another Servilius of relatively obscure origins, Gaius Servilius Glaucia. By Pollux, Gaius Marius, he can draft laws, that fellow! The setup is ironclad and novel, but it works. Back in the hands of the knights and so no consolation to governors, but workmanlike. Recovery of peculated property is now extended to the ultimate recipients as well as the original thieves—anyone convicted in the court cannot address any public meeting anywhere— men of the Latin Rights who successfully prosecute a malefactor will be rewarded with the full Roman citizenship—and there is now a recess inserted into the middle of the trial proceedings. The old procedure is a thing of the past, and the testimony of witnesses, as the few cases heard in it have proven, is now far less important than the addresses of the advocates themselves. A great boon to the great advocates.

And—last but not least—that peculiar fellow Saturninus has been in trouble again. Truly, Gaius Marius, I fear for his sanity. Logic is missing. As indeed I believe it is from his friend Glaucia. Both so brilliant, and yet—so unstable, so downright crazy. Or perhaps it is that they don't honestly know what they want out of public life. Even the worst demagogue has a pattern, a logic directed toward the praetorship and the consulship. But I don't see it in either of that pair. They hate the old style of government, they hate the Senate—but they have nothing to put in its place. Perhaps they're what the Greeks call exponents of anarchy? I'm not sure.

Anyway, the scales have recently tipped against King Nicomedes of Bithynia in the matter of the embassage from King Mithridates of Pontus. Our young friend from the remotenesses at the eastern end of the Euxine sent ambassadors acute enough to discover the secret weakness of all us Romans—money! Having got nowhere with their petition for a treaty of friendship and alliance, they began to buy senators. And they paid well, and Nicomedes had cause to worry, I can tell you.

Then Saturninus got up on the rostra and condemned all those in the Senate who were prepared to abandon Nicomedes and Bithynia in favor of Mithridates and Pontus. We had had a treaty with Bithynia for years, he said, and Pontus was Bithynia's traditional enemy. Money had changed hands, he said, and Rome for the sake of a few fatter senatorial purses was going to abandon her friend and ally of fifty years.

It is alleged—I wasn't there myself to hear him—that he said something like "We all know how expensive it can be for doddering old senators to marry frisky little fillies not out of the schoolroom, don't we? I mean, pearl necklaces and gold bracelets are a lot more expensive than a bottle of that tonic Ticinus sells in his Cuppedenis stall—and who's to say that a frisky young filly isn't a more effective tonic than Ticinus's?" Oh, oh, oh! He sneered at Piggle-wiggle as well, and asked the crowd, "What about our boys in Italian Gaul?"

The result was that several of the Pontic ambassadors were beaten up, and went to the Senaculum to complain. Whereupon Scaurus and Piggle-wiggle had Saturninus arraigned in his own treason court on a charge of sowing discord between Rome and an accredited embassage from a foreign monarch. On the day of the trial, our tribune of the plebs Glaucia called a meeting of the Plebeian Assembly, and accused Piggle-wiggle of having another try at getting rid of Saturninus, whom he hadn't been able to get rid of when he functioned as censor. And those hired gladiators Saturninus seems to be able to put his hands on when necessary turned up at the trial, ringed the jurors round, and looked so grim that the jury dismissed the case. The Pontic ambassadors promptly went home without their treaty. I agree with Saturninus—it would be a wretchedly paltry thing to do, to abandon our friend and ally of fifty years in favor of his traditional enemy just because his enemy is now far richer and more powerful.

No more, no more, Gaius Marius! I really only wanted to let you know about the triumphs ahead of the official dispatches, which the Senate won't rush to you in a hurry. I wish there was something you could do, but I doubt it.

"Oh yes, there is!" said Marius grimly when he had deciphered the letter. He drew a sheet of paper toward him and spent considerable time drafting a short letter of his own. Then he sent for Quintus Lutatius Catulus Caesar.

Catulus Caesar arrived bubbling with enthusiasm, for the hired courier who had carried Rutilius Rufus's Marius missive had also brought a letter from Metellus Numidicus to Catulus Caesar, and another from Scaurus to Catulus Caesar.

It was a disappointment to find Marius already aware of the two-triumph vote; Catulus Caesar had been dwelling rather voluptuously upon seeing Marius's face when he heard. However, that was a minor consideration. The triumph was the triumph.

"So I'd like to return to Rome in October, if you don't mind," Catulus Caesar drawled. "I'll celebrate my triumph first, since you as consul can't leave quite so early."

"Permission to go is refused," said Marius with cheerful civility. "We'll return to Rome together at the end of November, just as we planned. In fact, I've just sent a letter to the Senate on behalf of both of us. Like to hear it? I won't bore you with my writing—I'll read it out to you."

He took a small paper from his cluttered table, unfurled it, and read it to Catulus Caesar.

Gaius Marius, consul for the fifth time, thanks the Senate and People of Rome for their concern and consideration in respect of the matter of triumphs for himself and his second-in-command, the proconsul Quintus Lutatius Catulus. I commend the Conscript Fathers for their admirable thrift in decreeing only one triumph each for Rome's generals. However, I am even more concerned than the Conscript Fathers about the punitive cost of this long war. As is Quintus Lutatius. In respect of which, Gaius Marius and Quintus Lutatius Catulus will share one single triumph between them. Let all of Rome witness the accord and amity of the generals as they parade the streets together. Wherefore it is my pleasure to notify you that Gaius Marius and Quintus Lutatius Catulus shall triumph on the Kalends of December. Together. Long live Rome.

Catulus Caesar had gone white. "You're joking!" he said.

"*I?* Joke?" Marius blinked beneath his brows. "Never, Quintus Lutatius!"

"I—I—I refuse to consent!"

"You don't have any choice," said Marius sweetly. "They

thought they had me beaten, didn't they? Dear old Metellus Numidicus Piggle-wiggle and his friends—and your friends! Well, you'll never beat me, any of you."

"The Senate has decreed two triumphs, and two triumphs it will be!" said Catulus Caesar, shaking.

"Oh, you could insist, Quintus Lutatius. But it won't look good, will it? Take your choice. Either you and I triumph together in the same parade, or you are going to look like one enormous fool. That's it."

And that was it. The letter from Marius went to the Senate, and the single triumph was announced for the first day of the month of December.

Catulus Caesar was not slow to take his revenge. He wrote to the Senate complaining that the consul Gaius Marius had usurped the prerogatives of the Senate and People of Rome by awarding the full citizenship to a thousand auxiliary soldiers from Camerinum in Picenum right there on the field of Vercellae. He had also exceeded his consular authority, said Catulus Caesar, by announcing that he was founding a colony of Roman veteran legionaries at the small town of Eporedia in Italian Gaul. The letter went on:

> Gaius Marius has established this unconstitutional colony in order to lay his hands upon the alluvial gold which is mined from the bed of the Duria Major at Eporedia. The proconsul Quintus Lutatius Catulus also wishes to point out that *he* won the battle of Vercellae, not Gaius Marius. As proof positive, he tenders thirty-five captured German standards in his keeping, as against a mere two in the keeping of Gaius Marius. As the victor of Vercellae, I claim all the captives taken to be sold into slavery. Gaius Marius is insisting upon taking one third of them.

In answer, Marius circulated Catulus Caesar's letter among the troops of his own army and Catulus Caesar's; it had a laconic appendix from Marius himself attached, to the effect that the proceeds from the sale of Cimbric captives taken after Vercellae to the limit of the one third he had claimed for himself were to be donated to the army of Quintus Lutatius Catulus. His own army, he pointed out, had already been given the proceeds from the sale of the Teutonic slaves after Aquae Sextiae, and he didn't wish Catulus Caesar's army to feel entirely neglected, for he understood that Quintus Lutatius would—as was his right—be keeping the proceeds from the sale of his two thirds of the Cimbric slaves for himself.

Glaucia read out both letters in the Forum in Rome, and the People laughed themselves sick. There could be no doubt in anyone's mind who was the real victor, and who cared more for his troops than for himself.

"You'll have to stop this campaign to vilify Gaius Marius," said Scaurus Princeps Senatus to Metellus Numidicus, "or you're going to be slapped about again the next time you go into the Forum. And you'd better write to Quintus Lutatius and tell him the same. Whether we like it or not, Gaius Marius is the First Man in Rome. *He* won the war against the Germans, and the whole of Rome knows it. He's the popular hero, the popular demigod. Try to bring him down, and the city will unite to bring you down, Quintus Caecilius."

"Piss on the People!" said Metellus Numidicus, who was feeling the strain of having to house his sister, Metella Calva, and whichever lowborn lover she fancied.

"Look, there are other things we can do," urged Scaurus. "For one thing, you can run for consul again. It's ten years since you were consul, believe it or not! Gaius Marius will be running again, nothing surer. Wouldn't it be wonderful to saddle his sixth consulship with an inimical colleague like yourself?"

"Oh, when are we going to rid ourselves of this incurable disease called Gaius Marius?" cried Numidicus in despair.

"Hopefully it won't be long," said Scaurus, obviously not despairing. "A year. I doubt it will be more."

"Never, more like."

"No, no, Quintus Caecilius, you give up too easily! Like Quintus Lutatius, you let your hatred for Gaius Marius rule your head. *Think!* How much time during all his five eternal consulships has Gaius Marius actually spent in Rome herself?"

"A matter of days. What's that to the point?"

"It is the *whole* point, Quintus Caecilius! Gaius Marius is not a great politician, though I do admit he's got a wonderfully sharp brain between his ears. Where Gaius Marius shines is as a soldier and an organizer. I assure you, he's not going to thrive in the Comitia and the Curia when his world shrinks down to nothing else. We won't *let* him thrive! We'll bait him like a bull, we'll fasten our teeth in his carcass and we won't let go. And we'll bring him down. You wait and see." Scaurus sounded supremely sure.

Staring at these welcome vistas Scaurus was opening up, Metellus Numidicus smiled. "Yes, I understand, Marcus Aemilius. Very well, I'll stand for consul."

"Good! You'll get in—you can't not get in after we bring every ounce of influence we have to bear on the First and Second Classes, no matter how much they love Gaius Marius."

"Oh, I can't wait to be his colleague!" Metellus Numidicus drew out his muscles in a secretive stretch. "I'll block him every way I can! His life will be a misery."

"I suspect we'll have help from an unexpected quarter too," said Scaurus, looking like a cat.

"What quarter?"

"Lucius Appuleius Saturninus is going to run for another term as a tribune of the plebs."

"That's ghastly news! How can it help us?" Numidicus asked.

"No, it's excellent news, Quintus Caecilius, believe me. For when you sink your consular teeth into Gaius Marius's rump, and so do I, and Quintus Lutatius, and half a hundred more, Gaius Marius won't resist enlisting Saturninus to help him. I know Gaius Marius. He can be tried too far, and when that happens, he'll lash out wildly in every direction. Just like a baited bull. He won't be able to resist using Saturninus. And I think Saturninus is probably the worst tool a Gaius Marius could put his hands on.

You wait and see!" Scaurus said. "It's his allies will bring our bull Gaius Marius down."

The tool was on his way to Italian Gaul to see Gaius Marius, more anxious to form an alliance with Marius than Marius was with him at that stage; for Saturninus was living in the Roman political arena, whereas Marius was still living in a military commander's Elysium.

They met in the little resort town of Comum on the shores of Lake Larius, where Gaius Marius had hired a villa belonging to the late Lucius Calpurnius Piso, the same who had died with Lucius Cassius at Burdigala. For Marius was more tired than he would ever have admitted to Catulus Caesar, nearly ten years his junior; he packed Catulus Caesar off to the far end of the province to hear the assizes, and packed himself off very quietly to enjoy a vacation, leaving Sulla in command.

Naturally when Saturninus turned up, Marius invited him to stay; the two men settled down in welcome leisure to have their talks against the background of a lake far lovelier than any in Italy proper.

Not that Marius had grown more convoluted; when the time came to broach the subject, he attacked it straight on. "I don't want Metellus Numidicus for my consular colleague next year," he said abruptly. "I've got Lucius Valerius Flaccus in mind. He's a malleable man."

"He'd suit you well," said Saturninus, "but you won't pull it off, I'm afraid. The Policy Makers are already canvassing support for Metellus Numidicus." He looked at Marius curiously. "Anyway, why are you running for a sixth term? Surely with the Germans defeated, you can rest on your laurels."

"I only wish I could, Lucius Appuleius. But the job is not finished just because the Germans are defeated. I have two Head Count armies to discharge—or rather, I have one of six overstrength legions, and Quintus Lutatius has one of six very understrength legions. But I regard both armies as my responsibility, because Quintus Lutatius thinks he can just issue them with their discharge papers and forget about them."

"You're still determined to give them land, aren't you?" asked Saturninus.

"I am. If I don't, Lucius Appuleius, Rome will be the poorer in many ways. First off, because over fifty thousand veteran legionaries are going to descend upon Rome and Italy with a bit of money jingling in their purses. They'll spend the lot in a few days, and then turn into a perpetual source of trouble wherever they live. If there's a war, they'll re-enlist. But if there's no war on, they're going to be a real nuisance," said Marius.

Saturninus inclined his head. "I can see that."

"I got the idea when I was in Africa, and that's why I had the African islands reserved for veterans to settle in. Tiberius Gracchus wanted to resettle Rome's poor on the land in Campania to make the city more comfortable and safer, and to put some new blood onto the land. But Italy was a mistake, Lucius Appuleius," Marius said dreamily. "We need Romans of humble sort in our provinces. Especially veteran soldiers."

The view was so beautiful, but Saturninus didn't see it. "Well, we all heard the speech about bringing Rome's way of life to the provinces," he said. "*And* we all heard Dalmaticus's reply. But that's not your real object, is it, Gaius Marius?"

The eyes flashed beneath the eyebrows. "How very acute of you! Of course it's not!" He leaned forward in his chair. "It costs Rome a great deal of money to send armies to the provinces to put down rebellions and police the laws. Look at Macedonia. Two legions on permanent duty there—not Roman legions, admittedly, but they still cost the State money it could put to better use elsewhere. Now what if twenty or thirty thousand Roman veterans were settled in three or four colonies across Macedonia? Greece and Macedonia are very empty places these days, have been for a century or more—the people all left. Ghost towns everywhere! And Roman absentee landlords owning enormous properties, producing little, putting nothing back into the country, parsimonious about employing local men and women. And whenever the Scordisci come down across the border, there's war, and the absentee landlords bleat to the Senate, and the governor runs in different directions dealing with marauding Celts on the one hand, and irate letters from Rome on the other. Well, I'd put the land held by Roman absentee landlords to better use. I'd fill it up with veteran soldier colonies. More populous by far—and a ready-made garrison force in case of serious war."

"And you got this idea in Africa," said Saturninus.

"While I was doling out vast tracts to Roman men who will rarely if ever visit Africa. They'll put in overseers and gangs of grain slaves, ignore local conditions and the local people, keep Africa from going ahead, and lay it wide open to another Jugurtha. I don't want Roman ownership of provincial land to stop—I just want some parcels of provincial land to contain large numbers of well-trained professional Romans we can call on in times of need." He forced himself to lie back again, not to betray the urgency of his desire. "There's already been one small example of how veteran colonies in foreign lands can help in times of emergency. My first little lot I settled personally on the island of Meninx heard about the Sicilian slave uprising, organized themselves into units, hired some ships, and reached Lilybaeum just in time to prevent the city's falling to Athenion the slave."

"I do see what you're trying to achieve, Gaius Marius," Saturninus said. "It's an excellent scheme."

"But they'll fight me, if for no other reason than it's me," said Marius with a sigh.

A tiny shiver ran up Saturninus's spine; quickly he turned head and eyes away, pretended to admire the reflection of trees and mountains and sky and clouds in the perfect mirror of the lake. Marius was tired! Marius was slowing down! *Marius was not looking forward to his sixth consulship one little bit!*

"I daresay you witnessed all the squealing and shouting in Rome about my giving the citizenship to those wonderful soldiers from Camerinum?" Marius asked.

"I did. All Italy heard the racket," said Saturninus, "and all Italy liked what you did. Where Rome of the Policy Makers definitely did not."

"Well, and why *shouldn't* they be Roman citizens?" Marius demanded angrily. "They fought better than any other men on the field, Lucius Appuleius, and that's a fact. If I had my way, I'd confer the citizenship on every man in the whole of Italy." He drew a breath. "When I say I want land for the Head Count veterans, I mean just that. Land for the lot of them—Romans, Latins—*and* Italians."

Saturninus whistled. "That's asking for trouble! The Policy Makers will never lie down for it."

"I know. What I don't know is if you've got the courage to stand up for it."

"I've never really taken a good long look at courage," said Saturninus thoughtfully, "so I'm not sure how much of it I own. But yes, Gaius Marius, I think I have the courage to stand up for it."

"I don't need to bribe to secure my own election—I can't lose," Marius said. "However, there's no reason why I can't hire a few fellows to distribute bribes for the post of junior consul. And for you, if you need help, Lucius Appuleius. And for Gaius Servilius Glaucia too. I understand he's going to be running for election as a praetor?"

"He is indeed. And yes, Gaius Marius, we'd both be happy to accept help in getting elected. In return, we'll do whatever is necessary to assist you in getting your land."

Marius drew a roll of paper out of his sleeve. "I've done a little work already—just sketched out the sort of bill I think is necessary. Unfortunately I'm not one of Rome's greatest legal draftsmen. Where you are. But—and I hope you'll not take exception to my saying it—Glaucia is a lawmaking genius. Can the pair of you formulate great laws from my ill-educated scribbles?"

"You help us into office, Gaius Marius, and I assure you we'll give you your laws," said Saturninus.

There could be no mistaking the relief which coursed through

Marius's big fit body; he sagged. "Only let me pull this off, Lucius Appuleius, and I swear I don't care if I'm never consul a seventh time," he said.

"A seventh time?"

"It was prophesied that I would be consul seven times."

Saturninus laughed. "Why not? No one would ever have thought it possible that one man would be consul six times. But you will be."

The elections for the new College of the Tribunes of the Plebs were held as Gaius Marius and Catulus Caesar led their armies south toward Rome and their single joint triumph, and they were hotly contested. There were over thirty candidates for the ten posts, and more than half of that number were creatures in the employ of the Policy Makers, so the campaign was bitter and violent.

Glaucia, president of the current ten tribunes of the plebs, was deputed to hold the elections for the incoming college; had the Centuriate elections for consuls and praetors already been held, he would not have been able to officiate, for his status as praetor-elect would have disqualified him. As it was, nothing prevented his conducting the tribunate elections.

The proceedings took place in the well of the Comitia, with Glaucia presiding from the rostra, and his nine fellow tribunes of the plebs drawing the lots to see which of the thirty-five tribes would vote first through to last, then marshaling each tribe when its turn came to vote.

A lot of money had changed hands, some of it on behalf of Saturninus, but a great deal more on behalf of the anonymous candidates fielded by the Policy Makers. Every rich man on the conservative front benches had dug deep into his cashbox, and votes were bought for men like Quintus Nonius from Picenum, a political nobody of stoutly conservative heart. Though Sulla had had nothing to do with his entering the Senate, nor his standing for the tribunate of the plebs, he was the brother of Sulla's brother-in-law; when Sulla's sister, Cornelia Sulla, had married into the wealthy squirarchical family of Nonius from Picenum, the luster of her name inspired the men of the family of Nonius to try their luck on the *cursus honorum*. Her son was being groomed for the most earnest attempt, but the boy's uncle decided to see what he could do first.

It was an election full of shocks. Quintus Nonius from Picenum got in easily, for example. Whereas Lucius Appuleius Saturninus didn't get in at all. There were ten places for tribunes of the plebs, and Saturninus came in eleventh.

"I—don't—believe it!" Saturninus gasped to Glaucia. "I just don't *believe* it! What happened?"

Glaucia was frowning; suddenly his own chances to become a praetor seemed dim. Then he shrugged, clapped Saturninus on the back with rough comfort, and stepped down from the rostra. "Don't worry," he said, "something might change things yet."

"What can possibly change an election result?" Saturninus demanded. "No, Gaius Servilius, I'm out!"

"I'll see you shortly—here. Just stay here, don't go home yet," said Glaucia, and hurried off into the crowd.

The moment he heard his name called as one of the ten new tribunes of the plebs, Quintus Nonius from Picenum wanted to go home to his expensive new house on the Carinae. There his wife waited with his sister-in-law Cornelia Sulla and her boy, anxious to know the results, provincial enough to doubt Quintus Nonius's chances.

However, it was more difficult to leave the Forum area than Quintus Nonius had counted on, for every few feet he was stopped and warmly congratulated; a natural courtesy could not allow him to fob off his well-wishers, so he lingered in a forced detention, beaming and bowing, shaking a hundred hands.

One by one Quintus Nonius's companions dropped away, until he entered the first of the alleyways on his route home attended only by three close friends who also lived on the Carinae. When they were set upon by a dozen men armed with clubs, one of the friends managed to break away and run back toward the Forum, crying for help, only to find it virtually deserted. Luckily Saturninus and Glaucia were standing talking to some others near the rostra, Glaucia looking red-faced and a little disheveled; when the cry for help came, they all followed at a run. But it was too late. Quintus Nonius and his two friends were dead.

"*Edepol!*" said Glaucia, getting to his feet after verifying that Quintus Nonius was indeed dead. "Quintus Nonius has just been elected a tribune of the plebs, and I'm the officer in charge of proceedings." He frowned. "Lucius Appuleius, will you see Quintus Nonius is carried home? I'd better go back to the Forum and deal with the electoral dilemma."

The shock of finding Quintus Nonius and his friends lying extinguished in lakes of their own blood deprived those who had come to the rescue of their normal faculties, including Saturninus; no one noticed how artificial Glaucia sounded, including Saturninus. And standing on an empty rostra shouting to a deserted Forum Romanum, Gaius Servilius Glaucia announced the death of the newly elected tribune of the plebs Quintus Nonius. He then announced that the candidate who came in eleventh would replace Quintus Nonius in the new college—Lucius Appuleius Saturninus.

"It's all set," said Glaucia complacently later, at Saturninus's house. "You are now a legally elected tribune of the plebs, co-opted to fill Quintus Nonius's shoes."

He was not over-endowed with scruples since those awful events which had seen him dismissed from his post as quaestor at Ostia, but Saturninus was nonetheless so shocked he stared at Glaucia, aghast.

"You didn't!" he cried.

Glaucia put the tip of his index finger against the side of his nose and smiled at Saturninus from beneath his brows, a smile owning much fierceness. "Ask me no questions, Lucius Appuleius, and I'll tell you no lies," he said.

"The shame of it is that he was a nice fellow."

"Yes, he was. But that's his luck, to wind up dead. He was the only one who lived on the Carinae, so he was elected—in more ways than one. It's too hard to set something up on the Palatine—there aren't enough people on the streets."

Saturninus sighed, shrugged off his depression. "You're right. And I'm in. I thank you for your help, Gaius Servilius."

"Think nothing of it," said Glaucia.

The scandal was difficult to live down, but it was quite impossible for anyone to prove that Saturninus was implicated in a murder when even the dead man's surviving friend could testify that both Saturninus and Glaucia had been standing in the lower Forum at the time the deed was done. People talked, but talk was cheap, as Glaucia said with a sneer. And when Ahenobarbus Pontifex Maximus demanded that the tribunician elections be held all over again, he got nowhere; Glaucia had created a precedent to deal with a particular crisis which had never occurred before.

"Talk is cheap!" Glaucia said again, this time in the Senate. "The allegations that Lucius Appuleius and I were involved in the death of Quintus Nonius have no foundation in fact. As for my replacing a dead tribune of the plebs with a live one, I did what any true presiding officer of an election ought to do—I acted! No one can dispute that Lucius Appuleius polled in eleventh place, nor that the election was properly conducted. To appoint Lucius Appuleius the successor of Quintus Nonius as quickly and smoothly as possible was as logical as it was expedient. The *contio* of the Plebeian Assembly which I called yesterday gave my actions full-throated approval, as everyone here can verify. This debate, Conscript Fathers, is as useless as it is causeless. The matter is closed." Thus Gaius Servilius Glaucia.

Gaius Marius and Quintus Lutatius Catulus Caesar triumphed together on the first day of December. The joint parade was a stroke of genius, for there could be no doubt that Catulus Caesar, his chariot trailing behind the incumbent consul's, was very much the second lead in the production. The name on everybody's lips was Gaius Marius. There was even a very clever float put together by Lucius Cornelius Sulla—who as usual got the job of organizing the parade—showing Marius allowing Catulus Caesar's men to pick up the thirty-five Cimbric standards, because he had already captured so many in Gaul.

At the meeting which followed in the temple of Jupiter Optimus Maximus, Marius spoke with passion of his actions in awarding the citizenship to the soldiers of Camerinum and plugging up the Vale of the Salassi by planting a soldier colony at little Eporedia. His announcement that he would seek a sixth consulship was greeted with groans, gibes, cries of bitter protest—and cheers. The cheers were far louder. When the tumult died down he announced that all his personal share of the spoils would go to build a new temple to the military cult of Honor and Virtue; in it his trophies and the trophies of his army would be housed, and it would be sited on the Capitol. He would also build a temple to the Roman military Honor and Virtue at Olympia in Greece.

Catulus Caesar listened with a sinking heart, understanding that if he was to preserve his own reputation he would have to donate his own share of the spoils to a similar kind of public religious monument, rather than investing it to augment his private fortune—which was large enough, but not nearly as large as Marius's.

It surprised no one when the Centuriate Assembly elected Gaius Marius consul for the sixth time, and in senior place. Not only was he now the undisputed First Man in Rome, many were beginning to call him the Third Founder of Rome as well. The First Founder was none other than Romulus himself. The Second Founder was Marcus Furius Camillus, who had been responsible for the ejection of the Gauls from Italy three hundred years before. Therefore it seemed appropriate to call Gaius Marius the Third Founder of Rome, since he too had repulsed a tide of barbarians.

The consular elections were not without their surprises; Quintus Caecilius Metellus Numidicus Piggle-wiggle failed to carry the junior consul's poll. This was Marius's high point, and he won, even in the matter of his junior colleague; he had declared his firm support for Lucius Valerius Flaccus, and Lucius Valerius Flaccus was duly elected. Flaccus held an important lifelong priesthood, the position of *flamen Martialis*—the special priest of Mars—and his office had made him a quiet man, biddable and subordinate. An ideal companion for the masterful Gaius Marius.

But it was no surprise to anyone when Gaius Servilius Glaucia was elected a praetor, for he was Marius's man, and Marius had bribed the voters lavishly. What was a surprise was the fact that he came in at the head of the poll, and so was appointed *praetor urbanus*, the most senior of the six praetors elected.

Shortly after the elections Quintus Lutatius Catulus Caesar announced publicly that he would donate his personal share of the German spoils to two religious causes; the first was to purchase the old site of Marcus Fulvius Flaccus's house on the Palatine—it lay next door to his own house—and build thereon a magnificent porticus to house the thirty-five Cimbric standards he had captured on the field of Vercellae; the second was to build a temple on the Campus Martius to the goddess Fortuna in her guise of the Fortune of the Present Day.

When the new tribunes of the plebs entered office on the tenth day of December, the fun began. Tribune of the plebs for the second time, Lucius Appuleius Saturninus dominated the college completely, and exploited the fear the death of Quintus Nonius had provoked to further his own legislative ends. Though he kept denying strenuously any implication in the murder, he kept dropping little remarks in private to his fellow tribunes of the plebs which gave them cause to wonder if they might not end up as Quintus Nonius did, should they attempt to thwart him. The result was that they permitted Saturninus to do precisely what he pleased; neither Metellus Numidicus nor Catulus Caesar could persuade a single tribune of the plebs to interpose a single veto.

Within eight days of entering office, Saturninus brought forward the first of two bills to award public lands to the veterans of both German armies; the lands were all abroad, in Sicily, Greece, Macedonia, and mainland Africa. The bill also carried a novel proviso, that Gaius Marius himself was to have the authority to personally grant the Roman citizenship to three Italian soldier settlers in each colony.

The Senate erupted into furious opposition.

"This man," said Metellus Numidicus, "is not even going to

favor his Roman soldiers! He wants land for all comers on an equal footing—Roman, Latin, Italian. No difference! No distinguished attention for Rome's own men! I ask you, fellow senators, what do you think of such a man? Does Rome matter to him? Of course it doesn't! *Why should it?* He's not a Roman! He's an Italian! And he favors his own breed. A thousand of them enfranchised on the battlefield, while Roman soldiers stood by and watched, unthanked. But what else can we expect of such a man as Gaius Marius?"

When Marius rose to reply, he couldn't even make himself heard; so he walked out of the Curia Hostilia and stood on the rostra, and addressed the Forum frequenters instead. Some were indignant; but he was their darling, and they listened.

"There's land enough for all!" he shouted. "No one can accuse me of preferential treatment for Italians! One hundred *iugera* per soldier! Ah, why so much, I hear you ask? Because, People of Rome, these colonists are going to harder places by far than our own beloved Italy. They will plant and harvest in unkind soils and unkind climates, where to make a decent living a man must have more land than he does in our beloved land of Italy."

"There he goes!" cried Catulus Caesar from the steps of the Senate, his voice carrying shrilly. "There he goes! Listen to what he's saying! Not Rome! *Italy!* Italy, Italy, always it's Italy! He's not a Roman, and he doesn't care about Rome!"

"Italy *is* Rome!" thundered Marius. "They are one and the same! Without one, the other does not and cannot exist! Don't Romans and Italians alike lay down their lives in Rome's armies for Rome? And if that is so—and who can deny it is so?—why should one kind of soldier be any different from the other?"

"Italy!" cried Catulus Caesar. "Always it's Italy!"

"Rubbish!" shouted Marius. "The first allocations of land go to Roman soldiers, not to Italian! Is that evidence of an Italian bias? And isn't it better that out of the thousands of veteran legionaries who will go to these colonies, three of the Italians among them will become full Roman citizens? I said three, People of Rome! Not three thousand Italians, People of Rome! Not three hundred

Italians, People of Rome! Not three dozen Italians, People of Rome! *Three!* A drop in an ocean of men! A drop of a drop in an ocean of men!"

"A drop of poison in an ocean of men!" screamed Catulus Caesar from the steps of the Senate.

"The bill may say that the Roman soldiers will get their land first, but where does it say that the first land given away will be the best land?" shouted Metellus Numidicus.

But the first land bill, which dealt with various tracts Rome had possessed in her public domain for a number of years and leased to absentee landlords, was passed by the Plebeian Assembly in spite of the opposition.

Quintus Poppaedius Silo, now the leading man of his Marsic people in spite of his relative youth, had come to Rome to hear the debates on the land bills; Marcus Livius Drusus had invited him, and he was staying in Drusus's house.

"They make a great deal of noise out of Rome versus Italy, don't they?" Silo asked Drusus, never having heard Rome debate this subject before.

"They do indeed," said Drusus grimly. "It's an attitude only time will change. I live in hope, Quintus Poppaedius."

"And yet you don't like Gaius Marius."

"I detest the man. But I voted for him," said Drusus.

"It's only four years since we fought at Arausio," said Silo reflectively. "Yes, I daresay you're right, and it will change. Before Arausio, I very much doubt Gaius Marius would have had any chance to include Italian troops among his colonists."

"It was thanks to Arausio the Italian debt slaves were freed," said Drusus.

"I'm glad to think we didn't die for nothing. And yet—look at Sicily. The Italian slaves there weren't freed. They died instead."

"I writhe in shame over Sicily," said Drusus, flushing. "Two corrupt, self-seeking senior Roman magistrates did that. Two miserable *mentulae*! Like them you may not, Quintus Poppaedius, but grant that a Metellus Numidicus or an Aemilius Scaurus would not soil the hem of his toga on a grain swindle."

"Yes, I'll grant you that," said Silo. "However, Marcus Livius, they still believe that to be a Roman is to belong to the most exclusive club on earth—and that no Italian deserves to belong by adoption."

"Adoption?"

"Well, isn't that really what the bestowal of the Roman citizenship is? An adoption into the family of Rome?"

Drusus sighed. "You're quite right. All that changes is the name. Granting him the citizenship can't make a Roman out of an Italian—or a Greek. And as time goes on, the Senate at least sets its heart more and more adamantly against creating artificial Romans."

"Then perhaps," said Silo, "it will be up to us Italians to *make* ourselves artificial Romans—with or without the approval of the Senate."

A second land bill followed the first, this one to deal with all the new public lands Rome had acquired during the course of the German wars. It was by far the more important of the two, for these were virtually virgin lands, unexploited by large-scale farmers and graziers, and potentially rich in other things than beasts and crops—minerals, gems, stone. They were all tracts in western Gaul-across-the-Alps, around Narbo, Tolosa, Carcasso, and in central Gaul-across-the-Alps, plus an area in Nearer Spain which had rebelled while the Cimbri were making things difficult at the foot of the Pyrenees.

There were many Roman knights and Roman companies anxious to expand into Gaul-across-the-Alps, and they had looked to the defeat of the Germans for an opportunity—and looked to their various patrons in the Senate to secure them access to the new *ager publicus Galliae*. Now to find that most of it was to go to Head Count soldiers roused them to heights of fury hitherto seen only during the worst days of the Gracchi.

And as the Senate hardened, so too did the First Class knights, once Marius's greatest advocates—now, feeling cheated of the chance to be absentee landlords in Further Gaul, his obdurate enemies. The agents of Metellus Numidicus and Catulus Caesar circulated everywhere, whispering, whispering . . .

"He gives away what belongs to the State as if he owned both the land and the State" was one whisper, soon a cry.

"He plots to own the State—why else would he be consul now that the war with the Germans is over?"

"Rome has never subsidized her soldiers with land!"

"The Italians are receiving more than they deserve!"

"Land taken from enemies of Rome belongs exclusively to Romans, not to Latins and Italians as well!"

"He's starting on the *ager publicus* abroad, but before we know it he'll be giving away the *ager publicus* of Italy—and he'll give it to Italians!"

"He's calling himself the Third Founder of Rome, but what he wants to call himself is King of Rome!"

And on, and on, and on. The more Marius roared from the rostra and in the Senate that Rome needed to seed her provinces with colonies of ordinary Romans, that veteran soldiers would form useful garrisons, that Roman lands abroad were better held by many little men than a handful of big men, the bitterer the opposition became. It stockpiled rather than dwindled from too much use, grew daily stronger, more strenuous. Until slowly, subtly, almost without volition, the public attitude toward the second agrarian law of Saturninus began to change. Many of the policy makers among the People—and there were policy makers among the habitual Forum frequenters, as well as among the most influential knights—began to doubt that Marius was right. For never had they seen such opposition.

"There can't be so much smoke without at least some fire," they began to say, between themselves and to those who listened to them because they were policy makers.

"This isn't just another silly Senate squabble—it's too implacable."

"When a man like Quintus Caecilius Metellus Numidicus—who has been censor as well as consul, and don't we all remember how brave he was while he was censor?—keeps increasing the number of his supporters, he must have some right on his side."

"I heard yesterday that a knight whose support Gaius Marius desperately needs has spurned him publicly! The land at Tolosa he was personally promised by Gaius Marius is now going to be given to the Head Count veterans."

"Someone was telling me that he personally overheard Gaius Marius saying he intends to give the citizenship to every single Italian man."

"This is Gaius Marius's sixth consulship—and his fifth in a row. He was heard to say at dinner the other day that he would never *not* be consul! He's going to run every single year until he dies."

"He really wants to be King of Rome!"

Thus did the whispering campaign of Metellus Numidicus and Catulus Caesar begin to pay dividends. And suddenly even Glaucia and Saturninus started to fear that the second land bill was doomed to fail.

"I've *got* to have that land!" cried Marius in despair to his wife, who had been waiting patiently for days in the hope that he would eventually discuss matters with her. Not because she had either fresh ideas to offer or positive things to say, but because she knew herself to be the only real friend he had near him. Sulla had been sent back to Italian Gaul after the triumph, and Sertorius had journeyed to Nearer Spain to see his German wife and child.

"Gaius Marius, is it really so essential?" Julia asked. "Will it honestly matter if your soldiers don't receive their land? Roman soldiers never have received land—there's no precedent for it. They can't say you haven't tried."

"You don't understand," he said impatiently. "It isn't to do with the soldiers anymore, it has to do with my *dignitas*, my position in public life. If the bill doesn't pass, I'm no longer the First Man in Rome."

"Can't Lucius Appuleius help?"

"He's trying, the gods know he's trying! But instead of gaining ground, we're losing it. I feel like Achilles in the river, unable to get out of the flood because the bank keeps giving way. I claw myself upward a little, then go down twice as far. The rumors are incredible, Julia! And there's no combating them, because they're never overt. If I were guilty of one tenth of the things they're saying about me, I'd have been pushing a boulder uphill in Tartarus long ago."

"Yes, well, slander campaigns are impossible to deal with," Julia said comfortably. "Sooner or later the rumors become so bizarre that everyone wakes up with a start. That's what's going to happen in this case too. They've killed you, but they're going to keep on stabbing until the whole of Rome is sick to death of it all. People are horribly naive and gullible, but even the most naive and gullible have a saturation point somewhere. The bill will go through, Gaius Marius—I am sure of it. Just don't hurry it too much, wait for opinion to swing back your way."

"Oh, yes, it may well go through, just as you say, Julia. But what's to stop the House's overturning it the moment Lucius Appuleius is out of office, and I don't have an equally capable tribune of the plebs to fight the House?" Marius groaned.

"I see."

"Do you?"

"Certainly. I'm a Julian of the Caesars, husband, which means I grew up surrounded by political discussions, even if my sex precluded a public career." She chewed her lip. "It is a problem, isn't it? Agrarian laws can't be implemented overnight—they take forever. Years and years. Finding the land, surveying it, parceling it up, finding the men whose names have been drawn to settle it, commissions and commissioners, adequate staff—it's interminable."

Marius grinned. "You've been talking to Gaius Julius!"

"I have indeed. In fact, I'm quite an expert." She patted the vacant end of her couch. "Come, my love, sit down!"

"I can't, Julia."

"Is there no way to protect this legislation?"

Marius stopped his pacing, turned and looked at her from beneath his brows. "Actually there is. . . ."

"Tell me," she prompted gently.

"Gaius Servilius Glaucia thought of it, but Lucius Appuleius is mad for it, so I have the two of them clambering up my back trying to bend me over, and I'm not sure. . . ."

"Is it so novel?" she asked, aware of Glaucia's reputation.

"Novel enough."

"Please, Gaius Marius, tell me!"

It would be a relief to tell someone who didn't have any axe to grind save Marius's, he thought tiredly. "I'm a Military Man, Julia, and I like a Military Man's solutions," he said. "In the army everyone knows that when I issue an order, it's the best order possible under the circumstances. So everyone jumps to obey without questioning it, because they know me, and they trust me. Well, this lot in Rome know me too, and they ought to trust me! But do they? No! They're so set on seeing their own ideas implemented that they don't even listen to anyone else's ideas, even if they're better ideas. I go to the Senate knowing before ever I reach the awful place that I'm going to have to do my work in an atmosphere of hatred and heckling which exhausts me before I start! I'm too old and too set in my ways to be bothered with them, Julia! They're all idiots, and they're going to kill the Republic if they go on trying to pretend things haven't changed since Scipio Africanus was a boy! My soldier settlements make such good sense!"

"They do," Julia said, hiding her consternation. He was looking worn these days, older than his years instead of younger, and he was putting on weight for the first time in his life—all that sitting around in meetings rather than striding around in the open air—and his hair was suddenly greying and thinning. Warmaking was clearly more beneficial to a man's body than lawmaking. "Gaius Marius, make an end to it and tell me!" she insisted.

"This second bill contains an additional clause Glaucia invented specially for it," said Marius, beginning to pace again, his words tumbling out. "An oath to uphold the law in perpetuity is demanded from every senator within five days of the bill's passing into law."

She couldn't help herself; Julia gasped, lifted her hands to her cheeks, looked at Marius in dismay, and said the strongest word her vocabulary contained, *"Ecastor!"*

"Shocking, isn't it?"

"Gaius Marius, Gaius Marius, they'll never forgive you if you include it in the bill!"

"Do you think I don't know that?" he cried, hands reaching like claws for the ceiling. "But what else can I do? I've *got* to have this land!"

She licked her lips. "You'll be in the House for many years to come," she said. "Can't you just go on fighting to see the law upheld?"

"Go on fighting? When do I ever stop?" he asked. "I'm tired of fighting, Julia!"

She blew a bubble of derision aimed at jollying him. "Oh, pooh! *Gaius Marius* tired of fighting? You've been fighting all your life!"

"But not the same kind of fighting as now," he tried to explain. "This is dirty. There are no rules. And you don't even know who—let alone where!—your enemies are. Give me a battlefield for an arena anytime! At least what happens on it is quick and clean—and the best man usually wins. But the Senate of Rome is a brothel stuffed with the lowest forms of life and the lowest forms of conduct. I spend my days *crawling* in its slime! Well, Julia, let me tell you, I'd rather *bathe* in battlefield blood! And if anyone is naive enough to think that political intrigue doesn't ruin more lives than any war, then he deserves everything politics will dish out to him!"

Julia got up and went to him, forced him to stop the pacing, and took both his hands. "I hate to say it, my dear love, but the political forum isn't the right arena for a man as direct as you."

"If I didn't know it until now, I certainly do know that now," he said gloomily. "I suppose it will have to be Glaucia's wretched special-oath clause. But as Publius Rutilius keeps asking me, where are all these new-style laws going to lead us? Are we really replacing bad with good? Or are we merely replacing bad with worse?"

"Only time will tell," she said calmly. "Whatever else happens, Gaius Marius, never forget that there are always huge crises in government, that people are always going around proclaiming in tones of horror that this or that new law will mean the end of the Republic, that Rome isn't Rome any more—I know from my reading that Scipio Africanus was saying it of Cato the Censor! And probably some early Julius Caesar was saying it of Brutus when he killed his sons in the beginning of things. The Republic is indestructible, and they all know it, even as they're yelling it's doomed. So don't you lose sight of that fact."

Her good sense was placating him at last; Julia noted in satisfaction that the red tinge was dying out of his eyes, and his skin was losing its mottled choler. Time to change the subject a little, she decided.

"By the way, my brother Gaius Julius would like to see you tomorrow, so I've taken the opportunity to invite him and Aurelia to dinner, if that's acceptable."

Marius groaned. "Of course! That's right! I'd forgotten! He's off to Cercina to settle my first colony of veterans there, isn't he?" Down went his head into his hands, snatched from Julia's clasp. "*Isn't* he? Ye gods, my memory! What's happening to me, Julia?"

"Nothing," she soothed. "You need a respite, preferably a few weeks away from Rome. But since that's clearly not possible, why don't we go together to find Young Marius?"

That extremely handsome little man, not quite nine years old, was a very satisfactory son: tall, sturdily built, blond, and Roman-nosed enough to please his father. If the lad's leanings were more toward the physical than the intellectual, that too pleased Marius. The fact that he was still an only child grieved his mother more than it did his father, for Julia had not succeeded in either of the two pregnancies which had followed the death of his younger brother, and she was now beginning to fear that she was incapable of carrying another child to its full term. However, Marius was content with his one son, and refused to believe that there should be another basket in which to pile some of his eggs.

The dinner party was a great success, its guest list limited to Gaius Julius Caesar; his wife, Aurelia; and Aurelia's uncle, Publius Rutilius Rufus.

Caesar was leaving for African Cercina at the end of the eight-day market interval; the commission had delighted him, only one disadvantage marring his pleasure.

"I won't be in Rome for the birth of my first son," he said with a smile.

"Aurelia, no! *Again?*" asked Rutilius Rufus, groaning. "It'll be another girl, you wait and see—and where will the pair of you find another dowry?"

"Pooh, Uncle Publius!" said the unrepentant Aurelia, popping a morsel of chicken into her mouth. "First of all, we shan't need dowries for our girls. Gaius Julius's father made us promise that we wouldn't be stiff-necked Caesars and keep our girls free of the taint of plutocracy. So we fully intend to marry them to terribly rich rural nobodies." More chicken morsels suffered the same fate as the first. "And we've had our two girls. Now we're going to have boys."

"All at once?" asked Rutilius Rufus, eyes twinkling.

"Oh, I say, twins would be nice! Do they run in the Julii?" asked the intrepid mother of her sister-in-law.

"I think they do," said Julia, frowning. "Certainly our Uncle Sextus had twins, though one died—Caesar Strabo *is* a twin, isn't he?"

"Correct, he is," said Rutilius Rufus with a grin. "Our poor young cross-eyed friend positively drips extra names, and 'Vopiscus' is one of them, which means he's the survivor of twins. But he's got a new nickname, I hear."

The wicked note of gloat in his voice alerted everyone; Marius voiced the query. "What?"

"He's developed a fistula in the nether regions, so some wit

said he had an arsehole and a half, and started calling him Ses-
quiculus," said Rutilius Rufus.

The entire dinner party collapsed into laughter, including the
women, permitted to share this mild obscenity.

"Twins might run in Lucius Cornelius's family too," said Marius, wiping his eyes.

"What makes you say that?" asked Rutilius Rufus, sensing another snippet of gossip.

"Well, as you all know—though Rome doesn't—he lived
among the Cimbri for a year. Had a wife—a Cherusci woman
named Hermana. And she threw twin boys."

Julia's mirth faded. "Captured? Dead?" she asked.

"*Edepol,* no! He took her back to her own people in Germania
before he rejoined me."

"Funny sort of chap, Lucius Cornelius," said Rutilius Rufus
reflectively. "Not quite right in the head."

"There you're wrong for once, Publius Rutilius," said Marius.
"No man's head was ever better attached to his shoulders than
Lucius Cornelius's. In fact, I'd say he was the man of the future as
far as Rome's concerned."

Julia giggled. "He positively bolted back to Italian Gaul after
the triumph," she said. "He and Mother fight more and more as
time goes on."

"Well," said Marius bravely, "that's understandable! Your
mother is the one person on this patch of earth who can frighten
the life out of me."

"Lovely woman, Marcia," said Rutilius Rufus reminiscently,
then added hastily when all eyes turned on him, "At least to look
at. In the old days."

"She's certainly made herself very busy finding Lucius Cornelius a new wife," said Caesar.

Rutilius Rufus nearly choked on a prune pip. "Well, I happened to be at Marcus Aemilius Scaurus's for dinner a few days
ago," he said in a wickedly pleasurable voice, "and if she wasn't
already another man's wife, I'd have been willing to bet Lucius
Cornelius would have found a wife all by himself."

"No!" said Aurelia, leaning forward on her chair. "Oh, Uncle Publius, do tell!"

"Little Caecilia Metella Dalmatica, if you please," said Rutilius Rufus.

"The wife of the Princeps Senatus *himself*?" squeaked Aurelia.

"The same. Lucius Cornelius took one look at her when she was introduced, blushed redder than his hair, and sat like a booby all through the meal just staring at her."

"The imagination boggles," said Marius.

"As well it might!" said Rutilius Rufus. "Even Marcus Aemilius noticed—well, he does tend to be like an old hen with one chick about his darling little Dalmatica. So she got sent off to bed at the end of the main course. Looking very disappointed. And shooting a look of shy admiration at Lucius Cornelius as she went. He spilled his wine."

"As long as he doesn't spill his wine in her lap," said Marius grimly.

"Oh no, not another scandal!" cried Julia. "Lucius Cornelius just can't afford another scandal. Gaius Marius, can you drop him a hint?"

Marius produced that look of discomfort husbands do when their wives demand some utterly unmasculine and uncharacteristic task of them. "Certainly not!"

"Why?" asked Julia, to whom her request was sensible.

"Because a man's private life is his own lookout—and a lot he'd thank me for sticking my nose in!"

Julia and Aurelia both looked disappointed.

The peacemaker as always, Caesar cleared his throat. "Well, since Marcus Aemilius Scaurus looks as if he'll have to be killed with an axe in about a thousand years' time, I don't think we need to worry very much about Lucius Cornelius and Dalmatica. I believe Mother has made her choice—*and* I hear Lucius Cornelius approves, so we'll all be getting wedding invitations as soon as he comes back from Italian Gaul."

"Who?" asked Rutilius Rufus. "I haven't heard a whisper!"

"Aelia, the only daughter of Quintus Aelius Tubero."

"A bit long in the tooth, isn't she?" asked Marius.

"Late thirties, the same age as Lucius Cornelius," said Caesar comfortably. "He doesn't want more children, it seems, so Mother felt a widow without children was ideal. She's a handsome enough lady."

"From a fine old family," said Rutilius Rufus. "Rich!"

"Then good for Lucius Cornelius!" said Aurelia warmly. "I can't help it, I like him!"

"So do we all," said Marius, winking at her. "Gaius Julius, this professed admiration doesn't make you jealous?"

"Oh, I have more serious rivals for Aurelia's affections than mere patrician legates," said Caesar, grinning.

Julia looked up. "Really? Who?"

"His name is Lucius Decumius, and he's a grubby little man of about forty with skinny legs, greasy hair, and an all-over reek of garlic," said Caesar, picking at the dish of dried fruits in search of the plumpest raisin. "My house is perpetually filled with magnificent vases of flowers—in season, out of season, makes no difference to Lucius Decumius, who sends a new lot round every four or five days. And visits my wife, if you please, smarming up to her in the most nauseating way. In fact, he's so pleased about our coming child that I sometimes have deep misgivings."

"Stop it, Gaius Julius!" said Aurelia, laughing.

"Who *is* he?" asked Rutilius Rufus.

"The caretaker or whatever he's called of the crossroads college Aurelia is obliged to house rent-free," said Caesar.

"Lucius Decumius and I have an understanding," Aurelia said, filching the raisin Caesar was holding halfway to his mouth.

"What understanding?" asked Rutilius Rufus.

"Whereabouts he plies his trade, namely anywhere but in my vicinity."

"What trade?"

"He's an assassin," said Aurelia.

When Saturninus introduced his second agrarian law, the clause stipulating an oath burst upon the Forum like a clap of thunder; not a bolt of Jovian lightning, rather the cataclysmic rumble of the old gods, the real gods, the faceless gods, the *numina*. Not only was an oath required of every senator, but instead of the customary swearing in the temple of Saturn, Saturninus's law required that the oath be taken under the open sky in the roofless temple of Semo Sancus Dius Fidius on the lower Quirinal, where the faceless god without a mythology had only a statue of Gaia Caecilia—wife of King Tarquinius Priscus of old Rome—to humanize his dwelling. And the deities in whose name the oath was taken were not the grand deities of the Capitol, but the little faceless *numina* who were truly Roman—the Di Penates Publici, guardians of the public purse and larder—the Lares Praestites, guardians of the State—and Vesta, guardian of the hearth. No one knew what they looked like, or where they came from, or even what sex if any they actually possessed; they just—*were*. And they mattered. They were Roman. They were the public images of the most private gods, the deities who ruled the family, that most sacred of all Roman traditions. No Roman could swear by these deities and contemplate breaking his oath, for to do so would be to bring down ruin and disaster and disintegration upon his family, his home, his purse.

But the legalistic mind of Glaucia hadn't merely trusted to nameless fear of nameless *numina;* to drive the point of the oath home, Saturninus's law even dealt with any senator who might refuse to take the oath; he would be forbidden fire and water within Italy, and fined the sum of twenty silver talents, and stripped of his citizenship.

"The trouble is, we haven't gone far enough fast enough yet," said Metellus Numidicus to Catulus Caesar, Ahenobarbus Pontifex Maximus, Metellus Piglet, Scaurus, Lucius Cotta, and his uncle Marcus Cotta. "The People aren't ready to reject Gaius Marius—they'll pass this into law. And we will be required to swear." He shivered. "And if I swear, I must uphold my oath."

"Then it *cannot* be passed into law," said Ahenobarbus.

"There's not one tribune of the plebs with the courage to veto it," said Marcus Cotta.

"Then we must fight it with religion," said Scaurus, looking at Ahenobarbus meaningfully. "The other side has brought religion into things, so there's no reason why we can't too."

"I think I know what you want," said Ahenobarbus.

"Well, I don't," said Lucius Cotta.

"When the day for voting the bill into law comes and the augurs inspect the omens to ensure the meeting is not in contravention of divine law, we'll make sure the omens are inauspicious," said Ahenobarbus. "And we'll go on finding the omens inauspicious, until one of our tribunes of the plebs finds the courage to interpose his veto on religious grounds. That will kill the law, because the People get tired of things very quickly."

The plan was put into practice; the omens were declared inauspicious by the augurs. Unfortunately Lucius Appuleius Saturninus himself was also an augur—a small reward given him at the instigation of Scaurus at the time when Scaurus restored his reputation—and differed in his interpretation of the omens.

"It's a trick!" he shouted to the Plebs standing in the well of the Comitia. "Look at them, all minions of the Senate Policy Makers! There's nothing wrong with the omens—this is a way to break the power of the People! We all know Scaurus Princeps Senatus and Metellus Numidicus and Catulus will go to any lengths to deprive our soldiers of their just reward—and this proves they *have* gone to any lengths! They've deliberately tampered with the will of the gods!"

The People believed Saturninus, who had taken the precaution of inserting his gladiators into the crowd. When one of the other tribunes of the plebs attempted to interpose his veto on the grounds that the omens were inauspicious, that he had heard thunder besides, and that any law passed that day would be *nefas,* sacrilegious, Saturninus's gladiators acted. While Saturninus declared in ringing tones that he would not allow the veto, his bully-boys plucked the hapless tribune from the rostra and ran him up the Clivus Argentarius to the cells of the Lautumiae and kept him there until the meeting broke up. The second land bill was put to the vote, and the People in their tribes passed it into law, for its oath clause made it novel enough to intrigue the habitual attenders in the Plebeian Assembly; what would happen if it became law, who would resist, how would the Senate react? Too good to miss! The mood of the People was one of let's find out.

The day after the bill became law, Metellus Numidicus rose to his feet in the Senate, and announced with great dignity that he would not take the oath.

"My conscience, my principles, my very life itself depend upon this decision!" he roared. "I will pay the fine and I will go into exile on Rhodes. For I will not swear. Do you hear me, Conscript Fathers? I—will—not—swear! I cannot swear to uphold *anything* to which the very core of my being is adamantly opposed. When is forsworn forsworn? Which is the more grievous crime—to swear to uphold a law I set myself against, or not to swear? You may all of you answer that for yourselves. My answer is that the greater crime is to swear. So I say to you, Lucius Appuleius Saturninus, and I say to you, Gaius Marius—*I—will—not—swear!* I choose to pay the fine and I choose to go into exile."

His stand made a profound impression, for everyone present knew he meant what he said. Marius's eyebrows grew still, meeting across his nose, and Saturninus pulled his lips back from his teeth. The murmurings began; the doubts and discontents niggled, gnawed, amplified.

"They're going to be difficult," whispered Glaucia from his curule chair, close to Marius's.

"Unless I close this meeting, they'll all refuse to swear," muttered Marius, rose to his feet, and dismissed the House. "I urge you to go home and think for three days about the serious consequences should you decide not to take the oath. It is easy for Quintus Caecilius—he has the money to pay his fine, and plenty to ensure a comfortable exile. But how many of you can say that? Go home, Conscript Fathers, and think for three days. This House will reconvene four days from now, and then you must make up your minds, for we must not forget there is a time limit built into the *lex Appuleia agraria secunda.*"

But you can't talk to them like that, said Marius to himself as he walked the floor of his huge and beautiful house below the temple of Juno Moneta, while his wife watched helplessly and his normally saucy son hid himself in his playroom.

You just can't talk to them like that, Gaius Marius! They are not soldiers. They are not even subordinate officers, despite the fact that I am consul and they are mostly backbenchers who will never know the feel of an ivory curule chair beneath their fat arses. To the last one, they really do think themselves my peers—I, Gaius Marius, six times consul of this city, this country, this empire! I have to beat them, I cannot leave myself open to the ignominy of defeat. My *dignitas* is enormously greater than theirs, say what they will to the contrary. And I cannot see it suffer. I am the First Man in Rome. I am the Third Founder of Rome. And after I die, they are going to have to admit that I, Gaius Marius, the Italian hayseed with no Greek, was the greatest man in the history of our Republic, the Senate and People of Rome.

Further than that his thoughts never got during the three days' grace he had given the senators; round and round and round went his dread of the loss of his *dignitas* were he to go down in defeat. And at dawn on the fourth day he left for the Curia Hostilia determined he was going to win—and not having thought at all about what kind of tactics the Policy Makers might use to beat him. He had taken particular care with his appearance, unwilling to let the world see that he had walked the floor for three days, and he strode down the Hill of the Bankers with his twelve lictors preceding him as if indeed he truly did own Rome.

The House assembled with unusual quietness; too few stools scraped, too few men coughed, too few attendants scuffled and muttered. The sacrifice was made flawlessly and the omens were declared auspicious for the meeting.

A big man in perfect control, Marius rose to his feet in awesome majesty. Though he had given no thought to what possible tack the Policy Makers might take, he had worked out his own tack down to the finest detail, and the confidence he felt was written plainly upon him.

"I too have spent the last three days in thought, Conscript Fathers," he began, his eyes fixed upon some space between the listening senators rather than upon any one face, friendly or inimical. Not that anyone could tell where Marius's eyes were, for his eyebrows hid them from all but the closest scrutiny. He tucked his left hand around the front edge of his toga where it fell in many beautifully ordered folds from left shoulder to ankles, and stepped down from the curule dais to the floor. "One fact is patent." He paced a few feet, and stopped. "If this law is valid, it binds all of us to swear to uphold it." He paced a few feet more. "If this law is valid, we must all take the oath." He paced to the doors, turned to face both sides of the House. "But *is* it valid?" he asked loudly.

The question dropped into a fathomless silence.

"That's it!" whispered Scaurus Princeps Senatus to Metellus Numidicus. "He's done for! He's just killed himself!"

But Marius, up against the doors, didn't hear. So he didn't pause to think again; he just went on. "There are those among you who insist that no law passed in the circumstances attending the passage of the *lex Appuleia agraria secunda* can be valid. I have heard the law's validity challenged on two separate grounds—one, that it was passed in defiance of the omens, and the other, that it was passed even though violence was done to the sacrosanct person of a legally elected tribune of the plebs."

He began to walk down the floor, then stopped. "Clearly the future of the law is in doubt. The Assembly of the Plebeian People will have to re-examine it in the light of both objections to its validity." He took one small pace, stopped. "But that, Conscript Fathers, is not the issue we face here today. The validity of the law per se is not our first concern. Our concern is more immediate." One more little pace. "We have been instructed by the law in question to swear to uphold the law in question. And that is what we are here today to debate. Today is the last day upon which we can take our oaths to uphold it, so the matter of swearing is urgent. And today the law in question is a valid law. So we must swear to uphold it."

He walked forward hastily, almost reached the dais, then

turned and paced slowly to the doors again, where he turned to face both sides of the House again. "Today, Conscript Fathers, we will all take that oath. We are bound to do so by the specific instruction of the People of Rome. *They* are the lawmakers! We of the Senate are simply their servants. So—we will swear. For it can make no difference to us, Conscript Fathers! If at some time in the future the Assembly of the Plebeian People re-examines the law and finds it invalid, then our oaths are also invalid." Triumph filled his voice. "*That* is what we must understand! Any oath we take to uphold a law remains an oath only as long as the law remains a law. If the Plebeian People decide to nullify the law, then they also nullify our oaths."

Scaurus Princeps Senatus was nodding sapiently, rhythmically; to Marius it looked as if he was agreeing with every word spoken. But Scaurus was nodding sapiently, rhythmically, for quite a different reason. The movements of his head accompanied the words he was speaking low-voiced to Metellus Numidicus. "We've got him, Quintus Caecilius! We've got him at last! He backed down. He didn't last the distance. We've forced him to admit to the whole House that there is a doubt about the validity of Saturninus's law. We've outmaneuvered the Arpinate fox!"

Filled with elation because he was sure he had the House on his side, Marius walked back to the dais in real earnest, mounted it, and stood in front of his carved ivory curule chair to make his peroration. "I myself will take the oath first among us," he said, voice distilled reason. "And if I, Gaius Marius, your senior consul for the past four years and more, am prepared to swear, what can it possibly cost anyone else here? I have conferred with the priests of the College of the Two Teeth, and the temple of Semo Sancus Dius Fidius has been made ready for us. It's not such a very long walk! Come, who will join me?"

There was a sigh, a faint murmur, the hiss of shoes moving as men broke their immobility. The backbenchers began slowly to get up from their stools.

"A question, Gaius Marius," said Scaurus.

The House stilled again. Marius nodded.

"I would like your *personal* opinion, Gaius Marius. Not your official opinion. Just your personal opinion."

"If you value my personal opinion, Marcus Aemilius, then naturally you shall have it," said Marius. "On what?"

"What do you think personally?" Scaurus asked, his voice projected to every corner of the Curia. "Is the *lex Appuleia agraria secunda* valid in the light of what happened when it was passed?"

Silence. Complete silence. No one breathed. Even Gaius Marius, who was too busy racing across the awful wastes of the regions where his over-confidence had put him to think of drawing a breath.

"Would you like me to repeat the question, Gaius Marius?" asked Scaurus sweetly.

Marius's tongue flickered out, wet his hideously dry lips. Where to go, what to do? You've slipped at last, Gaius Marius. Fallen into a pit you cannot climb out of. Why didn't I see that this question was bound to be asked, and asked by the only truly great brain among them? Am I suddenly blinded by my own cleverness? It was bound to be asked! And I never once thought of it. Never once in all those three long days.

Well, I have no choice. Scaurus has my scrotum in his hands, and I must dance to his tug on my balls. He's brought me down. Because I have no choice. I now have to stand here and tell this House that I personally think the law is invalid. Otherwise no one will swear to uphold it. I led them to believe there was a doubt, I led them to believe that the doubt made the taking of the oath permissible. If I retract, I've lost them. But if I say I personally think the law is invalid, I've lost my own self.

He looked toward the tribunes' bench, saw Lucius Appuleius Saturninus sitting forward, hands clenched, face set, lips curled back from his teeth.

I will lose this man who is so important to me if I say I think the law is invalid. And I'll lose the greatest legal draftsman Rome has ever seen, Glaucia. . . . Together, we might have straightened the whole of Italy out in spite of the worst the Policy Makers could do. But if I say I think their law is invalid, I'll lose them forever. And yet—and yet—I must say it. Because if I do not, these *cunni* won't swear the oath and my soldiers won't get their land. That's all I can salvage out of the mess. Land for my men. I am lost. For I have lost.

When the leg of Glaucia's ivory chair scraped across a marble tile, half the members of the Senate jumped; Glaucia looked down at his nails, lips pursed, face expressionless. But the silence continued, moment after moment.

"I think I had better repeat my question, Gaius Marius," Scaurus said. "What is your personal opinion? Is this law a valid one, or is it not?"

"I think—" Marius stopped, frowning fiercely. "Personally I think the law is *probably* invalid," he said.

Down came Scaurus's hands on his thighs with a crack. "Thank you, Gaius Marius!" He rose and turned round to beam at those on the tiers behind him, then turned back to beam at those on the tiers opposite him. "Well, Conscript Fathers, if no less a man than our very own conquering hero Gaius Marius deems the *lex Appuleia* invalid, I for one am happy to swear the oath!" And he bowed to Saturninus, to Glaucia. "Come, fellow senators, as your Princeps Senatus I suggest that we all hurry to the temple of Semo Sancus immediately!"

"*Stop!*"

Everyone stopped. Metellus Numidicus clapped his hands. Down from the very back of the top tier came his servant, a bag burdening each hand so that he bent double and had to drag them across each of the six-foot-wide steps and down to the next with a crash and a chink. When the two bags rested near Metellus Numidicus's feet, the servant went back to the top and carried another two down. Several of the backbencher senators looked at what was piled against the wall, and signed their servants to help. The work went on more swiftly then, until forty bags were piled all around Metellus Numidicus's stool. He himself stood up.

"I will not take the oath," he said. "Not for a thousand thousand assurances from the senior consul that the *lex Appuleia* is invalid will I swear! I hereby tender twenty talents of silver in payment of my fine, and declare that tomorrow at dawn I will proceed into exile on Rhodes."

Pandemonium broke out.

"Order! Order! Order!" shouted Scaurus, shouted Marius.

When order did prevail, Metellus Numidicus looked behind him, and spoke over his shoulder to someone on the back tier. "Treasury quaestor, please come forward," he said.

Down he came, a presentable-looking young man with brown hair and brown eyes, his white toga gleaming, every fold perfect; he was Quintus Caecilius Metellus the Piglet, son of Metellus Numidicus Piggle-wiggle.

"Treasury quaestor, I give these twenty talents of silver into your keeping as payment of the fine levied upon me for refusing to swear to uphold the *lex Appuleia agraria secunda,*" said Metellus Numidicus. "However, while the House is still in assembly, I demand that it be counted so that the Conscript Fathers can be sure the amount is not so much as one denarius short of the proper sum."

"We are all willing to take your word for it, Quintus Caecilius," said Marius, smiling without a vestige of amusement.

"Oh, but I insist!" said Metellus Numidicus. "No one is going to move from this place until every last coin is counted." He coughed. "The total, I believe, should be one hundred and thirty-five thousand denarii."

Everyone sat down with a sigh. Two clerks of the House fetched a table and set it up at Metellus Numidicus's place; Metellus Numidicus himself stood with his left hand clasping his toga and his right hand extended to rest, fingertips lightly down, upon the table. The clerks opened one of the bags and lifted it up between them, then let its contents cascade in glittering clinking heaps near Metellus Numidicus's hand. Young Metellus signed to the clerks to hold the empty bag openmouthed to his right side, and began counting the coins, pushing them quickly into his right hand, cupped beneath the edge of the table; when the hand was full, he dropped its contents into the bag.

"Wait!" said Metellus Numidicus.

Metellus Piglet stopped.

"Count them out loud, Treasury quaestor!"

There was a gasp, a sigh, a ghastly collective groan.

Metellus Piglet put all the coins back on the table, and began again. "Wuh-wuh-wuh-one . . . tuh-tuh-tuh-two . . . thruh-thruh-thruh-three . . . fuh-fuh-fuuh-four . . ."

At sundown Gaius Marius rose from his curule chair. "The day is over, Conscript Fathers. Our business is not over, but in this House no one sits in formal session after the sun has set. Therefore I suggest we go now to the temple of Semo Sancus and swear our oaths. It must be done before midnight, or we are in violation of a direct order from the People." He looked across to where Metellus Numidicus still stood and his son still toiled at the counting—far from over, though his stammer had improved markedly when his nervousness evaporated.

"Marcus Aemilius Scaurus Princeps Senatus, it is your duty to remain here and supervise the rest of this long task. I expect you to do so. And I hereby grant you leave to take your own oath tomorrow. Or the day after, if the counting is still in progress tomorrow. "A glimmer of a smile was playing about the corners of Marius'smouth.

But Scaurus did not smile. He threw his head back and went into peal after peal of joyous, full-throated laughter.

Late in the spring Sulla came back from Italian Gaul, and called to see Gaius Marius immediately after a bath and a change of clothing. Marius, he discovered, looked anything but well, a finding which did not surprise him. Even in the very north of the country the events surrounding the passing of the *lex Appuleia* had not suffered in the telling. Nor was it necessary for Marius to retell the story; they simply looked at each other wordlessly, and everything which needed to pass between them on a basic level did so wordlessly.

However, once the emotional rush abated a little and the first cup of good wine was finished, Sulla did broach the more unpalatable externals of the subject.

"Your credibility's suffered shockingly," he said.

"I know, Lucius Cornelius."

"It's Saturninus, I hear."

Marius sighed. "Well, and can you blame him for hating me? He's given half a hundred speeches from the rostra, and by no means all to properly convoked assemblies. Every one accusing me of betraying him. In fact, since he's a brilliant speaker, the tale of my treachery hasn't lost in his style of translation to the crowds. And he draws the crowds too. Not merely regular Forum frequenters, but men of the Third and Fourth and Fifth Classes who seem fascinated by him to the extent that whenever they have a day off, they turn up in the Forum to listen to him."

"Does he speak that often?" asked Sulla.

"He speaks every single day!"

Sulla whistled. "That's something new in the annals of the Forum! Every day? Rain or shine? Formal meetings or no formal meetings?"

"Every single day. When the urban praetor—his own boon companion Glaucia—obeyed his orders from the Pontifex Maximus to instruct Saturninus that he couldn't speak on market days or holidays or non-comitial days, he simply ignored it. And because he's a tribune of the plebs, no one has seriously tried to haul him down." Marius frowned, worried. "In consequence, his fame keeps spreading, and we now see a whole new breed of Forum frequenter—those who come solely to hear Saturninus harangue. He has—I don't quite know what you'd call it—I suppose the Greeks have the word for it, as usual—they'd say *kharisma*. They feel his passion, I think, because of course not being regular Forum frequenters they're not connoisseurs of rhetoric, and don't give tuppence how he wiggles his littlest finger or varies the style of his walk. No, they just stand there gaping up at him, becoming more and more excited at what he says, and end in cheering him wildly."

"We'll have to keep an eye on him, won't we?" Sulla asked. He looked at Marius very seriously. "Why did you do it?"

There was no pretence at ignorance; Marius answered at once. "I didn't have any choice, Lucius Cornelius. The truth is that I'm not—I don't know—*devious* enough to see around all the corners I should if I'm to keep a pace to two ahead of men like Scaurus. He caught me as neatly as anyone could have wanted. I acknowledge the fact freely."

"But in one way you've salvaged the scheme," said Sulla, trying to comfort him. "The second land bill is still on the tablets, and I don't think the Plebeian Assembly—or the Assembly of the People, for that matter—is going to invalidate it. Or at least, I'm told that's how things stand."

"True," said Marius, not looking comforted. He hunched his head into his shoulders, sighed. "Saturninus is the victor, Lucius Cornelius, not I. It's *his* sense of outrage keeping the Plebs firm. I've lost them." He writhed, threw out his hands. "How am I ever going to get through the rest of this year? It's an ordeal to have to walk through the volley of boos and hisses from the region around the rostra whenever Saturninus is speaking, but as for walking into the Curia—I *loathe* it! I loathe the sleek smile on Scaurus's seamy face, I loathe the insufferable smirk on that camel Catulus's face—I'm not made for the political arena, and that's a truth I've just begun to find out."

"But you climbed the *cursus honorum,* Gaius Marius!" Sulla said. "You were one of the great tribunes of the plebs! You knew the political arena, and you loved it, otherwise you could never have been a great tribune of the plebs."

Marius shrugged. "Oh, I was young then, Lucius Cornelius. And I had a good brain. But a political animal I am not."

"So you're going to yield the center of the stage to a posturing wolfshead like Saturninus? That doesn't sound like the Gaius Marius I know," said Sulla.

"I'm not the Gaius Marius you know," said Marius with a faint smile. "The new Gaius Marius is very, very tired. A stranger to me as much as to you, believe me!"

"Then go away for the summer, please!"

"I intend to," said Marius, "as soon as you tie the knot with Aelia."

Sulla started, then laughed. "Ye gods, I'd forgotten all about it!" He got to his feet gracefully, a beautifully made man in the prime of life. "I'd better go home and seek an audience with our mutual mother-in-law, hadn't I? No doubt she's breaking her neck"—he shivered—"to leave me."

The shiver meant nothing to Marius, who seized upon the comment instead. "Yes, she's anxious. I've bought her a nice little villa not far from ours at Cumae."

"Then home I go, as fleet as Mercury chasing a contract to re-pave the Via Appia!" He held out his hand. "Look after yourself, Gaius Marius. If Aelia's still willing, I'll tie the knot at once." A thought occurred to him, he laughed. "You're absolutely right! Catulus Caesar looks like a camel! *Monumental* hauteur!"

Julia was waiting outside the study to waylay Sulla as he left. "What do you think?" she asked anxiously.

"He'll be all right, little sister. They beat him, and he suffers. Take him down to Campania, make him bathe in the sea and wallow in the roses."

"I will, as soon as you're married."

"I'm marrying, I'm marrying!" he cried, holding up his hands in surrender.

Julia sighed. "There's one thing we cannot get away from, Lucius Cornelius, and that is that less than half a year in the Forum has worn Gaius Marius down more than ten years in the field with his armies."

It seemed everyone needed a rest, for when Marius left for Cumae, public life in Rome simmered down to a tepid inertia. One by one the notables quit the city, unbearable during the height of summer, when every kind of enteric fever raged amid Subura and Esquiline, and even Palatine and Aventine were only debatably healthy.

Not that life in the Subura worried Aurelia unduly; she dwelled in the midst of a cool cavern, the greenery of the courtyard and the immensely thick walls of her insula keeping the heat at bay. Gaius Matius and his wife, Priscilla, were in like condition to herself and Caesar, for Priscilla too was heavily pregnant, her baby due at the same time as Aurelia's.

The two women were very well looked after. Gaius Matius hovered helpfully, and Lucius Decumius popped in every day to make sure all was right. The flowers still came regularly, supplemented since her pregnancy with little gifts of sweetmeats, rare spices, anything Lucius Decumius thought might keep his darling Aurelia's appetite keen.

"As if I'd lost it!" she laughed to Publius Rutilius Rufus, another regular caller.

Her son, Gaius Julius Caesar, was born on the thirteenth day of Quinctilis, which meant that his birth was entered in the register at the temple of Juno Lucina as occurring two days before the Ides of Quinctilis, his status as patrician, his rank as senatorial. He was very long and consequently weighed somewhat more than he looked to weigh; he was very strong; he was solemn and quiet, not prone to wailing; his hair was so fair it was practically invisible, though on close examination he actually had quite a lot of it; and his eyes from birth were a pale greenish-blue, ringed around with a band of blue so dark it was almost black.

"He's someone, this son of yours," said Lucius Decumius, staring into the baby's face intently. "Will you look at them eyes! Give your grandmother a fright, they would!"

"Don't say such things, you horrible little wart!" growled Cardixa, who was enslaved by this first boy-child.

"Gimme a look at downstairs," Lucius Decumius demanded, snatching with grubby fingers at the baby's diapers. "Oho ho ho ho ho!" he crowed. "Just as I thought! Big nose, big feet, and big dick!"

"*Lucius Decumius!*" said Aurelia, scandalized.

"That does it! Out you go!" roared Cardixa as she picked him up by the scruff of his neck, and dropped him outside the front door as smaller women might have dumped a kitten.

Sulla called to see Aurelia almost a month after the baby's birth, explaining that she was the only familiar face left in Rome, and apologizing if he was imposing.

"Of course not!" she said, delighted to see him. "I'm hoping you can stay for dinner—or if you can't today, perhaps you can come tomorrow? I'm so starved for company!"

"I can stay," he said without ceremony. "I only really came back to Rome to see an old friend of mine—he's come down with a fever."

"Who's that? Anyone I know?" she asked, more out of courtesy than curiosity.

But for a short moment he looked as if she had asked an unwelcome question, or perhaps a painful one; the expression on his face interested her far more than the identity of his sick friend, for it was dark, unhappy, angry. Then it was gone, and he was smiling with consummate ease.

"I doubt you know him," he said. "Metrobius."

"The actor?"

"The same. I used to know a lot of people in the theater. In the old days. Before I married Julilla and entered the Senate. A different world." His strange light eyes wandered around the reception room. "More like this world, only seamier. Funny! It seems now like a dream."

"You sound rather sorry," said Aurelia gently.

"No, not really."

"And will he get well, your friend Metrobius?"

"Oh, yes! It's just a fever."

A silence fell, not uncomfortable, which he broke without words by getting up and walking across to the big open space which served as a window onto the courtyard.

"It's lovely out there."

"I think so."

"And your new son? How is he?"

She smiled. "You shall see for yourself shortly."

"Good." He remained staring at the courtyard.

"Lucius Cornelius, is everything all right?" she asked.

He turned then, smiling; she thought what an attractive man he was, in a most unusual way. And how disconcerting those eyes were—so light—so ringed with darkness. Like her son's eyes. And for some reason that thought made her shiver.

"Yes, Aurelia, everything's all right," Sulla said.

"I wish I thought you were telling me the truth."

He opened his mouth to reply, but at that moment Cardixa came in bearing the infant heir to the Caesar name.

"We're off upstairs to the fourth floor," she said.

"Show Lucius Cornelius first, Cardixa."

But the only children Sulla was really interested in were his own two, so he peered dutifully into the baby's face, then glanced at Aurelia to see if this satisfied her.

"Off you go, Cardixa," she said, putting Sulla out of his misery. "Who is it this morning?"

"Sarah."

She turned to Sulla with a pleasant, unselfconscious smile. "I have no milk, alas! So my son goes everywhere for his food. One of the great advantages of living in a big community like an insula. There are always at least half a dozen women nursing, and everyone is nice enough to offer to feed my babies."

"He'll grow up to love the whole world," said Sulla. "I imagine you have the whole world as tenants."

"I do. It makes life interesting."

Back he went to gaze at the courtyard.

"Lucius Cornelius, you're only half here," she accused softly. "Something *is* the matter! Can't you share it with me? Or is it one of those men-only difficulties?"

He came to sit down on the couch opposite hers. "I just never have any luck with women," he said abruptly.

Aurelia blinked. "In what way?"

"The women I—love. The women I marry."

Interesting; he found it easier to speak of marriage than of love. "Which is it now?" she asked.

"A bit of both. In love with one, married to another."

"Oh, Lucius Cornelius!" She looked at him with genuine liking but not an ounce of desire. "I shan't ask you any names, because I don't really want to know. You ask me the questions, I'll try to come up with the answers."

He shrugged. "There's nothing much to say! I married Aelia, found for me by our mother-in-law. After Julilla, I wanted a perfect Roman matron—someone like Julia, or you if you were a little older. When Marcia introduced me to Aelia, I thought she was ideal—calm, quiet, good-humored, attractive, a nice person. And I thought, terrific! I'll have me my Roman matron at last. I can't love anyone, I thought, so I may as well be married to someone I can like."

"You liked your German wife, I believe," Aurelia said.

"Yes, very much. I still miss her in peculiar ways. But she's not a Roman, so she's no use to the senator in Rome, is she? Anyway, I decided Aelia would turn out much the same as Hermana." He laughed, a hard sound. "But I was wrong! Aelia turns out to be dull, pedestrian, and boring. A very nice person indeed, but oh, five moments in her company, and I'm yawning!"

"Is she good to your children?"

"Very good. No complaints there!" He laughed again. "I ought to have hired her as a nurserymaid—she'd have been ideal. She adores the children, and they adore her."

He was talking now almost as if she didn't exist, or as if she didn't matter as an auditor, only as a presence who gave him an excuse to say aloud what he had long been thinking.

"Just after I came back from Italian Gaul, I was invited to attend a dinner party at Scaurus's," he went on. "A bit flattered. A bit apprehensive. Wondered if they were all going to be there—Metellus Piggle-wiggle and the rest—and try to wean me away from Gaius Marius. She was there, poor little thing. Scaurus's wife. By all the gods in the world, why did it have to be her married to Scaurus? He could be her great-grandfather! Dalmatica. That's what they call her. One way of keeping them all straight, the thousands of Caecilia Metellas. I took one look at her and I loved her. At least I think it's love. There's pity in it too, but I never seem to stop thinking of her, so that means it's got to be love, doesn't it? She's *pregnant*. Isn't that disgusting? No one asked her what she wanted, of course. Metellus Piggle-wiggle just gave her to Scaurus like a honeycomb to a child. Here, your son's dead, take this consolation prize! Have another son! Disgusting.

And yet—if they knew the half of me, they'd be the ones disgusted. I can't see it, Aurelia. They're more immoral than I am! But you'd never get *them* to see it that way."

Aurelia had learned a great deal since she moved to the Subura; everyone from Lucius Decumius to the freedmen thronging the top two floors talked to her. And things happened—things the landlady was involved in whether she liked it or not—things which would have shocked her husband to his core did he only know. Abortion. Witchcraft. Murder. Robbery with violence. Rape. Delirium tremens and worse addictions. Madness. Despair. Depression. Suicide. It all went on in every insula, and concluded itself the same way; no taking these cases to the tribunal of the *praetor urbanus*! They were solved by the inhabitants, and a rough justice was dealt out in the most summary fashion. An eye for an eye, a tooth for a tooth, a life for a life.

So as she listened Aurelia pieced together a composite picture of Lucius Cornelius Sulla that was not so very far from the truth. Alone among the aristocrats of Rome who knew him, she understood from whence he had come, and understood too the terrible difficulties his nature and his upbringing had thrust upon him. He had claimed his birthright, but he was permanently branded with the stews of Rome too.

And as Sulla talked about one thing, his mind wandered among other things he didn't dare say to his listener: how desperately he had wanted her, Scaurus's little pregnant child-wife, and not entirely for the flesh or the mind. She was ideal for his purposes. But she was married *confarreatio* to Scaurus, and he was committed to splendid boring Aelia. Not *confarreatio* this time! It was too hideous a business to divorce; Dalmatica simply pointed up a lesson he had already learned in that respect. Women. He was never going to have the luck with women, he knew it in his bones. Was it because of the other side to himself? That wonderful beautiful glorious relationship with Metrobius! And yet he didn't want to live with Metrobius any more than he had wanted to live with Julilla. Perhaps that was it—he did not want to share himself. Too dangerous by far. Oh, but he had hungered for Caecilia Metella Dalmatica, wife of Marcus Aemilius Scaurus Princeps Senatus! Disgusting. Not that he normally objected to old men and child-brides. This was *personal*. He was in love with her, therefore she was special.

"Did she—Dalmatica—like you, Lucius Cornelius?" Aurelia asked, breaking into his thoughts.

Sulla didn't hesitate. "Oh, yes! No doubt of it."

"What are you going to do, then?"

He writhed. "I've come too far, I've paid too much! I can't stop *now*, Aurelia! Even for Dalmatica—if I had an affair with her, the *boni* would make it their business to ruin me. I don't have much money yet, either. Just enough to get by in the Senate. I made a bit out of the Germans, but no more than my proper share. And I'm not going to climb the rest of the way easily. They feel about me the way they feel about Gaius Marius, even though for different reasons. Neither of us conforms to their wretched ideals. Yet they can't work out why we have the ability and they don't. They feel used, abused. I'm definitely luckier than Gaius Marius. At least I have the blood. But it's tainted with the Subura. Actors. Low life. I'm not really one of the Good Men." He drew a breath. "Yet— I'm going to go right past them, Aurelia! Because I'm the best horse in the race."

"And what happens when the prize isn't worth it?"

He opened his eyes wide, astonished at her denseness. "It's never worth the effort! Never! That's not why we do it, any of us. When they harness us up to do our seven laps of the course, we race against ourselves. What other challenge could there be for a Gaius Marius? He's the best horse in the field. So he races against himself. So do I. I can do it. I'm going to do it! But it only really matters to *me*."

And she blushed at her denseness. "Of course." Rising to her feet, she held out her hand. "Come, Lucius Cornelius! It's a lovely day in spite of the heat. The Subura will be entirely left to itself—all those who can afford to leave Rome for the summer are gone. Only the poor and the crazed are left! And I. Let's go for a walk, and when we come back, we'll have dinner. I'll send a

message to Uncle Publius to join us—I think he's still in town."
She pulled a face. "I have to be careful, you understand, Lucius
Cornelius. My husband trusts me as much as he loves me, which
is a great deal. But he wouldn't like me to cause gossip, and I try
to be an old-fashioned kind of wife. He would be horrified to
think I *didn't* invite you to eat dinner with me—and yet if Uncle
Publius can come, Gaius Julius will commend me."

Sulla eyed her affectionately. "What nonsense men cherish
about their wives! You're not even remotely like the creature
Gaius Julius moons about over military dinners in camp."

"I know," she said. "But he doesn't."

The heat of the Vicus Patricii settled down on their heads like
a stifling blanket; Aurelia gasped and ducked back inside. "Well,
that settles that! I didn't think it was hot! Eutychus can run to the
Carinae for Uncle Publius, he can do with the exercise. And we'll
sit in the garden." She led the way, still talking. "Cheer up, Lucius
Cornelius, do! It will all turn out in the end, I'm sure. Go back to
Circei and that nice, boring wife. In time you'll like her more, I
promise. And it will be better for you if you don't see Dalmatica
at all. How old are you now?"

The trapped feeling was beginning to lift; Sulla's face light-
ened, his smile more natural. "A milestone this year, Aurelia. I
turned forty last New Year's Day."

"Not an old man yet!"

"In some ways I am. I haven't even been praetor yet, and I'm
already a year past the usual age."

"Now, now, you're looking gloomy again, and there really is
no need. Look at our old war-horse Gaius Marius! His first consulship at fifty, eight years over the age. Now if you saw *him*
poled up for the Mars race, would you pick him as the best horse
in it? Would you bet that he'd be the October Horse? Yet all his
greatest deeds he did after he turned fifty."

"That's very true," said Sulla, and did feel more cheerful, in
spite of himself. "What lucky god prompted me to come and see
you today? You're a good friend, Aurelia. A help."

"Well, perhaps one day I'll turn to *you* for help."

"All you have to do is ask." His head went up, he took in the naked balconies of the upper floors. "You are courageous! No screens? And they don't abuse the privilege?"

"Never."

He laughed, a throaty chuckle of genuine amusement. "I do believe you have the Subura hard cases all wrapped up in the palm of your little hand!"

Nodding, smiling, she rocked gently back and forth on her garden seat. "I like my life, Lucius Cornelius. To be honest, I don't care if Gaius Julius never gets the money together to buy that house on the Palatine. Here in the Subura I'm busy, fruitful, surrounded by all sorts of interesting people. I'm running a race of my own, you see."

"With only one egg in the cup and only one dolphin down," Sulla said, "you've got a very long way to go yet."

"So have you," said Aurelia.

Julia knew of course that Marius would never spend the whole summer at Cumae, though he had talked as if he would not return to Rome until the beginning of September; the moment his equilibrium began to right itself, he would be itching to get back to the fray. So she counted her blessings a day at a time, glad that the moment Marius returned to a rural setting, he shed both political *toga praetexta* and military cuirass, and became for a little while a country squire like all his ancestors. They swam in the sea off the little beach below their magnificent villa, and gorged themselves on fresh oysters, crabs, shrimp, tunnyfish; they walked the sparsely populated hills amid welters of roses cloying the air with perfume; they did little entertaining, and pretended to be out whenever people called. Marius built a boat of sorts for Young Marius, and got almost as much fun out of its instant imitation of a bottom fish as Young Marius did. Never, thought Julia, had she been quite so happy as during that halcyon summer at Cumae. Counting her blessings one day at a time.

But Marius did not return to Rome. Painless and subtle, the little stroke happened during the first night of the Dog Star month of Sextilis; all Marius noticed when he woke in the morning was that his pillow was wet where apparently he had drooled in his sleep. When he came to break his fast and found Julia on the open terrace looking out to sea, he gazed at her in bewilderment as she gazed at him with an expression he had never before seen on her face.

"What's the matter?" he mumbled, his tongue feeling thick and clumsy, a most peculiar non-sensation.

"Your face—" she said, her own whitening.

His hands went up to touch it, his left fingers as awkward as his tongue felt. "What *is* it?" he asked.

"Your face—it's dropped on the left side," she said, and choked on her breath as understanding dawned. "Oh, Gaius Marius! You've had a stroke!"

But because he felt no pain and no direct consciousness of any alteration, he refused to believe her until she brought him a big polished silver mirror and he could look at himself for himself. The right side of his face was firm, uplifted, not very lined for a man of his age, where the left side looked as if it were a wax mask melting in the heat of some nearby torch, running, drooping, slipping away.

"I don't *feel* any different!" he said, stunned. "Not inside my mind, where one is supposed to feel an illness. My tongue won't move around my words properly, but my head knows how to say them, and you're understanding what I say and I'm understanding what you say, so I haven't lost my faculty of speech! My left hand fumbles, yet I can move it. And there is no pain, no pain of any kind!"

When he refused with trembling anger to have a physician sent for, Julia gave in for fear that opposition would make his condition worse; all that day she watched him herself, and was able to tell him as she persuaded him to go to bed shortly after nightfall that the paralysis appeared to be about the same as it had been at dawn.

"That's a good sign, I'm sure," she said. "You'll get better in time. You'll just have to rest, stay here longer."

"I can't! They'll think I'm not game to face them!"

"If they care to visit you—which I'm sure they will!—they'll be able to see for themselves what's wrong, Gaius Marius. Whether you like it or not, here you stay until you get better," said Julia with a note of authority quite new to her voice. "No, don't argue with me! I'm right, and you know I am! What do you think you can accomplish if you go back to Rome in this condition, beyond having another stroke?"

"Nothing," he muttered, and fell back on the bed in despair. "Julia, Julia, how can I recover from something that makes me feel more ugly than ill? I must recover! I *can't* let them beat me, not now I have so much at stake!"

"They won't beat you, Gaius Marius," she said strongly. "The only thing that will ever beat you is death, and you're not going to die from this little stroke. The paralysis will improve. And if you rest, you exercise sensibly, you eat in moderation, you don't drink any wine, and you don't worry about what's happening in Rome, it will happen much faster."

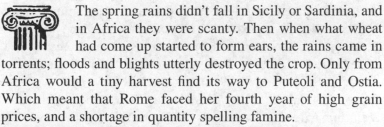 The spring rains didn't fall in Sicily or Sardinia, and in Africa they were scanty. Then when what wheat had come up started to form ears, the rains came in torrents; floods and blights utterly destroyed the crop. Only from Africa would a tiny harvest find its way to Puteoli and Ostia. Which meant that Rome faced her fourth year of high grain prices, and a shortage in quantity spelling famine.

The junior consul and *flamen Martialis,* Lucius Valerius Flaccus, found himself with empty granaries beneath the cliffs of the Aventine adjacent to the Port of Rome, and the private granaries along the Vicus Tuscus held very little. This very little, the grain merchants informed Flaccus and his aediles, would sell for upward of fifty sesterces per *modius,* a mere thirteen pounds in weight. Few if any Head Count families could afford to pay a quarter so much. There were other and cheaper foods available, but a shortage of wheat sent all foodstuffs up in price because of increased consumption and limited production. And bellies used to good bread found no satisfaction in thin gruel and turnips, which became the staples of the lowly in times of famine; the strong and healthy survived, but the old, the weak, the very young, and the sickly all too often died.

By October the Head Count was growing restive; thrills of fear began to run through the ordinary residents of the city. For the Head Count of Rome deprived of food was a prospect no one living cheek by jowl with them could face without a thrill of fear. Many of the Third and Fourth Class citizens, who would find it difficult anyway to buy such costly grain, began to lay in weapons to defend their larders from the depredations of those owning even less.

Lucius Valerius Flaccus conferred with the curule aediles— responsible for grain purchases on behalf of the State as well as for the storage and sale of State grain—and applied to the Senate for additional funds to buy in grain from anywhere it could be obtained, and of any kind—barley, millet, emmer wheat as well as bread wheat. However, few in the Senate were really worried; too many years and too much insulation from the lower classes of citizens separated them from the last Head Count famine riots.

To make matters worse, the two young men serving as Rome's Treasury quaestors were of the most exclusive and unpitying kind of senator, and thought little of the Head Count at the best of times. Both when elected quaestor had asked for duty inside Rome, declaring that they intended to "arrest the unwarranted drains upon Rome's Treasury"—an impressive way of saying that they had no intention of releasing money for Head Count armies—or Head Count grain. The urban quaestor—more senior of the two—was none other than Caepio Junior, son of the consul who had stolen the Gold of Tolosa and lost the battle of Arausio; the other was Metellus Piglet, the son of the exiled Metellus Numidicus. Both had scores to settle with Gaius Marius.

It was not senatorial practice to run counter to the recommendations of the Treasury quaestors. Questioned in the House as to the state of fiscal affairs, both Caepio Junior and Metellus Piglet said flatly there was no money for grain. Thanks to the massive outlays it had been called upon to make for a number of years outfitting and paying and feeding Head Count armies, the State was broke. Neither the war against Jugurtha nor the war against the Germans had brought in anything like enough money in spoils and tributes to rectify the State's negative financial balance, said the two Treasury quaestors. And produced their tribunes of the Treasury and their account books to prove their point. Rome was broke. Those without the money to pay the going price for grain would have to starve. Sorry, but that was the reality of the situation.

By the beginning of November the word had reached all of Rome that there would be no reasonably priced State grain, for the Senate had refused to vote funds for its purchase. Couched in the form of rumor, the word didn't mention crop failures or cantankerous Treasury quaestors; it simply stated that there would be no cheap grain.

The Forum Romanum immediately began to fill up with crowds of a nature not usually seen there, while the normal Forum frequenters melted away or tacked themselves onto the back of the newcomers. These crowds were Head Count and the Fifth Class, and their mood was ugly. Senators and other togate men found themselves hissed by thousands of tongues as they walked what they regarded as their traditional territory, but at first were not easily cowed; then the hissing became showers of pelted filth—faeces, manure, stinking Tiber mud, rotten garbage. Whereupon the Senate extricated itself from these difficulties by suspending all meetings, leaving unfortunates like bankers, knight merchants, advocates, and tribunes of the Treasury to suffer the besmirching of their persons without senatorial support.

Not strong enough to take the initiative, the junior consul, Flaccus, let matters drift, while Caepio Junior and Metellus Piglet congratulated themselves upon a job well done. If the winter saw a few thousand Head Count Romans die, that meant there would be fewer mouths to feed.

At which point the tribune of the plebs Lucius Appuleius Saturninus convoked the Plebeian Assembly, and proposed a grain law to it. The State was to buy immediately every ounce of wheat, barley, and millet in Italy and Italian Gaul and sell it for the ridiculously cheap price of one sestertius per *modius*. Of course Saturninus made no reference to the impossible logistics of shipping anything from Italian Gaul to regions south of the Apennines, nor the fact that there was almost no grain to buy anywhere south of the Apennines. What he wanted was the crowd, and that meant placing himself in the eyes of the crowd as its sole savior.

Opposition was almost nonexistent in the absence of a convened Senate, for the grain shortage affected everyone in Rome below the level of the rich. The entire food chain and its participants were on Saturninus's side. So were the Third and Fourth Classes, and even many of the centuries of the Second Class. As November edged over the hump of its middle and down the slope toward December, all Rome was on Saturninus's side.

"If people can't afford to buy wheat, we can't afford to make bread!" cried the Guild of Millers and Bakers.

"If people are hungry, they don't work well!" cried the Guild of Builders.

"If people can't afford to feed their children, what's going to happen to their slaves?" cried the Guild of Freedmen.

"If people have to spend their money on food, they won't be able to pay rent!" cried the Guild of Landlords.

"If people are so hungry they start pillaging shops and overturning market stalls, what will happen to us?" cried the Guild of Merchants.

"If people descend on our allotments in search of food, we won't have any produce to sell!" cried the Guild of Market Gardeners.

For it was not the simple matter of a famine killing off a few thousand of the Head Count; the moment Rome's middle and poorer citizens could not afford to eat, a hundred and one kinds of businesses and trades suffered in their turn. A famine, in short, was an economic disaster. But the Senate wasn't coming together, even in temples off the beaten track, so it was left to Saturninus to propose a solution, and his solution was based upon a false premise; that there was grain for the State to buy. He himself genuinely thought there was, deeming every aspect of the crisis a manufactured one, and the culprits an alliance between the Policy Makers of the Senate and the upper echelons of the grain barons.

Every one of the thousands of faces in the Forum turned to him as heliotropes to the sun; working himself into a passion through the force of his oratory, he began to believe every single word he shouted, he began to believe every single face his eyes encountered in the crowd, he began to believe in a new way to govern Rome. What did the consulship really matter? What did the Senate really matter, when crowds like these made it shove its tail between its legs and slink home? When the bets were on the table and the moment to throw the dice arrived, *they* were all that mattered, these faces in this enormous crowd. *They* held the real power; those who thought they held it did so only as long as the faces in the crowd permitted it.

So what did the consulship really matter? What did the Senate really matter? Talk, hot air, a nothing! There were no armies in Rome, no armies nearer to Rome than the recruit training centers around Capua. Consuls and Senate held their power without force of arms or numbers to back them up. But here in the Forum was true power, here were the numbers to back that true power. Why did a man have to be consul to be the First Man in Rome? It wasn't necessary! Had Gaius Gracchus too realized that? Or was he forced to kill himself before he could realize it?

I, thought Saturninus, gobbling up the vision of the faces in his mighty crowd, shall be the First Man in Rome! But not as consul. As tribune of the plebs. Genuine power lay with the tribunes of the plebs, not with the consuls. And if Gaius Marius could get himself elected consul in what promised to be perpetuity, what was to stop Lucius Appuleius Saturninus's getting himself elected tribune of the plebs in perpetuity?

However, Saturninus chose a quiet day to pass his grain bill into law, chiefly because he retained the wisdom to see that senatorial opposition to providing cheap grain must continue to appear high-handed and elitist; therefore no enormous crowd must be present in the Forum to give the Senate an opportunity to accuse the Plebeian Assembly of disorder, riot, violence, and denounce the law as invalid. He was still simmering about the second agrarian bill, Gaius Marius's treachery, Metellus Numidicus's exile; that in fact the law was still engraved on the tablets was his doing, not Gaius Marius's. Which made *him* the real author of land grants for the Head Count veterans.

November was short on holidays, especially holidays on which the Comitia could meet. But his opportunity to find a quiet day came when a fabulously wealthy knight died, and his sons staged elaborate funeral gladiatorial games in their father's honor; the site chosen for the games—normally the Forum Romanum—was the Circus Flaminius, in order to avoid the crowds gathering every day in the Forum Romanum.

It was Caepio Junior who spoiled Saturninus's plans. The Plebeian Assembly was convoked; the omens were auspicious; the Forum was inhabited by its normal frequenters because the crowd had gone off to the Circus Flaminius; the other tribunes of the plebs were busy with the casting of the lots to see which order the tribes were going to vote in; and Saturninus himself stood to the front of the rostra exhorting the groups of tribes forming in the well of the Comitia to vote the way he wanted.

In the conspicuous absence of senatorial meetings, it had not occurred to Saturninus that any members of the Senate were keeping an eye on events in the Forum, barring his nine fellow tribunes of the plebs, who simply did as they were told these days. But there were some members of the Senate who felt quite as much contempt for that body's craven conduct as did Lucius Appuleius Saturninus. They were all young, either in their quaestorian year or at most two years beyond that point, and they had allies among the sons of senators and First Class knights as yet too young to enter the Senate or senior posts in their fathers' firms. Meeting in groups at each other's homes, they were led by Caepio Junior and Metellus Piglet, and they had a more mature confidant-adviser to give direction and purpose to what might otherwise have ended up merely a series of angry discussions foundering in an excess of wine.

Their confidant-adviser was rapidly becoming something of an idol to them, for he possessed all those qualities young men so admire—he was daring, intrepid, cool-headed, sophisticated, something of a high liver and womanizer, witty, fashionable, and had an impressive war record. His name was Lucius Cornelius Sulla.

With Marius laid low in Cumae for what seemed months, Sulla had taken it upon himself to watch events in Rome in a way that, for instance, Publius Rutilius Rufus would never have dreamed of doing. Sulla's motives were not completely based on loyalty to Marius; after that conversation with Aurelia, he had looked very detachedly at his future prospects in the Senate, and come to the conclusion that Aurelia was right: he would, like Gaius Marius, be what a gardener would call a late bloomer. In which case it was pointless for him to seek friendship and alliance among those senators older than himself. Scaurus, for instance, was a lost cause. And how convenient that particular decision was! It would keep him out of the way of Scaurus's delectable little child-bride, now the mother of baby Aemilia Scaura; when he had heard the news that Scaurus had fathered a girl, Sulla experienced a shaft of pure pleasure. Served the randy old goat right.

Thinking to safeguard his own political future while preserving Marius's, Sulla embarked upon the wooing of the senatorial younger generation, choosing as his targets those who were malleable, able to be influenced, not very intelligent, extremely rich, from important families, or so arrogantly sure of themselves they left themselves open to a subtle form of flattery. His primary targets were Caepio Junior and Metellus Piglet, Caepio Junior because he was an intellectually dense patrician with access to young men like Marcus Livius Drusus (whom Sulla did not even try to woo), and Metellus Piglet because he knew what was going on among the older Good Men. No one knew better than Sulla how to woo young men, even when his purposes held no kind of sexuality, so it was not long before he was holding court among them, his manner always tinged with amusement at their youthful posturings in a way which suggested to them that there was a hope he would change his mind, take them seriously. Nor were they adolescents; the oldest among them were only some seven or eight years his junior, the youngest fifteen or sixteen years his junior. Old enough to consider themselves fully formed, young enough to be thrown off balance by a Sulla. And the nucleus of a senatorial following which in time would be of enormous importance to a man determined to be consul.

At this moment, however, Sulla's chief concern was Saturninus, whom he had been watching very closely since the first crowds began to gather in the Forum, and the harassment of togate dignitaries began. Whether the *lex Appuleia frumentaria* was actually passed into law or not was far from Sulla's main worry; what Saturninus needed, Sulla thought, was a demonstration that he would not have things all his own way.

When some fifty of the young bloods met at the house of Metellus Piglet on the night before Saturninus planned to pass his grain law, Sulla lay back and listened to the talk in an apparent idle amusement until Caepio Junior rounded on him and demanded to know what he thought they ought to do.

He looked marvelous, the thick red-gold hair barbered to bring out the best of its waves, his white skin flawless, his brows and lashes dark enough to show up (had they only known it, he touched them with a trace of *stibium*, otherwise they virtually disappeared), his eyes as glacially compelling as a blue-eyed cat's. "I think you're all hot air," he said.

Metellus Piglet had been brought to understand that Sulla was anything but Marius's tame dog; like any other Roman, he didn't hold it against a man that he attached himself to a faction, any more than he assumed that man could not be detached. "No, we're not all hot air," he growled without a single stammer. "It's just that we don't know what's the right tactic."

"Do you object to a little violence?" Sulla asked.

"Not when it's to protect the Senate's right to decide how Rome's public money is to be spent," said Caepio Junior.

"And there you have it," said Sulla. "The People have never been accorded the right to spend the city's moneys. Let the People make the laws—we don't object to that. But it's the Senate's right to provide any money the People's laws demand—and the Senate's right to deny funding. If we're stripped of our right to control the purse-strings, we have no power left at all. Money is the only way we can render the People's laws impotent when we don't agree with them. That's how we dealt with the grain law of Gaius Gracchus."

"We won't prevent the Senate's voting the money when this grain law goes through," said Metellus Piglet, still without a stammer; when with his intimates he didn't stammer.

"Of course not!" said Sulla. "We won't prevent its being passed, either. But we can show Lucius Appuleius a little of our strength all the same."

Thus as Saturninus stood exhorting his voters to do the right thing by the *lex Appuleia frumentaria*, the crowds no closer than the Circus Flaminius and the meeting as orderly as any consular could demand, Caepio Junior led some two hundred followers into the lower Forum Romanum. Armed with clubs and billets of wood, most of them were beefy muscular fellows with the slack midriffs which suggested they were ex-gladiators now reduced to hiring out their services for any sort of job requiring strength or the capacity to turn nasty. However, all the fifty present at Metellus Piglet's house the night before led the vanguard, Caepio Junior very much the leader of the pack. Lucius Cornelius Sulla was not among them.

Saturninus shrugged and watched impassively as the gang marched across the Forum, then turned back to the well of the Comitia and dismissed the meeting.

"There'll be no heads broken on my account!" he shouted to the voters, dissolving their tribal clumps in alarm. "Go home, come back tomorrow! We'll pass our law then!"

On the following day the Head Count was back in attendance

on the Comitia; no gang of senatorial toughs appeared to break up the meeting, and the grain bill passed into law.

"All I was trying to do, you thick-headed idiot," said Saturninus to Caepio Junior when they met in the temple of Jupiter Optimus Maximus, where Valerius Flaccus had felt the Conscript Fathers would be safe from the crowds while they argued about funding for the *lex Appuleia frumentaria,* "was pass a lawful law in a lawfully convoked assembly. The crowds weren't there, the atmosphere was peaceful, and the omens were impeccable. And what happens? You and your idiot friends come along to break a few heads!" He turned to the clusters of senators standing about. "Don't blame me that the law had to be passed in the middle of twenty thousand Head Count! Blame this fool!"

"This fool is blaming himself for not using force where force would have counted most!" shouted Caepio Junior. "I ought to have killed you, Lucius Appuleius!"

"Thank you for saying that in front of all these impartial witnesses," said Saturninus, smiling. "Quintus Servilius Caepio Junior, I hereby formally charge you with minor treason, in that you did attempt to obstruct a tribune of the plebs in the execution of his duty, and that you did threaten to harm the sacrosanct person of a tribune of the plebs."

"You're riding a half-mad horse for a fall, Lucius Appuleius," said Sulla. "Get off before it happens, man!"

"I have laid a formal charge against Quintus Servilius, Conscript Fathers," said Saturninus, ignoring Sulla as nobody of importance, "but that matter can now be left to the treason court. Today I'm here to demand money."

There were fewer than eighty senators present, in spite of the safe location, and none of significance; Saturninus glared at them contemptuously. "I want money to buy grain for the People of Rome," he said. "If you haven't got it in the Treasury, I suggest you go out and borrow it. *For money I will have!*"

Saturninus got his money. Red-faced and protesting, Caepio Junior the urban quaestor was ordered to mint a special coinage from an emergency stockpile of silver bars in the temple of Ops, and pay for the grain without further defiance.

"I'll see you in court," said Saturninus sweetly to Caepio Junior as thc meeting finished, "because I'm going to take great pleasure in prosecuting you myself."

But in this he overstepped himself; the knight jurors took a dislike to Saturninus, and were already favorably disposed toward Caepio Junior when Fortune showed that she too was most favorably disposed toward Caepio Junior. Right in the middle of the defending counsel's address came an urgent letter from Smyrna to inform his son that Quintus Servilius Caepio had died in Smyrna, surrounded by nothing more comforting than his gold. Caepio Junior wept bitterly; the jury was moved, and dismissed the charges.

Elections were due, but no one wanted to hold them, for still each day the crowds gathered in the Forum Romanum, and still each day the granaries remained empty. The junior consul, Flaccus, insisted the elections must wait until time proved Gaius Marius incapable of conducting them; priest of Mars though he was, Lucius Valerius Flaccus had too little of Mars in him to risk his person by supervising elections in a climate like this present one.

Marcus Antonius Orator had had a very successful three-year campaign against the pirates of Cilicia and Pamphylia, which he finished in some style from his headquarters in the delightfully cosmopolitan and cultured city of Athens. Here he had been joined by his good friend Gaius Memmius, who on his return to Rome from governing Macedonia had found himself arraigned in Glaucia's extortion court along with Gaius Flavius Fimbria, his partner-in-crime in the grain swindle. Fimbria had been convicted heavily, but Memmius was unlucky enough to be convicted by one vote. He chose Athens as his place of exile because his friend Antonius spent so much time there, and he needed his friend Antonius's support in the matter of an appeal to the Senate to quash his conviction. That he was able to defray the costs of this expensive exercise was due to pure chance; while governing Macedonia, he had almost literally tripped over a cache of gold in a captured Scordisci village—one hundred talents of it. Like Caepio at Tolosa, Memmius had seen no reason why he ought to share the gold with anybody, so he didn't. Until he dropped some of it into Antonius's open hand in Athens. And a few months later got his recall to Rome and his seat in the Senate reinstated.

Since the pirate war was properly concluded, Gaius Memmius waited in Athens until Marcus Antonius Orator was ready to go home as well. Their friendship had prospered, and they formed a pact to seek the consulship as joint candidates.

It was the end of November when Antonius sat down with his little army on the vacant fields of the Campus Martius, and demanded a triumph. Which the Senate, able to meet in the safety of the temple of Bellona to deal with this, was pleased to grant him. However, Antonius was informed that his triumph would have to wait until after the tenth day of December, as no tribunician elections had yet been held, and the Forum Romanum was still packed with the Head Count. Hopefully the tribunician elections would be held and the new college would enter office on the tenth day of the month, but a triumphal parade with the city in its current mood, Antonius was informed, was out of the question.

It began to look to Antonius as if he would not be able to stand for the office of consul, for until his triumph was held, he had to remain outside the *pomerium*, the sacred boundary of the city; he still held imperium, which put him in exactly the same position as a foreign king, forbidden to enter Rome. And if he couldn't enter Rome, he couldn't announce himself as a candidate in the consular elections.

However, his successful war had made him tremendously popular with the grain merchants and other businessmen, for traffic on the Middle Sea was safer and more predictable than in half a century. Could he stand for the consulship, there was every chance that he would win the senior position, even against Gaius Marius. And in spite of his part in Fimbria's grain swindle, Gaius Memmius's chances were not bad either, for he had been an intrepid foe of Jugurtha's, and fought Caepio bitterly when he returned the extortion court to the Senate. They were, as Catulus Caesar said to Scaurus Princeps Senatus, as popular a pair with the knights who formed the majority of the First and Second Classes as the *boni* could possibly ask—and both of them were infinitely preferable to Gaius Marius.

For of course everyone expected Gaius Marius back in Rome at the very last minute, all set to stand for his seventh consulship. The story of the stroke had been verified, but it didn't seem to have incapacitated Marius very much, and those who had made the journey to Cumae to see him had come away convinced it had not in any way affected the quality of his mind. No doubt of it in anyone's thoughts; Gaius Marius was sure to declare himself a candidate.

The idea of presenting the electorate with a pair of candidates eager to stand as partners appealed to the Policy Makers very strongly; Antonius and Memmius together stood a chance of breaking Marius's iron hold on the senior chair. Except that Antonius stubbornly refused to give up his triumph for the sake of the consulship by yielding his imperium and stepping across the *pomerium* to declare himself a candidate.

"I can run for the consulship next year," he said when Catulus Caesar and Scaurus Princeps Senatus came to see him on the Campus Martius. "The triumph is more important—I'll probably never fight another good war again as long as I live." And from that stand he could not be budged.

"All right," said Scaurus to Catulus Caesar as they came away from Antonius's camp despondent, "we'll just have to bend the rules a little. Gaius Marius thinks nothing of breaking them, so why should we be scrupulous when so much is at stake?"

But it was Catulus Caesar who proposed their solution to the House, meeting with just enough members present to make a quorum in yet another safe location, the temple of Jupiter Stator near the Circus Flaminius.

"These are trying times," Catulus Caesar said. "Normally all the candidates for the curule magistracies must present themselves to the Senate and the People in the Forum Romanum to declare their candidacies. Unfortunately the shortage of grain and the constant demonstrations in the Forum Romanum have rendered this location untenable. Might I humbly beg the Conscript Fathers to shift the candidates' tribunal—for this one extraordinary year only!—to a special convocation of the Centuriate Assembly in the *saepta* on the Campus Martius? We must do *something* about holding elections! And if we do shift the curule candidates' ceremony to the *saepta*, it's a start—the requisite time between the declarations and the elections can elapse. It would also be fair to Marcus Antonius, who wants to stand for the consulship, but cannot cross the *pomerium* without abandoning his triumph, yet cannot hold his triumph because of the unrest in our hungry city. On the Campus Martius he can present himself as a candidate. We all expect that the crowds will go home after the tribunes of the plebs are elected and take office. So Marcus Antonius can hold his triumph as soon as the new college goes in, after which we can hold the curule elections."

"Why are you so sure the crowds will go home after the new College of Tribunes of the Plebs takes office, Quintus Lutatius?" asked Saturninus.

"I should have thought you of all people could answer that, Lucius Appuleius!" snapped Catulus Caesar. "It's you draws them to the Forum—it's you up there day after day haranguing them, making them promises neither you nor this august body can keep! How can we buy grain that doesn't exist?"

"I'll still be up there speaking to the crowd after my term is over," said Saturninus.

"You will not," said Catulus Caesar. "Once you're a *privatus* again, Lucius Appuleius, if it takes me a month and a hundred men, I'll find some law on the tablets or some precedent that makes it illegal for you to speak from the rostra or any other spot in the Forum!"

Saturninus laughed, roars of laughter, howls of laughter; and yet no one there made the mistake of thinking he was amused. "Search to your heart's content, Quintus Lutatius! It won't make any difference. I'm not going to be a *privatus* after the current tribunician year is finished, because I'm going to be a tribune of the plebs all over again! Yes, I'm taking a leaf out of Gaius Marius's book, and with no legal constraints to have you yammering after my blood! There's nothing to stop a man's seeking the tribunate of the plebs over and over again!"

"There are custom and tradition," said Scaurus. "Enough to stop all men save you and Gaius Gracchus from seeking a third term. And you ought to take warning from Gaius Gracchus. He died in the Grove of Furrina with only a slave for company."

"I have better company than that," countered Saturninus. "We men of Picenum stick together—eh, Titus Labienus?—eh, Gaius Saufeius? You'll not get rid of us so easily!"

"Don't tempt the gods," said Scaurus. "They do love a challenge from men, Lucius Appuleius!"

"I'm not afraid of the gods, Marcus Aemilius! The gods are on my side," said Saturninus, and left the meeting.

"I tried to tell him," said Sulla, passing Scaurus and Catulus Caesar. "He's riding a half-mad horse for a fall."

"So's that one," said Catulus Caesar to Scaurus after Sulla was out of earshot.

"So is half the Senate, if only we knew it," said Scaurus, lingering to look around him. "This truly is a beautiful temple, Quintus Lutatius! A credit to Metellus Macedonicus. But it was a lonely place today without Metellus Numidicus." Then he shrugged his shoulders, cheered up. "Come, we'd better catch our esteemed junior consul before he bolts to the very back of his warren. He can perform the sacrifice to Mars as well as to Jupiter Optimus Maximus—if we make it an all-white *suovetaurilia*, that should surely buy us divine approval to hold the curule candidacy ceremony on the Campus Martius!"

"Who's going to foot the bill for a white cow, a white sow, and a white ewe?" asked Catulus Caesar, jerking his head to where Metellus Piglet and Caepio Junior were standing together. "Our Treasury quaestors will squeal louder than all three of the sacrificial victims."

"Oh, I think Lucius Valerius the white rabbit can pay," said Scaurus, grinning. "He's got access to Mars!"

On the last day of November a message came from Gaius Marius, convening a meeting of the Senate for the next day in the Curia Hostilia. For once the current turmoil in the Forum Romanum couldn't keep the Conscript Fathers away, so agog were they to see what Gaius Marius was like. The House was packed and everyone came earlier than the dawn did on the Kalends of December to be sure they beat him, speculations flying as they waited.

He walked in last of the entire body, as tall, as broad-shouldered, as proud as he had ever been, nothing in his gait to suggest the cripple, his left hand curled normally around the folds of his purple-bordered toga. Ah, but it was there for all the world to see upon his poor face, its old beetling self on the right side, a mournful travesty on the left.

Marcus Aemilius Scaurus Princeps Senatus put his hands together and began to applaud, the first clap echoing about the ancient hall's naked rafters and bouncing off the ruddy bellies of the terracotta tiles which formed both ceiling and roof. One by one the Conscript Fathers joined in, so that by the time Marius reached his curule chair the whole House was thundering at him. He didn't smile; to smile was to accentuate the clownlike asymmetry of his face so unbearably that every time he did it, whoever watched grew moist in the eyes, from Julia to Sulla. Instead, he simply stood by his ivory seat, nodding and bowing regally until the ovation died away.

Scaurus got up, smiling broadly. "Gaius Marius, how *good* it is to see you! The House has been as dull as a rainy day these last months. As Leader of the House, it is my pleasure to welcome you home."

"I thank you, Princeps Senatus—Conscript Fathers—my fellow magistrates," Marius said, his voice clear, not one slurred word. In spite of his resolve, a slight smile lifted the right side of his mouth upward, though the left corner stayed dismally slumped.

"If it is a pleasure for you to welcome me home, it cannot be one tenth the pleasure it is to me to *be* home! As you can see, I have been ill."

He drew a long breath everyone could hear; and hear the sadness in its quaver halfway through. "And though my illness is past, I bear its scars. Before I call this House to order and we get down to business which seems sorely in need of our attention, I wish to make a statement. I will not be seeking re-election as consul—for two reasons. The first, that the emergency which faced the State and resulted in my being allowed the unprecedented honor of so many consecutive consulships is now conclusively, finally, positively over. The second, that I do not consider my health would enable me to perform my duties properly. The responsibility I must bear for the present chaos here in Rome is manifest. If I had been here in Rome, the senior consul's presence would have helped. That is why there *is* a senior consul. I do not accuse Lucius Valerius or Marcus Aemilius or any other official of this body. The senior consul must lead. I have not been able to lead. And that has taught me that I cannot seek re-election. Let the office of senior consul pass to a man in good health."

No one replied. No one moved. If his twisted face had indicated this was in the wind, the degree of stunned shock every last one of them now felt was proof of the ascendancy he had gained over them during the past five years. A Senate without Gaius Marius in the consul's chair? Impossible! Even Scaurus Princeps Senatus and Catulus Caesar sat shocked.

Then came a voice from the back tier behind Scaurus. "Guh-guh-good!" said Metellus Piglet. "Now my fuh-fuh-father can cuh-cuh-cuh-come home."

"I thank you for the compliment, young Metellus," Marius said, looking directly up at him. "You infer that it is only I who keeps your father in his exile on Rhodes. But such is not the case, you know. It is the law of the land keeps Quintus Caecilius Metellus Numidicus in exile. And I strictly charge each and every member of this august body to remember that! There will be no decrees or plebiscites or laws upset because I am not consul!"

"Young fool!" muttered Scaurus to Catulus Caesar. "If he hadn't said that, we could quietly have brought Quintus Caecilius back early next year. Now he won't be allowed to come. I really think it's time young Metellus was presented with an extra name."

"What?" asked Catulus Caesar.

"Puh-Puh-Puh-Pius!" said Scaurus savagely. "Metellus Pius the pious son, ever striving to bring his *tata* home! And stuh-stuh-stuffing it up!"

It was extraordinary to see how quickly the House got down to business now that Gaius Marius was in the consul's chair, extraordinary too to feel a sense of wellbeing permeating the members of the House, as if suddenly the crowds outside couldn't matter the way they had until Gaius Marius reappeared.

Informed of the change in venue for the presentation of the curule candidates, Marius simply nodded consent, then curtly ordered Saturninus to call the Plebeian Assembly together and elect some magistrates; until this was out of the way, no other magistrates could be elected.

After which, Marius turned to face Gaius Servilius Glaucia, sitting in the urban praetor's chair just behind and to his left. "I hear a rumor, Gaius Servilius," he said to Glaucia, "that you intend to seek the consulship on the grounds of invalidities you have allegedly found in the *lex Villia*. Please do not. The *lex Villia annalis* unequivocally says that a man must wait two years between the end of his praetorship and the beginning of any consulship."

"Look at who's talking!" gasped Glaucia, staggered to find opposition in the one senatorial corner where he had thought to find support. "How can you stand there so brazenly, Gaius Marius, accusing me of thinking of breaking the *lex Villia* when you've broken it in fact for the last five years in a row? If the *lex Villia* is valid, then it *unequivocally* states that no man who has been consul may seek a second consulship until ten years have elapsed!"

"I did not *seek* the consulship beyond that once, Gaius Servilius," said Marius levelly. "It was bestowed upon me—and three times *in absentia!*—because of the Germans. When a state of emergency exists, all sorts of customs—even laws!—come tumbling down. But when the danger is finally over, whatever extraordinary measures were taken must cease."

"Ha ha ha!" said Metellus Piglet from the back row, this being an interjection in perfect accord with his speech impediment.

"Peace has come, Conscript Fathers," said Marius as if no one had spoken, "therefore we return to normal business and normal government. Gaius Servilius, the law forbids you to stand for the consulship. And as the presiding officer of the elections, I will not allow your candidacy. Please take this as fair warning. Give up the notion gracefully, for it does not become you. Rome needs lawmakers of your undeniable talent. For you cannot make the laws if you break the laws."

"I told you so!" said Saturninus audibly.

"He can't stop me, and nor can anyone else," said Glaucia, loudly enough for the whole House to hear him.

"He'll stop you," said Saturninus.

"As for you, Lucius Appuleius," Marius said, turning now to look at the tribunes' bench, "I hear a rumor that you intend to seek a third term as a tribune of the plebs. Now that is not against the law. Therefore I cannot stop you. But I can ask you to give up the notion. Do not give our meaning of the word 'demagogue' a new interpretation. What you have been doing during the past few months is not customary political practice for a member of the Senate of Rome. With our immense body of laws and our formidable talent for making the cogs and gears of government work in the interests of Rome as we know it, there is no necessity to exploit the political gullibility of the lowly. They are innocents who should not be corrupted. It is our duty to look after them, not to use them to further our own political ends."

"Are you finished?" asked Saturninus.

"Quite finished, Lucius Appuleius." And the way Marius said it, it had many meanings.

So that was over and done with, he thought as he walked home with the crafty new gait he had developed to disguise a tiny tendency to foot-drop on the left side. How odd and how awful those months in Cumae had been, when he had hidden away and seen as few people as possible because he couldn't bear the horror, the pity, the gloating satisfaction. Most unbearable of all were those who loved him enough to grieve, like Publius Rutilius. Sweet and gentle Julia had turned into a positive tyrant, and flatly forbidden anyone, even Publius Rutilius, to say one word about politics or public business. He hadn't known of the grain crisis, he hadn't known of Saturninus's wooing of the lowly; his life had constricted to an austere regimen of diet, exercise, and reading the Classics. Instead of a nice bit of bacon with fried bread, he ate baked watermelon because Julia had heard it purged the kidneys, both the bladders, and the blood of stones; instead of walking to the Curia Hostilia, he hiked to Baiae and Misenum; instead of reading senatorial minutes and provincial dispatches, he plodded through Isocrates and Herodotus and Thucydides, and ended in believing none of them, for they didn't read like men who acted, only like men who read.

But it worked. Slowly, slowly, he got better. Yet never again would he be whole, never again would the left side of his mouth go up, never again would he be able to disguise the fact that he was weary. The traitor within the gates of his body had branded him for all the world to see. It was this realization which finally prompted his rebellion; and Julia, who had been amazed that he remained docile for so long, gave in at once. So he sent for Publius Rutilius, and returned to Rome to pick up what pieces he could.

Of course he knew Saturninus would not stand aside, yet felt obliged to give him the warning; as for Glaucia, his election would never be allowed, so that was no worry. At least the elections would go ahead now, with the tribunes of the plebs set for the day before the Nones and the quaestors on the Nones, the day they were supposed to enter office. These were the disturbing elections, for they had to be held in the Comitia of the Forum Romanum, where the crowd milled every day, and shouted obscenities, and pelted the togate with filth, and shook their fists, and listened in blind adoration to Saturninus.

Not that they hissed or pelted Gaius Marius, who walked through their midst on his way home from that memorable meeting feeling nothing but the warmth of their love. No one lower than the Second Class would ever look unkindly upon Gaius Marius; like the Brothers Gracchi, he was a hero. There were those who looked upon his face, and wept to see it ravaged; there were those who had never set eyes on him in the flesh before, and thought his face had always been like that, and admired him all the more; but none tried to touch him, all stepped back to make a little lane for him, and he walked proudly yet humbly through them reaching out to them with heart and mind. A wordless communion. And Saturninus, watching from the rostra, wondered.

"The crowd is an awesome phenomenon, isn't it?" Sulla asked Marius over dinner that evening, in the company of Publius Rutilius Rufus and Julia.

"A sign of the times," said Rutilius.

"A sign that we've failed them," said Marius, frowning. "Rome needs a rest. Ever since Gaius Gracchus we've been in some kind of serious trouble—Jugurtha—the Germans—the Scordisci—Italian discontent—slave uprisings—pirates—grain shortages—the list is endless. We need a respite, a bit of time to look after Rome rather than ourselves. Hopefully, we'll get it. When the grain supply improves, at any rate."

"I have a message from Aurelia," said Sulla.

Marius, Julia, and Rutilius Rufus all turned to look at him curiously.

"Do you see her, Lucius Cornelius?" Rutilius Rufus the watchful uncle demanded.

"Don't get clucky, Publius Rutilius, there's no need! Yes, I see her from time to time. It takes a native to sympathize, which is why I go. She's stuck down there in the Subura, and it's my world too," he said, unruffled. "I still have friends there, so Aurelia's on my way, if you know what I mean."

"Oh dear, I should have asked her to dinner!" said Julia, distressed at her oversight. "Somehow she tends to be forgotten."

"She understands," said Sulla. "Don't mistake me, she loves her world. But she likes to keep a little abreast of what's happening in the Forum, and that's my job. You're her uncle, Publius Rutilius, you tend to want to keep the trouble from her. Where I tell her everything. She's amazingly intelligent."

"What's the message?" asked Marius, sipping water.

"It comes from her friend Lucius Decumius, the odd little fellow who runs the crossroads college in her insula, and it goes something like this—if you think there have been crowds in the Forum, you haven't seen anything yet. On the day of the tribunician elections, the sea of faces will become an ocean."

Lucius Decumius was right. At sunrise Gaius Marius and Lucius Cornelius Sulla walked up onto the Arx of the Capitol and stood leaning on the low wall barring the top of the Lautumiae cliff to take in the sight of the whole Forum Romanum spread below. As far as they could see was that ocean of people, densely packed from the Clivus Capitolinus to the Velia. It was orderly, somber, shot with menace, breathtaking.

"*Why?*" asked Marius.

"According to Lucius Decumius, they're here to make their presence felt. The Comitia will be in session to elect the new tribunes of the plebs, and they've heard that Saturninus is going to stand, and they think he's their best hope for full bellies. The famine has only just begun, Gaius Marius. And they don't want a famine," said Sulla, voice even.

"But they can't influence the outcome of a tribal election, any more than they can elections in the Centuries! Almost all of them will belong to the four city tribes."

"True. And there won't be many voters from the thirty-one rural tribes apart from those who live in Rome," said Sulla. "There's no holiday atmosphere today to tempt the rural voters. So a handful of what's below will actually vote. They know that. They're not here to vote. They're just here to make us aware they're here."

"Saturninus's idea?" asked Marius.

"No. His crowd is the one you saw on the Kalends, and every day since. The shitters and pissers, I call them. Just rabble. Denizens of crossroads colleges, ex-gladiators, thieves and malcontents, gullible shopkeepers bleeding from the lack of money, freedmen bored with groveling to their ex-masters, and many who think there might be a denarius or two to be made out of keeping Lucius Appuleius a tribune of the plebs."

"They're actually more than that," said Marius. "They're a devoted following for the first man ever to stand on the rostra and take them seriously." He shifted his weight onto his paretic left foot. "But these people here today don't belong to Lucius Appuleius Saturninus. They don't belong to anyone. Ye gods, there weren't more Cimbri on the field at Vercellae than I see here! And I don't have an army. All I have is a purple-bordered toga. A sobering thought."

"Indeed it is," said Sulla.

"Though, I don't know. . . . Maybe my purple-bordered toga is all the army I need. All of a sudden, Lucius Cornelius, I'm looking at Rome in a different light than ever before. Today they've brought themselves down there to show themselves to us. But every day they're inside Rome, going about whatever is their business. Within an hour they could be down there showing themselves to us again. And we believe we govern them?"

"We do, Gaius Marius. They can't govern themselves. They put themselves in our keeping. But Gaius Gracchus gave them cheap bread to eat, and the aediles give them wonderful games to watch. Now Saturninus comes along and promises them cheap bread in the midst of a famine. He can't keep his promise, and they're beginning to suspect he can't. Which is really why they've come to show themselves to him during his elections," said Sulla.

Marius had found his metaphor. "They're a gigantic yet very good-natured bull. When he comes to meet you because you have a bucket in your hand, all he's interested in is the food he knows you've got in the bucket. But when he discovers the bucket is empty, he doesn't turn in terrible rage to gore you. He just assumes you've hidden his food somewhere on your person, and crushes you to death looking for it without even noticing he's turned you into pulp beneath his feet."

"Saturninus is carrying an empty bucket," said Sulla.

"Precisely," said Marius, and turned away from the wall. "Come, Lucius Cornelius, let's take the bull by his horns."

"And hope," said Sulla, grinning, "that he doesn't have any hay on them after all!"

No one in the gargantuan crowd made it difficult for the senators and politically minded citizens who normally always cast their votes in the Comitia to get through; while Marius mounted the rostra, Sulla went to stand on the Senate steps with the rest of the patrician senators. The actual voters of the Plebeian Assembly that day found themselves an island in the ocean of fairly silent onlookers—and a sunken island at that, the rostra like a flat-topped rock standing above the well of the Comitia and the top surface of the ocean. Of course Saturninus's thousands of rabble had been expected, which had led many of the senators and normal voters to secret knives or clubs beneath their togas, especially Caepio Junior's little band of conservative young *boni;* but here was no Saturninian rabble. Here was all of lowly Rome in protest. Knives and clubs were suddenly felt to be a mistake.

One by one the twenty candidates standing for election as tribunes of the plebs declared themselves, while Marius stood by watchfully. First to do so was the presiding tribune, Lucius Appuleius Saturninus. And the whole vast crowd began to cheer him deafeningly, a reception which clearly amazed him, Marius discovered, shifting to where he could keep his eyes on Saturninus's face. Saturninus was thinking, and transparently: what a following was this for one man! What might he not be able to do with three hundred thousand Roman lowly at his back? Who would ever have the courage to keep him out of the tribunate of the plebs when this monster cheered its approval?

Those who followed Saturninus in declaring their candidacies were greeted with indifferent silence; Publius Furius, Quintus Pompeius Rufus of the Picenum Pompeys, Sextus Titius whose origins were Samnite, and the red-haired, grey-eyed, extremely aristocratic-looking Marcus Porcius Cato Salonianus, grandson of the Tusculan peasant Cato the Censor and great-grandson of a Celtic slave.

Last of all appeared none other than Lucius Equitius, the self-styled bastard son of Tiberius Gracchus whom Metellus Numidicus when censor had tried to exclude from the rolls of the *Ordo Equester*. The crowd began to cheer again, great billows of wildly enthusiastic sound; here stood a relic of the beloved Tiberius Gracchus. And Marius discovered how accurate his metaphor of the gigantic gentle bull had been, for the crowd began to move toward Lucius Equitius elevated on the rock of the rostra, utterly oblivious of its power. Its inexorable tidal swell crushed those in the Comitia and its environs closer and closer together. Little waves of panic began among these intending voters as they experienced the suffocating sense of helpless terror all men feel who find themselves at the center of a force they cannot resist.

While everyone else stood paralyzed, the paralyzed Gaius Marius stepped forward quickly and held out his hands palms facing out, miming a gesture which commanded HALT HALT HALT! The crowd halted immediately, the pressure decreased a little, and now the cheers were for Gaius Marius, the First Man in Rome, the Third Founder of Rome, the Conqueror of the Germans.

"Quickly, you fool!" he snapped at Saturninus, who stood apparently rapt, entranced by the noise emanating from those cheering throats. "Say you heard thunder—anything to dismiss the meeting! If we don't get our voters out of the Comitia, the crowd will kill them by sheer weight of numbers!" Then he had the heralds sound their trumpets, and in the sudden silence he lifted his hands again. "Thunder!" he shouted. "The voting will take place tomorrow! Go home, people of Rome! Go home, go home!"

And the crowd went home.

Luckily most of the senators had sought shelter inside their own Curia, where Marius followed as soon as he could make his way. Saturninus, he noted, had descended from the rostra and was walking fearlessly into the maw of the crowd, smiling and holding out his arms like one of those peculiar Pisidian mystics who believed in the laying-on of hands. And Glaucia the urban praetor? He had ascended the rostra, and stood observing Saturninus among the crowd, the broadest of smiles upon his fair face.

The faces turned to Marius when he entered the Curia were white rather than fair, drawn rather than smiling.

"And what a vat of pickles is this!" said Scaurus Princeps Senatus, unbowed as usual, but definitely a little daunted.

Marius looked at the clusters of Conscript Fathers and said, very firmly, "Go home, please! The crowd won't hurt you, but slip up the Argiletum, even if you're heading for the Palatine. If all you have to complain about is a very long walk home, you're doing well. Now go! Go!"

Those he wanted to stay he tapped on the shoulder; just Sulla, Scaurus, Metellus Caprarius the censor, Ahenobarbus Pontifex Maximus, Crassus Orator, and Crassus's cousin Scaevola, who were the curule aediles. Sulla, he noticed with interest, went up to Caepio Junior and Metellus Piglet, murmured something to them, and gave them what looked suspiciously like affectionate pats on the shoulder as they left the building. I must find out what's going on, said Marius to himself, but later. When I have the time. If I ever do, judging by this mess.

"Well, today we've seen something none of us has ever seen before," he began. "Frightening, isn't it?"

"I don't think they mean any harm," said Sulla.

"Nor do I," said Marius. "But they're still the gigantic bull who doesn't know his own strength." He beckoned to his chief scribe. "Find someone to run up the Forum, will you? I want the president of the College of Lictors here at once."

"What do you suggest we do?" asked Scaurus. "Postpone the plebeian elections?"

"No, we may as well get them over and done with," Marius said positively. "At the moment our crowd-bull is a docile beast, but who knows how angry he might become as the famine worsens? Let's not wait until he has to have hay wrapped round his horns to signify he gores, because it will be one of our chests he plugs if we do wait. I've sent for the head lictor because I think our bull will be bluffed tomorrow by a fence he could easily walk through. I'll have the public slaves work all night to set up a harmless-looking barricade all the way around the well of the Comitia and the ground between the Comitia and the Senate steps—just the usual sort of thing we erect in the Forum to fence off the area of combat from the spectators during funeral games, because they'll know the look of that, and not see it as a manifestation of fear on our part. Then I'll put every lictor Rome possesses on the inside of the barricade—all in crimson tunics, not togate, but unarmed except for staves. Whatever we do, we mustn't give our bull the dangerous idea that he's bigger and stronger than we are—bulls can think, you know! And tomorrow we hold the tribunician elections—I don't care if there are only thirty-five men there to vote. Which means all of you will go visiting on your ways home today, and command the senators in your vicinity to turn up ready to vote tomorrow. That way, we'll be sure to have at least one member of each of the tribes. It may be a skinny vote, but a vote it will be nonetheless. Understood, everyone?"

"Understood," said Scaurus.

"Where was Quintus Lutatius today?" asked Sulla of Scaurus.

"Ill, I believe," said Scaurus. "It would be genuine—he doesn't lack courage."

Marius looked at Metellus Caprarius the censor. "You, Gaius Caecilius, have the worst job tomorrow," he said, "for when Equitius declares himself a candidate, I'm going to have to ask you if you will allow him to stand. How will you say?"

Caprarius didn't hesitate. "I'll say no, Gaius Marius. A man who was a slave, to become a tribune of the plebs? It's unthinkable."

"All right, that's all, thank you," Marius said. "Be on your way, and get all our quivering fellow members here tomorrow. Lucius Cornelius, stay. I'm putting you in charge of the lictors, so you'd better be here when their head man comes."

The crowd was back in the Forum at dawn, to find the well of the Comitia cordoned off by the simple portable post-and-rope fencing they saw every time the Forum became the site of someone's gladiatorial funeral games; a crimson-tunicked lictor holding a long thick stave was positioned every few feet on the inside of the barricade's perimeter. Nothing nasty in that. And when Gaius Marius stepped forward and shouted his explanation, that he wanted no one inadvertently crushed, he was cheered as loudly as on the previous day. What the crowd couldn't see was the group inside the Curia Hostilia, positioned there well before dawn by Sulla: his fifty young members of the First Class, all clad in cuirasses and helmets, swords and daggers belted on, and carrying shields. An excited Caepio Junior was only their deputy leader, however, for Sulla was in command himself.

"We move only if I say we move," Sulla said, "and I mean it. If anyone moves *without* an order from me, I'll kill him."

On the rostra everyone was set to go; in the well of the Comitia a surprisingly large number of regular voters clustered along with perhaps half the Senate, while the patrician senators stood as always on the Senate steps. Among them was Catulus Caesar, looking ill enough to have been provided with a chair; also among them was the censor Caprarius, another whose plebeian status should have meant he went into the Comitia, but who wanted to be where everyone could see him.

When Saturninus declared his candidacy once more, the crowd cheered him hysterically; clearly his laying-on-of-hands visit on the previous day had worked wonders. As before, the rest of the candidates were greeted with silence. Until in last place came Lucius Equitius.

Marius swung to face the Senate steps, and lifted his one mobile eyebrow in a mute question to Metellus Caprarius; and Metellus Caprarius shook his head emphatically. To have spoken the question was impossible, for the crowd went on cheering Lucius Equitius as if it never intended to stop.

The heralds sounded their trumpets, Marius stepped forward, silence fell. "This man, Lucius Equitius, is not eligible for election as a tribune of the plebs!" he cried as loudly as he could. "There is an ambiguity about his citizen status which the censor must clarify before Lucius Equitius can stand for any public office attached to the Senate and People of Rome!"

Saturninus brushed past Marius and stood on the very edge of the rostra. "I deny any irregularity!"

"I declare on behalf of the censor that an irregularity does exist," said Marius, unmoved.

So Saturninus turned to appeal to the crowd. "Lucius Equitius is as much a Roman as any of you!" he shrieked. "Look at him, only look at him! Tiberius Gracchus all over again!"

But Lucius Equitius was staring down into the well of the Comitia, a place below the vision of the crowd, even those in its forefront. Here senators and sons of senators were pulling knives and cudgels from beneath their robes, and moved as if to drag Lucius Equitius down into their midst.

Lucius Equitius, brave veteran of ten years in the legions—according to his own story, anyway—shrank back, turned to Marius, and clutched his free right arm. "Help me!" he whimpered.

"I'd like to help you with the toe of my boot, you silly troublemaker," growled Marius. "However, the business of the day is to get this election over and done with. You can't stand, but if you stay on the rostra someone's going to lynch you. The best I can do to safeguard your hide is put you in the cells of the Lautumiae until everyone's gone home."

Two dozen lictors stood on the rostra, a dozen of them carrying the *fasces* because they belonged to the consul Gaius Marius; the consul Gaius Marius formed them around Lucius Equitius and had him marched away toward the Lautumiae, his progress through the crowd marked by a kind of parting of the people-ocean in response to the authority inherent in those simple crimson-corded bundles of rods.

I don't believe it, thought Marius, eyes following the parting of the people-ocean. To hear them cheer, they adore the man the way they adore no gods. To them it must look as if I've put the creature under arrest. But what are they doing? What they always, always do whenever they see a line of lictors marching along with *fasces* on their shoulders and some purple-bordered toga strutting at their rear—they're standing aside to permit the majesty of Rome the right of way. Not even for a Lucius Equitius will they destroy the power of the rods and the purple-bordered toga. There goes Rome. What's a Lucius Equitius, when all is said and done? A pathetic facsimile of Tiberius Sempronius Gracchus, whom they loved, loved, loved. They're not cheering Lucius Equitius! They're cheering the memory of Tiberius Gracchus.

And a new kind of pride-filled emotion welled up in Gaius Marius as he continued to watch that lictorial dorsal fin cleave the ocean of Roman lowly—pride in the old ways, the customs and traditions of six hundred and fifty-four years, so powerful still that it could turn a tide greater than the German invasion with no more effort than the shouldering of a few bundles of sticks. And I, thought Gaius Marius, stand here in my purple-bordered toga, unafraid of anything because I wear it, and know myself greater than any king who ever walked this globe. For I have no army, and inside their city I have no axes thrust into the rods, nor a bodyguard of swords; and yet they stand aside for the mere symbols of my authority, a few sticks and a shapeless piece of cloth rimmed with less purple than they can see any day on some unspeakable *saltatrix tonsa* parading his stuff. Yes, I would rather be consul of Rome than king of the world.

Back came the lictors from the Lautumiae, and shortly thereafter back came Lucius Equitius, whom the crowd gently rescued from the cells and popped back on the rostra with a minimum of fuss—almost, it seemed to Marius, apologetically. And there he stood, a shivering wreck, wishing himself anywhere but where he was. To Marius the crowd's message was explicit: fill my bucket, I'm hungry, don't hide my food.

In the meantime Saturninus was proceeding with his election as quickly as he could, anxious to make sure he got himself returned before anything untoward could happen. His head was filled with dazzled dreams of the future, the might and majesty of that crowd, the way it showed its adoration of him. Did they cheer Lucius Equitius, just because he looked like Tiberius Gracchus? Did they cheer Gaius Marius, broken old idiot that he was, because he'd saved Rome from the barbarians? Ah, but they didn't cheer Equitius or Marius the way they cheered *him*! And what material to work with—no rabble out of the Suburan stews, this crowd! This crowd was made up of respectable people whose bellies were empty yet whose principles remained intact.

One by one the candidates stepped forward, and the tribes voted, while the tally clerks scribbled busily and both Marius and Saturninus kept watch; until the moment when, in last place of all, it came time to deal with Lucius Equitius. Marius looked at Saturninus. Saturninus looked at Marius. Marius looked across to the Senate steps.

"What do you wish me to say this time, Gaius Caecilius Metellus Caprarius Censor?" Marius called out. "Do you wish me to continue denying this man the right to stand for election, or do you withdraw your objection?"

Caprarius looked helplessly at Scaurus, who looked at the grey-faced Catulus Caesar, who looked at Ahenobarbus Pontifex Maximus, who refused to look at anyone. A long pause ensued; the crowd watched in silence, fascinated, not having the remotest idea what was going on.

"Let him stand!" shouted Metellus Caprarius.

"Let him stand," said Marius to Saturninus.

And when the results were tallied, Lucius Appuleius Saturninus came in in first place for a third term as a tribune of the plebs; Cato Salonianus, Quintus Pompeius Rufus, Publius Furius, and Sextus Titius were elected; and, in second place, only three or four behind Saturninus, the exslave Lucius Equitius was returned as a tribune of the plebs.

"What a servile college we're going to have this year!" said Catulus Caesar, sneering. "Not only a Cato Salonianus, but an actual freedman!"

"The Republic is dead," said Ahenobarbus Pontifex Maximus, with a look of loathing for Metellus Caprarius.

"Well, what else could I do?" bleated Metellus Billy Goat.

Other senators were coming up, and Sulla's armed guard, divested of its accoutrements, emerged from the interior of the Curia. The

Senate steps seemed the safest place, though it was becoming obvious that the crowd, having seen its heroes elected, was going home.

Caepio Junior spat in the direction of the crowd. "Goodbye to the rabble for today!" he said, face contorted. "Look at them! Thieves, murderers, rapists of their own daughters!"

"They're not rabble, Quintus Servilius," said Marius sternly. "They're Roman and they're poor, but not thieves or murderers. And they're fed up with millet and turnips already. You'd better hope that friend Lucius Equitius doesn't stir them up. They've been very well behaved throughout these wretched elections, but that could change as the millet and turnips get dearer and dearer in the markets."

"Oh, there's no need to worry about *that*!" said Gaius Memmius cheerfully, pleased that the tribunes of the plebs were duly elected and his joint candidacy with Marcus Antonius Orator for the consulship looked more promising than ever. "Things will improve in a few days. Marcus Antonius was telling me that our agents in Asia Province managed to buy in a great deal of wheat from way up at the north of the Euxine somewhere. The first of the grain fleets should arrive in Puteoli any day."

Everyone was staring at him, openmouthed.

"Well," said Marius, forgetting that he could not smile in sweet irony anymore, and so producing a terrifying grimace, "all of us are aware that you seem to have a gift for seeing the future of the grain supply, but how exactly do you happen to be privy to this information when I—the senior consul!—and Marcus Aemilius here—Princeps Senatus as well as *curator annonae*!—are not privy to it?"

Some twenty pairs of eyes were fixed on his face; Memmius swallowed. "It's no secret, Gaius Marius. The subject came up in conversation in Athens when Marcus Antonius returned from his last trip to Pergamum. He saw some of our grain agents there, and they told him."

"And why hasn't Marcus Antonius seen fit to apprise me, the curator of our grain supply?" asked Scaurus icily.

"I suppose because—like me, really—he just assumed you knew. The agents have written, why wouldn't you know?"

"Their letters haven't arrived," said Marius, winking at Scaurus. "May I thank you, Gaius Memmius, for bearing this splendid news?"

"Indeed," said Scaurus, temper evaporating.

"We had better hope for all our sakes that no tempest blows up and sends the grain to the bottom of the Middle Sea," Marius said, deciding the crowd had now dispersed enough for him to walk home, and not averse to talking with some of its members. "Senators, we meet here again tomorrow for the quaestorian elections. And the day after that, we will all go out to the Campus Martius to see the candidates for consuls and praetors declare themselves. Good day to you."

"You're a cretin, Gaius Memmius," said Catulus Caesar crushingly from his chair.

Gaius Memmius decided he didn't need an argument with one of the high aristocracy, and walked off in Gaius Marius's wake, having decided he would visit Marcus Antonius in his hired villa on the Campus Martius and apprise him of the day's events. As he strode out briskly he saw how he and Marcus Antonius could pick up additional merit with the electors. He would make sure their agents went among the Centuries as they gathered to witness the declaration of the curule candidates the day after tomorrow; they could spread the news of the coming grain fleets as if he and Marcus Antonius were responsible. The First and Second Classes might deplore the cost of cheap grain to the State, but having seen the size of the crowd in the Forum, Memmius thought they might be very grateful to think of Roman bellies full of bread baked from cheap grain.

At dawn on the day of the presentation of candidates in the *saepta,* he set off to walk from the Palatine to the Campus Martius, accompanied by an elated throng of clients and friends, all sure he and Antonius would get in. Buoyant and laughing, they walked briskly through the Forum Romanum in the cold breeze of a fine late-autumn morning, shivering a little when they passed through the deep shade of the Fontinalis Gate, but positive that down on the sunny plain spread beneath the Arx lay victory. Gaius Memmius would be consul.

Other men were walking to the *saepta* too, in groups, couples, trios, but rarely alone; a man of the classes important enough to vote in the curule elections liked company in public, for it added to his *dignitas.*

Where the road coming down from the Quirinal ran into the Via Lata, Gaius Memmius and his companions encountered some fifty men escorting none other than Gaius Servilius Glaucia.

Memmius stopped in his tracks, astounded. "And where do you think you're going dressed like that?" he asked, eyeing Glaucia's *toga candida.* Specially bleached by days hanging in the sun, then whitened to blinding purity by copious applications of powdered chalk, the *toga candida* could be worn only by one who was standing for election to a public office.

"I'm a candidate for the consulship," said Glaucia.

"You're not, you know," said Memmius.

"Oh yes I am!"

"Gaius Marius said you *couldn't* stand."

"Gaius Marius said I couldn't stand," Glaucia mimicked in a namby-pamby voice, then ostentatiously turned his back on Memmius and began to speak to his followers in a loud voice which dripped homosexual overtones. "Gaius Marius *said* I couldn't stand! *Well!* I must say it's a bit *stiff* when real men can't stand, but pretty little pansies can!"

The exchange had gathered an audience, not unusual under the circumstances, for part of the general enjoyment of the proceedings were the clashes between rival candidates; that this clash had occurred before the open field of the *saepta* had been reached made little difference to the audience, swelling as more and more men came along the Via Lata from town.

Painfully aware of the audience, Gaius Memmius writhed. All his life he had suffered the curse of being too good-looking, with its inevitable taunts—he was too pretty, he couldn't be trusted, he liked boys, he was a lightweight—on and on and on. Now Glaucia saw fit to mock him in front of all these men, these voters. Oh, he didn't *need* to have them reminded of the old homosexual tag on this day above all others!

And understandably Gaius Memmius saw red. Before anyone with him could anticipate his intention, he stepped forward, put his hand on Glaucia's left shoulder, and ripped the pristine toga off it. Then as Glaucia spun round to see who was assaulting him, Memmius swung a wild punch at Glaucia's left ear, and connected. Down went Glaucia, Memmius on top of him, both pristine togas now grimed and smeared. But Glaucia's men had concealed clubs and cudgels about their persons; out they came swinging; Glaucia's men waded into the stunned ranks of Memmius's companions, laying about with furious glee. The Memmius entourage disintegrated at once, its members flying in all directions crying for help.

Typical of uninvolved bystanders, the audience made no move to help, just watched with avid interest; to do it justice, however, no one looking on dreamed that what he saw was anything more than a brawl between two candidates. The weapons were a surprise, but the supporters of candidates had been known to carry weapons before.

Two big men lifted Memmius up and held him between them, struggling furiously, while Glaucia got to his feet kicking away his ruined toga. Glaucia said not a word. He plucked a club from someone standing near him, then looked at Memmius for a long moment. Up went the club, held in both hands like a mallet; and down it came upon Gaius Memmius's strikingly handsome head. No one attempted to interfere as Glaucia bent to follow Memmius fall, and kept on beating, beating that head, handsome no longer. Only when it was reduced to pulp and brains and splatters did Glaucia cease his attack.

A look of incredulous and outraged frustration spread then across Glaucia's face; he flung the bloodied club away and stared at his friend Gaius Claudius, watching ashen-faced.

"Will you shelter me until I can get away?" he asked.

Claudius nodded, speechless.

The audience was beginning to mutter and move in upon the group, while other men were running from the direction of the *saepta;* Glaucia turned and raced toward the Quirinal, his companions following him.

The news was carried to Saturninus as he prowled up and down the *saepta,* canvassing persuasively for Glaucia's illegal candidacy. Covert yet angry glances told him how most of those hearing the news of Memmius's murder felt, and he was branded as Glaucia's best friend. Among the young senators and sons of senators a furious buzz was starting, while some of the sons of the more powerful knights gathered around their senatorial peers, and that enigmatic man Sulla was in the midst of it.

"We'd better get out of here," said Gaius Saufeius, only the day before elected an urban quaestor.

"You're right, I think we'd better," said Saturninus, growing more and more uneasy at the anger he could feel all around.

Accompanied by his Picentine henchmen Titus Labienus and Gaius Saufeius, Saturninus left the *saepta* in a hurry. He knew whereabouts Glaucia would have gone—to Gaius Claudius's house on the Quirinal—but when he got there Saturninus found its doors bolted and barred. Only after considerable yelling did Gaius Claudius open up and let the three friends in.

"Where is he?" Saturninus demanded.

"My study," said Gaius Claudius, who had been weeping.

"Titus Labienus," said Saturninus, "go and find Lucius Equitius, will you? We need him, the crowd thinks he's lovely."

"What are you up to?" Labienus asked.

"I'll tell you when you bring me Lucius Equitius."

Glaucia was sitting grey-faced in Gaius Claudius's study; when Saturninus entered he looked up, but said not a word.

"Why, Gaius Servilius? *Why?*"

Glaucia shivered. "I didn't mean to do it," he said. "I just—I just lost my temper."

"And lost us our chance at Rome," said Saturninus.

"I lost my temper," Glaucia said again.

He had stayed the night before the presentation of the curule candidates in this same house, for Gaius Claudius threw a party in his honor; more a creature than a man, Gaius Claudius admired Glaucia's boldness in challenging the provisions of the *lex Villia*, and thought the best way to show his admiration was to use some of his large amounts of money to give Glaucia a memorable send-off down the canvassing path. The fifty men who later accompanied Glaucia on his walk to the *saepta* were all invited to the party, but no women of any sort had been invited, and the result was a comedy remarkable only for its bibulousness and its biliousness. At dawn no one was feeling very well, yet they had to go to the *saepta* with Glaucia to support him; clubs and cudgels seemed like a good idea. Just as unwell as the rest, Glaucia gave himself an emetic and a bath, wrapped himself in his whitened toga, and set off with eyes screwed up against the thousand tiny hammers of a severe headache.

To meet the immaculate and laughing Memmius, his handsome head already held like a victor's, was more than Glaucia's frayed nerves could cope with. So he responded to Memmius's opposition with a cruel taunt, and when Memmius tore away his toga, Glaucia lost all control. Now the deed was done, and could not be undone. Everything lay in ruins around Gaius Memmius's shattered head.

Saturninus's silent presence in the study was a different kind of shock; Glaucia began to understand the enormity of his deed, its ramifications and repercussions. Not only had he destroyed his own career, he had probably destroyed the career of his best friend as well. And that he couldn't bear.

"Say something, Lucius Appuleius!" he cried.

Blinking, Saturninus emerged from his trancelike thoughts. "I think we have only one alternative left," he said calmly. "We must get the crowd on our side, and use the crowd to make the Senate give us what we want—safe office, a ruling of extenuating circumstances for you, a guarantee none of us will face prosecution. I've sent Titus Labienus off to fetch Lucius Equitius, because it's easier to sway the crowds with him there." He sighed, flexed his hands. "The moment Labienus comes back, we're off to the Forum. There's no time to waste."

"Should I come?" asked Glaucia.

"No. You stay here with your men, and have Gaius Claudius arm his slaves. And don't let anyone in until you hear my voice, or Labienus's, or Saufeius's." He got up. "By nightfall I have to control Rome. Otherwise—I'm finished too."

"Abandon me!" said Glaucia suddenly. "Lucius Appuleius, there's no need for this! Throw up your hands in horror at my deed, then put yourself in the forefront of the pack baying for my condemnation! It is the only way. Rome isn't ready for a new form of government! That crowd is hungry, yes. It's fed up with bungling government, yes. It wants some justice, yes. But not enough to beat in heads and tear out throats. They'll cheer you until they're hoarse. But they won't kill for you."

"You're wrong," said Saturninus, who felt a little as if he walked on wool, light, free, invulnerable. "Gaius Servilius, all those people filling our Forum are greater in numbers and power than an *army*! Didn't you see how the Policy Makers caved in at the knees? Didn't you see Metellus Caprarius back down over Lucius Equitius? There was no bloodshed! The Forum's run redder by far from the brawls of a hundred men, yet there were hundreds of thousands of them! No one is going to defy that crowd, yet it will never be necessary to arm them, or set them to beating in heads or tearing out throats. Their power is in their mass! A mass I can *control*, Gaius Servilius! All I need is my own oratory, proof of my devotion to their cause, and a wave or two from Lucius Equitius! Who can resist the man who runs that crowd like some gigantic siege apparatus? The straw men of the Senate?"

"Gaius Marius," said Glaucia.

"No, not even Gaius Marius! And anyway, he's with us!"

"He's not," said Glaucia.

"He may think he's not, Gaius Servilius, but the fact that the crowd cheers him the way it cheers me and Lucius Equitius will make the Policy Makers and everyone else in the Senate see him in the same light as they see us! I don't mind sharing the power with Gaius Marius—for a little while. He's getting old, he's had a stroke. What more natural than for him to die from another one?" asked Saturninus eagerly.

Glaucia was feeling better; he straightened in his chair and looked at Saturninus in mingled doubt and hope. "*Could* it work, Lucius Appuleius? Do you really think it could?"

And Saturninus stretched his arms toward the ceiling, vibrating confidence, a smile of savage joy upon his face. "It will work, Gaius Servilius. Leave everything to me."

So Lucius Appuleius Saturninus went from the house of Gaius Claudius down to the rostra in the Forum Romanum, accompanied by Labienus, Saufeius, Lucius Equitius, and some ten or twelve other close adherents. He cut across the Arx, feeling that he should enter his arena from above, a demigod descending from a region on high filled with temples and divinities; so his first sight of the Forum was from the top of the Gemonian Steps, down which he intended to walk like a king. Shock made him stop. The crowd! *Where was the crowd?* Gone home after the quaestorian elections of the day before, was the answer; and with nothing scheduled to happen in the Forum, it saw no point in coming back. Nor was a single member of the Senate present anywhere, with events of that day all occurring out on the green field of the *saepta*.

However, the Forum wasn't deserted; perhaps two or three thousand of Saturninus's less reputable rabble paraded up and down, shouting and waving their fists, demanding free grain of the empty air. Sheer disappointment brought tears very close to the surface; then Saturninus looked sternly at the hard-bitten men roiling around the lower end of the Forum, and made a decision. They would do. They would have to do. He would use them as a spearhead; through them he would draw the vast crowd back into the Forum—for they mingled with the members of that vast crowd, where he did not.

Wishing he had heralds to trumpet his arrival, Saturninus walked down the Gemonian Steps and strode to the rostra, his little band of followers shouting to the rabble to gather round and hear Lucius Appuleius.

"Quirites!" he addressed them amid howling cheers, holding out his arms for silence. "Quirites, the Senate of Rome is about to sign our death warrants! I, Lucius Appuleius Saturninus, as well as Lucius Equitius and Gaius Servilius Glaucia, are to be accused of the murder of a minion of the nobility, an effeminate puppet whose only purpose in putting himself up for election as consul was to make sure that you, People of Rome, continue to starve!"

The dense collection about the rostra was silent and still, listening; Saturninus took confidence and energy from his intent auditors, and expanded upon his theme. "Why do you think you have received no grain, even after I passed my law to give it to you for a pittance? Because the First and Second Classes of our great city would prefer to buy less and sell it for more! Because the First and Second Classes of our city don't want your hungry mouths turned in their direction! They think of you as the cuckoo in their nest, an extravagance Rome doesn't need! You are the Head Count and the lower classes—you're not important any more, with all the wars won and the loot from them safe in the Treasury! Why spend that loot filling your worthless bellies? asks the Senate of Rome, and refuses to give me the funds I need to buy grain for your worthless bellies! For it would suit the Senate of Rome and the First and Second Classes of Rome very, very well if several hundred thousand of Rome's so-called worthless bellies shrank to the point where their owners died of starvation! Imagine it! All that money saved, all those smelly overcrowded insulae emptied—what a green and spacious park could Rome become! Where you cramped yourselves to live, they would stroll in pleasure gardens, the money jingling in their purses and their bellies full! They don't care about you! You're a nuisance they'd be glad to be rid of, and what better way than an artificially induced famine?"

He had them, of course; they were growling in the backs of their throats like angry dogs, a rumble that filled the air with menace and Saturninus's heart with triumph.

"But I, Lucius Appuleius Saturninus, have fought to fill your bellies so long and so hard that now I am to be eliminated for a murder I did not commit!" That was a good one; he hadn't committed murder either, he could speak the truth and have the truth ring unmistakably in every word! "With me will perish all my friends, who are your friends too. Lucius Equitius here, the heir to Tiberius Gracchus's name and aims! And Gaius Servilius Glaucia, who so brilliantly frames my laws that not even the nobles who run the Senate can tamper with them!" He paused, he sighed, he lifted his arms helplessly. "And when we are dead, Quirites, who will be left to look after you? Who will carry on the good fight? Who will battle the privileged to fill your bellies? *No one!*"

The growl was now a roar, the mood of the throng was shot with potential violence, they were his to do with as he pleased. "Quirites, it is up to you! Do you want to stand by while we who love you and esteem you are put to death, innocent men? Or will you go home and arm yourselves, and run to every house in your neighborhood, and bring out the crowds?"

They began to move, but the shrieking Saturninus pulled them up with his voice. "Come back to me here in all your thousands upon thousands! Bring yourselves to me, and put yourselves in my charge! Before night has fallen, Rome will belong to you because it will belong to me, and then we shall see whose bellies are full! Then we'll break open the Treasury, and buy grain! Now go, bring the whole city to me, meet me here in the heart of Rome, and show the Senate and the First and Second Classes who really rules our city and our empire!"

Like a vast number of tiny balls shocked by a single blow from a hammer on the rim containing them, the rabble scattered in all directions at a run, screaming incoherent babbles of words, while Saturninus sank back on his heels, and turned on the rostra to face his henchmen.

"Oh, wonderful!" cried Saufeius, straining at the leash.

"We'll win, Lucius Appuleius, we'll win!" cried Labienus.

Surrounded by men pounding his back in euphoric glee, Saturninus stood royally and contemplated the enormity of his future.

At which point Lucius Equitius burst into tears. "But what are you going to *do*?" he blubbered, mopping his face with the edge of his toga.

"Do? What do you think it sounded like, you imbecile? I'm going to take over Rome, of course!"

"With *that* lot?"

"Who is there to oppose them? And anyway, they'll bring the giant crowd. You wait, Lucius Equitius! No one will be able to resist us!"

"But there's an army of marines on the Campus Martius—two legions of them!" cried Lucius Equitius, still sniffling and shivering.

"No Roman army has ever ventured inside Rome except to triumph, and no man who ordered a Roman army to venture inside Rome would survive," said Saturninus, contemptuous of this mean necessity; as soon as he was firmly in control, Equitius would have to go, likeness to Tiberius Gracchus or not.

"Gaius Marius would do it," sobbed Equitius.

"Gaius Marius, you fool, will be on our side!" Saturninus said with a sneer.

"I don't like it, Lucius Appuleius!"

"You don't have to like it. If you're with me, shut up the bawling. If you're against me, *I'll* shut up the bawling!" And Saturninus drew his finger across his throat.

One of the first to answer the call for help from Gaius Memmius's friends was Gaius Marius. He arrived at the scene of the confrontation not more than a few moments after Glaucia and his cronies had gone running to the Quirinal, and found a hundred toga-clad members of the Centuries clustered around what was left of Gaius Memmius. They parted to let the senior consul through; with Sulla at his shoulder, he gazed down at the pulped remants of head, then looked toward the place where the blood-stained club still lay bedaubed with fragments of hair and muscle and skin and skull.

"Who did this?" asked Sulla.

The answer came from a dozen men: "Gaius Servilius Glaucia."

Sulla blew through his nose. "Himself?"

Everyone nodded.

"Does anyone know where he went from here?"

This time the answers conflicted, but Sulla finally established that Glaucia and his gang had raced toward the Sanqualis Gate onto the Quirinal; since Gaius Claudius had been one of them, it seemed likely they were heading for his house on the Alta Semita.

Marius hadn't moved, hadn't lifted his head from his silent contemplation of Gaius Memmius. Gently Sulla touched him on the arm; he stirred then, wiping the tears from his face with a fold of toga because he didn't want to betray his left hand's clumsiness by hunting for his handkerchief.

"On the field of war, this is natural. On the Field of Mars beneath the walls of Rome, it is an abomination!" he shouted, turning to face the men crowding around.

Other senior senators were arriving, among them Marcus Aemilius Scaurus Princeps Senatus, who took one swift look at Marius's tear-streaked face, then down at the ground, and caught his breath.

"Memmius! *Gaius Memmius?*" he asked incredulously.

"Yes, Gaius Memmius," said Sulla. "Murdered in person by Glaucia, all the witnesses say."

Marius was weeping again, but made no attempt to conceal the fact as he looked at Scaurus. "Princeps Senatus," he said, "I am convoking the Senate in the temple of Bellona immediately. Do you concur?"

"I do," said Scaurus.

Some lictors were straggling up, their charge the senior consul having outdistanced them by several hundred paces despite his stroke.

"Lucius Cornelius, take my lictors, find the heralds, cancel the presentation of the candidates, send the *flamen Martialis* to the temple of Venus Libitina to bring the sacred axes of the *fasces* to us in Bellona, and summon the Senate," said Marius. "I will go on ahead with Marcus Aemilius."

"This has been," said Scaurus, "an absolutely horrible year. In fact, in spite of all our recent vicissitudes, I don't recall a year so horrible since the last year of Gaius Gracchus's life."

Marius's tears had dried. "Then we're overdue for it, I suppose," he said.

"Let us hope at least there will be no worse violence done than the murder of Memmius."

But Scaurus's hope proved vain, though at first it seemed reasonable. The Senate met in the temple of Bellona and discussed the murder of Memmius; sufficient of its members had been eyewitnesses to make the guilt of Glaucia manifest.

"However," said Marius firmly, "Gaius Servilius must be tried for his crime. No Roman citizen can be condemned without trial unless he declares war on Rome, and that is not an issue here today."

"I'm afraid it is, Gaius Marius," said Sulla, hurrying in.

Everyone stared at him. No one spoke.

"Lucius Appuleius and a group of men including the quaestor Gaius Saufeius have taken over the Forum Romanum," announced Sulla. "They've displayed Lucius Equitius to the rabble, and Lucius Appuleius has announced that he intends to supplant the Senate and the First and Second Classes with a rule of the People administered by himself. They haven't yet hailed him as King of Rome, but it's being said already in every street and marketplace between here and the Forum—which means it's being said everywhere."

"May I speak, Gaius Marius?" asked the Leader of the House.

"Speak, Princeps Senatus."

"Our city is in crisis," Scaurus said, low-voiced yet clear-voiced, "just as it was during the last days of Gaius Gracchus. At that time, when Marcus Fulvius and Gaius Gracchus seized upon violence as the only means of attaining their desperate ends, a debate took place within the House—did Rome need a dictator to deal with a crisis so urgent, yet so short-lived? The rest is history.

The House declined to appoint a dictator. Instead, it passed what might be called its ultimate decree—the *Senatus Consultum de republica defendenda*. By this decree the House empowered its consuls and magistrates to defend the sovereignty of the State in any way they considered necessary, and immunized them in advance from prosecution and the tribunician veto."

He paused to look about him with immense seriousness. "I suggest, Conscript Fathers, that we deal with our present crisis in the same way—by a *Senatus Consultum de republica defendenda*."

"I will see a Division," said Marius. "All those in favor will pass to my left, all those against to my right." And moved to his left first of them all.

No one moved to the right; the House passed its second *Senatus Consultum de republica defendenda* unanimously, which it had not done the first time.

"Gaius Marius," said Scaurus, "I am empowered by the members of this House to instruct you as Rome's senior consul to defend the sovereignty of our State in any way you deem fit or necessary. Furthermore, I hereby declare on behalf of this House that you are not subject to the tribunician veto, and that nothing you do or order done shall be held against you for future action in a court of law. Provided that they act under your instructions, this commission together with its indemnity is extended to the junior consul, Lucius Valerius Flaccus, and all the praetors. But you, Gaius Marius, are also empowered to choose deputies from among the members of this House who do not sit as consuls or praetors, and provided these deputies act under your instructions, this commission together with its indemnity is also extended to them." Thinking of Metellus Numidicus's face were he present to see Gaius Marius virtually made dictator by none other than Scaurus Princeps Senatus, Scaurus shot Marius a wicked look, but managed to keep his grin on the inside. He filled his lungs with air, and bellowed, "Long live Rome!"

"Oh, my stars!" said Publius Rutilius Rufus.

But Marius had no time or patience with the wits of the House, who would, he thought, wittify while Rome burned around them.

Voice crisp yet calm, he proceeded to depute Lucius Cornelius
Sulla to act as his second-in-command, ordered the store of weapons in the basement of the temple of Bellona to be broken out and
distributed to those who lacked personal arms and armor, and
told those who did own arms and armor to go home and get it
while they could still move freely through the streets.

Sulla concentrated upon his young bloods, sending them flying
in all directions, Caepio Junior and Metellus Piglet the most eager of all. Incredulity was giving way to an outrage almost too
great for mere anger; that a senator of Rome would attempt to
seize rabble-fueled power in order to set himself up as a king was
anathema. Political differences were forgotten, mere factions dissolved; ultra-conservatives lined up shoulder to shoulder with the
most progressive Marians, all with their faces set obdurately
against the wolfshead in the Forum Romanum.

Even as he organized his little army and those awaiting arms
and armor from their houses bustled mouthing imprecations here
and there, Sulla remembered her; not Dalmatica, but Aurelia. He
sent four lictors on the double to her insula with a message to her
to bar herself in, and a message to Lucius Decumius to make sure
neither he nor his tavernload of operators were in the Forum Romanum for the next few days. Knowing Lucius Decumius, they
wouldn't be in the Forum anyway; while the rest of Rome's rabble
were rampaging up and down the Forum making noise and beating up innocent passers-by, the territory they normally patrolled
was delightfully open to a raid or two, and no doubt that had been
Lucius Decumius's choice. Even so, a message couldn't hurt, and
Aurelia's safety he cared about.

Two hours later everything and everyone was ready. Outside
the temple of Bellona was the big open courtyard always known
as Enemy Territory. Halfway down the temple steps was a square
stone pillar about four feet high. When a just and rightful war was
declared upon a foreign enemy—and were there any other kinds
of wars?—a special fetial priest was called upon to hurl a spear
from the steps of the temple over the exact top of the ancient
stone pillar into the earth of Enemy Territory. No one knew how

or why the ritual had started, but it was a part of tradition, and so it was still observed. But today there was no foreign enemy upon whom to declare war, just a senatorial decree to obey; so no fetial priest hurled a spear, and Enemy Territory was filled with Romans of the First and Second Classes.

The whole gathering—perhaps a thousand strong—was now girt for war, chests and backs encased in cuirasses, a few sporting greaves upon their shins, most also clad in leather undersuits flapping fringed *pteryges* as kilts and sleeves, and all wearing crested helmets. No one carried a spear; all were armed with the good Roman short-sword and dagger, and old-fashioned pre-Marian oval shields five feet high.

Gaius Marius stepped to the front of the Bellona podium and spoke to his little army. "Remember that we are Romans and we are entering the city of Rome," he said gravely. "We will step across the *pomerium*. For that reason I will not call the marines of Marcus Antonius to arms. We ourselves can deal with this, we do not need a professional army. I am adamantly set against any more violence than is absolutely necessary, and I warn all of you most solemnly—the young among you particularly—that no blade is to be raised against a man with no blade. Take clubs and billets upon your shields, and use the flats of your swords only. Where possible, wrest a wooden weapon from one of the crowd, sheath your sword, and use wood. There will be no heaps of dead and dying in the heart of Rome! That would break the Republic's good luck, and then the Republic would be no more. All we have to do today is avert violence, not make it.

"You are my troops," he went on sternly, "but few among you have served under me in any army until this one. So take heed of this, my only warning. Those who disobey my orders or the orders of my legates will be killed. This is not an occasion for factions. Today there are no types of Romans. Just Romans. There are many among you who have no love for the Head Count and Rome's other lowly. But I say to you—and mark me well!—that a Head Count Roman is a Roman, and his life is as sacred and protected by the law as my life is, or your lives are. *There will be no bloodbath!* If I see so much as the start of one, I will be down there with my sword raised against those raising swords—and under the conditions of the Senate's decree, your heirs cannot exact retribution of any kind from me should I kill you! You will take your orders from only two men—from me, and from Lucius Cornelius Sulla here. Not from any other curule magistrate empowered under this decree. I want no attack unless I call for it or Lucius Cornelius calls for it. We do this thing as gently as we can. Understood?"

Catulus Caesar tugged his forelock in mock obsequiousness. "We hear and obey, Gaius Marius. I have served under you before—I know you mean what you say."

"Good!" said Marius cordially, ignoring the sarcasm. He turned to his junior consul. "Lucius Valerius, take fifty men and go to the Quirinal. If Gaius Servilius Glaucia is at the house of Gaius Claudius, arrest him. If he refuses to come out, you and your men will remain on guard without attempting to get inside. And keep me informed."

It was early afternoon when Gaius Marius led his little army out of Enemy Territory and into the city through the Carmentalis Gate. Coming from the Velabrum, they appeared out of the alleyway which led between the temple of Castor and the Basilica Sempronia, and took the crowd in the lower Forum completely by surprise. Armed with whatever they could lay their hands upon— cudgels, clubs, billets, knives, axes, picks, pitchforks—Saturninus's men had swelled to perhaps four thousand in number; but compared to the competent thousand who marched tightly packed into the Forum and formed up in front of the Basilica Sempronia, they were a paltry gang. One look at the breastplates, helmets, and swords of the newcomers was enough to send almost half of them running headlong up the Argiletum and the eastern side of the Forum toward the anonymity of the Esquiline and the safety of home ground.

"Lucius Appuleius, give this up!" roared Marius, in the forefront of his force with Sulla beside him.

Atop the rostra with Saufeius, Labienus, Equitius, and some ten others, Saturninus stared at Marius slack-jawed; then he threw back his head and laughed; meant to sound confident and defiant, it came out hollow.

"Your orders, Gaius Marius?" Sulla asked.

"We take them in a charge," said Marius. "Very sudden, very hard. No swords drawn, just shields to the front. I never thought they'd be such a motley lot, Lucius Cornelius! They'll break easily."

Sulla and Marius went round their little army and readied it, shields swung to the front, a line of men two hundred long, and five men deep.

And then: "Charge!" shrieked Gaius Marius.

The maneuver was immediately effective. A solid wall of shields carried at a run hit the rabble like an enormous wave of water. Men and makeshift weapons flew everywhere and not a retaliatory blow was struck; then before Saturninus's men could organize themselves better, the wall of shields crashed into them again, and again.

Saturninus and his companions came down from the rostra to join the fray, brandishing naked swords. To no effect. Though they had started out thirsting for real blood, Marius's cohort was now enjoying the novelty of this battering-ram approach, and had got into a rhythm which kept cannoning into the disordered rabble, pushing its men up like stones into a heap, drawing off to form the wall again, cannoning again. A few of the rabble were trampled underfoot, but nothing like a battle developed; it was a debacle instead.

Only a short time elapsed before Saturninus's entire force was fleeing the field; the great occupation of the Forum Romanum was over, and almost bloodlessly. Saturninus, Labienus, Saufeius, Equitius, a dozen Romans, and some thirty armed slaves ran up the Clivus Capitolinus to barricade themselves inside the temple of Jupiter Optimus Maximus, calling upon the Great God to give them succor and send that gigantic crowd back into the Forum.

"Blood will flow now!" screamed Saturninus from the podium

of the temple atop the Capitol, his words clearly audible to Marius and his men. "I will make you kill Romans before I am done, Gaius Marius! I will see this temple polluted with the blood of Romans!"

"He might be right," said Scaurus Princeps Senatus, looking extremely satisfied and happy in spite of this fresh worry.

Marius laughed heartily. "No! He's posturing like one of those defenseless little animals plumed with fierce-looking eyes, Marcus Aemilius. There's a simple answer to this siege, believe me. We'll have them out of there without spilling one drop of Roman blood." He turned to Sulla. "Lucius Cornelius, find the city water company engineers, and have them cut off all water to the Capitoline Hill at once."

The Leader of the House shook his head in wonder. "So simple! But so obvious I for one would never have seen it. How long will we have to wait for Saturninus to surrender?"

"Not long. They've been engaged in thirsty work, you see. Tomorrow is my guess. I'm going to send enough men up there to ring the temple round, and I'm going to order them to taunt our fugitives remorselessly with their lack of water."

"Saturninus is a very desperate character," said Scaurus.

That was a judgment Marius disagreed with, and said so. "He's a politician, Marcus Aemilius, not a soldier. It's power he's come to understand, not force of arms, and he can't make a workable strategy for himself." The twisted side of Marius's face came round to frighten Scaurus, its drooping eye ironic, and the smile which pulled the good side of his face up was a terrible thing to see. "If *I* was in Saturninus's shoes, Marcus Aemilius, you'd have cause to worry! Because by now I'd be calling myself the King of Rome, and you would all be dead."

Scaurus Princeps Senatus stepped back a pace instinctively. "I know, Gaius Marius," he said. "I know!"

"Anyway," said Marius cheerfully, removing the awful side of his face from Scaurus's view, "luckily I'm not King Tarquinius, though my mother's family *is* from Tarquinia! A night in the same room as the Great God will bring Saturninus round."

Those in the rabble who had been caught and detained when it broke and fled were rounded up and put under heavy guard in the cells of the Lautumiae, where a scurrying group of censor's clerks sorted out the Roman citizens from the non-Romans; those who were not Romans were to be executed immediately, while the Romans would be summarily tried on the morrow, and flung down from the Tarpeian Rock of the Capitol straight after.

Sulla returned as Marius and Scaurus began to walk away from the lower Forum.

"I have a message from Lucius Valerius on the Quirinal," he said, looking considerably fresher for the day's events. "He says Glaucia is there inside Gaius Claudius's house all right, but they've barred the gates and refuse to come out."

Marius looked at Scaurus. "Well, Princeps Senatus, what will we do about that situation?"

"Like the lot in the company of Jupiter Optimus Maximus, why not leave matters lie overnight? Let Lucius Valerius guard the house in the meantime. After Saturninus surrenders, we can have the news shouted over Gaius Claudius's wall, and then see what happens."

"A good plan, Marcus Aemilius."

And Scaurus began to laugh. "All this amicable concourse with you, Gaius Marius, is not going to enhance my reputation among my friends the Good Men!" he spluttered, and caught at Marius's arm. "Nonetheless, Good Man, I am very glad we had you here today. What say you, Publius Rutilius?"

"I say—you could not have spoken truer words."

Lucius Appuleius Saturninus was the first of all those in the temple of Jupiter Optimus Maximus to surrender; Gaius Saufeius was the last. The Romans among them, some fifteen altogether, were detained on the rostra in full view of all who cared to come and see—not many, for the crowd stayed home. Under their eyes those among the rabble who were Roman citizens—almost all, for this was not a slave uprising—were tried in a specially convened treason court, and sentenced to die from the Tarpeian Rock.

Jutting out from the southwest side of the Capitol, the Tarpeian Rock was a basaltic overhang above a precipice only eighty feet in height; that it killed was due to the presence of an outcrop of needle-sharp rocks immediately below.

The traitors were led up the slope of the Clivus Capitolinus, past the steps of the temple of Jupiter Optimus Maximus, to a spot on the Servian Walls in front of the temple of Ops. The overhang of the Tarpeian Rock projected out of the wall, and was clearly visible in profile from the lower part of the Forum Romanum, where crowds suddenly appeared to watch the partisans of Lucius Appuleius Saturninus go to their deaths—crowds with empty bellies, but no desire to demonstrate their displeasure on this day. They just wanted to see men thrown off the Tarpeian Rock, for it hadn't happened in a long time, and the gossip grapevine had told them there were almost a hundred to die. No eyes in that crowd rested upon Saturninus or Equitius with love or pity, though every element in it was the same who cheered them mightily during the tribunician elections. The gossip grapevine was saying there were grain fleets on the way from Asia, thanks to Gaius Marius. So it was Gaius Marius they cheered in a desultory way; what they really wanted to see, for this was a Roman holiday of sorts, was the bodies pitched from the Tarpeian Rock. Death at a decent distance, an acrobatic display, a novelty.

"We can't hold the trials of Saturninus and Equitius until feelings have died down a little," said Scaurus Princeps Senatus to Marius and Sulla as the three of them stood on the Senate Steps while the parade of flailing miniature men dropped into space off the end of the Tarpeian Rock.

Neither Marius nor Sulla mistook his meaning; it was not the Forum crowd which worried Scaurus, but the more impulsive and angry among his own kind, growling more fiercely now that the worst was over. Rancor had shifted from Saturninus's rabble to Saturninus himself, with special viciousness reserved for Lucius Equitius. The young senators and those not quite old enough to be senators were standing in a group on the edge of the Comitia with

Caepio Junior and Metellus Piglet in their forefront, eyeing Saturninus and his companions on the rostra very hungrily.

"It will be worse when Glaucia surrenders and joins them," said Marius thoughtfully.

"What a paltry lot!" sniffed Scaurus. "You'd have thought at least some of them would have done the proper thing, and fallen on their swords! Even my slack-livered son did that!"

"I agree," said Marius. "However, here we are with fifteen of them—sixteen when Glaucia comes out—to try for treason, and some very resentful fellows down there who remind me of a pack of wolves eyeing a herd of deer."

"We'll have to hold them somewhere for at least several days," said Scaurus, "only where? For the sake of Rome we cannot permit them to be lynched."

"Why not?" asked Sulla, contributing his first mite to the discussion.

"Trouble, Lucius Cornelius. We've avoided bloodshed in the Forum, but the crowd's going to appear in force to see that lot on the rostra tried for treason. Today they're entertained by the executions of men who don't matter. But can we be sure they won't turn nasty when we try Lucius Equitius, for instance?" asked Marius soberly. "It's a very difficult situation."

"Why *couldn't* they have fallen on their swords?" asked Scaurus fretfully. "Think of all the trouble they would have saved us! Suicide an admission of guilt, no trials, no strangler in the Career Tullianum—we don't dare throw *them* off the Tarpeian Rock!"

Sulla stood listening, his ears absorbing what was said, but his eyes resting thoughtfully upon Caepio Junior and Metellus Piglet. However, he said nothing.

"Well, the trial is something we'll worry about when the time comes," said Marius. "In the meantime, we have to find somewhere to put them where they'll be safe."

"The Lautumiae is out of the question," said Scaurus at once. "If for some reason—or at someone's instigation—a big crowd decides to rescue them, those cells will never withstand attack, not if every lictor we have is standing guard. It's not Saturninus

I'm concerned about, but that ghastly creature Equitius. All it will take is for one silly woman to start weeping and wailing because the son of Tiberius Gracchus is going to die, and we could have trouble." He grunted. "And as if that weren't enough, look at our young bloods down there, slavering. They wouldn't mind lynching Saturninus in the least."

"Then I suggest," said Marius joyously, "that we shut them up inside the Curia Hostilia."

Scaurus Princeps Senatus looked stunned. "We can't do that, Gaius Marius!"

"Why not?"

"Imprison traitors in the *Senate House*? It's—it's—why, it's like offering our old gods a sacrifice of a turd!"

"They've already fouled the temple of Jupiter Optimus Maximus, everything to do with the State religion is going to have to be purified anyway. The Curia has absolutely no windows, and the best doors in Rome. The alternative is for some of us to volunteer to hold them in our own homes—would you like Saturninus? Take him, and I'll take Equitius. I think Quintus Lutatius should have Glaucia," said Marius, grinning.

"The Curia Hostilia is an excellent idea," said Sulla, still looking thoughtfully at Caepio Junior and Metellus Piglet.

"Grrrr!" snarled Scaurus Princeps Senatus, not at Marius or Sulla, but at circumstances. Then he nodded decisively. "You are quite right, Gaius Marius. The Curia Hostilia it must be, I'm afraid."

"Good!" said Marius, clapped Sulla on the shoulder in a signal to move off, and added with a frightful lopsided grin, "While I see to the details, Marcus Aemilius, I'll leave it to you to explain to your fellow Good Men why we need to use our venerable meeting-house as a prison."

"Why, thank you!" said Scaurus.

"Think nothing of it."

When they were out of earshot of all who mattered, Marius glanced at Sulla curiously. "What are you up to?" he asked.

"I'm not sure I'm going to tell you," said Sulla.

"You'll be careful, please. I don't want you hauled up for treason."

"I'll be careful, Gaius Marius."

Saturninus and his confederates had surrendered on the eighth day of December; on the ninth, Gaius Marius reconvened the Centuriate Assembly and heard the declaration of candidates for the curule magistracies.

Lucius Cornelius Sulla didn't bother going out to the *saepta;* he was busy doing other things, including having long talks with Caepio Junior and Metellus Piglet, and squeezing in a visit to Aurelia, though he knew from Publius Rutilius Rufus that she was all right, and that Lucius Decumius had kept his tavern louts away from the Forum Romanum.

The tenth day of the month was the day upon which the new tribunes of the plebs entered office; but two of them, Saturninus and Equitius, were locked up in the Senate House. And everyone was worried that the crowd might reappear, for it seemed to be most interested in the doings of the tribunes of the plebs.

Though Marius would not permit his little army of three days before to come to the Forum Romanum clad in armor or girt with swords, he had the Basilica Porcia closed off to its normal complement of merchants and bankers, and kept it purely for the storage of arms and armor; on its ground floor at the Senate House end were the offices of the College of Tribunes of the Plebs, and here the eight who were not involved in the Saturninus business were to assemble at dawn, after which the inaugural meeting of the Plebeian Assembly would be conducted as quickly as possible, and with no reference to the missing two.

But dawn had not yet broken and the Forum Romanum was utterly deserted when Caepio Junior and Metellus Pius Piglet led their raiding party down the Argiletum toward the Curia Hostilia. They had gone the long way round to make sure no guard detected them, but when they spread out around the Curia, they discovered they had the whole area to themselves.

They carried long ladders which they propped against both

sides of the building, reaching all the way up to the ancient fan-shaped tiles of the eaves, lichen-covered, brittle.

"Remember," said Caepio Junior to his troops, "that no sword must be raised, Lucius Cornelius says. We must abide by the letter of Gaius Marius's orders."

One by one they scaled the ladders until the entire party of fifty squatted along the edge of the roof, which was shallow in pitch, and not an uncomfortable place to roost. There in the darkness they waited until the pale light in the east grew from dove-grey to bright gold, and the first rays of the sun came stealing down from the Esquiline Hill to bathe the roof of the Senate House. Some people were beginning to arrive below, but the ladders had been drawn up onto the Curia's roof too, and no one noticed anything untoward because no one thought to look upward.

"*Do it!*" cried Caepio Junior.

Racing time—for Lucius Cornelius had told them they would not have very long—the raiding party began ripping tiles off the oak frames between the far more massive cedar beams. Light flooded into the hall below, bouncing off fifteen white faces staring up, more startled than terrified. And when each man on the roof had a stack of tiles beside him, he began to hurl them down through the gap he had made, straight into those faces. Saturninus fell at once, as did Lucius Equitius. Some of the prisoners tried to shelter in the hall's farthest corners, but the young men on the roof very quickly became skilled at pitching their tiles in any direction accurately. The hall held no furniture of any kind, its users bringing their own stools with them, and the clerks a table or two from the Senate Offices next door on the Argiletum. So there was nothing to shield the prisoners below from the torrent of missiles, more effective as weapons than Sulla had suspected. Each tile broke upon impact with razor-sharp edges, and each weighed ten pounds.

By the time Marius and his legates—including Sulla—got there, it was all over; the raiding party was descending the ladders to the ground, where its members stood quietly, no one trying to escape.

"Shall I arrest them?" asked Sulla of Marius.

Marius jumped, so deep in thought had he been when the quick question came. "No!" he said. "They're not going anywhere." And he glanced at Sulla, a covert sideways look which asked a silent question. And got his answer with the ghost of a wink.

"Open the doors," said Marius to his lictors.

Inside the early sun threw rays and beams through a pall of slowly settling dust and lit up the lichen-grey heaps of tiles lying everywhere, their broken edges and more sheltered undersides a rich rust-red, almost the color of blood. Fifteen bodies lay squeezed into the smallest huddles or splayed with arms akimbo and legs twisted, half-buried by shattered tiles.

"You and I, Princeps Senatus," said Marius. "No one else."

Together they entered the hall and picked their way from one body to the next, looking for signs of life. Saturninus had been struck so quickly and effectively that he hadn't tried to hunch himself up protectively; his face was hidden below a carapace of tiles, and when revealed looked sightlessly into the sky, his black lashes caked with tile dust and plaster dust. Scaurus bent to close the eyes, and winced fastidiously; so much dust lay upon the dry-ing eyeballs that the lids refused to come down. Lucius Equitius had fared worst. Hardly an inch of him was not bruised or cut or swollen from a tile, and it took Marius and Scaurus many mo-ments to toss aside the heap burying him. Saufeius—who had run into a corner—had died from a shard which apparently struck the floor and bounced up to lodge itself like a huge fat spearhead in the side of his neck; his head was almost severed. And Titus La-bienus had taken the long edge of an unfractured tile in the small of his back, gone down without feeling anything below the colos-sal break in his spine.

Marius and Scaurus conferred.

"What am I to do with those idiots out there?" Marius asked.

"What *can* you do?"

The right half of Marius's upper lip lifted. "Oh, come, Prin-ceps Senatus! Take some of the burden upon your scraggy old carcass! You're not going to skip away from any of this, so much do I promise. Either back me—or be prepared for a fight that will leave everything done here today looking like the women's Bona Dea festival!"

"All right, all right!" said Scaurus irritably. "I didn't mean I wouldn't back you, you literal-minded rustic! All I meant was what I said—what *can* you do?"

"Under the powers invested in me by the *Senatus Consultum* I can do whatever I like, from arresting every last one of that brave little band outside, to sending them home without so much as a verbal chastisement. Which do you consider expedient?"

"The expedient thing is to send them all home. The proper thing is to arrest them and charge them with the murder of fellow Romans. Since the prisoners hadn't stood trial, they were still Roman citizens when they met their deaths."

Marius cocked his only mobile eyebrow. "So which course shall I take, Princeps Senatus? The expedient one—or the proper one?"

Scaurus shrugged. "The expedient one, Gaius Marius. You know that as well as I do. If you take the proper one, you'll drive a wedge so deeply into Rome's tree that the whole world might fall along with it."

They walked out into the open air and stood together at the top of the Senate steps, looking down into the faces of the people in the immediate vicinity; beyond these scant hundreds, the Forum Romanum was empty, clean, dreamy in the morning sun.

"I hereby proclaim a general amnesty!" cried Gaius Marius at the top of his voice. "Go home, young men," he said to the raiding party, "you are indemnified along with everyone else." He turned to the main body of his listeners. "Where are the tribunes of the plebs? Here? Good! Call your meeting, there is no crowd. The first business of the day will be the election of two more tribunes of the plebs. Lucius Appuleius Saturninus and Lucius Equitius are dead. Chief lictor, send for some of your fellows and the public slaves, and clear up the mess inside the Curia Hostilia. Give the bodies to their families for honorable burial, for they had not been tried for their crimes, and are therefore still Roman citizens of good standing."

He walked down the steps and crossed to the rostra, for he was senior consul and supervisor of the ceremonies which would inaugurate the new tribunes; had he been a patrician, his junior colleague would have seen to it, which was why one at least of the consuls had to be a plebeian, to have access to the *concilium plebis.*

And then it happened, perhaps because the gossip grapevine was in its usual splendid working order, and the word had sparkled up and down its tendrils with the speed of sunbeams. The Forum began to fill with people, thousands upon thousands of them hurrying from Esquiline, Caelian, Viminal, Quirinal, Subura, Palatine, Aventine, Oppian. The same crowd, Gaius Marius saw at once, which had jammed into the Forum during the elections of the tribunes of the plebs.

And, with the trouble largely over and a feeling of peace within his heart, he looked out into that ocean of faces and saw what Lucius Appuleius Saturninus had seen: a source of power as yet untapped, innocent of the guile experience and education brought, ready to believe some passionately eloquent demagogue's self-seeking *kharisma* and put themselves under a different master. Not for me, thought Gaius Marius; to be the First Man in Rome at the whim of the gullible is no victory. I have enjoyed the status of First Man in Rome the old way, the hard way, battling the prejudices and monstrosities of the *cursus honorum.*

But, Gaius Marius concluded his thoughts gleefully, I shall make one last gesture to show Scaurus Princeps Senatus, Catulus Caesar, Ahenobarbus Pontifex Maximus, and the rest of the *boni* that if I *had* chosen Saturninus's way, they'd be dead inside the Curia Hostilia all covered in tiles, and I'd be running Rome single-handed. For I am to Saturninus what Jupiter is to Cupid.

He stepped to that edge of the rostra which faced the lower Forum rather than the well of the Comitia, and held out his arms in a gesture which seemed to embrace the crowd, draw it to him as a father beckons his children. "People of Rome, go back to your houses!" he thundered. "The crisis is past. Rome is safe. And I, Gaius Marius, have great pleasure in announcing to you that a fleet of grain ships arrived in Ostia harbor yesterday. The barges will be coming upstream all day today, and by tomorrow there will be grain available from the State granaries of the Aventine at one sestertius the *modius*, the price which Lucius Appuleius Saturninus's grain law laid down. However, Lucius Appuleius is dead, and his law invalid. It is I, Gaius Marius, consul of Rome, who gives to you your grain! The special price will continue until I step down from office in nineteen days' time. After that, it is up to the new magistrates to decide what price you will pay. The one sestertius I shall charge you is my parting gift to you, Quirites! For I love you, and I have fought for you, and I have won for you. Never, never forget it! *Long—live—Rome!*"

And down from the rostra he stepped amid a wave of cheers, his arms above his head, that fierce twisted grin a fitting farewell, with its good side and its bad side.

Catulus Caesar stood rooted to the spot. "Did you hear that?" he gasped to Scaurus. "He just gave away nineteen days of grain—*in his name!* At a cost to the Treasury of thousands of talents! How dare he!"

"Are you going to get up on the rostra and contradict him, Quintus Lutatius?" asked Sulla, grinning. "With all your loyal young Good Men standing there getting off free?"

"*Damn him!*" Catulus Caesar was almost weeping.

Scaurus broke into peals of laughter. "He did it to us again, Quintus Lutatius!" he said when he was able. "Oh, what an earthshaker that man is! He stuck it to us, and he's left us to pay the bill! I loathe him—but by all the gods, I do love him too!" And away he went into another paroxysm.

"There are times, Marcus Aemilius Scaurus, when I do not even begin to understand you!" Catulus Caesar said, and stalked off in his best camel manner.

"Whereas I, Marcus Aemilius Scaurus, understand you all too well," said Sulla, laughing even harder than Scaurus.

When Glaucia killed himself with his sword and Marius extended the amnesty to Gaius Claudius and his followers, Rome breathed more easily; the Forum strife might be presumed to be over. But that was not so. The young Brothers Luculli brought Gaius Servilius Augur to trial in the treason court, and violence broke out afresh. Senatorial feelings ran high because the case split the Good Men; Catulus Caesar and Scaurus Princeps Senatus and their followers, were firmly aligned with the Luculli, whereas Ahenobarbus Pontifex Maximus and Crassus Orator were committed by ties of patronage and friendship to Servilius the Augur.

The unprecedented crowds which had filled the Forum Romanum during the troubles with Saturninus had disappeared, but the habitual Forum frequenters turned out in force to witness this trial, attracted by the youth and pathos of the two Luculli— who were fully aware of this, and determined to use it in every way they could. Varro Lucullus, the younger brother, had donned his toga of manhood only days before the trial began; neither he nor the eighteen-year-old Lucius Lucullus yet needed to shave. Their agents, cunningly placed among the crowd, whispered that these two poor lads had just received the news that their exiled father was dead—and that the long-ennobled family Licinius Lucullus now had only these two poor lads to defend its honor, its *dignitas*.

Composed of knights, the jury had decided ahead of time that it was going to side with Servilius the Augur, who was a knight elevated to the Senate by his patron Ahenobarbus Pontifex Maximus. Even when this jury was being chosen, violence had played its part; the hired ex-gladiators of Servilius the Augur tried to prevent the trial's going on. But the handy little band of young nobles run by Caepio Junior and Metellus Pius Piglet had driven the bully-boys from the scene, killing one as it did so. The jury understood this message, and resigned itself to listening to the Brothers Luculli with more sympathy than it had originally intended.

"They'll convict the Augur," said Marius to Sulla as they stood off to one side, watching and listening keenly.

"They will indeed," said Sulla, who was fascinated by Lucius

Lucullus, the older boy. "Brilliant!" he exclaimed when young Lucullus finished his speech. "I *like* him, Gaius Marius!"

But Marius was unimpressed. "He's as haughty and pokered up as his father was."

"You're known to support the Augur," said Sulla stiffly.

That shaft went wide; Marius just grinned. "I would support a Tingitanian ape if it made life difficult for the Good Men around our absent Piggle-wiggle, Lucius Cornelius."

"Servilius the Augur *is* a Tingitanian ape," said Sulla.

"I'm inclined to agree. He's going to lose."

A prediction borne out when the jury (eyeing Caepio Junior's band of young nobles) returned a unanimous verdict of *DAMNO,* even after being moved to tears by the impassioned defense speeches of Crassus Orator and Mucius Scaevola.

Not surprisingly, the trial ended in a brawl which Marius and Sulla viewed from a suitably aloof distance, and with huge enjoyment from the moment when Ahenobarbus Pontifex Maximus punched an intolerably jubilant Catulus Caesar on the mouth.

"Pollux and Lynceus!" said Marius, delighted when the pair settled down to engage in serious fisticuffs. "Oh, go it, Quintus Lutatius Pollux!" he roared.

"Not a bad classical allusion, given that the Ahenobarbi all swear it was Pollux put the red in their inky beards," said Sulla when a punch properly directed by Catulus Caesar smeared Ahenobarbus's whole face with blood.

"And hopefully," said Marius, turning away as soon as the brawl ended in defeat for Ahenobarbus, "that brings events in the Forum to an end for this hideous year."

"Oh, I don't know, Gaius Marius. We've still to endure the consular elections."

"They're not held in the Forum, one mercy."

Two days later Marcus Antonius held his triumph, and two days after that he was elected senior consul for the coming year; his colleague in the consulship was to be none other than Aulus

Postumius Albinus, whose invasion of Numidia had, ten years ago, precipitated the war against Jugurtha.

"The electors are *complete* asses!" said Marius to Sulla with some passion. "They've just elected as junior consul one of the best examples I know of ambition allied to no talent of any kind! Tchah! Their memories are as short as their turds!"

"Well, they say constipation causes mental dullness," said Sulla, grinning despite the emergence of a new fear. He was hoping to run for praetor in the next year's elections, but had today sensed a mood in the electors of the Centuriate Assembly that boded ill for Marian candidates in future. Yet how do I dissociate myself from this man who has been so good to me? he asked himself unhappily.

"Luckily, I predict it's going to be a mentally dull year, and Aulus Albinus won't be given a chance to ruin things," Marius went on, unaware of Sulla's thoughts. "For the first time in a long time, Rome has no enemies worth a mention. We can rest. And Rome can rest."

Sulla made an effort, swung his mind away from a praetorship he knew was going to prove elusive. "What about the prophecy?" he asked abruptly. "Martha distinctly said you'd be consul of Rome seven times."

"I *will* be consul seven times, Lucius Cornelius."

"You believe that."

"I do."

Sulla sighed. "I'd be happy to reach praetor."

A facial hemiparesis enabled its sufferer to blow the most wonderfully derisive noises; Marius blew one now. "Rubbish!" he said vigorously. "You are *consul* material, Lucius Cornelius. In fact, one day you'll be the First Man in Rome."

"I thank you for your faith in me, Gaius Marius." Sulla turned a smile upon Marius almost as twisted as Marius's were these days. "Still, considering the difference in our ages, I won't be vying with *you* for the title," he said.

Marius laughed. "What a battle of the Titans that would be! No danger of it," he said with absolute certainty.

"With your retiring from the curule chair and not planning to attend the House, you'll no longer be the First Man in Rome yourself, Gaius Marius."

"True, true. But oh, Lucius Cornelius, I've had a good run! And as soon as this awful affliction of mine goes away, I'll be back."

"In the meantime, who will be the First Man in Rome?" asked Sulla. "Scaurus? Catulus?"

"*Nemo!*" bellowed Gaius Marius, and laughed uproariously. "*Nobody!* That's the best joke of all! There's not one of them can fill *my* shoes!"

Joining in the laughter, Sulla put his right arm across Marius's togate back, gave it a squeeze of pure affection, and set their feet upon the road home from the *saepta*. In front of them reared the Capitoline Mount; a broad finger of chilly sun alighted upon the gilding of Victory's four-horse chariot atop Jupiter Optimus Maximus's temple pediment, and turned the city of Rome to dazzling gold.

"It hurts my eyes!" cried Sulla in real pain. But could not look away.

FINIS

AUTHOR'S NOTE

Essentially, this book is a one-woman band. I have done my own research, executed the maps and drawings myself and written my own glossary. Whatever flaws and errors the book contains must be laid at my door and no one else's. However, there are two people I would like to thank by name, most sincerely. The first is Dr. Alanna Nobbs, of Macquarie University, Sydney, Australia, who has acted as my classical editor. The second is Miss Sheelah Hidden, who traveled the world in search of source materials and books, talking to many authorities in the field, tracking down the whereabouts of portrait busts, and more. To the many others who shall be nameless due to lack of space, but no less highly regarded because of it, a warm and sincere thank-you also. And thanks to my husband; to my literary agent, Fred Mason; my editor, Carolyn Reidy; Jean Easthope; Joe Nobbs; and the staff.

Rather than append a long scholarly dissertation in defense of my hypotheses, I have chosen to incorporate a minimum of this within the Glossary. For those with sufficient background to be skeptical about my treatment of the relationship between Marius and Sulla during these early years, about the identity of Sulla's first wife, and about the number of daughters Gaius Julius Caesar Nepos had, I suggest you consult the Julilla entry in the Glossary, wherein you will find my thoughts on these matters. To check the facts about Martha the Syrian's prophecies concerning Gaius Marius, see Martha in the Glossary. And if you doubt the ancients knew what vintage wines were, look up wine. A discussion about the location of the Forum Piscinum and the Forum Frumentarium can be found under those entries. And so on. The Glossary is as full and accurate as space permits.

No bibliography is appended. First of all, because it is not usual to do so in the case of a novel. But more importantly, any bibliography would run to many pages. One hundred and eighty volumes of the Loeb Classical Library in my possession would be but a small beginning. I will only say, where possible, I have gone to the ancient sources, and have treasured the modern works of many fine historians, including Pauly-Wissowa, Broughton, Syme, Mommsen, Münzer, Scullard, and others. My scholarship will be obvious enough to those qualified to judge, without a bibliography. However, should any reader be interested, he or she may write to me in care of the publisher for a bibliography.

I beg the indulgence of Latinate readers, who will find some Latin words kept in the nominative case when vocative, dative, or other cases are in actual fact correct; and who will find family names, especially in the first half of the book, Anglicized in the plural. This has been done in order to make reading less confusing for what will be a largely non-Latinate audience.

A word about the drawings. I am so tired of people thinking Cleopatra looked like Elizabeth Taylor, Mark Antony like Richard Burton, and so forth, that I decided to supply my readers with genuine Republican Roman faces. Where possible, these are authenticated likenesses; where no such identification has been made, I have chosen an anonymous Republican Roman head of the right age and type, and given it a historical name. In this book, there are nine drawings of persons. Only two are authenticated—Gaius Marius and Lucius Cornelius Sulla. Of the other seven, Catulus Caesar is based upon an atypical portrait bust of Caesar the Dictator, and Gaius Julius Caesar upon an equally atypical portrait bust of a Marcus Aemilius Lepidus. Aurelia is taken from the full-length statue of a crone of impeccably Republican date; though the statue is weatherworn, the lady's bones bore a strong likeness to those of Caesar the Dictator. Metellus Numidicus, Marcus Aemilius Scaurus, Publius Rutilius

Rufus, and the young Quintus Sertorius are based upon anonymous portrait busts of Republican date. That only one woman has been included is due to the dearth of Republican-era female portraits; what few do exist, I have had to ration out, and keep them to illustrate women in whom I can see a likeness to some authenticated Roman man. There are, after all, more books to come!

The next book in the series is tentatively titled *The Grass Crown.*

GLOSSARY

ABSOLVO The Latin term employed by a jury when voting for acquittal of the accused.

Academic An adherent of Platonic philosophy.

adamas Diamond. The ancients knew it was the hardest substance, and employed it as a cutting tool when they could get hold of it. What diamonds were available came from Scythia and India.

Adriatric Sea Mare Adriaticum. The body of water separating the Italian Peninsula from Illyricum, Macedonia, and Epirus; it was contiguous with the Ionian Sea.

advocate The term generally used by modern scholars to describe a man active in the Roman law courts. "Lawyer" is considered too modern.

aedes A house of the gods which was not considered a temple because it was not used for augury at the time of its consecration. The temple of Vesta, for example, was actually an *aedes sacra* rather than a full temple.

aedile One of four Roman magistrates with duties confined to the city of Rome. Two were plebeian aediles; two were curule aediles. The plebeian aediles were created first (in 493 B.C.), to assist the tribunes of the plebs in their duties, but more particularly to guard the rights of the plebs in relation to their headquarters, the temple of Ceres. They soon inherited supervision of the city's buildings as a whole, and archival custody of plebiscites passed in the Plebeian Assembly, together with any senatorial decrees directing the passage of plebiscites. The plebeian aediles were elected by the Plebeian Assembly. Two curule aediles were created (in 367 B.C.) to give the patricians a share in custody of public buildings and archives, but the curule aediles were soon as likely to be plebeians as patricians. The curule aediles were elected by the Assembly of the People. All four from the third century B.C. onward were responsible for care of Rome's streets, water supply, drains, traffic, public buildings and facilities, markets, weights and measures, games, and the public grain supply. They had the power to fine citizens for infringements of any regulations connected to any of the above, and deposited the moneys in their chests to help fund the games. Aedileship—plebeian or curule—was not a part of the *cursus honorum*, but because of the games was a valuable way for a praetorian hopeful to accrue popularity.

Aedui A powerful confraternity of Celtic tribes who lived in central Long-haired Gaul. After Gnaeus Domitius Ahenobarbus in 122 and 121 B.C. subjugated their traditional enemies the Arverni, the Aedui became less warlike, steadily more Romanized, and enjoyed Roman patronage.

Aeneas Prince of Dardania, in the Troad. The son of King Anchises and the goddess Venus (Aphrodite), he fled the burning city of Troy (Ilium) with his aged father on his shoulders and the Palladium under one arm. After many adventures, he arrived in Latium and founded the race from whom true Romans were descended. Vergil says his son Iulus, was actually Ascanius, his son by his Trojan wife, Creusa, whom he brought from Troy with him; on the other hand, Livy says Iulus was his son by his Latin wife, Lavinia. What the Roman of Gaius Marius's day believed is really not known, as both Livy and Vergil wrote almost a hundred years later.

Aenus River The modern river Inn, in Bavaria.

Aetna Mons Modern Mount Etna. The famous Sicilian volcano was as active in ancient times as it is in modern, but the land around it was extensively used.

Africa In Roman Republican times, the word "Africa" was mostly applied to that part of the northern coast around Carthage—modern Tunisia.

Africa Province   The Roman province of Africa, which in the days of Gaius Marius was actually very small—basically, the outthrust of land containing Carthage. The Roman province was surrounded by the much larger Numidia.

ager publicus   Land vested in Roman public ownership. Most of it was acquired by right of conquest or taken off its original owners as punishment for disloyalty. This latter was particularly true in the Italian Peninsula. It was leased out by the State (the censors had the duty) in a fashion favoring large estates. The most famous and contentious of all the many pieces of Italian *ager publicus* was the *ager Campanus*, land once belonging to the town of Capua, and confiscated by Rome after various Capuan insurrections.

Agger   The double rampart and fortifications protecting the city of Rome on its most vulnerable side, along the Campus Esquilinus; the Agger was a part of the Servian Walls.

Alba Longa   Near modern Castel Gandolfo. The ancient center of Latium, and the original home of many of Rome's oldest patrician families, including the Julii. It was attacked and conquered by King Tullus Hostilius of Rome in the seventh century B.C., and razed to the ground. Its citizens were relocated in Rome.

Albis River   The modern Elbe, in Germany.

Alexander the Great   King of Macedonia, the third to be called Alexander. He was born in 356 B.C., and died aged thirty-three years. When he was twenty years old, he succeeded his father, Philip II, as king, and, haunted by the specter of the Persians, he resolved to render the threat of a Persian invasion of Europe nonexistent for all time. So in 334 B.C. he led an army across the Hellespont with the aim of subduing Persia. His odyssey between this time and his death of a fever in Babylon took him, always victorious, as far as the river Indus in modern Pakistan. His tutor as a boy was Aristotle. As he died without a true successor, his empire did not survive him as a possession of Macedonia, but he seeded many Hellenic kings in the persons of his generals, who divided most of Asia Minor, Egypt, Syria, Media, and Persia between them.

Allies   Quite early in the history of the Roman Republic, its magistrates began issuing the title "Friend and Ally of the Roman People" to peoples and/or nations which had assisted Rome in an hour of (usually military) need. In time, all of the Italian Peninsula not enfranchised with full Roman citizenship or on the way to enfranchisement by being given the Latin Rights was deemed to consist of "Allies." Rome assured military protection and some trade concessions, in return for armed troops supported by the Allies whenever Rome demanded them. Abroad, peoples and/or nations began to earn the title too; the Aedui of Long-haired Gaul and the Kingdom of Bithynia were deemed Allies. When foreign elements entered the picture, the Italian nations were simply called Allies, while the overseas nations used the full title "Friend and Ally of the Roman People."

Allobroges   The confraternity of Celtic tribes which occupied the lands south of Lake Lemanna between the crest of the western Alps and the river Rhodanus, as far south as the river Isara. They loathed Roman penetration into the area, and were obdurate foes of the Romans.

Ambarri   A sept or subsection of the confraternity of Celtic tribes known as the Aedui, in central Long-haired Gaul. They lived closer to the Arar (Sâone).

Ambrones   A sept or subsection of the Germanic people called the Teutones; they perished to the last man at Aquae Sextiae in 102 B.C. (see Teutones).

ambrosia   The food of the gods.

Amisia River   The modern Ems, in Germany.

Amor   Literally, "love." Because it is also "Roma" spelled backward, the Romans of Republican times commonly believed that "Amor" was Rome's vital secret name.

amphora, amphorae (pl.)   A pottery vessel, bulbous in shape, with a narrow neck and two large handles on the upper part, and a pointed or conical bottom which prevented its being stood upright on level ground. It was used for the bulk (usually maritime) transport of wine or wheat, its pointed bottom enabling it to be fitted easily into the sawdust which filled the ship's hold or cart's interior. It then sat upright during the journey, cushioned and protected. The pointed bottom enabled it to be dragged across level ground by a handler with considerable ease in loading and unloading. The usual size of amphora held about 6 American gallons (25 liters).

Anas River   The modern river Guadiana, in Spain.

Anatolia   Roughly, modern Asian Turkey. It extended from the south coast of the Black Sea (the Euxine) through to the Mediterranean, and from the Aegean Sea in the west to modern Armenia, Iran, and Syria in the east. The Taurus and Antitaurus Mountains made its interior and much of its coastline very rugged. Its climate was continental.

Ancus Marcius   The fourth King of Rome, claimed by the family Marcius (particularly that branch cognominated Rex) as its founder-ancestor; unlikely, since the Marcii were plebeians. Ancus Marcius was said to have colonized Ostia—though there is some doubt whether he did this, or captured the salt pits at the mouth of the Tiber from their Etruscan owners. Rome under his rule flourished. His one lasting public work was the building of the Wooden Bridge, the Pons Sublicius. He died in 617 B.C., leaving sons who did not inherit their father's throne, a source of later trouble.

Anio River   The modern Aniene.

Anna Perenna   One of the numinous gods native to Rome and owing nothing to Greece (see *numen*); possessed of neither face nor mythology, Anna Perenna was regarded as female. Her feast was held on the first full moon after the old New Year (March 1), and it was a very happy occasion for everyone in Rome.

Antiocheia, Antioch   The capital of Syria and the largest city in that part of the world.

Apennines   The range of mountains breaking Italy up into three regions largely isolated from each other: Italian Gaul (northern Italy of the Po Valley), the Adriatic seaboard of the peninsula, and the wider, more fertile plains and valleys of the peninsula's west coast. The range branched off the Alpes Maritimae in Liguria, crossed the base of the peninsula from west to east, then ran down the full length of the peninsula to Bruttium, opposite Sicily. Its highest peak rose to 9,600 feet (3,000 m).

aqua   An aqueduct. In the time of Gaius Marius, there were four such, supplying water to the city of Rome. The oldest was the Aqua Appia (312 B.C.), next was the Aqua Anio Vetus (272 B.C.), then the Aqua Marcia (144 B.C.), and finally the Aqua Tepula (125 B.C.). During the Republic, the aqueducts and the water they provided were cared for by water companies hired under contract by the censors.

Aquae Sextiae   Modern Aix-en-Provence. A spa town in the Roman province of Gaul-across-the-Alps.

Aquileia   A Latin Rights colony seeded in far eastern Italian Gaul to protect the trade routes across the Carnic Alps from Noricum and Illyricum; the date was 181 B.C. Provided soon after with several roads connecting it to Ravenna, Patavium, Verona, and Placentia, it quickly became the most important city at the top of the Adriatic.

aquilifer   Presumably a creation of Gaius Marius at the time he gave the legions their silver eagles. The best man in the legion, the *aquilifer* was chosen to carry the legion's silver eagle, and was expected to keep it safe from enemy capture. He wore a wolf skin or a lion skin as a mark of his distinction.

Aquitani, Aquitania   The lands of southwestern Long-haired Gaul between the Carantonus River and the Pyrenees, and extending eastward along the Garumna River almost to Tolosa were called Aquitania, and were occupied by a Celtic confederation of tribes called the Aquitani. The largest of the Aquitanian *oppida* was Burdigala, on the southern side of the mouth of the Garumna.

Arar River   The modern Sâone, in France.

Arausio   Modern Orange. A small settlement under Roman influence on the eastern bank of the Rhodanus River, in Gaul-across-the-Alps.

Arduenna   The modern forest of the Ardennes, in northern France. In the time of Gaius Marius the Arduenna extended all the way from the Mosa to the Mosella, and was impenetrable.

area Flacciana Marcus Fulvius Flaccus, an important adherent of Gaius Gracchus, was murdered together with two of his sons in 121 B.C. as part of senatorial suppression of Gaius Gracchus's policies. His lands and all his properties were confiscated postmortem, including his house on the Palatine, which was torn down and the land left neglected. This vacant block, which overlooked the Forum Romanum, was called the *area Flacciana.* Quintus Lutatius Catulus acquired it in 100 B.C., and used it to build a colonnade in which he installed the standards taken from the Cimbri at Vercellae.

Arelate Modern Arles. A town, possibly founded by the Greeks, in Gaul-across-the-Alps. Situated on the Rhodanus just above its delta, Arelate grew in importance after Gaius Marius built his ship canal.

armillae The wide bracelets, of gold or of silver, which were awarded as prizes for valor to Roman legionaries, centurions, cadets, and military tribunes.

Arnus River The modern Arno. Throughout its course, loop and all, it formed the boundary between Italy proper and Italian Gaul.

Arpinum A town in Latium not far from the border of Samnium, and probably originally peopled by Volsci. It was the last Latin Rights community to receive the full Roman citizenship, in 188 B.C., but it did not enjoy full municipal status in Gaius Marius's time.

Arx The more northern of the two humps which sit atop the Capitoline Mount of Rome.

as The smallest in value of the coins of Rome; ten of them equaled one denarius. They were bronze. I have avoided mentioning the *as* in the book because of (a) its relative unimportance, and (b) its identical spelling to the English adverb, conjunction, or preposition "as"—most confusing!

Asia Province The west coast and hinterland of what is now Turkey, from the Troad in the north to Lycia opposite Rhodes in the south. Its capital in Republican times was Pergamum.

Assembly (Comitia) Any gathering of the Roman People convoked to deal with governmental, legislative, or electoral matters. In the time of Gaius Marius there were three true Assemblies—of the Centuries, the People, and the Plebs.

The Centuriate Assembly marshaled the People in their classes, which were defined by a means test and were economic in nature. As it was originally a military assemblage, each class gathered in its centuries (which by Marius's time numbered far in excess of one hundred men, as it had been decided to keep the number of centuries in each class to a certain value). Its Latin name was Comitia Centuriata, and it met to elect consuls, praetors, and (every five years) censors; it also met to hear trials involving a charge of treason. The other two Assemblies were tribal in nature, not economic. The **Assembly of the People** allowed full participation of patricians; its Latin name was Comitia Populi Tributa, and it met in the thirty-five tribes among which all Roman citizens were divided. The Assembly of the People (also called the **Popular Assembly**) was convoked by a consul or praetor, could formulate laws, and elected the curule aediles, the quaestors, and the tribunes of the soldiers. It could also conduct trials. The **Assembly of the Plebs** or **Plebeian Assembly** was known in Latin as Comitia Plebis Tributa or Concilium Plebis. It did not allow the participation of patricians, and was convoked by a tribune of the plebs. The Plebeian Assembly had the right to enact laws (strictly, known as plebiscites), and conduct trials. It elected the plebeian aediles and the tribunes of the plebs. In no Roman Assembly could the vote of one individual be credited directly to his wants; in the Centuriate Assembly his vote was credited to his century of his class, and his century's total vote was credited as going whatever way the majority did; in the tribal Assemblies of People and Plebs, his vote was credited to his tribe, and his tribe's total vote was credited as going whatever way the majority of its members decided.

Asylum A part of the saddlelike depression which divided the two humps atop the Capitoline Mount; it carried the ancient meaning of asylum—that is, a refuge where a fugitive from any form of earthly justice or retribution could dwell without fear of arrest or detention. It was established as an asylum for fugitives by Romulus himself, when he was seeking a greater number of men to live in Rome than he could find by other means.

Athesis River   The modern Adige, in Italy.

atrium   The main reception room of a Roman private house; it mostly contained a rectangular opening in the roof, below which was a pool. Originally the purpose of the pool was to provide a reservoir of water for use of the household, but by the time of Gaius Marius, the pool was usually not used in this way; it had become ornamental.

Attalus III   The last King of Pergamum, and ruler of most of the Aegean coast of western Anatolia as well as Phrygia. In 133 B.C. he died, relatively young and without heirs closer than the usual collection of cousins. His will was carried to Rome, and there it was learned Attalus had bequeathed his entire kingdom to Rome. A war followed, put down by Manius Aquillius in 129 and 128 B.C. When Aquillius set about organizing the bequest as the Roman province of Asia, he sold most of Phrygia to King Mithridates V of Pontus for a sum of gold which he put into his own purse.

Attic helmet   An ornamental helmet worn by Roman officers, usually above the rank of centurion. It is the kind of helmet commonly worn by the stars of Hollywood's Roman epic movies— though I very much doubt any Attic helmet of Republican times was ever crested with ostrich feathers!

Atuatuci   Also known as Aduatuci. A confraternity of tribes inhabiting that part of Long-haired Gaul around the confluence of the Sabis and the Mosa, they appear to have been more German than Celt in racial origins, for they claimed kinship with the Germans called Teutones.

auctoritas   A very difficult Latin term to translate, as it means much more than the English word "authority." It carried implications of pre-eminence, clout, leadership, public and private importance, and—above all—the ability to influence events through sheer public or personal reputation. All the magistracies possessed *auctoritas* as part of their nature, but *auctoritas* was not confined to those who held magistracies; the Princeps Senatus, Pontifex Maximus, Rex Sacrorum, consulars, and even some private individuals could also accumulate *auctoritas*.

augur A priest whose duties concerned divination rather than prognostication. He and his fellow augurs constituted the College of Augurs, and numbered some twelve at the time of Gaius Marius, six patrician and six plebeian. Until the *lex Domitia de sacerdotiis* was passed by Gnaeus Domitius Ahenobarbus in 104 B.C., augurs had been chosen by those men already in the college; after that law, augurs had to be publicly elected. The augur did not predict the future, nor did he pursue his auguries at his own whim; he inspected the proper objects or signs to ascertain whether or not the projected undertaking was one having the approval of the gods, be the undertaking a meeting, a war, a proposed new law, or any other State business. There was virtually a manual of interpretation, so a man did not have to pretend he was psychic in order to be appointed an augur; in fact, the Roman State mistrusted men who did claim to have psychic powers, preferring to "go by the book." The augur wore the *toga trabea* (see that entry) and carried a staff called the *lituus*.

auxiliary A legion incorporated into a Roman army without its troops having the status of Roman citizens; a member of such a legion was also called an auxiliary, and the term extended to the cavalry arm as well. In the time of Gaius Marius, most auxiliary infantry was Italian in origin, where most auxiliary cavalry was from Gaul, Numidia, or Thrace, all lands whose soldiers rode horses, whereas the Roman soldier did not.

ave atque vale "Hail and farewell."

Baetis River The modern Guadalquivir. A river in Further Spain (Hispania Ulterior). According to the geographer Strabo, the valley of the Baetis was the most fertile and productive in the world.

Bagradas River The modern Mellègue. The most important river of the Roman African province.

Baiae The small town on the bay side of Cape Misenum, the northern promontory of what is now known as the Bay of Naples.

It was not fashionable as a resort during the Republic, but was famous for its beds of farmed oysters.

baldric The belt, either slung over one shoulder and under the other arm, or worn around the waist, which held a man's sword. The Roman *gladius*, a short-sword, was carried on a waist baldric, where a German long-sword needed a shoulder baldric.

basilica, basilicae (pl.) A large building devoted to public facilities such as courts of law, and also to commercial facilities, from shops to offices. The basilica was clerestory-lit, and during the Republic was erected at the expense of some civic-minded Roman nobleman, usually of consular status. The first of the basilicae was built by Cato the Censor, was situated on the Clivus Argentarius next door to the Senate House, and was known as the Basilica Porcia; as well as accommodating banking houses, it also was the headquarters of the College of Tribunes of the Plebs. By the time of Gaius Marius, it had been joined by the Basilicae Sempronia, Aemilia, and Opimia, all on the fringes of the lower Forum Romanum.

Belgae The fearsome confraternity of tribes inhabiting northwestern and Rhineland Gaul. Of mixed racial origins, the Belgae were probably more Germanic than Celtic; among them were the nations of the Treveri, the Atuatuci, the Condrusi, the Bellovaci, the Atrebates, and the Batavi. To the Romans of Gaius Marius's time, they were legendary rather than real.

Benacus, Lacus Modern Lake Garda, in northern Italy.

biga A chariot drawn by two horses.

Bithynia A kingdom flanking the Propontis on its Asian side, extending east to Paphlagonia and Galatia, south to Phrygia, and southwest to Mysia. It was fertile and prosperous, and was ruled by a series of kings of Thracian origin. Its traditional enemy was Pontus.

Boiohaemum Bohemia. Modern Czechoslovakia.

boni Literally, "the Good Men." First mentioned in a play by Plautus called *The Captives*, the term came into political use during the days of Gaius Gracchus. He used it to describe his followers—but so also did his enemies Drusus and Opimius. It then passed gradually into general use; in the time of Cicero, the *boni* were those men of the Senate whose political leanings were ultra-conservative.

Bononia   Modern Bologna, in northern Italy.

Borysthenes River   The modern Dnieper, in the Ukraine.

Brennus (1)   King of the Gauls (or Celts). It was Brennus who sacked Rome and almost captured the Capitol during his siege of it, save that Juno's sacred geese cackled until the consular Marcus Manlius awoke, found where the Gauls were climbing the cliff, and dislodged them; Rome never forgave its dogs (which hadn't barked), and ever after honored its geese. Seeing their city reduced to smoking rubble beneath their eyes and having nothing left to eat, the defenders of the Capitol finally agreed to buy their salvation from Brennus. The price was a thousand pounds' weight of gold. When the gold was brought to Brennus in the Forum, he had it reweighed on scales he had deliberately tampered with, then complained he was being cheated. The Romans said *he* was the cheat, whereupon Brennus drew his sword and threw it contemptuously onto the scales, saying, "Woe to the vanquished!" *("Vae victis!")* But before he could kill the Romans for their audacity in accusing him of cheating while they were buying their lives from him, the newly appointed dictator, Marcus Furius Camillus, appeared in the Forum with an army, and refused to allow Brennus to take the gold. In an initial battle through Rome's streets, the Gauls were ejected from the city, and in a second battle eight miles out along the Via Tiburtina, Camillus slaughtered the invaders. For this feat (and for his speech persuading the plebeians not to quit Rome thereafter and move permanently to Veii), Camillus was called the Second Founder of Rome. Livy doesn't say what happened to King Brennus. All this happened in 390 B.C.

Brennus (2)   A later king of the Gauls (or Celts). Leading a large Celtic confraternity of tribes, he invaded Macedonia and Thessaly in 279 B.C., turned the Greek defense at the pass of Thermopylae, and sacked Delphi, in which battle he was wounded. He then penetrated into Epirus and sacked the enormously rich oracular precinct of Zeus at Dodona, and sacked and looted the richest precinct of them all, that of Zeus at Olympia in the Peloponnese. In retreat before a determined Greek guerrilla resistance, Brennus returned to Macedonia, where he died of his old wound. Without Brennus to hold them together, the Gauls were rudderless. Some of them (the Tolistobogii, the Trocmi, and a segment of the Volcae Tectosages) crossed the Hellespont into Asia Minor, and settled in a land thereafter called Galatia. The Volcae Tectosages who did not go to Asia Minor returned to their homes around Tolosa in southwestern Gaul, bearing with them the entire loot of Brennus's campaign, which they held in trust against the return of the rest of Brennus's people; for the gold belonged to everyone.

Brundisium   Modern Brindisi. The most important port in southern Italy, and possessing the only good harbor on the whole Italian Adriatic coast. In 244 B.C. it became a Latin Rights colony, as Rome wished to protect its new extension of the Via Appia, from Tarentum to Brundisium.

Burdigala   Modern Bordeaux, in southwestern France. The great Gallic *oppidum* belonging to the Aquitani.

Caesarean section   The surgical procedure resorted to when a woman in childbirth finds it impossible to deliver her child through the pelvis. The abdomen is incised, the loops of bowel retracted, and the wall of the uterus cut open to extricate the child from within it. In this manner, so it is said, was Gaius Julius Caesar the Dictator delivered; the procedure still bears his family's *cognomen*. I have chosen to ignore the story, for the reason that we know beyond a shadow of a doubt that Caesar's mother, Aurelia, lived to be seventy years old, and apparently enjoyed good health up until the time of her death. The history of Caesarean section in antiquity was a grim one; though the operation was occasionally resorted to, and the child sometimes saved, the mother inevitably perished. The first truly successful Caesarean section that is well recorded occurred in Pavia, Italy, in April, 1876, when Dr. Edoardo Porro removed a healthy child—and uterus—from one Julie Covallini; mother and child survived and did very well.

Calabria　Confusing for those who know modern Italy! Nowadays Calabria is the toe of the boot, but in ancient times it was the heel.

Campania　The fabulously rich and fertile basin, volcanic in origin and soil, which lay between the Apennines of Samnium and the Tuscan (Tyrrhenian) Sea, and extended from Tarracina in the north to a point just south of the modern Bay of Naples. Watered by the Liris, Volturnus/Calor, Clanius, and Sarnus rivers, it grew bigger, better, and more of everything than any other region in all Italy. Early colonized by the Greeks, it fell under Etruscan domination, then affiliated itself to the Samnites, and eventually was subject to Rome. The Greek and Samnite elements in its populace made it a grudging subject, and it was always an area prone to insurrection. The towns of Capua, Teanum Sidicinum, Venafrum, Acerrae, Nola, and Interamna were important inland centers, while the ports of Puteoli, Neapolis, Herculaneum, Surrentum, and Stabiae constituted the best on Italy's west coast. Puteoli was the largest and the busiest port in all of Italy. The Via Campana, Via Appia, and Via Latina passed through it.

campus, campi **(pl.)**　A plain, or flat expanse of ground.

Campus Martius　Situated to the north of the Servian Walls, the Campus Martius was bounded by the Capitol to its south and the Pincian Hill on its east; the rest of it was enclosed by a huge bend in the river Tiber. Here on the Campus Martius armies awaiting their general's triumphs were bivouacked, military exercises and military training of the young went on, the stables for horses engaged in chariot racing were situated, assemblies of the Comitia Centuriata took place, and market gardening vied with public parklands. The Via Lata (Via Flaminia) crossed the Campus Martius on its way north.

Cannae　An Apulian town on the Aufidius River. Here in 216 B.C., Hannibal and his army of Carthaginians met a Roman army commanded by Lucius Aemilius Paullus and Gaius Terentius Varro. The Roman army was annihilated; until Arausio in 105 B.C., it ranked as Rome's worst military disaster. Somewhere between thirty thousand and sixty thousand men died.

The survivors were made to pass beneath the yoke (see that entry).

capite censi Literally, "Head Count." The *capite censi* were those full Roman citizens too poor to belong to one of the five economic classes, and so were unable to vote in the Centuriate Assembly at all. As most *capite censi* were urban in origin as well as in residence, they largely belonged to urban tribes, which numbered only four out of the total thirty-five tribes; this meant they had little influence in either of the tribal Assemblies, People or Plebs (see also Head Count, *proletarii*).

Capitol The Mons Capitolinus, one of the seven hills of Rome, and the only one more or less limited to religious and public buildings. Though the top of the Capitol contained no private residences, by the time of Gaius Marius its lower slopes boasted some of the most expensive houses in all Rome. Gaius Marius himself lived in this location.

Capua The most important inland town of Campania. A history of broken pledges of loyalty to Rome led to Roman reprisals which stripped Capua of its extensive and extremely valuable public lands; these became the nucleus of the *ager publicus* of Campania, and included, for instance, the fabulous vineyards which produced Falernian wine. By the time of Gaius Marius, Capua's economic well-being depended upon the many military training camps, gladiatorial schools, and slave camps for bulk prisoners which surrounded the town; the people of Capua made their living from supplying and servicing these huge institutions.

carbunculus The precious stone ruby; the word was also applied to really red garnets.

carcer A dungeon. The Tullianum's other name was simply Carcer.

Carinae One of Rome's more exclusive addresses. The Carinae was the northern tip of the Oppian Mount on its western side; it extended between the Velia, at the top of the Forum Romanum, and the Clivus Pullius.

Carnic Alps The name I have used to embrace that part of the alpine chain surrounding northern Italy at its eastern end, behind the coastal cities of Tergeste and Aquileia. These mountains are generally called the Julian Alps, the name Carnic Alps being reserved for the mountains of the modern Austrian Tyrol. However, I can find no evidence to suggest that some member of the family Julius of earlier date than Gaius Julius Caesar the Dictator had a mountain range named after himself, and so must assume that prior to Gaius Julius Caesar the Dictator, the Julian Alps were known by some other name. For want of ancient evidence (which is not to say it does not exist, only that I haven't found it), I have simply extended that name Carnic Alps to cover the Julian Alps as well.

Carnutes   One of the largest and most important of the Celtic tribal confraternities of Gaul. Their lands lay along the river Liger between its confluence with the Caris and a point on about the same meridian of longitude as modern Paris. The Carnutes owed much of their pre-eminence to the fact that within their lands lay the cult centers and Gallic training schools of the Druids.

Castor   The senior of the twin gods Castor and Pollux (to the Greeks, Kastor and Polydeukes), also called the Dioscuri. Their temple, in the Forum Romanum, was imposingly large and very old, indicating that their worship in Rome went back at least to the time of the kings. They cannot therefore simply be labeled a Greek import, as was Apollo. Their special significance to Rome (and possibly why later on they came to be associated with the Lares) was probably because Romulus, the founder of Rome, was a twin.

Cebenna   The highlands of south-central Gaul, lying to the west of the river Rhodanus. The Cebenna in modern terms would incorporate the Cévennes, the Auvergne, the Ardèche, and, in effect, all of the Massif Central.

cella, cellae **(pl).**   Literally, "room." Rooms in domestic households had mostly acquired special names distinguishing their functions, but a room without a name was a *cella*. The rooms inside temples were always *cellae*.

Celtiberians   The members of that part of the Celtic race who crossed the Pyrenees into Spain and settled mostly in its central, western, and northwestern regions. They were so well ensconced by the time of Gaius Marius that they were generally regarded as indigenous.

Celts   More the modern than the ancient term for a barbarian race which emerged from north-central Europe during the early centuries of the first millennium B.C. From about 500 B.C. onward, the Celts attempted to invade the lands of the European Mediterranean; in Spain and Gaul they succeeded, while in Italy and Greece they failed. However, in northern Italy, Macedonia, Thessaly, Illyricum, and Moesia, they seeded whole populations which gradually admixed with those peoples already present. Galatia, in central western Anatolia, was still Celtic speaking many centuries A.D. (see Brennus [2]). Racially the Celts were different from yet kindred to the later Germans; they considered themselves a discrete people. Their languages held certain similarities to Latin. A Roman rarely used the word "Celt"; he said "Gaul."

censor   The most senior of all Roman magistrates, though he lacked imperium, and was not therefore escorted by lictors. No man who had not already been consul could seek election as censor, and only those consulars owning tremendous personal *auctoritas* and *dignitas* normally bothered to stand. To be elected censor was complete vindication of a political man's career, for it said he was one of the very top men in Rome. The censor (two were elected at the same time) held office for a period of five years, though he was active in his duties for only about eighteen months at the beginning of his term. He and his colleague in the censorship inspected and regulated membership of the Senate, the *Ordo Equester* (the knights), and the holders of the Public Horse (the eighteen hundred most senior knights), and conducted a general census of Roman citizens, not only in Rome, but throughout Italy and the provinces. He also applied the means test. State contracts were let by him, and various public works or buildings initiated by him.

Centuriate Assembly   See Assembly.

centurion, Centurio, centuriones (pl.) The regular officer of both Roman citizen and auxiliary legions. It is a mistake to equate him with the modern noncommissioned officer; centurions were complete professionals enjoying a status uncomplicated by our modern social distinctions. A defeated Roman general hardly turned a hair if he lost military tribunes, but tore his hair out in clumps if he lost centurions. Centurion rank was graduated; the most junior *centurio* commanded a group of eighty soldiers and twenty noncombatants called a century. In the Republican army as reorganized by Gaius Marius, each cohort had six centurions, with the most senior man, the *pilus prior*, commanding the senior century of his cohort as well as commanding his entire cohort. The ten men commanding the ten cohorts making up a legion were also ranked in seniority, with the legion's most senior centurion, the *primus pilus*, answering only to his legion's commander (either one of the elected tribunes of the soldiers or one of the general's legates). Promotion during Republican times was from the ranks.

century A term which could apply to any collection of one hundred men, but which originally meant one hundred soldiers. The centuries of the Centuriate Assembly no longer contained a mere one hundred men, nor had military significance, but originally were indeed military. The centuries of the legions continued to contain one hundred men.

Cercina Island Modern Kerkenna. One of the islands of the African Lesser Syrtis, it was the site of the first of Gaius Marius's veteran soldier colonies. The father of Gaius Julius Caesar the Dictator was sent by Marius to organize the settlement of Cercina.

Ceres A very old Italian-Roman earth goddess whose duties chiefly concerned food crops, particularly cereal grains. Her temple, on the Aventine side of the Forum Boarium (and therefore outside the *pomerium*), was held to be the most beautiful temple in Republican Rome, and was built to house the cult of the Plebs in the days when Rome was controlled by the patricians and the Plebs often threatened to pack up and leave Rome, settle elsewhere; the first such mass desertion of the Plebs, in 494 B.C., was only as far as the Aventine, but that was far enough to win them concessions. By the time of Gaius Marius, the temple of Ceres was simply known as the headquarters of the Plebeian Order; it held the offices and records of the plebeian aediles.

Charybdis A mythical whirlpool variously located in the straits between Italy and Sicily, or near the Pillars of Hercules, or other places. Charybdis was always lumped with her companion, Scylla, a monster with a girdle of snarling dogs, who lived so close to Charybdis that no sailor could avoid the one without falling into the clutches of the other. In ancient times the saying "caught between Scylla and Charybdis" was the equivalent of our "between the devil and the deep blue sea," or "between a rock and a hard place."

chersonnese The Greeks' word for a peninsula, though they used it somewhat more flexibly than modern geographers. Thus the Tauric Chersonnese, the Thracian Chersonnese, the Cimbrian Chersonnese, etc.

Cherusci A confraternity of German tribes who lived in the area around the Amisia River (now the Ems) and the Visurgis River (now the Weser). Some segments of the Cherusci left this homeland about 113 B.C. to join the mass migration of the German Teutones and Cimbri.

Cimbri A very large confraternity of German tribes who lived in the more northern half of the Cimbrian Chersonnese until, in 120 B.C. or thereabouts, a massive natural disaster forced them to leave their homeland. Together with their immediate southern neighbors, the Teutones, they began an epic trek to find a new homeland—a trek which lasted nearly twenty years, took them thousands of miles, and finally brought them up against Rome—and Gaius Marius.

Cimbrian Chersonnese Modern Denmark, also known as the Jutland Peninsula.

Circei, Circeii The area, including Mount Circeii, which formed the coastal boundary between Latium and Campania. The town of the same name occupied the Tarracina side of the

Circeian Promontory, and was a popular Republican seaside resort.

circus   A place where chariot races were held. The course itself was long and narrow, and was divided lengthwise by a central barrier, the *spina*, the ends of which were conical stones called *metae*, which formed the turning points for the chariots. Bleacher-style tiers of wooden seats completely fenced it in. The seven laps of a race were monitored by seven eggs in cups, and seven dolphins; both were probably always there, but Agrippa certainly gave the Circus Maximus new and better dolphins. A race normally took about twenty-five minutes to complete. It is now thought that all four colors—red, green, white, and blue— were a part of the races throughout the middle and late Republic as well as during the Empire. I imagine four colors meant four competitors.

Circus Flaminius   The circus situated on the Campus Martius not far from the Tiber and the Forum Holitorium. It was built in 221 B.C., and sometimes was made to serve as a place for a comitial meeting, when the Plebs or the People had to assemble outside the *pomerium*. There were several temples within the Circus Flaminius, among them one to Vulcan, and the very beautiful, very famous temple of Hercules and the nine Muses.

Circus Maximus   The old circus built by King Tarquinius Priscus before the Republic began. It filled the whole of the Vallis Murcia, between the Palatine and Aventine mounts. It held somewhere between 100,000 and 150,000 people, even in Republican times; during the Republic, only Roman citizens were admitted, and there is ample evidence to suggest that freedman citizens were still classified as slaves when it came to admission to the circus; I imagine that freedmen were excluded because too many people wanted to go to the circus. Women were allowed to sit with men.

citadel   Properly, a fortress atop a precipitous hill, or that part of a larger fortified place occupying the heights, and surrounded by its own walls.

citizenship   For the purposes of this book, the Roman citizenship. Possession of it entitled a man to vote in his tribe and his class (if he was economically qualified to belong to a class) in all Roman city elections. He could not be flogged, he was entitled to the Roman trial process, and he had the right of appeal. At various times both his parents had to be Roman citizens, at other times only his father (hence the *cognomen* Hybrida). The citizen was liable to military service, though, prior to Gaius Marius, only if he owned sufficient property to buy his arms and support himself on campaigns beyond the very small sum he was paid by the State, usually at the end of a campaign.

classes The five economic divisions of property-owning or steady-income-earning Roman citizens. The members of the First Class were the richest, the members of the Fifth Class the poorest. The *capite censi* did not belong to a class.

client In Latin, *cliens*. The term denoted a man of free or freed status (he did not have to be a Roman citizen, however) who pledged himself to a man he called his patron (*patronus*). The client undertook in the most solemn and morally binding way to serve the interests and obey the wishes of his patron, in return for various favors (these were usually gifts of money, or positions, or legal assistance). The freed slave was automatically the client of his former master, until discharged of this obligation—if he ever was. A kind of honor system governed a client's conduct in respect of his patron, and was remarkably consistently adhered to. To be a client did not necessarily mean a man could not also be a patron; more that he could not be an ultimate patron, for his own clients technically were the clients of his patron also. There were laws governing the foreign client-patron relationship; concerning foreign client-kingdoms or states owning Rome as patron, there was a legal obligation to ransom any kidnapped Roman citizen, a fact that pirates relied on heavily as an additional source of income. Thus, not only individuals could become clients; whole towns and even countries could be clients.

client-king A foreign monarch who pledged himself as client in the service of Rome as his patron, or sometimes in the service of a Roman individual as his patron. The title "Friend and Ally of the Roman People" was a statement of clientship.

Clitumnus River   A river in Umbria, Italy.

clivus A street on an incline—that is, a hilly street. Rome, a city of hills, had many.

cloaca, cloacae **(pl.)**   A drain, particularly a sewer. There seems no doubt that a very extensive system of *cloacae* was put down very early on in Rome's history. Livy says that after the Gauls virtually demolished the city in 390 B.C., the rebuilding was not planned as it ought to have been, due to the Senate's fear that the Plebeian Order would move holus-bolus to Veii unless allowed to do precisely what they wanted. So where in the old city plan the streets had been wider, and followed the course of the main sewers, the new city saw narrower and more tortuous streets, and many buildings put on top of the main sewers.

Cloaca Maxima   The system of sewers which drained the Subura, the upper Esquiline, the Capitol, the Forum Romanum, and the Velabrum; it entered the Tiber between the Pons Aemilius and the Wooden Bridge (Pons Sublicius), but closer to the Pons Aemilius. The ancient river which formed its first tunnels was the Spinon.

Cloaca Nodina   The system of sewers which drained the Palatine, the lower Esquiline and Oppian mounts, the area of the Circus Maximus, and some of the Aventine. It followed the course of the ancient river Nodina and its tributaries, and entered the Tiber just upstream of the Wooden Bridge (Pons Sublicius).

Cloaca Petronia   The system of sewers which drained the Viminal, Quirinal, and Campus Martius, following the original course of the ancient river Petronia and its tributaries. It entered the Tiber just upstream of Tiber Island; from this point downstream, the Tiber was not used for swimming.

Coan   Pertaining to the island of Cos, one of the Sporades, and located off the coast of Asia Minor. The adjective "Coan" was attached to a famous export of Cos—Coan silk. This was not real silk, but wild silk (real silk did not reach the Mediterranean until the early Empire). Coan silk was much esteemed by prostitutes, to the extent that a prostitute was simply called a Coan.

cognomen, cognomina **(pl.)**   The last name of a Roman male anxious to distinguish himself from all his fellows having the same first and gentilicial (family) names. In some families it became necessary to have more than one *cognomen;* for example, take Quintus Caecilius Metellus Pius Scipio Nasica! The *cognomen* usually pointed out some physical or character idiosyncrasy—jug ears or flat feet or a humpback—or else commemorated some great feat, as in the Caecilii Metelli who were cognominated Dalmaticus, Balearicus, Numidicus. Many *cognomina* were heavily sarcastic or extremely witty. For the meanings of a number of *cognomina,* see pages 1110–1114.

cohort   The tactical unit of the Roman legion, comprising six centuries of troops; in normal circumstances, a legion had ten cohorts. It was customary to speak of the size of a Roman army under three or four legions in strength in terms of cohorts rather than legions.

college   A body formed by the association of a number of men having something in common. Thus, there were priestly colleges, political colleges like that of the tribunes of the plebs, religious colleges like that of the lictors, and work-related colleges. Certain groups of men from all walks of life (including slaves) banded themselves together in colleges which looked after the city of Rome's crossroads and conducted the annual feast of the crossroads, the Compitalia.

Comitia   See Assembly.

Comum   Modern Como, in northern Italy.

CONDEMNO   One of two words employed by a jury when delivering a verdict of "guilty." The other word was *DAMNO* (see that entry).

confarreatio   The oldest and strictest of the three forms of Roman marriage. By the time of Gaius Marius, only patricians still practised it—but by no means all patricians, as it was not mandatory. The *confarreatio* bride passed from the hand of her father to the hand of her husband, thus preventing her acquiring any measure of independence; this was one reason why *confarreatio* was not popular, as the other forms of marriage allowed a woman more control over her business affairs and dowry. The difficulty of divorce was the other cause of its unpopularity; divorce (*diffarreatio*) was a dismal, religiously and legally arduous business considered more trouble than it was worth, unless the circumstances left no other alternative.

Conscript Fathers   As established by the kings of Rome, the Senate consisted of one hundred patricians titled *patres*, which means "fathers." Then after the Republic was established and plebeians were admitted to the Senate, and its membership had swollen to three hundred, and the censors were given the duty of appointing new senators, the word "conscript" came into use as well, because the censors conscripted these new members. By the time of Gaius Marius, the two terms had been run together, so that the members of the Senate were addressed as Conscript Fathers.

consul   The consul was the most senior Roman magistrate owning imperium, and the consulship (modern scholars do not refer to it as the "consulate" because a consulate is a modern diplomatic institution) was considered the top rung of the *cursus honorum*. Two consuls were elected each year by the Centuriate Assembly, to serve for one year. The senior of the two—who had polled his requisite number of centuries first—held the *fasces* for the month of January, which meant he officiated while his junior colleague looked on. The first day of a consul's office was New Year's Day, January 1. Each consul was attended by twelve lictors, but only the lictors of the consul officiating during the month carried the *fasces* on their shoulders. By the time of Gaius Marius, consuls could be either patrician or plebeian, excepting only that two patricians could not hold office together. The proper age for a consul was forty-two, twelve years after entering the Senate at thirty. A consul's imperium knew no bounds; it operated not only in Rome but throughout Italy and the provinces as well, and overrode the imperium of a proconsular governor. The consul could command any army.

consular   The title given to a man who had been a consul. He was held in special esteem by the ordinary members of the Senate, was asked to speak ahead of junior magistrates, and might at any time be sent to govern a province should the Senate require the duty of him. He might also be asked to take on other duties, like caring for the grain supply.

consultum, consulta (pl.)   The proper term for a senatorial decree. These decrees did not have the force of law; in order to become law, a *consultum* had to be presented to the Assembly of the People or to the Plebeian Assembly, which then passed the *consultum* into law—or did not. However, many *consulta* did not go to one of the tribal assemblies, yet were accepted as law; such were senatorial decisions about who was to govern a province, or the declaration or pursuit of war, or who was to command an army. Foreign affairs were normally conducted through unratified senatorial *consulta*.

contio, contiones (pl.)   The preliminary meetings of all the comitial assemblies, whether to debate promulgated legislation or establish a trial at law, were called *contiones*. A *contio* could be called only by a magistrate having the correct power to convoke whichever assembly it was—a consul or praetor could convoke the Centuriate Assembly or the Assembly of the People, but only a tribune of the plebs could convoke the Plebeian Assembly.

contubernalis   The Latin term for a cadet, a subaltern of lowest rank in the military officers' hierarchy, but excluding the centurions; no centurion was ever a cadet, he was an experienced soldier.

corona   A crown. The term was generally confined to military decorations for the very highest valor. In descending order of importance, these crowns for various acts of bravery were:

Corona Graminea   The grass crown, awarded to a man who saved a whole legion, or—upon rare occasions—even a whole army.

Corona Civica   The civic crown, made of ordinary oak leaves. It was awarded to a man who had saved the lives of fellow soldiers, and held the ground on which he did this for the rest of the battle.

Corona Aurea   The first of the more minor crowns, which interestingly were intrinsically far more valuable than the top two (an indication that they were far newer). This gold crown was awarded to a man who killed an enemy in single combat, and held the ground for the rest of the battle.

Corona Muralis   A crenellated gold crown awarded to the first man over the walls of an enemy city when it was stormed.

Corona Navalis   A gold crown adorned with ship's beaks, awarded for outstanding valor during a sea battle.

Corona Vallaris   A gold crown awarded to the first man across the ramparts of an enemy camp.

cottabus   A game played in the dining room. The lees in the bottom of a man's wine cup were tossed into a large flattish bowl, and the winner was decided by the number of rays in the splash pattern, though exactly how it worked, we do not know.

cuirass   Two plates usually of bronze or steel, but sometimes of hardened leather, one protecting a man's thorax and abdomen, the other his back from shoulder to lumbar spine; the plates were held together by straps or ties at the shoulders and along each side beneath the arms. Some were exquisitely tailored to the contours of the torso; others were suitable for all wearers of average size and physique. The men of highest rank, especially generals, normally wore cuirasses beautifully tooled in relief, mostly of silver-plated steel or bronze, occasionally gold-plated; the general and his legates also wore a thin red sash around the cuirass about halfway between the nipples and the waist, ritually knotted and looped.

culibonia   A Latin obscenity interpreted by Dr. J. N. Adams as meaning a whore who offered anal intercourse; hence Publius Rutilius Rufus's pleasure in his own pun on *boni* in his letter, page 806.

culus   The basic Latin word for the anus.

Cumae   The first Greek colony in Italy, founded in the early eighth century B.C. It lay on the sea side of Cape Misenum, and was an extremely popular Roman Republican resort.

cunnum lingere   A very crude Latin obscenity, meaning to lick the female genitalia.

cunnus   A Latin obscenity at least as offensive to Romans as "cunt" is to us. It meant the female genitalia.

curator annonae The man responsible for regulating the grain supply from the provinces to Rome.

***curia, curiae* (pl.)** The *curia* originally was one of the thirty most ancient divisions of the Roman People, preceding the tribes and certainly the classes. These first Roman clans gathered in special meeting halls; each *curia* was headed by a *curio* or chieftain, elected for life. The *curiae veteres* or ancient meeting halls were clustered on the edge of the Palatium of the Palatine, adjacent to the Via Triumphalis. By the time of Gaius Marius, the *curia* was all but forgotten in the political and social organization of the People. When, as with the adoption of a patrician into a plebeian family, or the conferring of imperium upon a senior magistrate by a *lex curiata*, the thirty *curiae* were required under law to assemble, they were represented by thirty lictors.

Curia Hostilia The Senate House. It was thought to have been built by King Tullus Hostilius, the third of Rome's kings, hence its name ("meeting-house of Hostilius").

cursus honorum "The way of honor." If a man aspired to be consul, he had to take certain steps: first he was admitted to the Senate (either by seeking election as quaestor, or by co-optation of the censors, though the censors always had the final word in Gaius Marius's day); he had to serve as quaestor even if already a senator; after which he had to be elected praetor; and finally he could stand for the consulship. The four steps—senator, quaestor, praetor, and consul—constituted the *cursus honorum*. Neither of the aedileships (plebeian and curule) nor the tribunate of the plebs was a part of the *cursus honorum*, but most men who aspired to be consul understood that in order to attract sufficient attention from the electorate, they needed to serve as a tribune of the plebs or as an aedile. The office of censor, available only to those who had already been consul, was also separate from the *cursus honorum* (see also magistrates).

curule chair In Latin, *sella curulis*. This was the ivory chair reserved exclusively for men in senior magistracies; a curule aedile sat in one, but a plebeian aedile did not. The praetor and consul used curule chairs. They were the exclusive province of the magistrates who held imperium, as were lictors. In style, the curule chair was beautifully carved, with curved legs crossing in a broad X; it was equipped with very low arms, but had no back. The Roman in a toga sat very straight and allowed nothing to disturb the complicated massing of his toga on arm, back, and shoulders.

Cynic An adherent of the school of philosophy founded by Diogenes of Sinope. It was not a school in the Academic sense, nor was its rule of life of great complexity. Basically, the Cynic believed in simplicity and freedom from the thrall of possessions. Cynics completely mistrusted all human endeavors and worldly aspirations, deeming them self-seeking.

DAMNO One of the two words employed by a jury when delivering a verdict of "guilty." Presumably there was a reason why a jury would vote *DAMNO* rather than *CONDEMNO*; perhaps *DAMNO* was more vigorous, and was a way of recommending that no mercy be shown in sentencing the damned.

Danastris River The modern river Dniester, in Moldavia. It was also known to the ancients as the Tyras River.

Danubius River The modern Danube, Donau, or Dunarea. The Greeks, who called it the Ister, knew it was a very great river, but had not explored it beyond those inevitable Greek colonies around its outflow into the Euxine. Only its upper, alpine reaches were known to the Romans of Gaius Marius's day, though like the Greeks, they knew its course through Pannonia and Dacia in theory.

Delphi The great sanctuary of the god Apollo, lying in the lap of Mount Parnassus, in central Greece. From very ancient times it was an important center of worship, though not of Apollo until about the sixth or seventh century B.C. There was an *omphalos* or navel stone (in all likelihood, a meteorite), and Delphi itself was thought to be the center of the earth. An oracle of awesome fame resided there, its prophecies given by a crone in a state of ecstatic frenzy; she was known as Pythia, or the Pythoness.

demagogue Originally a Greek concept, meaning a politician whose chief appeal was to the crowds. The Roman demagogue preferred the arena of the Comitia well to the Senate House, but it was no part of his policy to "liberate the masses," nor on the whole were those who listened to him composed of the very lowly. The term was one employed by ultraconservative factions inside the Senate to describe the more radical tribunes of the plebs.

denarius, denarii (pl.) Save for a very rare issue or two of gold coins, the denarius was the largest denomination of Roman Republican coinage. Of pure silver, it contained about 3.5 grams of the metal. There were 6,250 denarii to the talent. It was about the size of a dime, or a threepence.

Dertona Modern Tortona, in northern Italy.

diadem The diadem was a thick white ribbon about 1 inch (25 mm) wide, each end embroidered, and often finished with a fringe. It was worn tied around the head, either across the forehead, or behind the hairline, and knotted beneath the occiput; the ends trailed down onto the shoulders. Originally a mark of Persian royalty, the diadem became the mark of the Hellenistic monarch after Alexander the Great removed it from the tiara of the Persian kings, as being a more appropriately Greek understatement than either crown or tiara.

dignitas A peculiarly Roman concept, *dignitas* cannot be translated as the English "dignity." It was a man's personal share of public standing in the community, and involved his moral and ethical worth, his reputation, his entitlement to respect and proper treatment. Of all the assets a Roman nobleman possessed, *dignitas* was likely to be the one he was most touchy about; to defend it, he might be prepared to go to war or into exile, to commit suicide, or to execute his wife or his son. I have elected to leave it in the text untranslated, simply as *dignitas*.

Dis An alternative name for Pluto, the god who ruled the underworld.

diverticulum, diverticula (pl.) In the sense used in this book, a road connecting the main arterial roads which radiated out from the gates of Rome—a "ring road."

Dodona A temple and precinct sacred to the Greek Zeus. Located among the inland mountains of Epirus some ten miles to the south and west of Lake Pamboris, it was the home of a very famous oracle situated in a sacred oak tree which was also the home of doves.

dominus Literally, "lord." *Domina* meant "lady," and *dominilla* "little lady." I have used these words to indicate the kind of respect servants would show to an English nobleman in addressing him as "my lord."

***domus, domi* (pl.)** Literally, "house." It was the term used to describe a city house or town house, and as used in this book is intended to mean the residences of those living privately rather than in apartments.

Domus Publicus This was a house owned by the Senate and People of Rome—that is, owned by the State. There were at least several such, and perhaps more—all, it would appear, inhabited by priests. The Pontifex Maximus, the Vestal Virgins, the Rex Sacrorum, and the three major *flamines—Dialis, Martialis,* and *Quirinalis*—lived in State-owned houses. All were apparently situated within the Forum Romanum. The evidence suggests that during Republican times, the Pontifex Maximus and the Vestal Virgins shared the same house (on the site of the much later Atrium Vestae, but oriented to the north); this was usually the one meant when the term "Domus Publicus" was used. The house of the Rex Sacrorum, located on the Velia, was referred to as "the King's house." I have drawn in the houses of the three major *flamines* on my map of central Rome in purely arbitrary positions, intended only to show where they might have been.

Dravus River The modern Drava, in Yugoslavia.

Druentia River The modern Durance, in France.

Druidism The major Celtic religion, particularly in Gallia Comata and in Britannia; its priests were called Druids. Druidic headquarters were located in the area of Long-haired Gaul inhabited by the Carnutes. A mystical and naturalistic cult, Druidism did not appeal in the least to any of the Mediterranean peoples, who considered its tenets bizarre.

Duria Major River The modern Dora Baltea, in northern Italy.

Duria Minor River The modern Dora Riparia, in northern Italy.

ecastor The exclamation of surprise or amazement considered polite and permissible for women to utter. Its root suggests it invoked Castor.

edepol The exclamation of surprise or amazement men uttered in the company of women, as sufficiently polite. Its root suggests it invoked Pollux.

Elysium Republican Romans had no real belief in the intact survival of the individual after death, though they did believe in an underworld and in "shades," which were rather mindless and characterless effigies of the dead. However, to both Greeks and Romans, certain men were considered by the gods to have lived lives of sufficient glory (rather than merit) to warrant their being preserved after death in a place called Elysium, or the Elysian Fields. Even so, these privileged shades were mere wraiths, and could re-experience human emotions and appetites only after a meal of blood.

emporium The word had two meanings. It could denote a seaport whose commercial life was all tied up in maritime trade (the island of Delos was an emporium). Or it could denote a large building on the waterfront of a port where importers and exporters had their offices.

Epicure, Epicurean An adherent of the school of philosophy founded by the Greek Epicurus during the early third century B.C. Personally Epicurus had advocated a brand of hedonism so exquisitely refined it approached asceticism on its left hand, so to speak; a man's pleasures had to be so relished and strung out and savored that any excess defeated the purpose of the exercise. Public life or any other stressful kind of occupation was forbidden. In Rome especially, these tenets underwent considerable modification, so that a Roman nobleman could call himself an Epicure, yet espouse a public career.

Epirus The Molossian and Thesprotian area of western Greece, isolated from the mainstream of Greek culture by the Gulf of Corinth and the high mountains of central Greece, for there were few passes into Thessaly or Boeotia. After the defeat of Macedonia by Aemilius Paullus in 167 B.C., some 150,000 Epirote people were deported, leaving the country depopulated and helpless. By the time of Gaius Marius, it was largely the fief of absentee Roman landlords who grazed vast herds for wool and leather.

Eporedia   Modern Ivrea, in northern Italy.

ethnarch   The Greek term for a city magistrate.

Etruria   The Latin name for what had once been the Kingdom of the Etruscans. It incorporated the wide coastal plains of northwestern peninsular Italy, from the Tiber in the south to the Arnus in the north, and east to the Apennines of the upper Tiber.

Euxine Sea   The modern Black Sea. It was extensively explored and colonized by the Greeks during the seventh and sixth centuries B.C., but behind its coasts in its upper regions both on the European side (Sarmatia) and the Asian side (Scythia), the land remained barbarian. Trade routes were many, however, and jealously guarded. Whoever controlled the Thracian Bosporus, the Propontis, and the Hellespont was in a position to levy duty or passage fees between the Euxine and the Aegean; in the time of Gaius Marius, this control belonged to the Kingdom of Bithynia.

faction   The term usually applied by modern scholars to Roman Republican political groups. These can in no way be called political parties, for they were extremely flexible, and their membership changed continually. Rather than form around an ideology, the Roman faction formed around a man of formidable *auctoritas* and *dignitas*. I have completely avoided the terms "Optimate" and "Popularis" because I do not wish to give any impression that political parties existed.

Fannius paper   A Roman Fannius who lived at some time between 150 and 130 B.C. took the worst grade of papyrus paper and subjected it to a treatment which turned it into paper as good as the best hieratical grade. The Brothers Gracchi used Fannius paper, which is how we know when Fannius must have invented his treatment. Fannius paper was far cheaper to buy than hieratical Egyptian paper, as well as easy to obtain.

Fanum Fortunae   Modern Fano, in Italy.

fasces These were bundles of birch rods ceremonially tied together in a crisscross pattern by red leather thongs. Originally an emblem of the old Etruscan kings, they persisted in Roman public life throughout the Republic and into the Empire. Carried by men called lictors, they preceded the curule magistrate (and the proconsul and propraetor as well) as a symbol of his imperium. Within the *pomerium*, only the rods went into the bundles, to signify that the curule magistrate had only the power to chastise; outside the *pomerium*, axes were inserted into the bundles, to signify that the curule magistrate also had the power to execute. The number of *fasces* indicated the degree of imperium—a dictator had twenty-four, a consul or proconsul twelve, a praetor or propraetor six, and a curule aedile two.

fasti The Latin word for "holidays," which has come to mean the calendar as a whole. The calendar was divided into *dies fasti* and *dies nefasti*, and was published by being attached to the walls of various buildings, including the Regia and the rostra. It told the Roman what days of the year he could use for business, what days were available for meetings of the Comitia, what days were holidays, what days ill-omened, and when the movable feasts were going to fall. With the year set at 355 days, the calendar was rarely synchronized with the seasons—save when the College of Pontifices took its duties seriously, and intercalated an extra twenty days every two years, after the month of February. Normally the college didn't bother, as Romans found it hard to see the point of the exercise. The days in each month were not calculated as we do, in a simple consecutive counting-off—March 1, March 2, etc.—the days were counted backward from one of three nodal points: the Kalends, the Nones, and the Ides. Thus, instead of March 3, a Roman would say "four days before the Nones of March," and instead of March 28, he would say "four days before the Kalends of April." To us, very confusing! But not to the Romans. See chart next page.

felix Literally, "happy in fortune," rather than our interpretation of the word "happy," which is more to do with the mood of the moment. Latin *felix* was inextricably tied to the goddess Fortuna—to *luck*.

MONTH	NUMBER OF DAYS	DATE OF KALENDS	DATE OF NONES	DATE OF IDES
January	29	1	5	13
February	28	1	5	13
March	31	1	7	15
April	29	1	5	13
May	31	1	7	15
June	30	1	5	13
Quinctilis (July)	31	1	7	15
Sextilis (August)	29	1	5	13
September	29	1	5	13
October	31	1	7	15
November	29	1	5	13
December	29	1	5	13

fellator   A very crude Latin obscenity which denoted the man on the receiving end—he whose penis was being sucked. It was considered a far more honorable situation than that of the man doing the sucking (see *irrumator*).

Ferentinum   Modern Ferentino, in Italy.

Firmum Picenum   Modern Fermo, in Italy.

flamen, flamines **(pl.)**   A priest in a special group who served the oldest and most Roman of gods. There were fifteen *flamines*, three major and twelve minor. The *flamines maiores* served (1) Jupiter, (2) Mars, and (3) Quirinus. Save for the *flamen Dialis*, none seems to have had very demanding duties, yet the three major priests received their housing at the expense of the State. This was undoubtedly because the *flamines* were Rome's most ancient priests.

flamen Dialis   The special priest of Jupiter, and most senior of the fifteen *flamines*. His life was not an easy one. He had to be a patrician, and married *confarreatio* to a patrician woman; both his and her parents had to be alive at the time he was appointed to the priesthood; and the position lasted for life. The *flamen Dialis* was absolutely loaded down with taboos and shibboleths—could not see or touch a dead body, could not touch iron, could have no knot on his person, could not use iron to cut his hair or beard, could not wear leather taken from an animal killed for the purpose, could not touch a horse, could not eat beans or any form of leavened bread. His wife, the *flaminica Dialis*, was almost equally constrained.

Florentia   Modern Florence or Firenze, in Italy.

flumen   The Latin word for a river. For this reason, the rivers on my maps are labeled as "Volturnus F.," "Isara F.," etc.

Fortuna   The Roman goddess of fortune, and one of the most worshiped deities in the Roman pantheon. There were many temples to Fortune, each dedicated to the goddess in a different guise or light. The favor of Fortuna mattered tremendously to politicians and generals, who all—including men as formidably intelligent as Gaius Marius, Lucius Cornelius Sulla, and Gaius Julius Caesar the Dictator—believed in her machinations implicitly.

forum   An open-air public meeting place for all kinds of business, public and private.

Forum Boarium   The meat markets, situated at the northern (Velabrum) end of the Circus Maximus. The word *boarium* meant "cattle," but by Gaius Marius's day, the meat markets vended all kinds of beasts and meats.

forum castrum   The meeting space inside a Roman military camp. It was located alongside the general's command tent.

Forum Frumentarium   The grain markets. My map situation for them is purely hypothetical, but my reasons are as follows: I do not believe that the private grain vendors (and there were many) conducted their activities in the same area as the public grain issue. The public grain was concentrated in two areas—one in the Porticus Minucia on the Campus Martius, where the aediles had their booths and offices, and issued the grain chits; the other the public granaries, which were located under the cliffs of the Aventine adjacent to the Port of Rome. We know that there were granaries along the Vicus Tuscus below the cliffs of the

Palatine, rebuilt by Agrippa during the principate, but probably privately owned during the Republic. Therefore I have located the Forum Frumentarium in the Velabrum, adjacent to the granaries of the Vicus Tuscus.

Forum Holitorium   The vegetable markets. They were situated right on the banks of the Tiber, half inside the Servian Walls, half outside, though they had probably originally lain entirely inside. This location favored those who grew on the Campus Martius and the Campus Vaticanus.

Forum Piscinum   The fish markets. Their location is a mystery, but we know from the grizzles of Cicero that the prevailing winds of Rome blew the smell of stinking fish into both the lower Forum Romanum and the Senate House. I have therefore located them just to the west of the Via Nova, in the Velabrum.

Forum Romanum   The center of Roman public life, a long open space devoted to politics, the law, business, and religion. By the time of Gaius Marius, I believe the Forum Romanum was free from stalls and booths unattached to the basilicae. The amount of political activity—not to mention legal activity—would surely have rendered free-standing structures in the middle of any concourse at peril, as well as most inconvenient. The close proximity of two big markets, the general Macellum on the far side of the Basilica Aemilia and the Macellum Cuppedenis beyond the Clivus Orbius, no doubt provided plenty of booth and stall space.

freedman   A manumitted slave. Though technically free (and, if his former master was a Roman citizen, a Roman citizen himself), he remained in the patronage of his former master, and had little chance to use his vote in the time of Gaius Marius, for he belonged to one of two urban tribes—the Suburana and the Esquilina. In some cases, freedmen of superior ability or ruthlessness managed to acquire great wealth and power, and so were able to vote in the classes.

freeman   A man born free and never sold into slavery (except as a *nexus* or debt slave—this was rare among Roman citizens during Gaius Marius's time, though still prevalent among the Italian Allies, victims of Roman greed).

Fregellae A Latin Rights community situated on the Via Latina and the river Liris, just over the border into Samnium. It was always very loyal to Rome until 125 B.C., when it revolted, and was crushed with singular cruelty by the praetor Lucius Opimius. Destroyed completely, the town never really flourished again. Rome replaced it with the town of Fabrateria Nova ("new made") on the opposite bank of the Liris.

Further Spain Hispania Ulterior, the further from Rome of Rome's two Spanish provinces. In the time of Gaius Marius, the boundary between Nearer and Further Spain was somewhat tenuous, but by and large, the further province encompassed the entire basin of the Baetis River, the ore-bearing mountains in which the Baetis and the Anas rose, the Atlantic littoral from Olisippo at the mouth of the Tagus to the Pillars of Hercules, and the Mediterranean littoral from the Pillars to the port of Abdera. The largest city by far was Gades, now called Cádiz, but the seat of the governor was Corduba.

Gaetuli A far-flung Berber people, nomadic in their way of life, who inhabited the regions behind the coast of North Africa, all the way from the Lesser Syrtis to Mauretania.

Gallia Comata Long-haired Gaul. Having subtracted the Roman province of Gaul-across-the-Alps, Gallia Comata incorporated modern France and Belgium, together with that part of Holland south of the Rhine. It was a huge, fairly low-lying, and heavily forested land of largely untapped agricultural richness, watered by many superb rivers, including the Liger (Loire), Sequana (Seine), Mosa (Meuse), Mosella (Moselle), Scaldis (Schelde), Samara (Somme), Matroma (Marne), Duranius (Dordogne), Oltis (Lot), and Garumna (Garonne). During the time of Gaius Marius, the bulk of Gallia Comata was hardly known, save for the campaigns of Gnaeus Domitius Ahenobarbus in 122 and 121 B.C. The inhabitants were mostly Celtic, except where Germanic tribes had invaded from across the Rhenus and racially mixed, as was the case with the tribes collectively called Belgae. Though all of the Gauls who wore their hair long (hence the Latin name for the country) knew of the existence of Rome, they studiously avoided contact unless unlucky enough to live on the borders of the Roman province. The Gallic way of life was rural, as much pastoral as agricultural, and they spurned urbanization, preferring to cluster in farmsteads and villages. They did build what the Romans called *oppida*, these being strongholds designed to protect the tribal treasures, the person of the king, and their grain. Religiously they were under the sway of the Druids, save for the most Germanic among them. On the whole the long-haired Gauls were not warlike insofar as that they did not pursue war as an end in itself, but they were fierce warriors. They drank beer rather than wine, were flesh eaters more than bread eaters, drank milk, and used butter rather than olive oil. Physically they were tall and well built, and tended to be fair or red of hair, and blue or grey of eye.

Gallia Transalpina   Transalpine Gaul, the Roman province I have called Gaul-across-the-Alps. I did this to avoid the hideous confusions for nonclassicist readers that are involved in the mine-field of Cis and Trans. Cisalpine Gaul, Transalpine Gaul, Cispadane Gaul, Transpadane Gaul—just too confusing for most people, so why get into it at all? Gaul-across-the-Alps was largely won for Rome by Gnaeus Domitius Ahenobarbus just before 120 B.C., to ensure that Rome had a safe land route for her armies between Italy and Spain. The province consisted of a coastal strip all the way from Liguria to the Pyrenees, with two inland incursions: one to Tolosa, in Aquitania, the other up the Rhodanus (Rhone) Valley as far as the trading post of Lugdunum (Lyon).

games   A Roman institution and pastime which went back at least as far as the early Republic, and probably a lot further. At first games, or *ludi*, were celebrated only when a general triumphed, but in 366 B.C. the *ludi Romani*, as the first games were called, became an annual event held to honor Jupiter Optimus Maximus, whose feast day occurred on September 13. It was not long before the *ludi Romani* occupied more than just that day; by the time of Gaius Marius they went on for ten days, possibly beginning on the fifth. Though there were a few rather half-hearted boxing and wrestling bouts, Roman games never possessed the athletic, physical, sports nature of the Greek games (very different!). At first they consisted mostly of chariot races, then gradually came to incorporate animal hunts, and plays held in specially erected theaters. On the first day of the games, there was a spectacular yet ostensibly religious procession through the circus, after which came a chariot race or two, and then the boxing and wrestling, limited to this first day. The succeeding days were taken up with plays in the theaters; tragedies were not popular, comedies were, and as the Republic wore on, farces and mimes became more popular than old-fashioned comedy. Then, as the games drew to a close, the chariot races reigned supreme, together with wild-beast hunts to vary the program. Gladiatorial combats were *not* a part of any games held during the Republic; these were confined to funeral games, and generally held in the Forum Romanum rather than in the circuses. They were put on privately, not at the expense of the State, as were the games. However, men ambitious of making a name for themselves among the electors dug deep into their private purses when aediles to make the games more spectacular than the allocation of funds from the State would permit.

The first games of the year were the *ludi Megalenses* in early April, followed immediately by the *ludi Cereri*, and with the *ludi Floriae* at the end of April extending into May. Then in July came the *ludi Apollinares*, early in the month. Then nothing until the *ludi Romani* in early September. On the Ides of October came the single day of the *ludi Capitolini*, games put on by a private college. The last games of the year were the *ludi Plebeii*, which occurred in early November, and ran for many days. Free Roman citizen men and their women were allowed to attend (there was no admission charge), with women segregated in the theaters but not in the circus; neither slaves nor freedmen were permitted.

garum   A highly esteemed and much loved flavoring essence made from fish by a process calculated to make a modern man or woman ill at the thought; apparently it stank, being extremely concentrated. However, the ancients adored it. There were many places around the Mediterranean and Euxine where *garum* was made, but the best *garum* was held to come from the fishing ports of Further Spain.

Garumna River   The modern Garonne, in France.

Gaul   See Gallia Comata, Gallia Transalpina, Italian Gaul.

gens, gentes (pl.)   A Roman family or clan owning the same name—Julius, Domitius, Cornelius, Aemilius, Fabius, Servilius, and Junius were all gentilicial names, for example. All the members of the same *gens* could ultimately trace their line back to a common ancestor. The term was feminine in gender, so in Latin it was *gens* Julia, *gens* Cornelia.

Genua   Modern Genoa or Genova.

Germani   The inhabitants of Germania, this being all the lands on the far side of the Rhenus River (the modern Rhine).

Getorix   A very Celtic name borne by several known Celtic kings. I have chosen it as the name of the unknown Celtic king who led the combined tribes of the Tigurini, Marcomanni, and Cherusci on the trek of the Germans. All we know of him historically is that he belonged to the tribe of the Tigurini, who were Celts.

gig   A two-wheeled vehicle drawn by either two or four animals, usually mules. It was very lightly and flexibly built within the limitations of ancient vehicles—springs and shock absorbers did not exist—and was the vehicle of choice for a Roman in a hurry because it was easy to draw, therefore speedy. However, it was open to the elements. Its Latin name was *cisia*. The two-wheeled closed-in carriage, a heavier and slower vehicle, was called the *carpentum*.

gladiator   A soldier of the sawdust, a professional warrior who performed his trade for an audience as an entertainment. An Etruscan inheritance, he always flourished throughout Italy, including Rome. His origins might be several: he might be a deserter from the legions, a condemned criminal, a slave, or a freeman who voluntarily signed himself up; but in all cases he had to have evinced an interest in becoming a gladiator, otherwise he was not worth the expense of training. He lived in a school (most of the Republican era schools were situated around Capua), was not locked up or locked in, nor ill-treated; the gladiator was a very profitable and attractive investment. His training was supervised by a *doctor*; the *lanista* was the head of the whole school. There were four ways he might fight—as a Mirmillo, a Samnite, a Retiarius, or a Thracian; the difference lay in the way he was armed. In Republican times he served for perhaps four to six years, and on an average fought perhaps five times in any one year; it was rare for him to die, and the Empire's "thumbs-up, thumbs-down" verdict was still far in the future. When he retired, he was prone to hire himself out as a bodyguard or bouncer. The schools were owned by businessmen who made very fat profits from hiring out pairs of gladiators all over Italy, usually as the main feature of funeral games; many senators and knights owned gladiatorial schools, some of them large enough to contain over a thousand men, a few even more than that.

Good Men   See *boni*.

governor   A convenient English word to describe the consul or praetor, proconsul or propraetor, who—usually for the space of one year—ruled a Roman province in the name of the Senate and People of Rome. The degree of imperium the governor owned varied, as did the extent of his commission. However, no matter what his imperium, while in his province he was virtual king of it. He was responsible for its defense, administration, the gathering of its taxes and tithes, and many other things.

Gracchi   Also known as the Brothers Gracchi. Cornelia, the daughter of Scipio Africanus and Aemilia Paulla, was married when eighteen years old to the forty-five-year-old Tiberius Sempronius Gracchus; the year was about 172 B.C., and Scipio Africanus had been dead for twelve years. Tiberius Sempronius Gracchus had been consul in 177 B.C., was censor in 169 B.C. and consul a second time in 163 B.C. When he died in 154 B.C., he was the father of twelve children, but they were universally a sickly brood, and only three of them did Cornelia manage to raise to adulthood, despite assiduous care. The oldest of these three was a girl, Sempronia, who was married as soon as she was of age to her cousin Scipio Aemilianus; the two younger were boys. Tiberius Gracchus was born in 163 B.C., and his brother, Gaius, not until the year of his father's death, 154 B.C. Thus both boys owed their upbringing to their mother, who by all accounts did a superlative job.

Both the Brothers Gracchi served under their mother's first cousin Scipio Aemilianus, Tiberius in the Third Punic War, Gaius at Numantia; they were conspicuously brave. Tiberius was sent to Nearer Spain as quaestor in 137 B.C., and single-handedly negotiated a treaty which extricated the defeated Hostilius Mancinus from Numantia, and saved his army from annihilation; however, Scipio Aemilianus considered the action disgraceful, and managed to persuade the Senate not to ratify the treaty. Tiberius never forgave his cousin-cum-brother-in-law.

In 133 B.C., Tiberius was elected a tribune of the plebs, and set out to right the wrongs the State was perpetrating in its leasing of the *ager publicus*. Against furious opposition, he passed an agrarian law which limited the amount of public land any one man might lease or own to 500 *iugera* (with an extra 250 *iugera* per son), and set up a commission to distribute the surplus of land this limit produced among the civilian poor of Rome. His aim was not only to relieve Rome of some of her less useful citizens, but also to ensure that future generations would be in a position to give Rome sons qualified to serve in the army. When the Senate chose to filibuster, Tiberius Gracchus took the bill straight to the Plebeian Assembly—and stirred up a hornets' nest thereby, for this move ran counter to all accepted practice. One of his fellow tribunes of the plebs (and a relative), Marcus Octavius, vetoed the bill in the Plebeian Assembly, and was illegally deposed from office—yet another enormous offense against the *mos maiorum* (that is, established practice). The legality of these ploys mattered less to Tiberius Gracchus's opponents than did the fact that they contravened established practice, however unwritten it was.

When Attalus III of Pergamum died that same year and was

discovered to have bequeathed his kingdom to Rome, Tiberius Gracchus ignored the Senate's right to decide what was to be done with the bequest, and legislated to have the lands used to resettle more of Rome's poor. Opposition in Senate and in Forum hardened day by day.

Then, as 133 B.C. drew to a close without a successful conclusion to his entire program, Tiberius Gracchus flouted another established practice, the one which limited a man to serving as a tribune of the plebs only once. He ran for a second term. And, in a confrontation with the senatorial forces led by his cousin Scipio Nasica, Tiberius Gracchus was clubbed to death on the Capitol, together with some of his followers. His cousin Scipio Aemilianus—though not yet returned from Numantia when it happened—publicly condoned the murder, alleging that Tiberius Gracchus had aimed at making himself King of Rome.

Turmoil died down until ten years later, when Tiberius Gracchus's little brother, Gaius, was elected a tribune of the plebs in 123 B.C. Gaius Gracchus was the same kind of man as his elder brother, but he had learned from his brother's mistakes, and was the more able of the two. His reforms were far wider, and embraced not only agrarian laws, but also laws to provide very cheap grain to the urban lowly, to regulate service in the army, to found Roman citizen colonies abroad, to initiate public works throughout Italy, to remove the extortion court from the Senate and give it to the knights, to farm the taxes of Asia by public contracts let by the censors, and to give the full Roman citizenship to all those having the Latin Rights, and the Latin Rights to every Italian Ally. Of course this program was nowhere near completed when his year as a tribune of the plebs came to an end, so Gaius Gracchus did the impossible—he actually secured his re-election as a tribune of the plebs. In the face of mounting fury and obdurate enmity, he battled on to achieve his program of reform, which was still not completed at the end of 122 B.C. So he stood for the tribunate of the plebs a third time. However, he and his friend Marcus Fulvius Flaccus were defeated.

When 121 B.C. saw his laws and policies attacked at once by

the consul Lucius Opimius and the ex-tribune of the plebs Marcus Livius Drusus, Gaius Gracchus resorted to violence. The Senate responded by passing its first ever "ultimate decree" to contain the growing lawlessness, with the result that Fulvius Flaccus and two of his sons were murdered, and the fleeing Gaius Gracchus committed suicide in the Grove of Furrina on the flanks of the Janiculan Hill. Roman politics would never again be the same; the aged citadel of the *mos maiorum* had been breached.

The personal lives of the Brothers Gracchi were dogged by the same thread of tragedy. Tiberius Gracchus went against his family's custom (which was to marry Cornelias of the Scipios) and married Claudia, daughter of Appius Claudius Pulcher, the consul of 143 B.C., and an inveterate enemy of Scipio Aemilianus's. They had three sons, none of whom lived to achieve public careers. Gaius Gracchus married Licinia, the daughter of his supporter Publius Licinius Crassus Mucianus; they had a daughter, Sempronia, who married Fulvius Flaccus Bambalio, and in turn produced a daughter, Fulvia, who became in turn the wife of Publius Clodius Pulcher, Gaius Scribonius Curio, and Mark Antony.

grammaticus　　Not a teacher of grammar, but a teacher of the basic arts of rhetoric, or public speaking (see rhetoric).

greaves　　Shin guards. Made of metal and strapped on behind the knees and ankles, they were not worn by Romans of any rank save the centurions, for whom greaves were a badge of office.

Hannibal　　The most famous of the Punic princes who led the forces of Carthage in their wars against Rome. Born in 247 B.C., Hannibal was taught to soldier in Spain as a mere child, and spent his youth in Spain. In 218 B.C. he invaded Italy, a shock tactic which took Rome by surprise; his crossing of the Alps (with elephants) through the Montgenèvre Pass was brilliant. For sixteen years he roamed at will through Italian Gaul and Italy, defeating Roman armies at Trebia, Trasimene, and finally Cannae. But Quintus Fabius Maximus Verrucosis Cunctator evolved a strategy which eventually wore Hannibal down: relentlessly, he shadowed the Carthaginian army with an army of his own, yet never offered battle or allowed his forces to be pushed into battle. Because Fabius Maximus was always in the vicinity, Hannibal never quite got up the confidence to attack the city of Rome herself. Then his allies among the Italians flagged, and Fabius's presence forced him further and further south after his hold on Campania was broken. He then lost Tarentum, while his brother Hasdrubal in the Umbrian north was defeated at the river Metaurus. Penned up in Bruttium, the very toe of Italy, he evacuated his undefeated army back to Carthage in 203 B.C. At Zama he was beaten by Scipio Africanus, after which, as the Punic head of state, he intrigued with Antiochus the Great of Syria against Rome. In the end he sought asylum with Antiochus, but after Rome subdued the King he fled again, seeking refuge with King Prusias in Bithynia. When in 182 B.C. Rome demanded that Prusias hand Hannibal over, he committed suicide. An unrepentant enemy of Rome, he was always admired and respected by Rome.

hasta   The old-fashioned, leaf-headed spear of the Roman infantry. After Gaius Marius modified the *pilum*, the *hasta* disappeared from the ranks.

"hay on his horn"   All ancient oxen were endowed with most formidable horns, and not all ancient oxen were placid, despite their castrated state. A beast which gored was tagged in warning; hay was wrapped around the horn he gored with, or around both horns if he gored with both. Pedestrians scattered on seeing an ox with hay wrapped round its horn, pulling a wagon through the streets of Rome. The saying "hay on his horn" came to be applied to a deceptively large and placid-seeming man after it was discovered he could turn and strike very suddenly and destructively.

Head Count   The term I have used throughout the book to describe the lowliest of Roman citizens, the *capite censi,* those who were too poor to belong to one of the five economic classes. All the censors did was take a "head count" of them. I have preferred "Head Count" to "the proletariat" or "the masses" because of our modern post-Marxist attitudes to these terms—attitudes entirely misleading in the ancient context (see also *capite censi, proletarii*).

Hellenic The term used to describe Greek culture after Alexander the Great expanded Greek influence so dramatically throughout the ancient world.

Hercules, Pillars of The narrow passageway between the Atlantic Ocean and the Mediterranean Sea was known as the Pillars of Hercules because of the presence of two huge rocky outcrops, one on the Spanish side called Calpe (modern Gibraltar), and one on the African side called Abydus.

herm A pedestal upon which originally the head of the god Hermes was mounted; it was traditionally adorned about halfway up its front side with a set of male genitals, the penis erect. By Hellenistic times it had become the custom to mount all busts upon herms, the term having come to mean a pedestal possessing male genitalia. A visitor to any modern museum owning ancient bust pedestals will note the presence of a square cavity about halfway up the front side; here there once proudly reared two testicles and an erect penis. The herms were defaced during Christian times.

Hippo Regius Modern Annaba, in Algeria.

Hispania Modern Spain. Also called Iberia.

Hispania Citerior See Nearer Spain.

Hispania Ulterior See Further Spain.

hubris A Greek word which is still used today. It means overweening pride.

hydra-headed monster A creature killed by Hercules. It had seven snaky heads, and when a head was cut off, it grew back again at once. Thus the term came to be used of any dilemma which seemed solved, only to grow back again.

Hymettan honey Honey gathered from the bees of Mount Hymettos, one of the hills around Athens. The reason the honey was so universally prized did not lie in the flowers the bees visited, but in the fact that Hymettan apiarists never smoked their hives when gathering the honey.

Hypanis River The modern Bug, in the USSR.

Icosium Modern Alger (Algiers).

Ilium The Roman name for Troy.

Illyricum   The wild and mountainous lands bordering the upper Adriatic on its eastern side.

Ilva   Modern Elba. It was rich in iron ore; this the Ilvans mined. They smelted the ore on Ilva to the bloom stage, then shipped the bloom iron "sows" to Pisae and Populonia for refining.

imago, imagines **(pl.)**   The beautifully painted and bewigged, most lifelike mask of a Roman family's consular (or perhaps praetorian) ancestor. It was made out of beeswax (those who have been to Madame Tussaud's will understand how lifelike a beeswax face can be), and kept by the ancestor's direct descendants in a dust-free cupboard shaped like a miniature temple. The cupboard—though prestigious families usually had more than one ancestor so honored, thus owned many cupboards—was placed in the atrium of the house near the altar to the household Lar and Penates. The mask and its cupboard were the objects of enormous reverence. When a man of the family died, an actor was employed to don the *imago* and impersonate the ancestor. If a man became consul, his mask was made and added to the family collection; occasionally a man who was not consul did something so extraordinary he was considered deserving of a mask.

imperator   Literally, "the commander-in-chief" or "the general" of a Roman army. However, the term gradually came to be given only to a general who won a great victory; in order to apply to the Senate for permission to celebrate a triumph, the general had to be able to prove that after the battle, his troops had formally hailed him with the title *imperator*. It is of course the root of the word "emperor."

imperium   Imperium was the degree of authority invested in a curule magistrate or promagistrate. Having imperium meant that a man had the authority of his office, and could not be gainsaid (provided that he was acting within the limits of his particular imperium and within the laws governing his conduct). It was conferred by a *lex curiata*, and lasted for one year only; extensions had to be ratified by Senate and/or people for promagistrates who had not in the space of one year completed their original commission. Lictors bearing *fasces* indicated that a man possessed imperium.

insula, insulae (pl.) Literally, "island." Because it was mostly surrounded by streets or lanes or alleys on all sides, apartment buildings became known as insulae. Roman insulae were very tall (up to 100 feet—30m—in height), and some were large enough to warrant the incorporation of several internal light-wells, rather than the normal one. Then as now, Rome was a city of apartment dwellers.

Iol Modern Cherchel, in Algeria.

irrumator A man sucking another's penis. Romans thought this the lowest form of sexual activity, indicating a servility, and moral self-abnegation no honorable man would condone (presumably it was not considered in such a harsh light when the *irrumator* was an *irrumatrix*—a woman). As Latin obscenities were graded, this was the worst one of all. The act itself was *irrumo, irrumatio*.

Isara River There were several rivers named Isara. One was the modern Isère (a tributary of the Rhodanus); another was the modern Isar (a tributary of the Danubius); yet another was the modern Oise (a tributary of the Sequana).

Isarcus River The modern Isarco, in northern Italy.

isonomia Originally this Greek word mean "equality." However, the sixth-century B.C. Athenian statesman Cleisthenes, popularly supposed to have evolved the form of government the Greeks called democracy, applied the tag *isonomia* to the concept of democracy.

Italia This name was reserved for the Italian Peninsula south of the rivers Arnus and Rubico, though it is doubtful if a Roman ever thought of the peninsula as a nation when he called it Italia.

Italian Allies Those people, tribes, or nations (they are variously described as all three) which lived in the Italian Peninsula without enjoying either the full Roman citizenship or even the Latin Rights. In return for military protection and in the interests of peaceful co-existence, they were required to furnish properly armed soldiers for the armies of Rome, and to pay for the upkeep of these soldiers. The Italian Allies also bore the chief burden of general taxation within Italy at the time of Gaius Marius, and in many instances had been obliged to yield part of their lands to swell the Roman *ager publicus*. Many of them had either risen against Rome (like the Samnites) or sided with Hannibal and others against Rome (like parts of Campania). Rome's most successful way of keeping the Italian Allies in their place was to implant "colonies" within their borders; these colonies consisted of a nucleus of Roman citizens and a community enjoying either the Latin Rights (most commonly) or the full citizenship, and they were of great influence in the lives and policies of the Allied states surrounding them. Naturally they tended to side with Rome in any of the multitudinous disputes and discontents which marred existence in the Italian Peninsula. To some extent, there was always some movement among the Italian Allies to throw off the Roman yoke, or to demand the full citizenship; but until the last century of the Republic, Rome was sensitive enough to act before this grumbling became too serious. The last great concession before the events leading to the Social War was a law passed by an unknown Roman politician about 123 B.C., which allowed the men who held magistracies in Latin Rights communities to assume the full Roman citizenship in perpetuity for themselves and their descendants.

Italian Gaul Gallia Cisalpina—that is, Gaul-on-this-side-of-the-Alps. I have called it Italian Gaul in the interests of simplicity. It incorporated all the lands north of the rivers Arnus and Rubico, on the Italian side of the formidable semicircle of alpine mountains which cut Italy and Italian Gaul off from the rest of Europe. It was bisected from west to east by the mighty Padus River (the modern Po), and there was a marked difference in the nature of the lands on either side of the Padus. South of the river, the people and towns were heavily Romanized, many of them possessing the Latin Rights. North of the river, the people and towns were more Celtic than Roman, and at the time of Gaius Marius, the number of Latin Rights communities were limited to Aquileia and Cremona only; Latin was a second language at best, if spoken at all. Politically Italian Gaul dwelled in a kind of limbo, for it had neither the status of a true province nor the benefits—such as they were—of the Italian Allies. In the time of Gaius Marius, the men of Italian Gaul were not recruited into the Roman infantry, even as auxiliaries.

iugerum, iugera (pl.)   The Roman unit of land measurement. In modern terms one *iugerum* was 0.623 (or five eighths) of an acre, or 0.252 (one quarter) of a hectare. The modern user of British imperial and American measure will get close enough in acres by dividing the number of *iugera* in two; the modern user of metric measure will be very close in hectares by dividing the number of *iugera* in four.

Iulus   The son of the Trojan hero Aeneas. Both in ancient and in modern times there is much confusion as to whether Iulus's mother was the Trojan woman Creusa or the Latin woman Lavinia. Vergil plumped for Creusa, Livy for Lavinia. What we do not know is which woman the *gens* Julia deemed Iulus's mother. Iulus was also called Ascanius, this definitely being the name Homer gives to Creusa's son. As Vergil was the official poet patronized by Augustus, a Julian, perhaps Augustus wished to have it known his Julian lineage was impeccably Trojan on both sides; what his great-uncle Caesar the Dictator thought is another matter, as Augustus tended to manipulate his divine great-uncle's human thoughts and deeds to suit his own ends. However, it really doesn't matter who was the mother of Iulus; the important thing is that the clan Julius implicitly believed they were the direct descendants of the son of Aeneas, and therefore also descended from the goddess Venus (Aphrodite), who was Aeneas's mother and Iulus's grandmother. If one considers that the time span between the arrival of Aeneas in Italy and the birth of Caesar the Dictator in 100 B.C. is about the same as the time span between the invasion of England by William the Conqueror and modern Englishmen claiming to be able to trace their lineage back to one of William's Norman barons, then perhaps the Julii Caesares could indeed trace their ancestry back so far.

Julilla   In this book, the younger daughter of Gaius Julius Caesar. There is really nothing to say that Caesar did not have two daughters; the fact that only one, Julia, is mentioned in the an-

cient sources is at best only negative evidence. I am endlessly
fascinated with what the ancient sources considered important
enough to report, and what they ignored as unimportant; and our
most contemporary ancient source, Cicero, wrote for the men of
his own time, so assumed that everyone knew many facts he
therefore didn't bother to mention. Julia lived to be an old woman,
and was one of the most admired and notable matrons of her day;
also, she was the one memorable wife of the great Gaius Marius,
and the mother of a son who also made his mark on Rome. Little
wonder then that her name has come down to us, whereas other
female offspring of Caesar and his wife, Marcia, might naturally
not be so notable. We know from Plutarch that Sulla's first wife
was a Julia, but he had three wives after her, though only the last
two obtain any real mention in the ancient sources. And, bearing
in mind the width of the rift which opened up between Marius
and Sulla later on, it is very possible Sulla in his memoirs (used as
a source by later historians like Plutarch) had little to say about
his Julian wife; Julia the widow of Gaius Marius was well and
truly alive when Sulla published his memoirs.

For the sake of a seamless story alone, I might be pardoned for
taking novelist's license and making a younger sister of Marius's
wife Julia the first wife of Sulla. But there is more to it than that.
Historical fact reveals that Sulla's early political and military career was strongly tied to Gaius Marius; look though one will,
there is nothing concrete during the years chronicled in this book
to suggest that Sulla and Marius were anything other than close
colleagues. All the inferences that Sulla tried to claim the credit
for winning the war against Jugurtha because he had personally
captured Jugurtha have their origin in two lots of memoirs published many years afterward—one, the memoirs of Sulla himself,
and the other, the memoirs of Quintus Lutatius Catulus Caesar.
At that stage, it behooved both men to diminish the reputation of
Gaius Marius. Yet when one looks at the intertwined careers of
Marius and Sulla between the years 107 and 100 B.C., it is impossible to infer from actual events that any enmity really existed at
that stage. On the contrary, actual events suggest rather that the

two men continued to be close colleagues, and trusted each other. If a feud existed between them thanks to Sulla's alleged claims he won the war against Jugurtha, why would Marius have taken Sulla with him to Gaul as his legate? Then, all of a sudden, Sulla pops up in Italian Gaul with Catulus Caesar, right about the time Marius was committed to battle with the advancing Teutones on the far side of the Alps. But not, I think, because of any falling-out with Marius; Catulus Caesar rashly sets off up the Athesis, and then a mysterious revolt breaks out among his troops, and back down the Athesis goes Catulus Caesar—who, instead of shrieking mutiny in Rome, sits tamely with his saved army in Placentia, and waits for Marius. Of Sulla in all this, not a word, yet he was Catulus Caesar's senior legate. One cannot claim it for certain, but it is just as logical to assume that Sulla was sent by Marius to prevent Catulus Caesar's losing an army Rome could not afford to lose, as it is to assume Sulla and Marius had fallen out.

Going back to the year 108 B.C., when Marius escaped to seek the consulship in Rome, he must have asked for Sulla's services as his quaestor personally, for when his year in Numidia was up, Sulla remained with Marius, the act of one personally committed to his general. Indeed, Sulla did not come home until Marius came home. He was Marius's named choice as quaestor. Yet how would Marius ever have come to know Sulla well enough to ask for him? They hadn't served in any campaigns together, there was a seventeen-year gap between their ages, and their life-styles were radically different, if one is to believe Plutarch. And Plutarch says Sulla's first wife was a Julia. If Sulla's first wife, Julia, was the sister of Marius's wife Julia, it answers many questions. Or it may have been that the two Julias were cousins and close friends. But for the novelist, plagued by the need to keep story and characters in as small a framework as possible given the size of this particular theme, to have them sisters is perfect. Thank you, Plutarch, for mentioning Sulla's first wife's name! Given the inarguable fact that family was foremost to a Roman, what could be more logical than that Marius and Sulla were closely related by marriage, and that the older man was beseeched by his wife's family to give the younger man a helping hand onto the first rung of the *cursus honorum*? Therefore, Julilla was born, the younger daughter of Gaius Julius Caesar, and wife of Lucius Cornelius Sulla.

Juno Moneta   Juno of Warnings, or perhaps Reminders. It was her gaggle of sacred geese which cackled so loudly they woke Marcus Manlius in time for him to dislodge the Gauls trying to scale the Capitol cliffs in 390 B.C. The mint was located inside the podium of her temple on the Arx of the Capitol; from this fact, we obtain our English word "money."

Juturna   One of Rome's native deities, and therefore numinous, having no image or mythology in the Greek sense (though later she acquired a mythology, mostly courtesy of Vergil). Juturna was a water deity, and had a pool and shrine adjacent to the Vestal Steps leading up to the Palatine. Its waters were thought to have healing powers, and so the shrine was visited by many pilgrims.

knights   The *Equites*, the members of the *Ordo Equester*. It had all started when the kings of Rome had enrolled the city's top citizens as a special cavalry unit provided with horses paid for from the public purse. At the time, horses in Italy of good enough quality were both scarce and extremely costly. By the time the kings of Rome had yielded to the young Republic, there were eighteen hundred men so enrolled, grouped into eighteen centuries. As the Republic grew, so too did the number of knights, but all the extra knights bought their own horses and maintained them at their own expense; the eighteen hundred men who held the "public horse," as it was called, were now the senior branch of the *Ordo Equester*. However, by the second century B.C., Rome was no longer providing her own cavalry; the *Order Equester* became a social and economic entity having little to do with military matters. The knights were now defined by the censors in economic terms, and while the original eighteen centuries holding the public horse remained at a hundred men each, the rest of the knights' centuries (some seventy-one) swelled within themselves in numbers, so that all men who qualified at the knights' census were accommodated within the First Class. Until 123 B.C., senators were actually still a part of the *Ordo Equester*; it was Gaius Gracchus who split them off as a separate order of three hundred men. However, their sons and nonsenatorial males of their families were still classified as knights.

To qualify as a knight at the census (held on a special tribunal in the Forum Romanum), a man had to have property or income in excess of 400,000 sesterces. Though it was not always observed, some censors insisted upon a parade of the eighteen hundred knights who held the public horse, in order to make sure these men were looking after themselves and their steeds properly. The parade of the public horse (when held) occurred perhaps on the Ides of July, with the censors sitting in state at a tribunal atop the steps of the temple of Castor and Pollux in the Forum Romanum, while each holder of the public horse solemnly led his mount in a kind of march-past before the censors.

From the time of Gaius Gracchus down to the end of the Republic, the knights either controlled or lost control of the courts which tried senators for minor treason or provincial extortion, and were at loggerheads with the Senate fairly regularly. There was nothing to stop a knight who qualified on the senatorial means test from seeking entry to the Senate; that, by and large, they did not aspire to the Senate, was purely due to the knightly love of trade and commerce, forbidden fruit for senators. The *Ordo Equester* (it was not called that formally until after Gaius Gracchus) liked the thrill of the business forum more than they liked the thrill of the political forum.

Lanuvium Modern Lanuvio.

Lar, Lares (pl.) Among the most Roman of all gods, having no form, shape, sex, number, or mythology. They were *numina* (see *numen*). There were many different kinds of Lares, who might function as the protective spirits or forces of a locality (as with crossroads and boundaries), a social group (as with the Lar Familiaris, the family's private Lar), an activity (as with sailing), or a whole nation (as with the public Lares of Rome). By the late Republic they were depicted (in the form of small statues) as two young men with a dog, but it is doubtful whether a Roman actually believed there were only two of them, or that they owned this form—more that the increasing complexity of life made it convenient to "tag" them.

Lares Permarini   The Lares who protected voyagers on the sea.

Lares Praestites   The Lares who watched over the State—also called the Public Lares.

Larius, Lacus   Modern Lake Como.

Latin Rights   An intermediate citizen status between the nadir of the Italian Allies and the zenith of the Roman citizenship. Those having the Latin Rights shared many privileges in common with Roman citizens: booty was divided equally, contracts with full citizens could be entered into and legal protection sought for these contracts, marriage was allowed with full citizens, and there was the right to appeal against capital convictions. However, there was no *suffragium*—no right to vote in any Roman election—nor the right to sit on a Roman jury. After the revolt of Fregellae in 125 B.C., the magistrates of Latin Rights towns and districts were entitled to assume the full Roman citizenship for themselves and their direct descendants.

Latium   The region of Italy in which Rome stood. Its northern boundary was the Tiber, its southern a point extending inland from Circei, and on the east it bordered the lands of the Sabines and the Marsi.

lectisternium   A propitiatory form of religious observance usually reserved for major crises. Images of the important gods arranged in male/female pairs were placed upon couches; food was offered them and great honor paid them.

legate, *Legatus.*   The most senior members of the Roman general's military staff were his legates. In order to be classified as a *legatus*, a man had to be of senatorial status, and often was a consular in rank (it appears these elder statesmen occasionally hankered after a spell of army life, and volunteered their services to a general commanding some interesting campaign). Legates answered only to the general, and were senior to all types of military tribunes.

legion The smallest Roman military unit capable of fighting a war on its own (though it was rarely called upon to do so); that is, it was complete within itself in terms of manpower, equipment, and function. By the time of Gaius Marius, a Roman army engaged in any major campaign rarely consisted of fewer than four legions—though equally rarely of more than six legions. Single legions without prospect of reinforcement did garrison duty in places like the Spains, where tribal rebellions were small, albeit fierce. A legion contained about five thousand soldiers divided into ten cohorts of six centuries each; it also contained about one thousand men of noncombatant status, and usually came with a modest cavalry arm attached to it. Each legion fielded its own artillery and matériel; if one of the consul's legions, it was commanded by up to six elected tribunes of the soldiers; if belonging to a general not currently a consul, it was commanded by a legate, or else by the general himself. Its regular officers were the centurions, of which it possessed some sixty-six. Though the troops belonging to a legion camped together, they did not mess or live together en masse; instead, they were divided up into units of eight men (the century contained only eighty soldiers, the extra twenty men being noncombatants).

legionary The correct word for a soldier in a Roman legion. "Legionnaire," which I have sometimes seen used instead, is more properly the term applied to a member of the French Foreign Legion.

Lemanna, Lake Modern Lake Leman, or the Lake of Geneva.

lex, leges **(pl.)** The Latin word for a law; it came to be applied also to the *plebiscita* (plebiscites) passed by the Plebeian Assembly. A *lex* was not considered valid until it had been inscribed on bronze or stone, and deposited in the vaults below the temple of Saturn; however, logic says that the law's residence in the temple of Saturn was extremely brief, as the vaults could not have contained anything like the number of tablets necessary to hold the body of Roman law, even at the time of Gaius Marius—especially not when the Treasury of Rome was also beneath Saturn. No doubt the tablets were whisked in and whisked out again to be stored permanently in any one of many places known to have been repositories of law tablets.

lex Appuleia agraria The first of Lucius Appuleius Saturninus's two land bills, which were aimed at giving land on the Roman public domain to the veterans of the Marian army. This first bill concerned lands in Greece, Macedonia, Sicily, and Africa. It would seem logical to assume that these lands had all been in the possession of Rome for some considerable time, and were not regarded as important.

lex Appuleia agraria (secunda) I have tagged this law as *secunda* purely as a matter of convenience, to distinguish it from Saturninus's first land bill without giving it its full Latin title, only an additional confusion for the nonscholarly reader. This second bill is the one containing the oath of loyalty, the one which provoked such extremely bitter opposition in the Senate. The reasons behind the opposition are still hotly debated in academic circles. I have chosen to assume that the reasons lay in the newness of the land concerned—Transalpine Gaul and Nearer Spain. There must have been many companies and large-scale pastoralists intriguing to have this very rich land given to them, especially considering that they probably hoped there was mineral wealth involved too; the West was traditionally rich in undiscovered mineral lodes. To see the lands go to soldier veterans of the Head Count must have been quite intolerable.

lex Appuleia de maiestate The treason law which Saturninus introduced during his first tribunate of the plebs. It removed control of the treason court from the Centuriate Assembly, in which body it was virtually impossible to secure a conviction unless the culprit confessed out of his own mouth that he had gone to war against Rome. This law concerned itself with degrees of treason, and provided for convictions in what might be called "minor treason." A special *quaestio* (court), hearing matters to do only with treason, was given to the knights, who were both jury and presidents.

lex Appuleia frumentaria Saturninus's grain law, which I have chosen to assume belonged to his second tribunate of the plebs rather than to his first. As the Second Sicilian Slave War had been by then going on for nearly four years, it is possible that the grain shortage in Rome was growing ever more acute. The law is also better situated in the second tribunate of the plebs because by then Saturninus was actively wooing the lowly.

lex Domitia de sacerdotiis　　The law passed in 104 B.C. by Gnaeus Domitius Ahenobarbus during his tribunate of the plebs. It took control of membership in the priestly colleges of pontifices and augurs away from the incumbent members, who had traditionally co-opted new members. The new law required that future members of both colleges be elected in a special tribal assembly composed of seventeen tribes chosen by lot.

lex Licinia sumptuaria　　The luxury law passed by an unknown Licinius Crassus somewhere after 143 B.C. It forbade the serving of certain foods at banquets, including the famous licker-fish of the Tiber, oysters, and freshwater eels. It also forbade the excessive use of purple.

lex Villia annalis　　Passed in 180 B.C. by the tribune of the plebs Lucius Villius. It stipulated certain minimum ages at which the curule magistracies could be held (presumably thirty-nine years for praetor and forty-two years for consul), and apparently also stipulated that two years at least had to elapse between the praetorship and the consulship, as well as that ten years must elapse between two consulships held by the same man.

lex Voconia de mulierum hereditatibus　　Passed in 169 B.C., this law severely curtailed the right of women to inherit from wills. Under no circumstances could she be designated the main heir, even if the only child of her father; his nearest agnate relatives (that is, on the father's side) superseded her. Cicero cites a case where it was argued that the *lex Voconia* did not apply because the dead man's property had not been assessed at a census; but the praetor (Gaius Verres) overruled this, and refused to allow the girl in question to inherit. Presumably the law was got around, for we know of several great heiresses (among them, Antony's third wife, Fulvia). In this book, I have had Cornelia the Mother of the Gracchi succeed in obtaining a senatorial waiver; another ploy possible if there were no agnate heirs was to die intestate, in which case the old law prevailed, and children inherited irrespective of sex. It would seem too that the *praetor urbanus* had considerable latitude in interpreting the laws governing inheritance; there was apparently no court to hear testamentary litigation, which meant the *praetor urbanus* was the final arbiter.

Libya That part of North Africa between Egypt and Cyrenaica.

lictor One of the few genuine public servants in the employ of the Senate and People of Rome. There was a College of Lictors—the number of members is uncertain, but enough certainly to provide the traditional single-file escort for all holders of imperium, both within and outside Rome, and to perform other duties as well. Two or three hundred may not be unlikely. A lictor had to be a full Roman citizen, but that he was lowly was fairly sure, as the official wage was apparently minimal; the lictor was obliged to rely heavily upon gratuities from those he escorted. Within the college, the lictors were divided into groups of ten (decuries), each headed by a prefect, and there were several presidents of the college senior to the prefects. Inside Rome the lictor wore a plain white toga; outside Rome he wore a crimson tunic with a wide black belt ornamented with brass; a black toga was worn at funerals. For the sake of convenience, I have located the College of Lictors behind the temple of the Lares Praestites on the eastern side of the Forum Romanum, but there is no factual evidence of this at all.

Liger River The modern Loire, in France.

Liguria The mountainous region lying between the Arnus and Varus rivers, extending inland from the sea as far as the crest of the Alpes Maritimae and the Ligurian Apennines. The chief port was Genua, the largest inland town Dertona. Since its arable land was scant, Liguria was a poor area; it was chiefly famous for its greasy wool, which made up into waterproof capes and cloaks, including the military *sagum*. The other local industry was piracy.

Lilybaeum The chief town at the western end of the island of Sicily.

Liris River   The modern Garigliano, in Italy.

litter   A covered cubicle equipped with legs upon which it rested when lowered. It also had a horizontal pole along either side, projecting in front of and behind the cubicle. Between four and eight men could carry it by picking it up along the poles. It was a slow form of transport, but the most comfortable one known in the ancient world.

Long-haired Gaul   See Gallia Comata.

Lucius Tiddlypuss   See Tiddlypuss, Lucius.

Lugdunum   Modern Lyon, in France.

Lugdunum Pass   The name I have used to indicate the modern Little St. Bernard Pass between Italian Gaul and Gaul-across-the-Alps. It lay at a high altitude, but it was known and had been occasionally used before the time of Gaius Marius. The Great St. Bernard Pass was also known, but was not used. Both passes were guarded in Italian Gaul by a tribe of Celts called the Salassi, who occupied the modern Val d'Aosta.

lustrum   The Latin word which came to mean both the entire five-year term of the censors, and the ceremony with which the censors concluded the census of the ordinary Roman People on the Campus Martius.

lychnites   A term used by Pliny the Elder to describe a precious stone found in western Numidia. It is now thought to have been tourmaline.

Macedonia   To a Republican Roman, a much larger region than the Macedonia of today. It commenced on the east coast of the Adriatic Sea below Dalmatian Illyricum, at a point about where the town of Lissus was; its southern boundary on this western extremity lay against Epirus; and its two major ports receiving Adriatic traffic from Italy were Dyrrachium and Apollonia. Bordering Moesia in the north, Macedonia then continued east across the great highlands in which rose the Morava, the Axius, the Strymon, and the Nestus; in the south it bordered Greek Thessaly. Beyond the Nestus it bordered Thrace, and continued as a narrow coastal strip along the Aegean all the way to the Hellespont. Access to and from Macedonia was limited to the river valleys; through the Morava, Axius, Strymon, and Nestus the barbarian tribes of Moesia and Thrace could—and often did—invade, chiefly the Scordisci and the Bessi in the time of Gaius Marius. To the south, the only comfortable access between Macedonia and Thessaly was the pass at the Vale of Tempe. The original inhabitants of Macedonia were probably Germano-Celtic; successive invasions over the centuries mingled this original people with others of Dorian Greek, Thracian, and Illyrian origins. Long divided by natural topographical barriers into small nations tending to war with each other, a united Macedonia came into being under the kings prior to Philip II; but it was Philip II and his son Alexander the Great who thrust Macedonia into world prominence. Following the death of Alexander, Macedonia was first exhausted by a struggle between rivals for the throne, then ran afoul of Rome; its last king, Perseus, lost to Aemilius Paullus in 167 B.C. Roman attempts to convert Macedonia into a self-governing republic failed, so in 146 B.C. Macedonia was reluctantly incorporated into the expanding Roman empire as a province.

macellum   An open-air market of booths and stalls.

magistrates   The elected executives of the Senate and People of Rome. By the middle Republic, all the men who held magistracies were members of the Senate (elected quaestors were normally approved as senators by the next censors); this gave the Senate a distinct advantage over the People, until the People (in the person of the Plebs) took over the lawmaking.

The magistrates represented the executive arm of government. In order of seniority, the most junior of all magistrates was the tribune of the soldiers, who was not old enough to be admitted to the Senate, but was nonetheless a true magistrate. Then came the quaestor; the tribune of the plebs and the plebeian aedile were next; the curule aedile was the most junior magistrate holding imperium; next was the praetor; and at the top was the consul. The censor occupied a special position, for though this magistracy owned no imperium, it could not be held by a man who had not been consul. In times of emergency, the Senate was empowered

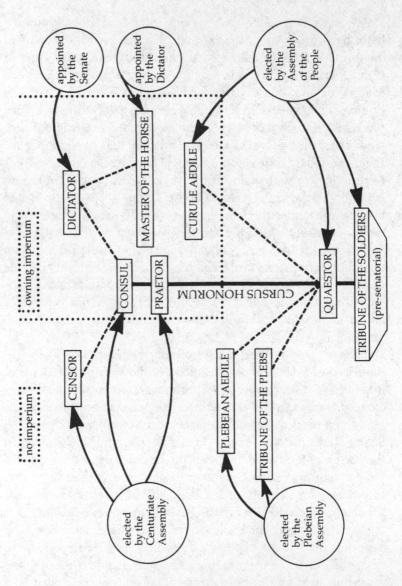

Roman Magistrates

to create an extraordinary magistrate, the dictator, who served for six months only, and was indemnified against answering for his dictatorial actions after his term as dictator was over. The dictator himself appointed a master of the horse to function as his war leader and second-in-command.

maiestas minuta   Literally, "little treason," so called to distinguish it from the kind of treason where a man abrogated his citizenship by going to war against Rome. Lucius Appuleius Saturninus first put *maiestas minuta* on the law tablets as a criminal charge, and set up a special *quaestio* or court to hear it during his first tribunate of the plebs in 103 B.C. The court was staffed entirely by knights, but the men tried in it were senators. After Saturninus's act, the old-style treason charge—called *perduellio*—heard in the Centuriate Assembly was virtually abandoned.

Malaca   Modern Malaga, in Spain.

Mamilian Commission   The special court set up by the tribune of the plebs Gaius Mamilius Limetanus in 109 B.C. It was empowered to inquire into the dealings between Jugurtha of Numidia and certain Romans, particularly magistrates.

maniple   The old tactical maneuvering unit of the Roman legion. It contained only two centuries of troops, and by the time of Gaius Marius had proven too small to contend with the armies Rome was now called upon to face. Marius eliminated it as a tactical unit.

manumission, manumit   Manumission was the act of freeing a slave. It literally means "sending from the hand." When the slave's master was a Roman citizen, manumission automatically endowed the slave with the Roman citizenship, and he took the name of his old master as his new name, adding to it his original slave name as a *cognomen*. A slave could be manumitted in any one of several ways: by buying his freedom out of his earnings, as a special gesture of the master's on some great occasion like a coming-of-age birthday, after an agreed number of years of service, in a will. Though technically the slave was then the equal of his master, in actual fact he was obliged to remain in his old master's clientship, unless this was formally dispensed with. He had little opportunity to exercise his franchise, for under the law he became a member of one of two of the four urban tribes—Esquilina or Suburana—and therefore found his vote worthless in tribal elections; his economic lowliness in almost all cases meant he was not made a member of one of the Five Classes, so he could not vote in Centuriate matters either. However, most slaves found the Roman citizenship highly desirable, not so much for themselves as for their descendants. Once a slave was manumitted, he was called a freedman, and was required for the rest of his life to wear a slightly conical skullcap on the back of his head; this was the Cap of Liberty.

Marcomanni   One of the three peoples who tacked themselves on to the German migration of 120 B.C. The Marcomanni were Celts closely allied to the Boii of Boiohaemum, and orginally lived around the headwaters of the river Albis (modern Czechoslovakia). They joined the Cimbri and Teutones in about the seventh year of the trek, 113 B.C.

Marsi   One of the most important Italian peoples. The Marsi lived surrounding the Fucine Lake, which belonged to them; they extended into the mountains of the high Apennines, and controlled the passes on the western—that is, the Roman—side. Their history indicates that they were always loyal to Rome, and did not side either with the Samnites or with Hannibal. They were extremely martial, affluent, and populous, and adopted Latin as their language fairly early. Their chief town was Marruvium; Alba Fucens, a larger and more important town, was a Latin Rights colony seeded on Marsic territory by Rome. The Marsi worshiped snakes, and were famous snake charmers.

Martha   The Syrian prophetess who predicted that Gaius Marius would be consul of Rome seven times before he had been consul once. She extracted a promise from Marius that he would bring her to Rome, where she lived as his guest in his house until she died, and regularly scandalized the city's inhabitants by appearing in a purple litter. It is my own novelist's license which added the second part of her prophecy, to the effect that a nephew of Marius's wife Julia would be a greater Roman than he; I needed to do this to make events in a later book more logical and reasonable.

Massilia Modern Marseilles. This superb seaport in southern Gaul-across-the-Alps not far from the mouth of the Rhodanus River was founded as a Greek colony in about 600 B.C. The Massiliotes, as its inhabitants were called, soon made cultural and trading inroads into Gaul, and were influential in Hellenizing those Gallic tribes which lived along their trade routes; this was especially true of the Volcae Tectosages of Tolosa, the Ligures of Nicaea and Portus Herculis Monoeci (modern Nice and Monaco), and some of the peoples who lived along the lower Rhodanus River. Massiliotes introduced the grapevine and the olive tree to Gaul. The city's inhabitants were quick to see the potential of Rome, and allied Massilia to Rome during the Second Punic War. It was Massiliote complaints about the depredations of the headhunting Salluvii of western Liguria which led to the famous Gallic expedition of Gnaeus Domitius Ahenobarbus in 122 B.C., and the founding of Transalpine Gaul (Gaul-across-the-Alps).

Mauretania Modern Morocco. In Gaius Marius's day, far western North Africa. The boundary between Numidia and Mauretania was the Muluchath River, about 600 miles (960 km) west of Cirta. The inhabitants of Mauretania were called Moors; they were Berbers racially. The capital was Tingis (modern Tangier). There were kings; during the time of Gaius Marius's war against Jugurtha, the King's name was Bocchus.

Mediolanum Modern Milan.

mentula, mentulae **(pl.)** The great Latin obscenity for the penis.

mentulam caco "I shit on your prick!"

merda A Latin obscenity referring more to the droppings of animals than to human excrement.

Metella Calva The sister of Lucius Caecilius Metellus Dalmaticus Pontifex Maximus and Quintus Caecilius Metellus Numidicus. She was married to Lucius Licinius Lucullus, and was the mother of the Brothers Luculli. She was one of the very few women of her time to earn a mention in the ancient sources; she had a lifelong penchant for choosing low-class lovers, and pursued her affairs in scandalous manner.

Middle Sea   My name for the Mediterranean Sea, which in the time of Gaius Marius had not yet acquired its later Latin name—"Our Sea." Properly, it was called Mare Internum.

Military Man   The *vir militaris*. He was a man whose whole career revolved around the army, and who continued to serve as a senior officer in the army beyond his obligatory number of campaigns. Such men entered the political arena relying upon their military history to recommend them to the electors; many of them never bothered to embark upon a political career at all, but if a *vir militaris* aspired to command an army, he had to attain the rank of praetor. Gaius Marius, Quintus Sertorius, Titus Didius, Gaius Pomptinus, and Publius Ventidius were all Military Men; but Gaius Julius Caesar the Dictator, the greatest military man of them all, was never a Military Man.

mime, Mimus   First a Greek theatrical form, the mime gathered its most enthusiastic followers in Rome, and kept increasing in popularity from the third century B.C. Where the actors in comedy and tragedy wore masks, and adhered to the strictly accented and metered script of the playwright, the actors in mime wore no masks, and evolved a technique closer to what we today might call ad-libbing. The repertoire of plots and situations was a stock one, but the individual performances did not contain formal memorized dialogue. Mime was considered vulgar, bawdy, poor theater, and much else by those who loved the proper theater of tragedy and comedy, but its snowballing popularity at the Roman games slowly banished formal drama to a poor second place. There can be no doubt that mime was very funny indeed. It seems to have survived in the stock characters of the commedia dell'arte—Harlequin's costume of patches and the jester's costume of patches closely resemble the *centunculus* of the mimetic fool, for example.

minim   A bright earth-red pigment with which the triumphing general painted his face, it would seem so that he looked like the terracotta-faced statue of Jupiter Optimus Maximus.

Minoan   *Not* a word the Romans would have used! It is the modern term (possibly coined by Sir Arthur Evans) to describe the civilization of Crete and Greece which existed during the second millennium B.C. I placed the term in Sulla's mouth during a conversation for the sake of clarity and convenience; for while the Romans knew of the civilization, what they called it, we do not know.

Mithridates   The traditional name of the kings of Pontus. There were six kings of Pontus surnamed Mithridates, the last of whom was by far the greatest. The royal house of the Mithridatidae (to give it its proper name) claimed descent from the old Iranian kings, particularly from Darius the Great, but the features of the men displayed on truly wonderful coins of Pontus are Germano-Thracian.

***modius, modii* (pl.)**   The measure of grain in Rome. One *modius* weighed 13 pounds (6 kg).

Moor   The word for a Berber of Mauretania.

Mons Genava Pass   What name the Romans actually gave to the modern Montgenèvre Pass through the Alps from the headwaters of the Dora Riparia in Italy to the headwaters of the Durance in France, I do not know. For the sake of a tag in the reader's mind, I Latinized the modern French name. This was the most consistently used of all the alpine passes, for it lay on the Via Aemilia/Via Domitia.

Mosa River   The modern Meuse (in Dutch, Maas).

Mosella River   The modern Moselle.

Muluchath River   The modern Moulouya.

Muthul River   A river in central Numidia. There is still great debate about the identity of the stream. I have made it a tributary of the river Bagradas, after the *Atlas of Classical History* (edited by Richard J. A. Talbert).

Mutina   Modern Modena, in Italy.

Narbo   Modern Narbonne, in France.

Neapolis   Modern Naples. It was one of the largest and most successful of the Greek colonies planted in southern Italy, though it fell under Roman domination by the end of the fourth century

B.C. In the Hannibalic troubles, Neapolis was wise enough to remain loyal to Rome, and so lost none of its lands to Rome. During the Republic, it was distinctly less important as a port than Puteoli, but it thrived nonetheless.

Nearer Spain The Roman province. In Latin, it was called Hispania Citerior. The territory embraced the Mediterranean coastal plain and mountainous foothills behind, from just south of New Carthage all the way north to the Pyrenees. The southern boundary between the two provinces was fairly tenuous, but seems to have run between the range of mountains called the Orospeda and the taller range behind Abdera called the Solorius. In Gaius Marius's day, the largest settlement was New Carthage (now known as Cartagena), because the Orospeda range behind it was honeycombed with productive silver mines the Romans had taken over when Carthage fell. Only one other part of the province was of much interest to its Roman governors: the valley of the Iberus River (the modern Ebro) and its tributaries, this area being very rich. The governor had two seats: New Carthage in the south, and Tarraco in the north. The nearer Spanish province was never as important to Rome as Further Spain.

nectar The drink of the gods. Apparently its base was honey.

nefas The Latin word for sacrilege.

Nemausus Modern Nîmes, in France. It lay on the western side of the salt marshes of the Rhodanus delta, and from the time of Gnaeus Domitius Ahenobarbus (ca. 120 B.C.), it was connected by a long causeway to the town of Arelate on the eastern side of the delta. Gaius Marius did much needed repairs to this causeway while waiting for the Germans in 104 B.C.

nemo The Latin for nobody or no one.

Nicomedes A name belonging to the kings of Bithynia. There were either three or four kings called Nicomedes; modern scholars differ about the number.

noble, *Nobilis.* The word used to describe a man and his descendants once the consulship had been achieved; it was an artificial aristocracy invented by the plebeians in order to further reduce the distinction of being patrician, since more plebeians reached the consulship during the last half of the Republic than did patricians. By the time of Gaius Marius, nobility mattered greatly. Some modern authorities extend the term *nobilis* to cover those men who reached the status of praetor without achieving the consulship. However, my feeling is that this would have demeaned its exclusivity too much, so I have reserved nobility for those of proven consular family.

***nomen, nomina* (pl.)** The family or gentilicial name—the name of the *gens*. Cornelius, Julius, Domitius, Livius, Marius, Marcius, Sulpicius, etc., were gentilicial names. I have not used *gens* very much in this book, as it takes a feminine ending; thus, it was not the *gens* Julius, but the *gens* Julia. Too confusing for non–Latin readers, English being a neutral language. Thus I have preferred to say "family Julius," and keep things simple.

Noricum What might today be called the eastern Tyrol and the Yugoslavian Alps. Its people were called the Taurisci, and were Celts. The main settlement was Noreia.

Numantia A small town of some four thousand Celtiberians, on the upper Durius River in Nearer Spain. It had successfully resisted a whole series of Roman armies and generals, starting with Cato the Censor in 195 B.C., and ending with Hostilius Mancinus in 137 B.C. Then in 135 B.C., Scipio Aemilianus was given the job of reducing it, and did so after a siege which lasted eight months. Jugurtha of Numidia, Gaius Marius, Publius Rutilius Rufus, and Quintus Caecilius Metellus Numidicus were all on Scipio Aemilianus's staff. When the town finally surrendered, Scipio Aemilianus literally tore it apart, dismantled it, executed or deported its people, and used it as an object lesson to the Celtiberians to show them that they couldn't win against Rome.

***numen, numina* (pl.)** Literally, "divinity" (but also "a nodding of the head"). *Numen* is a word used by modern scholars, rather than the Romans, to describe the peculiarly disembodied nature of the original Italian and Roman gods, if indeed they could be called gods. Spiritual forces might be a better description. These old gods were the forces which governed everything from rain and wind to the function of a doorway, to the proper siting of boundary stones or the element we call luck. They were faceless, sexless, and without a mythology. The word mostly used to describe them nowadays is the Anglicized adjective "numinous." As time wore on through the years of the Republic, and it became the mark of culture to subscribe to things Greek, many of the original numinous gods acquired a name, a sex, and even occasionally a face, but to call Roman religion a hybrid bastardization of the Greeks is to underestimate Rome grievously. Unlike the Greeks, Roman religion was so intimately tied to all the strata of government that one could not survive without the other; this dated back to before the kings of Rome, when all the gods were numinous, and it remained very much a fact until Christianization of the Emperors and their courts undermined the old religion of the Roman State. In the days of Gaius Marius, long before this State religion began to lose its hold, even the most brilliant and iconoclastic among the Romans subscribed scrupulously to religious matters, including men like Gaius Marius and Gaius Julius Caesar the Dictator. It was probably that numinous element in the religion which riddled even the most brilliant and iconoclastic Romans with superstitions.

Numidia   The ancient kingdom of middle North Africa which always lay to the west, south, and east of Carthage, and later of the Roman African province. The original inhabitants were Berbers, and lived a seminomadic life. After the defeat of Carthage, Rome and the Scipios encouraged the establishment of a regal dynasty, the first member of which was King Masinissa. The capital of Numidia was Cirta.

oakum   A crudely tamped together collection of fibers, in ancient times gathered from woolly seeds, maple "cotton," or the coarsest fibers of the flax plant. It was occasionally used for calking, but its main use was for lampwicks.

Odysseus   In Latin, Ulysses. King of Ithaca in days of legend. He was one of the main characters in Homer's *Iliad,* and the hero of Homer's *Odyssey.*

Olympia   The famous sanctuary of Zeus was not anywhere near

Mount Olympus; this Olympia was in Elis, in the western Peloponnese.

oppidum In the sense used in this book, a fortified settlement, usually atop a hill, and designed to protect the lower lands around it. I have confined the term to the strongholds of Gallia Comata— Long-haired Gaul.

opus incertum The oldest of several ways in which the Romans built their walls. A facing of irregular small stones mortared together was built with a hollow interior; this hollow was filled with a mortar composed of black pozzolana and lime mixed through an aggregate of rubble and small stones (*caementa*). Evidence suggests that *opus incertum* walls date back at least to 200 B.C.; in the time of Gaius Marius, the two younger ways of building walls had not yet replaced the tried and true *opus incertum*.

order, *ordo* In Roman terms, a social group having much the same family background and degree of wealth.

Ordo Equester See knights.

Oscan The language spoken by the Samnites, Lucani, Frentani, Apuli, Brutii, and Campani of peninsular Italy. It was allied to Latin, but very different. During the time of Gaius Marius, Oscan was still a living, widely spoken tongue. True Romans tended to despise those whose first language was Oscan.

Ostia Rome's closest seaport, situated at the mouth of the Tiber River, and in Rome's earliest days the location of the salt marshes which produced Italy's best—perhaps only—salt. It was a fortified town during the Republic, and became Rome's naval base during the Punic Wars. Bedeviled by silting-up and sandbars, Ostia was never a very satisfactory port, but its disadvantages did not prevent its being extremely busy. The swift and silt-dirty Tiber made it impossible for any but the smallest merchantmen to voyage up to the city of Rome; cargo was normally unloaded from large and medium ships in Ostia, and sent up to Rome by barge or lighter. Ostia contained granaries. It also had its own quaestor, who was responsible for overseeing the unloading and onward shipment of the grain supply, and responsible too for the levying of all customs and excise duties.

Padus River   The modern Po, in northern Italy.

Paeligni   One of the peoples of central peninsular Italy, allied to the Marsi and the Sabines.

Pamphylia   That part of the southern coast of Asia Minor lying between Lycia (opposite Rhodes) and Cilicia (opposite Cyprus). The extremely high Taurus Mountains plunged straight into the sea, giving Pamphylia a very rugged and inaccessible coastline. The interior was heavily forested with pines, but the whole region was rather poor in yielding a decent living for its people, who found that the most profitable enterprise—and the one to which their country was most suited by nature—was piracy.

pantheon   The word used in modern times to describe collectively the whole array of gods in a polytheistic system of religious belief.

papyrus   The pithy stalks of the Egyptian marsh papyrus were made into paper by a most painstaking and ingenious method; no species of papyrus other than Egyptian was ever successfully used to manufacture paper. The process whereby the plant was converted into a substance suitable for writing on is hard to date, but seems not to have been in general use prior to the first Ptolemy, about 322 B.C. There can be no doubt that the ever-widening availability of paper as a writing material from 300 B.C. onward was the single most significant contribution toward literacy in the ancient world. A process invented by a Roman Fannius (see Fannius paper) about 150 B.C., to convert poor paper into good, made writing paper even easier to get, as well as cheaper.

parchment   When King Ptolemy V Epiphanes of Egypt banned the export of paper from Egypt about 190 B.C., the shortage of a suitable medium for writing upon was so acutely felt that in Asiatic Pergamum a process was quickly evolved to produce a substitute for papyrus paper; this substitute became known as vellum, or parchment. The skins of very young animals, particularly lambs and kids, were washed, very carefully scraped, then polished with pumice and chalk. However, papyrus paper was soon put back onto the world market, and the Pergamum parchment industry could never have hoped to replace papyrus paper, for it was both more expensive and slower to make. Parchment was kept for the documents considered so important that they had to "last forever."

Pass of Brennus   The modern Brenner Pass. The name comes either from the first of the two Celtic kings named Brennus (see Brennus [1]), who invaded Italy through this pass, or from the tribe of Celts called the Brenni, who lived in the Alps around the pass. The lowest of all the alpine passes into Italian Gaul, it followed the valley of the river Isarcus, a tributary of the Athesis. That it was seldom used was because the lands to its north were inhospitable.

Pass of the Salassi   The modern pair of passes called the Little St. Bernard and the Great St. Bernard (see Lugdunum Pass, Salassi).

Patavium   Modern Padua, in northern Italy. The fastest-growing and most properous town in Italian Gaul.

paterfamilias   The head of the family unit. His right to do as he pleased with the members of his family unit was rigidly protected by the laws of the Roman State.

Patrae   Modern Patras, in Peloponnesian Greece. It lay outside the Gulf of Corinth on its southern (Peloponnesian) shore, and was the natural (that is, with regard to winds and sea currents) terminus for those voyagers to Greece from Tarentum or Sicily.

patricians   The original Roman aristocracy. Patricians were distinguished citizens before there were kings of Rome, and ever after kept their title of patrician, as well as a prestige unattainable by any plebeian (no matter how many consuls in his family had ennobled him). However, as the Republic evolved and the power of the plebeians grew in pace with their wealth, the special rights and entitlements of the patricians were inexorably stripped from them, until by the time of Gaius Marius they tended to be relatively impoverished compared to the families of the plebeian nobility. Not all patrician clans were of equal antiquity: the Julii and the Fabii were certainly some centuries older in their tenure of patrician status than the Claudii. Patricians married in a special form called *confarreatio*, which was virtually for life, and patrician women never were allowed the relative emancipation of their plebeian fellows. Certain priesthoods could be held only by patricians—Rex Sacrorum and *flamen Dialis*—and certain senatorial positions could be held only by patricians—*interrex* and the Princeps Senatus. At the time of Gaius Marius, the following patrician families were still regularly producing senators (if not consuls): Aemilius, Claudius, Cornelius, Fabius (but through adoptions only), Julius, Manlius, Papirius, Pinarius, Postumius, Sergius, Servilius, Sulpicius, and Valerius.

patron *Patronus.* Roman Republican society was organized into a system of patronage and clientship. Though perhaps the smallest businessmen and the ordinary lowly workers of Rome were not always participants in the system, the system was nonetheless very prevalent at all levels of society. The patron undertook to offer protection and favors to those who acknowledged themselves his clients (see client).

pectoral A small metal plate, mostly square but sometimes round, usually of bronze or iron (steel), worn on the chest as armored protection.

pedagogue *Paedagogus.* A teacher of young children. He was the man who instilled rudimentary education—reading, writing, and arithmetic. His status was usually that of slave or freedman, he lived within the family unit, and his nationality was more often than not Greek; however, he was required to teach in Latin as well as in Greek.

pedarius, pedarii **(pl.)** A senatorial backbencher (see also Senate).

Peloponnese The Isle of Pelops. It was that southern part of Greece which is connected to the "mainland" by a narrow neck, the Isthmus of Corinth. In the time of Gaius Marius, the Peloponnese was unimportant and underpopulated; as on the "mainland," many of its inhabitants chose to sell themselves into slavery rather than stagnate at home.

Penates The Di Penates, the gods of the storage cupboard. Among the oldest and most numinous of Roman gods (see *numen*), the Di Penates were worshiped in every Roman house in conjunction with Vesta (spirit of the hearth), and the Lar Familiaris, the special family representative of the Lares. Like the Lares, the Di Penates were depicted (in the form of bronze statuettes usually) as youths.

Penates Publici   Originally these were the royal Di Penates belonging to the King of Rome; during the Republic, the Penates Publici came to be worshiped as the caretakers of the public storage cupboard—that is, of the State's well-being and solvency.

People   Technically, this term embraced every Roman citizen who was not a member of the Senate. It applied to patricians as well as to plebeians, and the Head Count as much as the First Class.

Peripatetic   An adherent of the school of philosophy founded by Aristotle, but developed by his pupil Theophrastus. Unfortunately Theophrastus's immediate successors did not concern themselves with the written words of Aristotle, and gave the only copy of his works to Neleus of Scepsis, who took them home to Scepsis (a town in the Troad) and stored them in his cellar, where they remained forgotten for 150 years. The name Peripatetic was given to adherents of the school because of a covered walkway within the school that was used for strolling while the scholars conversed; it was also said Aristotle himself walked while he talked. By the time of Gaius Marius the philosophy was in disrepute, for it had quite lost the wonderful breadth of Aristotelian interests, devoting itself to literature, the criticism of literature, the writing of biographies in a florid and inaccurate style, and moral matters.

peristyle   An enclosed garden or courtyard which was surrounded by a colonnade.

Pessinus   A small city in eastern Phrygia, famous for containing the chief sanctuary and precinct of the Great Mother.

phalerae   Round, chased, ornamented silver or gold discs about 3 to 4 inches (75 to 100mm) in diameter. Originally they were worn by Roman knights as insignia, and also were the trappings of their horses. During the middle Republic they became military decorations awarded to cavalrymen, but by the time of Gaius

Marius they were also awarded to infantrymen. Normally *phalerae* given to soldiers for valor were mounted in sets of nine (in three rows of three) upon a decorated leather harness of straps designed to be worn over the mail shirt or cuirass.

Phrygia   One of the wilder and less populated parts of Asia Minor, synonymous to the ancients with nymphs, dryads, satyrs, and other mythical woodland folk, as well as with peasants so defenseless they were easily enslaved. Phrygia lay inland from Bithynia, south of Paphlagonia, and west of Galatia. Mountainous and heavily forested, it was a part of the Attalid empire of Pergamum; after the wars following the bequeathing of the Kingdom of Pergamum to Rome, the Roman proconsul Manius Aquillius literally sold most of Phrygia to King Mithridates V of Pontus, pocketing the gold for himself.

Picentes, Picentines, Picenum   Picenum was that part of the eastern Italian Peninsula roughly occupying the area of the Italian leg's calf muscle. Its western boundary was the high Apennines; to the north lay Umbria, and to the south and west Samnium. Since it had a good section of the Adriatic coast, it also had two busy seaports, Ancona and Firmum Picenum; the main inland town and chief center was Asculum Picentum. The inhabitants were originally of Italiote and Illyrian stock, but during the invasion of the first King Brennus, many of his Celtic tribesmen settled in Picenum, and intermarried with the original people. By the time of Gaius Marius, the Picentines were well admixed with the Celts, most particularly in the north.

pilaster   A column or pillar engaged within a wall, so that only a part of it showed on the outside of the wall.

pilum, pila (**pl.**)   The Roman infantry spear, particularly as modified by Gaius Marius. It had a very small, wickedly barbed head of iron that was continued as an iron shaft for perhaps three feet (one meter); this was joined to a shaped wooden stem which fitted the hand comfortably. Marius modified it by introducing a weakness into the junction between iron and wooden shaft sections, so that upon lodging in shield, body, or ground after throwing, it broke apart, and thus was of no use to the enemy. However,

Roman craftsmen within the legions could repair these broken specimens of *pilum* very quickly.

pipinna A little boy's penis.

Pisae Modern Pisa, in Italy.

Placentia Modern Piacenza, in northern Italy. It was one of the largest and most important towns in Italian Gaul, and was a Latin Rights colony from 218 B.C. Its importance increased enormously after the censor Marcus Aemilius Scaurus Princeps Senatus caused the building of a good road from the Tyrrhenian coast through Dertona to Placentia and the Padus Valley.

plebeian, plebs All those Roman citizens who were not patricians were plebeians—that is, they belonged to the plebs (the *e* is short, so the word "plebs" has the same *e* sound as "February"—it is not pronounced *pleebs*, as at West Point military academy). At the beginning of the Republic, no plebeian could be a priest, a curule magistrate, or even a senator. This situation lasted only a very short while; one by one the exclusively patrician institutions crumbled before the onslaught of the plebs, until by the time of Gaius Marius only a very few politically unimportant posts remained the province of the patricians. However, the plebs created a new nobility to distinguish the stars in its firmament from the rest, by calling a man who had attained the consulship a *nobilis* (nobleman), and ordaining that his direct descendants would also be noble.

plebiscite Strictly speaking, a law enacted in the Plebeian Assembly was not called a *lex* or law, but a *plebiscitum* (hence our modern English word "plebiscite"). From very early in the history of the Republic, plebiscites were regarded as legally binding, but the *lex Hortensia* of 287 B.C. made this a formal fact. From then on, there was virtually no difference at law between a *plebiscitum* and a *lex*. By the time of Gaius Marius, almost all the legal clerks who were responsible for putting the laws on tablets and recording them for posterity neglected to qualify whether they were recording a true *lex* or a *plebiscitum;* simply, they had all been classified in the minds of the clerks as laws.

podex The Latin obscenity—a mild one—for the posterior fundament or anus.

Pollux The "forgotten twin"—Castor's brother the boxer. Of the four children of King Tyndareus and his wife, Leda—born as quadruplets—two were sired by Tyndareus, and two by Zeus, who had ravished Leda in the guise of a swan. Castor and Helen belonged to Zeus; Pollux (Polydeukes) and Clytemnestra belonged to Tyndareus. Doomed always to be mentioned after his brother, very often Pollux was not mentioned at all. Romans called the temple of Castor and Pollux in the Forum Romanum simply "Castor's" (see Castor).

pomerium The sacred boundary of the city of Rome. Marked by stones called *cippi*, it was reputedly inaugurated by King Servius Tullus, and remained the same until the time of Sulla the Dictator. The *pomerium* did not exactly follow the Servian Walls, one good reason why it is doubtful that the Servian Walls were actually built by King Servius Tullus—who would surely have caused the walls to follow the same course as the *pomerium*. The whole of the ancient Palatine city of Romulus was enclosed within the *pomerium*, but the Aventine was not, nor was the Capitol. Tradition held that the *pomerium* could be enlarged only by a man who significantly increased the size of Roman territory. In religious terms, Rome herself existed only within the *pomerium;* all outside it was merely Roman territory.

pons A bridge.

pontifex The Latin word for a priest; it has survived to be absorbed unchanged into most modern European languages. Many philologists consider that in very early Roman times, the *pontifex* was a maker of bridges, these being deemed magical structures. Be that as it may, by Republican times the *pontifex* was a priest of special kind; incorporated into a college, he served as an adviser to Rome's magistrates in religious matters—for Rome's religion was administered by the State. At first all the *pontifices* had to be patrician, but in 300 B.C. a *lex Ogulnia* stipulated that half the members of the college must be plebeian.

Pontifex Maximus The head of the State religion, and most senior of all priests. He seems to have been an invention of the infant Republic, a typically masterly Roman way of getting around an obstacle without ruffling too many feelings; for the Rex Sacrorum (a title held by the kings of Rome) had been the chief priest. Rather than upset the populace by abolishing the Rex Sacrorum, the new rulers of Rome in the person of the Senate simply created a new *pontifex* whose role and status was superior to that of the Rex Sacrorum. He was called the Pontifex Maximus, and he was elected rather than co-opted, in order to reinforce his statesman-like position. At first he was probably required to be a patrician, but by the middle Republic he was more likely to be plebeian. He supervised all the various members of the various priestly colleges—*pontifices*, augurs, fetials and other minor priests, and the Vestal Virgins. In Republican times he occupied the most important Domus Publicus, or State-owned house, but shared it with the Vestals. His official headquarters (it had the status of a temple) was the little old Regia in the Forum Romanum.

Pontus The large state at the southeastern end of the Euxine Sea (the Black Sea).

Populonia A port city on the western, Tyrrhenian coast of the Italian Peninsula.

porta A gate.

porticus A roofed-over colonnade, either in the form of a long straight arcade, or a rectangle enclosing a courtyard (peristyle). It was commonly a place of business, public as well as commercial; the Porticus Margaritaria at the top of the Forum Romanum was named after the pearl merchants who had their shops or stalls therein; the Porticus Metelli adjacent to the temple of Jupiter Stator on the Campus Martius contained offices for the censors as well as many business offices; the Porticus Minucia, at the Circus Flaminius, held the grain supply offices of the aediles as well as business offices; the Porticus Aemilia, fronting onto the wharves of the Port of Rome, was a true emporium, containing the offices of those engaged in the import and export of goods.

Port of Rome The Romans simply called it Portus. It was that bank of the Tiber downstream from the Pons Sublicius or Wooden Bridge on the city side of the river, where wharves and emporia were built to take the constant barge and lighter and small merchantman traffic which came up from Ostia. Cargo unloaded from merchantmen in Ostia was here finally discharged for Rome. The Port of Rome lay outside the Servian Walls, and was confined to a fairly narrow strip of riverbank by the Aventine cliffs, in which lay the State granaries.

praefectus fabrum "He who supervises the making." One of the most important men in a Roman army, he was technically not a part of it, but a civilian appointed to the position of *praefectus fabrum* by the general. He was responsible for the equipping and supplying of the army in all respects, from its animals and their feeding to its men and their feeding. Because he let out the contracts to businessmen for equipment and supplies, he was very powerful and, unless a man of strong integrity, in a position to enrich himself.

praenomen, praenomina (pl.) The first name of a Roman man. There were very few of them in use, perhaps twenty at most during the time of Gaius Marius, and half of that twenty were not common. Each *gens* or family clan favored certain *praenomina* only, which further reduced the number available. A modern scholar can often tell from a man's *praenomen* whether or not that man was a genuine member of the *gens;* the Julii, for instance, favored "Sextus," "Gaius," and "Lucius" only, so a man called Marcus Julius was unlikely to be a true Julian of the patrician *gens;* the Licinii favored "Publius," "Marcus," and "Lucius"; the Pompeii favored "Gnaeus," "Quintus," and "Sextus"; the Cornelii favored "Publius" and "Lucius." Some families had *praenomina* peculiar to their families alone; "Appius" belonged only to the Claudii, and "Mamercus" to the Aemilii Lepidus. One of the great puzzles for modern scholars concerns that Lucius Claudius who was Rex Sacrorum during the late Republic; "Lucius" is not a Claudian *praenomen*, but as he was certainly a patrician, Lucius Claudius must have been a true Claudian; I have postulated that there was a branch of the Claudian *gens* bearing the *praenomen* "Lucius," and which traditionally always held the post of Rex Sacrorum.

praetor Praetorship was the second most senior rung on the

Roman *cursus honorum* of magistrates (excluding the office of censor, which was a special case). At the very beginning of the Republic, the two highest magistrates of all were called praetors. But by the end of the fourth century B.C., the word "consul" was being used to describe these highest magistrates. One praetor was the sole representative of this position for many decades thereafter; he was very obviously the *praetor urbanus*, for his duties were confined to the city of Rome (thus freeing up the consuls for engaging in war). In 242 B.C. a second praetor was created; he was the *praetor peregrinus*. There followed the acquisition of overseas possessions requiring governance, so in 227 B.C. two more praetors were created to deal with Sicily and Sardinia. In 197 B.C. the number increased from four to six, to cope with governing the two Spains. However, no more praetorian positions were created after that; in the day of Gaius Marius, the number of praetors still stood at six. There is, I must add, some debate about this: there are two schools of modern scholarly thought, one that it was Sulla as dictator who increased the praetors to eight, the other that the number was increased from six to eight during the time of the Brothers Gracchi. I have preferred to keep the number of praetors at six.

praetor peregrinus   I have translated this as "foreign praetor," because he dealt only with legal matters and lawsuits where at least one of the parties was not a Roman citizen. By the time of Gaius Marius, his duties were confined to the dispensation of justice; they took him all over Italy, and sometimes further afield than that. He was also responsible for looking after cases involving noncitizens within the city of Rome herself.

praetor urbanus   I have translated this as "urban praetor." By the time of Gaius Marius his duties were almost purely in litigation, and he was responsible for the supervision of justice and the law courts within the city of Rome. His imperium did not extend beyond the fifth milestone from Rome, and he was not allowed to leave Rome for more than ten days at a time. If both the consuls were absent from Rome, he was its senior magistrate and was empowered to summon the Senate to a meeting, as well as to organize the defense of the city if in danger of an attack. It was his decision whether two litigants might proceed to court; in most cases, he decided the matter there and then, without benefit of the full legal trial process.

primus inter pares   "The first among equals." This was the cry, the catch-phrase of all those Romans engaged in the political arena. It summed up the aim of a Roman politician—to stand at the forefront of his peers. By definition, this meant he had to have peers—men who were his equals in birth, experience, background, family, status, achievements, *dignitas*. It was a strong indication of the fact that the Roman nobleman did not want to be a king or a dictator, this being standing above all others, and having no peers. Romans loved the competition.

primus pilus   The centurion in command of the leading century of the leading cohort of a Roman legion, and therefore the chief centurion of that legion. He rose to this position by a serial promotion, and was considered the most able man in the whole legion.

Princeps Senatus   What today we would call the Leader of the House. The censors chose a patrician senator of unimpeachable integrity and morals—and high *dignitas* as well as high *auctoritas*—to fill the role of Princeps Senatus. Apparently it was not necessarily a title given for life, but was reviewed every five years when a new pair of censors entered office. Marcus Aemilius Scaurus was created Princeps Senatus at a relatively young age, having acquired the title, it would seem, while still actually serving as consul in 115 B.C. As it was not usual for a man to be appointed Princeps Senatus before being elected censor (Scaurus was not elected censor until 109 B.C.), Scaurus's winning the post was either a signal mark of honor for an extraordinary man, or else (as some modern scholars have suggested) he was in 115 B.C. the most senior patrician senator available for the job. Whichever was the case, Scaurus held the title until he died—and never stood in danger of losing it, as far as we can gather.

privatus   A private citizen, but used in this book to indicate a man who was a member of the Senate yet not serving as a magistrate.

proconsul   One serving with the status of a consul. This imperium was normally given to a man who had just finished his year as consul, and went still holding the status of a consul (that is, as a proconsul) to govern a province or command an army in the name of the Senate and People of Rome. A man's term as proconsul normally lasted for a year, but was commonly prorogued beyond the year if the man was engaged in a campaign against an enemy still unsubdued. If a consular was not available to govern a province stormy enough to warrant the appointment of a proconsul rather than a propraetor, one of the year's crop of praetors was sent to govern it, endowed with the imperium of a proconsul. The proconsul's imperium was limited to the area of his province or task, and was lost the moment he stepped across the *pomerium* into the city of Rome.

proletarii   Another name for the lowliest of all Roman citizens, the *capite censi* or Head Count. The word *proletarius* derived from *proles*, which means progeny, offspring, children in an impersonal sense, and was given to these lowly citizens because children were the only thing they were capable of giving Rome.

propraetor   One serving with the status of a praetor. This imperium was given to a praetor still serving his year in office, or to a praetor after his year in office was over, and was awarded to empower its owner to govern a province and, if necessary, conduct a war. Like the imperium of a proconsul, that of a propraetor was lost the moment he stepped inside the sacred boundary of Rome. In degree, the position was less powerful than proconsul, and was normally given when the province in question was peaceful. Hence, any war the propraetor engaged in had to be forced upon him; he could not seek it out.

prorogue   The act of extending a man's tenure of magisterial office beyond its normal time span. It applied to governorships or military commands, not to the actual magistracies themselves.

province, *Provincia.*   The sphere of duty of a magistrate or a promagistrate holding an imperium. By extension, the word came to mean also the place where the imperium was exercised by its holder—in other words, a territory or possession of Rome requiring the attention of a governor in local residence. By the time of Gaius Marius, all of Rome's provinces were outside Italy and Italian Gaul.

pteryges The leather straps which depended from the waist to the knees as a kilt, and from the shoulders to the upper arms as sleeves; they were sometimes fringed at their ends. The traditional mark of senior officers and generals of the Roman army, they were not worn by the ranks.

Punic The adjective applied to Carthage and its people, but particularly to the three wars fought between Carthage and Rome. The word is derived from the word "Phoenician."

Puteoli Modern Pozzuoli. By the time of Gaius Marius, Puteoli was Italy's busiest and most important port, and as an emporium had surpassed Delos. It was a very well organized and run city, and in spite of its port status still managed to remain an appealing seaside vacation spot for wealthy Romans. Its most prominent family was the family Granius, who apparently had ties to Gaius Marius and the Latin town of Arpinum.

quadriga A chariot drawn by four horses.

quaestor The lowest rung on the senatorial *cursus honorum*. At the time of Gaius Marius, to be elected quaestor did not mean a man was automatically made a member of the Senate; however, it was the normal practice of the censors to admit quaestors into the Senate. The exact number of quaestors elected in any one year is not known for this date, but was perhaps twelve to sixteen. The age at which a man sought election as quaestor was thirty, which was also the correct age for entering the Senate. A quaestor's chief duties were fiscal: he might be seconded to the Treasury in Rome, or to secondary treasuries, or to collecting customs and port duties (there must have been at least three such quaestors at this time, one for Ostia, one for Puteoli, and one for the other ports), or to managing the finances of a province. A consul going to govern a province the next year could ask for a man by name to serve as his quaestor; this was considered a great distinction for the quaestor and a sure way to be elected. In normal circumstances the quaestorship lasted for one year, but if a man was requested by name, he was obliged to remain in the province with his governor until the governor's term was brought to an end. Quaestors entered office on the fifth day of December.

Quirinus   One of the most Latin of all gods, Quirinus was the divine embodiment of a concept, an idea. Perhaps of Sabine rather than Latin origins, he had his home on the Quirinal Hill, where in the very beginning there had been a Sabine settlement. Later it became a part of Romulus's Latin city, and Quirinus the god was fused with Romulus the god. Just who Quirinus was, and what he was, no one knows; but it is thought he was the embodiment of the Roman citizenship, the god of the assembly of Roman men. His special priest, the *flamen Quirinalis,* was one of the three major *flamines,* and he had a festival of his own, the Quirinalia. In front of his temple there grew two myrtle trees, one representing the patricians, the other the plebeians.

Quirites   Roman citizens of civilian status. What we do not know is whether the word "Quirites" also implied that the citizens in question had never served as soldiers in Rome's armies; certain remarks of Caesar the Dictator might lead one to believe that this was so, for he addressed his mutinous soldiers as Quirites, and by doing so heaped such scorn upon them that they immediately pleaded for his pardon. However, much had changed between the time of Gaius Marius and the time of Caesar the Dictator. I have chosen to believe that at the time of Gaius Marius, the word "Quirites" was an honorable one.

Regia   The ancient little building in the Forum Romanum, oddly shaped and oriented toward the north, that served as the offices of the Pontifex Maximus and the headquarters of the College of Pontifices. It was an inaugurated temple, and contained shrines or altars or artifacts of some of Rome's oldest and most numinous gods—Opsiconsiva, Vesta, Mars of the sacred shields and spears (see *numen*). Within the Regia the Pontifex Maximus kept his archives. It was *never* his residence, though tradition had it that the Regia had been the home of Numa Pompilius, the second King of Rome.

Remus   Romulus's twin. Having assisted Romulus in founding his Palatine settlement and helped in the building of its walls, Remus was then killed by Romulus for jumping over the walls— apparently some kind of sacrilege.

repetundae Extortion. Until the time of Gaius Gracchus, it was not standard practice to prosecute provincial governors who used their power to enrich themselves; one or two special courts or commissions had been set up to prosecute particular governors, but that was all. These early special courts or *quaestiones* were staffed entirely by senators, and quickly became a joke, because senatorial judges and juries would not convict their fellow senators the governors. Then in 122 B.C. Manius Acilius Glabrio, boon companion of Gaius Gracchus, passed a *lex Acilia* providing a permanent extortion court staffed by knights, and empanelled 450 named knights as a pool from which the juries were to be drawn. In 106 B.C. Quintus Servilius Caepio returned *all* courts, including the extortion court, to the Senate. Then in 101 B.C. Gaius Servilius Glaucia gave the extortion court back to the knights, with many innovative refinements which were to become standard practice in every kind of court. The cases we hear of were all concerning governors of provinces enriching themselves, but it would seem that after the *lex Acilia* of 122 B.C., the extortion court was also empowered to try any case of illegal enrichment. There were rewards offered to citizen informants, and noncitizens who successfully brought a prosecution before the court were rewarded with the citizenship.

Republic The word was originally two words, *res publica*—that is, the thing which constitutes the people as a whole—that is, its government. We use the word "republic" today to mean an elected government which does not acknowledge any monarch its superior, but it is doubtful that the Romans in establishing their Republic thought of it in quite that way, despite the fact that they founded their Republic as an alternative to monarchy.

Rex Sacrorum During the Republic, he was the second-ranking *pontifex* in the pontifical hierarchy. He had to be a patrician, and he was hedged around with as many taboos as the *flamen Dialis*.

Rhea Silvia The daughter of Numitor, King of Alba Longa in the days before Rome existed. Numitor was deposed by his younger brother Amulius, and Rhea Silvia was made a Vestal Virgin so that she could never have children. But the god Mars saw her, and ravished her. When Amulius found out she was pregnant he locked her up until her confinement, then put the twin boys she bore into a basket made of rushes and threw the basket into the Tiber, at the time in flood. The basket washed ashore at the foot of the Ficus Ruminalis, the sacred fig tree near the later Steps of Cacus leading to the Palatine. The twins were found by a she-wolf, which suckled them in her cave nearby. They were rescued by Faustulus and his wife Acca Larentia, who raised them to manhood. The twins—Romulus and Remus, of course—then killed Amulius and re-established Numitor on the throne of Alba Longa. The other name of Rhea Silvia was— Julia.

Rhenus River   The modern Rhine. In ancient times, it was the natural boundary between Germania and its German tribes, and Gallia and its Gallic tribes. So wide and deep and strong was it that it was considered impossible to bridge.

rhetoric   The art of oratory, which both the Greeks and the Romans turned into something very close to a science. A proper orator spoke according to carefully laid-out rules and conventions which extended far beyond mere words; body movements and gestures were an intrinsic part of it. In the early and middle Republic, Greek teachers of rhetoric were despised, and sometimes even outlawed from Rome; Cato the Censor was an avowed enemy of the Greek rhetor. However, the Graecophilia of the Scipionic Circle and other highly educated Roman noblemen of the time broke down much of this Latin opposition, so that by the time of the Brothers Gracchi, most young Roman noblemen were taught by Greek rhetors; it was the Latin rhetors who then fell into disfavor. There were different styles of rhetoric—Lucius Licinius Crassus Orator favored the Asianic style, more florid and dramatic than the Attic. It must be remembered that the audience which gathered to listen to public oration, be it concerned with politics or the law courts, was composed of connoisseurs of rhetoric; they watched and listened in a spirit of marked criticism, for they knew all the rules and the techniques at first hand, and were not easy to please.

Rhodanus River The modern Rhone. Its large and fertile valley, inhabited by Celtic tribes of Gauls, came early under Roman influence; after the campaigns of Gnaeus Domitius Ahenobarbus in 122 and 121 B.C., the Rhone Valley up as far as the lands of the Aedui and Ambarri became a part of the Roman province of Transalpine Gaul—that is, of Gaul-across-the-Alps.

Ria Plutarch (writing in Greek) says that the name of Quintus Sertorius's mother was Rhea, but this is not a Latin gentilicial name. However, even today "Ria" is a diminutive of "Maria," which is indeed a Latin gentilicial name. It was the family name of Gaius Marius. The attachment of Quintus Sertorius to Gaius Marius from his earliest days in military service, right through to the days when Marius's conduct had become repugnant even to his loyalest adherents, makes me wonder about that enigmatic maternal name; Sertorius, says Plutarch also, was very devoted to his mother. Why then should not Sertorius's mother have been a Maria called Ria for short, and a blood relative of Gaius Marius's? To have her so answers many questions. As part of my novelist's license, I have taken the standpoint that Sertorius's mother was indeed a blood relative of Gaius Marius's. However, this is pure speculation; of proof positive, there is absolutely none.

Roma The Latin name of Rome.

Romulus The more dominant of the twins Romulus and Remus (see Remus, Rhea Silvia). After he built his Palatine town and killed his brother, Romulus gathered male citizens by establishing an asylum in the depression between the two humps of the Capitoline Mount, and there collecting refugees who seem largely to have been criminals. Female citizens he found harder to get, so he invited all the inhabitants of the Sabine settlement on the Quirinal to a feast, overpowered the Sabine men, and kidnapped the Sabine women. As a result, the Sabine settlement on the Quirinal became a part of Romulus's expanding city, and the damp, gloomy, marshy depression between the Palatine and the northeastern hills became an area of neutral ground where markets were established and public meetings held; its name eventually became the Forum Romanum. Romulus himself ruled for a long time. Then one day he went hunting in the Goat Swamps of the Campus Martius, and was caught in a terrible storm; when he didn't come home, it was believed that he had been taken by the gods, and made immortal.

rostra   The plural form of "rostrum," which was a ship's bronze or reinforced oaken beak. This fierce object jutted well forward of the bows just below the level of the water, and was used to hole an enemy ship in the maneuver called ramming. When the consul Gaius Maenius in 338 B.C. attacked the Volscian fleet in Antium harbor, he defeated it so successfully that he broke the power of the Volsci. To mark the completeness of his victory, he removed the beaks of the ships he had captured, and fixed them to the Forum wall of the speaker's platform tucked into the well of the Comitia. Even afterward, the speaker's platform was known as the rostra—the ship's beaks.

Rusicade   The port in closest proximity to the city of Cirta, in Numidia.

Sabatia   Also called Vada Sabatia. Modern Savona. A port on the Ligurian coast.

Sabines, Sabini   The Oscan-speaking people who lived to the north and east of Rome, from the outskirts of the city to the crest of the Apennines, more or less around the area of the ancient salt route to the Adriatic, the Via Salaria. Sabines were famous for their integrity, bravery, and independence. The chief Sabine towns were Reate, Nersia, and Amiternum.

Sabis River   The modern Sambre, in France.

sacrosanct   The tribunes of the plebs possessed *sacrosanctitas*—that is to say, their persons were inviolable; they could not be physically hindered or obstructed in the execution of their duty. This asset was given them by their masters, the Plebs, who swore an oath to uphold the inviolability of their special magistrates, the tribunes of the plebs.

saepta   "The sheepfold." In Republican times, this was simply an open area on the Campus Martius not far from the Via Lata, and in proximity to the Villa Publica; it possessed no permanent buildings, but was nonetheless the place where the Centuriate Assembly or Comitia Centuriata met. As Centuriate Assemblies normally called for a voting procedure, the *saepta* was divided up for the occasion by temporary fences so that the Five Classes could vote in their centuries.

sagum The soldier's heavy-weather cape. It was made out of greasy wool to render it as waterproof as possible, cut on the full circle with a hole in its middle for the head to poke through, and came well down the body for maximum protection. The best kind of *sagum* came from Liguria, where the wool was extremely suitable.

Salassi A tribe of Celts who occupied the great alpine valley of the Duria Major River, to the north and west of Mediolanum. Roman incursions into the Vale of the Salassi during the second century B.C. caused the people of the tribe to retreat, but to harden in their resistance to Rome. What attracted Roman attention was alluvial gold, found in large quantities in the bed of the Duria Major not far from Eporedia. However, those prospectors who ventured higher up the valley ran a palpable risk of Salassi attack. Gaius Marius strengthened the Roman presence by settling some of his soldier veterans at Eporedia, and slowly the Salassi withdrew into the high Alps, where they made it very difficult for the Romans to use the two passes they guarded.

saltatrix tonsa Literally, "barbered dancing girl." In other words, a male homosexual who dressed as a woman and sold his sexual favors.

Samnites, Samnium The Oscan-speaking people who occupied the territory between Latium, Campania, Apulia, and Picenum. Most of Samnium was ruggedly mountainous and not particularly fertile; its towns tended to be poor and small, and numbered among them Bovianum, Caieta, and Aeclanum. Aesernia and Beneventum, the two biggest towns, were Latin Rights colonies implanted by Rome. Throughout their history, the Samnites were implacable enemies of Rome, and several times during the early and middle Republic inflicted crushing defeats upon Roman armies. However, they had neither the manpower nor the financial resources to throw off the Roman yoke permanently. About 180 B.C., the Samnites were sufficiently sapped to be incapable of refusing new settlers in the persons of Ligurians removed from Liguria by Rome to lessen Roman troubles in the northwest. At the time it seemed to Rome a good move; but the new settlers were fully absorbed into the Samnite nation, and harbored no more love for Rome than did their hosts, the Samnites. Thus did Samnite resistance grow anew.

Sardinia One of Rome's earliest two provinces. A large island in the Tuscan (Tyrrhenian) Sea to the west of peninsular Italy, Sardinia was mountainous yet fertile, and grew excellent wheat. Carthage had controlled it; Rome inherited it, with Corsica, from Carthage. Riddled with bandits and never properly subjugated during the Republic, it became the least esteemed of all Rome's territorial possessions. The Romans loathed Sardinians, apostrophizing them as inveterate thieves, rogues, and oafs.

satrap The title given by the Persian kings to their provincial or territorial governors. Alexander the Great seized upon the term and employed it, as did the later Arsacid kings of Parthia. The region ruled by the satrap was called a satrapy.

Savus River The modern Sava, in Yugoslavia.

Scipio (1) (Scipio Africanus) Publius Cornelius Scipio Africanus was born in 236 B.C. and died around the end of 184 B.C. As a very young man he distinguished himself at the battles of Ticinus and Cannae, and at the age of twenty-six, still a private citizen, he was invested with proconsular imperium by the People rather than the Senate, and dispatched to fight the Carthaginians in Spain. Here for five years he did brilliantly, defeated every Carthaginian army, and won for Rome its two Spanish provinces. Despite bitter senatorial opposition, he succeeded when consul in 205 B.C. (at the early age of thirty-one) in gaining permission to invade Africa, which he did via Sicily. Both Sicily and Africa eventually fell, and Scipio was invited to assume the *cognomen* Africanus. He was elected censor and appointed Princeps Senatus in 199 B.C., and was consul again in 194 B.C. As farsighted as he was brilliant, Scipio Africanus warned Rome that Antiochus the Great would invade Greece; when it happened, he became his younger brother Lucius's legate, and accompanied the Roman army to the war against Antiochus. But at some time he had incurred the enmity of Cato the Censor, who embarked upon a persecution of all the Cornelii Scipiones, particularly Africanus and his brother. It would appear that Cato the Censor emerged the victor, for Lucius (his *cognomen* was Asiagenus) was stripped of his knight's status in 184 B.C., and Africanus died at the end of that year. Scipio Africanus was married to Aemilia Paulla, the sister of the conqueror of Macedonia. He had two sons, neither of whom distinguished himself, and two daughters; the older daughter became the wife of her cousin Publius Cornelius Scipio Nasica Corculum, and the younger Cornelia the Mother of the Gracchi.

Scipio (2) (Scipio Aemilianus)   Publius Cornelius Scipio Aemilianus Africanus Numantinus was born in 185 B.C. He was not a Cornelian of the Scipio branch, but the son of the conqueror of Macedonia, Lucius Aemilius Paullus, who gave him in adoption to the elder son of Scipio Africanus. His brother was given to the Fabii Maximi for adoption, as Paullus had four sons; the tragedy is that after Paullus gave up these two, his younger sons died within days of each other in 167 B.C., thus leaving him without heirs. Scipio Aemilianus's mother was a Papiria, and his wife was the surviving daughter of Cornelia the Mother of the Gracchi, Sempronia the sister of the Brothers Gracchi, and his own close blood cousin.

After a distinguished military career during the Third Punic War in 149 and 148 B.C., Scipio Aemilianus was elected consul in 147 B.C., though not old enough for the position, and bitterly opposed by many in the House. Sent to Africa to take charge of the Third Punic War, he displayed that relentless and painstaking thoroughness which was thereafter always to distinguish his career; he built a mole to close the harbor of Carthage, and blockaded the city. It fell in 146 B.C., after which he pulled it apart stone by stone. However, modern scholars discount the story that he ploughed salt into the soil to make sure Carthage never rose again, though the Romans themselves believed it. In 142 B.C. he was an ineffectual censor (thanks to an inimical colleague); in 140 and 139 B.C. he took ship for the East, accompanied by his two Greek friends, the historian Polybius and the philosopher Panaetius. In 134 B.C. he was elected consul a second time, and commissioned to deal with the town of Numantia in Nearer Spain; this small place had defied and defeated a whole series of Roman armies and generals over a period spanning fifty years. When Scipio Aemilianus came to deal with it, Numantia lasted eight months. After it fell, he destroyed it down to the last stone and beam, and executed or deported its four thousand citizens.

News from Rome had informed him that his brother-in-law Tiberius Gracchus was undermining the *mos maiorum*—the established order of things—and he encouraged Gracchus's enemies, especially their mutual cousin Scipio Nasica. Though Tiberius Gracchus was already dead when he returned to Rome in 132 B.C., he was commonly held responsible. Then in 129 B.C., aged forty-five, he died so suddenly and unexpectedly that it was ever afterward rumored he had been murdered. The principal suspect was his wife, Sempronia, Gracchus's sister, who loathed her husband.

By nature, Scipio Aemilianus was a curious mixture. A great intellectual with an abiding love for things Greek, he stood at the center of a group of men who patronized and encouraged the likes of Polybius, Panaetius, and the Latin playwright Terence. As a friend, he was everything a friend should be; as an enemy, he was cruel, cold-blooded, and utterly ruthless. A genius at organization, he yet could blunder as badly as he did in his opposition to Tiberius Gracchus; and though he was an extremely cultured and witty man of pronounced good taste, he was also morally and ethically ossified.

Scordisci A tribal confederation of Celts admixed with Illyrians and Thracians, the Scordisci lived in Moesia, between the valley of the Danubius and the highlands bordering Macedonia.

Powerful and warlike, they plagued Roman Macedonia implacably, and made life difficult for many a Roman governor.

Scylla   One half of the awful dilemma; the other half was Charybdis (see that entry).

Senate   Properly, Senatus. The Romans themselves believed that it was Romulus who had founded the Senate by giving it a hundred patrician members, but it is more likely to have been a foundation of the time of the less shadowy kings of Rome. When the Republic began, the Senate was retained as a senior advisory council, now three hundred in number, but still entirely composed of patricians. However, a few scant years saw plebeians also admitted as senators, though it took the plebeians somewhat longer to secure the right to occupy the senior magistracies.

Because of the Senate's antiquity, legal definition of its powers, rights, and duties was gradual and at best only partial. Membership was for life, which predisposed it to the oligarchy it very quickly became; throughout its history, its members fought strenuously to preserve their—as they saw it—natural pre-eminence. Under the Republic, membership was given (and could be taken away) by the censors. By the time of Gaius Marius, it had become custom to demand a property qualification of at least one million sesterces, though during the entire Republic this was never a formal law; like much else, it simply *was*.

Senators alone were entitled to wear a tunic bearing the *latus clavus* or broad purple stripe; they also wore closed shoes of maroon leather and a ring (originally of iron, it came to be gold). Meetings of the Senate had to be held in places which had been properly inaugurated, for the Senate did not always meet in its own House, the Curia Hostilia. The ceremonies and meeting of New Year's Day, for example, were held in the temple of Jupiter Optimus Maximus, while meetings to discuss war were held in the temple of Bellona, outside the *pomerium*.

There was a rigid hierarchy among those allowed to speak in senatorial meetings, with the Princeps Senatus at the top of the list in Gaius Marius's day; patricians always preceded plebeians of precisely the same status otherwise. Not all senators by any means were allowed to speak. The *senatores pedarii* (I have used the British parliamentary term "backbenchers" to describe them, as they sat behind those who did speak) were permitted only to vote, not speak. No restriction was placed upon a man's oration in terms of length of time or germane content; hence the popularity of the technique now called filibustering—talking a motion out. Sessions could go on only between sunrise and sunset, and could not continue if the Comitia went into session, though meetings could be convoked on comitial days of the calendar if no Comitia met. If the issue was unimportant or the response completely unanimous, voting could be by voice or a show of hands, but formal voting was by division of the House. An advisory rather than a legislative body, the Senate issued its *consulta* or decrees as requests to the various Assemblies. If the issue was serious, a quorum had to be present before a vote could be taken, though we do not know the precise number constituting a quorum in Gaius Marius's day; perhaps a quarter? Certainly most meetings were not heavily attended, as there was no rule which said a senator had to attend meetings on a regular basis.

In certain areas it had become tradition for the Senate to reign supreme, despite its lack of legislating power; this was true of the *fiscus,* for the Senate controlled the Treasury, true of foreign affairs, and true of war. In civil emergencies, after the time of Gaius Gracchus the Senate could override all other bodies of government by passing the *Senatus Consultum de republica defendenda*—its "ultimate decree."

Sequana River   The modern Seine, in France.

Servian Walls   Murus Servii Tullii or Tulli. The Romans believed that the walls enclosing the Republican city had been erected in the time of King Servius Tullius. However, evidence suggests that these walls were not actually built until after the Gauls under Brennus (1) sacked Rome in 390 B.C.

Servius Tullius   Or Servius Tullus. The sixth King of Rome, and the only King of Rome who was a Latin, if not a Roman. Though thought to have built the Servian Walls (which he didn't), he probably did build the Agger, the great double rampart of the

Campus Esquilinus. A lawmaker and an enlightened king, he negotiated a treaty between Rome and the Latin League which was still displayed carefully in the temple of Diana at the end of the Republic. His death was ever after a scandal, for his own daughter, Tullia, conspired with her lover, Tarquinius Superbus, to murder first her husband and then her father, Servius Tullius. He was cut down in a street off the Clivus Orbius, and Tullia then drove her carriage back and forth over her father's body.

sestertius, sesterces   The commonest of Roman coins, the sestertius was the unit of Roman accounting, hence its prominence in Latin writings of Republican date. Its name derives from *semis tertius,* meaning two and a half (*as*es). In Latin writing, it was abbreviated as *HS.* A small silver coin, it was worth one quarter of a denarius. I have kept to the strict Latin when referring to this coin in the singular, but in the plural (more frequently mentioned by far) I have used the Anglicized "sesterces."

Sibyl, Sibylline Books   Properly, Sibylla. An oracle. The Sibyl issued her prognostications in an ecstatic frenzy, as did most oracular priestesses. The most famous Sibyl lived in a cave at Cumae, on the Campanian coast. The Roman State possessed a series of written prophecies called the Sibylline Books, acquired, it was believed, by King Tarquinius Priscus; originally written on palm leaves (transferred later to paper), they were in Greek. At the time of Gaius Marius, these Sibylline Books were so revered that they were in the care of a special college of ten minor priests, the *decemviri sacris faciundis,* and in crises were solemnly consulted to see if there was a prophecy which fitted the situation.

Silanus, Silenus   The satyrlike face—ugly, leering, and flatly pug-nosed—which spewed water into Rome's public fountains as set up in stone by Cato the Censor.

sinus   A pronounced curve or fold. The term was used in many different ways, but for the purposes of this book, two meanings are used. One refers to the geographical feature we call a gulf—Sinus Arabicus (the Red Sea), Sinus Ligusticus (the Gulf of Genoa), Sinus Gallicus (the Gulf of Lions). The second refers to the folds of the toga as it emerged from under the right arm and was swept up over the left shoulder—the togate Roman's pocket.

Skeptic An adherent of the school of philosophy founded by Pyrrhon and his pupil Timon, and based upon the town of Scepsis in the Troad, hence the name. Skeptics did not admit that dogma existed, and believed that no man would ever master knowledge. In consequence, they disbelieved everything.

smaragdus Emerald. It is debatable whether the stone the ancients called emerald was our emerald, though those stones from Scythia may have been; the stones mined on islands in the Red Sea and a part of the private entitlements of the Ptolemaic kings of Egypt were definitely beryl.

Smyrna One of the greatest of the port cities on the Aegean coast of Asia Minor. It lay near the mouth of the river Hermus. Originally an Ionian Greek colony, it suffered an extinction of nearly three hundred years, from the sixth to the third century B.C. When re-established by Alexander the Great, it never looked back. Its chief business was money, but it was also a center for learning.

Sosius A name associated with the book trade in Rome. Two brothers named Sosius published during the principate of Augustus. I have taken the name and extrapolated it backward in time; Roman businesses were very often family businesses, and the book trade in Rome was already flourishing in Marius's day. Therefore, why not a Sosius in Marius's day?

spelt A kind of flour, very fine and soft and white, not suitable for making bread, but excellent for making cakes. It was ground from the variety of wheat now known as *Triticum spelta*.

steel The term "Iron Age" is rather misleading, for iron in itself is not a very usable metal. It only replaced bronze when ancient smiths discovered ways of steeling it; from then on, it was the metal of choice for tools, weapons, and other apparatus requiring a combination of hardness, durability, and capacity to take an edge or a point. Aristotle and Theophrastus, both living in the Greece of the fourth century B.C., talk about "steel," not "iron." However, the whole process of working iron into a usable metal evolved in total ignorance of the chemistry and metallurgy underlying it. The main ore utilized to extract iron was haematite; pyrites was little used because of the extreme toxicity of its sulphuric by-products. Strabo and Pliny the Elder both describe the method of roasting (oxidation) the ore in a hearth-type furnace; but the shaft furnace (reduction) was more efficient, could smelt larger quantities of ore, and was the method of choice. Most smelting yards used both hearth and shaft furnaces, and produced slag-contaminated "blooms" which were called sows. These sows were then reheated to above melting point, and compelled to take up additional carbon from the charcoal by hammering (forging); this also drove out much of the contaminating slag, though ancient steels were never entirely free of it. Roman smiths were fully conversant with the techniques of annealing, quenching, tempering, and cementation (this last forced more carbon into the iron). Each of these procedures changed the characteristics of the basic carbon steel in a different way, so that steels suitable for various purposes were made—razors, sword blades, knives, axes, saws, wood chisels, cold chisels, nails, spikes, etc. So precious were the steels suitable for cutting edges that a thin piece of edge steel was welded (the Romans knew two methods of welding: pressure welding and fusion welding) onto a cheaper base. However, the Roman sword blade was made entirely of steel, taking a cruelly sharp edge; it was produced by tempering at about 280°C. (Those readers who are old enough may remember carving knives or machetes made of nonstainless carbon steel, and remember with longing in our stainless-steel age how viciously sharp they were, and how easy they were to keep viciously sharp—these blades were very similar indeed to Roman ones.) Tongs, anvils, hammers, bellows, crucibles, fire bricks, and the other tools in trade of a smith were known and universally used. Many of the ancient theories were quite wrong: it was thought, for instance, that the nature of the liquid used in quenching affected the quenching; and no one understood that the real reason why the iron mined in Noricum produced such superb steel lay in the fact that it contained a small amount of manganese uncontaminated by phosphorus, arsenic, or sulphur, and so was the raw material of manganese steel.

stibium   A black antimony-based powder, soluble in water, used to paint or dye eyebrows and eyelashes, and to draw a line around the eyes.

Stoic   An adherent of the school of philosophy founded by the Phoenician Cypriot Zeno, in the third century B.C. Stoicism as a philosophical system of thought particularly appealed to the Romans. The basic tenet was concerned with nothing beyond virtue (strength of character) and its opposite, weakness of character. Virtue was the only good, weakness of character the only evil. Money, pain, death, and the other things which plague Man were not considered important, for the virtuous man is an essentially good man, and therefore by definition must be a happy and contented man, even if impoverished, in perpetual pain, and under sentence of death. As with everything Greek they espoused, the Romans did not so much modify this philosophy as evade its unpalatable concomitants by some very nice—if specious—reasoning. Brutus is an example.

Subura   The poorest and most densely populated part of the city of Rome. It lay to the east of the Forum Romanum, in the declivity between the Oppian spur of the Esquiline Mount, and the Viminal Hill. Its very long main street had three different names: at the bottom, where it became contiguous with the Argiletum, it was the Fauces Suburae; the next section was the Subura Major; and the final section, which scrambled up the steep flank of the Esquiline proper, was the Clivus Suburanus. The Subura Minor and the Vicus Patricii branched off the Subura Major in the direction of the Viminal Hill. The Subura was an area composed entirely of insulae, and contained only one prominent landmark, the Turris Mamilia, apparently some kind of tower. Its people were notoriously polyglot and independent of mind; many Jews lived in the Subura, for instance.

Suburana   The name of one of the four urban tribes, and one of the two into which newly enfranchised freedmen were placed (the other was the *tribus* Esquilina). In Republican times, this made Suburana one of the two largest in number of members of all the thirty-five tribes.

suffect consul   *Consul suffectus.* When an elected consul died in office, or was otherwise rendered incapable of conducting his duties, the Senate appointed a substitute called a *suffectus.* The *suffectus* was not elected. Sometimes the Senate would appoint a *suffectus* even when the consular year was almost over; at other times no substitute would be appointed even when the consular year was far from over. These discrepancies reflected the mood within the House at the particular time. The name of the *suffectus* was engraved upon the list of Rome's consuls, and he was afterward entitled to call himself a consular.

sumptuary law   A *lex sumptuaria.* This was a law which sought to regulate the amount of luxurious (that is, expensive) goods and/or foodstuffs a Roman might buy or have in his house, no matter how wealthy he was. During the Republic, sumptuary laws were often leveled at women, forbidding them to wear more than a specified amount of jewelry, or ride in litters or carriages within the Servian Walls; as several censors found out, women so legislated against were inclined to be a nasty force to be reckoned with.

suovetaurilia   This was a special sacrifice consisting of a pig (*su*), a sheep (*ove*), and an ox or bull (*taur*). It was offered on critical occasions to certain gods: Jupiter Optimus Maximus was one, Mars another, and others whose identities are not known. The ceremony surrounding the *suovetaurilia* called for the sacrificial victims to be led in a solemn procession before being killed. Besides the special occasions, there were two regular occasions on which a *suovetaurilia* was offered: the first occurred in late May, when the land was purified by the twelve minor priests called the Arval Brethren; the second occurred every five years, when the censors set up their booth on the Campus Martius and prepared to take the full census of every Roman citizen.

Syracuse   The capital and largest city of Sicily.

tablinum   The Latin term for the room kept as the exclusive domain of the *paterfamilias;* quite often his sleeping cubicle and a smaller cubicle used as a wardrobe or storage area opened off it. I have called it the study.

talent   A unit of weight defined as the load a man could carry. Bullion and very large sums of money were expressed in talents, but the term was not confined to money and precious metals. In modern terms the talent weighed about 50 to 55 pounds (25 kg). There is an imperial measure of our time called the quarter; it weighs 56 pounds.

Tanais River   The modern Don, in the USSR.

Taprobane   Modern Sri Lanka (Ceylon). The ancients knew it was a pear-shaped, very large island mass off the southeastern tip of India. It was a source of valuable spices like pepper, and of ocean pearls.

Tarentum   Modern Taranto. It lies on the Italian foot, and was founded as a Greek colony by the Spartans, about 700 B.C. The original terminus of the Via Appia, it lost importance once the road was extended to Brundisium, though it was always the port of choice for travelers to Patrae and southern Greece.

Tarpeian Rock   Its precise location is still debated, but it is known to have been quite visible from the lower Forum Romanum, and presumably was an overhang at the top of the Capitoline cliffs. Since the drop was not much more than eighty feet, the rock itself must have been located directly above some sort of jagged outcrop. It was the traditional place of execution for Roman citizen traitors and murderers, who were thrown from it, or perhaps forced to jump off it. I have located it on a line from the temple of Ops.

Tarquinius Priscus   Tarquinius the Old, the fifth King of Rome. Reputedly a Greek who fetched up in Caere, he became an Etruscan, and then emigrated to Rome. He is said to have drained the Forum Romanum, built many of the sewers, commenced building the temple of Jupiter Optimus Maximus, and built the Circus Maximus. He was murdered by the two sons of Ancus Marcius when they plotted to usurp the throne; Priscus's wife foiled the coup, though she could not avert the murder, and secured the throne for the sixth king, Servius Tullius or Tullus.

Tarquinius Superbus   Tarquin the Proud, the seventh and last King of Rome. He finished and dedicated the temple of Jupiter Optimus Maximus, but had more of a reputation as a warmaker than a builder. His accession to the throne was a lurid tale of murder and a woman (Tullia, daughter of King Servius Tullius), and his deposition was much the same kind of tale. An uprising of patricians led by Lucius Junius Brutus led to his flight from Rome, and the establishment of the Republic. Tarquin the Proud sought refuge with several local anti-Roman leaders in turn, and eventually died at Cumae. A curious story is told, of how Tarquin the Proud finished his war against the city of Gabii: when asked what he wanted done with Gabii's prominent men he said not a word; instead, he went into his garden, drew his sword, and lopped the head off every poppy taller than the rest; his son in Gabii interpreted the message correctly, and beheaded every Gabian man of outstanding merit. Few people today know the origins of the so-called Tall Poppy Syndrome, though the phrase is used metaphorically to describe the character assassination of men and women of superior ability or prominence.

Tarracina   Modern Terracina, in Italy.

Tarsus   The largest and most important city in Cilicia, in southeastern Anatolia.

Tartarus   That part of the underworld reserved for the punishment of the great sinners of the ancient mortal world: Sisyphus perpetually rolled his boulder uphill, Ixion wobbled around tied to his wheel, and Tantalus stretched in vain for food and drink. However, these were all men who for one reason or another had acquired immortality from the gods, and so could not be punished in the normal way, by death. Despite the deep discussions of men like Pythagoras, Plato, and Aristotle, the Greeks and Romans did not have a true concept of the immortal soul. Death meant the extinction of the vital principle; all which survived death was a shade, a mindless and insubstantial replica of the dead person. And to the great philosophers, the soul was—female! A butterflyish creature.

tata   The affectionate Latin diminutive of "father"—akin to our "daddy."

Taurasia   Modern Turin. The name seen on maps of ancient Italy is Augusta Taurinorum, but clearly this is the name bestowed on the city during the principate of Augustus. After considerable research, I came upon the name Taurasia, apparently the pre-Augustan city.

Taurisci The Celtic confederation of tribes which inhabited Noricum, the mountainous regions of the modern eastern Tyrol and the Yugoslavian Alps.

Tergeste Modern Trieste.

Teutones The confederation of Germanic peoples who had originally lived at the base of the peninsula called the Cimbrian Chersonnese, and who embarked upon a long migratory trek about 120 B.C. together with the Cimbri. The Teutones as a people perished at Aquae Sextiae in 102 B.C.

theaters In Republican Rome, theaters were forbidden as permanent fixtures. So they were made out of wood, and erected before each set of games incorporating theatrical performances. During the early years of the Republic, theater was felt to be morally degrading, a corrupting force, and this attitude persisted with only slight relaxation until the time of Pompey. Women were forbidden to sit with men. Public pressure, particularly from the lowly (who adored farces and mimes), had obliged the magistrates and Senate to condone theatrical performances; that the theaters were temporary was their protest. These wooden theaters were amphitheatrical in construction, and had proper stages and *scenae,* including wings, and concealed entrances and exits for the actors; the *scenae* (backdrops) were as high as the top tier of the *cavea* (auditorium). At the end of each set of games, the theaters were dismantled. Presumably the materials from which they had been made were auctioned off, and the money received put into a permanent theater-building fund (like other ancient cities, Rome was not well equipped with buildings large enough to store such items as dismantled wooden theaters holding up to ten thousand people).

Thermopylae The coastal pass between Thessaly and central Greece. The road was flanked by the Aegean Sea on one side, and cliffs on the other. However, it was by no means an ideal spot to defend, for the mountains above it contained routes whereby an army holding it could be outflanked. The most famous of these routes was the path called Anopaea, and the most famous defense of the pass was that of Leonidas of Sparta.

Thessaly Northern Greece; on the west it was bordered by the rugged mountains of Epirus, and on the east by the Aegean Sea. In the days of Gaius Marius, it was administered as a part of the Roman province of Macedonia.

Thrace Thracia. Loosely, that part of Balkan Europe between the west side of the Hellespont and a line just east of Philippi; it had coasts on both the Aegean Sea and the Euxine Sea, and extended north into Sarmatia. The Romans considered its western boundary as the river Nestus. Thrace never really got itself organized, and remained until Roman occupation a place of partially allied Germano-Illyrian-Celtic tribes long enough settled in the area to warrant the name Thracian. Both the Greeks and the Romans considered the Thracians utterly barbaric. After the wars of the Attalid succession in Asia Minor were settled about 129 B.C., the Aegean strip of Thrace was governed as a part of Macedonia. For Rome had built the Via Egnatia, the great highway between the Adriatic and the Hellespont, and needed to protect this vital land route, the quickest way to get an army from Italy to Asia Minor. Aenus (a port city at the mouth of the river Hebrus) and Abdera (a port city to the east of the river Nestus) were the two most important settlements on the Aegean; however, Thrace's largest city by far was the old Greek colony of Byzantium, on the Thracian Bosporus.

Tiber, Tiberis The city of Rome's own river. It flowed from the high Apennines beyond Arretium down to the Tuscan (Tyrrhenian) Sea at Ostia. Rome was situated on the Tiber's northeastern bank. The river was allegedly navigable as far up as Narnia, but in actual fact, its very swift current made upstream sailing difficult. Floods were frequent and sometimes disastrous, especially for Rome.

Tibur Modern Tivoli. In Republican times it was a small settlement on the Anio River where that stream tumbles abruptly from the mountains to the Tiber plains. In Gaius Marius's day Tibur did not have the full Roman citizenship.

Tiddlypuss, Lucius I needed a joke name of the kind people in all places at all times have used when they wanted to refer to a faceless yet representative person. In the U.S.A. it would be "Joe Blow," in the U.K. "Fred Bloggs," in reference to an aristocrat "Lord Muck of Dunghill Hall," and so forth. As I am writing in English for a largely non-Latin-reading audience, it was not possible to choose a properly Latin name to fill this function. I coined "Lucius Tiddlypuss" because it looks and sounds patently ridiculous, because it ends in "uss," and because of a mountain. This mountain was named in a Latin distortion after a villa which lay on its flanks and belonged to Augustus's infamous freedman, Publius Vedius Pollio. The villa's name, a Greek one, was Pausilypon, but the Latin name of the mountain was Pausilypus—a clear indication that Publius Vedius Pollio was loathed, for *pus* then meant exactly the same as English "pus" does now. Speakers of Latin punned constantly, we know. And that's how Lucius Tiddlypuss came to be.

Tigurini A confederation of Celtic tribes which occupied lands in modern Switzerland adjacent to the confederation of tribes called the Helvetii. In about the eighth year of the migration of the German Cimbri and Teutones, the Tigurini tacked themselves on in last place, allying themselves with the two other confederations which had also tacked themselves on—the Marcomanni and the Cherusci. Deputed in 102 B.C. to invade northern Italy on the eastern front, from Noricum across to Aquileia, the Tigurini-Marcomanni-Cherusci changed their minds when they heard about the defeat of the Teutones at Aquae Sextiae. They all returned to their original homelands instead, and so escaped the extinction which became the fate of the Teutones and the Cimbri.

Tingis Modern Tangier. The capital and principal royal seat of the Kingdom of Mauretania. It lay on the Oceanus Atlanticus, beyond the Pillars of Hercules.

Tingitanian ape The Barbary ape, a macaque, terrestrial and tailless. Monkeys and primates were not common in the ancient Mediterranean, but the macaque still found on modern Gibraltar was always present in North Africa.

toga   The garment only a full citizen of Rome was permitted to wear. Made of lightweight wool, it had a most peculiar shape (which is why the togate "Romans" in Hollywood movies never look right—Hollywood research, at least on ancient Rome, is poor). After exhaustive and brilliant experimentation, Dr. Lillian Wilson worked out a size and shape which produce a perfect-looking toga. A toga to fit a man 5 feet 9 inches (175 cm) tall and having a waist of 36 inches (89.5 cm) was about 15 feet (4.6 m) wide, and 7 feet 6 inches (2.25 m) long; the length measurement is draped on the height axis of the man, and the much larger width measurement is wrapped about him. However, the shape was *not* a simple rectangle. It looked like this:

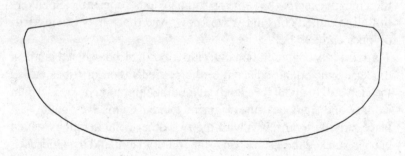

Unless the shape is cut as illustrated, the toga will absolutely refuse to drape the way it does on the togate men of the ancient statues. The Republican toga of Gaius Marius's day was very large (the toga varied considerably in size between the time of the kings of Rome and A.D. 500, a period of a thousand years). One final observation about the toga resulted from my own experimentation: I proved rather conclusively that the togate Republican Roman could not possibly have worn under-drawers or a loincloth. The toga itself completely disqualified the left hand and arm from performing any task at groin level, as to do so would have resulted in collapse of the multiple folds carried on the left arm, and necessitated the toga's entire redraping. But when the toga is properly draped, the right hand can part it with astonishing ease, push up the hem of the tunic, and perform the act of urinating from a standing position—provided, that is, there are no under-drawers or loincloths to fiddle with! I mention this interesting fact only because it is still said in some modern textbooks that the Roman man did wear some sort of nether undergarment. Well, if he was wearing a toga, he couldn't have; Republican Roman morality would *never* have condoned a slave's being called upon to help in this extremely personal activity.

toga alba (or *pura*)   The plain white toga. It was probably more cream than stark white.

toga candida   The specially whitened toga worn by those seeking office when applying for registration as a candidate (our word "candidate" comes from the *toga candida*). The candidate also wore his *toga candida* as he went about Rome canvassing, and when present at the polls on election day. Its stark whiteness was achieved by bleaching the garment in the sun for many days, and then working finely powdered chalk through it.

toga picta   The all-purple toga of the triumphing general, lavishly embroidered (presumably in gold) with pictures of people and events. The kings of Rome had worn the *toga picta,* and so too did the statue of Jupiter Optimus Maximus in his temple on the Capitol.

toga praetexta   The purple-bordered toga of the curule magistrate; it was also worn by men who had been curule magistrates, and by children of both sexes.

toga pulla   This was the mourning toga, and was made of wool as close to black as was possible.

togate   The correct English-language term to describe a man clad in his toga.

toga trabea   Cicero's "particolored toga." It was the striped toga of the augur, and very likely the *pontifex* also. Like the *toga praetexta*, it had a purple border, but also was striped in alternate red and purple down its length.

toga virilis   The toga of manhood. It was actually the *toga alba*, or *toga pura*.

Tolosa   Modern Toulouse, in France. Situated on the river plain of the Garumna River, Tolosa was the capital of the Gallic confederation of tribes called the Volcae Tectosages.

torc, torque   A thick round necklace or collar, usually of pure gold. It didn't quite form a full circle, for it had a gap about an inch (25 mm) wide, worn at center front. No doubt it was there so that the torc could be put about the neck, then bent inward; it was probably never removed. The torc was a mark of the Gaul or Celt, though some Germans did wear it also. The ends of the torc at the gap were mostly finished in a highly decorative manner, with knobs, twists, swirls, or animal heads.

tribe, *Tribus.*   By the beginning of the Republic, *tribus* to a Roman was not an ethnic grouping of his people, but a political grouping of service only to the State. There were thirty-five tribes altogether; thirty-one of these were rural, only four urban. The sixteen really old tribes bore the names of the various patrician *gens,* indicating that the citizens who belonged to these tribes were either members of the patrician familes or had originally lived on land owned by the patrician families. During the early and middle Republic, when Roman-owned territory in the Italian Peninsula began to expand, tribes were added to accommodate the new citizens within the Roman body politic. Full Roman citizen colonies also became the nuclei of fresh tribes. The four urban tribes were supposed to have been founded by King Servius Tullius, though the time of their actual foundation is likely to have been somewhat later, during the early Republic. The last date of tribal creation was 241 B.C. Every member of a tribe was entitled to register one vote in a tribal Assembly, but this vote was not of itself significant. The votes were counted first in each tribe, then the tribe as a whole cast a single vote. Which meant that in no tribal Assembly could the huge number of citizens enrolled in the four urban tribes affect the outcome of a vote, for there were thirty-one rural tribes, and each one of the thirty-one rural tribes was entitled to register its single tribal vote—even if only two members of a tribe turned up to vote. Members of rural tribes were not disbarred from living within urban Rome; almost all senators and knights, for example, belonged to rural tribes.

tribune, *Tribunus.*   An official representing the interests of a certain part of the Roman body politic. The word originally referred to those men who represented the tribes (*tribus—tribunus*), but, as the Republic got into stride, came to mean an official representing various institutions not directly connected with the tribes per se.

tribune, military *Tribunus militum.*   Each of the middle officers in the chain of command of a Roman army was classified as a military tribune. The most senior was the elected tribune of the soldiers (see that entry). If the general was not also consul, and did not therefore have the consul's legions, an unelected military tribune might command his legions. Unelected military tribunes also served as commanders of the cavalry squadrons.

tribune of the plebs   This office came into being not long after the establishment of the Republic, when the Plebeian Order was at complete loggerheads with the patricians. Elected by the tribal body of plebeians formed as the Concilium Plebis, or Plebeian Assembly, the tribunes of the plebs took an oath to defend the lives and property of members of the Plebeian Order. By 450 B.C. there were ten tribunes of the plebs; by the time of Gaius Marius, these ten had proven themselves a thorn in the side of the Senate, rather than merely the patricians, even though they were by this automatically members of the Senate upon election. Because they were not elected by the Whole People (that is, by patricians as well as plebeians), they had no actual power under Rome's largely unwritten Constitution. Their power resided in the oath the Plebeian Order took to defend the sacrosanctity—the inviolability—of its elected representatives. It was perhaps due to the tribal organization of the Plebeian Assembly that these representatives were called tribunes. The power of a tribune of the plebs lay in his right to exercise a veto against almost any aspect of government: he could veto the actions of his fellow tribunes of the plebs, or any—or all—other magistrates; he could veto the holding of an election; he could veto the passing of a law or plebiscite; and he could veto decrees of the Senate, even in war and foreign affairs. Only a dictator (and perhaps an *interrex*) was above the tribunician veto. Within his own Plebeian Assembly, the tribune of the plebs was truly all-powerful: he could convoke the Assembly; he could call the discussion meeting known as a *contio;* he could promulgate plebiscites, and even exercise the death penalty if his right to proceed was blocked.

During the early and middle years of the Republic, tribunes of the plebs were not members of the Senate, even after the middle years saw them empowered to call meetings of the Senate. Then the *lex Atinia* of ca. 149 B.C. laid down that a man elected a tribune of the plebs was to be automatically a member of the Senate. This meant that the tribunate of the plebs became an alternative way to enter the Senate; until the *lex Atinia,* the censors had reigned supreme. However, though by the time of Gaius Marius the tribunate of the plebs was recognized as a true and proper magistracy, it was not given imperium, and the authority of the office did not extend beyond the first milestone.

Custom had it that a man served only one term as a tribune of the plebs, entering office on the tenth day of December, and leaving it on the following December's ninth day. But custom was not legally binding, as Gaius Gracchus proved when he sought and secured a second term as a tribune of the plebs. The real power of the office was vested in the veto, which meant that tribunician function was more often obstructive than innovative.

tribune of the soldiers Twenty-four young men, aged from about twenty-five to twenty-nine years, were elected each year by the Assembly of the People to serve with the consul's legions as *tribuni militum*, or military tribunes. Being elected by the Comitia Populi Tributa, the Whole People, these military tribunes were true and proper magistrates. They were assigned to the four legions of the consuls, six per legion, and served as overall commanders. When the consuls had more than four legions in the field, the tribunes of the soldiers were rationed out among however many legions the consuls had under arms.

tribune of the Treasury *Tribuni aerarii*. There is a great deal of mystery about what the *tribuni aerarii* actually did. Originally they seem to have been the army's paymasters (not a very onerous job under the conditions of the old, pre-Marian army), but certainly by the time that Gaius Marius reformed the army, the *tribuni aerarii* had nothing to do with it, for pay was distributed by quaestors. I have theorized that the *tribuni aerarii* were civil servants. Though the Senate and People of Rome frowned upon bureaucracy, and strenuously resisted the growth in numbers of public employees, once Rome's territorial possessions began to accumulate, one branch of the SPQR at least demanded more and more bureaucrats. This branch was the Treasury (the *aerarium*). By the time of Gaius Marius there must have been a fairly large number of senior civil servants administering the many departments and duties of the Treasury (and this increased dramatically in the years after Gaius Marius). Money had to be exacted for many different taxes, at home and abroad; and money had to be found for everything from the purchase of public grain, to censors' building programs, to the minutiae like the urban praetor's pigs distributed throughout Rome at the time of the Compitalia. While an elected magistrate could issue orders about any or all of these things, he certainly did not concern himself with the actual mechanics. For these, there had to have been senior civil servants, men whose rank was somewhat higher than clerk or scribe; no doubt they came from respectable families, and were probably well paid. The existence of a class of them can certainly be supposed at the time Cato Uticensis (in 64 B.C.) made such a nuisance of himself when appointed Treasury quaestor, for it was obvious quaestors had long ceased to concern themselves personally with how the Treasury worked, and by 64 B.C. the Treasury was huge.

triclinium The dining room. In a normal family dining room (preferably, the room was square), three couches were arranged to form a U. From the doorway, if one was looking into the hollow center of the U, the couch on the left was called the *lectus summus*, the couch forming the middle (bottom end) of the U

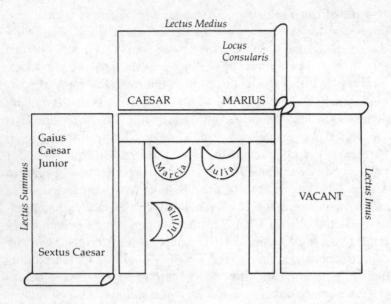

Caesar's dining room on the day he invited Gaius Marius
to dinner for the first time

was the *lectus medius*, and the couch forming the right side was
the *lectus imus*. Each couch was very broad, perhaps 4 feet
(1.25 m) or more, and at least twice as long, perhaps more. One
end of the couch had a raised arm to form a head; the other end
did not. In front of each couch, a little lower than the height of
the couch, was a narrow table running its length. The diners reclined on their left elbows, supported by bolsters; they were not
shod, and could call for their feet to be washed. The host of the
dinner reclined at the left end of the *lectus medius,* this being the
bottom end of the couch; the right hand end of the same couch,
at its head, was the place where the most honored guest reclined,
and was called the *locus consularis.* At the time of Gaius Marius, it was rare for women to recline alongside dining men, unless the women were of dubious virtue, and the dinner a men's

party. The women of the family sat inside the hollow center of the U on straight chairs, entered with the first course, and left as soon as the last course was cleared away; normally they drank only water.

Tridentum Modern Trento, in Italy.

Triocala The almost unassailable fortress town the rebel slaves of Sicily built in the ranges behind Sicily's southern coast. It was invested by Lucius Licinius Lucullus in 103 B.C., but did not fall until 101 B.C.

tripod Any device mounted on three legs. Oracular crones sat upon tripods. Sacrificial fires or augural fires were contained in tripod braziers. Tables were often tripods.

triumph The greatest of days for the successful Roman general. By the time of Gaius Marius, a general had to have been hailed as *imperator* by his troops, after which he was obliged to petition the Senate to grant him his triumph; only the Senate could sanction it, and sometimes—though not often—unjustifiably withheld it. The triumph itself was a most imposing parade which followed a rigidly prescribed route from the Villa Publica on the Campus Martius, through a special gate in the Servian Walls called the Porta Triumphalis, into the Velabrum, the Forum Boarium, and the Circus Maximus, after which it went down the Via Triumphalis, and turned into the Forum Romanum's Via Sacra. It terminated on the Capitoline Mount at the foot of the steps of the temple of Jupiter Optimus Maximus. The triumphing general and his lictors went into the temple and offered the god their laurels of victory, after which happened the triumphal feast.

triumphator The term for a triumphing general.

trophy The trophy was a suit of enemy chieftain's armor. In a practice instituted by the early Greeks, it was mounted on a frame made from a spear, fixed in the ground of the battlefield, and there dedicated to the gods who had assisted in the winning of victory. The Romans changed this practice by erecting a permanent monument on the battlefield, and carrying all the trophies back to Rome. There the trophies were displayed in the general's triumphal parade; afterward, they were dedicated to some chosen

god and set up permanently in the god's temple. Metellus Macedonicus built Rome's first marble temple (to Jupiter Stator) and
installed trophies in it; Gaius Marius built a temple to Honor and
Virtue, and installed his trophies in it.

Tullianum   Also known as Carcer. This one-roomed little
building had a chamber beneath it that served as Rome's only
execution cell. All the important prisoners who walked in the
general's triumph were led off as the parade began the ascent to
the top of the Capitoline Mount, and were strangled in the lower
chamber of the Tullianum. The term "strangling" does not seem
to mean bare hands were used, but a noose or garrote. The victim's body was then thrown into one of the sewer drain openings
in the walls of this lower chamber. It was equally lawful (though
not often done) to thrust the prisoner into the lower chamber and
leave him there to starve to death.

Tullus Hostilius   The third King of Rome, and a very shadowy
figure. A warlike man, he attacked, captured, and destroyed Alba
Longa, then brought its people into Rome and added them to the
populace; Alba Longa's ruling class became a part of Rome's pa-
triciate. Tullus Hostilius also built the Senate House, called the
Curia Hostilia in his honor.

tunic, *Tunica.*   This was the basic item of clothing for almost all
ancient Mediterranean peoples, including the Greeks and the Romans. As worn by a Roman of Gaius Marius's day, it had a rectangular body, without darts to confine it at the sides of the chest;
the neck was probably cut on a curve for comfort, rather than kept
as a straight edge continuous with the shoulders. The sleeves may
have been woven as rectangular projections from the shoulders,
or they may have been set in. Certainly it does not seem beyond
the skill of ancient tailors to inset sleeves, for there is mention in
the ancient sources of long sleeves, and these have to be set in. The
statues do not indicate that the tunics of men important enough to
have statues were simply joined up the sides with a gap left at the
top for the arms to go through, and the sleeves of the tunics
shown on military statues in particular look like proper short
sleeves. The tunic was either belted with leather or girdled with a

cord, and was always worn longer at the front than at the back, which was some 3 inches (75 mm) higher. Those of the knights' census wore a narrow stripe on the tunic, those of senatorial census a wide stripe. I believe these stripes were displayed on the right shoulder, rather than on the center of the chest. A wall painting from Pompeii displaying a man wearing a *toga praetexta* shows the wide stripe down the right shoulder of the tunic. So, I note, do the models employed by Dr. Lillian Wilson.

tunica palmata   The triumphing general's tunic, which may or may not have been purple in color, but was certainly embroidered all over with palm fronds.

Tusculum   A town on the Via Latina some 15 miles (24 km) from Rome. It was the first Latin town to receive the full Roman citizenship, in 381 B.C., and was always unswervingly loyal to Rome. Cato the Censor came from Tusculum, where his family had possessed the public horse of Roman knighthood for at least three generations.

tyro   In Latin, *tiro*. A novice, a beginner.

Ulysses   See Odysseus.

Utica   After the destruction of the city of Carthage by Scipio Aemilianus in 146 B.C., Utica became the most important city and port in the Roman province of Africa. Utica was the seat of the governor, and lay at the mouth of the river Bagradas.

Vale of the Salassi   The modern Val d'Aosta (see also Lugdunum Pass, Salassi).

Vediovis   A very Roman god, mysterious, and without a mythology. Nowadays he is thought to have been a manifestation of the young Jove (Jupiter); even Cicero was vague about Vediovis! Certainly he wasn't a happy god, was perhaps chthonic (associated with the underworld), and seems to have been the patron of disappointments. He had two temples at Rome, one on the Capitol, the other on Tiber Island; outside Rome he was not worshiped at all as far as we know, save at Bovillae, where some Julius erected an altar to Vediovis on behalf of the whole *gens* Julia in the year 100 B.C.

Vercellae   A small town in Italian Gaul. It lay on the north side of the Padus River, at the opening to the Vale of the Salassi. Outside it were a pair of small plains, the Campi Raudii, on which ground Marius and Catulus Caesar defeated the Cimbri in 101 B.C.

verpa A Latin obscenity used more in verbal abuse than as a sign of contempt. It referred to the penis—apparently in the erect state only, when the foreskin is drawn back—and had a homosexual connotation. On the literary and graffitic evidence, Dr. J. N. Adams discounts the word's meaning a circumcised penis.

Vesta A very old Roman goddess of numinous nature, having no mythology and no image (see *numen*). She was the hearth, and so had particular importance within the home and the family circle, where she was worshiped alongside the Di Penates and the Lar Familiaris. Her official public cult was equally important, and was personally supervised by the Pontifex Maximus. Her temple in the Forum Romanum was small, very old, and circular in shape; it was adjacent to the Regia, the Well of Juturna and the Domus Publicus of the Pontifex Maximus. A fire burned in the temple of Vesta permanently, and could not be allowed to go out under any circumstances.

Vestal Virgins Vesta was served by a special priesthood, the college of six women called Vestal Virgins. They were inducted at about seven or eight years of age, took vows of complete chastity, and served the goddess for thirty years, after which they were released from their vows and sent out into the community, and could marry if they wished—though few did, for it was thought unlucky. Their chastity was Rome's luck; that is, the luck of the State. When a Vestal was deemed unchaste, she was not judged and punished out of hand, but was formally brought to trial in a specially convened court. Her alleged lovers were also tried, but in a different court. If convicted, she was cast into an underground chamber dug for the purpose; it was sealed over, and she was left there to die. In Republican times the Vestal Virgins lived in the same Domus Publicus as the Pontifex Maximus, though sequestered from him.

vexillum A flag or banner.

via   A main highway, road, or street.

Via Aemilia   Built in 187 B.C.

Via Aemilia Scauri   Finished about 103 B.C. Its builder was Marcus Aemilius Scaurus Princeps Senatus, censor in 109 B.C.

Via Annia (1)   Built in 153 B.C.

Via Annia (2)   Built in 131 B.C. There is great debate about whether this was a Via Annia or a Via Popillia. I have marked it Via Popillia on my maps after a count of my sources produced one more Via Popillia than Via Annia.

Via Appia   Built in 312 B.C.

Via Aurelia Nova   Built in 118 B.C.

Via Aurelia Vetus   Built in 241 B.C.

Via Campana   No date is available.

Via Cassia   Built in 154 B.C.

Via Clodia   Built during the third century B.C., but of unknown certain date.

Via Domitia   Built in 121 B.C. Its author was Gnaeus Domitius Ahenobarbus.

Via Egnatia   Built perhaps around 130 B.C.

Via Flaminia   Built in 220 B.C.

Via Labicana   Too old to date.

Via Lata   Too old to date.

Via Latina   Too old to date.

Via Minucia   Built in 225 B.C.

Via Ostiensis   Too old to date.

Via Popillia (1)   Built in 131 B.C.

Via Popillia (2)   Built in 131 B.C. This road is also called the Via Annia, and there is still doubt as to which man was responsible for it.

Via Postumia   Built in 148 B.C.

via praetoria   The wide road inside a Roman military camp that ran between the camp's front and back gates.

via principalis   The wide road inside a Roman military camp that ran at right angles to the *via praetoria,* and connected one side gate with the other. The general's tent was located at the intersection of these two main *viae.*

Via Salaria   Too old to date. This was probably the very oldest of Rome's long roads. A branch road was built in 283 B.C., the Via Caecilia. Yet another branch road was built in 168 B.C., the Via Claudia.

Via Tiburtina   The old name for the first part of the Via Valeria, between Rome and Tibur.

Via Valeria   Built in 307 B.C.

vicus   A small city street, though not necessarily a short one. The word meant not so much the thoroughfare itself as the collection of buildings on either side of the thoroughfare; it originated as the word for a rural hamlet, where the buildings straggled down either side of one street. In any city, street names do not change through the centuries, save when a monarch or a politician honors himself by giving a street his name. Thus, in making my map of the city of Rome, I have used all the street names of Imperial Roman times that did not belong to new districts or Imperial town planning; the Vicus Insteius, Vicus lugarius, Vicus Tuscus, Vicus Patricii, Vicus Longus, and the rest must always have borne these names. Similarly with the Alta Semita and the hills like the Clivus Orbius, Clivus Patricius, Clivus Capitolinus, Clivus Argentarius, Clivus Pullius in Tabernola etc. It may be, however, that whereas we would say we lived *on* the Vicus Cuprius, a Roman would have said he lived *in* the Vicus Cuprius. Some of Rome's streets were named after the activities going on in them, like the Vicus Sandalarius ("street of cobblers"), Clivus Argentarius ("hill of the bankers"), Vicus Fabricii ("street of artificers"); others bore place names, like the Vicus Tuscus (Etruria); some simply described where they were going, like the Vicus ad Malum Punicum ("street leading to the Punic apple— pomegranate—tree").

Vienne, Vienna   Modern Vienne. The proper name of this trading post town on the Rhodanus River was Vienna, but it is usually called by its modern name, to save confusing it with Vienna, the capital of Austria.

villa   A country residence, completely self-contained, and originally having an agricultural purpose—in other words, a farmstead. It was built around a peristyle or courtyard, had stables or farm buildings at the front, and the main dwelling at the back, of the courtyard. By the time of Cornelia the Mother of the Gracchi, wealthy Romans were building villas as vacation homes rather than as farmsteads, and the architecture of the villa had changed correspondingly. Many of these holiday villas were on the seashore.

Villa Publica   The parklike piece of land on the Campus Martius, fronted by the Vicus Pallacinae, in which the participants of a triumphal parade were gathered together before the parade set off.

vir militaris   See Military Man.

Visurgis River   The modern Weser, in Germany.

Vocontii   A Celtic confederation of tribes dwelling along the Druentia River in Gaul-across-the-Alps; their lands bordered those of the Allobroges, who were to their north. They took great delight in preying upon Roman travelers on the Via Domitia as it crossed the Alps and wound down the Druentia toward the Rhodanus Valley.

Volcae Tectosages   A Celtic confederation of tribes occupying Mediterranean Gaul beyond the Rhodanus River, and extending all the way to Narbo and Tolosa (see also Brennus [2], Tolosa).

Volsci   One of the ancient peoples of central Italy. They had occupied eastern Latium, and were centered around the settlements of Sora, Atina, Antium, Circei, Tarracina, and Arpinum; their allies were the Aequi. By the end of the fourth century B.C., the Volsci had been so completely absorbed into the Roman system that their cultural and social identities had largely disappeared. They did not speak Latin, but a language of their own, akin to Umbrian.

wine, vintage wine   Wine was an intrinsic part of the life of both Romans and Greeks; in the absence of brewing or distillation apparatus, wine was the only beverage available that contained alcohol. This made it the object of great reverence (hence the gods of wine, Bacchus and Dionysos), and—usually—great respect. Many different varieties of grapes were grown to make wine, of the white and the purple kinds, and wines came in white and red.

By the time of Gaius Marius, Roman viticulture in particular was a highly educated business, and had outstripped Greek viticulture decisively. The Romans were always good with plants and planting, with gardens, and with growing; from the time her privileged citizens began to travel abroad, Rome was gifted with many imported plants, both new varieties of old friends and completely new friends. This could be said of the grapevine, certainly, always being added to with foreign importations.

Roman viticulture was expert at grafting, and knowledgeable about pest prevention. Asphalt, for instance, dredged out of the Palus Asphaltites (the Dead Sea) in Palestine, was smeared on the woody parts of grapevines to prevent the growth of smuts and moulds. When exactly ready, the grapes were picked, placed in vats, and trodden; the juice which oozed out of the vat at this time was reserved to make the best wine of all. Then, after treading, the grapes were pressed in presses similar to those known today in vineyards where mass-production techniques have not been introduced; this juice was made into ordinary wine. Then the grapes were pressed again, to produce a thin, sour, third-class beverage which retailed so cheaply it was drunk in large quantities by the lowly, and was also given to slaves; this was sometimes fortified to increase its alcohol content, by the addition of boiled-down must after the fermentation process. Fermentation took place with more or less care, depending upon the class of juice and the intent of the *vigneron*. Vats coated inside with wax (for the best wines) or pitch (which is a resin obtained from pines, so these wines took up some of the resin, and emerged tasting like a modern Greek retsina) held the juices for several months, during which they were skimmed frequently.

After fermentation, wines to be drunk at once were put into amphorae or (occasionally) skins. But those wines intended for additional maturation were first strained rigorously through sieves and cloths, then "bottled" in amphorae which were scrupulously stoppered and sealed from the air with melted wax; they were labeled with the year, the vineyard, the type of grape, and the name of the *vigneron,* and were stored in cool cellars.

Wooden casks were also used to store some of these better wines.

Most wines were intended to be drunk within four years, but those wines carefully sealed did not continue to ferment, only to mature, and some could take twenty years to reach their peak drinking moment. These of course were vintage wines. Then, as now, the oenologist reared his head and came out with his stock vocabulary of adjectives and adverbs; of connoisseurs there were many. One such was the great legal advocate Quintus Hortensius Hortalus, who when he died in 50 B.C. bequeathed the staggering number of *10,000* amphorae of wine to some unknown beneficiary; the amphora held 25 liters, or 6 American gallons, which means Hortensius had 60,000 U.S. gallons of wine in his cellar. It was not normal practice to drink wine neat—water was added, in varying proportions.

Roman women of Gaius Marius's time drank little wine; during the early Republic, if a *paterfamilias* so much as smelled wine on the breath of one of his womenfolk, he was considered fully justified in having her executed immediately. Despite the apparent continence of Roman wine drinkers, watering their intake as they did, alcoholism was as real a problem in antiquity as it is today.

Wooden Bridge   The name given universally to the Pons Sublicius, built of wood.

yoke   The yoke was the beam or crosstie which rested upon the necks of a pair of oxen or other animals when harnessed to draw a load. In human terms, it came to mean the mark of servility, of submission to the domination of others. There was a yoke for the young of both sexes to pass beneath inside the city of Rome, located somewhere on the Carinae; it was called the Tigillum, and perhaps symbolized submission to the seriousness of adult life. However, it was in military terms that the yoke came to have its greatest metaphorical significance. Very early Roman (or perhaps Etruscan) armies forced a defeated enemy to pass beneath the yoke; two spears were planted upright in the ground, and a third spear was placed across their tops to form a crosstie—the whole was too low for a man to pass beneath walking upright; he had to bend over. Unfortunately enemy armies adopted the idea, with the result that from time to time a Roman army was compelled to pass beneath the yoke. To do this was an intolerable humiliation; so much so that the Senate usually preferred to see a Roman army stand and fight until the last man was dead, rather than sacrifice Roman honor and *dignitas* by surrendering and passing beneaath the yoke. Even the ordinary people of Rome, including those as lowly as the Head Count, deemed passing beneath the yoke an utter humiliation, and clamored too to know why the defeated army hadn't fought until its last man lay dead.

PRONUNCIATION GUIDE TO ROMAN MASCULINE NAMES

To some extent, the pronunciation of classical Latin is still debated, but there are definite conventions among scholars. Liturgical Latin and medieval Latin are pronounced somewhat differently than classical Latin. None of which need worry the reader unduly. The aim of this little section is simply to offer guidelines for those readers without Latin.

One convention adhered to in pronouncing classical Latin is to sound the consonantal *v* like our English *w:* thus, the word *veritas* is properly pronounced *weritas*. But the rule is not hard and fast, even among scholars, so in the interests of reader comfort, I shall proceed to ignore it.

The diphthong *ae* should not be pronounced as in "say," but rather as in "eye"; this convention I have adhered to.

We have several more consonants in English than the Latin language did. The one which concerns the reader most is *j*. It has been customary in the English language for centuries to spell those Latin words commencing in consonantal *i* with a *j*. Thus, Julius should really be Iulius, and pronounced Yoo-lee-uss, *not* Joo-lee-uss. However, I have elected to go with English *j*.

The Latin *g* has only one sound, which I shall call *guh,* as in "gain"—"get"—"give"—"gone"—"gun." The other *g* sound in English, which I shall call *juh*, as in "ginger," is *never* used in pronouncing Latin.

Rather than adopt one of the current lexicographic systems of pronunciation, I have elected to use a phonetic system of my own, rhyming the Latin with some ordinary English word pronounced identically on both sides of the Atlantic as well as in the Antipodes—where possible!

And, last but by no means least, none of it really matters save to the purist. The most important thing is that the reader discover and enjoy the world of Republican Rome. Do not feel uncomfortable with the names. Latin is a major root of the English language, and that is a major help in itself. (Note: in some cases I have given the standard English pronunciation first, and put the more correct pronunciation in parentheses, in the lists below.)

The *Praenomen* (the First Name)

Appius	Ah-pee-uss (*ah* as in "pa," "ma"—*uss* as in "puss")
Aulus	Ow-luss (*ow* as in "cow")
Gaius	Gye-uss (*gye* as in "eye")
Gnaeus	Nye-uss (*nye* as in "eye")
Lucius	Loo-shuss (more correctly, Loo-kee-uss)
Mamercus	Mah-mer-kuss (*mah* as in "pa"—*mer* as in "her")
Manius	Mah-nee-uss (*mah* as in "pa")
Marcus	Mar-kuss
Publius	Pub-lee-uss (*pub* has the same *u* sound as "put")
Quintus	Kwin-tuss (*kwin* as in "twin")
Servius	Ser-vee-uss (*ser* as in "her")
Sextus	Sex-tuss (*sex* as in "sex")
Spurius	Spoo-ree-uss (*spoo* as in "too")
Tiberius	Tye-beer-ee-uss (more correctly, Tee-bear-ee-uss)
Titus	Tye-tuss (more correctly, Tee-tuss)

The *Nomen* (the Family or Gentilicial Name, Indicating the *Gens*)

Aelius   Eye-lee-uss (*eye* as in "eye"—*uss* as in "puss")
Aemilius   Eye-mil-ee-uss (*mil* as in "will")
Annius   An-nee-uss (*an* as in "tan")
Antistius   Ahn-tist-ee-uss (*ahn* as in "gone"—*tist* as in "fist")
Antonius   An-toh-nee-uss (*an* as in "tan"—*toh* as in "so")
Appuleius   Ah-poo-lay-ee-uss (*poo* as in "too"—*lay* as in "say")
Aquillius   Ah-kwill-ee-uss (*kwill* as in "will")
Atilius   Ah-tee-lee-uss
Aurelius   Or-ree-lee-uss (more correctly, Ow-ray-lee-uss)

Baebius   Bye-bee-uss (*bye* as in "eye")
Billienus   Bill-ee-ay-nuss (*bill* as in "will"—*ay* as in "say")

Caecilius   Kye-kill-ee-uss (*kye* as in "eye"—*kill* as in "will")
Caelius   Kye-lee-uss
Calpurnius   Kahl-purr-nee-uss (*kahl* as in "doll")
Cassius   Kass-ee-uss (*kass* as in "lass")
Claudius   Klaw-dee-uss (*klaw* as in "paw")—the English way
                  Klow-dee-uss (*klow* as in "cow")—the correct Latin way
Clodius   Kloh-dee-uss (*kloh* as in "so")
Coelius   Koy-lee-uss (*koy* as in "boy")
Cornelius   Kor-nee-lee-uss (strictly, Kor-nay-lee-uss)
Curtius   Koor-tee-uss (*koor* as in "poor")

Decius   Deck-ee-uss (*deck* as in "peck")
Decumius   Deck-oo-mee-uss (*oo* as in "too")

Didius	Did-ee-uss (*did* as in "bid")
Domitius	Dom-it-ee-uss (*dom* as in "tom"—*it* as in "fit")
Equitius	Ay-kwit-ee-uss (*ay* as in "say"—*kwit* as in "fit")
Fabius	Fay-bee-uss (strictly, Fab-ee-uss, *fab* as in "cab")
Fabricius	Fab-rick-ee-uss (*fab* as in "cab"—*rick* as in "kick")
Fannius	Fan-nee-uss (*fan* as in "tan")
Flavius	Flay-vee-uss (strictly, Flah-vee-uss)
Fraucus	Frow-kuss (*frow* as in "cow")
Fulvius	Full-vee-uss (strictly, Fool-vee-uss)
Furius	Few-ree-uss (strictly, Foo-ree-uss)
Gavius	Gah-vee-uss (*gah* as in "pa")
Granius	Grah-nee-uss (*grah* as in "pa")
Gratidius	Grah-tid-ee-uss (*tid* as in "bid")
Herennius	Her-en-ee-uss
Hortensius	Hor-ten-see-uss (*hor* as in "or"—*ten* as in "ten")
Julius	Joo-lee-uss (*joo* as in "too")
Junius	Joo-nee-uss
Labienus	Lab-ee-ay-nuss (*lab* as in "cab"—*ay* as in "say")
Licinius	Lick-in-ee-uss (*lick* as in "kick"—*in* as in "sin")
Livius	Liv-ee-uss (*liv* as in "spiv")
Lucilius	Loo-kill-ee-uss
Lusius	Loo-see-uss
Lutatius	Loo-tah-tee-uss (*tah* as in "pa")
Macrinus	Mah-kree-nuss (*mah* as in "pa")
Maelius	Mye-lee-uss (*mye* as in "eye")
Magius	Mah-gee-uss (the *g* as in "gear")

Mallius   Mah-lee-uss
Mamilius   Mah-mill-ee-uss (*mill* as in "will")
Manlius   Mahn-lee-uss
Marcius   Mar-shuss (more correctly, Mar-kee-uss)
Marius   Mah-ree-uss
Matius   Mat-ee-uss (*mat* as in "pat")
Memmius   Mem-ee-uss (*mem* as in "them")
Minucius   Min-oo-kee-uss (*min* as in "sin"—*oo* as in "too")
Mucius   Mew-shuss (more correctly, Moo-kee-uss)

Nonius   Noh-nee-uss (*noh* as in "so")
Norbanus   Nor-bah-nuss (*nor* as in "or"—*bah* as in "pa")

Octavius   Ock-tay-vee-uss (more correctly, Ock-tah-vee-uss)
Opimius   Oh-pee-mee-uss
Oppius   Op-ee-uss (*op* as in "top")

Papirius   Pah-pee-ree-uss
Perquitienus   Pair-kwit-ee-ay-nuss (*pair* as in "air")
Petreius   Pet-ray-uss (*pet* as in "yet")
Plautius   Plow-tee-uss (*plow* as in "cow")
Plotius   Ploh-tee-uss (*ploh* as in "so")
Pompeius   Pom-pay-ee-uss (*pom* as in "tom"—*pay* as in "say")
Pomponius   Pom-poh-nee-uss (*poh* as in "so")
Popillius   Pop-ill-ee-uss (*pop* as in "top"—*ill* as in "will")
Poppaedius   Pop-eye-dee-uss (*pop* as in "top")
Porcius   Por-shuss (more correctly, Por-kee-uss)
Postumius   Poh-stoo-mee-uss (*poh* as in "so"—*stoo* as in "too")

Rutilius   Roo-tee-lee-uss

Saufeius   Sow-fay-ee-uss (*sow* as in "cow"—*fay* as in "say")

Sempronius	Sem-proh-nee-uss (*sem* as in "hem"—*proh* as in "so")
Sergius	Sair-gee-uss (*sair* as in "air"—the *g* as in "gear")
Sertorius	Sair-tor-ee-uss (*tor* as in "or")
Servilius	Sair-vee-lee-uss
Siccius	Sick-ee-uss (*sick* as in "kick")
Sosius	Soh-see-uss (*soh* as in "so")
Sulpicius	Sool-pick-ee-uss (*sool* as in "fool"—*pick* as in "kick")
Terentius	Tair-en-tee-uss (*tair* as in "air"—*en* as in "ten")
Thorius	Thor-ee-uss (*thor* as in "or")
Titius	Tit-ee-uss (*tit* as in "fit")
Tullius	Too-lee-uss
Turpilius	Tur-pill-ee-uss (*tur* as in "fur"—*pill* as in "will")
Vagiennius	Vah-gee-en-ee-uss (the *g* as in "gear")
Vettius	Vet-ee-uss (*vet* as in "yet")

The *Cognomen* (the Last Name, Surname, or Distinguishing Name)

These names had definite meanings, so I shall give the meanings where we know them, as well as a guide to pronunciation.

Africanus	Ah-frick-ah-nuss	"of Africa"
Agelastus	Ah-gel-ah-stuss (the *g* as in "get")	"never smiles"
Ahala	Ah-hah-lah	unknown
Ahenobarbus	Ah-hay-noh-barb-uss	"red- or bronze-bearded"
Albinus	Ahl-bee-nuss	"whitish"
Augur	Ow-goor (*goor* as in "good")	"an augur"
Balearicus	Bah-lay-ah-rick-uss	"of the Balearic Isles"

Bambalio	Bahm-bah-lee-oh	unknown
Bestia	Best-ee-ah (*best* as in "rest")	"the beast"
Brocchus	Broh-kuss	"buck-toothed"
Brutus	Broo-tuss	"animal stupidity"
Caecus	Kye-kuss	"blind"
Caepio	Kye-pee-oh	"the onion vendor"
Caesar	See-zar (Latin, Kye-sar)	"a fine head of hair"
Caesoninus	Kye-soh-nee-nuss	unknown
Caldus	Kahl-duss	"lukewarm"
Calvus	Kahl-vuss	"bald"
Camillus	Kah-mill-uss	unknown
Caprarius	Kah-prah-ree-uss	"billy goat"
Carbo	Kar-boh	"burned out" or "cinder"
Cato	Kay-toh (Latin, Kah-toh)	"shrewd but up-tight"
Catulus	Kah-too-luss	"pup" or "cub"
Cicero	Siss-er-oh (Latin, Kick-er-oh)	"chick-pea"
Cotta	Kot-tah (*kot* as in "pot")	"wine splash"(?)
Crassus	Krass-uss (*krass* as in "ass")	"thick"
Cunctator	Koonk-tah-tor	"he who holds back"
Dalmaticus	Dahl-mah-tee-kuss	"of Dalmatia"
Dentatus	Den-tah-tuss (*den* as in "ten")	"born with teeth"
Diadematus	Dee-ah-dem-ah-tuss	"of a royal head-band"
Dives	Dee-vays	"the heavenly one"
Drusus	Droo-suss (*droo* as in "too")	unknown

Eburnus	Ay-boor-nuss	"made of ivory"
Fimbria	Fim-bree-ah (*fim* as in "him")	"hair worn in a fringe"
Flaccus	Flah-kuss	"big ears"
Galba	Gahl-bah	"potbelly"
Getha	Gay-thah	"from the ends of the earth"
Glaucia	Glow-kee-ah (*glow* as in "cow")	"grey-green"
Gracchus	Grah-kuss	"jackdaw"(?)
Laenas	Lye-nahss (sibilant ending)	"priestly mantle"
Lentulus	Len-too-luss (*len* as in "ten")	"tardy" or "slow"
Lepidus	Lep-id-uss (*lep* as in "step")	"a wonderful fellow"
Limetanus	Lim-ay-tah-nuss (*lim* as in "dim")	"of a boundary"
Longinus	Long-gee-nuss (the *g* as in "get")	"in the far distance"
Lucullus	Loo-kull-uss (*kull* as in "pull")	"a little grove of trees"
Macedonicus	Mahn-ked-on-ee-kuss	"of Macedonia"
Mactator	Mahk-tah-tor	"slaughterman"
Magnus	Mahg-nuss	"great"
Mancinus	Mahn-kee-nuss	"of a cripple"
Margarita	Mar-gah-ree-tah	"pearl"
Maximus	Mahx-ee-muss	"greatest"
Meminius	Mem-in-ee-uss (*mem* as in "hem")	"of the Gallic Meminii"

Merula	Me-roo-lah (*me* as in "met")	"blackbird"
Metellus	Met-ell-uss (*met* as in "get")	"a liberated mercenary"
Mus	Moos	"rat" or "mouse"
Nasica	Nah-see-kah	"nosy"
Nerva	Nair-vah (*nair* as in "air")	"stringy" or "tough"
Numidicus	Noo-mid-ee-kuss (*mid* as in "bid")	"of Numidia"
Orator	Oh-rah-tor	"the public speaker"
Orestes	Oh-rest-ays (*rest* as in "nest")	"mother died in birth"
Paullus	Pow-luss (*pow* as in "cow")	"wee one" or "trifle"
Philippus	Fill-ip-uss (*fill* as in "will")	"of Philippi"
Pipinna	Pip-in-ah (*pip* as in "hip")	"little boy's penis"
Piso	Pee-soh	"I grind down"
Porcella	Por-kell-ah	"piglet" or "little girl's genitals"
Postumus	Poss-too-muss (*poss* as in "boss")	"born after father died"
Pulcher	Pool-ker	"beautiful"
Ravilla	Rah-vill-ah (*vill* as in "will")	"talked himself hoarse"
Reginus	Ray-gee-nuss (the *g* as in "get")	"of a queen"
Rex	Rayx	"king"
Rufinus	Roo-fee-nuss	"of a red-haired family"

Rufus	Roo-fuss (*fuss* as in "puss")	"red-haired"
Ruso	Roo-soh	"a country bumpkin"
Saturninus	Sah-tur-nee-nuss	"of Saturn"
Scaevola	Skye-voh-lah	"left-handed"
Scaurus	Skow-russ (*skow* as in "cow")	"puffy feet" or "dropsical"
Scipio	Skee-pee-oh	"a ceremonial rod"
Serranus	Se-rah-nuss (*se* as in "set")	"of a saw" or "serrated"
Sesquiculus	Say-skwee-koo-luss	"an arsehole and a half"
Siculus	See-koo-luss	"of Sicily"
Silanus	See-lah-nuss	"ugly puggy face"
Silo	See-loh	"snub-nosed"
Stichus	Stick-uss (*stick* as in "kick")	slave's name (Greek)
Strabo	Stray-boh (Latin, Strah-boh)	"cross-eyed"
Sulla	Soo-lah	unknown
Tubero	Too-bear-oh	"hump" or "morally bad"
Varro	Vah-roh	"bandy-legged"
Vatia	Vah-tee-ah	"knock-kneed"
Verrucosis	Ve-roo-koh-sus (*ve* as in "vet")	"covered in warts"
Vopiscus	Voh-piss-kuss	"survivor of twins"

PRONUNCIATION GUIDE
TO OTHER NAMES
AND TERMS

Because the guide to pronunciation of male names should familiarize the reader with general Latin pronunciation, the list which follows is considerably abbreviated.

Achaeans	Ah-kye-ans
Achilles	Ah-kill-ees
Adherbal	Ahd-her-bahl
aedile	eye-deel (English, ee-dyel or ay-dyel)
Aedui	Eye-doo-ee
Aeneas	Eye-nay-ahs (English, An-ee-ass or Ay-nee-ass)
Aeschylus	Eye-skee-luss (English, Ee-skee-luss)
ager publicus	ah-ger (the *g* as in "got") pub-lee-kuss
Agger	Ag-er (*ag* as in "hag")
Allobroges	Al-oh-broh-gays (*al* as in "pal")
Ambrones	Am-broh-nays (*am* as in "ham")
Amor	Ah-mor
Anopaea	Ah-noh-pye-ah
Antigone	Ant-ig-oh-nay (*ant* as in "pant"—*ig* as in "pig")
Apulia	Ah-poo-lee-ah
aqua	ah-kwah
Aquae Sextiae	Ah-kwye Sex-tee-eye

Arausio	Ah-row-see-oh (*row* as in "cow")
Ariadne	Ah-ree-ahd-nay
Aricia	Ah-rick-ee-ah (*rick* as in "kick")
Arpinum	Ar-pee-noom (*oom* is "short"—like the *u* in "puss")
Atuatuci	Ah-too-ah-too-kee
auctoritas	owk-tor-ee-tahss (*ow* as in "cow")
augur	ow-goor (*ow* as in "cow"—the *g* as in "good")
Aurelia	Ow-ray-lee-ah (English, Awe-ree-lee-ah)
Baetis	Bye-tiss
Baiae	Bye-eye
Berenice	Bear-en-ee-kay (English, Bear-en-eye-kee)
biga	bee-gah
Bithynia	Bith-in-ee-ah (*bith* as in "pith")
Boii	Boy-ee
Boiohaemum	Boy-oh-hye-moom (*oo* sounded like the *u* in "put")
Boiorix	Boy-or-ix
Bomilcar	Bom-ill-kar (*bom* as in "tom")
Bona Dea	Boh-nah Day-ah
boni	bonny (as in Scots "bonny")
Brundisium	Broon-dis-ee-oom (*dis* as in "this")
Burdigala	Boor-dee-gah-lah (*boor* as in "poor")
Caelian	Kye-lee-ahn
Campania	Kam-pah-nee-ah (*kam* as in "ham")
campus	kam-puss (same then as now)
Capena	Kap-ay-nah (*kap* as in "tap")
capite censi	kap-it-ay ken-see (*ken* as in "ten")
Capua	Kap-oo-ah (*oo* as in "too")
carcer	kar-ker
Carinae	Ka-reen-eye (*ka* as in "can")

Celt	Kelt (as in "spelt")
Cercina	Ker-kee-nah (*ker* as in "her")
Charybdis	Kah-rib-dis (*rib* as in "crib")
Cherusci	Ker-oos-kee
Cilicia	Kill-ick-ee-ah (English, Sill-ish-ah)
Cimbri	Kim-bree (*kim* as in "him")
Circei	Ker-kay-ee
cloaca	kloh-ah-kah (*kloh* as in "so")
confarreatio	kon-fah-ray-ah-tee-oh
consultum	kon-sool-toom
contio	kon-tee-oh
corona	kor-oh-nah
cottabus	kot-ah-buss (*kot* as in "pot")
Croesus	Kree-suss
culibonia	kool-ee-bon-ee-ah (*bon* as in "upon")
Cumae	Koo-mye
cunnus	koo-nuss
curia	koo-ree-ah
cursus honorum	koor-suss hon-or-oom (*hon* as in "upon")
curule	koo-rool
Danaë	Dan-ah-ay (*dan* as in "can")
dignitas	deen-yee-tahss (sibilant ending)
domus	dom-uss (*dom* as in "tom")
Druentia	Droo-en-tee-ah
Epaphroditus	Ep-ah-froh-dee-tuss (English, Ep-afroh-dye-tuss)
Euxine	Erx-een (English, Yewx-een)
fasces	fass-kays (*fass* as in "lass")
fasti	fah-stee
Fauces Suburae	Fow-kays (*fow* as in "cow") Soo-boo-rye
Felix	Fay-licks

fellator	fell-ah-tor (*fell* as in "sell")
flamen	flah-men (*men* as in "ten")
flamen Dialis	flah-men Dee-ah-lis
flumen	floo-men (*floo* as in "too")
Fortuna	For-too-nah
forum	for-oom
Forum Boarium	Boh-ah-ree-oom
Forum Frumentarium	Froo-men-tah-ree-oom
Forum Holitorium	Hol-it-or-ee-oom (*hol* as in "doll")
Forum Piscinum	Piss-kee-noom
Forum Romanum	Roh-mah-noom
Gades	Gah-days
Gaetuli	Gye-too-lee
Gallia	Gal-ee-ah (*gal* as in "pal")
Gallia Comata	Com-ah-tah (*com* as in "tom")
garum	ga-room (*ga* as in "gap")
Garumna	Gah-room-nah
Gauda	Gow-dah (*gow* as in "cow")
gens	gens (the *g* as in "get"—word rhymes with "hens")
Germalus	Ger-mah-luss (the *g* as in "get"—*ger* as in "her")
Germani	Ger-mah-nee (the *g* as in "get"—*ger* as in "her")
Getorix	Gay-tor-ix (*ix* as in "six")
Halicyae	Hal-ee-kee-eye (*hal* as in "pal")
Hiempsal	Hee-emp-sal
Hispania	Hiss-pah-nee-ah
Hispania Citerior	Kit-er-ee-or (*kit* as in "sit")
Hispania Ulterior	Ool-ter-ee-or
hubris	hoo-briss
Iampsas	Yamp-sahss (*yamp* as in "lamp")
Iamus	Yah-muss

Icosium	Ee-koh-see-oom
Illyricum	Ill-ir-ee-coom (*ir* as in "stirrup")
imagines	im-ah-gee-nays (the *g* as in "gear")
imago	im-ah-goh (*im* as in "him")
imperator	im-pair-ah-tor
imperium	im-pair-ee-oom (English, im-peer-ee-oom)
insula	in-soo-lah
Iol	Yol (as in "doll")
irrumator	irr-oo-mah-tor (*irr* as in "stir-rup")
iugera	yew-gair-ah
iugerum	yew-gair-oom (*yew* as in "few")
Juba	Joo-bah
Jugurtha	Joo-gbor-thah (English, Joo-ger-thuh)
Julia	Joo-lee-ah
Julilla	Joo-lil-lah
Juturna	Joo-toor-nah
Lares	Lah-rays
Lares Permarini	Pair-mah-ree-nee
Lares Praestites	Prye-stit-ays (*stit* as in "sit")
Lautumiae	Low-too-mee-eye (*low* as in "cow")
Licinia	Lick-in-ee-ah
Lugdunum	Loog-doo-noom
macellum	mack-ell-oom (*mack* as in "tack")
Marcia	Mar-kee-ah (English, Marsh-uh or Mar-see-uh)
Marcomanni	Mar-koh-mah-nee
Marrucini	Mar-oo-kee-nee (heavy *r—mar* as in "tar")
Marsi	Mar-see
Masinissa	Mah-sin-iss-ah (*sin* as in "tin")
Mastanabal	Mah-stan-ah-bahl (*stan* as in "ran")
Mauretania	Mow-ret-ah-nee-ah (*mow* as in "cow")

mentula	men-too-lah (*men* as in "ten")
mentulam caco	men-too-lahm kah-koh
Metrobius	Met-roh-bee-uss (*met* as in "set")
Micipsa	Mick-ip-sah
Milo	Mee-loh (English, Mye-loh)
Misenum	Mee-say-noom
Mithridates	Mith-rid-ah-tays (English, Mithrid-ay-tees)
Muluchath	Moo-loo-kath
Myrto	Meer-toh
Nabataea	Nah-bah-tye-ah
Nabdalsa	Nab-dahl-sah (*nab* as in "cab")
Naevius	Nye-vee-uss
Narbo	Nor-boh or Nah-boh
Neapolis	Nay-ah-pol-iss (*pol* as in "doll")
nefas	neff-ahss (*neff* as in "left"—*ahss* as in "arse")
nemo	nay-moh
Nicopolis	Nick-op-ol-iss
Numantia	Noo-man-tee-ah (*man* as in "man")
Numidia	Noo-mid-ee-ah (*mid* as in "bid")
Ocelum	Ock-ell-oom (*ock* as in "sock")
Odysseus	Odd-iss-oos (English, Odd-iss-ee-uss)
Oedipus	Ee-dee-puss (American, Ed-ee-puss)
oppidum	op-id-oom (*op* as in "hop"—*id* as in "bid")
opus incertum	op-uss in-ker-toom
Oxyntas	Ox-in-tahss (*in* as in "sin")
Paeligni	Pye-leen-yee
Pamphylia	Pam-fee-lee-ah (*pam* as in "ham")
Paphlagonia	Paff-la-goh-nee-ah
papyrus	pap-eye-russ (*pap* as in "tap")
Patavium	Pat-ah-vee-oom (*pat* as in "cat")

paterfamilias	pat-er-fam-ill-ee-ahss
Patrae	Pat-rye
Penates	Pen-ah-tays (*pen* as in "ten")
Perseus	Per-soos (English, Per-see-uss)
phalerae	fal-er-eye (*fal* as in "pal")
Phrygia	Fridge-ee-ah
Picenum	Pee-kay-noom
pilum	pee-loom
Placentia	Plah-ken-tee-ah
plebs	rhymes with "webs"
podex	poh-dex (*dex* as in "sex")
pomerium	poh-mair-ee-oom
praefectus fabrum	prye-feck-tuss fab-room (*fab* as in "cab")
praenomen	prye-noh-men
praetor	prye-tor
praetor peregrinus	pair-egg-ree-nuss
praetor urbanus	oor-bah-nuss
primus inter pares	pree-muss in-ter pah-rays
Princeps Senatus	Prin-keps Sen-ah-tuss
Priscilla	Priss-kill-ah (English, Priss-ill-uh)
privatus	pree-vah-tuss
pteryges	terry-gays
Ptolemy	Tol-em-ee (*tol* as in "doll")
Ptolemy Apion	Ah-pee-on
Ptolemy Euergetes	Er-air-get-ays
Puteoli	Poo-tay-oh-lee
Pyrrhus	Pirr-uss (*pirr* as in "stirrup")
Reate	Ray-ah-tay
Regia	Ray-gee-ah (the *g* as in "gear")
Remus	Rem-uss (*rem* as in "hem"—English, Ree-muss)
Rhenus	Ray-nuss
Rhodanus	Rod-an-uss (*rod* as in "cod")
Roma	Roh-mah

Romulus	Roh-moo-luss
rostra	roh-strah
Rusicade	Roo-see-kah-day
Rutilia	Roo-tee-lee-ah
saepta	sye-p-tah
sagum	sag-oom (*sag* as in "hag")
saltatrix tonsa	sal-tah-tricks ton-sah (*ton* as in "upon")
Samnium	Sam-nee-oom (*sam* as in "ham")
satrap	sat-rap
Scordisci	Skor-disk-ee
Scylax	Skee-lacks (English, Sky-lacks)
Scylla	Skee-lah (English, Skill-uh or Sill-uh)
Servilia	Sair-vee-lee-ah (*sair* as in "air")
Servilia Caepionis	Kye-pee-oh-niss
smaragdus	smah-rag-duss
Smyrna	Smeer-nah (English, Smur-nuh—*smur* as in "fur")
stibium	stib-ee-oom (*stib* as in "crib")
stimulus	stim-oo-luss (*stim* as in "dim")
Subura	Soo-boo-rah
Sulpicia	Sool-pick-ee-ah
suovetaurilia	soo-of-et-ow-rill-ee-ah
Syrtis	Seer-tiss (*seer* as in "leer")
Taprobane	Tap-roh-bah-nay
Tarpeian	Tar-pay-ee-an
tata	tah-tah
Teutobod	Ter-toh-bod (*bod* as in "cod")
Teutones	Ter-toh-nays
Thermopylae	Ther-mop-ee-lye
torc	tork
tribuni	trib-oo-nee (*trib* as in "crib")
tribuni aerarii	eye-rah-ree-ee
tribuni militum	mill-it-oom (*mill* as in "will")
tribuni plebis	pleb-iss (*pleb* as in "web")
Tullianum	Tool-ee-ah-noom

Tusculum	Tuss-koo-loom (*tuss* as in "puss")
Tyrrhenian	Tir-ray-nee-an (*tir* as in "stirrup")
Ubus	Oo-buss
Ulysses	Oo-liss-ays (English, Yew-lissees)
Utica	Oo-tee-kah
Vediovis	Ved-ee-of-iss (*ved* as in "bed"—*of* as in "of")
Velabrum	Vel-ab-room (*vel* as in "sell"—*ab* as in "cab")
Velia	Vel-ee-ah
Vercellae	Ver-kell-eye
via	vee-ah
Via Aemilia	Eye-mill-ee-ah
Via Aemilia Scauri	Eye-mill-ee-ah Skow-ree (*skow* as in "cow")
Via Annia	Ah-nee-ah
Via Appia	Ah-pee-ah
Via Aurelia	Ow-ray-lee-ah (*ow* as in "cow")
Via Domitia	Dom-it-ee-ah (*dom* as in "tom"—*it* as in "sit")
Via Flaminia	Flam-in-ee-ah (*flam* as in "ham")
Via Lata	Lah-tah
Via Latina	Lat-ee-nah (*lat* as in "sat")
Via Nova	Noh-vah
via praetoria	prye-tor-ee-ah
via principalis	prin-kip-ah-liss
Via Sacra	Sack-rah
Via Salaria	Sal-ah-ree-ah (*sal* as in "pal")
Via Tiburtina	Tib-er-tee-nah (*tib* as in "crib")
vicus	vee-kuss
Vicus Patricii	Pat-rick-ee-ee (*pat* as in "sat")
Vicus Tuscus	Tuss-kuss (as in "puss")
Volcae Tectosages	Vol-kye Teck-toh-sah-gays
Volscian	Vol-skee-an

COLLEEN McCULLOUGH is the internationally acclaimed author of eighteen immensely successful novels. She lives on Norfolk Island in the South Pacific with her husband, Ric Robinson.